PENGUIN BOOKS

BELLE DU SEIGNEUR

'A massive, sprawling masterpiece, exuberant and pessimistic, which won the French Academy's Grand Prix du Roman in 1968 … It takes one's breath away metaphorically as well as literally' – Caroline Moore in the *Sunday Telegraph*

'Albert Cohen's alternatively lyrical, comical and tragic hymn to life and to love is one of the great monuments of the modern European novel … What makes it so immensely loveable is that all its characters, however deluded, ridiculous, rigid, or self-serving, are objects of the author's affection' – David Bellos in the *New Statesman*

'*Belle du Seigneur*, with its breadth of ambition, psychological lucidity and stylistic virtuosity, is one of the few great post-war French novels … a wonderfully funny work; a baroque, exuberant satire on the League of Nations, and a merciless dissection of middle-class hypocrisy' – Adrian Tahourdin in *The Times Literary Supplement*

'Impeccably translated by David Coward, these thousand glorious pages are a joy to read … a richly-tragi-comic novel of almost epic proportions' – Eva Figes in the *Jewish Chronicle*

Albert Cohen was born in Greece on the island of Corfu in 1895 and emigrated with his parents to France when he was five. He went to school in Marseilles and studied law at the University of Geneva. He became a Swiss citizen, spent a year in Egypt, published a collection of verse, edited *La Revue Juive* in Paris and then worked in the Diplomatic Section of the International Labour Office in Geneva. During the 1930s he devoted himself to his writing. After the fall of France he spent seven years in London as legal adviser to the Intergovernmental Committee on Refugees. He was responsible for drawing up the International Agreement of 1946, which provided travel documents for refugees. In 1947 he returned to Geneva and the United Nations, where he headed a division of the International Refugee Organization. After 1952 he resumed his literary work, determined to complete his novel-cycle, which had begun with *Solal* (1930) and *Mangeclous* (1938), and ended with *Belle du Seigneur* (1868) and *Les Valeureux* (1969). *Belle du Seigneur* was awarded the French Academy's Grand Prix du Roman. Albert Cohen died in 1981.

David Coward is Professor of Modern French Literature at the University of Leeds. He has written widely on the literature of France since 1700 and is the translator of tales by de Sade and Maupassant and of *La Dame aux Camélias* by Dumas *fils*. He was awarded the 1995 Scott Moncrieff Prize for his translation of *Belle du Seigneur*. A regular contributor to *The Times Literary Supplement*, he is currently writing a history of French literature.

Albert Cohen

BELLE DU SEIGNEUR

Translated and with an Introduction by
David Coward

PENGUIN BOOKS

TRANSLATOR'S NOTE

The French text used for this translation was prepared for the Pléiade edition (Paris, 1986) by Christel Peyrefitte and Bella Cohen. I am most grateful to Madame Cohen for many invaluable suggestions and her patient support. I claim as my own any blemishes which may have found their way into print.

PENGUIN BOOKS

Published by the Penguin Group
Penguin Books Ltd, 27 Wrights Lane, London w8 5tz, England
Penguin Putnam Inc., 375 Hudson Street, New York, New York 10014, USA
Penguin Books Australia Ltd, Ringwood, Victoria, Australia
Penguin Books Canada Ltd, 10 Alcorn Avenue, Toronto, Ontario, Canada m4v 3b2
Penguin Books (NZ) Ltd, 182–190 Wairau Road, Auckland 10, New Zealand

Penguin Books Ltd, Registered Offices: Harmondsworth, Middlesex, England

First published in France by Editions Gallimard 1968
This translation first published in Great Britain by Viking 1995
Published in Penguin Books 1997
1 3 5 7 9 10 8 6 4 2

ALBERT COHEN AND
BELLE DU SEIGNEUR

Albert Cohen was French not by birth but by adoption and conviction. He was born Abraham Albert Coen in 1895 on the island of Corfu, which since the sixteenth century had been a place of refuge for the persecuted Sephardic Jews of Spain and Italy. Ruled by Venice until Napoleon's victorious Italian campaign, Corfu became part of a British protectorate in 1814 and was ceded to Greece in 1864. Until 1919, when he became a Swiss citizen (and added an 'h' to his name as an affirmation of his Jewishness), Albert Cohen retained the nationality of his Turkish grandfather.

The Coens had long been leading figures in the island's Jewish community, which, however, declined sharply in the 1890s when accusations of ritual murder created severe anti-Semitic tensions. In 1900, as part of the exodus which followed (but also because the family soap business was in difficulties), Marco and Louise Coen emigrated to Marseilles, taking their only son with them. And there they stayed, buying and selling eggs for a modest living. Apart from a brief visit for his bar mitzvah in 1908, Albert Cohen never returned to Corfu, the 'Cephalonia' of his books. Yet from that visit he took away impressions as vivid as those left on Edward Lear, who was startled by the exuberance of springtime on the island. 'There is hardly any green left,' he wrote in April 1856, 'since an immense crop of marigolds, geraniums, orchises, irises, & cannonilla have come out . . . The hedges are *absolutely* pink, & in fact the whole thing is most absurd from its very oddity.' But, in addition to the lush vegetation, the sun and the limpid sea, there were human sights and sounds and smells which Cohen never forgot. The memory of narrow, bustling streets filled with extravagant talk and gestures, and the patriarchal gravity of his grandfather Abraham, who now led the Jewish community, were experiences which shaped the exotic mythology which fills a whole corner of his imaginary universe, rather as the Indo-China of Marguerite Duras's childhood underpins her fictional world. Cohen's barely-glimpsed Corfu, he said, was the seed from which he grew a baobab tree.

He was sent to a Catholic kindergarten and a state elementary school in Marseilles before moving on to the Lycée Thiers. There he met Marcel Pagnol, who was to remain a lifelong friend, and learned how to be French. But assimilation was not easy in the aftermath of the Dreyfus affair. On 16 August 1905, his tenth birthday, he stopped to listen to the patter of a street hawker selling stain-remover, who singled him out, called him a 'dirty yid', said all Jews were German spies and the secret masters of international finance, and told him to go home to Jerusalem. On that day, Albert Cohen learned what it was to be an outsider. But the experience was also an early intimation of his ambiguous cultural position, which finds obsessive expression in his books. He was caught between the extravagant style, warmth and moral certainties of his Jewish, oriental roots on the one hand and, on the other, the rationalist tradition of his adopted country, and his work was to be a quest for a way of reconciling multiple cultural tensions, of bridging the gap between East and West, the ideal and the real, the absolute and the limitations of the human condition.

But his childhood was not unhappy. If his relationship with his father was difficult, he was adored by his mother, who told him stories and encouraged him to believe that he was special. He also discovered literature, made the French language his, and, at sixteen, began a rather showy affair with an opera singer, which greatly impressed his schoolfriends. In 1914 he enrolled for a law degree in clean, neat Geneva – another culture shock after the dirt and bustle of Marseilles – and he began moving in cosmopolitan, wartime, student circles. He acquired new friends and a mistress, a Hungarian countess who doubtless bears some resemblance to the Countess Kanyo of *Belle du Seigneur*: all the women in his life were to find their way eventually into his books. In 1919 he married Elisabeth Brocher, the daughter of a Protestant minister, for whom he wrote *Paroles juives* (1921), a sequence of highly sensual poems which contain many of the themes to which he would later return – the greatness and degradation of the Jewish people, the need to embrace life and God like an eager lover, the brotherhood of man, and the supremacy of the Commandments of Moses, which stand like a beacon even to those who have no belief. It is a lush, lyrical incantation to which the nearest comparison is the Song of Solomon.

Cohen found few openings for his law degree in Geneva, and his only offer was a position in Egypt, where he lived for a year, separated from his wife and daughter. He returned to Geneva in 1921 determined to make his way as a writer. He had read widely, and his tastes were eclectic and highly personal. To the cool passion of Racine and Corneille he preferred the warmer tones of Dickens and Stendhal, and he distanced himself almost entirely from the great influences of the age, Marx, Freud and surrealism. He also admired writers as different as Proust (whom he later came to despise for his snobbery) and Paul Morand. In 1922 a first article in the prestigious *Nouvelle revue française* brought praise and contacts. Other articles followed, including a homage to Chaplin which reappears in modified form in *Belle du Seigneur* (chapter 87). But, as his literary career seemed poised to take off, tragedy struck. In 1924 his wife died of cancer. Cohen reacted by throwing himself into his work, which now took a new direction. He had met Chaim Weizmann by chance and, with his backing, became the editor of the short-lived *Revue juive* in 1925. Increasingly aware of the threat of fascism and anti-Semitism, which had spread even to the clean streets of Geneva, Cohen felt driven to defend the Jewish cause, recently revitalized by the Balfour Declaration. His work for the *Revue juive* gave him a high profile (Einstein and Freud were members of the editorial board) and confirmed his literary standing with its publisher, Gallimard, and with Jacques Rivière, the driving force behind the *NRF*, who had already offered him a contract for five novels. (They were never written: Cohen never wrote anything to order.) When the *Revue juive* ceased publication, Albert Thomas, director of the International Labour Office in Geneva, prompted by Rivière, offered Cohen work. It was his introduction to the world of the international civil service, to which he would subsequently return at intervals.

He also began to rebuild his personal life. He drew increasingly close to Yvonne Imer, a friend of his late wife. They were ideally suited, and it was to her that he dictated a play, *Ezéchiel* (1927), a number of shorter texts which he subsequently destroyed, and his first novel, *Solal*, which appeared in 1930. With her he perfected a working method which he never abandoned. He did not so much plan his books as cultivate them. He began by turning ideas over in his mind, jotting down possibilities and turns of phrase as they occurred to him, then spoke them for transcription on to paper. The result was revised and expanded and retyped, then revised and dictated again, a process which was repeated until the refinements of invention flagged. The result was a vast, untidy bush which was pruned and trimmed until a shape emerged. Cohen claimed that he never really finished any of his books: he merely abandoned them. In this sense, his art was a long patience. But it was also a patience shared, a complicity which stimulated him and gave him a first audience: a smile or a frown from his amanuensis determined the fate of many an irony or added yet another subtlety to character or action. He always dictated to women, and preferably the women he loved. Other men, he said, bring women flowers; he preferred to give his a book. Writing, when properly managed, was a kind of conjugal joy which constantly reinvented his relationships, providing a common intensity of experience which staved off boredom, which is the death of love. Had Solal and Ariane followed their creator's practice, their love might never have turned stale and lethal.

Cohen planned to marry Yvonne Imer. His flexible arrangement with the ILO guaranteed a modest lifestyle, and his literary prospects seemed set fair, and much fairer than his physical and mental health. He had caught tuberculosis in Egypt, was plagued by a variety of allergies and depressive moods, and was permanently obsessed by death. For all the infectious rumbustiousness of the Valiant, who make their first appearance in *Solal*, a dark shadow lay over Cohen's world; this deepened when, in June 1929, Yvonne Imer died suddenly of a heart attack, aged thirty-four. Cohen again sought refuge in his professional duties and his writing. *Solal* was a critical success, and *Ezéchiel* won the *Comoedia* prize for the best one-act play of 1930.

In 1931 he married Marianne Goss, the daughter of a Genevan architect, and was reunited with his daughter, Myriam, who had been raised largely by her mother's relations. They made a happy enough family, though Marianne proved not to be a soul-mate, nor was she a literary accomplice. This role soon passed to Myriam, with whom Cohen discussed each day's additions to his majestically growing accumulation of pages. These were typed by a secretarial assistant, Anne-Marie Boissonnas, whose father was to survive in the kindly figure of Uncle Gri. Until 1939 Cohen devoted all his time to literature, maintaining a very low profile. In 1933 *Ezéchiel* ran for ten performances at the Comédiè-Française, receiving mixed notices and a generally favourable reception. However, the public preview provoked strong reactions: members of the fascist leagues had come, as usual, to boo any celebration of Jewishness on principle, while some Jews in the audience, only too aware that Hitler was in the Reichstag, objected to the portrayal of the sturdy unkillability of the Jewish spirit as a crude and dangerous caricature. Cohen, essentially a shy man, had no stomach for a fight, was appalled by the furore, and never again wrote for the theatre. Instead, he disappeared from view and proceeded to amass materials for a novel which began where *Solal* had left off, feeling his way, pursuing the stream of his invention which turned into a river and then reached a delta, slow-moving but rich in alluvial deposits. By 1938, when Gallimard, who had been paying him an allowance against future royalties, intimated that some return would be in order, the manuscript had reached some three thousand pages. Cohen's answer was to extract chapters featuring the Valiant (whose antics made his daughter laugh) and take the tale of Solal up to the point where he goes forth to seduce Ariane. *Mangeclous* (1938) (translated as *Nailcruncher* in 1940) was well received, and the jacket announced a sequel, already entitled *Belle du Seigneur*, which was to be another thirty years in the making. Cohen had been virtually forgotten when it appeared finally in 1968 and won the French Academy's prize for fiction.

But the year of Munich was hardly the time for embarking on long-term literary projects. At the beginning of 1939 Cohen became Chaim Weizmann's personal representative in Paris, and in the spring he canvassed support for the establishment of an international battalion, the Jewish Legion – a proposal which was finally turned down by the French Foreign Office in November. When France was overrun in June 1940, Cohen realized that his connection with Weizmann made him particularly vulnerable, and he escaped with his wife and daughter to England, not without difficulty, by way of Bordeaux. In London, as official adviser to the Jewish Agency for Palestine, his main function was to liaise with various governments-in-exile. He met de Gaulle ('personally likeable and rather engaging'), who pledged his support for the Jewish cause. Cohen was even more impressed by Churchill, whom, like many, he regarded as the pugnacious, phrase-making spirit of freedom.

Churchill d'Angleterre (1943) was one of a number of long articles which Cohen published, some under the pseudonym of Jean Mahan, in wartime magazines designed to boost morale. Among the most significant of these were two reflective, autobiographical pieces which he later expanded and published as *Le Livre de ma mère* (1954) and *O vous, frères humains* (1972).

The first was prompted by the death of his mother in German-occupied Marseilles in 1943. His ambiguous feelings towards his father (to whom he had nevertheless dedicated *Mangeclous*) had not been resolved, but this elegiac memorial to his mother is made of aching tenderness, regret, self-reproach and total surrender. She had sensed that she was not Westernized enough for her successful son, who was ashamed of her strong accent and clucking attentions and whose books she did not understand. Yet hers was the perfect, selfless love that knows no limit. Though there are more fathers in the novels than mothers, Louise Coen walks abroad in them as the spirit of unreachable, absolute love and the life-giving source of the outlandish, passionate but noble and generous impulses of the 'valiant' Jewish tradition which she had passed on.

The second piece was a meditation on his acquaintance, on his tenth birthday, with racial hatred, which he does not attempt to explain in rational terms (as aggression born of collective fear, say, or as the equivalent of the territorial imperative of the animal world) but accepts as a fact of life – his life, and the life of Jews. Yet on the wider front the persecution which runs like a spiteful thread through the centuries of Jewish history, and was to culminate in the Holocaust, is itself subject to the greater power of death. But this is small consolation, for love and friendship are no less vulnerable, and human kindness is as fragile as the inhumanity of man to man. History and each person's experience surely demonstrate that exhortations to brotherly love will not suffice to soften hearts to true communion. If the only certainty is the knowledge that all are born to die, that we are brothers in death, then the only basis for moral actions is the recognition of our common mortality, a helpless, loving pity for all those, even those who injure us, who will inevitably grow old, wither and be cut down. We are all tomorrow's corpses.

Cohen remained in London after the war ended, detained by his appointment in 1944 as legal adviser to the Intergovernmental Committee on Refugees. He was responsible for drawing up a thirty-two-page travel document intended for refugees who were unable to obtain a passport. It was far superior to the old Nansen certificate (in existence since 1922), and the provisions on which it was based were eventually incorporated into the 1951 Convention on the status of refugees. It was, said Cohen with justifiable pride, 'my best book'. In 1946 he separated from his wife, and they divorced the following year when he returned to Geneva to work first for the International Refugee Organization, where he was appointed Director of the Protection Division, and then for the ILO, finally retiring from public life in 1952 to devote himself entirely to writing. In 1957 he was approached unofficially by the State of Israel, which had him in mind for an eventual ambassadorial role. He was tempted but eventually refused because he was determined to see his book through to a conclusion.

In 1955 he married Bella Berkowich, whom he had first met in 1943 and in whom he found a devoted companion and the ideal literary co-conspirator. It was to her that Cohen dedicated *Belle du Seigneur*. Work on his novel proceeded slowly, however, interrupted by long periods of serious illness, and Cohen lived a reclusive life punctuated by increasingly immediate intimations of his own mortality. It was not until 1967 that he submitted a 'monstrous' manuscript to Gallimard, who insisted on substantial cuts. Cohen reluctantly agreed, and the adventures of the Valiant which had originally followed chapter 11 appeared separately in 1969 as *Les Valeureux*.

When *Belle du Seigneur* was published, in 1968, it was hailed as a masterpiece of sustained invention and baroque power. Cohen was lionized by the press, and there was talk of the Nobel Prize. But, wary of the publicity machine, he jealously guarded his privacy until, in 1977, he was interviewed for the television literary magazine *Apostrophes*, which made him an unlikely star. His mixture of teasing guile, frailty and shrewdness appealed to a wide audience. But his last book, *Carnets 1978*, made no concessions to popular taste. He returned to his major preoccupations – death, the difficulty of faith, the eternal cruelty of man to man – but the bleakness was relieved by a gleam if not of hope then of wisdom. If the enjoinder to brotherly love has failed, we should look elsewhere and accept the 'universal irresponsibility' of men, who are what they are: not simply fallible, but mortal. Still waiting for a sign from the God he revered but could not believe in, Albert Cohen died in 1981, still keeping faith with the commonwealth of brotherly pity.

Belle du Seigneur is the longest episode of a single work which evolved slowly over four decades. The first instalment, *Solal*, is by far the most eventful. The story begins in about 1910, in Cephalonia, and tells how the thirteen-year-old Solal of the Solals, son of the island's unbending, patriarchal Chief Rabbi, resolves to escape the ghetto and fulfil his high destiny. When he is sixteen, he defies his father and elopes impetuously with Adrienne de Valdonne, the young wife of the French consul. The adventure does not last, but it widens his horizons and sets his feet on the road to the success which seems his by right. Solal has every quality: he is one of nature's aristocrats, as handsome as he is clever. But he is also driven by a sense of mission which he does not fully understand. When still in his early twenties, he is immensely rich, married to Aude de Maussane, who loves him, and is Minister of Labour in a French socialist government. Yet he senses that his success is built on the rejection of his Jewish roots – that is, of a whole area of human diversity. He tries to make amends – he fills the cellar of a mansion with needy Jews – but neither good works nor the love of Aude can redeem him. He begins to act erratically and descends into poverty and obscurity. Clutching his baby son, he kills himself, only to be mysteriously resurrected – to fight another day, perhaps, or because the fates have not done with him yet. 'The sun lit the tears, the defiant smile of the bleeding lord who now, overflowing with a lunatic love of earth and crowned in beauty, strode into the future, went forth to meet the miracle of his defeat.'

For Solal, Cohen has the same mix of affection and ridicule which Stendhal showed for Julien Sorel. His hero is also a restless, reckless spirit in search of the absolute. But while Julien is in love with love, Solal is in love with a god he cannot accept, and views himself as a Messianic figure pledged to making a world which has room for loyalty, love, Christians, Jews and all who are born to die. Cohen, whose own idealism was permanently undermined by an incapacity for faith, both shared this sense of mission and mocked it – and his jokes are very good indeed. For against the sombre history of the rise and fall of Solal must be set the 'Valiant', an unlikely quintet of middle-aged, garrulous, squabbling, picturesque cousins who, prefiguring Snow White's dwarves and the Marx Brothers, cut a considerable dash as comic musketeers.

Cohen was extremely fond of them, and introduced them to new readers on a number of occasions: he does so again in chapter 12 of *Belle du Seigneur*. 'Uncle' Saltiel is the senior member and acknowledged leader of the 'Valiant of France', so called on account of their attachment to the libertarian tradition of the Revolution of 1789 and to the florid, archaic language of the sixteenth century. United by friendship, they are constantly divided by their self-importance and bumbling incompetence. Saltiel, a failed inventor, is reduced to living by his wits: we first see him selling chestnuts on which he has inscribed verses from Deuteronomy. Naileater (so called because once, when a boy, 'he gobbled a dozen screws to assuage his inexorable hunger') is an engaging charlatan who displays endless ingenuity in devising hopeless money-making schemes, which range from setting up a university in his kitchen to a method for making shoes squeak properly so that everyone will know that they are new. Mattathias, the one-armed miser, keeps his own counsel and whatever money comes his way. Solomon, a little man with a big heart, is innocence on legs, the easily wounded conscience of the group. Michael, 'the giant', has a military bearing and a moustache which women find irresistible. The Valiant are physical, unreliable and tasteless; but they are also resilient, resourceful and endlessly optimistic: they are, in a word, everything which the popular imagination understands by Jewishness. In creating them, Cohen stands well outside the defensive tradition of much Jewish writing (from Zangwill to Bashevis Singer and Elie Wiesel) and makes no apology for the Valiant, who, for all their demented antics, represent good humour and sanity in a world which has forgotten how to live in joy. They, as much as the Law of Moses, are what Solal has denied.

When *Mangeclous* opens, ten years or so have passed. By means which are not explained, Solal has once more achieved a position of power and influence: he is now Under-Secretary-General of the League of Nations. He sends money to the Valiant and invites them to visit him in Geneva. Suddenly rich and swollen with their own importance, they make a grand tour of Europe, leaving a trail of chaos in their wake. Their adventures are as extravagant as Baron Munchausen's, and their Chaplinesque spirit is unquenchable. They join forces with Scipion Escargassas, a Tartarin from Marseilles, and Jérémie, a Jew who has been a guest of Herr Hitler's prisons, both of whom succeed in obtaining an audience at the Palais des Nations by posing as an Argentinian delegation. Solal is both amused and appalled by their absurdity, because once more he has reached a point of crisis. His idealism, which he feels like a physical need, founders on his inability to reconcile two contradictory propositions. Intellectually he is convinced that the world must be saved through Reason and the Law of Nations. But his instinct tells him that its salvation lies in Faith and the Law of Moses. But Reason and Faith are irreconcilable, and his loyalties swing wildly between their immediate manifestations – the League and the Valiant. Solal is at war with himself and turns away from the world of international diplomacy and base, self-serving functionaries towards what seem to be the greater certainties of his Jewish past. But while he never doubts the Law of Moses, he cannot believe in the God of his fathers. Moreover, he despises the fecklessness of the Valiant and the meekness of Jews like Jérémie, who will never inherit the earth however much they deserve to. He is no less aware that love of women is an eternal betrayal of love. Solal is a chemically pure idealist who lives in a comprehensively contaminating world.

Some readers may classify Solal's inner contradictions as classically Oedipal: he cannot relate to his father, whom he rejects, and feels guilt for ignoring his mother and abandoning Adrienne, a mother substitute, who is driven to suicide. Whatever the merits of such a diagnosis, Solal is certainly more easily understood if we think of him as a compulsive personality rather than as a man entirely in control of himself who tries consciously to develop a life consistent with his character. He is incapable of compromise, and there is in him more than a touch of masochism, even of the will to self-destruction. Like Buridan's ass, he finds himself between two equidistant piles of hay, incapable of making a choice between his Jewish and Westernized selves. In the event he chooses neither, but pursues the purity which eludes him with Ariane, the wife of the ineffectual Adrien Deume. She will be his partner in Perfect Love, the living proof that the will can overcome the spoiling power of existence. He knows he cannot fail to make Ariane love him, and the knowledge leads him to despise himself, Ariane and whatever purity they might one day achieve. His defeat may be magnificent, but it is inevitable. Yet though this defeat was announced at the end of *Solal*, Cohen was in no hurry to bring him to it. *Mangeclous* closes as Solal prepares for his campaign. He dons a white beard, blacks his teeth, and climbs into the filthy coat which he bought from Jérémie. Solal the contemptuous idealist is ready for battle.

Belle du Seigneur is Cohen's baobab tree in all its glory. He guides us through the tangled roots – the same characters reappear, the same ritual of revolt is re-enacted – but he also invites us now to linger over the lushness of the upper foliage, which is filled with new personalities, fresh dramas and wider dimensions. The action once more begins in early spring, with Solal taking his first extravagant steps in the long seduction of Ariane. Soon the Valiant, summoned once more by cheque, will arrive in Geneva, where their engaging but feckless optimism serves as a counterpoint to Solal's anguish . . .

But *Belle du Seigneur* is not a novel to be read for the plot. Though there are moments of high tension and drama, the forward march of the action is regularly delayed by diversions to the point where it seems as if Cohen was trying to see how slowly he could pedal his bicycle without falling off. For long periods time stands still (the action covers a mere twenty-seven months, in fits and starts), and the world which unfolds before us is oddly insulated against history.

There are few echoes of contemporary events – Mussolini's invasion of Abyssinia, the Spanish Civil War, the election of the Popular Front government in Paris – for *Belle du Seigneur* generates its own closed and claustrophobic atmosphere. A few cheeky taunts are lobbed at the 'square-jawed' Duce, but even the Hitler menace is evoked obliquely and, as in chapter 54, in allegorical terms. Cohen makes his opposition to Nazi brutality abundantly clear, but he ensures that we see it as merely the latest outbreak of the persecution to which Jews have been subjected throughout their history. Cohen's stance is moral rather than political, and this may explain why the story does not proceed beyond 1937 and into the war. Of course, it may simply be that in Cohen's mind his fictional world had assumed its definitive mood and shape by 1938. But, had he extended the time-scale, it seems reasonable to think that the horrors of the Holocaust could not have been kept at arm's length in quite the same way and that Cohen's generous, conciliatory humanism would then have been harder to sustain. As it is, he is able to stand back and point to the folly of intolerance and oppression without being accused of special pleading or of relying on Nazi atrocities to stir the reader's sympathies. Cohen's purpose was not to be achieved by locating the struggle for idealism in a particular setting, for he intended his message of tolerance to be timeless.

Paradoxically, this lack of historical specificity in no way diminishes the sense we have of the solid reality of the world of *Belle du Seigneur*. On the contrary, the minutiae of everyday living are lovingly re-corded through the eyes and thoughts of characters obsessed with their immediate selves and material things. Every corner of Cohen's immense canvas is filled with solid, intricate detail. He takes us behind the scenes at the League of Nations and politely exposes its pomposities in a series of blistering insiderly snapshots which will delight anyone who has experienced the workings of corporate organizations. He invites us to meet the ghastly Antoinette Deume, who needs no prompting to put on one of the finest bravura displays of middle-class bigotry and hypocrisy in modern fiction. Cohen not only creates a vast range of acutely observed types – from Mariette the maid to the henpecked Hippolyte and the self-serving Adrien Deume – but sustains them brilliantly over many chapters. Others, like the boot-licking Benedetti or the wild Rosenfeld, make briefer appearances, but are no less meticulously conjured. And governing all of them is Cohen's sharp eye for absurdity and his acute, unforgiving ear for the cliché, which surfaces remorselessly in the guarded, coded language of the League's servants, Mme Ventradour's sanctimonious mummery or Mariette's smug self-communings. The novel hums with voices, which are orchestrated into choruses, combined into duets, and above all set free in endless solos: few writers have dared take the interior monologue to quite such lengths. Cohen's comic talents span the widest range, from the ability to create a seemingly endless supply of sharply differentiated eccentrics, to the low farce of the Valiant and the highest social comedy.

The laughter, however, invariably has a dark edge to it. Cohen's bourgeois, like the denizens of the League of Nations, live empty lives with neither joy nor point beyond materialism, success and a grim determination to dominate others. It is a damning enough indictment, but Cohen's pessimistic picture of society is merely a prelude to a much profounder charge. Solal, moving freely through the well-fed, self-perpetuating, cosy world of middle-class cosmopolitanism, recognizes the bustle as a charade which sanitizes primeval forces. The physical strength of Neanderthal man has acquired a softer image – money and influence are its modern forms – but society still respects the animal power of nature, which is ultimately the power of one man to kill another. Strong individuals oppress the weak, and nations find philosophies to justify the annihilation of their neighbours. It is here that the Valiant come into their own. They grow older but they never change: they are the permanent standard-bearers of the Law of Moses, which provided mankind with the antidote to the law of nature. They find no difficulty in reaching accommodations with society and the world, whereas Solal's whole life has been an attempt to break free of patriarchal chains by inserting himself into history. He may have succeeded in worldly terms, but he knows that he has achieved nothing: his meteoric rise has brought him only disillusionment.

Rejecting his worldly success but incapable of believing in the God who framed the Commandments, he turns his back on public life. Still questing, he trusts to love to provide an alternative salvation. But here too disappointment awaits him. The poets are guilty of complicity with the animal in man, for they have linked love with physical beauty: if Vronsky had lost two front teeth, would Anna Karenina still have loved him to the depths of her soul? But, worse, women respond all too readily to the Neanderthal in man. Solal's last resort is his love of Ariane, who is a creature of flesh and blood and fallibly human. Through his long devotion to her, he discovers that love cannot be lived, that it is subject to the erosion of everyday life. Solal is destroyed by his inability to reconcile conflicting absolutes: God with the Law, the League of Nations with the cynicism of cosmopolitan values, and, most poignantly, love with life. He fails to save the world. He fails as Don Juan. He is a man nailed to the pursuit of an impossible goal, and as he ventures along the path of purity so the mood of the novel becomes darker and increasingly claustrophobic. The Valiant bow out, the satire fades, the social comedy disappears, until all that remain are despair, defeat and the victory of death. Solal, who wanted everything, ends by having nothing.

Solal is an example of the vanquished hero, who, Camus once remarked, is the only kind of hero possible in the twentieth century. But he is also a symbolic figure, the self-appointed Messiah who will reconcile Jews with Christians, East with West, man with woman, and man with his brothers in death. Solal is a new Icarus who has flown too near the sun. He falls, but in defeat he remains magnificently defiant: even in death he still clings to his hope for man and his belief in love. For his creator never loses faith with him. As an international civil servant, Cohen was more effective than Solal, and in his private life was uxorious to a degree. Yet he too, a Corfiote Jew who learned to be French in Marseilles and a citizen of the world in Geneva, lived his life at a busy crossroads. Unlike Solal, he was able to rise above personal tragedy and the suffering of his people and, out of the quarrel with himself and with others, made high art. The Solal cycle creates a strange, obsessive universe, as full of symmetries and repeated circular flourishes as a Persian carpet. For all its social reality, it is a world forever slipping into allegory. *Belle du Seigneur* has the epic grandeur of a descent into hell.

David Coward

BELLE DU SEIGNEUR

To My Wife

PART ONE

CHAPTER I

He dismounted and strode past hazel and briar, followed by the two horses which the valet led by the reins, through the crackling silence, stripped to the waist under the noonday sun, smiling as he went, a strange, princely figure, confident of coming victory. Twice, yesterday and the day before, he had been a coward and had not dared. Today, the first day of May, he would dare and she would love him.

In the sun-dappled forest, the still forest of age-old fears, he walked through the tangled branches, handsome and no less noble than Aaron his forebear, brother of Moses, walked on with sudden laughter, the maddest of the sons of man; laughing out of blazing youth and love, suddenly uprooting a flower and biting its head off, suddenly dancing a jig, a great lord in high boots, dancing and laughing in the blinding sun among the branches, dancing with grace, with the two unresisting animals at his heels, dancing with love and triumph while his subjects the forest creatures went heedlessly about their business, pretty lizards living their lives beneath the foliate bowers of huge mushrooms, golden flies tracing geometric patterns in the air, spiders rising out of clumps of pink heather to watch the movements of bugs with prehistoric probosces, ants grooming each other and exchanging signals before returning to their solitary tasks, itinerant woodpeckers taking soundings, lonely toads giving nostalgic tongue, shy crickets chirping, screeching owls strangely awakened now.

He halted and thereupon, after kissing the valet's shoulder, he relieved him of the case he needed for the deed to come, and ordered him to hitch the reins to a branch and to wait for him there, wait for him for as long as was required, until evening or later, wait for him until he heard the whistle. And when you hear the whistle, you must bring the horses, and you shall have all the money you could want, my word on it! For what I am about to attempt no man ever attempted before, do you hear, no man since the beginning of the world! Yes, brother mine, all the money you could ever want. Thus he spake, and he struck his boot with his crop for joy. Then he went striding towards his destiny and the house where the woman lived.

He stood before the opulent residence, built Swiss-chalet style of wood so highly burnished it looked like mahogany, and gazed up at the cupules of the anemometer as they turned slowly above the slated roof. Suitcase in hand, he carefully opened the gate and went in. In the birch-tree which hung its incandescent head, small birds kicked up a senseless twittering fuss in homage to this enchanted garden. To avoid the crunching gravel of the drive, he made a leap for the flower-beds where hydrangeas grew protected by outcrops of rockery. He reached the large bay window and there, hidden by the ivy, he watched. In the gold-wainscoted drawing-room hung with red velvet, she was sitting playing the piano. 'Play, my lovely, you have no idea of what lies in store for you,' he murmured.

He climbed into the plum-tree and pulled himself up on to the first-floor balcony, found a foothold on a stone pier and gripped a projecting wooden support with one hand, steadied himself, hauled himself up to the window-sill on the second floor, opened the half-closed shutters, pulled back the curtains, and sprang into her room. He was there, he was in her house, just like yesterday and the day before, only this time he would reveal himself to her and he would dare. Quickly now, make ready for the deed.

Leaning bare-chested over the open case, he took out an old tattered greatcoat and a moth-eaten fur hat and stared in surprise at the tie of the Order which his searching hand had found. It was crimson and very handsome. Might as well put it on since it was there. When he had tied it around his neck, he struck a pose before the swing-mirror. Oh yes, disgustingly handsome. An impassible face beneath a crown of raging shadow. Narrow hips, flat stomach, broad chest and, under the tanned skin, muscles like intertwining serpents. So beautiful, yet such beauty was destined for the graveyard, to be tinged with green here and yellow there, consigned to a coffin split by the damp earth. How the tables would be turned on all the women if they saw him then, silent and stiff in his casket! He smiled to himself, resumed his prowling, occasionally testing the weight of the automatic pistol in his hand.

He stopped and stared at his small, squat, ever-ready, ever-willing accomplice. It was already loaded with the bullet which later, yes much later ... No, not the temple, too much risk of ending up still alive but blind. The heart, then, but take care not to aim too low. The right place was at the angle formed by the base of the sternum and the gap between the third and fourth ribs. With a pen he found lying on a small table next to a bottle of eau-de-Cologne, he marked the spot and smiled. That was where the small star-shaped hole would appear, in a halo of black particles, a few centimetres from the nipple which so many nymphs had kissed. Why not shrug off the burden of living now? End his dealings with the ghastly human race, which was never happier than when hating and spreading slander? He was freshly bathed and newly shaved and would make a most presentable corpse – and a Knight of the Order to boot. But no: first attempt the impossible. 'Blessings upon thee if thou art truly as I take thee to be,' he murmured, while the piano below went on pouring out its delightful tinklings, and he kissed his hand, then resumed his pacing, a half-naked, absurd Knight, holding the bottle of Cologne to his nose, uninterruptedly breathing its fragrance. He halted by the bedside table. On its marble top, a book by Bergson and a box of chocolate fondants. No thanks, I couldn't. On the bed a notebook. He opened it, raised it to his lips and read:

'I have decided to become a great novelist. But this is my first shot at writing and I need the practice. It would be a good wheeze to write down in this notebook everything that comes into my head about my family and about myself. Then, when I've got a hundred or so pages together, I'll go back and use all the true things I've written for the start of my novel, pausing only to change the names.

'As I begin, I feel a thrill. I think I might have the sublime gift of creation. At least I hope so. So each day I shall write not less than ten pages. If I can't finish the sentence I've started or if I get bored with it, I shall write telegrammese. But of course I shall only put proper sentences in my novel. So here we go!

'But before I start, I must tell the story of Spot, the dog. It's got nothing to do with my family but it's a very fine story and shows the moral character both of the dog and of the English people who looked after it. Anyway, it's always possible I'll be able to make use of it in my novel too. A couple of days ago, I read in the *Daily Telegraph* (I buy it from time to time so as not to lose touch with England) that Spot, a black-and-white mongrel, was in the habit of waiting for his master every evening at six o'clock at his bus-stop at Sevenoaks. (Too many ats. Rephrase.) Now one Wednesday evening his master did not get off the bus. Spot did not budge from the bus-stop and waited by the side of the road all night in the cold and fog. A passing cyclist, who knew him and remembered seeing him a little before six the previous evening, noticed him again the next morning at eight, still sitting in the same place, patiently waiting for his master to come, the pet. The man on the bike felt so sorry for Spot that he shared his sandwiches with him and then pedalled off to inform the local inspector at the Sevenoaks RSPCA. The matter was looked into and it was learned that Spot's master had fallen down dead the day before in London of a heart attack. The paper gave no further details.

'I was terribly upset by the suffering of the poor little dog who had waited there fourteen hours for his master. So I sent a telegram to the RSPCA (actually, I am a Patron) saying that I was prepared to adopt Spot the dog and that they could send him to me by air at my expense. The same day I got a reply: "Spot adopted." I telegraphed back: "Spot adopted by reputable person? Send details." The answer, which came in a letter, was priceless. I shall copy it out to show just how marvellous the English are. This is how it ran. "Dear Madam, In reply to your query, I am pleased to be able to inform you that Spot has been adopted by His Grace the Archbishop of Canterbury, Primate of All England, who is, in our view, a perfectly reputable person. Spot ate his first meal in the Archbishop's Palace with relish. Yours sincerely."

'But now: My Family and Me. I was born Ariane Cassandre Corisande d'Auble. The Aubles are very top-drawer in Geneva. They came from France originally to join up with Calvin in 1560. Our family has provided Geneva with scientists, moral thinkers, frightfully distinguished, tight-lipped bankers, and a gaggle of Protestant ministers and moderators of the Venerable Company. And there was one ancestor who did something scientific with Pascal. Genevan nobility ranks second only to the English aristocracy. Grandmama was an Armiot-Silly-oh. There are the Armiot-Silly-ohs, who are very *comme il faut*, and the Armyau-Billy-ohs, who are definitely not. The second names, Silly-oh and Billy-oh, don't really exist at all, of course: they are used for convenience, so there's no need for anyone to go to the bother of spelling the last letters of Armyau and Armiot, which sound exactly the same. It's a shame, but our name is dying out. All the Aubles have snuffed it except Uncle Agrippa, who is not married and therefore without issue. And if I have children some day, they'll only be Deumes.

'Now I must say something about Daddy, Mummy, my brother Jacques and my sister Éliane. Mummy died when she bore Éliane. I'll have to change that sentence in the novel, it sounds silly. I don't remember anything about Mummy very clearly. She doesn't look very nice in her photos, her face very stern. Daddy was a minister and a professor of theology at the University. When he died, we were still very young: Éliane was five, I was six and Jacques was seven. The maid said Daddy was in heaven and that scared me. Daddy was very kind, very dignified, and I looked up to him. From what Uncle Agrippa has told me about him, he appeared cold because he was shy, but altogether a most scrupulous and upright person: he had that moral uprightness which is the glory of Genevan Protestantism. There are ever so many dead people in our family! Éliane and Jacques were killed in a car accident. I can't say anything about Jacques and dear Éliane. If I did, I'd only cry and then I wouldn't be able to go on.

'As I write, the radio is playing "*Zitto, zitto*" from the *Cenerentola* by horrible old Rossini, who was a silly man only interested in cannelloni, which he made himself. A moment ago, it was *Samson and Delilah* by Saint-Saëns. Even ghastlier. Talking of the radio, the other night there was a repeat of a play by somebody called Sardou, entitled *Madame Sans-Gêne*. Awful! How could anybody be a democrat after hearing the audience guffawing and clapping? The imbeciles positively hooted at some of the lines given to Madame Sans-Gêne, Duchess of Danzig. Such as, for instance, when she was at a court reception, she said in a plebeian accent: "'Ere we are then!" Can you imagine it? A duchess who was once a washerwoman and proud of it! And her tirade against Napoleon! I thoroughly despise this man Sardou. Of course, old Madame Deume loved it. Another thing that's horrible on the radio is the vulgar braying of the mob at football matches. How can anyone not despise people like that?

'After Daddy died, all three of us went to live with his sister Valérie, whom we called Tantlérie. In the novel, don't forget to describe her villa at Champel, with its walls crammed with bad portraits of a whole string of ancestors, verses out of the Bible and Views of Old Geneva. Tantlérie's brother, Agrippa d'Auble, also lived at Champel. I used to call him Uncle Gri. He's quite interesting but I'll describe him some other time. For the time being, I'll stick to Tantlérie. She's one character I shall certainly put in my book. While she was alive she did her best to show me as little affection as possible, though she was deeply fond of me. I am going to try to describe her properly, as though this were the start of the novel.

'Valérie d'Auble was very aware that she belonged to the Genevan aristocracy. In reality, the first of the Aubles was a draper in the days of Calvin, but that was a long time ago and there is no sin but has its pardon. My aunt was a tall, regal woman with handsome, regular features, who always dressed in black and professed the utmost disdain for fashion. Whenever she went out, she always wore a peculiar flat hat, rather like a large apple-pie, which had a short black veil hanging down behind. Her purple sunshade, from which she was never separated and which she held out in front of her like a walking-stick as she leaned on it, was famous in Geneva. She was given to good works and shared the bulk of her income among various charitable organizations, evangelical missions in Africa and an association for the preservation of the beauties of Old Geneva. She had also endowed bursaries for good behaviour for which pious girls were eligible. "Will you do the same for boys, Aunt?" She said: "I won't have anything to do with scallywags."

'Tantlérie was part of a group, which has now all but disappeared, of particularly strict Protestants who were called the Very Holy. To her way of thinking, people were divided into the elect and the damned, most of the elect being Genevan. There were a few elect in Scotland, though not many. But she certainly did not believe that being Genevan and Protestant was enough to save your soul. To find grace in the sight of the Almighty, you needed to fulfil five further conditions. First, you had to accept the literal inspiration of the Bible and consequently believe that Eve was made of Adam's spare rib. Second, you needed to be a member of the conservative party, then called, I believe, the National-Democrats. Third, you had to feel Genevan and not just Swiss. ("The Republic of Geneva is allied to various Swiss cantons, but beyond that we have nothing in common with those people.") In her eyes, the inhabitants of Fribourg ("Ugh! Papists!"), the Vaud, Neuchâtel, Berne and the rest of the Confederation were all as much foreigners as the Chinese. Fourth, you had to be connected with the "good families", that is to say, families like ours with ancestors who were members of the Little Council before 1790. Exceptions to this rule were ministers, though only *serious* ministers "and not these beardless young liberal flibbertigibbets who have the impertinence to go around saying that Our Lord was simply the greatest of the prophets!" Fifth, you should not be "worldly". This word had a very particular meaning for my aunt. For example, she viewed as worldly any minister who was cheerful or wore a soft collar or sporty clothes or light-coloured shoes, which she loathed. ("Tsk! I ask you! Brown boots!") Also worldly were any Genevans, however well-connected they might be, who went to the theatre. ("Plays are made up. I do not care to listen to lies.")

'Tantlérie had a regular subscription to the *Journal de Genève* because it was a family tradition and because, moreover, she "believed" she owned shares in it. Yet she never read this highly respectable paper and left it unopened in its wrapper because she disapproved not of its political views, of course, but of what she called its "unsuitable" bits, which included: the women's fashion page, the serialized novel at the bottom of page two, the offers of marriage, and the space given to Catholic affairs and meetings of the Salvation Army. ("Tsk! I ask you! Religion with trombones!") Also unsuitable were advertisements for corsets and "places of entertainment", an expression she used as a generic term for any suspect establishments such as music-halls, Palais de Danse, cinemas and even cafés. While I'm on this subject, in case I forget: her snooty disapproval the day she found out that Uncle Agrippa, who was dying of thirst, had on one occasion gone inside a café for the first time in his life and, taking his courage in both hands, had ordered tea. Oh, the scandal! An Auble in a place of entertainment! And while I'm still on this subject, say somewhere in my novel that as long as she lived Tantlérie never told the weeniest lie. "Live in truth!" was her motto.

'Being a very thrifty person, though she was also quite generous, she never sold any of her stocks and shares, not because she was attached to worldly goods but because she considered herself to be no more than the steward of her wealth. ("Everything which came down to me from my father must be handed on intact to his grandchildren.") I said earlier that she "believed" she owned shares in the *Journal de Genève*. In reality, not having much of a clue about financial affairs, she regarded her shares and debentures as necessary but base matters which should be mentioned as little as possible and considered them unsuitable subjects for her attention. She deferred blindly to Messrs Saladin, de Chapeaurouge & Co., bankers to the Auble family since the winding-up of the Auble Bank, an impeccably respectable firm, though she did suspect them of reading the *Journal de Genève*. ("But tolerance is my middle name: I quite understand that the gentlemen at the bank have to. They must Keep Abreast.")

'Naturally, we only saw people of our own kind, and all of them were madly pious. Within the *"crème de la crème"* of the Protestant tribe in Geneva, my aunt and her cronies formed a small clan of diehards. It was quite out of the question for us ever to have anything to do with Catholics. I have a memory of when I was eleven: Uncle Gri took Éliane and me for the first time on a trip to Annemasse, a small town in France not far from Geneva. In Tantlérie's two-horse open carriage driven by our coachman, Moses – also a strict Calvinist, despite his name – we two little girls were greatly excited at the prospect of at last seeing Catholics, a peculiar race of mysterious natives. As we bowled along, we sang to the tune of "Why are we waiting?": "Wee roff to see the Cath-er-lix, wee roff to see the Cather-lix . . ."

'But to get back to Tantlérie. Wearing her flat hat with the little veil at the back, she would sally forth at ten of a morning in her open carriage driven by top-hatted, top-booted Moses. She went off to inspect her dear city, to see if all was as it should be. If some imperfection offended her, a railing that had worked loose, a piece of ironwork that was threatening to fall down or a public fountain that had dried up, she would "pop in and see one of their lordships", which meant that she was about to give one of the members of the Genevan government a good wigging. The prestige of her name and her force of character, backed by her liberalities and connections, were such that their lordships always bent over backwards to keep her hat straight. An illustration of Tantlérie's Genevan patriotism: she once broke with an English princess who, though every whit as pious as she, had written a letter containing a joke about Geneva.

'By eleven she was back in her handsome villa at Champel, which, with her open carriage, was her only luxury. She was, as I've said, most charitably inclined, but spent hardly anything on herself. I can still see those black, very stylish dresses with a hint of train at the back, but they were all old, shiny and carefully mended. At noon the gong was sounded. At half past twelve it was sounded again and everyone had to go into lunch at once. Lateness was not tolerated. Uncle Agrippa, Jacques, Éliane and I had to remain standing while we waited for the arrival of the "chieftainess", as we sometimes called her among ourselves. Of course, we never sat down until she did.

'At table, after grace had been said, the conversation would turn on respectable subjects such as flowers ("with sunflowers, you must always bruise the ends of the stems if you want them to last") or the colours of setting suns ("I have always loved them so, I was so terribly grateful for the gift of such splendour!") or changes of temperature ("I felt rather cold when I got up this morning") or the latest sermon of a favourite minister ("it was thoroughly thought out and prettily expressed"). There was much talk too of the progress of evangelization in the Zambezi, which explains why I am very well up in the black tribes of Africa. For instance, I know that in Basutoland the King's name is Lewanika, that the Basutos call their country Lesotho and speak Sesotho. On the other hand, it was not the done thing to speak of what my aunt called "material things". One day I remember being scatty enough to say that I thought there was a mite too much salt in the soup. She frowned and froze me with these words: "Tsk, Ariane, really!" I got the same reaction another time when I could not prevent myself commending a chocolate mousse which had been served. I felt my heart in my mouth when she cast her cold eyes on me.

'Cold is right, but she was also profoundly good-hearted. She did not know how to show it though, or express it. It wasn't insensitivity but aristocratic reserve, or perhaps a fear of the carnal. Hardly ever a kind word, and on the rare occasions when she kissed me it was just a brush with the lips on my forehead. On the other hand, when I was ill she would get up several times a night and trot along in her old, regal dressing-gown to see if I had woken up or thrown the covers off. O darling Tantlérie, though I never dared call you that.

'I must remember to put somewhere in my novel the blasphemous things I used to say when I was little. I was very pious and yet when I was in the shower I couldn't help myself saying suddenly: "Mangy old God!" But then I would shout out straightaway: "No, no, I didn't say it! God is good, God is very kind!" And then it would begin all over again and I'd come out with more blasphemies. It made me ill, and I used to hit myself as a punishment.

'Another memory comes back. Tantlérie had told me that the sin against the Holy Ghost was the worst of all. So sometimes when I was in bed at night I couldn't resist the temptation of whispering: "I do sin against the Holy Ghost, I do!" Of course, I had no idea what it meant. But immediately afterwards I'd feel really scared and hide under the bedclothes, and tell the Holy Ghost that I'd only said it for a joke.

'Poor Tantlérie had no idea of all the anguish she caused Éliane and me. For example, she believed she was acting in our best spiritual interests by talking to us frequently about death, in order to prepare us for the only thing that mattered: life eternal. We couldn't have been more than ten or eleven when she was already reading us stories about model children expiring, their faces alight, with heavenly voices in their ears, going to their death rejoicing. Result: nervous wrecks, both my sister and me. I remember how terrified we were once when we read the text for the following Sunday in a Bible calendar: "Thou shalt die and be hid in the Lord." One of our little Armiot cousins had invited Éliane and me to tea for that Sunday, so I told her we weren't certain we'd be able to come because we might be hid in God instead. Ever since, though I suppose I haven't really lost my faith, I've always hated hymns, especially the one that begins: "In the land of eternal glory". I always feel miserable when I hear the assembled congregation sing it in church with the false joy and sickly exaltation with which they convince themselves they'd be only too glad to die, though in reality they ring up the doctor at the slightest scratch for him to come and make it better.

'More memories, scribble them down higgledy-piggledy, so I won't forget. I'll pad them out in the novel. Tantlérie, working at her embroidery on her tambour after morning and evening service. At church, we would often finish with the hymn "As pants the hart", which always gave me the giggles which I covered up. But Tantlérie did a lot of praying in her boudoir by herself, thrice daily and always at the same times, and we had to be ever so careful not to disturb her. Once I spied on her through the keyhole. She was on her knees with her head bowed and her eyes shut. Suddenly she smiled: it was a strange, wonderful smile, and it made a great impression on me. Also say somewhere that she wouldn't have anything to do with doctors, not even Uncle Gri. She believed in the healing power of prayer. When talking about her fear of the carnal, which I referred to earlier, mention the towels in her bathroom. She had different ones for different parts of her body. The one she used for her middle could never be used for her face. The unconscious fear of sin, the separation of sacred and profane. But no, I shan't say anything about the towel business in the novel; I wouldn't want to run the risk that people might laugh at her. I forgot to say she never read a novel in her life, for the same reason: she detested lies.

'Here I'll make a start on the telegrammese. After death of Jacques and Éliane, just Tantlérie and me at the villa, with Uncle Gri gone off to Africa as a medical missionary. My religious neurasthenia. I didn't believe any more or at least thought I didn't. That was called "the spirit drying up" in our circles. I decided to do an arts degree. At University, I met Varvara Ivanovna, a young Russian émigrée, shrewd and very bright. We soon became friends. I thought she was very beautiful. I loved kissing her hands, her pink palms, her thick hair. I thought about her all the time. In short, it was love.

'Tantlérie unhappy about our friendship. "A Russian! Tsk! I ask you!" (The "ask" very long and drawn out, like steam escaping.) She wouldn't let me introduce Varvara to her but didn't forbid me to go on seeing her, which was a lot. But one day the police came round asking questions about a girl called Sianova, who held a temporary residence permit. I wasn't home. From the policeman, Tantlérie made two appalling discoveries. First, that my friend had been a member of a group of Mensheviks, or some sort of Russian revolutionaries. Second: she had been the mistress of the group's leader, who had been deported from Switzerland. When I got back late that afternoon, she told me I was to have nothing more to do with a lewd hussy who was being watched by the police, and a revolutionary to boot! I defied her. Give up my Varinka? Never! After all, I was of age. That evening, I packed my bags. Mariette, our elderly maid, helped me. Tantlérie had locked herself in her room. She refused to see me, so I went. Could I turn all this into a novel? But to proceed.

'I went to live with my friend in town in a ghastly little furnished flat. I had very little money of my own, Daddy having lost almost every penny in some financial collapse known as a "crash". She and I were happy. We used to go off to the University together, me to Humanities and she to Social Sciences. Lived like students. The little eating places. I began using a touch of face-powder, something I'd never done at Tantlérie's. But I never wore lipstick and never shall. It's dirty and it's common. I started learning Russian so I could talk with her and we'd be closer. We slept together. Yes, it was love, but pure, or very nearly. One Sunday, I discovered through Mariette, who often used to come to see me, that my aunt was leaving soon for Scotland. This made me feel awful, because I sensed very strongly that it was the life I was leading that was in effect driving her into exile.

'A few months later, during the Easter vacation, Varvara told me she had tuberculosis and couldn't go to the University any more.

She'd kept it from me so I wouldn't worry but also to avoid making our financial situation any worse with rest cures in the mountains. I went to see her doctor at once and he told me that in any case it was too late to send her to a sanatorium and that she had a year to live at most.

'During that last year of her life, I didn't behave terribly well. Naturally, I'd given up my studies to devote myself entirely to her. I looked after her, made her meals, did the washing and ironing. But in the evenings sometimes I'd suddenly feel like going out and accepting invitations from University friends, usually foreign students, not young men and women from my own set. So now and then I'd go out to dinner or a student hop or the theatre. I knew she was very ill yet I didn't put up much of a fight when I wanted to get away for a while. Varvara, darling, forgive me, I was so young. When I'd get back, I'd feel ashamed and what made it worse was that she never grumbled. But one evening, getting back from a dance at two in the morning, I was wheeling out some excuse or other for being late, when she said quietly: "That's all very well, but I am going to die." I shall never forget the way she looked at me.

'The day after she died, I looked at her hands. One glance was enough for you to sense how heavy they were, like marble. The sheen was gone, they were a dull white colour and the fingers were swollen. It was then that I knew it was all over, that everything was over.

'After the funeral, the fear I felt in the tiny flat where she had waited for me to come back at night. So I made up my mind to move into the Hotel Belle Vue. Adrien Deume had just got a job at the League of Nations and since his parents had not then landed on him, he was living in that same hotel. One evening, it dawned on me that I had hardly any money left. Couldn't pay the week's bill. Alone in the world. Not a soul I could turn to. My uncle was in the middle of Africa and my aunt somewhere in Scotland. Anyway, even if I'd had her address, I wouldn't have dared write to her. The people in my set, cousins, distant relatives, acquaintances, had dropped me since I'd run away and started living with "the Russian revolutionary".

'I don't exactly know what happened after I took all those veronal tablets. I must have opened the door of my room, because Adrien, returning to his, found me stretched out in the corridor. He picked me up and carried me back into my room. He saw the empty pillbox. Doctor. Stomach wash. Injected with all sorts of stuff. I gather I was at death's door for several days.

'Convalescence. Adrien's visits. I talked to him about Varvara, about Éliane. He comforted me, read to me, brought me books and records. The only person in the whole world who cared about me. I was numb. The poison I'd swallowed had softened my brain. One evening he asked me if I'd marry him, and I said yes. I needed somebody who was kind, somebody to be on my side who thought a lot of me, though I fully realized that I had committed social suicide. Also that I had no money and was ill-equipped for life's battle, not trained for anything, not even fit to be a secretary. We were married before his parents arrived. His patience when I told him that I was scared of what goes on between a man and a woman.

'Shortly after I got married, death of Tantlérie in Scotland. Summoned by her lawyer to his office. By the terms of her will, though it had been drawn up after my scandalous elopement, I inherited everything, except the villa at Champel, which went to Uncle Agrippa. Arrival of Adrien's parents. Trouble with my nerves. For weeks I stayed in my room in bed reading, with Adrien bringing me my meals. Then I decided I wanted to get away from Geneva. He requested several months unpaid leave. Our travels. His kindness. My moods. One evening I sent him away because he was there and not Varvara. I called him back. He came, so gentle, so sweet. I said that I was a horrible woman but all that was over and done with now, that I'd be nice in future and that he was to go back to his work. We returned to Geneva and I did my best to keep my promise.

'When we got back, I invited my old girl friends round. They turned up with their husbands. That was the finish. Never heard from them again. They took one look at old Madame Deume and her pint-sized husband and that was that. True, my cousins, the Armiots and the Saladins in particular, invited me to things, but by myself, without a mention of my husband. Of course, I never went.

'I simply must put in old Monsieur Deume, of whom I'm quite fond, as one character, and also have old Madame Deume as another – as Bogus Christian Lady given to Pious Posing. The other day, this nasty piece of work asked me about the state of my soul and said she was at my entire disposal if I should ever want to have a serious talk with her. In her vocabulary, a serious talk means a discussion about religion. Once she had the nerve to ask if I believed in God. I said not always. Thereupon, setting out to convert me, she explained that Napoleon believed in God and consequently I ought to as well. All this guff is just her way of trying to get the upper hand. I loathe her. She is no Christian. She's the very opposite. She's a cow and a cat too. Now Uncle Agrippa is a true Christian. Good through and through, a saint. People don't come any better than true Protestants. Long live Geneva! Tantlérie was good too. Her faith was a bit Old Testamentish, but noble and sincere. And the way old Madame Deume talks is appalling. Instead of "lovely" she says "lervely". For "nice" she says "naice", for "middle" she says "middel" and "little" is "littel", and "perlease" for "please". And she sticks in unnecessary words whenever she can.

'In my novel, I must talk about her talent for making barbed comments with a smile. She always clears her throat before she does this. When she clears her throat I know there's some piece of sugar-coated spite in the offing. For example, yesterday morning as I was coming downstairs I heard the awesome clacking of her heels! She was on the first-floor landing! Too late for me to escape! She took me by the arm, said she had something interesting to tell me, led me off to her room, and asked me to sit down. She cleared her throat. Then that ghastly, luminous, child-of-God smile and she started: "Dear, I must tell you something terribly naice: I'm sure you'll be perleased. You'll never guess, but just now, before he went off to the office, Adrien popped in, sat on my lap, threw his arms around my neck and said: Mummy darling, it's you I love best in the whole world! Now wasn't that naice, dear?" I stared at her and then left the room. If I'd told her she made me feel sick I know exactly what would have happened. She would have put her hand to her heart, like a martyr about to be thrown to the lions, and told me that she forgave me and would even pray for me. She's wicked, but all the same isn't she the lucky one, because she's absolutely convinced that there's an afterlife and that she'll be there fluttering round Almighty God for all eternity. She even claims that she'll be glad to die, or as she says in her way: "to get her marching orders".

'With a view to my novel, a few more details. Old Madame Deume was born Antoinette Leerberghe in Mons, Belgium. Money troubles after the death of her father, a lawyer I think. When she was forty, short on curves and physical attractions but long on bones and warts, she succeeded in dragging nice but weak Hippolyte Deume to the altar. A former accountant in a private bank in Geneva, he was distinctly lower middle class and was originally from the Vaud. Born Belgian, she became Swiss by marriage to mild Hippolyte, who was short and wore a goatee and a moustache. Adrien is Antoinette's nephew. Her sister, that is Adrien's mother, had married a Belgian dentist called Janson. Both Adrien's parents died when he was very young, and his aunt bravely took on the job of mothering him. She had been a paid companion to a Madame Rampal who used to spend a large part of the year in the small Swiss town of Vevey, and from her she inherited a villa there. She converted it into a nursing home for religious and vegetarian convalescents. Wanting a change, Hippolyte Deume, then fifty-five and the owner of a nice little property in Geneva which earned him a pretty penny, went to stay there after the death of his wife. Antoinette made a great fuss of him and looked after him when he fell ill. When he was better, he brought her a bunch of flowers. The maid of forty summers swooned, fell into the startled arms of the diminutive accountant, and murmured that she accepted because she felt it was God's will. Through the influence of one of old Madame Deume's distant cousins named van Offel, some sort of high-up in the Belgian Foreign Office, Adrien, who was then studying for an arts degree in Brussels, was appointed to the Secretariat of the League of Nations in Geneva. I forgot to say that a couple of years before this the Deumes had adopted the little orphan who thus became Adrien Deume.

'I also forgot to say earlier that, after moving to Geneva, old mother Deume was overcome by a spiritual need to belong to the so-called Oxford Group, a religious sect. Ever since joining (she loves it because it's Christian names straight off, and, once in, a person can be on the most intimate terms with ladies who are definitely top-drawer), she has not stopped having "direction", which, in the Oxford jargon, means getting orders direct from God. As soon as she was admitted into the group, old Madame Deume began receiving direction to invite her sister-members to tea or to lunch. (She prefers to say "luncheon", which sounds better, though she pronounces it "lunching".) Since Cologny, where the Deume residence is situated, is a select suburb, the ladies received direction to accept. But on their first visit they encountered little Monsieur Deume, and subsequently received direction to turn down all further invitations. Only one, a certain Madame Ventradour, received direction to accept two or three subsequent invitations to tea. O Father, Aunt Valérie, Uncle Agrippa, noble Christian people, so genuine, so sincere, so pure! In truth, there is nothing morally finer than well-bred Genevan Protestants. That's enough for now, I'm tired. I'll go on with this tomorrow.'

The phone rang downstairs. He opened the door, crept out on to the landing and leaned over the banister. He listened. It was the old girl's voice for sure.

'No, Didi darling, no need to worry about being late. You can stay and have lunching at the Palais des Nations or go to that restaurant you like, the Perle du Lac, because there's been a big change of plan. I was just about to phone to tell you the great news. You'll never guess, darling, but Dada and I have just this minute been unexpectedly invited to lunching by dear Madame Ventradour! It's the first time we've been asked to a meal, and it will definitely cement the relationship, make it closer, less formal. As I was saying, it will mean a big change of plan, first because now I'm going to have to ring dear Ruth Granier at once to put off to tomorrow our tea-and-meditation which we'd arranged for this afternoon, and second because I had thought of having grilled red mullet for lunching and I'm not sure if it'll keep till tomorrow even in the fridge, and it would be a shame to eat it tonight, especially after the big lunching we'll be having shortly, still there it is, we'll have it tonight and tonight's quiche will do for lunching tomorrow since quiche keeps better than mullet. But getting back to the invitation, I simply must tell you how it came about, though I'll have to be quick, I've just got time, still it can't be helped, we'll get a taxi at the rank, I must tell you, you'll love it. Anyway just now, not ten minutes ago, I had the happy thought or rather a direction to ring dear Madame Ventradour to recommend a really heart-warming book to her about Helen Keller, you know, the wonderful littel blind girl who's deaf and dumb but always so terribly cheerful, because I think it's important to keep in touch, and then as we talked of one thing and another, never lowering the tone of course, she told me all about her domestic problems, you know she keeps a large staff, cook, kitchen-girl, a personal maid who trained in the very best houses, plus gardener-cum-chauffeur. Tomorrow she is to be hostess to a consul-general and his wife who will be staying with her for a couple of days and naturally she wants everything to be simply tippety-top. She had planned it so that today was set aside for the window-cleaning, and she's got thirty windows, twenty of them at the front of the house, but what should happen but the regular woman who comes in to do the heavy work was taken ill at short notice, you learn to expect it with that type, that's the sort of trick they pull and it's always at the last minute of course, they never leave you enough time to make other arrangements. Obviously, dear Madame Ventradour was at her wit's end, didn't know which way to turn. Then I had a happy thought, straight from the heart, and said I'd be only too glad to lend her my Martha for the whole of this afternoon for her windows, of which ten are stained glass, Japanese, in the modern style, you remember them from when we went there to tea in January. She was so grateful and accepted like a shot, couldn't thank me enough, she was terribly relieved. I'm glad I had that happy thought, a good deed never goes unnoticed. So I said I'd bring Martha round to her at once, the poor girl would never manage to find her way on her own to the splendid Ventradour estate. Then – she's such a spontaneous person – she gave a shriek, why not come to lunching with your husband! it'll be pot luck! Really, pot luck! everything is perfection in her house, nothing but the best according to Ruth Granier! And served according to the rules! So we've managed to land a proper invitation! What? One o'clock of course, you know, when the best people have lunching. I must say I'm very perleased I can make use of Martha this afternoon because otherwise she wouldn't have had much to do, nowadays with the washing-machine all the work is done by mid-morning, and then again it will bring her on to see how servants in a really good house do things. I made it clear to her that it'll be an honour for her to clean windows in a mansion. Of course, when we set off for the taxi-rank, we'll want her to walk a few steps behind us, on account of the neighbours. I'll ask her very naicely. Anyway, she'd feel uncomfortable walking with us, she'd feel out of perlace. Well, darling, with that good news I'll say goodbye, I must go and change my dress, then I've got to ring dear Ruth Granier and of course cast an eye over what Dada's going to wear and make a few suggestions, especially about soup, he makes a terrible noise with soup! By the by, Madame Ventradour very kindly asked after you and she was very interested by all I told her about your official duties, it's all right isn't it if I give her your best? What's that? I should say your regards? You're right, it sounds much more tasteful, she's such a refined person. Sorry, I didn't catch that. All right, as you wish. I'll tell her to come, she's playing the piano of course, wait a sec. (Silence. Then the voice again.) She asked me to tell you she can't come to the phone because she's in the middel of her sonata and can't stop. Yes, dear, that's what she said. Listen, Didi, don't bother coming home, have a quiet bite to eat at the Perle du Lac, at least you'll be looked after there. But now I'll have to hang up, must dash. Goodbye, then, darling, see you this evening, Mummy'll be here, she'll not desert her post, you know you can always count on her.'

Back inside the room, he lay down on the bed, inhaled the eau-de-Cologne while Schumann's *Scenes from Childhood* wafted up from the drawing-room below. 'Play on, my lovely, play, you have no idea of what lies in store for you,' he murmured, then suddenly he stood up. Quickly now, the disguise.

He slipped on the old faded greatcoat, which was so long that it reached down to his ankles and drooped over his boots. Next he put the moth-eaten fur hat on his head, pulling it down to hide his hair, which hung down in thin black snakes. Standing in front of the swing-mirror, he looked approvingly at his shabby accoutrement. But the most important part had still to be done. He smeared his noble cheeks with some sort of shiny gum, laid the white beard on it, then cut two strips of black tape, which he stuck over his front teeth, except for one on the right and one on the left, so that his mouth looked like an empty space flanked by two gleaming canines.

In the semi-darkness, he gave a greeting in Hebrew to his image in the mirror. He was an old Jew now, poor and ugly, though not without dignity. After all, this is how he would be one day. Even if he wasn't already dead and rotting, there'd be no handsome Solal in twenty years. Suddenly he froze and listened. Footfalls on the stairs, then Cherubino's aria. *'Voi che sapete che cosa è amor.'* 'Yes, my darling, I know what love is,' he said. He reached for the case, bounded across the room, and hid behind the heavy plush curtains.

CHAPTER 2

She entered the room humming the Mozart aria, made straight for the swing-mirror, kissed the image of her lips in the glass, and stared at her reflection. She gave a sigh and then stretched out on the bed, opened the book by Bergson, and riffled through it while she helped herself to chocolate fondants. After a while, she stood up and headed towards the bathroom which adjoined her sanctum.

There was a roar of running water, divers little peals of laughter, an incomprehensible girlish twittering and then a silence which was followed by the splash of a body decisively immersed, and then came a voice that was inflected gold. Parting the curtains, he approached the half-open door of the bathroom and listened.

'I adore water that's too hot, wait darling, no wait, we'll leave the tap trickling so it gets really boiling without our noticing, when I'm embarrassed they say I squint a bit, just for a second or two but the effect is charming, the Mona Lisa's got a face like a cleaning-lady, I can't think why everyone makes such a fuss about her, am I disturbing you Madame? not at all sir, but do turn round, I'm not fit to be seen just now, who have I the honour of addressing? my name is Amundsen Madame, that means you are Norwegian I imagine? yes Madame, how very, very nice, I love Norway, do you know Norway Madame? no but I simply adore your country, the fjords the aurora borealis those sweet seals and then I always used to take cod-liver oil when I was a girl it came from the Lofoten Islands I loved the label on the bottle, and your Christian name sir is what? Eric Madame, mine is Ariane, are you married sir? yes Madame I've got six children one of

them is black, how very nice please tell your wife she's very clever
but tell me sir do you like animals? of course Madame, I see that we
shall get along swimmingly sir, have you read that book by Grey
Owl? he's a Canadian half-breed an admirable man who dedicated his
life to the beaver I shall send you a copy I'm sure you'll like it, but I
can't stand white Canadians on account of that song of theirs you
know 'alouette gentille alouette alouette je te plumerai', I mean
saying 'gentille alouette' one minute and the next I shall pluck the
feathers off you it's disgusting, and anyway they pronounce it 'ploume-
rai' which is ghastly, they are so proud of their awful song it's
virtually their national anthem, I shall ask the King of England to ban
it, oh yes the King does anything I want he's very sweet to me, and I
shall also ask him to set up a great big reserve for beavers, do you
belong to the RSPCA? Alas no Madame, that's very bad you know I
shall send you an application form, I have been a subscribing member
since I was a little girl I insisted on being in it, and I've left a lot of
money to the RSPCA in my will, since you insist I shall call you
Eric but keep your back turned please, first names yes but familiarity
no, I must be careful not to knock the scab off because it will bleed
afterwards, I fell down the other day and grazed my knee and it's left
a little scab of dried blood and I really must remember not to knock
it off, I love picking the crust off but it only bleeds afterwards and
then it reforms and I pull it off again, when I was little I used to pick
the scabs off all the time picking them off was lovely but nowadays
picking's not allowed! oh it's not disfiguring it's just a teeny-weeny
itsy-bitsy scab and it doesn't make my knee look awful, when I'm
dressed I'll show you, anyway do you like cats? yes Madame I'm very
fond of them, I knew it Eric, nice people cannot help liking them, I'll
show you a photo of my little cat and you shall see what a splendid
creature she was, she was called Fluffy, a nice name don't you think?
it was me that thought it up, it just came to me the instant they gave
her to me, she was two months old angelic blue eyes a mossy little
ball of fluff and good as gold, she looked up at me and I was won
over at once, alas no Eric she is no longer in the land of the living, she
had to have an operation and the poor little thing couldn't take the
anaesthetic because she had a weak heart, as she died in my arms she
looked up at me one last look with those beautiful blue eyes, yes she

was in her prime, she was only two, never knew the joys of motherhood, and incidentally it was because she could not have children that after much heart-searching I allowed her to be operated on, I still blame myself even now, it's only recently that I've been able to bring myself to look at photos of her, it's dreadful isn't it how with time we come to feel less and less the hurt of losing someone we have loved deeply, to me she was a friend like no one else I ever knew, an exceptional soul with such delicacy of feeling and so terribly well-behaved, for instance when she was hungry she would rush off to the fridge in the kitchen to tell me it was her dinner-time and then she'd run back to where I was in the drawing-room and ask me to feed her so sweetly so nicely heavens she would make up to me with such good manners, opening and closing her little pink mouth sound-lessly she never miaowed such delicate, polite entreaties, yes a lovable companion an incomparable friend, when I was in the bath she would come and sit on the edge of the tub for company, sometimes we'd play I'd stick my foot out and she would try to catch hold of it, I don't want to talk about her any more it's too painful, tomorrow Eric if you want we'll go and see my squirrel, I'm worried about him he looked so sad yesterday, he's so sweet when he brings his little bits of bedding out to air in the sun or when he's taking the skin off his hazel nuts, I always give them to him without shells so that he doesn't break his teeth, Eric do you want me to tell you my ideal? oh yes Madame that would give me the greatest pleasure Madame, well my ideal would be to have a large estate where I could keep all sorts of animals, starting with a baby lion with great big paws, paws like fluffy-luffy-duffy balls of wool I'd touch them all the time and when he got big he'd never harm me, the secret is to love them, and then I'd have an elephant, a lovely old grandfather jumbo, if I had an elephant I wouldn't mind having to do the shopping I'd even go and buy vegetables in the market he would carry me on his back and pass me up the vegetables with his trunk and I'd put money in his trunk so he could pay the lady, and I'd also have beavers on my estate I'd have a river put in just for them and they could build their house in peace, it's terrible to think they are becoming extinct it makes me sad to think of it every night when I go to bed, don't you agree that women who wear beaver coats deserve to be put in jail? oh yes Madame absolutely, it's very nice talking to you Eric we agree about every-thing, and koalas, I'd have koalas too, they've got such sweet little noses, unfortunately they can only live in Australia because all they eat is the leaves of a special kind of eucalyptus tree, otherwise I'd have already had a couple brought over, that's me though, I love all animals even the ones people think are ugly, when I was little at my aunt's I had a tame very affectionate sparrow-owl quite a charming little person, she would wake at sunset and spit-spot would come and perch on my shoulder, if she wanted to look at me she swivelled her head without having to bodily move, though that ought to be to move bodily I think, she would stare without blinking her beautiful golden eyes and then suddenly she'd come even nearer and give me a kiss with her turned-down beak which looked like the nose of some old lawyer, one night when I couldn't sleep I thought I would go and talk to her for a while and she wasn't in the little house I had made for her in the loft, I spent a terrible night in the garden calling her name, Magali! Magali! alas I never found her, I'm sure she didn't leave me of her own accord because she was very attached to me, I'm convinced some bird of prey took her from me, anyway all her sufferings are over now, as long as they don't bury me alive, that scares me, I hear the sound of footsteps above my grave getting closer I scream in my coffin I call out for help I try to smash the lid, then the footsteps fade the living have not heard me and I can't breathe, but no I can breathe I'm in the bath, oh yes I love all animals, toads for instance, they make me feel sad, the croaking of toads in the night when everything is quiet is a noble kind of melancholy, true solitude, when I hear one in the night I feel a pang of nostalgia, the other day I found one with a broken leg poor thing he was dragging himself along the road, I put iodine on his leg, when I put a bandage on it he didn't struggle a bit because he knew I was caring for him, though his poor little heart was racing and he didn't even open his eyes he was so worn out, speak to me toad, come on smile for Mummy, he didn't move though he opened one eye and gave me such a beautiful look as if to say I know you're my friend, afterwards I put him in a cardboard box on some pink cotton wool so he would feel at home, and then I hid him in the cellar so that old Madame Deume wouldn't know, he's getting better thank God and he'll make it all right, I feel closer and closer to him, when I go down to the cellar to reset his bandage, he has this wonderful look of gratitude, oh and the old pavilion in the garden that nobody uses, I intend to transform it I shall make it my own private place where I can go to think, I'll put my toad there until he's well again, that way he can convalesce in nicer surroundings, perhaps he'll get so fond of me that he won't want to leave me ever, now I'm thinking a rude word but I shan't say it out loud, I'm cold run some more hot water please, that's enough thank you, it's a good thing I had these thick curtains put up in my room, makes it easier to believe the stories you tell yourself, my hermit-man is more believable in the dark, it was a mistake to have my wardrobe put here in the bathroom my dresses will be ruined, tomorrow get it put back in my bedroom that's settled then, yes become a famous novelist people will beg me to go and sign my books at charity sales but I shall refuse it's not my style, my legs are really beautiful other women's are all hairy a bit like a monkey's but me, oh no, I'm as smooth as a statue yes, darling me, you are very beautiful, and what about my teeth, would you believe Eric that my dentist thinks I've got marvellous teeth, each time I go he says Madame it's incredible there's never anything that needs doing on your teeth they are quite perfect, so you do realize how lucky you are dear man? only the truth is I'm not happy, fortunately we sleep in separate bedrooms, but in the mornings I hear him getting up he whistles the Belgian national anthem, the Aubles are old Genevan aristocracy and here I am now married into a lower-middle-class family, yes Eric you are absolutely right I've got a very good figure, my eyes are flecked with gold have you noticed? all the rest is unblemished, cheeks matt with warm tones, attractive voice, brow definitely not low nose a little on the large side but decidedly very fine, an honest unmade-up face and overall frightfully elegant, it's a terrible strain being a grown-up, presently I shall get my animals out it'll do me good, when we know each other better I shall let you see them, there are sheep ducklings a kitten made of green velvet but he's not at all well he's losing his sawdust polar bears wooden cows bears that aren't polar spun-glass dogs little bowl things made of corrugated paper you know the ones fancy cakes come in they're for bathing my bears in, sixty-seven animals all told I've counted them, the big bear is the king but I can tell you that the real king the secret king is the little elephant with one leg missing, his wife is the duck, the heir apparent is my little bulldog pencil-sharpener who sleeps in the scallop shell and looks for all the world like an English detective, but that's all silly little-girl stuff, now go away please because I'm about to get out of the bath and I don't want to be seen, bye-bye Eric, just between ourselves you are a bit of a fool all you can say is yes Madame, so go away, you're a silly young man, I am going to dress gorgeously for my very own, my private pleasure.'

Hidden once more behind the curtains, he watched admiringly as she reappeared, tall, with that marvellous face and that incredible figure, in a noble evening gown. Shadowed by her undulating train, she walked proudly round the room and from time to time darted furtive glances at the mirror.

'The most beautiful woman in the world,' she declared, and she approached the mirror, made a tender, pouting face and stood for some time gazing at herself with her mouth half open, which made her look surprised, even slightly crazed. 'Yes awfully beautiful in every department,' she concluded. 'Though that nose is a shade large, perhaps? Not at all. It's just right. Now for the Himalayas. On with the secret Tibetan headgear.'

Returning from the bathroom, wearing a Scots tam which did not go at all with the evening gown, she strode around her bedroom with the deliberate, heavy tread of the experienced climber.

'Well, here we are on the lovely old maternal mountains of the Himalayas, I'm scaling the heights of the land of night. It's empty of humans and here the last gods live on mountain-tops buffeted by awesome winds. Yes, the Himalayas are my motherland. Om mani padme houm! O jewel in the lotus! That's the set form of worship which we Tibetan Buddhists use. But here's Lake Yamirok or Yamrok, the biggest lake in Tibet! May the Gods be victorious! Lhai gyalo! Ah! prayer-flags: let us bow our head in reverence before them! Oh dear, I'm quite out of breath, a six-hour trek in this thin air, I can't go another step! Mind you, the ghastly side to being a Tibetan woman is that you're required to have several husbands. I've got four, which means four sets of gargling before bed, four sets of snores during the night and four times the Tibetan national anthem in the morning. One of these days I shall divorce all of my husbands. Oh, but I don't feel right, not right at all.'

She walked to and fro, arms crossed and hands on shoulders, crooning a lugubrious lullaby to herself, delighting in exaggerating its inaner flights, trying out a silly walk with her toes turned inwards. She halted in front of the mirror and pretended to be old and senile: eyes big and round, mouth wide open, tongue hanging out and toes still turned in. Having paid herself back, she smiled, became beautiful once more, put her Scots tam away, stretched out on the bed, closed her eyes, and began to day-dream.

'That's it! I'll settle myself with my old trick, here goes I'm knocking my head against the wall, crash, bash, that's good, and again ... harder, faster, head against the wall, like a cannon-ball, bang, that's the stuff, head's a bit cracked, but it's doing me good, very relaxing, ah that's better, great! nobody in the house but me, I'm free till this evening, I wonder if my toad will be better soon, he wasn't up to much this morning, that's it I'll put some more iodine on him, poor little thing so sweet so patient, he never complains but it must sting it can't be helped, when Mummy puts that nasty iodine on your leg it's for your own good, he's still so weak, I'll give him something to eat to build him up, I'll take him out into the garden with me when I've had my rest after lunch, you'll like that see if you don't, we'll have tea together, we'll have a picnic on the grass, or perhaps I'll become a fierce lion-tamer, I step into the cage wearing boots an intimidating crack of the whip my masterful eyes flashing fire and the twelve petrified lions back away like stags at bay oops make that beasts of prey and then the fantastic burst of applause, or better still a conductor standing sublimely in front of an orchestra and everyone claps and I barely acknowledge the applause I just stand there a bit disdainfully and then walk off looking very blasé, only it's not true, when I was ten or eleven I had to get up at seven o'clock so that I'd be at school at eight but I would set the alarm for six so that I'd have time for the heroic soldier I used to imagine I was nursing, I'll take a couple of aspireens, the two e's are to ease, they'll make me sleep, right? right, darling girl, but you are my little sweetie yes you is, don't need no old aspireens I'm sleepy enough, oh lovely it's dark, I can hardly see a thing, I love the dark, I feel closer to myself when it's almost pitch black, it's very nice in bed, by stretching my legs out right and left in my own bed I can feel what it's like to be by myself without lovey-dovey hubby, I have a feeling I shall go to sleep tonight in my evening dress, can't be helped, the thing is to get off to sleep, when you're asleep you aren't unhappy, poor Didi's sweet though, the other day he was all smiles when he brought me that diamond bracelet, but I was nice too I didn't tell him I don't like diamonds, very sweet but he keeps touching me all the time it's very irritating, I can move my arms and legs now but later on I'll be trapped in a coffin and there's earth above me can't breathe start choking, can't see how anyone can believe in the immortality of the soul, what's the use of having all those ministers of religion in the family? let's pretend there are ten pretty little koalas here in my room fast asleep in their cots with their little paws crossed over their chests and their lovely big noses looking so nice, I gave them all their eucalyptus leaves for supper before I put them to bed, I can't keep my eyes open it's the veronal I took last night still in my system I took too much, I ought at least to take off my pretty white satin slippers, but it can't be helped, too tired too sleepy, I can keep them on they won't bother me, that's enough talk now, good-night darling me, sweet dreams.'

CHAPTER 3

Sitting on the edge of her bed, she shivered in her evening gown. A madman, she was in a locked bedroom with a madman and the madman had the key. Should she call for help? No point: no one else in the house. He had stopped talking now. He was standing with his back to her in front of the swing-mirror, observing himself in his long greatcoat and the fur hat which was pulled down over his ears.

She shuddered. She saw that he was looking at her in the mirror now, smiling at her as he stroked that awful white beard. His pensive stroking was horrible. His toothless smile was horrible. No, don't be afraid. He himself had said she had nothing to fear, that he only wished to talk to her and then he would go. Even so, he was a madman and might be dangerous. He turned round abruptly and she sensed he was about to speak. That's it, pretend to listen as though you're interested.

'One evening at the Ritz, an evening decreed by Destiny, on the occasion of the Brazilian reception, I saw you for the very first time and loved you at once,' he said, and again he smiled his dark smile where two fangs gleamed. 'But how was it that I, poor and old as I am, should be present at such a glittering affair? I was simply there as a waiter, a waiter in the employ of the Ritz, serving drinks to ministers and ambassadors, a rabble of men who were once my kind in the days when I was young and rich and powerful, the days before my fall and slide into poverty. And on that evening decreed by Destiny at the Ritz, she appeared unto me, noble in the midst of the ignoble did she appear, awesome in her beauty, she and I and no one else in the crowd of smart operators and attention-seekers who were once my kind, we two alone were exiles, she as lonely as I and as heartsick and disdainful as I and talking to no one, having no friend but herself, but at the first flutter of those eyes I knew her. It was She, the Unexpected One so long awaited, revealed as the Chosen One on that evening decreed by Destiny, proclaimed by the first flutter of her long curved lashes. She, divine Bokhara, favoured Samarkand, an embroidery of intricate pattern. And who is She? Why, you!'

He stopped, looked at her, and once more there came that toothless smile, the abject badge of old age. She controlled the trembling in her legs, lowered her eyes so that she would not have to see that horrible, adoring smile. Endure it, say nothing, pretend to be sympathetic.

'Other men take weeks, months before they fall in love, and even then they love but tepidly, nor can they dispense with endless talk, shared tastes and crystallizations. All I needed was one flutter of her eyelashes. Say I am mad, but believe me. A flutter of lashes, and she looked at me but did not see me, and suddenly I beheld the glory of spring and the sun and the warm sea and the transparency of water near the shore and my youth restored and the world fresh-minted, and I knew that no one before her, not Adrienne nor Aude nor Isolde nor any who peopled my splendour and youth, I knew that they had merely prepared a way for her and were her handmaidens. No one came before her nor will come after her, I swear it on the Scrolls of the Holy Law when in solemn state they pass before me in the synagogue, arrayed in gold and velvet, the Holy Commandments of the God in whom I do not believe but revere, for I am absurdly proud of my God, God of Abraham and of Isaac, God of Jacob, and I thrill to my very core when I hear His name and His words.

'But now listen and you shall hear a marvel. Wearying of the ignoble crowd, she fled the room and the chatter of the seekers of contacts and sought voluntary exile in a small adjoining antechamber which was deserted. Who is She? Why, you! A voluntary exile like myself, and she did not know that I was behind the curtains watching her. Then, and listen well now, she went up to the mirror that hung in that antechamber, for she has a mania for looking-glasses as I do, it is the mania of sad and lonely people, and, alone and unaware that she was observed, she leaned forward and pressed her lips to the glass of the mirror. Our first kiss, my love. O my mad sister, loved at first sight, transformed into my beloved by that kiss administered by herself unto herself. Oh how tall and slender. Oh those long curved lashes in the mirror! and my soul flew out and clung to her long curved lashes. A flutter of eyes, the space of a kiss in a mirror, and she was revealed for ever. Say I am mad, but believe me. And that was all. When she had returned to the crowded room, I did not approach her, I did not speak to her, I did not wish to treat her like the others.

'Now hear another of her splendours. Late one afternoon, weeks later, I followed her along the shore of the lake. I saw her pause and talk to an old horse harnessed to a cart. She talked to it earnestly, considerately, my mad mistress, as though to a kindly uncle, and the old horse nodded its head sagely. Then it started to rain. She rummaged in the back of the cart and produced a canvas sheet which she threw over the old horse with such gestures, the gestures of a young mother. And then, listen carefully, she kissed the old horse on the neck and said, must have said, for I know her, my brilliant, crazy love, she must have said, indeed said that she was sorry but she had to go because she was expected back at home. But don't fret, she must have said, she said, your master will come soon and you'll soon be out of the rain in a lovely warm stable. Goodbye, darling, she must have said, she said, for I know her. And she walked away with pity in her heart, pity for that poor docile old creature which did what it was bid without protest, went where its master ordered and would even go to Spain if its master so commanded. Goodbye, darling, she said, for I know her.

'Day after day from that evening decreed by Destiny forth, such longing for her. Oh She of All Charms. How tall and slender and marvellous of face. Oh eyes of gold-flecked mist, eyes set too far apart, those thoughtful corners of her mouth and her lips heavy with pity and intelligence, oh She whom I love. The way she smiled, like a retarded little girl, when I hid behind the curtains of her bedroom and observed her and came to know her secret follies, a Himalayan mountain-climber wearing a tam with a cock's feather in it, queen of beasts which she took out of a cardboard box, revelling in her absurdities as I did, O my clever one, my sister, intended by fate to be mine alone, meant for me, blessed be your mother, your beauty unmans me. Oh the tender madness and terrifying joy when you look at me, the intoxication when you look at me. Oh night! Oh this love of mine inside me, eternally enclosed within me and perpetually released so that I may contemplate it, and then folded away once more and shut up and kept in my heart. Oh she who permeates my sleeping hours, so loving when I sleep, her tender complicity in my sleep. Oh she whose name I write with my finger in the air or, when I am alone, inscribe on paper. I doodle her name, carefully retaining all the letters, and I jumble them and make up Tahitian names, names for all her charms, Rianea, Eniraa, Raneia, Aneira, Neiraa, Niaera, Ireana, Enaira, all the names of my love.

'Oh she whose sacred name I speak during my solitary walks and patrols around the house where she sleeps, for I watch over her as she sleeps, and she does not know that I watch, and I speak her name in secret to the trees, and I tell them, for I am mad for her long curved lashes, that I am in love, that I love the woman I love who will love me too, for I love her as no one else could, and why should she not love me back, she who can truly love a toad, and she will love me, love me, love me, the paragon will love me, and each evening I shall wait yearningly for the moment when I shall see her again and I shall make myself handsome to please her, and I shall shave, shave myself so close to please her, I shall bathe, bathe for an age to make the time pass more quickly, and all the time I shall think of her, and soon it will be time, oh the wonder of it, the snatches of song in the car which will carry me to her, to she who waits for me, towards her long star-spangled lashes, and the soon look, the look in her eyes when I stand before her, she waiting at her door, tall and slender and dressed all in white, ready and beautiful for me, ready and fearful lest she mar her beauty if I should delay, and darting to her mirror to view her beauty, to see if her beauty is still there, still intact, and then returning to the door and waiting for me in a cloud of love, heart-stoppingly standing at her door under the roses, oh tender night! Oh youth that is mine once more! Oh the wonder when I stand before her! the look in her eyes! the love we share! and she shall lower her head to my extended hand, a simple country-girl now, and oh the wonder of her kiss upon my hand! and she shall look up at me and our eyes shall light up with love and we shall smile at loving so, you and I, and glory be to God.'

He smiled at her, and she shuddered and averted her eyes. Horrible, that toothless smile. Horrible, the words of love which had escaped from that vacant mouth. He advanced one step and she felt the danger come near. Don't cross him, say whatever he wants to hear, but O God make him go, let him be gone!

'Behold, I stand before you,' said he, 'I am come. I am old but await your miracle. Here am I, feeble and poor, white of beard, and of teeth I have but two, but no man will love you or know you as I love and know you, nor could another honour you with such love. Two teeth only, but I give them to you with my love. Will you receive this love of mine?'

'Rather,' she said and she moistened her dry lips and essayed a smile.

'Glory be to God,' said he, 'in truth glory, for here is she who redeemeth all women. Behold the first woman!'

He bent his knee before her, a gesture which made him look quite ridiculous, then stood up and came towards her, towards their first kiss, came with his dark smile that was the badge of old age, his hands reaching out to she who redeemed all women, the first woman, who suddenly recoiled, backed away with a coarse yelp, a yelp of fear and hate, collided with the bedside table, grabbed the empty tooth-glass and hurled it at that antique face. He raised his hand to his eye, wiped the blood away and stared at the blood on his hand. Then he laughed and stamped his foot.

'Turn away, you little fool!' said he.

She obeyed, turned round, stood still, alone with the fear that she was about to get a bullet in the back of her head. Meanwhile, he drew back the curtains, leaned out of the window, put two fingers to his lips and whistled. Then he rid himself of the old greatcoat and the fur hat, took off his false beard, removed the black tape which covered his teeth, and retrieved his riding-crop from behind the curtains.

'Turn round,' he ordered.

In the tall horseman with the wild, black hair and the sharp, smooth features, a dark, clean-cut diamond, she recognized the man her husband had from a distance whisperingly pointed out to her at the Brazilian reception.

'That's right, Solal, the height of bad taste,' he grinned toothsomely. 'Boots!', he said, pointing to them, and he thwacked his right leg for joy. 'And I have a horse waiting for me outside. There were two. The second, you poor fool, was for you, and we would have ridden away for ever side by side, young, with all our teeth, I have thirty-two, all perfect, you can check and count them, or you could have ridden pillion and I would have borne you off gloriously towards the happiness which is lacking in your life. But I don't feel like it now, and all of a sudden your nose is too big, and it shines like a lighthouse, and anyway it's just as well. I shall leave now. But first, female of the species, hear me! Female thou art and as a female shalt thou be done by. Vilely shall I seduce you as you deserve and as you want. When we meet again, and it shall be soon, in two hours I shall ravish you in ways that women love and cannot resist, foul and filthy ways, and you, love's great fool, shall be mine, and it is in this wise that I shall avenge the old and the ugly and all the poor innocents who could never fan your flame, and you will come away with me, in doe-eyed ecstasy. Meanwhile, stay here with Deume until it pleases me to whistle for you as I whistle for a dog!'

'I shall tell my husband everything,' she said. And she felt ashamed, foolish, shabby.

'Good idea,' he smiled. 'A duel. Pistols. Six paces so that he can't miss. Tell him he has nothing to fear. I'll fire in the air. But I know you. You won't say anything.'

'I'll tell him everything and he'll kill you!'

'I simply love dying,' he said with a smile, and he wiped the blood from the eye she had cut. 'Next time, doe-eyed!' he said with another smile and he climbed out of the window.

'Bully!' she shouted, and again felt ashamed.

He landed in the soft earth beneath, then straddled the white thoroughbred which, held by the valet, stood pawing the ground. Spurred on, the horse pricked up its ears, reared up and then broke into a gallop, and its rider laughed, for he knew that she was watching from her window. He gave another laugh, dropped the reins, stood in his stirrups and held both arms out wide, a towering image of youth, laughing and wiping the blood from the eye which she had cut, the blood which fell in streaks like living benedictions across his bare torso, behold the Knight of the Bleeding Countenance, laughing and urging his steed forward and speaking words of love into its ear.

Quitting the window, she stamped on the remnants of the shattered glass, tore page after page out of the book by Bergson, hurled her little alarm clock against the wall, and then heaved on the neckline of her low-cut gown with both hands so that her right breast fell out of the long tear she had made. That's it, go and see Adrien, tell him everything and tomorrow they'll fight a duel. Tomorrow, see the swine made ghastly pale by her husband's pistol, see him fall mortally wounded. When she was decent again, she went across to the swing-mirror and spent some time examining her nose in her reflection.

CHAPTER 4

Swinging his heavy walking-stick with the ivory raven's-head handle, all too aware of his cream spats and yellow gloves, replete after the delicious lunch he had eaten at the Perle du Lac, he strode along self-importantly, charmed by the thought of the toxins that had been burned off during his long post-prandial perambulation.

When he arrived outside the Palais des Nations, he paused to drink it in. Throwing back his head and breathing deeply through his nostrils, he admired its power and the salaries it paid. An official, he was an official for goodness sake, and he worked in a palace, an immense palace which was brand-new, the latest thing in palace design, old man, every modern convenience! And no income tax, he murmured as he made for the entrance.

Ennobled by the dignity of high social service, he acknowledged the doorman's salute with a paternalistic nod and set off down the long corridor, breathing in the gorgeous smell of floor-polish and giving somewhat feminine greetings to any superior he encountered. Stepping into the lift, he glanced at himself in the mirror. Adrien Deume, international civil servant, he told his reflection, and he smiled. Oh yes, quite brilliant, it had come to him yesterday, to think of starting a literary society. It was just the thing for increasing his list of useful contacts. All the big noises from the Secretariat would be on the committee, he decided as he got out on the fourth floor. Yes, having contacts with the big noises in gatherings that had nothing to do with admin and were on the classy and artistic side was a terrific wheeze for getting to know the right people. Offer the chair to the big boss and he could have fruitful little talks with him. And later on, when he was really in, a spot of astute manœuvring with a view to promotion to grade A!

'And that stinker Solal can be Vice-Chairman!' he sniggered as he opened his office door.

Once inside, his first glance, as always, was for his in-tray. O God! Four new files! With the twelve that came yesterday that made sixteen in all! And all for immediate action! Not a single one for information only! A charming welcome for someone just back from sick-leave. Fair enough, it had been a wangle, but VV didn't know that, he thought he'd really been ill. Really, no consideration! VV, what a bastard! (His boss, Jonkheer Vincent van Vries, Head of the Mandates Section, always signed his notes with his initials. Among themselves, his subordinates accordingly called him VV.)

'You swine!' he shouted at his boss.

Removing his peccary-skin gloves and his brown waisted overcoat, he sat down and at once began going through the four new arrivals in turn. Though the work that would subsequently have to be done was irksome, he enjoyed this first contact with a file. He liked tracing its fate and following its peregrinations in the comments scribbled on minute-sheets attached to the left inside cover where one colleague after another had noted brief views for each other. He liked rooting out the ironies, acrimonies and hostilities which lurked beneath the polite phrasing, and even, and this was a refinement of pleasure, detecting and savouring what he called Dirty Tricks or Stabs-in-the-Back. In a word, the arrival of a new batch of files, no sooner on his desk than avidly perused, brought him a whiff of the world outside and was always a stimulating event, a distraction, a diversion, which in a sense was not unlike the arrival of passing tourists who drop by on a jaded castaway on his desert island.

When he had finished reading file number four, he treated himself to the liberty of adding to the handwritten comment in the margin of the minute-sheet, next to a grammatical mistake perpetrated by an A-grade colleague, an anonymous and vengeful exclamation mark. He closed the file and sighed. That's the nice part over.

'To work!' he said when he had changed out of his outdoor jacket into an old one with shiny sleeves.

For the fun of it, he crunched a sugar lump with his front teeth. Then he took hold of his glasses by the crosspiece over his nose, whipped them off sharply to avoid damaging the legs, wiped the lenses with a piece of chamois leather which he kept in a tortoiseshell snuffbox, put them on again, picked up a folder without looking at the cover, and opened it. Ugh! Rotten luck: it was Syria (Jebel Druses), a file he definitely did not care for. Mental block on that one pro tem. Come back to it later. He closed it, stood up and, going across to Kanakis's office for a chat, swapped a few careful slanderous items with him on the subject of Pei, a Chinese who had just been made up to grade A.

When he returned some minutes later, he opened the Syria (Jebel Druses) file, rubbed his hands, and readied himself with some deep breathing. Right, to work! He marked his solemn decision by declaiming a snatch of Lamartine:

> O holy law, which levies universal toil
> In this wise are thy ways set:
> That he who would fructify the soil
> First must water it with his sweat.

Like a wrestler making ready for the fray, he rolled up his sleeves, hunched his back over Syria (Jebel Druses), and then closed the file again. He didn't seem able to connect with this one. Get back to it later when in the proper frame of mind. He stuffed it into the bottom right-hand drawer, which he called Limbo or sometimes the Lazar House. It was his repository for nauseous files which he could deal with only when he felt really up to it.

'Next please! First come first served! No favouritism!'

The second file, which he picked up at random, turned out to be N/600/300/42/4, Correspondence with the Association of Jewish Women in Palestine, which he had already glanced at last night. They were always whinging about the mandatory power! Hell of a cheek, really! After all, there was a world of difference between a group of sheeny women and His Britannic Majesty's government! Make them wait a month or two, that'll larn 'em. Better still, don't reply at all! There'd be no come-back: they're private not official. So off you go, get thee to the Boneyard! He pushed the file into the bottom left-hand drawer, which he kept for work which could be safely forgotten for ever.

He stretched and groaned, glanced smilingly at the wrist-watch he had bought last month but still fondly thought of as being brand-new. He examined the face and the back, rubbed the glass, and drooled at the thought that it was completely waterproof. Nine hundred Swiss francs, but it was worth it. It was even better than that snob Huxley's, he only said hello every other time you met him. Then his mind turned to his old Brussels chum, Vermeylen, poor sap, he had an arts degree and was currently teaching grammar to scruffy kids for starvation wages, something like five hundred Swiss francs a month.

'I say, Vermeylen, take a peep at my wrist-watch. It's a Patek Philippe, the best Swiss make, old man, a first-class time-keeper, old friend, guaranteed to keep perfect time, comes with a built-in alarm, see? if you want I'll set it off for you, and completely waterproof, you can have a bath without taking it off, you could even wash it in soap and water if you wanted, and none of your gold-plate, it's solid gold, eighteen carat, see the hallmark for yourself if you like, two thousand five hundred Swiss smackers, old bean!'

He snickered with pleasure and thought kindly of good old Vermeylen and his big steel pocket-watch. Poor Vermeylen, never had the breaks, a really good bloke, he liked him a lot. Tomorrow, he would send him a large box of the very best chocolates, the biggest size they had. Vermeylen would be delighted to sample them with his poor, sick, tubercular wife in their gloomy little kitchen. It was very nice to be nice. He rubbed his hands together at the thought of how pleased Vermeylen would be. Then he opened another file.

'Damn! Not the Cameroon Acknowledgement again!'

This Acknowledgement business was never-ending. He was fed up to the back teeth with acknowledging receipt of a French government report on this to-do about trypanosomiasis in the Cameroons! He couldn't care less about a lot of nig-nogs in the Cameroons and their sleeping-sickness! Still the Acknowledgement was urgent: there was a government involved. Absolutely must concoct something today. The bloody file had been toing and froing for weeks. It was VV's fault for sending it back to him so many times for amendment. And every time he had had to start from scratch. The last time was because of the insofar as. Ever since the Secretary-General's principal private secretary had told van Vries that he did not care for insofar as, VV had been on the lookout for insofar as. The mentality of a slave! What was it this time? He read his chief's memo: 'Dear Deume, Please modify the final paragraph of your draft. The word "you(r)" appears four times. What would the French government think of us? VV.' He reread the paragraph: 'I am most grateful to you. I hereby acknowledge receipt of your Report which, you may rest assured, will be forwarded as from you via the usual channels.'

'Oh, fair enough,' he admitted. 'Bloody Cameroon nig-nogs! Why don't they all just die of their sleeping-sickness and have done with it!'

Listless and moodily surrendering to his thoughts, he rolled his eyes and let his head sag to one side over his desk. He opened and closed the malignant file several times, and each time he swore violently. Finally, he straightened up, reread the paragraph he had to rewrite, and groaned. Right. OK. He'd do it at once.

'At once,' he yawned.

He got to his feet, made for the safe haven of the gents, a legitimate procrastination. To justify his presence there, at the streaming china stall, he tried and then merely pretended to go. When he'd finished, he looked at himself in the tall mirror. With one hand on his hip, he admired himself. This suit, light brown with small checks, really looked a treat, and the jacket emphasized his waist neatly.

'Adrien Deume, man of fashion,' he confided once again to the mirror, while he tenderly combed his hair which he lovingly and expensively washed every morning with eau-de-quinine.

Then he sallied forth with warlike tread. As he passed van Vries's office, he made a point of informing his hierarchical superior, though in a whisper and in terms totally lacking in refinement, that he was a bastard and his mother was a tart. Pleased with himself, he gave a schoolboy snigger which was his next-best thing to a laugh, a boiled-down, symbolic laugh which he managed by shutting his eyes and clearing the back of his throat. Then, as he had done yesterday, he stepped into one of the paternosters, which are doorless lifts that go endlessly up and down and are an invaluable expedient for bored civil servants. When he reached the fifth floor, he got out and stepped into the lift that was going down. On the ground floor, looking extremely busy, he jumped out and got into the lift that was going up.

Back in his coop once more, he decided to make up for lost time. To put himself in the mood, he conscientiously worked through his breathing exercises. (Because he thought so much of himself, he was always on the lookout for new ways of making his own dearly beloved person healthier. He was a great believer in tonics and tried a steady stream of them, at intervals of a few weeks, the latest always being so much more effective that the one before was promptly discarded. He was currently ingurgitating an English variety which he said was wonderful. 'This Metatone is terrific,' he told his wife: 'I've been feeling like a new man since I started taking it.' A fortnight later, he would drop Metatone for a miraculous multivitamin preparation. Virtually unchanged, his verdict then became: 'This Vitaplex is terrific. I've been feeling like a new man since I started taking it.')

'Perfect!' he said, as he exhaled for the twentieth and last time. 'Well done, old man. And now, to work!'

But first, a glance at the *Tribune*, just to keep abreast of things. He had the old porter well trained, right enough: he brought him the *Tribune* and *Paris-Soir* every day at four on the dot! Oh yes, he was that type, knew how to get other people to do as they were told. He opened the Genevan evening paper and mumbled his way through the headlines. General election in Belgium, a new victory for the royalist party. Excellent. Degrelle was a marvellous man. Yes, he felt he could connect with Degrelle, who'd soon rid Belgium of the mafia of Jews and freemasons. A disruptive influence, Jews. And Freud, with his crackpot ideas, no one knew where they stood any more! Right then, now to work!

He sat down at his desk, put petrol in his lighter, though, having been filled the day before, it did not need it, but he was fond of his little friend and liked taking good care of it. When he could not make this diversion last any longer, and needing to see a friendly face, he looked at himself again in his pocket mirror. He loved his round, childlike features, his earnest blue eyes behind the large horn-rimmed glasses, and he nodded approvingly at his small paintbrush moustache and his short, neat fringe of a beard, the beard not just of an intellectual but of an intellectual who was also an artist. Perfect. Was his tongue coated? No, all normal, as pink as could be wished for. Perfect.

'Not bad, Lord Deume. A fine-looking man. His missus has got nothing to complain about there.'

He put the mirror away in its crocodile-skin case and yawned. Tuesday today, a miserable day, a day without hope. Another three and a half days to get through. To console himself, he stared at his wrist-watch. In the privacy of these four walls, knowing he was not observed, he planted a small kiss on its face. 'Little pet,' he said. Then he thought of Ariane. Oh yes, he was the husband of a beautiful wife. He was in his rights if he wanted to touch any part of her, breasts, behind, as he wanted, whenever he wanted. A beautiful woman all to himself. Say what you will, marriage had its good points. Tonight, then, for sure. Still, for the time being, to work, since toil is the holy law. Where shall we start? O God, he had forgotten! The British Memorandum, of course! Comments needed, most urgent! That bastard VV! Always wanting things urgently! He riffled through the pages of the thick document. Two hundred pages, the swine! They seemed to have plenty of time to waste in the Colonial Office in London! What's the time? Nearly twenty past four. Just over an hour and forty minutes to go before six. He'd never have time to read two hundred single-spaced pages in an hour and a half, give or take a few minutes. What he liked was a fair stretch of time in front of him, at least four hours, so he could put in a good stint and know he could finish what he had started, that is, get some serious work done. Anyway, this rubbish had to be read straight through, so that he would have an overall view. And anyway, most urgent, even when underlined, didn't mean same day. God, two hundred pages! Perfidious Albion! Right, he'd read the stuff tomorrow morning, from start to finish!

'Agreed, *nem. con.* Tomorrow morning without fail. Nine o'clock on the dot, just watch me! Oh yes, when this Deume cove puts his mind to it you'd better look out! He'll make the windows rattle!'

He shut the British Memorandum. But its bulk dismayed him still. He pushed it into the Lazar House and then went tsk with his tongue.

To round off the afternoon, he needed some lightish task, something refreshing. Now let's see. The Cameroon Acknowledgement? No, that was too small, since he still had a good hour to play out. Put the Cameroons to one side instead, it'll fill a gap some time or other. Yes, but the Cameroon Acknowledgement was urgent too. In that case, do it in a while.

'Thassa ticket. In a bit,' he said in a funny accent to beguile the time, 'in a bit when we rin the proper framamind.'

But now that the British Memorandum was shut away, he was quite capable of forgetting it existed! And it had a top-priority rating. Now let's not have any slip-ups! He opened the Lazar House and took out the Memorandum, placed it bravely in his urgent tray, and congratulated himself. There. A clear indication that he was ready to show willing, that his mind was quite made up to deal with it first thing in the morning. It wasn't long before he masked its baleful presence by covering it up with his *Tribune de Genève*.

His mood brightened, he filled his pipe, lit up and drew on it. Excellent this Dutch mixture, highly aromatic, must send some to Vermeylen. Still sucking on the stem, he did some sums on a pad and amused himself by converting the gold-value of his salary into Belgian francs, then into French francs, in which it seemed enjoyably so much more. Amazing, really, what he earned! Ten times as many shekels as old Mozart ever did!

(The snigger which followed calls for a word of explanation. Just before the start of his sick-leave, he had read a biography of Mozart and had been extremely taken with the chapter devoted to the small amounts of money earned by the composer, who had died in poverty and been buried in a common pauper's grave. After making enquiries in the Economics Section about the purchasing power of various European currencies between 1756 and 1791, he had arrived at the conclusion that he, Adrien Deume, earned ten times as much money as the composer of *The Marriage of Figaro* and *Don Giovanni*.)

'In short, old Wolfgang Amadeus wasn't much cop at fending for himself!' he sniggered again. 'He'd have never been able to afford a watch costing nine hundred Swiss francs!'

Now launched on this tack, he did some more sums. The ceiling of someone on a grade A was sixteen times more than Mozart earned, a first embassy secretary ditto, a head of section twenty times more than Mozart, a minister with portfolio ditto, well more or less ditto, and an ambassador forty times more than Mozart! As for Sir John, hell's teeth, fifty times more than Mozart if you included the entertainment allowance! Or put it this way: the Secretary-General of the League of Nations was earning more than Beethoven, Schubert and Mozart put together! The League of Nations was some set-up! It certainly did things in style!

Highly delighted, he began whistling a sublime theme by the non-self-fending pauper, one of whose symphonies had been given a respectful hearing the night before and had been vigorously applauded by the gaggle of self-fending grade Bs and grade As, heads of section, ministers and ambassadors, all of whom were music-mad but money-wise.

'In short, my dear Mozart, you were had,' he concluded. 'Fine. Right. And now for a little thought about one's social life.'

Yes, a phone call to dear Penelope, Kanakis's wife, an absolute must. According to the etiquette in these matters, one should always thank one's hosts the day after one's been to dinner. This he now did. When his call to Kanakis's wife was finished, he gave a sigh. Oh dear, why did Ariane have to make him say all that guff about migraine, all because she couldn't stand the Kanakises, though they were delightful friends. Now for a careful call to Madame Rasset, who wasn't just anybody but the daughter, no less, of the Vice-President of the International Committee of the Red Cross! He had really got on awfully with her at the Kanakises last evening! Charm her? He had charmed her off her branch, anyone could have seen it a mile off. All the same, the Rassets hadn't been in touch with them for four months. And yet they'd been positively throwing invitations about for a couple of months now, having lots of interesting people round, even a princess according to Kanakis. And all because, of course, they had not reciprocated for the dinner they'd been to. Hence the reprisals. Though it was fair enough really. If the Deumes stopped introducing them to interesting people, why should they introduce interesting people to the Deumes? It was all Ariane's fault, who didn't care much for them either. But things would have to be patched up pretty smartly with the Rassets, who were money in the bank from a social point of view.

He dialled the number, cleared his throat, and got ready to put on his best cut-glass accent.

'Madame Rasset? (Then, in a hushed, muted, transmuted, confidential, ecclesiastical, circumspect, careful, winning, oily voice, which he imagined was the acme of social charm, he announced himself:) Adrien Deume here. (He was inexplicably proud of his name.) My dear Madame Rasset, how are you? I trust you got home safely last night. (This with a flirtatious edge:) Did you have sweet dreams? Was I in them?' (He poked out his tapering tongue and then retracted it sharply as he was in the habit of doing whenever he was giving his impression of a witty, sophisticated man of the world.)

Et cetera. He put the phone down, stood up, buttoned his jacket, and rubbed his hands. Whacko! The Rassets booked for dinner on Tuesday 22 May! Capital, capital. Oh yes, everything was coming along swimmingly on the social front! Rising like a rocket, old bean! The Rassets are frightfully well connected! 'Adrian Deume, star of the social scene!' he exclaimed and, for joy, he drew himself up to his full height, twirled round and round, clapped his performance, acknowledged the applause with a bow, and sat down again. Delighted with himself, he repeated for his own benefit the clever, cultivated morsels he had served up for la Rasset, and again his tongue darted out like pink lightning only to disappear at once after a quick wipe of his upper lip.

Excellent. Congratulations. And now for some thought to other couples to invite who would be on the same wavelength as the Rassets. The Kanakises, of course. They were owed. VV too, best keep in with the swine. He'd see about the other couples tonight when he got home, he'd look in his card-index of addresses. On the whole, it would be a good idea to mark the cards with little metal tabs of different colours according to social rank. For example, red for really top-drawer people. It would simplify the whole business of invitations. Reds would be asked only with other Reds, and Blues only with other Blues. If a B was promoted to grade A, all that was needed was to remove the Blue tab and substitute a Red one, and when the index was mostly Red he could get rid of the Blues altogether. Dump the Blues in the waste-paper basket!

'Right. That's enough time wasted. Now to work. But first a little wander round, just a couple of minutes to stretch the old legs and clear the tubes before we get back to it.'

In the grounds, he joined a group of four colleagues who had all stepped outside for the same purpose. He was immediately drawn into the conversation, which covered three issues of great moment. To begin with, there was the matter of mouth-watering travel plans for the fast-approaching holidays, which were outlined and listened to with equal absorption by the five civil servants, who communed in a delightful sense of caste and solidarity in privilege. Next, cordially colluding in their own good fortune and well-disposed towards each other because they all shared the same comfortable life, they elaborated, in a mood of charmed optimism, on the make of their next car, which they had already decided on.

Then, moving to the last subject, they talked heatedly of unfair promotions looming on the horizon. Garraud, a B in the Economics Section, spoke of the selection process for a grade-A post details of which had just been advertised. The qualifications required, in terms of nationality and linguistic competence, were so specific that it was as clear as day that the whole thing had been deliberately rigged for the benefit of Castro, the section's Chilean B. Everyone grew hot under the collar. It was a put-up job, it was obvious! And all because, of course, Castro was the darling of his delegation! 'Sickening, unadulterated favouritism,' exclaimed Adrien. Whereupon, Garraud declared that if Castro was appointed, then he would ask for an immediate transfer to another section! Work under somebody like Castro? Never! Yes he would, he'd get a transfer. And they would have no choice but to manage as best they could without him!

'Sorry, I have to go,' said Adrien. 'Duty calls. I've got a big job waiting for me.'

Back in his office, he stared at his fingernails and sighed. An incompetent like Castro! He laughed bitterly as he recalled the draft of a letter which the ignoramus had begun with an 'I write to officially state' and ended with a 'militate these drawbacks'! And they were about to make an ass like him a grade A with a leather armchair, a glass-fronted lockable bookcase and a Persian carpet! If they did, then the denizens of this rotten hole would have seen the lot.

Dipping from time to time into the box of fondants he had taken out of Limbo, he mused dreamily about whether he should buy a monocle. Huxley was terribly smart with his. Too bad if a monocle was less convenient than glasses, he'd just have to get used to it. Only how could he prevent his colleagues thinking he was making a spectacle of himself? One glimpse of him turning up one morning wearing one and they would laugh, especially for the first couple of days. Huxley was a different matter altogether. They had been used to seeing him with a monocle ever since he had first joined the Secretariat, and anyway he was related to Lord Galloway. Heller too was frightfully smart with his. Those two had all the luck. According to Kanakis, Heller was a baron, an ancestor of his having been raised to the peerage by the Emperor of Austria. Baron de Heller. Baron Deume: now that would be something!

'I'll have to find some dodge to help the monocle go down. Could I say my optician has discovered that my sight is weak in my right eye only? Maybe, though it's a shade premature. Wait until I'm an A, I'll have more nerve then. Anyway, a monocle might annoy that stinker Solal. What on earth did he do to manage to get himself appointed Under-Secretary-General? A Jew-boy born in Greece who now has French nationality, it's enough to make anyone puke! Obviously, the Jewish mafia! In any case, if it really is true that Castro's going to be put up to an A through sheer, rotten influence, then I'm not going to take it lying down! I'll stage my own go-slow, oh yes! And halve my productivity!'

When he had finished the last fondant, he gave a little whinny of pleasure. The day after tomorrow was the opening meeting of the Tenth Session of the Permanent Mandates Commission! He loved the sittings of the PMC. No need to stay stuck in an office, you could listen to the debates and feel at the centre of politics with all that string-pulling in the lobbies, all those confidential tip-offs, and no VV bothering you with draft letters or sending over more files, you could give your full attention to the Commission, it was fun, it was high drama, comings and goings, quick fetch a document, come back and sit at VV's right hand, whisper a word in the ear of some high-up on the Commission, smile knowing smiles, savour the double-dealing and above all chat on an equal footing, well almost, with the delegates during the recesses, hands in pockets, trickling over to VV to repeat something said in confidence by a delegate, in short it was high politics. Very subtle that move of his with Garcia. The really clever bit was getting hold of the latest slim volume of poems by the Argentinian delegate and learning one by heart.

'Ambassador, may I venture to say how very much I admired "The Galleons of the Conquistador"?' and he would go straight into a recitation of his putrid poem, intone it with eyes downcast, a big performance long on emotion, it should come across very sincere, in short lay it on thick and then something about how the French Academy honoured itself by honouring him, etc. He'll love it, we'll talk about books, we'll see each other again, we'll have lunch together, and at our third meeting I'll let slip I'm at the top of grade B! He'll have a word with Sir John and I'm in!'

He gave a stage snigger, like a triumphant villain in a play, then laid his head on the desk and groaned. Straightening up, he opened the Cameroon file. He leafed right through it unseeingly, turning his yawns into little tunes. He shut it, took out his lighter and flicked the wheel. Was the flame not just a trifle too low? He examined the wick, decided reluctantly that it was the right length, removed the flint, noted that it was worn right down, replaced it with a new one, humming the while. How satisfying to know that there was a new flint in one's lighter. 'You can't complain, I look after you,' he said to the lighter. Then he frowned. No, it was not certain that his Garcia ploy would work, not certain at all.

In fact his only real guarantee was a personal intervention by one of the bigwigs. Oh yes, the top men knew exactly how to work the promotions racket, manipulate the budget, arrange for posts to be transferred from one section to another and so forth. And the most suitable bigwig was Solal whose word was law throughout the organization. Give him five minutes and the swine could get you made up to a grade A. Hell's teeth! to think that your fate was in the hands of a yid!

'But how can I get him to do the necessary for me?'

He cupped his head in his hands, leaned forward again until his forehead was on the desk, and remained there for some time without moving, breathing in the depressing smell of the imitation-leather top. All at once he sat up. Aha! he exclaimed at the prospect opened up by an idea which had just emerged. Aha! how about toddling off and loitering in the vicinity of the Under-Secretary-General's office? If he hung around long enough he would be bound to see him pass by sooner or later. He would say good-morning or whatever and, who knows, perhaps the yid would stop and they might exchange a few words.

'Right. I'm all for it. It's worth a try. So, gentlemen, the matter is settled,' he declared as he stood up and buttoned his jacket with gusto.

No sooner said than done. He did his hair, combed his beard, looked at himself in his pocket mirror, straightened his tie, undid his jacket, pulled on it to improve the hang, refastened the buttons, and then left his office, gripped by a vague uneasiness.

'The battle for survival,' he murmured in the lift.

Getting out on the first floor, he had second thoughts. Was it dignified to hang about in the hope of meeting up with the Under-Secretary-General? His conscience came up immediately with the answer that it was his duty to fight. There were chaps who were As but didn't deserve to be. He did. Therefore, by trying to catch the eye of the USG, he was fighting for right. Besides, if he were indeed to be promoted to a grade A, he would be in a position to serve the cause of the League of Nations more effectively, for he would then surely be entrusted with serious political business, duties which were worthy of him. And in any case, with the higher salary, he could do a lot of good in smaller ways, like lending a helping hand to good old Vermeylen. And, not least, the honour of Belgium was at stake.

At peace with his conscience, he walked up and down in the corridor, checking from time to time that his flies were not undone. Suddenly he stopped in his tracks. If anyone saw him hanging about empty-handed, what would they make of him? He hurried back to his office, returned breathing hard with a fat file under one arm which made him look earnest and busy. Fine, but even so hanging around slowly still made him look idle. So he strode purposefully down the whole length of the corridor. If the USG did appear, then it would look as though he were rushing off to see a colleague with the redeeming file under his arm. Yes, but what if the USG should come by at the delicate moment when he had reached one end of the corridor and was turning to go back the way he'd come? In terms of probabilities, there was little risk of that happening. Anyway, if he were to be taken unawares at the critical instant when he was making his turn, an explanation would not be hard to find. That's it, he'd say he'd changed his mind, that before going to see X he had thought it would be better if first he went and consulted Y. Whereupon he embarked upon his frenzied toings and froings. He marched in hope and perspiration.

'Oh hello, Arianny, what a lovely surprise, how sweet of you to call. Excuse me just one second, darling.' (He pretended to speak to a colleague who had supposedly just come into his office, and in a superior voice, with his mouth close to the receiver so that his wife would not miss a word, he said: 'Couldn't possibly. I shan't have time to see you today. If I've a moment free tomorrow, I'll let you know.') 'Sorry, darling, that was Huxley wanting some information, you know, the one who rather fancies himself, but that sort of thing doesn't wash with me.' (Huxley, Solal's principal private secretary, was the best turned out but also the most overbearing Englishman in the whole Secretariat. Adrien had selected him as his victim because he knew for certain, alas, that he would never be invited to Huxley's house. So there was absolutely no risk of Ariane's ever noticing that he could be very pleasant to the snob in other circumstances.) 'Well now, darling, and to what do I owe the pleasure of hearing the sound of your lovely voice?' (A flash of his tapered tongue, pushed out and sucked back in at once, a habit he had copied from Huxley.) 'You want to come and see me here? How splendid! I'm delighted! Let's see, it's ten to five now. Take the car and try to come directly, will you? I'll show you my little Brunswick, you know, I told you about it, that improved pencil-sharpener with the handle you turn, I ordered one from Supplies before we went to Valescure, a porter just brought it. I haven't tried it yet but I think it's pretty good.'

There was no reply. She had hung up. He wiped his glasses. A funny girl, his Arianny, but what charm! Yes, kiss her hand when she arrived, that would be the refined smart thing to do. Then he'd usher her to a chair with a touch of the Quai d'Orsays. Annoyingly, all he had to usher her to was an ordinary straight-backed affair rather than a proper leather armchair. But 'I write to officially state'! And 'militate these drawbacks'! Patience, patience!

'Is that all you can say? But there is absolutely nothing I can do, old man, I've done my level best to get to meet that stinker Solal, confound him! What do you want me to do, it's not my fault if that swine Huxley happened to come by and give me a queer look, obviously he was wondering what on earth I was doing there clutching a thick file. So what did you expect? I had to clear off, there was nothing else for it. I'll have another go tomorrow, all right? Right. Fine. Now leave me alone. Anyway, I've got other things on my mind. I must see how our little Brunswick performs. Come on then, pet.'

Feeling quite excited, he put the first pencil in the slot, turned the handle gently, admired its smooth, well-oiled action, and then took the pencil out. A perfect point. The Brunswick was a good little worker, the two of them would get along like a house on fire.

'I love you,' he told it. 'And now for the next of the bunch!' he said, picking up another pencil.

A few moments later the phone rang. He withdrew the seventh pencil from the sharpener and picked up the receiver. It was the porter at the front entrance asking if a Madame Adrien Deume could come up. He replied that he was in a meeting and would phone the moment he was free. He hung up, poked out the end of his tongue, and then put it away again. Good for the image being in a meeting and making her wait a while!

'In a meeting,' he said, archly articulating, and he put the pencil back into the machine, gave it three turns, removed it, inspected it, decided it was done to a T, and pricked his cheek with it to test its sharpness. A marvel! He would do some more tomorrow. But now, get things ready. He moved the chair she would sit on to the right spot. Alas, it was humble and uncomfortable, a skeleton of a chair which had junior civil servant written all over it! And Castro was about to rise to a leather armchair for visitors! But to work. First better smarten up. To begin with, expunge all dandruff.

With his pocket mirror propped up against the *Statesman's Year-Book*, he brushed the collar of his jacket and then his beard, smoothed down his eyebrows, tightened his tie, inspected his nails and pronounced them clean, peered at his round cheeks and found a blackhead.

'We'll have a little squeeze of you, you little bastard.'

When the little bastard had been winkled out, he examined it with satisfaction then got rid of it by squashing it on his blotter. After a quick wipe of his shoes with a cloth, he emptied the ashtray into the waste-paper basket, blew his desk-top clean, opened three files to give the impression he was busy, and pushed back his chair. That's it, not too near the desk, leave himself room to cross his legs. Finally, he tucked his handkerchief into his left sleeve, as Huxley did. The Oxford touch, casual elegance, a hint of the queer, but a terribly fashionable queer. Titivations over, she could now be shown up, his meeting was over. No, on second thoughts don't phone the porter, go down and fetch her: that would be more gentlemanly, more British Foreign Office. And besides, she could be shown round the Palais, since this was the first time she'd been since the Secretariat was relocated here. She would be bowled over.

'Carried, let's bowl her over,' he said, and he stood up, buttoned his jacket, and inhaled great lungfuls of air to make himself feel manly.

CHAPTER 5

'Office of the French Under-Secretary-General,' murmured Adrien Deume, glancing with an apprehensive nod of his head towards a tall door. 'That's Solal, you know,' he added in an even lower whisper, as though saying the name aloud was to court danger or infringe some rule. 'They say it's fabulous inside, done out with Gobelin tapestries, a gift from the French government.' (He regretted the 'they say', which made him sound like an underling and showed that he had never yet set foot inside the sanctuary. To counter the effect, he cleared his throat in a soldierly sort of way and, putting on a spurt, stepped out determinedly.)

As they walked along corridors and climbed staircases, he introduced his wife to the splendours of his own beloved Palais des Nations. Self-important, behaving as though the place were in fact partly his, enamoured of his cushy but noble number and eager to stress its thrilling official character, he proudly pointed out the gifts from various countries – carpets from Persia, wooden figures from Norway, tapestries from France, marble statues from Italy, paintings from Spain and the rest of the offerings – and explained the exceptional qualities of each.

'Of course, the whole place is enormous, you know. Imagine, one thousand seven hundred doors, all with four coats of paint, which ensures that they show up perfectly white, I keep up with these things, as you'd expect, I often used to pop down while the work was being done to see how they were getting on, and, do you see, every door with its own chrome metal frame. And there are one thousand

nine hundred radiators, twenty-three thousand square metres of linoleum, two hundred and twelve kilometres of electric cable, fifteen
hundred taps, fifty-seven water hydrants and a hundred and seventy-
five fire extinguishers! It all adds up, doesn't it? It's enormous,
enormous. For instance, how many lavatories do you reckon we've
got here?'

'I've no idea.'

'Go on, say a number, how many do you think?'

'Five.'

'Six hundred and sixty-eight!' he said distinctly, with barely controlled pride. 'And they've got everything, but everything, you
know! Mechanized ventilation by fans which extract and replace the
air eight times every hour. Automatic flushing every three minutes to
cater for people who forget or are too lazy to bother. If you like, I
could show you round one.'

'Some other time. I'm feeling a bit tired.'

'Right-ho, fair enough, another time. But here we are! This is it!
After you, dear lady,' he said, pushing the door open. 'This is my
little *chez moi*,' he smiled, his throat tight with excitement. 'What do
you think of it?'

'It's very nice.'

'Obviously, it's not the de-luxe model, but it's a neat little set-up,
and practical too.'

Eager to show off its many excellent features and share its delights
with her, he explained the various amenities of his new coop, peering
at her to see the effect produced by each. He ended with a eulogy of a
metal cabinet, a most practical arrangement, with two hangers, one
for his overcoat, the other for his jacket, and a Yale lock, so no
chance of anything being stolen, and the dinky little drawer under the
top shelf, so convenient for keeping those personal odds and ends –
aspirins, iodine, indigestion tablets, petrol for removing stains. He
gave a little laugh. He had forgotten to show her the most important
item! What about his desk, then! It was brand new, as she could see,
basically almost exactly the same as the model issued to As, very
functional, really well designed.

'See? By turning the key in this middle drawer, I can also lock the
left-hand and right-hand drawers too, twelve all told. It's really

terrific, don't you think? And this key is a Yale too, which means the best.'

Basking happily in the esteem he had generated, he sat down in his chair, pointing out that it was the very latest swivel type which gave excellent support to the back, then propped his feet on the edge of the desk, like van Vries, and began see-sawing to and fro gently in his chair, also like van Vries. And rocking himself in his might and power, his hands clasped behind his head the way van Vries did, this future corpse found a suitable opening to say that during a recent discussion with his boss he had been pretty outspoken, fiercely independent and a master of the devastating comment. Suddenly struck by the thought that this same hierarchical superior might come in unexpectedly, he put his feet down and stopped see-sawing. His pipe on the desk offered a reassuringly manly substitute. He reached for it, knocked it out loudly on the ashtray, and opened his tobacco pouch.

'Damn and blast! I've run out of tobacco! Listen, I'll pop out and get some from the kiosk. I'll only be two minutes. Be back soon, all right?'

'Sorry, got held up, couldn't help it,' he said, bursting through the door, simply dying to tell her about the amazing thing that had happened. (He took several deep breaths to master his excitement and strike a suitably measured tone of voice.) 'Fact is, I just bumped into the USG.'

'The what?'

'The Under-Secretary-General,' he spelled it out, slightly ruffled. 'Monsieur Solal,' he added after taking in a new supply of air. 'USG is the normal abbreviation, I've told you several times. (A pause.) I've just had a talk with him.'

'So . . . ?'

He stared at her in amazement. A simple 'So . . . ?' was all she could say about a talk with Sir John's right hand! Clearly no sense of social values! Still, couldn't be helped, that was the way she was, always with her head in the clouds. Tell her about it now but, mind, be offhand, don't give the impression you attach any special importance to it. He cleared his throat so that his fantastic news wouldn't be spoiled by any huskiness in the telling.

'I've just had a conversation with the Under-Secretary-General of the League of Nations, a talk, quite unexpected. (A faint twitch of the lip, a weird urge to burst into tears.) We had a little chat, just the two of us. (A sharp intake of breath to stifle a budding sob.) He even sat down, which goes to show he was in no hurry to get rid of me. I mean, he really wanted to talk to me. He wasn't just being polite. He truly is amazingly intelligent. (A difficulty with his breathing, caused by the excitement, prevented his speaking in long sentences.) This is how it happened. I went down to the ground floor, right? When I'd bought my packet of Amsterdamer from the kiosk, it occurred to me, can't think why, to come back via the corridor which goes past the USG's office, or rather offices, an odd thing to do since it meant going the long way round. Anyway, just at that moment he comes out through his door dressed, you'll never guess, in riding clothes, as he does from time to time. He looks marvellous in them, incidentally. But it's the first time I've ever seen him wearing a monocle. Mind you, it was black, as if he was covering up some trouble with his eye. Apparently he had some sort of accident this afternoon, fell off his horse and knocked an eye. Kanakis told me, I met him as I was coming back up, he'd just been to see Miss Wilson, she's the USG's secretary, he's on very good terms with her, and she told him all about it in confidence. It only happened a couple of hours ago, he arrived on a horse with a valet in tow, it's a habit of his, he often comes on a horse and then the valet takes the horse back, he's terribly *comme il faut*, and the first thing she saw was his eye, which was bleeding, well the eyelid actually, a cut, he must have fallen on something sharp, but he wouldn't have it seen to, he just asked Miss Wilson to send out to an optician's for some black monocles, apparently you can buy them over the counter. The man's got style! (He gave a little charmed, appreciative smile.) Straightaway he thinks of a monocle! So amusing! Anyway, I hope it's not serious, the cut I mean. You know, he's in charge of everything here, he's the best. (Another admiring smile.) The black monocle suits him awfully well, makes him look arrogant, aristocratic, know what I mean? Kanakis is no fool, is he? He butters Miss Wilson up something chronic. It helps no end, you realize, to be on good terms with the secretary of one of the top brass, helps no end if you want him to see you quickly, or want to hear what's going on before other people do or get a confidential tip-off and so on and so forth. Anyway, getting back to the point, the USG was striding along pretty smartly when the tapers he had in his hand, sorry, papers, slipped and fell on the floor. I picked them up. Of course I'd have done the same for anybody, only being polite. But he paused and thanked me ever so nicely. "Thank you, Deume," he said. It wasn't what he said but the way he said it, see? He remembered my name, that's the main thing. I can tell you, I was thrilled to think he knows who I am, to feel he knows I exist. It's important, don't you see? That was when he sat down and pointed to a chair facing him, all very chummy. Because just outside his offices there's this small waiting-area, with chairs, very comfy chairs of course. And then, ever so nicely, you'd never believe how nicely, he asked which section I worked in, what particular line of thing I did, if I liked the work, in short took an interest in me. So you see that if I was a long time coming back it was well worth it. A conversation lasting very nearly ten minutes! Have you any idea of what the consequences, administratively speaking, could be? He was terribly unaffected, very friendly, went out of his way not to pull rank, the two of us just sitting there, face to face. He was absolutely charming to me. And I was quite at ease and chatted away. Just think, VV walked past and saw the USG and me chatting away like old friends! What a picture. VV will be hopping mad!'

'Why hopping mad?'

'Jealousy, of course,' he smiled and shrugged his shoulders in delight. 'Also it'll have put the wind up him. It's always dangerous for a head of section if a member of his staff is on good terms with one of the top brass. It can mean trouble for him! It's like this, the chap might say to the bigwig, quite casually, without seeming to mean anything by it, he might say what he thinks of his boss, drop a few hints, suggest how the section might be reorganized, blow his own trumpet, you know, show up his boss in a poor light, or he might even come out with direct criticisms, depending of course on how the bigwig is reacting, and not pull his punches if he has the feeling the big man is none too well disposed towards his boss, I mean the chap's boss, you know, VV for instance, I mean if he feels he needn't hold back. Know what I mean?'

'Of course.'

'But I know VV. He won't show how cross he is, and tomorrow he'll be all sweetness and light. It'll be my dear Deume this, my dear Deume that, if it's not too much trouble, I realize how terribly busy you are, and so forth, and all done with a smile! He's got the mentality of a slave. I'm a threat, so it's out with the kid gloves. Anyhow, we sat there chatting for quite a while, ten minutes or so! I did wonder whether I should ask him about the black monocle, enquire if he had something wrong with his eye. But I wasn't sure and didn't in the end. Do you think I was right?'

'Yes.'

'Yes, I think so too, it would have been a touch familiar. When it was over, he got up, shook my hand, a really nice chap, you know. Very decent of him to stop and talk to me, don't you think? Especially since he was on his way to see the SG, who had asked to see him, see? So on my account he kept Sir John waiting! What do you say to that?'

'That's good.'

'Good! I'll say it's good! Just think, a conversation with a bigwig who's on hail-fellow-well-met terms with Sir John! And, mark you, not a conversation in the USG's office, not an official conversation, but a chat in the corridor, with both of us sitting down in the same class of chair, a private chat, I mean, man to man! If that's not the start of a personal contact I don't know what is! Oh, but I'm forgetting the most important bit. You'll never guess, but when he got up to go he patted me on the shoulder, or rather on the back, well anyway near the shoulder but definitely on the back, quite a firm pat, very friendly. Now to me that pat was the nicest part of the whole thing, it was I don't know intimate, spontaneous, ever so chummy. And that coming from someone who has held ministerial office in France, and is a Commander of the Legion of Honour, I mean after all he's only the most important man in the Secretariat after Sir John! And don't go saying less important than the Deputy Secretary-General because it's not true, he's more important than the Deputy Secretary-General, who may outrank him but between ourselves . . . (After a wary glance around him, in a whisper:) between ourselves, he's got no influence, there are all sorts of papers which don't ever go to him, and he never complains, can you credit it? (He looked at her. Yes, she was definitely impressed by the pat.) But that's just between the two of us, all right? And of course, much more important than the other two Under-Secretaries-General, who are small fry in comparison. It's true: whenever anybody says the USG you know it's him they mean. And the consideration he gets shown! He's the only Under-Secretary-General with a principal private secretary! Do you realize what that means? (In an even lower whisper:) Just between the two of us, I'd even go so far as to say he's more important than the Secretary-General. Oh yes! Because with Sir John it's golf and then more golf and, that apart, just a figurehead, always says amen to whatever the USG decides! So you see how tremendously important that pat on the back was. (He smiled a dreamy, feminine smile:) And anyway the man oozes charm somehow. That smile of his, awfully disarming! And his eyes, so warm, so understanding. I can see why women fall for him. Even that black monocle suits him terribly well, makes him look, I don't know, romantic. And got up like that in riding clothes! Every inch the gentleman. Obviously not everybody in the Secretariat would dare turn up on a horse. Of course if a ... (He almost said "a spear-carrier" but changed his mind, so as not to do himself down.) ... a lower-grade civil servant tried it on, it would raise an eyebrow or two. Just imagine the fuss there'd be if VV turned up one morning in riding boots! But if the USG does it, no one gives it a second thought. Seventy thousand a year in gold equivalent, plus entertainment allowance! They say he's got a luxury suite at the Ritz, with two drawing-rooms. By the way, I might forget. To be on the safe side, I didn't say anything to Kanakis about my little chat with the USG. I mention this, you never know, just in case you ever come across him. Just think: two drawing-rooms! I bet he runs up a hotel bill and a half! Anyhow, he's definitely top-drawer, bags of style, very smart, terribly aristocratic. Still, that's not the point. He's got a brilliant mind. And then there's that charm of his, it's hard to define really, a sort of gentleness but mixed in with it a hint of cruelty, it's a well-known fact that Sir John thinks the sun shines out of him, you often see them chatting together on the friendliest terms, he always looks completely relaxed, they say he calls him John, really, can you imagine? By all accounts Lady

Cheyne thinks even more highly of him! And it's no secret that he's a Don Juan, all the girls in the Secretariat are mad about him. And Countess Kanyo, that's the wife of the Hungarian minister to Berne who died two years ago, she's his mistress, she's crazy about him, it's an open secret. Kanakis saw her here once kissing the USG's hand! Can you imagine that? She's tremendously cultured, it seems. Very beautiful, still young, about thirty-two or thirty-three, very stylish and immensely rich with it, they say,' he concluded proudly. (She brushed his cheek with one finger.) 'What are you doing that for?'

'Because you're so sweet.'

'Oh I see,' he said with a vague feeling of annoyance.

He was not entirely pleased to be sweet. He would have preferred to be an out-and-out man, with a pipe between his teeth and cold eyes, hard as nails. To show he was not as sweet as all that, he stuck out his jaw. For his wife's benefit, he did his impression of a man bent on living dangerously whenever he thought of it. He did not think of it often.

(If the tough guy, the he-man, the daredevil, was Adrien Deume's staple ideal, he also subscribed to other, quite different, archetypes as contradictory as they were interchangeable. On a day, for example, when he was dazzled by Huxley, he would try to cut a dash as the faintly effeminate diplomat, courteous but slightly cool, very man-of-the-world, the acme of sophistication, and the next day have no compunction about shedding that particular skin after reading the biography of some great writer. He would then become, as the case might be, exuberant and larger than life, or sardonic and disillusioned, or tormented and vulnerable, but never for very long, just for an hour or two. Then he would forget and revert to what he was: an insignificant little Deume.)

The dictatorial, over-jutted jaw made the back of his neck ache, so he allowed it to revert to a more pacific angle. He glanced at his wife and waited for her reaction, thirsting to talk so staggering an occurrence through with her, to discuss it at length and work out together what avenues it opened up.

'Well now, darling, what do you make of it all?'

'I think,' she said after a silence, 'that it's encouraging.'

'Exactly!' he said with a grateful smile, ready to run with the word. 'You've hit the nail on the head. You're right, it was an encouraging chat. I don't say we've got a close relationship exactly, not yet, but at least it's the start of something which might lead to a close relationship. A human contact, that's what it was. Especially since our encounter ended with that pat. (He blinked his eyes in an effort to reach a subtle definition, to get to the bottom, of that pat.) That pat was, how shall I put it, a signal which conveyed intimacy, liking. Especially since it was a solid sort of pat, you know, almost knocked me over. Anyhow, it all could be vitally important for my career, see?'

'Yes, I see.'

'Listen, darling, I've got to have a serious talk with you. (He lit his pipe so that he could introduce the topic properly, generate dramatic tension and above all drum up a sense of his own importance and say what he had to say with maximum persuasiveness.) Darling, I've got something rather important to say. (The "rather" was intended to convey the impression of a hard-boiled type not much given to extravagant turns of phrase.) It's this. Last night I didn't sleep terribly well and I began turning an idea over in my mind. I had intended to keep it until this evening, but I'd sooner tell you now because it's been preying on my mind. Anyhow, my idea is that we should make the most of the fact that Dada and Mummy are going away on Friday for a month, I mean make the most of it to start having a proper social life, not the occasional, random entertaining we've done up to now, but a full, properly managed social life, based on a maturely thought-out plan, a written schedule of dinners and cocktail parties. I've lots of ideas on the subject, especially since I have it in mind to distance myself from Dada and Mummy so I can be freer to operate. I'll tell you all about it later, and also about one or two large dinner parties I'm thinking of giving. But first let's talk about the cocktail parties, for that's the most urgent aspect of the problem. I think that we should put our heads together this evening and draw up a list of people to invite to our first formal party.'

'Whatever for?'

'O darling,' he began, making a great effort to be patient, 'because a man in my position ought to have a modicum of a social life. All my colleagues manage somehow to have twenty or thirty guests round for drinks. Kanakis has had up to seventy at his place, interesting people, the sort who draw a lot of water. We have been married for five years now and we've never yet organized anything together, not according to a plan worked out in advance. Top of the list are the parties we ought to return. If we don't return hospitality, people will notice and won't invite us again. The number of invitations to drinks we've been getting is already well down. It's a danger signal, and I'm becoming rather concerned about it. In this life, darling, you never get anywhere unless you have contacts, and cocktail parties are ideal places for making contacts. In one fell swoop you can ask a lot of pleasant people round who will return the invitation, which gives you an opportunity to get to know a whole lot of other people at a stroke, because the thing starts to snowball, and then you're in the position of being able to pick and choose which of your new contacts you want to invite next time, because you have to be choosy of course, you have to stick to the people you feel an affinity for, people you get along with. And bear in mind that, from the host's point of view, drinks cost less than a dinner party and the result is virtually the same. I say virtually because from a personal-contact point of view you can't really beat a dinner party, so we'll have to start asking people to dinner too, the type of people we get on with best. Dada and Mummy will have to be kept firmly out of all this, even before the parting of the ways which I have in mind for the very near future. But let's stick to the cocktails for now. On this issue I shall tell you exactly what I think. Well, my plan, which I have slightly revised and modified since I had that conversation just now, my plan is to kick off by asking the USG to our very first cocktail party. He's bound to come after that pat on the back. And if I can let it be known that he's coming, I can count on getting the cream not only of the Secretariat but of the permanent delegations as well! Don't worry, I shan't be bothering to invite any rabble. So. Operation USG: cocktails as opening gambit followed at a later date by a formal dinner party. Now isn't that a tasty dish to set before a king?' (One of Mummy's little turns of phrase which just slipped out, so full was his mind with what he was saying.)

'I don't like him very much. Why are you so keen on inviting him?'

'This, darling,' he said, with honeyed sententiousness which hid the first stirrings of annoyance, 'is how I answer that. One, top brass don't have to be nice to be invited. Two, I myself have always found the USG extremely pleasant. Three, if I am so keen to invite him, as you put it, it is for the very good reason that I take my orders from van Vries and van Vries takes his orders from the USG. Look, I've been stuck at the top of grade B for seven months and van Vries won't do a thing, you know, won't lift a finger to get me put up to an A! He refuses to do anything because he's gutless! He's gutless because he thinks to himself that putting me up for promotion might not go down very well upstairs and might therefore reflect back unfavourably on him. But, on the other hand, he'll do something when he finds out I'm in the USG's good books, and you can rest assured that if I am indeed so favoured I shall make a point of letting him know about it on the q.t.! But there shouldn't be any need for me to tell him, because when I throw my grand cocktail party he'll see the USG there and will draw the appropriate conclusions, and that means he will find the guts to put me up for an A because he'll feel his recommendation would get a sympathetic hearing and would not involve any danger to himself. Anyway guts isn't the word, he'll be pleased to do it, he'll fall over himself to recommend me without reservation, in terms of the warmest sincerity, in a shower of praise, because doing so will get him in with the USG. Do you see now how the thing works?'

'But you said yourself that your boss was annoyed because you were talking to that man.'

'No, no, darling, you don't understand,' he said cheerfully. 'I'm an old hand and I know my way about. Sure it annoyed him, sure he hates me. But I told you: that won't stop him smarming all over me. And when he knows we're on a sound friendly footing, that is, when I ask the USG round to my house and the USG dines with me at home, he'll go down on his knees before me, literally! I've made a good start with the USG but I'm going to have to strike while the iron's hot and build on the liking he did me the honour of taking to me, yes, honour, I'm not afraid to say it! But for that to happen he'll have to get to know me better. A cocktail party I invited him to would pave the way to a closer relationship, I could talk to him and he could size me up. Listen, personal contacts with your hierarchical superiors is the top and bottom of success. But personal contacts start in a chap's home, when you ask people round on equal terms. And it's only natural I should invite him. That pat on the back was pretty definite, you know. Inviting him to dinner straight off would be a bit much, a bit over the top. But a largish cocktail party would be a halfway house and would soften him up for a dinner eventually. Of course, the party would have to be a fairly lavish affair. Engraved invitation cards. You must be prepared to splash out when you have to. With RSVP in the bottom right-hand corner, you know, do the thing properly. And remember, if I'm keen to have the USG round at my place, it's basically only because I thought he was a really nice chap. He improves the more you get to know him. Of course, if he gives me a leg-up on the promotion front so much the better, but that's not the main thing. If I didn't like him, there'd be nothing doing, I'd never dream of inviting him, but I feel he's a kindred spirit, you understand. I'll tell you what I really think: it makes me sad for my country that apart from Debrouckère there isn't another Belgian on an A. Belgium deserves better than that. A country that's suffered so much has it owing to her! Her neutrality breached in '14, in spite of being guaranteed by the treaties of 1839! The destruction of Louvain! The agony of the German occupation! Anyway, this party, you can leave the whole thing to me, the hired waiters in white jackets, the drinks, sandwiches, canapés . . . All you would have to do would be to put on a stunning frock and be pleasant to everybody, including the USG.'

He paused, wiped his brow, and smiled: he could see it now! Yes, a top-notch cocktail party! The master stroke would be to have the Belgian ambassador who would be showing up soon for the Tenth Session. That's it, arrange to be introduced by Debrouckère and invite the ambassador for drinks. The dodge would be to tell the ambassador, as though it was all fixed already, that the USG would be there. The ambassador would be certain to accept – and then invite the USG mentioning that the ambassador would be coming! On the day, there'd be fifty cars parked outside the villa! Just picture it! The neighbours wouldn't know what had hit them!

Delightedly he crunched a sugar lump, nibbling at it like a rabbit.

He saw himself deep in conversation with the USG, both with cigars in their mouths and a Martini or a port cocktail in their hands, an exchange of pleasantries between equals. Just before the guests arrive, a tot of whisky to give him confidence and make him sparkle. No, don't bring up promotion straight away at the party, don't give him the impression that he was invited for a reason. Be patient. The top brass always got annoyed if people talked about promotion. Don't mention top of grade B until they were friends.

Oh yes, from now on a high-profile social life! New Year cards to all his acquaintances! But not to anybody below member of section! Expensive cards for As and above! And with a short handwritten greeting! It was money in the bank! Contacts, for God's sake! A man was only as good as his contacts! No: a man was the sum of his contacts! Top priority: rent a villa with cook and valet-cum-butler! Every day, quality guests for lunch and dinner, that was the secret of success! The butler buttling in white gloves! Big spending on these things was money in the bank! Very *haute cuisine* – more money in the bank! The Adrien Deumes keep a very good table! Knock down the wall between two rooms and have one huge reception room, nothing like it for making your name! And in the middle of the room, a grand piano, as a status symbol! And bridge once a week! With bridge, you not only made contacts, you kept them! And a sumptuously appointed guest bedroom! Whenever the Assembly was in session, whenever the Council met, invite the highest-ranking Belgian delegate to stay in his home! So much nicer than a hotel, Minister. And then one evening, after dinner, as they stroll in the garden, the sudden confidence dropped in a mild, wistful tone of voice, 'That's the position, my dear Minister, I've been stuck at the top of grade A for umpteen years now.' And then a sigh, just a sigh, that's all. And with the joint, fully coordinated backing of the principal Belgian delegate and the USG, behold Adrien suddenly promoted to the rank of adviser or even made head of section!

The tea-lady came in to remove the tray. He teased her, mildly flirtatious, about her perm. Then he apologized to Ariane for having to pop out for a few moments and left the room in an aura of cocktail parties to come, invitations back and milkable Belgian delegates sleeping in the guest room. He walked quickly along the corridor. He wanted to run, shout, kiss his hands with delight. So happy it hurt, biting back the squeals that queued up in his mouth, he felt madly pleased with himself. 'Adrien, you love, you treasure, I adore you,' he murmured.

'Pat on the back, pat on the back!' he said aloud in a deserted lavatory. 'Adrien Deume, the conquering hero!' he proclaimed in a voice of brass as he stood at the urinal where perpetual waters flowed.

Returning to his wife, he sat down gravely, clasped his hands behind his head, propped his feet on the edge of the desk, and again began see-sawing gently in his chair, like van Vries, but now also trying to make his face expressionless like the Under-Secretary-General's. But again, suddenly struck by the thought that VV might burst in at any moment, he put his feet down and stopped see-sawing. To make up for the loss of advantage he derived from his rakishly displayed feet, he pushed out his lower lip and chin once more, like the Italian dictator, and stiffened his neck.

'You know, on second thoughts, I honestly think we could go ahead and invite him to dinner straight off, or at any rate lunch, take the plunge, and not bother with the cocktail party, in the light of that pat on the back, do you follow me? It's an altogether nicer occasion than a party. Yes, best invite him to dinner, there's more time for conversation when the meal's over. I wouldn't mind making it a candlelit affair, like the ones the Kanakises give, it would lend a touch of class. Incidentally, we'll have to check and see if everything's in order at home, you know, dinner service, plates, knives, forks, different sizes of wineglass, tablecloths, napkins and so on and so forth. Because everything will have to be just right, he's used only to the very best, you know. (He resisted the temptation to insert a forefinger into one nostril and, as second best to giving his nose a good raking, settled for stroking it gently.) I say, this Hitler chap really is a beast, he's taking a pretty strong line with those poor Jews who are people like anybody else, with failings and qualities. Anyway, Einstein's a genius. But to come back to the question of the table, we've got a decision to make, assuming we do in fact invite the USG to lunch or dinner: there's a tablecloth problem. I wonder if we oughtn't to dispense with a tablecloth altogether because I have this feeling tablecloths for formal dinner parties are out nowadays. It's no good saying the Kanakises always have one, because what's set me wondering is that in *Art and Decoration*, you know, the glossy mag I persuaded Periodicals to order, I've seen photographs of top people's dining-rooms with tables made of precious kinds of wood, and they didn't have tablecloths, just a napkin under each plate, the effect was absolutely marvellous. Anyway we can talk about it when we've got more time.'

The ringing of the phone made him jump and brought his chin back to a less imperious angle. He sighed with a weariness born of impatience, said that there was no peace in this place, and picked up the receiver.

'Deume. Yes, sir. I most certainly do have it and I shall bring it up at once. (He got to his feet and buttoned his jacket.) That was VV, he gets on my wick, a dratted nuisance, wants the verbatim record of the Third Session of the PMC, damn it all I'm not the section archivist, that man is getting to be a real pain in the neck. (He unbuttoned his jacket and sat down again defiantly. To keep VV waiting for a few minutes was not to run much of a risk, and Ariane would see that he was not a slave at everybody's beck and call. He'd tell van Vries that it had taken him some time to unearth the verbatim record, which was old. Anyway, what the hell, there was the pat on the back.) So, high and mighty lady,' he went on, 'what do you reckon to this grand dinner party in honour of our beloved Under-Secretary-General?'

'I'll tell you . . .' she began, resolved to reveal the whole story.

'Just a moment, darling. I'll have to stop you there. I've just thought of something. (VV did not like to be kept waiting, and his voice had sounded rather sharper than usual. Besides, it would create a bad impression if he said he'd had to look high and low for the verbatim record. It would make him look like the kind of disorganized civil servant who can't find his way round his own files. He got up, opened a filing-cabinet, took out a document, and did up his jacket.) Listen, darling, on second thoughts, I'd rather go now. Though generally speaking I take a great pleasure in making old VV wait. But just for once I want to have a bit of peace to chat things over with you, so might as well get it over and done with at once. I'll be off then, but I'll be back straight away. What a bore! Right then, see

71

you shortly, all right?' he said with a smile, and headed for the door, slowly, to cover up the fact of his capitulation.

Once he was in the corridor, he set off at a run towards the rocket he felt was coming his way. Van Vries's tone had not been reassuring. Outside the door of his hierarchical superior, he prepared a smile, knocked gently, then turned the knob gingerly.

CHAPTER 6

He came in, casual in manner and whistling through his teeth. He sat down, drummed on his desk-top with his fingers, closed the three files, and smiled.

'What's up with you?'

'Nothing, nothing at all,' he said, all innocence. 'Just the opposite, everything's fine. Feeling a touch liverish, that's all,' he said after a moment's silence, and he got to his feet, pressed his hand to his right side and smiled again.

'Oh come on, you'll get round to telling me all about it in the end. Is it your boss?'

He collapsed into his chair and gave her a shipwrecked look.

'He threw the book at me. On account of the British Memorandum. Because I hadn't submitted my comments yet. How he thinks anybody can work in the middle of constant interruptions . . . (He paused, hoping she would ask questions. But she said nothing, so he went on.) He's going to put my shilly-shallying in my annual report, anyway what he calls my shilly-shallying. That means goodbye to my annual increment, and it could perhaps mean I'll get an official warning or even a reprimand from the Secretary-General. So that's how things stand. (His fingers drummed scales of stoical despair on his desk-top.) Naturally it's going to put paid to any chance of promotion, it'll be a black mark in my record. Stuck with it. Like Nessus's tunic, you know. But I've done my best, I told him I'd forward my comments tomorrow morning first thing. He said it was too late, and then he brought up the Cameroon Acknowledgement.

Scathing he was, really scathing. So there we are, it's a disaster. (Again he drummed out the tragic submission to destiny.) I wasn't going to say anything to you, no point you suffering too. (In silence, he glumly turned the handle of the pencil-sharpener.) Retaliation, that's what it is, I'm pretty sure it's because he saw me talking to the USG, it'll be his way of getting even. Jealousy – I told you, didn't I? It didn't take him long. (He looked at her, hoping for support.) You get something like that in your annual report and you're for the chop, curtains, a B for life. So that's it, I've had it, bang goes my future in the international civil service,' he concluded, with a brave smile.

'You're imagining things, it's not as bad as all that,' she said, sensing that he was deliberately exaggerating the seriousness of the situation as a way of extracting words of comfort.

'How come?' he asked eagerly. 'What do you mean?'

'If you let him have the work tomorrow, he won't be cross any more.'

'You think so? Do you really think so?'

'Of course. You can do it at home tonight.'

'Two hundred pages,' he sighed, and shook his head several times, looking like a chastened schoolboy. 'You do realize, don't you, that it'll take me all night?'

'I'll make you lots of black coffee. I'll keep you company, if you want.'

'So you really think it will all turn out all right?'

'Of course it will, don't be silly. Besides, you've got someone on your side now.'

'You mean the Under-Secretary-General? (He knew very well that was who she meant, but wanted to hear her say it. Moreover, he found it comforting to say the prestigious title aloud in full and through its majestic syllables conjure up the shadow of a guardian angel. A magical incantation, in other words.) The Under-Secretary-General?' he repeated, and he gave a wan smile, drew his chair closer, and with one hand clutched his wife's skirt.

'Who else? Judging by what you told me, he was very sweet to you just now.'

'That's right, the Under-Secretary-General,' he said with another smile. He reached mechanically for his pipe, sniffed at the bowl, which was now cold, and put it down again on his desk. 'You're right. Very sweet.'

'You said he asked which section you worked in?'

'Asked very nicely too, really, wanted to know what I specialized in, if I liked my work, took an interest. And he called me Deume.'

'And he asked you to sit down and you chatted.'

'Man to man. Never made me aware of the difference in rank.'

'And then there's the pat on the back.'

'Oh yes, the pat on the back,' he beamed, and he knocked his pipe out and refilled it.

'I believe it was a hefty pat?'

'Very. Just here, it was. I bet my shoulder is still red from it. Would you like to see?'

'No, don't bother. I believe you.'

'And coming from someone who is more important than the Deputy Secretary-General!'

'Or even the Secretary-General,' she said, going one better.

'Quite! Because Sir John, you know, is golf, golf and golf, apart from that he's just a figurehead who says amen to whatever the USG tells him to. So you see how important that pat on the back was!'

'I do see,' she said, and she bit her lip.

He lit his pipe, sucked in a sweet, calming lungful, then got up and paced around his small office, wreathed in a cloud of tobacco smoke, with one hand in his pocket and the other round the bowl of the pipe.

'I'll tell you shumthing, Arianny,' he said, without removing the pipe from between his teeth, which made him slurp his words like van Goelerkhen's fat wife, 'I'm shertain VV won't take it any further, hish bark'sh louder than hish bite, sho don't worry your head about it, and even if he putsh in a bad report on me it doezhn't bother me none, shee? I'm not schcared of the shwine, the mountain will bring forth a moushe! (He sat down again, propped his feet on his desk and see-sawed. His pipe, still airily clamped between his teeth, purred damply at intervals.) But the charm of the man! You musht have notished it at the Brajilian reshepchion. An indefinable miksh, don't you think? The impreshion hish mind'sh elshewhere when you talk to him, that short of shcornful tilt of the head, like a marble busht, and then all of a shudden that disharming shmile of hish, sho attractive. He'sh a real charmer. Anyway, Countesh Kanyo and I shee eye to eye on that, take it from me. Did I ever tell you about the woman who doesh for Petrechco?'

'No,' she said. (He put his pipe, now out, in the ashtray.)

'It's quite fascinating. I forgot to tell you. Yes, Petresco lives at Pont-Céard, not far from the Countess's château.'

'I've been to Pont-Céard. There's no château there.'

'Well, a rather splendid house, then. But that's beside the point. The woman who looks after Petresco is very pally with the Countess's personal maid, which means that Petresco has a pretty good idea of everything that goes on at the Countess's. He told Kanakis, who told me in strict confidence. Apparently the Countess waits in for the USG every night. (Privily, excitedly, slyly, guiltily, deliciously shocked by this titbit of rather scandalous gossip, he poked out his tapered tongue.) Apparently every night she dolls herself up to the nines, sumptuous dinner on the table, bowls of super-duper fruit, flowers, the whole shoot. She waits for him for hours. (He gave a perfunctory glance to right and left and lowered his voice to a whisper.) Apparently more often than not he doesn't show up. Every evening, she gets ready as if he's supposed to be coming, sits for hours by the window watching to see if he'll turn up in his Rolls, and then he doesn't. Highly significant, wouldn't you say?'

She stood up, read the title of the books on a shelf, and forced a yawn.

'Have you ever seen this baroness?'

'Countess,' he corrected her. 'Higher rank altogether. Old Hungarian aristocracy, oodles of diplomats in the family. Of course I've seen her, she's always at the Assembly, comes to meetings of the Council, committees, anywhere he's likely to be, can't take her eyes off him. It wouldn't surprise me if she were downstairs this very minute, hanging about in the lobby, especially since she knows all the best people, she would, wouldn't she, seeing that her father was such a high-up. What's the matter, darling?'

'Nothing. I don't much care for such goings-on. That's all.'

'Well, he's not married and she's a widow, so they're both free.'

'They should get married, then.'

'Some of the very best people have affairs, you know. What about Louis XIV and Madame de Maintenon?'

'That was a morganatic marriage.'

'All right then, Aristide Briand has been having an affair, everybody knows, but no one thinks the worse of him on that account.'

'I do.'

He looked at her, his eyes large and kindly behind his glasses. What was biting her? Better change the subject.

'So, great and high-born lady, you don't think too badly of my little *chez moi*? Obviously, there aren't any Gobelin tapestries on the wall like in the USG's office, but it's not too awful, is it? If you'd seen the offices they have in ministry buildings in Belgium, you'd realize how luxurious things are here. Besides, it's a pretty privileged set-up. In this place, we're on a Diplomatic footing, you know. Hours, for example. In the afternoon we generally make a start at three or even later, but if required we've got to stay on until easily seven, eight at night, as they do in the Quai d'Orsay or the Foreign Office. Here the atmosphere is very different from the International Labour Office, where everybody has to go at it hammer and tongs, I say "has to" but in fact they love it, it's another world, you know, all those trade unionists and left-wingers. Here the tone is Diplomatic Service and life's very pleasant. Look, I'll show you, I'll tot up the days when I don't work. (Highly pleased with himself before he had even begun, he took out a propelling pencil and a pad and ran his tongue over his lips.) To kick off, every month, there's the day's leave every official can take without having to send in a doctor's certificate, article thirty-one of Staff Regulations. I make the most of that, as you'd imagine. (He made a note.) So, twelve extra days a year off work.'

(This calls for a word of explanation. The said article thirty-one was intended to cover an indisposition unique to women, but the prudish men who had drafted the Staff Regulations had not dared be so specific. It followed therefore that male officials also had the right to be indisposed on one day every month without the requirement to supply medical evidence.)

'So,' repeated Adrien Deume, 'twelve extra days a year off work. Are you with me? (With his handsome gold propelling pencil and a relaxed, easy smile, he carefully noted the figure twelve.) Then twice a year I can wangle special sick-leave, as long as I can provide a doctor's certificate. Overwork, say. Incidentally, what they put on the last certificate was a peach. Reactive stress. Isn't that just marvellous? So, two lots of sick-leave, a couple of weeks apiece, say, no inching on. So, another thirty extra days off work! Thirty plus twelve makes forty-two, that's right, isn't it, agreed? Forty-two it is. (When he had written the figure down, he acknowledged it with a delighted "ta-ra!") Then we have the thirty-six working days of official leave a year, the normal leave, all above board, article forty-three of the Regulations. Right! But note they are *working* days!' he exclaimed excitedly. 'So in practice, it comes to more than thirty-six days off! There are five and a half working days in a week. That means that my annual leave of thirty-six working days turns out in fact to be forty-five days when I don't have to come in! We'd got up to forty-two extra days' leave. Add the forty-five for official leave and that brings us up to eighty-seven! That's correct, isn't it? (Eagerly:) Will you do the adding-up the same time as me, darling? (He passed her a piece of paper and a pencil. He was civility itself.) So, eighty-seven rest days! Next,' he whispered like a guilty but playful schoolboy owning up, 'there are the fifty-two Saturday mornings which should be worked in theory but never are, when Lord Adrien of Deume sits back and enjoys the good life! (Riding high on his buoyant mood and forgetting the need to maintain his dignity and manly, sober bearing, he let out one of his braying schoolboy laughs which emerged from a tremendous clearing of the throat.) It's all above board and you can't say different, what can anybody do in an hour or two? It really isn't worth traipsing in all that way from Cologny to the Palais for a couple of hours' work at most, because even chaps who come in on a Saturday are away by noon! There's no point. Anyway, VV never turns out on a Saturday, come Friday evening he shoots off in a plane to look after his VIPs from The Hague or Amsterdam, which means a lot of sucking-up. So why should I put myself out? So, fifty-two Saturday mornings amount practically speaking, note the practically, to twenty-six special little days off. Eighty-seven plus twenty-six, that makes a hundred and thirteen, unless my maths have let me down. Aren't you totting it up too, to check I've got it right?' he said anxiously. 'Oh well, please yourself. So we'd got up to a hundred and lovely thirteen. (Sticking his tongue out, he wrote the figure down.) One hundred and thirteen!' he hummed. 'Oh, and then we mustn't forget the fifty-two Saturday afternoons and fifty-two Sundays. But let's get this absolutely right: I've counted six of each in my official holiday already plus four of each when I was adding up my sick-leave. Are you with me?'

'Yes.'

'So let's say fifty-two Sundays take away ten, forty-two. We'd got up to a hundred and thirteen. So a hundred and thirteen plus forty-two takes us to a hundred and fifty-five rest days, plus fifty-two Saturday afternoons take away ten, forty-two, which gives us another twenty-one days off. A hundred and fifty-five plus twenty-one comes to a hundred and seventy-six days of little me sitting about twiddling the old thumbs! The diplomatic life! You can't beat it!'

'True.'

'And now we've got to add on bank holidays. Christmas, Good Friday and so on, a dozen public holidays, article forty-nine. A hundred and seventy-six plus twelve – one hundred and eighty-eight non-working days. That's the lot, isn't it?'

'Yes.'

'Oh but it's not, darling!' he exclaimed, his face lighting up, and he thumped the top of his desk. 'There are the bonus days they give us when the Assembly rises, what about them? It's two generally but three if it's been tough going. So a hundred and eighty-eight plus two, you see I'm being conservative, gives us one hundred and ninety. What do you say to that?'

'So,' she said.

'I'm sorry?' he said, taken aback.

'So.'

'So what?'

'Your so. The so you say all the time. I just said it before you did.'

'Oh, I see. Fine. (She had mixed him up. He did his sums again.) I got it right. So, one hundred and ninety days of restful respite. (He drew sunbeams all round the exquisite number of one hundred and ninety. Then all at once he unleashed a fiendish snigger.) Darling! there's more! (His hand smote the desk-top.) What about the official visits! The official visits, for God's sake! On average, two two-week tours a year, each involving two days' proper work, because, you know, when you're on an official visit you don't push yourself too hard, you're your own boss, no one breathing down your neck, you go at your own speed, and the work you do on a tour consists mainly of inviting a lot of people to slap-up meals. So, four days' actual work for both tours, that leaves us, and tell me if I've got it wrong, that leaves us a net gain of twenty-six days for rest and assorted play which, in jolly mood, we shall now add to the hundred and ninety we've brought forward! So, that gives two hundred and sixteen non-working days per annum!'

He looked up in triumph, exuding happiness so pure, so childlike, that she brushed his hand with her forefinger, overcome by something very much like pity. He stared at his darling wife, his eyes glistening with gratitude.

'Just a sec,' he whispered, 'I'll show you a secret.'

From the middle drawer, he produced a large sheet of squared paper covered with columns of microscopic figures which had been entered with exquisite care: they looked like columns of ants.

'It's a thirty-year calendar,' he explained, not without a hint of embarrassment. 'It took me weeks to do. Can you see, each column represents a year. Thirty columns of three hundred and sixty-five days. I've allowed for leap years of course. The days that are crossed off are the ones I've been here. Look, more than five years struck through already! It'll be terrific when I get down to here,' he said pointing to the bottom of the thirtieth column. 'So I've got a bit under twenty-five years still to go, around nine thousand days to cross out. I cross one out every day, you know. But there's a problem with weekends: when should I cross out Saturdays and Sundays? Which do you think? Friday evening or Monday morning? I say Friday evening because, as you know, for the aforementioned reasons, I don't come in on Saturday mornings. So, do I tick them off before or after? Which do you say? (She shook her head to indicate that she had no idea.) No, come on, which, in your opinion: Friday evening or Monday morning?'

'Monday,' she said, to be done with it.

Through his glasses, he shot her a grateful look.

'Yes, I thought Monday's best too. It gets the week off to a good start. First thing when I get here in the morning, bingo, I put a line through Saturday and Sunday! Two days less, out they go! As good as a tonic! (He sighed.) But, you know, the other solution, crossing them off on a Friday before I leave, has got something to be said for it too. Because then, do you see, I can get a kick out of crossing off three in one go: Friday, Saturday and Sunday! And it rounds off the week's work very nicely! Fridays I get away a little earlier than usual, free as a bird! (Pursed lips, rapid flutter of meditative breaths.) On reflection, I'll go for the Monday solution because of the tonic effect, and anyway you thought of it and I like the idea of doing something you thought of. (He smiled at her lovingly. It was simply grand being able to share everything with his wife.) Half a tick, I'm going to show you something. (He opened his index drawer and laid a tenderly proprietorial hand on the cards inside.) See this? All my mandated territories are here. Here,' he repeated with the pride of the good craftsman. (Fondly, his hand executed an erotic slide along his cards.) Everything having regard to. (He winced. Oh the hell with it, he wasn't writing a letter.) Everything having regard to the natives in my territories has been put on file by yours truly.'

'Are the natives well treated?'

'Of course they're well treated. Don't worry, they're better off than we are, they dance, they don't have a care in the world. I'd willingly swap places with them.'

'How do you know they're well treated?'

'Their governments send us reports.'

'Are you sure the reports are true?'

'Of course they're true. They're official.'

'And when you get them, what do you do with them?'

He gave her a puzzled look. What had got into her?

'We forward them to the Permanent Mandates Commission. And this here is my little machine-gun,' he added, gesturing towards his lovely stapler. 'I'm the only one in the section who's got this model.'

'What exactly does this Commission do to help the natives?'

'It studies the situation and sends congratulations to the mandatory Power on the civilizing action it has taken.'

'But what if the natives are badly treated?'

'Oh, that hardly ever happens.'

'But I read a book by Gide where he talked about abuses.'

'Yes, I know,' he said sulkily. 'He exaggerated the whole thing. Anyhow, he's a queer.'

'Ah, so there has been ill-treatment, then. If that's the case, what does this Commission do?'

'Well, it comments on the reports, says it has every confidence in the mandatory Power, expresses the hope that there will be no recurrence of similar incidents, and indicates that it would be grateful for any information which the competent authorities would consider appropriate to provide concerning recent developments. Yes, because if there are abuses or if repressive measures are taken – and in any case the press will report them more or less accurately – we always prefer to use the expression "recent developments", which is more suitable, less direct. Look, it's a genuine Bostitch! Forty staples a minute!'

'But what if the Commission's comments have no effect? What happens if the natives go on being maltreated?'

'Oh come on, what do you expect? We can hardly go around upsetting governments. Touchy chaps, governments. And besides, they contribute to our budget. But, generally speaking, things go very smoothly. Governments do all they can. We are on cordial terms with their representatives. Forty staples a minute, just watch,' he said, and he brought his fist down on his stapler.

Moved by the sacred spirit, frenzied and wild-eyed, fervent and warlike, he struck again. Implacably and quiveringly did he strike. Spectacles bouncing, scarcely human, exalted, he struck without mercy while outside, in the corridor, drawn from all directions, his assembled colleagues gave expert and delighted ear to the loud reports produced by the perspiring, ecstatic international civil servant.

'I'm going for a walk in the grounds,' she said. 'I'll be back in a few minutes.'

As soon as the door closed behind her, he pushed the stapler away, suddenly sobered. He oughtn't to have. What he'd been doing was manual work, secretary's work. Nor ought he to have taken her into his confidence and told her about his little wangles for arranging extra holidays. It made him out to be a minor cog, made him look like some sort of cheat. In short, he'd lowered his own stock. And all because of this need to share everything with her, to tell her everything, to enjoy everything together.

'I love her too much, that's my problem.'

He raised his right hand as though taking an oath. From now on, no more confiding, no more being so free and easy. It would go hard on him, but there it was. The important thing was to keep his wife's respect. Or perhaps, to combat the cross civil-servile image he'd just created, what if he were to tell her tonight or tomorrow that he'd been hallucinating, that he'd seen a lot of crabs running after him? That would counteract the effect. Hm. Perhaps not. That would be coming it a bit strong, she'd never buy it. So from now on, just be reserved, laconic, a mite distant, that was the way to be admired. When she came back, mention the plan for writing a novel, that would make up for the stapler. And mention casually that if it suited him to turn up at the Palais on any given morning at ten or ten thirty, as the spirit took him, there was nothing anyone could say, he was a senior official. That would help to make it up too. And also point out that L of N officials were much better paid than those in the ILO, who all had to be in on time and were kept hard at it all day. There was no comparison. You see, darling, we're on the same footing as the Diplomatic.

'And now, to work, let's get down to this Memo. Drat! Quarter past six! Where on earth has the time gone?'

CHAPTER 7

When she came back, he leaped out of his seat and kissed her on both cheeks.

'Listen! Something fantastic has just happened. But first let me get my breath back. It was a jolly good thing I hadn't gone home, he'll have been most impressed when he saw I was still here after normal working hours. And I owe it all to you, because you were so late coming back, thank God! Well anyway,' he said, spacing out his words to hide his breathlessness, 'not ten minutes ago, at twenty past six, his principal private secretary phoned me. The USG's, I mean. What if he hadn't caught me, can you imagine? I'm to see him in his office at quarter past seven – the USG's office, not his PPS's. Nineteen fifteen hours. (From the special pocket in his waistcoat, he took out his spare timepiece, then put it back without looking at it.) I went out into the grounds to look for you at once to tell you, but you weren't there, so I came back here. Doesn't matter. (He tried a cool, collected smile.) Is my suit all right?'

'Yes.'

'Any bits of fluff on it?'

'No.'

'Jacket creased? How about behind?' (He turned his back to her.)

'No.'

'The thing is, yesterday I forgot to put my working jacket on. Sitting down in it all day, well you never know. (He discovered a greasy mark on his jacket sleeve. "Drat! how horrid!" he murmured in his feminine voice. From his little drawer, he got out the bottle of

Détachol and rubbed the sleeve. But the look his watching wife gave him made him feel uncomfortable, and he put the stopper back in the bottle.) There, done it, spot's gone. Six thirty-three already, another forty-two minutes to go. Look, I think that all things considered I'd rather be left by myself to have a think about all this. Be an angel and wait for me downstairs, I mean on the first floor, in the little waiting-area just outside his office, you'll find it easily enough, it's just where there are always a couple of porters sitting around. That way I'll be able to . . . (He stopped. On no account say that then he would be able to see her one last time before going into the USG's office.) Because that way I'll be able to tell you how it went soon as I come out, see? I'll get there a little early. You be there at seven, five past at the latest, so we'll have a moment to talk, say a few last-minute things. (Without thinking, he inserted a sheet of paper into the stapling-machine, gave it a few half-hearted whacks, stared at the result and then at his wife.) Tell me, what do you think, what's he want to see me for?'

'I don't know.'

'You don't know,' he muttered vacantly. (He remained for a moment with his mouth open, then lit a cigarette, inhaled, then stubbed it out roughly in the ashtray to arm himself with courage.) 'Anyway, like I said, we'll meet up on the first floor at five past seven, better make that seven, just in case, so we'll have time to put our heads together if we need to. All right then, see you later, darling.'

The moment the door closed behind her, he made a leap for the bottle of Détachol, poured some of it on to his handkerchief, and dabbed vigorously at his sleeve. When the spot had disappeared, he trotted off to the bar, where, reeking of petrol, he ordered a couple of cocktails which he downed in quick succession. Cocktails were dearer here than in town. Couldn't be helped, needs must when the devil drives. Should he pop down and ask the duty medic for a Maxiton pill? Maxiton perked up the brain. But perhaps it wouldn't mix very well with the drinks. If in doubt, don't: better safe than sorry.

In his office, he examined the sleeve. Damn, a ring! He'd have to keep his arm out of sight as best he could, that's all. The summons was obviously about something important, but important in a good sense or a bad sense? What if he rang Miss Wilson to get some idea of what was in the wind? No, he didn't know her well enough, she was too discreet to give anything away to him. Should he say something to VV? No, that would be a ghastly floater. What if he'd been sent for because VV had reported his shilly-shallying and wanted to drop him in it? The British Memorandum? A verbal dressing-down from the USG before the formal warning or even a reprimand was officially issued? (He recited aloud the fatal passage from Staff Regulations.) Disciplinary measures will be notified in duplicate to the official concerned who shall return one copy, duly initialled! O God! He wiped his forehead with the handkerchief, which was still damp with petrol.

But soon the cocktails began to work and he took heart. No, VV would never dare report somebody he'd seen ensconced in an armchair chatting with the USG. And besides and of course there was the pat on the back! A real solid pat too, he'd nearly been knocked off his feet! It was pretty clear, really, all was well. Perhaps the USG was about to put an interesting proposal to him, maybe ask him to join his private office, where the real power lay. Hell's teeth, those cocktails were strong, he felt giddy. But it was not an unpleasant sensation, not unpleasant at all, he smiled, smugly satisfied.

'Yes, old man, he's sent for me to tell me something to my advantage, take it from me, old boy, you'll see, I bet my bottom dollar it'll all go off a treat. And anyway, I do have a brain, so let's have a plan of action. I go in, greet him with a little bow, not too low, though, and I give him a smile, just a small one, no grovelling. He tells me to sit down, I sit, I cross my legs and we chat. It'll all go swimmingly, you'll see. I'll turn the conversation round to the Jewish Agency for Palestine, that'll get him interested. No, it might get his back up, he might take it as an allusion. The most important thing, see, is for me to come across as sound, a touch of humour, a witty remark, be on the ball, drop in a Latin tag just to show I'm not just anybody. *Quis, quid, ubi, quibus auxiliis, cur, quomodo, quando.* And remember: you're nobody's fool. People take you at your own estimation. I shall be pleasant, yes, but with a hint of authority so he gets the idea that I'm quite capable of running a section. "My own view, Under-Secretary-General, is that the political nub of this particular issue could be summed up like this."'

That damned title of his, Under-Secretary-General, what a mouthful, must be careful not to trip over it. Say it as quickly as possible but taking care not to slur any of the syllables. Five to seven, time to take the vital precaution. Be as totally relaxed as possible so as to be in full possession of all faculties.

'And sharp about it!'

Parked in front of the white porcelain, legs splayed, an easy smile on his face, and eyes misty with alcohol, he began declaiming as he shuddered with terminal relief: 'Under-Secretary-General, I am happy to have been given this opportunity to outline my ideas for the regeneration of indigenous races.' He began this sentence again, replacing 'ideas' with 'own thoughts'. Thereupon, when he was good and finished, he double-checked that he was not improperly dressed in a particular sector of his attire. He even undid his buttons to be quite sure that he had done them up securely, made a point of noting consciously that each button was indeed firmly buttoned to avoid experiencing, just before being shown into the USG's office, any heart-stopping twinge of doubt.

'All done up, every last one,' he muttered. 'Inspected, noted and officially checked.'

Back in his office, he was again seized by panic. Should he draft a note in two parts? Lower-case a, possible replies if a dressing-down. Lower-case b, topics to develop if a non-dressing-down. Yes, on a slip of paper he'd keep hidden. No, three minutes past seven! Too late!

'Anyway he can't give me the push, I've got a permanent contract. The worst I can expect if VV really has reported me is a reprimand. From now on, all work to be carried out with immediate effect.'

In a fever of agitation, he combed his hair and brushed himself down. He wiped petrol fumes over his face again, then pulled his dress handkerchief further out of his top pocket, then tucked it in, then pulled it out again and pondered the effect in his reflection in the window pane. Only then did he leave his office, a sickly smile on his lips and feeling weak at the knees. Reeking of petrol, he was so preoccupied that it never even occurred to him to acknowledge colleagues he passed with a smile or a nod of the head according to

87

grade, his rule of thumb being that a person must be able to keep on the right side of everybody, that politeness costs nothing and may be money in the bank.

CHAPTER 8

On reaching the first floor, he filled his lungs with air and saw her sitting there. 'Fourteen minutes past seven, I'm on my way,' he said as he passed her without stopping, making straight for the head porter, who was lounging in a chair reading a detective novel with relish. 'Do you have an appointment?' asked Saulnier in a voice which managed to be both friendly and suspicious. The reply being affirmative, he smiled cordially, for he liked officials who had appointments. While Adrien turned to join her, he got to his feet and proceeded, like an affable priest, in a poetic aura of importance and authority, to announce Monsieur Deume to the principal private secretary. She took her husband's hand in hers to make him stop buttoning and unbuttoning his jacket. He did not even notice.

'What do your instincts tell you?' he asked.

He did not hear her answer, which anyway was negative. Seven seventeen. All at once he felt convinced that the USG must have got to hear about his regular absence on Saturday mornings. Seized by panic, he sat down beside her in one of the deep braided-leather armchairs which were a gift of the Union of South Africa. His knees trembled and he muttered to himself in a barely audible whisper that he was sitting on hippo hide, hippo hide, hippo hide. And then there was the matter of his sick-leave at Valescure. Perhaps someone had seen him playing roulette at Monte Carlo and had ratted on him.

Seven nineteen. When the porter came towards him he stood up, blinking rapidly in deference to this lowly being who saw the USG every day and was lit by the light of the master. 'This is it. Here I go,' he said to Ariane. 'You will wait for me, won't you?' He wanted to have someone there when he came out, after it was over, someone to give comfort or to constitute an admiring public as the case might be.

But Saulnier merely asked him to be patient, as the Under-Secretary-General was still in a meeting with the British ambassador, but it wouldn't be much longer now since the ambassador was shortly due to meet with the Secretary-General. Brushed by so much greatness, Adrien Deume gave Saulnier a humble smile and through a fog heard him speak of the glorious weather they had enjoyed that day, then of the pretty little country house he had bought at Corsier. Ah, nature! Nature was the only reality! You needed fresh air to be healthy, and peace and quiet too. The porter made a point of being friendly to this young man who was perhaps about to be attached to the private office. Adrien listened uncomprehendingly to the cordial chat put out by Saulnier, who, when he sensed he had acquired a future ally and possibly a protector, went back to his novel.

A few minutes later a discreet buzz unleashed the porter who jumped zealously to his feet and shot off with alacrity towards the Under-Secretary-General's office. He emerged almost at once, holding open the door of the Ark of the Covenant. 'Monsieur Deume,' he called with a gravity which combined benign graciousness with authority and accompanied it with a smile of ecclesiastical complicity which seemed to signify: 'We understand each other, we two, you know I have always had the greatest regard for you.' With his right hand he held the doorknob and, bowing slightly, with his left described a respectful circle by which he appeared to be telling the young man, clearly a high-flier, that he was delighted to allow him in – more, that it would be a positive pleasure to show him the way.

Rising immediately to his feet, Adrien Deume felt a twinge. God! He wanted to go again! No help for it, have to hold out. He buttoned his jacket one last time, doing it up for various reasons of which he was quite unaware – because when his jacket was done up he felt even more weirdly convinced that he cut a stylish dash; because whenever he tried on suits at his tailor's he always ended up thinking that a buttoned-up jacket showed off his figure better and made him look even more irresistible; because a jacket which is fastened is the ultimate protective coat; because, in a fight, the man who wears loose clothes is in the weaker position; because when he was six Adrien had been terrified by an aunt who had given him a dreadful telling-off when she found him doing 'naughty things' with the little girl from next door; because at this solemn juncture he dared not undertake one last check; and because, if by some mishap he were indeed not decent, his buttoned-up jacket would cover up the scandal.

Marching towards his destiny, he absently smartened his tie by primping the knot. Ignoring his wife, his mind blank with fright, and with a virginal smile on his lips and the pallor of death on his face, which with all his anguished strength he tried to make witty yet serious, refined but alert, cultured but determined, grave yet relaxed, respectful but dignified, a face that was interesting but more to the point already interested in the fine, substantive, fruitful views which deserved to be written down at once and become law, the same sacred views, that is, which were about to be uttered by his hierarchical superior to whose cause he was utterly devoted, as indeed he was to all causes and matters of international concern, the junior official, exuding an air of deference and worldliness, hurried towards the sacred shrine with a pleasant look of administrative keenness on his face and, in his loins, an incomprehensible, inconvenient urge which really was most unfair.

God! What a long way it was to the door! Hardly knowing what he was doing, his mind in a whirl, an all-too-willing slave-in-waiting, Adrien Deume quickened his step, believing utterly in international cooperation but equally prepared to give immediate and unconditional support to whatever other topics, human or divine, trifling or dire, would be pleasing in the sight of the Mighty One who held in his hands not only the plentiful manna of promotions, official visits and special leave but also the crackling thunderbolts of official warnings, cautions, reprimands, reductions of salary within the grade, demotion, removal from office and dismissal without notice. Reverential and apprehensive, irresolute, without a clear thought in his head, he passed through the portals, looked up, saw the Under-Secretary-General at the far end of his enormous office, and felt suddenly lost.

Saulnier closed the door reverently, withdrew a couple of paces and smiled at Ariane, who was obviously a delightful person since she was an appendage of a delightful and highly gifted official. Turning round, he suddenly noticed that the door was not quite closed. Galvanized into action, he pulled it to him with a mother's tenderness. With a brow like Jove, he took his irritation out on Octave, his assistant and butt, a long, thin, anaemic, slow-moving young man.

'You little bastard!' he whispered, his mouth twisted with hate. 'Why didn't you tell me? Have I got to do everything around here? I suppose it's no odds to you if the chief catches cold!'

And, unleashing another smile at Ariane, he trod hard on Octave's corn. Octave moved his chair uncomplainingly and went on in slow motion making animals out of twisted paper, which were, as was only right and proper, smaller than the ones made by his superior. She got up, asked the porter to tell her husband that she would be waiting for him downstairs in the lobby. Priest-like, Saulnier inclined his head in boundless comprehension, sat down, and wiped his forehead, for he felt tired. Then he ran his comb through his stubble-cut hair, over a sheet of paper intended to catch the dandruff. When enough had collected, he chortled and blew it all away. Taken with a playful urge to do some work, he inserted a pencil into a Brunswick, the large model, of which Octave proceeded to turn the handle. From time to time the head porter told his underling to stop, and he checked the point of the pencil. Finally, when it was just as he wanted, he raised his left hand, uttered a Napoleonic 'Halt!' and put the pencil on his desk.

'Three hundred and fifty!' he announced, for he kept count of the number of pencils he had sharpened since his arrival in the Secretariat of the League of Nations.

The door to the office opened, and Adrien, after courageously declining to walk through it first, then dared to obey. Followed by the eyes of the porters, whose paper animals were nowhere in sight, the two officials strolled round the waiting-area, the senior man talking and the junior listening with his head turned reverently towards Solal, who suddenly grasped his arm.

Chaste and shy, overwhelmed by this contact sublime, by so much kindness, his mind spinning deliciously in free fall, Adrien Deume walked on air at the side of his superior. He walked, and as he walked he worried that he would get out of step and fail to keep his feet synchronized with the august progress. Soulful and dazed, smiling and perspiring, stunned at having his arm grasped by a high-ranking hand and too bewildered to be sipping the sweetness of such close contact, he proceeded with smooth and dignified tread, listening for all he was worth and understanding nothing of what he heard. Bewitched and feminine, trembling and insubstantial, ethereal as a virgin seduced or a shy bride led to the altar, he floated on the arm of his superior, and his maiden's smile was delicately sexual. Intimate! He was on intimate terms with a chief! Personal contact at last! Oh happy the arm that had been grasped! It was the finest moment of his life.

CHAPTER 9

When he was alone again, Adrien Deume was approached by Saulnier who, smoother than ever, gave him Madame's message. Still wearing the sweet, melting smile which was intended for his hierarchical superior, the junior official went downstairs in a dream. When he reached the ground floor, still smiling, the spectral embodiment of happiness, he walked past his wife without seeing her. Her touch on his arm. He turned and recognized her.

'A,' he said.

He grabbed her arm and controlled an impulse to shout out his amazing exultation. Casting a fonder glance than was his wont in the direction of two belated diplomats who stood chatting together – for now more than ever was he one of them – he guided her towards the lift, forgot to let her go first, pressed the button, and closed his eyes.

'A,' he said again.

'What's the matter? Do you feel ill?'

'Made up to grade A,' he explained in a tight voice. 'No. Not here, not in the lift. In my office, just the two of us.'

'Well now,' he began, settling back into his chair and pulling at his pipe to get his feelings under control, 'well, it's like a fairy tale, it really is. But I must tell you everything, from the beginning. (He surrounded himself with smoke. Don't cry now, act the cool, all-conquering hero. Don't keep looking at her, for the admiration he would see in her eyes might squeeze out the sobs he felt building up in his stomach.) Right, in I go, super de-luxe office, Gobelins and so forth. There he was, very impressive behind this huge desk, face impassive, eyes that looked right through you, and then all of a sudden he smiled. I took to him like a shot, believe me, he's really most awfully charming. I feel as if I could go through fire and water for a chap like him. Well anyway, he smiled, but he didn't say anything. He didn't say anything for ages, a couple of minutes perhaps. I don't mind admitting I wasn't feeling a hundred per cent at my ease but, hell's teeth, I could hardly start talking to him while he was thinking, so I bided my time. And then all at once something quite extraordinary happened. He asked me, completely out of the blue, if I had anything to say to him. It shook me rigid, but of course I said no. He said that was what he thought. To tell you the truth, I didn't quite get what he was driving at, but no matter. So then, not being entirely stupid and in fact with pretty exceptional presence of mind as I'm sure you'll agree, I took the bull by the horns and said that as it happened I did have something to say to him, which was how happy I was to be given an opportunity to say what an honour it is for me to be working under him even if, I added cleverly, it was at several removes. Get the hint there about being appointed to his private office? Neat bit of patter I thought. Next we chatted about this and that, international politics, Briand's latest speech, with me keeping up my end of the conversation very nicely, a proper conversation in his fabulous office surrounded by the Gobelins, I mean a genuine conversation between equals, like it was a sort of social occasion. But hang on, that's not all, there's better to come. Suddenly he takes a sheet of paper and writes something on it. I look out of the window so as not to appear indiscreet. Then he hands me the sheet of paper. It was addressed to Admin. And do you know what was written on it? Well, I'll tell you! My promotion! (He breathed deeply, closed his eyes, opened them again, relit his pipe to choke off an incipient sob, took several puffs to protect his manhood and mask the twitching of his trembling lips.) It said: by decision of the Secretary-General, Monsieur Adrien Deume is promoted to grade A as of the first of June! Just like that! Then he asked for the paper back, signed it, and tossed it into his out-tray. I'd say he'd not even talked it over with Sir John! So it was a personal decision, bypassed the usual channels! What do you say to that?'

'It's wonderful.'

'You bet it's wonderful! Can you imagine? Pitchforked up to an A in one go! And remember I never asked for anything! Can you imagine what sort of bloke he must be, sizing a person up in a couple of minutes, because this afternoon, you know, I didn't talk to him for more than four or five minutes at the outside, but that was enough for him, oh yes, he saw what sort of chap he was dealing with and he drew his own conclusions! He's a very shrewd reader of character! And what a fine man! You know, there's a lot of anti-Semitism about but I must say I don't understand it, it's beyond me! A race that's produced your Bergsons, your Freuds and your Einsteins! (A quick draw on the pipe orchestrated by bubbling dottle.) Oh yes! He saw the sort of person he was dealing with! So, am I in line for congratulations?'

'Yes of course: many congratulations on your promotion. You deserve it,' she added after a pause.

Beside himself with delight, he gave a broad grin which accentuated the roundness of his face. Drops of sweat glistened in his wispy beard. He kissed her ecstatically, then blew his nose. How marvellous to have such a marvellous wife! He put his Détachol-perfumed handkerchief away and sat down in his chair looking very pleased with himself.

'I say, what a shame you didn't stay on the first floor and wait for me. You should have seen the pair of us when we came out of his office! Walking up and down, chatting, just like a couple of old chums, and him with his hand on my arm! Just think, the same hand that takes Sir John by the arm, that very hand held the arm of yours truly! Oh, I was forgetting, when he said goodbye he asked me to present his respects to you. Yes, he said his respects. I thought that was a nice touch, because he doesn't really know you at all. He's every inch the gentleman. (He tapped her lightly on the cheek.) So there we are, Arianny, come the first of June I'm an A. The first of June, it's to do with the budget, the A slot in question doesn't fall vacant for another month, it's Sundar who's going, he's off back to India to run the office there with the rank of director of course, a real cushy number, lucky devil! But an A! Just think what it means! Twenty-two thousand five hundred and fifty smackeroons in gold-equivalent a year, and that's just to start with, because there'll be annual increments to come, don't forget! And in terms of status it's a huge leg-up! Because being an A means having a Persian carpet, a padded leather armchair for visitors, and a lockable glass-fronted bookcase instead of the open shelves Bs are entitled to! Oh, all very senior civil servant! (He was very excited and began leafing through a file without realizing what he was doing, then shut it and opened another.) A leather armchair because, you understand, an A has to see a lot more visitors, it's a job with a definite political dimension, you know. Talks. Overviews. And now, you see, I'll be able to have a couple of modern paintings on the wall! An A can please himself! And not any of your figurative daubs either, they'll be abstracts! And an inlaid box on my desk with the best cigarettes for visitors! Oh very head of section! And beside it a signed photo of the USG! I'll have a quiet word and ask him for one. I mean, someone who walks me around holding my arm, you'd think I'd be able to ask for a photo at a suitable moment, wouldn't you?'

'Yes, maybe.'

'Only maybe?'

'I meant definitely.'

'Oh, I see. So you think it would be all right for me to ask him for a photograph of himself?'

'Yes, I think so.'

'Me too. And another thing, you know, when I'm dealing with members of the Permanent Mandates Commission, I shall be in an altogether stronger position. If I've got anything to say to Volpi – he's the chairman and a marquis – things will be on a different footing from now on. And then the official visits will start rolling in! Because they give As political jobs that call for tact and diplomacy, subtlety, the broader view. (He rapped his forehead.) Damn, I'm forgetting the most important bit! Seeing he was in the right mood, I struck while the iron was hot and invited him to dinner! To make sure he'd accept, I went so far as to say you'd be so happy blah-blah-blah, I even said that when you'd got to know I was seeing him you told me I had to positively insist that he came to dinner, in other words I played on his weakness for the distaff side. Pretty smart, wouldn't you say? I mean you've got to use a spot of diplomacy now and then. Whereupon he accepted – but not before the first of June, which is a month to go, said he wasn't free before then, as you can imagine people scratch each other's eyes out to have him! Unless of course he said June the first because that's my first day as an A, which would be extremely thoughtful of him, don't you think? Listen, we'll have to serve a different wine with every course. I've got a list of the best vintages in my card-index at home. And you, ducky, dressed to kill, evening gown, the lot, as befits the wife of an A! At dinner he'll be on your right, of course, and you'll be ravishing in a low-cut little number! Aren't you pleased, Arianny, to be having a really important person to dinner? Haven't you got anything to say?'

'I've a headache, I'd like to go home,' she said, and she stood up.

'But of course, I'll take you back straight away.'

'No, I need to be by myself for a while. I shan't be very well.'

He did not press her. He knew he had to tread warily when she said those fearful words: they were a warning signal, hoisted monthly, which heralded irritability, moodiness and floods of tears at the least provocation. No good trying anything on with her when she was like this, especially not the day before. Keep out of the way, say three bags full to everything, stay on the right side of her.

'Very well, darling,' he said, considerate and discreet, as we men always are at such moments, and, also like each one of us, O brothers mine, cowed by the imminent arrival of the mysterious dragon of femininity.

'You're right, angel, it'll do you good to go home and have a bath. Just as well you came in the car. You wouldn't maybe like to take a couple of aspirins before you go? I've got some here. No? All right, darling, as you wish. Look, I think I'll hang on here for a bit, it's five past eight but needs must. I really have to make a start on this blasted Memo. I'll be back late, eleven o'clock, even midnight, but it can't be helped. *Noblesse* grade A *oblige* and all that! (A quick in and out of the tongue.) Shall I walk you downstairs?'

'No thanks.'

'Fair enough. Right then, I'll say cheerio. Tell Mummy and Dada that I've had to stay on because something big's come up, but don't breathe a word about my promotion. I want to be the first to tell them.'

When his wife had gone, he got down to the British Memorandum. But on page four he straightened up. Should he keep the signed photo of the USG here, on his desk, or at home, in the drawing-room? If he put it on his desk it would shut VV up all right, but obviously it would go down tremendously well in the drawing-room at home, anybody dropping by would get a clear idea of the kind of circles he moved in. There was something to be said for both solutions. Should he ask for two signed photos? No, that would be over the top, it would look odd.

'Eureka!'

But of course! On evenings when he was expecting company, he'd take the photo on his desk home with him, smuggle it out in his attaché case, and put it up in the drawing-room before any of the guests arrived, and then he'd bring it back to his office the next morning! Two birds with one stone! How's the time going? Eight twenty-nine.

He shut the Memo. No, it was asking too much! He was appallingly hungry. He wasn't going to die of starvation just to keep his highness the VV's hat straight! There were far more important things in life than all this bloody waffle from the British Colonial Office. Like what Dada and Mummy would say when they heard! Get home, put on a tragic face, say he'd been demoted, say he was now just an assistant member of section, and then suddenly come out with the big news! Hugs all round! Mummy crying! Champagne! The Memo could wait! After all, four weeks from now he'd be an A! To all intents and purposes he was already an A! And nuts to VV! He'd let him have his comments, but in his own good time, on A Day! He picked up the phone and dialled the number of the porter's lodge.

'A taxi for Monsieur Deume immediately.' He gave the order in his haughtiest voice, then replaced the receiver with a flourish.

With his felt hat worn broadside, he left, slamming the door behind him. In the corridor, he ran into a B he knew, tremendously keen chap, just transferred from the ILO, who was stuck in his old routine and was usually still there until eight or nine o'clock of an evening. He gave him an unusually effusive greeting and managed to resist the temptation of blurting out the good news, though at considerable cost. But watch your step, you could never tell. Until a promotion had actually gone up on the Staff Movements notice-board, you couldn't count on anything, it could be rescinded. So meantime, mum's the word, button the lip, not a whisper to anybody that might stir up trouble and protests. There'd be plenty of time to crow after the first of June. He'd get rid of the Chrysler and buy a Cadillac! And a little Fiat for Ariane, all to herself! She'd been a brick today, she really had! Oh yes, women liked winners! Everyone knew that.

'See that?' he whispered to his reflection in the mirror in the lift. 'That, old man, is an A!'

PART TWO

Adrien Deume gave a contented sigh, pleased with himself for slotting his car between the two parked Cadillacs at the first attempt. He removed the keys from the ignition, checked that the windows were closed, got out, locked the door, tried the handle several times just to make sure, and gazed fondly at his car. Stunning motors, Chryslers! Amazing acceleration. Easy to handle yet so responsive. His sturdy walking-stick tucked under one arm and with the other holding the attaché case which was the badge of the distinguished civil servant, he moved off briskly. May the twenty-ninth today. Three days from now, the first of June, was A Day, with a starting salary of twenty-two thousand five hundred and fifty smackers in gold-equivalent, rising with annual increments to a ceiling of twenty-six thousand! Not to be sneezed at, old man!

Reaching the lobby, he walked casually over to the Staff Movements board, made sure that no one was watching him and, as on previous days, feasted his eyes on the thrilling words which announced his promotion. Dazzled and transfixed, overcome by wonder as before a divine presence, he stood gazing at them for several minutes, taking them in, making them his, staring at them until they made his head spin. Yes, it was him, really him: Deume, grade A, with effect from the first of June. Three days, and he'd be an A! Could it really be true? Yes! the promise was there, before his very eyes, solemn and official!

'Sweety-pie,' he said to the mirror in the lift which bore him up to his work.

Getting out on the fourth floor, he spotted Garraud in the distance and his mouth watered at the thought of the compliments which were about to come his way. But poor Garraud, who was just a B, did not have the courage to pretend and did an about turn so that he would not have to say how very pleased for him he was. On the other hand, the congratulations offered by Castro, recently promoted to an A, who he ran into a few moments later, were heartfelt. The two As, one newly minted and the other impending, chatted cordially, Castro complaining of dreadful migraines and Adrien promptly giving him the name of his own doctor, the best in Geneva, as was everything he had. Then they formulated a few careful criticisms of the upper echelons of the Secretariat and their permanent mania for reorganizing everything. The Cultural Section, which had been closed down last year, had just been reopened, presumably so that they could close it down again next year. They exchanged knowing smiles and shook hands warmly.

'Castro's a decent enough fellow, a likeable sort,' Adrien murmured as he closed his office door behind him.

Yes, add Castro to the list of people he should ask round soon. On the other hand, cross off all the Bs, who were now infra dig. Except Kanakis, the minister's nephew, and in any case he'd soon be put up to an A, the little swine. He opened his small cupboard to get his working coat, then changed his mind. No, a man who would be an A three days from now shouldn't be seen in an old jacket. An A should be dignified at all times. He turned on his axis, sat down, and thought about his good fortune.

'Promotion – and official, by God, it's up on the board, by God, there's no going back on it now, I really put one across them! I don't mind telling you now, old man, I had the collywobbles all the time until my promotion was put up on the board! You never know, do you, last minute manœuvrings behind the scenes and all that. But now, old man, it's up on the board, all signed and sealed! There's nothing you can do about it now, VV, you'll just have to lump it and look big. Besides, old man, the USG's coming to dinner at my house on the first of June. Hear that, VV? That's three days from now! Is he coming to dinner at your place? I very much doubt it! More coffee, Under-Secretary-General, old man? No, that's no good, much too familiar, it is only the first time after all. More coffee, sir? No that's not right either. More coffee? That's it, with a relaxed smile, as between people of similar background. The fly in the ointment is that Mummy and Dada will be there. Damn! What a rotten idea, bringing the date of their return from Brussels forward like that! They're bound to put their foot in it, Dada will for sure. Can't be helped, but at least it'll show the USG that I've pulled myself up by my bootstraps. But Ariane will be there and she'll make up for them. Now, let's get on with some work!'

Listlessly he reached for the British Memorandum and then pushed it away again. No, really, he couldn't face any kind of big job this morning, it was all a question of state of mind. He couldn't help it, it was outside his control. Anyway, it was almost twenty to eleven. Far too late to start on a task that size. He'd make up for lost time this afternoon. But mark you, old bean, from now on you get in on time every morning, never later than quarter past nine. Agreed, motion carried. But if for urgent and pressing reasons he should ever arrive exceptionally late, leave hat, stick and attaché case in the car. Then, once the front entrance was safely negotiated, behold the model civil servant! Also carried. Now for a bit of a stroll through the corridors, it might help him to think up some undemanding job, a pottering affair, which would be in tune with his frame of mind. Besides, perhaps he needed to go to the lavatory. He'd know when he got there. He left his office with a melancholy look in his eye, for he felt genuinely bad about not working, couldn't rid himself of the thought of the baleful, bulky British Memorandum which sat waiting for him on his desk.

In the lavatory, which was busy as usual, he found himself standing next to Johnson, Head of the Economics Section, who offered him a cordial greeting. An atmosphere of relaxed equality reigned in this place of easement, where the top men, stationed before the perpetual waters, gave friendly smiles to their subordinates who were suddenly become their peers and companions. From this semicircle of like-minded celebrants who stood gravely in their stalls, communing in quietude and occasionally giving an involuntary shudder of ultimate evacuation, there rose a mood of collusion, confederacy and concord, a union of souls, a cloud of male clubbability and veiled fraternity. Adrien emerged with new heart, resolved to put in a good stint.

'And now for the Cameroon Acknowledgement!' he said once he was back in his office. Sitting at his table, he proclaimed that universal toil was a holy law, then opened the Cameroon file with a flourish. Clapping his hands over his ears, he concentrated. How should he start? With 'I am pleased to acknowledge' and so on or 'I am most grateful' and so forth? To enable him to strike the right note, he closed his eyes. But there was a double knock on the door and Le Gandec came in, with his watering eyes and his lavallière. Eager to please and trying to be funny, he gave a military salute.

'Eleven hundred hours, General, the time is nigh,' he announced, and as he said the last word he screwed up his mouth so that he might be thought amusing and roguish. 'Fancy a coffee?'

'Spiffing notion,' said Adrien, who immediately shut the file and stood up. 'Let us sally forth and revitalize the inner man through the uplifting ministrations of the percolator.'

As they did every morning at the same time, they set out with martial tread towards their coffee-break. They were both happy, Le Gandec because he was being seen in the classy company of a future A, and Adrien because he always felt deliciously superior when he was with Le Gandec, who was a lowly assistant member of section. He found being with the poor sod stimulating, it made him feel sophisticated, a charmer, witty and outspoken, and he often liked to pretend that his mind was elsewhere to take the wind out of his humble companion's sails and force him to repeat his questions. In so doing, he merely inflicted on Le Gandec, who was a decent sort, the same mortifications as he was subjected to by Huxley, who was a great exponent of the insulting art of convenient deafness.

In the cafeteria, they chose the table where the section's two pretty secretaries were sitting. Excited by their presence, Adrien, with a gleam in his eye, ordered 'black coffee, please, very strong, to expand my brain power', made a couple of puns, and then quoted Horace to compensate. Basking in their admiration, he teased the two giggling juniors who felt highly flattered, acted up like a rogue male, impersonated Don Juan, took a sip out of one girl's cup so that he would know what she was thinking, and a flirtatious bite out of the other's cake. In a word, he shone, feeding on the deference shown by the other three, revelling in the sheer bliss of being a person of some importance. And so it was that at eleven twenty, feeling thoroughly perked up and after insisting on paying the girls' bill, he stood up suddenly, leader of the quartet, and gave the signal for the off.

'O holy law which levies universal toil, in this wise are thy ways set,' he said with a smile to the two secretaries.

Sitting at his desk, he puffed out his cheeks and amused himself blowing childish noises through his compressed lips. Then he lowered his head on to his blotter and waggled it from side to side, crooning a mournful dirge. Next he put one folded arm on the desk-top, laid his left cheek on it, closed his eyes, and began day-dreaming in a half-whisper, stopping from time to time to ingurgitate a fondant, with his head still hunched to one side on his arm.

'She behaved beautifully at our Heller Petresco dinner, VV had another engagement like oil he did! he's got it in for me on account of my promotion, I don't give a damn, not with that pat on the back behind me, Kanakis genuinely wasn't free, bloody annoying the Rassets didn't turn up because some aunt had kicked the bucket, that was genuine too I saw in the paper that she'd snuffed it, she certainly chose her moment, I admire her timing, learn bridge quick, that way you can invite higher-ups, "Oh Director, we're having a bridge party on Sunday afternoon, would you care to join us?" and then we're in, Meredith, next it's their turn to invite us back, bridge is the thing, no need to make conversation all the time, yet it puts your personal contacts on a friendlier footing and bridge-players are a much more refined, cultured sort, she's not always very easy to get on with these days, what was all that about when I said I wanted to phone Dietsch, what on earth's happened to stop him coming, pity, he knows ever so many people and anyway it impresses people if you can get the conductor of an orchestra she must have upset him, make two alphabetical card-indexes of the things you need when you go away on trips, index A things still to be packed in the cases, index B things already in, on each card write down the item that is to travel with symbols to indicate where the item is to be put, a red marker for items that are a must to take on even a short trip, black marker for items needed only for long journeys, then on the day of departure each time I put an item in the relevant case I take the card relating to the said item out of index A and I transfer it to index B, that way I've got a check, I'll make a start this afternoon, I'll indent for two metal card-boxes, anyway old man a figure like a goddess I can see her with no clothes on whenever I want and believe me it's a sight worth seeing, an adviser is a cut above an A, advisers' offices have two windows, and with two windows you really feel you're somebody, yes don't stew among the As, set your cap at adviser and make it snappy.'

He raised his head, looked around him vaguely, munched a biscuit to drive away a sudden intimation of his own mortality, and looked at his watch. Eleven fifty. Forty minutes to kill. Call in on the duty quack and have his blood pressure taken? No, best go for a turn in the lobby downstairs. The Sixth Committee was meeting today, a tremendously political body with heaps of terribly important people on it.

'Look lively, ducks, we're going to meet some big nobs.'

CHAPTER II

In the lobby, the ministers and diplomats circulated, gravely discussing, knowing-eyed, doubting not the high importance of their ephemeral concerns with ant-heaps soon to pass away, and no less convinced of their own importance, soberly exchanging futile points of view, ludicrously solemn and dignified, stalked by haemorrhoids, faces suddenly wreathed in beaming pleasantries. Affability as an obligation of rank, bogus smiles, courtesies delivered with a cruel curl of the lip, ambitions sugar-coated with the noblest of airs, calculated machinations and crafty manœuvrings, honeyed words and suspicious looks – the connivance and stratagems of tomorrow's dead men.

Like a beetling dockside crane, the leader of the Swedish delegation leaned wearily over Lady Cheyne, who, blithe spirit, sipped the tea in her cup then unwound her long, supple, nut-brown arms with unlovely ease. Lord Robert Cecil, garnished with large, elegantly degenerate ears, smiling and feeling the cold, round-shouldered, a tall, hunched vulture and romantic actor in a high wing-collar, was explaining an extraordinary golf shot to a diminutive French prime minister of radical persuasion and imposing girth, who understood nothing but listened with electoral attention. The young Marquess of Chester smiled smiles of sterling shyness and in a timid stammer offered well-bred suggestions, 'if I may say so', to Benès who, to be civil and to avoid compromising the loan, smiled back through teeth which were much too regular to be true. A towering, high-handed horse, Fridtjof Nansen, nodded approvingly at the man from *The*

Times, vigorously wagging his head and the drooping moustache that went with it to compensate for his straying attention. Lady Cheyne doled out the bounty of her graded civilities, matching them to the status of the persons with whom she conversed and beaming between the two lines which, running from her nostrils to the sides of her mouth, enshrined the contempt of the truly rich. Underlings listened to their betters with rapt attention. Peevish behind a goatee, a foreign minister repeated that it was quite out of ze queshiun and that his gumment would never continence. Beneath a turban of gold, his hands ashen and his eyes bloodshot, a lone rajah reflected. The accredited fly on the international wall, an American lady journalist, was interviewing another foreign minister who was saying that this year would be make or break and constitute a turning-point in international politics. The Bulgarian delegate, a nautch-girl run to fat in thick horn-rimmed glasses, ajangle with bracelets and brooches, a poetess with whom a shy young king had lost his innocence thirty years before, exuded sickly perfumes, quoted Bergson's 'spiritual supplement', and then drove home her point, mammaries pitching and rolling, to the Greek delegate whom she was holding by one button of his jacket in her eagerness to convince. Wherever she went, her nose peeling from too much sun, the Secretary-General's beautiful secretary left a trail of the fragrance of pear blossom. Young bulls, silkily multilingual, laughed dauntlessly. Hygienic and thoroughly scrubbed, her pince-nez attached by a ribbon to her bosom, the Danish delegate stood listening, virginal and pure, to a prime minister who, as he belatedly acknowledged the eager greetings of those around him, explained that this year would be make or break and constitute a turning-point in international politics, a view surreptitiously noted by an eavesdropping journalist. The Deputy Secretary-General closed one eye and puffed up his cheeks the better to decipher the hidden meaning of the formal civilities uttered by Titulesco, the beardless guardian of inner sanctums. Injecting a chummy note into his voice, Benedetti, Head of the Information Section, repeated his instructions to his one-armed aide, who was being watched from afar by his jealous secretary to whom he had been promising marriage for years. The almost white-skinned delegate from Haiti prowled, speaking to no one, gloomily carding the wool of his hair. Albert Thomas, irretrievably suburban, wagged a bright-red tongue through the lush growth of his Greek-patriarch beard, over which the lenses of his spectacles glinted mischievously. The Bulgarian delegate circulated, jangling with passionate intensity and spreading waves of cypress in the wake of her tremendous rump, then sprang at Anna de Noailles, who had just appeared looking deathly ill, and fell on her neck with loud cries. One of Luxemburg's ministers, dumbfounded at being taken seriously, cupped a hand to one ear and relished the remarks directed at him by the German delegate who had a twitch which exposed a set of terrifying canines. Two enemies walked arm in arm and as they went squeezed each other's biceps to bruising point. With rage in his heart, Poland's Foreign Minister, a consumptive condor, accepted the congratulations of the Liberian delegate. Spaak, pure in heart, believed implicitly in the good faith of a smiling Belgian ambassador whose head never stopped nodding approvingly. Hump-backed on a chair, with the butt of a dead cigarette glued to his pendulous lower lip, Aristide Briand informed a newspaper editor overcome by gratitude that this year would be make or break and constitute a turning-point in international politics, then looked around with lifeless eyes and with one drooping finger summoned an embassy secretary who, hardly believing his luck, hurried light-footedly forward, with the grace of a ballerina taking a curtain-call, bent down, lent a doting ear and relished the whispered order. Sunk in an overstuffed armchair and enjoying a long cigarette, Volpi, the new Chairman of the Permanent Mandates Commission, sat dreamily thinking up strategies guaranteed to raise him to the rank of Grand Officer.

Adrien Deume stepped modestly into the lobby, keeping a sharp eye open for any important personages he knew. Spotting the Marquis Volpi, he paused and pursed his lips as an aid to thought. Why not, what the hell, during the last session he had personally handed documents to him, even explained a point of procedure, and had been thanked effusively for his pains. Seize the moment by the tail, especially since the Chairman was sitting by himself, smoking a cigarette. So walk up to him casually, nod and present your respects, which would provide an excuse for starting a conversation, which might in turn be the beginning of a personal contact. Try to bring the talk round to Leonardo da Vinci or Michelangelo. He buttoned his jacket and bore down on his quarry giving no indication that he had seen him yet so that their meeting would seem to be an effect of chance rather than design. When at last he faced the prey he hoped to bag, he manufactured a sophisticated look of delighted surprise, smiled and bowed low, his right hand at the ready. The Marquis Volpi stared at him without responding and the young civil servant looked away, giving the impression that he was smiling at a delicious thought which had struck him, then took to his heels.

Having retreated to the safety of the far end of the room, leaning against the wall with his hands clasped behind his back, meek and despondent, watching for an opportunity to pounce and carry off a prize, Adrien Deume observed the political comings and goings, fascinated by the proximity of such desirably influential figures absorbed in substantive discussions who, with just one word in Sir John's ear, could magically transmute an A into an adviser. From a respectful distance he watched them with deference, nay, with a reverence that hurt, dewy-eyed and pleading, insignificant and scorned, stationed at the rich man's gate, where he caught whiffs of the life of power of which he was no part – of five-star hotels, entertainment allowances, exchanges of views and overall assessments. With his back against his wall, alone, a person of no importance, he smarted at not knowing any of the dignitaries who were there, within arm's reach, on display but not to be touched. He would have liked so much to go among them and shake hands, say hello how are you, nice to see you, chat to life's royalty, to be brilliant and come out with bright comments as witty as they were profound, and above all to be clapped on the back by an important person. Alas, he knew no one, not a single delegate who might have introduced him, not even a technical adviser to tack himself on to. Should he opt for the brazen, frontal approach and simply introduce himself to Spaak, who was a fellow countryman after all? He turned the possibility over and over in his mind, but did not dare.

At length, after waiting in hopes which remained unfulfilled, for he was not recognized or even noticed by any dignitary, he abandoned his crow's nest and went roaming further afield, with eyes peeled, but found nothing to harpoon. The big fish, the ministers and ambassadors whom he had never met, were too big for him. The rest, a shoal of which were backed up in a corner, were small fry beneath his consideration, interpreters, secretaries and facetious journalists who slapped each other wise-crackingly on the back, only too delighted to be misinformed three hours before the general public was. Alone and ignored, the correspondent employed by a Jewish wire agency smiled at the young civil servant with the complicity of the solitary and held out his hand. Without pausing, Adrien kept him at bay with a hurried hello and quickened his step.

He had his back against another wall when who should he see emerging from the Council Chamber but the Secretary-General, who was putting on a cordially jocular display for the Japanese ambassador, a tiny, wizened old party in gold-rimmed glasses, holding him by the upper biceps to demonstrate the sincerity of his feelings. Suddenly Adrien broke into a cold sweat, convinced that Sir John Cheyne had caught his eye and had frowned. Appalled by the idea that he had been observed paddling idly in this tide of pomp where he had no business to be, he about-turned and made for the exit at a pace which he hoped would seem determined and conscientious, modest but above reproach, the step of a man going about his business. Once he was safely in the corridor outside, he made off at a trot towards the reassuring haven of his office.

CHAPTER 12

Behold the Valiant, the five cousins and sworn friends, newly come unto Geneva, mark them well, these men of silver tongue, these Jews of sunnier climes and even finer words, proud to have remained French citizens within their ghetto on the Greek island of Cephalonia, and loyal to the old and noble country and the old tongue.

First, mark Saltiel of the Solals, uncle to Solal of the handsome visage, an old man of consummate kindliness, without guile, solemn, now seventy-five years of age, so engaging to see with his clean-cut, clean-shaven, pleasantly lined face, with his crest of white hair, the beaver hat tilted over one ear, the nut-brown frock-coat with the inevitable buttonhole, the breeches fastened by a buckle at the knee, the dove-coloured stockings, shoes held by more buckles of antic silver, his earring, the stiff schoolboy collar, the cashmere shawl which keeps his chilly shoulders warm, the flowered waistcoat, and his way of inserting two fingers between the buttons thereof, for he is smitten with Napoleon no less than with the Old Testament and – but tell no man – with the New.

And mark Pinhas of the Solals, whom men call Eater-of-Nails but also Commander-of-the-Winds, bogus barrister and unqualified doctor of medicine, tall and consumptive, with forked beard and tortured face, wearing as always a top-hat and a double-breasted frock-coat over the hairy chest beneath, but today sporting shoes with crampons which he has pronounced indispensable for getting about in Switzerland. So much for him.

Next mark Mattathias of the Solals, known as Gum-Chew but also as Widowman-by-Choice (wives being an expensive item), a tall, gaunt figure, unemotional and circumspect of manner, sallow of face, with blue eyes and pointed ears or rather twitching appendages permanently attuned to the rumour of profit. He has only one arm, for the right ends in a large brass hook with which he scratches the top of his shaven head when estimating how much each potential borrower is good for.

Now mark this perspiring, impressive man of fifty years, by name Michael of the Solals, gold-brocaded usher to the Chief Rabbi of Cephalonia, a gentle giant and devout chaser of skirt. On his island, when he walks through the huddled streets of the Jewish quarter, one hand on hip and the other clenching a bubble-pipe, it is his delight to sing in his deep bass voice and draw the submissive glances of the girls, who admire his immense stature and his large, dyed moustache.

And last, mark the youngest of the Valiant, Solomon of the Solals, seller of apricot-juice in Cephalonia, a sweet, chubby little thing a metre and a half tall, so engaging to behold, with his round, beardless face dotted with freckles, his turned-up nose and the quiff which stands permanently erect over his forehead. A cherub, always admiring, always respectful, dazzled by trifles and readily entranced. Solomon, pure in heart, my best and closest little friend, at times when life disgusts me.

'Well now, gentlemen,' began Uncle Saltiel, standing hand on hip and legs bowed. 'With the help of the tutelary goddess, I have obtained an electrical coupling of the apparatus which transmits the human voice, with the corresponding apparatus inside the League of Nations, and I have informed a refined voice of the opposite sex that I wished to have speech with my nephew. And then there burst forth, like a flower suddenly blooming, another female voice, yet more refined and melodious, luscious as Turkish delight, which proclaimed itself keeper of my nephew's privy secrets. To it I communicated the intelligence that we have this moment, this thirty-first of May, incontinently arrived in Geneva in accordance with the directions of my dear Sol, informing the same that our personal toilettes being completed by means of total immersion in the baths of the aptly named Hotel Modeste, we were at the entire disposal of His

Excellency, even adding, to bring a smile to those charming lips, that Solomon had anointed his quiff and forelock with vaseline in the foolish hope of making it lie down. Whereupon, on learning that I was an uncle on the mother's side, the voice like spun gold informed me that my nephew had delayed his return to Geneva, having been obliged to travel as a matter of urgency to divers capitals on secret business.'

'Did she actually say secret?' asked Naileater, somewhat put out.

'No, but the meaning was clear from her tone. He is to return tomorrow, and yesterday he was thoughtful enough to leave a verbal message for me, by the long-distance telephone!'

'All right, all right, we all know you're his pet!' said Naileater. 'Just give us the verbal message and let's have done with these interminable blatherings!'

'The nub of the communication transmitted by the refined lady, who must earn a handsome emolument if we may judge by her voice, is that I am invited to present myself, unaccompanied, tomorrow, the first day of June, at nine o'clock ante meridiem, at the first-class Ritz Hotel.'

'What do you mean unaccompanied?' said Naileater angrily.

'Unaccompanied, she said, and can I help it if he wishes to speak to me in private?' said Saltiel, who opened his snuffbox and took a delicate pinch. 'No doubt your turn will come within the next few days,' he added, not without a hint of malice.

'I see. So I had a bath for nothing,' said Naileater. 'Saltiel, you're going to have to make it up to me, because you needn't think that I braved the waters for my own good pleasure! If that's clear to you, I'm going out. I get edgy if I'm shut up inside too long.'

'Where are you going?' asked Solomon.

'I shall put on my white gloves and leave my card with the Vice-Chancellor of the University of Geneva, a simple courtesy which I must discharge as a former Vice-Chancellor of the Jewish and Philosophical University of Cephalonia which I founded with such success, as I believe you know.'

'What university?' asked Mattathias while Uncle Saltiel shrugged his shoulders. 'Its premises were your back kitchen, and you were the only professor.'

'My dear fellow, quality is much more important than quantity,' retorted Naileater. 'But enough. Let's have no more envy. What I've done is to make a visiting-card by cunningly writing my name so that it looks as if it has been professionally printed. I listed my previous functions, then wrote simply: "from one colleague to another, distinguished greetings", then added the address of our hotel should he in turn feel inclined to drop by and leave his card and invite me to share a polite conversation between Vice-Chancellors over a helping of the Swiss dish known as "fondue", which is made with cheese, garlic, white wine, nutmeg and a slurp of kirsch which must be added at the last moment. It will all depend on whether he's a man of breeding. Farewell, gentlemen.'

CHAPTER 13

The porter at the Ritz Hotel peered suspiciously at the dove-coloured silk stockings worn by the tiny old man who stood before him with a gold earring in one ear, a beaver hat in his hand and his mackintosh over one arm, while the three young bellboys sitting on a bench swung their legs and whispered veiled remarks to each other through barely moving lips.

'You have an appointment?'

'Appointment, my foot and my elbow!' came the cool reply from this bizarre personage, who proceeded to put his hat back on his head. 'Know this, O janissary, learn, O brown-uniformed, excessively gold-braided one, and be told that I am his uncle, that's the long and short of it; that it is none of your business whether I have an appointment or not, though as a matter of fact I have, made yesterday via the telephonic apparatus by the lady with the cultured voice for this very day, the first of the month of June, at nine o'clock ante meridiem, but I thought it would be better to come at eight, for that way we shall be able to drink our morning coffee together.'

'So you have an appointment for nine?'

In a transport of delight, with the nearness of his nephew making him overbearingly full of himself, Saltiel did not even hear the question.

'I am his uncle,' he went on, 'and should you require me to show you my totally genuine and absolutely unforged passport, you will see that my name is Solal, like his! His uncle, rightful brother to his own mother, who was also a Solal, but of the junior branch, which in reality is the senior line! But let's not go into that. And when I say his uncle, I really should say his father, for he has always preferred me to his natural sire! That's life, my friend, for the biddings of the heart are not ours to command! One person is born to be loved, another to be loved less well! This man becomes a chieftain in the League of Nations by the power of his brain, and this other a hotel porter eternally at the mercy of guests who arrive, and condemned to touch his cap to those who depart! May God comfort him in his lowly station! But here's the nub: I have come to see him before the appointed hour of nine because it is my pleasure to wish to drink the first cup of coffee of the day in his company, for I held him on my lap when he joined the Covenant, when he was but one week old, and because it is also my pleasure to converse with him on divers lofty subjects while luxuriating in his splendiferous surroundings, which I do, though not without resentment, for he is most assuredly being overcharged in this hotel where I note that the electric lights are still burning at eight o'clock in the morning, thus driving up the overheads. And who pays for it all? He does! The hand that reaches into his wallet steals from me! So if it's not too much of a strain, would you mind turning off all these lamps, for outside the sun shines as bright as in the land of the Pharaohs?'

'Who shall I say is calling?' asked the porter, who decided against ejecting this madman straight off since it could be true that he was a relation after all. With these foreign types you could never tell.

'Since you have to do something to earn your salary and justify the two golden keys on your collar, say that it is Saltiel of the Solals, his only uncle, who has stepped on to terra firma in one piece from a flying-machine chartered in London, whither I had ventured to study the manners and customs of the British in the wake of numerous other expeditions, some undertaken by means of locomotives, others on the wings of clouds, others still by maritime routes, with the constant purpose of increasing my knowledge and exploring the human heart. But now I am arrived in this place, summoned by my nephew and son of my soul! I have spoken. And now do your porterly duty!'

Picking up the receiver, the porter announced the arrival, listened to the reply, hung up, smiled pleasantly, and asked the visitor if he would be good enough to go up. At this, Saltiel crossed his arms, like an admiral.

'Find favour in the eyes of the King,' he intoned, 'and the haughty viper will sing with the humble voice of the canary! So it is with me, friend: gracious words for the affable, but beastly to beasts, a lion to hyenas! But we should show mercy to menials, so let us draw a veil over what has been! Tell me the number of his room.'

'Apartment thirty-seven, sir. I'll have a bellboy show you the way.'

At a sign from his superior, one of the bellboys stood up and Saltiel gazed curiously at the red uniform worn by the impeccably groomed adolescent: braided-gold epaulettes, buttons shining on the bum-freezer jacket, gold stripes on the trousers and sleeves. 'Bell-ringing at his age?' he thought. 'What strange customs they have here! And just look at him! Turned out like the Prince of Wales! Yet another charge on the overheads!' Biting his lip to keep a straight face, the bellboy indicated that he would lead the way. But, two metres before they reached the lift, Saltiel stopped, troubled by a sudden thought. All these underlings would now proceed to put it about that their illustrious client had an uncle who lacked polish and was therefore a member of a family of no distinction. Well, he'd show these Europeans that he knew how to behave and that he was perfectly at ease in the most exalted circles.

'No, after you,' he said with a pleasant smile to the diminutive lackey in white gloves, who had halted at the entrance to the lift.

The bellboy obeyed, crimson with suppressed mirth, and Saltiel followed him, his gait a mixture of glide and sway which seemed to him the very pineapple of the diplomatic manner.

'Return to your duties, child,' he said, when the lift stopped at the third floor. 'There is no need for you to come with me. I shall find the apartment, which is numbered, myself. Here are ten Swiss centimes for you. Buy yourself some sweeties or make an oblation thereof to your saintly mother, according to the dictates of your heart.'

He was shocked by the ingratitude of the impertinent youth who did not even pause to say thank you. All the king-sired child had done was to press one finger on a button of this vertical locomotive! So what did the princeling expect by way of a tip? He had got pennies, it was true, but they were Swiss pennies, in other words droplets of pure gold!

His indignation spent, he stood in the corridor and smiled, congratulating himself on having got rid of the Prince of Wales. Now he could take his time, prepare his entrance and make a good impression. He produced a looking-glass from his pocket and peered into it. The turned-down collar looked well, very clean and highly starched. A good thing he'd thought of running the iron over his frock-coat that morning. The red carnation in his buttonhole went nicely with the flowered waistcoat. Besides, didn't English cabinet ministers always wear a buttonhole? He smoothed his silky crest of white hair, then pulled his beaver hat down over one ear, for he had noticed that whenever his nephew dressed formally he wore his handsome top-hat slightly to one side.

'Yes, the titfer modestly tilted is altogether more modern, more rakish, and, by the by, commands attention.'

He lowered the little looking-glass until it was on a level with his knees. Yes, his breeches were held firmly in place by the buckles of antic silver. Last evening, Naileater had made disparaging remarks about these breeches which belonged to another age. Just jealous, of course. He had been wearing breeches all his life and he wasn't going to alter his habits now, not at his age. No, very presentable. He unleashed a long, simpering sigh. Just imagine, his nephew was there, on the other side of this door, thinking of him and waiting for him to come. Yes, as soon as he was inside he would embrace him and give him his blessing. He cleared a frog from his throat and, with his old heart beating loudly, he approached the enchanted door and knocked quietly. There was no reply. Taking his courage in both hands, he knocked louder.

The door opened and Solal, wearing a sumptuous dressing-gown, bent his head and kissed the hand of Saltiel, who felt suddenly weak at the knees. He was overwhelmed by the kiss bestowed on his hand and could think of nothing to say. He dared not embrace his nephew – in any case he was too tall – who stood looking at him with a smile on his face. To show a bold front, he rubbed his hands together and then asked Sol if he was well. The reply being in the affirmative, he rubbed his hands again.

'God be praised. I am very well too, thanks. What a splendid day it is,' he added after a moment's silence.

Eventually Solal took pity on his little uncle and cut short his embarrassment by kissing him on both of his perfectly clean-shaven cheeks. Saltiel returned the embrace, wiped his nose, murmured a blessing, looked all around him and beamed.

'Handsome drawing-room, son. May you long have the use of it, dear boy. But I see that the window is open. You must watch out for draughts, laddie, and remember that a dab of mentholated vaseline in the nostrils keeps colds away. Well now, Sol, all well with the politics? Are you pleased with the various nations?'

'They are behaving themselves,' said Solal soberly.

There was another silence, which Saltiel dared not break. Sol was probably turning important thoughts over in his head, preparing some difficult speech perhaps. He decided to let him be for a moment or two, so that he wouldn't lose his thread. He crossed his arms and stood quietly where he was, watching his nephew pace up and down the room. How tall he was! Just imagine, he had held him on his lap the day he was circumcised! Then he was a baby who cried; now he was a great lord, a leader of nations. Praise be to God who knew what He had been about! Yes, that must be the reason. If he wasn't saying much, it was because his mind was on his speech or busy mulling over a decision on which hung the fate of some country or other. And to think that that infernal Englishman, Sol's so-called superior, would go about telling everybody that it had been his idea all along and then take all the credit! This 'Under' affixed to 'Secretary-General' stuck in his craw: he just could not swallow it. When the devil would this blasted Englishman make up his mind to resign and leave the job to a man capable of doing it properly? Of course, he did not wish this useless Englishman dead, but if it pleased God to visit him with just enough arthritis to force him into early retirement, well, heigh-ho, it would be the will of the Almighty.

'Uncle. Dinner this evening. At the Deumes. Shall I go? Or stay away? You decide.'

'What can I say, dear boy? I'm not qualified to judge. If you want to go, then go you must.'

Solal opened a drawer, took out a bundle of bank notes, handed them to his uncle, who counted them and, when he was done, looked up at the source of such bounty with pride, his eyes ashine with brimming tears. Only a scion of a royal line would give you ten thousand Swiss francs as if it were a bull's-eye or a gobstopper!

'The blessing of God be on you, my boy. I thank you from the bottom of my soul. But I don't need money. I am too old to want so much. What would I do with it? Keep the fruits of your sweat, laddie, but not in a drawer, not even in a lockable drawer, for a key can be copied – such is the destiny of keys. Put these notes deep in your pocket and fasten it with safety-pins, for pockets yawn – such is the way of pockets. And now, dear heart, know that I never miss a thing: I have observed that you need to be alone to ponder the matter of this evening's dinner. So I shall take myself off downstairs and find me an armchair. I shall not be bored, never fear. I shall watch the people as they come and go, it's a hobby of mine. Send me word when you have done your pondering. So goodbye for now, eyes of mine, and God be with you!'

When he reached the lobby, his misgivings took hold of him again. Yes, he really had been a bit rude to the porter earlier on. The blackguard was perfectly capable of getting his own back on the uncle by taking it out on the nephew – by tearing up an important letter or committing God knew what other piece of underhanded villainy. It was absolutely imperative that he should work himself into the swine's good graces and spike his thirst for revenge.

He went over to the small office, leaned his elbows benignly on the counter, and said to the porter: 'My nephew has spoken to me about you. You stand high in his esteem.' Taken aback, the porter made gratified noises and Saltiel, shooting a bewitching smile at the now neutralized nasty, began casting about for an affable follow-up to consolidate this auspicious beginning. 'I take it you are a Swiss citizen?' The porter gave a grudging 'Yes', shocked that a League of Nations bigwig should be a nephew of this clown in breeches. Clearly, with foreigners you could expect anything, you never quite knew which part of the woodwork they crawled out of.

'My compliments,' said Saltiel. 'Switzerland is a wise and noble country, possessed of every virtue, and I most sincerely wish it a prosperous future, though it has no need of my wishes since it keeps a pretty firm hand on the tiller. And this hotel is excellently well run, where's the harm in leaving a few lights on, makes it more cheerful. (After a pause, he thought that one or two details about Sol might be of interest to this gloomy individual and complete the softening-up process.) Just consider, my porterly friend, that, like all first-born sons of the senior Solal line, my nephew's first name is Solal! It's a tradition! More specifically, on his Jewish birth certificate he is recorded as Solal XIV of the Solals, son of the revered Chief Rabbi of Cephalonia and a descendant of the High Priest Aaron, brother of Moses! Fascinating, isn't it? And that, pleasant porterman, is not all: my four cousins and I have the honour of belonging to the junior line! After several centuries, some highly agreeable, others less so, spent in divers provinces of France, we sailed away to the isle of Cephalonia in 1799, there to link hands with the senior line which had taken refuge therein in 1492 in the wake of the expulsion of the Jews from Spain! Cursèd be Torquemada! I spit on him! Listen, we five, of the lesser Solal lineage and known as the Valiant of France, received full French citizenship by the terms of the most agreeable decree issued by the National Assembly on the twenty-seventh of September 1791, and French citizens we have been proud to remain, duly registered by the consulate at Cephalonia, thrilled to speak the sweet tongue of the old country spiced with fustian vocables unique to the county of Avignon and known only to us, and honoured on long winter evenings to be dewy-eyed readers of Ronsard and Racine. But know this too, O porter of porters, that both Naileater and Michael saw service with the Hundred-and-Forty-First Infantry at Marseilles, the other three of us, myself included, having been judged unfit for military duties, which was a great disappointment, but there you are.'

The ringing of the telephone stopped his flow. The porter replaced the receiver on the hook and said that his nephew was asking for him. 'Very glad to have had this little chat. Be so good as to accept an aniseed ball,' said Saltiel, who proffered his little box of sweeties, gave a graceful bow, and departed, highly delighted by his little stratagem. From this moment henceforth, Sol was safe and dry! He had wound the porter round his little finger! It was with extreme affability that, having first proffered a liquorice allsort as being 'more suited to your age', he said no to the invitation to use the lift extended by the other potential enemy he had thus appeased, the princeling arrayed in red and buttoned in gold. This cage which went up and down did not appeal to him at all. The cable might snap, and he had his doubts about the life to come.

'Capital, this fine-blend coffee! Balm to my soul!' said Saltiel, and he poured himself a second cup, which he then sipped with the slurpings indispensable to a proper appreciation of its flavour. 'The tray, both coffee pots and the spoons are all silver, I can see the hallmarks, God indeed be praised. Ah, if only your poor mother could see you now surrounded by all this silverware! By the by, I omitted to tell you that following our visit last year, after we bade you farewell, we went, you'll never guess, unto a mountain named Salève, close by Geneva, it was Naileater's idea. Eight hundred metres it measures in the matter of height! My dear, the precipices! The cows left to wander about! Horns a metre long, as God's my witness! And with such a stupid, unfeeling look about them! All these Gentiles who pay good money to get themselves impaled on an Alp so that they can freeze to death and fall over cliffs when they're exhausted, well, it passes my understanding! Yes please, I'll have another cup of coffee if there's some left, there's no point in leaving any, they charge you enough for it. Thank you, my son, and may the Almighty watch over you and look upon you with gladsome eye. Ah, my boy, it makes me so very happy to know that you are here in Geneva, the small republic with a great heart, home of the Red Cross and righteousness! It's quite different from Germany! Incidentally, Naileater told me yesterday afternoon in the strictest confidence that he was thinking of buying rabid dogs from the Pasteur Institute so that he could release them secretly into Germany. The idea was that they would bite Germans, who would also get rabies, who would then bite other Germans, and so on and so forth until the whole cursed lot of them were biting each other. I absolutely forbade him to do any such thing, quite outrageous, pointed out to him that there's nothing German about us! Anyhow, we had a long discussion about it and in the end he conceded defeat! After that, I took a turn outside with Solomon, felt like a breath of lakeside air, and we strolled along together holding hands by our little fingers. Then we went to see the Wall of the Reformation. Quite magnificent. We doffed our hats before the four great reformers and observed a minute's silence, because Protestantism is a noble faith, and moreover Protestants are very honest people, very proper, it's a well-known fact. You should have seen Solomon, standing to attention like a soldier, very serious, holding his little boater in his hand. He even wanted us to observe an extra minute's silence. I find that Lord Calvin has something of our own master, Moses, about him, just a little something, of course, since Moses, our master, is beyond compare, he was the Almighty's only friend, He has never had another, so there's no contest! Still, I like Calvin very much, strict but fair, not a man to trifle with! Next, we went and had a look at the University, which is just opposite. There's a motto carved over the main entrance, I committed it to memory, I'll recite it for you, see what you think: "In dedicating this building to advanced study, the People of Geneva pays tribute to the virtues of Education, the ultimate guarantor of the rights of citizens." Now isn't that superb! Such a thought is the hallmark of a great people, believe me! I wiped a secret tear from my eye, I don't mind admitting. And Solomon took his hat off and was all for observing another minute's silence, this time, in front of the University! And there you have it, a full statement of how I spent yesterday. Oh, by the way, dear boy, this boss of yours, the Englishman, still keeping well is he?'

'Very well,' smiled Solal.

'Thanks be to God,' Saltiel said, and then sighed: 'And yet he is a man getting on in years.'

'He has the constitution of an ox.'

'Thanks be to God,' Saltiel said, and then gave a little cough. 'So, you are happy with world politics. But have a care: if this Hitler fellow asks you to lunch, don't go! Of course, if you absolutely have to accept because of your job, then go, but tell him your stomach's upset and you're not allowed to eat anything. I've just remembered, he keeps a cupboard full of all kinds of poisons. So don't eat anything if you do go, for the love of God, and if he gets angry, pay no attention. Let him get angry if he wants! Let him drop dead! A thousand curses upon him! The thing to do is to keep well in with the French and the English. When you write to them, butter them up, obedient servant and so forth. Anyway, my boy, what have you decided about your dinner this evening?'

'I shall go.'

'Lot of important people coming, I imagine?'

'She is beautiful and Ariane is her name.'

'Is she Jewish, son?'

'No. One last time shall I see her this evening and then it will be over, I shall let her be. Goodbye, Uncle.'

He placed the avuncular hat on the old man's head, kissed him on the shoulder, showed him to the door, and poor Saltiel, feeling lost, found himself in the dimly lit corridor. He walked slowly down the stairs, rubbing his nose and scratching his forehead. Clearly the boy was smitten, obsessed! How was it that only the daughters of Gentiles were pleasing to the boy's eye? First there had been that consul's wife, then the consul's wife's cousin, Aude, she was dead, may her soul rest in peace, and God knows how many others after her, and now there was this Ariane! No denying that all these blonde creatures were charming, but surely there were also plenty of Jewish girls who were charming, educated and fond of reciting poetry. What was it that they didn't have, apart from not being fair of hair?

With a lugubrious word to the porter, he went out into the street, where seagulls with an anti-Semitic gleam in their eye flew round and round shrieking stupidly, enraged by hunger. He paused at the lake. The water was wonderful, so clean that anybody would pay to drink out of it. These Swiss had all the luck. Setting off again, he addressed his nephew.

'Don't misunderstand me, my boy, I've got nothing against Christians, indeed I've always said that a good Christian is at least as good as any Jew on an off day. But, do you see, with a girl who is one of us you're part of the family, you can talk everything over with her, like brother and sister if you follow me. Whereas with a Christian girl, even the most delightful and sweetest-tempered of them, you would be well advised not to bring up certain matters if you don't want her vexed or offended. In any case she'll never understand our trials and tribulations the way we do. And besides, even if she is absolutely delightful, she'll always be watching you out of the corner of one eye, thinking something unpleasant about us when you're having a row, something not very flattering. Gentiles don't mean any harm, it's just that they have wrong ideas. They think badly of us because they believe they're right, poor misguided souls. I'll have to write a book to show them how mistaken they are. Besides, you know, every twenty or thirty years, that is in the lifetime of every man, something catastrophic happens to us. The day before yesterday it was the pogroms in Russia and elsewhere. Yesterday the Dreyfus affair. Today the utter beastliness of the Germans, and tomorrow God only knows what. You'll get through the hard times which are coming much better with a good Jewish girl by your side. Oh dear, why on earth did you send me away without giving me a chance to talk some sense into you?'

Lost in his thoughts, he walked on, rubbing his nose and scratching his forehead. To be sure, Sol had promised that he would let this Ariane girl be. But unfortunately he was smitten with her, he'd said so. So when he saw her tonight at dinner she'd be so willowy and blonde that he'd forget his resolve and pow! he'd look at her in a soul-stirring sort of way, he'd smile, he'd show his teeth, and the poor unfortunate girl would be ensnared, for he was winning and gentle and they liked that. For consider: had not the rogue, when barely sixteen, carried off the luscious wife of a French consul, as wide as she was tall? He sighed.

'Only one thing to be done: find one of our girls for him.'

He clapped his hands. Yes, put this Mademoiselle Ariane up against a virginal Jewish paragon with good looks, good health, expensive clothes, a taste for poetry, the piano, daily baths and modern-style skiing. When a suitable candidate was found, he'd praise her charms to his nephew, he'd overpower him with words, for his words would be like a needle in the hands of an expert etcher. Yes, baffle him with eloquence, marry him off whip and spur, and put a stop to all these silly notions!

'Forward march! First stop, the Rabbi's. Let's find out what he's got on offer!'

CHAPTER 14

At two o'clock that afternoon, Madame Deume and her adopted son
settled themselves in the drawing-room, she in a salmon-pink camisole
and he in plus-fours. Tied under their shoes were detachable felt soles,
the kind used to protect parquet floorings.

'Well now, darling, and how did it all go at the Palais on your first
morning as an A?' enquired the bony lady with the head of a
sententious dromedary. Under her chin hung a short ligament of skin
ending in a small adipose lump which was constantly on the move,
like a clapperless bell.

'Swimmingly,' said Adrien simply. He was determined to appear
nonchalant, as one to the manner born. 'Swimmingly,' he repeated,
'except that the lock on my glass-fronted bookcase turned out to be
faulty. Well, it did work after a fashion, but you had to try ever so
hard to turn it every time, so as you can imagine I told the little man
from Equipment what he could do with it and he sent up a locksmith
on the double. An A gets the full VIP treatment.'

'Of course, darling,' said Madame Deume approvingly, and she
smiled, her long upper incisors coming to rest at an oblique angle on
the soft cushion of her lower lip. 'Listen, I hope you'll make allowances for this poor excuse for lunching, just sandwiches, hardly the
thing to set before an A, but on a day like today I've had other things
on my mind, and anyway you'll have all the more appetite for dinner
this evening. (She stopped talking suddenly and played with her
adipose lump, a living trinket which she fingered in her more
meditative moments, savouring the feel of its spongy texture.) What's

the matter, Didi? You've got your worried face on all of a sudden. Is it on her account? You can tell Mummy.'

'It's that damned note on her door. Always the same old story – she's asleep and mustn't be disturbed. Nasty habit she's got into, taking those sleeping-pills.'

Again her hand strayed to the dangling meatball. She poked it with expert fingers, sighed, but decided this was not the moment for saying exactly what she thought. Not now, not on a red-letter day, when they were expecting the Under-Secretary-General of the League of Nations to dinner. Didi needed every ounce of his strength.

'It's not surprising, what she needs is an interest in life,' she could not prevent herself from saying even so. 'If only she could bring herself to do a few things around the house! It's staying in her room for hours on end reading novels that stops her sleeping, poor pet.'

'I'll have a serious heart-to-heart with her tomorrow when we won't have the invitation to worry about,' said Adrien. 'And you realize that the sleeping-pill was because it was midnight when we got back from the Johnsons'. Incidentally, I didn't have time this morning to tell you how the dinner went. Awfully smart, nothing but the best, there were eighteen of us. Faultless service. Everything in the very best of taste. I got invited on the strength of my A, of course. I'm somebody now, the Johnsons actually notice me. The USG was there, very sprucely turned out, but he hardly said a thing. Just exchanged a few words with Lady Haggard, who is pretty thick with the Johnsons, they're on first-name terms, the Johnsons calling her Jane at every opportunity. She's the one who's the wife of the British Consul-General, who in fact ranks as a full minister given how important his posting is in Geneva, it happens sometimes, anyway he wasn't there, had the flu. She's a looker, a lot younger than her husband, thirty-two at most, only had eyes for the USG. When we moved into the drawing-room, the biggest of them, because believe it or not there are three *en suite* . . .'

'The van Offels have three drawing-rooms *en suite* too,' broke in Madame Deume with a modest smile, and she exhaled noisily through her nose.

'So anyway, when we moved to the drawing-room, Lady Haggard sat down next to the USG and did nothing but talk to him, literally threw herself at him, and then, since the conversation got on to some cave or other the Johnsons have in the grounds, she offered to show him round it. Exactly what happened in the cave I couldn't say. Veil drawn over proceedings! And then, just as she was leaving, she offered him a lift in her car back to the Ritz since he hadn't brought his, perhaps it was being repaired, though I'd be surprised, since he's got a Rolls. What went on between them, well now, I'd sooner not speculate, least said soonest mended! I forgot to mention that among the guests there was also a counsellor from the Romanian legation, he was sitting on Madame Johnson's left with the USG on her right. So you see the kind of company my A gets me into!'

'Yes, darling,' said Madame Deume, happy for her adopted son's social success but inwardly seething at having no part of it and far from eager to be told about a world which behaved as though she did not exist.

'But that's enough of that. Tell me, Mumsy, there's just one little thing that bothers me. Poor Dada looked awfully low in his den after lunch. The way you sent him packing was a teeny bit obvious, you know.'

'Nothing of the sort. I put it to him very naicely that I needed a quiet word with you about the arrangements for this evening. I even called him "dearest Hippolyte", so I don't see how you can say that.'

'Yes, but he feels left out of things.'

'Not at all, he has his etiquette manual. Oh, I forgot to tell you, you won't credit it, but this morning he shot off to town bright and early to buy himself a guide to good manners and never told me, would you believe, never asked me what I thought. Oh no, his lordship wanted to confront me with a *fait accompli*. I know it comes out of his pocket money, but even so he might have shown a littel more consideration. But I've forgiven him and no bad feelings. It would have been something if it had kept him happy, but all blessed morning while you were out at the Palais, he insisted on following me around reading out bits from his book, I only listened with one ear, believe me, I had far too many other things on my mind.'

'Why not try to get him to join in a bit more. He never said a word all through lunch, the poor old boy obviously feels excluded.'

'But I do get him to join in. This morning I had him traipsing up and down the corridor. You can't beat felt soles for giving a parquet a good finish. He was only too glad to feel he was helping.'

'Fine. (He punctuated this monosyllabic comment by knocking his pipe out with the brisk flourish denoting the man of action which Madame Deume observed with admiration. Yes, Didi took after her, a true Leerberghe. All the same, she made a mental note: "Get Martha to give the ashtray a wipe over and tell her to hoover under the coffee-table.") Anyhow, Mummy, how far have we got with the arrangements? Our guest will be arriving at seven thirty. I should have said eight.'

'Why?'

'Because it's much more the thing. Dinner at the Kanakises' always starts at eight, same goes for the Rassets and the Johnsons too. The thing is I was a bit flustered, understandably so, when I dangled the invitation on the end of my line. (He was pleased with the image.) But too bad, what's done is done. What's important is that I'm the only one in the whole of my section to have the USG to dinner. Unless VV . . . no I don't think so. Anyway, fill me in about where we're up to with the preparations, what's been done and what's left to do, you know, a brief report on the state of play, to give me some idea of where I stand, but it'll have to be quick because it's already twenty past two and I have heaps of errands to do in town. If I could have swung it, I'd have taken the morning off too, but not with VV's temper the way it is these days. Between you and me, he just can't stomach my A, especially since he obviously sees me as a potential successor.'

'Yes, darling,' she said, gazing at him fondly.

'As it is, I was jolly lucky to get the afternoon off and I could hardly tell him outright it was on account of this dinner party for the USG, now could I, because that would have put me in his bad books once and for all.'

'Of course, dear, you're right. But what are these errands you've to do?'

'Candles for a start. We'll have a candlelit dinner. Lots of people are doing it nowadays.'

'But, darling, we have plenty of candles!'

'No,' he said in a categorical voice. (He relit his pipe and pulled masterfully on it.) 'They're the twisted sort, dreadfully *passé*. We've got to have straight ones, like they do at the Rassets. (Madame Deume's face turned to stone: the Rassets had never invited her to anything.) And there's something else. I'm going to change the wines. Goretta, if you please, sent me up a 1924 Bordeaux and a 1926 Burgundy. They're quite good vintages and he thought they'd pass muster. But I'm going to insist on Saint-Émilion 1928, Château Lafite, also 1928, and a 1929 Beaune, both excellent years, indeed I'd go as far as to say they are exceptional. (Recent expertise this, picked up from a book about wine he had bought the previous day.) Rather than phone, I shall call in myself and see to it that the order is changed there and then. They thought they could see me coming, but I'll show them exactly the sort of person they're dealing with!'

'Yes, dear,' said Madame Deume, tickled by her Didi's manly manner.

'And there'll have to be flowers.'

'But we have masses in the garden. I was just about to go and pick some!'

'No, we must have pukka flowers.'

'What sort of flowers, darling?' she asked, and she neatened her great big man's tie for him.

'I'll see. Maybe orchids. Or perhaps water-lilies we can put in a bowl of water in the middle of the table.'

'But wouldn't that look peculiar?'

'When Lady Cheyne gives formal dinner parties, she always has flowers floating in bowls in the centre of her table, Kanakis was telling me about it only the other day.'

'Does he get invited there?' she asked, pouncing like a tigress.

'Yes,' he replied after clearing his throat.

'But he's not senior to you, is he?'

'No, but his uncle's a minister. That opens doors.'

There was a silence during which Madame Deume again poked at her lump, suddenly dejected at the thought of the undistinguished husband which fate had wished on her. She sighed.

'You have no idea how difficult your poor Dada was all morning, following me around everywhere I went, reading out snippets from his etiquette book. In the end, I had to pack him off to the guest room, I've turned it into a naice littel snuggery for him since we got back so that I can get a bit of peace. If only he could take some of the pressure off you by running a few of your errands. But he's quite hopeless, poor man, gets everything mixed up. Anyway, you may not have an uncle who's a minister but you've got where you are on your own merits.'

She picked a speck of dust off her adopted son's jacket.

'Shush a minute! I'm thinking!'

She respected Adrien's inward communing and turned the silence to good use by running a finger over the top of the coffee-table. She inspected the fingertip. Good, Martha had done a thorough dusting. Through the open door wafted the voice of Monsieur Deume, who was declaiming a thrilling gem out of his etiquette book: '"When the guest unfolds his napkin, he sets his bwead down on his left"! Hear that, Antoinette?' She sang out: 'Yes, thank you!' Again the voice of Dada rang down: '"Bwead should be cwumbled with the fingers and never cut with a knife. Pieces may be bwoken off as and when wequired. On no account should morsels be pwepared in advance of need"!'

'There! He's been like that all morning. Do you realize the patience I've needed?'

'Listen, Mummy, I want this to be a really smart dinner party! So I've decided to let him choose the wines! Of course, the awfully in thing is to serve dry champagne all through dinner! I'm practically certain that's what he'll prefer and it'll impress him no end, you know. So, just as we're about to sit down to table, I'll say to him, all casual: "Which would you prefer, Under-Secretary-General, the classic accompaniment or just champagne?" I'll have to think about the wording. If he chooses champagne, the Bordeaux and the Burgundy will do for another time. Are you agreed that we shouldn't worry about expense?'

'Oh absolutely! Not for an occasion like this!'

'Champagne all through dinner is terribly smart! Best have six bottles so there's no danger of running out. In case he turns out to be a big drinker, though I don't think he is, still you never know. Oh, yes, that's it! Eureka!'

'Whatever's the matter, darling?'

He stood up, walked to the window, returned to his adoptive mother, and stood staring at her, hands in pockets, with a smile of triumph.

'I've had an idea! And if I say so myself, it's utterly brilliant!'

At this juncture, shuffling gracefully, Monsieur Deume appeared in the doorway, a small seal of a man with a goatee and large, round, prominent eyes which looked bewildered behind the lenses of his pince-nez. He said sowwy to intewwupt, opened his etiquette book at the page he was keeping with his forefinger, repositioned his pince-nez which hung round his neck on a ribbon, and started to read.

'"On being called to table, wait until the first course is served before starting to eat any bwead. It is not cowwect to begin nibbling one's bwead the moment one sits down. (He waggled his forefinger in the manner of the conductor of an orchestra waving his baton, to underline the following vital sentence.) It is also incowwect to eat large amounts of bwead between courses, as this displays an impetuosity of hunger and a lack of westwaint."'

'Quite, dear, very good,' said Madame Deume, while Adrien, who had sat down again, champed at the bit, simply bursting to come out with his brilliant idea. 'Now why don't you go up to your room?'

'Had half an idea that these tips might come in handy. (He decided to take the bull by the horns.) Seeing as how sometimes you eat bwead between courses.'

'Don't worry, dearest,' answered Madame Deume with a kindly smile, 'I am perfectly capable of behaving one way at home and in quite another in company. My father, thank the Lord, was much given to receiving. (This she said with a sharp intake of breath and a salival gurgle of colossal refinement.) Go and try on your dinner-jacket so there won't be any last-minute panics, it will give you something to do. I had to let it out – my dear father wasn't anywhere near as stout as you are. (Defeated, the seal made a noiseless exit on his felt skates. She turned towards her darling Didi.) You see the sort of thing I've had to put up with all morning? And now, dear, what were you saying about having an idea?'

'Here's my idea,' he declared and, getting to his feet to show just how epoch-making it was, he stood four-square before her, hands on hips in the manner of the Italian dictator. 'Right then, here goes.

Champagne is good. Very good. But he'll be the one who's calling the tune. But there is one thing I can settle myself: caviare! (He felt admiring eyes upon him and, nostrils flaring, he stuck out his chin.) Caviare!' he exclaimed and his spectacles flashed lyrically. 'Caviare! It's the most absolutely toppingest thing you can serve, and the most expensive! (He declaimed:) Caviare will be on the menu at the dinner hosted this evening by Monsieur Adrien Deume, an A-grade member of section, to honour his chief, the Under-Secretary-General of the League of Nations!'

'But it's horribly dear!' she quailed, all womanly frailty before the man in her life.

'I don't care a fig! I'm quite set on being on friendly terms with the USG! Besides, it's a way of keeping up our position in society! So don't worry about it, it's money in the bank!'

'But we're starting with a bisque, it's all planned. That's fish too!'

'I don't give a damn! We'll cancel the bisque. Bisque is winkles' water compared with caviare! Nothing is smarter than caviare! Melba toast, butter, slice of lemon! And caviare, mountains of it! "Care for a little more caviare, Under-Secretary-General?" It's not every day you have the most important man after Sir John round for dinner!'

'But darling, there'll be the lobster therdimor to follow.'

'Thermidor,' he corrected her.

'But I thought . . .'

'Thermidor, from the Greek *therme*, heat, and *doron*, gift or present. You will be careful, Mumsy, won't you, not to say therdimor this evening in front of our guest?'

'But there'll be far too many fishy things coming one on top of the other.'

'Caviare is never out of place! No, I shall not be moved! I shan't budge an inch! Caviare, caviare and I say again caviare! I will not sacrifice caviare to mere lobster! The thing is, Mumsy, at a formal dinner you eat just a little bit of everything. A few spoonfuls of soup, a mouthful of lobster. Trust me! The caviare will go down a treat! If there's one person round here who knows about these things, it's me! Anyway, if he doesn't fancy lobster, well, he'll say he doesn't want any! And to show I understand, I'll slip in a little joke. "The fare's a touch too sea-*faring*, Under-Secretary-General?" I'll work on the phrasing. Caviare, caviare! And none of your pressed rubbish, not the black stuff, for God's sake! It's got to be fresh, the grey kind, straight out of Stalin's larder!'

He strode fiercely round the drawing-room, thumbs hooked into his waistcoat, for there dwelt in him a god: caviare.

'I think that's Dada calling me. Just a moment, dear, I'll be back in a jiffy.'

In the hallway, she looked up at her husband, who was leaning over the banister, and asked him, with lethal sweetness, what he wanted.

'Listen, poppet, I'm sowwy to intewwupt. It's all wight by me if you won't say what's on the menu, it'll be a nice surpwise for me tonight, but there is just one thing I'd be gwateful to know: is there soup to start?'

'No. Soup is not served at formal dinners. (She had picked up this dictum the previous evening during a conversation with Adrien, who had got it on a visit to the Kanakises.) Look, I've still got quite a few important things to discuss with Didi and I need peace and quiet, the strain is giving me a terrible headache. Is there anything else you wanted to ask me?'

'No, thank you,' answered Monsieur Deume sadly.

'In that case, go on back to your room and try to occupy yourself by doing something useful.'

Old Monsieur Deume slowly climbed the stairs and sought the solace of the lavatory on the first floor. Sitting aimlessly on the padded seat, he folded a sheet of toilet paper into narrow parallel creases then opened it into a Japanese fan which he waved in front of his face while he brooded over his humiliation. After a while, he shrugged his shoulders, stood up and, arm raised in the fascist salute, sallied forth.

'Come along, let's get a move on,' said Adrien. 'Sum the situation up for me so that I can go with an easy mind. Make it a Note for Guidance, as it were.'

'Well, the drawing-room and dining-room have had a good going-over, polished and buffed from top to bottom. Everything's been vacuumed, including the curtains. Ditto for the hallway, and anywhere else our guest is likely to go. Martha has washed all the crystal glasses and the dinner set with the gold motif, you know, the Leerberghe service, it belonged to your grandfather. The knives and forks have been polished, likewise all the silver. I've checked them. So, it's all been done except the table, which hasn't been laid, but the butler will see to that, they have their own way of doing things. I've locked the dining-room. Obviously I'll have to unlock it when the man comes, but I shall put it out of bounds to Dada so that he doesn't get up to anything and upset the applecart. When we're finished here, in the drawing-room, I'll lock this door too.'

'And the downstairs loo? What if he wants to wash his hands before we go in to dinner?'

'I thought of that, naturally. All spick and sparkling, hand-basin, taps, mirror, toilet, everything spotless. I checked and I've locked the door, which means that for our *petits besoins* we'll have to use the one upstairs and, if it's just for a quick hands and face, the sink in the kitchen or your bathroom.'

'Have the towels been changed in the loo?'

'Really, dear, how can you ask! I've put out the brand-new ones, never been used before, I've had the iron run over them to take out the creases, oh, and new soap too, English, bought specially, the same kind as they have at the van Offels'.'

'Listen, Mumsy, I've thought of something. Is it quite pukka to let him wash his hands in the downstairs loo? He might be shocked. Wouldn't it be better to get him to go up to my bathroom?'

'Didi! You can't be serious! Whatever would it look like if we made him go up two flights of stairs just so he could wash his hands? Listen, it's quite simple. I'll hang my pretty piece of paisley with the silver thread over the toilet seat, you know, the present dear Élise brought me to be made up into a bedjacket. It'll cover the toilet and will look ever so smart.'

'Right, fair enough, but one more thing. You won't forget to unlock the loo door in good time, will you? It would be simply awful if we had to fetch the key and open up while he stood there waiting!'

'I'll unlock it at quarter past seven. I've set the kitchen timer as a reminder. By then there won't be time for anything to go wrong, Dada will be where I can keep an eye on him.'

'And the butler? Is that all laid on?'

'Insofar as it is humanly possible to say, yes. I phoned the agency again this morning to drum it into their heads that the man must be here without fail at half past five so that he has time to familiarize himself with the house, see that the table is laid properly and the rest of it.'

'Is he a dependable sort?'

'Well, a servant is always a servant and no more, dear. But the agency is reliable, it was recommended to me by dear Madame Ventradour. To be on the safe side, I've told Martha that she's not to let him out of her sight for an instant. Don't want anyone stealing the spoons.'

'And the caterer?'

'Bringing dinner at six. They said seven would be all right, but I said six so there'd be plenty of time to get back to them in case they're late. Their very best chef is bringing everything himself by van, and he'll stay on to keep an eye on the last-minute arrangements and ensure everything is properly reheated and see to the sauces. I'll phone them again at four to tell them six on the dot, not five past. I've written myself out a littel timetable, it's in my bedroom.'

'That all seems fine, I've got the picture now. But you won't mind if I make a suggestion? As well as setting the kitchen timer for quarter past seven, why not set another two, yours and mine? One for half past five and the other for six. Then if these two chaps aren't here on time we can phone up at once.'

'Very well, darling, that's a very good idea. O Lawks, that's him calling again!' ('Lawks': pious camouflage for 'Lord'.)

Going into the hall, they looked up. Monsieur Deume, trying to squeeze into his starched shirt, was whimpering in a voice which seemed to emerge from a deep dungeon: 'I cannot extwicate myself fwom this damned shirt. It's sticking to me all over!' After a series of dramatic swimming strokes, the little seal managed to poke his head out and, with a smile, said: 'Sowwy to intewwupt.' But only moments later, just as Adrien was opening the door on his way out, there came another cry for help: 'I can't do up my dwatted collar! I must have put on weight!'

'Didi, darling,' said Madame Deume, 'be an angel and give him a hand. It will be one thing less to worry about if he's ready in good time and there aren't any last-minute hitches.'

'All right, but I'll just toddle along first and see if Ariane's awake.'

'Keep smiling, Didi, don't weaken. And now I'm going for my nap, it's past my time, but I simply must, it's my duty, because today I shall need every ounce of strength I have if I'm to carry the heavy burden of responsibilities which I would have gladly shared with your darling wife. But there you are, one must be able to put oneself last and still go on loving others,' she concluded with a terrifyingly angelic smile.

With all the good grace he could muster, Monsieur Deume, in his tightly fitting dinner-jacket, stood perfectly still, doing what he could to be helpful to Adrien, who was trying to do up his detachable collar for him. But it wasn't easy. With his face turned heavenwards, the old gentleman muttered fiercely: 'Oh, if I could get my hands on the man who invented detachable collars, I'd wing his dwatted neck!' He arched his back with such enthusiasm that he upset a flower vase, which fell on the floor and shattered. The two men hurriedly hid the evidence. Surely she couldn't have heard anything, for the vase had fallen on the carpet. 'What's been broken up there?' called out Madame Deume. Monsieur Deume shouted down that it was only an armchair that had been knocked over and then unburdened his tortured soul to Adrien, who was now doing further battle with the collar-stud: should he bow to their guest before being introduced?

'No, only when I actually introduce you.'

'A low bow or just a nod?'

'Just a nod.'

'But I don't twust myself,' said Monsieur Deume, still standing rigidly to attention to make Adrien's task easier. 'I'll be so nervous when I see him standing there that I shan't be able to pwevent myself bowing stwaight off. At least I sincerely hope that bending forward or chatting over dinner won't make this confounded stud pop out. I mean, I've got to make some sort of contwibution to the chatter. Ouch! you're thwottling me!'

'There, got it. It's done.'

'Thanks, tewwibly good of you. But coming back to this nod business. What sort of angle do you think would be wight? If I lean forward like this, for instance, would that do the twick? There's something else too. In this wetched etiquette book, there's another bit that wowwies me. I'll wead it to you. (To avoid getting in the way of the bow Adrien was currently tying for him, the little seal raised his guide to good manners high above the head of his adopted son and read:) "In the dwawing-woom, a waised tone of voice gives an impwession of poise, bweeding and modernity." Do you think this would be a waised tone of voice?' he asked, and gave a strangled yelp.

'Possibly,' replied Adrien absently, for he was thinking of the strange way Ariane had answered him through the door just now.

'Or how about this?' yelled Monsieur Deume.

'Keep still, Dada, I can't finish tying your tie.'

'So you weally think it's not too loud like this, for instance?' bawled Monsieur Deume. (And to get into training for this strange social practice, he went on bellowing:) Under-Secwetawy-Genewal, Didi is tying my black tie for me!'

'What on earth is going on?' shrieked Madame Deume from downstairs. 'Why are you shouting like that?'

'I'm making polite conversation,' shouted back Monsieur Deume, who was in one of his bolder moods. 'It's a sign of poise and modernity! But sewiously, Didi, don't you think it'll seem a bit peculiar? I mean, if all five of us start shwieking our heads off like that it'll sound like a madhouse, that's how I see it. But there it is, since it's the done thing, I don't mind, only we won't be able to hear each other speak, that's all. Still, it's twoo: shouting like that does pep a chap up a bit, makes you feel important. (Adrien took off his glasses and ran his hand over his eyes.) What's up, Didi? Pwoblems?'

'She sounded very odd when she answered me through the door. I asked her which dress she was intending to wear for the dinner party. (He blew his nose, then stared into his handkerchief.) And she said: "Yes, yes, all right, I'll wear my smartest frock just for your chief's benefit!"'

'Doesn't seem too bad a weply to me.'

'It was the way she said it. She sounded annoyed, you see.'

With a characteristic gesture, Monsieur Deume smoothed the droop-ing wings of his moustache so that they joined forces with his goatee. He set his brain to work and cast about for something comforting to say.

'You know, Didi, young women sometimes get a bit highly stwung, but it doesn't last long.'

''Bye, Dada. I think the world of you, you know.'

'It's mutual, Didi. Don't wowwy your head about it. Beneath it all, she's a weally nice girl, take it fwom me.'

When his adopted son's car had gone, Monsieur Deume climbed back up to his den and locked himself in. He put a cushion on the floor, hitched up his trousers to ward off bagginess in the knees, knelt, clenched his false teeth together firmly, and prayed to the Almighty to watch over his adopted son and bless his dear wife Ariane with a child.

When he had finished his prayer, which was not the least admirable of all the prayers offered up on that day, and certainly finer than the pious requests formulated by his wife, this bearded seraph got to his feet certain in the knowledge that all would be well again nine months from now, or perhaps before, for the moment Ariane knew she was expecting a baby she would become sweet and gentle, no doubt about it. His mind at ease, he returned the cushion to its place, brushed his trousers, and settled himself in an armchair. With his bulging chameleon eyes glued to the pages of his etiquette book and his lips moving in studious silence, he stroked the birthmark which he called his big beauty spot and resumed his reading.

But he wearied of it quickly, closed the book, stood up, and looked round for something to do. Sharpen all the scissors in the house? A nice, easy job, all you needed to do was to cut up a sheet of sandpaper with a pair of scissors and the thing was done in a twinkling. Yes, but Antoinette would say now wasn't the time. Oh well, he'd do it tomorrow, when all this dratted business of the invitation, which required a chap to shout to be smart, would be over and done with.

He sat down again and yawned. Oh, how uncomfortable he felt wearing Monsieur Leerberghe's dinner-jacket. The sweet old man undid the top two buttons of the trousers, which were too tight for him, and gave his swollen abdomen a series of thwacks to pass the time as he pictured himself as a Negro chieftain summoning his tribe on the tom-toms.

CHAPTER 15

In the Rue du Mont-Blanc, passers-by turned their heads to stare at the little old man in the beaver hat, breeches and dove-coloured stockings, but were not unduly disconcerted, accustomed as they were to the fauna of the League of Nations. 'What shall we do?' wondered Uncle Saltiel as he shuffled along, stopping now and then to pat a child on the cheek before resuming his progress and his train of thought, head bowed and back bent.

'All things considered – yes.'

Yes, all things considered, what had to be done was to put up a first-class Jewish opponent against this Christian girl. But where was he to find one? He had not managed to see the Rabbi, who was ill, and at the synagogue all that fool of a beadle had on his books was the daughter of a butcher, that is, a girl who would not have an ounce of poetry in her and would hardly impress on the ski-slopes. How about giving Cephalonia a try? Now, let's see, what in the way of marriageable girls did they have back there? He went through the field, ticking them off on his fingers. Eight, but only two possibles. The great-granddaughter of Jacob Meshullam, who had a pretty dowry on her head and wasn't too bad to look at except for that missing tooth which unfortunately was in the middle of her smile. She could always be rushed off to a dentist, of course. Still, best not, it wouldn't do to fix Sol up with a fiancée with a false tooth. The only other choice was the daughter of the Chief Rabbi, but the little idiot had no dowry.

'But there, I don't suppose he really needs a dowry. According to my calculations, a gold napoleon drops into his trouser pocket every three minutes. Anyway, between you and me, those two girls are no oil-paintings, and this Ariane of his would wither them with a glance!'

In disgust, he jettisoned both candidates and made up his mind that the very next day he would go to Milan and cast an eye over the daughter of a prosperous jeweller of whom he had heard only good reports from a cousin from Manchester he had met in Marseilles. Now a jeweller was not to be sneezed at. On second thoughts, a jeweller's daughter was hardly Sol's type. She'd be plain, and all she'd be able to talk about would be rubies and pearls. Anyhow, jewellers' daughters were always fat, whereas this Ariane was a great beauty, for sure. Doe-eyed and the rest of it. So, to do battle with her, he was going to have to find a daughter of Israel as perfect as the moon in all its ripe and rounded fullness. Oh yes, only a Jewish beauty would do! Had not the Almighty forbidden His people to take the daughters of strangers to wife, Exodus thirty-four, verse sixteen?

'But where is she, this perfect creature of Israel? And how am I to find her?'

Still ruminating, he went on his way. A gendarme hove into view. He crossed the street on to the pavement on the other side, assuming an innocent, unconcerned air which almost got him run over. Naturally he hadn't done anything wrong, for he had always trod the path of righteousness, but with these damned policemen, you never knew. Outside Cornavin station he stopped dead in his tracks and smote his brow for he had just had the most wondrous idea.

'That's it, dear heart! Put an ad in the Jewish papers!'

In the third-class buffet, his hands shaking with impatience, he asked for 'clean writing-paper, a glass of lake water, if it isn't too much trouble, and a piece of Turkish delight'. This last request provoked a reaction of hostile irony in the waiter, so he settled instead for a black coffee, 'but with lots of sugar, if you would be so good'. After swallowing the first mouthful, he slipped on his old steel-rimmed spectacles with the scratched lenses which blunted his piercing gaze, then licked the point of a pencil which he found in a pocket of his frock-coat.

'Gird on thy sword, O mighty champion,' he muttered to himself, 'and mount thy charger to defend the purity of thy race!'

After tracing a few preliminary arabesques in the air, designed to conjure Inspiration, he began to write, pausing from time to time to nod approvingly or, with a highly self-satisfied air, to take a pinch of snuff from his snuffbox. When the great work was done, he read it over in a whisper, smiling with delight and admiring his handwriting. Oh yes, on the calligraphy front he feared no man!

'Bachelor Uncle seeks Wife on behalf of Nephew, Tremendously Handsome, Brilliant Position, higher than Ambassador (not in same class!). Thoroughly deserves Position plus Tie of Noble Order! Colour of tie withheld, discretion better part of valour. Just one small blemish on his amazing Good Looks: small scar over eye, fell off a horse, he tells me! Which proves he Rides! But aforementioned Scar a mere Trifle! A little white squiggle, hardly noticeable! But nothing escapes an Uncle's Eagle Eye! I mention the scar in all honesty! It's the only blemish! But such an attractive blemish! Otherwise, Magnificent Specimen. The successful applicant must be Healthy and without Hidden Defects! And Young! Must be Stunner! Eyes like a gazelle! Teeth like a flock of shorn sheep after dipping! Hair like a herd of goats on the slopes of Gilead! Cheeks like pomegranate halves! And the rest to match! And no Flightiness! No hanky-panky in the background with Tom, Dick and Harry! Uncle not amused by Goings-On! Must be of Highly Reputable, Honourable Jewish family! And God-Fearing, naturally! Virtuous and Sensible! With more than her fair share of Common Sense and able to give Sound Advice and Tick Him Off now and then! A spot of Ticking-Off won't come amiss as long as it is done nicely! Needs, in short, to be a Dove: pointless trying to pull wool over eyes and claiming to be Dove if not Dove, because Uncle is a Psychologist and will strain all applicants through the Sieve of Perspicacity! Dowry not essential since Nephew earns a Fortune! Money no object! What we seek is Virtue and Beauty! Reply to Poste Restante, Geneva, marking envelopes S.S.! Enclose recent photo, not old snap taken ten years ago, since Successful Applicant must be Young and Stunning! Also Good Housekeeper and careful with purse-strings! Not the sort to be forever buying Paris frocks! Still, a dowry would be no disqualification! Especially for the sake of the Young Lady, so that she can keep her Independence and is not put in the Humiliating Position of always pestering him, squawking for Money, saying I haven't got this and I haven't got that and I must have a New Hat! But Dowry not crucial. The main thing is that she must be Virtuous and Level-Headed! Also that she knows when to Keep her Mouth Shut and not make life Hell with Idle Chatter like some Well-Heeled Prattling Women do! All the same, she must be Educated and capable of keeping up an Intelligent Conversation! Music! Poetry and Verse! She should be a Modern Girl, but also go to Synagogue! And Pork must never darken their doorstep! And no Snails or Oysters either! Anyhow, they're not good for you! Nor should she be forever going on about what Well-Placed Connections she has, unlike some sisters of the faith! We simply must invite the Prefect's Wife, and so forth! She mustn't be always nagging at him, because he's a Well-Placed Connection in his own right and doesn't need Prefects! Whenever he meets Prefects, he spits on the floor! And she mustn't bother him about Stock Market Prices! It's unbecoming in a Lady! And none of your Theatre-Going and Dancing every night! And no dolling yourself up all the time! No lipstick! A dab of powder is quite sufficient! In short, a Perfect Young Woman!'

'That should knock this Ariane girl into a cocked hat!' he concluded.

Feeling suddenly tired, he supported his head on one hand, closed his eyes, and immediately fell asleep, for he was old. He woke again almost at once, reread his advertisement and saw that it would serve no purpose. Who could do battle with the most lustrous of Christian girls, a virgin like unto a full moon above a calm sea on a summer's night who doubtless knew whole reams of poems by heart? The answer — that was it! — was to turn this Christian girl into a Daughter of Israel! Right, he would see to it! He would talk meltingly to her, he would speak of the sanctity of the Commandments, of the greatness of the Prophets, of the tribulations of the Chosen Race, but above all he would explain that God was One and Indivisible, and lo and behold! she would see the light and become a true convert!

'Well now, Sol, I've given the matter careful thought and the answer's yes. Since it is your destiny, go ahead, marry the girl! Your happiness comes first, when all is said and done, and maybe it's God's will. Who knows, how can anybody know? After all, didn't our King Solomon marry wives who were not of our people? So it is agreed, and if you want, as your spiritual father as you put it in the splendid letter you wrote me, I always carry it around with me, you know, in my wallet, if you want, I'll speak to her parents, tell them that I give my consent, that I give my permission in my capacity as your spiritual father, and then ask for her hand on your behalf, it will be more suitable coming from me, and finally raise certain matters with them. I shall dress for the occasion, white gloves, buttonhole, everything as it should be. And, if you'll allow me, I'll have a little word in her ear when you're engaged, make her see things in the right light. And who knows, I mean with God's help, something good might come of it.'

Who knows, perhaps she'd even ask him to teach her Hebrew. He nodded his head with a smile at the prospect of pious conversations and delightful lessons in the sacred tongue. Every day, two hours of tuition, one devoted to Hebrew and the other to the Bible, with commentaries on the Sacred Commandments to dot the i's and cross the t's. She sitting beside him fervent and all ears, and he eloquent, inspired. How could she fail to be converted with that pretty face of hers? And then the wedding in synagogue, the happy couple standing side by side under the wedding canopy, she so sweet, with a blush on her cheek! He would have no difficulty surely in obtaining permission to celebrate the marriage instead of the Rabbi. Didn't he know as much as any rabbi? He could see himself drinking from the ritual cup, then offering it to Sol and the blushing bride, and finally pronouncing the blessing in Hebrew. He recited it in a whisper.

'"Mayest Thou delight this loving couple as of old Thou didst rejoice Thy handiwork in the garden of Delight. Lord our God, may there soon be heard in the cities of Judah and streets of Jerusalem the voice of joy and the voice of gladness, the voice of the bridegroom and the voice of the bride, the voice of wedding jubilation, bridegrooms in their festivities and youth in their festal song. Blessed art Thou, Lord, who rejoicest the bridegroom with the bride and who blessest their welfare!"'

He pulled out his handkerchief to wipe away his tears of joy, sniffed, then smiled. After the blessing, he would partake once more of the wine and offer it to Sol and the new bride, ravishing in white lace, then he would pour the wine away and smash the cup in memory of Jerusalem Lost. Later he would escort them to the train which would whisk them away on their honeymoon, and he would repeat his blessing. Yes, he would embrace the young woman, respectfully – she was his niece after all.

Leaving the station buffet, he ambled slowly along the Rue de Chantepoulet, head bowed and back bent, turning over pleasant thoughts in his mind. Make that a kiss on both cheeks. 'Thank you for everything, Uncle dear,' she would say. 'May God protect you, child, and mind you take care, don't do anything silly, and no jumping, especially after the third month.' And nine months after the wedding the first-born would arrive, and then a second, and a third. Two boys and a girl. Perhaps the second would be named Saltiel if the young mother was agreeable. Anyhow, he'd have to see. Trust in the will of the Almighty.

Lord! How mighty God was! The God of Abraham, of Isaac and of Jacob! This evening he would go to the synagogue to mark the coming of the sabbath and sing praises to the Almighty with his brothers and kiss the scrolls whereon the sacred law of Almighty God was writ! Oh the joy, the honour of belonging to the people which was the chosen of God! What grace and favour! Carried away, he stamped his foot three times, very hard, paying no attention to the curious, mocking stares which came his way.

Paying no heed to the curious, mocking stares, he walked on, invincible and praising the Lord, invincible and praising Him who was his strength and his tower, his strength and his tower, singing praises with all his heart, stamping his foot with all his soul, raising his hat now and then to any passers-by he liked the look of, smiling at them because God ruled sublime in his heart, then stamping his foot some more and singing the praises of the Almighty.

CHAPTER 16

The bedroom of Monsieur and Madame Deume senior, by day occupied exclusively by Madame, her mental fatigue requiring solitude and concentration.

Mixed smells: camphor, methyl salicylate, lavender and mothballs. On the mantelpiece, a gilt bronze clock surmounted by a uniformed standard-bearer valiantly dying for his country; a bride's posy under a glass dome; everlasting flowers; a small bust of Napoleon; a terracotta Italian mandolin player; a Chinese peasant sticking out his tongue; a small trinket case covered with blue velvet and decorated with sea-shells, a present from the Mont-Saint-Michel; a little Belgian flag; a miniature coach made of spun glass; a china geisha-girl; a fake Dresden marquis; a dinky metal shoe stuffed with pin-cushion velvet; a large pebble, a souvenir from Ostend. In front of the fireplace, a painted screen showing two puppies fighting over a croissant. On the walls, a huge fretwork heart inset with smaller hearts containing photographs of the van Offels, the Rampals, assorted Leerberghes, Hippolyte Deume at six months with no clothes on, Josephine Butler and dear Doctor Schweitzer; a selection of Japanese fans; a Spanish shawl; the chimes of Big Ben; verses from the Bible picked out in poker-work or luminous paint or sewn in satin-stitch; two oil-paintings, one of a small chimney-sweep playing marbles with a little pastry-cook's boy, and the other of a cardinal at lunch teasing a fluffy white cat. Over the head of the bed, an enlarged photograph of the first Madame Deume, plump and smiling, with the dates of her birth and death. Here, there and everywhere, little cloth tidies; pads under the lampstands; fringed lampshades; crocheted antimacassars; foot-stools, footmuffs and footwarmers; screens to ward off the cold and block insidious draughts; a set of brushes with tortoiseshell backs; glove boxes; an arrangement of green sponge with artificial flowers stuck in it; divers ferns; embossed pewter plant-pot holders; glassware by Gallé; a bald dwarf containing matches; paperweights; smelling-salts; marshmallow-flavoured cough lozenges.

Interminable and bony, prone on her bed, with her brown-warted hands crossed over her bosom, Madame Deume was taking her belated nap, snoring with the certainty of the just, her squinting teeth resting on the pallid pillow of her lower lip. Waking suddenly, she threw back the counterpane and, attended by her red-painted fingernails, got up, scantily, unattractively but sensibly clad, for, since the days still grew cool towards evening, she had thought it prudent to take off her calico bloomers and don a pair of man's loose woollen combinations which came down to her ankles and hung slackly about her. This garment, split fore and aft and lined inside, was of a mustard hue, a most practical colour, and the seat was strengthened by a patch of muslin decorated with mauve flowers.

After putting herself through a yoga routine to get herself in harmony with 'the Universal' (she had recently read a vaguely Buddhist book, had understood very little of it, but had been greatly taken with this Universal), she stretched out on the carpet, raised both legs, propped them on a low stool and relaxed. She then closed her eyes and bent her mind to thinking calming and constructive thoughts, which included the keen interest which God took in her. At four thirty she rose, for it was time to get ready since the butler would be arriving in an hour. After allowing her eye to linger lovingly over her ample hoard of household and personal linen ranged on the shelves of her mirror-fronted wardrobe, she put on a bright orange camisole, then a petticoat, and finally stepped into her new dress with the diamanté motifs. With Aunt Lisa's watch duly pinned to her chest, she poked a lavender-scented handkerchief into her chaste, flaccid sponge of a bosom, then round her waist looped a chatelaine from which hung an assortment of gold trinkets: a four-leafed clover, a number 13 enclosed in a square, a small horseshoe, a general's cocked hat and a tiny lantern. In full harness, she proceeded majestically down the stairs, more decorous than any queen mother.

After popping her head round the door of the kitchen, where she did not fail to bestow a gracious comment on the maid ('It's easy to see, my girl, what sort of home you come from') which was immediately followed by the customary smile which committed her inexorably to loving her neighbours, she went off to inspect the drawing-room, where all seemed shipshape. Even so, she moved three armchairs and pushed them closer to the settee to create a cosy corner. So. Herself and Hippolyte on the settee, their guest in the middle, in the best armchair, and Didi and his wife in the other two. Between the settee and the easy chairs would go the naice littel Moroccan coffee-table with the liqueurs, cigarettes and the good cigars. Yes, everything quite in order. She ran her finger over the low table and inspected it. No dust. When they were all sitting down, she would suggest coffee or tea and then they would chat. A good topic would be the van Offels. 'They're old friends, so very refined.' These preliminaries to a full dress rehearsal were interrupted by Monsieur Deume, who, from his eyrie on the first floor, asked if he could come down for a minute, adding that he wouldn't dirty anything: 'I'm still weawing my parquet-pwotectors.'

'What is it now, dear?' she said, already exasperated, as he came through the door and only narrowly avoided slipping on the over-polished floor.

'I've been weflecting and I weally think we ought to start with soup. Perhaps he likes soup.'

'Who?' she said, with a hint of sadism.

'Didi's boss, of course.'

'You could at least take the trouble to give him his proper title.'

'It's such a mouthful I always twip up when I twy to say it. Thing is, maybe he likes soup.' (The old hypocrite was thinking more of himself than of their guest of honour. He loved soup. He often said he was 'a wegular soup-fiend'.)

'I've already told you there wouldn't be any. Soup is common.'

'But we have soup evewy evening!'

'I'm talking about tone,' she groaned. 'One doesn't say soup, one says *potage*. One never gives important persons soup. Tonight we'll be having *potage bisque*.'

'Oh, I see. Is it nice?'

'It's what they serve kings and queens with.'

'And what's in it?' he asked, when his mouth had stopped watering.

'It can be made from all kinds of things,' she said prudently. 'You'll see tonight.'

Whereupon, taking his courage in both hands, he said that he would like to know exactly what was on the evening's menu. Yes, he wealized that he had asked particularly not to be told what there would be for dinner, so that he would be 'surpwised, like in a hotel when you're on your hols'. But the suspense was more than he could bear. He was delighted by her readiness to agree to his request. She opened a drawer and took out a long rectangle of stiff card.

'It's a surprise for Adrien, I just went ahead and ordered printed menus, had them engraved, do you see, with gilt lettering, which was an extra ten per cent, but well worth it. I had fifty done, five to put out on the table and the rest will keep in case we ever give other dinners for Didi's important friends, and if not they'll make a naice show. It cost the same for fifty as for five, might as well have whatever's going. You can have a look if your hands are clean.'

Potage bisque

Lobster Thermidor

Sweetbreads à la Princesse

Snipe Toasties

Foie Gras à la Colmar

Asparagus, Sauce Mousseline

Mixed Salad à la Pompadour

Meringue Glacée

Assorted Cheeses

Exotic Fruits

Bombe Glacée Tutti Frutti

Cakes and Biscuits

Café

Liqueurs

Cigars by Henry Clay and Upmann

Having perused the menu with an excitement which did not exclude a twinge of panic, he read it again more calmly, his lips moving over the words so as to fix them firmly in his mind, while she looked on, basking in the admiration which she felt sure she could see written all over her husband's face. She was proud of her brain-child. She had drawn it up by supplementing her inspiration from royal menus snipped out of newspapers, of which she had a collection. He felt that a compliment was called for, but he tempered his eulogy with a remark which immediately brought her eyebrows together.

'You don't think there's a bit too much? Lobster, then sweetbweads, then snipe followed by foie gwas. Isn't it a twifle on the heavy side? And later on, these two icy things, the mewingue and then the bombe.'

'Adrien approved the menu, that's good enough for me. Anyway, as you probably don't know, at formal and official dinners one eats just a littel of each course. A few spoonfuls of soup, a mouthful of lobster and so on. That's the correct thing.'

'Well, if Adwien's appwoved evewything, then it must be all wight.'

'Everything, that is, except the foie gras, because that's also a surprise from me to him. I ordered it myself and I shall pay for it with my own money, and believe me it doesn't come cheap, but it is the best, they had foie gras à la Colmar at the Élysée Palace in Paris when they gave a dinner for the Shah of Persia. So, as you see, we've got excellent precedents on our side. We'll serve the caviare right at the start, it isn't on the printed menu because Adrien has only just decided to have it, but it can't be helped. The Under-Secretary-General will take good note just the same.'

'And is it cowwect to put cigars on the menu?'

'They cost seven francs each. Didi told me they're the best money can buy in Geneva.'

'Fair enough. And what's this lobster something?'

'Thermidor. It's not an English word, it's Greek, came in at the time of the French Revolution. I do hope you're not going to say Lobster Something in front of our guest.'

'What's it made out of?'

'It's a complicated recipe. It was served to His Majesty the King of England at the royal castle at Laeken. But look, I've far too much to do to be telling you what goes into all these dishes.'

'Just one thing. How do you eat caviare?'

'Just watch what our guest does, and me too of course. I haven't got time to go into it now.'

'One vewy last thing. How shall we be seated wound the table?'

From a drawer she solemnly produced five small cards.

'It's another surprise for Didi. You see, when I was about it, I also ordered printed place cards with our names on them. In a while, when the table's set, I'll put them out according to precedency.' (She sucked on the word as though it were a chocolate, then gave one of her refined salival gurgles.)

'But the one for that chap has just got "The Under-Secwetawy-Genewal" witten on it. Why is that?'

'Because it's more correct that way.'

'And where are we going to put him?'

'In the place of honour.'

'Which is?'

'Always on the hostess's right. Anyone with manners knows that. (That salival gurgle again.) So he'll be on my right. You'll be on my left – that's the next place of honour. Ariane will sit next to him, since she's the wife. Always assuming, of course, that her ladyship decides to put in an appearance, and if she doesn't we'll be well rid. Adrien and I will see to the conversation. And Adrien will be next to you.'

'I'm not fussy about having the second-best place of honour, you know. Because if I do have it, I'll be diwectly acwoss the table from this chap and that means I'll have to make an effort to talk to him. Put Adwien on your left. That way he can talk to his boss, he'll be opposite him.'

'No, it's a matter of seniority, and the next-best place is yours by right, it's all settled, so we shan't mention the subject again. Well, there we are, I think that's you put fully in the picture.'

'Listen, in that book of mine, it says that soup-plates . . .'

'Say *potage*.'

'It says they mustn't be more than half full.'

'I know, dear, I know,' said Madame Deume, making a mental note of this useful tip. 'And now, I'd like to be left alone,' she added demurely.

He took this to mean that she wished to offer up a prayer, and left. Back in his den, he walked up and down reading his etiquette book. Suddenly, his face lost all its colour, for the manner recommended for eating asparagus in polite company was nightmarish. Absolutely petrifying. You had to pick the stuff up with a pair of tongs fitted with three rings into which you were supposed to insert the first three fingers of your hand! He went downstairs and listened outside the drawing-room door. Silence. She was undoubtedly still at her orisons. He decided to wait, and began pacing feverishly. He looked at his large pocket-watch every few seconds. When ten minutes were up he decided that she'd had plenty of time to say everything she wanted to say, and anyway God didn't need to have His ear bent quite so hard. Feeling none too sure of himself, he knocked on the drawing-room door and boldly poked his head round it. She was on her knees in front of the sofa and turned round with the startled air of a nymph surprised while bathing.

'What is it?' She gave a soulful and slightly martyred sigh, but was still too close to God not to forgive this trespass against the serene intimacy of the moment.

'Tewwibly sowwy to intewwupt, but listen, you've got to have tongs for the aspawagus!'

Levering herself up by means of the sofa, she rose slowly to her feet, as though taking her regretful leave of a secret assignation. She turned and gave him a look still suffused with celestial bliss.

'I know, dear,' she said with an air of sweet-tempered patience. 'When the van Meulebekes gave dinner parties, they were Belgian aristocracy, I was very close to them before I married, we always put out asparagus tongs. (Crooning inwardly, she looked back nostalgically to that brilliant time of her life, now long gone.) I bought a half-dozen the day before yesterday.'

'You think of evewything, my sweet. There's just one thing, though: I won't know how to use the dwatted wossnames, tongs.'

'Hippolyte, I do wish you'd perlease make an effort to speak properly.'

'What I'm afwaid of with this business of putting your fingers thwoo the wings is that I'll panic and forget which fingers you're supposed to use.'

'You can watch me and see how I do it,' she said, smiling radiantly like a saintly child of God who has resolved to be loving to all and sundry, come what may. 'And now, would you perlease mind letting me be? I still haven't finished,' she added, lowering her chastely adulterous eyes.

He left on tiptoe. On the landing, he paused to think, patting down the drooping wings of his moustache to consolidate his straggling goatee. No, there was no getting away from it: he'd never be able to cope with those tongs. The thing to do was to get Martha alone for a moment and ask her to put his portion of asparagus to one side for tomorrow.

'And tomowwow I guawantee I'll have a good old feed: I'll scoff the lot with my fingers!'

CHAPTER 17

Responding to her strident summons, his mind in a whirl, he rushed into the bedroom, where, arrayed once more in her bodice and striking a pose indicative of undeserved suffering, his wife was sniffing her smelling-salts.

'Whatever is the matter, my sweet?'

'I'll tell you what's the matter! That person you think the sun shines out of . . .'

'Me? I think the sun shines out of a person?'

'Yes, Lady Hoity-Toity! I've just been to see her! In a manner of speaking, that is, since she didn't even do me the courtesy of opening the door! She was playing the piano, naturally! I knocked politely, and do you know what she said? She said she couldn't open the door because she was in the nude! Her exact words! Can you imagine? Playing Chopin with no clothes on! Perhaps it's normal practice in Geneva among the aristocracy, going about naked at five o'clock in the afternoon! Yet I, Madame Antoinette Deume, née Leerberghe, swallowed the indignity of talking through a door! I put up with it for Didi's sake, because you can take it from me if there wasn't that poor boy to be considered I simply wouldn't stand for it, I don't care if she is an Auble! So, very naicely, I said: (She spoke in an angelic voice.) "Will you be ready soon?" You know what I'm like, soft as can be and not one to forget my manners. Well, do you know what answer I got out of this . . . person you go round smirking at all the time who is supposed to be so very charming? (She surveyed herself in the wardrobe mirror.) She said, and these are her exact words:

(Twisting her features into a horrible scowl and putting on a reedy voice.) "I don't feel very well. I don't know if I'll be able to come down to dinner this evening." And said it in a tone I couldn't possibly imitate, it's not in my nature. Lady Head-in-the-Air wasn't in it! And to think that there are Aubles who haven't got two pennies to rub together and, incidentally, won't have anything to do with her! Well, not Aubles exactly, cousins, but gentry for all that, at least so they say! Didn't I tell you the marriage would end in tears? All that money she makes him spend! Trips to the Riviera! The presents he buys her! When have I ever asked for presents? Mark my words, she'll be the ruin of him! Do you remember the business of the bathroom-just-for-her? When we bought the house, there were two bathrooms, ours on the first floor and another on the second for the newly-weds, and two was quite enough, thank you very much! But oh no, Madame wouldn't share with her husband, perhaps she finds the idea off-putting! Madame had to have her own bathroom! Acted up as if she was a princess! Separate bedrooms, separate bathrooms! The poor boy had to fork out four thousand three hundred and ninety francs for a third bathroom, which is what it came to in the end! When I think of all those poor people in India who live in the streets! Well? What do you think?'

'It's like you say, dear. You'd have thought a bwace of washwooms should have been ample.'

'Washroom is vulgar. Well-bred persons say bathroom, I've told you before, several times. It's a matter of being brought up properly, of background. But let's not go into that. And what about the expensive restaurants he takes her to? Have you nothing to say about that?'

He swallowed, gave a little cough, and did what was required of him.

'It's twoo that when you've got a home of your own you don't go eating out a lot in westauwants, there I'm absolutely with you.'

'She's a fine one, I must say! What good has she ever done him, I ask? I mean, for all the social advantages he's got out of her! To think that she's never introduced him to anybody, do you hear, not to anybody from her so-called upper-class circle! What do you make of that?'

'I'd say!'

'Express yourself properly. You'd what?'

'I'd say what you said.'

'Hippolyte, I'm sorry to have to say this but where this creature's concerned you're no comfort to me.'

'But, poppet, I am a comfort.'

'In that case, perlease say clearly what you think.'

'Vewy well. I'm saying clearly that you are wight.'

'Right about what?'

'That the way she behaves is a pwetty state of affairs,' the wretched man said, wiping his forehead.

'Well, it took you long enough! That poor boy let himself be talked into it! That's what comes of us not being there when he took up with her. Because you can take it from me, if I'd been there they'd never have got married in the first place! I'd have made the scales drop from his eyes in no time at all and he'd never have fallen into the trap!'

'I quite agwee,' said Monsieur Deume, and he promised himself that the very next day he would buy his daughter-in-law a present, an elegant ivory paper-knife, and slip it to her on the q.t.

'And what do you make of this business of not wanting to come down to dinner this evening?'

'I suppose if she's not feeling well . . .'

'If she wasn't feeling well, she wouldn't be playing Chopin in the nude! There you go again, always taking her side!'

'On the contwawy, dear . . .'

'I only hope that you'll think it's all right the day I start playing Chopin with no clothes on!'

'But I didn't say it was all wight.'

'Of course, I'm not an Auble! Oh no, I merely come from a family which was ever a stranger to scandal! Oh yes, I know a thing or two! (She sniffed hungrily at her smelling-salts and gave him a withering look.) One of those Auble girls got up to all sorts, and not so very long ago at that! I won't say what, I wouldn't dirty my mouth! ("And what about your sister and that chemist?" Monsieur Deume thought bravely to himself.) Anyway, she's not ill at all. She's only doing it to annoy us, to show that an Auble is not impressed by the fact that we've got an eminent visitor coming.'

'Who earns seventy thousand in gold-equivalent a year,' said Monsieur Deume, eager to say the right thing.

'That's beside the point. He is an eminent man. He'd still be eminent even if he wasn't earning a penny.'

'Natuwally,' nodded Monsieur Deume in agreement. 'Look, I'll go and have a word with Awiane myself.'

'That's right, run along and butter her up! I forbid it, do you hear! Never shall it be said that Monsieur Hippolyte Deume went down on bended knee and pleaded with a little snob who has one black ewe already in her family and . . . but never you mind, I know what I'm talking about! If she doesn't come down to dinner, we'll have to do without her, that's all! Thank heavens Didi'll be there to help out with the small talk.'

'And you'll be there too, poppet. There's nobody better at small talk than you,' said the cringing coward. 'You've got this gift for knowing the wight things to say. You could charm the birds out of the twees.'

She gave a delicate sigh, assumed her expression of refined melancholia, and put down the smelling-bottle.

'Right then, we won't give her another thought. She's not worth it. Come here and let me fix your tie, it's all crooked.'

'Tell me, why have you taken off your best fwock? You looked so pwetty in it.'

'I noticed it was creased at the back. Martha's ironing it for me now.'

Hearing a ring at the front door, she hastily donned a kimono which featured dragons spitting fire, and ran to the top of the stairs. Holding on to the banister rail with hands whose warts showed up like metal bolts, she leaned over and asked who it was. The maid, her hair dishevelled, visibly perspiring and wide-eyed, paused on the next-to-bottom step and said it was ''im about the dinner'. At that moment the alarm went off and Madame Deume remembered.

'You mean the butler?'

'Yes, mum.'

'Tell him to wait. Oh, and Martha,' she added in a whisper, 'don't forget what I told you. Don't let him out of your sight, do you hear?'

After a brief visit, for *petits besoins* to what she called the *buen retiro*,

she went downstairs just as the half-hour was striking by the Neuchâtel clock, one of the most prized possessions of Monsieur Deume,
who took enormous pride from the fact, so the story went, that
Napoleon had once checked the time by it when on his way through
Switzerland. Highly conscious of her superior social position, she
swept into the kitchen as majestically as a battleship. The instant she
set eyes on the butler, a stubble-cheeked man of fifty who was taking
his tailcoat out of a cheap suitcase, she knew him for an enemy and
made up her mind to bring him to heel there and then.

'Dinner must be served at eight. Our guest will be arriving at seven
thirty. He is Under-Secretary-General at the League of Nations.
When you open the door, you will show him all the deference due to
a person of his rank. (The butler stood impassively and she detected a
certain slyness in his manner. To put him in his place and show him
just who he was dealing with, she handed him one of the menus.
When he'd read it, he put it down on the kitchen table without a
word, his face as expressionless as before. How insolent could you get!
He could whistle for a tip!) Except for the caviare, which is not
marked on the menu and has been ordered separately, everything will
be brought at six by Rossi the caterers, they're very reputable.'

'I am acquainted with the establishment, Modom.'

'All the last-minute reheating will be seen to by the man from
Rossi's. So all you have to do is serve.'

'Quite, Modom. That is what I am paid to do.'

'You can begin setting the table now. A formal arrangement, of
course. We shall be five to dinner, including the Under-Secretary-
General. I've given the dining-room key to the maid, who will assist
you. Serviettes set out in the usual way, like fans.'

'I beg your pardon, Modom?'

'I said the serviettes are to be folded in the shape of fans, as they
always are when we entertain.'

'Folded like fans? Very well, Modom. But I would point out to
Modom that the fan arrangement has not been favoured for some
considerable time past. For luncheon, the napkin is folded once and
laid on the plate. At dinner, also folded once and containing the roll,
it is placed on the bread-plate to the left of the plate for the soup,
which is laid in advance. At least, such was the practice obtaining at

the residence of His Royal Highness the Prince Duke of Nemours, whom I had the honour of serving for ten years. But, if Modom insists, I am able to fold napkins into a variety of fancy shapes, fans, sunshades, wallets, bicycle wheels, swans and even, if required, cows. As Modom wishes. I am entirely at Modom's disposal.'

'Pooh! I don't attach any great importance to such trifles, myself,' said Madame Deume, purple in the face. 'Do whatever you wish. It's hardly worth bothering about.'

Her teeth well to the fore, she made an exit clothed in the pomp and majesty of She-Who-Owns-the-Place, corseted by dignity and head held high, and as she went she gave three little swishes with one hand over her hindquarters, a gesture which might have been a caress but was probably an automatic precaution designed to reassure herself that she had made herself decent and that her kimono had not remained hitched up behind in the wake of her sojourn in the room which her husband called variously 'the little nook' or 'the place where kings don't go on horseback'.

'Her menu's rubbish,' the butler said to Martha. 'I never saw anything like it. Bisque and then lobster, and apparently caviare as well! And sweetbreads and snipe and foie gras! They've shoved in every old thing any old how. You can tell at a glance that they don't know the first thing about the proper drill. A dinner must be carefully put together, it's got to be thought out proper. And fancy, a printed menu at a dinner for five! It's a hoot! And to cap it all they fetch me along here at half past five for a dinner that don't start till eight! Oh dearie me, the things you do see!'

His attention was caught by a framed notice hanging over the sink. He put on his glasses and peered at a small work of literature, handsomely copied out in Monsieur Deume's best hand, which, on instructions given by Madame, the maid was required to read each morning:

> In kitchen lowly as on vasty plain
> All live 'neath God's unwinking eyes.
> So stay not your hand nor grudge your pain,
> For God alone confers the prize:
> The health of those we hold most dear,

The sound of laughter in the home.
To work! sweet girl, no more to fear,
And learn to reap what thou hast sown.
                    (By Mme T. Combe)

'Is this poem intended for you?'

'It is that,' said Martha, who hid a toothless, shamefaced smile with her hand.

He sat down, crossed his legs, opened the paper, and started reading the sports page.

Fuming at the thought of the Duke of Nemours's napkins which she found difficult to stomach, she took up a position in the downstairs hallway with no other end in view than to find out exactly when the horrible little man would make up his mind to do what he'd been told. To avoid giving the impression that she was lying in wait to ambush him, she began tidying things which did not need tidying, inwardly seething at having to wait upon the good pleasure of a servant. She had been there for at least ten minutes and the creature still had not made any move to go and set the table! A fine example for Martha, who would conclude that orders could be disobeyed with impunity! Should she go back to the kitchen and tell him again? The lout was quite capable of saying that there was plenty of time, that it wasn't six yet. If he did, she would lose all credibility in Martha's eyes. Or should she phone the agency and ask them to send another man? They'd probably say they didn't have anyone else available. Besides, the phone was in the hallway and he'd hear the conversation, and that would make it even more impossible for her to settle his hash. Her hands were tied. She was at the mercy of this dreadful working-class person with the cheap suitcase! That snide reference to cows was obviously intended for her! There was a lot to be said for Signor Mussolini . . .

Once again the little round face with the staring eyes and the goatee appeared over the banister on the landing above and called down that discwetion was the better part of soup-taking, and that half-spoonfuls only was the wule. Determined to put a stop to this but not wishing to make a scene in public, she went up the stairs two at a time, grabbed her bewildered husband by the hand, and hauled him off to their bedroom. Shutting the door, she set about making him pay for both the butler and the ducal napkins.

'I've had just about enough of you!' she snarled through clenched teeth. 'You will be so kind as to make yourself scarce! Take off your felts, go outside into the garden, and stay there until I say you can come in again!'

But the poor man, so unceremoniously ejected, did not linger long in the open. If anyone walked past, what would they think when they saw him hanging about outside in a dinner-jacket? He repaired to a disused summer-house, shut the door, and found himself with nothing to do. To pass the time, he sat down on a wheelbarrow, where he made a pretty picture, and began humming 'O'er all our hills when morning sun', then 'Beat out, ye drums', followed by 'O mountains free', 'Airy peaks' and 'The old chalet'. When he had run through his entire repertory of patriotic songs, he decided to take a look round the cellar. There was always something interesting to do there. He sneaked a glance outside through the half-open door, made sure the coast was clear, and scuttled away.

In the cellar he did indeed find plenty of useful things to do. The jars of preserves were not stored in any logical order, so he rearranged them by contents and size. This took some time. Then he brushed down the cobwebs with an old broom. Finally he sat down on one of the cellar steps and told Antoinette exactly what he thought of her.

He cocked one ear. Yes, it was her. 'Hippolyte, where are you? Coo-ee! Hippolyte! Coo-ee!' That 'Coo-ee' was always a sign that she was in a good mood. He opened the door leading from the cellar into the garden, went outside, and put his best foot forward, as uncomplaining as a little chick and only too happy to be going indoors again. 'Here I am! Coming!'

She stood on the threshold of the front door, an imposing sight in her rustling evening dress, with the black velvet choker around her throat conferring undeniably dowager status, and welcomed him back with warmth, for she had been found pleasing in the sight of her mirror. So the matter of his recent spell in quarantine was not raised, and she even took him by the arm. This made him feel slightly ashamed after all the horrible things he'd said about her.

In the bedroom, without a hint of acrimony, she pointed out that he'd gone and got his dinner-jacket all messed up. So he told her about the tidying up he'd done in the cellar, and she nodded her approval. Her sweet mood even extended to brushing him down meticulously, and, as she did so, her adipose lump peeped out from under her choker and wobbled. He did not resist, and felt soothed. Antoinette had her good side too.

'You look scwumptious in that fwock, poppet. Makes you look just like a slip of a girl.'

She put on her saintly, wistful face and wielded the brush with renewed vigour.

'Did you know the caterer's man has come? A very naice young man, such good manners, definitely a cut above the usual type. Different kettle of fish altogether from the butler. Incidentally, I haven't told you the latest on him. He finally made up his mind to set the table . . .'

'You told him about doing the serviettes in a fan?'

'Oh that's been out for ages, dear, terribly old-fashioned. The correct thing nowadays is to have the napkin folded once with the roll inside and placed to the left of the plate for the soup, which is laid in advance. But to come back to that quite awful man. As I was saying when you interrupted, he made up his mind to set the table. Shortly after, I looked into the dining-room to see if everything was as it should be and what do I find but Mr Impertinence trying out my rocker! You know, Aunt Lisa's rocking-chair!'

'Never!'

'Turn round and I'll do your back.'

'So what did you do?'

'I sought direction.'

'And?'

'I received direction to do nothing, so as to avoid causing a fuss at the last moment, for it's far too late now to get someone else. It was what I'd been thinking myself! I had anticipated the will of God, from Whom nothing is hid! Oh Hippolyte, the things we have to put up with from the lower classes! There, now you're tidy again,' she said finally as she put the brush down.

'Thank you,' he said, and he kissed the hand of his wife, who, touched by this gallant gesture, resumed her faintly bereaved look.

'But the situation changed completely the minute Didi walked into the dining-room!' she blared suddenly. 'As soon as he saw the Man of the House, the bully was out of that chair in a flash and believe me he couldn't get back to the kitchen fast enough! Oh, Adrien's got presence, all right, he has authority! What a relief it is to me to have the support of the only virile member of the family!'

'So Adwien's back from doing his ewwands?'

'How dreadful, I forgot to tell you! Yes, when you were down in the cellar.'

'Has he been to see Awiane?'

'Yes, and by all accounts she has perked up no end and is this very minute getting togged up in her very best. That girl blows hot and cold! However. Adrien looks perfect in his new dinner-jacket, so distinguished. The poor boy's gone to ever so much trouble! He brought back all kinds of things. Enough candles to make it as bright as day! And six pewter candleholders to put them on! It will be a sight, like the theatre, you know, the sort of thing you see at big receptions! And flowers. Red, white and blue, because our guest is French. What a charming idea, don't you agree?'

'Oh first-wate,' said Monsieur Deume uneasily.

'And he's changed all the wines! He insisted he wanted a better quality! Oh no one puts anything over on Monsieur Adrien Deume! And take it from me, they didn't dare argue! Also six bottles of the best champagne and a big ice bucket, and of course ice to go in it! The poor darling has thought of everything! And caviare too! The best! And English bread for the Melba toast! He even remembered the lemons, you have to have lemon with caviare, it's the correct way to serve it. Incidentally, the caviare does not appear on the printed menu. Why don't you write it on, at the top, and make your writing look like printing? On second thoughts, perhaps not, he'll be able to see for himself that there's caviare. The caviare was a naice touch, don't you think?'

'Wather!' said Monsieur Deume.

'His chief will be thrilled. Still, Didi couldn't do any less for him.'

CHAPTER 18

'No I shan't go down I won't have anything to do with him I don't care if there is a row oh it's lovely lying here in the bath the water's too hot I love it too hot tumty-to tumty-tum pity I can't whistle properly like little boys do I adore being by myself holding them in both hands I love them I can feel their weight their firmness I'm crazy about them I think deep down I must be in love with myself when we were nine or ten Éliane and I used to walk to school together on winter days we would hold hands in the biting wind put on dirgy voices and sing that song I made up It's freezing hard the ice is on the pool And we two winkies are setting off for school that was it then we'd start again It's freezing hard oh a beautiful nude who was female and also male in one no that wouldn't be right on the other hand yes I will go down I'll behave badly at dinner I'll be rude to him I'll tell everyone about what he did I'll empty a jug of water over him yes who was male too I'd love to smoke a cigar just once to see what it's like watch your step it's a nasty word I won't say it I want to say it no I shan't say it shan't shan't tumty-to tumty-tum I fancy a chocolate when I eat a chocolate I look at it before popping it in my mouth before popping it in my mouth I turn it round and round and I take a small bite and then I take another bite and look at it some more and I turn it over and over and scrunch scrunch I chew and chew he brings me all those presents he smiles very nicely I'm often in a bad mood pray to God for help to make me a good wife but oh that animal look of his when he starts the animal stuff when he looks at me serious anxious like some short-sighted animal with designs on me I

167

mean when he wants to use me hideous idea funny thing though he always sneezes when he wants it whenever he's going to start on the animal stuff he never misses he sneezes twice atishoo atishoo and I tell myself here we go it's zoo time no escape he's going to do his gymnastics on top of me yet at the same time I want to laugh when he sneezes and at the same time I'm scared because it's about to happen he'll climb all over me one animal on top and another animal underneath but last time he started a silly new business he started nibbling at me which made me think of a pekinese playing it's horrible so why don't I simply tell him to jolly well stop his nibbling it's because I don't want to bally well offend him don't say jolly well and bally well but also because I'm fascinated by weird sights like when I'm on the bus and can't take my eyes off somebody with a horrible face and stare but possibly it's also because there's something cruel in me that makes me let him get on with it because then he looks quite ridiculous what oh what gives this man I do not know the right what right does he have to hurt me he hurt me especially at the beginning like a red-hot poker oh I don't bally well like men stop saying that and anyway what a silly idea how stupid can you get wanting to stick your that your thing into someone who isn't interested it just hurts her all that romantic guff in novels is all rot can there really be women around stupid enough to like such horrible things oh that dreadful canine snarl when he's on me how on earth can he get so carried away but at the same time I get this urge to laugh when he's rolling all over me he goes red in the face so busy preoccupied anxious he frowns and then that self-absorbed canine snarl can all that toing and froing be really that exciting it's ludicrous and anyway so undignified oh the oaf hurts me but he also makes me feel sorry for him poor man he perches over me so studious writhing away putting everything into it he has no idea I'm looking at him judging him deep down I don't want to humiliate him but each time it happens I can't stop myself saying Didi Didi to the beat to the rhythm of the pumping of the archings of the poor ninny crouching over me of the incredibly stupid and utterly pointless archings back and forth forth and back Didi Didi Didi I say over and over to myself I feel ashamed I loathe myself he's a nice enough boy but I can't help it and it goes on and on him lying on top of me Ariane d'Auble you'd think he was a madman or a savage oh it's all so ugly I'm sorry really so sorry poor darling oh that horrible canine snarl my marriage is all snarled up too and all this on account of how I didn't manage to kill myself irritable I feel irritable all the time and he never suspects a thing and I'm too sorry for him to tell him to get off on and on while I lie there defiled dishonoured and then finally the fit the ludicrous epileptic spasm of this international official who deals with mandated territories over me he shrieks like a cannibal because it's over and he seems to have liked it and then he collapses next to me panting it's over till next time no it's not quite over yet because now he snuggles up to me all sticky and adhesive and he starts saying tender things that make me feel sick that's even worse I can't stand it can't stand any more of it the business of his promotion the cocktail parties his upsets yet he's so pathetic poor lamb in his muddy little world a little more hot water now please that's enough thank you but he gets on my nerves careful as you go darling it's been raining and the roads are slippery drive slowly and then forever pestering me about wearing warmer clothes and worse his awful habit of touching me all the time it drives me crazy as if the nights weren't enough and also his mania for asking my advice all the time and so on and on the other day when he was brushing his teeth he appeared frothing at the mouth with toothpaste Arianny did you remember to take your tonic he's such a pain in the neck and that awful trip to Egypt with him taking notes about monuments and dynasties so he could show off when we got back and appear clever with those cretinous friends of his Kanakis Rasset Egyptian architecture is ghastly broken-down ruins rotten old columns stupid pyramids and people rave about it S is just as bad but in a different way I think I am quite abnormal I don't even know my times tables especially eight sevens and nine sixes for those I always have to do adding up I look up to my Daddy I really do grisly thought Daddy also sprawling on top of Mummy like an animal Daddy snarling and woofing aah aah how is it possible still everybody must do it since people are being born all the time Monsieur and Madame Henri are happy to enounce announce the birth of their little Henriette how do they have the nerve to admit it in public but everybody thinks announcing births is all very natural yes they all do woofing and nine months later they don't seem the least ashamed to

shout it from the rooftops even respectable people who go round
fully clothed by day not to mention government ministers who make
speeches in the League of Nations about world peace they look ever
so proper and serious keep all their clothes on by day and at night
they swarm naked all over their poor wives but nobody seems to
think it's ridiculous nobody laughs when they stand there with all
their clothes on announcing that in the name of their government et
cetera kings do it too and people bow down to them as if they didn't
and queens smile and wave as if they'd never been fumbled and
squirmed over I'm glad whip whip hooray horsewhip on his bare
back it raises pale welts jolly glad I didn't tell him about the beast
otherwise there'd have been a duel and poor Didi would have had his
chips poor Didi when people die the look in their eye goes up to
heaven and makes another star that's my lawful awful wedded
husband I don't like saying dear and darling it doesn't come naturally
to me I always have to make an effort though I bet Lady Haggard
didn't have to try very hard when they were in that cave Uncle Gri's
coming soon dearest Uncle he's a true Christian not like Old Mother
Deume who's not the genuine article Uncle Gri is a saint leave them
alone I loved Tantlérie she was a noble old soul and funny too listen
my girl only atheists and papists go into cafés she never wanted to
herself she wouldn't go to the theatre because theatre is just make-
believe those third-rate actresses interviewed on the radio always say
absolutely instead of just yes because they think absolutely sounds
more confident more definite more vivacious and wittier than yes
and then if they are asked about what play they're appearing in
next and there isn't one they won't admit it they say oh you know
what I need right now is to get away to the country for a complete
rest or else I've got something big coming up but I don't want to talk
about it because I'm a superstitious person or else they put on this sly
arty-smarty voice and say oh can't say mustn't let the cat out of
the bag just yet now for a bit more hot water I love it when it's
too hot the beast stays in hotels doesn't live in a house doesn't have
a home to call his own those actresses who show off on the radio
don't say outright that they've had a hit they say the pubic the public
was very sweet they always mention the name of the famous actor
who's been in the same play as them they always say he's a lovely

person and a good friend to show that he treats them like equals he's the original Wandering Jew and if they get asked about what part they've got in their next play they say oh I play one of those awful unfaithful wives or I'm one of those delightful very proper girls and they give one of their witty little giggles what a lot of rubbish I talk when I'm in the bath but worst of the lot are those singers with loud soulful voices and small brains obviously when she suggested the lift back in her car obviously they went back to his place in the Ritz and played mummies and daddies Didi gets very worried whenever I get back late he goes out in the road and waits for me you see darling I was dreadfully worried I was afraid you'd had an accident it gets on my nerves tsk tsk be careful not to mention it mind you it's odious oh dear us model wife from this day forth that Haggard bitch saying would you like me to show you the cave it's got stalactites fluttering her eyes talking to him holding her head on one side singsong voice being the helpless little woman asking questions thirsting for knowledge and then going into raptures whenever he said anything oh the unspeakably adoring look on her face Hail Caesar hell seize her pretending to be scared for his benefit I despise women I'm not very womanly in the Ritz naked disgusting when her husband was at home with flu it's horrid this urge to say rude words still I was brought up correctly maybe that's why I I aye-aye I'm the untamed unattainable maiden my costume the one I wore to the fancy-dress ball you know Diana the Huntress I've still got it darling Éliane it was you who designed it and made it up for me and the two of us went to the Armiots' ball do you remember you as Minerva and me as Diana I put it on sometimes when I'm feeling blue crescent moon on my head short tunic bare legs sandals with criss-cross straps and I walk round my room with quiver slung over my shoulder queen of the forest casting Actaeon to the starving hounds I I aye-aye like you very much the thoroughbred mares beloved of the winds in remotest Scythia are not more sad or more untamed than I on evenings when northerly breezes die away aye aye I suppose I could always take a rise out of Antoinette like when she says a naice lunching or pull her dangling lump and let it go to see if it shoots back like an elastic band it obviously would it would spring twang against her throat or else the blubbery string thing would snap a joy never to be tasted or turn a gun on her and make her dance a wild waltz but that's enough of that when I'm all by myself in my room I'm also Electra and her lament at Mycenae and Brünnhilde too am I abandoned on the isle of flames also Isolde pleading I'm also an idiot and Éliane too she could be a silly little goose at times like when she'd giggle in that shamefaced cheeky way of hers no matter now all the same it's true the plays we used to put on in the attic were quite ridiculous me as Phèdre consumed with passion Éliane as the confidante me as that stupid Desdemona she as Othello yes Desdemona's too stupid for words forever snivelling not a clue about how to look out for herself now me I'd have had Othello dirty nig-nog coon exactly where I wanted him don't you see it was Iago who set you up my dear you're such a fool you know I couldn't tell him he values his job far too much for that he'd be devastated he was so happy when the beast talked to him and so pathetic because his boss chewed his ear after that I didn't have the heart to spoil his promotion my nose is very alluring stupid clod and that stuff about going doe-eyed tip a jug of water over him when I go down filthy liar my nose is absolutely normal it's got character that's all while yours is enormous if a schnozzle that belongs in a synagogue is what that bitch Haggard likes then let her drool kisses all over it and good luck to her kissing it all over will keep her busy for at least an hour that is if she doesn't end up entangled on it like a fish on a hook sometimes Éliane would be Hippolyte sometimes Œnone Phèdre the S business was OK the once yes just about OK but thereafter definitely not OK I'm not normal but if I if it's because I wanted to be close to somebody anybody at least I've got that to look back on and also because of my stupid pride in wanting to be desired by somebody anybody S for sex disgusting word by somebody anybody who well just a bit divorce no the poor boy would be dreadfully hurt if only I had a wonderful grandfather to comfort me I'd go and see him in his house he'd live by himself in a house with pines all round it on a clifftop at the end of a long drive of strange trees my secret grandfather would stop playing his harmonium which would go on singing to itself for a moment or two he'd raise his smoking cap such a polite old man another helping of hot water please it's freezing in the bath she always says pearl ease I'd sit on his knee he'd run his wrinkled hand through his favourite granddaughter's hair no a grandmother would be best living in a house far from anywhere oh it's nasty it's wicked but I have a terrible urge to say that word shout it out loud shout it out of the window yes that is unless she doesn't end up caught on it like a fish on a hook the thing to do would be to take a horsewhip to him so that he'd scream with pain scream damn you scream yes so that he'd scream and beg me to stop tears running down his cheeks face all twisted with pain so funny I implore you I ask forgiveness on bended knee and I'll laugh just imagine he's there on his knees without his monocle he beseeches me hands together expression of abject terror but I go swish swish right across his face oooh he winces some more oh no you can expect no mercy from me and he can't get me I'll tie him up tight then I can horsewhip him in comfort as I help myself from a box of chocolate truffles a swish for him and a truffle for me yes I'll put a chain round his hands and his feet too and to be on the safe side a great big thick one about his middle fastened to the wall and swish swish he's pleading but I'm merciless there are tears running from his eyes swish swish on his tears no quarter the tears ran down the cheeks of Solal ben Ali Rum Baba but the plucky young woman went on lashing at him never letting up and over the ignoble face of Ali Rum Baba the red streaks turned into swollen livid welts and he pleaded piteously with her but the luminous girl undaunted flailed on and on swish swish that'll teach you to have such a big nose you beast said our sterling heroine with biting sarcasm there now he's had a damned good hiding can't take any more can't squeeze out any more tears mincemeat so I remove his chains take yourself off to the synagogue and get your cuts seen to by those men with the large noses and the little legs unfortunately his nose isn't all that big a drop more hot water please sweetie-pie thank you she fiddles with her dangly lump when she puts on her sweet and sainted face instead of saying different from she says different to and sometimes even different than and for please she says perlease or even police when she prays in that oily way she's really giving God his orders tells Him to make the sun shine and make sure she doesn't get ill and mind He helps Didi get on in his job and most of all she orders Him to order her to do the things she wants to do and when she asks Him if she should accept an invitation to be president of some charity or other you can

bet your boots that God will answer yes dear lady by all means accept
or again when she asks God if she is morally justified in going off on
a rest cure in the mountains God always answers no doubt about it
my dear Antoinette more than justified given all the mental strain
you have to put up with so God does everything she wants and she's
highly delighted with what He does for her the Lord is her handyman
she shall not want Uncle Agrippa isn't like that and her there while
her husband was home in bed with a temperature of over a hundred
and him too with his countess at her window his sad countess dolled
up to the nines waiting by her window every evening her entire life is
spent waiting and then midnight chimes and hope dies he won't come
now so she takes off her evening dress drops it on the floor poor
woman flops on her bed without bothering to take her face off and
she cries into her pillow all those flowers all that fruit for nothing and
tomorrow it'll be the same all over again but sometimes he turns up
on his horse and the brainless creature flings her arms round his neck
love-light in her eyes and the great black bird of love swoops down
on flapping wings but afterwards he insults her knocks her to the
ground kicks her Dietsch admired Maupassant who is horrible how
can people admire him there are heaps of horrible things that people
admire like Greek noses which make you look stupid or that idiotic
smile on the Mona Lisa why are there two 'm's in Mummy answer
all the better to mmunch you with dear I'm perfectly self-contained
thoughts racing in from all directions like lambs to the shepherd's fold
left to myself and it's enough it snuff anyhow I've got my hermit-
man to keep me company dear hermit-man he comes whenever I
want I feel tense on edge I'll go down and fetch him one good oh
calm down try and think of something else the wall trick no better
the high-jump right you are I'm standing on the seventh floor I jump
out of the window I've jumped I'm falling aaagh through space and
I've landed on the so so solid concrete splat not broken anything but
I'm aching all over and racked with pain but it's done me good and
now I'll try the scenario with the old buffer but close your eyes so it
seems more believable right it's a winter night snow silence ahead of
me there's this well-dressed gent he's got a bowler hat on and he's
walking along a road that winds up a hill I'm behind him I get out
my revolver close one eye take careful aim said gent falls down

noiselessly in the snow I tread on him he's all soft underfoot I feel calmer but it doesn't last it would take a whole string of little men like him that little delivery horse from the market garden is out at three a.m. in the cold and wet its joints still stiff with sleep it plods along gently head bobbing earnestly up and down obedient conscientious goes wherever its master wants it would go to and fro all night along the same road without protest if its master wanted it to poor little horsey oh the other night at the Johnsons' instead of saying it happened before I was married I said it happened before I was martyred fork folk no shut up it's dirty I won't say it folk no it's not nice oh very well just one more time but that's the last folk Daddy was foreclosed that's how he lost all his pennies Uncle Gri told me how do they foreclose anybody I imagine it's got something to do with banks but focus on foreclose what does it mean exactly focus foreclosed the words sound filthy listen Lady Haggard you bitch go and foreclose yourself there's a statue of a female sphinx just as you go into the Hôtel de Russie in the Rue du Mont-Blanc and when I used to go to piano lessons I'd always stop and stare at it a lioness sitting down with a woman's head and torso she had great big breasts which used to worry me I must have been thirteen I used to think about them in bed at night when Éliane and I were sixteen or seventeen we loved Romain Rolland's *Jean-Christophe* it was made for us two yearning pagan puritan Protestant girls there was music a vague and therefore alluring religion artistic sensuality rules for how to act nobly but especially there was that moronic musical genius Jean-Christophe we were just crazy about him two little idiots that was us Serge I never got too worked up you know that only happens with my hermit-man who et cetera though it did happen with Varvara too but I never realized that with Varvara what I felt was a sort of et cetera Serge is clever but not all that clever I sometimes think to myself that he talks rubbish kissing I've only ever liked kissing Varvara I liked touching her breasts I thought it was just to do with affection what a fat-head but with my hermit-man it works fine Old Mother Deume is uglier than a sunflower oh sunflowers are hideous but old women like them she says Naypoleon fork folk there I said it again whispered it so that's being only a bit rude my awful wedded husband yes awful's the word that stuff he wrote

175

was awful too before reading it out he said I hope you won't be bored and I said not a bit the very opposite and he said thank you darling because I really wrote this for you anyway here goes so settle yourself down comfortably he said comfortably so that I'd be all ears and not miss a word of his marvellous prose but maybe also so that I'd give him a charitable hearing and then he cleared his throat put his glasses on just to give his audience time to get into the mood and began reading it out reverently in a fluty singsong voice stress on the sibilants over the dentals dragging out the ends of words for effect every so often he'd glance up to see how I was reacting I listened with a smile on my lips and a stone in my heart poor boy whenever he sensed that my interest was flagging he speeded up but still droned on in the same too too sleep-making monotone poor boy it's dreadful I can't tell him if he ever found out it would be catastrophic I'm really quite fond of him when he got to page four he stopped to light his pipe but really he was fishing for compliments and then when he got to the end he was over the moon with the way I said how clever and he tried to oh he's so funny when he does that he's like an anxious bull in a hurry but what I really love is being alone and telling myself stories that aren't true while smoking a cigarette I love telling myself how I did or didn't and didn't is even worse if my cigarette goes out I leave it in my mouth unlit makes me look like an electrician I once heard a workman say forking hell in the street which filled my mind with luscious thoughts six nines are fifty-three no fifty-four still what's one between friends Tantlérie used to call moving-picture houses public houses quick more hot water stars are the eyes of the long dead whenever somebody dies the look in their eyes shoots up into the sky and turns into another star it's a fact when I was little I was frightened of Jesus because of the Last Judgement terrified it might happen any time that bat the other night perhaps her name was Pretty where are you flying to my Pretty bat where are you flying to I've one to care for two to care for three to care for sir she said I'm going round and round the garden and there in my claws I'll catch three fat gnats for my one two three batbrats dying's not such a bad idea the lake will still be there when I'm gone pity I didn't put his eye out while I was about it when I was little I used to say letters for lettuce I used to say Aïane has ate up all her letters oh I adored sleeping in Varvara's bed kissing her was out of this world so was the other thing but I never realized yuk I'm fed up to the back teeth with his unexpected upsets his personal contacts with the high-ups I've told that story about stars being the eyes of dead people twice oh if only I could go back to being the little girl who ate letters and when we used to go to the circus I always cried when the clowns came on screamed when they made the elephant kneel down I'd love to be quite flat imagine I'm flat and my hermit-man folds me once and then twice like a tablecloth and puts me in his little bag he's a man a smooth man not an hairy man and when we reach the spring in the shade he opens his bag and unfolds me and it's lovely I never do anything perhaps I ought to get a job poor people are very lucky they work all the time or maybe I'll found an order for saving fallen women it would be called the Sisters of Purity I'd be the superior of the order and the sisters would all be beautiful mission to make virtue attractive pretty uniform but hair tied back to suggest severe moral tone the usual inanity not much in my line pointing out the straight and narrow to secretaries with painted nails with half an inch of dirt under them and oh the conversations saying how they liked *Madame Bovary* because the film was ever so good and *Anna Karenina* because it had Greta Garbo in it yes a tiny horse no higher than my finger a pretty little thing with lots of muscles galloping round and round on the coffee-table then he comes to get his reward there my pet here's a sugar lump no you can't have it all it's far too big you won't be able to keep it down squirming self-absorbed preoccupied on top of me don't ever again beat time to his pumping by saying his Christian name or at least the shortened version don't ever think of Mummy and Daddy doing it oh I can't bear it ugh it makes me feel sick how is it possible that Daddy could ever still he must have because there was Éliane and then me Daddy squirming on top of Mummy it's too horrible parents ought never to perhaps that's why I loved Varvara so much it's odd that I hardly ever think about my brother a grand-mother is what I need the little sweet-natured wizened russet-apple sort living in a house miles from anywhere on top of a dune I'd go and see her and she would comfort me with milky coffee while the wind howled outside but we'd be snug and warm what's the matter Ariane I don't know Granny I'm unhappy I need what do you need darling what I need is a proper woman friend I could tell everything to and admire someone I could kill myself for and what I don't want is to be violated by a strange man yes my little sweetie I understand I understand but perhaps some day you will have a friend like that meanwhile have a choc don't feel like it Granny in that case go out and play for a while take your dolly for a walk no I want to be happy but when a person is as pretty as you are that person must be happy what use to me is being pretty I'm no good for anything I spend all my time day-dreaming that's all I do oh all my time telling myself make-believe stories it's not funny well why not get on with that thesis about Amiel don't fancy it Amiel was a silly boring old slug who went on and on about arranging a perfect marriage or else withdraw to a chalet in the mountains and look for God make that the Himalayas no too cold and anyway the air's too thin to breathe and anyway what would I find to do all alone up there in French novels the hero always washes his hands in the loo and never in the bathroom don't they ever wash properly oh that female smell of irises those flowers it's a bedroom for one woman and several men Old Mother Deume has all the luck she's looking forward to her life everlasting rejoicing at the prospect of flying off into the beyond in her mustard knickers I've seen them they're man's combinations saw them hanging up to dry in the garden she has all the luck because she'll never find out that there is no afterlife since once she's dead she won't know she's dead for good totally unresurrectable and that all her praying was an absolute waste of breath served no purpose whatever there go the toms they're after next door's cat I used to be horrified by the thought of cats mating but now I think it's quite fascinating male suitors doing battle slow-motion ballets Samurai warriors duelling it's all very intriguing there aren't any real battles it's all pretence and threats it's all grace and danger at the Johnsons' party everybody managed to drop an important name except he of the black eyeglass who hardly said a word pretending to be above it all looking bored silently mulling over supposedly profound thoughts oh what a crowd of morons there were at the Johnsons' all delighted to learn that the English minister lost his temper and thumped the table as if it was important they're just a bunch of menials leading empty lives but I am Fairy Vivacious and I have a domain all to myself with diddy little goats he hardly said a word in any event you'll never be received into high Protestant circles except perhaps by the servants' entrance because you're an imbesilent fool if they're so persecuted no don't say it it's not really fair the name is almost like something out of a chemist's take two capsules of solal I suppose it's terribly clever to show how bored you are but really how on earth could any woman be attracted by that creepy sinister type of man with eyes like a Turkish belly-dancer it's beyond belief I wouldn't like to meet him in a dark corner of a souk she put on a little girlie voice for his benefit and she leaned her head to one side when she suggested giving him a lift home she wanted to do disgusting things with him that Haggard woman's a bitch all evening at the Johnsons' she acted the helpless little woman asking him questions so that he could feel masterful did it to please him and whenever he opened his mouth she hung on to every word how on earth women can be attracted to men in general is beyond me such hairy arms and they all know better than the next one men have small breasts they're quite useless but they're fully formed complete with nipples women's are much more beautiful men have copied us but it didn't work we've borrowed nothing from them so we come out winners oh for a little baby who'd fall down I'd pick him up and after a bit he'd start crawling all over the carpet full of beans showing off and he'd find something on the carpet a box maybe and he'd pick it up in his little hands and hold it out to me 'ook Mummy 'ook he'd say that way those nocturnal cavortings would at least serve some useful purpose the blackest thoughts about my life come at me mostly when I'm cleaning my teeth they're quite quite useless so before starting to clean them I open a book and prop it up on the little shelf over the wash-basin and I read as I brush my teeth I read as I brush to keep my mind occupied to stop the black thoughts to blot them out well not blot them out exactly but at least to paper over them jump to it you bitch go and fetch when he drops his eyeglass on purpose oh how she loves it I feel as though my head's been stretched as if there's an arm stretching inside my head I suppose I could always kill myself I'd love to be able to kiss my breasts long kisses just there on the nipples but it's physically impossible I'd crick my neck right then it's decided I'll send for him but first get comfortable more hot water there that'll do and now close my eyes so there's just me let's have the full story don't change anything otherwise it won't work you can begin I'm in my domain I'm all by myself as usual spending the livelong day waiting for him I'm naked though that's only because it's more religious like that it's been weeks since he came I keep watch by the window suddenly I see him in a flowing white robe he's striding quickly along the dusty blinding road his bare feet don't seem to touch the ground now he draws near and I am there pure naked and not at all flat that's from another story he comes nearer still he's opened the gate he stands saint-like and royal he is my hermit-lord I fall to my knees his solemn faithful disciple he stands tall before me but does not look in my direction ignores me completely that's important he has to despise me a bit otherwise it doesn't work I am as nothing beside him just one kindly look the hint of a smile and then I am beneath his contempt shivers run up and down my back oh so kind and that single smile from this man of scorns and casting all care to the winds I am his handmaiden though between us there is an unspoken closeness because eventually he will agree to but for the moment he speaks of God but does not look at me for his eyes are fixed on some distant prospect he gives me knowledge of the path of truth and life and I in purity of heart give ear on bended knee he stops speaking he stands before me because he knows what must come to pass I am moved to tears I bow my head I give a curtsy of profound respect I get to my feet I go to fetch the pitcher of scented water scented oil would be more sacramental but it makes your hands all sticky it would be silly to have to rush away and soap it off in the middle of the ritual it would spoil the effect so make it scented water I get back from fetching it I stand there naked holding the pitcher in my hands me looking very religious and him utterly regal he pays no attention to me he mustn't then I kneel and slowly pour water over his bare feet all powdery from walking the dusty road and slowly I untie my hair which is very long and ritually I dry his holy feet with my flowing hair I take my time lots of time oh how good it feels he lets me do it because honour is his due I love doing it more more now I am kissing his feet he lets me he does not punish me for my forwardness my lips are glued to his holy feet long do I linger there and now I look up and behold he smiles oh wondrous smile of acceptance oh how I shake drawing close I go to him since he lets me yes I oh it's so good more more oh again O my lord and master more O great Lord in me.

CHAPTER 19

At ten minutes to seven, the three Deumes took their places in the drawing-room, grave-faced and dignified. When she had sat down, exuding mothballs, her cheeks aflame with the lavender water she had rubbed into them, Madame Deume declared that since their guest was not due to arrive for another forty minutes, at seven thirty, they should make the most of the time to put their feet up, sit back in their armchairs and relax, closing their eyes if they could. But these words of wise counsel were soon forgotten in a welter of nervous toings and froings and brittle smiles.

There was a great deal of sitting down and standing up. Severally they got up to move a table a wee bit closer, to open the plush curtains just a trifle wider, to push back a coffee-table, to rearrange the liqueur bottles by size, to put the curtains back as they were because they were far far better like that, to check if that was really a spot down there or just a shadow, to move an ashtray, to make more of a display of the cigar- and cigarette-boxes, for Adrien had an eye for creative disorder which he strove constantly to refine with the aid of his limited-edition de-luxe art books.

For her part, Madame Deume left the room seven times: to give orders to 'the domestics'; to make sure the hall did not smell of *potage bisque*; to dab a little more powder on her face; to cast a final look over the dining-room table and the downstairs lavatory; to straighten her choker; to remove any excess powder and smooth her eyebrows; and, finally, to take that last-minute precaution which was followed by the clank of a cistern and the rushing of mighty waters. When she returned, flapping her hand over her hindquarters, she advised both Hippolyte and Didi to follow her example, one after the other.

'What does your watch say?' she asked for the third time.

'Seven thirteen,' said Adrien.

'Another seventeen minutes,' said Monsieur Deume, who went on reciting to himself pieces of advice from his etiquette book.

Do not mop up the gwavy on your plate with a piece of bwead. Fine, that was an easy one. It should be left to the senior person pwesent to inauguwate the conversation. That was fine too. But if this chap didn't inauguwate the conversation did it mean that they weren't allowed to speak? It would be a weal wum do, a lot of people sitting awound looking at each other waiting for the chap to make a start. And what else was there? Ah yes, when guests are first intwoduced, the talk should be of common acquaintances. But he didn't have any acquaintances in common with the chap. Apart, that is, fwom Didi. They'd talk about Didi. But he couldn't keep going on the subject for long, except to say that he was extwemely fond of him. In his heart he knew they should have stayed on in Bwussels and not come hawing back to Geneva for this blessed dinner party. It was all her fault, she was simply itching for a chance to be a gwand social hostess.

'Didi, it is the case, is it not, that your wife will come down the moment he gets here?'

'Oh yes, Mummy, I've told Martha exactly what she's to do. She'll go up and call her the minute he arrives.'

'Talking of Martha,' said Madame Deume, 'it will be her job to answer the door, I've just been to tell her.'

'But why not the butler? It would be much smarter.'

'He'll see the butler soon enough since the butler will be serving dinner. But I also want him to have sight of the maid, housemaid rather, I'll get her to wear the littel embroidered apron and white cap I bought for her yesterday. Seeing as how we've got a housemaid and butler we might as well show them off. I've told Martha exactly what to do, how to open the door, how to say good evening, how to take his hat, how to show him into the drawing-room where we'll be waiting. (Old Monsieur Deume gave a shudder.) I also bought her a pair of white cotton gloves, like the ones at Madame Ventradour's.

I've already told her to put them on, so that she doesn't forget them at the last moment. She's such a scatterbrain. So, barring accidents, which can never be ruled out, everything is well in hand.'

'Listen, Mummy, I've had a thought,' said Adrien, who stopped his pacing and stood hands in pockets. 'There's something been bothering me: the hall, it looks rather bare. That abstract painting in my bedroom, I think I'll fetch it down and put it in the hall. It was done by an artist who's all the rage just now. It'll go well there instead of that engraving, which doesn't amount to anything much.'

'But Didi, there's no time!'

'It's all right, it's exactly twenty past seven. It's not going to take me ten minutes to do it.'

'But what if he gets here early?'

'High-ups never arrive early. Come on!'

'But at least I won't have you carrying that picture yourself, it's far too heavy. It's a job for Martha.'

At seven twenty-four, perched on a stool which had been placed on a chair, Martha was attempting to hang the picture, which positively churned with spirals and circles, while Madame Deume held her firmly by her thick ankles.

'Careful you don't fall!' shouted Monsieur Deume.

'What's the matter with you, yelling like that?' asked Madame Deume without turning round.

'Sowwy I'm sure,' said Monsieur Deume, who didn't dare admit that he was merely getting his socially acceptable raised tone of voice in trim.

At seven twenty-seven, as the picture was finally hung, the doorbell rang and Madame Deume gave a sudden start which sent Martha tumbling off her perch, while further down the hallway a voice bellowed: it was the exchange angrily informing the subscriber that the phone had been left off the hook. As Monsieur Deume helped up Martha, whose nose was bleeding, Adrien hurriedly put the chair and the stool back where they belonged, the doorbell jangled impatiently, the phone brayed, and, in the kitchen, the butler and the caterer's man from Rossi's split their sides.

'You see! He did come early!' whispered Madame Deume. 'Wipe your nose, you silly creature, it's bleeding!' she muttered to Martha who, panic-stricken, reeled round and round and snorted blood noisily into the handkerchief which was held out to her. 'There! That'll do, it's stopped bleeding. Go and change your apron, and be quick, it's got blood all over it! Get another apron! Smile! Apologize for the delay! Say you had a littel accident! Smile, girl, smile!'

The three Deumes scurried into the drawing-room, closed the door, and stood motionless, hearts thumping, forcing a steadfast smile, already shaping for the gracious welcome. 'You and your last-minute ideas about changing the pictures,' muttered Madame Deume. This said, she refashioned her smile to cover her fury. The door opened but it was only Martha, apron skew-whiff, who said 'It's the bomb, mum.' Madame Deume let out a 'Phew!' But of course, the *bombe glacée*! She had forgotten all about it.

'Are you waiting to take root, you stupid girl? Get along with you, and wash your face! And put your apron straight! Give me back my handkerchief! On second thoughts put it with the dirty washing, not in the bin, put it in the bag with the fine things! Go on, and comb your hair! As for you, Adrien, wanting to hang up pictures at the last moment, well, I just can't think what got into you! Still, it could have been worse. Let's hope she doesn't manage to break a leg. All we need now is for that girl to have an accident and we'd be saddled with her hospital bills. What's the time?'

'Seven twenty-nine.'

'One minute to go,' said Monsieur Deume in a constricted voice.

Madame Deume ran her eyes over her two men. Had they dirtied their clothes in the excitement? No, thank the Lord. Monsieur Deume was chewing the cud of fear. He was sure he'd make a mess of saying how delighted he was when Adwien intwoduced him. And he remembered that there was a lot of palaver in his etiquette book about pwinces and high dignitawies and how they were always at home whewever they went and by wights ought therefore to be put in the host's chair. This chap of Adwien's was a high dignitawy, so maybe he shouldn't be put on Antoinette's wight. Moreover there was the conversation over dinner. The book said that one should never discuss politics but talk about litewature instead. Now that was all vewy well but he didn't know the first thing about litewature and in any case the chap was pwobably pwetty keen on politics, given his job and so forth. But if they did start talking about litewature he'd listen and nod his head appwovingly, that's what he'd do. Besides, Antoinette didn't weally know an awful lot about litewature either, did she? Still, there'd be Adwien and Awiane.

All three went on just standing there, not having the courage to sit down and behave normally. They waited in silence, awkward under a veneer of ease. The minutes ticked by but the smiles stayed put. Eventually Madame Deume asked what time it was.

'Thirty-nine minutes past,' answered Adrien. 'When he rings,' he added, rigid with tension, in a voice barely audible through lips which hardly moved, 'I shall count to fifteen to give Martha time to open the door and take his hat. Then I'll go and greet him in the hallway, it's more friendly. You two can stay here in the drawing-room.'

'You must introduce me first. The hostess is generally supposed to take precedence,' whispered Madame Deume in a stiff-backed, starched undertone.

'Why on earth do you want him to intwoduce you?' breathed Monsieur Deume, no less rigid, with only his lips moving. 'You know he's Monsieur Solal because we're waiting for him. We've been talking of nobody else for the past month.'

'What's the time now?' asked Madame Deume without condescending to reply.

'Seventeen minutes to eight,' said Adrien.

'I make it sixteen,' said Monsieur Deume.

'I set my watch by the radio,' said Adrien.

He raised his hand and cocked an ear. The distant sound of an approaching car grew louder and rose above the sigh of the wind in the poplars. 'This is it,' breathed Monsieur Deume in a strangled voice which would have been more at home in a dentist's chair immediately prior to an extraction. But the car did not stop. Erect, their ears straining, studying each and every sound from outside, the three Deumes waited bravely on.

'It's the proper thing to arrive a littel late,' said Madame Deume. 'What's the time?'

'Eleven minutes to,' replied Adrien.

'Oh yes,' she went on, 'people with manners always arrive a littel late, in case the hosts aren't quite ready. It's a mark of thoughtfulness, of consideration for others. Quite different than the *hoi polloi*.'

Quite distraught, Monsieur Deume repeated 'different than the *hoi polloi*' to himself and soon it became fwent a hopoly, fwent a hopoly. All three remained on their feet, waiting in an aspic of beaming, dismal refinement.

Speechlessly slumped in their armchairs, they looked weary and listless. Old Monsieur Deume hummed inaudibly in an effort to appear natural. Adrien's right shoe, its toe perpendicular to the floor, trembled uncontrollably. With lowered eyes, Madame Deume inspected her long, squared-off fingernails, each with an unsightly five-millimetre white crescent inscribed by the penknife she had cleaned them with.

'How's the time going?' she enquired.

'Ten minutes past eight,' said Adrien.

'I make it eleven minutes past,' said Monsieur Deume.

'I told you, I set my watch by the radio,' said Adrien.

'You're quite sure he said seven thirty?' asked Madame Deume.

'Yes, but he did mention he might be a little late,' lied Adrien.

'I see, well that's something. Still, you might have told me.'

They resumed their waiting, feeling humiliated but hiding their discomfiture from each other. At twenty-three minutes past eight Adrien looked up suddenly and raised one hand. A car door slammed.

'This time it's him,' said Monsieur Deume.

'On your feet!' ordered Madame Deume, who, as she got up, smoothed herself down behind for one last check. 'Don't forget to introduce me first.'

A ring at the door. With a premature smile, Adrien straightened his tie and began counting, waiting till he got to fifteen before emerging to greet his glorious guest. He had got to twelve when a perspiring Martha, looking guilt-stricken, entered and announced to the trio of statues that it was a man for next door who'd got the wrong house.

'Send him packing,' said Madame Deume, now completely flustered.

When the maid had gone, all three looked at each other. Forestalling the question which was waiting in the wings, Adrien said it was almost eight twenty-five. He whistled under his breath for a moment then lit a cigarette, which he stubbed out immediately. More cars went by, but not one of them stopped.

'Something must have gone wrong,' said Old Monsieur Deume.

Madame Deume fingered her lump for a moment. Then she said: 'Adrien, go and phone him at the Palais. An hour late! It's really too much, I don't care if he is an important dignitary.'

'He won't be at the Palais at this time of night. We'd be better advised trying to reach him at his hotel.'

'Well, go and phone his hotel then, if that's where he lives,' said Madame Deume, and she added a quick intake of breath which signified that she found it very peculiar that such an important man should not have a home of his own.

'It's a bit awkward,' said Adrien.

Right! If the menfolk didn't have the stomach for it, she most certainly did! Trailing a strong whiff of mothballs in her wake, she stepped out decisively and headed for the telephone in the hall. For the entire duration of her conversation the two men stood quite still, saying nothing. Old Monsieur Deume stuck his fingers in his ears, so ashamed did he feel. For her return, Madame Deume wore an expression of considerable self-importance.

'Well?' asked Adrien.

'You're such a scatterbrain, Adrien Deume,' she said in a tone which was almost good-humoured. 'It was all a terrible misunderstanding. He said that you'd invited him for next Friday! All this trouble I've gone to for nothing! But he said he'll call round at ten, after an important dinner he has to attend, just as soon as he can get away, which is very decent of him, because it's bound to upset his plans. Really, Adrien, I cannot understand how you could be so careless!'

He did not argue, but he was not taken in. The USG's excuse was so thin it was transparent. Why only the day before yesterday he had left a note for Miss Wilson to give to the USG to jog his memory about the dinner party tonight, a reminder, he'd only done what the Hellers did. Fortunately he hadn't mentioned it to Mummy. The USG had forgotten, that was all. Yes, say nothing, it was much better to be thought absent-minded than to be classed as the sort of chap whose dinner invitations get forgotten. Pity, though, about the two hundred grams of caviare, especially since it was fresh. But he was coming, that was the main thing.

'Did you speak to him personally?' he asked.

'I got a valet first,' said Madame Deume with reverence, 'then I was put through to the Under-Secretary-General himself. He was quite charming, I must say, such a pleasant voice, very resonant, with a hint of depth to it, and so polite! To begin with we untangled the misunderstanding, then he made his apologies and said how very sorry he was, he put it so well, I mean, perfect *savoir faire*. It was a good thing I thought of telephoning when I did because I only just caught him, he was about to leave to go to an important function.'

'Is that what he said?' asked Adrien.

'Well I imagine it's an important function, since it's being given by the Argentinian delegation. Anyway, he said he'd make his excuses to the delegation, explaining about the misunderstanding, and he'd leave the moment dinner was over and come on to us. Really, charming beyond words! He quite won me over, and I don't mind admitting it! Besides, we should appreciate all the trouble he's putting himself to, I mean it's extremely good of him to come on here immediately after dining with members of the Argentinian government, it's awfully flattering for us. It's funny but I felt completely at my ease when I was chatting to him. I think I can say that we already know each other,' she concluded chastely.

'Sounds as if Argentinians have dinner wather late,' said Monsieur Deume, who was starving.

'The more formal the function, the later dinner is served,' said Madame Deume, the milk of her charity having been set flowing by her phone call. 'At least now we know how we stand, and it's a weight off my mind I can tell you. Everything's straightforward now, all cut and dried: he said he'd get here at ten on the dot. Now the first thing on the agenda is to get rid of that butler, I don't want to see his face here any more, we'll get Martha to lay on a light refreshment. Hippolyte, go and tell that bumptious littel upstart that dinner has been cancelled. Better tell the caterer's man too. Give them something so there won't be any unpleasantness, three francs apiece is more than enough, what with everything. Didi'll pay you back.'

'I daren't!'

'I'll go,' said Adrien, 'and while I'm about it I'll let Ariane know what's happened.'

'Poor Didi! You seem to get all the nasty jobs. Still, you are the man of the house. Oh, and send Martha to me in the dining-room, would you, perlease?'

Following his wife into the dining room, Monsieur Deume stared open-mouthed at the sumptuously laid table brave with flowers, candles and champagne. He caught a whiff of imminent bliss. They'd be able to tuck into a whole feast of good things and it would be just family, with no important guest there to keep an eye on them. And they could eat the aspawagus without having to use tongs! His great round eyes watered at the prospect, and he rubbed his hands.

'Shall we sit down now?'

'I should think not,' said Madame Deume. 'We'll have a bite to eat standing up, on the hoof. Martha, you can bring bread and cheese and the three ham sandwiches left over from lunching. Put it all on the sideboard and then you can start clearing away the table things. Come on, girl, get a move on. For now, just put everything in the kitchen. It will all need to be put away properly but I'll come along later and show you exactly what to do, and be careful with my tablecloth, fold it properly so that it doesn't crease. The dinner will do for the younger Rampals,' she said, turning to her husband. 'I'll phone them in the morning, first thing.'

'How do you mean, the Wampals? They're not in Geneva, are they?'

'Oh dear, what with everything that's been going on, I forgot to tell you. They phoned this afternoon to say they'd just arrived. As delightful as ever. I yearned to invite them there and then to come to dinner this evening. It seemed too good an opportunity to miss, and we could have made the most of the food we'd got in and at the same time it would have shown the Under-Secretary-General the sort of people we know.'

'Are they staying long?'

'Three or four days. They're here, you know, for the usual business. I mean they have no choice, given all those disgraceful taxes they're forced to pay in France. She mentioned it ever so amusingly on the phone. She said she'd end up with corns on her hands from all that snipping! You look as if you don't understand, but it's really quite simple, it was a reference to cutting dividend warrants off their bonds. With a pair of scissors, do you see? In those naice littel private areas they have in the strongroom at the bank. Anyway, as I was saying when you interrupted, I very much wanted to invite them for this evening, but, since Adrien wasn't in at the time and not knowing what he'd make of it, I didn't dare, because from his point of view he'd probably want to entertain his chief on an intimate basis this first time round, so I was noncommittal, said I'd call them back tomorrow, mentioned I was giving a large, very large, dinner party this evening, there's no harm in them knowing, and didn't know which way to turn what with having to get everything ready. So I'll phone them tomorrow morning first thing.'

'But won't evewything have gone all dwy by tomowwow, poppet?'

'I'll see to it that it doesn't. With the fridge, there's nothing to worry about. Everything will be just as good when it's warmed up.'

'I see,' Monsieur Deume murmured unenthusiastically.

'Such a sumptuous menu – and it couldn't have come at a better time, seeing as how the Rampals are nobility,' said Madame Deume for the benefit of Martha, who, however, did not register its significance.

'Old Fwench nobility,' added Monsieur Deume mechanically.

(For several generations past, Leerberghe parents had passed on to Leerberghe children a healthy regard for the Rampals, who owned properties in Belgium which had been administered by a succession of Leerberghe sons, their faithful liegemen. For a century and more, the Rampals' wealth, castle and hunting-grounds had been the subject of many a conversation around the Leerberghe hearth on winter evenings. When he was just three years old, comparing the Rampals to Adèle (the Deumes' maid at the time), little Adrien would cry with convincing solemnity: 'Dèle, poo! Ampal, nice, not poo!' As this makes clear, he was full of early promise. Madame Deume quickly communicated the infection to her husband, who could never mention the dazzling name Rampal to people he knew in Geneva without adding, with a little quake in his voice and eyes modestly lowered, that they were 'old Fwench nobility'.)

'Anyway, I'll have a word on the subject with Didi in the morning. I won't bother him tonight, so that he can give all his mind to his boss. If he thinks it would be better to invite his famous Rassets, though personally I've never clapped eyes on them, then he can decide to do that. But either way we shall be hosting a grand dinner party tomorrow night, either for the Rampals or the Rassets, or, failing that, for Madame Ventradour, I say failing that because she's not out of the same drawer, besides all that caviare for a single guest would be a waste. To be honest, I think I'd prefer the Rassets, it would be an opportunity to make their acquaintance in grand style. Come along, Martha, quick about it, and could we have a littel more vim, perlease? Oh and by the by, Martha, and pay attention to what I'm going to say. The gentleman will be coming at ten, but to be on the safe side I want you in white gloves standing smartly by the door in good time, so you're ready in case he comes early. Go and take up your position by the door at nine thirty. Stand up straight, don't forget your white gloves and mind you don't dirty them, and take good care of your apron too, it has to stay spotless. When the gentleman rings, you open the door with a smile, then you take his hat with a smile, but your smile must not be familiar but modest and . . . servanty. Then, when you've done that, you go to the drawing-room, where we'll be waiting, you open the door and in a clear voice and without smiling this time you announce the Under-Secretary-General of the League of Nations, the way it's done at grand receptions. Is that clear?'

'But Antoinette, Adwien said that he would go and meet him in the hall fifteen seconds after the doorbell wings.'

'You're right, I'd forgotten. Frankly I prefer it. Announcing guests calls for someone with a certain manner, a certain sense of occasion, a certain knowledge of how things are done. Poor Martha, you wouldn't have been up to it, would you, seeing as how in your lowly station such naiceties as receiving important persons do not loom large, I believe! It's not a criticism. It's hardly your fault that you come of humble stock,' she ended with one of her luminous smiles.

Adrien returned and said that Ariane was not hungry and would not come down until their guest had arrived. Monsieur Deume made for the sideboard, picked up a small piece of bread, and on it balanced a small piece of Gruyère. 'Hippolyte!' said Madame Deume disapprovingly. He didn't need to be told twice, put the bread and the cheese back where he had got them, and stood waiting until his wife had said grace. It was a bit thick, though, saying pwayers over a bit of cheese which, to boot, was to be eaten standing up!

'O Lord,' began Madame Deume, who parked herself in front of the sideboard with eyes closed, 'we thank Thee for granting and preparing with Thine own hands this evening which we are about to spend in the fellowship of the Under-Secretary-General of the League of Nations. Yes, thank you, Lord, thank you. (As she could not think of anything else to say, she repeated "Thank you" several times in a progressively affecting, melting voice to fill the silence while waiting for further inspired words to suggest themselves.) Thank you, thank you, oh thank you. We give Thee thanks too because Thou hast, in Thy wisdom, made the foot of our dear son to lie in the path of his superior. Oh grant that our wondrous companionship here this evening prove to be a plentiful fount of blessings upon our dear Adrien, and may he ever find his path strewn with opportunities for moral advancement and spiritual enrichment. Amen.'

To restore my spirits after this dose of Madame Deume, I propose to write a letter to Georges-Émile Delay, a Protestant minister at Cuarnens in the Canton of Vaud, a truly pure and good man, a real Christian, a brother. My Christian brother, as I call him in my heart.

CHAPTER 20

'Shall we retire to the drawing-room?' Madame Deume said grandly, crackling and rasping in her diamanté-encrusted shot-silk dress.

'Yes, let us wetire to the dwawing-woom,' repeated her diminutive husband, who, limping slightly, hands clasped behind his back, followed her lead and was followed in turn by Adrien.

They sat down. To an accompaniment of assorted twitterings, Madame Deume rooted out particles of ham which had stuck in her teeth. Then she asked the time. Both men reached for their pocket-watches and Adrien said that it was twenty minutes past nine. Monsieur Deume set his turnip back one minute.

'He told me quite definitely that he would be here at ten on the dot,' said Madame Deume once more.

'Forty minutes to go,' said Monsieur Deume.

'I'm so glad I thought of having Martha put a wave in her hair with the curling-tongs,' said Madame Deume. 'She really looks quite presentable in her linen apron and matching cap. Fortunately I took the precaution of buying two housemaid's aprons. If I hadn't, what with her bleeding all over the place, we'd have been in a pretty pickle! But it's all worked out naicely.'

Yes, she'd thought of everything. She had put Martha through her paces and made her repeat her tasks in order. A little rehearsal had been staged for her benefit, with Didi as the Under-Secretary-General ringing the doorbell, then coming in and handing over his hat, to which a walking-stick was added just in case, though Adrien had said that his chief was not a walking-stick man. As soon as their guest reached the drawing-room, Martha was to let Ariane know and ask her to come down. Then, exactly ten minutes later, she was to appear in the drawing-room with three different kinds of hot drink: tea, ordinary coffee and decaffeinated. Their guest would then choose. Next he would be invited to take a liqueur or, if he preferred, a glass of champagne. There would be plenty left over for no end of Rampals or Rassets. But if his chief preferred a herbal infusion, an eventuality ruled out by Didi, it could be quickly prepared, for they had all sorts in the house – verbena, camomile, lime-blossom, mint and aniseed. Yes indeed, everything was under control. She let her eyes wander round the room and gave a satisfied sigh.

'The drawing-room looks a picture,' she said. (She pronounced it piksher.)

While Martha, her hair waved, wearing her white gloves and impersonating a housemaid, stood at her post behind the door, ready to answer the call and quaking in her shoes, the three Deumes sat patiently, tactfully waiting. As tense as if they were visitors in their own home, they did not dare settle back comfortably in their chairs. Ears already cocked for noises off, they racked their brains for something to say and then exchanged a few words on vapid topics of conversation in desultory fashion, blowing on flames which died down again at once. Out of an obscure sense of their own dignity, they refrained from mentioning their guest now that his arrival was imminent. They were reluctant to admit that they had thoughts only for him and that their hearts swelled with pride at the idea of entertaining a person of such eminence, albeit at ten in the evening. However, from time to time a reference to the Under-Secretary-General got through. It was a way of intimating how very much at their ease they felt. But for the most part they opted for a silence pregnant with mutual regard and a paradoxically cheery gloom, Madame Deume checking to see if her nails were clean, or fluffing up her lace jabot, or unleashing a bountiful smile, her crooked yellow teeth resting affectedly on the soft cushion of her lower lip. Since their honoured guest had said that he would be in their midst at ten o'clock sharp, she was confident of success and radiated smug self-satisfaction. She was so happy that several times she expressed her love for her adopted son with a muted 'Coo-ee, darling!' which she punctuated with roguish pats on his hand. Adrien had brought home a photograph of Solal which he had cut out of a Paris daily, and to while away the time she said that their guest looked every inch a leader of men. It was the highest accolade she could bestow.

The time hung nobly on them, and already they felt they were fully paid-up members of the Under-Secretary-General's circle of intimates, and of the Rampal coterie too. Waiting was a delight, and they bided their time free of apprehension and well disposed to the world at large. Now and then one or other of them got up and wiped away a trace of dust, repositioned an occasional table or an ornament, checked to see whether the thermometer registered a temperature fit for a leader of men, closed the lid of the grand piano and then propped it up again because, on reflection, it looked better open for like that it struck a note of unstudied elegance. In turn, the two men went over to the window where, with back turned to the mistress of the house, they discreetly checked certain buttons.

'The drawing-room looks a piksher,' repeated Madame Deume, the smiling, confident hostess. 'Still, you know, Didi, there is one tiny improvement we could make one of these days: we could hang curtains over the bay, cotton rep with great big flowers, hand-painted of course, and behind them we could install subdued lighting which can be turned on at night when the curtains are drawn, that's how Emmeline Ventradour has it, it would look very artistic. We'd only switch on when we had guests. But we'll talk about it some other time. Yoo-hoo, darling!' she said this time to her Didi, and she playfully pinched his wrist then shook it this way and that.

When she had finished scouring her teeth with the help of further twitterings and the pocket toothpick loaned by her husband, and had given the alarming crescent under her fingernails another good scraping with Hippolyte's handyman's knife, she felt in the mood for a little of the conversation on elevated topics which she considered to be *de rigueur* at this point of the evening. Breathing minty waftures released by the lozenges she was sucking, she spoke of a book, 'so well written', entitled *The Story of My Life*, which she had made a point of displaying, for all to see, on one of those little trolleys which she called 'wheelie-trays'. She opened the volume, which the world owed to the pen of Queen Marie of Romania, and read out a sentence which had struck her forcibly: 'Blessèd, thrice blessèd, be the gift which God has granted me of feeling the beauty in things so deeply and of rejoicing in their beauty!'

'Now isn't that lervely! It's so profound!'

'Oh absolutely,' said Monsieur Deume. 'Pwofound's the word.'

'That was written by a queen, dear. Need one say more?'

All graciousness, she gave a delicate smile, for she felt at one with the Queen of Romania, an intuition fuelled by the imminent arrival of the Under-Secretary-General, a high dignitary most certainly on calling terms with the dear Queen, into whose ken she therefore felt she had somehow, by proxy, swum. She had a sense that evening of belonging in the same top drawer. Then she raised the matter of a photograph which she had seen in an illustrated weekly. It showed another queen, who, at some official ceremony or other, had not been afraid to ease one foot out of her shoe to rest it. Just like any other woman! Wasn't that lervely?

Then she drooled over a third queen, who had insisted on travelling by bus, just once, to see for herself, because she'd never been on a bus before! Imagine! On a bus! A queen who could afford coaches and expensive motor cars catching a bus! Wasn't that a lervely, a really lervely, thought! And what about the children of the English royal family, who'd wanted to take the tube, to see what it was like! Those littel princes on the Underground! Too sweet for words! she said with a tender smile. And, added Monsieur Deume, it was democwatic too. Returning to the queen who had caught the bus, Madame Deume quoted another moving incident in which she had been involved.

'While visiting some small town or other, she made a point of shaking hands with one of the Mayor's deputies, a crippled grocer who had been forced by his infirmity to stay in the background in a wheelchair. I mean, she went out of her way, *she* went to *him*, although he was yards away! A grocer! Such a kind thought! A lervely gesture! As I read about it in the paper, there were tears in my eyes! They say she has magnetic charm, and with it so tremendously at her ease with ordinary people! Now there's someone who thoroughly deserves to have been set on high! Mind you, the same goes for queens in general, they're all so sensitive, so . . . bountiful!'

Her stock of queens now exhausted, there was a silence. They coughed, cleared their throats. Adrien looked at his watch. Nine thirty-seven. 'Another twenty-thwee minutes,' said Monsieur Deume, stifling a nervous yawn. At least, he thought, the visit of this eminent dignitawy – cowwection, dweadful bore, he said to himself, to spite him – would be over by midnight, and then a chap could slip off quietly to bed without having to bellow out any more conversation in the waised tone of voice which showed that a person was socially accomplished, no more jabbewing on about this or that, no more waiting for this other cove to open his mouth first. Suddenly Madame Deume tappèd Adrien sharply on the knee.

'Listen, Didi, why don't you tell us a bit about our guest, I mean about his private side, his character, so we get to know him a littel. I'll start: does he believe in God?'

'Haven't a clue. All I know is a couple of things which show what an amazing chap he is. Castro was only saying to me this morning, oh I must tell Ariane, it was Lady Cheyne, who told Castro who often gets invited to her house, so it's authentic. By the by, I must have Castro round to dinner one of these days, he's a sound chap, ever so well-read.'

'Yes, yes, but what about these things you know?'

'First, there was this fire in a hotel in London. By all accounts he risked his life to rescue two women.'

'Oh, lervely!' exclaimed Madame Deume. 'That means he must believe in God!'

'And then here in Geneva there was a poor girl, a midget, who used to play the guitar in the streets, a beggar in other words. Well, he saved her from poverty, rented a little flat for her, and they say he even pays her an allowance, so now she doesn't have to beg any more, she does voluntary work for the Salvation Army. Quite simply, he completely changed the poor little thing's life.'

'Oooh, I just know that he and I are going to get on!' exclaimed Madame Deume.

'They say the two of them have been seen out walking together. Imagine it: him very tall and her very short, with stubby legs, in her Sally Army uniform.'

'Sounds a vewy decent sort,' said Monsieur Deume, smoothing the wings of his moustache to make them lie flat, 'wouldn't you say so, Antoinette?'

'I always commend charity,' she said. 'Though in his position I don't really think he ought to be seen with a person of lower social rank, especially a person who has been a professional beggar.'

For something to do, the old gentleman hummed quietly to himself, then from the waistcoat pocket of his dinner-suit produced a cheap, thin, black cheroot which he prepared to light, not because he felt like a smoke – he was too nervous about the introductions for that – but so that he would have something to cling to when their guest walked through the door. His wife removed the cigar from his mouth and put it away in a drawer.

'Brissago cheroots are common.'

'But I have one evewy evening after dinner!'

'And you are wrong to do so. It makes you look like a post-office clerk. Adrien, you will please turn the conversation round to *The Story of My Life*, which will bring us on nicely to Her Majesty the Queen of Romania, oh and you can mention dear Dr Schweitzer too. That'll give me a chance to get a word in. The *bombe glacée!*' she exclaimed, changing course without warning.

'What about it, Mumsy?'

'We can offer him the *bombe tutti frutti!*'

'But Mumsy, we can't possibly. You don't offer guests *bombe glacée* at ten o'clock at night. Whatever would he think?'

'Yes of course, you're right, Didi. But it's such a shame. It won't keep till tomorrow night, it will have melted by then, even in the fridge. We'll have to buy a new fridge, with a deep-freeze compartment, if we can get a good part-exchange on the one we've got. Hippolyte, go this minute and tell Martha she can eat as much of the *bombe glacée* as she wants, it'll be a treat for the poor girl and besides it will be a Good Deed.'

Monsieur Deume obeyed with alacrity and hurried away to bring the good tidings to Martha. In the kitchen, he made great inroads into the *bombe glacée*, shovelling it down until his teeth chattered. Returning to the drawing-room, disguising his shivers, he ventured to ask Antoinette if he could pour himself a small cognac, saying: 'I feel cold all of a sudden, can't think why.'

At nine fifty Madame Deume judged the moment had come to go up to her room and repair what was, in truth, the irreparable. After anointing her bangs with oil of heliotrope, she took a piece of cotton wool and dusted her face with a white powder called Carina, which she used only on special occasions and kept under lock and key in the secret drawer of her dressing-table. Then behind her ears she dabbed a few drops of Floramye, a forty-year-old fragrance. Alluring, with fresh heart, she went downstairs and made her entrance into the drawing-room, the perfumed embodiment of moral worth and social presence, wearing the doleful air of the truly refined.

'What's the time?' she asked.

'Three minutes to ten,' said Adrien.

'Just thwee minutes now,' said Monsieur Deume, holding himself stiffer than a candle.

They waited, not daring now to look at each other. Intermittently, to fill the vacuum, a sentence rang out hollowly with a remark concerning the temperature, or a comment on how efficient the flush in the downstairs lavatory had been since it had been repaired, or a comparison of the respective merits of the teas of China and Ceylon, the first having a more subtle aroma and the second more body. But hearts and ears were elsewhere. 'Yes,' Madame Deume recited inwardly for the benefit of the ladies she would see the following Monday at the next meeting of the sewing-circle in aid of the converts of the Zambezi, 'the other evening we sat up ever so late, oh a small private function, a family affair really, we had the Under-Secretary-General of the League of Nations round, just him, no one else. An intellectual treat! He's such a charming man, terribly naice and very unaffected, well he was unaffected with us at any rate.'

Ten o'clock was struck simultaneously by the Neuchâtel clock and the three other clocks in the house, all scrupulously kept to time by Monsieur Deume. Adrien stood up and his adoptive father followed suit. It was a solemn moment. The mistress of the house caressed her neck to ensure that her velvet choker was perfectly positioned, then adopted a pose of dignified expectancy, and smiled with the aforementioned doleful air which left her squinting teeth highly visible.

'Aren't you going to get up too, poppet?'

'The lady of the house remains seated when she receives a gentleman,' said his poppet, who, having spoken with the voice of authority, shut her eyes.

After running a comb through his wispy beard, Adrien suddenly decided that the de-luxe art books he had bought the day before would be better if arranged in a geometric order. Then he mixed them up again because on second thoughts they were better as they were, looked more intellectual. Madame Deume gave a start, and her adipose lump swayed like a gracefully dangling bauble.

'What is it?' she asked.

'Nothing,' said Monsieur Deume.

'I thought I heard a car.'

'Just the wind,' said Adrien.

Monsieur Deume opened the window. No, there was no car.

At ten minutes past ten it was agreed that the Argentinian dinner had probably started late, it was the sort of thing you had to learn to put up with from South Americans. Furthermore, perhaps the Under-Secretary-General had embarked upon some weighty discussion with the delegates, exactly the sort of thing that happened over the coffee and cigars. 'He could hardly get up and go just as some important decision was about to be taken,' said Madame Deume. 'Wather,' said Monsieur Deume.

At twelve minutes past ten, Ariane, in a black crêpe dress, finally put in an appearance. After issuing smiles to all those present, she enquired, with an innocent flutter of her eyes, if they were waiting for the Under-Secretary-General. She could jolly well see that they were waiting for him, replied Adrien, who made the muscles of his jaws stand out to lend his face a look of indomitable energy. There had been a minor misunderstanding, explained Monsieur Deume. At what time was the Under-Secretary-General coming? she asked, meticulously separating each of the syllables of the long title. About ten o'clock, replied Madame Deume tartly.

'I'll wait with you,' Ariane said pleasantly.

She sat down. She crossed her arms and observed that it was a trifle cold in the drawing-room. She crossed her legs. Then she stood up, asked to be excused for a moment, said she was going to get a fur wrap. When she returned, her mink stole over her shoulders, she sat down again quietly and stared at the floor. She sighed. Then, as good as gold, she crossed her arms again. A moment later, she unfolded them and yawned politely.

'If you're tired, why not go and have a lie-down,' said Madame Deume.

'How kind. I must admit I do find waiting here in the cold a little tiring and I am rather sleepy as a matter of fact. So I'll say good-night, Madame. Good-night, Da-Da, good-night Adrien. I do so hope your guest won't be long.'

At ten twenty-seven Adrien rearranged his art books symmetrically and then remarked that the wind was getting up. Monsieur Deume added that in his opinion there was a storm bwewing, that it had gwown noticeably cooler, and that it might be a good idea after all to light a few sticks in the gwate. Madame Deume said there wasn't any more wood in the cellar, and in any case lighting a fire on the first of June was quite unheard of. At half past ten she announced that her back was playing up. 'Shush! a car!' warned Monsieur Deume. But none of the cars that passed the house ever stopped. At ten thirty-two, a loud burst of the 'Marseillaise' played on the piano came from the second floor and rang throughout the house. This was followed by a slushy tune from the ballet *Coppélia*. 'An odd way of feeling sleepy,' commented Madame Deume.

At ten thirty-five old Monsieur Deume sneaked his fifth biscuit, smuggled it into his mouth, and let it dissolve secretly inside his closed jaws. He coped with the business of swallowing it as best he could. At ten forty he was on to his ninth, and this time managed the thing with rather more recklessness, for Madame Deume's eyes were now closed in silent martyrdom. From the second floor, the funeral march by Chopin crept lugubriously downstairs, while the silence in the drawing-room deepened, the wind moaned outside, Monsieur Deume masticated the decreasingly appetizing biscuits with cheerless pleasure, and, stationed by the door, the shivering Martha, dressed up like the maid in a farce, continued to stand guard. The wind increased in strength, and it was Adrien's turn to remark that a storm was brewing. Then the silence closed round them again and Monsieur Deume shuddered. Should he get his coat? No, it would only make her cross.

'By the way, Antoinette,' he asked a moment later, 'under what heading do we enter the cost of the dinner party in the household accounts?'

'It will be added to Adrien's personal contribution,' she said, and she stood up. 'Good-night. I am going to bed.'

At ten forty-five the drawing-room was empty save for two men and six biscuits. Monsieur Deume, now swaddled in his woollen greatcoat, suggested that it was time for bye-byes, adding that he had aching legs and an upset stomach. Adrien said that he would hang on for another few minutes, just in case. Monsieur Deume said good-night and made for the door, looking like sciatica personified. When he reached it, he turned and said: 'If you ask me, something wum's happened.'

After telling Martha she could go to bed, he made himself a scalding hot-water bottle for comfort, checked the assortment of locks and bolts on the front door, turned off the gas, and decided he would sleep in the guest room so as not to disturb Antoinette. In reality he went somewhat in awe of her this evening and preferred to keep his distance.

Monsieur Deume slipped blissfully between the cool sheets and surrendered to joys which, because they were modest and self-contained, were impervious to disappointment, ordering his toes to perform a refreshing little jig, rootling about with his feet for the hot-water bottle and playing little games with it, taking his feet off it to be cold for just a moment, putting one instep under it and raising it an inch or so, for a delicious little change. He was snug in his bed, so too bad if Adrien's chap hadn't come.

Suddenly, outside, brilliant bursts of lightning instantly extinguished, angry claps of thunder which rolled in waves, and the clatter of a violent downpour. 'A weal storm,' murmured the old gentleman and from the comfort of his bed he smiled. How well off a chap was under his own roof, snug in the shelter of this lovely home of theirs! Those poor tramps with no place to call their own, he thought, putting his feet on the hot-water bottle, which was just right, hot but not too hot. Yes, those poor unfortunate tramps, who were at this very moment raking the roads, sheltering under trees, poor creatures. He gave a sigh of genuine compassion, while in her bedroom next door his wife was examining, spread out on the counterpane, the bearer bonds issued by Nestlé, which she had told no one she had bought.

He plugged his ears with blobs of wax, a present from Madame van Offel, switched off his bedside lamp, and turned his face to the wall with a smile. Oh yes, he felt pretty fit. Good for another twenty years at least. Tomorrow he must tell Martha that he had a great deal of sympathy with the socialists. That way, if there was a revolution, she would be able to speak on his behalf. He smiled another smile. That white paint he'd put on the pipes in the kitchen had turned out very well. He'd been careful to use the best-quality gloss and given it three coats. In the morning, he'd check to see if the third coat was dry. Maybe it was dry already. Should he pop down now to see, just for a moment?

In the kitchen, wearing only nightshirt and slippers, he bent down over one of the pipes and ran his finger over it. Yes, dry as a bone! He beamed at the pipes, which beamed back dazzling white, and his heart went out to them.

Adrien stood in the middle of the drawing-room and undid his tie, downed a whisky, munched the last biscuit, and looked at his watch yet again. Ten past eleven. Better stay on for another couple of minutes. Oh he knew he wouldn't come now, but just in case he phoned. All the same, it would show a little courtesy to the family if he phoned to apologize or at least explain, dammit.

'Stood-up! And how! It's a bit thick! Unless he's dead.'

Obviously if he was dead then he had a perfectly valid excuse. If he was, then he'd have to go to the funeral, he owed him that much. When senior ranks were buried, there were opportunities for making useful contacts. But he wasn't really dead, he knew it in his bones, he wasn't the type to turn up his toes just like that, he still looked pretty young. What he couldn't make out, though, was that he'd definitely told Mummy he was coming. So what the dickens had gone wrong? Nobody had the right to pull a stunt like that! First he wasn't coming to dinner, and they'd got all that caviare in, for God's sake, then he gave his solemn word he'd be arriving at ten, and in the end, zero! Oh no, such behaviour was totally indefensible!

'Or perhaps he forgot the address?'

No, that didn't hold water. When you forgot an address, you looked in the phone book. So, unless he'd dropped dead, he had no excuse. Deep down, he knew he wouldn't phone. God Almighty, you couldn't go round playing fast and loose like that, even if you were the Pope. Still, he was an A. Hello, storm's over. An A. So there.

At a quarter past eleven, after a second whisky, he left the drawing-room, slowly climbed the stairs, punctuating each step of his way with an evil-sounding word while Mumsy's angry snores filled the silence. He stopped when he reached the second-floor landing. Should he go and talk it over with Ariane? It would be a comfort, he could work out with her what to do in the morning if the USG didn't call him in to offer an explanation and especially to ask him to convey his apologies to Mumsy and Ariane, who were ladies, dammit! An apology would save face. Yes, if by tomorrow lunch-time he had not been summoned by the USG, then ask to see him, it would be easy enough to arrange, he was well in with Miss Wilson, hadn't he brought her those almond cakes when he'd got back from Valescure? Should he knock on Ariane's door? She was probably asleep already and she didn't like being woken up. No, best not. Especially since she was being rather hard to please these days.

'The best thing, of course, would be that he's had a heart attack, apoplexy and so on. That would wipe his slate clean for not turning up. But even if he comes up with some fairy story, who gives a damn provided he does the honourable thing by the family, and by me too, he owes me that, to show he doesn't despise me. Hell's teeth, let him fob me off with some tale or other, that's all I want. So tomorrow, come straight to the point and ask if he was prevented from coming by a sudden indisposition. That'll suggest the kind of yarn he can spin and honour will be saved. Yes, but if I ask to see him after he's stood me up like this, won't it look as if I'm accusing him of something? Damn, damn, damn!'

In his bedroom, feeling thoroughly disheartened, he tossed his brand-new dinner-jacket on to a chair. He got into his old pyjamas and stood at the foot of the bed, his eyes fixed and staring, contemplating his unhappy lot. Surely he could go and wake her, it was a quite exceptional situation. He took off his pyjamas and put on a new pair, freshly ironed, shuffled into his new slippers, and ran a comb through his thin beard. It was twenty-six minutes past eleven. Yes, why not? He'd go.

'I mean to say, I am her husband after all.'

Stepping out of her bath, she dried herself quickly, because it was terribly important to be tucked up in bed before eleven thirty at the outside, for otherwise the results could be disastrous. (This little rich girl was descended from a long line of tender flowers accustomed to taking good care of themselves, who laid great stress on fatigue, on rest which overcomes fatigue, and on sleep which brings rest. One rule considered self-evident by the Auble clan was that if one retired for the night after eleven o'clock, one ran the risk of not sleeping, which was an abomination and a fate worse than death. The fear of going to bed late, transmitted from one generation to the next, verged on mania in Auble women, who led idler lives than their menfolk and were therefore more addicted to morbid introspection, more preoccupied by what they called the state of their nerves, and they took great care not to become overtired, forced themselves to go on frequent holidays, which did them good, they said, and above all never went to bed late. Which explains why of an evening, after dinner, the genteel drawing-room conversation was regularly interrupted by one of these ladies who, suddenly setting down her crewelwork or embroidery, would exclaim with an anguished start: 'Heaven! Look at the time! Twenty to eleven! There's just time to get ready for bed!' It goes without saying that next morning, at the breakfast table, the first thought of these ladies was to tell each other how they had slept, in a spirit of keen and kindly interest and a specialized jargon of fine detail and subtle distinctions such as: 'Yes, I slept well, perhaps not as well as I might have, anyway not as well as the night before last.' Throughout her childhood and adolescence, Ariane had scrupulously observed the sacred eleven o'clock rule, which Aunt Valérie had invoked on many occasions. She still went in childish awe of it. Yet ever since she had been of age, perhaps influenced by her Russian friend, she had come round to the view that as a grown woman she could put back her bedtime by half an hour. But if she was any later than eleven thirty she panicked at the likely prospect of a sleepless night.)

With a sigh of relief that she had not missed the deadline, she crept between the sheets at twenty-nine minutes past eleven and turned out the light at once. Lying in the dark, she smiled. There had been no ring at the door since she had come upstairs. So the beast hadn't come. Egg all over the collective Deume face.

'Serves them right,' she murmured, and curled herself up into a ball.

She was composing herself for sleep when there were two light taps on her door. It must be him. What did he want now? She decided not to answer. He would think she was asleep and give up. And a few moments later she did indeed hear him go back to his room and shut his door. Saved! Curled up once more, she shut her eyes again. Damn, he was coming back. Two knocks, louder this time. O God, why couldn't he leave her in peace? Might as well answer and get it over with.

'Who's there?' she said with a groan, pretending to wake with a start.

'It's me, darling. Can I come in?'

'All right.'

'You don't mind me disturbing you?' he asked as he entered.

'No,' she said, and she put on a ghostly, long-suffering smile.

'Don't worry, I shan't stay long. I'd just like to know what you make of it, I mean the fact that he didn't show up.'

'Dunno. He must have been prevented.'

'Yes, but it's odd, don't you think, that he didn't even phone to let us know, or send his apologies or anything. Say: what do you think I ought to do tomorrow? Should I go and see him?'

'Yes, go and see him.'

'But that might put his back up, it might sort of look like a criticism, as if I was asking him to explain himself.'

'Well don't, then.'

'Yes, but on the other hand I can't just leave things as they are. I mean, what sort of idiot would I look if I bump into him and he doesn't say anything? I mean, I've got my pride. What do you think?'

'Best go and see him.'

'Are you cross because I came?' he asked after a pause.

'No. But I'm feeling rather sleepy.'

'I'm sorry. I shouldn't have come. Sorry. I'll go now. Good-night, darling.'

'Good-night,' she smiled. 'Pleasant dreams,' she said. It was his reward for going away.

He got as far as the door then turned and came back.

'Look, can I stay for two more minutes?'

'Yes, of course.'

He sat down on the edge of the bed and took her hand. Ever the model wife, she arranged her lips in a fixed smile while he peered at her through his glasses with spaniel eyes and waited for her to comfort him. When the words he hoped to hear did not come, he tried to drag them out of her.

'You know, it's been a bit of a let-down for me.'

'Yes, I see that,' she said, and then reverted to her fixed smile.

'What would you advise me to do?'

'I don't know. Wait for him to apologize.'

'Yes, but what if he doesn't apologize?'

'No idea,' she said, and glanced towards the clock on the mantelpiece.

In the silence, he stared at her and waited. She thought only of the minutes which dropped one by one into the silence. If he stayed much longer the deadline would go by and she'd be in for a sleepless night. He had promised he would only stay for two minutes, but he'd been sitting there for well over two minutes just goggling at her. Why wasn't he sticking to his promise? She knew exactly what he was after: reassurance. But if she started being comforting they'd be there for ages. He would raise objections to her reassuring words to make her console him some more, and the whole business would drag on until two in the morning. His clammy hand on hers felt most unpleasant. Her subtle efforts to free herself failing to produce any effect, she said that she had pins and needles, took her hand away, and looked at the clock.

'I'll stay another minute and then I'll go.'

'Yes,' she smiled.

Suddenly he stood up.

'You're not very nice to me.'

She sat up in bed. How unfair! She had answered him nicely, she had gone on smiling at him, and here he was finding fault!

'In what way?' she asked, looking him in the eye. 'In what way aren't I nice?'

'All you want is to see the back of me, and yet you know how much I need you.'

These last words made her see red. Who was this man to be needing her all the time?

'It's ten to twelve,' she said pointedly.

'So what if I was to get ill and you had to keep watch by my bedside, how would you manage then?'

She had a sudden vision of herself sitting up all night by his bed, and she was filled with fury against this man who never gave a thought to anyone except himself. She put on her stoniest expression, unyielding and hard. She had turned into a crazed ice-maiden, incapable of thinking of anything beyond her threatened sleep, so terrorized was she by the prospect of a night of insomnia. He repeated his question.

'I don't know! I don't know!' she shouted. 'I have no idea what I would do. But what I do know is that it's eight minutes to midnight! Why choose the middle of the night to start a question-and-answer session? And why bring up all this rubbish about falling ill? (She felt an urge to say that there were nurses to look after the sick, but thought better of it.) Now I'll never get to sleep, thanks to your selfishness!'

She glowered with hate at this man who saw fit to need her at midnight. Oh, this awful passion of his for depending on her for every little thing!

'Darling, don't be mean, be nice to me. I'm so unhappy.'

Again she turned her implacable face to him, the face he knew so well, and he was suddenly afraid. It was the face of a heartless woman and it belonged to his wife, she whom he had chosen above all others, his companion through life. He sat down on a chair next to the bed and, gathering his thoughts together, forced himself to dwell on his misery: perhaps he could make himself cry. In a little while tears duly came, and he turned towards his wife to ensure that she got a good look at them, to make the most of the wetness of his cheeks. She averted her eyes, for women do not care much for men who weep, especially if they are the cause of the problem.

'Darling, be nice to me,' he repeated to keep her attention, for it was important to maximize the return on his tears while they still flowed, before they evaporated.

'What do you mean when you say I'm not nice?'

'You're not being very nice just now.'

'It's not true, I am nice!' she exclaimed. 'I am very nice! You're the one who's not nice! It's midnight!'

Maddened by the thought that all was now lost, that she wouldn't sleep that night and that tomorrow she'd feel as limp as a rag, with a crushing migraine, she leaped out of bed wearing only her pyjama jacket, walked up and down the room in a fury, looking unusually tall on her long, bare legs. Crushed in advance, and anticipating the recriminations which were sure to come, he slumped over the edge of her bed. This made her angrier still. What gave this man the right to sit down on the bed, her bed, the bed she'd slept in when she was a girl? In a rage, she picked up a pencil and snapped it in two. Then turning to her oppressor, incandescent with indignation and determined to defend the victim she felt herself to be, she prepared to do battle by buttoning up her short jacket and began to protest. She was a good protester.

'It's shameful, it's outrageous,' she began, to get her hand in and build up a head of steam while waiting for inspiration and a suitable theme. 'So, you don't think I'm very nice! Is it because for the last half-hour I've been sitting here meek and mild, like Patience on a monument? Is it because I didn't say anything when you broke your promise, though I knew I probably shouldn't sleep? Yes, broke your promise! You said you'd only stay for two minutes. You lied to me, you lured me into a trap! You've been here half an hour and I've not complained once that you've failed to keep your solemn word! (He looked up at her helplessly. Failed to keep his solemn word! The way she had of putting things! He hadn't given any solemn word, and she knew it. But what was the use of trying to defend himself? Whatever he said, he'd be shot down in flames.) No,' she went on, 'I never complained, the very opposite, I smiled ever so sweetly, and that's what you call not being nice: I smiled! That's right, I went on smiling for half an hour hoping that you'd realize what horrible torment you were putting me through, hoping and hoping that sooner or later you'd show a little mercy, a drop of pity, a glimmer of love!'

'But you know I love you,' he murmured, with head bowed.

'But why should you feel pity for your slave?' she continued, ignoring everything that was not grist to her mill.

'Keep your voice down,' he begged. 'They'll hear!'

'Let them hear! Let them know how you treat me! Yes, why should you pity a slave?' she went on again, quivering with warlike fervour, for here she had hit upon a high-yield theme. 'A slave has to put up with anything! If it so pleases her master to wake her at one o'clock in the morning, she must bend the knee! If it is her tyrant's whim to keep her up talking all night, she must bow her head! And woe betide her if she does not hide her tiredness and her need for sleep! Woe betide her if she does not knuckle under or dares to close her eyes! She'd be accused of being selfish, of not being nice! Woe betide her if she has the guts to want to be treated like a human being and not like a dog who can be woken up at any hour of the night! And why am I guilty of the crime of wanting to sleep? So as to be ready to serve you tomorrow, at first light! Because a slave must always be ready, always available! Such a view of marriage is down-right disgraceful! A wife is her husband's chattel! She doesn't even have the right to be called by her own name! She must bear the mark of her husband's ownership like a brand burned across her forehead! Like an animal! If there's anybody here who is selfish it's you, because you claim the right to need me at any time during the night! You're the one who's mean, because you've got the nerve to insist that I should undertake here and now to sit up all night by your bedside if you ever fall ill, whatever you're ill with, even if it's something trivial! So be it, I will be your servant, your skivvy! But even a skivvy has the right to sleep!'

Blithely pursuing her theme, she next dealt with various aspects of her martyr's life. After recalling his crimes against femininity, which she had already brought up in previous scenes, she then moved on, with the requisite wealth of dates and places, to enumerate, for the benefit of the poor bewildered male, other misdemeanours which he now learned he had committed during the course of their marriage. Indefatigable, nothing like a limp rag but firing on all pistons, she strode up and down in her red polka-dot jacket which left her thighs bare, paced feverishly, her words warmed by a sacred flame and strengthened too by the exultation of victory, while her spouse, stunned and left reeling by the power of her avenging eloquence, could only stand by and watch open-mouthed as his unsuspected sins were clearly marshalled and paraded before him.

They constituted a heavy indictment. Like the best orators, she was sincere, for she believed every word she said. Stirred by a noble indignation, she was utterly convinced of the rightness of her cause. It was her greatest strength, and, admirably sustained by a mixture of aggression and sarcasm, it enabled her to crush her much less skilful opponent. But she was also clever. As skilfully as the ablest of prosecuting counsels, she set out her case in blacks and whites which strengthened it immeasurably, eliminating anything which might count against her and imparting the required twists, warps and amplifications to the words and actions of her guilty husband. And all her unfairness was spoken in good faith, for she was honest.

He listened in a daze to her tireless outpouring and he knew that she accused him unjustly, with only a semblance of right, as always. But he also knew that he would never convince her she was wrong, that he had neither the talent nor the stamina for it, that he was far too wretched to be able to defend himself properly. All he could do was to repeat – because it was the truth – that she was being mean and unfair, to which she would respond endlessly and always victoriously.

No, he simply wasn't up to it. Her fire-power was the greater. He laid down his arms and left her without saying a word, which rather impressed the young woman and sent her husband's stock up several points.

It was true. The poor man was just not up to it. Throughout the whole of that terrible month of May, each time he'd tried to stand up to his wife, each time he had put a cast-iron case to prove that she was in the wrong, she had not budged one inch. She always got the better of him in any argument, because she interrupted and talked him down so that he was left, a speechless bystander, to watch helpless and hopeless as the various charges in the indictment were wheeled out before him; or else because she steamrollered him with unsubstantiated but extremely telling thrusts, such as describing his plain, honest arguments as 'a tissue of clever fibs and quibbles'; or because she sidetracked him and mixed him up; or else because she deliberately ignored everything he said and simply went on piling up grievances which, because they were incomprehensible, were also irrefutable.

The best he could manage, if he ever succeeded in making her listen to his side of things and got her on the wrong foot, was to see her wriggle out of reach by seeking refuge in the tears and sufferings of the helpless, ill-used wife, or by refusing to answer and looking stony-faced if he begged her to admit her faults, or by resorting to the 'I-don't-know-what-you're-talking-about' tactic, a ploy she was capable of repeating indefinitely if he restated his thesis and began once more to explain, as conscientiously and as clearly as he could, exactly in what ways she was to blame. (This was a bee in the poor man's bonnet: he believed in the clarifying power of explanations. It would have been far better for him if he'd never become a husband, for that was his only sin.) Whenever he attempted this, she would let him prattle on without trying to interrupt, but then, when he had finished and was looking at her with hope in his eyes, convinced that this time he'd explained things clearly and made her see them from his point of view, she would simply stand her ground and again scream that she didn't know what he was talking about, couldn't for the life of her see what he was driving at!

And woe betide him if he let himself be goaded by such patent but triumphant pretences, woe betide him if he were to bear down on her with fists clenched, woe betide him! For then she called him a brute, a wife-beating coward, screamed with terror, with genuine terror too, which was quite diabolical of her, and shouted for help and roused the neighbours. One night, shortly before the Deumes had got back, just because he had told her to stop shouting and had raised his arm, though he had absolutely no intention of hitting her, she had ripped off her pyjama top and run out into the garden, stark naked with rage. The following night, because he had gone so far as to raise his voice a little and tell her she was mean to him, she had paid him back by shrieking that he was a monster, a tyrant, a torturer, by tearing off a piece of the wallpaper, then by going downstairs and locking herself in the kitchen, where she had stayed put until four in the morning while he trembled with fear at the thought that she might put her head in the gas-oven.

And that was not all, for she had other weapons in her armoury which the poor devil knew only too well: reprisals for the morning after. These included headaches, sit-down strikes in her room, swollen eyes offered as evidence of tears shed in solitude, a whole battery of ailments, stubborn sulks, an embattled loss of appetite, fatigue, forget-fulness, dejected airs – the complete, fearsome panoply of the helpless but quite invincible female.

CHAPTER 22

A suicide would be best. Fire the pistol but not just anywhere, not into the wardrobe with the mirror nor at the ceiling. Aim for somewhere where it wouldn't do too much damage, like the bed, aim for the bed. The bullet would end up in the mattress without causing too much harm. The noise would bring her running and he'd explain that his hand had been shaking and the shot had been deflected. Then she would see what sort of dance she led him and how miserable she was making him.

'No, it won't work.'

No, it wouldn't work. In spite of their wax ear-plugs, Mummy and Dada might hear the shot. And even if they didn't, how would he explain the hole in the bedcovers, the sheets and the mattress? Especially since Mummy had eyes in the back of her head. How about a heart attack, the kind where you couldn't breathe, brought on by suffering? No, he wouldn't know how to fake it, it was too difficult. Anyway, a choking fit wouldn't make enough noise, no-where near enough to make her come. Don't talk to her for several days, even try not eating? That wouldn't work either. Mummy would catch on straight away that something was up and would start asking questions and then there'd be an almighty fuss. No, the only real solution was to do his level best to stop loving her. Yes, be resigned to living without love, tell himself that she was a stranger with whom he had to go on living, but not to expect anything more from her, and immediately alter his will and leave everything to Mummy and Dada.

He had just sat down to write his last will and testament when there was a light knocking at his door. He glanced up at the mirror, took off his glasses, and opened the door. A noble penitent in a white silk dressing-gown stepped forward, a priestess robed in sweetness, who said she was sorry she had behaved badly, had lost her self-control, her head.

'No, I'm the one who was in the wrong,' he said. 'I shouldn't have come so late. Say you forgive me, darling.'

Back in her room, as she stood at the foot of her bed, he found her so touching in repentance that he folded her in his arms. Feeling her breasts firm against him, he whispered in her ear. She got into bed and closed her eyes so that she would not see him taking off his pyjamas. He turned back the bedcover, lay down beside her, and gave two sneezes. Here we go, she thought. Woof-woof time. How very, very stupid she'd been to feel sorry for him, how could she have been so brainless as to go and ask his forgiveness? And now she was going to have to pay for it.

In the circumstances, Adrien Deume moved effortlessly from continence to the eagerness of a bull in a hurry. Still, a few weeks previously he had read the *Kama Sutra*, which had taught him the importance of certain preparatory manœuvres. Accordingly, without further ado, he began nibbling his wife. Ah, the pekinese routine now, she thought, and she could not resist the temptation of yapping doggily inside herself. She was cross with herself for wanting to laugh, though she kept her giggles firmly under control while the newly elevated grade A diligently busied himself with his nibbling. All the same, she felt ashamed but still went on yapping to herself, woof-woof, woof-woof. After further fondlings, studiously rendered as per the Indian manual, what was inevitable came to pass.

Stretched out beside her, perfectly relaxed now, he whispered tenderly and spoke fine and noble thoughts, while she struggled to keep the lid on her wrath. Oh no! It was a bit thick, it really was, coming the idealist and man of feeling now that he had taken his pleasure with her, the cheek of him, thinking that he could pay her off with a mouthful of poetry and high-flown sentiments after dragging her through the mud of his bestiality! He had drunk his fill of her: why couldn't he just sleep it off quietly?

And another thing. He was lying much too close. He was sweating and sticky, and each time she moved away he snuggled up closer and drooled out more lovey-dovey goo, squirming cannibal one minute, recumbent leech the next, he had a nerve! And what gave him the right to take root beside her, what right did he have to go on clinging to her now that he'd got what he wanted, now that she was no more use to him? He'd had his epileptic fit, so why wouldn't he just go away? Horrible thought: she was just something to be used. O Varvara, so smooth, so silky, lying in Varvara's arms had been exquisite.

'It's going to be so lovely sleeping next to you,' he smiled, smugly gorged, drowsily digesting his satedness. 'It's odd, though,' he said with a yawn. 'I only seem to be able to sleep if I curl up like a hunting-dog.'

Fascinating, thanks for telling me. The man-dog has stopped panting and is now just hanging around, kicking his heels. A stranger in my bed, naked and clammy, a stranger who calls me darling and expects me to darling him back. And stupid with it, a stupid idiot who hasn't the first clue about anything. Now he's inspecting that big mole he's got on his stomach, plays with it, feels it. How strange that I should feel such loathing for this poor inoffensive man, quite bizarre that I should hate him because he feels his mole, strokes it. Now, having got himself all hot with all that stupid squirming, he's thrown off the covers as far as his knees, thereby shamelessly exposing his sex, his horrible sex. Oh the fear, the terror of his sex so obscenely exposed, but he's rather proud of it, oh it's ugly and vulgar and, yes, canine. O Varvara, my lost darling. Now he moves one of his legs, below the knee, because he can never get to sleep unless he jerks that leg.

Oh yes, she was quite aware of how impossible she was, that she was odious. She felt sorry for him, he made her feel sorry for him, and there were heaps of times when she quite liked him, but right now she felt she wanted to kick him because he kept jerking his right leg. Should she let him sleep in her bed? It would be her good deed. But he'd snore, and then she wouldn't sleep. O Varvara. Besides, if she let him stay all night, as had happened many times before just because she felt horribly torn between pity and loathing, then he'd wake up in the morning and make the joke he always made: 'Heavens! There's a woman in my bed!' And he'd look to see if she was amused. She forced herself to stroke his forehead.

'Listen, I'm worn out and I'll never be able to sleep unless I'm by myself.'

'Of course, darling, I'll push off, you need your beauty sleep. But it was good, though, wasn't it?' he whispered in the noble communion-of-twin-souls and shared-secret-just-between-us mode.

'Yes, very good.' (Go away, clear off, she thought.)

He got out of bed, put his pyjamas back on, and kissed her hand. Under the cover of darkness she scowled. A kiss on the hand after being brutalized like one animal by another animal! He left on tiptoe, for he was afraid that Mummy might be on the spy.

Once more in his own room, he winked at himself in the mirror and beat his chest with both hands. 'Very good' was what she had said. Very good, he sniggered. She'd said it herself.

'But that's the sort of fellow I am, old man,' he said to his reflection.

CHAPTER 23

Next morning she was up early and in the best of spirits. She hurried in to say good-morning before she had her bath, and kissed him on both cheeks. Oh yes! he thought, the physical side of things was important to women. They needed it, you see. It was ages since she'd kissed him with such warmth. Oh yes, gentle as a lamb! He'd make a note of it.

While she poked her head out of the window to fill her lungs with garden air, he expanded his chest and gave himself a metaphorical pat on the back for kissing her hand last night before leaving. Paying his respects to the lady after sexual congress was a nice touch, made him look considerate, very gentlemanly, after all she was the junior and he the senior and dominant partner. It was true, I grant you, quite true, that she hadn't shown her feelings much last night when, you know, but she'd enjoyed it in silence, he'd felt it, oh yes, she'd loved it all right. It was just that she wasn't the demonstrative sort, she was aristocratic, expressing her feelings didn't come easy to her, it's what they call womanly modesty. Besides, hadn't she said it had been very good? It was quite an endorsement, you know, that she who was ordinarily so reserved should have actually come out with that, it showed she'd really enjoyed it. Oh yes, the quiet, demure type, but she didn't turn her nose up at it. She loved it, in spite of all that butter-wouldn't-melt-in-my-mouth stuff, loved it, old man, said she thought it was very good! Right then, there'd be more where that came from! But what should he do now? Ask her if she'd slept well, say he hoped she wasn't too tired, with a knowing smile?

He was weighing the pros and cons of this when the imperative of social intercourse suddenly reasserted itself and chased away thoughts of the other sort. The international civil servant saw off Don Juan and he began to chew on his fingernails.

'I shouldn't worry about the fact that he didn't show up,' she said, rejoining him.

He tapped the end of his tongue with his forefinger.

'That's all very well, but all the same it's a worry not knowing what to make of it. I mean to say, he stood us up something chronic, for God's sake!'

'He'll apologize, you'll see.'

'Oh, I don't expect he will.'

'What's worrying you exactly?'

'What's worrying me is that it's damned awkward for a chap when there's any unpleasantness between him and his chief. I feel very uneasy about it, that's what.'

'It'll all sort itself out, you'll see.'

'You really think so?'

The way he kept tapping his tongue with his forefinger was pitiful to see. She decided to wheel out the big battalions.

'You shouldn't worry about little things like that. What's important is your own work. Your real work, nothing else matters.' (This brought an uneasy flush of embarrassment to her cheek.)

'You mean my writing?'

'Of course,' she said, feeling awkward under the grateful look he shot at her. 'In any case, your A is in the bag.'

He smiled. She was right. So the USG hadn't turned up: that didn't mean they could take his A away from him. And come to think of it, what more could the USG do for him at the moment? Nothing. He could hardly expect to be made head of section for another two years at least. And between now and then, he'd have time to form a clear picture of how the land lay.

'Look, darling, I'm going to have to love you and leave you. I know it's Saturday, but I must put in an appearance at the Palais this morning. I feel a moral obligation, you see. I mean to say it's only my second day as an A. And besides, he might send for me to explain about last night.'

Lying in his bath, he whistled to himself. Of course, she was absolutely right, for God's sake! The Secretariat was just a job, it paid the bills. But his life, his real life, was Literature, just you wait and see! When he got to the office, he'd sit down and definitely come up with a sure-fire subject for a novel. Now let's see, what would be original?

Two hours later, ensconced in the drawing-room, she knitting and he updating his file of recipes and handy hints, Madame and Monsieur Deume were on to their third post-mortem of the events of the previous evening.

'Well, let's hope he'll have the decency to send a formal note with his apologies,' concluded the dromedary. 'Not that it matters greatly, for our acquaintance extends to the van Offels and the Rampals, who are a definite cut above him. And, you know, I was never entirely convinced about him, because he is a foreigner after all, and with foreigners you never quite know where you are.'

'It's twoo. Foweigners aren't liked anywhere. They're not welcome in any countwy. Just goes to show there's no smoke without fire.'

'Besides, he's Jewish. Don't you remember Jacobson, that chemist my poor dear sister was involved with? She paid for her littel mistake. It was lucky for the family that they were able to arrange matters satisfactorily, before it showed, so that she could marry that very naice Monsieur Janson, a widower, slightly round-shouldered he was, a hunchback really, but quite *comme il faut*. Fortunately I had direction never to say a word to Didi. Poor boy, if he ever suspected the truth. Thank God, he has Leerberghe blood in his veins.'

'What happened to the chemist?'

'Struck down, carried off by meningitis just days after he'd led her astray. "As the whirlwind passeth, so is the wicked no more," Proverbs ten, verse twenty-five. So you see, you've always got to watch where you put your feet when you're dealing with Jews.'

'But the Apostles were Jews, you know. Besides . . .'

'Yes, but that was a long time ago,' Madame Deume interrupted. 'Incidentally, to your handy hints you could add an idea which dear Emmeline Ventradour passed on to me the other day. With all the other things I've got on my mind, I might forget. (Curiosity whetted,

Monsieur Deume leaned forward, pencil at the ready.) When you're using the washing-machine, before you put in anything delicate, camisoles with lace trimming or fine doilies or good linen hankies or scarves that don't like rough handling, first place them in a pillowcase to protect them from the action of the paddles. Wasn't that sweet of her? I mean to say, she didn't have to tell me about her littel trade secret. So as a way of thanking her I passed on mine about woolly combs that have gone at the knees, the kind I wear in winter.'

'What's this secwet? I don't know what you do with them,' exclaimed Monsieur Deume, ever on the lookout for new knowledge.

'Well, out of the top part which is still serviceable I make short drawers which I wear in the in-between seasons, spring and autumn. Then I unpick the areas around the knees which are worn, wind the thread into a ball, and give it to one of those poor unfortunate women who rely on my charity. But of course the legs I keep, if they're in good condition: I knit a border that goes round the top and for the bottom I make a foot with wool in a shade that more or less matches, and I end up with a pair of socks for you. You've already got three pairs like that.'

'I had no idea!' said Monsieur Deume ecstatically.

He was readying himself to jot down these new hints when Ariane came in. She was wearing a radiant smile, which intrigued Madame Deume and delighted Monsieur.

'Good-morning, Madame. Morning, Dada. I hope you slept well, Madame.'

'Oh so-so,' replied Madame Deume, not without a certain coolness of manner.

'Me too. Just so-so,' said the minor courtier, anxious to stay on the right side of the ruling establishment.

'I wasn't feeling at all well last night,' said Ariane. 'To try and get rid of my headache, I played the piano for a while and I'm afraid I must have disturbed you. Please accept my apologies.'

'There is no sin but has its pardon,' said Madame Deume impassively.

Thereupon, Ariane said she had taken advantage of the fact that she'd been up for hours to give Martha a hand in the kitchen. She'd be up and about early tomorrow too, that way she'd have time to brush all of Adrien's suits. She apologized for rushing away so soon but she wanted to bake Adrien a fruit cake using a recipe she'd just found in a religious magazine, which should therefore be excellent. She left the room wearing the same smile. Madame Deume cleared her throat, then played with her lump in silence.

An hour later this model young woman was back in the drawing-room sewing in the company of the Deumes, who were doing the household accounts, which were set out under various headings. From time to time Madame Deume glanced up sharply at her daughter-in-law.

'What do you think, Awiane, that business last night, you know Adwien's chap not coming, what was behind it?' asked Monsieur Deume, while his wife looked on stony-faced and unconcerned.

'Perhaps he was taken ill suddenly.'

'I sincerely hope he was,' said Madame Deume.

Then the talk turned to such pleasing subjects as the effects of tetrachloride on greasy stains and the efficacy of prayer on warts. Ariane agreed wholeheartedly with everything, and then asked Madame Deume for her advice. What should she do to produce a finer knit than you got with garter stitch, one which would be pleasantly slack?

'I suggest you try moss-stitch,' said Madame Deume. 'One plain, one purl, then, in the next row, one purl, one plain. You can take that as a basis for all other patterns. For instance, instead of changing the order every row, you can change every other row.'

'Thank you so much, Madame. I'm sure I'll find that such a help. It's an age since I did any knitting. If you have any other tips you could pass on, I'd be most awfully grateful.'

'Well, if you're that out of practice, I'd advise you to start by tackling something small so you don't get tired of it, something for the baby of a needy mother, bootees, for instance.'

'I was thinking of making a cardigan for Adrien,' said Ariane, with eyes demurely lowered.

'In that case, it's not moss-stitch you want! It's stocking-stitch! Still, if you're really set on moss-stitch, there's no reason why you shouldn't,

I suppose. It's worth a try. But if there's one piece of advice I have for you it is this: be sure to buy all the wool you need while you're about it. Otherwise you may find yourself in a pretty pickle because you can't get any more of exactly the same shade. There's nothing more annoying. To be on the safe side, buy a littel more than you need.'

'What good advice, Madame! I really can't thank you enough for all your help.'

'And another thing. If you are a littel rusty, practise knitting without looking at what you're doing. There's nothing better for bringing you on.'

'I'll do my best. But now it's time I was going. I've a few things I must do for Adrien. Is there anything you want while I'm out?'

'As a matter of fact there is something. You could pay the telephone bill for me. I shan't have time myself this afternoon. I'm going to Coppet to call on the Rampals, such dear people, the younger Rampals, that is.'

'Old Fwench nobility,' said Monsieur Deume. He smoothed his moustache as though he were wiping it clean, then sniffed with considerable self-importance.

'Of course, you're not up to date with events. Yesterday, that is Friday, I received a delightful phone call from the Rampals, who are in Geneva for a few days, they have to settle some business at the bank. I had a word first with Didi and then called them back this morning and invited them to dine here this evening. You do appreciate that we,have to use up all that food we got in.'

'Oh yes, Madame, absolutely, you're so right.'

'Unfortunately, I just missed the boat, as dear Corinne Rampal junior so wittily put it. She went on to say that she would have loved to give us precedence but in the meantime they'd had to say yes to lots of other invitations – such dear people, so in demand – and they were booked for lunching and dinner until Tuesday next, and Tuesday evening they leave for Paris, but that merely meant putting off the pleasure until they come again in December, when the next dividend warrants fall due. But, to make up for it, dear Corinne was sweet enough to ask me over to see them this afternoon in the splendid place they have at Coppet, seeing as how she won't be swamped by bank business after lunch because the banks will be closed by then.

For tea. Ladies only,' she smiled, revealing her long, slanting teeth, and she added one of her refined salival gurgles. 'Oh, I'm so looking forward to seeing dear Corinne again! Such an old soul, you know, and so inward, she cares for many poor persons who receive her charity, she quite spoils them, you know, she gives them shoes that have hardly been worn, and are they grateful? She's a truly good person, I love being with her, we have such deep discussions, we're so attuned inwardly, in that superb drawing-room of hers at Coppet, it's twelve metres by seven. I must say I feel a great deal closer to her than to her dear husband, with whom I have never been intimate, he's extremely courteous and pleasant of course but obviously a littel on the reserved side, I mean, he is a diplomat after all! Where was I? I've lost my thread. Oh yes, when Adrien realized we couldn't get the Rampals, he didn't stand about dithering, he took the bull by the horns, and so before he went off to the Palais this morning the dear boy just picked up the phone and rang his friends the Kanakises at their home so as he would get the both of them, because his wife was included too, to say yes. So it's all fixed. Once Didi starts something, he doesn't shilly-shally, it's all arranged, a dinner party, here, tomor-row night, Monsieur Kanakis is the nephew of a minister, you know.'

'Of the Kingdom of Gweece,' said that lover of detail Monsieur Deume, who proceeded to persuade the wings of his moustache to swell the ranks of his goatee.

'It's extremely fortunate they were able to come tomorrow at such short notice, and accept what must have seemed a rather point-blank invitation, don't you think?'

'It's worked out quite splendidly, Madame.'

'But you really should have seen how perfectly at his ease Didi was when he was speaking to Madame Kanakis, he called her "dear lady", I mean the manner, all the graces of a man of the world. And I must say it's a load off my mind, my dinner is saved, it would have grieved me if we'd had to eat up all that expensive food ourselves, especially the caviare. And we'll be able to use the printed menus too. When he'd done that, Adrien also phoned the Rassets but, aha!, most mysterious, he got no answer! He rang me just now from the Palais, because he tells his Mummy everything, he does, he rang to say he'd tried to phone the Rassets several times but kept getting no reply, I think they must be away, probably off on their travels, it's a pity, Madame Rasset is the daughter of the Vice-President of the Red Cross.'

'International Committee of the Wed Cwoss,' corrected Monsieur Deume.

'Oh, that's a real shame,' said Ariane.

'Especially since it would have been a right royal occasion, seeing as how we have rather a lot of everything. We'll just have to keep plying the Kanakises with caviare, that's all. It doesn't keep.'

'That's a good idea,' said Ariane.

'From one point of view, it's a pity, caviare is so expensive. But it's better than throwing it away, because at least we'll be giving someone pleasure, don't you agree, Ariane?'

'I do indeed, you're quite right. Isn't there anything else I can do for you, Madame?'

'Well you could get me a pound of tea, English broken-leaf, nine francs twenty-five, oh and a pound of coffee, Colombian.'

'It's got more body than Bwazilian,' said Monsieur Deume.

'Only too delighted,' said Ariane.

'Thank you very much, Ariane,' said Madame Deume, who, on an impulse, reached out and took both her wondrously transmogrified daughter-in-law's hands in hers. She gazed at her with a strongly spiritual expression on her face. 'You can also get me a pound of Palmina margarine. It's a lot cheaper than butter for cooking.'

When Ariane enquired if she was absolutely sure there wasn't anything else she could do for her, Madame Deume asked her, if it wasn't too much of a bother, to call at lost property and hand in a bunch of safety-pins which she'd found on a tram the day before yesterday, there must be a couple of dozen all told, brand new, probably been dropped by some unfortunate working-class woman, and the thought of it was preying on her mind. Ariane said it was no bother at all, because as it happened she was going to the Place du Bourg-de-Four in any case to ask about a cookery class she was thinking of putting her name down for. Madame Deume made a mental note and gave an angelic smile.

'If you're going in that direction, perhaps you'd be very kind and call on Madame Replat who is someone I met at the ladies' sewing-guild, as it happens she lives at number six, Place du Bourg-de-Four, it won't take you much out of your way, and tell her I told her a lie, I'm sorry to say, though not on purpose of course, but I feel very bad about it, and I'd rather get it off my chest, perhaps it's part of the reason why I haven't been sleeping well. I told her that Saint-Jean d'Aulph was nine hundred and forty metres above sea level. And when I went to check last night I was a hundred metres out! Saint-Jean d'Aulph is only eight hundred and forty metres above sea level! Would you mind telling her that?'

'Not at all.'

'Thank you, my dear, thank you very much. You see, I cannot live with a lie. For instance, when I write to friends I could never say "best wishes from Hippolyte" without asking him first! And if he was out I wouldn't dream of sending his regards, not even if I was writing to his oldest friends! Honesty is the best policy is what I say, in littel things as well as in big things. Thank you once again, dear,' smiled Madame Deume, and the lenses in her spectacles glinted with love.

When her daughter-in-law had gone, she looked at her husband, who looked back at her with an expression of neutrality, neither for nor against, on his face. Inwardly he was aquiver with delight, so proud was he of Ariane, the darling girl. But you never knew, and prudence was the best policy.

'What do you reckon?' she asked.

'Well, I weckon . . .'

'Let's hope it lasts. To my mind she's been thinking about religion. You'll have noticed that she got that recipe for her fruit cake out of some religious magazine, I wonder which, but anyway it's a good sign. Do you remember she asked me if she could have the small room downstairs and turn it into a sitting-room where she could put her piano and so on? I said no, because that room is a godsend to me for keeping all sorts of bits and pieces in. But no matter, she can have it. I'll tell her at lunching that it's hers. Oh, it'll be a hardship for me, a great trial, but I do believe that once it's done I shan't regret the sacrifice.'

CHAPTER 24

Feeling remiss for not yet having said his morning prayers, Uncle Saltiel hurriedly washed his hands, sang the three praises, and then, draping the ceremonial shawl over his head, intoned the prescribed verses of Psalm thirty-six. He was about to put on the phylacteries when the door suddenly burst open to reveal, skimming on his crampons, Naileater.

'Comrade and cousin,' quoth he, 'behold I am come into your august presence to speak, in confidence, plain words of good sense intended for your ears only. Here beginneth the nub. Loyal friend and companion of my vicissitudes, how long shall the present torment last?'

'What torment?' asked Saltiel calmly, and he proceeded to fold his prayer-shawl.

'Give ear to the utterance of my tongue and you shall be enlightened. I summarize: travelling from London by aerial conveyance, we made land here in Geneva as dawn's rosy fingers reached out on the thirty-first day of May, and today is Tuesday the fifth of June. Am I correct? Do you hold another view? Then the motion is carried. Therefore have we been five days in Geneva and I have yet to set eyes upon your lord and nephew! But you, with vested egotism, have met with him every day and yet you have not made me privy to the secret of your conversation, doubtless finding in this procedure some paltry pleasure which flatters your sense of superiority. All you deigned to do was to come with mysterious intent last night and wake me, thus disturbing my innocent sleep, with the aim of informing me with satanic glee that you had just spent several delightful hours in the company of the aforementioned lord, and of announcing in an aside, the brevity of which cut me to the quick, that he is to call on us this morning at ten, here in our auberge, a word of German origin. Eschewing all animosity, forgiving those who trespass against me, and strangling in my bosom the lion of indignation and the hyena of envy, I made shift to smile with blameless heart and pure, filled to the brim with the disinterested joy of at last seeing your nephew who, after all, is also linked to me by the bond of blood. With my heart ablaze with impatience, I have awaited his coming since the break of day.'

'Why since the break of day if he said ten o'clock?'

'Because I have a temperament of fire! And now it is ten thirty and I have not seen as much as this nephew's little finger! And so the days pass, dismal and unproductive! It cannot go on! I cannot go on, kicking my heels like this in my Slough of Despond! Since I have been in Geneva's fair city, what have I accomplished that is sufficiently grandiose and pungent to warrant transmission to future generations? Nothing, my friend, nothing, except for one prettily handwritten visiting-card left at the home of the unmannerly Vice-Chancellor of the University of Geneva, a man of no refinement, who did not even return a word of thanks! To put it in a nutshell, I languish, my life is trickling away in this city of interminable waiting where stupid gulls shriek their spite! For five days, my friend, I have been leading a life which has no meaning, no poetry, no noble aspiration! I direct my steps through a Slough of Despond, I peer through shop windows, I eat and I sleep! In short, I lead a purely animal existence, devoid of creativity, repercussions, adventure, bereft of unexpected advantages, stripped bare of even one illustrious action! And so, when evening falls, having nothing to do or achieve, pale-cheeked and hollow-eyed, I take myself off to my bed at a dismally early hour, at dusk, when night begins to descend, trailing its wake of widow's weeds! Now what sort of life is that, I ask you? I will say it bluntly: your nephew has neglected us, and it sets my fingertips atingle. He gave a promise, he has not kept that promise and I judge him severely! He is deficient in family feeling: that is my verdict! How do you say?'

'What impudence! And who are you to judge him? Where are your diplomas? What high office do you hold?'

'Sometime Vice-Chancellor!'

'And foot doctor! Can you not understand that he has doubtless been faced with some last-minute world-shattering issue this morning? Deficient in family feeling, my foot and my elbow! And what of the three hundred gold napoleons of inconceivable weight which he forced on me last night, to be divided equally between the five of us, as I informed you the moment I returned to our hotel? And of course you insisted on having your share, sixty napoleons, then and there, did you not, O grasping man, O devouring lion!'

'It was done in all innocence. I merely wished to slide them under my pillow and fill my ears with their sensuous tinkling as I slept.'

'Deficient in family feeling, eh? And the sixty napoleons? The coinage is current in Switzerland.'

'Current coinage and also legal tender, I agree. But what good to me are napoleons and their gladness if I lack the joy of creating, acting and being admired? What I need is a life of excitement filled with argument and schemes! I need to live a little before I die! Be reasonable, Saltiel, and try to understand my anguish. We are in Geneva, city of grand receptions, and I am invited to none of them! Tell me, is it your nephew's intention to keep me in a gilded cage and drive me to pernicious anaemia? I can stand it no longer, I am buffeted by clouds of inertia and my life of solitude is turning me into a skein of dried seaweed.'

'And what conclusion, O man of words, do you draw therefrom?'

'I conclude that we are idiots, myself excepted. And that since your nephew has not come to us, we should go to him, in his castle of the nations!'

'No. He would be most aggrieved were we to arrive unannounced. I shall have parlance with him via the electrical circuit and shall remind him that we are waiting.'

'But if he comes here, where's the pleasure?' groaned Naileater, revealing his true thoughts. 'Surrounded by ministers and ambassadors, that's how we should see him, our hearts swelling with pride, because our hearts thirst for ministers and ambassadors, that is, for important persons! They cry out for animated conversation with the aforementioned eminences! Come now, Saltiel, let us live dangerously! Let us go forth and pay him a visit in his enchanted palace of influence! Let boldness be our friend! Let us set a *fait accompli* before him! Was not my grandfather cousin to his grandfather? Moreover, dear friend, there are rich employments for the asking in this League of Nations, golden opportunities! Who knows what Fate might have in store for us if we repair thither today? Perhaps I might strike up a friendship with Lord Balfour! I have read in this city's public print that the Count of Paris, scion of the forty kings who created France in twenty centuries, is currently in residence in Geneva! He may at this very moment be at the castle of nations and I would like to meet him and earn his good opinion with a few well-chosen royalist remarks, for I am ever mindful to take all requisite precautions just in case the monarchy of France be one day restored! Believe me, Saltiel, your nephew would be delighted to see us arrive unannounced and his tongue would explode with joy, you have my word on it! Let us sally forth, Saltiel, come, feast your eyes on your nephew, observe him enthroned in his all-importance, that your chest may swell and mine too!'

He spoke on, spoke at length, and in the end poor Saltiel allowed himself to be persuaded, because he was an old, enfeebled man in the seventy-fifth year of his age and because he loved his nephew. And so he got up on trembling legs and immediately a beaming Naileater flung open the door and bawled to Solomon and Michael who had been loitering in the corridor awaiting the outcome of the negotiations.

'Time, gentlemen, to show a ceremonial leg!' he bellowed. 'Order of the day: we are to pay a call on His Excellency! Solemn accoutrements and evening dress shall be worn! Let us do honour to our beloved island and let us by our appearance dazzle all those Gentiles, like small suns! To this end, my dears, spend freely of the napoleons which our uncle has in his keeping for you from the liberal hands of Solal the Munificent! He who is not awesome in his habiliments shall not be permitted to gaze upon ministers and ambassadors! I have spoken! For my part, armed with my sixty pocket napoleons, and before the best shops shut their expensive doors, I shall hie me to town, there to procure new apparel, tasteful accessories and ditto fripperies, disbursing freely, sparing no expense, counting not, gladly paying up whatever the price, the sky being the limit! Go forth, apples of my eye, and do likewise!'

At two o'clock that same afternoon, Naileater stood hand on hip admiring himself in the small mirror in his hotel room. New frock-coat with silky lapels. Starched shirt. A spotted lavallière adding a touch of dash. Panama hat, given the heat. Sand-shoes, for he had tender toes. Tennis-racket and golf club in the manner of English diplomats. Gardenia in his buttonhole. Intellectual pince-nez solemnized by a black ribbon on which his long teeth chewed with gay abandon. And to complete the outfit, the crowning surprise, kept in reserve in the pocket of his coat to be produced at the right moment, which was immediately before he was presented to Lord Solal. Yes, prudence required that good Saltiel, who was inclined to be pernickety, be confronted by a *fait accompli*.

Enter, moments later, Mattathias and Michael. The latter had opted to retain his uniform of synagogue usher: waistcoat gilded with small buttons and braid, fluted Greek kilt, Turkish slippers with turned-up toes and red pompoms, and tucked into the wide belt the damascened butts of a pair of antic pistols. Naileater nodded approvingly. Excellent, Michael would pass muster as his aide-de-camp! On the other hand, Mattathias had done no more than remove the piping from his undertaker's suit (which he had acquired in Cephalonia from one of his debtors who had been the beneficiary of the will of a relative who had worked for an undertaker) and had furthermore stuck on his head a Havana hat which he had found on the London–Geneva flight. Rather lacklustre was Mattathias, thought Naileater, but it was no bad thing, the contrast would make him to shine the more brightly. The two cousins were amazed by the jet-black glint of his forked beard, so he explained that not having been able to put his hand on his brilliantine, he had instead used a spot of boot polish, which was every bit as good.

Meanwhile, Solomon put in an appearance, blushing in the outfit which he had just bought from a shop called 'The Prodigal Son'. Not having found anything small enough for his size, he had decided on the first-communion suit which an assistant, who was either very astute or a wag, had warmly advised. He was particularly proud of the white armband with the silk fringe of whose religious significance, like the other three Valiants, he was sublimely ignorant. He also took inordinate pride from the little Eton jacket, which had no tails and stopped short at his waist, and which Naileater immediately dubbed a 'bum-freezer'.

Finally Saltiel appeared, and Naileater was delighted to observe that he had kept to his nut-brown frock-coat. Perfect. He would shine brightest, he would appear superior, Western: everyone would assume that he was the leader of the delegation. Saltiel inspected the cousins with a Napoleonic eye in which Michael alone found favour.

'Solomon, take off that armband, it's meaningless. Mattathias, don't wear a hat at all if that's the best you can do. And you, Naileater, why the fancy dress? The frock-coat is fine, you can keep that. But get rid of the rest of the abominations. Otherwise I shall take steps and you won't be allowed in.'

His tone was such that Naileater had no choice but to obey. The tennis-racket, the golf club, the Panama and the sand-shoes were exchanged, respectively, for a morocco briefcase, a walking-stick with a gold handle, a grey topper and patent-leather pumps, and these accessories he was obliged to rush out and purchase without further ado, Saltiel being adamant. But in the matter of the lavallière, the gardenia and the pince-nez, Naileater stood firm, spoke bitterly of despotism, and complained that the intention was to impugn his honour. For the sake of peace, Saltiel gave in.

'Full steam ahead for the palace of delights and seat of greatness!' cried Naileater.

The cab drew up outside the front door of the Palais des Nations. Naileater got out first. Casually tossing a gold louis to the driver and showing the way to the rest of the Valiants, he strode into the entrance hall, empty now in early afternoon, and headed immediately for the lavatory. To the stupefaction of his cousins, he emerged moments later with the sash (First Class) of the Legion of Honour slung diagonally across his chest. To silence possible protests, he immediately set about neutralizing Saltiel.

'Behold! A *fait accompli*! No good losing your temper, it's too late now! You can't make a scene here, so you can't spoil my royal little game! Anyhow, my decoration is not only thoroughly deserved but is actually authentic, for it was bought in Paris, and a pretty penny it cost too, from a specialist outfitter's whither I secretly repaired before we left for Marseilles. So hold your peace, gentlemen, and put your best foot forward. Let he who is with me follow where I lead! Fall in behind the sash, red, First Class!'

On the first floor, Saulnier shot to his feet, dazzled by the sheer calibre of the sash, though he was well used to the strange fauna of exotic delegations. A head of state, President of some small South American republic, he thought, slightly taken aback however by the blue lavallière with white dots and the peculiar garb worn by members of the retinue. But the sash and the fear that he might put his foot in it outweighed all other considerations. So he forced a chilly smile and waited.

'A delegation,' said Naileater, twirling his gold-handled cane. 'Come to parley with the honourable Solal!'

'Your Excellency has an appointment? I take it you are expected, Mr President? (In reply, the Sash (First Class) merely gave a disdainful smile and twirled his cane in the opposite direction.) Who shall I say is calling, Your Excellency?'

'I am here incognito,' replied Naileater. 'Negotiations. Political secrets. It will be enough, O liveried underling, to give him the password, which is Cephalonia. Now go, make haste!' he barked, and the porter scurried off.

On his return, Saulnier, breathing heavily, informed His Excellency the President that the Under-Secretary-General, currently in a meeting with Monsieur Léon Blum, had requested His Excellency and the other gentlemen to be good enough to wait a few moments. He led the strange band into the small antechamber reserved for the use of distinguished visitors.

'But hear this, my good man. I shall wait no longer than five minutes,' said Naileater. 'It is a rule which I have always observed in my official life. Convey this intelligence to whomsoever it may concern.'

The moment the door closed, Saltiel raised the forefinger of authority and commanded the impostor to remove instanter the sash to which he had no right. 'At once, knave!' Naileater gave a leering, sneering smile but did as he was told, for he sensed that the all-powerful nephew might not take too kindly to the sash (First Class), which, in any case, had already served its purpose. Besides, best not risk making difficulties with Léon Blum, whom he might be meeting shortly: as Prime Minister it was more than likely that he knew personally everyone who had been so honoured by France. He took off the sash, kissed it reverently, put it away in his pocket, and, with a wink at Saltiel, sat down.

'And now, gentlemen,' said Saltiel, 'let silence and good manners be your watchwords, for on the other side of that quilted door two great minds are even now discussing the happiness of mankind. So I do not want to hear a mouse stir or a pin drop!'

Awed by the splendour of the room, the Valiant fell silent. Solomon crossed his arms to show his good breeding. Michael cleaned his fingernails with the point of one of his daggers and did not protest when, feeling in need of a smoke, he had his cigarette snatched from his lips by a grimly silent Saltiel. Mattathias inspected the furniture, felt the wool in the carpet, and did sums in his head.

In the silence, Saltiel smiled. Perhaps Sol would introduce him to Monsieur Blum. If he did, and if the atmosphere were conducive, he would respectfully point out that workers in France really seemed to be going in for far too many strikes. He might even advise Monsieur Blum not to stay on too long as leader of the Cabinet, to avoid attracting jealousy and envy. Jews in politics should stay out of the limelight, it was safer. Minister, yes, but Prime Minister was too much. They'd have their turn later when, God willing, Israel was reborn. Be that as it may, he was soon to see Sol in his magnificent office, and, who knows, perhaps Sol might even bark a few orders down the telephone in full sight of the admiring cousins. He glanced up at them with a delicate, affectionate smile as he sat anticipating the imminent joy of being ushered into the presence. And, who knows, perhaps Sol would kiss his hand while the others watched in wonder. And so he mused on, while Solomon worked out a greeting in verse to recite when the moment came, and Naileater, less assured now that he was sashless, gave a series of nervous yawns which all ended in a squeak.

The door opened and the Valiant got to their feet. Solomon forgot his greeting in verse and the hand of Saltiel was indeed kissed. Whereupon the tiny old man took out a squared handkerchief and blew his nose in it, feeling weak at the knees. Sol gestured them to sit, and the Cephalonians sat down, Solomon feeling quite overcome by the softness of his armchair, which almost swallowed him whole.

'Good discussion was it, Sol, with the Prime Minister?' enquired Saltiel after a brief clearing of the throat.

'We talked of state secrets which I am not at liberty to divulge,' said Solal, who knew exactly which answer would go down best.

'Quite right, O High Excellency,' said Naileater, eager to contribute his pennyworth and be seen in a good light. 'If I may say so with all due deference, quite right.'

'And tell me, Sol, you and the Prime Minister parted on good terms?'

'We embraced.'

His uncle feigned deafness to make him say it again, so as to be quite sure that all present had heard. He coughed and observed the effect on the four shining faces of the Valiant.

'So you and the Prime Minister embraced, did you? Very good. Very good indeed,' he said loudly for the benefit of Mattathias, who was sometimes a little hard of hearing. 'And tell me, my boy: the Vatican City. It seems to me to be very small, quite insignificant, and I am grieved for His Excellency the Pope, who looks a kindly sort of man. Couldn't the League of Nations see its way to making his patch just a tiny bit bigger? I mean to say, he is a sovereign prince after all. I raise the matter so that you might give it a little thought as and when. You see, I feel a great warmth for His Holiness. Anyhow, if you were able to do something, it would be a good deed well done. Well now, son, so you, as I learned yesterday, have been made a Commander by Léopold II, Leopold the Opulent, he of the Congo. I forgot to mention it, gentlemen,' he said, turning to the silent cousins. 'Which means you are twice a Commander, once for the French and once for the Belgians. I have always had a great respect for Belgium, a country distinguished by great common sense. By the by, my boy,' he added, affecting an air of innocence, 'has the President of the Republic by any chance recently offered you something in the

Legion of Honour higher than Commander? No? How very odd. But there, I never did much like his face.'

When Solal wondered if they might wish to partake of some refreshment, Saltiel suggested a small black coffee, if it was not too much trouble. Solomon was bold enough to say that he liked strawberry cordial, then, red with shame, dabbed at his forehead with a handkerchief. Michael stated his preference, which was for the yolks of two eggs beaten up in cognac. First parking his gum on the arm of his chair, Mattathias said he was not thirsty but would accept the equivalent in cash and buy himself a drink in town later.

'And for my part, Highness,' said Naileater, 'I require, with all due deference, very little. A couple of slices of cooked ham, which is the pure and Jewish part of the pig. With a blot of mustard and soft rolls, if it can be managed.'

'Pay no attention to these unschooled morons!' cried Saltiel, who could contain himself no longer. 'O cursèd crew! O men of little breeding! From what manner of mannerless mothers did you spring? Where do you think you are? In a station buffet or some tavern? Sol, if you can find it in your heart to forgive them, a small coffee for each and nothing else! (With arms crossed and feeling perfectly at home, he glared at each of the uncouth cousins in turn.) Strawberry cordial, indeed! Egg yolks! Equivalent in cash! As for this other unspeakable oaf! Wanting ham, like some Freemason!'

'O tiger-hearted uncle,' muttered Naileater. 'A harmless, inconsequential *petit déjeuner* and he takes it out of my mouth!'

A few moments later, Miss Wilson – to whom Solal had seen fit to introduce the Valiant, with all due ceremony and a detailed explanation of how exactly they were all related – set down five cups of coffee in front of these shocking visitors and went out without saying a word, more bottomlessly strait-laced than ever, so bottomless and so straight in fact that Naileater went so far as to ask, in the case of so obvious a virgin, which was the front of her and which the back. At this, Saltiel withered him with a look. This was the very last time that he'd bring this hell-hound to respectable places! The hell-hound, encouraged by the way Solal smiled, crossed his legs to show a quick flash of patent-leather pump, sniffed at his gardenia, stroked his beard, which left his fingers black, and began to speak.

'My dear Excellency,' he asked with a crafty, insinuating air, 'do you by any chance have an opening here for a superlatively able principal private secretary?'

'I grant,' said Solal, 'that you'd make the smartest PPS I ever had.'

'It's a deal, Excellency!' interrupted Naileater, and he sprang to his feet. 'I accept the post! The thing being agreed in principle, the contract, though verbal, is taken as read and shall be binding on both parties. I thank you from the depth of my bowels! You can let me have your firman at your leisure, for I have every confidence in your good faith and know that your word is your bond! Until we meet again, then, Excellency,' he said as he made for the door. 'You may rest assured that I shall prove worthy of your trust!'

'And where do you think you are going, you miserable oaf?' cried Saltiel, barring his way.

'To announce my appointment to the press,' said Naileater, 'to meet my staff, initiate an overview or two, exchange views, give orders, offer assurances of my support, and levy one or two taxes!'

'I forbid you to leave this room! Sol, you must stop this man blackening your good name! Explain to him that he hasn't been appointed to anything! Principal private secretary, indeed! Can't you see that he'll create havoc? Sit down, son of Satan! Sol, this man brings perdition in his wake! Promise that you won't appoint him!'

'I can't promise that because I've already appointed him,' said Solal, to leave Naileater one crumb of comfort. 'But since you so wish it, Uncle, I hereby countermand it.'

Under his breath, Naileater wished a plague of boils on Saltiel, but drew immediate comfort from the thought of the visiting-cards he would order at once which would feature the mention: Sometime Principal Private Secretary at the League of Nations! So he crossed his arms and eyed Saltiel beadily. Meanwhile Solal was writing, for he had hit upon a way of brightening Saltiel's declining years.

'Uncle, what would you say if I asked you to undertake an official visit on behalf of the League of Nations?'

Saltiel turned pale. But he managed to maintain his composure and answered that he was at the entire disposal of an organization which had long stood high in his esteem and that if his meagre talents and so forth. He was very pleased with his answer. After a careless glance in

Naileater's direction, the untroubled glance of a man well accustomed to success, a man of infinite unflappability, he asked with beating heart exactly what the visit entailed. It was explained to him that the rabbi of Lausanne had recently informed the Secretariat that he was organizing a series of lectures on the League of Nations. As it happened, the first was being delivered this very afternoon, at four thirty. It would be a friendly gesture if the League of Nations were to send a special representative who, empowered to act on its behalf and duly accredited by the present letter, would honour the lecture by his presence and convey the warmest wishes of the Secretary-General. Would Uncle Saltiel agree to go to Lausanne?

'I am ready, my boy,' said Saltiel, rising to his feet. 'Lausanne is close by Geneva. I shall leave at once and take the train. Give me the letter of accreditation. Thank you. Farewell, my son, I must away to the station with all convenient speed.'

'Wait,' said Solal. He picked up the telephone, gave an order in English, replaced the receiver, and smiled at the tiny old man. 'Uncle, you will be driven to Lausanne in an official car, which will bring you back to Geneva once your mission has been completed. The car is waiting. The porter will show you the way.'

Again Saltiel turned to Naileater, and gave him a cool victorious stare. Holding his letter patent in his hand, he offered to take the cousins with him, as advisers, though it was to be clearly understood that he alone, as the authorized representative, was empowered to speak to the rabbi. All the Valiant agreed to this, with the exception of Naileater, who, folding his arms across his chest once more, informed Saltiel that he was not accustomed to serving in a subordinate capacity and that furthermore the idea of an official visit to a mere rabbi, who in all likelihood was a total ignoramus, was to his sense a complete and utter waste of time.

From his window, Solal watched the departure of his uncle, for whom a liveried chauffeur, holding his cap in his hand, opened the door of the Rolls. The League's accredited agent stepped briskly into it, head bowed in the manner of cabinet ministers who have much on their minds, and was followed by Mattathias and Michael, who sat opposite him, while Solomon sat in the seat next to the driver. When the car had driven off, Solal smiled at his good deed. The official visit was a minor affair which could not possibly go wrong, and even if Uncle blotted his copybook the rabbi would understand. Among Jews, accommodations were always possible.

'Highness,' said Naileater gesturing towards the leather chesterfield, 'let us sit on yonder couch of privy counsel and talk together in confidence now that there are none here present save men of the world. Highness, I have a question which, if I may speak frankly, I should like to put to you. Could you not see your way to conferring some minor title upon my person so that I might retain my rank? For example: you are assistant governor of the world, so couldn't you make me a law lord complete with wig and a black cap for wearing on the head when sentencing guilty persons to death? No? Not to worry, Highness. And how many Under-Secretaries-General are there?'

'Three.'

'Couldn't you make your English master see his way to having four, four being a lucky number, and, if he's the sort of man who understands these things, you may intimate with crafty insinuendo that I'd be prepared to share the salary with him? If you did, say we'd go halves: tell him a fifty-fifty split so that he gets the message. No? Not to worry, Highness. Adversity has never got the better of me. How about this: since I am a sometime principal private secretary, could I not at least be paid a modest pension which I could draw regularly during my lifetime and which would thereafter pass to my three little orphan children? No? Pity. Then may I suggest another little scheme. The League of Nations has the power to grant diplomatic immunity which prevents any prying by customs officials, is that not so? Well, I am prepared to organize a simple, innocent little smuggling operation, which I could manage nicely in my capacity as a diplomatic courier. What do you say, Highness?' he asked, and he tapped his nose with his forefinger. 'No? I understand your scruples, which do you honour. Let us now drop a subject which I never raised.' (This nephew of Saltiel's, he thought, has a hide like a rhinoceros.)

Solal rang again, for he felt an impulse to torment Miss Wilson by inflicting the further presence of his impossible relative on her. When she materialized before him, he had of course to find something for her to do. So he asked her to send him a stenographer, while Naileater, eyes glued to the ceiling, racked his brains for even riper schemes. A Russian princess appeared almost immediately, man-killing and sinuous, equipped with an eye-catching rump and a small shorthand typewriter. Garnished with long lashes, she sat and waited, her eyes fluttering and her breasts thrust forward, always a good idea.

'Ready?'

'I'm always ready,' she smiled.

'A letter, addressed to Madame Adrien Deume at Cologny.'

While she took his dictation, the finger-tapping princess smiled without taking her eyes off him, in part to demonstrate her mastery of the shorthand typewriter, but also because she was keen to climb the ladder of promotion, to intimate that she was his to command for all manner of non-stenographic tasks. Meantime, Naileater gave his impersonation of the soul of discretion who makes a point of not listening. To this end, he remained standing, eyes fixed on the ceiling, his grey top-hat in his hand, the perfection of stillness: dignified, understanding, solemn and honourable. But of course, he did not miss a word of the letter.

When he had finished, Solal asked the princess to give the letter when typed to Saulnier, who would bring it to him for signing. Furious at being deprived of the opportunity of bringing it herself and of wiggling her hips at him some more, she gave a gracious smile and proceeded to wiggle towards the door. As she went, she was plotting (a) to invite the Deumes, with whom the Under-Secretary-General was on such good terms, to her very next cocktail party, and (b) to go out of her way to be pleasant in future to young Deume whenever she was called to his office to take dictation.

'Highness,' resumed Naileater, fanning himself with his topper, 'is there not at least some privilege, conferred by your munificent bounty, which I who held you in my fond arms when you were an infant might yet enjoy, a diplomatic passport, say, or a special pass? Or might I not in turn be allowed the advantage of a mission, which I should carry out with the dignity of the elephant, with the reliability backed by manufacturer's guarantee of a faithful dog, and with the quickness of the hunted deer or, alternatively, the promptness of the eel, which, though forbidden by our religion, is excellent when suitably smoked? For instance, dear nephew of my good friend Saltiel, I am prepared to volunteer personally to deliver the letter which you have just dictated and of whose import I am ignorant, having forced myself not to listen, into the hands of my lady Deume! As it pleases your Highness! Do let me have a little mission too! For pity's sake, dear brother in religion, else human solidarity will be no more than a vain and empty word! High Excellency, an unforeseen, intestinal imperative forces me to take a hurried leave. I shall return forthwith. Meanwhile I remain respectfully yours in guile,' he grinned and with a gracious bow he went, tenderly holding his abdomen with both hands.

Minutes later, furnished with several new arguments, he was back. He found Solal poring over the letter which Saulnier had just brought in. He stood and waited discreetly, suddenly saddened by the thought that the King of England would soon cease to be Emperor of India. A terrible shame! Such a splendid title! This Gandhi was an impertinent upstart! But there, what could you expect of a man who hardly ever ate? Solal signed his name and looked up.

'Intestinal insurrection quelled, Highness. Actually it was a false alarm. You can't always tell with bowels. And, while I'm on the subject, may I take this opportunity to congratulate the League of Nations on its lavatories! Sumptuous, palatial, places of true enchantment! If we had their like on Cephalonia I would happily spend the rest of my life there! With that said, I now launch into my moving peroration, which shall be brief! Highness, please understand that when I return to Cephalonia and people ask me what I accomplished in Geneva I shall die of shame! For what in truth will I tell them? There will be nothing to say, Highness! Nothing!' he repeated, and he held his head in both hands. 'The day before yesterday, weary of my enforced idleness, I journeyed to Berne, a small capital full of vast women who wear black and consume large cakes. Was I not there subjected to the humiliation of being turned away by an imbecile in the pay of the government to whom I had intimated my not unflattering desire to take out Swiss nationality, while not of course ceasing to be French, even unto offering to pay the appropriate fee according to his convenience and requirements! "Now look here, what wrong have I done? And why so censorious?" I shouted at him, ablaze with indignation. "Come now, state your price!" But he was immovable! O exalted Highness, grant that I too might have my own official visit! I ask it for three reasons. Firstly, that I may be avenged on this government clerkling and make his ears to glow when I inform him of my appointment and say unto him: "Now you see who you missed having as a fellow citizen!" Secondly, that I do not lose face with Saltiel! Thirdly, that the mission you entrust to my keeping shall be as honey on my tongue as I speak of it to the assembled population of the green-girt isle where you were born! It was five o'clock in the morning. Dawn was already glazing the distant sky with pink, and the horizon was thronged with freshly minted effulgencies! I was there, anxiously seated on the steps of the palace of the venerable Chief Rabbi who sired you, yes I was there, like a faithful dog, fists pressed to my temples, awaiting in anguished anticipation the announcement of a happy deliverance! And how can I describe what I felt when at last I learned of your dear entry into this world, how should I count the tears of joy I shed at that moment? Have I not softened your heart, Highness? Then listen further to what I say! Kings are fortunate indeed, Excellency, for they are always held in the spotlight at the centre of the world's stage while I remain constantly in the shadows! My heart bleeds when I read of sumptuous receptions, the King greeted with the national anthem, the crowd applauding and moronic soldiers presenting arms! And when he is received by the Pope, what pomp! Swiss guards, princes arrayed in black, smiling cardinals in a row, and such courtesies shown by the Pope to the King! No one dances attendance on me! Not for me the love of the crowd, soldiers bearing arms, or kindly popes! But I would dearly love to have arms presented in my honour! I would take the salute graciously and then retire for a friendly but suitably respectful word with the Pope. Tell me, whatever did this King do to earn all the honours he enjoys in life? Answer: he got himself born! Was I not born too, and born richer far than he, with a greater capacity for joy and despair, more noble of heart, more splendid of brain? And afterwards, mark the sumptuous dinner given by the Pope to honour the King: a thousand candles and endless smoked salmon! But for me, poor Eater of Nails that I am, I have cockroaches in my cellar and, to appease my hunger, a plain dish of boiled potatoes consumed while I shed bitter tears over the menu for their dinner! And when their browsing and sluicing are done and the King is brimful of smoked salmon, the thick part is best because it isn't as salty, the Pope gives him a paternal pat on the cheek, asks him if he wouldn't like just a little more smoked salmon or another helping of squashy chocolate cream cake, and then presents him with the grand cross of some order or other, as if the lucky devil – born of a seed just like me – didn't have a chestful of decorations already! And then there are magnificent toys for the King's children, though they aren't anything like as clever as my own three treasures who get nothing given to them by the Pope, not even a salted pistachio! And then the Pope escorts the King to the door with ceremonious attentions and kissings of cheeks! If I went to see the Pope, would he show me out personally and kiss my cheek? Yet am I not a man born of woman, like the King? Mark these tears, mighty Effendi, mark them well while they are wet, before they evaporate, before they dry on cheeks aflame with the consumption which spares not its prey! The conclusion of my homily, lovely Lord, is therefore to beg you to charge me with a League of Nations mission which will drag me from the shadows and put an end to the injustice which has dogged my life, for being a great man is less important than appearing to be one, and incidentally it would enable me to silence Saltiel when he returns from Lausanne, he'll go around screaming like a seagull to the four winds that he's been made a head of mission, nay even a chargé d'affaires, for that is something which in all reason I cannot be expected to tolerate! Ah, but you smile, Highness! I feel that you are swayed! Oh, blessings be upon you!'

And he was indeed smiling at Naileater, who was of his family, of his people, and he loved him, claimed him as his own, gloried in him as proudly as in the greatest and noblest of his race, men with a mission, sublime and as numberless as the sands on the shore of the sea of centuries. He loved everything in his people, willed himself to love everything about them, their failings and their splendour, the pitiful among them and the princes. For such is love. Perhaps he alone in all the world loved his people with the love that is true, the love that sees through eyes of sadness, eyes that know. Yes, he would display this sorry specimen to the daughter of the Gentiles so that she would learn whence he, Solal, came. He held out the letter to Naileater, who promptly took it. Now in a position of strength, with the letter safely tucked away in the pocket of his frock-coat, the sponge sat down, crossed his legs financially, and spoke in a quite altered, extremely businesslike voice.

'And now, if you will, we must settle the material details, gentle, genial Excellency. I refer to the little matter of expenses, so that I may do you honour, to wit: car allowance, opera hat better suited to the occasion, silk socks, sum set aside for a haircut.'

'But you no longer have any hair worth cutting, Naileater.'

'Oh yes I have, Excellency, I've still a few hairs left, very fine and quite visible close to! So let's see, scalp massage at the barber's, shampoo of beard, manicure, costly unguents designed to send forth diplomatic waftures, large selection of ties so that I may lay them out on my bed and choose the best, assorted vestimentary refinements, in short improvements which dandify! I am in your hands, Excellency, for I shall incur many expenses.'

'O Bey of Liars, O Prince of Impostors! You know very well that you will incur no expenses whatsoever,' said Solal.

'Great Lord,' began Naileater after a fit of self-induced coughing intended to give him time to come up with a reply, 'your perspicacity has stopped my cough dead in its gristly tracks and, struck dumb with shame, I humbly confess! You are right: I shall incur no expenses whatsoever! Therefore I thank you for the unexpected conferment of titles which, though unlovely, yet contain a promise of a happy outcome, and I await penitently the granting not of innocently mendacious expenses but of a handsome gift from the generous hand of affection which opens hearts and repays kin in kind!' He smiled and was irresistible, entrancing and suddenly utterly feminine. With three fingers, he blew a kiss to the great lord. 'Thank you, and may blessings drop upon you,' he said, reaching for the banknote. 'Is the young woman beautiful?' he asked with a fond, paternal smile, wanting to end on a note of intimacy.

'How do you know she's young?'

'Put it down, Great One, to my long acquaintance with the human heart, and a quivering sensibility. Well, Excellency, is she beautiful?'

'Incredibly. The letter will allow me to see her one last time. After that, never more.'

'May I say, Highness, that I don't believe a word of it?' replied Naileater knowingly. He bowed then left the room, fanning himself with the banknote.

Outside, holding the precious letter in his hand, he pondered ways of saving himself the taxi fare to Cologny. One good idea might be to flag down the first car that came along, explain that he'd forgotten his wallet, and say that he was on a mercy mission to a brother-in-law, as dear to him as his own brother, who was being operated on at that very moment, for removal of a kidney, in a clinic at Cologny! Perhaps not: all things considered, he wouldn't save himself much that way. Besides, he didn't have to worry about saving anything. His Excellency had given him a thousand-franc note and he still had several gold louis left. So, take one of those taxis yonder and drive straight to Cologny! But first stop by the hotel to pick up the tennis-racket and golf club, which would make a good impression on the young woman. And change hats, wear the black topper, which was more finely attuned to official protocol. Perfect! He began walking, whistling to himself as he went, grey top-hat set at a jaunty angle and cane twirling, master of his fate and captain of the universe: a head of mission.

On the corner of a street, sitting on a collapsible chair with his back to a garage wall, a blind man was playing palsied music on an accordion to which no one was listening. Naileater paused, searched his pockets, tossed a gold louis in the bowl which the beggar's poodle was holding in its jaws, walked on, stopped again, consulted his instinct, did an about turn, added the banknote, and stroked the dog. Then, in plenipotentiary haste, he set off at a run, lavallière flying in the breeze, towards the taxi rank. But why on earth were all these fools staring at him in that curious way? Hadn't they ever seen a frock-coat?

CHAPTER 25

On opening his front door, Monsieur Deume recoiled at the sight of the astounding apparition, a tall figure in formal dress, his chest bisected diagonally by the grand sash normally worn only by Presidents of the French Republic, who handed him his top-hat.

'Cloakroom,' said Naileater. 'My topper must be deposited in the cloakroom, in accordance with what the English call the diplomatic drill via the usual channels,' he explained to the inwardly panicking little man with the goatee whom he read, at first glance, as one of nature's innocents. 'And take care now, don't damage it, it's brand-new. How are you? I myself am exceedingly well. In my person, my good man,' he went on at an amazing rate of knots while continuing to twirl his golf club, 'you see before you the principal privy secretary of my august master His Excellency Solal of the Solals, and in the social vortex that is London I am yclept Sir Pinhas Hamlet, ABC, GHQ, QED, DDT, such an agreeable habit the English have of putting letters after one's name, it gives one a certain importance, but I also hold the office of Grand Marshal of the King's Household, thereby attracting cabals and jealousies beyond number, and furthermore I rank joint first among peers of the realm, yes, my good man, I, whom you see standing before you, and moreover I am sole and legal owner of half of Shropshripshire wherein, bounded by a river the name of which slips my memory for the moment, is situate my splendid private and personal estate which goes by the name of Gentleham Hall, Gent's for short, famed for its stupendous castle proudly bristling with forty bell-towers, revered seat of my forefathers, where, settled of a morning in a Louis XIV armchair beneath a picture painted by an old master, I indulge myself unstintingly with repeated helpings of bacon and eggs, after which, full to my brimmy-brim-brim, I always put in an hour riding around Gent's on a dapple-grey charger, oh Shropshripshire of my oligarchical youth! noble Shropshripshire where I attended to my studies dressed in a fetching Eton jacket, white collar and top-hat, the habit of which, as you will observe, I have kept to this day, but come, my good man, cast not your eyes down in this shamefaced manner, be not froward with me, and furthermore I have received the Order of the Garter, I'm wearing it now under my trousers, my favourite club is the Crosse and Blackwell's Marmalade, I drop in for little chats with the Archbishop of Canterbury, Cantab to his chums, and a dozen lords of the realm who are my equals, my peers and my friends, my regular address is number ten, Downing Street, and I may also be reached next door at number eleven, the home of the Chancellor of the Exchessor, my good friend Lord Robert Cecil, whom I call Bob and invariably address in English as I do my gracious sovereign the Queen, whom I accompany in my grey topper to the fashionable racecourses which we both love, Royal Ascot, the Derby at Epsom, Epsom Downs, ups and downs, that is the question, Bank of England and House of Lords in tomato sauce, fish and chips in Buckingham Palace, yours sincerely, God save the King, don't you agree?'

'I . . . er . . . don't quite follow,' said Monsieur Deume with a bemused smile which pleased the Gentleman of Gent's and earned him a pat on the back.

'Do not take it to heart, young man, it's a little foible we English aristocrats have of suddenly breaking into a tongue which, though made glorious by Shakespeare, remains unintelligible to persons of small schooling. Rest assured that I think none the worse of you and let us come to the point forthwith. I have here a letter, which I extract from the recesses of my frock-coat, sent by my lord and master, he who is a prince in his own palace, he whose lordly vassal I am. You may examine the official envelope, which is blazoned with its place of origin and source most high, to wit, the three words League of Nations embossed thereon regardless of expense! You may look, but you must not touch! As you see, it is addressed to the lady wife of Adrien Deume Esquire. Now that proofs of my veracity have been furnished, hie thee to this lady and inform her that I shall wait here for her to present herself in person so that I may proceed to deliver the said missive into her hands according to due protocol and also indulge in a little light banter in the best possible taste. (Delighted with his performance, he fanned himself with his tennis-racket.) Stay not but go in search of her without further humming and hawing!'

'I'm most awfully sowwy, but she's out shopping.'

'Very well, I shall decide upon what course of action to take when I have seen the lie of the land. To begin with we must become acquainted. Who are you? The butler in mufti?'

'I am Monsieur Deume. The father-in-law,' came the fearful reply. A gulp followed hard on its heels.

'Ah! A member of the family? What medals have you got?'

'I'm sowwy to say I haven't got any,' said the old man, moistening his lips and essaying a sheepish smile.

'I can see why you are sorry,' said the Garter. 'Nevertheless, I shall trust you, and into your keeping shall I give the letter for the lovely lady designated by name thereon. When she returns, give it to her and mind you don't dirty it or dare to open it in her absence by means which are contrary to post-office regulations and public order. Have you got that?'

'Yes.'

Naileater ran his eye over the unimposing figure who stood before him motionless and deferential, holding the letter with his fingertips for fear of crumpling it. What should he do now? Borrow ten francs for his taxi fare back and explain that persons of rank never carried money since doing so might be construed as vulgar? No, he was far too nice an old party for that. Suddenly an idea stirred in the deep waters of his brain. To entice it forth, he gave his furrowed pate a thoroughgoing rub and, behold!, it arose therefrom, freshly watered and bathed in beauty.

'The conveyance of the letter merely constitutes part one of my mission,' he said. 'There is more – and better – to come. Since in the event he was unable to be among you himself to break bread last evening for reasons of state, as he casually informed me in a moment of friendly badinage, as well he might, with the member of his inner circle that I am, my sovereign lord has mandated me to the same end, to wit, the breaking of bread in accordance with the practice of good company, please consult the manuals of protocol at the chapter entitled: "Concerning the Envoy Plenipotentiary: On Sipping and Supping". To abridge, His Excellency has entrusted to me, the above-mentioned, as his representative, a browsing mission and a sluicing mandate, which means in plain language more readily intelligible to the *hoi polloi* that I am here to ingest the odd morsel or two in his stead so that I may render him an account of same and report back. This is the correct form in official circles and among well-informed sources. My master had it in mind to dispatch me hither to partake of luncheon among you, which would have been more suitable, but we were delayed at the eleventh hour by a pressing summons to cheer up the poor old Emperor of Ethiopia who was crying his eyes out. But rest assured: I shall refresh the inner man in symbolic manner only. So, Father-in-Law, if you are not conversant with tea parties of the third party or if you feel constrained by avarice, I can very easily go away empty and unreplete. It was a gracious gesture by my master designed to favour you with an honour. What do you say?'

'I am most honoured, Mr Pwincipal Pwivate Secwetawy,' said old Monsieur Deume, who had by now regained something of his composure.

'Just call me my Lord.'

'Very honoured, my Lord, and thank you so much, but alas I am alone in the house, for both ladies are out and what's more we've been maidless since yesterday, she had to go home, feeling unwell, which obviously means I'm afwaid that in the matter of tea I'm going to have to ask you to wait a while.'

'A lacklustre start to the proceedings,' said Naileater, and he stuck his little finger in one ear and waggled it vigorously. 'My dear fellow, I see that the fashionable at-home is not exactly second nature to you. But no matter. I am a tolerant man. I shall direct your untutored steps and together we shall repair to the kitchen and see what's in the offing. Excellency I might be, yet for all that I care not a fig for protocol and shall help you to the utmost of my ability, since aristocrats are always able to make common cause with common

251

folk. So cast out these black thoughts and, dispensing with ceremony, let us draw up a menu fit for teatime. But bring me my top-hat. There is a chill lurking in this gloomy hallway.'

Wearing his top-hat, he stepped into the kitchen, followed by Monsieur Deume, whom he instructed to sit while he studied the possibilities. Removing his frock-coat for greater freedom of movement but with the great sash (First Class) of the Legion of Honour still athwart his chest, he made for the fridge and attempted to open it. Monsieur Deume hurriedly explained, not without embarrassment, that his wife had had it fitted with a lock to which she alone held the key. He was really, truly sorry about this. Reading between the lines, Naileater consoled him with a pat on the cheek and said that they'd manage nevertheless.

'Worry not, my dear fellow. I shall now proceed to search the premises and shall achieve my ends. I have had a great deal of practice at this sort of thing.'

The disconcerted little seal watched the toings and froings of the whistling Garter as he set about a methodical search, opening drawers, peering into cupboards, and announcing his discoveries one after the other. Three tins of sardines! One of tuna-fish! Pretty unexciting fare for an hors-d'œuvre, but no matter! A loaf of bread, not started! Coconut biscuits! A pot of jam! A tin of Milanese tripe! Another of cassoulet!

What a rum do, thought Monsieur Deume. Clearly, all wealthy English aristocrats were eccentrics to a man, he'd always heard as much. This chap was eccentric all right, but he was also important, that much was written all over him, the way he carried on, the way he talked, and then there was the decoration, the same as the one worn by the President of France. So let him get on with it, don't cross him, especially since doing so might harm Didi's chances. Oh dear! It must be the excitement.

'I'm sowwy, my Lord. I won't be vewy long.'

'Take your time, my dear chap. While you're gone, I'll warm up the tripe and the cassoulet.'

In what he called 'the little nook', Monsieur Deume sat and pondered. Really, it was a rum do. He was an odd chap, of course, but a decent enough type for all that, seeing the bright side, willing to lend a hand. Definitely out of the top drawer though, high-handed yet not at all toffee-nosed, and a way with him of putting people at their ease. Still, he would never have dreamed that an English lord would have known what to do with tripe and cassoulet, and fancy him rummaging through cupboards, and with such good humour too. These Englishmen really took the biscuit. Concocting tea parties out of tins, it was most peculiar. But there, it was true the English liked large breakfasts, so perhaps the principle extended to tea as well. A tea party for a third party, that was weird too, but it was a well-known fact, was it not, that people in important positions sent representatives to funerals, weddings and official dinners, he'd read about it in the newspaper. But that was as may be, it would have been better if this chap had come to the dinner party of the third party last night, when he'd have found everything ready for him, and not turned up unexpectedly today like this. Obviously all these important men were so busy that they did everything in a hurry, when they could fit it in. If only Antoinette had left the key to the fridge, he would have invited the chap to eat up the remains of the caviare. Still, best let him get on with it, for Didi's sake especially.

Returning to the kitchen, which was now filled with the pleasant aroma of the tripe and the cassoulet, he found the Garter, still in shirtsleeves and top-hat, cutting thick wedges of bread while keeping an eye on the two saucepans, the contents of which he stirred from time to time with a wooden spoon. The table, arrayed in the best damask cloth, was set. Everything was ready, places laid, serviettes daintily folded, crystal glasses, sardines and tuna in the hors-d'œuvre dish, and even flowers in the middle of the table, yes, the flowers from the drawing-room! There was no denying it: his Lordship, not a man to let the grass grow under his feet, had thought of everything. But what would Antoinette say if she happened to come back?

'Could I help you to cut the bwead, my Lord?'

'As you were, Father-in-Law, just sit you down and don't fret. Anyway, 'tis done. Twelve slices should be enough to be going on with. But there won't be any butter on them, a state of affairs we can fairly lay at the door of your lady wife and her wretched key.'

'Yes, I'm twuly sowwy about that,' said Monsieur Deume. He bowed his head, guilty by association.

'Never mind, let's say no more about it. These unpretentious coconut biscuits, though quite elderly and lacking the bite which is their principal charm, enhanced by this rather runny strawberry jam, she used too much water and not enough sugar, will make a democratic dessert. Of course, when I breakfast at George's I fare rather better. Noodles with garlic, stuffed aubergines, chopped liver and onions, lamb's-foot salad! Because George knows that I dote on lamb's feet served with a vinaigrette sauce and lots of onions. When I say George, I refer to my noble British sovereign, whom God preserve! Please stand up as a mark of respect! Thank you, you may sit down again. As to the bold, long-drawn blast of wind which I have this moment emitted, be not amazed. It is a custom of the English court and indicates to the host that the guest feels utterly at home and perfectly at his ease. But come, take up your serviette and let us begin by attending to the fruits of the sea!'

'But I should be boiling the kettle for the tea.'

'I see that you are not *au fait* with these things,' said Naileater. 'In circles *à la mode*, no one drinks tea at teatime! The fashion nowadays is for Bordeaux! There are several bottles in that ill-favoured little cupboard there, be a good fellow and open one! I'll make a start and you can catch me up,' he smiled, and he tied his napkin round his neck then gave a contented sigh. 'Ah, dear friend, how happy I am for once to be breaking bread in a humble cottage far from my feudal Shropshripshire mansion!'

Having downed his first glass of Bordeaux, he laid into the sardines and tuna, demolishing them noisily, pausing only to refill his glass and invite his chum Deume to feel free, refresh the inner man, for goodness sake, and take a glass or two, for who knew what generalized cancer fate held in store for them? Thus exhorted, the old gentleman did justice to the hors-d'œuvre and the Bordeaux. Without waiting to be told, he opened a second bottle the moment the steaming saucepans were brought and emptied directly into soup-dishes by the Principal Private Secretary, who had girded himself with Martha's white apron in order to protect the great sash of the Legion of Honour. Their faces gleaming, the two messmates drank deep and tucked into the tripe and cassoulet, switching delightedly from one to the other, exchanging many a grin, bursting into merry song and swearing eternal friendship.

Over dessert, his mood of exultation turning to gloom, Monsieur Deume, with his face smeared with jam and speaking in veiled terms, disclosed certain disappointing aspects of his married life. At this, Naileater recommended the use of a stout stick every morning, then proceeded to tell such amusing anecdotes that the little seal almost choked on his laughter. They drank each other's health, called each other by their first names, with young Hippolyte chortling and chuckling for no reason whatsoever, then haranguing his glass, which was no sooner empty than refilled, and even on two occasions tickling his lordship under the arm. He had never had such a high old time, and new horizons opened before him. And if Antoinette showed her face, why, he'd let her have a few good swipes with his stick!

'Come, old friend,' exclaimed Naileater, throwing his arms around him, 'let's drink with stout hearts and make the most of the time we have on this earth! A murrain on racial discrimination! I shall even go so far as to pay homage to Lord Jesus, son of the Lady Mary, provided that you, good old Hippolyte, pay homage to Lord Moses, God's bosom companion. So here's to Christians, I say, for there's good in all of them! Upon which note, though of different faiths yet sworn friends unto death, let us drink up and sing and thankfully embrace, for this is a day of rejoicing and friendship is the spice of life!'

CHAPTER 26

On this same afternoon, Benedetti, Head of the Information Section of the Secretariat of the League of Nations, had assembled fifty or so of his dearest friends at the cocktail party which he hosted each month. Of the modest gaggle of ideas contained in Benedetti's tiny brain, the most firmly rooted was the principle that in this life it was vitally important to have many friends and contacts, to return all invitations, and to make no enemies. Hence the monthly drinks parties held in his enormous drawing-room. Enormous it certainly was, yes, but on to it was tacked a minute and quite hideous bedroom which overlooked a small, dark yard. Appearances, that was what counted.

His important guests, holding frosted glasses into which they peered at floating ice-cubes, reacted according to their several temperaments with anger or gloom when approached or buttonholed by a guest less important than themselves and consequently of no use to them in their efforts to climb the social and professional ladder. Staring vacantly, their minds preoccupied by strategic thoughts, feigning attentiveness to some bore who, highly delighted with his capture, oozed charm and warmth, they mounted a holding operation to contain such unproductive company until something better came along, that is, a more profitable prize in the shape of someone, anyone, who outranked them. They tolerated the buttonholing because it provided them with the passing pleasure of flexing their power and exercising their talent for benign contempt, or else because it enabled them to save face by rescuing them from isolation, a fate even more appalling than being seen talking to a subordinate, for not knowing anyone was the greatest of social sins. Besides, exchanging conversation with an underling was not of itself discreditable as long as it was done in a tutelary and sufficiently offhand sort of way, for a brief conversation could be construed as charity. But it was not a good idea to let matters get out of hand. The chat should be cut short quickly, and then promptly followed up by a rehabilitating discussion with a person of superior rank. Which explains why the important guests, mumbling their vague yeses and quites, kept their anxious, restless eyes on the buzzing throng and, without seeming to, maintained a periodic, three hundred and sixty degree sweep, hoping in the glare of their revolving lighthouse beam to catch sight of a choice fish, a Superchief, to be harpooned without further ado.

Beneath the laughter, the smiles and the affable pleasantries lay a deep ground swell of serious endeavour, a mixture of unease and vigilance, as each guest watered the seed of his worldly interests. Swirling the ice in his glass or forcing a smile, but inwardly dispirited and dismayed by the inevitable underling presently trying his patience, each Important Person stood ready to make his nuzzling approach to a More Important Person, who had at last been located but was, alas, in the clutches of some tiresome, hated rival. Keeping watch on his future prey while pretending to listen to the Unimportant Person clinging stickily to him, he remained on full alert, eyes bright with stratagems and inattentiveness, prepared to dump the Other Ranker after a hasty 'We must talk again soon' (never make enemies, even of the small fry) and, like an expert hunter who knows exactly when to strike, ready to make his play for the More Important Person who would, he sensed, be free any second now. Which was why he never took his eyes off him for a moment and cocked a smile ready for use. But the More Important Person, no fool he, had scented danger. Abruptly disengaging himself from his current hanger-on and pretending not to catch the eye or see the smile of the merely Important Person, the lovingly covetous eye and the serfish smile as yet no more than a hint of what encouragement might make it, the More Important Person, giving the impression that he had noticed nothing, slipped quietly away and was immediately lost in the drinking, masticating crowd, while the thwarted Important Person, disappointed but not downhearted, dismayed but tenacious and firm of purpose, readied himself, now that he was rid of his own bootlicker, to start and pursue a new prey.

But having escaped the danger of social devaluation, the More Important Person now came up skilfully upon an even more important person, a Most Important Person in fact, only to discover, alas, that he was surrounded by a crowd of fawning courtiers. His eyes already glistening with deference, his face aflame with modesty and surrender, he in turn steadied himself to fire his harpoon at the first possible moment, though without losing his dignity, not out of pride and self-respect, but because making oneself cheap is invariably prejudicial. He waited for the chance to pounce, the moment when the Most Important Person would at last shake off the circle of beaming admirers. In his heart was hatred for his rivals, who seemed rooted to the spot, warmed by the sun of power. Gentle and patient as a seal crouching by a hole in the ice hoping for a fish to surface, he waited and set his social skills the task of finding the kind of amusing, spirited conversational gambit which would engage the attention of the Most Important Person and draw his friendly interest. From time to time he would lock the object of his desire in his gaze, willing him to give a sign of acknowledgement, hoping for a distant smile which would allow him to step forward in the most natural way in the world and, quivering with girlish excitement, join the knot of vassals. But senior men rarely acknowledge their inferiors.

Since their inferiors, tomorrow's corpses every one and all diligently applying themselves to the business of success, were vaguely aware of the boredom (variously gracious – 'I see, most interesting, well done, congratulations' – or preoccupied – 'Perhaps, yes, possibly, it's an idea worth following up' – or frankly hostile – 'I've no idea, I haven't had time') of the superiors they were trying to impress; and since, for their part, these same More Important Persons did not always manage to strike up a conversation with Most Important Persons – either because every Most Important Person was already being monopolized by other incipient corpses no less intent on making a favourable impression and wondering how best to book him for their next cocktail party, or else because of the dearth of Really Important Persons ('Honestly,' some of the guests would complain when they got home, 'honestly, darling, Benedetti's show was appalling, nobody worth talking to, just a crowd of hangers-on, perhaps it's time we dropped him') – a profound, unstated gloom ruled this roost loud with clucking laughter and the twitter of chit-chatting voices. There was gaiety on every lip. But the eyes were anxious and restless.

And yet the gloom was not universal, for there present were Equals who, sensing their mutual equality, derived some satisfaction from talking to each other, though it was obviously very much a second-best and hardly comparable with the spoils to be got from a conversation with a superior, but what was the alternative? Antennae quivering, casually, and in oblique asides, two Equals, or at least two men temporarily giving each other the benefit of the doubt, dropped and swapped the names of important contacts by way of intimating how they ranked, where they stood in what they called the pecking order. If the outcome proved positive, the less equal of the two would extend, or try to extend, an invitation to the other in order to expand his own stock of contacts, but also – and more so, for the socializing classes are insatiable – to be invited in turn to the other's home, there to meet more Equals or better still Superiors to whom he would extend, or try to extend, invitations for exactly similar ends. And so on and so forth.

Not one of these well-dressed mammals endowed with the opposable thumb had come in search of intelligence or human warmth. All without exception were driven by an urgent quest for contacts, whose social value they assessed by the number and quality of scalps collected. Thus a converted, homosexual Jew (who knew all there was to know about the kinship, marriages and health of everyone who counted in pan-European high society, where he had finally gained a footing after twenty years spent plotting, cajoling and being snubbed) was highly gratified to note that the person with whom he was talking was on visiting terms with an exiled queen who was 'absolutely adorable and terribly gifted musically'. When he had pigeon-holed his new acquaintance, he decided he was worth cultivating and as such invitable: so he invited him. It is such flummery which fills the waking hours of these poor excuses for human beings who all too soon will expire and rot and lie stinking in the earth.

Sometimes, in this gilded cage, sex occupied the high ground, attenuating or even supplanting the dominant social imperative. Over there, discreetly in a corner, a bald ambassador (who for forty years had deferred in servile flattery to his superiors so that he might steadily rise and eventually, wizened and with a colon riddled with bacilli, achieve Importance) was talking animatedly to a young interpreter, equally inane in four languages, who was endowed with breasts which had yet to fall and a grotesque rump significantly enhanced by a skirt chosen for its tightness: so decreed the lifeplan of this simpering kitten now basking in the exercise of her temporary power. For the action of the sexual is fleeting, while the social urge is sovereign and enduring.

Thirsting for contacts and personalities, a Greek lady journalist, acting clever and cute, said 'Hello, cousin' to a Russian princess to be chummy, shrieked at the correspondent of *The Times* 'Hi there, O Great One, I adored your piece in yesterday's paper,' then moved off to prowl in the purlieu of a pair of ministers who were taking themselves rather seriously. The bald ambassador, having succeeded in making a date with the owner of the large rump, was listening gravely to a porkling named Croci, a plenipotentiary minister of minor standing. He felt intense dislike for this upstart, who made unduly much of being addressed as Excellency, so he feigned a mind preoccupied with higher things as a way of making him repeat his questions. Having thus taken the wind out of his sails, he would then reply with exaggerated courtesy or even not reply at all but instead come out with a question on an entirely unrelated subject. Close by, a flaccid, bovine redhead, never once dropping her smile, was quietly berating her husband, a tall, stooping ape of a man with woolly hair and an anguished expression, for not having dared approach a high commissioner now in the clutches of Mrs Crawford, an American millionairess who, in a space of mere months, had managed to bag all the big names in international politics by the simple expedient of offering sumptuous hospitality, for when good things to eat are set before the good and the great they come running. Countess Groning's teeth were wreathed in friendly smiles. She extended her hand with mathematical precision, unleashed a guttural 'How do you do' and, hungry for secrets, asked a delighted Benedetti if it were true that the English delegate had really thumped the table with his fist during the private sitting of the Council. The reply being affirmative, she closed her eyes in political ecstasy while she savoured the titbit. A fat Lebanese lady who had bought a husband who was a fool but also Baron de Moustier – she was the President of a Literary Society founded by herself as a method of extending her range of top-drawer acquaintances – was talking excitedly about a lecture given by a duke who was also a French Academician which she had attended with the express purpose of accosting him afterwards so that she could say henceforth that she knew the duke, such a dear, unaffected, approachable man, and say it casually, as was only right. Meanwhile, overcome at finding himself in conversation with the impassive Guastalla, an incompetent but well-connected marquis who, because nobody knew what to do with him, had been appointed special adviser to the Secretary-General, Petresco promptly began talking about his holidays, which he would possibly be spending with the Titulescos, who had an estate at Sinaia, but it got so damnably hot there in summer that he had not finally made up his mind even though the minister had repeated his invitation several times. At this, an amiable smile appeared on the lips of the marquis. Whereupon, seizing her chance to be unconventional, Madame Petresco clapped her hands like some spoilt brat or self-willed schoolgirl and shrieked that she wanted to go and stay with dear Titu and nowhere else, who cared if it got hot at Sinaia, with dear Titu and nowhere else, with her boyfriend Titu and nowhere else, so there! And she went on clapping her hands wilfully and screeching the name of her Titu to impress the impressive Guastalla. Abandoned by a minister for the disabled who owed his entire political career to his wooden leg, a husband and wife who could not stand each other but were at one in their determination to scale the social heights readied themselves to mount a joint attack on the ambassador of a small, newly created state, an ex-journalist with dandruff who was staring at himself incredulously in a mirror. Weighed down with ten heavy rings, an aged English poetess looked on in scorn and splendid isolation while she fiddled with her comforting medieval hat from which hung a long black train, the sort worn by Catherine de Medici and queen mothers given to poisoning. Noticing Solal, Croci the minister made a beeline for him, saying how happy he was to have this opportunity of exchanging a few words with such a dear friend. In reality, he had only turned up in the hope of landing some snippet of ephemeral political information which he could pass on to Rome and thereby raise his stock. Adopt a high profile, wangle an ambassadorial appointment, rise up the ladder from which all topple and fall into the waiting hole below. To get rid of him, Solal invented a tip which he passed on in confidence to the porkling, who made an avid mental note, Adam's apple bobbing wildly. Mouthing courtesies, he went on his way, elated and accompanied by an undiagnosed cancer. The lift was slow in coming and he took the stairs at a run in his impatience to share his knowledge of this vital item of political jiggery-pokery with his minister. Now he'd get his embassy! Quick, encode the telegram and mark it 'Top Secret. For the Exclusive Information of His Excellency'! No, wait a minute, why not fly direct to Rome? An ironclad reason for a meeting with the supremo in person! Having at last got the bald ambassador to herself, Baronne de Moustier was quoting, in a voice made resonant by a large population of nasal polyps, a *pensée* perpetrated by the dear duke, such an unassuming, approachable man, to the effect that it is as important to be a good gardener as it is to be a worthy duke and peer. What a beautiful thought, and how true! she drooled, turning a heart-warming smile upon the ambassador, who, however, not one to be fooled by a scheming woman, cut her off brusquely and sidled up to Lord Galloway, to whom the Romanian delegate, casting prudent looks in all directions, was saying that she had it from an unimpeachable source that in Council the day after tomorrow the Italian delegate would speak not of national revendications, like last year, but of national aspirations, a subtle but crucial distinction which heralded a turning-point in fascist policy, she affirmed, as she stood, regally, categorically bejowled, with her tiny hand on her vast hip like the proprietress of a pot-house. Overhearing her, an eavesdropping journalist gave a start and hurried off to telephone this astounding scoop to his paper, bumping as he went into an elderly professor from the University of Zurich, who, in the hope of being awarded the Legion of Honour before he died, was keeping a sharp lookout for the French cultural attaché, while Madame Petresco, eager to show off her social graces, circulated saying 'Delighted to meet you', adding a 'ch' to 'meet' the way Lady Cheyne did. 'Marry in haste, repeat at leisure,' said the Greek lady journalist, trying to be witty and chic for the benefit of Baronne de Moustier, who gave her a sullen glare and, paying no further attention to a little schemer who was nothing and nobody, fixed her eyes on the inaccessible Lady Cheyne, with whom Countess Groning was enthusiastically discussing Lord Balfour. Dear Arthur! Such a wonderful person and a really great man of course, she had spent a delightful week at his place in Scotland. Yes, she was to dine with him and Anna de Noailles this evening, dear Anna was a genius and what a wonderful friend!

Four guests, painfully aware of their insignificance, did not even dare try to make contacts. They were untouchables, and they clung together and spoke in whispers. They knew that they were pariahs and that pariahs they would always be, but would never have dreamt of admitting it, and they formed a supercilious, jaded little group. Though they were beyond the pale, they sought to capture the moral high ground by making sarcastic remarks about the glittering guests they so envied. These sad lepers, whose cynicism had been thrust upon them, cowered with tribal solidarity in a corner by a window, put on a brave show, and stuffed themselves with sandwiches. They were obscure subordinates of Benedetti: the secretary with eczema from the Information Section, the Portuguese registrar, a Belgian clerk and a typist who looked like a small, fat muskrat. Benedetti had asked them to his party because it was another of his principles that persons in authority should look to their popularity and be loved by those, however humble, who worked under them. But he only invited the four outsiders once a year, and was in no doubt that they would know their place, which was near the window.

★

To comfort herself, the secretary with eczema again brought up the subject of her father, who had been a consul somewhere in Japan and as such had once had the honour of putting up a member of the French Academy named Farrère whose complete writings she had had bound up into a set. Two or three times a week she wheeled out her father who had been a consul and her Academician called Farrère. But there, does not each of us have a social hobby-horse which we ride when given half a chance, some small redeeming laurel crown which we hoist to our brow at every conceivable opportunity?

The most wretched of all the guests was Jacob Finkelstein, doctor of social sciences, a small, underfed man who worked as an ill-paid correspondent for a Jewish press agency. Benedetti invited him once a year too, so as to avoid antagonizing the Zionists, for, like all anti-Semites, he had a morbidly exaggerated idea of their influence in the United States. He invariably invited along some such impossible person who was not seen again for another year. Thus diluted, these dreadful people never impinged on what Benedetti, who prided himself on his literary turn of phrase, called the 'ambiance' of his parties.

No guest talked to Finkelstein, a social nothing who was not only no use to man or beast but, more damningly, could not harm a fly. He was not dangerous, *ergo* he was not interesting, not the sort who called for careful handling, not someone you need like or pretend to like. Even the four pariahs by their window kept their distance from his degrading, low-caste presence. Ignored by all and having no other Jews to talk to, the wretched leper decided that acting like a man in a hurry would enable him to show a bold front, and his involvement in the reception consisted of elbowing his way firmly through the chattering mob at regular intervals. Head lowered, as though dragged down by the weight of his nose, he would charge across the immense room from one end to the other, occasionally crashing into other guests, saying sorry, though his apologies fell on deaf ears. Launched on his series of lightning, slanting runs, he camouflaged his isolation by giving the impression that it was desperately urgent that he get to someone he knew who was waiting over there, at the far end of the room. It was a gambit which deceived no one. When Benedetti came across him and could not pretend he had not noticed, he kept him at arm's length with a merry, preventive 'All right?' and immediately left him to his unremitting ambulations. Whereupon the doctor of social sciences and supercharged Wandering Jew set off once more, retraced one of his pointless journeys through this land of exile, and with the same haste headed for the buffet and a comforting sandwich, which was his only social contact and the sole right he enjoyed at the reception. For two hours, between six and eight, poor Finkelstein subjected himself to forced marches of several kilometres, which he would not mention to his wife when he got home. He loved his Rachel and kept his griefs to himself. Why these unremitting charges? And why stay so long among these unfeeling people? Because he clung to his annual invitation, because he would not admit defeat, and also because he went in hopes of a miracle: a conversation with another human being. Poor, inoffensive Finkelstein, who wore your heart on your sleeve, a Jew dear to my heart, I hope you are in Israel now, among your people, among our brethren, and touchable at last.

At seven thirty, Sir John Cheyne, Secretary-General of the League of Nations, put in an appearance looking several sheets to the wind. Suddenly metamorphosed into a ballerina, Benedetti pirouetted hurriedly to meet him with love-light in his eye. The flame of his love was in no way simulated, for Benedetti was so driven by social ambition that he genuinely admired, nay doted on, any person of importance who might prove useful to him. Only sentiments which are sincere may be expressed effectively, that is, in a way which yields the maximum return. Moreover, one is left with a clear conscience. Far too big a bastard to be dishonest, Benedetti was quite convinced, even when privately admiring himself in his mirror, that he was genuinely fond of the Secretary-General and truly believed him to be a great man. He had been just as lovesick and just as reverential in his regard for the ex-Secretary-General. But when the previous incumbent had resigned, Benedetti had forgotten him instantly in his new enthusiasm for Sir John, whose photograph had immediately appeared in his office, ousting that of his predecessor.

★

By now, Sir John was chatting with Benedetti, with one hand placed firmly on his arm. The great man's touch made the bondsman thrill with infinite gratitude. Like Adrien Deume a few weeks previously, he walked like a fluttering virgin on the arm of the chief he loved, flustered by so much kindness and simplicity, proud and maidenly-modest, sanctified by the hand of the master, raising his eyes from time to time and casting a look of religious awe at his liege. For beneath his self-interested love for the lord of all lurked love of a different hue, a terrible, genuine and disinterested love, the abject love of power, the feminine worship of strength, a naked, animal reverence. But enough, more than enough, of this ghastly crew. I have seen my fill.

CHAPTER 27

Madame Deume sat in her room at her escritoire, where, warding off starvation with cruelly crunched cracknels, she was catching up with her correspondence. She had just appended her signature to a final letter, to married friends in Lausanne, and had closed with her favourite envoi, which ran: 'Home is where the hearth is. We both send our very best wishes.' (She had been using 'home is where the hearth is' ever since she had read it at the end of a letter from Madame Rampal. 'It's original,' she was wont to say, 'it's succinct, and it says what it means.' To which her husband invariably replied: 'It's a pwetty thought. Has a wing to it.')

Having duly licked the envelope, she took up her knitting while Monsieur Deume perched on a chair and placed his spirit-level on the top of the mirror-fronted wardrobe to see if it was sitting four-square. Damnation, it wasn't straight! Quick, find a wedge to go under the left side! Stepping down off the chair, he rubbed his hands, only too happy to have something useful to do. Madame Deume, getting to a straight bit of her knitting which was easy to do, suddenly waxed conversational.

'What were you doing downstairs just now? You were gone for ages.'

'I was cleaning out the water-jug fwom yesterday. I managed to get wid of that nasty deposit with coarse salt and vinegar, and then I finished it off by swishing it wound and wound with my finely cwushed eggshells and a little water. You'll see, it's come up all bwight and shiny!'

'Honestly, dear, you'd make someone a wonderful wife,' she said with a condescending smile, and she gave her mouse of a spouse a little pat on the hand, then yawned. 'Wednesday already, how time flies, it doesn't seem like three days since we had the Kanakises here. The dinner went off terribly well, don't you think? The memory of it is pure gold.'

'Oh quite, couldn't agwee more,' said Monsieur Deume, who was busily rummaging through his toolbox.

'And, don't forget, Madame Kanakis telephoned the very next morning to say she wouldn't have missed it for worlds, said it had been so nice meeting me, really a most proper person, thoroughly conversant with the rules of society, has them at the tips of her fingers, one senses immediately that she has a fine soul, I enjoyed her company immensely.'

'I'm sure you did,' said Monsieur Deume. (But he hadn't, at all: she was one of those forceful women, very superior, and besides she'd prattled on and on about music no one else had ever heard of. Ah, this looks like a useful wedge, just the right thickness.)

'And then Monsieur Kanakis. What a charming man, such manners, truly the *crème de la crème*. Did you notice him kiss my hand?'

'Yes I noticed,' said Monsieur Deume, who was now on his knees in front of the wardrobe.

'Such a lervely touch, one senses that he has an aura. Anyway, we managed to get shot of everything we ordered from Rossi's, though there's still some foie gras and caviare left.'

'Well done,' said Monsieur Deume, whose mind was entirely taken up by the effort of tapping his wooden wedge daintily home with a hammer.

Clambering back up on to the chair and putting his spirit-level on the top of the wardrobe, he noted that it now showed true. 'Spot on,' he murmured, and his eye lingered fondly on his initials which only last night he had etched in poker-work on the handle of his little hammer. He got down and put the spirit-level on the marble-topped bedside table. What the dickens! The bedside table wasn't plumb either! How had he gone on for all these years with a bedside table that was out of kilter? Especially since there could have been nasty accidents, you know, seeing that it was a bedside table. Quick, something to put under it. Wood was no good. Too thick.

'Antoinette, you wouldn't have a little bit of cardboard I could put under the leg of the bedside table? It's not stwaight.'

'Now you've gone and made me lose count,' she said, and she stopped knitting. 'You always start talking to me at the wrong moment, it's most disheartening. No, I don't have any bits of cardboard,' she said, to punish him.

He tiptoed out. Returning in the same manner, he slipped a piece of card folded in two under one leg of the bedside table, which he then tested. The result was satisfactory. Disconcerted by his instant success and at a loss for what to do next, he clasped his hands behind his back and stood watching his wife, who had put her knitting to one side and was now savouring the small but comforting pleasure – known only to the already comfortable who do not have to worry about tomorrow – of cutting the pages, prior to perusal, of a work entitled *Inner Freedom,* a present from Madame Ventradour. She was looking forward with joy to making a start on it later, when she had a quiet moment this evening, especially seeing that dear Emmeline had told her that it was such a wholesome book, the sort that provided food for thought. Yes, tonight, when she was in bed, with her feet on a lervely hot-water bottle. Sensing that she had cooled down, he ventured to ask a question.

'Antoinette, what are we going to do about the Gwuyère that doesn't taste of anything?'

'Take it back to the grocer,' she said, and she went on cutting. 'I'm certainly not going to be left with a pound of tasteless Gruyère on my hands. And make him give you the money back, it's two seventy-five.'

'Yes, but he'll give me cwoss looks if I weturn it.'

'Perlease, Hippolyte, be a man for once.'

'Couldn't you take it?'

'No. I've got my stiffness again.' (Whenever she did not feel like working or preferred to leave some disagreeable chore to somebody else, she genuinely felt her right leg go stiff.)

'Well, couldn't we send the new girl who's starting tomowwow morning?'

'No. You can go,' she said, and she twiddled the little tuft of hairs which sprouted from the mole on her chin, then gave a sigh of relief. 'I must say, though, I'm very glad to be rid of poor Martha. With that back of hers, there's no telling where it could all have ended.'

'To be fwank, I'd wather have kept her on till she was better, and got the doctor to her and evewything.'

'But you must see that she would never have got well here. At such times it's up to one's family to rally round. She'll be able to take things easy and be looked after by her loved ones, who will shower her with care and be at her beck and call, poor dear. State of mind is tremendously important for a healthy body. If she is happy in her mind, her back will get better all the more quickly. And if she does have to have an operation, it's only right and proper that the family should bear their share of the responsibility. The annoying thing, though, is that we'll have to put up with this new daily until Mariette gets back. I must say I was not best pleased by Mariette's telegram. We agreed she could have heaps of time off, until the first of July, to look after that sister of hers. And when we wired her, what did we say? We asked her to come back three weeks before the date we'd agreed on account of this business of Martha and her back.'

'Twoo, but she couldn't, because her sister's got pneumonia.'

'It's always the same with domestics. I see it as a lack of tact and loyalty. I mean to say, here's someone who is supposed to be devoted to Adrien's wife and for years and years was in the service of Mademoiselle Valérie d'Auble. I should have thought she'd have shown more consideration. Anyway, I wonder if her sister is really as ill as she makes out. The lower classes are such mollycoddles, they give in at the first sign of suffering. I've had bronchitis myself more than once, and I never made as much fuss.'

'Yes, but her sister's got double pneumonia.'

'Bronchitis and pneumonia are six of one and half a dozen of the other. But let's drop the subject. Such utter lack of principle is beyond me. Do let's talk about something else. Now, on the business of Monsieur Solal's precious letter, the more I think about it the less gratifying it seems. In the first place, it was addressed to her, though I would have thought it more natural if he had written to me, but there it is. Besides, I don't care at all for the tone. Do you remember how it starts? Just apologies, and not even sincere apologies either, though it would have been only good manners. And then "Perlease convey my apologies to all concerned" is a reference to you and me. He could at least have mentioned my name, seeing as how I spoke to him on the telephone. And then he talks about a sudden indisposition without saying what it was exactly. I find it all very offhand, I must say. What do you make of it?'

'The fact is,' said Monsieur Deume.

'And he sends his regrets, but he couldn't even go to the bother of saying they were heartfelt.'

'I'll second that,' said Monsieur Deume.

'And he ends with plain good wishes, not best. I know she's young and so forth, but really! And the way he invites them to dinner, at his hotel, giving them just the one date, Friday the eighth of June at eight o'clock, which is the day after tomorrow. It's a case of take it or leave it. What do you think?'

'Well, I weckon he's a vewy important man and obviously . . .'

'I know all that,' she sighed. 'But even so, manners are manners. And why didn't he invite us too? Do you think that's correct?'

'Maybe he doesn't know we live with Didi.'

'He is perfectly aware that we do! Because I introduced myself over the telephone that evening, and I even said my husband and I or something of the sort. You mustn't think I mind in the least, first because I'm used to staying in the background, and second because in any case we won't be here the day after tomorrow, and third because I can well do without hotel cooking, thank you very much. But it's his manner I don't care for. Still, he did send his apologies, and so appearances have been kept up.'

'Besides, he's the chap who fixed Didi's pwomotion.'

'He gave him his due and no more. (To underscore her point, she voraciously resumed her knitting. She finished a row then scratched the inside of her ear with the free needle.) And as for that wife of Didi's, talk about a flash in the pan! All her fine resolutions have died a natural death, vanished in a puff of smoke! Saying she was running errands for him, pressing his trousers and so forth, all that's gone with the wind! She spent all yesterday afternoon sunbathing in the garden in full view of passers-by! Carrying on like that will hardly send our stock up with the neighbours! And I see that she hasn't even cut the pages of *Watch and Pray*, which I gave her to read! That's all the thanks I get for giving up my small room downstairs so that Madame could turn it into her sitting-room! Imagine, her own private sitting-room! And none of her usual sloth in the way she set about it! She bucked up her ideas and took no time at all to set up shop with all those awful old bits and pieces belonging to her aunt, I wouldn't have them if they were given! That ancient threadbare carpet! She even had her piano brought down! And brought down at Didi's expense, of course! And not answering when I asked her ever so naicely how she was, spiritually speaking. The conceited, impudent hussy! Haven't you got anything to say for yourself?'

The downstairs telephone rang. Only too grateful for the diversion, Monsieur Deume rushed off to answer it. He returned gasping for breath, for he had climbed the stairs three at a time, and said Madame Ventradour was on the line. Madame Deume hurried off.

As the door closed behind her, he collapsed into an armchair. That phone call was providential. If it lasted any length of time, it would give her something else to think about and maybe she wouldn't go on any more to him about Ariane. No, he couldn't and wouldn't say nasty things about her just to keep Antoinette's hat straight. Not after Ariane had been so sweet to him yesterday when she'd got back just after that English chap had gone, she'd been a brick, taken charge, quick! hide the empty tins, hurry up! tidy up the kitchen, spit-spot! take a taxi to town and buy replacement tins and more bottles of the same Bordeaux! And she'd given him excellent advice about the letter, just say it had come and leave it at that. Fortunately Antoinette had got home late from Madame Gantet's. He'd have really caught it in the neck if she'd come back and found him and the Englishman there together up to their eyes in Bordeaux and cassoulet, singing their heads off! The Englishman was a very decent sort, though, and they'd had a merry time of it. They'd even embraced when it was time for him to go. Come to think of it, he'd never had a real friend in his life. He wouldn't have minded seeing him again, except that he was a lord and therefore several cuts above him. Well at least their tea party would be a memory to treasure. He blew his nose and stared into his handkerchief, folded it, and forced himself to think about something else. Yes, he'd buy a magnetic screwdriver, it would come in very handy. What on earth was she telling Madame Ventradour? Noiselessly he opened the door, leaned over the banister, and listened.

'What a pity, dear, you missed Jeanne Gantet's littel talk, she's such an intellectual person, never at a loss for words. She spoke to us about the link between science and religion, it involves all sorts of things one never normally thinks of, such as the telephone, for instance, which enables us to ask a friend with greater religious experience for spiritual support in some faith-shattering moral crisis, or again the railways, religious congresses could not be held without them! or the radio, which puts out such comforting programmes! We were all absolutely spellbound! It was definitely one in the eye for unbelievers who say that there aren't any links between science and religion! Anyway, I'm so pleased everything is going well for you. But I must tell you, dear, that we've been through thick and thin here these last few days! It never rained but it poured! First, the sink in the kitchen got blocked, pouring chemicals down didn't do the trick and in the end we had to call the plumber! And then Martha's gone, went the day before yesterday. I didn't catch that. Oh no, I didn't send her packing, she left of her own accord. You see she'd been having trouble with her back ever since she fell when trying to hang a picture, you know what these girls are like, always getting ideas into their heads, that's right, she was trying to hang quite a large picture the other evening while we were waiting for a supper- or rather dinner-guest, as a matter of fact it was the Under-Secretary-General of the League of Nations, a very dear friend of Adrien's. Martha, poor thing, could barely drag herself about, and naturally her work suffered as a result. So, feeling very sorry for her, I advised her to go home to her family for a rest, to return to the fold and get good and well again there. Besides, I had made it perfectly clear to her from the beginning that I was engaging her on a purely temporary basis, only until such time as Mariette came back. Not that she's any great loss. For a start, she was dreadfully clumsy in her work in spite of all the trouble I took to train her, and, since she'd never learned how to behave, I didn't get very far in my efforts to teach her naice manners. For example, she had this mania for knocking before entering the drawing-room. How many times did I point out in the kindest possible way that it's only on bedroom doors a correctly brought-up person knocks before entering! And tactless! Would you believe that one day I found her crying her eyes out, so naturally I asked what was the matter and even held her hand to encourage her to speak up for herself, and can you imagine what she told me? She had the impudence to say she was homesick for her cows! Of course, I forgave her with all my heart, for I never lost sight of the fact that she came of humble stock. But I do hope that the serious talks I had with her will prove a blessing on her, the poor littel thing was religiously quite backward. Anyhow, I did my level best to raise her spiritual consciousness, especially by praying with her, yes I did! We'll have someone else as of tomorrow, she doesn't seem anything to write home about and she'll be mornings only, seeing as how she does somewhere else in the afternoons. But in view of the fact of how difficult it is finding domestics nowadays we should be grateful for whatever God sends us in the way of servants, even if the quality leaves much to be desired. Naturally, as soon as poor Martha decided to go off and get well wherever it was she came from, I wired reply-paid to Mariette, who is if you recall in Paris and is in any case due to resume her duties here on July the first, asking her in the light of events to come back and start work with immediate effect. We received a telegram saying she couldn't come seeing as how her sister, who is a concierge, has come down with double pneumonia, and that she won't be in a position to return before the beginning of July. Really, it's always the same with servants. We are at their absolute mercy. But, dear, there I go, prattling on, and I haven't yet told you the big news! You won't believe it, but we're off to Brussels the day after tomorrow! Relations of mine, the van Offels, of the Château van Offel, have sent for me urgently! Yes, I got a letter by the midday post yesterday from dear Élise van Offel, that is the younger Madame van Offel, literally begging for my help! Her mother-in-law has had a stroke, one side is completely paralysed, and they've taken her in because she was in such a bad way. But Wilhelmine van Offel, that's Madame van Offel the elder, the one who's been struck down, can't get on with any of the nurses and has been positively clamouring for me, seeing as how I once looked after her many years ago. Heeding only the promptings of my heart, I was naturally prepared to drop everything and go to her at once, taking Hippolyte with me, of course, he can't do without me, but there weren't any sleepers until the day after tomorrow. When I travel overnight I always take a sleeper, it's a firm family principle. So we booked both of us on the Friday-night train nineteen francs forty-five, excuse me nineteen forty-five, a quarter to eight that is. It will get us into Brussels at ten to nine on Saturday morning, God willing and barring accidents, which can always happen. We'll probably be away for three months, or perhaps a bit less, depending on how her condition develops, for at best, or so the doctor says, the poor dear will be promoted to glory by the beginning of August at the very latest. There's no knowing how it will all turn out, it's in the hands of the Almighty, to whom all things are known. Be that as it may, I cannot leave dear Élise in the lurch, incidentally her maiden name was van der Meulen, the family was very big in refining. Oh yes, naturally there'll be a nurse, I'll be there principally to provide spiritual comfort but also to tell the nurse what to do. I'll put the time to good use, though, I'll catch up with my knitting and shall make a point of getting on with some more socks for my husband, who goes through them at a terrible rate, I can't think how he manages it. Sorry? No, no. What I do is the heel first, then I knit the feet in two parts up to the place where you decrease. I knit up two pieces of the right length because, do you see, the instep doesn't get much wear, so when the sole needs replacing all I have to do is a new underside and decreases, that way I save both time and wool. But tell me, dear, I've just had a thought, I'd love to see you before we caviare, sorry, slip of the tongue, I meant to say before we leave here. We'd be ever so perleased if you were able to come to lunching tomorrow, Thursday. Thursday's no good for you? Well perhaps Friday, then, the day we leave? You have a lunching engagement? Well in that case there's nothing for it: you'll have to come on here for an early supper. You can? Wonderful, I'm delighted. But listen, dear, do come early so that we can squeeze in a good heart-to-heart. Now let's see, our train goes at nineteen forty-five, which is a quarter to eight. Would you like to come at four? We'll sit down to table at half past five sharp, so it will have to be high tea, in the circumstances you won't mind taking pot luck. I'll see you on Friday then, dear, I'm so looking forward to it, and thanks again for your useful tip about using pillowcases for delicate things, I've already tried it and it protects them wonderfully! I'll pass on good wishes from Hippolyte, who is right beside me making signs that I'm to give you his best. I'd have passed on my Adrien's too if he'd been here, but it's wicked to tell untruths, isn't it dear? Let's just say that if he had been here he would certainly have wanted me to convey his very best to you. But I must let you get on, dear. I'll see you at four the day after tomorrow, I'm so looking forward to it, and in the meantime I send you a joyful smile!'

When she got back to her room, Madame Deume sat down in the Voltaire-style armchair, picked up her knitting, put it down again almost at once, and gave her husband a pale-blue look. He shivered and assumed an innocent expression.

'Did you notice there was something up with Didi this morning? Oh, he did his best to hide it, but a mother's heart is never deceived. Oh yes! I know exactly what the matter was! It was because yesterday she wouldn't go with him to the big reception given by Monsieur what's-his-name Benedetti! That girl's a nasty piece of work! (She crunched a cracknel: it exploded in the sinister, frightening mouth of her self-regard.) I guarantee that when we sit down to dinner – if, that is, Madame condescends to put in an appearance – I guarantee that when I tell her we're having Emmeline Ventradour over the day after tomorrow for high tea she won't say a word, just to show that Princess High-and-Mighty is simply not interested in such things. (Dental twitterings to accompany the removal by suction of fragments of cracknel.) Anyway, you can take it from me that the Ventradour estate is in a different class altogether in terms of size from that tiny place of her aunt's, which in any case was snatched from under our very noses, seeing as how it was left to the uncle so that my poor Didi wouldn't get his hands on it! And she had the barefaced nerve to tell me that she thought it was only right! Still, I have a duty to love her and I shall pray for her!'

CHAPTER 28

Responding with a conditioned reflex to the sound of the buzzer, Miss Wilson made an exactly judged entry and halted two metres short of the Louis XVI desk. Fifty-something, proper, deficiently hindquartered, convinced of the utter rightfulness of her existence, exuding overpowering waftures of lavender orchestrated with the harmonics of Pears soap, she waited in silence, perpendicular and efficient, and netted him with her frank, green, fearless, irreproachable, devoted and vacuous stare.

Turning his head away to avoid her eyes which made him uneasy, for it was the look worn by the uncomplicated and the sensible, he asked her to call the heads of section to a meeting. She acquiesced gravely, deferential but self-contained, then turned on heels as flat as her behind, and made her exit, borne up by her certainties, strong in her faith in God and King, sustained by her implacable uprightness, by the sure promise of a place in the ever-after and by the cottage she had already bought in Surrey, where she would live when she retired and snip her roses with sharp secateurs between cups of tea (strong, no sugar), held in high regard by all and sundry, pally with the vicar's wife, irreproachable and happy in her little cottage, which she would leave only when, still a virgin and with her large feet first, she was summoned directly to heaven. Her place was among life's fortunates and she had faith. He, on the other hand, belonged nowhere, a man of solitude who believed in nothing. The only way out: suicide. But in the meantime, on with the farce of the daily meeting.

★

The six heads of section sat waiting in the committee room around a long table, notepads before them, smoking and courteously flashing expensive lighters at their neighbours, exchanging pleasantries and heartily detesting each other. Jonkheer van Vries, secretly despising his colleagues who were commoners and lacking in the social graces of which he believed he had more than his fair share, contributed little to the conversation. (He was particularly proud of his familiarity with the stratospheric social niceties, such as knowing that some great names like Broglie or Cholmondeley were pronounced in unexpected and quite delightful ways, or that some dukedoms were sovereign and others not. Furthermore, saying 'my tuxedo' rather than 'my dinner-jacket' filled him with a delicious sense of superiority. These and other insiderly trivialities together with his acquaintance with a versifying countess who, though constantly at death's door, was socially very astute and gave large parties, plus the fact that he was received by a particularly dim-witted queen-in-exile, were the *raison d'être* which sustained this sorry specimen of humanity, with his great pop-eyes and his perpetual highly perfumed aura of Russian Leather.)

The heads of section stood up when Solal came in. He surveyed them and knew them for what they were. With the exception of Benedetti, who plotted against him underhandedly, they were all on his side, that is to say, they settled for a prudent smile, occasionally tinged with approval, when they heard someone speak ill of him.

He motioned them to be seated and said there was only one item of business, which had been put on the agenda at the request of the Secretary-General and drafted by Sir John personally, to wit: 'Action to be taken to promote the goals and ideals of the League of Nations'.

None of the section heads had any more idea of what form such action should take than did Sir John, who expected his subordinates to tell him what he wanted. Nevertheless, they all took turns and spoke volubly, the rule of rules being never lose face, always appear to be on top of things, and at all cost never admit to not understanding or not knowing what to do.

And so they rambled on boldly, brightly, without any clear idea of which issues they were supposed to be discussing. While his colleagues, who all quickly tired of lengthy comments other than their own, drew geometric doodles on their notepads and then glumly proceeded to improve them with curlicues, van Vries droned on for ten minutes to the effect that it was essential to draw up a plan of action which was not simply systematic but concrete. Next, Benedetti spoke to two points which were in his view crucial: firstly that, in his opinion, for what it was worth, what was required was a programme of action rather than a plan of action, he repeated, a programme, the difference, he believed, was capital, at least in his book it was; and secondly, that the programme of action should be conceived as a specific project, he was not afraid to nail his colours to the mast, a project that was specific.

The other heads of section nodded in agreement, and all acknowledged the absolute necessity of having a specific project. Specific projects were always in good odour in the Secretariat. It was not clear what value 'specific' added to 'project', but a specific project looked altogether more pondered than a penny-plain project. In reality, no one knew the difference between a project and a specific project, and nobody had ever bothered to ask what the precious adjective meant and what purpose it served. People were only too happy to talk about specific projects and left it at that. When a project was said to be specific, it immediately acquired a highly esteemed aura of mystery, became a marvel pregnant with the promise of fruitful action.

Next to take the floor was Basset, Head of the Cultural Section, who pointed out the need to work closely with the relevant voluntary organizations. But everything should be open and above board! interjected Maxwell, Section Head of Plans and External Liaison, and it had to be made crystal clear from the word go that the Secretariat would retain overall control of the specific project! That was all very well! cried Johnson, but the whole matter craved wary walking, and nothing should be done without the full agreement of the member states! To this end, the first and indispensable step would be to circulate various governments with a questionnaire, the responses to which would serve as the basis on which the specific project that was to constitute the programme of action would be drawn up. Orlando considered that their best option would be to contact the Education Ministers of member states with a view to setting up a programme of school talks on the theme of the goals and ideals of the League of Nations.

Returning to the charge, Basset – his real name was Cohen, surname of the descendants of Aaron, brother of Moses, but the little stinker had chosen to hide behind Basset – argued that 'since the specific project is to provide for a programme of action which must be not only systematic and concrete but also coordinated, it follows that special action is required to establish the parameters of coordination on the one hand between the various sections of the Secretariat and, on the other, between the Secretariat and the various intergovernmental agencies, so as to avoid crossed wires, arguments about who is responsible for what and general duplication, and that the specific project should lay down as its ultimate objective, after consultation with the relevant governments, the creation within the Secretariat of a new section with particular responsibility for promoting the goals and ideals of the League of Nations. I thank you for your attention,' he said and he bowed his head, no less proud of his little speech than he was of being a faithful little basset. His colleagues backed the principle that a new section should be created, for they were all aware of the reorganizing fever which periodically gripped the Secretary-General. Like a little boy with a Meccano set who never wearies of making and unmaking things, old man Cheyne was never happier than when taking his fine box of tricks apart and then putting it together again, closing this section down, dividing that one into two, inventing some brand-new one, though it was always on the cards that he would go back to the old structure within a matter of months.

Anxious to shine in the presence of their silent chief, this fine body of men went at it with a will and improvised enthusiastically, conjuring up in the strange language of the Secretariat 'avenues to be explored', 'the consensual accord to be sought on the repartition of responsibilities both in the organizational and the operational contexts', 'perceived models of approach to this problem', 'the published track record of the specialized agencies', 'the provision of back-up equipments which governments, if approached in a spirit of cooperation, might be incited to take on board', 'past experience which gives a favourable inference to a high profile vis-à-vis the urgent need for concrete action', 'the penury of viable alternatives', 'practically non-existent difficulties', 'the convergent vocation of recent interventions in Council debates'. And so on and so forth, the whole interlarded with confused and contradictory proposals which were all conscientiously noted by the stenographer, who could not make head nor tail of any of them, for she was an intelligent girl.

Suddenly there was a silence. The waters had been so muddied that no one knew quite where they were or what had been decided. Maxwell saved the day by mooting the usual lazy face-saver, the setting up of 'a working party to explore avenues and to present, to an ad hoc committee to be constituted at a later date and composed of members delegated by national governments, the draft of a specific project setting out concrete proposals which shall form the broad framework of a long-term programme of systematic and coordinated action designed to promote the goals and ideals of the League of Nations'.

Kicking himself for not having thought of suggesting this himself, and most anxious to make a good impression, van Vries proposed that, on the basis of the discussion which had just taken place and the recommendations made, a note for guidance should be 'drafted and forwarded to the as yet unconstituted working party which would serve as both its broad brief and its terms of reference'. Proud of this little piece of sabotage and delighted to land a rival with a nasty chore, he suggested that Maxwell might care to look after drafting the note for guidance, which needed to be done quickly so that it could then be submitted to Sir John for his approval.

'Excellent. We are all in agreement,' said Solal, and he bit his lip again. 'Maxwell, go to it. Thank you, gentlemen.'

When he was alone, he pictured what would happen next. Maxwell would send for Mossinsohn, currently on temporary transfer to Plans and External Liaison, and tell him that the whole stenographic record of the meeting contained all he needed to draft a note for guidance, that the work had been virtually done for him and that all he, Mossinsohn, had to do was to lick the thing into shape and get it down to a reasonable length. It shouldn't take him more than an hour or two. 'Go to it,' he too would say, 'it's a piece of cake, though do take care, be alive to the political dimension and steer clear of anything that might offend national susceptibilities, aim for the flexible approach, avoid anything that might upset governments, keep it general, blur the edges, and let me have it first thing tomorrow morning.' And the unfortunate Mossinsohn would go to it all through the night, stayed with coffees innumerable. In the end, fogged down by the inconsistencies in the verbatim record, despairing of ever getting to the bottom of their mysteries, he would simply make up what the six heads of section had decided and concoct a suitable note for guidance out of his own head. And so an insignificant Jew without friends at court, employed as a temporary clerk at five hundred francs a month, would dictate the decision which Sir John Cheyne KCB, KCVO would then proceed to take.

'Miss Wilson, would you ask van Vries to come and see me?'

Tall, neurasthenic and horsy, his red hair parted in the middle, the Head of the Mandates Section, shoulders drooping and guilty in advance, entered in fear and dread of the dressing-down which was always on the cards. Solal waved him to a chair and, letting his gaze wander, asked him if he was satisfied with young Deume. Van Vries manufactured a minor coughing fit to give him time to come up with the right answer. Deume, whom he loathed as much for his reputation as a man of letters as for his sloth and chronic lateness, had recently been made up to an A by direct selection. *Ergo* the little swine was well regarded in high places. *Ergo* say nothing but good of him.

'Very satisfied. An excellent official. Punctual, lots of ideas, works well with colleagues.'

'I'd like you to send him on an official visit now and then.'

'As it happens, I was thinking along those self-same lines myself this very morning,' van Vries lied quickly. 'In fact, I was just about to send you a note recommending that he should be sent to Paris and London to make contact with the relevant ministries. There's nothing like the personal touch for creating an atmosphere of trust and collaboration. Moreover, he'll be able to bring back very useful information, since information is always easier to gather on the spot. I also had half a mind to suggest that he should then be sent on to two areas which pose particularly delicate problems, I mean of course Syria and Palestine.'

When he had finished, he coughed respectfully and waited with a look of devotion on his face. Solal gave his approval, and van Vries went away elated at having got through the interview unscathed. Once in the corridor, he stepped out straight-backed and exuding authority once more. It had all turned out well, he'd be rid of Deume for two, no three months. Mossinsohn, the temp, a workhorse if ever there was one, would make an excellent replacement.

CHAPTER 29

'I tell you, old man, that went down a treat,' he said, buttoning his trousers while the cleansing cascade boomed round the pan of his favourite lavatory. 'Congrats, old bean,' he added, and he emerged feeling an urge to frisk and gambol like a puppy celebrating duty done in the tender morning grass.

Outside in the corridor, he wondered what he could do now. His daily dose of sodium cacodylate had been administered by the duty nurse. His morning coffee had been duly drunk. All that remained now was to get down to work. That Danish nurse was an absolute corker. 'To work, to work,' he hummed as he pushed his office door. No sooner was he settled at his desk than he opened his newspaper and stared at the kindly face of the new Pope, who had been elected the previous day.

'Now that's what I call promotion!' he murmured to His Holiness. 'Still, I haven't done too badly myself!'

When he had folded his paper, he looked dotingly round his office, which was the office of an A, digging his feet into the Persian carpet so that he felt its reassuring presence, allowing his eyes to linger fondly on the glass-fronted lockable – ah yes, lockable – bookcase filled with fine volumes from the library which were quite useless but were bound and therefore looked decidedly smart.

'And if they ask for them back, sucks to them, I'll say I have to have them on permanent loan! A chap's got to be able to stand up for himself in this hell-hole!'

Delighted with his invigorating cacodylate, which he got given free, gratis and for nothing, and feeling as breezily fit as any man ought who enjoys trouble-free digestion, he moved the picture of his wife on his desk slightly to one side with the most gratifying results. With it angled thus, he would not be the only one to get the full benefit. Any B he invited to take a pew in his leather armchair would see it too and could sit and admire. In the antique silver frame, she looked very high-society, dress revealing just enough, a beautiful woman. And she was his wife, dammit all, and he could get his hands on her whenever he felt like it. Pinching his nostrils between thumb and forefinger, he gave a delighted, nasal 'quack-quack'. The photo was a brilliant move, very senior-civil-servanty. Pity they had no children. A picture of a pretty little girl in a nice dress would have been very section-headish. But there it was. At any rate, he'd reorganized his office jolly well since being put up to an A. The non-figurative painting on the wall suggested the cultivated official who needed an artistic environment. The box, also of antique silver, was another good idea, a useful status symbol.

'I lift the lid and shunt it towards any Bs who trickle respectfully along with a request for information. "Cigarette, Carvalho?" "Cigarette, Hernandez?" Best of all, old man, would be to have a personally signed photo of the USG: "To Adrien Deume, with all good wishes." Or perhaps warmest regards. Warmest regards would be tickety-boo! Just imagine the expression on VV's face as he came in and read it! Yes, except that I don't know him well enough yet. Watch your step, old man, no mess-ups, don't get impatient, bide your time! The signed photo will depend on how our personal relationship develops. But for starters, tomorrow, the evening of Friday the eighth of June, dinner at the Ritz as guests of the USG! Me in bib and tucker and she in her best evening frock! That's right, m'dear fellow, dinner with the Under-Secretary-General of the League of Nations! I was bursting to tell VV, it took every ounce of my self-control to stop myself blurting it out! No, let's wait until we're on really close terms with the USG. Agreed, not a word to VV until my position is unassailable. His letter to Ariane struck just the right note. "Please convey my apologies to all concerned." Prettily said, eh? And on top of that he sent her his good wishes. Say what you like, I've come a long way in a short time. (He went through his "quack-quack" routine again.) If all goes well tomorrow night, I won't mess about, I'll go ahead and organize a party and ask him to come. On second thoughts, make that an invitation to dinner, especially now that Mummy and Dada are going away tomorrow evening and won't be back for at least two months. Come to think of it, it was just as well he couldn't come the other evening, stroke of luck! That's it, invite him to dinner! I'll simply be returning his invitation, right? Just him, Ariane and me in the quiet of our own home. Butler in white gloves. Quack-quack. But the main thing for the moment is to make a good impression tomorrow night. Take a couple of Maxitons an hour beforehand, at seven, to make certain I'm on the top of my form. I'll be cultivated, witty, amusing. If he laughs, if he sits up and takes notice, we're in, Meredith! And remember, don't be late! No fooling around, is that clear? His letter says eight. So come eight o'clock tomorrow night on the dot, enter Lord Deume of A Grade, preceded by his delightful wife. She's in a good mood these days, thank God, and has been since, well, you know. Women need it. Now that's all very well, chum, but you're going to have to sparkle and catch his eye. To which end go home this afternoon and fetch back here everything you've got on Mozart, Vermeer, Proust, and swot it all up between two and six so you'll be able to draw on a supply of well-informed, freshly minted views on the aforementioned so you can amaze him with your wealth of knowledge. The thing is to get to that moment when all of a sudden he sits up, gives me an old-fashioned look, and says to himself: "This young Deume's a dark horse, must see more of young Deume." Oh, and don't forget to ask him if he's been to the Picasso exhibition, it'll give me a chance to hold forth. (He sniggered. Smart move, memorizing those three wizard sentences from that review of the Picasso show. They'd have the most electrifying effect.) But say them slowly, as if I'm searching for my words, as if I'm making it up as I go along. Damn! What if he doesn't like Picasso? In that case I'll be shooting myself in the foot if I come out with my three sentences! Test the water first, find out whether he likes Picasso or not, all right? Agreed. You'll see, everything will be fine on the night. Keep the tone lofty, shove in a few "albeits", "explicates" and "assume responsibility for our acts". Yes, and also make a list of other suitable topics which will permit displays of culture and wit. Deep thoughts, but keep 'em light. That's the ticket, make him laugh, but don't lower the tone. If he laughs, it's the friendship stakes! Because if he laughs, horizons open up, signed photo and the move up to adviser! Because get this straight: I've no intention of letting my A grow whiskers! Because I'm already starting to feel fed up with being an A when Petresco, for God's sake, has been pitchforked up to adviser! Still, I suppose it's not really surprising, he keeps a photo of that minister of his, Titulesco, on his desk. It makes you sick. Favouritism, that's what it is. Petresco's a nasty piece of work. Now I've seen just about everything in this dump. Oh yes, old bean, you heard, adviser! And sharp about it! But to pull it off you're going to need to get his respect and his friendship. Objective: earn his respect and friendship. Scribble list of conversational topics on piece of paper you can take a peep at in case mind goes blank. If that happens, a quick peer under the table, all casual-like. Set your mind at rest, old man, not only shall I be brilliant but I'll have Ariane there for back-up, looking stunning and driving him crazy. No, scrub the Maxiton, it can have side-effects, just a little whisky for courage during those first ten minutes. I'll keep the large signed photo here on my desk, it'll be my safe conduct in dealing with VV. Don't talk about promotion over dinner, not even a hint, that'll be a feather in my cap. It's in my interest to act disinterested. But look here, old sport, that's enough chatter for now. Don't let this go any further, but you haven't done a stroke all morning.'

Feeling a twinge of guilt and dreamily twirling his secret teetotum, then playing with his cornelian marbles which went click-click, and beguiling his gloom by banging his stapler in slow motion, none of which gave him any pleasure, for his sloth pained him like a wound, he tried to find excuses for himself. There were no two ways about it, working on Thursdays was enough to give anyone the hump. Because, dammit, Thursday was practically the end of the week, you felt you didn't have a decent run at anything, there was no incentive. Still, he had a good hour still to go and he supposed he ought to do something to earn his pittance, it was a matter of professional conscience. He parked his marbles and the teetotum next to his two magnets (another clandestine possession which gave him hours of harmless fun) and opened the Cameroon file.

'O holy law, which levies universal toil, In this wise are thy ways set,' he intoned, and he unscrewed the cap of his pen.

At that moment the phone rang. He swore crossly and screwed the top back on his pen. God in heaven, there was never any peace in this place! He snatched at the receiver and said his name in an aggressive tone of voice. It was van Vries. 'Yes, sir,' he said meekly, 'I'm on my way.' Damn! There he is, just getting into the swing of it, on the point of setting to with a will, and he gets disturbed! Absolutely no chance of getting on quietly with his work! Really, what a madhouse!

'Stir your stumps! There's no rest for the wicked,' he muttered as he stood up.

What did VV want now, he wondered in the corridor. Was it to be a telling-off? He stopped, unfastened his jacket, and scratched his head. VV must have spotted him sloping off to the cafeteria with Kanakis. Rats to that, he couldn't care less! Wasn't he having dinner with the USG tomorrow night? He did up his jacket again and yanked and tugged it till it was straight. Besides, he was an A now. But standing outside the door of his boss's office he knocked quietly and entered like any B.

'Sit down,' said van Vries, who, after a quick sideways glance in his direction and without raising his head, went on with what he was writing.

It was his usual gambit and it served the multiple purpose of maintaining his authority, satisfying a minor sadistic streak, and making his inferiors pay for the mortifications he suffered at the hands of his superiors. Moreover his risk-free rudeness went some way to compensating him for not having made the Diplomatic. (Now if he had been a diplomat, just think of all the Broglies and Cholmondeleys he could have rubbed shoulders with, easily and naturally, without any effort or strain on his part.) So whenever he summoned one of the members of his section, it was his practice to keep him waiting for periods which varied according to the character or contacts of the person concerned, the pretext more often than not being that he was finishing off a note on the minute-sheet of a file. (Van Vries's notes were greatly admired by his fellow heads of section but made his staff tear their hair. He was a past master of the art of saying nothing. He was pathologically circumspect, and quite capable of stringing together a dozen sentences which seemed pregnant with meaning but, on close examination, meant nothing at all and therefore did not commit him to any point of view. It was this buffoon's very special talent that he could take pages and pages to say nothing.)

On this particular morning he judged it prudent to inflict only a brief wait on this scheming little squirt who had mysteriously wormed his way into the good graces of what he called the 'celestial spheres'. He put down his pen, raised his large, sickly eyes, and aimed a friendly, welcoming smile at the little swine to whom he owed the humiliation of seeing one of his subordinates promoted by direct selection, over his head, without his knowledge, without his even being consulted beforehand, which would have saved face.

'How are you, Deume?'

Adrien replied that he was well and, reassured by this opening salvo, sat back more comfortably in his chair, while at the same moment the door opened admitting a trolley pushed by a tea lady. Van Vries offered him tea, and he said yes please. But this sign of consideration from his boss did not wash away the gloom he felt at the sight of the teapot: heads of section had a right to a pot of tea, whereas other section staff were entitled only to a cup. He made up his mind to raise the matter that same day with Castro and one or two other As. That was the way: a collective note from As to Supplies and Equipment with a view to putting an end to a scandal and being granted teapot privileges. Their teapots needn't be as grand as section heads' teapots, if that was what it took, but teapots they would have, by God! And besides, a collectaneous note would provide opportunities for meeting As he didn't know yet, whom he could then invite home.

The trolley lady reappeared with another cup, poured the tea, and went away. As she left, van Vries, stepping completely out of character, made a humorous remark about her which extracted from his subordinate the obeisance of a gale of laughter. (Adrien Deume often laughed uproariously, for reasons which varied according to the standing of the person he was with. When he was outranked, it was to prove by a show of irrepressible hilarity just how much he'd enjoyed the joke. With his equals, he simply howled!, which was his way of getting himself thought of as a thoroughly good sort, pals with everyone and as frank as he was open. With women, and with his wife in particular, his explosive, hearty laugh was intended to make him look manly, a force of nature.) Having established a cordial atmosphere with his witticism, for anyone who is in receipt of favour must be handled with kid gloves, van Vries swivelled in his chair, put his feet on his desk, and clasped his hands behind his head, striking an attitude he intended as eloquent of the relaxed leader of men but which among themselves his subordinates dubbed his 'Egyptian-dancer pose'.

'I have decided to send you on an official visit,' he began in a lofty tone of voice which reassured him of his existence. (A pause for thought. Should he refer to his conversation with the Under-Secretary-General? Best not, on the whole. If this pipsqueak Deume were to discover that the idea had come from such a height, his head would swell and he'd be more difficult to handle. Besides, it was incumbent upon him to maintain the aura of the section head who made his own decisions. However, just to be on the safe side, for everything gets out sooner or later, he added a minimum of truth:) 'I've had a word with the upper echelons. (Allow a pause to savour the last words which pleased him immensely.) The upper echelons agree. So I'm sending you to Paris and London. Come to think of it, you'd better go to Brussels as well, though Belgian mandates aren't really your province. But the fact that you're Belgian will make it easier for you to establish contact. You'll round off with a detailed study visit to Syria and Palestine, our two most sensitive mandated territories. Your visit must not exceed twelve weeks, unless something unexpected crops up, in which case you will be able to obtain, at the appropriate moment, permission to extend your stay in accordance with the relevant procedures. Officially, your role will be to gather information useful to the section from the relevant ministries in all three capitals and also from the high commissions of Syria and Palestine. At the same time, and this is the unofficial and not least important part of your visit, you will make every effort to meet leading figures in these ministries and high commissions and establish friendly, personal contacts in a mood of trust and cooperation.

Among other matters, you will allude, with all the requisite tact and judgement, to . . .'

Et cetera. Van Vries rambled on vaguely about the political dimension and among other things recommended Deume to avoid offending the legitimate susceptibilities of duly constituted national authorities, to convince them of the sympathetic interest with which the Secretariat of the League followed their tutelary endeavours, which were as generously assumed as they were difficult to execute, and which constituted a major contribution to civilization, and above all to approach all questions with the said authorities in a flexible frame of mind which took account of the political imponderables which were always so crucial.

'Flexibility, my dear Deume, flexibility and still more flexibility.'

After a quarter of an hour, handing over Adrien's travel warrant, van Vries rang down the curtain on what he called his 'commandments' or sometimes even his 'precept', then stood up. With a smile and a cordial handshake, he wished his dear Deume fair winds and a successful outcome, promising himself that one of these fine days he would put a spoke in this young upstart's wheel.

CHAPTER 30

'Sweetie! I'm so glad to have got through to you, I was afraid you might have gone out! Listen darling, something's happened that'll have tremendous repercussions for my career in the service! I've been given a twelve-week official visit! A political tour, calling for tact and judgement! The only fly in the ointment is that I've got to leave tomorrow night! It's short notice, still I didn't dare say anything, it's a golden opportunity from the career point of view. Just think of what an official visit of this calibre will look like on my file, it'll stand me in tremendous stead later on, you do understand that, don't you, but we'll talk about it when I get home. So, anyway, I'm off to Paris tomorrow night, but the train doesn't go till twelve fifty, which means that dinner with S is still on: that's S as in Suzanne, get it? It'll be fine if I leave the Ritz half an hour after midnight, that'll give me heaps of time, it's not far to the station. I've already got my warrant. I've just been down to the Travel Section, they'd already been notified by V . . . , Monsieur van Vries. They're wonderful! First-class sleeper, single of course, already booked! Suite ditto at the George V with bathroom and political, sorry, private toilet. Hotels don't come any better than the George V, it's the tops, super de-luxe, four hundred and nine rooms, I looked it up in the Michelin. And another thing: Monsieur van Vries said I can have the day off tomorrow to get everything ready. Fortunately I've got my packing index, you remember, I showed it to you, my card system for everything I need to take with me according to length of time away. Another good thing is that you don't need special injections for the Middle East. So all I need do is call in at the Palais tomorrow afternoon to pick up my official letters of introduction, signed by Sir John – no less! – and also my Thomas Cook tickets. And *non solum* that, *sed etiam* my letter of credit, which Finance has ordered in a great rush from the Crédit Suisse. Oh and darling, I've something else I must tell you, but I'm going to use nods and winks so try to take the hint. Look, I don't really believe that a certain person would have taken an initiative of this importance off his own bat, whatever he says to the contrary, you see who I'm getting at, starts with one of the last letters in the alphabet. The way I see it, the idea came from way up. Looks to me like the real source of the thing can be traced back to somewhere in the vicinity of Suzanne! Get it? The Suzanne we're having dinner with tomorrow night. But we'll talk about that later. Hey, I'm forgetting the most important bit. Listen, I have an idea we'll be dining in his suite. I'll tell you what makes me say that. I have it on good authority from a well-informed source, beginning with the letter K, whom I swore to secrecy before mentioning tomorrow night's dinner, that he has a full suite at the Ritz, full meaning not just bedroom and bathroom of course but also a sitting-room and a dining-room as well! A dining-room! Just imagine what his weekly bill for that little lot must come to! Moreover, I hear he's got an Annamite servant, nothing to do with the hotel, it'll be his man, his personal valet! I think this valet must have a room in the hotel too, but I wasn't able to find out about that. So, I put these two bits of info – drawing-room and valet – together and I come up with the near certainty that we shall be having dinner in his suite. Anyway, we'll know for sure tomorrow night. But how are you feeling, darling? Good, splendid. Must take care and have an early night so that you're all bright-eyed and bushy-tailed for tomorrow. I say, you wouldn't fancy coming with me on my visit? Paris, London, Brussels! Syria, Palestine, the mysterious Orient! You see, with my living expenses plus my entertainment allowance, we could just about manage it without having to put our hands in our own pocket. No? Oh all right, whatever you say. I would have loved to have you along, of course I would, but it's entirely your decision. Right, I'd better ring off now because I've mounds of work to get through, so I'll stay here for lunch, but I'll get home early so I can make a start with the packing tonight. Monsieur van Vries says it's fine for me to leave a little earlier this afternoon as soon as I've got shot of what I've got left to do. So cheerio, darling, see you soon.'

He replaced the receiver and gave a childish smile. By God, he'd been having nothing but luck of late, the luck of the Irish! He'd been an A for a week, was dining with the USG tomorrow night, after which he was off on an official visit at ten to one in the morning!

'In my first-class sleeper, I take off my dinner-jacket, put it in my trunk carefully so that it doesn't crease, I get into my pyjamas and slip into lovely bed! And a single sleeper too, old sport! I don't have to watch the pennies! I'm one of life's royals!'

He gazed at one of life's royals in his pocket-mirror, made admiring faces at his reflection, told it he was Adrien the Well-Beloved, a real brigand, a success-merchant first class! The only snag was those twelve weeks without her. How could he imagine not seeing her each evening when he got back to his hotel? Three months, still it would go by quickly. Besides, think of the home-coming, she in his arms and him cutting a dash as the negotiator just back from the Middle East, tanned and trailing clouds of glory! In the meantime, on his first night in Paris, which would be the day after tomorrow, in the George V, he'd be tucked up in bed by eight with a detective novel and he'd order himself a feast of a dinner, only things he liked, rich hors-d'œuvre with Vire chitterlings, followed by pig's trotters, stuffed or just simply grilled, grilled was just as good, with puréed potato and a mustard sauce, and a whole heap of other tasty items and a very good wine, he'd have to see their wine list, and to finish off a great big helping of fruit cake, and he'd have it all served in bed, they had specially designed trays, and wouldn't he just relish getting outside that little lot while reading his detective story! The high life! He stood up, spun round twice to get the real feel of his coming tour.

'And now for something to eat. I'm starving. Let's away!'

Out in the corridor, he strode along quickly, his step light with happiness, monarch of all he surveyed. Good God, when one of the top brass made you up to an A by direct selection and to boot invited you to dinner like that without prompting, there was no denying that you had most definitely clicked! Suddenly, in his mind's eye, he had a picture of himself at tomorrow night's sumptuous table sitting on the

USG's left: witty and debonair, smoking a rakish cigarette, admired by his boss, who was amazed by all the things he came out with about Proust and Vermeer. Who knows, the day might come when he'd drop the 'sir' or even call him plain 'Solal', forget the formalities, over brandy and fat cigars. 'Listen, Solal.' Who gave a damn about VV? VV wasn't dining with the USG! And who really gave a damn about all that literary stuff? It was a whole heap smarter being a diplomat in the field who put up at the George V and had his own toilet!

In the canteen, his lips twitching with excitement, he forced himself to be calm as he broke the news that he was going off on an official visit. He shook hands all round. He felt the greatest sympathy for these poor swine who would be staying behind cooped up in their little offices, hunched over their monotonous tasks, while he would know the spangled life of night-sleepers, palaces and five-star blow-outs with VIPs! When questioned, he was discreet with his answers, saying it was just a fact-finding tour, giving no details, but somehow implying that his mission was confidential. When there was no more to be said on the subject, he took a lively interest in the current burning issue, which was: who would replace the Head of the Disarmament Section, who had just been made minister of war back home?

Returning to his office, he lit the expensive cigar which he had bought to celebrate his official visit, inhaled a cloud of victory with an expansive gesture, and decided that he was not in the right frame of mind to deal with an Acknowledgement, which was in any case routine business and beneath the notice of a negotiator. In his position, he could get away with murder! Chewing on his cigar like an authentic man of action, he picked up the Cameroon file and wrote on the minute-sheet inside the front cover: 'Monsieur Le Gandec. For action, please. A.D.' That was the way! Now, what time was it? Twenty to three. Obviously it was still a bit early to leave. But what the hell! He had his bags to pack and, dammit, he was dining tomorrow night with the USG!

'Stir your bones, we're off!'

He locked the drawers of his desk and ensured they were secure by tugging on the handles one after the other, paying special attention to the Lazar House and the Boneyard. When he'd finished, to make sure he'd remember checking everything and thus be free of all worries on that score during the three months of his tour, he declared aloud, to drum it home: 'Locked, checked, rechecked, double-checked, signed, sealed and delivered by the undersigned.' He combed his hair, brushed his suit, and set his felt hat at an angle, for the raffish effect. It was a lovely feeling to be sloping off at quarter to three in the afternoon while all those without benefit of official visit were left like convicts chained to their desks to sweat over their files! He cast a last look over his desk! Hell and damnation, the British Memo!

'I'm sick of the sight of you,' he told it.

What should he do? Pass it on with the other thing to Le Gandec for comments? Hm. That would be taking things a weeny bit far and make himself an enemy. But he certainly wasn't going to sit down and stay shut away indoors lapping up hundreds of pages on a lovely day like this! Without even bothering to sit down, he leaned over the file and wrote on the minute-sheet: 'M. van Vries. I have read this important document with the keenest interest. It is a full and satisfactory statement of the current situation in Palestine. Consequently, I see no reason why it should not be approved in toto by the Permanent Mandates Commission. A.D.'

With an unsavoury word to speed it on its way, he gaily tossed the British Memorandum file into his out-tray and left, free as air, his stout walking-stick under his arm, a man with a mission, his eye alight with self-importance, blissfully happy, aware with every atom of his being that he was on the up and up, that he had the backing of the powers that be, and that he had his feet firmly under the social table, and never dreaming for one moment that he was born to die.

CHAPTER 31

A dumpling with chubby lips, nose like a parrot, and dead eyes, old Madame Ventradour, when shown into the drawing-room by Ariane, who had answered the door to her, flung herself upon her dear Antoinette, embraced her, shook Monsieur Deume's hand limply and young Adrien's firmly: she diagnosed Presence in him. When she was seated, she rearranged the front of her dress with its cameo and whalebone-stiffened bodice, took a moment to recover her breath, apologized for being late, and told of the dreadful happenings which had quite dislocated her day.

First there was her watch, which had suddenly stopped this morning, at ten past nine. That meant she had been forced to fall back on her stand-by, to which she was not used. Then dear Jeanne Replat, who came every Friday unfailingly at eleven on the dot, because before sitting down to table it was their custom to spend at least half an hour together in religious meditation, well, would you believe it, dear Jeanne Replat had arrived late for the very first time in her life, oh it wasn't her fault, but still she was frightfully late, she'd arrived at ten past twelve, which meant that they had not been able to start their meditation until twelve fifteen, which meant it had only lasted ten minutes, which in turn had left her thirsting spiritually and put her entirely out of sorts. And then, of course, instead of sitting down to table at noon as usual, they had not begun lunch until half past twelve, well twenty-eight minutes past to be exact, which had done nothing for the roast potatoes, which were hard and dry. So, instead of going for her nap at one as usual, it had been five and twenty to two before she'd been able to take herself off, which had completely thrown her off course, turned everything upside down, so that she had no idea where she was with her plans, her whole timetable being now in a shambles. Not to mention that her regular baker had not delivered her breadsticks, which always came on Tuesday and Friday mornings, and she'd had to send out for some in a hurry from the nearest bakery, but their breadsticks were distinctly odd and had made her feel quite peculiar. So, after her nap, to get to the bottom of it, she'd gone round to her regular baker's herself to ask what he meant by it, but unfortunately he wasn't there and the girl at the counter couldn't explain, so she had been forced to wait for the baker himself to get back. In the end the whole thing was cleared up, it was the fault of the new delivery-woman, a foreigner, a Frenchwoman who wore lipstick, who had been given a good telling-off there and then, and quite right too.

'Antoinette, do you really forgive me for coming so late?'

'But Emmeline, you weren't late at all, truly you weren't.'

'But I was, dear, I know I was. I got here at twenty to five instead of four o'clock as promised. I failed to keep my word and I feel dreadfully ashamed. But you know, the maid I've got just now, a little chit from Berne, has been leading me a merry dance.'

Listening to Madame Ventradour you got the impression that she was permanently knee-deep in domestic staff who were all midgets, for every maid she had ever employed was invariably described as 'little'. During the time since Madame Deume had met her at the sewing circle, Madame Ventradour had, in succession, gone through a little Spanish girl, a little Italian girl, a little girl from the Vaud, a tiny little thing from Aargau and, the most reprehensible of the whole lot, this little chit from Berne, who was the reason why she was late. When she had run through the chronicle of the little chit's misdemeanours, she produced a smelling-bottle from her reticule and inhaled. Ah, these servants would be the death of her!

'Listen, darling,' said Madame Deume turning nobly towards Adrien, 'dear Emmeline won't mind, I'll tell her about everything that's happened, but I do think that your wife and yourself should really be running along now. You have your packing to finish off and you've both to get changed, you'll just have time. I'll put you fully in the picture, Emmeline dear.'

After kissing Madame Ventradour's hand – he did it to impress her – Adrien said his farewells. He embraced Monsieur Deume, then Madame Deume, who held him lengthily clasped to her flaccid person and begged him to write as often as possible. 'Even if they're short letters, just to let your Mummy know that everything is going well for her Didi.' Ariane took her leave of both the ladies and of old Monsieur Deume, who was overjoyed because he and his daughter-in-law had a secret. Yes! They'd both already said their goodbyes away from prying eyes, just the two of them! And they'd embraced! She'd even given him a photo of herself and said he should keep it safe and not show anyone else! He smiled at the memory of it while Madame Deume, once the young people had gone, explained to dear Emmeline that Adrien had been invited with his wife to a 'grand dinner party' given by an influential person and that afterwards he was going away this very evening because he was being sent 'on a mission of high diplomacy to talk about problems with important people'.

'And now, dear, if you're not too put out by the novelty, we'll go in to table straight away. Oh, I know we've heaps of time, our train doesn't go until seven forty-five, but since you said you were agreeable to high tea I skipped ordinary tea altogether and I must confess that I'm feeling positively faint with hunger. Besides, if we eat early we'll have plenty of time for girl-talk afterwards while Hippolyte is looking after the last-minute arrangements. It's not quite five and our taxi is ordered for seven fifteen. We've got two hours all to ourselves for a good chat.'

'But my car is here, dear, I could get my chauffeur to drive you to the station, it would be no trouble since it's on my way. Except of course that your cases might damage the upholstery, but no matter, I'll not have to mind that. Some day I may even be glad I made the sacrifice, at least I'll try my very best to be.'

'Thank you, dear, thank you from the bottom of my heart, but I should never forgive myself, and besides your motor car is rather old and might not cope with the strain of our combined weights. Which reminds me, Didi's going to buy a new Cadillac when he gets back from his trip. They really are a superb motor. But now, let's sit ourselves down at table. Please excuse the absence of staff, but I did explain how we were fixed, what with poor Martha going off like that, Mariette leaving us in the lurch, and the temporary woman who's filling in only able to come mornings. That's why everything is already out on the table except for the *potage*. So if it's all right with you we'll move to the dining-room. Hippolyte, give dear Emmeline your arm.'

Madame Ventradour sat down cheerfully. She took out her slimming breadsticks, the trusty ones bought from the dependable family baker, put them down on her right, patted them tenderly, gave one of her chubby smiles, and cast her quickly reviving eyes over the delights spread out before her. Madame Deume apologized again, just cold offerings, the best she could manage in the circumstances, but then struck a bantering note as she asked her husband if he'd be the maid. Not needing to be told twice, for he had been thoroughly drilled beforehand, Monsieur Deume sprang into action.

He returned bearing the steaming soup-tureen. He served the *potage*, giving himself a double helping, his eyes wide with anticipation. But, just as he was about to dip his spoon into his *potage*, Madame Ventradour suddenly clapped one hand to her heart and emitted a wail like a mortally wounded bird. The penny dropped immediately and Monsieur Deume bowed his head in shame: how dreadful, he'd almost started without waiting for grace! Dear Emmeline, mettlesome as always, seized dear Antoinette's hand.

'I'm sorry, dear, so sorry, do forgive me if I offended you. I would never dream of forcing you to do anything that upset you!'

'But you know very well, dear, that we always say grace and that it does not upset us in the least. On the contrary, thanks be to God!' said Madame Deume. 'It was just that poor Hippolyte forgot himself momentarily, that's all.'

'You must forgive me, say you forgive me!' said Madame Ventradour turning to Monsieur Deume. 'Forgive me for offending you!'

'No offence taken, weally, Madame.'

'Oh say you forgive me! I was in the wrong, I blame myself! (Her voice grew ravaged, yearning, wanton:) But it's such a great joy for me, you know, a very great joy, oh yes, Lord, to speak with Thee.

(Noticing that she was slipping into her praying mode, she got a grip on herself.) Such a great joy to speak with Him before partaking of what He in His great Goodness has been pleased to set upon my table! Giving thanks is such a comfort,' she said in a damp voice. 'I ask you all to forgive me for having shocked you so!'

'But dear,' said Madame Deume, who considered that Emmeline was taking things rather too far, 'there's absolutely nothing to forgive!'

While Monsieur Deume stared at his now less than flamboyantly steaming *potage,* Madame Ventradour, undaunted in her distress, persisted with her pleasant little game, made further requests for forgiveness, but no she could not! she absolutely could not dispense with grace before a meal! She could not bear to be deprived of His spirit! Oh, forgive, forgive! In her hiccups, she grabbed the startled Monsieur Deume by the arm, closed her eyes, and looked as though she were at her last gasp.

'I feel unwell, forgive me! . . . my smelling-salts! . . . would you? . . . in my reticule . . . it's on the hall table . . . forgive me! . . . a small bottle . . . forgive me! . . . hall table . . . small bottle . . . forgive me! . . . table . . . bottle.'

When she felt she had bottled and tabled for long enough and had taken a good sniff at the said little green bottle, she revived and, like a convalescing angel, aimed a smile at Monsieur Deume, who was staring glumly into his *potage.* ('I wonder if it's the will of God that I seem always to be eating food that's gone cold on account of their pwayers.') Out of courtesy, Madame Deume asked dear Emmeline to say grace. Still husky-voiced, Madame Ventradour said she would do nothing of the kind, that she would surrender that great joy to dear Antoinette, and added that she didn't mind in the least not saying grace. She was the kind of person who, whenever she claimed that she didn't mind in the least, had to be understood as meaning exactly the opposite. She was of course hoping that Madame Deume would return the compliment and let her say grace. But dear Antoinette did not insist, for dear Emmeline went in for interminable graces, the equivalent of sermons, which she used to unload all the doings of her day to an accompaniment of sighs and other plaintive suspirations. So she dipped her nose towards the cream of wheatgerm and closed her eyes. Madame Ventradour followed suit in taking the mystical plunge, while old Monsieur Deume rested his head on both hands so that he could concentrate properly, for he found it difficult to derive any great pleasure from these perpetual communings with the Divinity. ('Nothing wong with it on Sundays, in fact I quite like it, but not thwee times a day!') The unhappy man focused his mind, resisting a strong urge to scratch the back of his neck, and concentrated, but could not quite resist peeping through half-opened fingers at his *potage*, which now had stopped steaming altogether and was surely lukewarm. ('Hang it all, I'm pwetty certain God cares for us without it being necessawy for us to be asking Him to do so all the blessed time, and anyway He's supposed to know evewything, so what's the point of going on at Him explaining things He alweady knows?')

Madame Deume, who knew she was performing in front of a professional, launched into a high-grade prayer, her meatball bobbing up and down as she proceeded. When two minutes were up, Monsieur Deume stealthily slipped his forefinger under his soup-dish to see how hot it was. Madame Ventradour was also tiring quickly, though she was not fully aware of the fact. This ghastly old bigot who was quite capable of praying at you for half an hour always found that other people prayed for far too long. At this point, just as Madame Deume was in the middle of reporting to the Lord on Juliette Scorpème's dreadful problems, Madame Ventradour, who was nothing if not spontaneous, gave a tragic little cry and pressed her hand to her heart. Dear Juliette had problems? And she had heard nothing about them!

'Sorry, dear. Forgive me. Do carry on.'

She closed her eyes again, did her best to listen, but a thought went round and round inside her head: she must not forget to ask exactly what kind of problems Juliette was having. In the end, she managed to shoo away these worldly notions, closed her eyes tighter, and tried to lose herself in the living words of the grace. But she could not help thinking that poor Antoinette did not vary her set expressions over-much. Her orisons lacked what Madame Ventradour liked best: spontaneity, the unexpected, the pungent turn of phrase. Her religious palate had been desensitized and required constant pepper and spice. For example, she bought a new Bible once every five years so she could taste afresh the pleasure of underlining comforting passages, nodding her head in agreement as she went. Truth to tell, the practice of daily observance tried Madame Ventradour's patience rather, though naturally she was not aware of it. But this was why, when confronted by the first sermon of a new entrant to the ministry or a talk given by a Negro evangelist or a lecture delivered by a Hindu prince, she was all ears for that hint of ginger which she needed if she was to believe that religion could thrill.

Madame Deume, suddenly remembering the seven forty-five, moved into a higher gear, briskly thanked the Almighty for having given them this day their daily bread, which in her case was this evening jollied along by caviare, foie gras in aspic, one of Rossi's roast chickens, Russian salad, a selection of cheeses, pastries and fruit. The Almighty does us proud. Sometimes.

'The Gantets must be worth a pretty penny,' said Madame Ventradour.

'I wouldn't say pennies was the right word,' Madame Deume corrected her. 'Two drawing-rooms *en suite*. A littel more chicken? Not even a littel more skin? I think perfectly browned skin is the best part of the animal. Perhaps a littel cheese, then? No? Well let's move straight on to dessert. Hippolyte, you can finish up your meringue and lend a hand, I've got my stiffness. Get a move on, it's six now, you've got just an hour and a quarter to do all your last things. And remember, I won't have that taxi kept waiting. Come along, clear the table and take all the things into the kitchen and put them down tidily so the daily won't find everything in a mess tomorrow morning, whatever would she think? Put the leftovers in the fridge but not the cheese, it ruins it, or else wrap it up in tin-foil first, make sure you close the kitchen shutters properly, all the others are done, and turn off the gas at the main, and then get a move on with my cases, except the one with my dresses of course, I packed that myself seeing as you wouldn't know how, my poor back's still aching. I've laid out all the rest of the things I'm taking with me on the bed and the tables, and you can pack them naicely in my two cases, you're quite good at that, making the most of the space and being careful with anything delicate, and don't forget to fold my tartan travelling-rug properly and put my two umbrellas through the straps. Oh botheration, what with everything I've had to think of I've forgotten to put the dust-sheets over the settee and the armchairs, so you can do it. When you've shut the cases, bring them down yourself, taxi-drivers demand outrageous tips for doing it, and take them outside, it'll save us time. On second thoughts, don't put them outside, best not risk it. Leave them in the hall, just by the door. Now come along, and put a littel vim in it, if you perlease!'

'Do you want me to do the washing-up as well?'

'Yes, but do it last thing and only if there's time, and be careful not to splash your clothes.'

'Did I tell you I've waterpwoofed the luggage labels in case it wains. I waterpwoofed them by wubbing them all over with a candle.'

'That's very clever, I'm sure, but now go, don't just stand there doing nothing, make yourself useful. You can get the table cleared away quickly and give us some peace and quiet, because we want to have a littel chat, just we two ladies. But you can leave the pastries. Dear Emmeline, do help yourself. Another Japanese fancy or a meringue? I shall have a rum baba, I can't resist them.'

While Monsieur Deume was clearing away, the two women smilingly put away an amazing number of cakes while discussing last Sunday's sermon, which had been a two-hander, shared by two preachers. It was a good idea for bringing in the young people, said Madame Deume. After a third chocolate éclair, Madame Ventradour agreed. The notion of sermons given by two ministers was rather bold, but she wasn't against new ideas as long as they were sensible.

When nice Monsieur Deume had gone, bearing his last load of plates and cutlery, the two ladies spoke on a variety of interesting subjects. To begin with there was the matter of that delightful woman who had that delightful house set in those huge and quite delightful grounds. Then there was the ingratitude of the poor who rarely showed their appreciation of all one did for them, always wanting more, and besides had never learned to hold out their hands with any degree of humility. Then they talked of the impertinence of the younger generation of servants, 'They give themselves airs, now-adays they insist on having an afternoon off in addition to the whole of Sunday, though they don't have the same demands on their time as we do, when you think of all the trouble we take to train them, and they're harder and harder to come by, one has such difficulties in getting hold of them, they're not interested in going into service any more, they prefer to work in a factory, they've lost the love-thy-neighbour spirit altogether, because it is my contention that respectable persons who have a spiritual need for servants surely count as neighbours.'

Next Madame Deume spoke glowingly of a Mademoiselle Malassis of Lausanne, 'quite a catch, the parents' apartment has a frontage with fourteen no sixteen windows, and of course not a stain on her character'. Then she evoked the splendours of the Kanakises, the Rassets and of His Excellency the Under-Secretary-General. Upon dear Emmeline's enquiring how the dinner for their gentleman from the League of Nations had gone off, dear Antoinette turned a deaf ear, was sparing with details, and limited her remarks to stating that he was an eminent man and that she had found great pleasure in conversing with him, though she did not mention the fact that the conversation had taken place over the telephone.

Finally they got on to their pet topic of the comings, goings and doings of various queens of whose affairs they kept abreast, from their engagements, outfits and times of rising to even what they had for breakfast, which generally started with grapefruit. They began with Queen Marie-Adelaide, their favourite, whose children were quite delightful. No less delightful was the interest she took in horses and horse-racing, which was so awfully smart. Besides, said Madame Deume as she munched the last of her apple in a gruesome detonation of smug conceit, dear Marie-Adelaide possessed the supreme art of always looking radiant, simple and natural, she had such a winning personality, hadn't she?

'They say she sometimes parts her curtains and watches ordinary people as they pass by in the street, apparently she tries to imagine the lives commoners lead, so as to feel closer to them, for she really does take an interest in simple folk! I think that's so naice, don't you? There's ever such a lervely story that's told about her son George, that's the eldest, he's eight now, gracious how quickly time flies, it seems only yesterday he was in that beautiful cradle of his, with the royal crest on it, well now, littel Prince George, you know him, the one with the curls, he'll be King when he comes of age, she's been Regent of course since the King died, well anyhow they say that littel Prince George was at the station waiting for the train to take him to one of their superb châteaux in the country, he completely forgot who he was and started running up and down the platform like any common boy, now wasn't that lervely? And then he caught sight of the stationmaster with his flag who was about to give the signal for another train which was about to leave, and he went up to him and said: "Perlease may I wave the flag?" He really said "perlease"! Now isn't that naice coming from a littel prince! The stationmaster was quite taken aback, didn't know which way to turn, because he's not allowed in any circumstances to hand over his flag to another person, it's against the rules, but dash it all, he said to himself, he is a prince, so he gave the flag to the littel Prince but apparently the littel Prince didn't know how to wave it properly! It made your heart ache to see it! Everybody had tears in their eyes. Just as lervely is another adventure the littel Prince had. He was coming out of the palace and, seeing as he doesn't miss a thing, it's in the blood, the eye of a born leader as they say, he noticed that the bootlaces of one of the palace guards had come undone, he pointed this out and apparently the guard said to him: "I'm very sorry, Your Royal Highness", that's right because he must be addressed as Your Royal Highness even though he's only eight, "I'm very sorry, Your Royal Highness, but I'm not allowed to bend down, I haven't been given permission, I must stand to attention all the time!" Well, it seems the Prince bent down, got on his knees, and laced up that private's boots with his very own hands! You have to have royal blood to behave with such simplicity! Quite wonderful! Because he could easily have said: "I'm a prince and I order you to bend down!" It seems Marie-Adelaide absolutely forbids people to cheer the littel Prince and Princess as they drive through the streets in their carriage. But I will say that unaffected she may be, but she has her dignity! Apparently a high-ranking aristocrat once said "your father" to her, to which she replied simply: "You mean His Majesty the King!" The aristocrat didn't know where to put himself! Still, I think he got what was coming to him, don't you? I'd even go so far as to say that I think she should have turned her back and ignored him and left him to stew! Emmeline,

I've just thought of something. Did you read the piece about littel Laurette in yesterday's paper?'

'No, dear. What did it say?'

'I absolutely must tell you all about it, a lervely story. Well now, she's a littel girl, just twelve years old, and her father's a plain, honest mason, and yet she has such sensitivity of feeling, as you'll see. Now when the King of Greece and his gracious Queen landed in Geneva in their superb aeroplane, there standing in the front row of the important dignitaries who had turned out to give them a right royal welcome was littel Laurette wearing a simple dress and holding a bouquet of roses in her hand! Now I'll tell you how it came about that she was given such a high honour. Littel Laurette, who of course positively dotes on the young Queen of Greece, was so happy when she heard that a young prince had been born who would continue the dynasty, she was so overjoyed that she plucked up the courage to write to Her Majesty saying ever so sweetly how happy she was and how much she admired her! Whereupon Her Majesty promised littel Laurette that she would see her for sure when she came to Switzerland! And that's how littel Laurette had the honour of giving flowers to a queen! Isn't that quite lervely? That littel girl might be from a humble home but she has a fine soul! And she'll grow up to be a fine person too! And what a memory for her to treasure for the rest of her life, to have been kissed by a queen!'

After this the two ladies aired their views on the romance between Edward VIII and Mrs Simpson. It was odious, a commoner setting her cap at the throne! exclaimed Madame Deume. She should know her place and stay in it! If a princess became a queen, that was only right and proper, she was of blood royal, it was the prerogative of rank, but for a person of the middle class to ... er ... to, well, the barefaced nerve! And what was one supposed to think of a king who let himself be trapped? The poor Queen Mother must have really been through the mill, and she so very proper, such a noble heart! Oh the tears she must have shed in secret! And what of poor Princess Eulalie with her democratic principles who had married a commoner? She wouldn't be happy for long, oh no, it was quite unthinkable! A princess could not possibly be happy with someone who was not of royal blood! An interior decorator too, it was appalling! Someone who had mixed with artists and other such bohemian riff-raff! Really, what on earth was the matter with all these princesses to make them so keen to marry commoners? Couldn't they see that their behaviour was a betrayal of dynasty, and a betrayal of the people too, which was to say of all the subjects in the realm? Their duty was to keep their place, stay in the rank where God had set them! Really, she preferred not to think about these ill-advised marriages, it was too painful. And so, turning to a more comforting topic, she asked dear Emmeline if she had happened to see the article about the wonderful gesture made by a princess who was next in line to a throne?

'You didn't? Then I'll have to tell you all about it, because it's too too sweet. Well now, Princess Mathilda, she's the one who's next in line to the throne, was in the aeroplane that was taking her to the United States, or was it Canada, I can't remember which, anyhow she was flying off on a state visit. As was only right and proper, a special cabin had been fitted out for her, no expense spared, it had a real bed, it was a proper bedroom in fact, with adjoining private bathroom of course. Well, anyhow, all of a sudden she comes out of her de-luxe cabin, calls to the air-hostess who of course had been assigned to wait exclusively on Her Royal Highness, and says to her: "Would you like me to show you my gowns and my jewels?" Naturally the air-hostess said yes and stepped ever so shyly into the de-luxe cabin, crimson with excitement and delight! So Her Royal Highness showed her all her evening gowns embroidered with precious stones, her ropes of pearls, her diamond necklaces, and her magnificent emerald diadem which of course has been in the royal family for generations, showed her the whole lot, simply, without affectation, woman to woman. By the finish, apparently, the air-hostess was positively sobbing with gratitude. I must say that as I read the article I had tears in my eyes myself. I think it's so beautiful! A royal princess showing all her marvellous things to that poor girl, not much better than a maid really, who'd never seen anything like it, but she'll always be able to say that for once in her life, if only for just a few moments, she knew the joy of being surrounded by all the trappings of high society, taste and wealth! Oh, it's wonderful! Only a person who is a princess and next in line to a throne could ever imagine doing anything so spiritually beautiful! Now that truly is what loving your neighbour means!'

She would have continued with her eulogy of princessly souls and hearts next in line to thrones had not Monsieur Deume appeared, panting with the effort of lugging heavy suitcases down the stairs, and announced that the taxi had arrived.

CHAPTER 32

Entering her room after doing up his new dinner-jacket, he found her standing in front of her long swing-mirror looking ravishing in her evening gown. He gave a jokey bow.

'I prostrate myself at your feet, noble lady. Right then, everything's all in order. My bags have been booked on to the twelve fifty. Don't you think it was clever of me to go down to the station? Now I can be easy in my mind. I wouldn't have fancied checking them in at the last moment. The man in the luggage office tried to make difficulties, said I was too early and so on. I said League of Nations, and that shut him up. They didn't open anything in customs, I just showed them my official identity card: stopped them dead in their tracks. Oh, I forgot to tell you. I've insured my luggage. I think I did right. After all, two francs per thousand isn't exactly going to break the bank. Actually, it came to fifteen francs all told, but now I can be easy in my mind. I hung on to the taxi, of course, it's waiting downstairs, I told the driver we'd be off directly. Oddly enough, it's the same driver who came for Mummy and Dada. It's a fact. Just as I was coming out of the station they were getting out of their taxi, which I of course commandeered, very fortunate really, because there weren't any others about, and the same porter who had carried my luggage took theirs too! Terrific coincidence, really! But look here, darling, I'm not too happy that after tonight you'll be here in the house all by yourself for months. There'll be nobody except for the daily woman, and she'll only be coming in mornings. What worries me most, though, is the night-time. Darling, tell me you'll take good care to see that the shutters are properly secured at night, you really will, won't you? And bolt the front door as well as locking it? Say you really promise!'

'Yes, I promise.' (Really, she murmured to herself.)

'I say, it's twenty-five to eight already! Still, we're not far behind schedule really. Shall we go? Better to be early than late. If we are a bit early we can always hang about in the lobby for a few minutes. Oh, you won't forget your new cigarette-case, will you? It's jolly nice, isn't it? Solid gold, you know, the best they had in the shop. Happy with it?'

'Yes, very happy, thanks,' she said, arranging a lock of hair over her forehead.

'Shall we go down, then?'

'Yes, just a moment,' she said, still staring at herself in the mirror.

'You are quite perfect,' he said, in the hope of cutting this last-minute inspection short. 'To my mind, the only thing that wouldn't come amiss would be a little wipe of lipstick.'

'Don't like lipstick,' she said without turning round. 'I never use it.'

'But couldn't you just this once, darling? I mean, we are going out. Just a touch?'

'Anyway, I haven't got any.'

'I thought of that, darling. I bought you a selection so you could choose the one you liked best. Here.'

'No thank you. This dress is too tight on the hips.'

'Nonsense, darling.'

'Besides, it's a ball-gown. It's not right for a dinner party.'

'That doesn't matter, it looks really nice. You've never worn it before. Such a shame, it suits you to a T.'

'It makes me feel uncomfortable.'

'In what way?'

'The neck's too low. It's indecent.'

'Absolute rot, take it from me, your neckline is no lower than the ones they have on other low-necked dresses, it's very, er, dressy, that's all.'

'Very well, I'll keep it on and look indecent, since that is your command.'

'I think you look terrific in that dress,' he said, to jolly her along.

She did not hear, for she was busy running through the silent routine of feminine artifice in her mirror, taking a few steps back, a few steps forward, pointlessly smoothing her smooth hips with her hands, sticking out one shoe, hitching up the hem of her skirt to see, with eyebrows knit and lips pursed, if it might have been an idea, if it might have been better to have had it not quite so long, the silent, frowning answer being all things considered no, the length was exactly right the way it was. He noticed that her legs were bare, but thought it wisest to say nothing about this. Top of the agenda was not to get to the Ritz late. Anyway, her legs were so smooth that his boss wouldn't notice. In any case, she looked stunning in that dress and, the main thing, was ready to leave. A new turn of phrase came into his mind, and he made immediate use of it.

'You look as pretty as a princess, you know.'

'My breasts are half bare,' she said, still with her back to him but looking directly at her husband in the mirror. 'Only the nipples are hidden. Doesn't that bother you?'

'But darling, they're not half bare. It's more like a third.'

'If I lean forward, it's half.'

'Then don't lean forward. Anyway, plunging necklines are considered perfectly suitable for evening wear.'

'And would you mind if it was considered perfectly suitable to show the whole lot?' she asked, and in the mirror she gave him another direct, masculine look.

'What on earth are you getting at, for goodness sake?'

'The truth. Do you want me to make them pop out when I meet this man?'

'Ariane!' he exclaimed, appalled. 'Why are you saying such horrible things?'

'Very well, I'll only show him the top half,' she said coolly. 'The bit that's suitable and seemly.'

There was a silence and he looked at the carpet. Why did she go on looking, staring, glaring at him like this? For God's sake, at the smartest balls the most fashionable women wore low necklines. So what? The best plan would be to change the subject, especially since it was now seven forty-two.

'Shall we go, darling? We've just enough time.'

'I'll go, and I'll bring my half-moons with me.'

'Look, you will be nice to him?' he asked, after forcing a little cough.

'What am I supposed to do for him?'

'Just be a little bit nice, that's all, join in the conversation, be pleasant.'

'It's no good, I've made up my mind. I shan't be coming,' she said with a smile to her mirror.

She turned round quickly. Her dress flared. He stared at her open-mouthed and he felt the flesh on his cheek crawl. Two thousand francs, two thousand francs for the cigarette-case, and this was the thanks he got!

'But why, in hell's name? Why?'

'Because I don't feel like being just a little bit nice.'

'Darling, I beg you! Look, don't spoil this dinner party for me! What sort of fool will I look like if I turn up by myself? Darling, my whole career is on the line here! It's now fourteen minutes to eight, you can't do this to me at the last minute! For heaven's sake, have pity! See some sense!'

She looked at him, at his wispy beard, at the dinner-jacket which fitted too well, as he begged and pleaded with a hint of a sob, probably manufactured, in his voice, wringing his hands, his lower lip pendulous and trembling, just like a baby about to burst into tears.

'I won't go,' she repeated, and with the same twirling flare of her dress she turned back to her mirror. 'Come along, look sharp, otherwise you'll be late and he'll tell you off. Come on, go and make some more personal contacts, get yourself another pat on the back, a nice hefty pat, that's how you like them isn't it, a real personal contact! Go on, tell him you're stuck at the top of your grade! Give him your doe-eyed look!'

'You're horrible, absolutely horrible!' he shouted, and he saw her watching him in the mirror, eyes gleaming with savage glee. 'Damn you!' he shouted and left, slamming the door behind him.

She smiled at her reflection and stepped back so that she could see herself full-length. The neck of her dress was so daringly low that waggling her shoulders to the right and then to the left was enough to make her breasts spill out, one after the other. Through half-closed eyes she examined them: they were resolute and primed.

'In doe-eyed ecstasy,' she murmured.

CHAPTER 33

'It's nice like this stretched out on the floor no cushion under my head it relaxes me better than bed, can't really imagine dying, funny me being so fond of lying on the floor staring up at the ceiling with my mouth open and then letting my crazy thoughts wander well pretending to, I love it, just as the rising tide seeps into the dry crumbly sand and then recedes leaving it grey and heavy and damp, so a tide of tears rises inside me and floods into my eyes and makes them all red and then the tide recedes sinks down inside me leaving my heart as heavy as the wet sand, that's not bad I must write it down, I think it would be really smart to have a white crêpe evening dress with cape effect framing a deep neckline and the hem arranged in such a way that the whole thing swings and sways with me as I walk, delicious sleeping together with our arms around each other, I'll never stop loving my Varvara if you've loved someone you'll go on loving them forever *semel semper*, oh yes clever-clogs I know a bit of Latin I doubt if you can say as much you probably know Arabic and Turkish, I really let him have it, he begged and begged the poor boy was almost in tears I was quite beastly all the things I said the pat on the back the personal contacts, I can't very well let him go away for three months remembering me sneering at him, I'll have to put it right, so best go to this Ritz thing since he so set his heart on it he'll be so pleased to see me when I get there I'll say my migraine's better I'll be nice to him I'll sit down beside him, I'll be polite to the man for Adrien's sake darling do you really promise terrific coincidence really, according to old Ventradour God is an ever-present help to her in all things so why doesn't He send her a better class of maid why does He go on bombarding her with cheeky little chits actually she thanks God for the nice things He does for her and is too polite to mention any of the unpleasant things from which He fails to preserve her in His capricious unfathomable ways, instead of saying seeing that Antoinette always says seeing as how for which I would gladly throttle her, yes with that foul man I'll be polite on account of Adrien his career and the rest of it, it will be a sacrifice a chance to redeem myself, polite but frosty, the brute will understand that Adrien was my only reason for coming, I'll go with him to the station, I'll say thank you for the gold cigarette-case it's far too heavy but naturally not a word on that score kiss him several times on the platform just before he gets on to the train, stay on the platform until the train starts moving, smile and wave my hand, in short do the necessary so that he goes away bearing fond memories, right then go and have a bath but I'm so comfy like this on the floor not dressed talking to myself I love talking to myself, in any case I larrupped horsewhipped him all over his bare back it bleeds it raises welts good thing whack I didn't say anything about the brute otherwise awful wedded husband would have been forced to challenge brute to duel result poor Didi dead, that wouldn't have been fair at all, turn up with just a dab of powder and nothing else, how can they bear to put red varnish on their nails it's disgusting, say headache's better but be frosty to the man, what a moron dressing up in that stupid disguise, hey don't put your legs in the air like that, it's not ladylike, poor sweet he'd have been devastated if he'd had to go off on his travels without seeing his wifey again the younger Madame Deume, Madame Deume junior, I don't even know my registers, that's what they say for it in Switzerland, I talk Swiss sometimes, in France they say multiplication tables which is better, I know the easy ones like twice three and three times four, I have these crazy urges to say rude words it's because I was brought up properly, the ones I don't know are the horrible ones seven eights and nine sevens, with them I have to do adding up, when I get there dinner will be over, because I refuse to be the guest of Ali Rum Baba out of the question, it's enough that I should turn up for the sake of my awful wedded to make amends, I'm glad I nearly knocked his eye out, old Mother Deume trying to make an impression at the Kanakises' dinner party but unable to think of anything to say to the said Kanakises who were so snooty and clubby and the literary conversation was entirely over her head too, so bending over her plate she pecked away with a smile on her face smiling with a knowing look on her face a look that implied she was thinking of something highly amusing, a knowing delicate little smile suggesting the height of sophistication, the smile of a countess lost in her own thoughts which were so fascinating so perky-bright that she had no time for other people's chatter, suggesting the height of self-sufficiency, but in reality utterly humiliated and suffering torments at the thought of not being able to contribute to the lively conversation which was in fact quite quite inane, her breasts must be awful can't stop thinking about them, always go for soft materials plain colours not patterns, stick to black anthracite grey white avoid brown and beige at all costs, come along have a quick bath then get ready look my best so that he, to please him, so that he carries away a pleasant memory of me on his train, poor boy he deserves it, quick your bath, the thoroughbred mares beloved of the winds in remotest Scythia are not more sad or more untamed than you on evenings when northerly breezes die away, I love those words, yes leave him with a pleasant memory, a bath with sweet-smelling bath salts, the white silk dress, do hair carefully, and then ring for taxi, Aix-en-Provence remember the hot-water springs with mossy green beards, the caryatids, the carved oak doors, the little grinning figures on the roofs at the ends of the fluted bronze gutterings, me and Éliane when we were little we dug a hole in Tantlérie's garden, a secret hidey-hole, we wrote down the instructions showing its location in a Bible, so many centimetres longitude north of the japonica, in it we put bits of glass chocolate paper an old key photos of both of us some coins a peacock feather what we called 'sea-biscuits' in case of famine a chocolate bear a curtain ring we said was a wedding ring for when I grew up, and when we'd filled the hole in we quarrelled and I hit Éliane and then we made up we kissed and made up and we used the blood from her nose to write a tragic letter about the sinking of the three-masted schooner *The Shark*, we collected the drips from her nose in a spoon then we dipped a pen in it and took turns to write, I wrote I'll dig up the buried treasure on our desert island the day I get married and I'll put the ring on my loving husband's finger, and then we wrote resolutions, we wrote the words backwards so that they were secret, resolutions about going in for spiritual uplift, that was an expression we knew because Tantlérie used it a lot, and afterwards we reopened the hidey-hole to put the tragic letter in, I'm bored, once upon a time in Arabia there was once really it's true there was a great big huge elephant and it's quite true a tiny little midget ant, and Nastrine the Ant said hello great big huge elephant and the elephant who had a short tail and big ears William I think he was called and the elephant said O tiny little weary midget climb up on my back I won't get tired honest and I'll carry you home and Nastrine said oh thank you nice great big huge elephant you are very kind you know and then the ant said oh I haven't a clue what the ant said down with Jews perhaps oh the whip lashing and the back flinching, the head sinking into shoulders and the nails sinking into palms, the blood dripping thickly and the hate feeding on itself which might be love and the foot that loses its footing and the endless falling falling whatever am I saying now for that bath don't go in a hat wear the white dress white goddess sort of yes it's long and full and long and full is altogether much more elegant than tight and narrow also much more stylish neckline not too low quite severe really except for the bare arms of course my thrilling golden arms and my very long white gloves setting off the gold of my arms delicious white satin slippers in a word tasteful and perfect shan't wear tight and narrow ever again only long and full in satin or crêpe oh the poor boy will be so pleased to see me again I was utterly bitchy to him bitchy bitchy very witchy but stay by his side until his train goes blow him kisses with my hand as the train starts good-evening how are you I just wanted to say hello I haven't got much time I've got to join my husband at a do given by some horrible man from the L of N come come you're not being very sensible.'

CHAPTER 34

'Two hundred francs a day if it's a penny, maybe more, I mean to say an entire suite, with de-luxe drawing-room and, so Kanakis reckons, dining-room as well, but that can't be right, he just wanted to give the impression he was in the know, but even so a whole suite of rooms, and in a five-star hotel, no it must add up to more than two hundred a day plus the extras which don't come cheap in five-star hotels breakfast meals in the restaurant laundry barber taxes tips, and on top of that wages and expenses for the personal valet and the chauffeur, the Annamite valet kitted out with a white linen jacket smart as smart the whole lot must cost at least, but we can work that out later when there's more time, of course he can afford to do himself proud on the money he gets, I mean take the restaurant bill he just signed without even looking at it, and the hundred-dollar note he gave the head waiter as a tip can you credit it, all in all dinner went off rather well, it was downstairs in the restaurant, still perhaps Kanakis is right perhaps there is a dining-room too but in that case why the restaurant, probably more practical for two the service is quicker, perhaps he only uses the dining-room for official dinners, anyhow the dinner went off a treat he took it well when I spun that tale about a headache and how sorry she was she couldn't make it, he might have been cross but no, just a smile as he looked at me and he said 'Of course', but what did he really mean by that, still the whole thing couldn't have gone better, really super-duper dinner-do, though I wasn't in the right frame of mind to make the most of it, I must say he turned on the charm for me, even the business of leaving me here by myself while he's changing into his dressing-gown, you might say that was a bit odd and you'd be right, but it was also considerate very decent of him treating me like a friend, and downstairs just now he couldn't have been more attentive did I like this and did I prefer that, marvellous dinner too, the *cuisine* couldn't have been more *haute*, but when we play the return fixture he won't regret it, when I get back from my official visit we'll lay on a slap-up do for him, we can think about it we've plenty of time for that, meanwhile I've eaten too much, it was his fault, he ordered half the menu and it was really all just for me, he hardly touched a thing, just smoked and drank champagne, but I was obliged to stuff myself, could hardly do otherwise, just to be polite.'

He was having trouble digesting all that rich food: caviare, then lobster au gratin, then quail conserve, then venison as well, the works. Basically, the reason he had eaten so much was the silence. At least if she'd been there the table talk would have been easier. Moreover, he had bolted his food: he put that down to nervousness. Right, he'd have to get busy with the bicarb when he got to his sleeper, there was some in the case he'd packed with the things he needed on the journey, ask the guard for a small bottle of Vichy. He really oughtn't to have called her horrible and said damn you. That was going too far. She was a woman and women get moody, probably she was about to be off colour, or, in her words, to get the dragon. Heigh-ho, he would write her a nice letter from Paris. Yes, it was that awful silence in the restaurant, but ever since we came upstairs the USG has been extremely kind, couldn't have chatted more amicably. So very nice of him to talk about the place where he was born. Odd idea, though, being born on Cephalonia.

'But the best bit of all, old bean, was when he said the two of us might go there together some day.'

How was that for chalking up a personal contact! If they ever made the trip together, that would be the time to bring up the reorganization of the section, tell him about everything that didn't work, especially the documentation side. The thing would be a lot easier when the two of them were stretched out side by side on the sand facing the sea. Lying there on the sand, he'd feel free to speak his mind, say frankly what he thought of VV, his lack of dynamism, he'd be able to voice all his criticisms while he and his boss were getting a tan in the sun like the best of pals. Atmosphere of intimacy and trust, administrative shop not on the agenda. Keep it on the personal level, see. Golly, he's certainly taking his time putting his dressing-gown on, though. Soon as he gets back, be self-assured, sparkle like billy-oh. But careful, go easy on Picasso, test the waters first, start by giving pros and cons then proceed according to the chief's reactions. If necessary, forget the three sentences from the article. But there was no denying it, it was really nice of the chief to say they'd go swimming together in Cephalonia. What a marvellous thought, a super-chief and a mere A swimming together in the sea, shouting to each other, joking! And then stretched out on the sand, chummy as anything, chatting and letting the sand run through their fingers.

'Following which, old bean, bounced up to adviser! I tell you, it's in the bag!'

He got to his feet, impressed by the sumptuous heavy black silk dressing-gown which gaped over a bare chest and reached down to a pair of bare feet encased in slippers. At a gesture from Solal, he sat down again in his armchair, minding his Ps and Qs, captivated, sucking saliva with faint, deferential suspirations, crossing his legs and then uncrossing them while the Annamite valet, smiling brownly, served coffee and cognac. To fill the silence, the young official picked up his cup and sipped his coffee fastidiously, taking care not to slurp the contents. He accepted a silently proffered cigarette, lit it with trembling hands, took several pulls on it while shooting covert glances from time to time at his host, who was fiddling with a string of amber beads. What on earth was going on? Why wasn't he saying anything? So pleasant only a few moments ago and now not a dicky-bird.

Paralysed by the silence, proof horrible and positive that his boss was bored with him, Adrien Deume could think of nothing to say. His face froze into a fixed smile, the refuge and recourse of the weak who try to please and find favour, a continuous, feminine smile of which he was quite unconscious, a smile which was at once a sign of submission, a display of ready-and-willingness and an indication of the pleasure he took in the company, even the silent company, of his superior. He smiled and was unhappy. To exorcise the silence and fill it, or to appear natural and at ease, or to give himself courage and come up with something to say, he downed his cognac in one tragic swallow, Russian-style, which made him cough. O God! What could he talk about? Proust was off, he'd talked about him downstairs over dinner. Ditto Mozart and Vermeer. He daren't bring up Picasso, too risky. He could not for the life of him remember any of the other conversational topics he'd carefully written down, duly numbered, on his scrap of paper. His face assumed a mildly constipated expression as he tried to activate his memory, but it was no use. Moving one hand to his hip, he could feel the life-saving sheet of paper, he felt it there, rustlingly alive in the pocket of his dinner-jacket, but how could he get it out without being seen? Say he wanted to wash his hands and take a quick peep at it while he was out of the room? No, too embarrassing, and it would only make him look boorish. The silence was now terrifying, and he felt it was all his fault. He inspected the bottom of his empty glass with absorbed interest, screwed up his courage, and looked up timidly at his superior.

'I believe you write. I'd like to hear about it,' said Solal.

'I scribble a little,' Adrien told him with a mincing smile, overwhelmed by such flattering attention and with eyes suddenly moist with gratitude. 'I mean, I do as much as my professional duties leave time for. So far all I've perpetrated (he gave a delicate little smile) are a handful of poems, in my spare time, of course. A slim volume, published last year, in a limited edition for private circulation only. Just for my own amusement and, I hope, for the amusement of a few friends. Poems with a vocation to express rather than to communicate. (Pleased by this noble turn of phrase, he sucked in another gobbet of refined spittle and then decided to strike a great blow.) I'd be delighted if you would allow me to offer you a copy, with my compliments, imperial format, on Japanese paper. (Encouraged by a nod of acquiescence, he resolved to press home his advantage and strike another great blow while the iron was hot.) But I'm seriously thinking of writing a novel. In my spare time, of course. It will be unique of its kind, I think, it won't have a plot and, in a way, it won't have any characters either. I absolutely reject all traditional forms of fiction,' he concluded, suddenly throwing caution to the winds under the impetus of the cognac, and he poked out his tapered tongue and then put it away again.

There was a silence and the poor, foolhardy wretch sensed that his chief had not been impressed by this outline of his novel. He grabbed his glass, raised it to his lips, realized it was empty, and put it down again on the table.

'Actually, I haven't finalized anything in my mind. I might still come round to a more classic form. In point of fact I'm thinking of a novel about Don Juan, a character who has haunted me for ages, obsesses me, and has to some extent taken me over. (A glance, just testing the water, at the impassive Solal.) But ultimately what really interests me,' he smiled timidly, 'is my work in the Mandates Section, which I find absolutely absorbing.'

'A novel about Don Juan. Sounds very interesting, Adrien.'

The young official gave a start. His Christian name! This time, he'd made it! Personal contacts!

'I've been turning it over in my mind. I've made quite a lot of notes,' the future novelist said eagerly, transported by enthusiasm for the greatness of his subject which had suddenly been revealed to him.

Yes, he'd made it! He could already see the signed photo. Don't speak, wait for him to ask questions. The chief was thinking about Don Juan; he sensed he was about to ask him something. Not an adviser straight off, of course. Maybe next year. Meanwhile get stuck into *Don Juan* since the chief was so interested. When he got back from his official visit, draft a couple of chapters and canvas his opinion. That would provide opportunities for friendly chats, perhaps even discussions where each of them defended his point of view. 'Oh no, Adrien, that won't do, I don't agree, it doesn't fit in with the Don's character.' Now that's what you called a personal contact! Well now, he'd steered a canny course after all.

'Tell me about what happens in this *Don Juan* of yours,' Solal said, breaking the silence and taking a cigarette, which Adrien, lighter levelled, immediately lit for him. 'What does he do in your novel?'

'He seduces,' said Adrien cleverly, and he gave himself a pat on the back for coming up with such a thumping answer. (But was it too brief? Add a few details about Don Juan's character? Make him elegant, witty, cynical? But perhaps that didn't fit in with the USG's idea of Don Juan. Had his answer been thought a smidgen offhand?) 'Of course, sir, if there's any advice you could give me, I'd be most awfully grateful. For example, some aspect of his character which you see as being central?'

Solal smiled at this creeping crawler who was tying himself in knots to impress. Very well, toss him a small bone.

'Have you built in a measure of primordial contempt?'

'Well, er, no, not as such,' said Adrien. (He was about to ask: 'What on earth is primordial contempt exactly?' but this question seemed far too casual, so he opted for a wording that was less direct.) 'When you say primordial contempt, what quite do you have in mind?' he said unctuously, so as to avoid any possible hint of disrespect.

'Don Juan has very little regard for any of the virtuous women he meets,' began Solal.

He stopped and sharpened his nose with thumb and forefinger while Adrien adopted the all-eared pose of eager listener. With his neck craned forward the better to catch the pearls about to fall, his expression made keener by half-closed eyes designed to give him that air of hanging-on-your-every-last-word concentration, his chin cupped in his right hand for the contemplative look, his legs intellectu-ally crossed, his face lined by attentiveness as though by age, the deferential curve to his backside running all the way down to the tips of his toes, everything about his appearance bore witness to intense mental application, fervent expectancy, an understanding spirit only too anxious to be convinced and all too ready to agree, plus the anticipated thrill of an intellectual feast, though not forgetting loyal devotion to the cause of Administration.

'Very little regard,' Solal resumed, 'because he knows that whenever he decides, alas, every woman, however proper and socially respect-able, is his for the bedding and will arch her back for him and wriggle like a fish. And why does he know this?' he asked Adrien, who adopted a knowing air of guile but took good care to say nothing. 'But that's enough of that. It's too appalling, and anyway it's not worth discussing.'

Adrien cleared his throat several times to banish a feeling of discomfiture. Women arching their backs and wriggling like fish! The chief was coming it a bit strong. Probably the champagne.

'Very interesting,' he said at length, doing his best to inject a fervent gleam into his eye. 'Very interesting. Very,' he added, for he found it impossible to think of a more specific comment. 'I'm quite sure I'll find your insights which you have been kind enough to let me have extremely valuable.'

He almost added that he was most grateful to receive them, a turn of phrase engrained in his mind. He invariably used it to acknowledge receipt of statistics forwarded from various colonial offices, which in his draft replies he always described as very interesting before immediately and definitively consigning them to his little Boneyard, for these statistics were normally inaccurate and contained many errors of addition.

'Not worth discussing,' repeated Solal. 'Anyway, what does he want with these women? Their breasts? That's a joke! What does he want with breasts that invariably droop and sag? In the papers, you see hundreds of adverts for anti-droop contrivances, mammary-pouches, or whatever they're called!'

'Brassières, sir.'

'They all wear them! It's a confidence trick! What's your view, Adrien?'

'Well, er, I mean to say . . .'

'That's exactly what I think,' said Solal. 'And furthermore they're so pathetic with their silly little hats, can't be right in the head, and all that mincing and waggling their hips on their high heels, and their behinds sticking out in those tight-fitting skirts, and how they come to life when they're talking to each other about clothes! "Can you believe it, she went and had a suit made by a dressmaker. My dear, it's ghastly, I blushed for her! A suit's a very tricky thing, especially the jacket, men are much better at it, really. A dressmaker won't get the cut right, she'll stick a haystack of pins everywhere!" And if you're rash enough to offer the tiniest criticism of her new dress she turns very nasty, you become her enemy, she looks at you with hate in her eyes, or else you've brought on her neurasthenia and she feels persecuted and wants to die! So no more women! I've done with them! And there again, you're forced to go on lying beside them when what Michael calls the usual thing is over, and they coo in that lovey-dovey way and they kiss your shoulder, they always do that, afterwards, it's a sort of mania they have, and they expect treats as a reward, for you're expected to say nice things to show your gratitude like how positively divine it was. Really, they could at least leave me in peace to purge my shame! So no more women! If I were to have all my teeth out, perhaps they'd leave me alone, and good riddance! But alas, there is no hope for me, she haunts me,' he groaned, and he stretched his arms out. 'Adrien, dear Adrien, stay me with flagons, comfort me with apples: for I am sick of love. No, not sick of love, but she haunts my soul. (Elated by the dear Adrien, which was incontrovertible proof of a truly personal contact, but alarmed by the flagons and apples, the young official essayed a look of understanding and sympathy.) You don't mind my calling you Adrien?'

'Not at all, sir, on the contrary. I . . . er . . .'

'You must not call me "sir", call me "brother"! You and I are brothers-in-man, doomed to die, soon to lie beneath the sod, you and I, docile and parallel!' he proclaimed joyfully. 'Come now, drink this champagne which is as dry as you and as imperial as she! Drink, and I shall tell you how I am haunted by She-Who-Puts-out-Eyes, She-Who-Holds-Me-in-Her-Spell, She-of-the-Long-Starlit-Lashes, cruelly absent Neiraa. Drink!' he ordered Adrien, who did as he was told, choked and spluttered. 'No, dear friend, no, loyal Polonius, it is merely drunk I am with love! With love! And so drunk that I want to take you by your beard and whirl you round and round above my head for the space of an hour, because I love her so much and because I love you so much too! Oh I know I'm not expressing myself well, for I am naturalized since little time! But drunk with love am I,' he said with a distracted smile, 'drunk with love, but the awful part of it, you see, is this: there is a husband, a poor wretch, and if I take her from him he will suffer. But what else can I do? But I must tell you all about her, the charms of her person, her long curved eyelashes, her lonely soliloquies and the Himalayas which are her motherland. I must tell it all to you, it's a physical need, for you alone can understand, and into the arms of the Almighty we commit ourselves! Yes, I shall tell you everything, tell you of the loving that we will share, she and I, but first I must take a bath, I'm hot. Be back soon, good, kind Adrien!'

Left to himself, young Deume gave his schoolboy snigger. Chief's completely round the bend. The parallel corpses, the flagons and the apples, that was the champagne talking. What a mishmash! And what was that about She-Who-Puts-out-Eyes? And why Polonius?

'And that business of grabbing me by the beard because he loved me so much! It's a hoot! Tight as a lord! Never mind, he said he loved me, and do you realize what that means? On the personal-contacts front, it's the tops!'

He frowned. The Himalayas which were her motherland? Hang on, yes, this woman was the wife of the Indian delegate! Yes, that's it, of course, she's from Nepal, which is slap-bang in the middle of the Himalayas! Anyway, the name he'd called her by sounded distinctly Indian. Oh yes, the wife of the leader of the delegation! And come to think of it she had heaps of charms to her person, beautiful eyes, long eyelashes, that was her right enough, she was beautiful and she was from Nepal! Well now, was the Indian delegate in for a cuckolding or was he not! Because if it was charm you wanted, the chief had oodles of it, there was no getting away from that! Hard cheese, Indian delegate! But the important thing was that the above-named, Deume Adrien, was now in extraordinarily thick with the USG, thick as thieves, for God's sake! Telling him about his love-life amounted to a cast-iron guarantee of imminent promotion! You alone can understand me! Well, that was a compliment and a half. So, when he got back from his tour, he'd ask him out to dinner in some ultra-smart restaurant, just the two of them, just two pals, no need to have Ariane along, make it a stag affair. We're off! Swedish hors-d'œuvre, smoked salmon, Belon oysters, hot woodcock paté, or else foie gras in pastry, or maybe duck galantine, or perhaps a lobster soufflé, he'd see, but there'd definitely be crêpes Suzette to finish with, plus assorted tales of love-life! And as much dry imperial pink champagne as the chief could drink! Waiter, another magnum! And remember to order the coffee well before the dessert, really good coffee took twenty minutes to make. And when the brandy, Napoleon, the best, was setting the finishing touches to the work begun by the dry imperial, hilarious drollery all round: then would be the time to fly a kite, when he too could slot his Christian name in. Surely he could tell a chap he was on first-name terms with what he really thought about VV's incompetence? His criticisms would be courteous in form but devastating in content. Anyway, VV would be retiring shortly. Say! How about if he slipped in a reference to VV's latest bloomer as soon as the USG had finished going on about his Himalayan beauty? No, too soon. *Chi va piano va sano.* Wait till he got back from his tour. For now, just prepare the ground by attracting maximum goodwill. So when he got back a few moments from now and started going on about the love of his life, listen, act understanding, be the sympathetic friend, encourage him to waffle on, it was child's play, right? But don't smile all the time, he'd gone overboard with the smile in the run-up to the thick-as-thieves turning-point, you blunted the effect if you smiled all the time. Every three or four minutes, just a smallish smile to show he was paying attention, that he was sympathetic, while remaining his own man, an equal. Hello! Quarter to ten! He'd be back soon in his dressing-gown. The dressing-gown was another very good sign: it made the contact decidedly personal.

'Well I never! The Under-Secretary-General about to do the dirty on the leader of the Indian delegation!' he chortled to himself, and from the back of his throat he unleashed one of his silly schoolboy sniggers.

Shortly after this the phone rang, and Solal, arriving at a rate of knots, answered it and said yes, the lady could come up. He replaced the receiver and then he laughed, and he danced, sparkling with joy, he danced with one hand held on his hip and his dressing-gown yawned revealing his nakedness. '*Ay mi paloma,*' he crooned, and then he stopped. Turning, he came up close to the husband, took him by the arm, and kissed him on the shoulder, still sparkling with joy.

''Tis my Himalayan girl,' he said.

CHAPTER 35

'Where's my husband?' she asked the moment she stepped through the door, while he was still greeting her, hand to lips, hand to forehead.

'He's just this instant left for the Palais. I'll explain. Please don't you try to explain anything: I know everything. Oh yes I know: hated the thought of seeing me, came in the end even so, because you didn't want to hurt his feelings, and if you didn't tell him about my unspeakable behaviour your only motive was to avoid a scandal which would damage his career. "You see, sweetie, it all went swimmingly with the chief, he says 'old man', calls me Adrien." That's what he'll say when you're alone together. So make your mind easy. What are you thinking?'

'I'm thinking how odious you are.'

'You're right,' he said with a pleasant smile. 'And now I shall explain. When they told me you were here, your husband offered to leave so I could be alone with my Himalayan beauty. I asked him to stay, but he was determined to be discreet, told me he had some urgent piece of work to finish. I insisted he should stay. However, he said he was very sorry but he was not going to obey my orders. What more could I have done? Nguyen showed him out and you missed seeing him. Since we're alone together, I shall now proceed to seduce you.'

'You're vile.'

'Utterly,' he said with a smile. 'But three hours from now you will be doe-eyed, just as I promised. Oh yes. Seduced. And by the despicable means which all women like and you deserve, you Putter-out-of-Old-Men's-Eyes. The day I came to you as an old man I was ready to whisk you away on the horse I had waiting outside, but tonight I find you unattractive. In fact, now I've got a chance to see that lumpish nose of yours in a good light, I am appalled.'

'Beast!' she said.

'Look, I'll have a little bet with you. If in three hours from now you aren't madly in love with me, I shall appoint your husband head of section. Scout's honour. I swear it on the head of my uncle. Do you accept? If you would prefer to leave now, you are at perfect liberty to do so,' he added after a pause, and he gestured towards the door. 'This way out for noses. I hope yours will get through without too much of a squeeze.'

'Bully,' she snarled, her jaw muscles taut.

'Well? Are you going or do you accept the bet?'

'I accept the bet,' she said, looking him directly in the eye.

'Sure of herself,' he said with a smile. 'But there's one condition. From now until one in the morning, you will not speak a word. Agreed?'

'Yes.'

'Word of honour?'

'No need. When I say yes, I mean yes.'

'Ditto when you say no. So, come one in the morning you will be doe-eyed. Come twenty to two you and I off to station, off our heads, off to sun and sea. What are you thinking? This was coming, you know, it had to be. Come on, say what you're thinking. Make it quick, while you've still got time. For at one in the morning you will look at me with ecstasy in your eyes. Come along, out with it.'

'Filthy Jew!' she said, and she gave him a quick, mean look, like a bad-tempered little girl.

'I thank you in the name of your Jesus, who was circumcised when he was one week old. Not that all that matters. We scorn your scorn. Blessed art Thou, Eternal, our God, Who chose us from all peoples and exalted us among all nations. So say we on the eve of our Passover. Shocked by the dressing-gown? Usually they don't mind my dressing-gowns. Women are much more tolerant than men because they're less conventional, especially the young ones. The other good thing about them is that once they start getting passionate they turn into Jew-lovers. You'll see. I shall only be a moment. Meanwhile, do powder your nose. It shines.'

When he returned, hair untidy, tall and slim in a white silk dinner-jacket, he stood in front of the mirror, knotted the tie which as a Commander of the Order he was entitled to wear, gave himself an approving once-over, then turned to her to see what effect he was producing. As she did not react in any way, he made as if to check a half-smothered yawn and then placed a sheet of paper, folded in two, on a coffee-table.

'Your husband's promotion. You can give it to him if things don't work out as planned. Head of the Disarmament Section. He'll be quite useless in the job, though no more useless than anybody else. My compliments, your nose has stopped shining. I think this dinner-jacket looks well on me, don't you agree? Yes, suits me very well, thank you.'

He picked up a rose, breathed its scent deeply, and then tossed it behind him. Holding a string of sandalwood beads, he strode round the room, then paused in front of the mirror and tapped his chest. The right place was at the angle formed by the base of the sternum and the gap between the third and fourth ribs. But come the moment, quite possible not find right spot with gun-barrel, probably be nervous as he made a start on the preliminaries. So mark the correct site beforehand, have a little blue spot tattooed there. Suddenly the phone. He picked it up.

'Good evening, Adrien. No, you're not disturbing me. Yes, and I shall also need to have your comments. Take your time. No, I told you, you're not disturbing me in the least. I haven't started on the seduction. By the way, don't forget to put Don Juan's primordial contempt in your novel. As I told you, his contempt derives from his certain knowledge that in three days or even three hours, if he so wishes, the proud and proper lady sitting so primly in her armchair will start cooing in that special, moronic fashion and will adopt assorted positions in bed which are hardly compatible with her current dignity. Just a matter of using the right tactics. So he doesn't have a great deal of respect for her to begin with and he finds it ludicrous that she should try to appear so respectable as she sits in her armchair, ridiculous that she should be offended by his dressing-gown, ludicrous and ridiculous because he knows that if he can go to the bother he'll soon have her wriggling like a fish in the usual way, a panting, animal servant of the night, naked and bucking under him, poor Don Juan, now sweetly moaning, now lustily thrusting, and invariably with the whites of her eyes showing, like a saint in ecstasy. Oh, were there a woman who would not succumb to seduction, one who would be mine for fine and noble reasons, I would trail my head in the dust all my days! Hence the primordial contempt, which, however, is maintained only at the cost of ever-open, ever-bleeding regret.

'I feel a strange compulsion to confide in you, my dear Adrien. Oh, to what pretences, to what shams am I driven by other people! For I must live, but not as a blear-eyed, down-at-heel teller of truths! For when you tell the truth, people turn very nasty and they'd have me kicked out if I ever said openly that our work is a farce and our illustrious League a house of clowns. But I need money. Not because I have a cash-box for a heart but because I am absurdly sensitive to the point where I faint in an unheated room and cold water numbs my fingers, even in summer. Besides, I have no wish to put my head on their block. They are without mercy for those who have no money. I know, I've experienced it. But above all Under-Clown-General I remain so that I do not become a poor man, with a poor man's soul. Poverty degrades. A poor man grows ugly and takes the bus, washes less, smells of sweat, watches the pennies, loses his natural nobility, and can no longer feel good, honest contempt for anything. You can despise, genuinely despise, only what you possess, what you control. Goethe despised more genuinely than Rousseau.

'Didn't catch that. Further thoughts on Don Juan? Well, for example, he never really listens to the people he talks to, because he is too busy assessing what they are like by watching them, which is much more revealing. But he remains eternally separated from others, even from those he loves. He sees them but he has no sense that they are real and distinct from himself. They are figments of his imagination, figures in a dream. He is eternally alone, he does not belong with them, he merely pretends that he does. What else? The constant awareness of his mortality, his mania for order, which reassures him, the attraction of his own death at three in the morning. The attraction of failure, too. Last year, in London, there was a young duchess or something along those lines. He'd just been introduced and she was drawn to him at once. They took themselves off to a side-room, away from the others, to chat, or rather to make a start on business which is invariably concluded in a bed. He felt an irresistible urge to touch the bone at the basis of the duchess's spinal column, a bone which is called the coccyx. This he did as she was about to sit down. He told her that he had wished to feel what was left of the tail of the duchess's distant ancestors. She did not approve of his interest.

'More again? In spite of the ill he speaks of them, he is at his ease only with women. With men, he has to stay on his guard and appear clubbable. But women do not criticize him, they accept him as he is, find that his dressing-gowns are unexceptional and his strings of beads perfectly natural. Like mothers. In summer, when he spends a few days with Isolde, she evinces no surprise whatsoever at his habit of strolling through the grounds wearing a tussore dressing-gown be-cause of the heat, a pith helmet as a protection against the sun, riding boots to ward off the mosquitoes, he is afraid of mosquitoes, swatting loathsome horseflies with a horsetail fly-whisk. She is indulgent and finds it perfectly natural that he should kit himself out like some African chieftain. But of all the women he knows, the one he likes best is little Edmée, a Salvation Army midget with twisted legs, who is his friend.

'Oh yes, Adrien, seducing them is easy. So easy in fact that when I was young I managed to bag one of my very own. It's a complicated story involving twin brothers – I was both – one clean-shaven and the other sporting a false moustache. I'll tell it to her tomorrow as we look out over the purple Cephalonian sea.

'And you must also explain Don Juan's mania for seduction. For in reality he is chaste and not particularly interested in bed-sports, finding them monotonous, primitive and, to be frank, comical. But he cannot avoid joining in if he wants women to love him. That's how they are. They insist on it. And he needs to be loved. Firstly, it stops him thinking about death, helps him forget that there is no afterlife, no God, no hope, no meaning, only the silence of a senseless universe. That is, through the love of a woman, he clouds his thoughts and cloaks his despair. Secondly, it is a bringer of comfort. When women worship him, they console him for the absence of oneness with his fellows. Such is his greatness: its attendant lady-in-waiting is yclept Solitude. Thirdly, they also console him for not being a king, for he was made to be king, born a king, effortlessly a king. He cannot be a king, and he will not stoop to be a political leader. For to be chosen by the masses he would first have to be like them, ordinary and unexceptional. So he elects to rule over women, women are his kingdom, and he will choose only those who are noble and pure, for where is the pleasure in subduing the unclean? Besides, the noble and the pure make far better bed-servants. Horrible man, she's thinking, which is a good sign.

'But the prime mover in his mania is the hope that he will fail, that one of them will at last resist him. Alas, he never fails. He thirsts for God, yet each of his sorry victories confirms that the chances of God's existing are small. One after the other, none of these noble and pure women can wait to fall flat on their backs. Yesterday they wore the face of the Madonna. Today, their tongues are in his mouth, proving yet again that there is no absolute of virtue and that therefore the God he longs for steadfastly refuses to exist, and there is nothing I can do to change that. But I'm going to have to ring off now, Adrien. I have to seduce the woman who is here listening to me, hating me. But never fear, mine she will be! Caught in my snares will she be! For fate decreed that I should be born Solal XIV of the Solals, a man with no first name, for no first-born of the older branch of the Solals is ever named, truly caught in my snares will she be, for by what name will she call me in the heat of passion? Oh yes, Deume, with the avenging glee of sorrow shall I seduce her, and on wings of love shall she and I, this very night, fly to a luxuriant isle while you slumber peacefully in your sleeper. Goodbye, and forgive me.'

He hung up and sat without moving. If no tattooer available in Geneva, try Marseilles. He could get the address of one in any bar on the Vieux-Port. The important thing in life was to be guaranteed a quick and sudden death. He turned and faced her.

'Your husband's a very lucky man, you know. He belongs. He has a country he can call his own, he has friends, kindred spirits, beliefs and a

God. But me, I'm always alone, a stranger, eternally watching my step. Sometimes I grow weary of having no one to depend on but myself, of having to rely on my sole ally: my intellijewishness. Sometimes I long to be a nobody, a nobody who belongs, who feels he is part of things, someone ordinary whose passage from cradle to grave is eased by social ties which make him a member of the community. It's crazy, but I wish I were a village postman, a road-mender, a policeman, somebody everyone knows and says hello to and likes, the sort who spends his evenings in the café playing cards with his friends. But I am always alone, I have only women to love me, and I wear their love like a badge of shame.

'The shame of owing their love to my handsome face, my sickening handsome face which sets the eyes of my darlings aflutter, my despicable handsome face whose praises they have been shrilling since I was sixteen. They'll be well and truly had when I'm old and my nose drips or, better still, when I'm six feet under consorting with roots and silent slithery worms, green and desiccated in a coffin split by damp earth, oh no they won't find me such a juicy proposition then, and it'll serve them right, I rejoice at the prospect. Handsome. It means such and such a length of meat, such and such a weight of meat, a full set of mouth ossicles, thirty-two of them, you can check them out later with a little mirror like the ones they have at the dentist's, so that the merchandise is fully guaranteed, before we set off, off our heads off to the sea.

'If I possess the appropriate length and weight and ossicles, she will be an angel, a cloistered nun of love, a saint. But if I do not, then I'd better look out! I can be a fount of goodness, a genius. I can worship the ground she walks on. But unless I can offer her a hundred and fifty centimetres of meat, her immortal soul will be unmoved. She will never love me with all her immortal soul, nor will she ever be an angel for me, a heroine ready to undertake any sacrifice.

'Look in the personal columns of the newspapers and you'll see how much importance young, yearning women attach to the centi-metres of the man of their dreams. "Look here," say the adverts, "what we want is meat at least a hundred and seventy centimetres long, and it's got to come complete with tan!" And if whoever answers can only produce a shorter length, they spit in his eye. Suppose all I can

offer is a poor hundred and fifty centimetres – make that cent*imeatres* –
but nevertheless try to tell her I love her to distraction. Her heart
will turn to stone, she'll look down her nose at my shortfall before
turning it up in disgust!

'Oh yes, if I'm thirty-five cent*imeatres* short she won't give a damn
about my soul, nor will she ever fling her arms round my neck to
protect me from a gangster's bullet. Ditto if I'm a genius but deficient
in ossicles! They long for the union of souls but are awfully keen on
those little bones! They pine for unseen spiritual realms, but those
ossicles have got to be highly visible!' he exclaimed gleefully, though
there was sadness in his eye.

'And they insist on quantity! At the very least, all front teeth have
to be present and correct! If there are two or three missing, those
sweet angelic creatures will be quite incapable of appreciating my
spiritual qualities and their souls will remain unmoved! If I don't have
those two or three little bones a few millimetres wide, there's no hope
for me, I'm doomed to be alone and loveless! If I dare speak to her of
love, she will throw a tooth-glass in my face in the hope of knocking
out an eye! "What," she'll say, "no little bones in your mouth? And
you have the impertinence to love me? Get out, you wretch, and
here's a kick to help you on your way!" Conclusion: don't be good,
don't be clever – pretend will do – but weigh the requisite number of
kilos and have a full complement of grinders and cutters!

'So I ask you, what value should I attach to a sentiment which is
entirely determined by half a dozen little bones, the longest of them
no more than a centimetre or two? Ah! you're thinking: oh, the
blasphemer! Well, would Juliet have loved Romeo if Romeo had had
four incisors missing and a great black gap in the middle of his
mouth? Of course not! And yet his soul would have been the same
soul and his character the same character! So why are they forever
telling me that what really count are soul and character?

'But I am naïve to go on about these things! They know it all.
What they want is that it should never be brought out into the open,
they want false coin, they want to hear those fine and noble words
which I regard as personal enemies. Instead of one hundred and
eighty cent*imeatres* and ossicles, they'd much rather have honeyed
talk of nobility and manliness and winning smiles! So away with their

carping! A fig for their scorn! And let them not whisper that I am base and self-interested! If anyone is self-interested, it's not me!

'Absolutely nothing escapes the notice of the pretty little creatures! When you meet them for the first time, their lips speak of Fioretti and St Francis of Assisi but their eyes list your assets and judge. Without appearing to, they notice everything, including the number and quality of your little toothbones, and if you've got one or two missing, all is lost! Yes, quite lost. But if, on the other hand, you look the least palatable, they know at a glance that you have eyes which are brown with just a hint of green and a few flecks of gold, though you yourself were never aware of the fact. They are the world's best scrutineers.

'But that's not all. They don't stop at your face! They want the whole package! At your first meeting, with those big, blue, angel eyes of theirs, they've already undressed you. You don't know it and they don't realize it either, because they won't even admit their X-ray probings to themselves. They all go in for this instant undressing, even the virgins. They are specialists, and they know at a glance what you are worth in meat under your clothes, if you have big enough muscles, a large chest, flat stomach, narrow hips, how much fat on your bones. For if you've got any fat on you, even the teeniest hint of flab, the game's up! An innocent couple of pounds of excess fat on your belly and you're written off, they don't want to know!

'On top of which, they go for you, tenacious as the counsel for the prosecution, and they will not commit themselves unless they're absolutely sure of their facts. Which is why, in the course of a genteel conversation in which nature and little birds feature prominently, they manage in the most casual way to quiz and prod, find out if you are the physically vigorous sort, if you like being out in the fresh air, if you're keen on sport. In the same way, the female of the tiny insect known as the empis will not plight her troth unless the male can demonstrate his athletic prowess! The poor devil must be able to carry on his back a little ball of something or other three times his own size! It's a fact! And if they find out that you ride or climb mountains or water-ski, they've got their guarantee and they proceed to think the sun shines out of you, safe in the knowledge that you are good for fighting and breeding. But naturally, since they are above such things and proper and middle-class, they never think base thoughts. They cover them with noble words, and, instead of talking about slim waists and good breeders, they say how charming you are. Nobility is a matter of the words you use.

'It's despicable. For what is this handsomeness which they all pursue with their fluttering eyes, what is this male beauty which means being tall, having hard muscles and teeth that bite, what is it if not the outward sign of youth and rude good health, that is of physical strength, that is of the ability to fight and to do violence to others which is the real test of strength, of which the ultimate expression, sanction and deepest root is the power to kill, the ancient power of the caveman? It is this power which draws the unconscious minds of these sweet, God-fearing, oh-so-spiritual women! That's why they'll chase anything that wears a uniform. In other words, before they can fall in love, they have to sense the potential killer in me, believe that I am someone who is capable of protecting them. You want to say something? You have my permission.'

'If you're right, then why don't you go and find yourself some humpbacked old hag and tell her you love her?'

'Aha! Clever are we? All right, I'll tell you why. Because I am a miserable male! I accept that hairy men are carnivorous creatures! But not women! I cannot accept that of Woman, in whom I believe! Not my pure angels! To be constantly reminded of the fact that women, with their melting looks and noble gestures and modest blushes, require me to be handsome before they give me their love, the only divine sentiment we know on earth, that is my torment and my despair! I cannot accept it because I cannot stop respecting them! Such is my nature, eternally born of woman. And I feel ashamed for them when they look at me and size me up and weigh me in their balance, when they use those eyes of theirs, yes their eyes, to sniff at the scales of my scaliness! Ashamed when I see their eyes acquire a sudden serious glint of interest, when their eyes fill with respect for my meat! Ashamed for them when I see them captivated by my smile, the one small part of my skeleton which is already visible!

'And as to admiring the beauty of women, who shall demur? For it is the promise of tenderness, a kind and loving heart, and motherhood. Those nice girls who want nothing more than to care for the sick and rush off to the front to be nurses when there's a war on warm the heart, and I am morally entitled to love their meat. But I cannot stomach the horrible attraction women feel for male beauty which signifies physical strength, courage and aggression, in other words man's animal qualities! That is what makes them unforgivable!

'Oh I know, this is a pathetic prelude to a seduction. It's quite absurd of me to expatiate at such length on standards of male physique and the power to kill, and I'm not done with these things yet. It would be much cleverer of me to talk to you about Bach and God and then ask you, virtuously, if we could be friends. Who knows, you might say yes nobly, with eyes demurely lowered, and you would fall pure into the trap at the end of which there is always a bedroom. But I cannot, I will not seduce the way they want! I have done with such ignoble games!'

He sat down and coughed once to make her look up at him, but her head remained bowed, which annoyed him. He whistled under his breath and wondered if his diatribe against women who adored gorillas had not been prompted by anger because he knew that the shameless creatures could be attracted by other men. For, in plain terms, he wanted all women for himself. He shrugged, undid his Commander's tie, played with it listlessly, and raised his eyes to heaven to take God as his witness that the wicked woman sitting there was not looking at him on purpose. To comfort himself, he lifted the lid of a small box, opening it just wide enough to insert two fingers. Just like a sultan stealing into the harem unannounced, she thought. Absently, he took the first cigarette he touched and she thought: the sultan has chosen his favourite for the night, without looking, because he likes surprises. He struck a match, forgot to light his cigarette, burnt his fingers, and dropped both the match and the cigarette in disgust. She checked a nervous laugh. The favourite has been spurned, she thought.

'Ashamed too that I owe her future love to my exalted but despicable job, which I got by ruse and the ruthless elimination of the competition. Ex-minister, Under-Clown-General, a Commander of some order or other, I don't recall which, or rather, I do remember, I just said that for the effect. A bit of an actor,' he smiled sweetly. 'Yes, that's me! Solal, fourteenth of the line of the Solals, slumming it as

Under-Secretary-General of the League of Nations, an abject big buzz in the humming, honeyless hive alive with bumble-bees, Under-Bumble-Bee-General, and Under-Fly-on-the-Wall-General. Tell me, what on earth am I doing standing elbow to elbow with all those tailor's dummies, the politicians, the ministers, the ambassadors? They haven't a soul between them. They are all stupid and cunning, dynamic and sterile, so many bobbing corks swept along by the current which they think they command, always so chatty and affable in the corridors and lobbies, backslapping, always an arm round the shoulders of the dear friend they heartily detest, but all busily doing each other down and setting out their own stalls with a view to rising up the ladder of influence from which they will soon topple and fall into the waiting hole below, silenced at last in their wooden coffins, but in the meantime putting up smokescreens, soberly discussing the Locarno Protocol and the Kellogg Pact, treating all the passing inanities with the profoundest gravity, giving their most serious attention to great political issues which are invariably either sordid family intrigues or shabby parochial squabbles, but these cretins take it all so seriously because they take themselves seriously, pompous-eyed, hands in their trouser pockets, the rosette of some honour or other in their buttonhole, and a white handkerchief peeping out of the breast-pocket of their jackets. And every day I take part in this farce, every day I pretend I'm a part of it, I too discuss gravely, I spout unadulterated twaddle, and I too strut with my hands in my trouser pockets and that political, international look in my eye. I despise the whole merry-go-round but I hide my contempt because I've sold my soul for a suite at the Ritz, silk shirts, a Rolls, three baths a day and my despair. But enough of that.'

He walked to the window and looked out over Geneva tranquilly illuminated below, across at the lights shimmering on the French bank and down at the gently swaying swans on the black lake, asleep with their heads tucked under their wings. Then he was standing before her again. He watched her for a moment, and smiled at the poor weak creature who was born to die.

'Do you ever give a thought for all those future corpses now walking along the streets and pavements, so rushed and busy that they aren't even aware that the earth in which they will be buried exists and lies waiting for them? They are tomorrow's dead men, and they laugh and fume and boast. And the laughing women are also food for worms, though today they brandish their breasts at every opportunity, flaunting them, making absurd mountains out of milky molehills. Future corpses all! Yet they fill their short span of life with cruelties and write "Death to Jews" on walls. And what if you travel the world and speak to men? What if you try to persuade them to pity one another, try to make them see that they are soon to die? It doesn't work. They like being cruel. It is the curse of the teeth that bite. For two thousand years there have been hatred, calumny, plotting, intrigue and war. What new weapons of destruction will be invented in the next thirty years? They are talking apes, and in the long run they will wipe each other out and the human race will be killed by cruelty. So a man might as well find comfort in the love of a woman. But being loved is so easy, so dishonouring. The same old inevitable strategy, and the same old base motives: meat and the social factor.

'Ah yes, the social factor. She is far too noble-hearted to be a snob, perish the thought, and she genuinely believes she attaches not the slightest importance to my Under-Clownship-General. But her unconscious is riddled with snobbery. But there, so is everyone's: we all worship power. She says nothing but inwardly protests, thinks I have a vulgar mind. She is utterly convinced that the things that matter to her are culture, civilized behaviour, delicacy of feeling, honesty, loyalty, generosity, love of nature and the rest of it. But, you poor fool, can't you see that all these noble conceits are signs and symbols of membership of the dominant class, and that is precisely why, deep-down, secretly, unwittingly, you set such store by them? In reality, it is knowing that a man is a member of the club that makes him so attractive to a pretty, empty-headed woman. Of course, she won't take my word for it. She never will.

'Clever remarks about Bach or Kafka are the tell-tale passwords, for they show that a man is a member of this exclusive club. Hence all those lofty conversations which mark the first stage of love's way. He says he likes Kafka. She, poor fool, is ecstatic. She believes he has a fine intellect, whereas in reality he has no more than a fine social status. The ability to talk about Kafka or Proust or Bach comes under the same category as having good table manners, as breaking your bread with your fingers instead of cutting it with a knife or not eating with your mouth open. Honesty, loyalty, generosity and love of nature are also signs of social status. The privileged have money to burn: why shouldn't they be honest and generous? They lead swaddled lives from the cradle to the grave and society shows them its pleasant face: why should they cheat and lie? And the love of nature is not high on the slum-dweller's agenda: it takes money. What is civilized behaviour if not the manners and vocabulary of the upper classes? If I say so-and-so "and his lady wife", I am thought common. The expression, which was considered civilized enough a couple of centuries ago, has only become vulgar since the working classes got hold of it. But if it were accepted practice in high society to say so-and-so "and his lady wife", you would think me a dreadful churl if I said so-and-so "and his lady" instead. So, honesty, loyalty, generosity, love of nature, civilized behaviour and all the rest of the twaddle, are no more than badges of membership of the ruling class, and that is why you attach such importance to them from what you claim to be the purest motives. Which, of course, merely shows just how much you worship power!

'Yes, power. Because their wealth, marriages, friendships and connections give the members of this class the power to harm others. From which I conclude that your respect for culture, that prerogative of the ruling élite, is ultimately and profoundly no more than a secret, unconscious respect for the power to kill. I see you smile. People always smile and shrug their shoulders. The truth I tell is not pleasant to hear.

'The worship of power is universal. Note how underlings bask in the sun of their leader, observe the doting way they look upon their chief, see them ever ready with a smile. And when he utters some inane pleasantry, just listen to the chorus of their sincere laughter. Yes, sincere. That's the most awful part of it. For underneath the self-interested love your husband has for me exists another, perfectly genuine and selfless love: the abject love of power, a reverence for the power to destroy. Oh that fixed and captivated grin of his, the obsequious civilities, the deferential curve of his backside as I talked to him. The moment the dominant adult male baboon steps into the cage, the younger, smaller, adolescent males get down on all fours, assuming the welcoming, receptive position of females, adopting the position of voluptuous vassalage, paying sexual homage to the power of destruction and death, the moment the dominant fearsome adult male baboon steps into the cage. Read up on apes and you will see that what I say is true.

'Baboonery is everywhere. The worship of the military, custodians of the power to kill: baboonery and the animal reverence for strength. The thrill of respect when the heavy tanks roll by: baboonery. The crowd which cheers the boxer who is about to demolish his opponent: baboonery. The crowd urging him on to the kill, "Go on, flatten him!": baboonery. And when he has knocked his man out, they are proud to touch him and slap him on the back: "It's what sport's all about!" they yell. The adulation given to the stars of cycle racing: baboonery. And the transformation brought about in the bully trounced by Jack London who, because he has been well and truly thrashed, forgets his hate and from that day forth venerates the man who bested him: more baboonery.

'Baboonery is everywhere. The crowds who cry out to be enslaved, who shake in orgasmic ecstasy when the square-jawed dictator, custodian of the power to kill, makes his appearance: baboonery. Their hands reaching out to touch the sanctifying hand of their leader: baboonery. Discreet, ecclesiastical, ministry baboons who stand behind their minister as he is about to sign the treaty and rush forward bearing blotting-paper and feel honoured as they beatifically dry his signature: such loyal little baboons! The gushing smiles of the ministers and ambassadors as they gather round the queen as she kisses the little girl who offers her a bouquet of flowers: baboonery. Baboonish too Benedetti's smile the other day at the Sixth Committee while old Cheyne read out his speech. The swine had on his fat face a smile which the thrill of veneration made, so to speak, pure, virginal and delicate. But that smile also signified that in loving the supreme chief he was really loving himself, for he felt that in some way he was part of the adorable Greatness which stood there droning on and on.

'Baboons, the morons who call on the Italian dictator and then come and tell me rapturously about the brute's charming smile, "such a warm smile underneath," they all say in female surrender to the strong. Baboons, the people who swoon over some small act of charity attributed to Napoleon, the same Napoleon who said: "What are five hundred thousand dead to me?" They all have a weakness for strong men, and the smallest crumb of sweetness that falls from the table of the mighty is balm to their souls and they are bewitched. In the theatre, their eyes moisten as they watch some stiff old martinet of a colonel unbend and turn unexpectedly into a kindly old party. Oh the slaves! On the other hand, the really good man is always treated as though he is not quite right in the head. In plays, the villain is never ridiculed, but the good man often is and audiences laugh at him. And is there not more than a hint of contempt in the words "there's a good chap" or "he's a good sort"? And surely it's a dead give-away that earthly possessions are called "goods".

'Baboonish worshippers of power, those American girls who stormed the railway carriage in which the Prince of Wales was travelling, kissed the cushions on which he had parked his behind, and gave him a pair of pyjamas to which each had contributed a few stitches. They did: it's a fact. The baboonery of the gale of laughter which convulsed the Assembly the other day when the British Prime Minister made a joke and the Chairman almost choked himself to death on it. It was a silly joke, but the reception given to jokes is in direct proportion to the standing of the teller, and the laughter is no more than the acknowledgement of power.

'Snobbery, which is the desire to be sucked into the ambit of the powerful, is baboonery and reverence for power. If the Prince of Wales forgets to do up the bottom button of his waistcoat, or if, because it's raining, he turns up the bottoms of his trousers, or if, because he has a boil under his arm, he raises his elbow when he shakes hands, the baboons fall over themselves to leave their bottom waistcoat buttons undone, order turn-ups for their trousers, and give overarm handshakes. And this fascination for the idiotic love-affairs of princesses: more baboonery. If a queen has a baby, all the ladies simply can't wait to find out how much the brat weighs and what his official title will be. But the real depths of baboonism are plumbed by the dim-witted dying soldier who asks to see the queen of his heart before he breathes his last.

'The feminine urge to follow fashion, which simply means aping the powerful and wanting to be counted in the ranks of the strong, is baboonery. The habit of the great and the good, kings, generals, diplomats and even members of the French Academy, of wearing a sword which is the badge of the killer: baboonery. But the height of baboonery is the way people express their respect for He who is respectable above all things and their love for He who is Love, for they dare to say that He is Almighty: this is an abomination and an acknowledgement of their odious veneration of Might, which is nothing more nor less than the power to inflict hurt and, in the final analysis, the power to kill.

'It is worship of the lowest, animal kind, and its vocabulary shows it for what it is. Words associated with Might are rooted in respect. A "great" writer, a "powerful" book, "elevated" sentiments, "lofty" inspiration. And behind them lurks the eternal image of the doughty, strapping war-dog and potential killer. On the other hand, adjectives denoting weakness are invariably expressive of contempt. A "small" mind, "low" sentiments, a "feeble" book. And why should "noble" and "chivalrous" be terms of praise? They are a hangover from the Middle Ages. Then only nobles and knights exercised real power, by force of arms, and they were doers of harm and killers of men and therefore respectable and admirable. Humanity caught napping! To express their admiration, the best the little people could come up with was two epithets redolent of feudal society in which war, that is murder, was the goal and supreme honour in the life of man! In medieval sagas, nobles and knights do little else but slaughter and butcher, and around them guts spill out of bellies, skulls crack open and ooze brains, and horsemen are cleft in twain, right down the middle. How noble! How chivalrous! Oh yes, the baboons were caught napping! For they linked moral beauty to physical might and the power to kill!

'All they love and revere is Strength. To occupy a high position in society is strength. Courage is strength. Money is strength. Character is strength. Fame is strength. Beauty, the outward show and guarantee of health, is strength. Youth is strength. But old age, which is weakness, they loathe. In primitive tribes, the old are clubbed to death. When good middle-class girls cannot find a husband, they advertise in the newspapers and in their adverts they always make a point of stating that they have direct Expectations soon to be realized, which means that their mummies and daddies will soon drop dead, thank God. And I myself am repelled by old women who always insist on sitting next to me on trains. It never fails. Whenever some bearded old hag heaves herself into my compartment, she always makes a beeline for me, attaches herself to me like a limpet, while I hate her in silence and try to put as much space as I can between myself and her repulsive person which is soon to die. And when I stand up I do my level best to step on her corns, unintentionally of course.

'What they call original sin is nothing more than the vague, shameful awareness we have of our baboonish nature and its disgusting affects. Just one out of countless examples of this base nature: smiling. Smiling mimics animal behaviour which we have inherited from our ancestors the primates. When one homuncule smiles at another, he is signalling that he comes in peace and will not bite, and to prove it he bares his teeth inoffensively for him to see. For us descendants of the brutish beasts of the Stone Age, showing our teeth without using them to attack has become a peaceful greeting, a sign of meekness.

'But enough. Why am I bothering with all this? I shall now begin the seduction. It's child's play. In addition to the two basic requirements, the physical and the social, all we need now are the right tactics. A matter of playing the right cards. At one in the morning, you in love. Come twenty to two, you and I off to station, off our heads, off to sun and sea, and maybe at last moment you left in lurch on station platform, to pay you back for the old man. Do you remember the old man? Sometimes at night I wear his long robe, dress myself up as my ideal Jew, with beard and poignant ritual ringlets and fur hat, dragging my feet, bending my back, artlessly waving my umbrella, an aged Jewman, noble since the start of time, O love of my life, transmitter of the Law, O redeeming Israel!, and I walk through the streets at night, to be mocked, proud to be mocked by them. But now: tactics.

'First tactic: give the subject notice that she is about to be seduced. It's an excellent way of stopping her walking out on you. She stays because it's a challenge, because she wants to see pride take a fall. Tactic number two: demolish the husband. That's in the bag. Tactic number three: wheel out the poetic gambit. Behave like a haughty aristocrat, a romantic spirit unhampered by social convention, and back it up with sumptuous dressing-gown, sandalwood beads, black monocle, a suite at the Ritz, and attacks of liverishness, carefully disguised. All of which is designed to allow the little fool to work it out for herself that I belong to the miraculous race of Lovers, the antidote to a husband who takes laxatives, and the Gateway to Life Sublime. The husband, poor devil, cannot hope to be poetic. No one can keep up the pretence twenty-four hours a day. Constantly on view, he is forced to be himself, his pathetic self. All men are pathetic, including seducers when they are alone and not play-acting for the benefit of some stupid, starry-eyed female. Pathetic, the lot of them, and I most pathetic of all!

'When she gets home, she will compare her husband with her supplier of poems and she will despise him. Every little thing will generate contempt, even her husband's dirty washing. As if Don Juan didn't put his dirty shirts in the laundry basket! But the stupid little fool, who only ever sees him when he is on stage, performing, always at his best, freshly bathed and elegantly spruced, imagines that here is a hero whose shirts never get dirty, who never has to go to the dentist. But he goes to the dentist, of course he does, just like any husband. But he never admits it. Don Juan is an actor who is never off stage, he is camouflaged, he disguises any physical shortcomings and does in secret everything a husband does openly and unaffectedly. But because he does these things in secret, and because she has no imagination whatsoever, he appears to her to be some sort of demigod. Oh the filthy, nostalgic look in the eye of the soon-to-be-unfaithful little fool! Oh her mouth gaping to catch the noble words of her Prince Charming, who has intestines ten metres long like everyone else! Oh the little numskull who fills her head, which is in the clouds, with thoughts of magic and lies. Everything about her husband irritates her. His radio and his harmless custom of listening to the news three times a day, poor sweet man, his slippers, his rheumatism, the way he whistles in the bathroom, the noises he makes when he cleans his teeth, his innocent mania for calling her by tender, baby names, like pet and petal or plain darling at every possible opportunity, a habit which has lost its charm and turns the knife in the wound. What Madame requires is an endless supply of sublimity.

'So she arrives home. Brief moments ago the seducer had hung garlands upon her, called her the goddess of the forest and Diana returned in human form, and here she is with a husband who turns her into a pet, and this makes her feel cross. Brief moments ago, sweet and captivated, she had listened eagerly as her seducer filled her head with elevated topics of conversation – painting, sculpture, literature, culture, nature – and she had responded with delight: in other words a couple of bad actors hamming it up. Whereas now the poor husband asks her in all innocence what she makes of the behaviour of the Boulissons, who came to dinner two months ago, since when, silence, not a peep out of them, nor invited back either. "And to cap it all, I've just been told they've had the Bourrassuses round to their place! You realize they only got to know the Bourrassuses through us! In my opinion we shouldn't have anything more to do with them. What do you think?" And so on and so forth, including the touching "You know, petal, everything was just fine and dandy with the boss, he calls me by my Christian name." In short, not many sublime moments with her husband, no pretentious exchanges of shared tastes for Kafka, and it dawns on the little fool that she is ruining her life with her snoring clod of a spouse, that her humdrum existence is not worthy of her. For she is as stupid as she is vain.

'But the funniest part of it all is that she resents her husband, not only because he is not poetic but also and especially because she cannot behave poetically with him. She might not know it, but she blames him because he is witness to the petty indignities which she suffers daily: her sour breath first thing in the morning, her rumpled hair which would not look out of place on a circus clown or some drink-sodden old hag, and all the rest of it, not forgetting perhaps her evening dose of liquid paraffin or her prunes. Living cheek by jowl with toothbrushes and slippers, she feels that she has been knocked off her pedestal and she lays the blame squarely at the door of the poor unfortunate husband who soon reaches the end of his tether. But come five in the afternoon, behold her process in triumph when, freshly laundered, with hair set and dandruff-free, more exultant and not less proud than the winged Victory of Samothrace, she goes forth with lively step to meet her noble, secret stomach-churner, and as she goes she sings Bach chorales, glorying in the knowledge that soon she will be performing sublime and beautiful things for her knotter-of-intestines, and that she will in consequence feel as immaculate as a princess in her hair-do which has really turned out most awfully well.

'On the day they married, Jewish women strict in the faith used to shave their heads and wear a wig. I like that. An end to beauty, thanks be to God! But take, on the other hand, the most glamorous star of the silver screen. She believes she is irresistible. She offers herself in alluring poses, which invariably feature her rump. Now because she is no more than the sum of her beauty, that devil's claw, all I have to do to punish her for her looks is to imagine that she has been given a strong enema and has the squits, and she immediately loses her charm and any hold she had over me! She can live in the lavatory for all I care! But a Jewess in a wig never loses her aura, for she has chosen to live on a level where no physical imperfection can undermine her. I've lost my thread. What was I saying about the little fool?'

'She realizes she's ruining her life.'

'Bless you,' he said, and with thumb and forefinger sharpened his aristocratic scimitar of a nose as though to sharpen his thoughts, and then his expression melted. 'Yes, there is nothing so noble as holy matrimony, the union of two human beings who come together not through passion, which is carnality, animal ruse and transience, but in tenderness, which is the image of God. Yes, a union of two miserable creatures doomed to sickness and death who seek the sweet joy of growing old together and being the only family each of them knows. "Brother and sister shalt thou call thy wife," says the Talmud. (He suddenly realized he had made up the quotation and went on more warily.) Verily, verily, I say unto you, the action of a wife who squeezes her husband's boils and tenderly drains the pus therefrom weighs more heavily and is finer by far than all the bucking and fishy writhings of Anna Karenina. So praise to the Talmud and shame upon adulterous women, for they have an animal itch and are only too ready to rush off, off their heads, off to the sea. Yes, animal. For Anna is in love with the body of that oaf Vronsky, that's the simple truth of it, and all her fine words are a smokescreen which hangs like lace over his meat. Do I hear voices accusing me of interpreting existence from the viewpoint of the materialist? But if some malfunction of the glands had made Vronsky fat and put thirty kilos of flab on his belly, the equivalent of three hundred packets of butter each weighing a hundred grams, would she have fallen in love with him the moment they met? Meat rules. There's no more to be said.

'Tactic number four: the strong-man ploy. Seduction is a game that's played dirty! The cock cockadoodles to let her know that he's a thug, the gorilla beats his chest, boom-boom, and soldiers have it made. "*Die Offiziere kommen!*" cry the young women of Vienna, and it's out with the comb. Strength is their obsession, and they miss nothing which seems to signal its presence. If he stares unblinkingly into her eyes, she feels deliciously stirred, her legs turn weak at the gorgeous threat he represents. If he settles back authoritatively in his armchair, she reveres him. If he's the laconic, English-explorer type who takes his pipe out of his mouth to say "Yes", she reads hidden depths in this "Yes" and admires the way he bites on the stem of his pipe and the disgusting noise the dottle makes in the bowl. It's virile and it thrills her. The seducer may talk rubbish, but if he talks self-confidently, in a manly voice, deep-throated and husky, she will gaze at him with eyes wide and moist, as though he had invented a new kind of relativity of even wider ramifications. She picks up everything: his walk, say, or that way he has of suddenly turning round, from which she deduces from deep inside her pretty little head that he is aggressive and dangerous, thank God. And to cap it all, to attract her, I am required to dominate and humiliate her husband, though it makes me feel shame for me and pity for him. Yes, I was ashamed when I had him on the phone just now, ashamed of the nauseating tone of superiority I put on for your benefit, which is indispensable if you want to do the husband down and ruin his credibility in the eyes of the little fool.

'Now all I have to do to seduce a dog is to be nice to him. A dog isn't particularly impressed by strength. But with women it's different, they demand it, they want danger, they find it attractive. Oh yes, it's the danger in strength, the power to kill, which attracts and excites them, for they are baboons. I once knew a girl, came of a good family, a family known for piety and noble sentiments, a pure young thing, who fell madly in love with a musician who was a hundred and eighty centimeatres tall but also, alas, quiet and shy. Being unable to change him into the genuine, dynamic article but determined to fall deeper and deeper in love with him, she tried injecting doses of artificial virility into his bloodstream so that she would be thrilled by the result and thus love him even more. So during the innocent walks they took together, she would say from time to time: "Jean, be more assertive!" One day, in the same spirit, she presented him with an English pipe, the short-stemmed kind, the sort smoked by sea dogs or English detectives, and she would not let him be until he stuck it in his mouth then and there while she watched delighted and fulfilled. The pipe excited her. But the very next day she met an army lieutenant at a smart social do. The moment she saw his uniform and his sword she immediately fell head over heels in love, her blood beat at the open door of her soul, and she saw clearly that defending one's country was an even finer thing than making music. You see, a sword is a good deal more exciting than a pipe.

'Strength, strength, that's all they talk about. And what is strength if not at root the age-old, ape-old ability to brain your prehistoric neighbour in a quiet corner of the virgin forest which bloomed a hundred thousand years ago? Might is the power to kill! I know, I've said it before. Well I'm saying it again, and shall go on saying it until the day I die! Read the adverts these genteel girls put in the paper, attractive appearance, with direct and soon-to-be-realized Expectations, as they phrase it. Read them and you'll see that what they want is a gentleman who is not simply as long as possible but also dynamic, with a strong character, and the thought of it makes them open their eyes in wonderment as though it were a fine and great thing, whereas in reality it is utterly repellent. Character!' he exclaimed sorrowfully. 'Character! They admit it! These hussies with their angel faces admit that what they want is a tall, dark, strong man with a firm jaw who chews gum, a beefy man, a manly man, a conceited cock who is always right, a man who speaks his mind and never changes it, a man of stubborn, unyielding heart, a man who can hand it out, a man, in other words, who is capable of murder! Character is just another name for physical strength, and the man with character is a substitute product, the social, ersatz version of the gorilla. Gorillas! Can we never get away from gorillas?

'They throw up their arms in protest and claim that I do them an injustice, since they want their gorilla also to be a moral creature! They insist that their meaty, beefy gorilla who has Character, that is, a potential killer, should speak fine words and talk to them of God, and that they should sit down together and read the Bible in the evening, before they go to bed. A feeble alibi which is also the height of perversity. And that's how these scheming creatures can, with a clear conscience, both cherish the hairy chests and murderous fists and also lap up the cool eyes and the pipe! Pig's trotters smothered in whipped cream! Mutton dressed up in flowers and paper frills as in a butcher's window! False coin circulating endlessly and everywhere! But instead of a hundred and eighty centimeatres they say handsome or dashing and in their adverts speak of good appearance! And for savage and cold-eyed bully-boy who can scare the delicious daylights out of us they say dynamic, has Character! Instead of wealthy and ruling class they say refined and cultured! And for fear of death and the selfish hope that slim hips will endure forever they say spirit, the hereafter, life eternal! I know that you hate me. Heigh-ho. Glory be to truth!

'There's no getting away from it, they're palaeolithic. They are the palaeolithic descendants of the low-of-brow females who meekly followed the squat caveman and his axe of flint! As far as I can tell, while he was alive no woman, not one, ever loved great Jesus, the man of sorrows, as a man. "Not manly enough," wailed the daughters of Galilee. They surely despised him for turning the other cheek. On the other hand they stood open-mouthed and wide-eyed at the spectacle of the square-chinned Roman centurions. Oh their admiration which makes me feel sick for them, their odious preference for the silent, upright Martin Edens who specialize in the right hook to the jaw.

'For the loves of my youth I feel only horror. Then, I loathed being loved for the carnimalities of my manhood which they forced me to perform, which they expected of me, hated being loved for what the brainless hen finds pleasing in the odious cockerel. To attract them, I rode a high horse, though haughty I was not. I beat my chest, though I certainly was not strong, thank God. But that was how they wanted me, and, although I was ashamed, I needed their love, however ill-gotten.

352

'Strong! Strong! The word is never far from their lips! I've had it drummed into me constantly. "You are so strong!" they would say, and I felt ashamed. One, more intense, more female than the rest, even drooled: "You're such a *brute!*" which made me appear even stronger still and catapulted me into the divine ranks of the great apes. I ached with shame and self-disgust. I was humiliated by such bestiality and felt an urge to shout and scream and tell her I was the weakest man that ever walked this earth. Had I done so, she would have dropped me like a hot potato, and I needed her warmth, the warmth which they give only when passion rules, the divine mothering bestowed by women in love. And so, to keep her warmth, which was what mattered most to me, I bought her passion by posing as her gorilla and, with lead in my heart, I pranced unrestrained, sat down authoritatively, crossed my legs as arrogantly as I could get away with, stated my views tersely, and brooked no reply.

'And so it was always gorilla time, though I would have much preferred her just to be by my bedside, sitting in an armchair, while I lay still and prone and held her hand or the hem of her skirt, and she crooned a lullaby. But oh no! I had to be wayward and dangerous, with Character on permanent display, constantly prancing and feeling foolish, the fool of her admiration. I do not say these things with a light heart. I would have been happy to find such warmth in men, to have had a friend to embrace when we met, to stay and talk with late into the night, even until the dawn. But men care little for me, I make them feel uncomfortable, they do not trust me, I do not belong, they sense that I am a loner. And so I was driven to seek warmth from those who give of it freely.'

Standing before the mirror above the mantelpiece, he removed his black monocle, inspected the scar on his eyelid, and wondered if he should burn his thirty thousand dollars in the presence of the Amalekite to teach her a lesson. No, better to burn the money when alone some evening, for the sheer hell of it, first draping his shoulders with his long silk prayer-shawl ennobled with tassels and striped with blue, his tent and his home. He turned abruptly and drew close to the daughter of Gentiles, beauty in long curved eyelashes, who looked at him in silence, true to her word.

'How they've made me suffer these twenty years with their babooneries. Babooneries,' he repeated, held in thrall by the word, suddenly transported to a cage at the zoo, peering in vacantly. 'Consider the baboon in his cage. Watch how he dons his virility to please his babooness, see how he beats his chest like jungle drums, observe how he struts with head held high like the colonel of a parachute regiment. (He strode round the room, hammering on his chest to be a baboon. With head held high, he looked elegant and innocent, young and carefree.) Then he rattles the bars of his cage, and the melting, captivated babooness realizes that he is a brute, that he is assertive, that he has Character, that she can rely on him. And the harder he rattles the bars, the more convinced she feels that his soul is fine, that he is morally reproachless, a chivalrous, loyal, honourable baboon. That's feminine intuition for you. And so the bedazzled babooness goes up to the baboon, waggling her hindquarters – they all do it, even the most virtuous, they're all keen on displays of rump, hence tight skirts – and with eyes chastely lowered she asks him meekly: "Do you like Bach?" Of course, he loathes Bach, a heartless robot and geometer of mechanical variations. But to impress, to show that he has a fine soul and belongs in the very best of baboonish circles, the wretch has no choice but to say that he positively dotes on the old bore and his works for long-distance wood-saws. Are you shocked? So am I. Then, still keeping her eyes demurely lowered, the babooness says in a sweet voice full of deep conviction: "Bach brings us closer to God, don't you think? I'm delighted we share the same tastes." It always starts with shared tastes. Don't they always begin with an opening salvo of Bach, Mozart and God? It strikes a proper conversational note, provides a respectable alibi. And two weeks later the trapeze is flying over the bed-springs.

'So the babooness continues her elevated conversation with her nice baboon, delighted to discover that his thoughts on all subjects – sculpture, painting, literature, nature, culture – coincide exactly with her own. "I'm also fond of folk-dancing," she says next, unleashing a flutter of eyelashes. And what exactly is folk-dancing? And why on earth do they rave about it? (He was so anxious to tell her, to convince her, that his sentences clashed and scattered grammar to the winds.) Folk-dancing, lot of strapping louts jigging showing how indefatigable how they'd dig a field go on for ever without dropping.

Of course, they never admit the real reason why they've been bowled over and they hide behind more fine words. They'll tell you that what they really like about the dancing is the folklore, the traditions, the national pride, the marshals of France, the homely country people, the *joie de vivre*, its sheer vitality. Vitality, my foot! We know what vitality really means, and Michael could explain it to you better than I can.

'But at this point a longer baboon is let into the cage, and he thumps his chest with much more gusto and a noise like thunder. The first baboon and apple of an eye but a moment ago keeps his mouth shut, for he is less long and nowhere near as lusty. He abdicates and, in deference to the greater ape, drops on all fours and adopts the female posture as a sign of vassalage. This sickens the babooness, who immediately develops a mortal hatred for him. Your husband a while ago, in the silences, his endless, fawning smile, that refined and humble sucking of saliva. Or, as I spoke, bent double to catch my every word. All that too was a feminine homage to the power to inflict hurt, of which the capacity to murder is the ultimate root: I say it yet again. Likewise the melting, virginal smiles on faces which verge on the loving when the King lays the first stone! Likewise the adoring laughter which greets the witticism, though it is not in the least witty, uttered by any great and powerful man! Likewise the ignoble reverence of the ministry official meticulously, scrupulously pressing the blotter upon his minister's signature on the last page of the peace treaty! Oh the perpetual duet sung by humankind, the same sickening baboonish tune: "I am greater than you. I know I am not as great as you. I am greater than you. I know I am not as great as you. I am greater than you. I know I am not as great as you." And so it goes on, constantly, everywhere! Baboons every one! Ah, I do believe I said all this a moment or two ago, about your husband, the adoring laughter and the ministry officials. So sorry! But all these contemptible little baboons are enough to addle anyone's brains. I see them everywhere, all busy displaying, like rutting animals.

'And just like me at this very moment, the great ape in his cage holds forth boomingly, his gestures marked by vitality. He speaks masterfully to the babooness, who watches him with great, round, wondering eyes. "Such charm!" she whispers to an old friend, another babooness, who sits fanning herself. "He has such a gentle smile. I just know somehow that he is a very good person, deep down." And spiders! Do you know anything about the habits of spiders? The female requires her husband to demonstrate his strength by showing how well he can jump! Like this. (With one standing jump, he cleared the table. Ashamed at having made a spectacle of himself, he lit a cigarette and exhaled furiously.) Scientific fact, I can get the book for you, if you want. And if the spider does not leap about and whizz off in all directions, then it's no go. The soul of spiderwoman casts him adrift while she heads off to the sea with a brand-new spiderman who, having been in the state of love for but a few days, prances and pirouettes fit to make her swoon with pleasure. The new one is a dark-skinned spiderman! For you should realize they adore dark-skinned spidermen, though this is a secret and they only whisper it to each other at night, by the light of the moon, when they are far away from their white spiderhusbands. And then, on the shore of the silky, low-lapping sea, poor spiderman is required to jump heights of five or six or even seven centimetres, which he does, and she worships him!'

He stopped, gave her a kindly smile, for he was enjoying the spiders and had forgotten the gap between the third and fourth ribs. In high spirits, he tossed his Commander's tie high into the air and caught it as it fell.

'And then, tragedy strikes! A third spiderman turns up who can outjump her dark-skinned spiderman! Spiderwoman says to herself that Mister Rightspiderman, a spiderman to make her soul o'erflow, has come along at last! Divorce! Third marriage! Departure off her head off to a new sea with her new spiderman! Honeymoon in Venice, where the little fool whinnies her fill about the stones and the colours, thanking her lucky stars that she is a Nartist, which means she screws up her eyes to get the full effect of the marvellous yellow bit in that corner of the picture and make out the rest of its myriad wonders, while all around her troops past a cheap hotelful of heifers being herded through their cultural transhumance, and the stay in Venice goes off like a charm because of poetry, and poetry because of many banknotes and a suite in the best *palazzo*.

'But when six weeks have gone by and the poor third husband is jumping through fewer hoops and has turned seedy and conjugal and is wearying of the physiological, when his thoughts turn again to his social life and to getting back to work and to inviting the van Vrieses to dinner, and when he begins to talk about promotion and his rheumatism, then all of a sudden it dawns on her, and how noble the illumination, that she has made a mistake. It never fails to come, that I've-made-a-ghastly-mistake moment. She makes up her mind to speak to him in her most dignified manner, and, to mark the solemnity of the moment, she perches a tall, golden turban on her head. "Dear third spiderhusband," says spiderwoman, clasping her little hairy forelegs together, "let us be worthy of each other, so let us part on an edifying note, without vain recriminations. Let us not with pointless name-calling defile the noble memory of our past happiness. I owe you the truth and the truth is, dear, that I do not love you any more." That never fails to come either, the I-don't-love-you-any-more moment. "It would be base of me to pretend," she goes on. "The fact of the matter, dear, is that I have made a mistake. I believed with all my heart and with all my soul that you would be my eternal spiderhubby. But alas I must tell you that a fourth spiderman has become important in my life." They love saying "important in my life", which sounds much nobler than "sleeping with". Then pretty spiderwoman goes on, her sentiments continually gaining altitude: "You see, I love him with all my heart and with all my soul, for he is the spiderman of spidermen, a rare spirit possessing Character of the very highest quality. He was placed on my path by God. Ah, what agonies I suffer, for the blow I have struck you will prove fatal, surely? But what choice have I? I can neither live a lie nor speak untruths, for my mouth must remain as pure as my inner being. So farewell, my dear, and think sometimes of your little Antinea." A variant: as she concludes her oration, she might suggest one last little bout in bed, just to show she is still genuinely fond of him and also to leave him with a happy memory. But most often, she ends with: "Come, be strong, and let us remain good friends."

'I hate her!' he shouted, banging the table with his fist, which made the glasses on it rattle. 'I hate her because she will never admit that it all came about because Spiderman IV is brand-new and makes a pleasant change from Spiderman III. Oh no! They always speak of their new love as having been decreed by heaven, as being ineluctable, adorable and mysterious, and involving soul-searching in the highest! And so, with a flourish of her soul and a waggle of her rump, she flees into Egypt with spiderman number four who will be a disappointment to her the day she realizes that he too can come down with diarrhoea just like a husband.

'And the empis! He has to perform feats of strength too, poor devil. The empisette is adamant. But I have mentioned her already. Well, what about the canaryess, then? Before the canaryess will agree to allow the earth to move prior to laying subsequential little eggs, she insists that her poor canary spouse must leap about and go through his athletic paces, that I should warble louder than other canaries, that I should act like an apache and roll my shoulders and do the java like a gangster and let my wings hang down menacingly! Alas, poor me! And if I try to be pleasant she turns into a raging fury and scratches my eyes out!'

He paused. Swinging his string of sandalwood beads round and round on his finger, he pictured himself first coming out of the tattooer's shop in Marseilles, then lying on the floor of a hotel room, impassive for all time, his arms spread wide under the lamp which has burned all night, arms outstretched and a hole above the nipple in a halo of black particles. No, not a hole, because shot fired point-blank. The gases from the detonation would have entered the hole, causing the skin to burst and leave a wound like a starred cross. He turned and faced her.

'I have used terrible words which I regret after I have said them: palaeolithic and babooness. I have used them and cannot help repeating them because it makes me so angry that women are not as they deserve to be and as they are in the inmost recesses of my heart. They are angels, and I know it. But why does the palaeolithic cast its shadow over the angel? Listen and I will tell you my secret. Sometimes in the middle of the night I wake suddenly, sweating with terror. How is it possible that they who are gentle and tender, my ideal and my religion, how is it possible that they can love gorillas and the things gorillas do? I lie awake at night amazed that women, who are marvels of creation, eternally virgins and eternally mothers, who originate in a world quite distinct from the place whence men come and are man's superior, it appals me that women, the annunciation and prophecy of the beatific human race which will one day come to pass, humanity made human at last, women, demure-eyed creatures whom I adore, grace made flesh, gentleness incarnate and spark visible of the godhead, it fills me with revulsion that they should surrender to might, which is the power of life and death, it fills me with disgust when I see them brought so low by their worship of brutes, it poisons my nights and I do not understand nor will I ever accept that it must be so! They are infinitely superior to the odious thugs and bandits who attract them, don't you see that? And it is an incomprehensible paradox which torments me that my divinities should be drawn to cruel, hairy men! Yes, divinities! Was it women who invented clubs, arrows, spears, swords, Greek fire, mortars, cannon and bombs? No, the perpetrators were the brutes, the virile men they have loved! And yet they worship one of my race, the prophet with the sorrowing eyes who was Love! What am I supposed to make of that? I can make nothing of it.'

He picked up his string of beads, stared at it as though trying to make some sense of it, put it on the table, murmured a pleasant 'Thank you' to no one in particular, and hummed a Passover hymn. Suddenly, aware that she was looking at him, he raised a hand in friendly greeting.

'Aude. She was my wife. During the last phase of our marriage, because I had dropped out of society, because I had put aside the mask of he-who-succeeds, because I was no longer a miserable government minister, because I had no money and had grown an absurd beard and walked in saintliness, because I had given up playing my role of strong man, because of all this, when I told her how sick in heart I was to see her love lose its lustre, how racked I was to see myself humbled by her contempt, me! the lord she once had loved with all her soul, when I said that, oh her silences and her impermeable face, her stony face, and oh the day in our shabby room when, in an effort to find favour in her eyes by washing the dishes, I dropped a plate and, fool that I was, apologized, oh her horrible, petty, impatient contempt, her woman's contempt! I was poor and therefore weak. I was no longer important, no longer a loathsome conqueror. Clinging ridiculously to hope, I told her it broke my heart to know I was no longer loved, for I was sure that if she understood what I was saying she would gather me up into her arms. And so I waited for her gentle words, waited, slack-mouthed with unhappiness. I hoped, I believed in her. "Aren't you going to say anything, darling?" "I have nothing to say," said the female in answer to the poor male, the vanquished male. Turned to stone, implacable because I had begged for help, because I needed her, the female said again: "I have nothing to say" with the moronic disdain of some remote empress who is irritated beyond endurance by the pauper who begs for her love. And this was the same woman who, in the early days, had asked nothing better than to be a slave to my shining, conquering hero.'

He lit a cigarette, inhaled a long lungful of smoke to stifle a sob, smiled, and repeated his friendly salute.

'Fifth tactic: cruelty. Cruelty is what they want and cannot do without. In bed, the moment we woke, they would always start pestering me about my handsome, cruel smile, my attractive, ironic smile, when all I wanted was to spread her toast with butter and love and bring her tea in bed. I repressed all such impulses, that goes without saying, for the breakfast tray would have singularly cooled her passion. Instead, hapless man that I was, I would curl my lip and show my toothbones in a cruel smile to make her happy. The things poor unhappy Solal has had to endure from them! One night, after a bout of the sport which they find so astoundingly fascinating, she duly billed and cooed a sweet nothing along the lines of "my meany-weany lover-man who was so horrible to me yesterday". And said it gratefully, do you hear? That was how Elizabeth Vanstead thanked me for all the cruel whims I was obliged, against my better nature, to inflict on her, oh yes, thanked me, while she kissed my bare shoulder. Horrible!'

He paused, breathing hard, wild-eyed, a caged tiger, while she stared at him. Elizabeth Vanstead, daughter of Lord Vanstead, the most eligible undergraduate in the whole of Oxford, on everyone's list, so haughty and so beautiful that she had never dared speak to her. Elizabeth Vanstead, naked, with this man!

'No, no, it's too sickening, I can't take any more. I'd prefer to have the love of a dog. Oh I know, I'm repeating myself. It's a habit of my race, a passionate people in love with their truths. Read the prophets and you'll find holy men repeating themselves everlastingly. To be loved by a dog I wouldn't have to shave myself close or be handsome or need to prove my strength. All I'd have to do is be kind. I'd need do no more than pat him on his little head and tell him he's a good dog, and me too. He'd wag his tail and he'd love me true with his soft eyes, he'd love me even if I were ugly and old and poor and rejected by mankind and had no identity card and no Commander's tie, he'd love me even if I had none of the thirty-two toothbones which self-respecting jaws should have, he'd love me, oh marvel of marvels, even if I were tender and weak with love. I think very highly of dogs. Tomorrow I shall seduce a dog and will devote the rest of my life to it. Or perhaps I should try being a homosexual? Best not, I wouldn't fancy kissing anybody with a moustache. And that, of course, is the measure of woman: a creature who, incredibly, actually likes kissing men. Horrible thought!'

Suddenly he gave a start, for he had noticed a fly on the wall, one of those disgustingly large metallic bluebottles he was afraid of. He crept quietly over to the wall and saw that, no, it was just a mark on the wallpaper. Relieved, he smiled at the woman, folded his arms, began a little jig, and smiled again, for all at once he felt inexpressibly happy.

'Like to see how well I can juggle? I can juggle with six separate objects. That's difficult, because of the differences in weight and size. For example, a banana, a plum, a peach, an orange, an apple and a pineapple. Shall I ring for the waiter and get him to bring fruit? No? Pity.'

He strode round the room, slim, tousle-haired, pretending that his mind was far away, carefully cultivating his personal magnetism, absurdly swinging his Commander's tie. Facing her once more, he offered her a cigarette, which she refused, then a box of chocolate fondants, which she also refused. He gave a resigned shrug and once more began to speak.

'I tell myself stories in the bath too. This morning I reported my own funeral to myself. It was delightful. To my funeral have come kittens in pink ribbons, two squirrels linking arms, a black poodle in a lace collar, ducklings in muffs, sheep wearing shepherd's hats, goats dressed in georgette, pale-blue doves, a little weeping donkey, a giraffe in a bathing costume circa 1880, a rough-pawed lion-cub crunching a lettuce-heart to show he is really a kindly soul, a musk-ox exuding sterling good cheer, a little short-sighted rhinoceros looking so sweet with its horn-rimmed specs and gold-painted horn, a baby hippopotamus with an oilcloth bib to stop it getting mess all over itself when it eats, though it never finishes all its soup. Also seven puppies who are the best of friends, wearing their Sunday best, proud of their sailor-suits and the whistles hanging on a cord round their necks. They drink raspberry cordial through straws and then put one paw to their mouths to conceal a yawn because they are bored at my funeral. The smallest puppy has patent-leather shoes and is dressed up like everyone's idea of a pretty little girl, with lace bloomers showing, and he skips with a rope to draw admiring glances from his mama, who is chatting respectably to a lady grasshopper with cold eyes who is dreaming of marsh and pond. This grasshopperess is very devout and dotes on royal births and the coronations of queens. As he skips, the bonny little puppy, panting for breath, rapidly recites a little poem so that his mama will say how clever he is. When it's finished, he clings to her skirt and looks up at her eagerly, expecting kisses and compliments, but she tells him in English that she's busy, "Mummy is very busy, dear," and she doesn't even look at him, for she is too busy listening to the tittle-tattle of the grasshopperess, who is knitting, so the little puppy starts skipping some more and recites his poem again while nearby a small armadillo, sick with jealousy, also proceeds to improvise a poem for his aunt. At my funeral there are also Jewish noses which walk around on little legs, a midget called Nanine who practises her *entrechats* watched by seven kittens, an unmarried rabbit reciting a prayer, a sad baby fawn, and chicks in satin suits and top-hats which are too small for them who confer standing up in a miniature coach: they're a squad of rabbis, the holiest chick in triple satin being the Chief Rabbi. Shall I go on?'

'Yes,' she said, without looking up.

'There is also a pekinese who every so often, to get respect, says "It is undeniable" and "I assume", and also a beaver who digs the hole to put my heart in, my overcombustible heart, and a koala bear with a Tyrolean hat who reads out my funeral oration and stumbles over the words, and my little cat Kitty in widow's weeds who blows her nose in mischievous grief but her veil catches in the prickles of a grave-faced hedgehog I once met in the canton of Vaud who is weeping sincerely while my little cat untangles herself from his prickles and goes and sits on a grassy grave and studiously washes her face in the warm sunshine, stopping suddenly to stare at the dwarf ponies decked out with feathers and turbans who, as their contribution to the solemn celebrations, feel obliged to paw the earth with their front legs and then rear up on their hind legs. There is also a little monkey in a velvet fez who plays a polka on an accordion because there's no organ, while a demented kitten who doesn't understand a thing about what's going on, goes on the rampage like an Arab stallion to attract attention, a very nasty stallion at that, recklessly charging at anyone anywhere, ears martially pricked and a plume stuck in its behind, convinced that it is terrorizing the ducklings who swap sweeties in a shower of giggles. And that's it: the funeral procession which follows my heart on its way to its last resting-place. It's delightful, it's delectable, it's a great success. And now my heart has been buried and is no longer with me. The cemetery is deserted and everyone has gone home, except for one fly sitting on my grave, rubbing its forelegs together and looking very pleased, and me, standing there empty and pale. A penny for your thoughts?'

'How does the little puppy's poem go?' she asked, after a pause during which she looked at him in silence.

'"Little pupply to his mummy says When I'm big I'll save de King On my toes a braid of gold On my head a clof of satin In my mouf a little pipe To draw on And de good King says: give Free little bones Free little breads To dat brave little pupply." He has a speech impediment, you see, he explained seriously. He can't say puppy, he says pupply, and he can't say th, he says f and de.'

'And what about the little armadillo's poem?'

'"Harrymadillo to his auntie said Hurry don't dally auntie or I'm dead Rummage around beneath my coat I need my auntie's antidote For I've gone and swallowed some armoured plate Hurry don't dawdle it really won't wait."'

'Is little Kitty a real cat?'

'A real cat, but she's dead. It was for her that I rented the house at Bellevue, because she wasn't happy here at the Ritz. I rented a whole house just for her, so she'd have trees to climb and sharpen her claws on, a paddock full of the good smells of nature, where she could run about and hunt. I had the drawing-room furnished especially for her with a sofa, armchairs and a Persian rug. I loved her. She was a very choosy, snooty, middle-class cat who had her ways and liked her comforts, very capitalist-minded when she sat in her armchair, but definitely an anarchist who hated doing what she was told when I told her to lie down, an angel with kleptomaniac tendencies, always looked serious even when she was at her friskiest, purred like a factory, a very feminine little thing, all purr and fur, a quiet little lady with whiskers, one minute all sugar and spice curled up in front of the fire and the next aloof and dignified, as in myth and fable.

'Ah Kitty, with whom I could be tender and absurd, an adolescent, without having to fear what anyone might say. Kitty! My fluffy Kitty! Her face seemed smaller when she felt like being sentimental, she would close her eyes with tender complicity, half-close them in ecstasy because I told her, for the hundredth time, that she was a nice pussy. Kitty, fur ruffled and dreaming in the sun, offering her little nose to the sun, living the good life in the sun, oh her precious, empty eyes! Kitty, looking so studious when, on a sudden impulse, she licked herself clean in the sun, licked her back leg, which she raised high in a way which made you think of a double-bass player, stopping abruptly to peer at me in sudden bewilderment, trying to understand or maybe just thinking, puzzled, her thoughts put to flight by the scorching sun. When I returned from the world of men, it was a relief to be away from those mean-minded monkeys in black coats and striped trousers and back with her again, for she was always ready to do as I said, to trust me, to card the wool on the knees of my trousers, to ingratiate herself by nuzzling my hand with her impassive head, her pretty head which thought no ill of me, my never-for-an-instant-anti-Semitic sweetie-pie.

'She knew over twenty words. She understood "Go out", "Beware of the dog", "Eat", "Fish-paste", "Nice liver", "Be good" and "Say hello" – which I had to pronounce "Say yellow" and to say hello she would rub her head against my hand. She understood "Fly", a word which meant anything that flew, and when she heard it Kitty my huntress would make a dash for the window in the hope of catching something. She understood "Naughty cat" but never agreed with me and always protested. She understood "Catch" and "Come". She did not always come when I said "Come", she was too independent. But she always came running if I said "Catch", all smiles, obliging, dancing attendance like the senior sales-assistant to some fancy dress-designer. Whenever I said "You've hurt my feelings", she miaowed tragically. If I said "It's all over between us", she went and hid under the sofa and suffered. But I always winkled her out of there with a walking-stick and cuddled her. Then she'd give me a cat-kiss, a single lick on the hand with her rough tongue, and then we'd both sit down and purr.

'The poor little thing was left entirely to her own devices all day long in that big house. Her only company was the gardener's wife who came morning and evening to put food out for her. When she got too bored and missed me, she would do something naughty like scratching and clawing the Bible left open on the drawing-room table. It was a cabalistic rite, an incantation, a spell, designed to make me appear in a puff of magic, to make the friend she could not do without suddenly materialize. Her tiny brain worked on these lines: whenever I do something naughty, he always scolds me, so he must be here somewhere. It was no more absurd than prayer is.

'When I came home to see her in the evening after the day's Under-Clowning, she'd come bounding down the hallway the minute she heard the miracle of the key in the lock, after which we rowed like any married couple! "I've been so miserable," her pathetic contralto miaowings said. "You leave me by myself far too much, it's no life for me." Then I'd open the fridge and take out some raw liver, cut it up with a pair of scissors, and everything would be all right again. The perfect romance. I was forgiven. Her tail quivering with impatience and joy, she'd purr like a steam engine, rub her pert little face against my leg, which was her way of saying how much she loved me and how kind I was to cut up her liver. When the liver was ready in her saucer, I preferred not to give it to her straight away. I'd meander through the hall and the drawing-room, and she would follow me everywhere, making a great occasion of it, grand as a marchioness, processing ceremoniously, half model child and half royal mistress, suddenly garbed in her party best, her noble, fluffy tail

upright and quivering, she would pad softly after me, dancing attendance in the form of the sweetest minuet, as quick in her cupidity as in
her affection, her eyes raised to the holy saucer, so loyal and faithful
and ready to follow me to the ends of the earth. My sweet little
bogus joy, my Kitty.

'When I'd get home and she happened to be outside, at the far end
of the paddock, she'd run towards me like a mad thing the minute
she saw me, come hurtling down the slope like a meteor, and it was
love. When she reached me, she'd come to a sudden stop, walk
slowly round me and be friends, regally, coquettishly and impassively,
with her sumptuous tail gloriously raised in joy. She'd walk round
me twice, come closer, curve her tail round my boots, tilt her head to
look up at me, arch her back and put on the charm, and then open
her little pink mouth, which was her delicate way of begging for her
dinner.

'When she'd finished eating, she'd go into the drawing-room for
her nap, settle herself into the best armchair, which was also the most
claw-marked, and doze off with one of her soft, furry paws over her
closed eyes to shut out the light. But suddenly, though she was
apparently fast asleep, her ears would prick up and twitch in the
direction of the window and some interesting noise outside. Then she
would get up, moving instantly from sleep to a state of eager
anticipation, frightening and beautiful, with her attention focused on
the intriguing sound, and the next moment she was away. Leaping on
to the window-sill and pressing herself against the bars, she'd stay
there perfectly still for a moment, poignantly concentrating, her eyes
fixed on some invisible prey, uttering faint growls of feline desire,
irregular, plaintive miaows. Then, gathering herself in readiness and
steadying herself on her back legs ready for the off, she'd spring
through the bars of the window. A-hunting she was gone.

'She loved sleeping near me. It was one of her aims in life. If she
were outside on the terrace, sunbathing or twitching greedily as she
watched a sparrow, and she heard me lie down on the sofa in the
drawing-room, she would leap up, burst through the open window,
and make a faint scuttering on the parquet floor with her claws. She'd
jump up on my chest and trample me, delicately raising and lowering
her paws, and make a comfortable nest for herself. When she'd

finished her little ritual dance, a relic perhaps from the forests of prehistory when her ancestors used to spread dried leaves for a bed before settling down to sleep, she'd stretch out on my chest, snuggle down in utter bliss, looking all of a sudden very long and every inch a princess, and the little outboard motor in her throat would start up, in first gear to begin with but soon moving into top, and we would drift off happily together. She used to put one paw on my hand, to make sure I was still there, and when I told her she was a nice cat she'd give me a little stab in the hand with her claws, without hurting me of course, just enough to say thank you, to indicate that she'd understood, to let me know that the two of us got on fine, that we were friends. That's the end. I'm not doing any more seducing.'

'All right, don't. But tell me the other tactics. Pretend you're telling a man.'

'A man,' he said, suddenly wonder-struck. 'Of course! You are a young cousin of mine, very handsome, who has come to ask how to bamboozle some dim girl. Call him Nathan. Men's talk! Lovely idea! Let's make a start. Where was I?'

'Cruelty.'

'Ah yes, cruelty. I understand you, Nathan, I do. You love her and you want her to love you, and you can't very well decide to love a dog instead just because a dog deserves your love more than she does. You've no choice: seduce her. Use your technique, do your horrible worst, sell your soul. Force yourself to be clever and cruel and she will love you a thousand times more than if you were a good little Deume. If you want to be loved with passion, pay the squalid price, stir the dung-heap where love's marvels grow.

'But have a care, Nathan. Don't come on too strong at the start, before the guinea-pig is properly infatuated. Your hold over her is still flimsy, and anything too obviously callous would put her off. They still have a modicum of common sense at the beginning. So use tact. Keep a sense of proportion. Just let her feel that you have a potential for being cruel. You can make her sense your capacity for cruelty by saying something nice and then staring at her a shade too insistently, or you can flash the famous Cruel Smile or use sharp little ironies or be mildly rude, for instance by telling her that she has a shiny nose. She will be furious but deep down she'll like it. It's a sordid business: you have to repel in order to attract! Alternatively, look impassive all of a sudden, behave as though your mind were on other things or feign deafness. Not answering a question she has asked by pretending to be thinking about something else will unseat but not displease her. It's a metaphorical slap in the face, a hint of cruelties to come, a foot in the sexual door, an assertion of masculine detachment. Moreover, by showing a lack of interest, you will strengthen her determination to attract your attention, to lure and please you. It will also serve to impress on her an obscure sense of respect. She'll say to herself, no, not say, she'll vaguely feel that you're in the habit of not paying too much attention to all those women who throw themselves at you, and that will increase your appeal. He has exquisite manners, she will think, but he could turn nasty if he wanted to. And this she will relish. Don't blame me: I'm not to blame for the way they are. The attraction of cruelty is squalid, for it is the egg of power. Whoever is cruel is sexually potent, capable of making others suffer but also, so says the innermost self, of giving joy. A lord who exudes the merest whiff of brimstone attracts them, and a dangerous smile makes them feel deliciously flustered. They adore men with a satanic cut to their jib. To them, the devil himself is enticing. Cruelty has a terrible glamour.

'And so, as the seduction begins to unfold, be prudent, take it step by step. But once she's hooked, you can set to work with a will. After the first act of what is curiously called love, it will even be advisable, provided everything has gone off well and been enthusiastically received by the poor, whimpering creature, advisable to tell her openly that you are going to make her suffer. While the sweat is still wet on her and her arms hold you tight, she'll tell you she doesn't mind, that any pain you cause her will still be a form of happiness to her. "As long as you love me," she murmurs, looking at you with candid eyes. They all have the courage to put up with suffering, especially before they've actually tasted any.

'When it gets to where passion rules her every moment, be openly, masterfully cruel. But don't overdo it. Keep a firm grip on things. Salt is an excellent condiment, but too much spoils the broth. So be heartless and gentle in turns, and don't forget the frolics, for frolics are compulsory. Recipe for a passion cocktail: be the enemy she loves, and sprinkle occasionally with barbarities so that she remains on a permanent amorous footing, feels permanently anxious, is always wondering what dreadful thing is going to happen next, is constantly tormented by jealousy, always longing, hoping that things will be patched up, and savouring each unexpected little act of tenderness. To sum up: don't let her get bored. Anyway, making up always adds spice to the frolicking. When you've been especially cool or beastly to her, just smile and she'll be so softened up that she'll melt with gratitude and rush off to tell her best friend all sorts of marvellous things about you and say that deep down you're really good and kind. Give women a callous man and they'll always manage to say that deep down he's really a very warm human being. They reward him for being cruel by fixing a crown of goodness on his head.

'And so, as long as you want her to go on loving you with all her heart and with all her soul, you must tread carefully and always take particular care to turn up late for trysts and meetings, just to keep her on hot bricks. Or now and then, when she's waiting for you, all set to go, meticulously primped and preened and not daring to move in case she spoils the effect, you should phone at the last moment and say you've been prevented from coming, though you're dying to see her. Or better still, don't phone and don't go. Touch of the lash: she'll be utterly miserable. What was the point of washing her hair, setting it and having it turn out so well since her blue-eyed, cruel-eyed boy has not come? What was the point of the new dress which suits her so well? The poor little thing cries and, because she is alone, blows her nose like a trumpet, and wipes it again and again on a stack of little hankies, and dabs at her eyes, which are swollen with tears, and puts her thinking cap on and invents a new explanation with each handkerchief she soaks. Why hasn't he come? Is he ill? Doesn't he love me as much? Is he with that woman? Oh, she's so clever: she knows how to get round him! Of course, she can afford to buy expensive tailor-made clothes! That's it! He must be with her! But only yesterday he was telling me . . . Oh, it's not fair! After all the sacrifices I've made for him! Et cetera, et cetera, and the rest of the usual cardio-lyrical litany. And next day she's sobbing on your shoulder and saying: "Cruel, cruel darling, I cried all night long. Oh, never leave me, I can't live without you." And there you have the squalid lengths to which she forces you to go if you want her to love you truly, madly!

'But, Nathan, when you see her clinging to you damp-eyed and crumpled, have a care not to allow your natural generosity of heart to get the better of you. Never abandon the little acts of cruelty which quicken passion and keep it burnished bright. She will complain, but she will love you. Should you make the unfortunate error of ceasing to be a brute, she won't hold it against you exactly but she will begin to love you less. First, because you'll have lost a part of your attractiveness. Second, because she'll be as bored with you as she would be with a husband. Whereas with a brute to love she's never bored, she observes him closely for signs of calmer waters, makes herself pretty to earn his approval, looks at him with imploring eyes, and hopes he'll be nice to her tomorrow. To put it in a nutshell, she suffers, and she finds suffering interesting.

'And so it comes to pass. Next day, he behaves exquisitely and she is in paradise, and there she basks, relishing every moment, in a state of bliss where the pale flowers of boredom never grow, because at every moment she fears that paradise might suddenly vanish. This way her life is varied and storm-tossed. Squalls, cyclones, sudden lulls, rainbows. See to it that she has intervals of happiness, but even more moments of suffering. That's how to manufacture a love that is sacred.

'The appalling thing, Nathan, is that this same sacred love, bought at such sordid cost, is the wonder of the world. But it means signing a pact with the devil, for he who would be sacredly loved shall lose his soul. They have made me pretend to be cruel, and for that I shall never forgive them! But what choice did I have? I needed them, so beautiful in sleep, needed the way they smell of fresh-baked bread when they sleep, needed their adorable, effeminately masculine ges-tures, needed their modesty which seamlessly becomes wondrous compliance in the dusky shadows of the night, for they are surprised or frightened by nothing which is done in the service of love. Needed the look in her eyes when I arrive and she waits, heart-stoppingly standing at her door beneath the roses. Oh night! Oh joy! Oh the wonder of her kiss upon my hand! (He kissed his hand, stared at the woman who watched him, and smiled in his soul's fullness.) And again and most of all, oh manna dropped by angels, needed the inspired tenderness of which they give freely only when they love truly, madly – and they love truly, madly only men who are callous. Ergo, use cruelty to buy passion and passion to buy tenderness!'

He juggled with a damascene-bladed dagger, a gift from Michael, put it down on the table next to the roses, looked at the young woman, and felt a surge of pity. Bursting now with youth and vigour and sumptuously twin-prowed, yet soon to lie unmoving under the earth, never more to share the joys of springtime, the first blooms of the year and the clamour of the birds in the trees, never more to know joy as she lies stiff and solitary in her stifling coffin, her airless coffin made of wood, of wood which was already a fact of existence, which was ready and existing somewhere. 'My poor doomed darling,' he murmured. He opened a drawer, took out a pretty little plush teddy-bear with spurred boots on its feet, a sombrero on its head and a winning, wistful expression on its face. He held it out to her. She declined with a nod and added a faint 'No thanks.'

'Pity,' he said, 'it was kindly meant. Tactic number six: vulnerability. You must of course, Nathan, be virile and cruel. But if you want to be loved to perfection you must also bring out her maternal side. Beneath your bullish exterior she must be made to discover a hint of weakness. Beneath the brashness of the man, they ask nothing better than to discover a little boy. A trace of human frailty from time to time – but it shouldn't be overdone – will please them immensely and melt their hearts. So be nine parts gorilla to one part orphan and you'll have them eating out of your hand.

'Seventh tactic: primordial contempt. This must be signalled from the outset but never articulated in words. They are extremely touchy about matters of vocabulary, especially in the early days. But when scorn is expressed in certain inflections of the voice or a special breed of smile, they sense its presence at once: they like it, it disturbs them. Deep inside them, a voice says that this man scorns because he is used to being loved, accustomed to holding women cheap. In short, a master before whom all women are as skittles. "Me too!" cries the voice inside them, "I want to be a skittle!" I shall get that dog to love me tomorrow. We'll go out together every day. He'll be so happy to be out walking with me, trotting on ahead but stopping all the time and turning round to see where I've got to, to be quite sure that the treasure I represent is still there, and suddenly he'll come running back and jump up at me with front paws outstretched, and he'll dirty me all over in the nicest possible way. What woman would do as much?

'Tactic number eight: consideration and compliments. If their unconscious relishes contempt, their conscious mind demands consideration. This tactic is important, especially at the start. Later on, it can be dropped. But during the process of seduction she will adore being raised on high by a man who scorns all other women, and will exult in the knowledge that she alone has found favour in his sight. So to your underlying contempt you should add a veneer of admiration which you will express in words so that she thinks: "Here at last is a man who understands me!" For they love being understood, though they have no very clear idea of what this means. Question her when, so noble and so wistful, she comes out with the famous line about having a husband who does not understand her. Try to find out what she means by being understood, and you will be appalled by the messiness of the answer.

'So, to begin with, pay her effusive compliments. Don't be afraid of laying it on thick. They'll believe anything. Appealing to their vanity is a sure way of getting them on the hook. Are they vain? Of course they are, but more important they are also very unsure of themselves. They have a bottomless need to be reassured, because each morning they look in their mirror and discover endless blemishes: hair that's dull and too dry, unwelcome dandruff, enlarged pores, ugly toenails, especially the little one, which is crooked, the little piggy with the runty nail on the end of it. So you see what sterling service you can render by putting them up there on a pedestal! Very unsure of themselves. Hence their chronic hunger for new dresses, which make them feel new and newly desirable. Oh, those absurdly long, painted nails, their silly plucked eyebrows, the slavish way they follow the laws of fashion. Tell them the fashion this year is for skirts with a large hole in the seat and they just can't wait to get into a skirt which bares their backside to the breeze. Compliment her on everything, even the ridiculous disaster of a hat she insists on wearing which sits on her head like a permanent judgement. To her, compliments are as rich in oxygen as a new dress: she inhales them and regains her bloom. So renew her faith in herself and she won't be able to live without you, even if you don't succeed in subduing her completely at your first meeting. She'll think of you each morning when she wakes. She'll repeat the nice things you said as she fiddles with her fleece, an activity which seems to stimulate her power of concentration. Incidentally, you mustn't be afraid of a touch of smut now and again. It brings down the barriers. Once she knows that you know she has a secret fleece, which you can perfectly well imagine to be blonde or auburn or dark, her defences will start to crumble.

'Ninth tactic, which is related to number seven: sexuality by suggestion. When you meet her for the first time, you must ensure that she senses in you the male of the species confronting the female. One useful tip: commit violations of her person, but of a minor sort so that she has no grounds for complaining. In any case, since no breach of propriety has taken place, she won't dislike it. For instance, into the gap between two respectful sentences you could let slip, sort of casually, a "dear" or similar, for which you would apologize at once. Best of all, look her straight in the eye with a hint of scorn, a trace of condescension, and a suggestion of desire, indifference and callousness: they make an effective mix and come cheap. To wit: the odious heavy-lidded glance, the proprietary stare, the calm, ironic look which is faintly amused and disrespectful though what you say is perfectly civil, a look of veiled familiarity. Then her unconscious cries out: "Hosanna! Here is Don Juan in the flesh! He does not respect me! He knows how to treat a girl! Hallelujah, I feel the most delicious commotion and cannot resist him!" You see all the contradictions? He's strong but vulnerable, disdainful but admiring, deferential but also strongly sexual. And each tactic makes its opposite shine more brightly and increases its attraction.

'And hear this too, Nathan. Do not be afraid to stare at her breasts. If you say nothing, all is well. She will guess that you desire her and will not be offended. Only words offend. Inwardly, as you face her discussing some respectable topic of conversation, silently sing to her the song of your desire.

'Let the song be in your eyes, the song of her breasts. Oh breasts so terrible, breasts so near, twin glories of womankind, double peaks of plenty, unknown and disquieting, seen from afar but unexplored as yet by hand of man, near yet forbidden, cruelly revealed because revealed too little and too much, angel domes, sweet pillows plumped with disconcerting power, crop ripe for picking, twin wonders of torment, young and proud, one on the right, one on the left, oh your twin trials, oh fruits proffered by a willing sister, oh juice-heavy fruits hanging within a hand's reach.

'So shall say your eyes, Nathan. For pity's sake, bare them, your eyes will say, uncover them, for she shows them yet shows them not, conceals without concealment, and this she does deliberately. Oh cruel tease who breathes too deep and as she breathes they rise, prosper and are perfect, oh cursed woman of my heart! Oh why does she not let them go free, for you want to live a little before you die, why does she not release them and offer them and their nipples to you, sublimely risen and emancipated, so that you may touch and know their weight and their benison. Please, your eyes will say, make her peel back the cloth which cloaks yet not quite hides them as they loom mightily armed and presumptuous. Let her unveil them, show them to you now, show them frankly and honestly. Begone, O ye coversome raiments which tempt and forbid and drive a man mad with desire! Enough, be done with this sorry charade! The trees and the lake which you see yonder will still be there when Death's pale rider sweeps you up in his arms, bears you away for ever towards the damp kingdom where breath is stopped. Quickly now, those lips, your eyes will say, cover her with your touch, cover her with your body and know her, live and gloriously die in her while you die too on those lips.

'You are alone in the world, Nathan, without kindred spirits, and she is yours by right in her noble, sunlit youth! Oh the flatness of her belly, the delicious hollow above her navel: exquisite, I swear! So beautiful, so feminine! Golden her youth, concave her belly, luscious her legs, her long, silky legs! Oh potency of woman! Oh firm thighs beneath her insufferable dress which again she pulls down modestly, or rather obsessively, oh rampant hips, oh agonizing roundness, oh sweet haven of her lap, oh her long curved lashes, oh soon her languid capitulation! Oh yes my love, so your eyes will tell her, oh yes! I desire you and am no more than my desire, which reaches out for you and for your secret, the secret beneath your dress, which exists beneath your dress.

'That is what your eyes will tell her, and more besides, while you talk civilly of Bach. And if you dance with her, do not be afraid to render a silent homage to her beauty. Nor are they offended as long as the words you speak remain respectful. So says Michael. In any case, the most modest of them always manage not to be aware of what has passed between you. And when you stop dancing, get back to Bach.'

The telephone. He picked up the receiver, held it to his head like a revolver, and then put it to his ear.

'Hello, Elizabeth. Come dancing with you? Why not, Elizabeth! Wait for me at the Donon. No, I'm not alone. The one I told you about, the one you knew at Oxford. Of course not, you know you are the only woman in my life. See you soon.'

He replaced the receiver and turned to face her.

'Note well, dear coz, that tactic number ten is the element of competition. Waste no time. Set the pace at your very first meeting and she will follow like a sheep. You must find a way of letting her know (a) that you are loved by another woman who is awesomely attractive and (b) that you were on the verge of falling in love with this other woman but now you've met her and she is the only one, supreme wonder of all her gullible kind, and this may of course be quite true. When you've got this far, you're well on the way to success with the little ninny, for she is a kleptomaniac like all her kind.

'And now she is ready for the final gambit: the declaration of love. Use all the stale old clichés you like, but attend to your voice and its fire. A grave tone is recommended. Naturally, you must make her feel that she is ruining her life with her awful lawful spiderman, that life with him is unworthy of her, at which point you will observe her yield a martyr-style sigh. This is a special kind of sigh, produced through the nose, and it means: "Oh, if only you knew what I've had to put up with from that man, but I shall say nothing, for I am a person of refinement and infinite discretion." Naturally, you will tell her that she is the only one, that she is unique, for they insist on this too, that her eyes are windows which offer a glimpse of the godhead. She won't understand this but will find the thought so beautiful that she will close the aforementioned windows and feel that with you life would be one perpetual round of extramarital bliss. For good measure, mention that she is the fragrance of lilac and the softness of night and the song of rain falling on a garden. Keep it cheap and cheerful and you will observe her far more deeply moved than if she heard the same words sincerely spoken by an old man. They'll swallow the whole bag of tricks as long as there is a deep and throaty throb in your voice. Go to it with all guns blazing so that she feels that life with you would be a paradise of eternal carnimalities, which they call living intensely. And don't forget to talk about setting off to the sea off your heads, they love it. Off to sea off your heads: remember these six words. Say them and the effect is miraculous. You'll see the poor wretch quiver. Choose a hot place, sumptuous surroundings, lots of sun, that is, ensure association of ideas with joyous physical congress and the high life. Off is the crucial word, for their vice is wanting to be off. The minute you mention going off, she shuts her eyes and opens her mouth. She's firmly on the hook, and you can gobble her up and wash her down with a cup of sadness. It's over. Here are the papers containing your husband's promotion. Love him and give him fine children. Goodbye.'

'Goodbye,' she said softly, but did not stir.

'Do you remember the poor words the old man spoke? Oh the wonder of it, the snatches of song in the car which will carry me to her, to she who waits for me, towards her long star-spangled lashes, and the soon look, the look in her eyes when I stand before her, she waiting at her door, tall and slender and dressed all in white, ready and beautiful for me, ready and fearful lest she mar her beauty if I should delay, and darting to her mirror to view her beauty, to see if her beauty is still there, still intact, and then returning to the door and waiting for me in a cloud of love, heart-stoppingly standing at her door under the roses, oh tender night! oh youth that is mine once more! oh the wonder when I stand before her! the look in her eyes! the love we share! and she shall lower her head to my extended hand, and oh the wonder of her kiss upon my hand! and she shall look up at me and our eyes shall light up with love and we shall smile at loving so, you and I, and glory be to God.'

'Glory be to God,' she said.

And then she bowed her head and her lips alighted on the hand of her lord, and she raised her head, looked at him, to virginity restored, holily gazed upon his face of gold and night, as upon a sun. With a bewildered smile on his trembling lips, he stared at the hand which she had kissed and raised it close to his eyes. What proof could he give her? Take Michael's dagger, pierce his flesh, and swear by the blood which coursed out of him? But that would make a mess of his dinner-jacket, it was his best, and he should have to leave her while he got changed! Heigh-ho, forget the dagger, stay with her for ever and ever, and Glory be to God, Glory be to God.

She gazed on, not daring to speak for fear of tarnishing the majesty of the moment, and besides perhaps her voice would break. Piously believing, devoutly young, she gazed gravely upon her lord, gazed upon him wildly, hardly breathing, icy-cold, trembling with fear and love, with the ache of happiness on her lips.

From the ballroom rose a summons, Hawaiian guitars reluctantly releasing their long, pure lamentation, a lament from the heart, a long-drawn, sweet lament, liquid to liquidate the soul, an infinite keening of farewell. Then he took her by the hand and they left the room. Slowly they descended. Solemnly did they go.

CHAPTER 36

Solemnly gyrating among the loveless couples, with eyes only for each other they danced, with eyes feasting on the other, solicitous, intense, engrossed. Blissful in his arms, happy to follow his lead, oblivious to her surroundings, she listened to the happiness coursing through her veins, glanced up at intervals to admire herself in the tall mirrors on the walls, was elegant, heart-stopping, exceptional, a woman loved, who now and then drew back her head the better to see him as he whispered wondrous words which she did not always understand, for she was too busy drinking him with her eyes, but invariably greeted with all her soul and an approving nod, as he whispered that they were in love, which prompted a faint, tremulous laugh, but of course! that was it! in love! as he whispered that he was dying to kiss and bless her long curved lashes, but not here, later, when they were alone, and then she said they had all their lives before them, and suddenly she was afraid she had displeased him, that she was too sure of herself, but no, oh joy! he smiled and held her close and whispered that every evening, yes, every evening they would be together. Jolted in his sleeper, he reproved himself for behaving like a brute, for being a brute and calling her horrible. After all, if she didn't like the chief, there wasn't much she could do about it, it was hardly her fault, was it? She had her good points. Just the other day, at the tailor's, she had been sweet enough to help him choose the material for his suit and had taken the whole thing very seriously. Most likely she would be sleeping soundly now, she looked so pretty when she was asleep. 'Sweet dreams, darling,' he said in his swaying

378

bunk, and he smiled just for her, and closed his eyes so that he would fall asleep with her. The gypsy band stopped and they paused without releasing each other while the rest of the unexceptional dancers, who let their partners go the moment the music died away, clapped their hands for more but clapped them in vain. But at a look from Solal, Imre, the pock-marked first violinist, winked back with a smile of complicity, mopped his glistening brow, and struck up majestically while, watched by the seated spectators, the odd couple resumed their dance with the gravity of love, and were soon attended by Imre fiddling wildly in a flurry of flapping sleeves and holding in his teeth the banknote Solal had given him. Leaving in her wake a trail of floating streamers which waved like slow multicoloured kelp, she let go his hand at intervals to smooth down her hair but to no avail, oh never mind, and perhaps her nose was shiny too, oh who cared, for she was his lovely, he told her so. Fair and her lord's beloved, she whispered to herself, and she smiled a beatific smile. But he couldn't get off to sleep and he wondered if she'd remembered to turn off the gas. It worried him her being in the house all by herself, with no one coming in except the daily who could only manage mornings, because Mariette wouldn't be back to work for almost another month, and it wasn't just the gas, there was also bolting the front door, most likely she wouldn't remember to do it last thing before going up to bed, and then the vitamins she took in the morning, she'd probably forget them too, oh worry, worry. Cheek to cheek, she and he, secretly, slowly turning. Oh but she, he murmured, is made of delights, a Himalayan climber in a Scots tam, queen of her porcelain zoo, the half-baked smile on her face when she was alone, the way she walked round her bedroom with toes turned inwards to make herself look silly, revelling like him in her absurd antics, pulling divinely funny faces, her own court jester, day-dreaming in her bath, friend to the sparrow-owl and protector of toads, she, his mad sister. Laying her cheek against the shoulder of her lord, she closed her eyes and asked him to tell her again, blessed in the knowledge that she was known, known better than she knew herself, that she was mocked and lauded by he who was her soul's brother, the only human being in the world who really knew her: this was love in all its glory, to be loved by a man, next to which Varvara was nothing, less than nothing, a heap of unimportance now gone for ever. Tilting back her head, she noticed that his eyes were blue and green with flecks of gold, luminous against the tan of his face, eyes which spoke of sea and sun, and she clung to him in gratitude for those eyes. Official visit, by God, with scale of allowances, by God, including climate allowance, by God, won't be long before it's the George V, by God, on a diplomatic ticket, by God. On arrival in Paris, give her a ring and remind her, gas, bolts, shutters, vitamins, et cetera. No, not on arrival, he might wake her. Leave it until eleven, right? And later on drop her a line confirming reminders. Draw up a list of things she mustn't forget on a separate sheet of paper, number them, underline items in red, a list she can pin on the wall of her room. Or perhaps suggest that she should put up at a first-class hotel until Mariette gets back, the Ritz for example, hang the expense, that way she won't be in the house on her own, so no chance of her forgetting to bolt the door. No, not the Ritz, she might bump into the chief, she didn't seem to have much time for him, she'd be quite capable of walking past him without saying hello. Whispers of their love hung over the dance. Yes, every evening of their lives, she thought happily, and she smiled at the glorious thought of getting ready for his coming every evening, singing as she made herself beautiful for him, oh the wonder of waiting every evening at the door beneath the roses, waiting in an exquisite new dress, and kissing his hand every evening when he came tall and clothed in white. 'You are beautiful,' he said, 'awesome in your beauty,' he said, 'a solar beauty ringed with eyes of mist,' he said, and he held her close and she closed her eyes, slightly ridiculous, full of grace, delighted to be awesome, elated to be thought solar. Blast, I'm not going to get to sleep, it was the gratin, I had too much. So phone at eleven, not before, don't want to go waking her up. Morning, darling. Sleep well? Everything went off swimmingly last night. I'll start with the dinner, caviare and the whole shoot. You want the whole shoot? Well I'll tell you. Caviare, as I said, then lobster au gratin Edward VII, quail conserve, haunch of venison chasseur, stuffed crêpes à la Ritz, the works, nothing but the best. Yieldingly turning in his miraculous arms, she asked him at what time he would come every evening. 'At nine,' he said, bowing his head to breathe the fragrance of her, and she said nine was good but knew not that she was born to die. The wonder of nine o'clock! At nine he would be there, every evening of their lives. So a nice long bath at eight and then get dressed quickly. Oh the enchanting prospect of making herself beautiful for him, elegant for him. But how oh how was it possible, and only a short time ago, she'd hardly got through the door, that she'd said those two dreadful words to him, and yet at this moment no one else but he existed. Ask to be forgiven for saying those two awful words? No, too difficult to manage while dancing, not now, later, and then explain everything. Explain what exactly? Oh forget it, forget it, just look at him, drown in his eyes. I ate a bit too much of the gratin and the quail, and a bit too much of the venison and, let's face it, of the caviare too, but it was only to show my appreciation, just being polite, see, and besides it gave me something to do while he wasn't saying anything, and on top of that he hardly ate anything at all and it made me feel awful to think that the waiters would come and take away all those delicious things only half eaten, and so beautifully presented too, and such generous helpings, you know, heavens, inside the quail there was a stuffing literally coal-black with truffles, if you please, so naturally I rather indulged myself. Solemnly turning in the suddenly blue-tinted semi-dark, she pressed to her lips the hand of this man she did not know, proud to be so bold. Upstairs, when I was ranting on about power and the gorillas, he thought suddenly, it was my power and the gorilla in me that she admired. No matter, we are animals, but I love her and am happy, he thought. 'Oh wonder of loving you,' he said. 'When did you know you loved me?' she dared to ask. 'At the Brazilian reception,' he murmured, 'where I saw you for the very first time and loved you at once, noble in the midst of the ignoble did you appear, you and I and no one else in the crowd of smart operators and attention-seekers, we two alone were exiles, you as lonely as I and as heartsick and as disdainful as I and talking to no one, having no friend but yourself, and at the first flutter of your eyes I knew you, knew you as the Unexpected One so long awaited, knew you at once for the Chosen One on that evening decreed by Destiny, proclaimed at the first flutter of your long curved lashes: you! divine Bokhara, favoured Samarkand, an embroidery of intricate pattern, O garden on a distant shore.' 'How beautiful,' she said, 'no one has ever talked to me like that before.' But they were the same words that the old man had spoken to her, he thought, and he smiled at her, and she worshipped his smile. The same words, but the old man had no teeth and you did not hear him, he thought. Oh derision! Oh pity! But she loves me and I love her, so glory be to my thirty-two toothbones, he thought. Anyway, as I was saying, tummy's upset, but what can you expect, it nettled me, especially since bills at the Ritz are pretty steep, oh and you'll not believe this but he signed the bill without even looking at it, because they let special customers sign their bills, he must have a monthly account with them, I didn't actually see how much it came to, he had his elbow in the way, but it must have cost the earth, especially since he'd ordered only the most expensive things on the menu plus a magnum of Moët dry imperial rosé, no less, it's the best, a whole magnum, we hardly touched it, and of course the whole lot goes on the bill whether it's been eaten and drunk or not, but the last straw was the hundred-dollar tip he gave the head waiter, naturally they hang on his every whim, a hundred-dollar note, I joke not! I saw it, saw it with my very own eyes, 'One Hundred Dollars', the words were spelled out on it, it fair took my breath away, can you imagine throwing that much money down the drain, though it's true that with his salary, but even so, in any case I'm jolly glad I got through all their gratin à la Edward VII, well nearly all, and I went at it a bit strong with the crêpes too, with the result that it all became rather indigestible, repeated on me, touch of acid, fortunately I'd remembered to pack the bicarb, so my idea works, I mean having filing-cards for the things I want to take with me when I go away, for now I'm sure not to forget anything. Other men take weeks, months before they fall in love, and even then they love but tepidly, nor can they dispense with endless talk, shared tastes and crystallizations. All I needed was one flutter of your eyelashes. Say I am mad, but believe me. A flutter of lashes, and you looked at me but did not see me, and suddenly I beheld the glory of spring and the sun and the warm sea and my youth restored and the world fresh-minted, and I knew that no one before you, not Adrienne nor Aude nor Isolde nor any who peopled my splendour and youth, I knew that they had merely prepared a way for you and were your hand-maidens. No one came before you nor will come after you, I swear it on the Scrolls of the Holy Law when in solemn state they pass before me in the synagogue, arrayed in gold and velvet, the Holy Commandments of the God in whom I do not believe but revere, for I am absurdly proud of my God, the God of Israel, and I thrill to my very core when I hear His name and His words. To help the bicarb down, I asked the sleeping-car chappie for a small bottle of Évian, it's very handy having these sleeping-car chaps around, they'll get you anything you want at any time of day or night, marvellous isn't it, all you have to do is ring, of course you have to tip them when you get to your destination, but it's worth it. I've taken three lots of bicarb, because as heartburn and acid indigestion go I've had a right old time of it, but that's hardly the point, the point is that it all went off a treat from the word go, you know. Over dinner, lively conversation, I was perfectly at my ease, Proust, Kafka, Picasso, Vermeer, it just turned out like that, sort of without me wanting it to, I don't mind saying I was brilliant on Vermeer: biography, character of the man, main works, plus remarks about technique and museum locations, he must have seen I knew my onions. Sitting at their gently lit table, they smiled at each other and only they existed. She looked at him and ached with a desire to stroke the luxuriant curve of his eyebrows with her finger, to reach out and circle his wrist with her hand and feel its slimness, but not here, not in front of these people. She looked at him and admired the imperious gesture with which he summoned the head waiter, who came running, obese but twinkle-toed, listened with an approving expression on his face, took the magnum out of the ice-bucket, swaddled it as though it were a baby, popped the cork, filled the two glasses with episcopal unction, then retired in a cloud of benign discretion, hands clasped behind his back, watchful and hundred-eyed, while in the meantime Imre and his band, jerking their heads triumphantly, broke into a ghastly tango and couples followed each other on to the floor, there to take ship under respectful sail upon the beautiful blue stream of dreams. She looked at him and admired the way he barely acknowledged the nod of the principal Japanese delegate, who wheeled ceremoniously and warily by, carefully pressing first his knee and then his sharp-edged femur against the thigh of his secretary, who was flattered and smiled poetically. She admired everything about him, even down to the heavy silk of his cuffs. Babooneries, he thought, but he did not mind, for he was happy. 'Your hand,' he said. In noble subjection she held it out, and suddenly observed that it was beautiful. 'Move your hand,' he said. She obeyed, and he smiled with pleasure. Oh wonder, she was exquisite, she was alive! 'Ariane,' he said, and she shut her eyes. Ah, they were in perfect harmony now. You'll hardly credit it, but Waddell was also at the Ritz, having dinner with someone who looked awfully important, I couldn't tell you who it was, tall chap with red hair, somebody from the British delegation I imagine, when I get back I'll ask Kanakis. Very well-connected is friend Waddell, he's a special adviser you know, never actually does anything of course, a bit special on the personal habits front too if you see what I mean. Waddell's a horrible snob, it must have set him right back on his heels to see me there having dinner with the Under-Secretary-General, chatting away like old pals. Take it from me, that tongue of his will ensure that everybody but everybody at the Palais will be in the know tomorrow. His highness the VV will go green at the gills! There are a lot of people who won't like it, of course, but it'll give me a very definite edge! From now on, I shall be someone with clout, get it? He stood up and said he was going to fetch presents to give her. She frowned tenderly, pursing and thrusting out her closed lips, her first show of female petulance. 'Come back soon,' she said, and she watched as he walked away while from the orchestra, like a human voice, rose the despairing complaint of a musical saw, like the sobbing of a serene madwoman or a siren abandoned, watched as he walked away, he who from this time henceforth was her portion of earthly happiness. 'Chosen at the first flutter of your long curved lashes,' he had said. 'It's true, I do have beautiful eyelashes,' she murmured. Suddenly she frowned. Which dress had she worn to the Brazilian reception? Oh yes, the long black one. She breathed in relief. Thank God, it was one of her best Paris numbers. She pictured herself wearing the dress which suited her so well and smiled. Like I was saying, lively chat over dinner, Waddell couldn't take his eyes off us, just couldn't get over it, knocked the stuffing right out of him. Must have been hard for him to take, not half! Anyway, the chief, ever so smartly turned out, awfully grand, but very polite, consulting me about the menu and so forth, he's unbelievably charming, I love watching him fiddling with his beads, it's a Middle Eastern custom, apparently. You know, when I get back I'm going to get myself a white dinner-jacket like him, white dinner-jackets in summer are very much the thing nowadays, you can take it as read that he's well up on the sartorial front. He set down her presents before her: his emerald necklace, his rings and the little teddy-bear with the sombrero. 'For you,' he said earnestly, and so pleased did he seem that she felt a maternal pang of pity. She opened her handbag and held out the handsome solid-gold and platinum cigarette-case which had been a present from her husband. 'This I give to you,' she said. He pressed it against his cheek and smiled at her. They were happy, they had exchanged gifts. After pudding, we went up to his suite, wow! you should have seen it, a superb drawing-room, period furniture, coffee served by his man who doubles as his chauffeur, or so Kanakis says. Then he got interested in a literary venture I've been mulling over, a novel about Don Juan, I've got a few ideas on the subject, I'll tell you all about it some time, I've come up with some terrific angles on Don Juan, primordial contempt and why he's so obsessed with seduction, won't go into it now, I'll explain later, it's rather complicated but I think it's new stuff, you know, original. So he started paying attention to what I was saying, asking questions, I mean pally as anything, elective affinities and all that, calling me by my Christian name, saying old man, honestly, I was firing on all pistons. He doesn't say old man to VV but he says it to Lord Adrien Deume! And you won't credit this but he even went so far as to tell me in confidence that he's in love with the wife of the leader of the Indian delegation! not in so many words, mark you, but I could read between the lines, put two and two together from clues he dropped, you see how chummy things were between us. Between you and me, things started to get a bit weird, he said he didn't want to make a play for this gorgeous Indian piece, but I egged him on because I don't give a toss for the Indian delegate, see, he can play footsie with his wife as much as he likes. Whispered echoes of their love in the sickly-sweet waltz now unfurling its slow, drawling refrain. Head reaching down to her, breathing the scent of her, he asked her to say something, said he needed to hear her voice. Waking from the torpor in which the fusion of souls had left her, she looked up at him like a gentle-eyed dog, looked up at him so wondrously tall, looked up and saw his adorably white teeth above her. 'Say something extraordinary,' he asked. 'We two,' she said, lost in the wonder of canines and incisors. 'Say more,' he asked. 'My eyes in doe-like ecstasy,' she smiled, and she held this stranger close. And in the middle of everything the porter phones to ask if this gorgeous Indian bint can come up. At this I put the wheel hard over, I don't mess about, I suggest I should take myself off to the office and immediately start preparing a summary of the British Memorandum, you know, the famous Memo, I told you about it, a great wodge of stuff I didn't have time to finish off given all the extra work there's been, but he said no need, said he didn't want to chase me away to the Palais, said I could stay, just being polite of course, so I said bluntly: 'I'm sorry, sir, but I'm not going to obey your order.' This answer seemed to go down pretty well. 'More,' he asked. 'Let's go away, we two,' she said, and she leaned her head on the shoulder of her slowly swirling partner. 'Go where?' he asked. 'Far away,' she sighed. 'Perhaps to the land where I was born?' 'Where he was born,' she smiled, filled with a beatific vision, 'oh yes, I'm so glad you were born. And when shall we go, we two?' 'This morning,' he said, 'in a plane all to ourselves, and this afternoon we shall be in Cephalonia, you and I.' Eyes aflutter, she looked at him, looked at the miracle of him. This afternoon, she and he, standing at the sea's edge, hand in hand. She inhaled, and caught the tang of the sea and its smell of life. 'Off our heads, off to the sea,' she smiled, and she swirled in time to the dance, with her head lovingly sanctuaried against him. Well, I left by the back stairs so I wouldn't bump into her, because it's a luxury suite, you know, with a separate service entrance, anyhow off I shot in a taxi to the Palais where I concocted a minor masterpiece for him, a super-duper summary, complete with super-duper personal comments, just came to me in the heat of inspiration, I was going at it hammer and tongs, felt I was carving out my future, highly political comments, repercussions, nuances, allusions and so forth, made the most of the opportunity, in short, snatched victory from the jaws of defeat: One, because my comments are very neatly turned so he'll see I've got it upstairs, Two, because I did him a personal favour by leaving him alone with his sultry siren, thereby generating gratitude and friendship, and

Three and not least, because doing a piece of work for one of the top brass without going through the usual channels sets you up, you know, gives you a direct line to the establishment, and VV can't do a thing about it, that's the beauty of it, this kid Adrien's a smart operator all right! Responding to a signal from the big spender, Imre headed towards their table, not hurrying himself unduly but stopping off here and there on the way like a free man. When he got to them, he doffed his bow in greeting then resumed his playing, improvising for his personal and private pleasure, shaping cadences of *furioso* which unexpectedly faded into regal passages of *lusingandos* and lush expanses of *piangevole* as he reached out for an absolute of tenderness, his cheek nestling lovingly into his fiddle which yielded an aching, dying fall to which he listened with orgasmically closed eyes. 'Wake up, Imre, that's enough,' said Solal. He obeyed, though he could not quite stop his fingers from gently strumming the strings. 'Imre, you're a good fellow. I want you to know that I am about to run away with Madame.' The gypsy fiddler greeted the good news by letting his bow glide slowly and deliberately across the strings, then inclined his head to the fascinating lady. With his fiddle supported only by his clenched chin, he poked the ends of his iron-curled moustache with his bow and asked what was the noble lady's pleasure. 'Your most ravishing waltz,' said Solal. 'Your wish is my command!' said Imre. The fly in the ointment was that I couldn't hand over my little masterpiece to him personally at the Ritz, which is a pity, it would have cemented relations, but I could hardly disturb him, not when he was with his sultry lady, so I put the summary and my comments in an internal envelope, wrote his name on the front, and sealed it with a gummed label marked 'Confidential', but just to be on the extra-safe side I didn't leave it in my out-tray, because VV sticks his nose into everything and would be quite capable of opening it to see what I was sending to the super-chief, 'Confidential' or not, or rather because of the 'Confidential', and equally capable of keeping it to himself, the swine, he's so jealous, anyway I'm not stupid, so I trotted along, looking as though butter wouldn't melt in my mouth, and quietly popped it into the chief's personal messenger's in-tray, chap named Saulnier, that way no one's the wiser and it's a cert that it won't be intercepted by his high and mightiness VV, I plead self-defence, m'lud. Impelled by the gravity of their desire, they orbited like stars. What kinds of trees were there on Cephalonia, asked this daughter of wealth, this consumer of nature's beauties. With a faraway look in his eye he reeled off the names of the trees he had so often recited to others, ran through the list of them: cypress-trees, orange-trees, lemon-trees, olive-trees, pomegranate-trees, citron-trees, myrtle-trees, mastic-trees. Reaching the limit of his knowledge, he went on, inventing lemonella-trees, tuba-trees, circass-trees, prune-trees and even puple-trees. Wonderingly she inhaled the vanilla-sweet fragrance of his miraculous forest. So tomorrow morning, phone to tell her to be sure to be nice to the chief if she ever bumps into him. 'Listen, darling, if the Kanakises ask you round to their place, which is more than likely since they now owe us an invite, and the chief happens to be there, because Kanakis told me he was intending to ask him and the Greek ambassador, old Kanak's got his head screwed on the right way, don't you act grouchy with the chief, mind, talk to him a bit, talk to him a lot if you want, but for heaven's sake be nice, you can be very nice if you choose, because he treated me very decently, you know, I guarantee that this time next year I'll be an adviser.' The luck of the Irish, he smiled, and he peered benevolently at the mole just above his navel, then rolled himself into a ball on his narrow bunk, burying his face in his pillow, enjoying its smell and relishing the expense-account first-class sleeper now whisking him off towards official delights. On the dais, Imre was perspiring and pining with a will, while the second fiddle lobbed brief, servile, mechanical phrases which his leader proceeded to amplify gaudily, lifting his chin when he got to the thrilling moments. As she turned and whirled, she whispered that she'd have no time to buy summer dresses in Geneva, though on his island it would be very warm and, to be seen with a lord such as he, she'd have to change her dress at least twice a day. 'The dresses worn by peasant girls on Cephalonia will look just right on you,' he said. She gazed at him in admiration. This man knew everything, ironed out all problems with such ease. 'We shall buy three dozen,' he said. Thirty-six dresses, glory be! this man was surely great! 'What will our house be like?' she asked. 'White, by a purple sea,' he said, 'with an old Greek serving-woman to attend to every-thing.' 'To everything,' she said approvingly, and she clung to him.

Captivatingly clothed in grace, light as snow and slowly turning, she looked up once more to see herself dancing in the tall mirrors where she existed exquisitely, gazed up at the fair and beloved of her lord, so elegant in a peasant dress embroidered in red and black, attended by a kindly, barefoot, old Greek woman on an isle of delight girt with myrtle-, mastic- and circass-trees.

CHAPTER 37

On this night, their first night, together in the little sitting-room which she had so wanted to show him, they stood at the open window looking out over the garden, breathing the star-spattered night, listening to the softly stirring leaves of the trees which whispered their love. Hand in hand, the blood coursing creamily in their veins, they stared up at the glorious heavens, gazed up at their love enshrined in the pulsating stars which shone down blessings from on high. 'Always,' she murmured, awed by his presence in her very own room. And then, aiding and abetting her happiness, invisible upon its branch, a nightingale sang its wild entreaties, and she squeezed the hand of Solal so that they might both share the unseen piper now striving, contriving to proclaim their love. Suddenly it stopped and there was only the innumerable silence of the night and from time to time the vibrant whirr of a cricket.

Gently she freed herself and went to the piano, like a noble but absurd vestal, for she knew that she must play for him and sanctify with a Bach chorale this their first hour spent alone together. Seated before the black and white of the keys, she waited a moment, head bowed in honour of the music soon to be. Now that she had her back to him, he picked up a silver-handled mirror lying on the table, beheld the face of a man who was loved and smiled at him. Oh the perfect teeth of youth!

Oh sparkling teeth, oh joy to be alive, oh this young and loving woman and the tedium of her te deum offered as an oblation! Piously she played for him, her face aglow with faith, transfixed. On the stool as she played, her full hips swayed and swayed him, moved and moved him, for they were his, they were promised.

He watched her and he knew, reproved himself for knowing, knew that she was ashamed, though perhaps she was not fully aware of it, ashamed of having danced too close to him at the Ritz, ashamed of her ecstasy at the prospect of running off to the sea with him, and he knew that the moment they had entered her little sitting-room she had felt an obscure need to atone. There was atonement in the star-gazing, the 'Always', the chaste squeeze of his hand so different from the Ritz where she had snuggled so close to him, in the respectful hearing given to that overpraised warbler the nightingale, cliché thou ever wert too, not bird. Atonement too in the chorale, which was designed to purify the surge of love, to infuse it with soul, to show her that she was brimful of soul so that she might taste the joys of the flesh without shame.

When the last chord had died away, she remained motionless on her stool, head bowed over the keys, honouring the sounds which had died away. After this bridging interval, which brought her from the celestial spheres back down to earth again, she turned to him and gave him her heart with a serious, almost imperceptible smile. She's not very bright, he thought. She stood up, but resisted an urge to sit by him on the faded silk of the sofa. Instead, she deposited her hind-quarters in an armchair and sat expectantly, waiting for his comments on the chorale. In the garden, a nocturnal woodpecker took soundings. Solal said nothing, for he loathed Bach, and she put his silence down to an admiration too deep for words, and felt a thrill of pleasure.

Intimidated by the silence but also because he was tall and slim and so elegantly arrayed in white, she crossed her legs, pulled down the hem of her dress, struck and held a poetical pose. Darling girl, he thought, moved by her weakness and her pathetic attempts to please. Feeling awkward under her reverential gaze, he lowered his eyes. She gave a start when she saw the scar. Oh she would kiss his eye, erase the hurt she had caused him and ask his forgiveness. She cleared her throat so that her voice would be pure and true. But he smiled at her, and she stood up.

Near to him at last, at last the flecks of gold so near, nestling at last in the haven of his shoulder, at last he held her. She drew back her head to see him more clearly, then brought her face closer, opened her lips like a flower in bloom, opened them reverently, with her head tilted back and eyes languishing, blissful and accessible, a saint in ecstasy. Goodbye chorale, goodbye nightingale, he thought. On solid ground now that she's got the soul routine out of her system, he thought, and he rebuked himself for harbouring this demon inside him. Oh yes, it was patently obvious, if he'd been four front teeth short there'd have been no enthralled 'Always', no nightingale, no chorale. Or if teeth all present and correct but out of a job and in rags, again no 'Always' nor nightingale nor chorale. Nightingales and chorales were for the owning classes. But never mind, she was his true love, so hold your tongue and keep your damnable psychology to yourself!

On the sofa of faded silk, the sofa which had once belonged to Tantlérie, they tasted each other's sweetness, mouth on mouth, eyes closed, drinking long and deep, oblivious, assiduous, insatiable. At times she pulled away to see and know him, gazed at him in adoration with wild, staring eyes, and inwardly spoke two words of Russian to him, the language she had learned for love of Varvara which now enabled her to tell a man that she was his. '*Tvoya zhena*,' she said to him in her heart of hearts as in her hands she held his stranger's face, then drew close and surrendered, while outside two cats raucously broadcast their love. '*Tvoya zhena*,' she said to him in her heart of hearts with each pause, each time they paused to draw breath, said it in her heart of hearts so that she might feel more deeply, more humbly, that she was his and dependent on him, feel it primitively, like a bare-foot peasant with the smell of earth in her nostrils, feel that she was his woman and his servant who from that very first moment had bent her head and kissed the hand of her man. '*Tvoya zhena*,' and she surrendered again and they kissed, with the haste and fury of youth, in quick, repeated surges, or according to the unhurried rituals of love, and then they stopped, looked at each other and smiled, breathless, glowing, easy, and then came the questions, then began the litany.

Sacred, obtuse litany, wondrous canticle, joy of poor human kind doomed to die, love's sempiternal two-voiced unison, the eternal love-duet which makes the earth to multiply. She told him over and over that she loved him. She asked him, for she knew the miraculous answer, asked him if he loved her. He told her over and over that he loved her. He asked her, for he knew the miraculous answer, asked her if she loved him. Love's first burgeoning, so tedious to others, so engrossing to those concerned.

Tirelessly crooning their duet, they declared their love for each other, and their banalities filled them with transports of delight. Closely embracing, they smiled, almost laughed aloud for joy, kissed then broke off to proclaim the wondrous tidings all too quickly confirmed by renewed collisions of lip and tongue in hungry exploration. Conjoined lips and tongues, the language of the young.

Those first moments of love, the kisses of those first moments, awesome chasms of their fate, oh those first embraces, there on this sofa handed down by generations of the stern and the dead, their sins tattooed upon their lips. The eyes of Ariane, her eyes now raised in reverence, her eyes now devoutly closed, and her unskilled tongue suddenly, marvellously proficient. She pushed him away so that she might look at him, her mouth still open though the kiss was done, to see and know him, see this stranger who was the only man in her life. 'I am your woman, '*tvoya zhena*,' she said falteringly, and if he made to break free she held him closer still. 'Never leave me,' she faltered, and they raised their cup to life, to their intertwined lives.

Those first moments. Oh kisses, oh pleasure found by the woman on the lips of the man, rising sap of youth, sudden truces, and they gazed at each other entranced, then, breaking the spell once more, kissed each other furiously, fraternally on cheeks, on forehead, on hands. 'Tell me, is this not God's doing?' she asked with a bewildered smile.

'Tell me, do you love me? Tell me you love only me. Tell me there is no one else,' she said, and she injected golden inflections into her voice to please him, to swell his love for her, and she kissed the stranger's hands, then laid her hands upon his shoulders and pushed him back, then sealed her adoration with a look of divinely sulky petulance.

Those first moments, this night of their first embraces. She yearned to break free of his embrace, go upstairs to her room, fetch gifts and lay them at his feet, but how could she bring herself to abandon him, abandon his eyes, abandon his dark lips? He held her, and because he held her so close it hurt, but it was such sweet hurt, and she told him once more that she was his woman. 'Your woman, your woman,' she said madly, proudly, while outside the nightingale resumed its fatuous serenade. Overwhelmed by the thought of being his woman, her cheeks lit up with tears. He kissed the tears on her cheeks. 'No, on the mouth,' she said, 'kiss me,' she said, and their mouths met in frenzy, and again she leaned back in his arms to adore him. 'My archangel, my fatal attraction,' she said, though she scarcely knew what she said, smiling, melodramatic, tawdry. I'll be your archangel and fatal attraction for as long as you want, he thought, but I cannot forget that you only talk of archangels and fatal attractions because I have thirty-two teeth. But I adore you, he thought immediately, and God be praised for my thirty-two teeth.

Those first moments. Kisses of youth, loving supplications, absurd and tedious petitioning. 'Tell me you love me,' he said, and, seeking a firmer purchase on her lips, he leaned on her, leaned on her thigh, and at once she brought her knees together, closing her knees in the presence of the male. 'Tell me you love me,' he said again, insistent with his crucial question. 'Yes, yes,' she answered, 'all I have to give you is a paltry yes,' she said, 'yes, yes, I love you as I had never hoped to love anyone,' she panted between kisses, and he inhaled her breath. 'Yes, darling, I love you. I love you yesterday, today and always, and it will always be today,' she said, husky-voiced, hare-brained, unhinged by love.

★

Those first moments. Two strangers suddenly, wondrously close, lips toiling, tongues searching, tongues ever questing, tongues reaching out and blending, tongues jousting, joining, loving, hating, the sacred toil of man and of woman, saliva mixing in mouths, mouths feeding on each other, on the food of youth, tongues conjoined in impossible desire, glances, ecstasy, the living smile of two mortal souls, wet-lipped murmurings, pet-name calling, childish kisses, innocent kisses on the corners of eyes and mouth, new beginnings, sudden surging explorations, saliva exchanged, let me kiss you, kiss me, kiss me again, tears of happiness, salt tears tasted, love exacted, love declared, oh the wondrous tedium of it!

'O my love, hold me close, I am yours in all purity,' she said. 'Who are you, what did you do to overwhelm me completely, body and soul? Hold me, hold me closer, but spare me tonight,' she said. 'In my mind I am already your wife, but not tonight,' she said. 'Go, leave me, leave me to think of you, to think about what is happening to me,' she said. 'But say, please say you love me,' she stammered. 'O my love,' she said, blissfully, tearfully, 'there was no one, my love, no one before you, and there will never be another. Go, my love, leave me, leave me alone so that I may be closer to you,' she said. 'No, no, don't leave me,' she begged, holding him fast with both hands, 'all I have in the world is you, I could not go on living without you,' she begged, wild-eyed and clinging to him.

Love and love's temerity. Lamp suddenly extinguished by his hand and she afraid: why? what would his desire be? Breasts bared to the night, a faint luminescence of breasts, a man's hand on a breast gleaming with moonlight, a woman's sweet shame, expectant lips half open, afraid and happy in subjection, trepidation and sweetness, a man's face bending over, boldness in the dark, boldness enjoined by love, boldness permitted by she who surrenders, yields and soon actively consents, oh her long-drawn sighs and moans, the self-same sounds that she will make in the hour of her certain death, oh her deathbed smiles, her pale face in the moonlight, her dazzled eyes the eyes of the living dead, suddenly revealed to herself, perplexed and fulfilled, running her hands through the hair of the man now nuzzling her breasts, her hands slyly caressing, hands playing an accompaniment to her happiness, grateful hands, light hands which said thank you, I love you, and asked for more. Love, thy sun shone bright this night. Their first night.

PART THREE

CHAPTER 38

Oh first days of their loving, the making shift to be beautiful, the crazy compulsion to be beautiful for him, the joys of waiting, the moments of his coming at nine and she invariably at the door waiting, at the door beneath the roses round the door, in the Romanian dress he liked, white it was with wide sleeves nipped at the wrist, oh those early days, the wild greetings when they saw each other again, the loving evenings, the never-ending hours spent gazing at each other, talking to each other, oh the joy of gazing at each other, telling each other everything about themselves, embracing, and when he left her in the small hours, left her in a star-burst of kisses, he came back sometimes, an hour later, two minutes later, oh the wonder of seeing her once more.

Oh his passionate homecomings, 'I can't live without you,' he said, returning, and for love's sake would kneel before her just as she for love's sake knelt before him, and then the kisses, she and he, transfixed, sublime, embrace upon embrace, a great black flapping of winged kisses, deep and endless kisses, oh their closed eyes, 'I can't live without you,' he'd say between the kisses, and he stayed for hours on end, for he could not, no he could not live without her, stayed until the dawn broke and the birds began their gossip, and it was love, he in her, victoriously, and she receiving and with all her soul approving.

New dawns, eagerly awaited morrows, eternally fresh-coined wonder of being beautiful for him, handsome for her, oh blissful reunions, the hours of jubilation, the joy of being together, of talking endlessly together, of being perfect and admired, the hostile interruptions of desire, tender adversaries probing, each seeking to fuse into the other.

Ariane: who would wait for him at her door, fair of form in her white linen dress. Ariane: the outward form of a goddess, the mystery of her beauty which unmanned her lover. Ariane: her arch archangelic face, the turned-down corners of her mouth, her high-minded nose, her walk, her breasts, which were both pride and challenge, her tender petulant lips when she set her eyes upon him, the sudden flare of her skirt when she turned and ran to him, came running to ask him, with lips outstretched, to ask him if he loved her.

Oh the joys, all their joys. The joy of being alone, but joy too in being with others, the joyful complicity of exchanging glances in the presence of others, of knowing they were lovers in the presence of others who did not know. The joy of going forth together, the joy of going to the cinema and holding hands in the dark and looking at each other when the lights came up, and then returning to her house the better to love, he filled with the pride of her, and passers-by turning their heads as they passed by, and the old suffering to see such love, such beauty.

Ariane, nun of love. Ariane and her long huntress legs. Ariane and her gaudy breasts, which she gave him, loved to give him, and she lost herself in his sweetness. Ariane, who would telephone at three o'clock in the morning to ask if he loved her and say that she loved him, and they wearied not of this marvel that was their loving. Ariane, who walked him home, then he walked her home, then she walked him home again, and they could not be parted, could not, and then the bed of love would open for them, handsome and affluent couple, the vast bed where she said that no man else before him and no man else after him and she wept tears of joy beneath him.

'You are fair,' he would say. 'I am fair, fair for my lord,' she would smile. Ariane: the sudden frightened look in her eye when, masking his love, he feigned coolness so that she would love him more. Ariane, who called him her joy and her pain, her tormentor and her Christian-baiter, but also her soul-brother. Ariane the ebullient, Ariane of the twinkling toes and perpetual sunshine. Ariane, inspired sender of telegrams a hundred love-words long, sender of many telegrams so that her loved one travelling far away should know within the hour, should know soon how much, how constantly his loving beloved loved him, and one hour after dispatching the wire sat reading her rough copy, reading the telegram at the same time as he, to be with him and also to savour the happiness of her beloved, the wonder of her beloved.

Her jealousies, goodbyes for ever, reunions, tongues intertwined, tears of joy, letters, oh the letters of those early days, letters sent and letters received, letters which, together with the preparations she made for the one she loved and the waiting for his coming, were the honey of their love, letters painstakingly penned, striven for through discarded drafts, letters penned painstakingly so that each thing which reached him from her was admirable and perfect. For him, the rush of blood in his heart when he recognized her handwriting on the envelope, and he would take the letter and keep it with him wherever he went.

Letters, oh the letters of those first days, letters from the loved one travelling far away, the times she waited for the postman to come, she would walk along the road to watch for his coming and, quickly now, the letter. At night, before sleep, she would prop it by her bedside to know that it was near as she slept and also to know that it would be the first thing she saw next morning, the letter which she read and reread on waking and then bravely let it lie, kept well away from it for hours on end so that she could come to it fresh and again feel all its savour, the treasured letter in which she buried her face so that she might believe she could detect the fragrance of her lover, and inspected the envelope too, studied the address he had written and even the stamp he had licked, and if it were firmly stuck straight in the right-hand corner then that too was proof of his love.

*

Solal and his Ariane, soaring naked at the prow of their tossing ship of love, princely commanders of sea and sun, immortal figureheads on the prow of love, and they looked at each other without end in the glorious lunacy of their beginning.

CHAPTER 39

The hours of waiting, oh joy, the waiting hours from early morning through the day-long day, the waiting for the evening hour, oh joy of knowing all the livelong day that he would come at eventide, at nine o'clock, and it was a foretaste of bliss.

The moment she woke, quickly she opened the shutters to see if the weather would be kind this evening. Yes, it would be fine, the night would be warm with countless stars which they would look at together, and there would be the nightingale which they would hear together, and she would snuggle up close to him as on that first night, and then they would go walking and strolling in the woods, walking arm in arm. Whereupon she walked around her room, one arm linking, anticipating. Or she might switch the radio on and if in the early morning it blared out a military march she would parade with the regiment, hand to temple by way of a salute, because tonight he would be there, so tall, so slim, and oh the way he would look at her.

Sometimes she would close the shutters, draw the curtains, lock her bedroom door, stuff earplugs in her ears so that she would not be distracted by outside sounds, which this pretty creature, in her pedantic way, called hostile constrainers. Prone in the dark and the silence, she would close her eyes and smilingly tell herself what had happened last night, all the things they had said and done, tell it over to herself as she lay curled and coiled, going into details, adding comments, treating herself to a feast of chatterage, as she put it, and then she would tell herself about what would happen tonight, and at such moments it was not unknown for her to stroke her breasts.

Sometimes, before she got up, she would sing to herself, quietly, so that the cleaning-woman would not hear, sing Bach's Whitsun hymn into her pillow, replacing the name of Jesus by the name of her beloved, which, though it made her feel uneasy, was such a delicious thing to do. Or else she spoke to her dead father, told him how happy she was, and asked him to give his blessing to their love. Or else she wrote the name of the man she loved in the air with her finger, wrote it ten or twenty times. And if she had not yet had her breakfast, her stomach would rumble suddenly and she grew angry with the rumble. 'Will you be quiet!' she would shout at the rumble. 'It's so sordid! Shut up, I'm in love!' She knew of course that she was being stupid, but acting stupidly was absolutely lovely when she was by herself and free.

Or else she might decide on a session of thorough lookage and scannage. But first she had to be purified, which meant taking the bath required by the ritual, but remember, swear on your honour, that when you're in the bath you won't start telling yourself about what it will be like tonight, otherwise you'll be at it for hours and it'll hold up the ritual. So, quickly now, into the bath with you, think of him, session of lookage and scannage coming up! Hopping on one leg because she was happy, she made a dash for the bathroom. Standing by the bath, which took an age to fill, she gave the Whitsun hymn everything she had:

> O my believing soul
> Be proud now and content
> For see! there comes thy heavenly king.

After her bath she went through the same ritual as for the chatterage. Shutters closed, curtains drawn, bedside lamp lit, blobs of wax stuffed in her ears. The world outside ceased to exist, and the ceremony could now begin. With the photographs spread out on the bed, but laid upside down so there was no way she could peep, she lolled beside them, picked out the photo she liked best, of him on a sandy beach, covered it completely with her hand, and then began the feast of lookage and scannage. First she uncovered his bare feet. Good-looking feet, of course, but not wildly fascinating. She raised her hand a smidgen and revealed his legs. Better, much better already. Should she go higher? No, not all at once, wait until she could wait no longer. And so, a fraction of an inch at a time, she moved her hand, uncovering as she went, feasting her eyes. It was him, he who would be here tonight. And his face, see his face now, the fount of her joy, his face, her pleasure and her pain. That's enough, don't look for too long. If you looked for too long, you lost the feeling. Still, the face was the most important, though the rest was too, the rest of him, even the bits that, quite. Him and everything about him, and she a nun in the service of her lord.

She wriggled out of her bathrobe and looked from her naked man to her man's naked woman and back again. 'O Sol, I do wish you were here,' she sighed, and she switched off the lamp and thought of this evening, of the moment of his coming, of their mouths. But she did not, would not, forget that she loved him as and for what he was: him, and the look in his eyes. And then would happen what would happen, a man and a woman, the blessed weight of him, her man. With lips half open, moist-lipped, she closed her eyes and drew her knees together.

The hours of waiting, oh joy! After her bath, after breakfasting, the wonder of dreaming of him as she lay snugly rugged on the lawn, or face down with her cheeks in the grass and her nose pressed to the earth, the wonder of remembering his voice and his eyes and his teeth, the wonder of humming to herself wide-eyed and rather overdoing the imbecility so that she might feel more acutely the sensation of languishing idly in the smell of grass, the wonder of telling herself how her lover-man would come tonight, of describing it to herself as though it were a play in a theatre, of telling herself what he would say to her and what she would say to him. Really, she mused, the most exquisite moments were when he was not there but was coming and she was waiting for his coming, but also when he has gone and has left me remembering. Suddenly she stood up and ran around the garden, surprised by a fearful joy, and gave a long whoop of happiness. Or leaped over the rose-hedge. 'Solal!' she cried each time she leaped. Like a mad thing.

Sometimes of a morning, when absorbed in some solitary task, earnestly picking mushrooms or raspberries, or sewing, or reading a book of philosophy which bored her, but she had to improve her mind for him, or guiltily but avidly perusing the agony columns or the horoscope of a woman's magazine, she would overhear herself fondly murmuring two words without intending to or without thinking of him. 'My love,' she would overhear herself say. Then she would say to her absent lover-man: 'You see, my darling, even when I'm not thinking of you, something inside me thinks of you.'

Then she would go indoors, try on dresses, try to make up her mind which she would wear tonight, and she would gaze at herself in her mirror, wallow in the admiring way he would look at her tonight, strike goddess-like poses, imagine that she were him looking at her, trying to imagine what he would really think of this or that dress. 'Tell me, do you love me?' she asked him in her mirror, and she would make a precious, pouting face which, alas, was wasted. Or she might write him a letter, for no reason, simply to be with him, to be doing something that involved him, to speak to him in graceful, intelligent sentences and be admired for them. She would send her letter by express, or she might take a taxi and deliver it personally to the Palais and hand it to the porter herself. 'It's very urgent,' she would say to the porter.

Or else, overcome by a powerful urge to hear his voice, she would telephone, but not before evicting any potential frogs in her throat and practising a few golden inflections of her voice, and ask him liltingly in English if he loved her, saying it in English on account of the cleaning-woman with the flapping ears. Then, still in English and heavenly-voiced, she would remind him unnecessarily about tonight at nine, ask him if he could bring that photo of him on a horse and also if he would lend her his Commander's tie, it was so pretty, thanks awfully, would inform him that she loved him and again ask if he loved her, and, his answer proving satisfactory, she would smile into the mouthpiece like a child opening a Christmas present. When the call was over, she would put the receiver down, her left hand still clutching at a lock of her hair, tugging at it as she used to when she was a little girl mortified at having to speak to a grown-up. Then she would let go of her hair and when her fluttering heart returned to normal would smile again. Yes, she had carried it off well, no catches in her voice and no tripping nervously over her words. Oh yes, she had pleased him! Hooray! Hooray!

One Sunday, in the middle of a call to him at the Ritz, her voice had suddenly roughened and she hadn't dared clear her throat to unclog it because that would have made a squalid noise and disgraced her and he would love her less. Without further ado, she had hung up abruptly, evicted a large family of frogs, tried a few words to make sure that her voice was once more in heavenly trim, then had rung back, calmly explained that they had been cut off, asked him if he'd looked at her photograph the moment he woke up, and what was he wearing, oh a dressing-gown, which one? And did he love her? 'I'm so glad, I do too, madly, and you'll never guess, my love, I popped into a church just now so I could think of you, a Catholic church, because a Catholic church is the best sort of place for thinking. By the way, would you like me to wear my Romanian dress tonight or the wild silk? The Romanian? Fine. Unless you'd prefer the red one I think you said you liked. You'd rather the Romanian? Sure? You're not tired of it? The Romanian it shall be then. Tell me: do you love me?'

When the phone call was over, she sat without moving, still holding the receiver, delighted with him and highly pleased with herself. I've suddenly remembered something else. On another occasion, as she was phoning, she felt a sneeze coming on. She hung up on him so that he wouldn't hear the degrading sound of the sneeze. But that's enough of that.

Hours of waiting untouched by tedium, for there was so much to do for him, so many preparations she could get on with the moment she was free of the watchful eye of the cleaning-woman, whom she christened the ninny, who left at the beginning of the afternoon when she had finished her work. Alone at last and free to do as she liked, amorous Ariane immediately went and checked her sitting-room, where she would take him tonight, and was never happy with the way the ninny had left it looking. So, wearing a swimming-costume, she would set to with a will, sweeping, polishing, waxing the floor, wiping everything in sight like any uncombed housewife, brushing the armchairs and the sofa, the precious sofa for tonight, dusting every visible surface though there was no need, running the vacuum over the faded pink Persian carpet, arranging her flowers then pausing to look at them, hiding her copy of *Vogue*, displaying two or three dull but quality tomes on the sofa, Heidegger or Kierkegaard or Kafka, that sort of thing, putting a few logs in the hearth just in case, burning a piece of paper in the grate to be quite sure the chimney was drawing properly, working out a system of subdued lighting which would encourage cosy intimacies, moving the armchairs, popping into the kitchen to iron a dress already ironed by the ninny which she wanted to wear tonight, toing and froing, occasionally thinking about the letters from her husband which she had left unanswered, tossing her mane like a mare bothered by a horsefly and from time to time singing, with feeling, some silly refrain she had heard on the radio. '*Paaarlez-moi d'amooour,*' she crooned, deliberately choosing a voice which made her sound like some lovesick factory girl. Never mind, she liked it. 'Me wits is turning,' she said. 'But there, isn't that what us girls is for?'

When the man on the radio spoke of political overviews and frank and cordial discussions which afforded hope of an easing of international tension, she listened in open-mouthed amazement. So there really were people who took an interest in such things, whose life it was! 'Pack of fools' she said to them, and she stopped the man on the radio dead in his tracks. In reality, there was only one matter of any importance: getting herself ready and being sure that he would find her attractive. Or else, if the Sunday sermon was on the radio and the preacher said that people should devote themselves to the service of the Lord, she concurred wholeheartedly. 'Yes, my darling, to your service!' she exclaimed, and she rearranged the flowers with renewed zest.

Suddenly, for no earthly reason, as she rummaged through a drawer, she would say: 'How are tricks, then?' Realizing that she had been speaking to him, she would cover her sacrilegious mouth with one hand, shocked but really quite proud of her boldness.

All at once she would stop working, decide it was time for fun, sit at her writing-table, write the name of the man she loved twenty or thirty times, and then his other names, Lalos, Alsol, Losal. Or else, she would stand in front of her mirror and say she loved him, say it in a variety of tones of voice so that she could decide which was best and use it tonight. Or else, wearing a black silk dressing-gown and his Commander's tie round her neck, she played at being him, the better to be with him. 'I love you, Ariane,' she said in a deep man's voice, and on the glass of the mirror kissed the lips which he would kiss tonight.

A cigarette-end which he had discarded last night. She lit it, and oh the bliss of inhaling smoke from the sacred butt! Or else she wanted to see the look on her face when she had kissed his hand last night, to see if it had pleased him. Standing before the mirror, she leaned forward while she kissed her hand, which made it rather difficult for her to get much of a view, but she managed it by straining her eyes until the whites showed. Or else, still standing in front of the mirror, she repeated snatches of things she had said the night before. 'Keep me by you, keep me by you always,' she said, and the words brought her close to tears. Or else she opened her dressing-gown, looked at her breasts in the mirror, her breasts which he would kiss tonight. 'Congratulations,' she said to her breasts, 'you are my glory and my prop,' she told them. 'He's a lucky devil, say what you like!' she concluded. Or else she dropped her dressing-gown on the floor, eager to see her nakedness objectively, in the mirror. 'A stunner, the girl's a stunner,' she said. 'Do you realize just how privileged you are, my good man?' she asked him through her nose, pinching it between two fingers, which made her sound like her aunt.

★

One afternoon she slipped into an unbleached linen dress which buttoned all down the front, and closed the shutters. In the luscious gloom, she undid the buttons down to her waist, flapped the bodice like wings, and promenaded, whispering to herself that she was the winged Victory of Samothrace come to life. 'Darling, I think you're the absolute tops,' she told the mirror. 'After him, you're the one I love most in the whole world.' Feeling rather guilty, she made herself decent, curtsied to the King of England, showed him to a chair, and then sat down herself. Crossing her legs, she exchanged a few words with His Majesty, asked him to ban that dreadful Canadian song about plucking poor alouette, yawned, felt proud of her teeth, undid the top of her dress, produced one opulent breast and on it, with a fountain-pen, wrote the name of the man she loved.

Abruptly serious and conscious of her responsibilities, she plastered her face and neck with the grey mud which was called a beauty mask, sat as though turned to stone in the service of love, without speaking or singing, for fear of cracking the dried slime, now and then doing her nails but drawing the line at varnishing them which she thought vulgar and fit only for Catholics. Next came washing her hair. 'Tonight, tonight,' she murmured under the lather, hands scrubbing, eyes closed.

At eight in the evening she had her last bath of the day, which she left as late as possible so that she would be a miracle of pure hygiene when he arrived. In the bath, she played at sticking her toes out of the water and waggling them, imagining to herself that they were her ten children, five little boys on the left and five little girls on the right, pretending to scold them and telling them to have their baths quickly and then go straight to bed, and then she put them back in the warm water. After this, she told herself more stories, told herself that he'd be there an hour from now, very tall, with those eyes of his, and she would look at him and he would look at her, and he would smile at her. Oh how absolutely wonderful it was to be alive!

I'll stay in the bath a little bit longer, but not more than five minutes now, do you hear, yes, all right, five minutes, I promise, and then get dressed quickly, he's probably shaving now, hold it there, that'll do, you're quite handsome enough as it is, be careful you don't cut yourself, come quickly, jump to it, jump in my bath, there's heaps of room, and if there isn't we'll manage somehow, 'cos I know a trick.

Emerging from her bath and still naked, she made a dash for the phone and told him to be on time. 'Darling, it's so awful when you come late, I start worrying you've had an accident, and besides my face gets totally ruined if I have to wait for you. So please, darling?' she smiled, and she hung up and then brushed her teeth one last time. Impatient, toothbrush in hand, her mouth unrinsed and foaming with toothpaste, she again sang the Whitsun hymn and the coming of a heavenly king.

Next on the agenda, with all its attendant angst, was the crucial business of getting dressed. Wouldn't it be better to wear the other dress, the severe one with the pleats, on second thoughts no, how about the red, which would be very fetching in subdued lighting? But then she knew in a sudden illumination that she would only feel right if she wore the little tussore two-piece. Ah, clothes were a state of mind too, anyway he'd said how much he'd liked the tussore only the other day, besides that way she'd be able to wear a blouse, a blouse was so much more convenient if, all you had to do was, whereas with the pleated dress, which had such a high neck and buttoned at the back, stupid thing, there was such a palaver if, but with a blouse it was straightforward if, because blouses unbuttoned down the front.

Oh I love it when, when he, when he kisses them and it goes on for ages and ages, I literally dissolve. Come on, you out there, didn't anyone ever kiss you like that? And if no one ever did, then it's your loss, you can sulk and fume till you're blue in the face, but me I love it, yes it's awkward if you're wearing a dress that only unbuttons a little way down the back, you have to take it off, and it would be me who'd have to do the taking off, it would be like a visit to the doctor's, I'd be so embarrassed I wouldn't know where to put myself, whereas a blouse – or should I say shirt? I've never known the

411

difference – can be unbuttoned without my knowing, really, it's much more decent, especially if the light's not too strong, though if Tantlérie were to, I suppose I wallow in being a woman, and there you are, can't help it.

Dressed now, she proceeded to give herself a final, objective inspection, took three or four paces towards the mirror to try out a few natural, relaxed moves, then retreated to get the effect, placed the back of one hand on her hip to give herself confidence, then experimented with poses and smiles, tested different combinations of faces and voices, the phrase recurring most frequently being 'No, I don't think so', because that made her appear sure of herself, a touch supercilious. Then she sat down and tried to stay absolutely still so as not to disturb her perfection. Anxiously she listened for the sound of a car, lit a cigarette to make her look poised, then extinguished it so as not to stain her teeth or make her breath smell, found sitting down tiring, and besides it was creasing her skirt, best step outside. At the door, surrounded by the warm night, she waited, afraid she might perspire, because if she did it would be awful: her nose would shine.

CHAPTER 40

He lay in his bath and mused that at this very moment she was probably covered in lather too. However eagerly he looked forward to seeing her soon, he could not help feeling that it was ridiculous for two pathetic human beings, simultaneously, and three kilometres apart, to be cleaning and scrubbing themselves, as they might scour pots and pans, just to please each other, like actors making up before walking on stage. Actors, that's what they were, absurdly play-acting. He had been acting the other night when he had gone down on his knees to her. She had been acting too when she had held out her hands like some lady paramount and feudally bade him rise, acting with her 'You are my lord, I proclaim it with trumpets', clearly fancying her chances as a Shakespearian heroine. Tawdry lovers condemned to act out noble parts. Their pathetic need to feel that they were different. He shook his head to drive out his demon. Enough! Torment me no more, an end to derision, malign not my love and let me love her with a pure heart, let me be happy!

He was now out of his bath, which he had deliberately prolonged to abridge the time of waiting until he saw her once more. Naked and oh so smoothly shaved, smooth-cheeked for her, he danced, danced for the joy of seeing her soon, danced like a Spaniard, with tiny, neat steps, one hand on hip, clicking the fingers of the other, suddenly stamping his heels or shading his eyes with one hand, desperately seeking a glimpse of the woman he loved, then danced like a Russian, squatting and kicking his legs out in front of him, straightening up and clapping his hands, unleashing ludicrous warlike whoops, leaped, whirled, dropped into the splits, got up again, gave a cheer because he would be seeing her soon, smiled at himself, loved himself, loved her, loved the woman he loved. Oh, if he had ever felt alive it was now and for ever!

In the taxi which carried him to her, he sang deliriously, and the sound of the engine covered his singing, and he urged the driver to go faster, to carry him like the wind, and he promised him prodigious sums, even said he would kiss him when they arrived, then he sang again of going to her, sang with such satanic glee that once he had flung his finest ring out of the window into the passing cornfields, and he sang and he sang and he sang endlessly that he was going to her, oh song of impatience and fearful joy, oh preposterous canticle of youth, and he sang and he sang and he sang, endlessly sang the triumph of being loved, and he looked at the man who was loved reflected in the windows of the taxi, was proud of his teeth, proud he was handsome, handsome for her, victoriously going towards her who waited, and lo! he saw her from afar, waiting at her door beneath the roses, oh glory, oh wondrous sight: 'Lo! behold the woman who is loved, unique and full of grace, glory to the Lord, the Lord in me,' he whispered.

CHAPTER 41

Their first evenings together, rapture of conversations interrupted by a myriad kisses, chaste interludes, the fascination and delight of telling the other about themselves, of learning everything there was to know about the other, of pleasing the other. She talked eagerly to him about her childhood, about the games she'd played with Éliane, about the little song she'd made up which they'd sung on the way to school, told him about her uncle and her aunt and Varvara, told him about Magali her owl and Fluffy her cat, two delightful little souls prematurely torn from her tender affections, showed him old photos and homework she'd done as a girl, even gave him her private diary to read, only too happy that he should know all about her, hold sovereign rights over her, or else she told him gravely about her father, and he put on an attentive, respectful expression to see her breathe more deeply, for she gloried in his respect, which justified their love and made it right.

The miracle, as they talked, of seeing herself with him in the mirror, of knowing that this was for ever, that he was with her and was hers. The miracle of sharing everything with him, of making an oblation of her most secret self, her adolescent passions, her day-dreams, the sometime hermit, now dead, the well-dressed gent she'd gunned down and left in the snow, her trick of soothing her nerves by banging herself against the wall, oh the miracle of feeling that he was her soul-brother who understood her completely, understood her better than she understood herself. Yes, the miracle too of being brother and sister, and of laughing together.

415

She told him what kinds of music she liked, and occasionally got up and played examples on the piano for him, and she gazed at him when she had finished, relieved if he liked them too, and she would kiss his hands. If he did not like them, she suddenly found them less beautiful, realizing that he was right. Oh this need to feel at one with him, to like only what he liked, to know what books he liked so that she could read them and like them too.

Endless talking, friendly suspensions of carnimalities which comforted her and were to her mind living proof that they were joined in spirit and not simply in body, the never tarnished joy of talking about themselves, of being clever and intelligent and handsome and noble and perfect. Two actors absorbed in outcharming each other, striving and strutting, he thought once more, but what did it matter, it was bliss, for everything about her delighted him, even her good-little-girl-I'm-watching-the-birdie-for-the-photographer-man smile whenever he said something nice about how beautiful she was, even her Genevan accent and vocabulary delighted him. He loved her.

One morning she invited him for dinner that evening at eight. It was the first meal they had eaten together. So proud to have got everything ready all by herself, and especially proud of her sorrel soup, which she carried gravely to the table. 'Darling, I made it myself from start to finish, the sorrel is from the garden, I picked it this morning.' Highly pleased with the thought that she was feeding her man, thrilled by her mental picture of the wife and servant genteelly ladling out the soup. The pleasure of watching him eat. She felt like a home-maker; she approved. She approved of him too. Good table manners, she thought as she watched him. Her pleasure too in the role of sensible wife. When he asked for a third piece of chocolate cake, 'No, darling, three pieces are too much,' she said sententiously. That same evening he cut his finger slightly, very slightly. Oh how happy she was to tend his hurt, to put iodine on it and swaddle it in a bandage which she sealed with a kiss, like a tender mother.

CHAPTER 42

One evening when their love was young, he asked her what she was thinking. She turned abruptly, making her skirt flare dramatically, a manœuvre she felt sure would please him. 'I'm thinking how enchanted I am to have met you,' she said. 'Enchanted,' she repeated, delighted by the sudden taste of the word on her tongue. She laughed, walked up and down, knowing that he was staring admiringly, feeling her dress hug her in all the right places. 'And now what are you thinking?' he asked. 'I'm thinking how sorry for myself I am, because the rest of my life will be spent trying to please you, wearing heels that are too high and skirts that are too tight, twirling my dress like I did just now, like Mademoiselle de La Mole in the book, it's quite appalling and I make myself sick, I'm turning into a regular female, it's dreadful.' She knelt and kissed his hand. Deplorable, this urge to be forever falling on her knees. 'Say you'll keep me, keep me by you always,' she said.

How beautiful she was kneeling, looking up at him, with both arms round his hips in the attitude of one who prays, his poignantly slim hips, the hips of her man. 'Let me look at you,' she said, and she drew back to see all of him, checked every feature and smiled, oh perfect teeth of youth. She must weigh sixty kilos, of which forty are water, he thought. I am in love with forty kilos of water, he thought. 'What are you thinking about?' she asked. 'I'm thinking about Kitty,' he said. She asked him to tell her again, because she loved listening to him talk about his sweet little cat, now, alas, no more. So he told her the first thing that came into his head, said that sometimes Kitty was fat and moody, sometimes slender and as friendly as an angel; sometimes she went on purring for as long as it took to eat her dinner, with her little head in her dish; sometimes as good as gold, eyes raised, patient, perfect; and other times as old as time and dreaming of days long ago. 'More,' she said. So he told her that Kitty demanded constant stroking because she was never free of the atavistic fear of danger, and stroking relieved her anxiety. If she was being stroked, she couldn't be in danger. 'I want to have my anxiety relieved too,' she said, and she snuggled up closer. Held by him, she tilted her head and half-opened her lips like a flower in bloom, and they drank each other's sweetness, painstakingly, deeply, lost to the world, and this was the grave and suddenly passionate language of youth, a long, lubricated struggle as lips and tongues conjoined. 'Lower,' she ventured in a barely audible whisper.

'Lower,' she sometimes ventured in a whisper when the mouth-kissing was done, shamed by her boldness, and she sometimes undid the top of her dress herself, and then he would lean forward and reach down to her bare breast, and she would close her eyes at once so that she would feel her shame less intensely, detach herself, know nothing, nothing but the magic of the night which opened to receive her, heedful of the honey that dripped in the night, yielding and deliques-cent, dumbly eavesdropping on exquisitely expiring ecstasies, on occasion breaking the silence with a moan of endorsement, on others giving him encouragement and thanks by slowly, uncertainly stroking his hair, sometimes whispering 'The other one now.' 'I love you,' she would add hurriedly, to reclaim her dignity and inject a modicum of soul, and then would moan once more, eyes closed, thoughts scattered, carnimal, her breath rasping and slavering in her throat, in the enchantment of his hovering over her other breast. Oh make him go on and on like this, don't let him move on too soon to the rest, she ventured to think.

When he pulled away to look at her so beautiful in her nakedness, she did not stir, her lips still open and head thrown back, smiling and dazed, happy in the knowledge that she was defenceless and entirely at his mercy, awaiting the resumption, and then velvet night came down again and it was filled with the exquisite torture of her crouching lover. But suddenly she gripped him by the shoulders, pulled him down on her and told him: now.

First nights of their loving, long, stumbling, fumbling nights, desire perpetually reviving, limbs intertwined, secrets whispered, brief and ponderous collisions, turbulent storms unleashed, Ariane submitting, altar and victim, at times nipping her lover's neck with plaintively sharp teeth. Oh her eyes showing white like a saint in ecstasy, and she would ask if he were happy in her, if he were content in her, and ask him to keep her by him, keep her by him always. First nights of their loving, mortal flesh colliding, sacred rhythm, primal rhythm, backs arching, backs lunging, deeply thrusting, rapid, dispassionate thrusting, male implacability, she passionately endorsing, suddenly flexing, reaching towards the male.

All passion spent, she would gently stroke his naked shoulder, grateful, eyes shadow-ringed, and speak to him of what she called their union, tell him whisperingly the bliss he had given her, and whisper even lower as she asked if he had been made happy by her. Then it was his turn to comment, quite aware of the absurdity of their dithyrambic exegeses, but he did not care, for he had never known another woman as desirable as she. He loved those tender interludes, her caress, their affectionate talk, the way they embraced, like brother and sister. Human contact restored, he thought, and he nestled against her while she bewitched his hair.

In these interludes their mood was bright, they were amused by trifles, and both laughed loud when she told the tale of Angeline, a farm-girl from Savoy, who pretended to be sorry for her cow so that the clever creature would respond with a gloomy moo. Ariane took both parts. First she was Angeline saying: 'Poor Buttercup, who's been smacking Buttercup, then?' (To give the story its proper flavour, you really had to sày 'Pore' and 'Boottercoop'.) Then she was the cow, answering with a martyred moo. The best part of the story was when the cow answered. Sometimes they mooed together, to emphasize just how smart that old moo-cow was. As you see, they weren't hard to please. They were bright, they were friends, laughing at little things, laughing if he told her about a kitten pretending to be afraid of a chair, or if he admitted that he was terrified by big, buzzing bluebottles which glinted like green metal, or if he said how cross he was when he heard people come out with the cliché about butterflies being pretty, they were horrible, soft, squashable, flying caterpillars, each one packed with nasty lymph, with wings in the worst possible taste which looked as though they'd been painted on by elderly unmarried ladies from another epoch. Oh how happy they were together, like brother and sister giving each other innocent pecks on the cheek. One evening, as they lay next to each other, when she asked him to make up a poem starting 'I know a land across the sea', he did so immediately. 'I know a land across the sea Where blooms the gillyflower; The people there smile charmingly Every minute of each hour. The tiger there is mild as grass, The lion gentle as a lamb, And to all the hoary tramps that pass Ariane gives buttered bread and jam.' She kissed his hand, and he was ashamed to be so worshipped.

If he lit a cigarette at the conclusion of a joust, she felt sad, as though lighting a cigarette was an act of disrespect for her, or even an act of sacrilege. But she let it pass without mention. They can be tactful at times.

Sometimes he fell asleep beside her, exuding trust. Her heart warmed then, for she loved to see him as he slept, loved to watch over him while he slept the sleep of a stranger on whom she gazed with curious pity, a stranger who was now her whole life. I have a stranger in my heart, she thought, and silently she spoke words to him, the wildest of words, the most holy of words, words which he would never hear. My son, my lord, my Messiah, she ventured inside herself to say, and when he woke she was seized by the joy that women know in the madness of their loving, oh superiority of womankind! She hugged him close, kissed him hard, entranced by the thought that he was alive, and he kissed her too, deliriously, suddenly terrified by the bones of her skeleton which he could feel beneath her pretty cheeks, and once more he kissed her beautiful young breasts which death would stiffen, and desire would flood back, desire which she welcomed, venerated. 'Take your woman,' she said.

'My master,' she would say, reverently beneath him, and she wept tears of happiness as she bade him enter. 'My master,' she said once more, words of gloriously appalling taste, and he was shamed by such exaltation, but oh how absolutely wonderful it was to be alive! 'Your woman, I am your woman,' she said, and she would take his hand. 'Your woman,' she repeated, and to know that this was so she told him to use her as he pleased. 'Use your woman as you please,' she loved to tell him. Perspiring beneath him, sobbing beneath him, she said that she was his woman and his servant, lower than grass and smoother than water, told him over and over again that she loved him. 'I love you yesterday, today and always, and it will always be today,' she said. But if I'd had two teeth missing that night at the Ritz, two pathetic ossicles, would she now be there, at her orisons, beneath me? Two ossicles weighing three grams apiece, which made six grams. Her love tips the scales at six grams, he thought, leaning over her, stroking, adoring.

First nights of their loving, oh their noble, wild conjoinings, their furious loving, oh beneath his weight Ariane suddenly transmogrified, possessed, transported, Ariane frenzied, frightening, groaning in terrified anticipation, in cautious expectation, watchfully awaiting the coming of imminent ecstasy, Ariane closing her eyes to hasten its coming, her piteously whimpered signal that ecstasy was near, her pleas to her lover: 'Together, my love, wait, wait for me, my love, now, now, O my love,' she would crazily say, and he plummeting through black skies, alone oh so alone, with death quivering in his bones, and life at last in spurting spasm and groan of triumph, his wondrously spent life escaping, his life in her at last, in her fulfilled, in receipt of such abundance, happy in her, beating the rhythm to feel it more intensely, he surrendering above her, she lying like a great blood-red flower which had bloomed beneath him. 'Oh stay, stay,' she implored, gentle and beguiling, 'do not leave me', and she held him closer, breathed his sweetness, held him close so that he would not go, to keep him by her, gentle and beguiling.

CHAPTER 43

One night, when he said it was time for them to part, she clung to him, said it wasn't late, begged him to stay, told him in French and then in Russian that she was his woman. 'Don't go, don't leave me,' she said in golden entreaty. He longed to stay, but it was important that she be kept thirsting for him, crucial that she never associate his nearness with lassitude or surfeit. He felt ashamed for stooping so soon to shabby stratagems, but it had to be so, he had to be the one who was pined for, the one who went away. In this wise did he sacrifice his happiness to the overriding requirements of their love. He stood up and switched on the light.

Through lips still swollen with loving, she said he mustn't look at her, and went to the mirror which hung above the mantelpiece. When she had straightened her dress and repaired her ravaged hair, she said he could look now, and gave him a pleasant, urbane, courteous smile, as though her brazen shamelessness had never been. He kissed her hand in a gesture of deference, which was gratefully received, for they love to be respected when the moans and the sweet, damp name-calling are over. After another ruling-class smile, she reminded him of the old Russian custom of sitting down a moment before one took one's leave. He sat, and she sat on his knee, closed her eyes, and opened her lips.

In the hall, she asked him to stay one minute more. 'No,' he said with a smile. Impressed by the calmness of his refusal, she looked up at him and her eyes worshipped until they hurt. She walked him chastely to the waiting taxi and opened the door for him. Ignoring the driver, she leaned forward and kissed his hand. 'Until tomorrow, at nine,' she reminded him in a whisper, then closed the door, and the taxi began to move. An instant later she was running after it, shouting to the driver to stop. Through the lowered window, she apologized breathlessly. 'I'm sorry, I got it wrong, I said tomorrow but it's four in the morning, so it's tomorrow already, anyway what I mean is that I'll be waiting for you tonight, so I'll see you tonight at nine, all right?' Standing there in the blue moon-washed road, shivering in her creased dress, she watched her destiny disappear into the night. 'God keep you safe,' she whispered.

When she got back to her sitting-room, she made straight for the mirror so that she would not be alone. Yes, she could say tonight already, and there'd be a tonight every day, and every tonight would have its tomorrow. She curtsied to the beloved of her lord whom she beheld in the mirror, then tried out various faces to see how she had looked to him at the end of their night, imagined once more that she was him looking at her, beseeched, offered her lips, and liked the effect. Not bad, not bad at all. But if she added words she would get an even better idea. 'Your woman, I am your woman,' she told her mirror, ecstatic and genuinely moved. Oh yes, that's a look and a half, definitely a touch of the St Teresa du Bernins. He must have been bowled over by it. And when they were kissing and snorkelling nineteen to the dozen, what did she look like then, with her eyes shut? She opened her mouth, closed her left eye, and stared at herself with the right. Difficult to tell. This merely made her look one-eyed, which rather spoilt the enchantment. Pity, now I'll never know what I look like during the performance. How awful me saying performance, because with him just now it was all so serious. Anyhow, if I want to know what I look like when it's all happening, all I have to do is to not quite close my eyes tight and peep through the slits. But on second thoughts there's no point, because when it's all happening he's got his head so close to mine that he wouldn't see anything anyway, so it's a waste of time.

★

She sat down, took off her shoes, which were too tight, wiggled her toes, gave a sigh of relief, and yawned. 'Phew! peace at last and good riddance,' she said. 'Don't have to be charming any more now that Sir has gone, his nibs, his boobiness, Simple Simon, oh yes, dear, we mean you. Sorry, darling, just said it for a joke, though perhaps a teeny-weeny bit also because I'm too much under your thumb when you're here, it's to get my own back, you see, to show you there are limits, to keep my self-respect, though all the same it's very nice to be all alone and by myself.'

She stood up, made faces to relax, and walked round the room. How wonderful to be able to pad about without shoes, in bare feet, without heels, even though it wasn't a very elegant thing to do, marvellous to be able to move her toes and not to have to be sublime and Cleopatra and awesomely beautiful all the time. And now for a bite to eat, lovely. 'Because, darling, I don't like saying this, but I am starving. I do have a body too, you realize. Though I expect you know that,' she smiled, and she walked airily out of the room.

She went to the kitchen and opened the fridge. Rhubarb pie? Absolutely not, it might be all right for women with bad skin in vegetarian restaurants but not for her. She needed protein, by God's guts, as Corisande d'Auble, mistress to Henry IV, probably used to say. Well, how about some of this sausage, just bite lumps off it, don't bother cutting slices? No, really, not after a night like tonight. Thin bread and butter and jam would be more suitable, more poetical, more appropriate after recent events. No, not enough bite. So she decided to have a large ham sandwich. It was an agreeable compromise.

When she'd made the sandwich, she ran out into the garden to eat it in the cool of daybreak, now festooned with the gabble of waking birds, and she swanked as she walked up and down, saucily hipped and gloriously legged. Chewing hard, brandishing her ham sandwich and proclaiming to the risen sun that she was fair and beloved of her lord, she took long strides barefoot through the dew-wet grass and smiled broad smiles, and the sandwich held aloft was a pennant of happiness, a flag of love.

*

Back in her sitting-room, she sneezed. Who cared, since he wasn't there? When her nose tickled again, she sneezed very loud on purpose, saying 'Atishoo!' very distinctly and dramatically. She even went as far as to allow herself the pleasure of peering into the mirror and observing the sorry, snivelling expression of a face which has sneezed. And now, upstairs with you and wipe that nose, and quick about it! In her bedroom, she stood in front of her swing-mirror to blow her nose so that she could watch herself make a noise like trumpets. A pleasant enough sight, but hardly mouth-watering. Never blow your nose when he's there.

She tore down the stairs whistling, ran into her sitting-room, and immediately made a wonderful discovery. On the carpet under the sofa was a cigarette-case, the gold case which belonged to the archangel! She smiled knowingly. Obviously they had gone at it hammer and tongs on the sofa. Lovely hammer and tongs! She picked it up, promised it that they would sleep together, filled it with cigarettes, only too happy to be doing something for him, and besides it was a start to the preparations for tonight. In the ashtray were the butts of the three cigarettes he had smoked. She picked out one and put it between her lips. 'Ariane Cassandre Corisande d'Auble, opener of car doors and picker-up of fag-ends!' she declared.

With the sacred fag-end between her lips, she examined the armchair he had sat in, gazed fondly at the impression he had left behind him. The sight of it made her tingle, but it could not be preserved indefinitely, since the ninny would be here in a couple of hours to tidy the sitting-room. Never mind, there'd be others. 'We have a whole lifetime of impressions in front of us!' she proclaimed. But there was the sofa too, and everything that had happened on it. No identifiable imprints of him on the sofa, which was too mussed up for her to detect anything particular in the mixed his-and-her spoors they had left in their amorous wake, in the bumps and hollows and petrified waves of their sea. Oh, how wonderful it would be to be cast away on a desert island with him for the rest of their lives! She genuflected briefly to the sofa, the altar of their love. And now, let's smoke a proper cigarette, and we'll hold it between our third and fourth fingers, just like he does!

When she'd smoked the cigarette, she looked at herself one last time in the mirror. Her darling body, which had lately acquired an importance it never had before. 'O my precious,' she said to her body, 'I'm going to take fantastic care of you, you'll see!' She whirled round abruptly and shouted that she was a scarlet woman! This gave her the idea of dialling old Madame Ventradour's number. Disguising her voice, she informed the old lady that she had a lover then hung up. And now, a quick bath and then quick to bed!

'Look lively, you stupid idiot,' she scolded herself once she was submerged in the warm water, 'get a move on. It's almost six in the morning and you must get some sleep, otherwise you'll look like some wrung-out old fright of thirty, with a corrugated face, like a fortune-teller, and he'll run away in horror, but let's see now, go through the list of last things, note left for ninny so that she doesn't wake me up, front door locked, also shutters of lovely sitting-room fastened, don't want to get strangled by burglars, must stay alive, my life has become very precious, I have a body which now serves some useful purpose, with S it didn't mean a thing, it was on account of being miserable with the awful lawful, but no one before you, no one after you, I do so love my lovely young breasts, I do think I'm rather good-looking, the others have beardy legs, mossy sometimes, poor things, I feel really sorry for them, but that's their problem, listen sweetie, time for a couple of minutes chatterage? no, out of the question, it'll be much nicer when you're tucked up in bed all snug and comfy, but just check the current state of play, I've brought up everything I need from downstairs, the archangel's cigarette-case, hand-mirror in case I need it urgently in bed, and then I'll run through what it'll be like tomorrow night, correction tonight, run through everything down to the smallest detail, what I'll wear, what I'll say to him, what he'll do to me, amazing really the erotic potential of a well-brought up young lady like me, not to mention my complete amorality, because when you come to think of it I gave him the solid-gold case that Didi gave me as a present, poor Didi of

426

course, but there you are, it isn't my fault you know, anyway he won't be back for weeks and weeks, there's heaps of time.

She stood up and plied the soap vigorously. Anyway, she'd only married him because he'd asked her so insistently and because she was unhappy, besides, she hadn't known what she was doing with the poison from the overdose still in her system, and that surely meant that her consent was invalid. He really shouldn't have pressurized her the way he did. What he'd done was to take advantage of her in her weakened state, well more or less. So roll on tonight at nine!

Wearing only her pyjama top, which left her backside naked, and a pair of red slippers, she hopped one-footed into her bedroom and knelt at the old prayer-stool which had belonged to her aunt. Suddenly catching sight of herself in the swing-mirror she felt uncomfortable. This jacket's a bit short, but there hadn't been time to put the trousers on. No matter, God wasn't bothered by little things like that, and anyway He knew what she looked like with no clothes on. After the concluding amen, she jumped into bed, where Jean-Jacques was waiting: he was the bald teddy she'd had since she was a little girl, the chubby, one-eyed companion of her nights. When she was settled in, she nipped her lips with the archangel's cigarette-case and embarked on chatterage.

'Come on, Jean-Jacques, don't look at me like that, do you mind, you know that nothing's happened to change the way I feel about you, so please let's not have a scene, I ought to have made myself a hot-water bottle, not that it's cold but it would have been snuggly, the chatterage would have been cosier if I had one, but never mind, for his cigarette ends I won't say fag-ends any more, it's vulgar, I'll say stubs, it's a much more dignified word to use for any cigarette of his, even though it's been smoked right down, I must tell him the real name of my teddy, I've only ever said it to teddy himself, you know, I always tell everybody else his name is Patrice, but with you, my darling, I can't have any secrets, he'll like that, though obviously there is one secret I'll never tell him, incidentally on that first evening when I played that Bach thing he must have been staring at my profile, I wonder what I looked like from the side, come on, sweetie, let's have a dekko.'

She switched the light back on, got out of bed, dragged a low table which she pretended was the piano-stool in front of the long mirror, sat her bare backside on it, and thought. Now let's see, he had been on her right, so he had seen her right profile. Adopting a rather uncomfortable posture, with one hand running over an imaginary keyboard and her little looking-glass in the other, she peered at her profile reflected in the swing-mirror. Not bad at all. But then her right side was her best. Seen from the right, her nose was perfect, couldn't want for better. Then, swinging round so that she had her back to the mirror, she peered into her looking-glass and inspected the reflection of her hips in the mirror behind her. Not bad, except that her behind moved too much as she played. 'Yes, too much wobble in the rear end, I'll have to do something about that.' But perhaps he'd liked it. Yes, he might well have. Now time for beddy-byes. On her way back to bed, she gave the Mexican bear, Solal's present to her, a snooty pat on the back. 'How're tricks, Pedro?'

'Right, I shan't get out of bed again, perhaps I might buy one of those girdles, no they make you feel imprisoned, and anyway a curve or two doesn't do any harm, if God made us with curves it was so we should make the most of them, right then, chatterage, we'll have it all out, just between us two girls, with no man to butt in, but this time we'll start with the end and work backwards, so, beginning with the end, at the height of the revels he pulled back, I begged, don't leave me, don't leave me, saying darling darling shamelessly to him, quite natural in the circumstances, am I a fallen woman, no I'm a risen woman, because from one point of view I was practically a virgin, so there I was adorable and alluring but it was no use he was adamant, then I stood up to make myself presentable, fortunately he didn't watch while I was straightening the top of my dress, I would have been humiliated if he had, smart move bringing up that old Russian custom, gained two minutes and two minutes are always worth having, the last kisses sitting down, three I think, but they were long ones, very speleological, then saw him to taxi, why a taxi since he has a Rolls and a chauffeur because he's a tremendously important person, perhaps because a taxi is more discreet, he lives like a lord, keeps taxis waiting for hours and hours, last night it was from nine until four, seven hours, but it's none of my business, anyway car door open, he surely likes it when I salaam and kiss his hand, and then me running after him rectifying, not tomorrow night at nine but tonight at nine.'

She stopped abruptly. Heart thumping in chest, hot flush stealing over face, difficulties with breathing. It had suddenly dawned on her: one blunder after another. First blunder was her eagerness to open the taxi door for him. Second blunder, running after the car like some panicking, giddy little under-maid. Third blunder, the meek way she'd walked beside the car as it slowed, the subservient way she'd spoken to him while she tried to get her breath back, while the car was still moving. Like some pathetic beggar-woman asking for money. And in aid of what? So she could pass on the absolutely brilliant insight that today was tomorrow. He'd never forget that. O God, if only she hadn't done it! O God, it would have been so easy to wait till morning and then phone to put him right about which night. But oh no, first fussing like a halfwit, then behaving like something out of a circus. Knocked clean off her pedestal. No more being worshipped. Watching the sky hand in hand, the you-are-my-lord-I-proclaim-it-with-trumpets, all that noble stuff and you finish up like some galloping housemaid. 'Not at all, believe me, you're letting this get out of proportion, you're imagining things. Just think of the loving things he said, remember how eager he was, remember our kisses, no, everything's fine.' Maybe, but the noble, magic moments had all been before her circus routine, so they didn't count any more. The circus routine had spoilt everything. Oh, she wasn't fit to live. Too impulsive, couldn't wait to be happy, always putting her foot in it. That Hungarian countess would never have run after the taxi.

'Now come on, keep a cool head,' she cautioned herself, getting up and sitting on the edge of the bed, where she contemplated her feet and the holy mess she was in. Yes, think it through coolly. Actually she hadn't burned any bridges. Life was full of ups and downs.

Impressions passed. What she had to do now was blot out the bad impression, cover it up with a good one, regain his respect. Tonight be a miracle of grace and dignity, use the grand manner when serving the tea, be a bit distant, wear your best, in short, redeem yourself. She stood up suddenly and wrung her hands. But no, it was quite hopeless! She gave a shudder. Moistening her dry lips, she pelted down the stairs and made a grab for the phone which was ringing in the hall.

Returning upstairs, she rushed across her bedroom and kissed herself in the mirror. Oh what a wonderful man to ring her up like that just to hear her voice! And without any prompting on her part he had said that it had been adorable of her to run after the taxi like that! Which was true, if you thought about it, quite attractive in a helter-skelter sort of way. Made her sound like a bewitching adolescent. Spontaneous, that was the word! In short, image untarnished, and now back to bed! She jumped between the sheets, snuggled down, and pulled the covers up to her chin.

'Adorable, did you hear, so you see I was right when I said you were imagining things, shall we have a go at describing him? oooh yes please, wait until I tuck myself in properly, there, that's better, well to start with he's tall, taller than I am, that's how it ought to be, I suppose women are all factory-girls under the skin, but why didn't he make love to me tonight, why stop at just kissing, tell me why, just kissing, and also rampaging over my young breasts of course, though naturally I'm far too much of a lady to go round dropping hints, well let's hope that tomorrow night oops sorry tonight, but we must pop into a church one of these days we'll kneel down and hold hands, but we'll go riding together too, and water-skiing, he's bound to be a marvellous water-skier, don't you think, yes I do, anyhow the night before last, to make up for it, there were two crowning moments, actually I keep a score, isn't it awful, I want the sitting-room cleaned from top to bottom please and give it a good hoovering please, I'm expecting an old school friend she's just back from Australia, pack the ninny off straight after lunch so I can be free to manœuvre safe from prying eyes and unspoken comments, and then get my sitting-room exactly as I want it, do you think I should try a session in a beauty parlour, no, I wouldn't dare, all those cheeky assistants with their painted faces who fuss over you and anyway they might make me look a fright, but if he's called away on an official visit I'll give it a try because if it doesn't work I'll have time for repairs, down with, death to the, no, absolutely not, the very opposite, put out some fruit in my sitting-room, on second thoughts don't, makes it too obvious you've gone to a lot of bother, too servile, just ask him if he wants some and then go and fetch it, the point of having fruit is that if you eat an apple or whatever just before the kissing and snorkelling and so forth your tongue's lovely and fresh and tastes nice, though mine never tastes anything but nice even with no fruit to help, just a sec that's a double negative or something, if it's hot wear your rustic, the striped dress with the square neck, or better, the linen one that unbuttons all down the front, slip it on at ten to nine so it isn't creased on second thoughts it's a morning dress really, so pick a dress for a summer evening but keep it as simple as possible, or better still my semi-formal two-piece which isn't too dressy, the nice thing about it is that you can take the jacket off and you've got a dress with a low neck, not too low actually, still if you lean forward a bit it might do if, but look, I'm going to have to get to the bottom of this countess business, has she really gone away for good, the other day at the Ritz when he was showing me a new shaving-brush he'd bought he looked so like a little boy while he was telling me all about his marvellous shaving-brush, how the bristles never came unstuck, he was so keen, I felt so grown-up in comparison, I absolutely adore him but at the same time I feel this fear, this aversion to, spit it out, male desire, but not all the time, just sometimes, but sometimes he just steamrollers me, the female of the species poleaxed by a tough and clever brain, I'm sure I couldn't come up with half the things he says, women are always a bit on the dense side, still I'm quite capable of taking him down a peg or two on the quiet, such as saying you're a show-off or your ideas are so confused. I never did that with Varvara, I was always very indulgent with her, I love him much more, but with her there was this understanding, I like it when he takes my clothes off, when I want him most I come over all coy, I just huddle coyly in my corner, sometimes I long for his lips when he has that detached far-away look on his face, also when he's dressed I like putting my arms under his jacket and squeezing him to show him that he belongs to me, but most of all I like it when, but I can't possibly say it out loud, basically I think that I that as far as what goes on at night in bed is concerned I have absolutely no moral sense at all, that's the way it is perhaps when decent women, I do believe that whatever he asked me to do in the dark I'd do, of course I would, provided the words weren't, oh I'm a mess, poor darling me, always waiting, heels too high and skirts too tight, the rest of them are a lot worse than me with their little hats and earrings, why do I feel this awful need to be humble, I make myself sick, all the same the first thing I'll do when he comes tonight will be to make a dive for his hand, pawing at him, licking, ugh! I hope you won't stay too long tonight, dear, because I find you rather trying, it would be marvellous if I could say that to him, oh and then there's that worshipping kiss which I invented all by myself, well all right there may be plenty of other pretty women who've also invented it, oh but the nicest part really is when he's not there and I'm waiting, also when he's gone and I'm remembering, another kind of shameful kissing is when I sort of sniff him as if I were a female monkey, no there's nothing shameful or monkeyish about it, oh that's enough of that, go to sleep now, when I play the piano my behind moves on the stool, maybe I do it a little bit on purpose, basically I'm a lesser mortal, oh I adore the Trio Number One in B flat major by dear old Schubert, so plump and kindly in his big glasses, yes I must ask him if he can whistle, hey handsome! know how to whistle? I feel this need for him all the time, this need to lie bewitched and mindless in his arms, I expect I get on his nerves because I'm always phoning him, he said that each night as he goes to sleep he thinks of me, that's real love for you, the other evening when I scolded him for the horrible thing he said that night at the Ritz about breasts being a joke and always drooping he asked me if I would forgive him, said mine were the most beautiful in the whole world, actually that's true, I wouldn't wish their like on my best friend, so that's that sorted out, line drawn under it, oh but I don't have a best friend, also when I said that he'd said the sport that they find so astoundingly fascinating and Don Juan thinks it's ever so comical, there again his answer was quite satisfactory, there's no sin but has its pardon, thwack with the lash on his back and there are red marks and then they turn into raised white welts, I'd love to, and then again I told him he'd said at the Ritz about not liking to be kissed on the shoulder afterwards, his reply was just as perfect, actually I'm rather pleased he doesn't like the others doing that to him, but does he honestly like it with me, of course he does, take it from me, when he arrived on his horse I went to meet him, he got off his horse, I felt all embarrassed as he watched me walking, incidentally kissing was quite different with S, I never felt anything with poor S, but I mustn't tell him I love him so often, I'm no good at all at keeping up my feminine mystique, be disconcerting, blow cool, forget to turn up to dates, tell him sorry can't see you tomorrow, try a touch of the how-nice-to-see-you-hope-you're-well, in short be the kind of woman who knows how to sweep a man off his feet, remote and regal, the kind that says oh maybe I don't know with a slightly blasé look on her face, the type that murmurs a languid possibly, the sort that answers you all weary and haughty, the disdainful sort with a long green cigarette-holder and eyes half shut, thinking enigmatic thoughts, agreed, motion carried, and you shall see what stuff I am made of my fine fellow-me-lad, yes change my personality completely, but not tonight, start tomorrow, I can't whistle properly, how do boys manage it, yes it would be lovely if he folded me, put me in a case and then when he needed me he'd get me out and unfold me, such a sweet idea, wish I was a little girl alone in a big house on the edge of a wood, a house with a low roof hidden under a cloak of Virginia creeper with patches of red in it, and I'd be as virginal as the creeper, though without any red blotches, and I'd show him the house, I'd take him to see the terrace which has a balustrade all round it the little goldfish pond the stone seat the lawn the Chinese summer-house and the big lake edged with mysterious trees, I'm giving you all this, darling, it's all yours darling, and I am yours too, for all the days of our life, my love.'

She closed her eyes so that she would see him, she took his hand so that she should sleep next to him, and smiled at the thought of tonight at nine. On legs that ceased to be, she walked into waters of blackness, her lips pressed to the gold cigarette-case. It was her time of happiness, the time of happiness of a future corpse.

CHAPTER 44

The next night, when she was all ready in a dress which she was wearing for the first time, he phoned to say he had been detained at the Palais by an unexpected meeting but would come without fail the following night. Whereupon, collapse of pretty party, sobbing face down on sofa. All the trouble she'd gone to, and for nothing! And her dress, which was quite divine on her! And she'd been looking her absolute best tonight!

Suddenly she was on her feet. She tore off the divine dress, ripped it into pieces, trampled the pieces, and kicked the sofa. The beast! He was doing it on purpose, it was a tactic to make her want him more, she was sure of it! Seeing him tomorrow was no good at all, she wanted him tonight! Oh, she'd pay him back tomorrow, she'd give him a taste of his own medicine! Beast!

In the kitchen, half-naked, she consoled herself with jam, black-cherry jam, of which she ate large quantities with a soup-spoon. Then, feeling nauseous with jam, she started to cry and toiled upstairs to the top floor, sniffing as she went. She stood in front of the bathroom mirror and, to make her grief bearable, made herself ugly. She mussed her hair and, liberally scattering face-powder and scrawling lipstick over both cheeks, gave herself a face like a clown.

At ten o'clock, he phoned again, said the meeting hadn't lasted as long as he'd thought it would and that he'd be there in twenty minutes. 'Yes, lord, I await thy coming,' she said. The instant the phone was back on its hook, she whirled and twirled and kissed her hands. Quickly now, a bath. Quick, clean that stuff off your face, do your hair, make yourself beautiful again, slip into a dress almost as divine as the other, hide the torn one, tomorrow she'd burn it, no it would smell too awful, in that case she'd bury it in the garden! Hurry, hurry! Her lord was on his way, and she was his beloved!

CHAPTER 45

One evening, just before nine, she decided that waiting for him outside, at the door, made her look cheap. Well then, she'd wait inside and answer the door when he came, but no hurrying, mind, walk slowly, taking deep breaths, that way she would remember who she was, that way also she wouldn't get there all out of breath. Yes, good, self-control, show him politely into the sitting-room. There, make conversation, then suggest a cup of tea. It was a good idea to have set everything out ready in the sitting-room beforehand, that way she wouldn't look like the maid bringing the tea-tray. Yes, she hadn't forgotten anything, teapot plus cosy, cups, milk, lemon. At the right moment, stand, pour tea slowly, then ask, and mind no crawling, milk or lemon. She tried it. 'Milk or lemon?' No good, it was all wrong, much too hockey-sticks, made her sound like a Girl Guide leader. She tried again. 'Milk or lemon?' Yes, that was fine. Pleasant, and not the least crawly.

When the bell rang, she made a dash for the door. But when she got as far as the hall she did an about-turn. Had she removed all the powder? She returned to her sitting-room, parked herself in front of the mirror, and peered at herself blankly. In the end, with the blood thumping in her ears, she sprang into action, scurried away, almost tripped, and opened the door. 'How-nice-to-see-you-hope-you're-well,' she said, and said it every whit as naturally as a soprano in an operetta attempting a passage of *parlando*.

★

Breathing with difficulty, she led him into her sitting-room. Her lips locked in a fixed grin, she motioned him towards one armchair, sat herself in another, pulled her dress well down over her knees, and waited. Why didn't he speak? Had she offended him? Perhaps she hadn't got all that powder off. She ran her hand over her nose and suddenly felt that she wasn't at all pretty. Should she say something? Her throat felt congested, and clearing it would make a horrid noise. Little did she know that he was merely adoring her embarrassment, that he wasn't saying anything because he wanted to make the moment last.

With trembling lips, she offered him a cup of tea. He accepted dispassionately. Tense and uneasy, her cheeks ablaze, she poured tea on the table, into the saucers and occasionally even into the cups, apologized, then held out the little milk-jug in one hand and the lemon slices in the other. 'Silk or melon?' she asked. He laughed, and, screwing up her courage, she looked up at him. He smiled, and she held out both hands. He took them, and got down on his knees before her. In a moment of inspiration, she went down on her knees to him too, and did it with such grace that she knocked over the teapot, the cups, the milk-jug and every last slice of lemon. Kneeling, they smiled, and their teeth gleamed, the teeth of youth. Kneeling, they were ridiculous, they were proud and they were handsome, and it was bliss to be alive.

CHAPTER 46

On another evening, as he was not saying anything, she sat quietly, without moving, respecting his silence. But when she observed him opening and closing his empty cigarette-case, she stood up and walked slowly to her tulip-wood writing-desk. Her tread was measured and harmonious, for her desire was to be perfect.

Bearing a cigarette-box which she had taken out of the writing-desk, she returned to him solemnly, priestess-like, hips barely moving. Poor sweet, he thought, for though his head was bowed he saw her. With a discreet smile, she placed the box of Abdullahs in front of him and, like a graceful slave, opened it. He took a cigarette, which she lit with the gold cigarette-lighter he had given her on that first evening. Then, happy to have been of service, she slowly returned, with a swagger of hips, to her armchair. She sat down, crossed her noble legs elegantly, modestly pulled down the hem of her skirt, and froze in a poetic pose. I adore you, he thought, touched by her pathetic effort to find grace and favour.

Sitting there staring at her delicate hands which had once more pulled and smoothed the hem of her dress, she looked the very image of perfection. And then, when everything about her was just right, what should happen alas, but a tickle started in her nose which warned her of the imminent arrival of a sneeze. 'Back in a jiffy,' she said, leaping to her feet, and she left the room in a rush, forgetting to wiggle her hips.

★

Stifling the disastrous urge, she took the stairs four at a time, pinching her nose between thumb and forefinger. When she reached the landing, she hurtled into the Deumes' bedroom, slammed the door behind her, and sneezed four times. Then, with a series of discreet snuffles which would not be heard, she wiped her nose in a check handkerchief which she found in a drawer and threw under the bed once she'd finished with it. But now what could she say to explain her absence? That she'd left the room to blow her nose? She would rather die first! She turned this way and that, looking around her in desperation. In the end, on the table, next to a book entitled *The Home Handyman's Treasury of Practical Tips*, her eye settled on a small photograph of herself in a leather frame. She grabbed it and left the room, though not without first taking a peek at herself in the wardrobe mirror, to check.

'Just popped upstairs to fetch a photograph of myself,' she said when she got back to her sitting-room. 'I'll give it to you when you're leaving, but you're not to look at it until you get home. That way, the taxi will be taking you back to where I'll be.' She inhaled deeply through her nose, pleased at the way she'd put it. Rehabilitated and little knowing that he had heard her explosive sneezes, she sat down again feeling decidedly poetic.

CHAPTER 47

Sometimes they spent their nights in his suite at the Ritz. She loved going there to see him, loved the idea of his waiting for her, of not having to worry that the horrid man might be late. In the taxi which ferried her to him, she loved to dream that she was Little Red Riding Hood off to visit the wolf, keeping her wits about her just in case she met her grandma on the way.

In the early hours, she would get dressed, kneel at the foot of the bed where, fatigued by love, he lay dozing, and magic him, as she put it, bind him with a spell of chaste caresses, which mostly meant stroking his feet patiently, rhythmically, and she would tingle as she pictured herself a slave kneeling at the bed of her king. She never went home before making absolutely certain that he was asleep, and she always left a short note for him to find when he woke. Her messages were written in a straggly hand, for they were scribbled in the dark, and she left them on his bedside table where he would see them on waking.

'I feel as tender and as proud as a mother when you let me magic you, like when I fluttered my hands over your back just now, like a dragonfly. Beloved, I resisted the urge to kiss you all over. Sometimes I think you have no idea of how much I love you. Sweet dreams, my love.'

'For heaven's sake, darling, don't smoke so much tomorrow. Please, not more than twenty. Fiddle with your beads instead. And don't be cross if I tell you to have lunch tomorrow. And no making do with just a starter, mind. Your little nanny-goat's knocking her head against a brick wall: what does she have to do to make her lovely billy see sense? Sweet dreams, my love.'

'Darling, I simply must tell you that the love you give me is a deep, deep sky where I discover new stars every time I look. I'll never stop seeing stars, it's endless and everlasting. Sweet dreams, my love.'

'Darling, you've made a real woman of me. All the dry leaves and dead wood have just fallen off, and when I'm with you I am simple and whole. Believe me when I say that a barefoot Romanian peasant with her dangling plaits could not look at her man with eyes more trusting, more adoring. O Sol, Sol, if only you knew how much love, how much crazy longing for you there is in your little peasant's your little girl's heart. Sweet dreams, my love.'

CHAPTER 48

One night he felt an overpowering urge to go back, to see her. No, he mustn't, he should let her sleep, he'd have to make do with the photo he had, the one of her he liked best. Oh, those legs, those long, huntress legs of hers, which would always run to where he was on spurs of love. Oh, her Romanian dress with embroidery circling hem and waist and running up and down the arms. Oh, her hands, which only moments ago had gripped his shoulders as they drank each other's honey. Oh, the mystery of happiness, a man and a woman drinking each other's sweetness. And here were her breasts beneath her dress, hidden from others but consecrated his. Hallelujah, here were her face, her soul, her very being, nostrils flaring, lips persecuted by his love. Yes, at first light, send a bellboy out to buy a magnifying lens, a strong one, and take a closer look at those lips which were made to yield to his. But what could he do till then? Sleeping was out of the question, he loved her far too much to sleep. But he could not be alone, he loved her far too much to stay by himself. Drive out to Pont-Céard and see Isolde. 'Isolde, Countess Kanyo,' he declaimed with a pride which was entirely bogus. '*Isolde, Kanyo grofnö*,' he declaimed again, in Hungarian.

Sitting on Isolde's lap, he ran his finger over the fine crow's-feet now beginning to appear around her lustrous eyes. His darling was getting old. He felt easy with her, for she was discreet and comforting. He stroked her hair, but kept his distance from her lips and looked away to avoid seeing her breasts, which her gaping dressing-gown left exposed, for the sight made him feel faintly queasy. Ah, how he would love to explain the wonders of Ariane to her, share them with her! His Isolde was good and kind. He knew that if he told her how happy he was she wouldn't make a scene, but there would be worse. There would be that look of hers which he knew of old, the same look there had been in her eyes when he'd told her about Elizabeth Vanstead, a look of mild reproach, the mildly crazed look of the unhappy and the helpless, the brittle smile and faded expression of a woman of forty-five who no longer dared to show herself in the harsh glare of the noonday sun. No, out of the question. He could not possibly tell her about Ariane.

To surrender to thoughts of Ariane as he lay in the arms of Isolde, he had shut his eyes, pretending to be asleep, while she stroked his hair and hummed a strange lullaby to herself. Sleep, my precious, my little precious, she hummed, and she knew then that he would leave her one day, knew that she was old, and she smiled at him helplessly, poignantly aware of the unhappiness which lay in wait for her but feeling only tenderness for the cruel man who was still for the moment hers. She watched him and was suddenly almost happy. For as he slept she could love him completely, without interference from him.

He opened his eyes, blinked as though he had just woken, and yawned. '"Daughter of Minos and of Pasiphaë,"' he intoned dreamily. 'I love that line. Who wrote it?' 'Racine,' she said, 'you know: "Ariane, dear sister, pricked by what dart of love . . ."' 'Of course, Ariane,' the hypocrite said, 'Ariane, the divine nymph who is in love with Theseus. She was very beautiful, wasn't she? Willowy, virginal, had a royal nose like all those lovelorn women in classical literature. Ariane. A lovely name, I do believe I am in love with the name.' Careful now, she would soon smell a rat. And so, gesturing vaguely, he explained that he had drunk a great deal of champagne at the Donon with the English delegates. 'Bit tight,' he smiled, tender and contented, but he was thinking of the woman asleep, far away at Cologny. She kissed him. He felt afraid and averted his lips. 'You look tired,' she said. 'I'll undress you, I'll put you to bed, I'll massage your feet to send you to sleep. Shall I?'

★

Sitting on the edge of the bed, she massaged his feet. Supine, he watched her through half-closed eyes. Proud Isolde, Countess Kanyo, now a humble pummeller of feet, and happy with the role. Still in her dressing-gown, she worked conscientiously, varying the movements of her hands like a professional, kneading, rubbing, smoothing, then switching to the toes, which she twisted this way and that. The unhappy woman was proud of her skill as a masseuse. She had even taken lessons so that she could serve him more perfectly.

Completely absorbed in what she was doing, striving like a good and faithful servant, pausing now and then to apply the talcum powder, she went on and on massaging while behind his eyes, which were closed once more, he saw his vivacious, pirouetting, sunlit girl, his Ariane. He bit his lip guiltily. Should he tell her to lie by his side and force himself to kiss her mouth, in other words stop treating her like a masseuse? Later, perhaps. He couldn't bring himself to do it now, not straight away. Poor, good-hearted sweet. Yes, he loved her like a mother, and he hated her like a mother. And yet there had been a time when he desired her. Forty-five she was now, poor darling, or maybe more. The skin on her neck was grainy, beginning to stretch. Her breasts sagged. 'How's the massage?' 'Fine, darling, fine.' (Should he add that it was exquisite? No, fine was quite adequate. Keep exquisite for later.) 'Would you like me to manipulate them for you?' 'Please, darling. That would be exquisite.'

Then began the manipulation. Her left hand gripped his heel, while with the right she skilfully but quite unnecessarily twisted and waggled his bare foot. Her lips were set in a faint smile of concentration or possibly pride at his having said that it would be exquisite. For his part, he was ashamed. He hated his foot. He felt pity for the noble face so studiously bent over his loathsome five-toed extremity, which was not worthy of such reverence. On and on she worked, pitiful, demeaned, her sumptuous dressing-gown messy with streaks of talcum. Should he tell her to stop? But if she stopped, what would they do?

She straightened and caught him in her almond, semi-oriental eyes,

fixed him with her gentle, warm eyes. 'Shall I do the other one now?'
'Yes please, my darling,' he said, pleased with the possessive, which
made a welcome variant, and then went one better: 'Yes, sweetheart,'
he said. She gave him a smile of thanks for those last words, which
were more gratifying than 'darling'. O unhappy woman who was
content with the tiniest crumbs, who snapped up the most unconsid-
ered trifles and was comforted! Oh if only he could speak the tender
words which rose fully formed on the tip of his tongue! But he could
not, and all the while, still manipulating silently, she waited to hear
words of love. Discreetly she waited for them to come, but he found
none which rang true. It would be so simple if he could only feel
desire for her. Then there would be no need for words. He would
manipulate her body in silence and all would be well, for nothing
reassured her quite as much. But, alas, all he could give her was
words. The male was defectively programmed in this respect. Eventually he plucked up courage and looked at her gravely. 'Listen,
sweetheart. (She stopped massaging and lifted her head, more pathetic
than a dog begging for a sugar-lump.) Sweetheart, there's something
I must say: I love you more now, far more, than in the old days.'
Sheepishly he looked away, but this impressed Isolde and convinced
her that he was sincere. She leaned forward, kissed his bare foot, and
resumed her manipulation, the happy fool of his manipulation. Oh
yes, a fool who believed she pleased him by tweaking and pulling his
feet. Happy, yes, but the effect of mere words could not last.
Tomorrow he would have to find new, more passionate words.
Besides, words were no substitute for the other which she was
expecting, the cursed other which was the only irrefutable proof. But
how could he perform the other with she of the scrawny neck? Oh
the bane of the flesh. Ah yes, he too hungered for meat.

She looked up and asked what he was thinking. 'I'm thinking about
you, Isé.' What else could he say? She stopped massaging and reached
for his hand. Sensing danger, he stretched out his foot. Thereupon she
resumed her task, but after a moment switched her attention to his
calf. More danger. What should he do now? Talk politics to her?
Hardly the moment, not at two in the morning. Now she had
reached his knee and clearly had further designs. Oh what a tragic

445

farce! And most farcical of all was that the need to be sexually massaged was entirely in her mind. She needed to know that he loved her, to be quite certain. How damnably males were programmed, for the urge to be kind was no part of it. 'A little more on the foot, darling, do the foot again, it's so relaxing. (What else could he do to cast out the demon? That's it! The novel! Never mind if it was a weird thing to ask at two in the morning.) Sweetheart, I'd like to hear some more of the novel you read from the other day, it was gripping stuff, anyway I love you to read aloud to me. You read so well,' he added, for good measure.

Holding the book in her left hand and continuing to knead his bare foot with her right, she put on her very best reading manner, disguising her accent, putting drama into the dialogue, and using different voices for each character. It set his teeth on edge. Should he ask her to stop? If he did that, it would be danger time again! Her Hungarian accent was overlaid by a veneer of over-refined English and it grated on his ears. Of course, if it had been the other who spoke with a Hungarian accent he would have thought it entrancing. Ask her if she wanted to go to the cinema? But then he'd have to talk to her during the intermissions. Anyway, you couldn't go to the cinema at two in the morning. So this is what lay in wait for him from now on each time he called on her in the afternoon, for his evenings were set aside for the other, who, poor gullible goose, suspected nothing, what lay in store for him were visits to cinemas and compulsory chats in the intermissions, or else foot massages, novels read aloud, and being forced to come up with fresh words of love, the misery of not desiring her, the torment of constantly sensing what she desired, what she humbly, silently demanded of him. And in him a constant feeling of guilt, of pity. He would feel pity when she sang Hungarian folk-songs to him, always the same songs, he knew all her songs by heart. He would feel pity each afternoon at five when she suggested ringing for the maid to bring tea, suggested it with an oddly innocent hope, with incurable optimism, as if tea would magically inject life into the living death which she refused to face squarely. Her poor, absurd faith in the miraculous power of tea taken together while they 'nattered', as she put it to make the ceremony sound more exciting than it was. But what would they natter about? He knew everything there was to know about her. He knew how fond she was of those dreamy, proper, refined, languid, unhurried, winning, tiresome or, to put it another way, upper-middle-class English women novelists. He also knew that she loved all sorts of flowers whose names he didn't know and that the Bach she loved was not Johann Sebastian but another one who was every bit as robotic.

'The other foot now, please, darling.' Yes, she was kind and gentle, but also depressing and not particularly good at anything. Whereas his Ariane was great fun, a little crazy and quite unpredictable. Like the way she'd described hens only yesterday: she'd said they were puffed up balls of panic, gossip on two legs, said they were always thinking about feathering their nests. And the way she'd talked about the injured toad she'd looked after in the cellar. He remembered what she'd said about the toad: its gorgeous, golden, flecky eyes, such a lovely expression, scared and yet trusting, and it looked ever so grateful when she talked to it and so dainty when it used its fingers to eat with. And when she'd told him about the way toads croaked, she'd said it was a song of regret, the call of a soul. And the day she'd spotted a sparrow on the lightning-conductor on top of the house singing its little head off and looking ever so comfortable, she'd said it was calling to all its little friends to tell them that sitting up there was as good as being on a sofa, it was lovely. And the heat of her kisses. But with this one, who read to him, he had only to attempt the lightest touch, out of pity, and she instantly assumed an expression like the Virgin Mary. Besides, he'd found out that she went to beauty salons to have her face descaled or something. What did this descaling involve? Perhaps it winkled tiny scaly creatures out of each pore? Ariane, clear skin, the delicious curve of her lips, and no lipstick. Not like this one, who was still pummelling his feet with hands which ended in painted nails, talons almost, talons dipped in blood. Ariane: her childish delight when he praised her beauty, shaping her mouth perfectly as though she were sitting for a photographer. The evening she'd given him sorrel soup, how proud she'd been of feeding her man. And the afternoon he'd come on a horse, she had been overjoyed at his unexpected visit, and she had run to meet him smiling far too broadly, it was a ridiculous smile, so wide and so earnest that it had made him laugh, the smile of a little girl on cloud nine or the grin of some clumsy, impish djinn incapable of staying still long enough to look dignified. But when would this one stop slapping his feet?

'Shall I go on reading?' 'Yes please, darling.' 'And massaging?' 'Please, darling.' And if she overdid it with the leg-stroking, take avoiding action. The gambit that never failed was the simulated liver flare-up. Oh she came to life then, positively bloomed at the idea of busying herself in his service. She applied burning compresses with appalling zest and scuttled off every few minutes to the bathroom for fresh supplies, which she brought back at a gallop. And how proud of herself she was when, with his skin burned bright red and unable to stand any more scalding compresses, he said the pain had gone away. Yes, the only happiness he was capable of giving her now was to convince her that she could be of use to him. So feign illness each time he came to see her. Result: something for her to do and think about without danger to himself. Next time, for a change, he'd try a frozen shoulder on her. He could already see her shooting off to a chemist's and rushing back breathlessly clutching jars of anti-rheumatic creams and ointments. Oh if he could only kiss her unfearingly on the cheek and talk to her of Ariane, tell her everything, share Ariane with her. But it was out of the question. She wanted him to herself, to monopolize him. But that was it for now. His feet had been mauled about quite enough for one day, thank you very much.

When he pulled his foot away, she said 'Shall I stop now?' 'Yes, darling.' 'You should sleep now, it's late. I want you to rest properly, so I'll leave you the bed and I'll sleep in the guest room.' He knew that these last words were spoken in the hope that he'd ask her to stay, to sleep by his side. It was no go. Never again. But if he agreed to let her sleep by herself she'd be utterly miserable, and tomorrow morning her eyes would be red and puffy. So leave. But where could he go? Wake up little Edmée and talk to her of Ariane? No, it would be too cruel to hold forth about his great love to a poor midget who, to boot, was a member of the Salvation Army. There was nothing for poor, lonely, glum Solal to do but go back to the Ritz. He told her he had some urgent work to do for Sir John. Besides, the taxi was waiting. He dressed and kissed her on the cheek. Sensing that she was expecting something more passionate, he improvised a coughing fit to muddy the waters and left hurriedly, his hat pulled down over his eyes, looking and feeling guilty.

In the taxi, he suddenly remembered the fine lines around her eyes. Withered on the vine, yet she had been still beautiful at the start of their affair. Age was so unfair, but there was also the lonely life she had led at Pont-Céard, she had lost a little of her bloom each day as she waited for him to come. She would soon be old. Yes, go away with her somewhere, anywhere, tonight! Give up Ariane. Spend the rest of his life with Isolde. He tapped the glass and asked the driver to take him back to Pont-Céard. How happy his Isolde would be!

Moments later, he tapped again and wound down the glass. 'Brother,' said he to the driver, 'my beloved lives and breathes at Cologny. Take me to her, for I am drunk with love, and what does dying matter? Oh the fatal attraction of that moment when first I saw her one evening descending the steps of the University, a goddess and my betrothed, a goddess, her footsteps dogged in the night. Accordingly, dear brother, ferry me roaringly, carry me most expeditiously to my beloved, and I shall make you happier than you ever were before, you have the word of Solal, fourteenth of the name!' Thus he spake, and he sang to the stars which twinkled through the window, sang in exaltation, for he was going to see her, and dying did not matter at all.

449

Her jealousies, the goodbyes forever. At night she took a horsewhip to herself as a punishment for thinking of him, and for days on end gave him no sign that she was alive. Waiting for her, waiting for her by the telephone which stubbornly, cruelly refused to ring, his heart missing a beat whenever the lift stopped at the third floor of the Ritz, for perhaps it was her, but no it was never her, and at last the phone would ring and she would come tonight. Whereupon the ludicrous charade of newmaking himself handsome.

The instant she walked through the door she fell into the brute's arms, seeking his mouth. But when the first ardour had cooled, suddenly seeing a picture in her mind of him with her, she plied him with questions. He answered that he could not desert Isolde, that if he saw her now it was as a friend. 'Liar!' she screamed, and looked at him with hate in her eyes. Oh the thought of him kissing that woman exactly as he kissed her! 'You brute! You wicked man!' she screamed. 'You do not fear God!' she screamed in the approved Russian manner.

After prophesying, in a sudden rush of virtue, that women would be his ruin, she leaped out of bed, dressed briskly, like a woman who meant business, declared that this time they were through and that she would never see him again, and then slipped on her gloves with steely determination. All this inflexible preparing to leave was designed to give her an excuse to stay, but with honour untarnished. And to show also just how unshakeably set she was on leaving him for ever, her unshakeability being telegraphed especially in the energetic way she buttoned up her jacket, the hem of which she then proceeded to pull down, an operation which required several attempts since she was never quite satisfied with the result, it seemed. Resolute preparations too because she hoped that if he saw that she was really intending to go, and if she spent enough time getting ready, then in the end he'd beg her to stay. Throwing himself into the spirit of the thing, he fully endorsed the idea of a clean break and encouraged her to go. Both of them brazened it out, though inwardly both were afraid, for this time the other might be deadly serious, mind made up, and yet at the same time, and quite paradoxically, both were absolutely certain that when it came to the point there would be no separation, and this gave them the strength to threaten and the determination to end the affair.

When there was nothing left to button up, pull down and straighten, no more powder to be meticulously applied to the face of stone in the mirror, she had no alternative but to leave. At the door, she would put her hand on the knob and turn it slowly, hoping that he would see that this time she meant it and at last beg her to stay. If he remained silent, she would say goodbye in a sombre voice to make him suffer and provoke an entreaty; or she might say in even more solemn tones: 'Goodbye, Solal Solal!', which was a degree more striking, for the best effects soon palled. Or, with the polite understatement which conveys iron resolution, she might say: 'I'd be grateful if you would not write to me or telephone.' If she sensed that he was suffering, she was quite capable of walking out on him immediately and not giving him any sign of life for days on end. But if he smiled, if he kissed her hand politely, thanked her for the memorable hours she had given him and opened the door for her, she would slap both his cheeks. Not just because she hated him for not suffering and for not preventing her from leaving, nor because she herself was suffering, but also, no, especially, because she did not want to go and because slapping his face would allow her to spin things out and thus enable her to work her way to a reconciliation, either because the face-slapping provided her with a decent excuse for saying sorry and staying or else because it might provoke the desired reaction, to wit, some roughness on his part, the kind which might well induce a flow of feminine tears which in turn might elicit a male request for forgiveness followed by undeniable and mutual tokens of affection.

Sometimes she would go, slamming the door behind her, and then come back immediately and start to cry, with her arms around his neck, boohooing that she could not, she absolutely could not live without him, and blowing her nose. But more often, to justify coming back, she called him names, shrugging her shoulders indignantly with a movement which made her breasts heave most attractively, said nasty things, and she was an expert at saying nasty things. But beneath the anger lay the deep joy of being near him once more.

At other times there was swooning. This needs to be explained. So that she had an excuse for staying and waiting for the miracle which would make everything right and reduce him to begging her not to leave him and promise never to see his countess again, she would feel faint, collapse in a heap, then get up and start ranting that he did not love her, or, as a variant, that he loved her so little that she was ashamed for him, before collapsing again, distressed and weak, like a disappointed little girl.

Oh youth, oh the noble swoonings for love! Oh the marvel of her, gorgeously evening-gowned, fainting and rising and collapsing, and of him, adoring her and inwardly comparing her to one of those celluloid toy clowns with lead behinds which always return to vertical, and she, love's wounded tigress, falling and rising and falling and wanting to die, feline and felled, so beautiful in her tears and so golden of voice, her glorious legs laid bare, and sobbing, and her opulent hips rhythmically rising and falling, and what had to be came to pass. And her face was clean-cut and androgynous, the pure face of ecstasy, and her eyes turned piously to the seventh heaven of earthly delights. 'Your woman,' she moaned.

CHAPTER 50

With the anaemic smile of the unhappy, she stared at the suitcase she had just packed any old how, as though she were in a dream. It was the case she had taken with her three years before, at the start of their affair, when she had travelled to Paris to be with him, travelled with such high hopes. Come along, stand up, shut the case. But she could not do it, was shaken by a fit of the helpless little sobs of the sick in body, and she sat on the case to fasten the straps. When she had done them up, she did not have the strength to stand, and remained seated, her arms dangling at her sides. Noticing a run in the stocking on her left leg, she shrugged. Too bad. She didn't have the heart.

Facing the old woman in the mirror – old Isolde, who had been kept on for pity's sake but kept at arm's length – she winced, undid the top buttons of her dress, and pulled at her brassière, snapping the straps. Worn-out, poor things. She luxuriated in their flaccidity, pressed them with her hands to emphasize their sag. Ah yes, they were not as firm now, and it was all over. They had dropped three or four centimetres, and it was over, love was finished. They had gone soft on her, and love was finished. She took her hands away to see them in all their decadence, waggled her shoulders to see them bounce this way and that, found the sight comic, found the sight tragic. Each evening for years she had waited for him, not knowing if he would come, each evening she'd dressed up for him, not knowing if he would come, each evening had made her house immaculate for him, not knowing if he would come, waiting each evening by her window and watching, not knowing if he would come. And now it was finished. And why? Because her two top pockets were less well filled than the top pockets of his other woman. When he'd been ill, the nights she'd spent caring for him, nights spent lying on the floor, on the carpet, by his side. Would this other woman know how to look after him? Should she phone and warn her about his allergy to pyramidon and antipyrine? Never mind, let them get on with it. He was fond of her, of course, he'd done his best on the rare occasions when he did come, complimenting her on being so elegantly turned out, showing an interest in her clothes, telling her she had beautiful eyes. All old women had beautiful eyes, eyes were their best feature. And now and then a peck on the cheek or even the shoulder, through her dress. Fabric was neutral, didn't make anyone feel sick. Kisses for old women. Caresses for old ladies. Obviously he found her repellent. He'd been pathetic, so embarrassed when he could no longer avoid telling her about his other woman, he'd been so sad to cause her pain. So sad. But on that evening there'd been real kisses for *her*.

Once more she waggled her breasts at the mirror. One to the right, one to the left! Swing, O ye aged globes! She'd been born too soon, that was it. Her father had been in too much of a hurry. And those bags under her eyes, the skin too slack under her chin, that dry hair, those bulges in all the wrong places, and the rest of the proofs of God's goodness. She buttoned the top of her dress, sat on her case again, smiled at the little girl she had once been who did not have bulges in the wrong places, who was fresh-faced, a bit scared, scared of a picture in a book she'd been given as a prize which showed a black man lurking behind a tree. When she was tucked up in bed at night and got to the black man, she would shut her eyes and turn the page quickly. That little girl hadn't known what was lying in wait for her. For what was happening to her now had always been there, waiting for her in her future.

She cupped her breasts in both hands and lifted them. Now that's how they used to be. She let them drop and gave them a smile. 'Poor things,' she murmured. He would use the pen she had given him to write to his woman. Ariane, my only one. Of course she was his only one! Her mammaries were in first-class shape, weren't they? Your turn will come, dear. Her old body was obscene, it made her sick too. Get thee to a cemetery, to a hole in the ground, you stinking carcass! 'You gruesome old woman,' she told the mirror. 'Why are you old, you gruesome old woman. You don't fool anyone with that dyed hair!' She blew her nose and found an odd satisfaction in seeing herself in the mirror disgraced, sitting on a case, blowing her nose. Come on now, stand up, life must go on, phone.

Shaken and jolted in the taxi, she stared at her hands. It was the first time she'd gone out without having a bath. Disgraceful, she smiled. Hadn't had the strength, you were always alone when you washed, so alone when you towelled yourself dry. Anyway, what was the point? It had happened. Disaster had struck. Punished for the crime of being old. She moved closer to the window. Versoix. The people outside, in the midst of life, striding along, washed and clean, each with a purpose. His woman was young, and she too had a purpose: she would see him tonight. Come on, make ready for tonight, scrub yourself clean-clean-clean so you don't stink. I too did all that for him every day for three years. He would be sad when he read the letter, but it wouldn't stop him, you know, tonight. Their two tongues snaking, ugh! She opened and shut her mouth to taste its coating of bitterness, and suddenly felt like tea. After all, there were still things which gave zest to life. A cup of tea, a good book, music. All eyewash, of course. Oh the damnable need to be loved, which never left you, however old you were. What would happen about Pont-Céard, after? The furniture, her things, who would look after all that?

Creux-de-Genthod. Pigeons in the road. Two pigeons tenderly billing and cooing. What stupid poems her French governess had made her learn. She was called Mademoiselle Deschamps. Spring is coming, spring is coming, Birdies build your nests, Weave together straw and feather, Doing each your best. Two big cows were lying down, One was white and one was brown. There'd been something between her father and Mademoiselle Deschamps. She remembered her father's Jewish estate-manager, always went cap in hand, always bowing and scraping, he had a horrid face. Bela Kun was Jewish too. It was Bela

Kun who had got Uncle Istvan, General Kanyo, who was a count, shot. Her father would never have allowed Jews inside his house.

Genthod-Bellevue. Geneva soon, not long to go now before the station. At the start of their affair, when she'd gone to Paris to be with him, she'd found him waiting for her at the barrier, tall, hatless, his hair dishevelled, looking rather absurd standing next to the ticket-collector. She recalled his smile when he had caught sight of her, the way he'd taken her arm. She had been surprised to see him on the platform, it wasn't his style to wait for trains at stations. In the hotel, the Plaza, he had undressed her immediately. Her dress had split across the top, he had carried her to the bed, and she, the fool of her forty-two years, had been so happy and so proud. But she was old then, already old, so why had he bothered? Why couldn't he have let her alone? All the effort she had made for three years to make herself attractive. What had been the good of going to all those beauty parlours? Hair went on growing on the legs of corpses for several days. As far as she was concerned, it could grow. Here's the station, gateway to nowhere. Stir yourself, life must go on.

The driver had been so absurdly overtipped that, impelled by a sense of class solidarity, he gave the nod to a porter, who, taking the hint, rushed forward, grabbed her bag, and asked which train. Not knowing what to say, she licked her lips. 'Marseilles, lady?' 'Yes.' 'The seven twenty. You can just make it. Got your ticket?' 'No.' 'You'll have to get a move on, then. Can't afford to hang about. I'll wait for you by the train. First class, is it?' 'Yes.' 'Best foot forward, lady, you've only got four minutes, it's the last window along. Look sharp!' Alone in the world, mastering an urge to be sick, she set off at a run, hat askew, repeating Marseilles, Marseilles to herself as she went.

An hour after the train got in, she left the hotel, ran across the Canebière, almost got herself knocked over, turned down a narrow street, and pulled up short in front of a poodle tied to an iron railing next to a grocer's waiting for its mistress who had gone inside. It waited anxiously, fretting, restless, pulling on its lead, trying to see into the shop. When would she come? Why was she so long in there? Had she forgotten him? Oh he suffered torments! Whimpering with almost human distress, straining with all his might, trying to inch forward, he tugged relentlessly on his lead, chafing to be near his cruel mistress, to make her come more quickly, waiting, hoping, suffering. She bent down and stroked him. He was unhappy too. She crossed the road again, went into a chemist's, and asked for veronal. The man peered at her dishevelled hair through his spectacles and asked if she had a prescription. No? In that case, he could not let her have veronal. She said thank you and left. Why had she said thank you? Because I'm a loser, that's why. Then on to the Rue Poids-de-la-Farine. She was glad she'd said in the letter she'd written him that she was going back to Hungary, that way he wouldn't worry. The main chemist's. Same refusal. The woman in the white coat suggested Passiflorine, a herbal sedative. Yes please. She paid, left the shop, looked right then left, left the Passiflorine at the foot of a wall, and stared at it for a moment. Why couldn't he have let her alone? Should she go to a doctor's for a prescription? She didn't have the strength, she was so tired. Rent a little furnished flat with a gas cooker? But where would she find one? She didn't have enough life in her. Even to die you needed to have life. In England, rooms in provincial hotels always had gas rings. Ought she to go to England?

She stopped. In the window of a shop, a sweet little basset-hound lay on straw behind wire netting, looking bored and mournful, nibbling one paw. Couldn't be more than a year old. She stroked the glass of the window. Delighted, the puppy stood up, leaned its front paws against the window, licked the glass just where the lady who was making a fuss of him had put her hand. Inside the shop, parrots, monkeys, a flock of assorted little birds, an old woman with hair that had been hacked rather than cut, and a young effeminate-looking man in slippers sporting a fringe and a white silk scarf. She went in, bought the basset, a pretty collar and a lead, and then left, holding the little dog in her arms, already aquiver with love.

Another chemist's. She went in. Surely a woman with a little dog would not arouse suspicion. Yes, the basset inspired confidence, but try to look cheerful, stroke him, say I'm having a lot of trouble getting to sleep, I'd like some strong sleeping-pills, but easy now, act cautious, they're not dangerous are they, how many is it safe to take, is a whole one too much? I'd like twenty, I live out of town, you see. But first ask for face-powder, dither about the shade, the man wouldn't suspect anything if she dithered about the shade.

Leading the dog on the leash, she walked out of the shop and discreetly poked her tongue out at the chemist. She'd pulled the wool completely over their eyes! Oh no, they weren't the only ones who could look out for themselves. 'Properly speaking, I really ought to ask you for a doctor's prescription, but you seem a responsible sort of person. Do be careful, though, they're very strong, don't take more than one at a time, and not more than two over a period of twenty-four hours.' She'd managed to smile and say she had absolutely no wish to die. The amber eau-de-Cologne had helped. 'Pulled the wool right down over their eyes. And all thanks to you, my little darling. Let's take that nasty lead off and you can trot along all by yourself, my little Boulinou.' Happy to be off the leash, the dog shook his collar to ease his neck, raced some distance ahead, came back at a run, and fell in behind her, full of himself, feeling important because someone loved him and knowing in whom he believed. Oh the great heart of little dogs.

He was now trotting along in front of her once more, independent, freed from the durance vile of the pet-shop window, wagging his tail, happy as the mayor and corporation, but stopping from time to time to turn round and make sure his new friend was still there, for how could he live without her, then running back to stare at her and get a pat on the head, which he enjoyed immensely, then running off to have fun and games, sniffing out fascinating smells and, having found one that was absolutely first-rate, turning round again so that she would take note, then racing back to tell her about the smell, at ease with himself and the world, then shooting off again and knowing that she was following, which meant that everything was fine, oh and how about a winkle, yes why not, always a pleasure, especially since here's a tree that's positively asking for it, then scurrying back to tell the nice lady all about it, he couldn't imagine anyone nicer, and looking up at her with such earnest sincerity, then scampering off again, tail held at an optimistic angle, leading the way while she followed staring so hard at the ground that she bumped into a child. 'Can't you look where you're going!' shouted its mother. Panicking, she hurried away, followed by the basset, who was delighted by this new game. Oh, he was having a lovely time with his friend!

In the Allées de Meilhan she sat down on a bench. Above her head the leaves of a plane-tree scarcely stirred. All this would go on without her. Trees and flowers would go on being, and she would lie in the earth all alone. It would be ideal if you could die without the bother. The bother was the worst part. Let them try it, they'd find out how easy it is. Will my name be in the papers? Only in the Marseilles papers, which meant he'd never know. She wiped her nose and stared into her handkerchief. That snot there was life. She felt a need to urinate. So her works were still functioning. She felt her abdomen. Soon she would no longer be able to touch her poor body which was still doing its duty, its duty to go on living. Across the way were a couple of lovers. Kiss him, kiss him, you little fool, you'll see where it gets you. Wagging his tail in passionate devotion, Boulinou looked desperately up at her, hoping for an affectionate word. The word did not come, so he jumped up on to the bench, sat down beside her, and worked his nose into the crook of her arm. 'My love,' she said to him.

Her room at the Hôtel de Noailles. The waiter has just set down the tray of cold meats. Ham, chicken and roast beef. The basset in his chair is on his best behaviour, as grave and attentive as a parishioner in his pew, trying very hard to be good so that he will be rewarded with the luscious treats which he can smell and is ogling with churchgoing eyes. He looks from the bountiful lady to the viands and back again with respectful fervour, afraid that he is not quite a good doggy, but holding out his front paws and waving them mildly in a show of well-mannered but very real hunger. Look here, is she going to come across with the goods or is she not? If she doesn't want any, that's fine, that's her business, but if she's not going to give him some

459

it's a bit thick, what with him being absolutely ravenous. He makes a diffident, begging gesture with his right paw, containing with some difficulty the urge to help himself, for he must make a good impression. At last! she's got the message, and about time too! He snatches the slice of ham she holds out to him and gulps it down quick as a flash. Ditto with three more slices of ham. This is getting a bit monotonous. The old girl has absolutely no imagination. He puts out one paw and then another, eyes glazed with the effort of trying to make her understand that he is ready to have a stab at the chicken and the beef. She rings. The waiter comes and picks up the tray. Devastated, Boulinou looks at him beseechingly and does a little agitated jig. Hang on, what about the beef and especially the chicken, chicken is my favourite! You can't do this to me! What's got into the old girl? Never saw the like! But heigh-ho, so be it, she gives the orders around here. Now he looks at her and gives a discreet little whine. He has had something to eat, for which many thanks, but his soul still hungers. He would like to be stroked, life really isn't worth living if you don't get stroked. A dog cannot live on ham alone. He raises both front paws and leans them on the kind lady. She shies away. The only creature in the whole wide world who loves her is a dog. She shuts him in the bathroom.

She woke with a start, looked up at the ceiling-light which was still burning, and thought of the basset which she'd returned to the pet-shop the previous evening. Feeling woozy, she roused herself, sat on the edge of the bed, caught a glimpse of herself in the mirror, still dressed and with hat askew over one ear. Her watch on the bedside table said seven o'clock. She would stay in bed. Bed was pleasant, even when times were bad. Even so, she got up after a while and drew the curtains. Outside was life, out there were happy people. There was nothing attractive about the old hag in the mirror, with her slits of eyes, prominent cheek-bones, dry hair and overfilled teeth – there was even a bridge in the back of her mouth. That weekend at Ouchy. It was at the start of their affair. On the Sunday afternoon, after they'd walked together along the edge of the lake, she had even refused him a kiss and had run off laughing. And now, just a foolish old woman alone in Marseilles who had fallen asleep still wearing her hat. 'Rotten old God,' she said aloud.

She took her hat off, sat at the table, folded a sheet of hotel notepaper in two and then in four, opened it out, took up her pen, and unscrewed the cap. She would leave a letter for him and say that he had nothing to blame himself for, that he wasn't responsible, that he was entitled to be happy. No, best not a letter, best not run any risk of compromising him. She opened the bottle of pills, counted them, picked up her pen, drew a cross which she turned into a diamond to which she added scalloped edges, and suddenly felt the lust for life return. Of course! The answer was to go back to Switzerland, rent a chalet in the mountains and live there quietly. She'd retrieve the basset, which would make pleasant company for her, and take a train to Geneva, though she wouldn't stay there any longer than she could help, to minimize the risk of meeting him, stay just long enough to get some cash from the bank. Then she'd go to Lausanne, where an estate agent would find her a chalet to rent. In Lausanne she'd buy books, records and a radio. Everything will work out fine, you'll see if it doesn't. A comfortable chalet, a nice little dog, books, pottering in the garden. Nothing more to do with love, good riddance, no more having to do something about those blue veins in her legs. And now have a bath, take a fresh hold on life. She upended the pill-bottle and yanked the lavatory chain.

Stepping out of the bath, she dried herself taking good care not to look at herself in the mirror, and rubbed herself down with eau-de-Cologne. It was pleasant to smell nice and feel clean. That too was another sign that life was returning. She put on her bathrobe, opened the window, stepped out on to the narrow balcony, put her elbows on the parapet, and suddenly he was there, tall, hatless, hair tousled, laughing as he tried to catch her, tried to catch her and snatch a kiss, and she leaned over, leaned over a little more so that he wouldn't catch her, and the top of the rail hurt her stomach and, hands reaching out, she screamed into the void where a black man watched and waited, and then there was another scream, and then there was the unyielding pavement just by the bespattered newspaper stand.

CHAPTER 51

Not wishing to leave anything to chance, she would first make rough copies, two or three and sometimes more. The latest version passing muster, she would wash her hands to avoid any risk of dirtying the writing-paper, a tinted parchment, wash them thoroughly, thrilled by the thought that she was a vestal purifying herself before performing a ritual.

Sitting at her table, or even kneeling on the floor, an inconvenient position but one which gave her a heady feeling, she would unscrew the top of her best pen, which had an angled nib and made her handwriting look faintly masculine. After a couple of florid but perfectly legible practice runs to get herself warmed up, she would rest her right hand on a sheet of blotting-paper to keep the fine parchment clean, and then begin her letter, poking out the tip of her tongue and wiggling it daintily in time to her thoughts. So intense was her search for perfection that it was not unusual for her to tear up a page which was almost finished because of one badly written word or a tiny smudge which she had just noticed. Or again she might decide to write out the same page two or three times so that she could choose the one which best pleased her eye. When, after much consulting of the dictionary, she was finally done, she would read the letter aloud to get the full effect, read it with mesmeric inflections of her voice, enhancing each especially well-chosen word or expression with dulcet emphasis, pausing at intervals to admire the style, indulging herself with encores of sentences which she thought particularly well turned, imagining that she was him receiving her letter so that she would have a clear sense of the impression it would make on him.

Once she forced herself to write in a most uncomfortable position, stretched out on the sofa, so that she could enjoy beginning her letter 'I'm writing this lazily stretched out on our sofa', which had voluptuous connotations, shades of Madame Récamier. Another time she wrote him a note in his presence which he was on no account to read until he got home, and she'd deliberately refrained from licking the envelope with her tongue, which would have been vulgar, but instead went through a most fetching rigmarole using her decorously moistened forefinger to wet the gum. She had been altogether less decorous on the sofa only minutes before.

When her lover was away on official business, she kept a rough copy of every letter she sent so that she could read it through on the day and at the exact time when she estimated he should have received it. In this way she had a sense of being with him and was thus able to appreciate the admiration which he must certainly be feeling for her. One evening, sensing that she was in touch with him, she was rereading the end of a letter which she considered particularly well turned ('I hold you close and feel our two hearts in counterpoint throb to a single beat'). She inhaled deeply, like a craftsman content with his handiwork. Awfully good that line about two hearts throbbing contrapuntally. His countess couldn't have come up with anything like that, not in a thousand years. Taken herself off back to Hungary, thank God. The order of the words hearts in counterpoint throb also had a definite ring to it. Suddenly, she bit her lip. It was all wrong, because it assumed that he was facing her! His heart, which is on the left, would obviously be opposite my right side, where my liver is, not my heart. For the image to work, his heart would have to be on his right since mine is on my left. That's ridiculous, he isn't a freak for goodness sake. What should she do? Correct it by telegram? No, that would make her sound weird. Oh, I'm always putting my foot in it! As an aid to reflection, she pushed the end of her nose up with her thumb and had a reassuring thought. Yes, of course, it could be maintained that he isn't standing exactly opposite me, that's it, he's facing me but well to the west, which gives left side against left side and therefore heart to heart, it's not beyond the bounds of possibility. Anyway, there's a case to be made for it. So let's not worry our heads. Noticing her teddy on his knees on the prayer-stool, she called him a psalm-singing little bigot and moved him to an armchair. 'What! Sleep in the same bed as me? Oh no, darling, that's quite out of the question and has been ever since my gentleman started calling. I'd find it embarrassing, honestly I would. You're far better off in your armchair. Come along now, relax, good-night, sweet dreams.'

Three times a day, long before the post was due, she was out on the road waiting. When there was nothing from her traveller, she gave the postman a pleasant smile though there was death in her soul. When there was a letter, she opened it at once and scanned it quickly. A speedy once-over, just running her eyes over it. She stopped herself taking it in, for she had no wish to get the full gist. All she wanted was to be reassured that nothing terrible had happened, that he wasn't ill, that his return to Geneva had not been put back. A proper reading would come later, when she got indoors. Duly reassured, she would run back to the house and the proper reading, run with her breasts gently bouncing, biting her tongue as she ran to prevent herself from shouting her happiness out loud. 'Darling,' she would murmur to the letter. Or possibly to herself.

In her bedroom. The usual routine. Door locked, shutters closed, curtains drawn, earplugs to shut out noises off, all the not-love noises. Bedside lamp lit, she lay down and arranged her pillow. No, don't read it just yet, make it last to stretch out the pleasure. First, just a peep at the envelope. A nice, thick envelope, not one of those with a horrible lining inside. Fine. And he had stuck the stamp on very neatly, not upside down but straight, in exactly the right place, with love, also fine. Yes, proof positive that he loved her. She held the letter at arm's length and stared at it without reading it. That was how, when she was a little girl, she had used to look at Petit-beurre biscuits before eating them. No, don't read it yet, hang on a bit longer. It's ready and available, but wait until I'm positively bursting to read it. Let's just glance at the address. He thought about me when he wrote my name, and because he had to put Madame which sounds all very respectable and decent he might well have been thinking of me with no clothes on, looking beautiful, he's seen me like that from every possible angle. And now for a peek at the notepaper, the back, not the side with the writing on. Very nice, exquisite, could be Japanese vellum. No, the paper isn't perfumed. It smells wholesome, perfectly clean. Manly paper, that's what it is.

Suddenly she could contain herself no longer. There followed a very close, tortoise-paced reading, more a textual analysis really, with pauses for thought and for mental pictures, eyes closed and a smile part foolish part divine on her lips. To give the more tender and impassioned words their full impact, she would at moments cover the paper with both hands so that only the wondrous sentence was visible. She would hypnotize herself with the sentence. Then, to get the true feel of it, she would declaim it or maybe pick up a mirror and say it softly at herself. And if he wrote that he was miserable without her she was happy and laughed. 'He's miserable, he's miserable, and a good job too!' she would exclaim, and she would read his letter again, read and reread till she could no longer understand what it said and the words lost their meaning.

Most often she resisted the temptation, for she knew that reading a letter too often spoiled it and meant that you ceased to feel the effect. So she would fold it away and swear honour bright that she'd let it alone and wouldn't look at it again until tonight. Between now and then the sap would rise again in the letter and that would be her reward for waiting, and she'd read it cosily tucked up in bed. She would smile, day-dream, lift her skirt a few inches and look lovingly at her legs. 'Want to see any more, darling? It's all absolutely yours.' She lifted her skirt a little higher and looked.

One evening she decided that fingers weren't much good for hiding. She hopped out of bed, took a clean sheet of paper, cut a small rectangle in it with a pair of scissors, and resumed her reading. Yes, that worked heaps better. Only three or four words were visible through the little window at any given moment and the effect was even more fantastic, the words seemed so much more alive. When she got to 'the most beautiful woman', she leaped out of bed and made a dash for the full-length mirror so that she could see this beautiful woman. Yes, it was quite true. But her beauty was wasted since he wasn't there. She made ugly faces in the mirror to make up for the absence of the man she loved. Stop it, that was quite enough of pulling faces, it could harm the skin or even weaken the muscles underneath. To repair any possible damage, she smiled an angelic smile.

CHAPTER 52

O Youth, O ye of tousled mane and perfect teeth, disport yourselves on that shore where love is for ever, where love is never not for ever, where lovers laugh and are immortal, O ye the elect, who ride a quadriga whipped on by love, gather now rosebuds while ye may and be as joyful as once were Ariane and Solal, but have pity for the old, for old you soon will be, with a nose that drips and hands that shake, hands mapped with swollen, knotted veins, hands with russet mottled, the rueful russet of dead leaves.

How beautiful this August night, a night still young, unlike me, says one I know who once was young. Where are they now, those nights he knew, this man who once was young, those nights that he and she once shared, and into what heaven, what hereafter, did they vanish, and on what wing of time?

On such nights, says he who once was young, we went into the garden, vainglorious with love, and she looked at me, and we went our way, brilliant with youth, slowly stepping to the illustrious music of our love. Why, O God, why is the sweet-scented garden no more, why do nightingales not sing now, why is there no arm in mine, no eyes turning to me and then raised to heaven?

Love oh love, the flowers and fruit which she sent him every day, love oh love, the foolish youthful fancy to eat of the same grape together, grape after grape together, love oh love, adieu beloved until tomorrow, love oh love, kisses and leave-taking and she walked him home and he walked her home and she rewalked him home and their destination lay in the great love-scented bed, love oh love, nights and nightingales, dawns and sempiternal larks, kisses tattooed on lips, God between their conjoined lips, tears of happiness, I love you and I love you, tell me you love me, oh the telephone tones of his beloved, her golden inflections, so tender, so plaintive, love oh love, flowers, letters, waiting, love oh love, so many taxis bearing him to where she was, love oh love, telegrams, off to the sea off their heads, love oh love, her inspired fancies, tenderness beyond belief, your heart, my heart, our hearts, such momentous silliness. O love, O sometime queen of my heart, is it for you or for my youth that I weep asks he who once was young. Where is the witch who will restore my black anthems so that I dare look again upon the sometime queen of my heart and not love her? But there is no such witch and youth nevermore returns. You could die laughing. It's a scream.

Others stay themselves with honours, with books or talk of politics. Others again, fools that they are, take comfort in the pleasures of fame or of being in control or of dandling their grandchildren on their worthy knees. But, says he who once was young, I cannot resign myself, I want my youth back again, I want a miracle, I want the fruit and the flowers of the queen of my heart, I want never to be tired, I demand the black anthems which once crowned my head. The old man's got a nerve! Right then. Make him a shiny new coffin and shove him in it!

Your jasmined breath, O lost youth of mine, is headier now than in the time of my youth, says he who once was young. You are gone for ever, youth of my youth, my youth which was but yesterday, and my back aches, and my aching back may signal the beginning of my end. My back aches and my brow is fevered and my knees fail me and I should see a doctor. But I prefer to see my task through, says he who once was young. Press on, says he, make haste, crazy, gentle journeyman who grimly garners hapless harvests, make haste, for the birds of understanding will soon still their song, press on, cast off your lassitude for night creeps on apace, come garner what crop you may.

Take heart, says a voice, faint like the voice of his mother. And to you, O men, farewell, he says. Farewell, bright-hued nature, soon I shall go to earth for all eternity, farewell. All things considered, it wasn't much fun.

I stand alone upon my ice floe, says he who once was young, broken-bodied and already dying on the ice floe which carries me oh I know whither through the night, I hold up my feeble hand and bless the young who on this night grow drunk on words of love beneath the infinite, hushed music of the spheres. Alone I stand upon my ice floe, and yet the rustle of spring is still in my ears. I am alone and old upon an ice floe, and night has fallen. So says one who once was young.

Farewell, O shore of youth upon which an ageing man now gazes, O forbidden shore where dragonflies are little beams from the eye of God. O queen of my heart, says he, you who were beautiful and noble and no less wayward than Ariane, my queen whose name I shall not speak, we dwelt upon that shore and there were we brother and sister, my best loved queen, the sweetest and the unquietest, the noblest and the slenderest, my bubbling, spinning, sunlit queen, haughty, arrogant, inspired, enslaved, and I would that I could have commanded all the voices of the wind to tell all the trees of the forest that I was in love, that I loved the one I loved. So says one who once was young.

There is a silence in the cemetery where sleep the sometime lovers. Oh they are quiet now, poor dead dears. No more waiting now, no more nights of ecstasy, no more damp bucking of young bodies. That is now consigned to the place where all must sleep. All pronely laid, these regiments of silent, unfleshed, grinning dead who once were quick and lively lovers. Sad and solitary, the lovers and their mistresses lie in God's good acre. The spellbound moans of the mistress stupefied with pleasure, her sudden undulations, her eyes turned holily heaven-ward, eyes closed to savour the pleasure, the noble breasts she gave you, all consigned to earth. Lovers, get ye to your earthy burrows!

In the midnight cemetery, gaunt and silent gentlemen with no noses, with mouths that leer and jawbones as impassive as their deep, hollow eye-sockets, rise from their burrows and bonily dance, staidly dance. Noselessly, they cut a jig in slow but indefatigable motion, tarsus and metatarsus rattling and clattering like false teeth, keeping time to the tune played on a shepherd's pipe which a diminutive cadaver, wearing a yellow fez with a feather in it and perched on diamond-studded dancing-pumps, holds to the gaping cavern that once was a mouth.

To the sound of *The Skaters' Waltz*, the gentlemen and their ladies dance and sometimes skip, jawbone to jawbone, cavern to cavern, teeth to teeth, lovingly entwined, and the desiccated dancers, the claws of the gentlemen's hands upon the shoulder-blades of their partners, all grin silently on hearing the unexpected strain of *Auld Lang Syne*, and one who wears the peaked cap of an officer clamps his humerus more firmly round the twenty-four ribs of his paramour and presses her to his sternum while an owl laughs stagily and a ladybones who was Diana, the bubbling, spinning, sunlit queen, the sweetest and the unquietest, haughty yet a slave in moments of moaning surrender, Diana, this lady now a bag of bones, with a wreath, poor wraith, of roses on her head, essays a tentative, clicking, clacking pirouette behind a bush.

PART FOUR

CHAPTER 53

'Work? I've got through stacks of work since I got back day before yesterday just like I promised that bitch Antoinette old Face-Ache I would, I told her I'd be back the minute my sister's swollen legs went down but of course it took longer than I thought seeing as how I'd said the start of July going on what the doctors had said and it's not my fault if they got it wrong, they always get it wrong though they never make mistakes when it comes to sending you bills and that's a fact, you can take it from me, it's not my fault 'cos I'm always as good as my word unless something special crops up, anyhow on the sixth of August, the minute the swelling went down, one-two one-two I'm on that train and the minute I land back spit-spot on with the job and I've done stacks since the day before yesterday and the place needed it around here I can tell you, sit yourself down, take the weight off your feet, I like talking even when I'm by meself, it keeps you company when you're working, specially like now when I'm polishing up the silver sitting down comfy sipping a nice cup of coffee, Madame Ariane says when I'm doing the silver I pull that many faces I look like I'm hopping mad at somebody, p'raps it's true and all, 'cos obviously I'm not looking in no mirrors when I'm doing my silver, the opposite's true, I love these silver things because it all belongs to Madame Ariane she got it from Mademoiselle Valérie who left it to her, so as I was saying, work, I've done stacks and stacks, there's not many of your young chits of girls would have got through half as much as old Mariette not that I've always been old mind, I may be little and roly-poly these days and that many wrinkles anybody'd say

I was an old apple left in a cellar, well past sixty, but there wasn't many like me around when I was twenty and good-looking and the rest of it, but now, poor Mariette Garcin, the dustbin is all you're fit for, never mind all the work I've got through, you should have seen the state the kitchen was in when I got back day before yesterday, sink like the back of the grate and two tins of elbow-grease before it was got clean again, dirt in all the corners, dishcloths all sticky and slimy like they'd never been rinsed through and the smell you never smelled anything like it and everything moved out of its proper place, shifted about all tipsy-tivy, of course it was all the fault of the girl they had to stand in, Putallaz they call her, I'll tell you about her in just a minute, the kitchen was a right mess, and so when I got back here home again from Paris day before yesterday, my sister's legs being a lot better, I was so upset seeing the kitchen in such a state, 'cos I always liked to see it looking nice and tidy and sparkling like the inside of a jeweller's shop, it took me all me strength and grit, cleaning all the windows and glass all over the house with a shammy, the whole lot, getting it all clean again, not stopping for a minute to catch my breath there being so much mess everywhere, not that it was any surprise seeing that when young Martha left it was that piece Putallaz who got her place instead, now there's one don't give a toss, just comes in mornings, I got her number, always with a fag in her mouth, painted up to the eyeballs and puts no vim into it when she sweeps the floor, just a quick once-over with the mop which don't get anything up at all, talk about half-hearted, sweeping it all into the corners if only you could have seen the corners, goes shopping in her slippers, stays ages jawing in the grocer's, always gossiping she is, she must have been vaccinated with a grammyphone needle, all she ever thinks about is feeding her face and drinking, she's a chicken-cemetery on legs, and unpleasant with it, getting up on her high hobby-horse soon as look at you, oh I got her number all right, and every evening it's off to the pictures or dancing and at her age too she's well past forty, and before ladymuck Putallaz there was that poor Martha who come after me when I left, nice enough but a real good-for-nothing, eyes in her behind she had, I done my best to train her up before I went off on account of my sister's phlebitics, family comes first of course, poor thing they put her in a what they call a cradle-splint, her legs being all swelled up and her various veins bursting and couldn't move a muscle all bandaged up she was, caretaker she is in the Aga Khan's villa, twenty rooms it's got, now that's a job, they weigh him in Africa and give him his weight in gold and diamonds, comes to a tidy sum though it's not fair with him being swelled up extra heavy, a right hippopotomouse, they say he's like the Pope to the blackies over there, but he makes sure he takes things easy, believe me, forever going off travelling and having a fine old time in the best hotels, wears a white topper to the races, gets pushed about in a wheelchair, I seen his picture in the paper, always got chorus-girls and suchlike hanging round him and he don't turn his nose up at any of them according to what my sister told me, it's a fact, always young they are, one in partickler, she's on the films, got a mouth the size of an oven, it's just as well she's got ears to stop it otherwise it would go on for ever, anyhow it's the high life all right and luxury when there's poor devils who got nothing, not even a room to lay their head or a clean shirt and bellies that's all puckered they're that hungry, well-meaning was Martha, that's my replace-ment, quite nice, but not much between the ears, not a clue about being organized, always scared stiff of Antoinette who goes about like she was God in heaven giving out orders with a smile, the upshot being that in between the time Martha left and ladymuck Putallaz came the house got all run-down, the silver got all discoloured, Madame Ariane isn't up to much when it comes to keeping an eye on things, it's a gift, you've either got it or you haven't, yes I will have some more, the milkpan'll have kept it nice and hot, come on Mariette, my treat, this one's on me, I like slurping my coffee you can taste it better that way, Madame Ariane reckons with my glasses on I get this sly look in my eyes when I'm drinking my coffee, and she says I got nice hands, like a little kiddy's, oh Madame Ariane if you'd have seen me when I was twenty, anyroad this coffee's reely good, you can't beat a good cup of coffee for giving you a bit more go for the job in hand, that Paris doctor told me I ought to give it up, seems I got blood-pressure in my arm according to that thing they put on you, but I just don't care, and anyway them doctors always look very knowing but they don't know that much, oh dear me no, except they know how to send a bill, they're pretty good at that, I'd have come back to work sooner only just when my sister was getting over her legs she gets pewmonia and they shoves this tube down her gullet so she could breathe, and then there was this fibrous tumour I had, so hospital for me, very nice them hospital doctors, specially the little dark one with curly hair, everyone was very complimentary about my fibrous tumour, thought it was wonderful, seems they never ever saw a bigger one, four kilos it weighed and you see when it's as big as that they say it can get all twisted up sometimes, anyroad thought the world of me did the doctors, looked after me like royalty specially after Madame Ariane when she found out and traipsed all the way to Paris on purpose, stayed a whole day, wanted them to put me in a room by myself, a private room they call it, but I told her not to bother but she insisted, she paid for everything, so you can tell she's fond of me, the family is very good with illness, take my niece, the one who got married, she gets monthlies that last fifteen mebbe twenty days then it stops for months on end and you start thinking that's it, she's going to have a kiddie, but not a bit of it, it's just a clot blocking her insides up and then it starts all over again talk about a running tap, they say clots is caused by little growths, the doctors said she ought to have her womb and tubes all taken away, and on top of that she's got this constricted yewteris, all the husband's fault according to my sister, they say God made us all in His image, well He can't be much of a sight to look at, all women's insides ought to be opened up, anything wonky should get took away and they should fit us with zips for when there's other bits of bubble and squeak that got to come out, still I suppose in a way my fibrous growth was a bit of luck 'cos without it I'd have been back sooner and then I'd have had to traipse all the way back to Paris again 'cos my sister got her swelling back when they thought it was all over and done with and it was hospital for her again, anyroad she's been put to rights now, I only hope it lasts, she is my only sister after all, Madame Ariane said she thought my frizz was very fetching, I say kiss-curl, it's nicer, all I use to get it like that is a wet finger, it sets off my forehead, it's a bit saucy-like, but it suits me, now getting back to the Aga Khan I grant your communists and all that lot could be right when it comes down to it but I'd never go along with them taking my savings off of me, never, not after working my fingers to the bone for fifty years keep off the grass I just wouldn't have it I just wouldn't, I know what they oughter do, but the government's too busy feathering their own nests, what's wanted to my way of thinking is that there should be ordinary folk, fair enough, but they should have enough to see them right when they're old and past it, then some folk in the middle, fair enough again, you got to have shops and business, but not people at the top so rich they got more money than they know what to do with, your Aga Khan and American millionaires and princesses of this and that like what you see in magazines, got too much of everything, necklaces and priceless pearls that they don't care if they get stolen, they just laugh like they was saying oh it don't matter tuppence to me, there's plenty more where they came from so I'll go out and buy some more, always dancing, riding horses with that look that says the world owes me a living, now that's more criminal in the eyes of the Lord up above than a thief, often it's not the man's fault, brought up poor, father always in a temper coming home fighting drunk, and what did your princesses ever do in life that was any use except that the king gave the queen a good poking one night, and the upshot is that every blessed thing is owed to her ladyship the princess, always going off to posh balls but would she ever polish a floor or do a wash for you? don't even rub her own stockings through when she gets home, it don't take a minute, but oh no, it's always high jinks in country houses, never steps out of a train unless it's on to a red carpet rolled out just for her, mustn't forget to worship the soles of her shoes, everybody gotter pay their respects as if she didn't have a crack if you follow me just where the rest of us girls have got one, that's what I think so there, then the papers say the queen of this or that is expecting in September, they crawl and kowtow and never so much as a nudge or a wink, it would never come into their heads to say it all come about 'cos the king gave the queen a good poking back in January, but don't go thinking I came back to work here, leaving my poor sister lower than ever she is, five different sorts of medicine she got on the table by her bed, no I didn't come back on account of that cow Deume with her buck teeth that look like a kiddies' slide, Madame Poison is what I call her to myself, says she'll pray for you, always going on about religion but talk about underhand she stabs you with them smiles of hers, thinks she's posh and a nob, now Mademoiselle Valérie, I was in service with her for twenty years, now she was real upper-crust, she'd met the Queen of England and curtsied when she was presented once a year what an honour! but Madame Poison is a jumped up nothing, no breeding, can't tell a Bordeaux glass from the glasses you should use for fine wines, oh no I'd never have put meself out and come back for her nor for that darling son of hers that snooty Didi that walks right past me as if I wasn't there, puts on airs all holier-than-thou, wears fancy white spats over his shoes not that they make him any nicer, and that wispy beard! but if I did put myself out it was partly for Monsieur Hippolyte's sake, he's a lamb, you can't help feeling sorry for him, but mostly I came back on account of Madame Ariane being my best friend, mind you being French I don't take naturally to Switzerland, in France we're used to variety, there's always something different, but Switzerland is all peace and quiet it gets monotonous, so it was for Madame Ariane, we're ever so fond of each other, you could say I'm a bit like a second mother to her since she's an orphing poor thing, there's no one she loves more than me, it's a fact, I've known her since she was a baby in nappies, in the summer I'd give her a bath in a wooden tub in the garden with warm water, the sunshine was good for her, when I got back the other day you should have seen her, she threw her arms around me before I'd even got out of the taxi, she was all smiles when she saw me, but what really pleased me was how changed she looked, last year before I went to Paris when my sister swelled up there was times when she looked sad, she didn't say much, was always doing her scribbling, I put it down to her marriage, p'rhaps Didi wasn't making her happy, he's not much of a ladies' man, dear me no, now if you'd met my late hubby, ever so good-looking a hundred kilos of real man and arms as white as a woman's, what a change has come over her! happy and singing she is, take this morning now, she was up early, popped in and gave us a kiss in the kitchen, wanted to know if the weather'll be as nice tonight as it is this morning, transformed that's what she is, dead chirpy, singing *La Vie en rose* in the bath, you know the one about when he takes me in his arms, I reely like that song it's about true love and being young and the man you love, what's up with you Mariette talking to yourself for company silly old fool, but one thing's for sure I won't stay here to sleep, no fear, I like my freedom too much, and the face Madame Poison had on her when I told her I'd be looking for a place of my own in the village, Cologny village that is, and when I was in Paris on account of my sister's swelled-up legs I paid my rent regular, on the nail, so as I'd have my own place waiting for me when I got back, so that of an evening when I finish doing for Madame Ariane and the washing-up's done I get away early seeing as how Madame Ariane also likes a bit of peace to read those books of hers and play the piano, anyhow by half past seven I'm behind my own front door, one room and a kitchen, very nice, getting on with my knitting and reading the paper, couldn't want for more, come round and see me some Sunday afternoon for coffee you'll see how nice I got it, my hubby did fretwork, very artistic, Madame Ariane's father was a toff too, the Rev d'Auble they called him, out of the top drawer he was and not short of a bob or two, always very proper, a fine-looking man, and with him being so clever with books and studying, the government in Geneva asked him to be a professor and learn his ideas to the young ones training to be ministers, what an honour, Madame Ariane's mother was upper-crust too, you should have seen who came to her funeral, and his funeral too a bit later, they said it was heart but he died of grief he did if you ask me it was losing Madame that did for him, with her it was Mademoiselle Éliane's purple fever after she had the baby, she's the young one passed away when she was eighteen, a real beauty, but I always preferred Mademoiselle Ariane, you can't help your feelings, unless Monsieur's death had something to do with him losing all his money after that bankruptcy business in America though mebbe not, ministers of religion aren't supposed to care about money, but anyroad they let on that all he had left was the wages he got for being a minister, but Mademoiselle Valérie stayed very comfortable though she handed a lot over to them church ladies who used to come round and suck up to her, strict but fair was Mademoiselle Valérie, she used to have big dinner parties sometimes, with me looking after the cloaks and feeling pleased as punch in my cap and an apron with embroidery on, and only nobs with titles got invited, they didn't talk loud but even if they did it was still all very grand, Mademoiselle Valérie like a queen in the middle of them, a smile turn her head another smile, but never

gushing oh no, always dignified, you should have seen her, and that's
how I got a start with her after Monsieur's death when she took the
children in, Monsieur Jacques who was the oldest he was eight,
Mademoiselle Ariane was six, Mademoiselle Éliane five, no I tell a lie,
Monsieur Jacques was seven, he wasn't born till two years after they
got married, they weren't in no hurry, p'raps they didn't know what
to do, ministers of religion may be clever you know but when it
comes to all that love stuff they're more backward than forward,
p'raps on their wedding night they got down on their knees by the
bed to ask the Good Lord up above to give them a few tips on how
to go about it and p'raps he didn't tell them right, that's enough it's
not funny, but coming back to Madame Ariane it's almost like she
was my own daughter with me looking after her ever since she was
little, bathing her, putting talcum on and that, I even used to kiss her
little behind when she was a baby, so you can appreciate I wouldn't
know where to start telling you how good she's been to me, only
yesterday she gave me a brand new cocodrile handbag as a present,
must have cost the earth, and I'd hardly got out of the taxi day before
yesterday after coming back on the train when she was wanting to
carry that heavy case of mine just imagine, and her with hands like a
princess, reely loves me, telling me I wasn't to wear myself out,
saying she'd have her tea dinner they call it for half past six so I could
get off at half past seven, ever so kind and thoughtful, there's just one
thing I got against her, which is that she married that Didi, how that
happened I'll never know, Mademoiselle Valérie's niece, can you
imagine, but that apart it's all smiles and consideration, now there's
just the two of us I give her whatever I fancy to eat, if it's sole and I
fancy sole sole it is, and if I got an upset tummy it's a bit of veal in
white sauce, I got a free hand, and never a sharp word with me,
things are very easy between us, though she's very ejucated, got no
end of diplomas, and you should see the way she eats, she don't make
a noise like you and me, don't slurp, it's breeding does that for you
and being in high society, when her aunt was alive you should have
seen her, talk about graceful, riding the horse that Mademoiselle said
she could have, won a prize for horse-riding when she was seventeen,
the best lady horse-rider in Switzerland she was, but since she got
married that's all finished, no more horses, no more hobnobbing with

high society, it grieves me, they've choked the life out of my little girl, the wasters, there's no side with her, sometimes she kisses my hand and her being who she is and copping all that money from her auntie being her only niece, and clean! you'd never believe how many times she has a bath, sometimes two or three a day without a word of a lie, so she's not likely to be the sort to go clarting up her mouth with lipstick, never even uses powder, once I told her to put a bit on and she smiled but didn't answer, she's got a lovely figure front and back, no problems in that department, you should see for yourself, she's got a behind like a statue, Cupid's cushion I call it, I bet that husband of hers don't get scratched in bed, full is what her figure is but not too full, just full in all the right places like a beautiful woman ought to be, and it makes me ill to think it should be that wet fish with his straggly beard that has it all to hisself, I'm sorry if I'm speaking out of turn but I'm French and the sort who always speaks her mind, I don't think it's fair she should waste her youth on Didi, he don't deserve it, and to be perfectly frank I'd much sooner she took up with some man or other, and I'm not afraid to say it though the Good Lord might hear, she deserves some good-looking chap, the sort of chap who'd be worthy of her, such as one of them toffs with a title that used to come when Mademoiselle Valérie was alive, but young of course, with plenty of go in him, but she's not the carrying-on type I'm sorry to say, she'd never do anything to catch the eye of anybody like that, they like painted faces giggly girls and wiggling behinds, but it's not her style, or p'raps it just don't appeal to her, p'raps she's not interested in men, clever people get funny ideas you know, and then again she's always got her head in a book, reads in the bath, reading in the bath's ever so bad for you, reads when she's washing, I seen her once with a book propped up against the taps leaning over to read it standing up in the bath while she soaped her pretty parts all over, you can take it from me or not as you like, she even reads when she's cleaning her teeth, she turns the pages of her book toothbrush going like billy-oh making pink splashes all over the shop, and it's poor old Mariette what's got to clean it all up, everybody's skivvy is what I am, sometimes when I'm making her bed I come across books in it, p'raps she reads when that Didi's doing his stuff in bed, now that's enough of that, don't make me larf, to my way of thinking she don't fancy her husband doing his stuff all that much, so as to this business of having some chap instead of Didi it's no go, books books books, never lets up, it's just the same with her piano, she don't go in for anything catchy, it's always the sort of thing organs play at funerals, nothing with a nice tune, so it's Didi piano and books, it's no life for a healthy woman, not that I got anything against reading of course, it passes the time, I read a book meself when I was in the women's hospital in Paris, but enough's enough, and there again I blame religion, though I'm Catholic of course, but she was brought up a Protestant and you know what that means, behaving respectable and no smut, on this question of religion I think they should have just one, when it comes down to it all religions want the same thing, and when you think of it the sensiblest thing would be to have the religion of the Jews because it's got only the one God, no more to be said, no old fuss and arguing about this and that, the only thing is they are Jews after all, you mustn't go thinking from what I been saying that I played fast and loose with my hubby 'cos no one could ever say that, I never even thought of looking round for anybody else, model wife is what I was, but he was worth it that's why, well that's the polishing done with, *paaarlez-moi d'amooour*, whisper those old sweet nothings again.'

CHAPTER 54

Perched on a ladder with a lantern in one hand, the tiny creature examined herself in the mirror on the wall, made faces at her reflection, then rouged her lips, powdered her square face, smoothed her large soot-black eyebrows, licked her finger and with it wet her beauty spot, smiled at herself, finally climbed down, and ran towards the far end of the cellar, along walls oozing with damp and bristling with long nails. When she reached the prone man, she struck an elegant pose with one hand on hip and, smiling clever smiles, hummed a tune. He shuddered, sat up, leaned against the wall, and passed one hand over his blood-soaked forehead.

'May God guard you in the coming week,' she sang softly in a contralto voice. 'And tell me, kind sir, what is your name and how good the family from which you came?'

As he stared at her without answering, fascinated by her head, which was supported by no visible neck, she shrugged her shoulders and turned away. Sweeping her short train behind her with a flourish, she began walking to and fro impulsively, perched on her high-heeled dancing-shoes, making the flounces of her yellow satin dress flare, and cooling herself furiously with a fan made of feathers.

'Not that I care, you know, I have absolutely no wish to get married,' she said. She had come close to him again and was still fanning herself in a jangle of charms and armlets. 'But, really, the ingratitude! Apart from the fact that I got dressed up like this for your benefit, it was I who saw you through the ventilator looking dead, you could have been shamming or perhaps you weren't, and it was I who ran and told my uncles, and they went out when the blond beasts had gone, rushed out at once to bring you in here, and bring you they did! And so here you are, quite safe! This is my father's house. He was a wealthy antiques dealer and I am his only heir, but I shall marry a famous doctor so that I can wave my fan in the best drawing-rooms! I shall bewitch him by singing songs which tell how he will find sweet bliss in my cradling arms! Of course my sister is beautiful too, but I'm not afraid of competition because she's blind and anyway her brain isn't quite what it should be! And in any case the doctor will get a double dowry, because my back's not straight! You shall see my sister presently! She is still asleep in a cellar which she has all to herself! She is very beautiful, and I'm proud of her even though I'm quite tiny! But no one must look upon her! She is sacred! Ambivalent! My feelings are ambivalent! I know a lot of words! Ask me any difficult word and I'll tell you what it means! I know explanations for everything! With just one glance I can tell you what a person is like! It's fear, do you see? And my sister is even more beautiful than you are! And if you don't like it then lump it, kind sir! Now that's cleared up, I, thanks to my double-dowered doctor, shall be received in the very best drawing-rooms, I shall be respected and important, and I shall fan myself quite furiously! Oh yes, I know that all men are born free and equal before the law, but that doesn't last long! So there! Give it a year or two and you'll see! They won't be satisfied with beating us or making us lick their dirty floors clean with our tongues or stringing us up with our hands behind our backs – hang on, I'm going to shout the next bit – with pulling our fingernails out or putting hot irons on our flesh or holding our heads under water! Give it one year, three years, and they'll be doing much worse! Their iniquity will reach up into heaven itself, said my uncle-in-religion, also known as my uncle-in-majesty. They will commit acts of great horror!' she yelped, and she fanned herself, then whirled round and yelped once more: 'They have the backing of the entire population! My uncle told me! Read the papers, find out for yourself! And when the sabbath day comes round do you know what my uncle-in-religion and my uncle-in-business do, even though our suffering is great? Well listen! They look at each other and try to laugh a little, for the sabbath is the Lord's day, the day of peace, and we must be happy!

That's what my uncles are like! So respect them! They even taught me a prayer! I shall recite it to you very quickly, so listen carefully! I shall begin now. "But we are Thy people, we are the children of Thy beloved Abraham with whom Thou didst make a covenant upon Mount Moriah; the descendants of Isaac who was offered up as a sacrifice; the posterity of Jacob, Thy first-born son whom, in Thy love and for the joy he gave Thee, Thou hast called Israel! Praise to Thee, O Lord who hath chosen us above all peoples to be the receptacle of Thy holy Law! And so, in the mischief of morning and the despair of eventide, we proclaim how joyful we are, how fortunate our lot and how pleasant our fate!" (Breathless with having recited so quickly, she paused to rest, put one hand on her heart, and smiled a kindly smile at him.) Isn't it a beautiful prayer! Sometimes when I say it my nose turns quite red because I'm so proud I want to cry! I'm going to try laughing too on the sabbath! I shall tickle myself under my arms to make myself laugh in our cellar, our beautiful cellar! It's dark and full of nails! There are nails everywhere! Big nails for big tribulations and small nails for small tribulations! They were put there by my uncle-in-business! Fingernails torn out, one nail! An ear sliced off, another nail! It's a way of passing the time, a consolation! There are lots of nails, maybe a hundred! We shall count them together! You've got to take your fun wherever you can, you've got to forget! I'd love a cracknel biscuit! I'd crunch it and run at you lunging and sliding and laughing to make you afraid! Give it one year, three years! The Germans are a terri, terri, terrifying people!' she screamed suddenly at the top of her voice. 'But only we know how terrifying! Beasts, beasts, beasts is what they are! They like killing! Oh yes, they may dress like men but they are beasts all the same! You shall see what they'll do to us, you shall, you shall!' she shouted, pointing a finger at him threateningly. 'So start quaking now! They do it because they hate our Law! They are beasts. They love forests and ambushes in forests, like real beasts which hide behind trees and jump out and go for your throat! Aaaargh! They aren't afraid in the forest, oh no, they sing in the forest! Two thousand years ago we had our prophets! Two thousand years ago they were wearing helmets decorated with the horns of beasts! My uncle-in-majesty told me so! I have a crooked back but I am a daughter of man! There, I think I've explained it all to you now! Oh say fine things to me, speak comfortable words! You can't think of any? Never mind, let's have a laugh instead, let's enjoy life! Sing "May God guard you in the coming week." Show that you were brought up properly. Repeat the words back to me, for today is the holy day! "May God guard you in the coming week." Say it now!' she cried, and she twirled her imitation-pearl reticule.

'May God guard you in the coming week,' he muttered.

'Very good, and because you said it nicely you find favour in my eyes, which are large and delightful, as you cannot deny! And when a person has a pair of delightful eyes and knows how to make up her face, that person always finds that the shoe fits and what does it matter if he or she is slightly humpbacked and has no neck? Having a humpback makes you see things more clearly! The shoe fits, what a splendid turn of phrase! I was brought up like a lady, you know! I had a French governess when I was a very little girl thanks to all my father's money! Elegantly raised in a rich world of silk and brocade! No expense spared to turn me into an accomplished young lady who would grow up to be a model wife completely at home in the language of Racine! And omniscient too! For example, did you know that cats use their sharp spiky whiskers to scratch with? You didn't! It's no good lying! You said a few things in French when you were unconscious from having been knocked on the head and so I'm talking in your language! That way I can show how clever I am! Piano, violin, of course, and I also play the guitar while fluttering my eyelashes and took elocution lessons and can dangle baited glances! I know ever so many words!' she sang as she whirled around, making her dress balloon out and revealing her crooked but muscular little legs. 'I have only one little fault, which is rather attractive actually, and that is I sometimes rush around screaming with fear and if there's a nice person handy I swarm all over and kiss whoever it is, but in a half-perverse half-winning sort of way! Oh, I'm also fond of gristle, so soft and yet so chewy! Gristle is perverse too! Otherwise, elegance is the word for me! Oh if you could see me of a morning dressed in a pink wrap edged with monkey fur and slippers the same colour trimmed with swansdown! If only you saw me in a feather boa, or in my summer outfit with boater pulled right down over my eyes, stiff detachable collar, and assorted little charms and trinkets! The earring is still in the ear that was cut off! And the best would be if you could hear me sing of passionate love and sweet promises!'

She adjusted the sky-blue bow in her hair, ran a wet finger over her eyebrows, stood on a stool, put one hand on her hip, and, craning her large head forward, sang with the passion and smiling lips of a soprano: 'Why do you doubt your happiness – For I love you? – Why do you speak with bitterness – For I love you?'

'There, that was just to give you an idea,' she smiled, stepping down off the stool. 'What do you think? (In the silence, she noisily crunched a sugared almond which she had produced from her reticule.) You won't say? Much good may it do you! I pick my large, fine teeth with a sharpened matchstick, and the perfume I use is called Rêve de Paris! I don't care what you say, perfume is the charm of woman! My heart won thine on that mad day,' she sang, lowering her eyes majestically. 'By the way, when my uncle-in-majesty, ignoring the dangers, went out the other day on religious business, for you have no idea how great our God is, it's quite simple really, His like does not exist, well I peeped out through the gap and I saw the beasts pulling his beard out! They were laughing, and in their laughter were stupidity and power, but my uncle-in-religion stood his ground like a king and stared right back at them, and in his eyes were grandeur and silence! Oh I was proud of him! They also like pulling out our fingernails. They are Germans! Listen, from now on you're going to be my plaything! I adore talking in languages I know, and I get bored being locked up in the dark when my uncles go off through the underground passage to the other cellars to see about food and diamonds, diamonds are vital, and to study the Law! Vital, absolutely vital! They can be hidden! You can take them with you wherever you go! I've two uncles, one uncle-in-religion and one uncle-in-business! I love talking, and my tongue is garnished with intelligence! It speaks all the French words a person could want!' she said as she whirled round with a great flourish of her yellow dress. 'Which means that I am quite perverse and can see at a glance what the other person is thinking, I'm terribly well educated and speak various languages, each with the best accent, so that I can cross frontiers without any trouble at all! But what kind of fool are you, going out into the street dressed like a Jew in a long robe and wearing phylacteries! It was a good thing the beasts got you and cut those notches in that manly chest of yours! Let it be a lesson to you! (Here she fanned herself furiously.) Didn't you know that the sons of God's chosen people must stay hidden behind closed doors because of the beasts outside? In Berlin as it is today, everything is topsy-turvy! People in cages and the beasts free to roam! I can speak all the French words anyone could possibly want! I know all the rules of grammar, and my participles all agree! And hadn't you heard that when they go marching past they sing songs about how happy they are when Jewish blood spurts beneath their knives? *Wenn Judenblut unter'm Messer spritzt!* Spurt! Spurt! You see, I really do know a lot of French words! There's something missing between my head and my shoulders, I realize that, but they, with their blue eyes and their oompah bands, love blood and will kill us all, you'll see! My uncle-in-majesty told me! They dress like men, but they love killing, it's what they like best, and they're happy when there's blood, but we are human beings aren't we? Praise Moses our master! Come on, praise him! Or else I'll bite! It's all right, don't make me laugh, you'll be the death of me! I only said it to scare you! Oh yes, they'll kill the very last one of us! But in the meantime we aren't dead yet, we are warm and snug, and I adore being alive and chatting! This house belonged to my father, and in this genuine Renaissance chest there is an ear which the beasts cut off for fun while they shouted *Heil* and the name of that German who barks like a dog! It's the authentic ear of my dear mother! I keep it ceremoniously in brandy, next to my trousseau, which is complete, three hundred and sixty items, finest linen every one! Sometimes I pick up the jar and kiss it so that people can admire me! (She made loud kissing noises.) Sometimes I shake the jar so that the ear comes alive! I'll show it to you later, when I trust you! Oh yes, there is a high price to pay to be the chosen of God! Diamonds are vital, absolutely vital, for with them we can buy the secret collaboration of some of the beasts, and then we can go on living a little longer! Come on, you say something! When all is said and done, they didn't kill you! (She rummaged through a yellow pouch hanging at her waist and thrust a small looking-glass at him.) Take a look! You see, it's only blood! And not much of it either! But I digress! (She drew closer and said confidentially:) Once, it was midnight, I went to the lavatory and my neck slipped down inside my body! You should never go to the lavatory at midnight, because that's the time when nasty people push your neck down inside you! It doesn't matter, though, having brains makes up for anything! I'm terribly happy! I've got someone to be with and I can talk as much as I like! It's not the sabbath today, you know, but there you are, in our situation, which is hardly a novelty for our people, you have to tell lies! (Again she came close to him.) I was born small! My mother did it on purpose to get her own back!'

She picked up a guitar lying on a ceremonial throne and plucked the strings petulantly with a mixture of radiant smiles and roguish glances. Then she put it back and fanned herself more furiously than ever.

'The fact is I don't know anything about you, and it's really terribly sweet of me to talk to you so openly, though I hide what must be hidden. I don't know where you come from nor from what mother's belly you emerged. So quickly now, your name! If you don't tell me, God only knows what I'll do! Come on, out with it, what is your name under Israel?' she screamed, stamping her little foot encased in satin. 'Introduce yourself correctly according to the rules! Quickly, your name! Midgets can be very dangerous! They bite, so take care!'

'Solal,' he said, and he raised his hand to his forehead covered in blood.

'That's all right, I know the name! A family of some renown! But I should tell you that one of my Russian forebears in the time of the tsars was Director of the Russo-Asian Bank with the titular grade of state councillor which was the equivalent of the rank of general! So don't come the high and mighty with me! And now your first name, out with it! The nice name the girl who marries you will use!'

'Solal.'

'There's no accounting for taste and I don't care either way!' the midget shrieked, tossing her flat hair, which fell back in a crudely cut fringe over her eyes. 'That's her business! Anyway, you'll get over it and you'll stay with us! They didn't hurt you very much really! Oh I know they marked your chest with their spidery swastikas, but scratches are hardly worth bothering about! You can't put scratches in

489

a jar! (She held her nose between two fingers and said in a nasal voice:) Look here, cover that manly chest of yours! I don't want to see it! (She put both hands over her eyes, but peeped through her fingers as he gathered the folds of his robe over his torso on which German crosses, now black with dried blood, had been notched.) They cut your flesh and beat your head and nose and eyes, but that's nothing compared to what it'll be like soon! My uncle-in-religion said so! (To help her think, she twisted and untwisted locks of her hair.) And do you know what? The peoples of other countries won't lift a finger to help us! They'll be only too happy to let the Germans do the job for them! But we aren't dead yet, we're warm and snug! Oh it's lovely! (She cracked a walnut with her teeth.) And I am Rachel and my father was Jacob Silberstein, the wealthiest antiques dealer in Berlin! Before all this we used to live upstairs in a magnificent, sublime, spacious shop!' she screamed, stressing the sibilants. 'But we aren't stupid, not stupid at *all* (she bellowed the word), and when my revered father, who gave me my life of woe, felt the black wind blow he pretended to go away! That's right, pretended to leave Berlin, you idiot! You need to have a couple of ears cut off, otherwise you'll never be smart! Pretend, we've got to pretend, we're always going to have to pretend! But with the connivance – I told you I knew a lot of words – with the connivance of the man who owns the building, he belongs to the same nation as the beasts but he's very keen on dollars, everything was brought down here, and here we came and hid! That's why we need dollars, lots of dollars! It's their fault, not ours! So that's how it is, we keep out of the way here, and in winter the stove stands tall and cosy and we are safe when evil walks abroad at night! The evil of night!' she ululated as she gestured with her hands. 'Talking of beds, I must go and make mine. The couch on which I lie!'

She winked, snapped her fan of ostrich feathers shut, and, her tiny muscular rump swaying as she went, strode off self-importantly towards a child's bed made of carved gilt wood. As she shook the sheets and blankets, she explained in a singing voice full of expression that Jacob Silberstein was a wealthy antiques dealer. Out of the corner of her eye, she watched to see the effect she was producing.

'Look at my things! They're all mine, because I am sole heir! Genuine period furniture, paintings by great masters complete with official provenances! And if you won't have any of them for free then buy them with money! I know how much they all cost and what they're worth! Being fair of face, I could sing their praises to you if you like, one lovely face to another! But if you had any sense you could have them for nothing after a sensible talk with my uncles. (As he remained silent, she tapped the ground with her foot.) They found you in the street and they brought you in! You should be grateful to them! What more do you want me to say? They picked you up and brought you in! Or maybe it was me who brought you in, because I had an eminently respectable purpose in mind. Think about me instead of thinking about yourself! Blood looks very nice on you, it's like velvet on your handsome face! Besides, I can speak several languages perfectly, without any trace of a foreign accent, which means that we can handle the police in any country you care to name! I also manage a house expertly! I can salt and wash and brush oil on meat before cooking it! That way there's no blood! And I sweeten my tea with cherry jam! I'll let you have a taste, and you must try my stuffed carp too! Furthermore, a good wife ought to know how to remove the dried blood from her husband's face and she must be ready to go away with him to escape from the police and have money hidden next to the skin, like a shield against the wicked! Having said that, the period of the engagement is the best time of life, and people who get engaged are happy indeed! Give me a moment to freshen up my face and then you'll see!'

And again she applied lipstick to her mouth and powdered her square face, smiling at him all the while, baring her teeth, making the muscles in her jaw stand out.

'Well, what do you say?' she asked, and she gave him a playful tap with her fan. 'Only the eyes count really! And don't laugh at my hump! It's like a royal crown on my back! And don't start getting ideas about proposing to my sister who is beautiful! Oh very well, so I'm not sole heir! That's how I am, sometimes I cheat when it suits me! But if she's tall and beautiful and has a generous heart she also walks in her sleep, which is only fair! But now, Jew, wait for me here, but talk loud to keep me company and stop me from feeling afraid!'

She ran towards the far end of the cellar, stopped at the ladder, picked up the lantern, and came back with it, uttering a long cry as she did so. Breathing hard and with one hand on her heart, she told him with a child's smile that she'd only just made it. Then she took him by the hand and together they walked past the paintings which hung from the weeping walls. She held the lantern high, mentioning the names of the artists, and as they came to each picture she ordered him with a dig of her heel to admire what he saw. But when he stretched out his hand to lift the veil which covered the last painting, she shook violently and took him by the arm. 'It's not allowed,' she screamed, 'you're not allowed to look at She with the Child! You could go to the stake for it!' Drawing him close to her, she led him past the antique bric-à-brac, suits of armour, mounds of fabrics, ancient dresses, mappa-mundis, glassware, rugs and statues, making faces as she prattled on about them and said how much they were worth. All at once she paused in front of a tall metal statue and scratched herself furiously.

'That's the German Virgin, the Virgin of Nuremburg!' she announced grandiloquently. 'It's hollow! They used to put us inside and the long spikes in the door closed on the body of the Jew! But most of the time they used to burn us alive! In every German city, Wissembourg, Magdeburg, Arnstadt, Koblenz, Sinzig, Erfurt, they were proud to call themselves Jew-roasters! *Judenbreter* was their word for it in those days! Oh I'm frightened of them! They burned us alive in the thirteenth century! They will burn us alive in the twentieth! There is no salvation for us, have no illusions on that score! They love their nasty leader who barks like a dog and has a moustache! They all agree with him! Bishop Berning agrees with him! He said all the German bishops agree. My uncle told me, my uncle-in-highest-majesty! Now step this way!'

His mind reeling but led on by the dwarf-woman, who periodically turned and leered at him, he walked past chests, armchairs, cabinets and grounded chandeliers, meekly following her while the clocks ticked against each other and the wax figures smiled as they watched them pass in the dark. Once again she halted suddenly, stroked a stuffed owl with orange eyes and large eyebrows which was also watching them, and then raised her lantern over a sarcophagus containing a mummy.

'Pharaoh was no different!' she said. 'He slew us, even unto the last of us! They destroy us, and then they all die too!'

Saying nothing and with his head still throbbing, he smiled proudly, became like her, and was aware of it. Suddenly the touch of her damp little hand revolted him, but he did not dare push her away, fearing she might turn on him unexpectedly. She halted in front of a wrought-iron screen, raised her lantern, smacked her lips, and gestured dramatically to an old court coach, the gilt was cracked and flaking and here and there it was black with smoke, but it sparkled with many-faceted mirrors and was decorated with cherubs holding flaming torches.

'It's a souvenir, a reminder of my grandfather, the miraculous rabbi! The famous Rabbi of Lodz! He was driven at night through the Jewish quarter in this very coach! It has no roof, because he stood up in it to bless the people! A royal coach! I'm so proud I could bite you! It will be used for my wedding! I can say wedding in seven languages! If anybody tells you my blood pressure is high, don't believe a word of it! I get ideas, that's all!' she clamoured, and she waved her little hands in gestures of spiteful glee. 'But I want to show you something – there's no need to be frightened, because they are safely tethered!'

He stood back and let her walk on, for he suddenly realized that if she stayed at his rear she might be tempted by the back of his head, start screaming with fear, go for his neck and bite him perhaps. 'Hurry,' she said, and she dragged him roughly after her. Behind the coach lay two doleful, emaciated horses. They were tethered together. The head of one rested on the beaten earth floor, its tongue half-protruding. The other worked its elongated human features, and its shadow swung uncertainly from one wall to the other.

'These are my grandfather's horses!' she announced. 'My father decided to keep them until the very end of all their days! Out of respect! Before that they lived in the stables upstairs, but now they too hide down here with us, poor old things! They're called Isaac and Jacob! But that's more than enough of that! Take a look at yourself!' she cried in a wild frenzy, once more holding out her mirror to him. 'That's what living outside can do to you, idiot! Into the cellar with you, Jew! You'll be all right with me, but I should tell you that my troth is already plighted to a baron whom I chose in preference to

Nathaniel Bischoffsheim, who is too young! I like them when they're ripe and ready, like Camembert, slightly soft to the touch! Furthermore, brandy pickles ears, a fact you might remember if some day you find yours on the floor! At Lodz there was a pogrom when she was pregnant with me, so she took her revenge and I was born little! Anyway, I can take or leave anything you tell me! So it's entirely up to you, and of course anyone who lies in his teeth won't have teeth for long and what girl would want you with no teeth? Surely you know that a person will never amount to much without a pair of well-stocked jaws? (She smiled broadly to show off two rows of fine teeth and put one hand on her hip.) They say I'm a midget, but people take an interest in me! Just ask Rothschild or Bischoffsheim! Anyway, it was written that you would end up confused in the head! Don't deny it, my little wheedling pet, a moment ago you were trying to catch Jacob's shadow on the wall! I saw you and nearly choked laughing! Listen, I'll tell you a secret! When I'm alone I harness Isaac and Jacob to the coach, then I get in, take the reins, and drive round the cellar! A real little queen! Just now when I said "walks in her sleep" I was being considerate, to avoid saying "blind"! Or if I get lonely, when everybody else has gone off to cellars elsewhere to buy things or have chats and they leave me because I'm too small and have a hump and no neck, I try to sleep so I don't have to think. Sleeping dogs have no fleas! Come on, look sharp, get up into grandfather's coach! Quick now, or I'll pinch you!'

She opened the door, which sparkled with multiple mirrors, pushed him inside with both hands, forced him on to the seat, climbed up beside him, and sat down. She swung her little legs contentedly, stopped suddenly and motioned him to be quiet.

'Can you hear them outside? Those clowns are happy when they've got a band to march behind. Whereas here we are sitting in a royal coach! Oh beautiful cellar of mine, oh high destiny, oh nails that I love! But now, do you feel like having a bit of fun? We've got masks for the Feast of Lots, they were bought before I was born! I'm terribly young, you know! You want a good laugh? We've got games for the Feast of Lots! Look!' she cried in a ringing voice, and, bending down, produced from under the seat a paper crown decorated with imitation rubies which she put on her head. 'On the Feast of Lots, I was always

Queen Esther, I was so graceful, the apple of my father's eye! Here, take this false nose and rejoice! Ignoramus, do you know in what you shall rejoice? I'll tell you: in the death of Haman! Sometimes I behave horribly, because it's not very nice being small. So I say "I like them ripe" or "I'll bite you", but it isn't true, it's just the laughter showing through the tears. And perhaps I was wrong when I said that other nations will be pleased. Let's wait and see! In any case, I don't trust Poland! Don't look at me stupidly like that! Hurry up, put your false nose on!'

He did as she asked and she clapped her hands as he stroked the grotesque cardboard appendage, stroked it proudly. He gave a sudden start on hearing a knocking which rose from the depths, three knocks, then two. She patted his hand self-importantly, told him not to be afraid, that it was Jews in the cellar in the next house asking for the trapdoor to be opened, a crowd of bores who often came looking for news or food. She got out of the coach and waddled off, holding her train aloft and her little rump swaying.

'I'll make you wait and wail, you've got no manners!' she shouted as she perched above the trapdoor. 'I'm very busy laughing and powdering my face! I'll open up in an hour from now, and not a minute before! Silence, Jews!'

Seated beside him once more in the coach, in sober mood, Rachel the midget was plucking the strings of another guitar from which she drew sad strains and from time to time glanced at him shrewdly. He gazed upon her and felt pity, pity for this tiny deformed creature with the large eyes, the beautiful eyes of his people, pity for the crazed little being who was both the culmination of age-old fears and the misshapen fruit of those fears, pity for her hump, and in his heart he felt a reverence for her hump, which was made of fear and the sweat of fear, sweat transmitted from one age to the next in the expectation of sorrow, the sweat and despair of a hunted people, his people and his love, an ancient people marked by genius but crowned with grief, the science of majesty and disillusionment, his mad old King striding alone through the storm bearing its Law, a jangling harp through the dark hurricane of the ages, and the immortal sound of its ecstasy of grandeur and persecution.

'I'm ugly, aren't I?' she asked, and with her tiny hand she touched her fringe with the heart-rending gesture of a sick monkey.

'You are beautiful,' he said, and he took her hand and kissed it.

Without speaking now, they sat holding hands in the ancient coach, he wearing his false nose and she with her paper crown on her head, brother and sister, holding each other tightly by the hand, a queen and a king from some sorry carnival at whom the two horses gazed sadly as they shook their chaste, professorial heads.

And then the midget removed her crown and put it on the head of her brother whose eyes were closed, and she covered his shoulders with the silk prayer-shawl, and placed in his hands the sacred scrolls of the Commandments. Then, climbing down shakily from the coach, she untethered the listless horses, backed them into the shafts, harnessed them, covered them with velvet cloths embroidered with gold and ancient characters, a curtain from the Ark of the Covenant, while the left-hand horse, the older of the pair and swollen-jointed, looked on approvingly, melancholy but majestic, and the right-hand horse raised its head in joy and whinnied a summons.

Then from the shadows she appeared, tall and marvellous of face, sovereign Virgin, Jerusalem made flesh, beauty of Israel, hope in the night, a sweet mad creature with sightless eyes, advancing slowly, folding in her arms an old doll over which from time to time she lowered her head. 'She's made a mistake,' whispered the midget: 'she thinks she's cradling the Law in her arms.'

All at once again there came a loud clamour from outside, and simultaneously the tramp of jackboots rang out beneath the song of the Germans, hymn of venom, hymn of German joy, joy of the blood of Israel spurting beneath German knives. '*Wenn Judenblut unter'm Messer spritzt*,' sang the young hopes of the German nation, while from the neighbouring cellar rose another song, hymn of praise to the Lord, sombre hymn of love, which rose out of the mists of time, the song of David my King.

And there, standing beneath the ventilator outside which the German jackboots tramped past, draped in the ample prayer-shawl with its bar of blue and its hanging tassels, relic of a noble past, the King, crowned with sorrow and bloody-browed, raised aloft the Holy Law, glory of his people, presented it to the worshippers of might, of the might which is a licence to murder, held it against the bars past which, mechanical and victorious, the young hopes of the German nation paraded, singing their joy at Jewish blood spilt, proud in their strength, proud in their strength in numbers, cheered by sweating girls with blonde plaits and arms inanely held high, gross sexual creatures excited by the spectacle of so much jackbooted manliness.

Indefatigable, son of his people, he held aloft the Law accoutred in gold and velvet and crowned with silver, gloriously raised it high and proffered the heavy, imprisoned Law, Law of justice and of love, the honour of his people, while outside, glorying in their power of death, pride of the German nation, to the sound of fife and drum and clashing cymbals, endlessly singing their joy in the blood of Israel which spurts beneath their knives, the torturers and killers of the weak and the defenceless marched past.

CHAPTER 55

'Dearie me! Mariette you poor old thing! I'm at my wits' end all I do is sit and sigh I don't even fancy a coffee no more, it's been going on like this for two days now, she's changed, she don't say a word and I can't make it out, I daren't ask why, it was the day before yesterday when she started on with the glums, the day after that day when she was so happy, that's right, it's two days she's been this way, Mary Magdalene at the foot of the Cross don't come into it, just has one bath of a morning though she usually has two or three, can't be bothered to get dressed, just stays in bed with books that she don't even read, staring up at the ceiling as if she was waiting for something, I know 'cos naturally I peep through the keyhole, I feel it's my duty seeing that she's an orphing, not talking or singing and I always used to love listening to her, stops in bed doing nothing, there's something fishy going on but what it is I've no idea, if she was the type I'd say she was crossed in love, but I don't think so, I'd have noticed, it's like I say, stays in bed not eating, a terrible sight to see, anything wrong Madame Ariane I've said two or three times thinking that she'd tell me what was up, but all she says is I'm tired I got a headache, and that's my lot, and by the look of her I can tell it's no good asking, she'd only get cross if I started ferreting, could be it's her nerves, her father had nerves, there was days on end when he wouldn't say a word, always thinking thoughts he was, but poor old me I just carry on as best I can, sometimes I say daft things to make her laugh but she don't laugh, yesterday morning to take her mind off things I says Madame Ariane how'd you fancy a little ride down to the Côte d'Azur to see the sea, she always loved the sea she did, and the country, all that sort of thing, though speaking for myself, you know, I never reckoned much to the sea, you can't get washed proper in it, it don't give you much of a lather, anyroad that's the sort of thing I've been telling her, but she shakes her head and says she's ever so tired, the same old tune over and over and not eating enough to keep a sparrow alive, listen I'll give you a for instance, last night I made a little bit of something for supper, just a few starters, to tickle her appetite, and I took it up to her in bed with the little invalid table, very handy is that table, it folds away when you're not using it, radishes, olives, sardines, a nob of butter and with it a nice bit of sausage that cousin of mine sent me from Nanteuil though she'd be better off paying me back the money she owes me, a helping of tuna in mayonnaise with paprika to cheer it up, grated celeriac in mustard sauce, all nicely set out, black olives the biggest I could get, puff-pastry boats, all artistic like, with funnels on to make her laugh and anchovies inside, hard-boiled eggs in mayonnaise arranged like a baby's face for a bit of fun with capers for eyes and a red-pepper mouth, Parma ham, in a word a selection of nibbles to tickle her fancy, flowers on the tray, no trouble spared to take her mind off things, and also I was forgetting the most important bit, smoked salmon that I went specially to that expensive shop in town to get, they're rogues and thieves but they got good stuff, speak as you find, two hundred grams, best quality, the thick part, not too salty, you don't have to eat it all up Madame Ariane, just what you fancy, but she didn't fancy any, all she had was some tea, so in the end I had to finish it all up by meself, made me feel real down in the dumps, mustn't let good food go to waste, and just now when I took her up her breakfast in bed she didn't even look up, drawing things on the bedcovers she was, here's a nice hot cup of coffee for you Madame Ariane, wait a sec and I'll put you another pillow so you're comfy, and she stares at me as if I wasn't there, a few sips of black coffee and that was it, just a mouthful, and what do you say to some nice croissants Madame Ariane, no thanks, Mariette, I'm not hungry, but Madame Ariane you don't have to be hungry to eat a little croissant, they melt in your mouth, it's not proper food, no thanks Mariette dear, and she looks up at the ceiling as if to say I don't want nobody talking to me, I want to be left alone, now to my way of thinking there's something seriously wrong there, I told her go and see the doctor, she didn't even bother to answer, you can't get through to her she's in such a mood, yes Mariette dear she says to me, poor lamb, though I'd much sooner she called me an old bag and ate something, I say Madame Ariane because I always called her Mademoiselle as long as her aunt was alive, on account of Mademoiselle Valérie never wanting me to say just plain Ariane when she got a bit older, you have to know your place, anyroad it's come to be a habit with me, first it was Mademoiselle and then of course Madame, but for all that she's still my little girl, me being a widow and never had children, she filled a gap, she was a sort of daughter to me I mean, because them nieces of mine aren't up to much, always chasing men, always stuffing their faces, whatever that pair haven't got it isn't a good appetite, but we'll see at lunch-time, perhaps she'll fancy a bite to eat then, I'll do her lamb chops, be best to keep it simple p'raps, with creamed potatoes and a nice bit of crispy salad with tarragon in, there's nothing like tarragon for giving a salad a lift, shape yourself Madame Ariane I'll say, just two small chops to keep your strength up, that doctor, the one that had the surgery I used to do for, he always said not eating is bad for the system, clogs it up, gives you swollen glands, that's what the doctor told me, anyhow I'd better shake meself and get a move on, no offence but you're holding me up, so nice to have seen you, ta-ta, thanks for coming, always lovely to see you, why don't you call round at home tonight, we'll have a cup of coffee.'

'If you'll hush a minute I'll tell you the whole story, there've been developments, she's got a boyfriend, you see I wasn't far out yesterday when I told you there was some man behind it, all that being sad and not talking, true as I'm standing here silly cow that I am I never suspected a thing, what with her being Mademoiselle Valérie's niece and having me on saying that she had headaches, but when I remembered how she was always asking me if the postman had been yet the penny dropped and I thought oho there's love-lines crossed here, you remember, I told you, she's not a one who can teach her grandmother to suck eggs, so there you are, but to begin at the beginning, this morning eight o'clock, just as I was making a start on the kitchen windows, the rain had made them ever so dirty, there comes a knock at the door, terrygram it was, I took it up at once of course, straight away, I went up them stairs so fast I nearly broke a leg, well the minute she reads the terrygram she jumps out of bed so fast you'd have thought she was an acrobat in a circus, and quick as a flash she's away to her bath, shouting there's no time to explain, she got to go out quick, she'll tell me what it's all about later, but she'd put her terrygram in her pyjama pocket, the top's too short, makes her behind look like an angel's from heaven, anyhow, just as she was zooming off whoosh to the bathroom like a scared rabbit, the terrygram falls on the floor, I think about it telling myself there's a responsibility on me to know what's in it, since she's only young and got no father or mother, so's I can give her advice and help her if it was bad news though it didn't look much like that what with the way she went leaping off for her soak, scalding she has it, you wonder how a body could stand having it so hot, she comes out looking like a lobster, anyway to cut a long story short, after I phone for the taxi she shouted from her steaming hot bath that I had to get for her, ooh I hate phoning, you got to yell if you want them to understand what you're saying, it always gives me a turn, though I'm past *the* turn I'm happy to say, anyway as I was saying after phoning I went back upstairs and had a bit of a read of the terrygram while she was in the bath, felt it was my duty, and guess what, poor Didi's out on his ear, probably never satisfied her, it had to come, the terrygram was from the boyfriend saying he'll be back on the twenty-fifth, ever so lovey-dovey, I'm itching with impatience tell me you're itching too, that's how it went word for word, well not quite word for word exackly, it didn't say he was itching, it said it much more fancy, ever so romantic, but that's what it meant, anyway in for a penny, I have a bit of a rummage through the papers in her drawer while she's still in the bath to see if I can find out what it's all about, I am responsible for her don't forget, she didn't tell me what the taxi she went off in was for but it was clear as daylight it was to go turtle-doving, oh come soon darling I can't wait no more, anyhow, getting back to the notebook, the one I read in her drawer to find out what it was all about with the very best of intentions, it was all about love, went on about the boyfriend, goings on like in a play, I love him, I love him, my own love, stuff like that, went on about kisses and crazy carryings-on, of course I didn't read much of it 'cos it was a scrawl just like when the doctor writes you a prescripshun, anyhow, they met when I was away in Paris and they saw each other of an evening, of course with that Putallaz creature pushing off every day at lunch-time they could kiss and cuddle with nobody to interfere, I ask you, and me thinking she was a saint or similar, poor Didi, I know I don't reckon much to him with his walking-stick and his skimpy overcoat ever so toffee-nosed, but you can't help feeling sorry for him, to my way of thinking he just didn't have a clue, it's a fact, so then we had all that business of being ever so sad and not talking, it's all there in her notebook, and then the boyfriend goes away all unexpected-like for a couple of days and don't come back when he said he was going to come back and he don't give her no news and she don't know where he's got to, so then she gets frantic and phones her darling's hotel her darling's office, can't find out where he's gone to, in the terrygram he explains how he can't explain why he didn't come back on the day he said he would and how he can't explain neither why he won't be coming back till the twenty-fifth, which is not for another eleven days yet, very hush-hush, politics, in her notebook, the one I had a quick read of where she wrote it all out, saying how terribly unhappy she was, before the terrygram come that is, not hearing anything about her sweetheart, thinking about doing herself in if it went on much longer, I'd love to see what this lucky beggar of hers looks like, he must be handsome enough to give you shivers up your back judging by what she says about him in them jottings in her notebook, but all the same what a slyboots not saying a word to old Mariette, a real minx, it would have been nice if she'd cried her heart out to me, I'd have told her there there, never mind Madame Ariane, he'll write to you soon you see if he don't, men don't think, not like women, but she didn't tell me and I'd not forgive her if I was on my deathbed, though of course I'm pleased she's happy like a woman should be, got a taste of joys I know so well, like the song says, but she'll keep it all to herself, you'll see, she won't tell me anything instead of us talking it over nice and cosy, her asking me what to do woman-to-woman, 'cos she's all I got really, my nieces are so coarse, and 'cos that's how things stand I won't read her stuff, cross my heart, I'll not read her letters and her notebook, I'll make myself a nice cup of coffee and I'll have a look at that novel I've got on the go it's much more interesting, and when she gets home I'll be stand-offish, that'll teach her, what a minx though, and me always saying how she was pure as a angel, though if there's blame I don't blame her, you're only young once and it don't last, anyway no good complaining, that's life, all the same what a snake in the grass hiding her big romance from me like that, she had no need to, I'd have been only too glad to know she was getting out of her rut with some good-looking man, she's entitled, 'cos that Didi's got what was coming to him, and besides the heart's the little tinkling bell on the heavy necklace of life, as the song goes.'

CHAPTER 57

In the wondrously lurching taxi which bore her along, she reread the telegram, lingered over the best parts, smiled at them, made approving noises in a voice that was now exalted, now sublime. 'Yes, my love,' she told the telegram, and she bit her hand to stifle the cries of joy which clamoured for release. Then she began again and read it over with all her soul, scarcely looking at it so well did she know what it said. She held it away from her to see it better, she brought it close, breathed it in, pressed it to her cheek, her eyes glazed with ecstasy, and she crooned senseless words to herself, lordy and phew and tra-la-la, and pip-pip and oompah and diddle-de-dum.

When the taxi stopped outside the post office, she gave the driver a hundred-franc note, fled before he had a chance to thank her, and went up the steps three at a time. Inside the main hall, she stopped and turned round several times on the spot. Which window dealt with telegrams? She located it and made a dash for it. One of her stockings had parted from her suspender and hung down her leg in creases.

Standing before a sheaf of blank forms, she opened her handbag. One thousand three hundred francs. Should be enough. She unscrewed the top of her pen, smiled at a small dog which looked cross and bored, rumpled her hair to put herself in the mood, and, already into her stride, began writing:

'Solal c/o Thomas Cook, Place de la Madeleine, Paris

'Thank you so much exclamation marks my love I have been so

unhappy but I won't have any word of reproach from me to you since I know now that I'll be seeing you soon stop I accept all I've had to go through I accept that you not due back till 25th I accept that you didn't tell me what prevented you returning on 9th as promised I accept that you didn't inform me of what you are doing and where you're going since you told me that you'll only be in Paris till this evening I suppose job makes all these secrets necessary stop I only ask one thing of you which is take train since too many accidents by aeroplane wire what time train arrives Geneva 25th and what time you will come by after all you should drop by the minute you get to Geneva even before going to Ritz but you will probably want to shave and make yourself handsome which is ludicrous you always look handsome too handsome stop I withdraw the too stop I'd like you to be at my house at 9 oh oh oh stop those ohs are for happiness stop I was so miserable between 9 Aug evening and 14 Aug morning stop the first night I phoned Ritz every hour and every time they said you weren't back stop the next days all that awful waiting for postman and awful phonecalls to Ritz and L. of N. stop just now in taxi blissfully sang stupid songs like on radio you know there's never been a love like ours stop thank you for not being able to live without me but in your telegram there is a very before beautiful but not before elegant should I conclude you do not think I'm really elegant stop during all that time when I didn't know what was happening and whether or not you had left me I couldn't bear to reread your letters but soon when I get home I'll spread your letters all over my bed and read them again lying down with nothing on because it's very hot stop when you come you shall do what you like with me I'm embarrassed because the telegram clerk will read this but no matter I won't look at him when he's counting the words stop please will you look at the polestar every night at 9 exactly for three minutes and I'll look at it too for three minutes at 9 that way our eyes will meet way up there and we'll be together stop the polestar only if there are no clouds of course stop if too cloudy try next night same time same place stop but remember that's 9 Swiss time so if in a country where time different look at polestar at time corresponding to 9 o'clock Switzerland stop my darling boy I'm afraid all of a sudden you might not know where it is in the sky stop the polestar is situated in Ursa Minor which is like a kite and the polestar is right at the end of the tail stop you can also locate it via Ursa Major also known as the Wagon which is close to Ursa Minor stop the polestar is on the continuation of a line that goes through the two stars which represent the back wheels of Wagon stop sorry for telling you all this but I've noticed you don't always know much about nature and I don't want to miss our nightly communing stop darling I beseech you if you can't find the polestar by yourself please do think of getting someone who does know to help you stop if you go to America in the next few days you'll find the polestar there too I found out I phoned the Observatory before leaving stop sometimes I realize it's quite true that part of me must be backward I've still got a fontanelle like babies do stop please don't smoke too much not more than twenty a day and if it's cold at night don't go out without a coat stop sorry for being so interfering stop I've never worn a wedding ring but I'm going to buy one and I'll put it on when I'm by myself and be your wife before God stop cannot for life of me think why you're in Paris for such short stays and why you won't give me the address of a hotel where I could phone you or even come and see you because after all you do stay in hotels even if you are in a different town every day stop so it will be ten days from tomorrow and on 24 Aug I'll be in bed telling myself I'll be seeing him tomorrow and then we'll do this and that stop I am yours I am whatever you want your child your friend your brother and on 25 Aug your wife with lots of dots stop I was so unhappy I cried I didn't get up I wasn't hungry but now I'm hungry especially for your arms around me holding me so tight I'd be most wonderfully black and blue stop on 25 Aug there'll be tea the best but I shan't spill a drop even if I'm kneeling down like the evening I knelt before my Prince of Night stop send me another telegram and tell me you love me and what time you arrive on 25 Aug darling stop every time you think of me over the next 11 days tell yourself at this very moment she's loving you and waiting for you it'll be true every time Ariane her Lord's own.'

The really ghastly part was having to deal with the telegrams clerk who, being old, would read her completed forms resentfully. How appalling to have to stand in front of him like a defendant in the dock while he counted the words and criticized them silently. Still, nothing for it. Do it quickly. Catching her foot in her left stocking, which had now come down around her ankle, she fell forward, got up, checked her teeth. Nothing broken. Thank you, God. Closing her eyes to make herself invisible, she hitched up her skirt, fixed her stocking, and then made quickly for the clerk's window, where she directed a ravishing smile at the grog-blossomed nose of the disgusting old man in the hope of buying his indulgence.

When she had paid, still blushing red with embarrassment, she broke free at a run, tore down the steps her face twitching with shame, entered a grocer's shop across the street, emerged with a packet of biscuits, hailed a taxi, and gave the driver her address. The moment she got home, she opened the packet and told the biscuits they were about to be eaten. Best get accustomed to the idea, turn adversity to good account. Use the eleven days to ensure she would be the height of elegance, especially given the fact that in his telegram he had said elegant not very elegant. So look through her clothes, get rid of anything that was below par, and order one or two new things from that new dressmaker everyone was saying was ever so good. That way the time would pass more quickly. 'August the twenty-fifth,' she whispered to the first biscuit.

CHAPTER 58

Mariette was in her kitchen fiddling with her kiss-curl as she read *Chaste and Blighted*, a novel loaned to her by next-door's maid, who looked like a long black grasshopper, flatulent in tendency and ceremonious in manner. She had got to the proud reply of the heroine, who was poor but honest, and turned the page with such eagerness that she knocked her coffee bowl on to the floor. Boil up some glue, she told herself in an even tone of voice designed to proclaim her independence and show that she was not a woman to be upset like that for a mere trifle.

Armed with brush and pan, she swept up the debris and tipped the lot into a bucket, said lordy it was better than a broken leg, sat down again, and went on with her book. She had just got to the bit where the wicked marquis gets his comeuppance when the creaking of the front door made her shut her book, which she pushed hurriedly into her work-basket under some half-finished knitting. 'Miss Slyboots is back, you just wait to hear what I got to say to her, she's not going to get away with it,' she muttered, and she reached for a broom so that she would look busy.

'Oh, so you're back, Madame Ariane, I didn't hear you. I hope the terrygram wasn't bad news?'

'No, not bad news. (A pause.) It says we're going to have a visitor in the next couple of days.'

'Well now, that's all right then, because there was me thinking something had happened to Monsieur Adrien and that you was upset seeing as how you shot off like that in such a great hurry. I expect your visitor is a lady?'

'No.'

'Perhaps a gentleman then?'

'A friend of my husband's. And of mine too, of course.'

'Oh yes, I'm sure,' said Mariette, carrying on sweeping studiously. 'It's a real shame, though, Monsieur Adrien being away on his trip. He'd have been so pleased to see this friend of his. A friend of your husband, that's nice, very nice. Anyhow, I can see you're over the moon about it. It's written all over your face.'

'Yes I am. I haven't seen him in ages, and of course I'll be happy to see him again, very happy I should say. I do like him most terribly.'

'In this life, you got to like people. It's nature's way. Liking people is what makes life worth living. And anyway it'll be something for you to do. Having a bit of a chat will be a lot better for you than lounging about in bed by yourself, thinking. Pity Monsieur Adrien's away. Still, I'll give this whole place a good going over, just you see if I don't.'

'Thank you, Mariette. As a matter of fact, I would like everything to be impeccable. Oh, by the way, I called in to see Gentet on my way home. His men will be coming to paint the ceilings and the woodwork.'

'What, the whole lot?'

'No, just the hall and my little sitting-room.'

'Which is to say the main bits. But while you're on, you ought to make the most of it and do out your bedroom too. It could do with it, don't you think?'

'Perhaps. I'll see.'

'Them painters will leave mess all over the floor. Never mind, after they've been and gone I'll make everything as clean as a new pin so it'll be as implacable as you could wish for. Is this gentleman good-looking?'

'Why do you ask?'

'Dunno, just curious, I'll be glad to have a visitor round the place, it'll make a change, so I'd be more pleased than not if he was good-looking. I like men with looks.'

'He's not bad,' smiled Ariane. 'It's rather that he's intelligent and well-read. I like talking to him.'

'That's right, there's nothing like a bit of a chin-wag, specially if you take a shine to the other person. I always say you got to make the most of life, because when you get old it's too late. When I get past it I'm going to tell the sister in the hospital to give us a good thump on the head with the water-jug and get it over and done with, and it won't bother me none if they don't plant me six feet under. They can throw me out with the sweepings if they want! I'd rather spend my money now and have a bit of fun, go to the pictures or treat meself to one of them pistachio cakes with kirsch in, rather than have other people spending it on a coffin for me that I'll never know I'm in anyway. (She put in a few vigorous strokes with her broom.) Oh dearie me yes, they can sweep me away when I'm dead, chuck ole Mariette down the stairs, dump ole Mariette in the gutter! And what would this visitor of yours do? He wouldn't do writing, would he?'

'He's one of the most important men in the League of Nations,' said Ariane, who immediately produced a diversionary yawn.

'Of course he is,' said Mariette. 'One of their high-ups. Must be ever so clever. He'll be Monsieur Adrien's boss, then. All the more reason for brightening the place up with a lick of paint so that it all looks nice for when he comes. Monsieur Adrien will be ever so pleased that you'll be rolling out the red carpet for his boss. Always pays to get in good with the bosses. Oh, there's twelve striking. Shall I do the lunch for one o'clock?'

'No, start it now, I'm hungry.'

'It's the fresh air, it's done you good to go out. And what'll you be wearing to impress the gentleman when he comes calling, seeing as how he's so important and all?'

'Haven't a clue. I'm going to have a quick bath. While I'm doing that, you can set the table, I'm ravenous,' said Ariane with a pirouette which sent her dress whirling, and she went. On the stairs, she gave a quick burst of the air of the Whitsun hymn at the top of her voice.

Whereupon, lifting her skirts with the pockets fastened by safety-pins where she kept her modest savings, the little old woman danced a wild, improvised cancan and sang: 'You need sy-hympathy, sy-hympathy, just sympathee.' Punctuating her jig with the words, tossing her head back and raising her stumpy fat legs like a circus horse, she continued galloping on the spot while upstairs the lovesick maiden in her bath rent the air again with Bach's glorious notes and announced the coming of a heavenly king.

CHAPTER 59

Wearily, moronically, exuding an aura of sexuality, the regally strutting, belly-thrusting, eyes-on-the-prize models paraded one last time under the strict eye of the diminutive dressmaker, who executed an elegant half-turn and beamed at the customer.

'Well, dear lady, I think we are agreed on all points. (She looked away, appalled by the "dear lady".) Today is the fourteenth. So we shall arrange a first fitting for Friday the seventeenth and a second on Wednesday the twenty-second, since everything must be finished and delivered on Saturday the twenty-fifth by eleven o'clock at the very latest. We shall have our work cut out but we shall not fail you, our sole aim being always to please. The styles you have chosen are absolutely you, terrifically chic, and will look stunning on. And now, Madame, if you will forgive me . . .'

Primped and perfumed and highly pleased with himself, Volkmaar bowed then went on his hip-rolling way, leaving his chief sales assistant to bring up the matter of the account. This Mademoiselle Chloé, a platinum blonde with a fearsome chin, did with consummate discretion. Ariane coloured, murmured that she had not given the matter a thought, adding that her bank was very likely closed by now.

'Oh yes, Madame, banks shut at five,' said the sales assistant in a tone of sententious gloom shot through with the imperceptible hint of a rebuke.

'It really is too annoying, but what can I do?' said the customer guiltily, while Chloé looked away questioningly towards the podgy purveyor of high fashion, who blinked to signal acquiescence, for the client in question was of the naïve-but-honest variety.

'No rush, Madame,' said Chloé. 'Tomorrow morning will do fine,' she crooned, as if she were talking to a baby. 'We open at nine. Good-day, Madame. No, please allow me, I'll close it behind you.'

When she got out into the street, Ariane stared at the ground and ran through her purchases in her mind. First, the two evening dresses, the white crêpe, very simple, and the gold lamé, the 'Juno' model, Volkmaar had called it, rather grand, awfully elegant. And the two rustic linen suits, one white with the spencer and the blue one with the roomy cardigan-style jacket, mother-of-pearl buttons, three-quarter sleeves and fob pockets. The cardigan was a darling, she had quite fallen in love with it. (She smiled at the darling cardigan.) And the light-grey flannel two-piece was divine too, very classic, boxy, flap pockets and tailored collar. She'd feel good in it. The 'Cambridge', it had been called by the moronic creature who had modelled it and, incidentally, worn it rather well.

'Yes, my lord, I shall wear the "Cambridge" and shall be pleasing in your sight.'

She halted, with the sudden feeling that the neckline on the gold lamé was cut too low. The red-haired girl who had worn it had shown a good three-quarters of her bosom, and one breast had all but jumped out when she did that quick turn. Slowly she walked on, pensive, head down. When she reached the lake she stopped again, riven by two other blunders which were far worse. Just two fittings was madness! No dress was ever right at the second fitting!

'It was also crazy to agree to wait until the twenty-fifth, the day Sol gets back, to have everything delivered. There are bound to be things that aren't right, and there won't be enough time for the alterations. Even supposing I take them back before twelve on the Saturday, they'll only have the afternoon to put right whatever's gone horribly wrong, and that's assuming they are open on Saturday afternoons, in any case they'll do it in a rush and they'll send me back a horribly botched job and I won't have anything to wear when he arrives, well nothing except for my old rags. And all because Piglet and Chloé were such bullies. But there you are, vulgar people always intimidate me. And the way they kept talking all the time got me all mixed up, in the end I was saying yes to everything just to get it over with and leave and not have to listen to any more dear-ladying. Basically I'm a coward, that's it, not equipped for life. No, but just a minute, you've got to do something about it, you've got to go back and see Piglet. No backing down, put up a fight. That's it, fight for his sake, so he thinks I look elegant. O my love, I've suffered agonies, I had no idea what was going on. Why did he take so long before wiring? Yes, fight! But first let's work out what I'll say to Piglet, stating my reasons. Draw up a battle-plan, write a summary so you're not left high and dry, there's a café, you can write it there, yes, come along.'

But once inside, her courage failed her, for the men looked up from their cards and stared. She turned round, pushed the revolving door too hard. It caught her in the small of the back and propelled her on to the pavement, where she saw, heading towards her, a friend she had known since before she was married. So that she wouldn't have to say hello, she took refuge in a stationer's, where, to justify her presence, she purchased a fountain-pen. A small cat sidled up to her. She tickled it in the approved manner, forehead first, under the chin next, then asked how old it was, what sort of character it had and its name, which, disappointingly, was Tiddles. Feeling that she had fallen among friends, she exchanged stories about cats with the proprietress, strongly recommended raw liver, an indispensable source of vitamins, said goodbye to Tiddles, and left with a smile on her face.

'On reflection, there's not much point writing it all out, all I need do is tell myself what I'm going to tell Piglet, sort of dress rehearsal. Basically, the main thing is to insist on three fittings, all close together. Friday the seventeenth, Tuesday the twenty-first, Thursday the twenty-third, no Wednesday the twenty-second, so as to leave a good margin in case of slip-ups. Ask calmly, act as if you're convinced you'll get your way. Yes, because everything depends on your inner attitudes. Don't say "I would like", say "I want", and say it firmly and categorically. "Monsieur, I want three fittings, and everything must be finished by the morning of Friday the twenty-fourth." Tell lies, never mind, it's self-defence. Yes, tell him unexpected developments, circumstances beyond my control, absolutely must leave on the evening of Friday the twenty-fourth, that is a day earlier than planned. Consequently, I must have everything absolutely but absolutely ready for the Friday morning without fail. Got to be firm with him. Look him straight in his piggy little eyes. And don't let him arrange to deliver it at Cologny, say you'll call in and collect everything yourself on the Friday morning. Friday morning I arrive, supposedly to collect the dresses and suits by car or taxi, and while I'm in the shop tell them straight, as if it had just occurred to me, that come to think of it I'd like to try everything on once more. That's it: be brave. They won't dare say no. That'll make a fourth fitting on the sly. If, when I try the things on, I find other faults that need to be put right, I ask for the alterations to be done for Friday afternoon, by six at the latest. If there's anything that's still wrong, tell more lies, no option, say I've put off going until Saturday evening, whereupon more alterations and dresses perfect, finished by Saturday at twelve or two. The advantage of spinning a yarn about going away on Friday evening is that it leaves me a margin of twenty-four hours to get everything spot on. Lying's wrong, of course. But, beloved, I lie for you. To sum up, be firm, don't weaken for any reason. I'm negotiating from a position of strength, since I haven't paid them anything on account. If Piglet won't play ball, say I'm cancelling the order, in which case grab a plane for Paris and try those de-luxe *haute couture* boutiques where they do off-the-peg lines, after all I do have a figure like a model's, so I'm not the least at Piglet's mercy. Oh, just one other thing: change the neckline on the gold lamé.'

Outside the canopied entrance to the dress shop, her courage failed her and she didn't dare go inside. It was no good denying it, she was afraid of people who were in trade, common people who did not like you and passed judgement. No, she did not have the courage to face the whole gang of them with their hypocritical, smirking faces – Volkmaar who thought it refined to say dear lady, the heavily made-up sales girls who criticized you silently, Chloé who thought herself so smart with her signet-ring on her little finger, and the rest of the vulgar tribe of models who behaved like man-eating, sensual princesses and had mothers who most likely were concierges. Better to phone. Feel braver when they can't see you.

In the phone-box, she scribbled the gist of what she wanted to say on the back of her husband's latest letter, postmarked Jerusalem but still unopened, like all the others. Damn, you'd better open them or, if you can't bring yourself to do that, wire him at the address on the back of the envelope and say: 'Thanks fascinating letters stop Read and reread them' etc. Concentrate, you can think about that tonight. After propping the envelope in front of her against the back of the phone-box, she dialled the number, sneezed, and made a face when she heard Chloé's voice.

'Oh hello, this is . . . (Awkward saying she was Madame Adrien Deume.) I was in the shop a little while ago. I'm ringing to say that . . . (She bent down to pick up the envelope which her sneeze had blown away, but failed.) On second thoughts, I'll pop in. (Out of the question to say that she was phoning from across the road.) I'll be with you in a quarter of an hour.'

She rang off quickly so she wouldn't hear the reply, and wandered through the narrow streets. When thirteen minutes were up, she turned on her heel, having made up her mind to be firm. Courage. In this life, success came to those who paid no attention to other people's opinions and rode roughshod over anything that stood in their way. Yes, be forthright, she told herself as the gold-braided porter pushed the door for her. But once inside the perfumed, mellowly lit salon, she was struck by the full enormity of both the things she was asking. So that they would not be held against her, and also to keep Volkmaar sweet, she began by saying that she would like another suit. He bowed before a customer who was clearly made of money.

'But before I decide anything about the extra suit,' she said, a warm flush creeping across her face, 'I'd like a small alteration to the gold-lamé dress. Yes, on reflection I think I'd rather not keep the plunging neckline. I'd prefer to have it come higher on the neck.'

'Round the neck,' said Volkmaar gloomily. 'Very well, dear lady, we shall make it round-necked. And what sort of material are we thinking of for our suit?'

'First I have something else to ask you. Unforeseen circumstances oblige me to bring forward the date of my departure, and I now have to leave on the Friday evening. (Volkmaar assumed an impassive expression.) I've just this moment heard. So I shall need everything I've ordered for the morning of Friday the twenty-fourth, noon at the latest, because I cannot possibly be expected to pack at the very last moment.'

'Ah?' was the only comment offered by Volkmaar, who was well accustomed to the time-worn gambit of the new date of departure.

'I realize it doesn't leave much time,' she said with a timid smile.

'Not much, Madame.'

'It was unavoidable, couldn't be helped.'

'Hardly any time at all,' said Volkmaar, sphinx-like and sadistic.

'I'd . . . (Say pay? Best not. Might offend him.) I'd be . . . happy to meet any extra charge you felt necessary to hurry things along.'

He pretended he had not heard, closed his eyes momentarily as though giving the matter his fullest attention, and began pacing round the shop while she looked on anxiously.

'It's a large undertaking, dear lady, but we shall manage it, even if we have to keep our workrooms open all night. Very well, everything will be finished for midday on Friday the twenty-fourth. As for the extra charge, perhaps you would have a word with Mademoiselle Chloé.'

She murmured that she was extremely grateful. Then, deliberately avoiding his eye and breathing with some difficulty, she recited: 'I'd like three fittings. The first on Friday of this week, and the other two on Tuesday and Wednesday of next week.'

While her breathing returned to normal, he assented with a bow, having made up his mind that this customer, whom he had marked down as easy meat, would be made to pay through the nose.

'And now Madame's suit,' he said. 'I have several pretty little numbers to show you. (He turned to a tragic, tubercular girl with huge eyelashes.) Josyane, bring down the Dormeuil that's just in, the Minnis twelve-thirteen and the shot cretonne by Gagnière.'

'There's really no need, I'm very taken with that flannel there on the table.'

'Excellent choice, dear lady. An exquisite cloth, and the charcoal grey is entrancing. And what style does Madame prefer? I could see Madame in a very short jacket, gathered at the waist, with a belt in the same material and high pockets. Or perhaps wide lapels and a scooped neckline to emphasize the bust? Chloé, would you ask Bettine to model the Caprice and Patricia the Androcles?'

'There's really no need,' she said, anxious to be gone and stop being a dear lady. 'Make the suit exactly like the other which is also flannel.'

'Very well, dear lady. Would you note that down, Chloé? A second Cambridge in the charcoal-grey Holland. First complete fitting on the afternoon of Friday the seventeenth. Madame shall have top priority. All other orders will be put back. Good-day, dear lady.'

Free at last and happy to breathe air which was not heavy with perfume, she decided she had earned a reward in the shape of several cups of tea. But just as she reached the teashop she knew in a sudden flash of intuition that the lamé dress would be horrid with a high neck. The idea of wanting to restyle a high-fashion dress like that, a garment which had after all been very carefully designed, was quite absurd. That beast Volkmaar ought never to have agreed to it. The round neckline was a stupid idea. A round neck! Round your neck. Noose round your neck, hang you by the neck until you're dead, dead, dead! Volkmaar was a beast. She kicked a pebble which was doing no one any harm. Once she had the dresses, she'd send Volkmaar an anonymous letter saying he had breasts like a woman.

'This time I'll phone.'

In the phone-box, she dialled the number after first propping the sacred telegram in front of her, to give her strength. But when she heard Chloé's voice she hung up and beat a hasty retreat. She halted abruptly when she had got as far as the tearoom. God! the telegram! She ran back and dashed into the glass-sided phone-box. It was still there! 'My love,' she said to it.

Be firm, yes, she would go, five uncomfortable minutes and it would be over and done with. I've been thinking. Leave the lamé dress as seen, that is with the deep neckline. Or should she say that she was cancelling it because it would be far too hot in summer. Yes, cancel, that would make her appear less undecided, more feet-on-the-ground.

At midnight, unable to sleep, she switched the light on and once more picked up the mirror. Terrific hair, oh yes. Light-brown, but with a wonderful golden sheen, like burnt hazel and gold. Fantastic nose too, marvellously attractive, though perhaps it was a teeny bit bigger than was usual. And the overall effect? She was beautiful. Even the swans had stared as she strolled by the lake after leaving Piglet's shop. But what was the good of being beautiful when he wasn't there?

'One: the white crêpe, which actually is extra to requirements since I've got something similar already, so that was a bad move. Two and three: the two heavenly rustic linen outfits. Four: the little light-grey flannel suit, absolutely tickety-boo, I'll feel wonderful in it. Five: the charcoal-grey flannel, stuck with it because I couldn't say no, it's absolutely ridiculous because it's a winter weight, let's hope there'll be some cold days. The kiss on that first night, the kiss on his hand, set the tone for our love. I am his slave, that's what I am. I make myself sick loving him the way I do, but it's divine. Next the dresses I ordered to get myself off the hook for cancelling the gold lamé. Six or seven: the black velvet, can't make my mind up about it, we'll see. Seven or eight: the sporty affair, twelve wooden buttons all the way down the front and back, not bad. Eight or nine: the linen one that laces up, I love it, it's a sort of fine sailcloth almost, it'll be grand swanning around like a galleon. All right, so I dropped a few clangers, but there's always some waste. So let's see, how many outfits is that? Eight or nine? No matter, we'll see how they turn out at the fittings. What absurd lengths to go to, just so he'll find me attractive. Mustn't ever let up, have to go on being attractive all the time, what a comedown. Tomorrow you absolutely must open Adrien's letters. Quarter past midnight. Hooray, that's one day gone, only another ten to go. Yes, the people chosen of God. Shall I convert? Anyway, I shall have to ask him to forgive me for those two words, I'll write and say sorry, I couldn't possibly tell him to his face. O my love, come now, she sighed, throwing the covers back. See, my love, I am yours, completely yours, and ready.'

CHAPTER 60

Next morning, she walked through the patrician portals of the house of Saladin, de Chapeaurouge & Co., bankers to the Aubles for more than two centuries. After exchanging a few friendly words with the aged porter she liked because he kept a tame raven which had a taste for *café au lait*, she made for a till manned by a counter-clerk who, observing her come in, had already checked the state of the account of this niece of an old and valued customer recently passed away.

'How much money may I withdraw?'

'Exactly four thousand francs, Madame. There's nothing more to go in until the first of October.'

'That's fine,' she said, and she displayed her teeth for his benefit. 'Funny, really, because as it happens I have an account to settle which comes to exactly four thousand francs.'

She signed the slip, collected the cash, asked after the raven, listened with a delighted smile as she was told all about it, and left, while the counter-clerk with the long ears straightened the comforting carnation in the buttonhole of his jacket. He wore a fresh one every day. It made him feel like a gentleman.

In the street, she reflected that it would be ridiculous to pay money on account since she already knew how much the final bill would come to. Eight thousand five hundred francs in all, Mademoiselle Chloé had said, including the extra charges. Might as well pay the whole lot straight off and then she could put it out of her mind. Yes, trot along to de Lulle's, where she surely had bigger holdings than with Saladin etc. & Co. She'd need to squeeze four thousand five hundred francs out of them. On second thoughts, best ask for a bit more, since there were lots of other things she'd need to buy, given that her lord would be coming back soon.

'At least fifteen thousand and be on the safe side.'

As she proceeded up the olde worlde street, she smiled as she recalled something Tantlérie had often said to Uncle Gri: 'Of course, Agrippa, I have the fullest confidence in de Lulle's. They are a very good family and have for generations been sound members of the Consistory. But I do not feel at ease in their bank, which is too modern, too grand. It even has a lift, tsk, really.' Dear Tantlérie, so undemonstrative when she was alive but so affectionate in her will. She remembered the words: 'With the exception of my villa at Champel, which I leave to my dear brother Agrippa, I bequeath the whole of my estate to my beloved niece, Ariane, née d'Auble, whom I commend to the protection of the Almighty.' Ariane, née d'Auble, that is what unbending Tantlérie had said: even in her will she could not bring herself to recognize her ill-advised marriage.

She halted outside the de Lulle bank, fished out the telegram she had received that morning, looked at it, but did not read what it said. Everything was now settled. He would take the train on the twenty-fifth just as she had asked him to. He would get in at seven twenty-two and would be with her at nine. Hallelujah! And between now and then they both had an appointment with the polestar every evening, also at nine. No, don't read the wire again now, don't extract the last drop of juice. Tonight, in bed, after the polestar-gazing, she'd read both of them again, the one she'd got yesterday and the one that had come this morning.

She frowned as she walked into the silent de Lulle building. Yes, tomorrow without fail, open and read all of Adrien's letters. Now that's out of the way, just enjoy being happy. She smiled at the cashier, another old acquaintance, a long, ascetic vegetarian with a Jesus beard, of whom Tantlérie had greatly approved because he believed the Bible was the inspired word of God. Having dealt with a lady customer with a face like an old pekinese with eczema, who waddled away with one hand tragically gripping the opening of her handbag, he straightened his clip-on tie in honour of the Auble inheritance and gave her a friendly, welcoming look.

'How much money is there in my account?'

'Unless I am very much mistaken, approximately six thousand francs, Madame,' said the salt-of-the-earth cashier, who knew the current state of the accounts of all his high-class customers like the back of his hand.

'I shall need more than that,' she said, and she smiled. (Why did Ariane smile so much in her two banks? Because she was comfortable in banks, which were very pleasant places, they made a person feel so at home. Bankers were very nice people, always ready to be of service and give you all the money you wanted. For Ariane, née d'Auble, money was the only kind of goods which could be obtained free of charge. All it took was a signature.)

The cashier looked at her unhappily over his glasses. In addition to being saddened, as he always was, when a client asked him for sums greater than were justified by her 'receipts', he was afraid that this eccentric niece was about to ask him to sell some of her shares. He loathed receiving instructions to sell, especially from young, inexperienced women customers. Though only a humble, modestly paid counter-clerk, a man of ingrained habits and many scruples, he felt a curious affection for the daughters of the well-to-do who had inherited money. He longed for them to prosper, and grew dispirited when he sensed that they were on the way down. A sort of underfed watchdog, resigned to his modest station in life, his joy was to stand guard over the wealth of the wealthy. So he asked his heiress, who, though of eminently respectable family, had little understanding of money matters, if she could not possibly wait until October, when large receipts were due. He adopted his most persuasive tone to beg to inform her that at that time her account would contain more than ten thousand francs.

'Oh, I need more than that,' she said with a smile. 'Besides, I can't wait.' (The mild-mannered cashier shrugged his shoulders wearily.)

'In that case, Madame must assign shares as collateral, or else authorize an instruction to sell. (The young woman did not like the word collateral. It sounded as though it might be something complicated, involving lawyers and wills, that sort of thing.)

'I'd prefer to sell,' she said, with a winning smile.

'How much does Madame wish to sell?'

To gain time, she asked how much her shares were worth in (she hesitated, for a true Auble never willingly allowed the graceless, sacred word to pass her lips) money. The cashier went away despondently and came back with the head of investment shares, a tanned and dynamic young man who greeted her somewhat less deferentially than usual.

'Approximately, what you have currently in your portfolio comes to, comes to, comes to. (He opened the file and perused it rapidly while she wondered what on earth was this portfolio which she'd never heard of. Bankers probably kept customers' stocks and shares in handsome, large, leather-bound portfolios. One of these days she must ask the nice cashier to show her.) Comes to, comes to something in the region of two hundred thousand francs.'

'I thought it was more,' she said timidly. 'Just a bit more.'

'The fact is, Madame, the estate of the late Mademoiselle d'Auble included a high proportion of French stocks, and even some Austrian and South American issues. (These last two adjectives were pronounced with considerable distaste.) Moreover, the Dow-Jones index has fallen dramatically these past few days.'

'Oh I see,' she said.

'So, two hundred thousand francs, in round figures. The markets are very unstable just now.'

'Quite,' she said.

'Do you wish to sell the whole lot?' (The cashier closed his eyes.)

'Oh no, I shouldn't want that.'

'Half?' asked the man of action. (This new generation, thought the cashier. No respect for anything.)

She thought for a moment. It would be an excellent idea if she could get her hands on a sufficiently large sum so that she wouldn't have to be forever waiting for those miraculous receipts they were always going on about. Especially since it would be September soon, and she'd have to start thinking about her winter wardrobe. And after that . . . But she did not follow her train of thought, which trickled into the sand.

'Half, Madame?' repeated the impatient young man.

'A quarter,' said the cautious young woman.

'In that case, we'll sell American Electric, Florida Power and Light,

Campbell's Soup and maybe Corn Products, there aren't many of those. Is that your wish, Madame? (His voice was martial, almost gleeful. The cashier moved away so as not to witness the slaughter.) We shall also sell Nestlé, Ciba, Eastman Kodak, Imperial Chemical and International Nickel! (His voice, in sacred ecstasy, rose in a hymn of victory.) Is that your wish, Madame?'

'Yes. Of course. Thank you. Tell me what I have to do.'

'Just sign the authorization to sell which I shall have drawn up. Do you stipulate a reserve or best price?'

'Which is better?'

'Now that all depends, Madame. According to whether you're in a hurry or not.' (She did not understand, but best price seemed more comforting.)

'I'd rather best price.'

'We shall also offload these South American bits and pieces and the Danube-Save-Adriatic. Is that your wish, Madame?'

Moments later, she had signed the authorization and was feeling a little cross with herself for making a mess of her signature. Without bothering to count the notes, which plunged the cashier ever deeper into gloom, she stuffed the ten thousand francs which had been advanced on account into her handbag and left. In the Rue de la Cité she moved off slowly with a smile on her face. At nine o'clock, a date with the polestar. They would be together at nine this evening.

CHAPTER 61

Two days later, at four in the afternoon in the teashop where she was treating herself to a reward for a protracted session with Volkmaar, she was struck, just as she took her first sip of tea, by an absolute certainty. The jackets of both the suits she had just tried on were too tight! Dear God, both flannel suits, and she had particularly set her heart on them! Abandoning tea and toast, she rose hastily, knocked her cup over, scattered five francs on the table, and set off hotfoot back to the torture chamber, where the two jackets, still only half-finished, were tried on again, taken off, put back on, compared with the version modelled, and discussed. The outcome of a rather muddled conference was the lame conclusion which dressmakers are always hearing.

'So, you will see to it that both jackets are neither too roomy nor too tight. (She pronounced the words as clearly as she could to be certain that her message was getting through. She was completely absorbed in the matter in hand, and invested these petty proceedings with great intensity and grimness of purpose, just as when she was a little girl she earnestly, with brows knit, built sandcastles on the beach.) Neither too roomy, then, nor too tight. Still, you could make them just a little bit roomy, though of course they mustn't be too roomy, I mean fairly close-fitting but not too tight, not cramped.'

'Ease and elegance combined,' said Volkmaar, who was immediately rewarded with a doting look.

'And as to length, we'll stick to what I said, two centimetres shorter than on the model. But I wonder if a centimetre and a half wouldn't be better. Yes, it would. Just a moment, I'll take a look, just to be absolutely sure.'

She slipped on the jacket which had been modelled, turned the hem up a centimetre and a half, shut her eyes to virginize her retina, opened them, and bore down on the triple mirror, smiling a little to look natural, to appear in the jacket as she would appear to him, in the life. After this, she took a few steps backwards then again advanced towards the mirror as naturally as could be, staring at her feet and imagining that she was out for a walk, and then suddenly glancing up, hoping for a blinding, incontrovertible revelation, the shock of truth, forcing herself to forget the fact that the hem of the jacket was turned up, making herself ignore the fuzzy edge of her temporary alteration and imagine that she was wearing a jacket which was 'the finished article'. She decided with the utmost impartiality that it looked well, very well.

'Shortening it by a centimetre and a half will be perfect,' she said. (Victorious, she filled her lungs with air, thoroughly convinced and satisfied. A centimetre and a half was an absolute, a figure decreed by God Himself.) 'So not two centimetres, is that clear? (Furrowed brow, head bent in thought, concentration, anxiety.) You don't think shortening it by one centimetre would perhaps be better? No, let's stick to one and a half.'

'Absolutely,' said Volkmaar with a bow, having made up his mind to make the jacket two centimetres longer. 'Good-day, Madame.'

She did not dare go back to the teashop, because of the cup she'd upset, and instead went into a café. When she had drunk her tea she sighed, for another worry had begun to gnaw at her. Piglet hadn't made a note of anything. He was bound to forget what had been decided. Horrible, unprincipled little man. She asked for something to write with and jotted down a summary of the alterations which had been decided. As a PS, she added: 'As agreed, the front edges of the two Cambridge jackets to be ever so slightly rounded. A sort of right angle with the corners just a little bit blunt. But I shall leave it to you if you think on the other hand that it might be better to make the corners perfectly round. In that case, please ignore the sketch below.'

★

But her note would get there too late if she sent it through the post. So bristle up your spirits and take it to the beast yourself. It wouldn't be much fun looking him in his little piggy eyes. But was she going to let herself be beaten? She put her best foot forward, swept through the doors, told Piglet she'd written a little note so that everything would be clear, held out her sheet of paper, and fled. Safely back in the street, she pulled a somewhat sheepish schoolgirl face to cover her shame, cast out her fear, and convince herself it was all over. She had done her duty. Now it was up to Piglet to get on with it. He had her note.

However, an hour later she was hunched over a table in the post office in the Rue du Stand, writing to Volkmaar instructing him not to shorten the two Cambridge jackets but to leave them exactly the same length as the version which had been modelled.

CHAPTER 62

'Thursday, 23 August, 9 p.m.

'From Ariane, to my Belovèd whom I love truly.

'Belovèd,

'There is no point to this letter because you won't read it until you're back in the Ritz where I shall deliver it myself in the morning. But I needed to be doing something for you, to be with you. Even so, perhaps it's not entirely pointless after all, because this way I shall in a sense be there at the Ritz the day after tomorrow to welcome you home. I would have loved to meet you at the station but I know you don't like being met.

'I'm writing to you in my kingdom, that is, a little summer-house at the bottom of the garden at the back of the house where the gardener employed by the previous tenants used to lurk. I've turned it into my Dreamy-House. No one else is allowed in. I'll show it to you, I do so hope you'll like it. There are holes in the floor, which is worm-eaten, the paint is flaking on the ceiling, and the paper is peeling off the walls. I feel completely at home here. There are spiders' webs everywhere you look, but I leave them alone because I like spiders and wouldn't have the heart to spoil their delicate creations. I've also got my lovely little desk here, the one I had when I was in school, and at this moment I'm using it to write to you. I don't know if desk is the right word, perhaps I should say table. It's a kind of combination of the two, sloping desk-top and seat with a back all in one, if you see what I mean.

'It was on this table affair that I used to do my homework with my sister Éliane. Two little girls in red slippers and identical little frocks. We giggled, played games, dressed up in the attic, quarrelled, got ever so cross, you're horrible, I shan't speak to you ever again, then we made up, you're not cross, Éliane? And that song I made up, when we were little girls maybe nine and ten, we used to put on dirgy voices and sing it as we walked along the road to school hand-in-hand on winter mornings. I think I told you about that song. "It's freezing hard the ice is on the pool And we two winkies are setting off for school."

'Facing the table is the cupboard I've made into a shrine for my sister. On the top shelf I put photographs of her, which I can't bear to look at now, and the books she loved. Among them is the volume of poems by Tagore which we used to read for all we were worth, little mystics of fourteen and fifteen that we were. In the cupboard, which I've just opened, is one of Éliane's dresses on a hanger, her best, which I've never had the heart to give away. Perhaps it still carries traces of the fragrance of her beautiful body which was stopped in full flight.

'Darling, last night I was reading a book and all of a sudden I realized I wasn't taking anything in but was thinking of you. Darling, I've had my little sitting-room and my bedroom redecorated. The men will be putting the final coat on tomorrow. I don't care if saying it makes me sound cheap, but I had it repainted for you. Also for you: a Persian carpet, a large Shiraz, I do hope you'll like it. The colours are green, pink and gold, all gloriously delicate and washed-out.

'Darling, I'm in a complete tizz about the new clothes I ordered. I don't know if you'll like the ones which have turned out all right, because I know now that some of them haven't, but I didn't dare say anything to the man who runs the shop and just pretended I was satisfied. They need so many alterations that they won't be ready until Saturday, the day you get back. I'm trusting to Providence! Listen, darling, you must underline *must* tell me which dresses you don't like, don't hold anything back, then I'll know not to wear them, at least not when I'm seeing you. Thanks in advance.

'Darling, I've a pain in my ankle because I went over on my foot the other day running to rescue your telegram, which I'd unforgivably left in a phone-box. But I wouldn't want you to think I've become some sort of cripple. So let me make it quite clear that my ankle is not swollen and I'm not limping. It'll be a thing of the past by the day after tomorrow and I shall have a perfectly normal ankle.

'I realize I should try to be more feminine and not be forever saying how much I want to please you, not be forever telling you how much I love you. In fact I ought really to have sent you just a very brief wire, along the lines of OK for 25 August, as basic as that, or better still Not OK for 25 August. If I was a real woman, I wouldn't be sending this letter to you who never find time to write to me. But I'm not a real woman, I'm just a little girl who is no good at feminine wiles, your little girl who loves you. You see, I could never send you a telegram saying I haven't got time to write.

'And now I shall tell you what I did yesterday and what I've done today. Wednesday afternoon, after my session at the dress-shop, I went over to Jussy to see some very nice people I've known for ages who have a farm there. I wanted to say hello but also to ask them to let me lead their cow to pasture, Brunette she's called, and I've known her since I was a little girl. They said I could and I got myself a great big stick, that's the way it's done. Giddy-up, Brunette! Then after, just as I was bending down to pick a few gorgeous mushrooms, I heard myself muttering, unconsciously, quite mechanically: "Oh my love." Brunette and I stayed out until seven o'clock.

'I got back here at eight. At five to nine I scooted out into the garden to look at the polestar. I hope you were watching. I had a feeling you were. Then I went for a walk in my forest. Got back quite late. Went to bed and reread your telegrams, but not over and over, so they wouldn't lose their freshness. Then I looked at a photograph of you, in segments, but did not let myself linger. I go easy on your photograph too, save it up, so it doesn't wear out. I put it under my pillow, to have it there while I was sleeping. But I was afraid it might get bent. So I took it out again and propped it up on my bedside table where it would be the first thing I saw when I woke up. By half past eleven I was feeling sleepy, but I kept my eyes open until midnight so it would be Friday and there'd only be one more day of waiting for you.

'And now for what I did today. This morning, after bathing in water, I stayed bathing in the sun for ages in the garden, just by the wall, thinking about you because I wasn't wearing very much. Lying there, it was as if my body, which in the sun was as hot, as heavy, as dense, as hard as the wall, could no longer tell, as it felt the touch of the wind's fingers all over, in a wisp of hair or a quiver of thigh, where it ended and the wall began. That last sentence is a bit flowery, I realize that. Just an attempt, and a pretty feeble one at that, to please you. Poor Ariane, what a comedown. Next I went out and walked round town aimlessly. Stopped outside the window of a gunsmith's, my eye drawn by a pile of Spratts. I had this terrible urge to go in and buy dog-biscuits, I had this craving for them when I was little, they must be scrumptiously hard. But I resisted the temptation, because a person who happens to be the one you love does not go round nibbling dog-biscuits. So just a little bit further along I bought some liquorice laces. So I could eat them unobserved, I went behind an arch of the Pont de la Machine. They tasted awful, and I chucked the whole lot into the Rhône. As I was crossing the Quai Besançon-Hugues, I almost got knocked down by a car. The driver shouted at me and said I was a moron. I told him I didn't believe him.

'What else did I do? Oh yes, the pen-and-paper cat (I mean the one in the stationer's) whose acquaintance I made the other day. I went back to see him, because he's a pet and ever so well-behaved. I thought he'd looked a bit down in the mouth that day, so I took him a packet of fortified granules made of liver and dried fish. He seemed to like them. After that, I went and stared at your hotel and the windows of your suite. And then I had this itch to have lunch in your hotel restaurant. I nearly fell as I went in, because I tripped over the carpet. The food was very good, and I ordered two puddings. All through the meal, a rather handsome man stared at me the whole time or very nearly!

'Darling, I stopped writing briefly to draw you a picture of Ursa Major and Ursa Minor on the attached sheet. The red dot is the polestar. Keep it. You'll be able to take it with you when you go away on other official visits. As I left the restaurant, I stopped at the reception desk of the hotel and asked if I could look at one of their suites, supposedly so I could tell this girlfriend of mine who was due to arrive in Geneva any day now what they were like. Just as I thought, they said they didn't have any suites vacant at that moment.

So rather cunningly I asked if I mightn't take a peek at a suite occupied by a guest who was away, hoping they'd show me yours. Alas, they said no. So my cunning plan didn't work. After that I thought I might like to go to the pictures, but the cinema was showing one of those soppy, romantic films. The leading man is never half as handsome as you, and it makes me cross to see the heroine turning all soppy over him. Besides, they go in for far too much kissing, and I find that very irritating. Instead I took a taxi and had myself driven to the Palais des Nations. I stayed watching the windows of your office. Then I went to the park to see our bench. But the most nauseating couple were occupying it, kissing for all the world to see. I beat a hasty retreat.

'From there I went and mooched glumly through the streets, feeling more alone without you than ever, handbag swinging, down in the dumps. Bought a book of beauty hints and another about international politics so I shouldn't be an absolute duffer. Then I got a tram to Annemasse, which is a little town in France a stone's throw from Geneva, but of course you know that. I left both books on the tram! Now I'll tell you why I went to Annemasse! I went there to buy a ring! I never fancied wearing one before, but now I want to. I liked the idea of buying it in France, it was more secret, more of a private thing just between us two. Darling, I told the jeweller at Annemasse that the date of my wedding was fixed for the twenty-fifth of August!

'While I'm on the subject of Annemasse, a childhood memory comes back to me. Oh sorry, I already told you about it one evening. But I've remembered something else, this time from when I was an adolescent. When I was fifteen or sixteen, I used to look up naughty words in the dictionary, such as embrace, loins, passion and others I can't mention. I don't need to do that any more.

'I'll carry on saying what I've been doing today. When I got back to Geneva, ring on finger, I bought you an absolutely gorgeous dressing-gown, the biggest size they had, and said I'd take it with me, because I wanted to spread it out on my bed. Next I bought twelve Mozart records, which I also refused to have delivered though they weighed a ton. After that I went and got weighed in a chemist's. Appalled by how much weight I'd put on. Had I got fat without noticing? Then I realized it was because I was still holding both sets of records, which were terribly heavy. Walked out of the chemist's humming: "Oh my love, I'm yours for ever." Aren't I silly?

'Got back to Cologny at half past five. Removed ring to avoid questions, for Mariette knows jolly well I never wear one. Had a go at Hegel, doing my best to understand. Then as a reward allowed myself a shameful peep at a woman's magazine: looked through the agony column then studied my horoscope to find out what's in store for me this week, though naturally I didn't believe a word of it. After that I tried to draw your face. The result was grisly. Then I looked you up in the *International Organizations Year-Book*. Then I cut your face out of one of several photographs I have of you and stuck it on a postcard of the Apollo Belvedere, over the head. Ghastly. Then I wondered if there was anything I could do for you, like knit something. No, too too tasteless.

'I went downstairs to see how they were getting on with decorating my little sitting-room. Mariette was there, and I had to put up with her in one of her medical moods. She launched with gusto into a recital of various ailments which had laid assorted nieces and cousins low. Going on and on about illness is her idea of fun, her dismal way of having a good time. I tried to stop her by saying it was better not to dwell on such depressing matters. Her eyes glazed over, she got quite carried away, and she didn't even hear what I said but just went on and on describing various operations, dragging out all the family insides for my benefit.

'Darling, a few days ago my uncle turned up in Geneva, just got back from Africa, where he's been working as a medical missionary. I'll tell you why he's come and why he's gone straight back into practice when I see you, so as not to make this letter longer than it need be. I'll describe him to you in telegrammese to hurry things along.

'I've changed places. I'm lying face down on the floor to write, it's ever so cosy. Right, I'll make a start. Agrippa Pyrame d'Auble. I've always called him Uncle Gri ever since I was a little girl. Aged sixty. Tall, thin, close-cropped white hair, drooping moustache, innocent blue eyes, monocle because he's short-sighted in one eye. When embarrassed, keeps screwing monocle in and out while Adam's apple bobs up and down. Looks like Don Quixote. Ancient green-tinged black suit. Detachable wing-collar and starched tubular oversleeves. Badly knotted white tie. Big boots with hobnails so they won't need resoling, which does away with a complication, he says. But he isn't the least bit miserly. On the contrary. But he has few needs and never bothers to look after himself. In spite of said threadbare suit and hobnails, looks terribly distinguished. The day after he got back, I managed – and it wasn't easy – to get him to buy himself a new suit. Wouldn't hear of anything made to measure, being loyal to an old shop, called The Prodigal Son, where they sell off-the-peg clothes. I took him there like a lamb to slaughter. Has few material needs, though he lives in a grand house. The contradiction is only superficial. As last male survivor of the Aubles, he believes he has a duty to his name to live in surroundings worthy of his forebears. It's a small failing. But what saint is without blot?

'I forgot to say that he has the Legion of Honour and other medals too. But for all his decorations, none of which he ever asked for, he is very shy, especially with bumptious people. It's fascinating to watch him hold out his hand when he's being introduced to someone. Elbow tucked well into his sides, he holds it out gingerly as though the other person is about to stick it into a vat of boiling oil. He often makes me think of a little boy lost, yet, though he has nothing of the grand manner and self-confidence of the eminent doctor, that is precisely what he is, and very highly regarded by his colleagues. He discovered something terribly important called the d'Auble syndrome. The Academy of Medicine in Paris elected him a corresponding member, which is supposed to be a great honour for a foreign doctor. The minute news got out that he was back in Geneva, the *Journal de Genève* published a very flattering article about him.

'I'm sitting down at the table again, because writing lying down was giving me a pain in the back of my neck. Darling, I do miss you so. Darling, we will go away together, won't we? I want to see the countries I love with you. We'll go to England, for instance, see the country around Norwich. You'll love it there, the plain stretching away endlessly, the wide sweep of the horizon, the great wind blowing, woods with avenues like cathedral naves, hills softened by bracken, and, far off, the sea. We'll roam through the deepest parts of the woods, we'll walk softly on thick moss, and pheasants will cross our path and squirrels will jump out of the trees. And then we'll stand on the cliff edge and look out to sea with the wind in our faces and we'll hold each other by the hand.

'But getting back to my uncle. I also omitted to mention that he is a past President of the Calvinist Consistory and a past Vice-President of the National Democratic Party, which is the party which decent people belong to. He is deeply religious, and I respect his faith because it is true and noble. It's the very opposite of Old Ma Deume's bigotry. Now I'll explain why he went to Africa. Some years ago, when he learned that there was a shortage of medical missionaries in the Zambezi, he decided to go out and offer his services free of charge to the evangelical missions there. At his age and though not a well man, he gave up a thriving medical career to care for the blacks and bring them what he calls, in his sweet phraseology, the Good News.

'If I dared tell my uncle that I know you and see you often, I'm sure he'd never guess there was anything untoward going on between us. With a kindly twinkle in those smiling blue eyes of his which see no evil, he'd say he was happy for my sake that I'm "such good pals" with a man. And that's why I'll never be able to bring myself to tell him about you. It isn't that he's slow on the uptake, the very opposite. The simple fact is that he's an angel. He's so honest himself that it would never cross his mind that I might be capable of hiding the truth from him. He's a real Christian, a kind of saint, so full of goodwill to all men, always ready to love and understand and see things from the other person's point of view, having eradicated all love of self and always putting others first. And so generous. Of the money he charges his rich patients – and he only sends bills to the rich ones, that is, when he remembers to send out bills at all – he just keeps the bare minimum necessary to maintain his modest style of living. All the rest goes to the poor and to charitable causes.

'When I was little, every time he came to Champel to see my aunt he used somehow to sneak a pile of chocolate money into the drawer of my table, which was delicious, especially in winter, when I used to put it out on a radiator to get soft. Last night he paid me a visit here at Cologny. Well, after he'd gone, I happened to open a drawer and found a pile of the same chocolate money in it!

'Darling, I suddenly have this memory of hot sunny afternoons in my aunt's garden loud with insects buzzing. Lying on the terrace, a skinny little thing of twelve, I was staring at the hot air, which shimmered. The cat was padding warily through the grass, and it was then that the miracle began. The terrace, which was paved with small slabs, turned into a deserted plain strewn with fearsome rocks like giants who'd had a spell cast on them and been turned to stone, while beyond the grass was the jungle and out of it, with fearsome stealth, emerged a little-girl-eating tiger. Then the scene would change and become a world heaving with little people. From under the eaves, spice-laden caravels set sail for overpopulated cities near the *chaise longue*; and dozens of pretty little horses, no bigger than your thumb but perfectly formed, galloped round and round the watering-can.

'Another memory comes back from when I was fourteen and my uncle had come for the holidays to Champel, to the house he now lives in, my aunt left it to him in her will. One night I couldn't sleep and, feeling hungry, I went to his bedroom to wake him up so he could keep me company, and we both went ever so quietly downstairs to the kitchen, he in his dressing-gown and me in pyjamas, for a secret midnight beano, and we talked in whispers because we were afraid of what Tantlérie would say. It was wonderful. But I dropped a plate and it made a fearful racket. We were both petrified at the thought of being found out by my aunt. I was terrified and dug my fingernails into my cheeks, while Uncle Gri automatically switched off the light, though that wouldn't have done us any good at all if Tantlérie had woken up. I can see us now picking up bits of broken plate, which he took back to his room and hid in his case.

'And now I must tell you about his car. It was born in 1912, does about ten miles to the gallon, make unknown, presumably because the manufacturer never dared admit responsibility or else killed himself in a fit of guilt after letting it see the light of day. It's a frightening creature and has all sorts of ways of its own. Sometimes it sort of jogs on the spot then staggers off down the road and then stops and starts jogging up and down again. He won't get rid of it and buy a new one. It's a matter of filial respect, because his juggernaut was given to him by his father when the century was young, at the time he was first starting up in practice. "I know she's on the temperamental side," he told me, "but I know how to handle her, and anyway I'm used to her."

'And now Euphrosine. She worked as Aunt's cook and wouldn't hear a word said against her. When his sister died, my uncle thought he was in duty bound to go on employing Euphrosine. When he decided to go to Africa, she went to live with some nephews of hers and my uncle arranged for an allowance to be paid her. Last Saturday he made the mistake of going along and asking how she was. She begged him to take her back into service, moaning about her nephews, who, she said, treated her shamefully. Feeling sorry for her, he agreed and presented me with a *fait accompli*. So Euphrosine turns up at the house at Champel next morning. Very bad move. The old witch is over seventy, and age has withered her faculties. Anyway, she didn't last. Two days after she arrived at the Champel house, she announced that she was exhausted and took to her bed. So, since the day before yesterday, she's been having a fine old time of it, staying in bed all day, and poor Uncle Gri has been fetching and carrying for her. Yesterday I engaged a daily until we can get a proper maid.

'Just one more thing and then I'll stop. For years my uncle has been working on three manuscripts. A book called *Things and People of Old Geneva*, a translation of *The Aeneid* and a biography of Calvin. The last mentioned is rather dull. When he reads pages out to me, I open my eyes very wide, lost in wonder, and he's happy.

'One other thing about him. Now and then he comes out with a sentence in English, especially if he's ill at ease, because he seems to think he can hide behind English. But he does it not just out of a feeling of awkwardness but also because he loves England. Saying a few words in English gives him confidence, reminds him that the country he reveres exists. The Aubles have always been great Anglo-philes. For instance, it was a family tradition to pack its young off to England or better still Scotland, where the religious atmosphere is more fervid. They'd stay a year or two and then come back, some-times betrothed to a young Honourable but invariably mad about England and the greenness of its lawns. These Anglophile leanings are shared by the whole Calvinist establishment in Geneva, which has more in common with the United Kingdom than with the rest of the

Swiss cantons. Anyway, my uncle never says he's Swiss but Genevan. So now you know him. Please try and like him.

'I thought about you a long time this morning when I woke up, lying there in bed, too long perhaps. I hope you won't understand what that means. But afterwards I just thought about your eyes. Sometimes they have a far-away look, and I love that. Or else they can seem full of childish delight, and I love that too. Or else icy and hard, which is awful but I also love that. Tomorrow I'll get a train timetable so I can follow your progress on Saturday. Aha, he's at Dijon now, now he's at Bourg, now he's got to Bellegarde, yummy! Darling, please do take care of yourself, *n'est-ce pas*? Don't smoke too much, please. Not more than twenty a day! Darling, I'll close now because it's ten to nine. I'm going out into the garden loving you.

'Here we are, back again. I stayed watching the polestar from nine minutes to nine until ten past, tilting my head back till it hurt, fighting off dizziness and not taking my eyes off the distant, twinkling light which is our rendezvous in the sky, trying to see your face looking back at me. If I went out at ten to nine and stayed watching it for twenty minutes, it was to be on the safe side because your watch might be fast or slow and I didn't want to run the risk of missing you. Actually it was just as well I did, because it wasn't until four minutes past that I felt your presence and our eyes met up there. Thank you, my darling. But put your watch right, please, it's four minutes slow.

'The pretty little blue beads I've just sewn in the shape of a corolla are supposed to be a myosotis, and I shouldn't need to remind you that the myosotis is more usually called the forget-me-not. It wasn't easy to sew them on without tearing the paper, even though I used a very fine needle. It's strange: a few weeks ago I didn't know you, and now, just because our lips met one night, you are the only person alive, the only one who matters. It's a mystery.

'Yesterday evening I sat in front of the mirror for ages trying to get an idea of how I would look to you the day after tomorrow. I have such a lot to do the day after tomorrow. I shall have to get up good and early.

'I'm back with you. I just went over to the window for a moment to listen to the silence of the night in the garden now pricked by glow-worms. In the distance, in the aristocratic part of Cologny, an amorous cat was wowling – in vain, because its owners, the Chapeau-rouges, won't let it plight its troth before the return of a tom named Sarasin, who is very clean and very well cared for and absolutely reliable in every way but who, unfortunately, is currently away on matrimonial duty at the residence of another lady cat, named d'Aubigné.

'I realize that everything I've written is intended to make me out to be intelligent and charming, to please you, kind sir. Poor, pathetic me, I feel so sorry for myself. But it doesn't matter, doesn't matter at all, as long as you love me. But you must feel sorry for me too, for I am utterly at your mercy. I write to you too much, I love you too much, I tell you I do too often. And more than all the rest is the tenderness I feel, darling, when you're asleep and you snuggle up close to me, so off your guard and trusting. Then inside of me I tell you *moy dorogoy, moy zolotoy*. O my love, if only you knew how completely you are my love! When I was at my wits' end because I had no news of you, I gave myself a deadline and when it was up I was going to kill myself with two tubes of barbiturates and slit wrists in the bath.

'Yours.

'My very dearest darling, I've just reread this letter. If I've gone on for so long about my uncle, it was because I've already told you a lot of beastly things about Ma Deume. Now I want you to understand, by comparing her with my uncle, that she is the exact opposite of a Christian, a caricature of the real thing. Your true Christian is my uncle, who is all kindness, all purity, all selflessness, all generosity. And if I talked a lot about him, it was also because I wanted you to like him and, in the person of this great Christian and great Genevan, to like and respect Genevan Protestantism, which is a most estimable moral commonwealth whose virtues he embodies so well. Yes, he is a kind of saint. Rather as I think your uncle must be.

'Last night, before going to bed, I put on my secret wedding ring. After turning out the lights, I stroked it, turned it round on my finger so I could feel it there, and went off to sleep so happy, my own darling's wife. The four Russian words I used earlier mean my precious, my treasure. Darling, I wrote Belovèd at the start of my letter on purpose. I think it looks much better with an è.'

CHAPTER 63

Maroon, with savaged mudguards and standing oddly tall on woebe-gone wheels, she threw a tantrum in the Avenue de Champel, jogged up and down, then weaved away erratically, leaving a snaking trail of black oil in her wake. One moment consumed by fury and the next pensive and musing, but with bonnet permanently festooned with belching vapours which spurted like sea water from the blow-hole of a whale, she turned at length into the Chemin de Miremont, where her master strove manfully to coax her to a halt. After backfiring three times and discharging an angry squawk, she yielded, though not without exacting a terrible revenge in the form of a final squirt of oil which spattered a pleasant-natured little bulldog as it went about its lawful occasions.

Tall and gaunt, with shoulders stooping and moustache drooping, Ariane's uncle extricated himself from the clutches of the beast still snorting with hate, extinguished both oil-burning headlamps, gave the bonnet an amiable pat, doffed his Cronstadt to the neighbours' maid, and pushed the front door open.

In the hall, which was a litter of books, he smoothed down the drooping ends of his moustache and scratched his close-cropped dome. Hm, yes, he was awfully late. What would she say? He climbed the stairs, knocked gently on a door on the landing, and went in. Euphrosine opened one eye, poked her hairy chin over the bedclothes, and grumbled that it was a fine thing to be kept waiting for her supper until all hours like this. Inserting his monocle then removing it immediately, he said he was sorry but he'd had to stay with his last patient, who was seriously ill.

541

'I'm ill an' all,' the old girl muttered, and she yanked the bedclothes over her sprouting chin. 'I gotter have a cheese omelette, with four eggs in, that's wot I gotter have. Oh yus!'

When he returned with the tray, she spurned the omelette and said she wanted another one that was more runnier. For the first time, he stood his ground, pointed out calmly that the omelette was perfectly edible, and said she wasn't going to get another one. She tried to make herself cry, but, observing that this got her nowhere, craned her head towards the plate and proceeded to stuff its contents into her mouth, pausing occasionally to cast a sly, leering look in his direction.

When she'd finished her dessert, he tucked her in again, patted her pillows, and, carrying the tray, went off to the kitchen, where he dined on a boiled egg and an orange and was interrupted three times by the ringing of Euphrosine's bell. On the first occasion it was on account of crumbs in the bed – which in her gaga-speak she called 'pricky-prickies'. On the second it was to demand her herbal tea – which she drank out of the spout of the teapot. And finally because she wanted her face wiped with a flannel damped with eau-de-Cologne. After which she snuggled up to the wall and pretended to go to sleep.

At two in the morning, the ringing of the telephone startled him into wakefulness. Holding the receiver to his ear, he smiled at Madame Dardier, who apologized for disturbing him but her baby had been crying for more than an hour and, what with all this talk of diphtheria, didn't he think? She was really very sorry to disturb him at such an inconvenient time. Not at all, he said reassuringly, he was glad of the chance to get out of the house, it was such a pleasant night.

'*Et vera incessu patuit dea,*' he muttered as he hung up.

Quite wonderful, the passage where Aeneas recognizes his mother, Venus, who has appeared in the guise of a young huntress. Wonderful, but very tricky to translate. In flowing nightshirt, he sat motionless for a while trying to find a rendering worthy of the original. Suddenly remembering the screams of baby Dardier, he dressed hurriedly, carefully smoothed down the ends of his long moustache,

542

and went out. Standing by his car while the bells of St Peter's chimed a thin snatch from *The Village Soothsayer*, he shook his head and thought of the delightful Dardiers. A fine family, large and very close-knit. Relative newcomers to Geneva, of course, but very well-connected. Pity no Dardier had sat on the Little Council under the old regime. It would have completed the family's moral credentials very nicely.

After lighting the lamps, he poked the starting-handle into the front of the car and heaved on it, using both hands. Upon a whim, having decided for once to act normally, the capricious old rattletrap roared into life first time. Whereupon her owner climbed up into the lofty driving-seat, seized the wheel, and the monster, already spewing fumes through divers orifices, but not before executing a preliminary solo featuring castanets, bounded forward with a noise like elephants. Proud of his prompt start and feeling that among drivers he was an old and steady hand, Agrippa d'Auble gave the bulb of the ancient hooter a triumphant squeeze.

'Now let's see. *Et vera incessu patuit dea.*'

All at once the vehicle mounted the pavement, for the solution had just come to him. Yes, simply say: 'By her progress was she revealed a true goddess.' Perfect. It was elegant and caught the succinctness of the original. Wait a jiffy, no, not perfect after all. The 'true' was heavy. Perhaps he should suppress 'true' and say 'revealed a goddess'? Yes, but *vera* was in the text. Say that by her progress was she truly revealed? He declaimed this new version aloud to get the full effect. No, the adverb was leaden. How about 'By her progress was she revealed a veritable goddess'? No, that sounded lame, and come to think of it 'progress' was clumsy. Why not just say 'gait' and have done with it?

In her progress (or gait), the bucking motor ran the goddesses of antiquity a very poor second in the gracefulness stakes, and weaved along the Rue Bellot driven by chance, for the Latinist's mind was on perfection. Then all at once it abandoned its wayward slaloms and steamed dead ahead, for he had found the answer.

'And her gait revealed her to be a goddess!' he announced loudly, and he beamed with innocent pleasure.

That was it! Ignore the *vera*! You had to know when to be

unfaithful! 'True' tacked on to 'goddess' served no purpose, since goddesses are always true, that is from the pagan standpoint, of course. The fact was that Virgil had only inserted *vera* for reasons of metre. *Vera* was a padding-out word and was useless in a translation, no it was worse, it was positively detrimental.

'And her gait revealed her to be a goddess!' said the kindly doctor, rolling the words around his tongue.

While he pressed the Dardiers' doorbell, he smiled at the goddess of the graceful gait. He never suspected for a moment that he was in love with the young bare-kneed huntress who had appeared to Aeneas, and that his painstaking translation was a way of paying respectful court.

On his return to Champel, he felt too exhausted to hang his clothes up, and threw them over the back of a chair. Getting into his nightshirt, which was trimmed with red embroidery, he slipped between the sheets and gave a contented sigh. After all, it was only three in the morning. He had four solid hours of sleep before him.

'For Thine is the kingdom, the power and the glory, for ever and ever,' he murmured. Then he closed his eyes and drifted off to sleep.

Toing and froing in the large drawing-room at Onex, her apple-pie bonnet sheltering beneath her open parasol, his sister Valérie repeated that someone was ringing the doorbell and told him to go and see who it was. He rubbed his eyes, realized that she was mistaken, that it was the phone. What time was it? Four o'clock. He picked up the receiver and recognized the rich, golden voice at once.

'Uncle Gri, I can't sleep. Look, would you be an angel and come round to keep me company?'

'You want me to come out to Cologny at this time of night?'

'Yes, please, I do so need to see you. But I don't want you to come in your car, it's bound to conk out and I'd worry. I'll phone and they'll send a taxi to pick you up. We'll have a nice long talk.'

'Yes, we'll talk,' he said, closing his eyes to snatch a little more sleep.

'And I'll get back under the covers and you'll sit by my bed, won't you?'

'Certainly,' he said, and he sat back against his pillow.

'And you can read a book while you hold my hand, and that'll send me off to bye-byes. But you'll have to take your hand away very quietly, bit by bit, so as not to wake me up.'

'Very well, dear girl, bit by bit. I'll go and get dressed now.'

'Listen, Uncle Gri, I'm terribly happy because I've got a friend, a girlfriend, I like very much, she's due to come the night after tomorrow, she's tremendously clever, you wouldn't believe how clever, and such a noble mind.'

'I see,' he said, completing a yawn which he disguised as best he could. 'And is she a Protestant?'

'No, not a Protestant.'

'Catholic?'

'Jewish.'

'Oh, I see, capital, capital. They're God's chosen people, you know.'

'That's right, Uncle Gri, God's chosen people, I'm sure they are! Listen, we'll have breakfast together, nice and cosy, and I'll tell you all about my friend. Her name is Solal.'

'Capital, capital. I know a Solal in Paris. First-rate cardiologist.'

'Tell me, Uncle Gri, how far have you got with your Calvin book?'

'I've finished chapter twenty,' he said, suddenly springing to life. 'It's all about Idelette de Bure, an excellent widow with several children, whom Calvin married in 1541, using Bucer from Strasburg as go-between, after rejecting the candidate suggested by Farel as unsuitable. On the other hand, Idelette won his heart by dint of her modesty and sweet nature. The rather touching thing is that he was the best of fathers to the children she had had by her first marriage. Alas, her daughter Judith, who married in 1554, committed adultery in 1557 or 1558. Hardly thinkable is it, the Reformer's own stepdaughter an adulteress!'

'Yes, it's awful!'

'It grieved him no end.'

'Yes, it's awfully sad, it really is. But anyway, best foot forward, I'm going to ring for the taxi.'

'I'll get a move on then,' he said, and he got out of bed, a tall figure in his long nightshirt.

Twenty minutes later, wearing the new suit he'd got from The Prodigal Son and a panama hat secured by a cord attached to the top button of his waistcoat, he was smiling blithely in the taxi, raring to go, feeling bright as a new pin and sniffing the coolest-before-dawn air. Already the blackbirds were singing their joyful little song to a world in which it was a pleasure to be alive.

He crossed his legs, smiled at the thought of Ariane, who looked like the goddess who had appeared before Aeneas, the huntress with the bare knees. How delightfully enthusiastic she had been when she'd told him about this Solal girl, who was in all likelihood a relative of the cardiologist and therefore of good stock. Darling Ariane, so pretty, the image of her grandmother about the time of her marriage. What a pity he had not thought to bring the latest pages of his manuscript. The sweet girl had shown such interest. The other evening she'd been most taken with the chapter on the doctrine of predestination, he'd noticed that most particularly. And, just now, her indignant reaction when she'd heard that Calvin's stepdaughter was an adulteress was genuinely heartfelt. She was truly dear Frédéric's daughter. 'No doubt about it,' he said, nodding his head. Well, in the absence of his manuscript, he would read her chapter thirteen of the first epistle to the Corinthians, so wonderful and so affecting, and afterwards they'd discuss it together. He looked up at the sky and smiled, certain of one sublime truth. Dear old Agrippa, good and gentle Christian, I loved you and you never suspected. Dear Geneva of my youth and long-dead joys, proud republic and noble city. Dear Switzerland, land of peace and gentle living, upright hearts and tranquil minds.

CHAPTER 64

'Here's your coffee, though I don't s'pose you taste coffee like this every day of the week, and get these croissants ate up while they're still warm from the oven, but look lively now, shift yourselves, and mind you don't go getting no splashes on my wallpaper, silk it is, cost the earth, so don't you go ruining it.'

She stood there, her podgy hands folded across her stomach, leering at the two deckyrators, who were young and a sight for sore eyes, as they tucked in with a will. Good lads as painters went, they'd even brought along a couple of buffing-pads so as they could put the shine back in the parky floor when they was done with their daubing. As they went back to work, she sat down on a stool and started shelling peas, keeping an eye on every stroke of their brushes, sensuously luxuriating, and feeling ever so pleased for Madame Ariane, who'd be over the moon when she saw her little sitting-room all gleaming, like one of them bijou places, you might say.

Towards the end of the morning, a delivery van brought a parcel and she guessed what was inside. She attacked the string with gusto, eager to bask in reflected glory. She took a handsome dressing-gown out of the box and held it against herself.

'Pure silk. Top quality. I bet your girlfriends can't afford anything as smart as this! When you got money you can do anything! Oh, and there's something else, I was forgetting. Seeing as how you've finished your painting you can come with me, I got something to show you. (In the dining-room, where the Shiraz intended for the little sitting-room had been put for safe keeping, she parked one hand on her hip

547

and launched into a commentary.) It's what they call a Sheerage, that's its name, it comes from somewhere down Algeria way, just look how fine it's wove, all hand-made, them coons certainly know what they're doing, you gotter hand it to 'em. Now if it was me I'd've kept the small one where it was before, it belonged to Mademoiselle Valérie, most likely it was a Sheerage too, but it's her business, if you pay the piper you can call the tune, like Monsieur Pasteur used to say, he's the one who invented the rabies, like wot dogs get, because the family's not short of the ready, they're real nobs, oh is it twelve already, must start thinking about something to eat for me, no need to bother about Madame Ariane, she's gone over to see her uncle, he's a doctor, got my nosebag ready last night, the peas is for tonight.'

The pleasure of her company having, as she had hoped, been requested, she thought it was ever so nice, as she chatted away and was heard with respectful attention, to be sharing the deckyrators' dinner with them: sausage and tinned tuna. Say what you liked, she was very fond of this sort of thing, company, conversation, a sort of picnic really, it reminded her of her young days. To be polite but also to show willing, she cheered the meal up with a leg of mutton, a *ratatouille niçoise* and a strawberry flan, all of which she'd prepared the night before with precisely this in mind. From under her apron, where she had hidden it, she even produced a bottle of the Châteauneuf-du-Pape which was Adrien Deume's pride and joy.

When they'd had coffee, Mariette and her two volunteers applied polish to the floor and then three buffing-pads sprang into action. Excited by the in-out in-out of their implements and with the sense of communal endeavour rather going to her head, she began humming a song from her youth, whereupon the chorus was taken up, all together and in time to the rhythm of the pads, by all three, their feelings quite running away with them:

> Star of love and love's sweet light,
> Star of joy and sweet caresses,
> See how lovers and their lasses
> Spoon by day and swoon by night.

But the singing stopped abruptly when the door opened and Ariane appeared. On her face was stamped all the propriety of the ruling class, while the proletariat stood before her, motionless and shamefaced. At this time of day she, who as Solal's horizontal naked slave was ready in the shadow-filled night to do anything in the service of love without protest, reverted to the vertical, social persona of a dignified Auble, cool in manner and imposing.

When the furniture had been put back in place, gratuities had been distributed and the decorators – accompanied by Mariette who had insisted on sending them on their way – had gone, Ariane gazed gloatingly round her little sitting-room. The furniture was set off magnificently by the white of the woodwork. The long swing-mirror, which the decorators had brought down from upstairs, looked extremely well here, and it was in exactly the right spot, opposite the sofa. Both she and he would feel closer now, because they'd be able to watch each other in the mirror. And the Shiraz was wonderful. He'd love the subtle harmonies and delicate shades, the washed-out greens and pinks.

She took a long, deep breath of sheer pleasure, while at the same instant a seventy-year-old manual labourer named Louis Bovard, who did not own a piano or even a small Persian carpet, too old to find gainful employment and all alone in the world, threw himself into the lake in Geneva without pausing to admire the subtle harmonies of its delicate shades. For the poor have no taste, no eye for beauty or anything which elevates the soul, and in this respect are quite, quite different from Queen Marie of Romania, who, in her memoirs, blesses the gift which God apparently granted her 'of feeling the beauty in things so deeply and of rejoicing in their beauty'. How very thoughtful of God.

Meanwhile Mariette was wiping her nose in the kitchen. Well, that was goodbye to the good times with them two young chaps, no more little chats and jokes. But her disappointments, though acute, were generally short-lived, so she splashed her face with water, rearranged her kiss-curl – rearranging her kiss-curl always cheered her up – and then scooted off to rejoin Madame Ariane.

She found her trying on the silk dressing-gown in the swing-mirror, putting it through its paces with her usual drill: to wit, walking towards the mirror, stepping backwards, then forward again with a smile, then tightenings and slackenings of the cord, poses various with leg out and leg in, turns partial and complete, assorted seated poses, each accompanied by suitable crossings of the legs, the fullness spread wide then drawn in again, and divers other dumb-shows of the same sort. Concluding that the dressing-gown was rather stylish, she gave Mariette a friendly smile and, thoroughly gratified, drew another deep breath through her nostrils, while Louis Bovard's filled with lake water.

'It's ever so smart on you. Makes you look like a statue, it's them folds that does it,' said the old servant meditatively, with her hands together.

'A teeny bit long. It'll need to be taken up two centimetres,' said Ariane.

After one last tightening of the cord round her middle and one last grateful look at the dressing-gown, she took it off, stood there in her nakedness, and then got into her dress, which she slipped over her head. Will you just look at her! Mariette said to herself, no vest, no petticoat, just her panties she calls them, and only a dress to her back, it's asking for trouble, sure as eggs, it's bronchitis for her come the first cold snap, still she's strong as a ox, which is just as well.

'If you wanted, and the two of us set to, we could take it up straight away, Madame Ariane. You could start one end and me the other, but we got to tack it first to make sure we're doing it right, I'll go and fetch what we need.'

She returned bearing needles, thread and a measuring-tape, and they sat down side by side on the sofa and made a start, chattering animatedly. At intervals they stopped talking and sucked their cotton, screwed up their eyes, and threaded their needles before settling back to the time-honoured task discharged by centuries of rapt and docile slave-wives: pursed- and sober-lipped did they ply their needles in a silence broken only by the gurgle of saliva swallowed by the twin seamstresses as they concentrated on their stitches.

Working quickly, her spectacles glinting with concentration, Mariette felt that they were two friends working happily together with one mind and a single cause, that they were allies and confederates. And, besides, there was just the two of them, nice and chummy, without any Deumes to bother them, specially not Antoinette, God Almighty in skirts, with her smile of what was supposed to be kindness but was in actual fact pure poison, always coming it over you, a nobody reely, goodness knows where she'd been dragged up, and as to this hem that had to be taken up right away, that was a job she liked on account of it being a dressing-gown for courting in, and very pretty in it she'd look too when her gentleman friend came calling, but he'd better realize how lucky he was, this chap of hers. She wanted to hold the hand of the beautiful creature who sat sewing at her side and say how happy for her she was about tomorrow night. But she didn't dare.

Instead, snapping her thread with her teeth, she made do with quietly humming: 'Star of love and love's sweet light, Star of joy and sweet caresses.'

Mariette was over the moon, and what a shoal of pleasures there followed in this conspiratorial hour! When the hem was tacked up, quick, see how the edge looked on Madame, oh the dressing-gown suited her to a T, it clung to her behind, but sh! mum's the word on that score. When the edging had passed muster, quick, rush off to the kitchen to fetch finer needles, quick, kill two birds with one stone, brew up some coffee they could drink together later, quick, fill the thermos, she loved filling the thermos because it reminded her of outings, then quick, hurry back and get on finishing the hemming-up, this was what life ought to be like, a bit of excitement, not like the humdrum way the Deumes plodded along, dull as ditchwater were the Deumes, forever thinking about ordinary things, always tapping the blessed barometer, whereas with Madame Ariane it was all romance and wild flings, the sort of thing young people needed if they wanted to stay healthy, still it was a poor lookout for Didi all the same, but it couldn't be helped, love's not ours to command, love's a wayward bird that grows up wild, as the saying goes.

'That was a reely lovely idea of yours, Madame Ariane, having the place deckyrated, and the big Sheerage smartens it up no end, a real little snuggery, just right for entertaining and conversations and such, all that's left to do is the windows and I'll make them shine a treat, you'll see, I've already taken the net curtains down and got the newspaper and vinegar ready, you can't beat newspaper and vinegar for windows, makes them shine like the crown jewels, and the curtains will come up lovely too, I'll use soapflakes for them, net dries in no time, just leave it to me, everything'll be perfick, I'll give the door a wash too, I mean the front door, it's the first thing he'll see when he rings, but I won't use soap 'cos soap brings off the paint, just warm water, but the dusting I'll leave till tomorrow, it's hardly worth doing today, it only comes back, dust's a thorn in the neck, I'll give the place a dust just before I leave tomorrow, which will be near enough to seven o'clock, and I'll give the parky a last going over too so everything's implacable when he comes to call, he'll find everything spickly-span, just you leave it to me, I'll take care of everything, he'll love it, you'll see if he don't,' the old woman concluded excitedly, for she had entered into the spirit of their romance.

'I'll leave you to finish the hem, Mariette, I've an appointment with Volkmaar. He's been very understanding and agreed to an extra fitting.'

'You go, Madame Ariane. Cheerio – and don't drive too fast.'

When the hem was finished, Mariette reached into her petticoats and produced Madame Ariane's surprise, which she set down on the piano-top, an artistic creation of her own design which she had made out of a leftover blob of china clay in the far-off days when she worked in a pottery. She stepped back to admire the stubby vase in the shape of a ruined tower featuring a lamb with a pig's face and a fat lady who for some reason was kneeling outside the doorway to the tower. Oh, Madame Ariane would be reely pleased, seeing as how it was all hartistic like. Also hand-made.

Leaving her medieval tower to its own devices, she closed the door, picked up the silk dressing-gown, put it on, announced to a man she did not know that she loved her husband and nobody else, and that was the top and bottom of it. She unleashed a look of utter disdain, and in a muted voice sang that once there was a star of love, a star of joy. But, catching sight of herself in the mirror, she saw that she was old and the strange man suddenly vanished. And so, taking off the dressing-gown, she found comfort, as old women do, in admiring herself on a restricted-area basis, by focusing on features which had retained their charm. Looking no further than hands, she had hands that would compete in any company. He used to say she had little hands, like a doll's. And her nose had stayed bonny, not a wrinkle in sight. She licked her finger, stuck her kiss-curl down, and examined it fondly. Hey-up, this was no good, gotter make a start on them windows. She began swabbing with all the ferocity of the dedicated.

'Oh yes, they're always very understanding when it's your money they're after, but you can't make her see it, she spends money like water, she won't have it that her precious Forkman butters her up something chronic, oh no, she don't care what she spends as long as her Mr Magic thinks she's beautiful, so there's pots and pots of cash for Forkman, what would poor Mademoiselle Valérie think if she could see her money going down the drain? quick: gotter buy one of them clinging dressing-gowns that he can take off her the minute he comes, quick: gotter have a Algerian rug, quick: gotter have the deckyrators in, no thought for nobody except him, even puts fags out ready on the table, and all that sun-bathing so she can go coffee-coloured all over, that's all your modern misses are interested in, it clings all right, specially around her behind, but whisht! I didn't tell her that nor will I, might make her feel ashamed, quite likely she won't wear it tomorrow night, but you got to with men, it points them in the right direction, anybody'll tell you that, men love behinds, it's the way they are, anyway there's not many got a behind like her, love-cushions I call them, it was grand just now when we was sat sewing side by side because I'll tell you straight I don't like routine, I like surprises, a bit of fun, I don't know if you follow me, what I mean is anything to get me out of a rut, he's coming at nine tomorrow night, he said so in the terrygram, oh yes, I read it all, she's hopeless at hiding papers, so come ten to nine I'll be hiding across the street waiting to get a proper look at him, sh! mum's the word, there'll be right goings-on tomorrow night, so get your glad rags on, and to think she's Mademoiselle's niece, not that I blame her mark you, it's only yuman nature, anyway it was bound to happen, stands to reason what with that wet dishcloth husband of hers, and her a healthy girl, pretty as a poppy blowing in the summer breeze, got a good shape on her, lady-bumps like marble knobs, poor Didi, but there it is, from the minute he was born he was destined to marry a wife who carries on, poor man, and then that skimpy beard of his and him always fussing over her and giving her presents and saying Arianny this and Arianny that and looking at her with eyes like a spaniel, always please and thank you and sorry and I hope you're not too tired, he might as well say go ahead, make a monkey out of me, be unfaithful and quick about it, poor devil, instead of asking her all the time if she's tired he should have tired her out a bit more hisself, she wouldn't have gone looking elsewhere then, but I will say her fancy man is good-looking, oh yes, no two ways about that, I could gobble him up meself, I seen a picture of him sitting on a horse that she leaves trailing everywhere even the bathroom, dark and handsome, gives you goose-pimples, I'm not keen on fair hair meself, it's a bit sickly, and you can bet your boots he don't waste time saying please and thank you and asking if she's tired, it's obvious he's the one that makes her tired with his toings and froings, and that's the size of it, she don't take after her auntie, I'd swear Mademoiselle Valérie never got up to tricks and mind you she must have been a pretty little thing when she was young, but keeping your mind on religion all the time calms you down, now getting back to Didi, it breaks my heart to think what'll happen when he finds out, 'cos he's bound to one of these days, but there you are, I got a soft spot for her, known her since she was a baby, I even used to call her Ariane without any Mademoiselle in front of it, even said Riri sometimes, but you see I had to leave Mademoiselle Valérie when she was twelve on account of my sister being so bad she couldn't manage, had her yewteris upside down and hovaries all over the shop, and when I came back, 'cos I missed her so much, she was already going on sixteen, a young lady, and her aunt told me I had to say Mademoiselle Ariane, and with her being so strong-willed I didn't have no choice, and then I got used to it, and nowadays it's Madame, but sometimes when I'm tucked up in bed I still call her Riri, how's it all going to end I ask, even a watched pot will boil over in the end, did you see the pretty vase I gave her as a surprise for her night of passion? I made it meself, done it in the kiln, when I was at the pottery I was on the hartistic side, always one for having heaps and heaps of ideas, it's a gift, you either got it or you haven't got it.'

CHAPTER 65

'She can be a real madam sometimes, and to show you just how contrary she can be I must tell you the tale of the lobster, no hang on, shut up a minute, it'll make you larf, the day I got back from Paris I brought this lobster for her as a present, a surprise, weighed a ton and very lively, it kept shifting about in its basket on the train, now when I told her I was going to cut it up while it was still alive so I could do it 'Merican style it's delicious done that way she lets out this horrible scream and shuts her eyes, I won't let you won't let you, she screams, you'll hurt it, so to calm her down I says right then I'll cut its head off first so it don't feel a thing, that made her yell some more as if it was her head that was going to be cut off, so, all kind and patient like, I says right I'll put it in boiling water, you should have seen her, talk about a paddy, she went white as if somebody was after her honour, but Madame Ariane that's how it's always done, for it to be fit to eat you gotter kill it live, that's the way with lobsters, they was meant to have their heads cut off or be dropped in boiling water, what else are you supposed to do with lobsters, put them to sleep like in horspital with chloryform? anyway a lobster don't suffer, it's used to it, you can cut off its head and it won't complain, but it was no good, you should have seen her, a real tigress, and here's the best bit, she took the lobster which was still alive and kicking, drove it by car to the airport, put it on the plane for Nice and left a tip so somebody could chuck it back into the sea, no shut up don't make me larf, the driver of the aeroplane must have thought it was his lucky day 'cos sure enough you can bet your boots he'll have ate it up hisself 'Merican style, and besides there was the tip to buy a nice bottle of wine to go with it, no but seriously she's a real lady, always does the proper thing, believes everybody else is like her, so she and her money are soon parted, but coming back to her fancy man, he's a burocrat, that means he does writing about politics, but he's diddy Didi's big boss and a dab hand at wife-stealing, now according to what she says about him in her notebook he's as handsome as they come, oh yes I had a quick peep in her notebook, it's not me being curious or nosy, it's just so I know, so I'm in the picture, seeing as how I got her best interests at heart, she's like a daughter to me, besides it's tempting fate the way she just leaves her notebook lying around in that suitcase of hers, it's not my fault if she don't lock it, in the circs you got no option reely, specially when she's in the bath, and she's always in the bath you've no idea, if she likes doing fish imitations there's nothing to stop her, she's her own mistress, according to what she tells me she's over the moon on account of her chap is coming tonight, and do you know why she stays so long in her bath which she has ever so hot? I do, 'cos another woman can understand how she feels, it's so that she can imagine what it'll be like tonight with her darling boy, get along with you I been young meself, there isn't much she can teach me about being in love, and she don't fool me by trying to make out how I'm tired and saying I ought to get off home early today, four o'clock she said, pretending to be so concerned, but reely she was itching for me to go, it's all play-acting so she can have plenty of time to doll herself up without me being there to see her or more's the point to catch a sight of him, also so that they can get up to all sorts in peace, poor Didi, but Madame Ariane I could pop back and bring the tea in tonight for you when you got your gentleman visitor here it'll save you the bother, no thanks Mariette dear you need to rest up she says the little fibber, right you are, I'll take meself off at four like she says, but sh! mum's the word, just before nine, 'cos he'll be coming at nine like it says in the terrygram, just before nine I'll hide across the street and have a look at her Prince Charming, Mariette dear, she said, it was nice of her to say that and besides she's an orphing, and that Didi don't amount to a bag of beans, not if it's a man you want.'

CHAPTER 66

All that remained now was to try on the white crêpe dress and the four suits. She pointed out that the dress was a little too full round the hips, for she was most anxious that her stately rump should be clearly and visibly profiled, yet, being a well-brought-up young woman, had no wish to say so directly or even acknowledge it to herself. The dressmaker reassured her. She did not believe him, but out of weakness said nothing. Too late for alterations now.

It took her just one glance to know that the pale-grey suit was not a success. She decided she didn't want to see it ever again, and gazed at the clock the whole of the time Volkmaar was inserting pins with a view to one final alteration which, however, would be quite pointless since she had already made up her mind to give Mariette this obscenity which made her look like a factory-girl with a hump.

'And now, dear lady, the delightful charcoal grey.'

In a daze she stared at the jacket which was too pinched, at the lapels which were clownishly wide at the top and idiotically narrow at the bottom, and at the overstuffed shoulders which would have been more at home on something from the ready-to-wear department. At last the penny dropped. The clothes she had seen modelled were perfect because they'd come from Paris, but this moron hadn't even been able to copy them correctly. She pretended to let her mind be put at rest by Volkmaar, who said a once-over with the iron would cure the problem or kept pulling the parts he'd messed up, which made everything right for a few seconds. To confuse her and divert her attention from the two suits which were clearly disasters, he made flattering comments about Madame's heavenly figure, which made her feel sick. Why didn't the little squirt with breasts like a woman just keep his remarks to himself?

'And now, dear lady, the two heavenly numbers in the rustic and we'll be done.'

Meekly she allowed him to try them on her one after the other. Even more ghastly than the two flannel suits. What was the use of complaining? There was nothing he could do to put things right in a matter of hours. Anyway, he wasn't up to it, he hadn't the first idea about tailoring a suit. Oh why had she ever decided to have anything to do with a jackass like him? Why hadn't she just gone out and bought something off the peg? O God! When a person was on the brink of doing something really stupid, *that* was the moment when she might just as easily not have done it at all!

'Yes,' she said, 'that's fine. Thank you.'

When Volkmaar had gone, she sat down. Crying wouldn't help. Besides, the dresses hadn't turned out too badly, well at least one or two hadn't. Only the suits were a disaster. She'd burn them tonight, the moment they were delivered. No, burning was too fiddly and it would make a stink. Better to cut them up and bury them in the garden. That way it would be as though they had never existed, and she could simply put them out of her mind. Later on she'd go to Paris and order ten suits if she had to, yes ten, so that at least two or three would turn out well. If you wanted to dress well, you had to accept a certain level of wastage. But the linen lace-up dress was very nice, a kind of duck of sorts really, but so fine, so light.

'My ducky dress,' she said with a smile, highly delighted with the adjective, which she had made up all by herself.

She took off her petticoat, panties, stockings and the brassière which she'd worn as protection against Piglet's prying eyes. Yes, take everything off, it was so hot today, at least thirty in the shade. Stripped to the skin, she got into the darling dress with the criss-cross laces up the front, so soft and white, so generously scooped-out at the neck and so divinely sleeveless, a dress fit for a heroine, and those wonderful folds surely belonged on a statue. Oh she felt just right in it! Yes, not wearing anything under it was a good idea. It really was stiflingly hot. And besides, what a lark to go round cocking a snook at people in the street, knowing that they didn't know!

She took the lid off a cardboard box, took out a pair of white sandals which she had bought earlier, and smiled at them fondly. Bare legs and sandals were perfect with her ducky dress. She stuffed her petticoat, shoes, panties and stockings into the box. Good riddance. She'd tell the suit-butcher to send it on to Cologny along with her old dress and the rest of the order. In the triple mirror, all three Arianes in their ducky dresses were striking and tall: three sweeties.

CHAPTER 67

Victorious in her ducky dress, blithely she sailed down the street, a white galleon of youth, striding long and smiling, acutely aware of her nakedness beneath the fine linen, aware of her bare skin cooled by the caress of the breeze. Know that I am beautiful, O ye at whom I choose not to look, take heed and behold a happy woman. Tall did she walk, and gloriously in her hand did she hold the railway timetable in which, occasionally pausing, she followed the progress of the train which was carrying him to her. What bliss to be in love, how fascinating to be alive.

She ground to a halt, feeling suddenly very angry with a cat which had crossed the road so close to the wheels of a car that the silly thing would surely get itself run over one of these days! But she had better watch out for cars too, didn't want to go getting herself killed today, mustn't be damaged now. Today she was very precious. Roll on tonight! She set off again, keeping single-mindedly to the middle of the pavement. The two men she cannoned into turned round, mesmerized, but she was already far away. She caught the shoulder of a third, and because he smiled at her she knew that he knew that she was happy, for she was going to the man she loved, to her love beyond compare. Yes, they all stared, they all knew, and they all endorsed her happiness.

Over her head, a cloud. If rain tonight, they wouldn't be able to stroll through the garden hand in hand. Almighty God, I've been so looking forward to it, please make it fine tonight. What I want is the floor of heaven to be thick inlaid with patines of bright gold. Tonight, offer him tea, avoid strong drink, too depraved, make it tea, like you'd give a brother just back from his travels, a very-good-quality Ceylon with white tips. No, that cloud up there like a pink-and-white baby isn't going to amount to anything. Little cloud, be good, don't get any bigger. Please, pretty please.

A goddess reared up before her in the glass of a jeweller's window. She admired the fullness of the lower lip and the warm intelligence of the mouth, the corners of the mouth so thoughtfully modulated, the gilded cheeks glowing as it were with an inner translucence, the dark-gold mole on her cheek, the flaring nostrils thirsting for life and investing the chaste expression of the whole face with a secret irony. 'Hail, Ariane full of grace, the Lord is with you,' she murmured.

When the lake hove into view, she gave it a nod of greeting. Oh the warmth when he slept by her side! The terrace of a café: a crowd of stupid men who did not love and were reading newspapers, a shoal of ditto women who were not loved and to make up for it were ingesting huge chocolate ices smothered in large quantities of whipped cream. O God, what was the point of that fat old woman with the flat-faced pekinese? Get thee to a cemetery!

Three o'clock already. In six hours she would see him. Off home with you spit-spot and start getting ready, get tremendously ready so that he shall be presented with the most beautiful woman on this earth. A week from today, next Saturday, Wispy-Beard would be back. She shook her head, like a mare troubled by a horsefly. She'd deal with that later on, for today was a day of consecration. The crack of a whip made her start, for she felt responsible for the fate of all horses. She turned and checked. No, he hadn't been maltreated, and besides he looked well cared for and wasn't wearing blinkers either, always a good sign.

Quai Gustave-Ador. She hurried along the shore of the blue and pink lake, naked under her fluttering dress, which flared now and then like wings beating in the draught of her breezy progress. A couple of road-menders stopped digging to stare at the tall girl with the parted lips who bore down on them. She paid them no attention, her high breasts falling and rising to the rhythm of her abundant, easy step. 'Well slung,' one of the road-menders said. She smiled, and walked a little faster.

Chemin de la Côte. Little flowers lit up the grass. She walked on, finding everything quite delectable. Switzerland was a wonderful place, and those three cows over there, perhaps they were sisters, were extraordinarily delightful. 'You pretties,' she said. 'Tonight!' she proclaimed to the proud poplars and the poppies in the breeze-waved cornfields. When she got home she'd burn her arm with a cigarette-end for a proof. See, my love, how I've suffered for your sake? Hurry, hurry!

Love's march of triumph, the exhilarating stride of the huntress. It was quite simple, wonderful and clear: she would see him tonight. And in her mind she raised her sword in greeting archangelical, and her gratitude flew up into the firmament like a skein of turtle-doves. Tonight! Tonight: she would see his eyes and his impetuousness and his way of turning suddenly to drink deep of her with hot eyes, and she would be defenceless and would melt. Tonight! Tonight: take him by the hand, enclose his heart-meltingly slender wrist, then she snug against him and their lips and her breasts and she naked and looked at. Oh the wonder of being looked at and found beautiful.

Love's march of triumph. Tonight! Oh the consecration and the hallowed weight upon her, and his precious face leaning over her, and the interludes when lips renewed their contact and at long last her joy, her moans. His woman, she was his wife and she worshipped him, his wife, his nun of love, his vassal and his vessel, fulfilled by the oblation of her depth, by the knowledge of him in her, happy in her who was doe-eyed with the happiness of knowing that he was in her, the cloistered nun of her lord. Yes, she was in love, at last she was in love. On the ice floe a wild rose had bloomed.

★

Love's march of triumph. She walked on quickly, opulent and serene, puissant and no less happy than the Queen of Sheba. Tonight! Oh make shift to please him, listen to his voice, and suddenly he would say nothing and she would be filled with fear because his face would be stone, but afterwards he would smile and she would swoon with rapture as she beheld such enchantment, which soared above and beyond his beauty. His smile, his teeth, oh best of the sons of man! And a little cruel too sometimes, though there was no harm in that. 'You will be my love always,' she told him. 'Death? What's death?' she exclaimed.

Love's march of triumph. Those bushes there made her heart sing, as did that police station, and this cow which was licking its calf as though plying a trowel. This copse stirred her senses, and that glen looked friendly, and all creation sent her into raptures, but especially did she enrapture herself. 'I am wonderful,' she said, and she walked on still faster.

Love's march of triumph. Yes, wonderful, because he had chosen her above all other women, chosen her at the first flutter of her long curved lashes, while he was the handsomest, the craziest, oh wonder of him dressed up as an aged relic, the most desperate, oh the words he had spoken that night at the Ritz, arrows of bitter truth, yet the most loving, the saddest, oh his eyes, the gayest, oh his lips, the proudest, the tenderest, the loneliest, a king without a people.

Love's march of triumph. Wonderful? Most certainly. Was this not conceit? Why not, it was a day for conceit. Only ugly women are modest. That's it, yell at the first woman she met. Yell: my teeth are perfect! Yell: I dare you to show yours! Yell: I dare you to point out the man you love, that is if you dare to without feeling ashamed! A raucous rooster clamoured in the distance and she halted, wondered if chickens ever sneezed, laughed because she was in love, and went on her way.

Love's march of triumph. In this hour when the sun shone bright and hot, she went on her way victorious, lips parted, smiling like a statue, and her divers claims to superiority came to her in bursts and warbles. What were all those other women good for? For plucking their eyebrows and shaving their legs. For wearing brassières with bones to hide their shame. For having their teeth filled, for burbling on about their yearnings, for varnishing their nails with horrible red for the benefit of horrible men, for reading a novel so they could talk about it and pretend to be cultured. Anyway, more often than not they just read the reviews, which they trotted out in drawing-rooms. And did ever woman receive such a telegram? Oh her darling who could not live without her and languished with waiting? 'And I too languish!' she told him. She quickened her step again, hands stretched wide to gather the wind, and she shrieked in a panic of happiness. 'My darling!' she shouted silently, for no one's benefit but her own.

The triumphal march of the tall nymph, striding long, confident of tonight, proud of her enslavement. Suddenly she stopped, struck by wonder. She was a woman who belonged to a man, his property. Oh the wonder of being the woman of a man, the prey of a man, a man's frail chattel. 'Thank you, God,' she said. She paused by a tree, stripped away the resin which oozed from the trunk, smelled its virile tang, the tang of life, held it for a moment between her lips before discarding it, smiled enigmatically, and then went out into the colossal sun, perspiring and happy. Life, this at last was life!

Love's march of triumph, the long march of Ariane now like unto a goddess as she skirted cornfields which waved in the hot wind. Out of a dip in the road, three honey-tressed virgins appeared, three little Swiss farm-girls who walked as bold and nervous as wagtails and broke into unexpected snatches of song with miraculous, instinctive assurance. But when they passed her they fell silent because she exuded the majesty of bliss, fell silent and nodded to the rippling gold and tan goddess, who smiled and sailed on. 'Tonight!' she proclaimed a little further along to a fifth cow, which was unable to grasp this startling intelligence and continued grazing. 'Stupid cow!' she told it, and, head held high, went on her way.

A march of triumph, stepping out by the side of a lord taller than she.

Grave-faced and halo-haired, drunk with health, intoxicated by so glorious a day, sun-kissed and bursting with all the hormones of youth, her hand in the hand of her lord, she walked on, striding long, beloved of her lord, her dress flapping and flaring in two beating wings. The snap of her dress as she walked was the flap of a wind-jammer bearing down on a fantastic island, and love was the wind which filled her sails. The snap-and-flap of her dress was exhilarating, the wind on her face was exhilarating, the wind on her face and her head held high.

Love's march of triumph. On she walked, proud, absurd, inspired. Ideas teemed in the recesses of her brain, thrilling ideas which, fanned by her heart's blood, spread like a peacock's tail, thoughts which would have been quite exquisite had she a mind to see them. But she had no time. She was going to make herself beautiful, was going towards the man she loved, proud and trusting, and in her wake followed melodies as golden as she who was their big sister, airs which were happy, absolutely carefree and as pure as springtime, Oh the white flowers dancing in the tall grass, such loving harmonies, so certain of the power of their spell, so serene and full of grace.

Love's march of triumph. Regally did she go, transformed by love as were in olden times her sisters of yore who now countlessly sleep the sleep of the earth, walking ever on, immortal in her progress, governed in her progress like the stars in their motions, legions launched by love on perennial trajectories, solemn Ariane, barely smiling, walking to an accompaniment of such celestial music, love, sweet love in love's beginning.

CHAPTER 68

Prone in the grass of the lawn, she reread the telegram while the little birds who lived in the cherry-tree exchanged friendly greetings, like schoolchildren at playtime, and a blackbird on the roof whistled because the country was a pleasanter place than the city, and a sparrow puffed its feathers and took a dust-bath just in front of her, its wings aquiver. 'He'll be here tonight at nine,' she announced to the quivering puff-ball, which greeted the news with indifference. So thoughtful to have remembered, the minute he had got back to Paris, to confirm that he would be coming, in spite of being so terribly busy. Such important missions, and secret too, most probably. 'He is a Very Important Person,' she explained to the sparrow, which had straightened up, pleased to be clean, and was looking at her with interest, leaning its head prettily to the right, wondering what to make of her.

'You are my lord. I proclaim it with trumpets.'

Revelling in the sacrilege and because she was happy, she repeated her oath of vassality in accents severally English, Italian and Burgundian, and then in the quavery voice of an old lady in an advanced stage of senility. She yawned, lit a cigarette with her last sulphur match. Terrific these French matches, you could strike them on anything, even the sole of your shoe like the men of the mountains did, and when you'd lit one the fumes went up your nose, very enjoyable. Next time she went to Annemasse she'd buy a dozen boxes.

No, don't smoke, don't want to be reeking of tobacco tonight at nine, when . . . She tossed the cigarette away, made up a story to herself that she was a cow, and mooed to prove it. On reflection, she decided she wasn't a cow at all but the friend of a black and white cow which was very sweet, clean and well-brought-up, followed her everywhere, and was called Flora. 'Come on, moo-cow, sit down by me and chew your cud nicely.' She patted her knee, which she pretended was the head of her moo-friend, noted the absence of horns, and explained to herself that it was a very young cow. 'I say, Flora, he's coming tonight.' She yawned again and chewed a blade of grass. Oh damn the cow, which couldn't sit still and had wandered off to graze. 'Flora! Will you come here at once! Come here, and if you're good I'll take you to the botanical gardens tomorrow, I'll show you flowers from the mountains, it'll be an education.'

To make it sit still, she sang it a Mozart aria in Italian, asked if it understood Italian, seeing that it hailed from Savoy. 'No,' said the cow. So then she explained what '*Voi che sapete che cosa è amor*' meant: 'You who know what love is'. 'And do you know what love is? No? Poor cow. That's because you're just a poor cow. But I know. And now push off, I don't want to see you any more. I'm going to start getting ready.'

In her small sitting-room, she knotted the crested tie he had given her round her neck, gave a military salute in the mirror, then played at twirling round and suddenly sinking to her knees to make her ducky dress balloon up around her. Then she went into the kitchen to see if there was any chocolate left. There was just one bar. Back in her sitting-room, she decided to make it last a long time by letting it melt in her mouth, forgot what she had decided, and polished it off inside two minutes. 'Never mind,' she chanted in a singsong voice, and then she stretched out on the sofa, for a preview of what was to come tonight. Four thirty. He'll show up at nine, that is four and a half hours from now. Two hundred and seventy minutes, two hundred and seventy little waits. The answer would be to get ready in a very meticulous sort of way so that the two hundred and seventy minutes would be just long enough. Yes, draw up plan of action, allotting so many minutes for each stage of the titivations. Bath and get dried. Shampoo hair and dry with the hot-air thingummy. Face-pack with the new formula as given in that stupid woman's weekly. Pop in and check this and that in the sitting-room and hall. Try on dresses, compare, give serious thought, eliminate progressively, and make final choice, allowing ample time for the whole operation. Out of all of Volkmaar's dresses which had just been delivered, there were at least several possibles. Allow for extra bath, possibly. Sundry other preparations to include time-wasting, sessions in front of mirror, practice runs in the smiles and expressions department, final touches to hair, bursts of song, pauses to make happy faces, unforeseen eventualities and disasters.

When she'd finished scribbling her plan of action on the back of the telegram, she totted it all up and found a preparation time of two hundred and thirty minutes. What time was it now? Twenty-five to five. Which meant he wouldn't get here for another two hundred and sixty-five minutes. Which meant a balance of thirty-five minutes of doing nothing. Which meant thirty-five minutes of waiting proper, since she'd be fully occupied the rest of the time. A wait of thirty-five minutes wasn't too long, she'd managed the thing rather well. Damn! She still hadn't opened the letters from the awful lawful. Best read the last one at least. You never knew.

His long letter was addressed from the Château van Offel, Brussels, and was dated Wednesday 22 August. She ran her eyes over it, skipping whole passages, singling out the odd sentence or two here and there.

'My sweetest darling Arianny,

'Been in Brussels a couple of hours and am settled in the luxury guest room which Monsieur and Madame van Offel have been kind enough to make available to me where I've just sat down to write this letter on a genuine Empire table.' Skip the next bit. 'So here I am, almost at the end of my diplomatic travels. And to think that only yesterday I was in Jerusalem! With aeroplanes, distance doesn't mean a thing any more.' How true, but let's move on. 'Darling, thanks for the loving telegram which reached me in Jerusalem. I must say, though, I would have rather had a nice long letter giving details of what you do each day, but I know how much my Arianny hates writing.' Too right. And on we go. 'In earlier letters I gave you all the relevant gen about my four weeks in Palestine as I went along. All I need do now is to bring you up to date about these last few days, because I've been much too taken-up by my all-absorbing official duties to pen the thrice-weekly missive as promised, for which I duly weep and wail and gnash my teeth. But on second thoughts I won't give you an update now, because these past few days have been the high point of my trip and have brought me two tremendous accolades in Palestine, the first being a wide-ranging review of the situation with His Excellency the High Commissioner himself, and the second an invitation to lunch at His Excellency's palace. It grieves me not to tell you all about it all here and now, because I really was highly honoured, but I do so want us to discuss and enjoy it together. And if I put my accolades down on paper it'll spoil the effect. Besides, you can't write down all the little details which build up the atmosphere. So the story of the two accolades will have to keep until we see each other! And now I turn to the last and most delicate part of my visit, our major concern being not to ruffle the legitimate susceptibilities of governments.' We can skip all that. 'I hope you haven't found the foregoing too dull, but whom can I tell about my struggles and my hopes if not my wife and companion through life?' Poor Didi, but on we go. 'You are my dearest wife, and I have missed you so! It's been sheer hell for me to be on the receiving end of so much flattering official attention without having you by my side to enjoy it with me. And I expect you've been in the dumps all these weeks, my little deserted wife.' Skip and skip. 'I enclose a photo taken in London, in the hope that a picture of me will be a foretaste of the real thing. The young man with me is Baron de Baer, First Secretary in the Belgian Legation, I had lunch at his house, a very nice chap.' Blah-blah. 'And so, my little geisha, for the above reasons, job *oblige* but also because I'm stuck with social and family obligations, I'm unfortunately going to have to stay on in Brussels for another ten days, until Friday 31 August inclusive. So I'll have to wait until Saturday 1 September for the joy of seeing my Arianny again, whom I so much look forward to telling about everything I've achieved, because honestly, modesty apart, I shall return very much the conquering hero!' Blah-blah-blah. 'Darling, just keep telling yourself that the separation is almost over and that very soon now we'll know the bliss of seeing each other once more. Until that marvellous moment comes, I'll hold you tight to my manly bosom.'

She tossed the letter into a drawer together with the photograph without even giving it a second glance. Should she phone him this instant in Brussels and say nice things to him? No, that would clash too horribly with the titivations. Much better to send him a telegram tomorrow. Ought she to open the other letters? There were far too many of them. She pulled out the drawer, retrieved the photo, and studied it. Poor lamb with that round head of his, proud as punch to be standing next to a real diplomat. The trusting look on his face made her cringe, and his assumption that she was sitting around waiting impatiently for him was cringe-making too. She put the photo back in the drawer. So now she knew: he'd be back in exactly one week. That left seven days of happiness with Sol, and then she'd see. Anyhow, she wouldn't think about that today.

In the bathroom, she squeezed toothpaste on to the brush, embarked on a conscientious dental scouring, then stopped to consult the railway timetable. The train would arr. Bourg in ten minutes. Good, she had plenty of time. Best foot forward! Brush thoroughly for at least five minutes. Suddenly she removed the brush from her mouth. Sometimes trains were derailed, leaving injured passengers trapped groaning under axles! Without pausing to rinse out her mouth, she spoke to the Almighty in accents clouded by the foaming toothpaste.

'O Lord, let tomorrow'sh trainsh all crash, let hundredsh and hundredsh of people be killed, if shuch ish Thy will, but let everything go shmoothly today, pleashe. Dearesht, shweetesht Lord,' she added to butter Him up. (She rinsed her mouth and went on with her prayer, which, like all prayers, was shamelessly mercenary.) 'Do this for me, Lord,' she trilled in her most alluring, feminine voice. 'You know how much I love You. Please make it all right for tonight, won't You? O Lord, watch over my friend's train,' she ended, on a chaste note, 'friend' seeming to her the most suitable word to use when addressing God. (She straightened up and held her nose with two fingers so that she sounded like a clergyman delivering a sermon.) 'Dear brothers and sisters, I will now pass beneath the waters of my bath, accompanied by both my rather ample bosoms. But first grant me leave to take another peek at my lover-man's picture, but just five seconds' worth so it doesn't go stale on me and stays fresh and heart-stopping. There, that'll do, put it away. And now for another little dekko at the telegram that came today, to pep me up a bit. Let's see what he says.'

She unfolded the square of green paper and read it in a dramatic, stagy voice, with actions. The wonderful last word made her knees go weak. Oh the joy, the glory, and the ecstatic cherubim singing on high beneath the wings of great angels bearing sounding harps, oh wonderful man! He had signed it simply 'Yours'! Just 'Yours'! How beautiful! But then she scowled. Perhaps 'Yours' was a word he'd just scribbled down without thinking, like a bank-manager putting 'Yours etc.' at the bottom of a letter? No, that couldn't be, he must have intended something by it! The word said what it meant, and it meant that he was hers, hers alone, her chattel, her property. 'Yours,' she whispered, and she took a deep breath. Now for that bath. Run the hot water.

'Come along, get a move on, stupid,' she told the tap.

She put the photo, the telegram, the train timetable, the little bear with the Mexican hat and her father's watch on a stool next to the bath. And, because there was no one there to laugh at her, she kissed the telegram and the timetable. And if the nuns who'd been listening to her sermon didn't like it, well yah-boo-sucks to them! When the water had been tested and pronounced just right, she undid the tie with the crests on, dropped her ducky dress on the floor, got into the bath, stretched out, gave a series of contented sighs, stuck her foot out of the water, wiggled her toes, and pretended they were five little boys coming home from school. 'Look sharp now, go and wash your hands and faces,' she told them, and the five little boys ducked back under the water. Then she made swimming movements with her arms and was transported to the sea. Next, with one hand, she patted the bottom of the bath to make bubbles, which tickled as they rose between her thighs. Then she stuck her foot out again, waggled her toes, ordered them to keep still, have their bath like good little boys, and then trot straight off to school, holding hands nicely.

'And if you don't come home with good marks, you'll be for it!'

Now for a thorough soaping. No, hang on, not straight away, bide a while first, she had hours and hours in front of her. She rowed gently with the palms of her hands on the green water which shivered with rings of sun, and thought the little waves she made were awfully pretty, like younger sisters of the proper waves of the ocean, where they'd all certainly end up together soon. Switching tack, she told herself that two pretty little light-blue parakeets were perched on one of the taps, the cold one, not the other one, which was too hot and would burn their little feet. Tweet-tweet, my pets, are you all right, are you happy? Me too, very, you can't possibly imagine how tremendously all right and happy I am! Suddenly serious, she hailed the marvellous coming of tonight by chanting the tune of the Whitsun hymn, substituting, not without a qualm or two, the name of the man she loved for the Sacred Name:

> O my believing soul,
> Be proud now and content,
> For see! there comes thy heavenly king,
> Solal is near: his praises sing!

But now, get down to it. Standing up with legs apart, singing and whistling by turns, shooting glances now and then towards watch and timetable, which were soon liberally sprinkled with water, she proceeded to the important business of cleansing her body, soaping herself ardently, frowning with concentration, rinsing herself off and resoaping herself, and pumicing her feet. Though she was doomed to die, she spared no effort, worked with a will to make herself perfect, like a conscientious craftsman, with her tongue poking out.

'Whew, it wears you out being in love,' she announced as she slipped back into the suds.

After blowing the pumice-stone to make it sail along by itself, she pulled out the plug, refilled the bath with clean water into which, as a reward, she poured scented bath salts. Yes, she had to feel frantically good: too bad if that meant behaving like the Catherlix do. Lying lusciously prone, it occurred to her that she was stupid to have had her bath as early as this. By the time he got there, she'd be showing the effects of several hours' decay of her flawlessness. Heigh-ho, she'd see how things went.

'Yours.'

She closed her eyes so that she could hear the most beautiful word on earth loud and clear, pronounced it in various ways until she was glutted with it, and all the while she contemplated her naked body under the flattering, insidious water. Chanting a singsong, wordless dirge, she felt the weight of her hot, firm breasts, stroked her nipples, sighed, ran more hot water to make herself comfortable, smiled at the two faithful parakeets who sat slinkily on their tap, dinkily raising their legs one after the other, exercising their toes to relax them. She closed her eyes, grew torpid, and let her mind wander.

CHAPTER 69

While his wife in Geneva was letting her mind wander in the bath, Adrien Deume, in the railway station at Basle, stood with his elbows leaning on the open window of his first-class compartment, feeling important and enjoying the sensation. Aware that lesser mortals in the commuter train drawn up alongside were staring, he adopted the nonchalant, superior air of one accustomed to travelling in luxury, the world-weary manner of a bored grandee, a cross between Lord Byron and Talleyrand.

Four mournful blasts of a whistle signalled the off, and there was a groan of protesting metal, and the engine emitted a long, valedictory hiss, and the whole train shuddered, staggered under a series of concussive impacts, began to move, and soon was hastening on its way with studied respiratory application, like an overgrown school-boy chanting French verbs. Deprived of his admiring audience, Adrien Deume sat down and flicked through the timetable. Next stop was Delémont at five fifty. Perfect. Then Bienne, Neuchâtel, Lausanne and finally Geneva at eight forty-five. A ten-minute taxi ride and he'd be at Cologny. Which meant that by nine o'clock tonight he'd be holding her in his arms.

He rubbed his hands briskly and looked around him with an air of satisfaction. Very nice, these first-class carriages. But remember now, a quarter of an hour before getting into Geneva, just after Nyon, go to lavatory, wash face, scrub nails, give beard good comb, give coat good brushing, especially the collar, which showed the dandruff, in a word make self presentable. To put a shine on his shoes, he could wipe them on the plush of the seat. It wasn't allowed, but what the hell. To smack him on the BTM, they'd have to catch him first! What a surprise for Arianny, who wasn't expecting him for another week! A surprise and a half, by jingo! Running his tapered tongue over his lips, he savoured in advance her delight and astonishment. To pass the time, he murmured what he was going to say after he'd kissed her.

'You see, darling, I couldn't resist it. Yesterday, right out of the blue, I suddenly had this feeling that I couldn't bear to wait another day longer. So I made a beeline for Sabena, unfortunately there wasn't a seat left on the plane, I played the ranking-official card but it did no good, couldn't budge them, fully booked up, never mind, decided to catch this morning's train. I did think of wiring you, but then I thought it would be nicer to give you a surprise, right? So who's a happy Arianny, then? A surprise and a half, right, duckie? Mummy was none too pleased, you know, but who cares, I mean is a chap entitled to pop back and see his missus after they've been separated for three months or is he not! You are glad to see me, aren't you? Half a mo, I'll give you your presents now.'

He yawned and in a whisper babbled o' grand titles. Baron Adrien Deume. Count Deume. General Sir Adrien Deume. He gave another gaping yawn and, getting up, cast around for something else to while away the time. He stood by the window, which he lowered, and leaned out. The rushing air made him blink and look stern and astute. The telegraph wires looped up down, up down, retreated, separated into a continuous line, their poles brave with white teacups dipping and rising, and trees sped towards him with cinematographic abruptness before careering backwards, heads bowed, to rejoin the green lights of signals left far behind, and all the while, too fast for eyes, the gravel of the other track flashed by between rails streaked with dazzling shafts of sudden illumination.

The engine gave a despairing, demented whinny, and he turned away, sat down on the red plush seat, gave a contented sigh, and smiled at his wife. What splendid breasts she had on her. Like marble, old bean, if you only knew, and I'll be making the most of them tonight, just you see if I don't. Yes, the moment he got in, he'd kiss her, hold her tight, then upwards and onwards to bed, his or hers, didn't matter. No, make it hers, it was bigger. Undress her quickly, tell her to lie down, and forward charge, like the Light Brigade! Basically, women loved it. Anyhow, for God's sake, he'd had his conjugalities cut off for three months, and it was more than flesh could bear! Afterwards, he'd get up and smoke a relaxing pipe, which was something he liked doing after performing his marital duty, and he'd open the case of presents! He could see it now! She'd clap her hands for joy! And then he'd tell her all about his official tour, the interview with the High Commissioner (a Lord, for goodness' sake!), and then the lunch with the High Commissioner (and a field marshal to boot, for goodness' sake!), and then he'd show her the photos he'd had taken with the top brass, show her everything, she'd be fascinated, she'd be proud of her hubby.

'Find it fascinating, do you, my little chickadee? I've come out of it rather well, even though I do say it myself. Carried all before me! I think that what went down best was that I didn't conduct myself like a civil servant, let alone a senior civil servant, but pitched the thing on a higher level, slipping in literary asides, Latin tags, very much the man of the world, if you see what I mean. Good. Fine. Tell her how I came through with flying colours in Syria and end with the big finish, i.e. Palestine, because that was the high point, she won't know what's hit her. Start with the personal contacts made in the bureau of the High Commission, the information gathered, the first visits by top people at my hotel, definitely make a point of telling her about the hotel, a hotel and a half, darling, the King David no less, the best, a top-class establishment. I had a full set of rooms, what they call a suite in these five-star places, i.e. drawing-room, bedroom and de-luxe bathroom. A suite definitely has an edge, because if some top nob comes to see you you don't have to go downstairs and entertain him in one of the public rooms, you can have him come up and receive him in your very own drawing-room, do you see what that means, it puts you in quite another class, it means you're somebody. Absolutely, you can take it from me: when you've got a suite at the King you know you're somebody! Oh yes, it's known locally in the best circles as the King, that's what people say. Of course it was bathroom with lavatory, which was a convenience, no need to go wandering outside along the corridor. Can't get by any more without my own lavatory. Either you're a diplomat or you're not is what I say. Especially since things could have been better from a digestive-functions point of view, all those slap-up dinners, you know, and having to venture out into the corridor three or four times a night would have been no fun, no fun at all. But the tummy-wobble problems can wait till tomorrow, when we'll have time to discuss them properly, we'll work out what if anything needs to be done after we've seen how things go between now and then, because the situation seems to be improving, markedly so, for example just three times today whereas yesterday it was seven, if you please! By the by, the plan I drew of my rooms at the King was jolly good, wasn't it? Of my suite, I should say. I had the dickens of a job with it, you know. Getting the measurements down on paper, setting it all out to scale, it took me a whole day. But 'nuff said, that brings me to my last days in Jerusalem, which were, if I say it myself, the high point of the entire tour. Can you picture it, Madame Adrien Deume, your lord and master being granted the honour of an audience with His Excellency the High Commissioner? I mean, he's only the most important man in those parts! A field marshal, mark you, the highest rank in the British military establishment. The audience lasted half an hour, would you believe! Atmosphere jolly friendly, well perhaps not friendly exactly, but definitely cordial. His Excellency was terribly pleasant, took an interest, quizzed me about my functions (not the digestive sort, of course!), asked questions about the work of the Mandates Section, he was altogether charming, and I sat there in an armchair very much at my ease, chatting man to man you might say, with His Excellency saying that it was his earnest wish that we should work together, close cooperation was what he said actually, and then paying tribute to the disinterested and difficult work of the L of N, and on top of that, listen to this it's very important you'll see why in just a moment, on top of that asking me to convey in person his good wishes and very best regards to Sir John, and so on and so forth. So, all in all, everything went off like a dream. I think I can say, without false modesty, that I was a definite hit.'

Ponderous, urgent, consumed by its purpose, the train lurched, gave a sudden cry of despair, and hurtled bone-shakingly into the tunnel with a crazed shriek of terror. A white eyelid closed immediately over the half-shut window and smoke billowed into the compartment. Victims of man, the stones and rails of the tunnel bounced their loudly echoing protests against the black, oozing walls, like martyrs bellowing their anger, boomingly cursing the hulking, obstreperous, panicking intruder, which hurried on, bustling, rocking, lunging in its headlong course. At the end of the tunnel the wrath abated, though a few echoes still reverberated against the smoke-blackened walls, where they were suddenly calmed by white smoke and all fury vanished along with the walls.

Delivered and assuaged now that it was free of the darkness and the hell, the train emerged once more into gentle countryside, awkward and eager, resuming its steady rhythm through the verdant fields and the rediscovered smell of grass. Lulled by its muted clanking, borne smoothly onwards, Adrien Deume stroked the soft red plush of the seat and smiled at his naked wife, who sat next to him.

'And now I come to the high point. Believe it or not, but the evening of the day I had my audience with the High Commissioner, a special messenger shows up with an invitation to lunch with His Excellency: proof positive of the first-class impression I had made! And the invitation was for the next day, a Sunday. Apparently invitations to Sunday lunch are a special mark of favour with the English. It was printed on beautiful vellum and had the official arms of Great Britain embossed on it in gold, with an engraved text requesting the pleasure and so forth, though of course my name was written in ink, in a fine, round hand, I've kept it to show you. Terribly impressive, as you'll see. It had my Christian name too. And an Esq. But to proceed. Anyway, next day at one on the dot I'm standing outside the residence, dressed up to the nines. I give the sergeant of the guard *carte blanche*, to wit my invite, and immediately he snaps to attention, salutes me smartly, and lets me pass. Looking supremely unconcerned, I proceed to the main steps and there, take note, both sentries present arms! You see, dear Madame, the sort of treatment your hubby gets! I would have liked you to have been there. Or to be there, if you prefer. After fifty-seven varieties of stone staircases and vast antechambers, an aide ushers me into an imposing room. His Excellency stands up as I enter. Like I told you, he's a field marshal. His Excellency Field Marshal Lord Plummer. We shake hands, I give an imperceptible little bow, thanking him for the honour and so forth, maintaining air of unconcern, projecting image of young diplomat thoroughly at home with protocol. Naturally, I kissed the hand of Lady Plummer, who arrived shortly after me, deep bow this time, it all went off very well. Next, cocktails, stuffed olives, conversation on a range of political, economic and social matters. After this a flunkey appeared and informed Lady Plummer, Her Ladyship he said, that luncheon was served. General exodus towards dining-room, with me offering Lady Plummer my arm and consequently being first in! Fortunately the aide had taken me aside and tipped me the wink in advance. Heavens, if you could have seen me ceremoniously leading the way with the wife of an English field marshal! Superb dining-room, impeccable standard of service, we are waited on by Arabs two yards tall in dazzling white djellabas with red-silk sashes round their middles, table sparkling with crystal, tableware engraved with the official arms of Great Britain! You felt the sheer power, had a sense of being part of the inner circle. I tell you, it took my breath away. Tomorrow I'll read you my notes in full, they're very detailed, how I behaved over lunch, who the other guests were, every one a luminary of the first water, yet it was little old me who got to escort Lady Plummer in! (He poked out his tapered tongue, then withdrew it immediately.) But I'll tell you about it all properly tomorrow, the various courses, I've noted them all down, the topics of conversation, all in English of course, and my contributions, which I think I can describe without false modesty as rather witty but subtle, a mix of Gallic charm and diplomacy! And sat on the right hand of Lady Plummer! But I'll save all that for tomorrow, my notes are very detailed, I wrote them up the moment I got back to the King, while my memories were still fresh. Just one other thing, the lunch I had subsequently with the aide, a delightful young captain, old titled family, Eton and Oxford, spoke marvellous French, highly cultured. I invited him to lunch at the King the following day. We drank champagne from start to finish! Anyhow, in the course of the conversation, I happened to mention, without any ulterior motive, that I was fed up at the prospect of having to wait another week for a seat on the plane, of course I said upset not fed up. He gave a mysterious, reserved sort of smile, you know, very old

English aristocracy. I didn't realize what that smile meant till the following day, when he rang me at the King to inform me, hold on tight, to inform me that one of the seats officially set aside for the use of the bureau of the High Commission was mine if I wanted it, on a flight that very evening. Imagine that! A VIP seat! For the record, that means a Very Important Person. Takes your breath away, doesn't it? But at least it gives you some idea of what pull and influence can do, that's what it's all about, you don't get anywhere if you haven't got connections and contacts. But I'll fill you in on the rest tomorrow. By the by, you have kept all my letters, haven't you? Because I stuck in a lot of local-colour stuff as a reminder for when I write up my official mission report. Good, capital! Because they'll come in handy for padding out the notes I took after each meeting. I hardly need say that I intend to cook up a report and a half. It'll create a stir, you can take that from me! Of course, I'll tart it up here and there, you know, the usual putting flesh on dry bones. Now, administratively speaking, I should be reporting to VV, who is then supposed to decide whether there are grounds for passing it on upstairs. So according to protocol the only name I should put at the start of my screed is VV's and nobody else's. But I know VV of old, he can't stand to see members of his section making a splash, especially if he feels they are potential rivals and therefore dangerous. So if I stick just his name down he'll hush my report up, because he'll realize it's just the sort of thing to get me noticed, he won't pass it on to higher authority, he'll just sit on it! Which means that, after giving the matter serious thought, I've decided to put a spoke in his wheel by taking the bull by the horns, and shall send my report straight to the top, through the usual channels of course, that is, by putting his name at the top of the report, then the name of my good chum Solal who has overall charge of the Mandates Section, and then Sir John's, no less! Yes, darling, Sir John himself, and that's final! Good wheeze, isn't it? Now don't go telling me I've no business sending my report to Sir John since according to regulations reports of official visits never go directly to him! Because I've got my answer ready if VV sticks his oar in! There are always exceptions! The fact is Lord Plummer, who is a field marshal for goodness' sake, which is the highest rank in the British military establishment, Lord Plummer, I repeat, High Commissioner for Palestine, KCMG, CB and so forth, personally asked me to convey his very best regards to Sir John! So I am duty-bound to convey same! That's my story and I'm sticking to it! I am therefore fully authorized to send my official report to the most senior of my superiors! QED. Anyway, VV will work it out for himself and I won't hear a squeak out of him and you can rest assured that he'll be too scared not to forward it! Lord Plummer! How about that!'

He yawned, stood up, and leaned his forehead against the window. A horse on a knoll peered sadly at the grass, then on a doorstep a little girl held a baby on her knee, a wall flashed past roaring like an angry sea at the lurching train, haystacks retreated rapidly, a peasant with a pitchfork on his shoulder stood by a gate as still as a scarecrow, and the mangy wagons of a goods train trundled by.

He sat down again, yawned, and stared at his nails. Buff them up ten minutes before they got into Geneva. She must have got a sheaf of invitations to cocktail parties now that he was an A. The question was, knowing what she was like, had she gone to the parties? She hadn't said anything about parties in her letters. Nor was there any word of the Kanakises, who after all owed them a dinner. Perhaps they were waiting for him to get back. In any case, must return the USG's invitation, to keep the contact going, and do it soon, make the most of the fact that Mummy and Dada weren't in Geneva. The USG was bound to accept, seeing that he had invited them first. Kill two birds with one stone and ask the Petrescos, who drew a lot of water. They wouldn't have to be asked twice, because he'd mention that the USG was coming. No, on second thoughts, not the Petrescos, he didn't want competition, and in any case Petresco, he of the confident, man-of-the-world air, was quite capable of hogging the conversation over dinner.

Matter-of-factly, the ticket-collector walked past chanting the name of the next station in a non-human voice. Five forty-five. Five minutes from now, Delémont, and three hours from now, Geneva! After all, she was his wife, for goodness' sake, and dammit he'd been deprived for three months, even though he'd been tempted at Beirut, but tarts weren't his style, besides there was always the risk of catching something unspeakable, so no thank you very much, not his style at all.

'Got this terrible urge, old bean, and I'm telling you now that I shan't be saying no to a spot of conjugal duty tonight! Believe you me, the bedsprings will be going like the Hallelujah Chorus! The minute I'm back, old man, I'll start my approach, I won't bother over-much with the formalities even if she holds back, because she's always been like that. Mind you, it isn't that she doesn't want to deep down, but she never shows it, it's a question of modesty with her, of reserve, respectable woman and all that, you see, also a matter of aristocratic distance, because, old man, without wishing to offend you, your wife and mine are chalk and cheese. No, don't poke your head out of the window, because of smut-in-eye. They say Swiss trains will soon be powered by electricity, it'll be cleaner, won't get so dirty. Splendid. Excellent.'

Five forty-seven. Two minutes nearer her. At nine, Cologny. At nine fifteen, Ariane naked, just for him. Five forty-eight. Delémont in one minute. 'Go to it, get a move on,' he told the train.

CHAPTER 70

Six o'clock I've heaps of time Yours Yours O my love why can't you
be here with me in this scrumptious hot bath it would be lovely just
the two of us never mind if a bit cramped for both we'd make
enough room somehow we'd think of a way the way that's as old as
Adam yes I know I've said all this about getting into the bath with
me before I keep repeating myself Eve was the first stupid woman to
say nobody understands my Adam no one realizes how wonderful he
is or put it another way all the things I say about you my darling I
wonder if chickens sneeze or at least if they do sometimes they're
perfectly entitled to catch cold aren't they thirty years from now I'll
be no it's too horrible never mind I won't be old tonight there's heaps
of time I feel oh so crazily tender when he's asleep so vulnerable his
face shines with a grace that is beyond the beauty of man I feel crazy
too when I catch a glimpse of his wrists so slender sometimes I feel
suddenly sick with myself for loving him so much now what was I
saying ah yes Yours Yours I wallow in Yours Yours yes but perhaps
if he hadn't met me he'd be wiring Yours to Elizabeth Vanstead to be
honest I wouldn't mind if all her teeth dropped out no steady on not
a gummy mouth that's not a nice thing to wish on anybody so just
let her lose a couple one of her front teeth would do just enough to
make her a teeny-weeny bit repulsive I find myself too attractive I
like looking at myself let's face it I fancy myself if it wasn't him there
would be somebody else and if the somebody else was an explorer I'd
be crazy about the Amazon or if he was a biologist about pickled flies
in jars no that's not true there's no one but him he's the only one

anyway believing that is an article of faith do Catholics really believe
in all the things they believe in why is it that you say everyone must
remember to take his hat off even when everyone includes women
too it's not fair why is it that you can't say everyone must remember
to take her hat off why is God always a man that's not fair either
what a pathetic spectacle me just now scrubbing myself down nothing
but a slave who lives to please her master woman's lot is unfair
always waiting and hoping and titivating what have stupid men got
that we haven't we're pathetic always having to be pretty and elegant
and fragile and demure and waiting and accepting and he takes me
too much for granted getting into Geneva at seven twenty-two and
not showing up here until nine and all because Mr Too-Big-for-His-
Boots wants to look his best maybe an hour in the bath and a very
close shave that's your feminine side showing my lad and no less
feminine are those peeps in the mirror you peep in the mirror a shade
too often it's a weakness dear and so stagy with his dressing-gowns far
too elegant and too long yes dear that's what we're like we slaves we
say nothing we look doe-eyed but we don't miss a trick only we're
very tolerant got the message have you dear what awful trouble
Stalin goes to all the time he has to keep an eye on everything trust
nobody have people spied on and killed and all for the stupid
exhausting fun of being in charge when he sees me home in the car I
always kiss his cuffs before saying good-night because they're so well
tailored and finest silk worship of might which is the power to kill
you see my dear I'm a good pupil I'd like him to whip me on the
back very hard so it raised stripy welts red to begin with then white
like a brand to show I belong to him I want it to hurt to make me cry
out with such pain that I beg him to stop but no he goes on yes beat
me more my darling aim lower no further down further yes that's it
hit me hard first the right cheek then the left it's because I was
brought up properly that I say right cheek left cheek the special ones
at the base of my spine beat them hard please beat them till the blood
flows oh thank you thank you darling get into the bath I am your
earth and you are my master and my ploughman plough me good
that's enough of that it's not healthy to think about ploughing
especially when you're in the bath no I don't think they can sneeze
there's a spot on the top of my head that's still tender it's the

fontanelle all babies have one I've still got mine another feminine thing about Bigboots is that he doesn't want me to meet him at the station because he's never properly shaved when he gets off the train Bigboots wants to be seen looking his best but you're always handsome too handsome when I'm not there he'll get to the Ritz at twenty to eight at the latest shall I ring him at twenty to eight no hearing his voice on the phone would be like having a preview of part of him it would be a damper on the lovely shock of seeing all of him walk through the door suddenly his voice his expression and all the rest if I ring it'll spoil the magic of his entrance it would be like eating before a meal just a small piece of cake *paaarlez-moi d'amooour* tell me again you love me it's silly but I like it feel like yawning go on then yawn aaah it's not the same when I touch them angels are a pain their music must be like César Franck only worse they're eunuchs with wings and I feel sick when I think of the spot where their wings are attached to their shoulders if I was in heaven I could never bear to touch that spot I think it must be hard and soft like a part of the chicken that's difficult to carve Antoinette is vulgar when I was little Uncle Gri always used to stand up when Tantlérie came into the room and thereafter if he saw that she wanted to go out he'd open the door for her and she would respond with an acknowledgement you know a little smile or a murmured thank you when the Kanakises came to dinner whenever Antoinette was at a loss for something to say because Kanakis and Didi were going on and on about books she'd never heard of she'd lean over her plate and jab with her fork with an amused clever smile on her face a witty flippant smile like a countess lost in her own thoughts as much as to say if I'm not saying anything it's solely because my mind's full of ultra-sophisticated *pensées* do people lean their heads against windows to think better in real life or is it just characters in novels we've got the message Herr Kafka you're a genius but for heaven's sake put a sock in it thirty pages of your genius are quite enough for anyone to see just how boring a genius you are though nobody would dare say so out loud not under the present reign of terror I'll smooth his eyebrows I'll reach my hands under his jacket to hold him fast and feel him close to me hold him tight so he can't run away he gets these moods seems so distant at times he makes me tremble with love I am his fair and his beloved he said so in the telegram Herr Kafka we've got your drift which is about feeling guilty when you've done nothing wrong but you do go on it gets tedious basically guilty-but-innocent is in fact the big Jewish theme it's the tragedy of the Jew I am fair and beloved of my lord I must tell him in case he's in an accident to put a note in his wallet saying they can contact damn my name's Deume all the fuss they make about Lindbergh after all he's only the driver of a taxi with wings who can joggle a joystick basically I get very cross about anything that does not sing Sol's praises and trumpet the greatness of his talents that's how silly women in love are they're forever bleating my Adam my Tom my Dick my Harry and they all say nobody else understands him I'm the only one who does my Adam my Tom my Dick my Harry is a genius they're pathetic the whole stupid gang of women in love Proust is marvellous but what a ghastly little snob all that hysterical flattering of Anna de Noailles and being entranced by aristocratic names like Oriane and Bazin and Palamède he drools reverently over them the little name-licker I haven't written much to the awful lawful but when I did write I was very nice to him geniuses know that genius means persistence morons believe it's a gift we'll go and put flowers on his cat's grave together Sol dresses perfectly and his table manners are *très comme il faut* that evening at the Ritz when I gave him my cigarette-case he pressed it against the scar on his eyelid surely that meant he forgave me for shying that glass at him men used to frighten me especially that certain something men have but not any more to redeem those two words I spoke I'll convert and become a good Jewish girl he's right how is it possible that intelligent people on our side can believe such stupid things it's the fear of dying that makes them so stupid oh it was such a fine and noble thing to want to be loved disguised as a horrible old man he said the dress I wore to the Brazilian reception when he fell in love with me at the first flutter of my eyelashes was very beautiful so I'll have another made just like it oh oh I'm freezing in this bath a drop more hot water please that'll do thanks when he gets here tonight try and hang on to reserve as long as poss keep your distance be pleasant but a shade stand-offish so he gets worried a touch of the ice-queen listen to what he says in such a way that he starts feeling uneasy answer along the lines of I don't know and maybe in a blasé sort of tone and then after a quarter of an hour of making him suffer suddenly come over all eager and loving another good ploy might be to leave the front door open so that he discovers me sitting down all regal and not getting up and holding out my hand for him to kiss he doesn't have such an effect on me when I'm sitting down or again I could be strolling in the garden and when I see him in the sitting-room looking lost because there's no one there I make my entrance all unconcerned no I couldn't I'd be far too excited I'd rush in like a dying duck and fall over my feet so the thing to do is to fling myself into his arms the moment he appears and eat him up with doe-eyed kisses the very first night after the Ritz quite unexpectedly there was a lot of wild kissing and tonguing on the sofa how awful doing that with someone I didn't know I was taken completely aback by those first kisses I always thought that kissing was just lips the thing should be made a great deal clearer in novels they say burning kisses and so on but I'd never have believed this other way was possible I used to think it was lips on lips and that was that but no you open your mouth three exclamation marks and then there's pandemonium and confusion of tongues as they say in the Old Testament my God if anybody had told me that some day I'd love to feel my I can't say the word mingling with the I can't say it of some man I'd never have believed it you must be mad I'd have said is it something that just he does or do other people do it too I wonder if Mummy and Daddy ever no surely not but Catholics probably do or maybe it's something he invented himself I was ashamed at first when his I can't say the word mingled with my I can't say it yes so ashamed but I persevered it was so amazingly intimate a thing to happen between a gentleman and a lady who hardly knew each other and were all of a sudden rummaging around in each other's mouths exploring gobbling yes I was terribly ashamed but pretty soon I stopped feeling ashamed and started to think it was nicer by the minute just think if Tantlérie had seen me I was every bit as good at it as he was and I'd never had any lessons either I got the hang of it straight off there were tons of kisses that first evening maybe five hundred all told and every one delicious tsk Ariane really I was in my element snorkelling away miles deep kissing like that is sublime but it also makes you want to laugh when you're alone and think about it afterwards because kisses like those can cause the most ridiculous kerfuffle yes I think you could call them have you anything-to-declare kisses because it's a bit like having some lunatic customs man poking around frantically in your suitcase quick quick turn everything upside down not a minute to lose I'm a funny sort of person even when I'm being perfectly serious inside I've simply got to have a giggle and say things such as kisses being like a crazy deranged rampaging customs man going round in a flap rummaging through your suitcase to see if you're trying to smuggle anything I think I'd curl up and die if he ever heard me babbling like this but when I'm with him I'm quite different I'm poetic and yet I'm just as much myself as I am at this very minute a drop more hot water please I wonder if a lot of snorkelling goes on generally do other people do it too if so it's too galling for instance a queen doing it with the king it's fine when we do it but not other people for it to be all right both parties must be very good-looking imagine Antoinette doing it for example I mean it would be horrendous is there a word for these eating kisses going-through-customs kisses cavern kisses snorkelling kisses fruity kisses that's it fruity kisses is just right because deep-down the world tastes so fresh when you're in love oops you sound like a silly factory-girl I was horribly embarrassed that first evening in the dark when he leaned over my neck well actually a bit lower it was awful but also awfully marvellous scatter a few improving books here and there on the sofa make it look casual leave one open to suggest me-reading-the-*Essays*-of-Montaigne-while-waiting-for-him sort of style no perhaps not Montaigne evokes crabby old schoolmarm best make it Kafka but if he asks questions he'll know I've only read a couple of pages I'd better get stuck into the complete works of Kafka at once buy a few Heideggers and something by other crashing old bores and also read a history of philosophy I've got an incentive now to improve my mind can't think why but I've suddenly got this urge to tell myself all about our first evening together yes go on tell us all about that first evening here goes in his drawing-room at the Ritz when he said goodbye I suddenly turned into something out of a Russian novel Nastasia Philipovna obsequiously salaaming and kissing his hand shut your eyes for a mental picture of what happened then he whispered glory be to God people say glory be to God when they're being very serious did he say it just for something to say or does he really believe in God when I kissed his hand I really meant it if there is no life hereafter all the true believers will never know whether it's true or not once they're dead they have all the luck no it wasn't him who said it was all a load of rubbish he's far too polite too sardonic I'm the one who says it's all rubbish anyway I withdraw the word rubbish I shouldn't have said salaaming O my love I'm not laughing at you please believe me it's just the way I go on you must believe that even if deep-down I'm very respectful I only say these things when I'm by myself because it's the way I'm made you can take it or leave it or take it please you do see it's just a cover because basically I'm rather shy then afterwards we danced in the ballroom at the Ritz he said awesome in your beauty then he said his soul flew out and clung to my long curved lashes sort of like a fish on a hook oh thinking back it wasn't very nice of me to have given him that cigarette-case which was a present from my awful lawful who is not my anything really but I'd forgotten that it was a present from the awful lawful but anyway since he gave it me as a present it was mine and I was perfectly entitled to do whatever I liked with it Didi poor pet what's happening to him is quite dreadful after the Ritz we came on here in his car yellow chauffeur white uniform huge blue Rolls who cares odd he can't drive obviously being ferried everywhere in a palanquin all the time is more his style his love perpetually released so that he might contemplate it and then folded away once more and shut up and kept in his heart I love that folded away Varvara would never have said that oh he's a brute but nice underneath while the rest are nice but brutes deep down fancy being in love with Varvara what a peculiar idea basically she was ordinary and sentimental and affected it's dreadful she's dead I should respect her memory she would never have gone on about baboons and spiders with her it was girly-talk and pretty-pretty stuff all the time in a little while I'll simply have to take a peep at my ravishing long curved lashes remember never buy accessories such as belts gloves handbags without first checking to see that everything matches read the Old Testament again though it's an awful bore a pink animal in ribbons a gardener's wife with her child a young lady with white cats hot water please you would not be seeking me had you not already found me that's a notion which makes people drool but personally I don't think it's at all profound actually I think it's rather silly with more sleight-of-word than truth to it a little girl named Lucie all alone in a tent in the middle of the African bush she wore pretty pyjamas with vertical red and green stripes she had a very small jaguar for a friend and she used him for a hot-water bottle in bed that cat of his ought to have been called Fluff not Kitty and then its kitten could have been called Fluffy I knew a cat called Fluffy which looked so drab and scruffy it spilt its milk and made a fuss and so I called it Blunderpuss what a nerve saying doe-eyed to my face and afterwards I danced all abject and only too happy to be doe-eyed such darling nerve there's something else I should do which is to say sorry for throwing the glass still how was I to know it was him never mind what's done is done the greatest leaders make mistakes so put it down to experience least said soonest mended after the Ritz we came back here little sitting-room gazed at the sky together me afloat on honey played the chorale awfully well when I'd finished turned round prettily and faced him charming serious sincere he was deeply moved I could feel it remember not to have it cleaned by just anybody there's a shop that specializes in cleaning suede in that little street I move around too much when I play the piano it shows up in my behind I must be more careful perhaps get myself a girdle that way curves less visible no you feel imprisoned besides it's bad for the circulation and then when he holds me close his hand strays down to well sometimes not always and I wouldn't want him to find elasticated fabric down there that wouldn't be much of a welcome and anyway what's a few curves curves are part of the female anatomy men like er well let's say hips and so do I too I think they're attractive but breasts much more so especially mine which are marmoreal it's tasteless to say marmoreal but when you're by yourself you can afford to be a weeny bit vulgar it's fun Solal is my bestest friend oh how I love him exclamation mark he loves me like a tender brother oh how he loves me exclamation mark here below relations friends and everything else may pass but he goes on for ever and by his grace he never wearies of me oh how I love him three exclamation marks now for the sofa on that first night the sofa came after the chorale he and I sitting on the sofa he being a man and me a woman so a man and a woman together and him in a white dinner-jacket all slim his black hair all tousled eyes so clear shoulders at least a kilometre wide and me sitting next to him looking quite adorable he draws near and I draw near too careful be sure you picture it accurately now first just lips then more than lips then snorkel snorkel me with my eyes shut performing like an old hand as if I'd been doing it all my life then getting very keen and acquiring a taste for it wanting more and beginning again twin mouths exquisitely tormenting and tormented frenziedly intertwining at deep-sea-diving depths oh it was glorious and when it was over we began again and yet before he came along and I was at the pictures and they showed a man's hand on the back of the girl's neck and her closing her eyes in ecstasy I used to say to myself I could never no it would make me laugh well I can tell you I didn't feel a bit like laughing when you think about it the way women like men is definitely odd our kisses weren't aren't in any way lewd or depraved they're just the way we have of expressing our love of saying I am him and he is me be careful not to keep him too late tonight make cut-off point one in the morning sharp I'm responsible for seeing he keeps in good shape that's my job now it's not the smoochy stuff I care about what matters is that he knows I love him and I know that he loves me so kisses are very important but they must be more than just physical our souls must seek each other and mingle by means of our kisses oh oh oh and then in the dark you know when he leaned over my my let's just say chestworks I felt the sweetness of his love not lust when he smokes he holds his cigarette between his third and fourth fingers I hold mine the same way oh be honest there was a hint of lust in the dark I was vanquished and deliciously ashamed and then I wasn't ashamed at all there I was a jelly entirely at his mercy like a grateful native girl obviously it all came as a bit of a shock that very first evening we had kissing with tongues first and then that other business in the dark but if I went along with it from the word go it was because I had absolute trust in him and anyway if I'd played up and created like some posturing nymph surprised while bathing it would have been as good as admitting that something improper was going on basically until now what I've been is a sort of virgin periodically raped by awful lawful I used to let him do it because I

591

felt sorry for him also sort of raped by S too and I used to let him do it because I was his friend and respected him but also out of vanity oh yes the stupid pride of knowing that I was desirable O Sol I'm sorry for hiding my pathetic little affair with S from you but I wouldn't want you to think that I've ever loved anyone else I've never loved anyone but you I am your maiden your virgin only with you do I S was nothing to me nothing he was a mistake it only happened because I was unhappy unhappily trapped in marriage I don't want you to despise me I don't deserve that I don't want to lose you eternity is each evening each moment I spend with you my lord which is why dying doesn't matter when it's me that touches them it's not the same thing as when he touches them and that goes to show that there's definitely something soulful about it something spiritual and proper anyway to do the things he does when he when he well anyway I'd need to have a bendy neck like a giraffe why do giraffes have such long necks perhaps it's so they can see their enemies coming miles away but how come their necks got to be so long perhaps it came about by accident perhaps there used to be several kinds of giraffes some with titchy necks touch my neck well anyway the ones with titchy necks couldn't see their enemies coming in time and got gobbled up by lions there aren't any giraffes like that left now only the ones with long necks survived or perhaps it wasn't an accident perhaps the longness came about gradually perhaps fear made them crane their necks which got longer and longer and mothers passed it on to their daughters not that I give a tuppenny damn coming back to that first evening fortunately I never wear a bra otherwise it would have been an uphill struggle especially for a first time it would have created the most awful tangle first I'd have had to undo it then take it off like in a doctor's surgery or at least pull it down which would have been terribly embarrassing he'd have had to wait until the performance was all over and I'd have died of shame while it was in full swing and besides it would have been undignified common a sort of striptease whereas in the event it all happened without my even noticing thanks to bra-less state or anyhow more or less it was all rather unreal and fortunately it was dark O God I wanted to talk about how noble it was and here I am going on about bras whereas it was holy after all that's what love your neighbour means fortunately he didn't look when I stood up and did up the top of my dress I would have felt humiliated he's taller than I am which is right that's how it should be I'm talking more and more like a shop-girl I love having to look up at him I love feeling very small that's how it is deep down we girls are all alike it's only our vocabulary that's different tell me sweetie is he good-looking I should say he is the Apollo Belvedere is a repulsive midget in comparison he's nice but he can be a brute at times that's what's so marvellous oh damn he said a lot of things at the Ritz about that sort of attitude but there it is there are times when his heartless smile makes me weak with happiness and there's that stony face of his which makes you behave like some fawning doll just so he notices you and becomes approachable I'd say one metre eighty-five I always thought Jews were all short his physical size is a reflection of his moral stature anyhow he's very handsome not handsome like your pretty young men but handsome because his noble soul shines through I've heard that all the girls in the L of N are crazy about him who told me that oh yes I think it was the awful lawful when he walks by the hussies all stare at him with their tongues hanging out like thirsty dogs the decent ones look away so they won't be tempted to stare poor things being stuck with the kind of husbands they've got you can well understand it when I was a Girl Guide I used to look up words in the dictionary for instance copulation it didn't help much I had a grasp of the general idea but there were details which escaped me before there was you I never kissed anyone the way I kiss you but you kissed lots of women you should have waited for me it makes me sad but at the same time I'm proud to think he has been so loved but they'd better lay off now I'll have to burn myself a bit to punish me for saying those two words burn myself just above my belly-button no you never know it's got to be a place that's well out of sight so burn myself on the sole of my foot with matches that way it'll hurt when I walk but it won't be visible it had to happen to me of course to fall head over heels for a Jew five centuries of Protestantism and that's where it's got me must remember tonight that my right side's my best but what shall I do if he sits on my left if he does say I'm a bit deaf in my left ear and tell him to sit on my right are you crazy or what make yourself out to be some sort of old crock no never out of

the question if he sits on my left get up as if I'm going to fetch
cigarettes and sit down again on my good side to ensure he's on my
right a simple elegant solution I get awfully silly when I'm by myself
rotten old cow she says insure instead of ensure rotten old cow she
says domestics instead of servants put some logs ready in the hearth
just in case it gets chilly if it does turn off the lights the two of us
sitting on the floor in the dark in the light of the dancing flames the
golden reflections on my face pull hem of skirt well down I'm glad
he likes his uncle so much it's very reassuring I love the way his uncle
gives him his blessing it's biblical I felt so thrilled and proud during
one lull between kisses it must have been around kiss number two
hundred I really admired what he said about his uncle but at the same
time I was wondering if he didn't want to any more but then it all
started up madly again we'll go into a church together and we'll hold
hands I should have gone to a beauty parlour but I'd have had to face
all those made-up trollops in their blue overalls and anyway they
might have made a mess of me mustn't forget to put out grapes and
peaches in my sitting-room they're useful because well anyhow in a
while try on the Volkmaars lay out the four that look best on me
then try them again just the four this time rule out half compare the
two winners and select supreme champion if none of them will do
you'll still have the ducky dress the neck's just low enough so it
should be all right provided all goes as planned I mean a girl has
to think of everything but it wasn't really my fault he begged me
after my suicide attempt went down on bended knee to marry him he
took advantage of my state wasn't in my right mind which means my
consent was not valid but when it's him it's divine so it must be
psychic which is a comfort the kisses must also be psychical but also
exquisite still you've got to admit that to the detached observer the
spectacle of wilful hungering mouths prodding churning would seem
highly comical and probably repulsive a couple of carnivores mouth-
in-mouth twin tongues unflaggingly snaking braided like initials
trying to intertwine and not succeeding but persisting nevertheless
and the result is uproar deep and probing yes exactly like a rampaging
maybe deranged customs official furiously ferreting through your
case and mixing up everything inside now that's enough there's to be
no more about customs officials God what sort of woman am I I

worship my lord and here I am up to my neck in water talking
sacrilege I really am beyond the pale what I've been saying is
abominable fruity kisses are absolutely divine but seriously darling I
do treat them as sacrosanct and give them with all my soul so when
he comes tonight countless divine kisses on sofa me pinned down
under him as he leans down and on with the divine fruity kisses all
flavours such as raging peach raspberry we're suddenly in calmer
waters then off we go again on another ride on love's raging
roundabout and then it's furious pineapple urgent apricot unruly
grapes passionate pear demonic apple and suddenly it's cherry and
sweet decelerating strawberry easy easy now O brother of my soul O
Jan of Janistan me at the end of my tether mouth hanging open just
letting it happen we're still in a heap on the divine divan and then
there'll be pauses and I'll be deliciously drained dry my head on his
shoulder like any mushy girl and then he'll take me in his arms and
I'll feel more and more gormless and helpless and protected by the
minute in other words absolute bliss and once more my lips will
meet his lips juices flowing though I've centuries of Aubles in me and
then him squeezing till it hurts a man and a woman and me unable to
hold out any longer and wanting him so much to take my clothes off
and look at me it's very nice being looked at when you've got no
clothes on I love it and I let him do whatever he likes inside my
mouth it's his kingdom oh yes and other parts of me are also his
kingdom his property his garden and I'll want him to take the
initiative and he'll sense it and then it'll be the other thing you know
leaning over my chestworks I mean over one of my smosob if you
must know that's right smosob smosob I say words backwards when
I'm too embarrassed to say them forwards anyway there I am like
some compliant queen being given her due it's heavenly begging him
to go on and on and on the right one then left then right again and
me grateful groaning purring politely in other words inarticulate
thanks and gently stroking my darling's divine and tousled hair so
that he knows I approve and am so very thankful and oh God don't
let him stop oh I'm so primitive and then all at once I say I can't wait
any longer and crave consecration I like a noble victim stretched out
on the altar oh his narrow garden let him in let him stay I hold him
there I urge him in oh stay for ever my beloved stay cloistered in

your nun of love oh when he is in me and I'm not ashamed to say it because it's so fine so noble oh oh when he's in me time has no meaning oh and when he finds release in me arching bucking release which I feel in me I look at him and time has no meaning and I acknowledge that someday one autumn evening I shall die perhaps of cancer this I accept because when he exults in me I exist outside time oh I am made happier by the joy I give him than by the pleasure I take from him oh my love tell me you are happy in me oh stay stay that's enough of that I forbid it because it's all getting disgusting no not disgusting my darling love but you do see it's intolerable especially in water water's dreadfully subversive oh my darling please come and be happy in me no but really put your foot down change the subject if only on account of those two poor little angels perched on their tap you're letting them hear things they're too young to know about darling don't despise me it just comes over me it has a will of its own I swear I feel ashamed of being so physical but I didn't used to be that way inclined at all when I'm talking to him say just that way not that way inclined but it's not wrong to be physical when love's your religion oh oh oh as she chanted a threnody the ravishing girl cupped her breasts and touched the nipples damn not the same thing at all she exclaimed giving way to dreadful rage and growing incensed because he was not there she devoured a large bar of scented soap like yes a black lizard yes that's much smarter and in conversation casually bring up analogies between Pascal and Kant so that he can see what stuff I'm made of take up riding again he must see me on a horse a Greek cruise me dressed in white and blue leaning over the ship's prow and he by my side watching me like mad and me with a far-off look in my eye oh when I look at him I'm just a native girl standing before a settler or rather a Romanian peasant with long plaits and bare feet gazing adoringly at her man a good thing to try would be to hold your nose and eat granulated sugar yes dearie we adorable creatures get hiccoughs when we're by ourselves on original sin he said that properly speaking it was oh I don't know what anyhow it was something to do with man's animal origins in other words a sense of guilt anyway I don't give a damn but you've got to pretend to take an interest when he asked for some photos of me when I was little I rushed off like some silly serving-girl I brought him my album he loved the photo of me when I was twelve knee-socks bare legs and ringlets he thought Daddy was very handsome said he looked scrupulous thoughtful I explained that the ring on my little finger with the Auble arms was Daddy's signet-ring which I had cut down to fit me he kissed the signet-ring Daddy it was as if he was asking your permission to love me that grey-flannel suit of his wonderfully cut he's the sort clothes always look well on doesn't wear his jackets waisted black tie with white polka dots women's dressmakers never get suits right they're always a bit approximate always overemphasize the waist I'll be firm about my next suit I'll say no nipping in at the waist got that my man darling I'm not afraid of you my man last night in bed I called him a cretin but you see darling you do bully me and it's rather nice to call you names back when I was little I used to stand outside toyshops and make magic signs I thought that perhaps when I got home the dollies I'd seen in the window would be there waiting for me no more Hungarian countesses no more Vansteads good riddance I wanted to tell him about my magic signs the day he went away but he came close and I couldn't my mouth was otherwise engaged so how could I say anything I get too passionate at night when I'm with him I'm afraid he'll think I'm awful call me medical names when he's being very attentive that is to say when he kisses my hand instead of hum you know what anyway when he's being attentive my conscious mind is ever so proud but my unconscious is another matter now mind you make jolly sure that his countess stays put in Hungary if we've adopted a rather formal way of speaking to each other most of the time it's really to heighten our appreciation of the more intimate er less formal moments sometimes when he looks at me the ends of both smosob get so hard that it's embarrassing they must show through my dress I worry in case they'll poke right through the material why am I becoming so dreadfully feminine I'd rather like to be a man but only in one department the rest I'd keep feminine hips breasts in fact the combination would be the perfect human being don't be silly everything is fine as it is don't change a thing let a man be a man and a woman a woman what sickens me is that I am so humble it started with my Russian salaaming it set the tone for our relationship yes it sickens me but I like it too it's funny I act like a woman in love when I'm with him oh yes I put it on and yet it's genuine too he is my god then next moment he's a happy little boy proudly showing me his new shaving-brush and I come over all maternal and turn into jelly oh the night before he went away oh when a good woman is in love a man can twist her round his little finger we women don't have any real moral sense at all if he wanted me to do something that's wrong though I can't think of an example let's just say something really infernal I just know that I'd do it remember to put out the fruit make it peaches have a bite of one just before he comes essential preparation for snorkelling and when he's here in intervals between snorkelling find way of taking another bite of peach as if your mind's elsewhere make out it's some kind of little female caprice all casual and delightful and pert the real point being to keep breath sweet and desirable and scents of garden indoors on second thoughts forget the peach peaches are too complicated it would have to be peeled first and that would make my fingers sticky and I'd make a mess and I'd drop bits and he'd notice and I'd lose face make it a grape now and then a grape would be much more discreet I could just pop one into my mouth on the sly without his seeing hello six twenty-five *Così fan tutte* gets tiresome when all those pretty young men and pretty young ladies start warbling quartets when I give Mariette her wages she always sort of bubbles in that way she has she comes over all friendly perks up no end not that she's close-fisted but for her holding her hand out for money is an absorbing ritual a fascinating ceremonial the way Mariette went on at the decorators was basically flirty a typical case of the glad eye the sort of thing working-class women do it always starts with that's men for you he must have liked it when I did my Romanian-peasant-girl-with-dangling-plaits number when you serve the tea don't put out biscuits because there's a reason oh what the I'll say it out straight here goes it's because biscuits leave might leave soggy little bits in my mouth and later on during snorkelling operations he'll find them and it would be a total fiasco I wouldn't be able to look him in the eye after that I've got a very literal mind but I can't help it and yet I am his completely his nun of love O darling the other day I called round to see Penelope Kanakis just so I could talk about you but to avoid arousing suspicion I said awful things about you O darling I said arrogant obnoxious heartless and

Penelope said she quite agreed the bitch I could have throttled her I left after a few minutes of very frosty chat and went on to Sigismonde de Heller's with the same thought in my mind I so needed to talk about you I also said that you're not as good-looking as people say Sigismonde objected violently she said all sorts of marvellous things about you clearly she's a person who improves with knowing just a little more hot water please thanks now darling I want to tell you how I kept you by me last night in a dark corner of the church how both our hearts swelled on hearing the joy of the fugue and we bowed our heads together when the grave-toned chorale growled and then we went out into the ill-lit square and we walked slow-stepped and you spoke of the organ and of God and I listened and I loved you on the wireless the minister said Thy kingdom come and I said Amen but I was thinking of your return do you remember that evening in your suite with the crowd of people and I was supposed to be just another guest it was wonderful to be making polite conversation like two civilized strangers and know that soon we'd be naked together but our eyes spoke of love and I blew you a kiss without anyone else being any the wiser wonderful to feel the caress of your hand when you offered me a cigarette we were exalted and raised above the crowd of conjugal mortals wonderful to take my leave of you and know that I would soon return when the others had gone oh hold me close I am yours in all purity with every fibre of my being you're a silly woman pull yourself together Debussy is ghastly so wishy-washy that old record of horrendous Yvette Guilbert she rolls her r's pronounces each word so carefully by that I mean she gives each word a silly spiritual charge if I ever get a cold I won't tell him that way I won't lose face I'll phone and say I want to be alone no don't phone write so he won't hear my voice all bunged up and nasal I'm sorry but I need to be alone that way he'll be miserable and he'll love me more so the unfortunate fact that I've caught cold and won't be seeing him will be put to good purpose another useful dodge when I'm supposed to go round to see him at the Ritz would be to ring up at the last moment and say I can't come or alternatively turn up late and to ensure I do turn up late have another bath just before leaving oh that'll make him really miserable do you remember the day I came to one of the L of N committees to see you doing your stuff you were ever so impressive jabbering away in English do you remember I sent you a note saying I love you and you read it with a face like stone and I was in seventh heaven watching you with a face like stone but afterwards you chatted pleasantly to Sir John hello said I to myself he can be very pleasant hello said I to myself he's got a boss and that's him and then when you'd finished speaking everyone clapped I whispered he's my man and his stony face lights up only for me and I suddenly had this crazy urge to go up to him in front of all the delegates and ask him to give me a fruity kiss I mean to say all those fully clothed serious people must get up to all sorts at night yes it's true when he's not with me I love him even more because when he's there he cramps my style and I can't love him properly besides things quickly turn all steamy when he's there and then I forget all about him I'm freezing a drop more hot water please thanks that's enough when I'm about to write him a letter I practise first before getting down to it in earnest I try different sizes and styles of writing then I place a blotter under my right hand to keep the paper clean and with my left I support one luscious breast I lean over the opening of my dress and breathe in the smell of my nakedness which rises with my body heat don't tell him that because unclean words should never pass a woman's lips especially during the day darling I want you to know that though I might seem passionately interested in what goes on between the sheets all that sort of thing comes a poor second in my book no don't tell him that he might be offended darling about that weekend we spent together at Ouchy in the Hôtel Beau Rivage you mustn't forget that I am my aunt's niece I wasn't used to hotels with quite so many stars do you remember this is the life for me I said strutting up and down proudly oh yes it would be wonderful to live with him in a hotel and never see anyone else that day I spotted him walking down the street I crossed to the opposite pavement because I wasn't sure if I was perfect enough to be seen oh that night at Ouchy as I lay in bed waiting while he took his bath I groaned I begged him to come quickly I felt oddly disturbed by this image I had of a woman waiting in a shameless state of nature waiting for the male in love with her own body which she contemplated as she waited oh when he takes me I say your servant your woman and I cry because I'm happy hollow-eyed inspired oh darling the day you came on horseback just as you were about to go I clung to your stirrup like the wife of the knight setting off for the crusades oh darling do you remember once it was three in the morning we'd just separated you'd just got back to the Ritz I phoned to ask if you would return to me and you came back so eagerly he must see how well I can ride too that'll be one in the eye for him you may do what you want with me take a horsewhip to my back or even lower down but you mustn't leave any permanent marks I love it when he looks at me when I'm naked sometimes when I'm by myself I like imagining that he's taking me by force or that I'm chained up and he's this male on the rampage I can't get away from him and he does the most dreadful things to me I don't see any objection to a spot of male savagery it suits me down to the ground why are you saying such awful things I despise you no don't despise me because I don't mean it it's just thoughts pure as the driven snow that's me I like singing hymns I thirst for your nearness holy lord of my faith in my great weakness what would I do without you every day every hour come to me Sol and stay oh stay by me and in the morning at the Beau Rivage after shaving he came and we had breakfast together it was wonderful there was a little blob of shaving-cream behind his ear which made me want to cry and then I drew his dressing-gown aside smooth tanned chest narrow hips and oh those clear greeny-blue eyes and also wakey-wakey it'll be seven o'clock soon look alive get out of bath look sharp dry yourself.

CHAPTER 71

'Best foot forward, try on dresses in sitting-room!'

Wearing bath-wrap and raffia sandals, she pitched all eight of Volkmaar's boxes down the stairs, helping them on their way with her foot because it was seven twenty-five and his train had already got in and in just a few minutes from now he'd be at the Ritz. But when she reached the foot of the stairs she told herself that it was quite absurd to be worrying her head about trying on dresses at the last moment when she had the stunning white linen number which wasn't creased or grubby. So the ducky dress it would be, and she could try on the others tomorrow, when she'd have plenty of time, her mind was always clearer in the morning.

'All right with you, darling girl? It's all right by me. But listen, should I phone him at his hotel after all, just a quick ring, to hear his voice? Oh please, do let me phone! No, darling, be sensible, I've already told you: a phone call would be like eating before a meal, a foretaste which would take the edge off seeing him again, and seeing him again must be a magic moment. So be patient, hold firm, and take Volkmaar's rubbish back to your room.'

Balancing four boxes on her head, she mounted the stairs, telling herself that she was a slave-girl in ancient Egypt carrying stone blocks for the great pyramid. When she reached the first floor she removed both the wrap and the sandals to add authentic local colour and so that she was a genuine naked Nubian slave-girl whose slinky walk quickened the blood of the Pharaoh, who, encountered by chance on the landing, promptly asked her to be his fair Pharaohess and Queen of Upper and Lower Egypt. She thanked him and said she'd think about it and would give him an answer later, after she'd had another bath, with fresh water, that's right dear, an odourless bath, because all the bath salts she'd just used smelled much too strong.

In her room, she put down the boxes and reached eagerly for her hand-mirror to check that all was well. All was well. She kissed her hand, smiled at the Pharaoh, who had followed her in, for he was anxious to know what her reply would be. She said that, having given the matter considerable thought, she was unable to agree to his request and went back downstairs, as Nubian as ever, to fetch the remaining boxes. On reflection, she really ought to have explained to Rameses the Bloated that she had given her heart to Joseph, a son of Israel and Prime Minister of Egypt. She'd tell him when she got upstairs.

Standing at the window, lulled by the pleasant jolting and gratified by the strenuous efforts made on his behalf by the train which was carrying him back to the good life at Geneva, Adrien Deume stared passively at the fleeing green meadows, the rapidly retreating corn-fields sucked up into the tornado which also made the trees keel over, and the telegraph poles which were joined by wires that drew the eye up and suddenly down. He lowered the window, through which damp, green smells immediately blew in, then a succession of distance-markers flashed past and a forest scuttled away bearing its secrets with it and a river glinted then promptly vanished, another train passed in the opposite direction, and he felt the heat of the engine as it hurtled by, wild, angry, full of breathy desire, leaving in its wake the staccato lights of the coaches, and then Adrien's train, stung to the quick, bolted as four gleaming rails shot away to the right. Must be doing a hundred and twenty kilometres an hour, he thought. Whereupon, determined to jot down an impression for his novel while it was still fresh in his mind, he took out his loose-leaf notebook and gold propelling-pencil. After staring for some time at the endlessly absconding countryside with eyes half closed to increase observational efficiency, he wrote down that the train was rattling along at breakneck speed and shut his handsome notebook.

He closed the window and strolled along the corridor. His first-class coach was completely empty, there was no one with whom he might have exchanged a few words. Hands in pockets, he yawned, proud of his ability to keep his balance, then hummed a tune, went into the lavatory for something to do, came out again, smiled at the waiter from the restaurant car, who, ringing his bell, bore down on him announcing the first service of dinner, and informed him that he would prefer to wait for the second service between Lausanne and Geneva. 'I'll be feeling more peckish by then,' he explained amiably. 'Ah,' said the waiter who went on his way reflecting on his daughter's leukaemia. Odd chap that, thought Adrien. For something to do, he staggered through the connecting section which smelled of wool grease and went observing among the third-class passengers. All along the corridor, which smelled of garlic and oranges, he allowed himself the moral indulgence of feeling sorry for all these poor folk who plied themselves with sausage, salami and hard-boiled eggs and huddled together on their hard seats. 'So sad,' he sighed happily.

Wearing her light linen dress and white sandals, she closed the shutters of her sitting-room, drew the curtains to create an atmosphere conducive to the solemnity of the occasion, switched on the reading-lamp, set it down on the occasional table, and looked at herself in her hand-mirror to check if she looked good in this light. The result was considered unsatisfactory. The source of illumination was too low and it made her face look hard and her eyebrows too thick.

'Makes me look like a Japanese mask.'

She put the lamp on the piano, sat down, had another look in her mirror, and scowled in disgust. Only half her face was lit. Now she looked like a Greek mask. Try putting the lamp high up, how about on top of the bookcase? She sat down again, peered at herself for a third time, and was satisfied. The diffused glow, which was almost as effective as concealed lighting, made her features look even and regular, like a statue's. Good, that's settled. But, when he came, be sure to sit on the sofa facing the long mirror. She tried it out for size. Yes, very good, because that way she'd be able to monitor progress in the mirror without his noticing, keep a regular check on the state of her face and the folds in her dress, which she could then adjust if necessary. Such a good idea to have had the long mirror brought down. And, since he would obviously come and sit next to her for the you know what et cetera, she'd be perfectly placed to glance up at her reflection during interludes to straighten her hair et cetera.

'On top of which there's another advantage. If I play my cards right and keep a weather eye open, maybe I'll be able to watch us billing and cooing, which would be too too divine, *n'est-ce pas?*'

Ogling herself in the mirror, her dress having worked itself up over her knees in the heat of passion, she pouted her lips in complete surrender. She resumed a more becoming pose, then clapped her hands in delight. Yum-yum! not much longer to wait! And now imagine you're him and try and work out if he'll like what he sees when he comes. She got up, stood close to the long mirror, smiled at it and stared approvingly at the face that he would admire when he came. For fun, she forced a squint then pulled dreadful faces so that she might exult in the contrast and in the rediscovery of her beauty when she stopped. Come to think of it, she reflected, she didn't really need him at all. She was alone now, and she was perfectly happy.

'Yes, sweetie-pie, but that's only because he exists at the Ritz.'

She kissed her lips on the cold smoothness of the mirror, admired her eyebrows, and was sorry that she couldn't kiss them too. That would be a job for him when he came. Oh the thought of him! In fearful joy she pinched her cheeks, pulled her hair, shrieked, and jumped up and down. And there would be such kisses, the ripe fruits of their love! She returned to the mirror, poked out her tongue diffidently, and then withdrew it at once, feeling ashamed. She stretched.

'Why doesn't he get a move on!'

But now down to serious matters. Start checking. The roses, all red ones, were fine. Three bunches, a dozen in each bunch, were quite enough. More and it would look as if she were grovelling. She ran one finger over the table. Not a speck of dust. Now the thermometer. Twenty-two Centigrade, the ideal temperature for you know what. She smoothed away an unsightly hollow in the cushion of the sofa, raised the lid of the piano, propped a Mozart sonata on the music stand and checked the magazine rack. All in order, no rubbish there. The *Vogues* and *Marie-Claires* were safely hidden in the kitchen. And now add a touch of intellectual tone. On the piano she put Pascal's

Pensées, and on the sofa a volume by Spinoza, which she left open. That way when he arrived he'd think she'd been reading a serious book while she waited. No, that wasn't right, it would be a lie. Besides it was dangerous to leave the book lying around, even unopened. It wasn't as if she were well up on Spinoza. Knowing about polishing spectacle lenses and pantheism was hardly enough. If he ever brought the subject up, she wouldn't exactly shine. She put the *Ethics* firmly back on the shelf.

What else was there? On the little table, next to the bowl of best grapes, she set out packets of cigarettes, English, American, French, Turkish, so that he could choose. She opened then closed each packet in turn. If they were left open, it would create an impression of overeagerness, make it shamingly clear that everything was intended for him. Fine, nothing more to be done here. After casting a glance all round, she left the room.

What could she do to smarten up the hall? Put down one of Tantlérie's rugs? No, out of the question, it would mean fetching one up from the cellar, and that was dangerous. Too risky: her nails might get broken, her dress might get dirty, maybe she'd twist an ankle, given the state of those steps. The last thing she needed tonight was a sprain. The easiest solution was not to turn on the lights when he rang. The Deumatitis wouldn't be noticeable in the dark, and she'd show him directly into her little sitting-room.

Damn! Clean forgot about the odourless bath! Seven forty-two already! There was still time, but only just. Right, extra-quick dip with plan of battle! Soap self while counting to sixty, no, make that fifty-five! On reaching fifty-six, rinse off lather, stop when get to sixty-six! Dry with towel, sixty-seven to eighty!

'Come along, darling, I'm going to give you a bath. Give me your hand.'

Back once more in his compartment, he felt himself every inch an A. Relaxing in his plush seat, he yawned, smiled at his wife, and wound his watch, which did not need winding. Quarter to eight. Lausanne in fifteen minutes. To make the most of the luxury which was placed at his disposal free of charge, he laid his head on the middle cushion, a fat sausage held in place by two straps. By God, you wouldn't find

Vermeylen travelling first-class! Poor Vermeylen, he'd forgotten to contact him, he would have very much liked to tell him all about his official visit. It was rather nice to think that the train was working so hard on his behalf, making such efforts for him, good old Adrien Deume, who was moving through space without moving a muscle, without lifting a finger, like a little king of creation. With his eyes closed and his head rocking deliciously on the cushion, he began in an undertone to draft the letter he would write tomorrow.

'Dear Mumsy, I send a loving kiss and hope you're not cross with me for deciding to bring forward the date of my return to Geneva so suddenly, but you must see Mumsy that it wouldn't have been fair now that my diplomatic mission to Brussels is over actually it finished yesterday to let another week go by without seeing my poor wife who must be feeling pretty bored all by herself, come on Mumsy smile for your ickle Didi, you'll never guess but I met someone awfully interesting, just as we were leaving Brussels this well-dressed chap got into my compartment and I sensed at once that here was someone I could get along with, very casually I glance at the visiting-card dangling from the handle of his case and I see that the person in question is Monsieur Louis-Lucas Boerhaave Director-General of the Belgian Foreign Office which means that he outranks Monsieur van Offel, my intuition hadn't let me down it's the little undefinable things that enable you to pick out distinguished persons, adopting the ploy of asking if he was bothered by my cigarette because as you can imagine I would never have dreamt of smoking my pipe in such company I struck up a conversation and it all went off very nicely, that's the advantage of travelling first-class you meet such interesting people, I should say that to start with he answered with a certain coolness but when he found out that I'd been staying for a few days with the van Offels who are socially on a par with him he immediately thawed and was tremendously friendly because he'd got me pegged, naturally I managed to slip in something about my lengthy official visit, in short he sensed that he was up against someone from his own social background, we chatted pleasantly about this and that, international situation, books, I found it most enjoyable, he's a very cultured man he reads Virgil in the original quotes bits of Greek but he likes a joke, for example we were talking about places to stay in

Switzerland and he said there were inexpensive but very pleasant little hidey-holes in Gruyère and he didn't mean the cheese, we had a good laugh about that, unfortunately he got out in Luxemburg and I was sorry to see the back of such a charming man I mean I had taken a real shine to him, he ranks with ambassadors and will be part of the Belgian delegation to the Assembly in September he'll be assistant delegate while Monsieur van Offel will be merely a technical adviser, we exchanged cards and I told him we'd be delighted to have him to dinner when he came to Geneva in September, so it's all fixed, pity we don't have a guest room that's bigger and especially more elegant, a decent guest room is the key to personal contacts, if we had one that was really decent I might have offered it to Monsieur Boerhaave there and then, which would have put us on an instant close footing, in fact we ought to have two guest rooms like the Kanakises do, then we could have both Monsieur Boerhaave and Monsieur van Offel to stay, we'll have to discuss it some time, don't forget to convey my warmest wishes and my thanks to Madame van Offel for her delightful hospitality along with my sincerest regards to Monsieur van Offel, and be sure you use the words "warmest wishes" "delightful hospitality" and "sincerest regards", they'll be noted and appreciated, I'm counting on you Mumsy not to leave this letter lying about on account of the comparison in terms of rank between Monsieur Boerhaave and Monsieur van Offel, the last named might perhaps take umbrage, but on the other hand you can mention casually that I got on very well with Monsieur Boerhaave.'

He gave a great yawn, stood up for something to do, staggered out into the corridor, pressed his face to a window, stared at the telegraph poles which went down like dominoes, at the grass less garish now in the gathering dusk, and at the mountains which stood out against the still light, still blue sky. He closed his eyes and prodded his stomach to check if it was upset. It wasn't, but all the same he'd best keep away from the restaurant car because the hors-d'œuvres he'd eaten at lunch still lay heavy on him. Pity, it would have made the time pass more quickly. He'd have something light to eat when he got home. Home sweet home.

'Hello, darling! How are you? Glad to see me?'

★

Crumbs! Nine minutes past eight! She stood up hurriedly and soaped herself, counting rapidly. At fifty-six she suddenly collapsed back into the warm water, which splashed in all directions. She shut her eyes so that she would not see the devastation. Then, plucking up courage, she turned her head carefully by small, fearful instalments towards the dress she had hung over the stool, and finally opened one eye. Her light linen ducky was dripping with soapy water! Ruined! She was done for! O God, it would have been so easy not to have flopped into the bath, such a simple thing to have taken three seconds longer and got back in patiently, in a civilized manner! Oh for a miracle! If only she could turn back the clock one minute and not have rinsed herself yet and been able to submerge herself gently!

'Damn you, water!'

She made herself cry, and lashed out with her foot at the damned water. What should she do now? Rub the dress through quickly, then rinse and iron it? Sheer madness! It would take at least three hours for it to be dry enough to iron! But hold on, all was not lost, there were the rest of Volkmaar's concoctions. She got out of the bath, dripping wet but determined to put up a fight and save her love.

In her room, naked and only half dry, she got out Volkmaar's dresses and suits and threw the empty boxes, which got in her way, out of the window. Too bad, strolls in the garden with him were off the menu, boxes *causa*. Blast, the swing-mirror wasn't there. Try the lot on in the bathroom. To be able to see herself in the mirror she'd have to stand on the stool. She set off at a run, laden with a jumble of clothes.

No point even thinking about the four suits, none of them were any good. Heave-ho! And she tossed them one after the other into the bath, where they became waterlogged and slowly sank. Alternately climbing on to the stool then stepping off it, she tried on the dresses. The white crêpe was too full, though she'd told the stupid oaf over and over. One, two, three! And she drowned it with the unhinged smile of the desperate. As to the so-called sporty number with wooden buttons, there was absolutely no point in trying it on, it was the beastliest of the whole bunch, that much she'd realized at the last fitting but had been too cowardly to say anything! She had been as cowardly at the dressmaker's as she had been at the registry office when the man had asked her if she took you know who to be her awful wedded husband. Husband a fiasco, dresses a fiasco! This vile rag was much too short, and besides the stupid material was rough, stiff and heavy, she'd positively melt in it. Give it the old heave-ho! Into the drink! And now for the black velvet, her last hope. It was a fright! A long fatuous sack, and to boot it gaped at the neck even when she was standing perfectly straight! A neckline that gaped when you leaned forward was perfectly in order, but one that positively ballooned when you were standing up! Volkmaar was a swine! Oh, if she could she'd cut off his nose in slices, and each time she cut a slice she'd wave one of his dresses in his face! Away with you! Into the bath you go, black velvet! She watched it as it foundered and joined the others. Oh what a mess. My God! Twenty-five past eight!

'Keep cool. Look through the old ones.'

From the wardrobe in her room she took the white dress she had worn at the Ritz. Nothing doing, it was obvious that it had been worn, it was all creased. And she'd had weeks and weeks to get it washed and ironed! Damn Mariette, who should have thought! Never mind, slip on the white linen skirt and the sailor top. No, too awful. All those dresses she had ordered, all those stocks she had sold so that she could end up wearing a morning outfit at nine at night! She went back to the wardrobe and riffled frantically through all the clothes on their hangers. Keep calm! Cool head! How about the green? It was old but possible!

Back in the bathroom, she stood on the stool, held the dress against her nakedness, and inspected the result. The green made her look waxen, like a lemon. Overwhelmed by misery, she did not even think about drowning the offender, took it back with her to her room, where she stood by her bedside table, turned the photo of Sol to the wall so that she wouldn't have to see him, lit a cigarette, and then stubbed it out at once. Noticing a length of string left over from one of Volkmaar's boxes, she picked it up, started pulling at it, trying to snap it, yanking and tugging, twisting it this way and that in a flurry of nerves. Half past eight. Sunk, she was completely sunk, she did not have a thing to wear, and when he rang the doorbell, and he would be ringing it soon, she wouldn't be able to answer the door and he'd go away. She yanked the string, disaster staring her in the face, hauled on the rope of her misfortune. 'Sunk, sunk, sunk,' she chanted to beguile and numb her unhappiness and be lulled by it. She picked up the green dress, gripped one end between her teeth, and pulled hard on the other. The material tore with a protesting groan.

'Now where's that got you, you moron, you imbecile, you silly silly cow,' she snarled, hating herself.

She dropped the dress, kicked it away, picked up the string, and dazedly resumed her grim sport, pulling it this way and that and mouthing meaningless words which smothered her wretchedness. She brandished her fist at heaven, which was to blame, and then collapsed in a heap on the bed. Sunk, she was completely sunk, she had nothing to wear.

'Stupid cow! Rotten old God!'

Suddenly she sat up, jumped off the bed, grabbed a key, and ran out of the room. As she used to when she was a little girl, she mounted the banister and slid down it, the feel of the wood against her bare skin reminding her that she was wearing nothing. No matter, there was never anybody about outside at this time of night. She raced through the garden, which was littered with Volkmaar's boxes, darted into her Dreamy-House, opened the wardrobe, snatched Éliane's dress and sandals, and ran back indoors, ambered by moonlight.

She stood in front of the mirror, shut her eyes, and put on the silk dress which still carried the scent of Éliane. Then she opened her eyes and gasped. The dress looked even better on her than the linen ducky! A revelation! A Greek statue! And now for the gilt sandals! Breathless, she fastened the straps, smiling as she did so at her bare legs, which went awfully well with the noble folds of the dress. Oh Samothrace, oh Victory, oh all the birds of the air that flew on fluttering wings of innocence!

Motionless in front of the mirror, she worshipped her new-born soul in this dress of silk so pure, so white, then moved her arms, her legs, to see and admire the way it hung and clung. Oh her darling! Oh she who was his alone! Euphorically, for he would find her beautiful, she smiled at herself in the dress which had once robed the beauty of one who now lay rotting in earth. Absurd in her youth in front of the long swing-mirror, she sang the air of the Whitsun hymn once more, sang the coming of a heavenly king.

The ticket-inspector proclaimed the imminence of Nyon, and Adrien opened the window and leaned out. Working-class houses came into view, and a girl at a window waved her hand. The engine gave a long hysterical whoop, and its billowing smoke was understained by the glow of fire, and more rails glinted and went forth multiplying, and stationary trucks rolled past looking lonely and bored, and then the station arrived, and the train faltered, blew off steam, and finally sighed to a stop in a concatenation of jolts fore and aft while the rails squealed like a beaten dog. 'Nyon,' intoned a voice of fathomless melancholy outside.

He stood up, lowered the window, and smiled with satisfaction. Eight thirty. The time to the minute given in the timetable. Jolly well done! These Swiss trains were spot on. Did you a power of good being on trains that arrived on time. Right then, here we are in Nyon, last stop before Geneva. Geneva in twenty mins. When the train sets off, make self presentable. Brush clothes, remove dandruff, comb hair, give nails a thorough scrub.

The engine shrieked like a mad woman, and the wheels groaned then made up their minds after a series of jolts, back-trackings and much clanking of tortured metal, and the train chugged on its way. Eight thirty-one, exactly as per the timetable. Due into Geneva Cornavin at ten to nine! Ten minutes by taxi to Cologny! He rubbed his hands savagely. At nine o'clock, that is twenty-nine minutes from now, he would see his wife and be happy! By the stars, he'd take her up a cup of tea and a half tomorrow morning!

'Morning, slinky-boots,' he murmured, making his way to the lavatory to make himself handsome for her. 'Sleep well, pet? Get a good rest? Here's a nice cup of tea for my sweetie!'

CHAPTER 72

Turning her back on the shipwrecked dresses, she put the finishing touches to her hair with untold strokes of her comb, first bold and expansive, then minute and subtle, circumspect, barely perceptible, a sequence of enigmatic pats and impalpable caresses executed in pursuit of an absolute of such infinitesimal perfection that only a woman could comprehend their relevance or appreciate their purpose. And all to a generous accompaniment of smirks, trial smiles, steps backward, frowns and long, searching looks. Pronounced stunning by self after a final impartial scrutiny, she glided out of the bathroom with soul refreshed and certain of her destiny.

But when she reached her sitting-room a fresh inspection was necessary, because it was here, in this light, that she would be seen by him. Half past eight, she had heaps of time. So, parking herself in front of the long mirror, she embarked on a ruthless quest for imperfections, undertook a meticulous close-range inspection of her face, and emerged from the grilling acquitted of all charges. Everything in order, no further action required. Lips excellent, no shine to nose, hair studiously disarranged, teeth glowing, thirty-two smilers firmly mounted, all present, correct and dazzlingly white, breasts, an indispensable item, as and where they should be, one on the right, the other on the left. Her nose was a bit big, of course, but that was part of her charm. Anyway, his nose wasn't exactly small either. She reset a wisp of hair over her brow, shook her head to rectify the rectification and make it look natural. Then, keeping her left sandal flat on the floor, she angled the right so that the outer side showed and the inside remained pressed to the carpet, her intention being to see if, in a pose which she imagined set her off to advantage, the dress really looked good on her and was neither too long nor too short.

'Heartiest congrats,' she concluded, and she dropped a curtsy to her reflection.

Still feasting her eyes on herself, she essayed a sweet smile and judged the result a success. Then, using her little looking-glass, she inspected her back in the long mirror, noted that all was perfect, especially in the hindquarter division. In the matter of her profile, remember to show the right side.

'Come on,' she cried, suddenly delirious with glee, 'get your skates on, fat-head, yes, I mean you, Solal, that's right, you absolute fat-head!'

Revelling in the sacrilege, she raised one hand to her mouth to cover a shocked grin. Then, after a further dab at the same wisp of hair and a final adjustment, she walked to and fro in front of the mirror, glancing into it slyly for glimpses of herself in motion. The dead girl's dress showed her hips much too blatantly, her sumptuous hips of which she had been ashamed once upon a time, disclosed much too clearly the light, lilac-scented, curved pubic arch. A bit blush-making, too revealing, too much on display. Heigh-ho, everything was his by right.

'Should I take just a peep at them? Just a little one, then, so I know what kind of impression they'll make on him. After all, if he's entitled to see them, why not me too? I mean, they are mine.'

After making herself decent once more, she again inspected the thermometer. Perfect. Good job there was no need to light a fire, the heat would have made her cheeks go all scarlet. Should she take a stroll in the garden to fill her mind with suitable thoughts? No, walking about might well spoil her face. The most sensible course was just to sit down and move as little as possible so as not to mar her perfection.

She sat in an armchair, holding her hand-mirror to ensure that the rose of her beauty did not wilt, and kept a watchful eye on her complexion for worrisome signs of deterioration. Paying particular attention to her nose, which she feared might well begin to shine in the warmth, she sat still and straight, like a model pupil, not stirring and hardly breathing to avoid spoiling her exquisiteness, a sacred idol which was yet fragile and beset by multiple dangers, scarcely moving her head and preferring to swivel her eyes whenever she glanced up to see the time by the carriage-clock. At intervals, still peering into her hand-mirror, she pouted her lips sensuously, or rearranged a fold in her dress, or raised one hand to her hair, to straighten, though without appreciable effect, some minutely errant strand, or inspected her nails, or lovingly contemplated her gilt sandals, or rectified another fold, or tried a smile which was altogether finer and subtler, or studied her teeth again, or checked the time, trembling all the while lest her beauty might fade as she waited.

'This light is no good at all. Too harsh. It's the white lampshade that's wrong. I'm already starting to look a bit red. By the time he gets here it'll be even worse, I'll look like a farmer's widow who's just put away an enormous dinner.'

She went out and came back clutching a red silk scarf which she draped over the lampshade. Standing on an armchair, she gazed round the room and felt better. The light was just right now, mysterious and suffused. Sitting down again, she consulted her hand-mirror and liked what she saw. The new light had banished the flush from her cheek, which was now clear and pale, like jade. Yes, fine, sort of enigmatic chiaroscuro effect, terribly Leonardo da Vinci. Twenty to nine. 'Another twenty minutes,' she murmured, breathless with excitement. Why couldn't the beast come a bit early? At this instant she was quite perfect. Smoke a cigarette to calm nerves? No, might stain teeth. Anyway, if there were to be fruity kisses it wouldn't do to reek of tobacco. Incidentally, when he rang, don't forget to eat a couple of quick grapes before answering, just one or two to keep mouth fresh, indispensable for snorkelling.

'And even when he's here, munch a surreptitious grape or two from time to time, taking care he doesn't see you, or, if he does, making it seem all very casual, though really it will be to maintain oral freshness. Awfully petty this, of course, but what do you expect, I'm a woman and a realist, the point being that it's absolutely crucial that he should find unadulterated pleasure in you know what. At this moment my mouth is a little dry because I'm excited. But he'll think that the freshness of the grapes comes from me, an amazing, natural freshness. That's how it is: a girl's got to think of everything.'

The packets of cigarettes closed like that made the place look like a tobacconist's. To open them all would obviously be taking things too far, but opening just a couple would do the trick, it wouldn't make it look as though she were falling over herself to please him. How was that? Yes, very good, much more friendly, altogether cosier. And now a ticklish question. What sort of welcome should she lay on for him when he came? Wait for him at the front door? No, that would suggest overkeenness and make her look like a housemaid. Wait for the bell to ring and then open the door? Yes – but what then? She stood up, again made her way to the long mirror, and held out her hand to it with a hostessy smile.

'Good-evening, how are you?' she said in her most breathily aristocratic voice.

No good, that made her sound like an overeager Scoutmistress. Besides, that 'how are you?' wasn't exactly romantic. How about leaving it at good-evening, and lingering over eeevening in an untamed, whispery sort of way, with a hint of sensuality thrown in? 'Good eeevening,' she said, trying it out for size. Or perhaps she could just hold her hands out and not say anything at all, as though there were not words enough to express the moment, and then collapse into his arms like a bird with a broken wing? That was a possibility. Of course, saying 'Good evening, how are you?' when he got there would have the advantage of establishing a suitably disturbing contrast between the respect for social convention shown by the question and the aforementioned collapse and the subsequent hungry kiss which would have to follow immediately if full advantage was to be taken of the grapes.

'No, not feminine enough. Wait for him to make the first move.'

She moistened one finger, rubbed a mark on her left sandal, inspected her nostrils in the hand-mirror, checked them for come-hitherness by making them dilate, and redirected a dozen hairs to the right. This light was definitely too dim, he wouldn't be able to see her properly. It was too red, it was oppressive, ambiguous and really quite *louche*. That was because the silk round the lampshade was double. Just make it the one layer. She climbed on to the armchair once more and made the change. The lighting was unassailably respectable now, with no hint of bawdy-house or lewd dancehall.

Nine minutes to nine. She improved the arrangement of a few of the roses, removed one which was wilting, and put it away in a drawer. Then she repositioned one of the vases and put another at a safer distance, because it was too near the sofa and might get knocked over. Seven minutes to nine. She munched two grapes and moistened her lips. Everything was now under control.

Six minutes to go. She had thought of something a little while back. What was it? Ah yes, don't draw his attention to the new rug, don't give the impression that one had gone to a great deal of bother for his benefit. He must think that it all looked divine without being able to put his finger on why. That way she wouldn't lose face. If he did notice the new rug, react casually. 'Do you like it? Yes, it's not bad.'

Oh no! The cigarette packets were all full! He would realize she'd bought them specially for him. How shaming to show so obviously that one danced such attendance on him. She half-emptied all five packets. Where could she put the cigarettes she'd removed? Crikey, four minutes to nine, he might be here any time now! She threw the cigarettes under the sofa. No, that wouldn't do. If he sat down in any of the armchairs he'd see them for sure! She hitched up her dress to avoid creasing it, got down on hands and knees, and collected up all the cigarettes one by one. Throw them out of the window? No, if they did go for a stroll in the garden after all, he'd see them there. Hide them upstairs! The coolness of the evening reminding her she wasn't wearing any panties, she headed for the stairs at a run, both hands full of cigarettes. How stupid! She was always forgetting her panties! From now on, hang a sign on the handle of her bedroom door with the word panties followed by an exclamation mark.

When she reached the top floor, she gave a sudden start, felt her heart leap, and the blood surged to her face, which promptly turned scarlet. The doorbell! She flung the cigarettes into the bath, rushed into her bedroom, grabbed a pair of panties, and wasted time telling herself that it was a waste of time putting them on. Heigh-ho, forget the panties!

On the first-floor landing, she did an about-turn, went back up to check with the mirror in the bathroom. Damn, why had her nose chosen this of all moments to start shining? Where was the face-powder? Never mind, talc would have to do! She dabbed her nose with it, decided it made her look like a clown, reached for a towel, and removed the talc as the doorbell rang again. Shout down that she was coming? No, that would scatter the magic.

She tore down the stairs, suddenly noticed that she was holding a pair of pink panties in her hand, and dashed away and stuffed them into the bookcase behind Spinoza. Disregarding the impatient jangling of the bell, she took one last look at herself in the mirror, forcing herself to be calm so that she could take proper stock. Not disastrous. In fact distinctly presentable.

'All right,' she murmured, 'I'm coming.'

Good. The fact that he was ringing meant he hadn't gone away. Feeling weak at the knees, she headed for the door to Wonderment, opened it with an exquisite smile, and recoiled. Holding a suitcase in one hand and his thick walking-stick tucked under his arm, there stood her husband, Adrien Deume, with his wispy beard, his horn-rimmed glasses and his good-natured grin.

CHAPTER 73

That same evening, squatting in the grass of a meadow in the vicinity of the *Casa* Deume, Naileater, Solomon and Mattathias silently watched as Michael, his back to a hayrick and one leg folded under him, magnificently bedizened with furbelow and engraved silver cartridge-belt, sat languidly smoking his gurgling hookah while the glowing embers sputtered in the gold-brown tobacco bowl. Weary of waiting, Naileater resumed.

'Come, Michael, O man of mischief and tormentor of our souls, O monstrous issue of Leviathan, O clandestine getter of one hundred and one bastards, will you not break your silence and will you not reveal for what purpose we are gathered here in nature's tedious bosom, lit by the light of a wood fire? Do not think that we shall with patience bear our fate much longer while you sit forever, with your eyes closed, smoking like a sultan! Come now, quit your English reticence and be forthcoming! What is this secret mission? What manner of plot have you hatched? What are we doing here at a vesperal ten fifteen by the light of a full moon? And what is the meaning of the two dangerous white horses which you tied to yonder tree without so much as a word of explanation?'

'And why have you not sent away yon mobile, internal-combustion-engined conveyance, which, though self-propelling, eats money and has a relentlessly ticking clock?' demanded Mattathias, pointing with his gleaming harpoon-hook at the taxi parked on the roadside with its lights extinguished. 'And why the madness, unknown in rhyme or song, of ordering its guide and shepherd to wait? Have we no legs? In any case, I say to you now that I have no intention to disburse, in whatever degree, even unto the smallest of quotients, the Swiss monies which figure in remorselessly rising succession upon the face of the clock of exploitation!'

'Come, Michael, unlock the portals of your eloquence, tell us your secret!' commanded Naileater.

'Yes, explain yourself, dear Michael of ours, because it pains us to walk in the path of ignorance!' begged Solomon.

Michael closed his eyes by way of signalling his refusal, then opened them again, revived his flagging water-pipe with a few fresh embers, inhaled deeply of the smoke, which he then proceeded to send out in small puffs which he contemplated from a lordly height.

'Speak! I have been asking you to speak for aeons of time!' cried Naileater. 'If it is my death you want, then out with it! You cannot seriously think that I am the sort of man who can long tolerate living when I know that there is another who knows something I don't?'

'And I, Simple Solomon, walk in deeper darkness still!' said Solomon, gesturing diffidently. 'All I know, victim that I am, is that this morning I was yet in Athens in the pleasant company of your good selves, dear cousins all, ready to take joyful ship at Piraeus, port of Athens, and sail away to the fair isle of Cephalonia where we were born and which is without compare, and also to a reunion with my revered wife, also without compare, nurturing the great joy of clasping her to my heart after so many sojourns in divers lands, when worthy Saltiel was struck by a sudden desire and bowel-stir of sweet emotion to feast his eyes once more on lord Solal, the nephew of his soul, and this tender and loving uncle forthwith ordered our immediate departure upon the wings and winds of the air! So come, poor Solomon, obey! Obey, O hapless man, and give up the enticing prospect of seeing your wife once more!'

'Well spoken, tiny one,' said Naileater. 'But I would remind you that your wife has one tooth only, though it is true that it is a handsome tooth, and firm. But pray continue your babble, for you interest me!'

'And so, uprooted like a flower, without pausing to attend to my morning devotions at the synagogue, and risking death most abrupt, I was forced to take wing by flying-machine and come with you unto this city of Geneva! And now I find myself in the dark middle of nowhere, exposed to the ravages of a sore throat induced by the nocturnal cool, and comprehending not, poor unhappy wretch that I am! O Michael, O cousin of the same aboriginal loin, a Solal as I am myself, tremble lest I too should succumb in the arms of the angel of death! O my friend, take pity on my ignorance and throw me the weeniest word of explanation!' concluded Solomon, holding his hands together and raising his eyes to Michael, who yawned to show just how little he thought of the diminutive petitioner.

'Be silent!' said Naileater, pushing the little man to one side. 'Hold your peace, O dregs of the spoon and scourings of the macaroni pot! And you, Michael, hear me! What is the meaning of this cruelty, the twin of which is yet unborn? Will you not take pity on me? Was I not made to suffer enough by the grief and tribulations inflicted on me in London by a fair lady of noble extraction? Have I not had my fill of suffering ever since I set my toes once more upon the soil of the land of William Tell? Do you discount entirely the pain I felt when, on stepping out of the distance-eating flying-machine this afternoon, we observed that our beloved cousin Saltiel had been suddenly struck down low by jaundice of the deepest yolk and were obliged to install him in the finest clinic in Geneva at fifty francs a day full board, exclusive of any fearsome bills issued by the pea-brain of a consultant?'

'And this same poor uncle instructed us to conceal his illness from the lord his nephew who was not to be worried,' broke in Solomon, 'and instead enjoined us to inform him that he had been unexpectedly obliged by a matter of business to remain in Athens, a most thoughtful mark of consideration!'

'Close your inconsequential orifice, O little toenail, or should I say mere clipping of same?' ordered Naileater. 'Let him speak who has words to speak and the gift of speaking! That said, I now pick up my thread of argument, hand on heart. I was, I believe, telling of my sufferings. O Michael, O true Bengal tiger, I ask you again: Have I not suffered enough? Will you set at nought my feelings of humiliation when, admitted into the presence of the nephew of Saltiel, albeit not until eight o'clock this very evening, we conveyed to him his uncle's heroic stratagem, to wit, that he had remained in Athens, at which the said nephew dismissed my good self, Mattathias and Solomon, incomprehensibly singling you out to be alone with him while, like an outcast, tail between my legs and withered by an unwarranted slur which turned my heart to miry blackness, I left, accompanied by the cousins here, in deepest penitence and severest loss of face, to await your return, which we hoped would be both prompt and fraternal, in the hotel noticeably lacking in running water, where we indeed waited upon your coming, though not without first having laid in a provision, with you in mind no less than myself, of much drink and mouth-watering viands courtesy of the Jewish grocer-cum-victualler from Salonica who stays open until midnight and from whom I purchased, counting not the cost and with money no object, for expense means nothing to me, because death is my constant companion as are the torments which will necessarily precede it in the shape of spasms, choking fits, lacerations of the chest and divers gargly rattles, which is why I spit on coin of gold both *seriatim* and *privatim*, from whom I purchased, as I was saying, his entire stock of ready-to-eat fare, including a consignment of luscious squid just in from Marseilles which he fried in a vast sizzling pan in my presence! Such crispy, crunchy squid which cry out: "Come, ye hearts of oak, come feast on us!" Do you set at nought the generosity which, though consumed by an equine hunger, led me to ordain that all should await your coming so that the said squid should be eaten in your company, in the comradeship of the family bond? In conclusion and fourthly, did not my cup run over when, upon your returning to the hotel, an event which did not occur until as late as approximately a quarter past nine, I, though faint with hunger and gripped by a fever of curiosity, enquired courteously, concernedly and considerately as to the reason for your mysterious tardiness, only to receive a new blow to my authority, influence and honour by your returning the impertinent reply that you had been for a short walk with Saltiel's nephew, which answer you gave with a heart-stabbing absence of detail designed to ride roughshod over my dignity! Was ever man treated more unjustly? O cruel fate! O mother of mine who now lie mouldering in your grave, why did you bring me into this harsh world?'

Striking a tragic attitude, he drew one hand across his glistening brow to wipe away his sorrow.

'You have a way with words, O learned one,' said Solomon.

'I am perfectly well aware of that. But to continue my oration. What happened then, O Michael? You bade us go with you on a secret mission, the nature of which you cruelly refused to divulge despite my tender entreaties, though you promised to explain all when we reached the theatre of operations where the plot was to be executed. To this I acquiesced. More, I humbly bowed my head and armed myself with patience while you attended to your toilet, endless ablutions and sprinklings of perfumes accompanied by warbling of mindless love-songs and the application of the pomade yclept Hungarian to your dyed moustache, the ends of which you raised and fixed in place by means of a fine but absurd net which remained anchored to your ears for some considerable time.'

'Moderate the roar of your flatulence, for pity's sake,' said Michael, 'for I can barely hear what you say.'

'I always break wind when I am upset, dear Michael. But, to resume, we embarked on this mission, bearing the victuals in high hopes of a convivial repast after unveiling of said secret!'

'I know all that. Why bother to tell me?'

'Because there you have the exordium, the necessary prolegomena and indispensable ingredient of any speech, the marrow of eloquence and heart of the edifice of the orator's craft, that's why! And so, armed with viands which thus far had profited us not, we came with you in this self-propelling conveyance (and I burdened, to boot, with my London telescope, which, though cumbersome, I brought along just in case), in total ignorance of the true purpose of our nocturnal foray! Righteous, bewildered but trusting in your promise to explain all when the hour was ripe, I resigned myself to knowing nothing, not even the reason why an oil-fired carriage should be conveying us bouncingly to our first stop at the place called Bellevue, in which neighbourhood, so you told us – for, say I with a sneer, it would appear you know everything pertaining to the circumstances and events of the life of Saltiel's nephew – in the neighbourhood of which, I say again, was situate his auxiliary castle. There you conveyed to a drowsing servant a note signed by His Excellency, bade the stable doors be opened wide, and there, in inexorable silence, you saddled two palfreys, both magnificent but equally bereft of reason, and we stood by and watched bewildered while, tight-lipped as ever and showing no compassion for my thirst for explanations, you held the reins of one, climbed upon the back of the other, O heathen, and bade the captain of the hired vehicle to lead the way and ferry all of us, your hookah included, unto this present place! Well now, friend, here we are, and I put an oliphant to my lips and summon you to remember your oath! Come, explain yourself! Tell me why I am here, I who know nothing of your plotting and who am of less use than a plenipotentiary minister and more sterile than an ambassador! Has not this faithful account of my torments moved, swayed and disarmed you?'

He closed his eyes, gulped like a runner breasting the tape, held out an imperious hand to Solomon, demanded his handkerchief, wiped the perspiration from his forked beard, undid the buttons of his frock-coat, dabbed at his streaming chest, which was matted with grey hairs, and pocketed the handkerchief. Proud of his speech and of the mouths of his cousins which hung open, he crossed his arms and turned to Michael with a magnanimous smile.

'Having now soberly summarized my principal arguments, I leave the philippic and move on to the peroration, with due change of register and the requisite injection of emotional appeal. Dearly beloved Michael, apple of my heart, O scion of a generous-hearted people, grant my wheedling request and preserve the life of a father for the sake of his dear babes! You cannot be unaware that when an unsolved enigma rises to the brain it may unleash a fatal brainstorm otherwise known as meningitis? What would then become of my poor orphans so cruelly deprived of a much-loved father? Oh tears, oh the weeping, oh the wailing of children! Given which, gentle Michael, would you not agree that, out of earshot of both these cousins, if such is your wish, in most scrupulous confidence, friendly conference and heartfelt effusion, would you not agree that the two of us should discuss your secret mission amicably, so that you may have the benefit of my advice and the churnings of my brain while I, on the other hand, may learn this succulent secret and discourse thereon at length and thus soothe my throat and sweeten my tongue?

I need hardly say that this cherished secret so affectionately shared would be kept entirely to myself until the day I die, inclusive, you have my word on it! And now, O janissary, harken to what I say! I have been your friend and cousin for more than half a century and my love for you has no bounds, but unless you divulge, at least to me, the purpose of our presence in these nocturnal surroundings, together with the reason for these horses and yonder waiting motor, know *primo* that I shall expire of unslaked curiosity, which would be a shame, and besides you have absolutely no right to cause my death in the prime of my days! Know *secundo*, O lion of Abyssinia, that not only will my ghost return to curdle your blood but furthermore I shall send two anonymous letters, one to the Captain of Customs at Cephalonia with details of your smuggling career and the other to the Christian Attorney General of the isle of our birth informing him in no uncertain terms of your ignoble dalliance with his daughter, which would mean the scaffold for you, and I shall be there munching toffees as they chop off your head. And know at the last that I shall never speak to you again as long as I live! So, what are we doing here and what is this earth-shattering affair?'

'Come, speak,' said Mattathias.

'It is our nature to want to know secrets,' explained Solomon.

Having thus summed up the situation with plain common sense, little Solomon gave his mind to the matter of his health. To this end, he turned up the collar of his tiny sheepskin coat to protect his precious throat, then tied two large handkerchiefs horizontally across his round, freckled face, making himself look like a half-grown Tuareg, to ward off night chills so apt to inflame the teeth. Confident that he had done all that was necessary to prolong his life on this earth, he waited upon the unfolding of these absorbing events, with a pleasant smile on his lips and hands quietly held behind his back, while nevertheless keeping a close watch on the grass around him for any vipers which were quite likely to be lurking there.

'Kill me,' begged Naileater, suddenly falling to his knees. 'Strangle me, dearest Michael, but speak! Wring my neck, if that is your wish! Here, take it, it is yours!' he said, still on his knees, holding his chin high and proffering his throat. 'Throttle me, friend, choke me, but tell all as you squeeze my life away. For this secret which I do not know is driving me insane! It turns my blood to vinegar and makes me more helpless than any of my poor, dead, sucking babes! O Michael, look kindly on your very dear friend, who now waits on bended knee in expectation!'

Aquiver with passionate sincerity, he waited for death to strike as he knelt in supplication, hands extended prayerfully and neck still held in pious offering, staggered by the depth of his sacrifice and sneaking a glance to see what effect it was having on the three watchers. After a long silence, Michael stood up, drew his damascened dagger from his wide belt, tested its edge on a fingernail, and pointed it at his cousins.

'Comrades,' he said, 'this is a blade of well-tempered steel and, as points go, its point is sharp indeed. Whoever dares to follow me with a view to spying on my secret purpose will get the taste of it in his belly and his blubber. So if any of you has such an intention, let him now, for the last time, call upon the Oneness of our God.'

Having thus spoken, he sheathed his dagger and from the recesses of his gold-braided jacket produced a sheet of paper folded in four, which he pressed piously to his lips to deepen the enigma and inflame the curiosity of the cousins. Then, holding it in his dangling hand, he set off, lady-killingly rolling his hips, in the direction of the Deumes' house, broad-shouldered and tall, while Naileater, on his feet now and brandishing his fist, hurled abuse in an abundance matched only by its virtuosity, wishing, *inter alia*, that he might live to be a hundred, but eyeless, and vainly pleading for charity from his bastards.

CHAPTER 74

'Now that the first part of my mission has been successfully accomplished, I shall tell the secret,' said Michael, on rejoining the cousins. 'But first, Naileater, give us something to drink.'

'With all convenient speed! I have an eye to it!' exclaimed Naileater. 'To hear is to obey, dear friend!'

He immediately uncorked a bottle of retsina and filled the glasses which the cousins held out to him. So that he might enjoy Michael's tale without impediment, Solomon removed both anti-inflammatory handkerchiefs and his tiny coat. However, as a protection for his throat, which he insisted was delicate, he wrapped his neck in one of those ghastly white tippets made of goat-fur which good little middle-class girls used to wear at the end of the last century.

'My throat is now safe from besiegement,' he said to Michael. 'You may speak, O man of valour!'

'Come along, Michael, unstop your mouth or I shall burst!' exclaimed Naileater. 'I stand impatiently on the frontiers of impatience, to the point of entirely forgetting all that mouth-watering fare contained in yon hampers! Be expeditious with your tale and we shall dine when it is told, when our curiosity is satisfied!'

'No, we shall dine first,' said Michael.

'But you will not forget your promise?'

'I swear it by the living God!'

'Oh how delighted I am to hear it!' cried Solomon. 'Oh how my heart sings! At pudding-time, we shall know the secret!'

'No,' said Michael. 'After the pudding.'

627

'After the pudding! So be it!' cried Solomon. 'O my dear friends, after pudding, our souls shall be enriched by knowledge of this great secret! Rapture the like of which you have never known, mark my words!' he squeaked, and he waggled his little legs like knitting-needles.

'You sound happy as a baby in its cot,' said Michael.

Naileater, who was goodwill incarnate, for disclosure was imminent, transformed himself into an impromptu butler. Removing the frock-coat which covered his naked torso, he spread it on the grass for a tablecloth, set out on it the assorted victuals, and, like some hairy-chested master of ceremonies, announced them by name as they emerged from the two hampers.

'Four pairs of botargos, of which I, exercising my right to the lion's share, commandeer half! Anyone against? Motion carried! One dozen large, fried, crispy squid, perhaps a touch on the tough side, but all the more delectable for that! Eight for me, because squid is my all-consuming passion! A large clutch of eggs hard-boiled for a whole day in water flavoured with olive oil and fried onions so that the flavour soaks well in! Of this I was assured by our noble grocer-cum-victualler and co-religionist, whom God preserve, amen! Tomatoes, peppers, succulent olives and raw onions for nibbles! Aromatic cheese fritters also simply begging to be gobbled up! Twenty-eight meat-and-pinenut patties! Large ones! Stuffed gooseneck to be consumed with love! Beef sausages guaranteed kosher, the little darlings! Roasted, guiltless kid to be eaten with the fingers and pilau rice, which I shall roll into little balls and then gently pop down my gullet! Six bots retsina, two being already earmarked for my good self! Deliciously chewy honey fritters, quantities of Turkish delight and sesame nougat to close the proceedings and accompany eructations of satisfaction! And finally, for incidental gratification, roasted pumpkin seeds, fried chick-peas and salted pistachios designed to quicken the thirst and destined to be most ambrosially crunched during the unbuttoning of the secret! Come, gentlemen, to table! Let there be eating and drinking and gnashing of teeth!'

Sitting in a circle on the grass under the hayrick, the Valiant stuffed themselves to the limits of brimfulness, masticating manfully and exchanging smiles. When the groaning board had been picked clean,

Michael sat cross-legged, loosened his cartridge-belt, removed his Turkish slippers to be comfy, stroked his bare feet, and cleared his throat.

'The hour of disclosure has struck in your lives and several fates,' he proclaimed.

'Harken!' cried Solomon.

'Silence, O pea-brain!' thundered Naileater. 'And a cancer upon your wagging tongue!'

'But I only said it so that everybody would listen and not talk!' protested Solomon.

'Close and padlock your mouth, oaf!' ordered Naileater. 'We are all ears, dear Michael! Please proceed and speak your divine speech!'

'But first, I will put a question to you, O Naileater. Why do your masticating jaws never stop working day and night?'

'On account of vitamins, coz. Plus, I would add, frequent visits of black dog which call for consolation. To me, eating is really more a need of the spirit than a function of the body! And now, O great one, open the door of the secret and speak your courteous, finely chiselled speech! Say on!'

'Ahem,' began Michael. 'This morning we were, as you recall, in Athens, where, suddenly moved by a desire to see the face of his lord and nephew, the revered Saltiel impulsively resolved that we should leave by flying-machine.'

'I thought my hour had come,' noted Solomon.

'O hoary-moustached old sinner, why do you expatiate on matters of our common past with which we are as well acquainted as you yourself?' said Naileater indignantly. 'Come to the point! Explain what we are doing here with two horses and an oil-fired conveyance!'

'Just a moment, dear Michael, don't start yet. I must just answer a call of nature,' said Solomon.

'A second cancer upon your importunate bladder, O postponer of disclosures!' bawled Naileater.

'I'll go over there, to be polite, but I'll be back in a jiffette,' said Solomon, and he went, but not without first taking his leave with a graceful bow.

'Pay no attention to the insignificant little tick and his unseemly interruption,' said Naileater. 'Start without him!'

'We shall wait for him,' said Michael. 'Why should I deprive the poor little fellow of the pleasure of knowing the secret?'

Having spoken, he played with his toes to pass the time, then yawningly crooned a love-song. Meanwhile, Mattathias chewed his gum and did sums with a pencil, and Naileater entertained himself and calmed his nerves by waggling the toes of his large, bare feet.

'Mission accomplished,' sang out Solomon as he returned. He looked highly pleased with his little self. 'That didn't take long, did it? I do assure you it couldn't wait, for I drank large quantities of fizzy lemonade at the hotel! And very good lemonade it was too! I shall take some back for my dear wife! That's better! Now I'm light as a feather! But I felt horribly scared behind that tree by myself! I was afraid dead persons would jump out and get me! But now it's over, thanks be to God, and I am back safe with my dear cousins!'

'Come, O janissary of our hearts, speak!' cried Naileater. 'Speak your nectareous words, for our ears are open to the fullest setting of their apertures!'

'Now hear this, O friends and frisking kidlets,' began Michael, 'give ear and know, you who hear me, who have been my trusty vassals over years of the span of time, be apprized that the matter concerns an affair of the heart and that lord Solal is fired with passion and embroiled in dalliance!'

'Is she pretty?' asked Solomon.

'As a water-melon,' replied Michael.

Convinced by this and with eyes that glistened with admiration, Solomon ran his tongue over his lips.

'An authentic rose of Araby and like unto the moon in its fourteenth day!' he said. 'He will marry her, you see if he doesn't, mark my words!'

'Out of the question,' said Michael. 'She comes already provided with a husband.' (At this, the tuft of hair on Solomon's head rose all by itself, like virtue outraged.)

'Fine, he's positively incandescent with passion, agreed,' said Naileater. 'But what connection is there between said passion, these two horses and the backfiring vehicle? And what were you up to just now, when you visited yonder house and forbade us to follow under pain of having our bellies slit open in the manner of the Japanese?'

'Merely carrying out the first part of my mission according to orders honourably received,' said Michael. 'I shall explain everything in due course, for each event must be told in order and in its own time. The nub, then, is a bed matter involving a charming creature ready supplied with a deceived husband.' (Solomon covered his ears, but left a tiny gap.)

'You've said that once!' said Naileater. 'Proceed with your exposition and stop being so pompous!'

'When, through the bond of friendship, I was privileged to see him alone in his apartments, he confided to me that he had arranged a secret tryst with the delightful creature for this evening, at nine o'clock. I besought him to allow me to go with him, for I have a tooth for such adventures. Besides, did I not, in the time of his youth, aid and abet his carrying-off of the tall and ample spouse of a consul?'

'Get to the point!' cried Naileater.

'I found favour in his eyes, for he is extremely fond of me, and he did me the glory and honour of accepting. And so, travelling at unbelievable speeds in his long, white conveyance, we reached this place a little after nine, and I escorted him to a door not far from this spot but which you cannot see since it is hidden by trees. Now just as he was raising his hand to ring the jangle-box, the door opened and the delicious filly appeared, and well endowed she was, fore and aft, an indispensable requirement. After I had twirled and retwirled my moustache and directed passionate oglements towards one who was as lovely as a pasha's daughter, I withdrew to a discreet distance, which was yet not so far away that I could not see with my eyes and hear with my ears, though I let it be understood by my demeanour that I was both deaf and blind. They began with a kiss which appeared to me to belong, in fencing parlance, to the category known as the inside reverse double columbine, but to that I would not like to swear. Then the gorgeous girl spoke, expounded an exposition, and I was privy to everything. And oh, my friends, in a voice of such sweet harmony!'

'But what did she say in this voice of celestial euphony?' asked Solomon, who had unstopped his ears.

'The vixen, a true daughter of Satan like all her kind, explained that on hearing the approach of the horseless carriage and in consequence divining the imminent arrival of he who was the idol of her heart and limbs, she immediately informed her petty half that she had a mind to prepare an infusion which the Gentiles call by the name of tea. Whereupon, under the pretence of repairing to the kitchen, she ran out into the garden which we had that moment entered! Such was the explanation which I heard while maintaining my pretence of deafness,' concluded Michael, and he began picking his teeth with a match to raise the interest and tension to a new pitch.

'Proceed without further ado, by the prophets!' Naileater besought him. 'Proceed, for I am as a man racked upon a white-hot gridiron!'

'Next, after a second embrace of a type not wholly visible to me in the gloom but which was in all likelihood a *touché* in tierce with grapple and follow-through, the fair filly said that as soon as she could slip the vigilance of her walking disaster, who is soft as wax and as clinging as tar, she would communicate with her treasure tomorrow by means of the speakoduct so that they might delight in their bodies together upon a couch of silk.' (Solomon reblocked his ears.)

'And is that how the she-devil expressed it?' asked Naileater.

'No, she used words scoring high in respectability and poetry, but I have told you what she had in the recess of her brainpan. Ah, dear cousins, what ingenuity these ladies of Europe display on behalf of any man suitably equipped with the wherewithal to turn night into joy!'

'An end to these general observations!' cried Naileater. 'Proceed with the particular!'

'Next, upon her enquiring who I was, he beckoned me to come near and introduced me as his liegeman and confidant.'

'You are speaking exceedingly well today,' said Naileater.

'That is because the fumes of youth are rising on my tongue. Having thus been introduced, I knelt on the ground and kissed the hem of her raiment, whereupon she immediately gave me a winsome smile. (Ears unblocked, Solomon sighed.) A smile of great warmth, for she was doubtless impressed by the breadth of my shoulders and the braid on my uniform. For make no mistake, the ladies of Europe love the outward show and promise of manliness. But to abridge.

The two love-birds separated after much flowery speech on the part of her graciousness, for the ladies of Europe, mark you well, are fond of uttering words of high nobility and virtue to mask the desires and itches of the flesh.'

'You are shrewder than I took you for,' said Naileater.

'I am well versed in these matters,' said Michael. 'But now you must know that, on returning to his hotel wherein dwells Wealth, I courteously taxed the lord with his patience and appealed to his honour as a man! What, said I, such a pot of peanut butter, so warm, so smooth, and attended by the requisite quartet of globularities, and Your Lordship is content to wait until the morrow to take his pleasure of it? In short, I proposed that he should allow me to steal away the agreeable creature so gently born and let me do the deed without him, so that the glory of the day would be mine alone! I am versed in these matters, said I, and such business restoreth my youth. Submitting to my arguments, he concurred, even to the point of giving me his authority to bring you all along, and he handed me a letter to convey to the queen of his heart. Great indeed is the favour shown me by my magnificent lord. Accordingly, I repaired thither a short while since and took up position under the window of the room wherein she was feigning to give ear to her poor ox, who held forth on serious matters instead of performing with her the principal business which exists between any man and woman, for example repeating, poor fool, divers conversations which he had held with principals and ministers, a topic of no interest to a well-endowed young woman yearning for more solid fare. Through a crack in the shutters, I saw her biting her lip to choke a yawn and bar its exit from her closed mouth, and then reverting to her frozen smile while the husband she was deceiving talked on with relish and fascination of important personages. But abruptly halting his flow, he had the gall to divulge to her the commotion of his vitals and his pressing need of latrines, a need which should always be veiled, for nothing is better calculated to cool a woman's ardour. When the unmanly oaf had accordingly left the room, I tapped on the window, which she opened, evincing no surprise on seeing me since I had already been introduced to her by her paramour. I knelt and offered up the letter of empowerment which charged me with bringing her this night to a place of dancing and epicurean sorbets known as the Donon, dancing being a most suitable preliminary to the main item of business.'

'He must be mad!' muttered Mattathias. 'God only knows what they'll charge him for a plain sorbet!'

'In the missive he spoke also of all three of you, so that she would not be surprised when confronted by your divers ways and miens.'

'What did he say about me?' asked Naileater eagerly.

'That you are a genius of sorts, an observation which greatly surprised me.'

'Why of sorts?' said Naileater indignantly. 'But posterity shall decide. As for your surprise, O bullock-brain, pray keep it to yourself!'

'And me? What did he say about me?' asked Solomon.

'Will you be quiet!' bawled Naileater. 'Let him speak who is empowered to speak! So what reply did she make to the missive?'

'She returned her answer in a melting voice, and devoutly did I listen as she said that she would certainly meet her lord this night, but at an hour unspecified, for she could not tell when she would be alone once more. Yes, alone is what she said. Now, friends, marvel at such delicacy! Another would have said: "I cannot tell when I shall be able to rid myself of my encumbrance." Or perhaps: "I shall get away the instant my abomination begins to snore." We are dealing here with a person of perfect manners. Note further that although she performs the principal business, to wit, the unmaking of beds, with our lord, she discoursed in tones of formal courtesy throughout their interview in the garden. That is the way of high-born ladies, princesses and duchesses: in bed they squirm and frolic, but out of it are all correctness and ceremony. And so, having given me her answer, she again held out her hand for me to kiss, and I departed, but not before putting one hand on my hip and aiming an ardent oglement in her direction. And now, Solomon, charge our glasses!'

Seated in a circle, their thirst slaked, the Valiant made free of the salted pistachios. In the august silence of the night was heard the sound of munching, while a nightingale complained in vain.

CHAPTER 75

'But why the horses?' asked Solomon, when all the pistachios had gone.

'One's for her and the other one's for me,' said Michael.

'But why *horses*?'

'Have you not heard tell, O ignorant son of an ignorant father, have you not heard tell that in matters of gallant dalliance a woman is never stolen away except on the back of a horse, especially if the lady in question is married?'

'No, I did not know that,' said Solomon. 'But now I do, so, pray, do not be angry.'

'Besides, the lord was delighted when I suggested horses.'

'But I am not the least delighted,' said Mattathias, 'and I pronounce Saltiel's nephew to be off his head! I say he is not worthy of his high office, nor of the dollars he banks! I tell you, he is quite mad!'

'While you are saner than sane,' said Michael, 'though it does not sweeten your temper any.'

'That's as may be, but why the carriage which emits fumes from its backside?' asked Solomon.

'In case she does not care to get on the horse.'

'Quite right,' said Solomon. 'A matter of courtesy, so that the lady may choose according to her preference. And she is very beautiful, you say?'

'Complexion like pink soap. And furthermore she appeared to me well suited to pelvic exhilarations, for she is as firm and as supple as perfectly cooked Italian macaroni, and has, in the matter of her fore and her aft, a decided advantage over the female of the elephant. Hindquarters like a pair of overstuffed pillows! Ah, our lord certainly knows how to pick them! A dromedary ripe for bedding! Truly she is a pasha's daughter and a honeyed waffle! And a mouth made for kisses in the category of the quadruple overhead arabesque! (Solomon recoiled, and his hair stood on end.) On the other hand, as I stood there peeping through the gap in the shutters, I saw her abomination and was able, by observing his nose, to deduce that he was a man of small endowment and consequently inferred that she must hate him heartily. For it is well-known that women like big noses, which are a sign of power and a promise of size. But you may set your minds at rest: she will contrive to rid herself of her ox and at any moment you shall observe her come, trailing sinuous undulations in her wake. I tell you that it will be so because I know her kind well.'

'When a wife is on coupling bent, A husband shall not prevent,' improvised Naileater, and he smiled in acknowledgement of his own talent while Mattathias stopped chewing his gum to spit in disgust and Solomon held his head in both hands, torn between admiration for such a beautiful lady and his veneration for the Ten Commandments.

'A water-melon,' sighed Michael, dreamily watching the coils of smoke curl up from his nostrils.

'Look, you can talk about water-melons till you're blue in the face,' said Mattathias, 'but meantime, on account of your water-melon, the price clock fitted to the steam-driven coach ticks remorselessly on and Swiss francs drop into the money-pouch of the Gentile who commands the hellish, horseless conveyance. Ah, that's the job to have! You sit behind the guiding control doing nothing, and each minute that passes begets more centimes for you!'

'Ne'er in my life did I see a more delicious mount for riding nor such configuration for dalliance and bed-sport,' mused Michael. 'She puts me in mind of a red-headed woman I once knew in the Cephalonia Palace Hotel who was quite perfect at one thing, her only fault being that she talked English to me the whole time during the performance of that very thing.'

'But look here,' Solomon broke in, 'if she is the wife of a husband, how can she possibly agree to be taken to this place of sorbet, there to trip a light fantastic with another man?'

'That is what the ladies of Europe are like,' said Michael. 'O my friends, if all the deceived husbands in Europe wore lamps on their hats, mercy, what illumination we should see!'

'That's quite enough philosophizing,' yawned Naileater. 'Could anyone please indulge me with a few pistachios, if any such remain?'

'No!' exclaimed Solomon. 'No, I am convinced that she will not leave her husband! Since she is beautiful, she must therefore surely be virtuous! Devil take it, she's married, and what else can she want?'

'New thews and jam on it,' said Michael.

'Oy, oy, oy!' groaned Solomon. 'Why are you doing this to me? Why must I listen to such things? Is it not enough that today I have already been made to fly through the air, and so high that my soul departed my mouth? Oy, oy, oy!'

'Stop your oy-oying! You make my ears tingle as with little worms awiggling,' said Naileater.

It was all too much for Solomon. He had agreed to travel on the wings of the wind, he had spent the entire journey with his eyes shut reciting psalms, he had spent two mortal hours with fear gnawing at his vitals, filled with a presentiment that the pilot was about to faint or the wings drop off, and for what? To hear tell of horrors to make the wickedness of Babylon pale into insignificance!

'But does this mean that the poor husband will lose his wife, his joy and his trust?' he asked, and he spread his little hands wide.

'He can croak for all I care!' said Michael, confirming the crescent of his moustache. 'For such are the wages of husbands.'

'That's not true!' cried Solomon.

'And if he makes trouble for the pretty filly, I shall personally tear out his cuckold's horns and ram them into his underemployed groin!'

'Shame on you, you blackguard!' exclaimed Solomon. 'I am on the side of decency! That, in a nutshell, is where I stand. And I take refuge in the Almighty, who is my strength and my tower! And He is a holy God, so there! Verily I say that lord Solal does not well in this matter! Why does he, who is so intelligent, the son of a chief rabbi and a descendant of Aaron, stoop so low? Ah my friends, what is there more beautiful than marriage and conjugal fidelity? You look at your wife, you smile at her, you feel no shame, and God is well pleased! If you are troubled, you can unburden yourself to her when you get home at night and she will comfort you, she will say that you mustn't worry, that you're just being silly. And you are happy. And you both grow old together gracefully. That is what love is. If there is anything more beautiful, my friends, pray tell me what it is!'

'Especially,' said Mattathias, 'since all these adulterous fillies involve a considerable outlay on flowers.'

'But it is a providence that the uncle knows nought of the sinfulness of the nephew,' said Solomon. 'God, in His great goodness, has visited him with a bout of jaundice which detains him far from this place.'

'Let a barricade be built around all this idle talk!' ordered Michael. 'Whatever the lord does is well done, and virtue is a dish fit only for the small of nose! Oh what would I not give to be in his shoes, for the woman is the veritable fragrance of jasmine and as sound as a cockerel's eye!'

'And more majestic than an English man-of-war!' said Naileater, partly for the ring of the expression and partly because he was bored.

'And having the coolness of cherries,' added Solomon illogically.

'And with a cheek I could nibble even though I did not hunger,' said Naileater, 'though it would go down better with a brace of cucumbers.'

'For my part,' said Mattathias, 'I find in her neither cockerel's eye nor coolness of cherries, and I'd rather make do with the cucumbers without the cheek. I tell you, all this is a hanging matter.'

'It is true that the husband might well put in an appearance brandishing pistols,' said Naileater for the benefit of Solomon, who immediately stood up, brushed his tennis trousers, and put on his tiny coat lined with goat-fur.

'I'm feeling the cold rather, and moreover I have a headache, which is why I shall now say farewell and return to our hotel.'

'O chicken-heart!' cried Michael.

'Chicken-heart is correct, and I'm proud of it!' answered Solomon, his two little hands bunched bravely into fists. 'And I'm quite right, since it is fear which tells me when there's danger and keeps me alive! And what is better than being alive? I have already told you, my dear friends, I wouldn't say no to being locked up in prison for good, provided I could go on living for ever! And I'd have you know, Michael, that the timid are invariably meek and kindly folk and pleasing in the eye of the Almighty, while you, with your revolvers and built like the ox who is chief of the herd, are muscleman and Muslim-man, so there! Furthermore, I am just as brave as you, though only when there is no alternative! And now, having returned my answer to this blackguard here, I take my leave of you both, dear cousins, and shall return to town, where a man is much better off than in the country!'

But, tenderly restrained and embraced by Michael, he gave up the struggle, only too well aware that flight was impossible and in any case how would he find his way now, after midnight, along roads which were strewn with stones and alive with ghosts? Best hide, for the husband might at any moment realize what was afoot and set off in pursuit of his young wife, armed with a blunderbuss to prevent her visiting the place of dancing and sorbet! Yes, devil take it, he'd better hide, for a stray bullet soon finds a billet! Let the thought be father to the deed! Having crawled on all fours into a pile of lopped branches close by the hayrick against which his cousins were sitting, he begged Michael to cover him with leaves. Thus disguised as a forest, he calmed down. He remained silent for a while, but then a small voice emerged from the shrubbery.

'O mighty scion of Jacob,' said the little voice, 'why does not lord Solal love the daughters of our people? Are they not queens in their homes, and do they not anoint their hair with perfumed oils upon the holy sabbath day? What have Gentile girls got that they haven't?'

'They recite poems to him,' sniggered Naileater.

'How odd, but I always imagined that must be the case,' said the little voice after a moment's reflection.

'But when he is unwell', went on Naileater, 'they stop reciting poems to him, because when he is unwell he sickens them! So they put two fingers in their mouths and whistle and they say to the hotel menial who comes running: "Take this carcass away, remove it from my sight!" That is what they do. That is how they conduct themselves!'

'But if you aren't ill, what delights await you!' retorted Solomon, creeping out of his leafy refuge. 'A young lady who recites poems to you all day long, why, it is a wondrous thought!' he announced, and he stood with eyes turned heavenward, clenching his little fists. 'You get out of bed in the morning and without further ado your ears are filled with a poem which is as peach-juice descending into the stomach of your soul!'

'Naileater,' said Michael, 'is this tale of the carcass and the whistling an established fact or an invention of your brain? It goes without saying that our lord is not the least unwell, thanks be to God, but were he at some point to experience an ache in his lumbar region, would she not instead apply a poultice?'

'Damn the poultice!' cried Solomon. 'Devil take the poultice, provided that when I rise in the morning . . .' (But remembering that he was Solomon, a simple seller of apricot-water, he fell silent.)

'Since you fancy the idea so much, O human-headed ant,' said Naileater, 'what is there to prevent you from snatching this whistling spouter of poems out of the arms of lord Solal?'

'I'm too little,' explained Solomon. 'She wouldn't give me a second glance, don't you see? The Almighty, whose name is blessèd, fashions his creatures according to his good pleasure.'

'Why is everyone so interested by all this talk of love?' yawned Mattathias. 'I'd much rather hear about an end-of-year financial statement which showed a healthy profit.'

'Why are we so interested?' said Michael aggressively. 'Can you not conceive, O unfledged egg, you son of a lily-spermed father, have you no conception of what delights await them on this hot and sultry night? Do you not comprehend, O mule-brain, that inflamed by the dance they will repair to the hotel wherein dwells Wealth, there to spend pleasuresome hours together, she as naked as the day she was born, stretched out upon a couch of silk, her eyes lozenged with blue mascara and her bosom as white as the snow that sits on a branch, spiced and aromatic and mettlesomely displaying her quadruple globularities on which a man may founder, ripely primed upon her gold-fringed sheet, and then the lord . . .'

'Don't go on!' pleaded Solomon.

'And then, having matched moist kiss with moist kiss and gambol with gambol, the lord will also lie down upon the bed, with no fig-leaf other than his hands, and then she, amply and illustriously proportioned, reaching the limits of her jubilance and burning with an itch, will laughingly reach out and remove the fig-hands of the favoured of her soul to inspect and savour the opulence of the male, savour his treasure with a smile of wonder all over her fair face! (Outraged, Solomon dropped into a fighting crouch, flailed with his little fists to limber up, then began pummelling at the ribs of the janissary, who, without losing his good humour and serenely unaware of the blows raining on his sides, let him get on with it and calmly continued.) And she will approve and will think well of him for being more abundantly equipped in a certain department than the husband she deceives, and she will unfurl her soul! (Giving up the unequal struggle, Solomon stopped punching and stuck his head into the hayrick.) For never forget, that certain department is a woman's life entire, her goal both by day and by night! And doubtless it is a department in which her husband does not please her, and therein lies the secret of her melancholy moods, her ill-temper, marital discord, contempt and ultimately divorce, for God made some as I am, but others made He puny and woebegone and like unto wax which grows more flaccid the more it is handled! (Appalled and not knowing where to put himself, Solomon half buried himself in the hay.) Yes, she will unfurl when she sees such mettle and such power, she will clap her hands, and she will know the lunging, plunging, puncturing force of his mettle, its ingress and its egress and its instantly rejoined congress, and then shall they enter the lists where man and woman do hard and lengthy battle, and she will be tender and acquiescent, with a rhythm in her loins, reaching out with her man-questing loins, and he shall find delight in his bucking, perspiring mount, and both shall call a truce to partake of good food and better wine and then will resume their lovely war and their indefatigable toings and their untiring froings, and the despairing retreats and ecstatic advances will continue until the time of dawn and the time of blood which is the sign, as the *cognoscenti* will know, that even the strongest man can go on no longer!'

'Say on, Michael!' cried Naileater, 'for your subject gives wings to your tongue and verily it confers upon you a way with words of which I did not believe you capable. I shall listen to you with the ears of respect.'

'No! Make the black-faced blackguard hold his tongue!' cried Solomon.

'What more shall I say, Naileater old friend,' said Michael, 'except that the lord will do right to make her earth move and roughly use her during their night of love divine? For in this mortal life there is no other truth but bareback riding. All else is tinsel and taradiddle. For a man's life lasts no longer than the blink of an eye and is followed by everlasting putrefaction, and with each day that passes you take one more step towards the hole in the ground in which you will moulder numb and mute with no company save that of the same fat white worms as dwell in flour and cheese, and they will slowly, surely creep into all your orifices, there to feed. And so, my friends, I ride boldly each night of my life insofar as it is given to me so to do, that I may die at peace having discharged my duty as a man, for, mark my words, it is what women expect of us, it is the sole object of their brief lives and the only thought in their heads. Above all, it is the will of God that we should serve and satisfy them, and it was for this purpose that He made and created us. And if He put in us the hunger for meat, the thirst for wine and the need for sleep, it was so that this meat, this wine and this sleep should be distilled into dense seed which we must needs bestow on the poor females who await its coming! For my own part, dear lords and cousins, having no plans for rogering this night and consequently failing in my duty and my obligation, I feel presently oppressed by a great sadness, this I tell you candidly, for who knows how many beautiful women desire the approach of the male on this hot and sultry night? But where are they to be found?'

'Though pleasant in form, your utterance calls forth my profound-est strictures in the matter of content,' said Naileater, 'except for the passage concerning everlasting putrefaction, which was apposite, true, legitimate, based on sound argument and most agreeable.'

'Yes, my liegemen,' said Michael, 'all women desire night-riding, hard, clean and protracted! Even royal princesses desire it!'

'That's a lie,' cried Solomon from the middle of his hayrick. 'They are pure!'

'They've all got behinds!' retorted Michael.

'And the appurtenances thereto pertaining!' sniggered Naileater.

'That's a foul slander!' cried Solomon. 'Shame on you both, you blackguards! May your eyes lose their sight!'

'Hear me, O little one,' said Michael, 'and listen well, for I shall now tell you what a king does to his queen as he turns her this way and that!'

'Get thee behind me, Satan!' cried Solomon, emerging from the hayrick and stamping his foot. 'Behold, the worm turns! For I am tired of being the universal butt of all! This morning it was the flying-machine! This afternoon, in the hotel, Naileater took great pleasure in telling me about all the diseases which may some day visit my body, top, bottom and middle, plus all the operations that surgeons may perhaps perform on me and how in the end I shall die and how my face will be twisted by agony just before I do! It's not fair, for I am always nice to everybody! And now it's even worse, for this blackguard Michael speaks ignobly of unclean things, from which God preserve! What did I ever do that you should use me so cruelly? Listen to me Michael, O blackguard, O black of face, O man unworthy to belong to our saintly nation, O dishonour of Israel, hear me! If you persist in your unseemliness, I shall flee into the night and the heart of darkness where brigands hide behind trees and no matter if I am murdered, for I refuse to stay and listen to your vileness! I say long live virtue and morality and the chasteness of wives! So just put that in your pipe and smoke it! Moreover, I shall tell Uncle Saltiel everything, and he will make you know your shame and will even lay his curse upon your head! And quite right too! And make no mistake, his curse is efficacious, for he is a man of great saintliness, a true Jew, while you are a Muslim, and that's a fact! And if you should ever dare to set foot inside our synagogue I shall drive you out with whips!'

'O little man,' said Michael, and plucking a stem of grass he began to chew it while he smiled at old memories. 'O man of virtue,' he went on, 'since you protest so warmly, pray tell me how it is that you have children and by what miracle they came to be in the belly of your wife!'

'We used always to put the lights out,' said Solomon, blushing, eyes downcast. 'Besides, did not the Almighty, whose name be praised, enjoin us to go forth and multiply? So we have no choice. And anyway, it's perfectly respectable. That is what marriage is for.'

After a long silence punctuated by yawns, for the hour was late, Naileater declared that, since they had nothing further of interest to discuss or eat, he would take a nap for the sake of his lungs until such time as the heatheness should put in an appearance.

Stretched out in the grass, with his top-hat on his large feet to protect them against vipers, he fell into a sleep in which he was garlanded with roses by the Queen of England, who whispered in his ear and suggested that he should succeed her husband, who was just then strolling in the garden and whose head was suddenly crowned by a flowerpot which had fallen from the central balcony of Buckingham Palace.

CHAPTER 76

'That's all very well,' said Mattathias, 'but it's now ten past midnight and the shameless jade and daughter of Belial, chiefest of all the demons, has not come, and still the conveyance of ruination stands yonder, horrendously waiting. The last time I looked, the pocket-emptying counter had already clocked up forty-two Helvetic francs. The woman ought to be stoned. In sooth, a heartless creature. Forty-two gold francs of eighteen carats apiece! That's more than eight thalers!'

'No matter, for the lord has furnished me with a well-stocked purse,' said Michael.

'When I see money spent, I feel ill,' said Mattathias, 'even if it's somebody else's money.'

'I do believe that what reconciles our Mattathias to the thought of dying is that when he's dead he won't have to pay any more taxes,' said Naileater. 'Moreover, I know why he never keeps spices in his house: it's because if he suddenly succumbed in the dread arms of the angel of death there would be some salt or pepper left, and that would be a waste, money down the drain! By the by, Michael, what is my role in this affair, and why was I not given authority to parley with the heatheness?'

'It is none of my doing if the lord preferred to enlist the support of a fine figure of a man, one who is a connoisseur of oglements.'

'But what do I stand to gain from a business which may possibly cost me my honour?'

'The lord will surely give you thousands.'

'In that case, count me in, lost honour and all,' said Naileater. 'Anyway, what is a sense of honour if not the despicable fear of what people might say, a truth which makes the tragedies of Corneille look pretty damned silly! But if there are bags to be carried, I shall not carry them. It would demean my standing as a man of intellect.'

He yawned, cracked the knuckles of both hands, and wondered if it was worth digging a trench so as to give the husband a run for his money if he decided to attack. But his optimism was restored by the discovery of a remnant of nougat, and he began chanting a psalm in his resonant voice, beating time with his large bare feet.

'All the same,' said Solomon, rubbing his nose, 'all the same, it's not right. If she were just some slip of a girl and there was marrying business in the air, then even if the parents were against it I'd say aye! But she's already married!'

'Furthermore,' said Mattathias, 'if she were to come into money from some old aunt, he wouldn't stand to gain a penny, since in the eyes of the law they wouldn't be married!'

'You could let me handle the case,' said Naileater.

'What? And see all the money vanish into your pocket!' said Michael.

Naileater gave a smug leer and roguishly made corkscrews in his beard with his finger. Yes, perhaps he might well make the money vanish into his pocket, and why not? All the best lawyers did it, for God's sake! But then he grew bored, stared at his veined and hairy hands, and yawned gloomily. What was he doing here playing second fiddle in these green pastures reserved for the use of the lowly, grazing beasts of the field?

'The ideal solution,' said Solomon, 'would be if the lord were to run away instead with the husband, on the best of terms, like friends, go touring, and the two of them could enjoy themselves, spend their time together in honest pursuits, that's what I say, speaking as a good Jew. Who needs women?' he added, with scant thought for the logic of his train of thought.

'Sometimes you say quite sensible things, O sprout of the bean,' said Naileater. 'My friends, what would you say if we could earn ourselves a sackful of moral credit by redirecting this young woman's feet into the paths of virtue? This we would do by dangling a choice plum in front of her.'

'Has your brain curdled?' said Solomon indignantly. 'You're not suggesting that she'd ever give up her heart's delight for a plum! You can't seriously believe that to a handsome lord she would prefer a ripe victoria or a juicy greengage?'

'A figure of speech,' said Naileater with all the weariness of the man of superior intellect.

'For my own part,' said Mattathias, 'I say categorically that to make her forget Saltiel's nephew we'd need to get her interested in some good, solid commercial or preferably banking proposition, brokered through New York.'

'That's just what I was going to say!' exclaimed Naileater. 'O Mattathias, O you of the red hair, you have taken the idea out of my mouth, where it lay basking in my saliva! A commercial proposition was exactly the kind of plum I had in mind, I swear! No, I won't swear, because it's God's truth! O companions in affection and in the length and breadth of time, this is what we shall do, so listen carefully! The instant we see the hussy coming, undulating, anointed with oils of cinnamon and holding her little finger in the air, we shall speak words of censure and make her feel shame for her sinful undulations! And when I have struck her with my prophetic fire I shall stroke my beard and put on my satanic but genial smile, and I shall give a little bow, assume a paternal tone of voice, with just a hint of an English accent to give her confidence, and propose the setting-up of a limited company for the purpose of founding a newspaper carrying advertisements costing one sou per line which we should sell for five francs per issue because the advertisements in it will be so riveting! Naturally the capital will be hers and the idea mine, so fifty per cent of the profits will be for me, twenty for you and thirty for her and her husband! To my sense it's a much more agreeable prospect than reciting poems at her lover-man under three palm-trees in Nice! Now that's my idea of living! And let's have an end to all those obnoxious embracings in tierce with grapple and follow-through!'

'It's not a bad idea at all,' said Mattathias, stroking his ginger goatee with his harpoon. 'And I do believe, Naileater, that she'd be even more interested if the paper were to charge an extra ten per cent every time an advertisement produced a positive result.'

Sitting on the grass, rinsed blue by the moon, Mattathias and Naileater argued at length before compromising on a figure of five per cent. Then it was settled, declared Naileater. As soon as the heatheness arrived, he would stand up, put the proposition to her with full panoply of moral argumentation, and would surely win her over! So it would all turn out well, and, instead of foolishly running away after love, she would join forces with the Valiant and her husband, and even, if she insisted, with lord Solal, and start up a profitable newspaper business with telephone and headed stationery, and that would put a stop to all this preposterous love business! Any losses would of course be borne by the husband, and the newspaper would have an all-white telephone, because the shameless jade was mad about poetry! What else could she possibly want? She would even be appointed Chairwoman of the Board of Directors and have her name printed on the headed stationery, as long as it was understood that only he could sign! Furthermore, they would get her to buy a refrigerated railway truck which she could then hire out to the countries of Europe! There were millions to be made that way! Enthusiastic but bashful, Solomon spoke up and suggested that the lady herself might be invited to recast the advertisements as verse, which would prevent her brooding and to some extent be a substitute for the pleasures of love. Michael, a connoisseur of the female heart, hummed and yawned and let the ignoramuses burble on.

'And do you know what I'll do after Saltiel's nephew has been deserted by his poetess?' said Naileater. 'I'll send a wire to my two daughters telling them to come, and, smiling irresistibly, I'll put it to him that he might care to choose one to be his lawful companion in life, either would do, I don't mind which, as long as he says yes to one of them! And then I'll be his father-in-law, and just think of the lovely cushy job I'll be able to wangle for myself in the famous League of Nations! Just you wait! When you come to see me in my office, I'll be sitting at my desk with a telephone to my ear, giving orders right and left, hat tipped to one side, large as life! And my office will be next door to my own son-in-law's!'

'Don't be absurd,' said Michael. 'You don't think that he's going to give up so easily on this choice piece of mattress-fodder, young and supple and supplied with all the curves a man could ask for? You don't seriously think he'd look twice at either of your daughters, not even to pick his teeth with?'

Naileater, immediately convinced, sighed. Ah yes, it was quite true, his two long daughters were like a couple of upturned carrots, both as pointed as they were dim, and all they ever did was snivel. Heigh-ho, so it was goodbye to a top job in the League of Nations. His lads, now, were a different kettle of fish altogether from those two stupid girls! He smiled, and his soul went forth to his three lovely boys, and upon a sudden he sensed that some day they would all be roaring millionaires and darlings of Parisian high society, of that there was no doubt. Oh, he would ask nothing of them, not even a farthing in pecuniary assistance, he would let them alone to enjoy their dollars. All he wanted was to see all three richly married, each riding in a long motor car, and then to die in peace. 'Yes, my pretty pearls,' he muttered, and wiped away the figment of a tear. Then he felt hungry.

'My dear Solomon,' he said, 'I don't suppose you have any salted pistachios left which, out of friendship to me and your own natural kindness, you could see your way to donating to my cause?'

'Alas, my dear Naileater, I am pistachio-less: I gave them all to you.'

'In that case, drop dead,' yawned Naileater.

'You don't mean that,' said Solomon with a smile, 'because I know you love me, and last year when I was sick and like to die with a temperature of a hundred and five you sat up all night by my bedside and you even cried, I saw the tears! So there! But tell me, old friend, you who know everything, how does a man get a young woman of unimpeachable morals to understand that he has been pricked by Cupid's dart? I mean, what is the proper procedure and manner of it?'

'Generally speaking, you inform her by registered post, making sure you get a receipt as proof of delivery.'

'But what does one say in the letter?'

'Generally speaking, you say this: "Adorable girl, I have the honour of informing you by the present of today inst. that, beguiled by your modest bearing and the judiciousness of your spoken remarks, I shall, this evening, setting aside all other matters, hasten to deliver my flame by hand to your very own front doorstep."'

'That's not bad,' said Solomon. 'But if it was me I'd rather say that I loved her with all my soul and with intention honourable.'

'And she'd just laugh at you,' said Michael.

'I don't agree,' said Solomon. 'She'd think I was very nice, because girls warm to the respect of an upright heart. And now I'm going to answer another call of nature,' he said in conclusion, and he scurried away.

'Naileater, how did you end your letter?' asked Michael.

'Deliver my flame by hand to your very own front doorstep.'

'Yes, that might do, I suppose. But, if she's married, it would be a good idea to add: "unbeknownst to your clod of a husband", to make her laugh. A woman who laughs is ripe for the plucking. But why bother with a letter at all? Just ask her to dine on strong salted meats, followed by red mullet with chillies and she'll be on fire before you reach the pudding.'

'You are, alas, not far wrong,' said Naileater. '"Fishy dishes and strong salt meat Will fan the flames and raise the heat; For did not Venus, or so they say, Rise from the waves one sunny day?" That's how I put it in my *Treatise of Medical Poetry*.'

'Or else,' said Michael, 'I place a golden guinea between my teeth in her presence and I bite it clean in two, whereupon she goes mad for me. Or again, if I'm dancing with her, I give her to understand by means of a certain manifestation of my physiology that I find her attractive. This never offends women as long as it is accompanied by words of subtle import and bottomless respect.'

'It's true, the blood of the Arab does run in your veins,' said Naileater, suddenly repelled by Michael's thick lips. 'But hold your peace now. Our little friend returns.'

'One o'clock in the morning,' announced Mattathias.

He stood up and said it was more than a man of parts could bear, that he was being roasted on a slow spit by the debt rising remorselessly on the clock which ticked in Helvetic francs. Having extracted a promise of reimbursement from Michael, he wandered over to the taxi-driver, reluctantly handed over the sum registered by the meter, heartily wished him broken bones on his road to perdition, and furnished him with unexpected details concerning the morals of his female relations, both close and collateral.

CHAPTER 77

Perched atop the hayrick and once more wearing his frock-coat, Naileater, a full metre above the ground, regardless of danger, was discharging the function of lookout. Now shading his eyes with one hand, now peering through his marine telescope, he swept the horizon, ready to give the signal the moment the lady hove into view.

'Land ho!' he cried suddenly in a half-choked voice.

Whereupon Michael hurried into the forest where the two horses had been tethered, while the watchman, gripped by emotion of the strangest kind, carefully climbed down from his hummock. So there was such a thing as love after all, he thought. The tall, beautiful figure now approaching was headed in the direction of happiness, docile and compliant, drawn by the prospect of happiness, was walking towards the happiness of love.

'Atten . . . shun!' he bellowed, and broke wind to clear his mind, to feel at his best, and to ensure that his command of his rhetorical powers was free of all material concerns.

Not wishing to have anything whatever to do with the adulterous she-devil, Mattathias drifted away, while Solomon, whey-faced with shyness but obeying the order, stood motionlessly to attention. When she halted before them, like a statue of youth, the little man's face turned scarlet, he lost his head and he gave a low bow. 'Delighted, Your Excellentness,' he managed to say. For his part, Naileater strode nobly forward, kindly-eyed, hand on heart, already putting a value on the ermine wrap which she carried over her arm.

'Sir Pinhas Wolfgang Amadeus Solal,' he said by way of introduction, then removed his hat with a wide gesture, 'my *nom de plume* being Naileater, gentleman of leisure and no stranger to soap, friend of humanity at large and humble relation of lord Solal, whom I dandled on my knee when he was one week old on the occasion of his circumcision, by which I intend no unseemly allusion, that would be entirely misplaced, and in whose name and by the right of proxy invested in me, implicitly or tacitly, as you wish, I bid you welcome in fervent words inspired by the Song of Solomon, chapter six, verse ten, to wit, Who is she that looketh forth as the morning, fair as the moon, clear as the sun and terrible as an army with banners? Or, to put it another way, How do you do? Sir Pinhas, I repeat, honourable gentleman and thinking reed, a man noble in Israel and customarily attired in fashionable tails but tonight in frock-coat only by reason of this sojourn in dank nature's bosom, former vice-chancellor and a galloping consumptive since my tenderest youth! (He manufactured a dramatic gale of coughing and then proceeded, with a smile, to remark upon it, thus:) Proof positive of the truth of my allegations! Furthermore, in a PS, I declare twelve small infants who have been humbly starving to death for many years! In short, behold an unhappy father and gentleman, to suffering condemned!'

Having spoken, he bowed again with a flourish of his top-hat. She looked on bemused, her eyes moving between these two eccentric apparitions: the long, thin streak of Byronic gloom with the bare feet, and the small, round figure frozen in mid-obeisance as though he were looking for worms in the grass and doubtless thinking that in the circumstances this posture was a reasonable way of maintaining his dignity.

'Peace be with you, adorable Highness,' Naileater resumed, 'and may no care gnaw your vitals in the matter of your cordial but honourable tryst at the delightful house of dancing. The underling with the moustache has even now taken himself off with a view to procuring for Your Grace a mode of hippic locomotion, or should I say a hippic mode of locomotion, to convey you whither your heart desires, and you may set your mind at rest, for soon you shall have dancing and sorbet in abundance! So nothing presses, for there is but one indispensable thing in life, which is charity, the giving of alms to the poor, that sad class of humankind to which I have the painful misfortune and honour to belong,' he concluded with a woebegone smile which revealed his long-in-the-tooth fangs as he held out his inverted hat like a begging-bowl.

Assuming a pose of modest but dignified expectation, he then fell silent, while Solomon, who had slipped away unnoticed, was now standing some way off, bent over in the grass, absorbed in a mysterious task. Observing that nothing was forthcoming and that his topper remained innocent of coinage of any kind, Naileater resorted to a new tactic in his attempt to soften the heart of this daughter of Gentiles who was decidedly of the stingy variety.

'A beautiful night, is it not, dear lady?' he went on. 'In sooth, a velvety night, made for the languid labours of love, which leads me, not without tact and with all due reverence, to express my sincerest wishes that your sorbets be delicious and your prancing pleasant, in short that you may have all the joys which your heart quite properly desires. (He sighed with feeling.) Youth must have its fling of pleasures, be they legitimate or not, and I am a tolerant and understanding man, say I with a paternal wink. I am all the more broad-minded in my views for having standing before me Youth at its zenith and Beauty taken to such a pitch that I should have no difficulty in comparing Your Hoity-Toityness to the mare which once drew Pharaoh's chariot, or better still to a fresh young gooseneck generously stuffed with pinenuts. (She bit her lip to suppress her giggles.) Besides, I have observed that generosity is invariably the companion of grace and beauty! (He coughed and waited. What on earth was the matter with the girl that she should stare at him thus without saying a word? He decided to pluck the patriotic string.) Ah, dear lady, how happy I am to be here in this Geneva of yours, Geneva which is my third or fourth home, whose citizens I admire so much for their charitable instincts! As for the few fleeting moments of discomfort which you inflicted on Michel Servet, such things happen, *errare humanum est*. So we'll say no more about it! But coming back to the matter of charitable instincts, what, for example, could be finer than your Red Cross? The very thought brings tears to my eyes! *Inter arma caritas!* Verily, it is a noble motto! Still, I would add that to my sense charity should also be shown in time of peace! In short, fair lady, I'll put my cards on the table and say in all frankness that if I deserted

Uncle Saltiel, whom I left groaning in his bed of sickness laid low by jaundice, and came unto this place so far removed from urban comforts, it was certainly with the intention of presenting you with the respects and charmed greetings of an honourable man but also, I freely confess, crippled as I am by lack of the ready, in the hope of lawful pecuniary gain!'

He stressed these last three words, because quite clearly the heatheness was not terribly quick on the uptake. Replacing his top-hat on his head, he stood and waited, arms crossed and bare feet set wide apart. Was the miserly tightwad going to make up her mind or was she not? It was at this juncture that Michael returned, leading the two horses by the reins. Bustling Naileater out of his way, he dropped on one knee before her beauty and kissed the hem of her dress. Then, rising to his feet, he took her around the waist and, holding her more closely than was strictly necessary, lifted her on to the white horse and sat her on it side-saddle.

Only then did she say to Naileater: 'I'm sorry, I haven't any money on me.'

'Don't let that stop you, dear Highness!' he exclaimed forcefully. 'I also accept banker's drafts and promissory notes, which are highly convenient forms of payment, and I have about my humble person the necessary paper and pencil! Over and above which, my poor daughters shiver with cold, and the chattering of their crooked teeth can be heard as far away as the stronghold of the podestàs,' he added, with a wheedling look in his eye and one hand on the ermine wrap, which he chastely fingered. 'The wretched girls have always longed for warm raiment. They talk about it at night in their dreams. The upshot of which, dear benefactress, is that they would bless your open palm and God will reward you a hundredfold,' he ended, snatching away the wrap, which Michael immediately wrested from him and restored to the lady on the horse. 'Damn you to hell, you interceptor of ermine!' screamed Naileater. 'And the devil take the lewd bones of your grandam too!'

She stroked the neck of her horse, took a firm hold of the reins, and handed the fur wrap back to Naileater, who gestured his thanks by placing one hand to his heart and then raising it to his lips, after which he winked cheekily at Michael, who was now sitting astride the other mount, his water-pipe tucked underneath his arm. It was at this moment that Solomon suddenly reappeared like a small tornado, clutching with both hands a bunch of poppies which he held out, gasping and puffing, to the lady on her horse. Then, as his two cousins looked on in amazement, he began, in a voice half-choked with emotion, to recite a dainty little poem of his own devising which made mention of 'flowers, fairest work of nature's art, The very emblem, lady, of your heart'.

When he had finished, the sweet little man in his sheepskin coat stood on the tips of his toes to receive his reward. Leaning down, she picked him up and gave him such a kiss that he felt as though his soul would fly away on the wings of bliss. Set down once more on terra firma, he ran off quickly and, to give unimpeded expression to his delight, began running round and round in circles with all the concentration of a circus horse, while the lady on the white palfrey, attended by the janissary, cried out with a joy so unconfined that it was almost awesome, uttered a protracted whoop of gladness, a song of youthful praise, heedless of the reins and with arms spread wide, before vanishing into the shadows of the night.

Then Solomon, who was still galloping round and round, gave vent to his pride and joy. He had been kissed, but the others had got nothing! They, poor fools, did not know that he had been planning his master-stroke for the last hour and had composed his pretty poem with much counting of syllables on his fingers! With arms raised, he frolicked and capered and yelped until he was fit to choke that Solomon had won, that Solomon had been kissed, while Naileater, the ermine wrap slung carelessly over his shoulders, was refusing to sell it to Mattathias and was inwardly devising a scheme whereby he could sue Michael for damages on the ground that he had inserted a spoke into his wheel.

'You saw it, Naileater?' asked Solomon, when he had returned to earth once more. 'She kissed me!'

'Yes, just as if you were a toddler of three,' said Naileater. 'If I were in your boots I'd be ashamed.'

Whereupon, consumed by sudden passion, he whipped the wrap from his shoulders and kissed it ardently, his eyes starting out of their sockets. Murmuring words of tenderness to it, telling it that he would turn it into three pretty little capes for his three pretty little boys, clutching it to his bosom, he waltzed with it on his great, wanton, erratic feet. And there in the moonlight, under the astounded gaze of his cousins, he whirled and gyred interminably with the white fur wrap, the tails of his frock-coat flying, gracefully whirled and leaped and skipped, his bare feet entrechating.

CHAPTER 78

Waking at seven, he stretched and smiled because he was home again, in his own bed, which was so much more comfortable than any hotel bed, an old friend really, on top of which no need to worry if everything was clean. Home, sweet home again. And next door, only yards away, was his wife! His wife, for goodness' sake! He'd be seeing her soon and they'd chat just like old friends. Yes, he'd tell her more about his mission.

'If only you'd seen how interested she was, old bean, quizzing me about my interviews, especially about the one with the High Commissioner, a Field Marshal, I don't suppose you come across many Field Marshals, do you, old man? And then when I told her I'd begun my novel about Don Juan, made a start on it when I was away on my official travels, got three chapters under my belt already, forty pages in all, she wanted me to read it out to her. You should have seen the pair of us, old sport, me in my silk dressing-gown reading, because before starting I changed into my dressing-gown, it's a Sulka, my dear Vermeylen, bought it in Paris, in the Rue de Castiglione, it's *the* shop you know, anyway if you could have seen me reading in my ultra-stylish dressing-gown, gave me that sophisticated look, you know, leading-man-of-letters stuff, and she listening deferentially, hanging on my every word, dead keen, fully entering into the spirit, if you follow me. Oh yes, old friend, marriage is the thing! (He emitted a series of short, sharp yawns and then hummed his "Home, sweet home again".) I say, Arianny, two hundred kilos of documentation! What do you say to that! I must find a way of making damned sure Monsieur Solal is put fully in the picture. Know what I'll do? As an appendix to my report, I'll draw up a complete list of all the documentary material I've brought back with me, it'll run to pages and pages single-spaced. Of course he won't read all of it, but he can't fail to be impressed by the quantity. Naturally anything that qualifies as documentation has been sent on directly to the Secretariat, but if you're interested you can come along to the Palais sometime and I'll show you the whole lot. By the by, I've brought back masses of photos, of native dances put on in my honour and of me standing next to high-ranking officials, I'll show them to you. There's one taken in Paris where this head of section in the Colonial Office is holding me by the arm, ever so matey, and him being a very big gun indeed, you know, marvellous chap, just about to be pitchforked up to Director-General, I'll show you that one, it'll interest you, though I must say we were both a bit squiffy after that dinner at the Lapérouse. I'll stick all the photos in a special album, with a note in white ink under each one, and *natürlich* the date. So you like my three chapters, do you? Now if you've got any criticisms to make, don't hold back, honestly I'd be very interested, I'm not above criticism, you know. Forty pages! It's starting to mount up! I've got about another two hundred to go. I've worked it out: forty thousand words. To my mind, forty thousand words is the right length for a novel, not too long and not too short. I've decided to call it *Juan*, my first thought was *Don Juan* but I felt *Juan* would be more original, everybody's got so used to *Don Juan*. Listen, the more I think about it, the more I reckon it would be a good idea to invite Monsieur Solal here as soon as possible because then I could fill him in about my official visit. A face-to-face is much better than a report, it's more sort of reciprocal, and besides with a report you never know whether your stuff's been read seriously or not, while with a conversation, they're bound to listen to what you say. Don't you agree? But coming back to my novel, I was really bucked, you know, that you particularly liked the passage about primordial contempt, and also the bit where he explains why he has this mania for seducing women. Those are two themes I'm particularly keen on, in fact they've been haunting me for ages. Yes, tremendously bucked, because really, you know, everything I write is intended for you. I really believe I've hit the jackpot with this novel. What I need now is a transfer to Paris, to our office there. If I had a big flat in a smart part of town and scattered the invitations about right, left and centre, I'd make loads of personal contacts. Then next stop the big literary prizes, like the Femina or the Interallié, see? 'Cos getting to know people, making friends, is the pathway to success. And now, Vermeylen old man, we shall rise and make her some tea. But mind you don't make a noise, mustn't wake her before taking up her tea. She loves her morning tea. (He gave a delicate, dreamy smile.) In fact she's mad about anything English, she picked the habit up in England. Three years at Oxford, old bean, in a fashionable women's college where they only admit really high-class girls. I don't think your wife could say as much for herself, now could she? Morning tea! I'll explain what it means, old bean. It's a cup of tea you drink first thing when you wake up. But I shall make it in a teapot, because sometimes she fancies a second cup and also because I'll have some too, it's such bliss being there sipping together. Very strong tea, a little milk, no sugar, that's the English way. Breakfast comes later, after you've had your bath, that's how the best people do it. She's not a bit like your wife, you know. She's not the type to whinge about the cost of living or sit at home darning socks. No, old man, she is pure delight, poetry in motion! So now you know. Ready! Steady! One, two, three, and away we go!'

He crept cautiously down, avoiding the creaking middles of the stairs, keeping close to the banisters. When he got to the bottom, he winked at his mackintosh, which was hanging in the hall. Yippee, happy days were here again! In the kitchen, he put the kettle on, rubbed his hands, and hummed a snatch of Mozart:

> With willing marriage kiss,
> In Hymen's temple true,
> Strew our path to wedded bliss
> With flow'rs of every hue.

Rather! The path to wedded bliss! Morning, sweetie-pie! Did my little sweetie-pie sleep well, then? Here's some nice tea for my sweetie-pie! He loved watching her drink her tea, still soggy with sleep, she seemed such a baby. If she woke up full of beans and didn't want to go back to sleep after her cup of tea, he'd suggest an outing and an early start.

'Listen, Arianny, I've had a spiffing idea. It's such a marvellous day, can you guess what I'm going to suggest? Give up? Well, I vote we get our skates on this morning! At nine o'clock we'll hop in the car and drive out into Savoy, what do you say? I've heard there's this marvellous restaurant at Talloires, three stars in the Michelin, which can't be bad. It's where all the biggest names in politics go when they want a slap-up do, you know, Briand, Stresemann and the rest of them, so it must be pretty good. So what do you say to treating ourselves to a gourmet lunch at Talloires? What do you reckon to that? No, watch it, don't say "reckon to that" say "Does that tempt you?" But if she'd rather go back to sleep after her morning tea, heigh-ho, we'll make it later in the day. Hello, kettle's boiling. Warm the pot first, go by the book. Right, I've warmed the pot. Jolly well done, old man. Now put the water back in the kettle, absolutely essential water be at one hundred degrees Centigrade, or should we say Celsius? Perfect. Quick now, two heaped spoonfuls of tea, no make it three, no expense spared is the management's motto. And now, look slippy, pour the water, then on with the nice fat cosy and allow to stand for the regulation seven minutes. Got what it takes, old man, showed a real interest in my official trip, if you could have seen the way she listened. Between you and me, I would have rather, I felt you know, dammit all, I'd been deprived of home comforts for months, I wouldn't have said no to a spot of conjugal duty, believe me, but when it came down to it, when I began my move, she made it perfectly clear, not tonight, Josephine, carried it off nicely but firmly, oh she wasn't being deliberately awkward or anything, it was the surprise of seeing me back so unexpectedly, a week before I was due, it was the shock, she'd thought I wouldn't be arriving till the thirty-first of August, it knocked the stuffing out of her and brought on a terrible migraine, so obviously she was hardly in the mood for, you know, so as far as the two-backed beast was concerned, nothing doing, you can whistle for it, and all very understandable of course because I realize now that I was a brute turning up unannounced like that, I thought she'd be pleased, a nice surprise for her, but women are fragile creatures, very highly strung, awfully delicate, old man, you have no idea. But she'll be none the worse off for waiting. Her migraine will certainly have gone by this morning and there'll be twanging of bed-springs in the old town tonight, you can take it from me! Still, she'd have every right to be cross with me for turning up on the doorstep without warning, but no, not a bit of it, she was very sweet, didn't chunter, just kept on asking questions about my trip. But what really got me, old man, was that notion she had of trying a dry-run with a view to August thirty-first. Her best frock, the flowers, the red lights, the whole thing set up just to give her an idea of how she'd have everything organized for when I got home on the thirty-first. A dress rehearsal, she called it. Now if that ain't love, old man, then I dunno what is! Only she could dream up something as romantic as that. And what about this scheme of hers for having her little sitting-room completely redone and the woodwork repainted for my benefit, isn't that love? I tell you what, from now on we'll be able to do our entertaining in that little sitting-room, much cosier than the drawing-room. Let's go into the sitting-room, my dear Under-Secretary-General, we'll be more comfortable there. It'll be one in the eye for the Kanakises too, we could invite them when we have the USG over. Perhaps we should call it The Den, much smarter than sitting-room. Come off it, old bean, the Kanakises are definitely out, you must be mad. It would be utter folly to give Kanak an opportunity to make a personal contact with the USG. Invite the USG by himself or with a few hand-picked guests, people from outside the firm, not members of staff, because those little swine would be only too glad of a chance to ask him round to their own dos. Oh by the way, Arianny, I forgot to tell you. Last night, when the train stopped at Lausanne, I bought a copy of the *Journal de Genève* and what did I find but that Petresco and his wife are dead, car accident, it happened on a level crossing. So it was just as well I didn't invite them here with the Kanakises after all, it would have been totally unproductive from my point of view since they're both dead now and, as far as personal contacts go, there wouldn't have been any mileage at all in it for me. Of course, it means that there's an A slot going begging, I wonder who'll get it, I shouldn't be at all surprised if . . . but we'll have to wait and see. Hey, this is no good, you're wasting time, get yourself upstairs and make yourself irresistible. My poor heart's going pit-a-pat at the thought of seeing her. I'd even go so far as to say it's going pat-a-pit.'

Back in the kitchen, wearing clean pyjamas, hair brilliantined, wispy beard neatly combed and nails clean, he looked admiringly at himself in Mariette's mirror. Prince Charming in person. And now for a few thoughts about tactics.

'Let's have a little ponder about what the best approach would be. We go into her room. Right. If she's sleeping, a state which all the indicators would appear to lead human wit to anticipate, we creep up on her quietly and wake her with a tender kiss on the forehead or the cheek, according to the position of her head, or even possibly on the lips! *Fortuna audaces juvat!*'

He leered at the prankish thought which had suddenly popped into his head. Yes! Play the same trick on her as Dada did on Mummy. After the kiss, he'd look serious and tell her he'd read an article about how good camomile was for you and so, instead of tea, he'd thought it would be better for her to make a nice camomile infusion. She'd pull a face but, when she saw it was tea after all, how they'd laugh! No, on reflection, as stunts go it wasn't as funny as all that, so just say he'd brought her tea, as usual. 'Here's some tea, lovely tea for my sweetie-pie, a nice morning cuppa!' Motion carried.

When he got to the first floor, he put the tray down on the ground, knocked quietly, and was not at all surprised to get no reply. The poor lamb was probably fast asleep, so wake her gently. Stick to the forehead for the kiss. Holding the tray in both hands and leaning on the handle with his elbow, he opened the door slowly, said he'd brought tea, lovely tea for his sweetie-pie. On the bed, which had not been slept in, was a single sheet of paper folded in four. The tray slipped from his nerveless fingers and tea spilled all over the carpet. He unfolded the paper and soaked the front of his gorgeous striped pyjamas with his urine.

CHAPTER 79

Hunched on the sofa in the little sitting-room with the shutters closed, he twisted his hair around his finger then untwisted it again. The flowers and the cigarettes had been meant for the other man. No doubt about it, yes, the pair of them on this sofa, facing the long swing-mirror which had seen everything. But damnation, she had agreed to marry him, so how come? She'd bought tonics for him, and at mealtimes she always reminded him to take them, so why?

He got up, left the room, wandered through the hall, brushed past the lapels of his mackintosh, stopped by the barometer, and tapped it. They'd have fine weather for their trip. Italy, perhaps, the land of love. 'With willing marriage kiss, In Hymen's temple true, Strew our path to wedded bliss With flow'rs of every hue,' he murmured as he shuffled into the kitchen.

He sat down at the table, unfolded the letter, rolled it into a cone, then unrolled it, tried to smooth it flat, and was reminded of how, when he was a little boy, he used to spend hours covering his exercise books. He little knew then what lay in store for him. Slack-jawed, he looked up and stared at the galvanized clothes-line which ran from wall to wall. It was perfectly straight, absolutely taut. He had put it up himself. He'd never be able to take any pleasure from looking at it ever again.

There were biscuits on the table. He grabbed two and munched them slowly. The soggy biscuity mess in his mouth tasted of calamity. He pointed a forefinger at the fridge. They'd chosen it together when they were first married, one Saturday afternoon. As they left the shop, she'd linked with him, spontaneously, and they'd walked along arm-in-arm, husband and wife.

And now she was with somebody else, somebody who could touch her whenever he wanted, and she would let him. Yet she was still his wife, she still bore his name. He rolled the letter into a cone again, unrolled it, and read it aloud.

'Sunday morning, six o'clock,

'My poor darling, I feel dreadful at the thought of you sleeping peacefully, not knowing yet. You're so good, it's awful putting you through the mill like this. When I left him a little while ago to come back here, I was intending to talk to you and explain, but when I got to the door of your room I just couldn't face it. Forgive me for keeping it from you last night, it was all too much for me. He was due back from a trip too, and it was him I was expecting when you showed up. I would like to have written a long letter to make you see that I can't help myself. But I promised him I'd be back very soon, because we are getting an early train, at nine this morning.

'Just now, as I got back, I stopped for a moment by your mackintosh hanging in the hallway. Seeing it made me feel queer and upset. I patted the lapels and noticed that the middle button had nearly come off, so I sewed it back on. It was very comforting to me still being able to do something for you. I looked in the fridge. There's everything you need for today. Heat up your dinner, don't eat it cold. Go back to work tomorrow and have your lunch with your colleagues. Don't stay home in the evenings, go out and see friends, and above all wire your parents to come home at once. Forgive me, but I need to be happy. He is the love of my life, the first and the last. I'll write after we get there.

'Ariane'

He got up, opened the fridge, picked up a cheese flan, and bit into its icy heart. He, him, he, him, as if he was the only man on earth. And how kind of her to think of letting him know that they'd be leaving at nine o'clock. Should he phone the station to find out where the train went? Wasn't he even entitled to know where she was going or whom she was going with? All the same, she might have told him who the man was. This flan's not up to much. And the nerve of her, saying 'my darling'.

He raised his eyebrows in stern judgement, then turned the gas taps on, shut them off, walked up and down with one arm bent just like on the day when they had strolled arm-in-arm and she had linked with him, hadn't needed to be prompted. He rounded his arm some more, so that he could picture it more clearly, raised his eyebrows again, and moved off, shuffling his feet with the right-on-my-side dignity of the weak who have been wronged. Pausing by the pile of clean linen which had been left on a chair, he picked up the laundry-book and ran his eye down the list. Just household linen. Obviously her things were too delicate and Mariette washed those. Ticking each item off against the list, he checked through the pile and put every-thing away in the sideboard. Six sheets? Rather a lot for a fortnight. Of course: must have been all on account of her man. He, him, he, him. Spotless sheets every time, of course. Really, the very idea of doing it in his house, between sheets which had been a present from Mummy, on Mummy's wedding present to them! Actually, Mummy'd be glad. Really taut, that line. These new screw stretchers were far superior to the old rack-and-pinion sort.

He struck a match, laid it on the table, picked it up just as it was about to go out, turned it round, and managed to rekindle the flame. Victory! She'd come back to him! But he was really quite aware that his lucky strike was a trick of fate, a hope doomed to disappointment.

'From now on, indifference.'

He opened the sideboard and inspected the shelf of preserves. He'd tarry a while with these jars, which were lined up like whores in a brothel waiting for a client to take his pick. That's it, try a little humour. Peach jam? Too sweet. Plum? Too common, a bit infra dig for an A. Cherry? Yes, interesting taste, with just a hint of tartness. So cherry jam it was, motion carried *nem. con.* Little cherries, I'm going to gobble you all up. That's more like it, don't take it all so seriously, be strong in adversity. He stamped his foot to be strong, hummed the toreador's song from *Carmen*, then dug into the jamjar with a fork which did service as a sieve so that he got just the cherries and left the runny stuff behind. So she was happy, was she? Well so was he, and yah-boo-sucks to her.

'Look, I'm scoffing jam!'

He pushed the jar away, reached for a tin, and unscrewed the lid. Deuced handy for camping, really hermetically sealed. This much at least he had left, something solid you could depend on which never played fast and loose with you. Twenty francs for rolled, boned shoulder of lamb was a bit steep, the man was obviously coming it pretty strong. He added two exclamation marks to the butcher's bill and put the stub of the pencil in his pocket. Shoulder of lamb was very nice, tender, a touch on the greasy side perhaps. He, him, he, him. He was glad he'd sent Mariette away when she'd rung the front-door bell. The old cow was clearly in on it.

'Now let's get dressed and go out.'

A stroll followed by lunch in town. On guard, toreador! That's it, go out. Lightweight suit, blue tie. When she tied his tie for him, she always gave him a little pat on the cheek afterwards. Last night it was this other man she'd been waiting for. And he, like a complete idiot, had gone and read his manuscript out to her! The freshly painted woodwork and the new carpet had been for her lover-man. The carpet must have cost three thousand francs at least. Money down the drain. He'd hardly ever seen her with no clothes on, and when it happened she always covered up straight away and said it made her feel embarrassed. But she wouldn't be embarrassed with this other man. Stark naked, and she'd touch him, you know, and it wouldn't make her feel the least bit sick.

'A tart, that's what.'

No, she wasn't a tart, she was a respectable married woman. That's what was so awful about it, a respectable woman who was prepared to do disgusting things with a man. Should he call a cab in due course, go to the station and ask which platform it was for the nine o'clock train? Perhaps she'd feel sorry when she saw what a good sport he was by the way he'd pass them their bags through their carriage window. He wouldn't say a word, he'd just look at her with eyes glistening with tears, such pathetic eyes, and perhaps she'd get off the train. He murmured: 'Adrien, my darling, I'm not going, I'm coming back to you.'

But she wouldn't come back. The other man played a cool hand. He was a lover, made her jealous probably. Whereas he had always been straight with her. From him she'd got nothing but sincere affection and consideration. And she'd made him pay for it. Oh yes, sincere affection, the affection of a dupe, the consideration of a hoodwinked husband. He scraped out his nose in Mariette's little mirror, inspected his haul, rolled it into a ball, and flicked it away. What did such things matter now? Anyway, as a deserted husband, he was entitled. Go upstairs now and take off these sodden pyjama trousers, which were making him feel cold. Perhaps it was Florence, and perhaps they were staying in the same hotel, the one where they'd spent their honeymoon, overlooking the Arno. Maybe in the same room, and she'd let him touch her and she'd touch him back without feeling the weeniest bit sick. He raised his eyebrows. He'd always trusted her completely. Why would she want to write to him from there? To tell him how many times they'd done it since they left? It was his mackintosh she'd felt so sorry for, but he could up and die for all she cared. Stop, that's enough of that.

'I'm ordering you to go upstairs and get dressed.'

In his room, he knelt before the unmade bed and prayed to God to make her come back to him. Then he got up and stared at his hands. Of course, his prayers wouldn't do any good, he was well aware of that. He went over to his bedside table. Next to his wristwatch, she smiled out of her antique silver frame. He turned the photograph to the wall. He'd been so delighted when he'd found the frame in the antique shop. Quick, rush off home to show her and put her picture in it! Quarter past eight. He fastened his watch on his wrist. At least if he knew where she was at this moment he could phone, he would beg her to put off her departure so that they could talk things over together, like friends, he would tell her to wait and see if she was sure she couldn't live without this man.

'Darling, wait, wait and see if you really can't live without him.'

A little while ago he'd been too hot. Now he was too cold. He put an overcoat on top of his pyjamas. The trousers would dry soon enough, no need to change. He stared into the wardrobe mirror and hated the way he looked, especially the beard. He had a round head, a husband's head. He opened the drawer of his bedside table, took out his automatic, and read the words engraved on it. Manufactured By National War-Arms, Herstal, Belgium. He slipped it into the pocket of his overcoat. She'd been frightened when he'd shown it to her one morning when he brought her tea. 'But it's a must, darling, when you live in the country.' Whereupon she had told him to mind what he was doing with it and be careful. She'd been fond of him in those days. It was a pleasant time of the day, her morning tea in bed. 'Here's a nice cuppa for my sweetie-pie!' Once, when he'd brought up the tray, she'd winked at him, for no reason, just to show that they were good pals, that they got on together. Standing in front of the wardrobe, hands joined in supplication, he asked her to come back, then, recalling a song from one of Dada's old records, he sang the refrain softly, deeply moved by its entreaty: 'Please return, come back to me, Life's not worth living Now you're not near, So please return, my dearest dear.'

Some time later he was aware of being in the bathroom. He'd had it put in for her. Four thousand francs. Especially for her, because she'd wanted a bathroom next to her bedroom. 'I want to be alooone,' she'd said. What was this mania she had of mispronouncing words? He'd never know what all these dresses and cigarettes were doing in the bath. Still, they were a reminder of her presence. Nor would he ever find out what was behind the torn dress on the floor of her room, the green dress he'd bought for her, in Florence actually. That morning the weather had been superb, they'd left the hotel and she had held his hand. The same hand which, tonight, in bed . . . But she was still Madame Adrien Deume, dammit! Morally speaking, she wasn't entitled to her passport any more. What would they think in the hotel when they saw that her name and the other man's were different? Oh, he was perfectly aware why he was here in her bathroom. It was to see her things, to be with her. Yes, here was her toothbrush. He held it under his nose, to get the smell of her, but he resisted the temptation to open his mouth and clean his teeth with it.

'Still, there's nothing she can blame me for.'

When she had her period, she wasn't easy to deal with. On those days he'd always taken great care not to cross her. 'Well if that's what you think, darling, then so be it, it's entirely up to you. Has my sweetie-pie got a pain, then? Anything I can do to help? What about an aspirin. Want me to make you a hot-water bottle?' She called her time of the month the 'Days of the Dragon'. When they came round, she was remote and he felt a little scared of her. He respected her suffering and was genuinely sorry for her. The new man wouldn't give a toss, he certainly wouldn't look after her, he was a lover. All those rubber hot-water bottles he'd used to get for her, scalding hot, and he always let the air out before screwing down the stopper. 'Here you are, darling. This'll do your tum-tum good.' By day four he was happy because she had almost stopped hurting. She must have resented him a great deal for fussing over her on those days. It must have irritated her when he asked where it was hurting, whether she had a pain in her tum-tum or a headache. Really, he'd always had a pretty good idea, but he'd never been able to stop himself dancing attendance. But you could bet your life that this other man wouldn't be asking questions when she was like that, nor would he call her sweetie-pie. And she respected and loved him. Whereas she despised her husband for behaving like a nursemaid. Moreover, perhaps she'd resented him just for knowing she had a pain in the stomach. A whole stack of things which he now understood for the very first time. I'm starting to wise up at last. In such a hurry to be off that she'd forgotten to take her toothbrush, comb and powder. They'll buy all that in Florence, at a chemist's, holding hands. In the old days she never used powder. This powder would be for the new man's benefit. The gossip in the Secretariat, the looks he'd get from colleagues. Most likely her man was tall. Where had she met him?

He picked up the comb and, peering into the mirror over the hand-basin, carefully made a parting in his hair and then covered it up again. What if he went to the station and offered to fight? Hm. This man of hers was probably a lot stronger than him and would break his glasses and he'd end up looking silly. But if she thought he looked silly perhaps she'd feel sorry for him and get off the train just before it left. He up-ended the box of face-powder into the bath and snapped the handle of the toothbrush in half. 'Dishonourably discharged for treason,' he murmured. That's enough of that, now get yourself downstairs.

In the kitchen, he opened the shutters to let in some courage, picked up the bottle the milkman had left on the sill, poured milk into a pan, and lit the gas. The day he'd made her an egg-nog because she had a cough, she'd said he was a pet and he'd been terribly chuffed. A pet, but also a cuckold. All cuckolds were pets. All pets were cuckolds. She most certainly wouldn't be telling her new man that he was a pet.

He leaned out of the window. A pair of lovers in their Sunday best were doing filthy things with their mouths. They laughed. 'Just you wait and see, my bucko, she'll leave you in the lurch too one of these fine days.' He turned away so he wouldn't see them any more, noticed that the milk had boiled over, turned off the gas, and slowly emptied the pan into the sink. She had sewn the button back on his mackintosh and then she'd made a beeline for the kissing and the rest of it. She'd been so proud of sewing that middle button back on. But if another button came loose tomorrow, he could whistle for it.

He washed his hands in the sink to wash away his unhappiness, to make a fresh start. Tomorrow was Monday, back to work, dictate the report on his official visit, dress his window, resume contact with the USG. From now on it was naked ambition and nothing else. He reached for a walnut from the fruit-dish, cracked it between his teeth, and left the kitchen. In the hall, he halted by his mackintosh and yanked on the middle button until it gave.

'Go up and have a bath.'

But it was into her room that he went, after knocking on the door. This was the room where they had talked together, where he had brought her tea. On the floor lay the green dress, the teapot, the two cups, various lengths of string, shoes, and her big fluffy teddy-bear with its legs in the air. Patrice, she called it. Sometimes, when he brought the tea, she was clutching Patrice, having slept with him all night. None of these shoes had trees in them. How many times had he told her how essential shoe-trees were? Her sun-glasses were on the floor too. When she wore them she looked just like a film star going about incognito and he'd felt oh so proud. On her bedside table was another bear, a small one, with boots on. He'd never seen this chap before.

Over the back of the armchair was the dress she'd worn last night. He spread it out, arranged the folds. She ought to have told him, ought to have trusted him. He would have let her go on meeting this other man, but at least she would still have been here, near him, he could have seen her every day, she would have had all her meals at home, well almost all, she would have been there each evening when he got back from the office, well almost every, because there'd be times, of course, but no one would have known except the three of them. He stroked the dress. He talked to it.

'Darling, I'd have arranged everything for you.'

Four minutes to nine. He opened the shutters and looked out. Not a soul in sight. No car bringing her back to him. He turned, gave a shoe a feeble kick, picked up a piece of string, and went back to the window. Three minutes to nine. They'd be in their compartment now, their cases stowed away on the rack above their heads. De-luxe cases. He saw her gloved, elegant, happy, sitting next to him.

Standing at the window, he fiddled with the string. Tangling and untangling it, pulling and yanking on it, he allowed his eyes to wander between the empty road and the empty sky. Nine o'clock struck one floor down. The train had set off, was now carrying her away from him for ever. Sunk, he was sunk.

'Sunk, sank, sink, sonk,' he muttered, tugging at the string, straining every sinew to snap it. 'Sunk, sank, sink, sonk,' he muttered over and over, for when the human spirit is brought to a certain pitch it invariably finds some pathetic way of beguiling its distress, of playing some ghastly game such as tugging at a piece of string and saying nonsensical words, inventing some piece of tomfoolery to make the unhappiness bearable, so that life can go on.

CHAPTER 80

Shivering in his coat, he spent the rest of the day in a daze, going up and down stairs, walking into rooms, switching on lights, opening and shutting drawers, looking at himself in all the mirrors so he did not feel alone, switching off lights, moving on, sitting on the stairs to flick through a book he'd come across in Dada's room, getting up suddenly, resuming his wandering, sometimes talking to himself, saying 'Hello, darling' to her, or 'Night-night, darling', now humming a tune, now murmuring to himself with a little smile that he was a cuckold, the Wandering Cuckold.

When it was nine in the evening, he went into her room, opened the door of the wardrobe, stared at the dresses on their hangers like corpses on a gibbet, leaned in, and filled his nose with their fragrance. She'd be in Florence by now, already in bed with her new man, they couldn't wait. The truth of the matter was that she'd never wanted him, always reasons why she couldn't, too tired, headache. He raised his eyebrows and turned on the radio. A well-fed voice informed him that suffering was spiritually enriching. Of course, it was Sunday. He turned the radio off and opened the drawer where she kept her little handkerchiefs. So pretty when she blew her nose. His foot brushed against the fluffy teddy-bear on the carpet. He picked it up.

'Come on, we're off to the loo, I want to go.'

He went down one flight, holding Patrice by the hand, and entered the bathroom. He put the teddy and Dada's book on the white lacquer stool facing the pedestal, for company. He lowered the mahogany-effect seat, hitched back the folds of his overcoat, undid the cord of his pyjama trousers, and sat down. Odd, being late like this. Generally speaking he was regular as clockwork, went every morning soon after waking. It was the emotional shock which must have clogged him up. Travelling made him constipated too. So did anything out of the ordinary, really. 'Just carry on as though she'd never existed,' he told the bear, and stood up. When all the formalities had been completed, he pulled the chain, gazed at the tumult of rushing, mighty waters, went on watching until the porcelain returned to white and immaculate. Quite: time healed all wounds.

'I'll get over it, you'll see.'

Sitting down again, he took a sheet of lavatory paper, folded it in narrow parallel creases, then made it into a fan which he waved in front of his face. Sunday breakfast together. She was very fond of butter. The amount of bread and butter she could put away! And then they'd talk, like good chums. He had meant something to her in those days, he was her husband. When she came back from picking mushrooms, she simply couldn't wait to show him her swag. That long intake of breath as she stood there proudly, waiting for him to say how well she'd done. At times like those she was just like a little girl. None of that would mean a thing to other people, but to him it was divine. Nevermore. She happy in Florence; he all alone sitting on a lavatory seat. He sniffled. Holding his drooping pyjama trousers with one hand, he got up, went across to the mirror over the hand-basin, stared at his tears and muttered.

'I remember days gone by and do weep their passing.'

He blew his nose on a piece of lavatory paper then pulled the chain, although there was no need, seeking comfort in the efficient working of the flush. It wasn't exactly enough to constitute a goal in life. He picked up the comb which lay on the glass shelf and sat down again on the seat, though he did not feel a need. When he was a little boy and Mummy scolded him, he used to shut himself in the lavatory to cheer himself up. He got to his feet. On legs shackled by his pyjama trousers, which had fallen round his ankles, he shuffled over to the mirror to see the little boy he once had been, whom he recognized under the wispy beard, Didi aged eight, a good boy, a happy boy, who had worked hard at school, had embarked on life's journey with hope, had had no idea of what lay in store for him, and had worked so very hard for his exams. He looked on himself pityingly, shook his head, gave Didi a gentle smile, a woman's gentle smile.

. 'Poor boy,' he told the mirror.

Keep busy, pick up the threads. Smoke his pipe? No, he only smoked his pipe when he was happy, when she came to see him in his office. He'd imagined he cut rather a fine figure then, poor fool that he was, hadn't had any inkling of what was cooking. Awfully clinging, that dress last night. Especially round her behind. It had clung for her new man. He stroked his cheek in the mirror. Well somebody still loved him, somebody stroked his cheek. He poked his tongue out, to see if it was coated. Yes, somebody still worried about him. Spotting a blackhead on his nose, he squeezed it, inspected the little worm of grease on his fingernail, and squashed the little bastard into nothingness. Touting her behind to whoever-he-was, that was her goal in life from now on. He removed the stopper from the bottle of cologne and breathed its fragrance to rekindle his lust for life. Then he washed his hands. Who could tell, perhaps when the soap was nearly used up, when it was a thin, flat disc, she might come back. In two months, or three. Hurt, disappointed, she would seek sanctuary in his arms, and he would hold her close and comfort her. Trying to mimic the voice he would never hear again, he murmured: 'He made me so unhappy. I've come back to you.'

Sitting down again, he tore a sheet off the roll, made it into a tube which he put to one eye, like a telescope, then let it drop on the floor. No, he wouldn't change his will, too bad if this other chap did gain by it. That would make her see the calibre of the man she had deserted. He tore off more sheets of lavatory paper, one by one. She loves me, she loves me not, she loves me, she loves me not, she loves . . . him. Yes, that was clear from the letter. Talked about 'him' all the time, 'he' this and 'he' that, went on about her new man. So in love that she couldn't see how cruel she was being.

It was a very cruel letter. Stroking the lapels of his mackintosh was cruel. His lapels were the only thing of his which she stroked now. Saying 'my darling' was cruel. Cruel, saying that there was everything he needed for today in the fridge. But if there wasn't anything in the fridge tomorrow, her darling could run up a shutter and die for all she cared. She might feel awful about putting him through the mill, but that wouldn't stop her, you know, tonight with her man. Have lunch with his colleagues! As though that would make everything all right! It was the unfeeling charity of the heartless. So she needed to be happy! And what about him? Didn't he need to be happy?

He unfolded her note, underlined the cruelties, and put exclamation marks in the margin. Pity he didn't have cancer. If he had cancer she wouldn't have left him, he'd have had another two or three good years with her. Downstairs, on the little table in front of the sofa, was the propelling-pencil he had given her. It was cruel to have left it there, for it had seen all the disgusting things she had done with her man on the sofa. He arched his eyebrows and smiled faintly. For with one stamp of his heel he had pulverized the propelling-pencil and had spat on the sofa. Served them right. See, that's what I've come to!

'I'm hungry,' he told the teddy-bear. 'Let's fetch something to eat.'

When he got back from the kitchen, still holding Patrice under his arm, he put an old copy of a woman's magazine, a hunk of bread and a whole garlic sausage − Mariette's favourite snack − on the stool. Loosening his pyjama trousers, he sat down, removed the skin from the sausage, which he wrapped in lavatory paper so that his fingers would not get all messed up, bit into it, and smiled at the teddy on the stool facing him. Feeding his face was company, a comfort. Sitting on the lavatory eating garlic sausage was pretty disgusting, though. Who cared? Nobody loved him, so he was entitled.

Hunched over the magazine, sausage in one hand and bread in the other, he read the adverts as he munched. The Modern Way to Monthly Hygiene. Femina Tampons Being Worn Internally Are Undetectable. Femina Tampons Are Super-Absorbent. Her new man wouldn't be making any hot-water bottles for her, that was for sure. The World's Most Exciting Bra, Will Not Sag or Stretch. For That Attractive Shape, Superb Uplift, Ideal For The Smaller Bust, Be The Most Popular Girl In Town. The bitches! That's all they ever thought about.

'I was too nice. That's what cooked my goose.'

Oh, he'd had the occasional inkling, which was why he would come on strong and manly, but it never lasted, he couldn't keep it up, he always forgot. He was a weakling, no good saying otherwise, and that was the root of the matter. Sometimes, when she was being impossible, he would lose his temper, and then, afterwards, he would go and say he was sorry and next day he'd bring her presents. What was he supposed to do now with the presents he'd brought her from Syria and Palestine? Some fellows had all the luck, the ones who were strong all the time, didn't need to try, didn't know they were doing it. Waiters in restaurants never came when he called, he always needed several stabs at it, but was that his fault? Was it his fault if he scared easily, if he was afraid of not pleasing, if he smiled when a superior talked to him? It was all due to hormones. He had defective glands, and she'd made him pay for it. Raising his fist, which still held the stump of the garlic sausage, he bellowed menacingly at the ceiling.

'No God! There is no God!'

The sausage was all gone. If he could only spend all the time eating he wouldn't feel so bad. There was a horrible taste of garlic in his mouth. He wiped his sausage-greasy hand on his pyjama coat. Being dirty was a sort of way of getting his own back. That dress had clung everywhere. Her behind. Her new man would be making the most of it now. Here he was thinking piggish thoughts, that was how low he'd sunk. Being unhappy made you think piggish thoughts. So be it, then, he was a pig, a sausage-eating pig. So much for God. He tore off a sheet of lavatory paper, wrapped it round the comb, hey presto, the harmonica of his youth, and he growled out the theme of wedded bliss across the thin, vibrating paper. 'With willing marriage kiss, In Hymen's temple true, Strew our path to wedded bliss With flow'rs of every hue.' He stopped, ran the comb through his hair, pulling it down over his forehead, sweeping it straight back, and then repeating the operation.

Ensconced on his solitary throne, he went on combing and uncombing his hair. Now and then, for a change, he twisted it between thumb and forefinger, making it into a kind of knot which he screwed tight and then suddenly combed out, deriving sensual pleasure from tearing out whole tufts, masochistically maiming himself. Or again, he would open his pyjama coat and run the comb through the hairs on his chest, while dipping at random into Dada's book

677

which lay open on his knees, and signally failing to take in any of the different ways of removing stains. But reading helped further to deaden his unhappiness. After a while he returned to his hair.

Still plying the comb backwards and forwards, he read on, moving his lips to give each word its shape, to force it into his mind, to make it mean sense. She was terribly keen on whipped cream, and when her plate was empty she used to scrape away at it with her spoon, like a little girl. Would her new man notice, would he love her the more for it? He stood up, bare-buttocked, gave another heave on the chain, though there was still no need, to fill the silence of the house, to hear the sound of reality, so that he did not feel alone.

He sat down again while the cistern refilled, and resumed his obsessive combing with a sense of humiliation. But why not? Fiddling with his hair was all the fun he had left. You needed a little fun to bear the misery, to go on living, he knew that now, any kind of fun would do, even if it wasn't much fun, even if it was stupid. Besides, when he was combing his hair and twisting it into knots and pulling it out by the roots, he did not feel so lonely. He was in dialogue with his hair. He had a relationship with his hair. His hair was company.

Sitting there fiddling with his locks, his companions in misery, he mulled over old joys. The morning tea he used to bring her in bed on Sundays. He would come in holding the cup feeling pleased as Punch. 'Morning, sweetie-pie. Did my little sweetie-pie sleep well, then? Feel rested? Here's a nice cup of tea for my sweetie-pie!' She would be so fast asleep that at first she'd open just one eye, looking dazed, and he loved her terrifically when she looked at him with one eye. Darling, darling girl. And then she'd sit up, open the other eye, and hold the cup with both hands, fuddled with sleep, hair sticking up like a clown, a very pretty clown.

He murmured: 'Here's a nice cup of tea for my sweetie-pie!'

And she would say 'Goody' as she took the cup, 'Oh thanks,' she'd say, and she would hunch over the cup and his heart would be riveted on her face as she drank. He would watch carefully to see if she liked the tea he had made for her and waited on her approval. 'That's nice,' she would say after the second or third sip. 'Nice tea,' she would say in her waking-up, little-girl voice. And then he, proud of having made a nice cup of tea, gratified by this small thing which made her happy, would watch the happiness on her face as she drank, still half-asleep, a coddled baby-doll, while he stood with hand braced to steady the cup if it tilted too far. 'Goody! And when I've had this I'm going back to sleep,' she'd say.

'Goody! And when I've had this I'm going back to sleep,' he murmured.

When she was done, she would hand the cup back to him. 'I'm going to snuggle down again now,' she'd say, and she would face the wall, turn over on her side, pull the covers up to her chin, and curl up into a ball, and it was an agreeable thing indeed to see her curl up into a ball. 'Have a good rest, darling, sleep tight, I'll bring you up breakfast later on, in an hour, all right?' With her mouth pressed into her pillow, she'd say: 'Yes'. Sometimes she said: 'Yeah', because she was so sleepy, and she'd curl up into an even tighter ball. Seeing her curl up like that, seeing her so snug, made him feel good. Before he went, he always leaned over for another look at her face and packed the bedclothes firmly round her back to make her even more comfortable. Once, when he'd brought her morning tea, she'd said he was a good husband.

'So why, for God's sake, why?' he muttered, and he tweaked his pubic hairs, tried to pull them out.

After morning tea, when she'd had her bath, it was time for her breakfast, which he brought to her in bed, only too happy to wait on her and sucks to the way Mummy glared when they passed on the stairs. Everything set out nicely on the tray: toast, butter, jam. The slices of toast she could put away! And he was so pleased to see her lay the butter on thick, on account of the vitamins. He would watch her eat, loved watching her eat, watching her build up her strength. Sometimes he'd play a trick on her as he came in. He'd say the gardener's donkey was very sick, or that Mariette had broken a leg, so he could enjoy telling her straight away that it wasn't true, so he could see her smile, so he could make her happy.

After breakfast she'd light up a cigarette, and the smoke always got into her eyes. Oh, what pretty faces she'd pull! And then they used to chat like old pals, husband and wife together, they'd talk about everything under the sun. When she told him about her pet owl or her cat, she'd get so excited. She was so sweet then, interrupting her tale to see if he was listening appreciatively. Sometimes she would read out stories about animals faithful unto death. She got carried away, was so innocent, and interrupted her reading to see if he liked the tale, to see if he was joining in, to make him see for himself just how faithful that old elephant was. He always made a great show of being interested, to keep her happy. Sometimes she told him about her childhood, how when she was a little girl she used to say 'letters' instead of 'lettuce'. They'd go on chatting endlessly, they were friends at breakfast time. He was her husband, she was his wife, and it was good, it was what life was all about.

'Please return, come back to me, Life's not worth living Now you're not near,' he hummed softly, still sitting on the mahogany-effect lavatory seat, trousers undone, buttocks bared, hands joined in prayer.

God, how he used to love phoning her from the Palais, to say hello, for no reason, to hear her voice, to know what she was doing at that moment. And when VV got up to one of his nasty manoeuvres, quick, he'd phone home and ask her to come down to the office, and just knowing that she'd soon be there made him feel better. From the stool where it sat with its legs splayed, the teddy-bear watched him with equanimity.

'A couple of fat-heads sitting face to face.'

Cruel, she was so cruel. But what was the good of calling her cruel? It wouldn't make her come back. It wouldn't stop her, you know, with him. Weak, that's what he was, weak, that was the size of it. Serve him right, he'd been punished for being weak. Without getting up, he pulled the chain, shivered as his buttocks were splashed by the rushing waters, ran the comb through his hair once more, brought it low over his forehead, and then swept it back. Strong men and dictators never fiddled with their hair, nor did they stay perched on a lavatory seat for hours on end. But that was all he was capable of doing.

Losing interest in the comb, he felt for the loading-clip. Six bullets. The first one, being on top, was fully exposed to view. So small and yet quite a little number, eh, sweetie-pie? He inserted the clip, removed the safety-catch, pulled the loading-mechanism and then released it. Right you are, the first bullet was in the spout. That line in the kitchen, absolutely taut, dead straight, a pleasure to behold. He'd managed to put it up awfully well, he liked looking at it whenever he went into the kitchen, he'd made a definite success of it. He was attached to it, but there it was, he'd have to say goodbye to it now. Oh yes, the first one was in the barrel for sure. Did you sleep well, sweetie-pie? No, got thoroughly pleasured, more like. The hell with it, who gave a toss about her? She went to the lavatory like everyone else, didn't she?

The answer, that's it, was the outside world, where life was real, other people. Get out and about, yes, go to a nightclub, the Donon, for instance, it was where everyone went. First have a bath, then monkey-suit, taxi and voilà, the Donon. His new dinner-suit, the one he'd worn to dinner at the Ritz. Quick now, into the bath. He smiled to perk his spirits up. He got to his feet, pulled up his trousers, and stamped his foot to put the pep back into his system.

'Right. Take a bath. Salvation lies in the bath.'

Lying in the bath, he felt his unhappiness like a pain. All alone in the water, making himself clean to no purpose and for nobody's benefit. In the old days, whenever he'd got spruced up it had always been for her. All alone in the water, while the two of them would be asleep in each other's arms. Or perhaps they weren't asleep. Perhaps they. Perhaps at this very moment. Oh yes, and with that face of hers which was so pure, so childlike when she got worked up about one of her animal stories. Would they take precautions? But he felt his unhappiness even more intensely when, after mechanically shampooing his hair, he ducked his head under the water to rinse off the suds and stayed under for several seconds, ears blocked, as he always did. God, how alone he was here in the water, in the silence. He was drowning in unhappiness in water, all alone, submerged in water, with his eyes open. He lifted his head to breathe, then plunged beneath the surface once more, to be in deep water, to be at the rock-bottom of his misery.

Wearing his dinner-jacket, his trousers with the silk stripe lowered round his knees, buttocks bared and once more ensconced on the mahogany-effect lavatory seat, he pored over the first photograph he'd ever taken of her, when they were engaged. Just before the shutter clicked, she'd said that as she looked into the camera she would be thinking how much she loved him. His throat felt tight, his eyes were dry, as, with wispy beard quivering and hands like ice, he stared at that beautiful face which said 'I love you' and would go on saying it every time he looked at it. Phone up Kanakis and ask him to come round? Out of the question, it was too late, it was eleven o'clock at night, what sort of fool would he look? Anyway, Kanakis couldn't care less if he was unhappy. After a funeral, everybody went off and fed their faces.

'The Donon it is, then.'

But he would come home and not find her there! Who was he to say goodbye to in the morning, and good-night at bedtime? Each night, after they'd said good-night, he used to shout through the wall from his bedroom, to be near her still, even if it was at one remove, he'd call good-night again. He'd sing out good-night several times. 'Sleep tight, darling, good-night, good-night, sleep tight, see you tomorrow.' Love-calls, that's what they were. Whenever there was a beautiful piece of music on the wireless he'd call to her right away, he couldn't possibly listen to anything beautiful unless she was there to share it. He stood up again. Getting tangled in the trousers of his dinner-suit, which were now wrapped around his ankles, he shuffled over to the wash-basin mirror, took a long look, and gave himself a smile. So that was despair: smiling at yourself in a mirror when you were all by yourself alone.

'What am I going to do?' he asked the mirror.

All those school lessons he'd learned so carefully, staying up until eleven o'clock, even midnight. 'Time for bed now, Didi, it's late,' Mummy used to say. But he wanted to be top in Recitation and switched the light on again when she'd gone and got up at five in the morning to go over the test-piece. What had been the point? And the pleasure he'd taken in starting new exercise books in back-to-school October. The care, the love with which he had written his name, form and subject on them. What had been the point? Herstal, Belgium. Once, when he'd brought her morning tea, she'd winked at him for no reason, because they were friends, to say how well they got on together. He winked at the mirror. His eyelids lived, they obeyed.

Sitting on the seat once more, he removed the safety-catch on the Browning, put it back on again, ran his fingers through his sweaty hair, inspected his fingers, and wiped them on the jacket of his pyjamas. He was afraid. Runnels of perspiration trickled down his beard and collected under his chin. He was afraid. He took the safety-catch off again. Even if you wanted to die, you still had to make a living gesture, you had to pull the trigger. Forefinger squeezing the trigger, then moving once more so that it need never move again. That was what it boiled down to, a forefinger with a mind to act. But not him, he was young, he had the whole of his life before him. He'd soon make adviser, then head of section. Tomorrow he'd dictate his report. On your feet now, ring for a taxi, then the Donon. That's right, the Donon.

But first let it rest against your temple for a moment, just to see what it was like when a person made the decision. Not that he was such a case, oh no, he wasn't that stupid, he was young and had the rest of his life before him. He only wanted to see, that's all. To go through the motions, to feel what it was like, to get an idea of how it was done. Yes, that was how it was done, you put the barrel against your temple, so. Not that he'd do it, his forefinger simply wouldn't want to. With him it was just testing. He'd never, oh no, he wasn't the sort, he wasn't a fool. Sleep well, darling, had a good rest? Once, she'd winked at him.

She winked at him, and his finger made up its mind. 'Time for bed now, it's late,' a voice whispered in his ear as he subsided slowly. His forehead came to rest on the stool between the legs of the teddy-bear, and he stepped back into the warm bedroom of his childhood.

PART FIVE

Here in the hotel at Agay they had no thought but for themselves, no thought save for discovering all there was to know about each other and, between conjunctions of alarming frequency, for telling all there was to know about themselves. Identical nights, sweet fatigues, welcome cessations of love's labours, and she would let her fingers run over the bare shoulder of her lover-man to give him thanks or bind him in her spell, and he would close his eyes and smile his delight. Locked in each other's arms, they rested from their momentous labours, fell asleep in a murmur of tender words and fascinating exegeses, surfaced from sleep to join their lips or cling more closely or fuse muzzily, still only half awake, or to take furious, carnal knowledge of the other in a sudden stirring of loins. After which, sweet slumber returned. Symbiotically. How could they sleep if not together?

Come the dawn and he would leave quietly, taking care not to wake her, and go back to his room. Sometimes, opening her eyes, she protested. 'Don't go,' she moaned. But he would tear himself free of her weakly restraining arms, speak reassuringly, say he would come back soon. There was a reason for his early-morning leave-taking: he did not want to be seen as anything less than perfect, not shaved and not freshly bathed. He was also afraid that when she went to take her bath he would hear the appalling preliminary, the thunder of the lavatory flushing in ruinous tumult.

Shaved and bathed and wearing his dressing-gown, he would phone and ask if he could come. 'Give me a few minutes,' she would say. Groomed and bathed and wearing her white morning gown, she would open the bathroom window to clear the air, then close the door behind her, pause momentarily to check the face of She-Who-Was-Loved, nod with satisfaction, note the shadows under her eyes with pride, straighten the curl over her forehead, and then phone to say that she was ready. And he would come, and there was wonder as they stood and drank with their eyes, demigods, poetic and clean-scrubbed, clad in the priestly robes of love.

Masking the badges of love, she would ring for the head waiter, who appeared almost at once bearing the large tray. And then unfolded the scherzo of breakfast ingested with smiles, a sprightly appetite and an unquenchable desire to please He-Who-Was-Loved, whose toast was buttered by her own fair hand. When, duly summoned, the head waiter returned to remove the tray, they both averted their eyes, he because he was mortified at the thought of being served by an unfortunate forced to be in harness so early in the day, she because she felt uncomfortable in her all-too-revealing morning gown. She stared at the carpet to make herself invisible.

When the door closed, she would draw the curtains, and then was performed the allegro of the return to bed, the resumption of kisses, meandering talk and childhood memories. They had so much to tell each other. Oh the joy of those moments of friendship free of desire! Sometimes, with a look of tender reproach, she would show him those badges which she had masked moments before, and demand that he make amends by delicate kissings of her emblems of love, which she was proud to bear. There is absolutely no point in telling what happened next, though they found it absorbing.

In late morning she would ring for the chambermaid, give her a radiant smile, and ask her to do both their rooms. Then, after flashing another toothy signal of neighbourly love at the elderly maid, who was to die a few months later of chronic myocarditis, she would leave and join Solal, who was waiting for her below, outside the hotel. Then they would make for the beach nearby, arrogant and handsome in their bathing-wraps, heedless of the stares of the genteel.

When they reached the sea, she would shrug off her wrap and sprint away, glorying in the knowledge that he worshipped her, a fleet-footed nymph on the gleaming, soft sand, arms outspread to catch every shred of breeze, and she would plunge into the waves and call to him. They swam side by side, sometimes starting fights which made her laugh in a mood of rediscovered childhood, laugh so much that the salt water went up her nose. Then she would beat a hasty retreat so that she could not be seen blowing her nose with her fingers, and then she would rejoin him, and then there were races or competitions to see who could stay under water longest. When their games were over, they lounged in the sun on the now empty beach. Afterwards it was the showers for them, clean water raining down on their tall bodies which sometimes pulsed and joined.

They would be back by two and order lunch in their sitting-room, because they preferred not to go down to the restaurant, hating the idea of meeting the other hotel guests. Sitting at the table in the French window which overlooked the dazzling sea, they would laugh at little things, because a little birdie had stopped its pecking on the balcony and was staring at them, with head to one side and beak raised in surprise, or because, when the hors-d'œuvres finally came, she announced that she was pitifully hungry. He watched admiringly as she ate ravenously yet daintily, with her mouth closed, as she unselfconsciously set about satisfying her healthy woman's appetite, an exhibition which boded well for the jousts to come.

The elbow of the *inamorata* nuzzled the elbow of the *inamorato* and proclaimed their love with each intrusion of the waiter, who seemed more than happy to serve them even though the hour was late. His keenness thrilled her. She interpreted it somehow as a promise of a future oozing with bliss. Delightedly, she put his attentiveness down to the sheer charm of the man she loved. She also fondly imagined that the hotel staff were quite starry-eyed to see them so much in love and had fallen in love with their love, that they were the most willing accessories and revered them as the Prince and Princess of Passion. She had no concept of the efficacy of generous tipping.

Over the pudding, their lips met, and sometimes these labial encounters were complicated by the business of sharing a grape which she held out to him with her teeth. Life like this is perfect, she thought. In the intervals between the kissing, she gazed upon him, treasuring the thought that he was hers, admiring all the things, including juggling with oranges, that he could do. Being a slave to sex, he thought, is softening her brain. But he loved her, and was happy.

After coffee, they took refuge in Ariane's bedroom, leaving the waiter to clear away. There, with blinds lowered, she went to the bathroom to slip into something more comfortable, emerged freshly powdered and underarms perfumed, and beckoned with an inviting look or a word. 'May it please my lord to share the bed of his servant,' she'd said to him one day, pleased with the biblical ring of the invitation. Inwardly squirming, he had smiled and obeyed.

In the evening sometimes a taxi whisked them off to the Moscow, Cannes' Russian restaurant. There, elegantly turned out and heavy-eyed, they started with blinis and caviare while back at Agay the elderly, cardiac maid shuffled about busily in slippers, hastening the hour of her death by tidying both their bathrooms and remaking the ravaged bed. Sitting side by side, they avoided touching, each guarding their secrecy, and behaved with the utmost respectability. Wearing her social face, she firmly refrained from calling him by any of her private, intimate names. She insisted on a certain tone because it heightened her sense that they were votaries of a priestly cult, and convinced her that they were star-blessed lovers.

But they did not go often to Cannes. Most evenings at about ten, after a stroll along the beach where, with a final heave, the beating sea deposited its exhausted waves on the sand which instantly swallowed them up, they would return to the hotel to be greeted by the devoted smile of Paolo, the lift-man, a small, shy Italian, fat and woolly-haired, who could not believe his good luck at having a decent job and his good fortune at having landed one at the Royal. He quivered with dog-like pleasure whenever he saw the gentleman and his beautiful lady. Delirious with dedication, proud to be of service, he would leap into action and open the lift door ceremoniously. As they went up, he never took his eyes off them, targeted them with ingenuous smiles, and politely sucked back his spittle to show that he had been properly brought up, so eager to please, so happy in his lowly but important station which allowed him to see the good and the great at close quarters and, in a sense, to associate with them. When they reached their floor, this good and simple man opened the door with all due deference, then stood to attention. She always rewarded him with one of the radiant smiles which she distributed so liberally, and then promptly forgot all about him.

Behind closed doors once more, they found the dinner left by the waiter on the sitting-room table swathed in blankets and an eiderdown to keep it hot. They would sit down and she would serve him, filling his glass with burgundy, pressing him to a little more meat, discreetly endeavouring to feed her man.

One evening in late September, as she imperiously forked a second hunk of meat on to her lover's plate, he looked away, embarrassed by the attentions which she lavished on him. What would she do next? Rub down his coat with a handful of straw? Polish his hooves? Come to think of it, he mused, she had recently begun to enjoy trimming his nails for him. But he looked at her again, and, seeing her humble and submissive and respectful of his silence, he felt a surge of tenderness. She was his handmaiden, she had sacrificed everything for him without a thought for what people might say, she lived only for him, and in him was all her hope. Suddenly he pictured her lying in her future coffin, white and stiff, and he ached with pity. Whereupon he kissed the hands which served him, her hands, which still lived.

One evening early in October, after dinner, she sat with her legs revealingly crossed and spoke to him of music, then of painting, a subject of which he knew nothing and moreover despised, and on which he was consequently driven to make loud whinnies of sincere but perfunctory approval by means of energetic tossings of his mane. Saying that she was tired, she turned out the ceiling light, draped a red scarf over the bedside lamp, and stretched out on the bed.

In the semi-darkness, she watched him through half-closed eyes and smiled, and suddenly he was afraid of her smile, for it was a smile from another world, a dark and potent world, was afraid of this woman who lay in wait for him, afraid of her tender eyes, afraid of their unwavering beadiness, afraid of her smile so single-minded in its purpose. Supine and soft in her web of spells, she wore her expectant smile in the dim, diffused red glow, and beckoned silently to him, a loving, terrifying magnet. He got up, and stepped into the world of women.

Impaled beneath his weight, she enveloped him, held him fiercely with arms and clutching thighs which were thongs to bind his back, and he was afraid to be thus held and harnessed, afraid of this woman beneath him who was a stranger to him, who was bewitched by lust, possessed, an ecstatic prophetess gripped by the holy frenzy of orgasm, who suddenly looked up at him with a beatific, crazed smile, wanting everything, dangerously wanting everything he had to give, wanting his strength to feed on, his air to breathe, offering the kiss of the vampire, wanting to imprison him in her dark world.

Appeased and re-entering the world of human speech, but still keeping him in her, gripping him inside her, she spoke in a voice that was soft and low. 'Darling, together always, loving always, that is what I want,' she said with one of her crazed smiles, and he shuddered, the captive of she who held him fast.

CHAPTER 82

One evening in late October, as he stepped into her room, he was assailed by a voice, a pure lily-white voice, singing Cherubino's aria, '*Voi che sapete che cosa è amor*'. With eyes ashine, she watched as the surprise registered on her lover's face, then she sat down beside him and they exchanged kisses while via the gramophone a Viennese soprano told them, courtesy of Mozart, what a thing their love was. When the music died away, she stopped the record. He praised the melody, duly admired Mozart, and said what a clever girl she'd been to buy a gramophone. She breathed deeply, proud to be clever, and then excitedly told him all about it, putting on her good-little-girl face as she always did when he said nice things to her.

'Got the idea in a flash of inspiration, I thought you'd like it, so I rushed off to Saint-Raphaël to buy one. Unfortunately it's the wind-up sort. It was just a little shop and they didn't stock any of those new turntables that work by electricity. It doesn't matter, though, does it? I've already bought twenty records, Mozart, Bach and Beethoven. It was a good idea I had, wasn't it?'

'Absolutely first-rate,' he smiled. 'We'll play them all to celebrate our being here for two months.'

She held out her lips to celebrate their sixtieth day of untrammelled love. She then expatiated on the Mozart aria, twice saying that it was adorable. To show an interest, he asked her to play it again. All eagerness, she wound the handle, blew on the record to remove any specks of dust, and carefully lowered the needle. The adorable aria began again, she went back to her place and nuzzled up to Solal's shoulder. Locked in each other's arms, they listened to all twenty double-sided records. She got up at frequent intervals to rewind the spring, then returned to him and gazed into his eyes while the records played on, to share the music, to see if he liked it. She provided a running commentary for each piece and he nodded approvingly. It was '*Voi che sapete che cosa è amor*' which brought the proceedings to a conclusion in the late afternoon of their sixtieth day.

'You who know what love is,' she translated in a whisper, and her cheek reached for the cheek of her love.

At seven forty she unveiled a second surprise. For that evening, she had ordered a special dinner, a semi-gourmet menu, which would be served at eight. There would be Russian hors-d'œuvres, then lobster *à l'américaine*, followed by all sorts of other goodies. And dry champagne! He told her all over again how clever she was. She demanded a kiss as a reward, said 'Thank you, kind sir' when she got it, explained that when she'd returned from Saint-Raphaël she'd made a point of having a personal word with the chef to make absolutely sure that everything would be just right and that there'd be no stinting on the hors-d'œuvres, because he was so fond of them. Such a nice man, the chef, so obliging. Besides, he loved cats, always a good sign.

The following day, which was the twenty-seventh of October, there was yet another surprise. For dinner she wore a marvellous, boldly plunging evening dress which revealed the small of her back. She had bought it secretly in Cannes that very morning. At midnight, when the twenty double-sided records had been played, he said that he was tired and took his loving leave. She asked him to promise he wouldn't laugh, but she had this urge to wash him all over in his bath. Say I can? You will let me? And so it came to pass, and she bathed him with handmaidenly ritual. After which she undressed and asked his permission to join him in the tub.

During the evenings which followed, they were served in their rooms with fine dinners specially ordered by Ariane, whose heart was gladdened by his evident pleasure. After coffee, Mozart's sublime aria swelled regularly round them, while noble words and deeds of tenderness passed between them and were interrupted on occasions by the grating cackle of jazz music to which commoner souls downstairs were dancing. When this happened, she pulled free of him and waited for the vulgar music to end.

One evening in early November, as she put down the book from which she had been reading aloud, she suggested a walk. He refused with a brief squinting blink of an eye and said it was raining outside. Then she said she would show him the family photograph album, which she happened to have brought with her. It had photos of her father, her mother, Aunt Valérie, Uncle Agrippa, Éliane, various grandparents and assorted great-grandparents. He made comments and admiring noises, and when she closed the album he suggested a trip to Italy — Venice, Pisa, Florence. They could leave tomorrow, catch the morning train. She got to her feet, clapped her hands, and said she'd start packing her cases that very minute.

CHAPTER 83

That day, after lunch in their sitting-room, they repaired severally to their rooms, undressed and got ready. Naked under a white silk dress, she completed her ablutions and titivations by spraying perfume here and there. Meanwhile he, naked under his red dressing-gown, shame-facedly scrubbed his nails. After a few moments the Mozart aria struck up and he gave a start. It was the summons. For she no longer phoned now, she put a record on instead. It was more romantic.

Yes, the summons. He was to report at once for love. She-to-Whom-Great-Debt-Was-Owed had sent for him, was summoning him to make her happy. Come now, prove to me that I was right to choose a life of solitude with you, she would say under cover of 'You who know what love is'. Today was November the twenty-sixth. Three months had already passed since they'd left Geneva, three months of chemically pure love. Agay first, then Venice, Florence and Pisa, and now Agay again, where they'd been for a week. If she noticed that today was November the twenty-sixth, there was a danger that the twenty-sixth of August would have to be commem-orated with romantic effusions and de-luxe coition.

He put down the nailbrush and the soap and peered at himself, close-shaven and disgustingly clean in his dressing-gown. So this was to be his life from now on: to be a daily object of desire, to display for sexual purposes. She had changed him into a peacock. Not to put too fine a point on it, both he and she lived like animals. But at least animals had seasons for pairing and mating. Not them: they were at it all the time. Constantly scrubbing himself, shaving twice a day, being handsome all the time, such had been his sole purpose in life for three months.

'Yes, all right, I'm on my way, I'm coming,' he told the Mozart aria, which, as he knew it would, was being encored.

Two o'clock. Outside a bitter wind was blowing. This meant he was sentenced to be confined to the love-nest. What on earth were they to do until it was time for dinner? What could he think up? These last few days there'd been scenes which had livened things up a bit and given them something to think about, but it had taken too much out of her. So he was going to have to find something else.

Perhaps they might slip away to Italy again? He hadn't the heart for it. Besides, even if they went to Venice they'd still be the same people when they got there. Moreover, at every train journey's end her nose was silted up with smoke. He did his best not to stare, but he couldn't help it, for his eyes were drawn to the grisly sight of her blackened nostrils. Of course when they checked into the hotel she washed them clean along with the rest of her, but those last few hours in the train, when the poor innocent girl, smiling nobly, displayed her sooty nostrils, were more than he could bear. He felt a crazy urge to take his handkerchief and give her nose a thorough clear-out. Really, she must have special nostrils which attracted every sooty particle that passed by, and he was allergic to smoke-attracting nostrils.

'Come on, chaps, over the top.'

Enter the peacock, he said to himself as he opened the door to the love-nest, where, immaculate in the dress which she had just ironed herself, she greeted him with a heavenly smile which she immediately followed up by dropping a kiss on his hand. The gesture was now merely part of the ritual, he thought. But, oh, the sacred brush of her lips on his hand that night at the Ritz had been the willing gift of her soul.

'A little music?' she suggested.

Touched by her clumsy but evident eagerness to please, he said he'd like that. So she rewound the gramophone and minced Solal's heart. Another Mozart aria filled the room and she slowly drew near, a priestess of such grave demeanour that he felt afraid and retreated imperceptibly before her advance, while at the same time he checked a nervous urge to laugh prompted by the ceremonial flexing of her masseters. For these days whenever she came near him with Intentions, as a way of showing her love or signalling her desire she invariably clenched her teeth as though she were about to bite. This made the muscles of her jaws stand out and brought on an attack of incipient giggles, which he controlled as best he could. Inspired by Mozart, she held out her lips, on which he immediately fastened, only too happy to avoid the looming paroxysm of nervous laughter and, like her, giving an imitation of the keenest pleasure. But she was not aware that she was imitating anything. All through the kiss, which he prolonged because he could not come up with anything to say, he was thinking that in the Geneva days the idea of having music as an accompaniment to kissing had not been deemed necessary. Then their love had made music enough.

When the peculiar suction which glues male and female together was finished, he turned on the wireless, hoping against hope for a play or a talk. But immediately a brainless, drooping female crooner begged him to speak to her of love, to say old words of tenderness. He switched her off and made up his mind that he would have this one, who was there. It would use up an hour, because once he'd given her the reassurance she wanted he could pretend to go to sleep. So get on with it. Take off her damned dress and make a start on the preliminaries.

At two thirty-five, having received due homage, she was stroking his naked shoulder. He raised his eyebrows in resignation, like a victim whose sufferings go unnoticed. Now it was time for the ritual, the ritual enactment which followed the gymnastic display, to which women attached such curious importance. This mania they had, once the loving convulsions were over, for switching to Sentiment by means of the tender charade of running their fingers lightly over the neck of their stallion. That was it exactly. She was stroking his withers, rubbing his coat, so to speak, patting him as a way of saying thanks very much for giving her such an exhilarating ride. Poor misguided girl, who thought she could bind him in her coils with such romantic chivvying! Actually her sweet post-coital attentions were torture. Moreover, she was lying far too close for comfort, and he could feel her skin moist and sticky. He backed away, and as their bodies separated there was a faint sound as of a cupping-glass released.

But now she was clinging to him once more. Clinging for love, of course. To draw away again would be ungracious. So make the best of it, suffer it, be a limpet, be kind, love this neighbour who was decidedly too neighbourly. I am odious, he thought, oh yes, odious, for this transition from sex to sentiment is a beautiful thing and I should respect her for it, but I am a brute. Yesterday, for fun and because he thought she'd like it, he had chased her along the deserted beach, and she had screamed shrilly like a frightened little girl, she'd run around and skipped in that silly way of hers, waving her arms about like dislocated wings, beating them clumsily, and suddenly she had turned hysterical and strangely gangling, suddenly she was a tall girl at the awkward age, and the sight had sickened and repelled him, he had felt degraded, diminished, he had had the impression that he was chasing a large female canary. Oh yes, I'm a brute. Yet I love her as I have never loved anyone before, and I feel such aching tenderness for her when I see signs of youth passing from her face, the portents of old age to come, of old age which will inevitably come, and I shall not be there to watch over her, over you, my love, my precious love, and, just like you, when I'm in the bath I find myself unconsciously whispering 'my treasure', and that means you, my love, my poor love.

'Penny for your thoughts?' she said.

He knew very well what she wanted. She wanted accolades, a super-flattering review of their recent gallop together, she wanted to hear him say that it had been so et cetera, that he'd never et cetera, the whole couched in the deeply irritating 'it was bliss' mode, which was nobler and less technical than the other words for it. He did the necessary, proceeded to provide the analysis which she wanted and which resulted in a grateful and particularly sticky application of bare skin. Having made up his mind to be as perfect a lover as she could wish for, he bore it without flinching while she continued her maternal combing-and-currying with her walking fingers, which were now skiing down his shoulder in slaloms which made his flesh creep in the most appalling way.

All in all, the best course was to pretend to go to sleep. That way he'd have a break, wouldn't have to be poetic. So he settled down, closed his eyes, and pretended to grow drowsy, but this merely encouraged her to stroke him more lightly still. With curlicues and flourishes worthy of the most meticulous craftsman, and glorying in the abundance of love and pleasure with which she believed she had so recently supplied him, she lay there ministering to him, patient and gooey-eyed, an unwearying priestess, his gracious handmaiden, patting him soothingly to beguile him into sleep, while through the open window there wafted the primeval smell of the sea, the lazy, muffled murmur of the sea.

But this new, improved variety of stroking was even worse than the regular kind, for it was accompanied not only by aggravated goose-pimples but also by the most devastating tickling sensation, and he had to bite his lip to prevent himself quaking with laughter. To put a stop to it without offending her, he heaved a sigh suggestive of deep sleep in the hope that she would get the message and realize that there was no need to go on ravishing his senses. And, thanks be to God, stop she did.

The pressure of her lover's arm on her shoulder was painful, but she stayed quite still so as not to wake him, and she watched him as he lay with his cheek on her breast, proud that she had lulled him to sleep, proud to feel him nestling up to her so trustingly. He was hers, he was sleeping innocently by her side. The cramp in her arm was painful, but she did not stir, glad to suffer for his sake, and she stroked his hair gently. What if I was bald, he thought, would she stroke my smooth pate? She watched him breathing peacefully, tousled-haired, watched over him. He's my little boy too, she thought, and she felt a thrill of tenderness. You've been fooled, lady, he thought.

Suddenly he felt guilty. He opened his eyes, went through the motions of waking, and snuggled up to her. She did not dare mention cramp but half propped herself up in the hope that he'd remove his arm of his own accord. He picked up her hand and kissed it, and she drew a deep breath, deeply moved by the thought that this man, who had possessed her body only moments before, respected her. 'Would you care for some fruit?' she asked, savouring the formality of the question, for she was naked by his side. Good idea, he thought, because whenever she fed him fruit he had the bed to himself. He said thanks, yes, he would. 'I'll get it for you this instant!' she said with gusto. He sharpened his nose with two fingers, embarrassed by her haste. 'But, please, you mustn't look, because I'm not decent.'

Being accustomed to such odd, sudden onsets of modesty, he shut his eyes and then opened them again almost immediately, drawn by the spectacle. Whenever he saw her from the back as she paraded in the nude, he invariably felt a twinge of pity. Beautiful when prone, she was faintly ridiculous when walking around naked, touching and ridiculous, because she seemed bland and defenceless and so vulnerable, pursued by two swaying, swelling half-moons at the base of her spine, hemispheres of frailty, too full as are all the bulbous curves of woman, absurdly inflated and quite unsuited for the struggle. Mesmerized and guilt-ridden, he watched as she bent down and gathered up her dressing-gown, and he felt pity, an immense, loving pity, as though confronted by a kind of physical infirmity, pity for that too smooth skin, the too narrow waist and those inoffensive twin globes.

He lowered his eyes, ashamed of finding anything to laugh at in the sweet and trusting creature who served him so devotedly. 'I love you,' he said again to himself, and he gazed adoringly on the poignant moons, the sacred moons of woman, the overpowering insignia of female superiority, dual orbs of loving warmth, twinned divinities of loving goodness. 'Yes, I love you, ridiculous though you are,' he said to himself, and he moved his legs this way and that, scouring the sheet, revelling in delicious single occupancy.

Emerging from the bathroom, restored to decency and once more every inch a niece of Mademoiselle d'Auble, she knelt by the side of the bed and held out the bunch of grapes she had just washed for him. With towel at the ready, she watched as he fed on the luscious fruit, observing him like a passive but vigilant sentry, doting, taking pleasure in the pleasure of her grown-up boy, hanging on his every gesture, and in so doing causing him acute embarrassment, and he too felt like asking her to shut her eyes and not look. When he had finished, she wiped his hands for him.

When she had dressed and done up her hair, looking more than ever like Ariane Cassandre Corisande, née d'Auble, she had rung for tea and was already on her fourth cup. As he watched her sip, he could not help thinking that in an hour or so from now she would ask him, with the same well-bred smile, if he would be good enough to leave her for a moment. He would grant her wish at once, and, instants later, from the poor girl's bathroom, would come the baleful tinkling of the lavatory flush. And that, in a nutshell, was the life of passion. In his room, he would cover his ears considerately, but it was no good, for the plumbing in the Royal was quite spectacularly vigorous. In due course he would be musically recalled by means of a Mozart record or something by Bach the Boring, and he would have to make love again. And that, in a nutshell, was the life of passion.

What's to do now? he wondered as he stood by the rattling window-pane which was buffeted by the fiercely gusting wind. What can I do to make the poor girl happy? The poor waterlogged girl, with a pint of tea inside her, sat quietly expectant, respectful of his silence. Order more tea? Perish the thought. There was a limit to the amount of tea even an Anglophile like her could drink. Try chatting. But what about? If he said he loved her, he wouldn't be telling her anything she didn't know already. Anyway, he'd told her that three times only a few moments ago, once before sex, once during and once after. She knew he did. Besides, talking about love no longer had the same glamour as in the old days in Geneva. Then, each time he'd told her he loved her it was a heavenly surprise for her and her eyes opened wide and her whole face lit up. Nowadays, whenever he brought up this loving business, she greeted the well-known fact with an artificial smile which was as lifeless as any wax dummy's, while her unconscious grew more and more bored. Their words of love had become good manners, a polite ritual, gliding over the linoleum of habit. Should he kill himself, and have done with it? No, that would mean leaving her alone.

So come on, say something, unglue yourself from this window. But what should he say, what could he say? They'd said it all, they knew every single thing there was to know about each other. Oh the voyages of discovery of those early days! It was because they didn't love each other any more, fools would say. He silenced the fools with a glare. Not true, they did love each other, but they spent all their time closeted together, closeted with their love.

Alone, that was it, they'd been alone with their love for three months, with nothing but their love to keep them company, had done nothing else for three months but make themselves beautiful for each other, with only their love to bring them together, incapable of speaking of anything but love, incapable of doing anything but make love.

He peeped out of the corner of his eye. She-Who-Was-Owed sat patiently, sweetly waiting, waiting for happiness. Come on, pay your dues, be the marvellous lover for whose sake she had sacrificed everything, make it up to her for abandoning a life of respectability, for knowing what misery she had caused her husband. Come on, you debtor, give her an interest in life, provide fresh joy. Come on, use your imagination, be author and actor.

Yes, talk to her, and sharp about it! But what about? He hadn't done anything. Who about? He never saw anyone. Should he tell her why he hadn't done anything, why he never saw anybody? Should he tell her that he'd been dismissed from the service? Tell her that his French nationality had been withdrawn? Admit that he was nothing, nothing but a lover? No, he mustn't. His social standing had been one of the contributory factors in the love she had for him, and still was. Moreover, he could not possibly deny the poor girl the pride she had in him. So keep up the lie about having been given extended leave. She'd find out in the long run, of course. Well, he'd meet that when he came to it. He'd kill himself.

Bed her again? Didn't feel like it. He couldn't be doing it all the time, now could he? In any case, though she might not be aware of it, she had begun to take less pleasure in their coupling. But she was a stickler for it all the same. For to be desired was to be loved. It was absurd, but that's how women were. If ever a day or two went by without her making him jump through the hoop, without her tapping his barometer, without a damned tilt in the lists, she started to worry. Of course she was far too refined and discreet to bring the matter up openly, or even make oblique reference to it. But he could sense her unease. Which was why life had to be one long round of passion punctuated with proper proofs of same, under pain of Hurting Her Feelings. Does he still love me as much as he used to? and the rest of it. A sweet and biddable handmaiden, but dreadfully demanding. Poor thing, she was saying nothing, just sat there waiting meekly, respecting his silence. He'd have to give her something to think about. But what? He could hardly go on wanting her twenty-four hours a day. So what could they do to pass the time until dinner? If this silence went on, she was quite capable of suggesting a walk. She had a mania for wanting to go walkies with him the minute a freezing wind got up. What possible pleasure did she see in trudging about in silence, putting one foot forward then the other, and then repeating the process, with the silence still unbroken, for he could never find much to say during these ghastly slow-footed forward marches into the teeth of a bitter wind. Get her to read to him, that would be the simplest solution.

'Let's have some more of that novel you were reading to me yesterday, darling. I'd like to know what happens next. Besides, you read so well.'

So there it was, he was in charge, he was the master of the ship of their love, he was thinking, while she read from a clever, slim French novel, paying particular attention to enunciating clearly, taking great pains with the dialogue, varying her intonation, putting on a silly gruff voice when it was the hero talking, touchingly concentrating on giving a perfect performance, but also thoroughly irritating. Yes, he was in charge, responsible for stage-managing each day's long-running farce of love, for dreaming up fresh scenarios daily to keep her happy. The worst thing about all this was that he genuinely cared for the poor girl. But they were always alone, and all they had for company was their love.

That damned wind-up gramophone. The day she'd come back with it from Saint-Raphaël, so excited, he had shuddered inwardly. It was the first leak in their ship of love. The Mozart aria was a vitamin supplement. Whenever that hellish 'You who know' blared out, she felt that her love was being given a new lease of life. Mozart, a purveyor of sentiments which the heart no longer manufactured for itself. Another dire symptom of love's vitamin deficiency was the way she had of resorting to lesser stimulants. Initially she had been very reserved with him when there were other people about, but now, when they were at the Moscow, she kissed him in public. The exhibitionism of it excited her. As did what transpired, on more than one occasion, beneath the sequestered pine-trees. And communal ablutions in the bath. And the bold cavorting in front of the mirror. It was all designed to ward off anaemia. Heigh-ho. And now she was putting on her voice of Jove again because it was the young hero who was talking. Living this life of love in a goldfish bowl was softening her brain. Where was the crazy, clever girl he had known in Geneva?

'Have a rest now, darling, don't read any more.'

He came over, sat down facing her, made a few lacklustre remarks about the novel, but soon recognized that simpering look of genteel misery he associated with well-bred women who have no idea just how bored they are. He stopped talking. To be sure, she still loved him madly, but in her unconscious she was obviously thoroughly sick of their stupendous passion! He, on the other hand, was not the least bored, for he had something terrible to occupy his mind: he was observing the slow wreck of their ship of love.

He looked at her. Oh the way she smiled, frozenly, like a set of false teeth, the way she sat there prim, flawless and quite lifeless: everything about her cried out that she was terminally bored, though no doubt she would prefer to call it feeling off colour or being depressed for no particular reason. She bit her lip, and he realized that she had been just in time to stifle a yawn. No, it was not stifled entirely, for by dilating her nostrils she managed to yawn inwardly. He had to act quickly, for her sake, for love of her. He looked her in the eye, to prompt a question.

'What are you thinking, darling?'

'I was thinking how bored I am,' he said. (Should he add 'with you'? No. It wasn't necessary.)

She paled. It was the first time he'd said such a thing to her. To finish what he had started, he set about producing a repressed yawn which was all the more significant for being covered up. Whereupon she burst into tears. At this, he shrugged and left her.

Back in his room, he allowed himself a smile in the mirror. His angel girl had come to life again. There had been a quickening of interest in her eyes which he had not seen for days. Whenever he said that he loved her, told her she was beautiful, she flashed him one of her set, denture smiles. But the spark he had just seen in her eyes was genuine, had struck real fire. His darling girl had come to life again. Oh, if all it took to make her happy was to be nice to her all the time he would have gladly danced around her like a whirling dervish and told her over and over, morning, noon and night, how much he adored her, only too eager to cram her with sweetness, to serve her, even unto brushing her clothes and polishing her shoes. But non-stop tenderness cloyed and was unmanly, and women did not care for it. They needed rapture, they cried out for the roller-coasters and toboggans of passion, delicious shifts from misery to joy, they wanted anguish, sudden bliss, waiting, hope and despair, the whole damned passion-shoot with its grisly bevy of alarums and theatrical life-goals. Well, he had given her a life-goal. From now on she would be on constant alert, she would keep a wary eye on him, wonder whether he was bored with her, and that would be plenty for her to think about. That is to say, she would take over his role. And tomorrow, if a vigorous carnal going-over were to follow a moment of tenderness which followed a moment of cruelty, the said going-over would be all the more keenly appreciated. Oh the misery of it, this obligation to be cruel to be kind. Solal, the unwilling tormentor.

He went outside and listened at her door. He could hear her sobbing. He smiled again. The poor girl was in tears, she was fully occupied, she had more important things on her mind now than how to stifle yawns. Praise be, she was crying, was more conscious than ever of how much she loved him, of how she never grew tired of being with him. He tiptoed back to his room. Saved! He was saved! But, more than that, he had saved her! After a while there was a quiet knock and a small voice spoke through a blocked nose on the other side of the door. 'Listen, the weather's nice now,' said the little voice. He rubbed his hands. The manœuvre had worked! Her head was filled with a need to get on the right side of him. She had a goal in life. 'So?' he said, exaggerating the tetchiness in his voice. 'Wouldn't you like us to go out?' said Little Damp Voice. 'No. I'd rather go out by myself,' he said. 'My treasure,' he said to her inwardly, and he stroked the wood of the door behind which she had come to life once more.

Outside, he traipsed through scenery which gave him the horrors: the sky was too blue, the trees were dry and dusty, and the rocks were razor-sharp. He felt elated and aimed kicks at stones. At this minute she was acutely aware of exactly how much she missed him, and shortly she would be so happy when it was safe again for him to be nice to her. As he sauntered along, he imagined he had met a man of God who spoke words of reproach to him, saying that he never behaved like that to his own dear wife, that he made her happy.

'Hold it there, Parson, you're talking through your hat,' said Solal. 'If your wife is happy, there are ten reasons for it and, of those ten, nine have nothing whatsoever to do with love. To wit: her place in the social order which she owes to you and the respect she enjoys thereby, her attendance at church sewing-bees, your common friends and your at-homes, what you say about the people you have to deal with, your children, the things you tell her about your work, the contribution she makes to your ministry, the pleasure she gets out of visiting the sick, the kiss you give her when you get home each evening, the prayers you say on your knees together at the side of your bed. What's that? She likes a roll in the hay with you? But of course she does: civilized and fully dressed by day, naked and biological by night, though not every night. And she enjoys it because of the sheer contrast, because the pair of you who were so proper and so properly dressed only moments before suddenly turn into nakedly sexual beings. But we two, we two poor specimens, behave like animals all the time.'

Fine, then. This evening, soon, when he got back, she'd have a few intensely lived hours, he would smile at her and she would fling her arms round his neck, and she would cry tears of happiness and there would be de-luxe kisses, kisses from the depths of her soul, kisses from the old Geneva days, and she would say that she never felt bored with her darling, even though he was a beast, and she would believe it utterly. Praise be. Fine. An evening of bliss lay waiting just around the corner, of bliss for the pair of them. But what about tomorrow? Could he really go on telling the poor girl each and every day that he felt bored when he was with her?

CHAPTER 84

The next day, she suggested they might have lunch downstairs, in the hotel restaurant, just this once of course, it was so much more pleasant taking their meals in their rooms but just for once it might be amusing to take a peek at their respectable fellow guests, rather as if they were in the theatre in fact. They went down in high spirits, arm in arm.

All through lunch she made ironic remarks about people's faces, made guesses about what they did for a living and what they were like. She was proud of her Sol, so elegant, so unlike the rest of the browsers and sluicers here present, proud of the looks she got from their wives, who were all perfect frights. One, however, found favour in her eyes, a rather handsome woman in her forties with red hair, who was reading a newspaper propped up against a water-jug and had a little dog with her which was sitting as good as gold on a chair.

'The only likely proposition in the whole place,' she observed. 'English, I'd say. I haven't seen her before. Her little Sealyham is a pet. Just look at the way he looks at his mummy.'

In the lounge where coffee was served, they perused a magazine together. Close by them, two couples who had just checked in, sensing they might be social equals, had struck up a conversation. After a preliminary exchange of pleasantries, they had dusted down their antennae and proceeded to probe each other's social standing, casually slipping into the conversation details about their respective professions and connections. Reassured, recognizing fellow denizens of the same ant-heap when they saw them, they blossomed and bloomed, communed loudly, and trumpeted their delight: 'Well, well! Isn't it a small world! Of course we knew them, we used to see a great deal of them! What a pity they left! Such lovely people!'

Further along, two other husbands, who had also been sniffing each other out by dropping the prestigious names of lawyers and bishops, were talking motor cars in the face of constant interruptions from the younger of the wives, a doll-like creature with a moon face who bore a striking resemblance to the wife of Petresco and, like Petresco's wife, was doing her adorable, skittish number, shrieking at frequent intervals, as she bobbed up and down and clapped her hands like a little girl, that what she wanted was a Chrysler, she did, a nice Chrysler, so there! All these people were aquiver to run with their kind, itching to be happy clots and lumps in the collective porridge. In silence, holding hands, the two lovers read on, noble and remote. Suddenly, she stood up.

'Let's go. They're making me feel ill.'

In their loving-room, they listened to the new records they had bought, discussed them, and then there were kisses. At two thirty he said he had a headache and wanted to lie down in his room, so they arranged to meet again for tea. Left to herself, she went back downstairs.

She found a chair in the lounge and flicked through a pile of tourist guides on a table, while, next to her, happy future corpses were making noisy plans for outings and the podgy doll again ran through her pretty-little-girl routine. Jumping up and down and clapping her hands, sillier than an American majorette, the oh-so-spontaneous little kitten again told her husband that she wanted a Chrysler, she did, a nice Chrysler, so there, highly delighted not only to be seen to be so headstrong but also to let their new friends know, by means of her endlessly reverberating childish refrain, that she and her husband were more than able to afford a Chrysler, thank you very much. But when Ariane got up and left she stopped her antics, and the conversation lapsed and gave way to whispers.

Ariane walked slowly along the gravel drive, where the woman with red hair was also strolling. Going up to the little dog, which was sniffing busily around, she bent down and stroked him. Smiles were offered, views on the attractions of Sealyhams were exchanged – jealous but loyal – then on the weather, so warm and it was the twenty-seventh of November too, quite extraordinary really, even for the Riviera.

Eventually they sat down in cane chairs under a sickly, dust-laden palm. Ariane made further enquiries as to the character of the little dog, which, having taken due note of all the ambient smells and judged them to be of no interest whatsoever, rested its chin on its front paws, heaved a great bored sigh, and pretended to go to sleep, but kept one eye half open on the progress of an ant.

The conversation having been carried on in English, the lady with the red hair confessed to being amazed by the perfect accent of her new acquaintance, who at once proceeded to evoke the wonderful years she had spent at Girton, Cambridge, and thereafter at Lady Margaret Hall, Oxford. A gleam of renewed interest flickered in the eyes of the Englishwoman at the mention of these women's colleges, both so exclusive and attracting only students from the very best circles. She looked fondly at her new acquaintance. Lady Margaret Hall! Really! But how fascinating! Wasn't it a small world! Barbara and Joyce, dear Patricia Layton's twins, Viscountess Layton, you know, absolutely, were currently up at LMH and were very happy there, such a wonderful place. But look, she said with a smile, it's the hols after all, and a person might quite properly dispense with etiquette and introduce herself. She was Kathleen Forbes, wife of the British consul-general in Rome. After a momentary hesitation, her acquaintance also gave her name and said that her husband was an Under-Secretary-General at the League of Nations.

Whereupon Mrs Forbes became ebullient and utterly charming. Under-Secretary-General! Really! But how fascinating! Eyelids fluttering and with a fond look suffusing her face, she declared that she adored the League of Nations, a wonderful institution where so much wonderful work was done to promote international peace and mutual understanding! When people understood each other, they would love each other, now wasn't that so? she said with a smile, and her eyelids fluttered more exquisitely than ever. Sir John was such a kind man, and Lady Cheyne was so accomplished, so considerate. Actually, one of her nieces had just got engaged to a second cousin of dear Lady

Cheyne! All at once her beating eyelids turned into butterfly wings and she grabbed Ariane's hand. But of course! She remembered now! Her cousin, Bob Huxley, worked in the Secretariat! Madame Solal must surely know him, for he had spoken a great deal about Monsieur Solal last year, had sung his praises! But how fascinating! Her husband would be delighted to meet Monsieur Solal, because he too took the keenest interest in the League of Nations!

In response to a polite question from Ariane, Mrs Forbes, like a silvery trout safely returned to its native waters, said that she had been at Agay since the day before yesterday but that her husband would not be arriving until that afternoon, perhaps with dear Bob in tow. Yes, he'd had to make a detour to call on his dear friend Tucker, that's Sir Alfred Tucker, the Permanent Under-Secretary at the Foreign Office, who was alas receiving treatment in a clinic which, as it happened, was in Geneva. 'A very, very dear friend,' she concluded with a dying fall and a modicum of melancholy tinged with coyness. But she had felt desperately run-down and had not had the strength to make the stopover at Geneva. After the social whirl of Rome, which was simply too wearing, all she had wanted to do was to get to the good old Royal, where she felt thoroughly at home, though its clientele was not of course entirely congenial nor very interesting, save naturally for a few exceptions, she added with a sweet smile, but it was so marvellously situated, perfectly heavenly surroundings. From one point of view it could be considered an advantage to stay in an hotel frequented by people of quite dissimilar backgrounds to theirs, because it meant that one could enjoy one's privacy. Oh yes, after the social round in Rome, which made such inroads into one's time, she so enjoyed this chance to relax and respect one's physical being, she said with an intellectual smile. Oh, were she free to follow her own tastes, she would gladly turn her back on the social whirl and settle for a hermit's life of solitude, indulge her passion for nature, and be nearer God, with only a few good books for company. But it was the duty of the wives of holders of official positions to sacrifice themselves and to some extent assist their husbands, she affirmed, giving her companion in executive matrimony a sweet smile. And in addition to the ghastly social round, which was so invasive, there was also the requirement to keep abreast, was there not, of anything that was of interest from the intellectual point of view – *vernissages*, concerts, lectures, social problems, the books which people were talking about, not to mention tedious staff problems when, as she was, one was expected to maintain a certain social style. Oh yes indeed, she was only too happy to be a simple body for these two weeks, to bathe in the dear old Med and play a set or two of tennis every day. By the by, perhaps Madame Solal would care to make up a mixed foursome with them tomorrow? And perhaps Monsieur Solal might like to join them?

So it was agreed between them that they should meet outside the hotel at eleven next morning. Having had her social appetites whetted by the reserve and refinement of the Under-Secretary-General's delightful wife, Mrs Forbes took her leave, her teeth bared affectionately, then retired, followed by her little dog, quite delighted with the catch she had landed.

CHAPTER 85

The following day, a little before four o'clock, they went down to take tea in the small lounge of the hotel and sat down by the window overlooking the terrace, which she opened so that they might enjoy the balmy air. Seeing him blink, she drew the curtains to take the edge off the sun's brightness. When she had drunk her first cup of tea, she said that anyone would think it was April, not November. This was followed by a silence. To fill it, he suggested they should give marks out of twenty to the clothes she had bought in Cannes. The conversation got under way immediately, and they saw eye to eye on giving top marks to the evening dress in that truly ravishing deep pink. An evening dress, he thought, what was the point? For what reception, official dinner or ball was it intended?

They moved on to the other items and she argued fiercely, not suspecting for a single moment what pity he felt to see her falling so easily for the lure. As she hesitated between a seventeen and an eighteen for the ruby cardigan, he felt an urge to kiss her on the cheek. But no, they were lovers. They were sentenced to lips.

When everything had been given a mark, she suggested a stroll along the shore. 'The sea, the ever changing yet unchangèd sea,' she said, quoting Valéry for his benefit. Not particularly taken with artiness of this kind, he smiled appreciatively then said he had a headache. She immediately suggested aspirin, and got up to go for some. He refused the offer, saying that he would rather lie down for an hour or two, and asked her if meantime she would pop over to Saint-Raphaël and buy some more records. He had a yen to hear the Brandenburg Concertos.

'I think they're wonderful!' she said, getting up again. 'But I'll go to Cannes to be sure of getting all six. I've just time. There's a train in a couple of minutes.'

He stood, ashamed to be fobbing her off like this, she so innocent, so pleased to be making herself useful. To give her a cud of happiness to chew while she was on the train, he said in a voice oozing sincerity that just now, upstairs, they had made wonderful love together. She looked up at him gravely and kissed his hand, and he ached with pity, tried to think of some other way of making her happy, to give her something to look forward to, some little goal for when she got back.

'Later on I'd like you to try on your new dresses again for me, one by one. You look so marvellous in them.'

She gave him a heart-meltingly grateful look, breathed deeply, revived by this draught of admiration, said she'd have to get a move on if she wasn't to miss her train, and was off. He watched her run for all she was worth, so eager, poor girl, to fetch records he didn't want. But at least he had given her something to think about. He'd have to come up with some fresh ideas when she got back, after she'd finished trying on the dresses. She'd been very disappointed that morning when he had told her that Forbes had rung to postpone their game of tennis. She had already got into her shorts, was raring to go and very happy. Was the Forbes woman really ill?

He sat down again, took a swallow of lukewarm tea, and looked at the time. She'd be on the train now, thinking about him, happy to be fetching new records for him. Remember to gush later on when she tried on her frocks.

A hum of voices. He stubbed out his cigarette, peered through the gap in the drawn curtains, and recognized the Englishwoman with the red hair, la Forbes, bursting with rude good health, being gracious to a very tall woman in her fifties with an immensely long chin, in whose company she shortly sat down on the cane divan just under his window. He edged closer.

Oh yes, Mrs Forbes exclaimed, she knew Alexandre de Sabran very well. He had spoken to them frequently of his uncle the Colonel, who was military attaché at Berne! Wasn't it a small world! Who would ever have thought that here at Agay she would be talking to the aunt of dear Alexandre of whom she saw so much in Rome, whom she positively adored, and who both for herself and her husband was quite simply Dear Sacha, an absolutely delightful boy who, by the by, was enormously highly thought of by the ambassador, she had it from the dear ambassador's own lips! This very evening she would write and tell Sacha that she'd had the pleasure of making his aunt's acquaintance! So Colonel de Sabran was presently observing the Swiss army on manœuvres, was he? But how fascinating! Obviously, as military attaché, it was part of his official duties, she said with a smile as she sucked on a social barley-sugar. Oh the army, she positively adored the army! she sighed, and she fluttered her eyelashes. The army! Honour, discipline, ancient traditions, chivalry, an officer's word his bond, cavalry charges, mighty battles, field marshals deploying brilliant tactics, men dying like heroes! There was no finer career! If only she'd been a man! What was nobler than to lay down one's life for one's country! For there would always be war, nothing would stop it, the League of Nations could talk until it was blue in the face. And would the Colonel be joining her soon? she asked, with a look ablaze with sympathetic interest. In three days! Her husband and she would be delighted to meet him and give him the latest about Dear Sacha.

Whereupon she suggested that Madame de Sabran might care for some refreshment, enquired as to her preferences, summoned a waiter with one forefinger, ordered China for Madame and very strong Ceylon for herself, asked for very hot buttered toast to be brought in a napkin, and never once did she so much as glance at the man. Having thus reminded him of the base clay of which he was made and of the fact that he existed solely to wait upon the wives of military attachés and consuls-general, she turned dreamily to her congenial companion, who was a colonel's lady and an authentic baroness. After alluding briefly to dear Sir Alfred Tucker and Viscountess Layton – a rare soul if ever there was – she cleared the decks for harpooning-stations. How wonderful it was to be at Agay, simply to follow one's physical rhythms, to be able at last to play tennis every day, to be free for a little while of the tiresome social round which, when all was said and done, was so banal, didn't Madame de Sabran agree?

'By the by, would you like to make up a tennis foursome with us? Shall we say tomorrow, at eleven?'

Madame de Sabran, highly conscious of the gulf which separated the diplomatic service from the consular, acquiesced with muted enthusiasm and a thin smile. Her lack of enthusiasm thrilled Mrs Forbes, for it was an indication of the size of the catch she had landed, and her covetousness was increased thereby. She directed a fawning smile at Madame de Sabran, who stood up and said she would be back in a moment. Sure in the knowledge of her twenty-four social carats, she made a stately exit.

On her return, with eyes of blue ice and looking for all the world like a supercilious giraffe, she peered from a disdainful distance at the podgy doll-woman who was going through her set routine in the lounge, bouncing up and down and clapping her hands together. Placing one hand along her scrawny rump in the manner of Madame Deume the elder, the baroness satisfied herself that her skirt hung properly, then sat down and congratulated Mrs Forbes on her excellent command of the French language. To which Mrs Forbes of the red hair replied modestly that she couldn't honestly claim any credit for that because she had always talked French with her nanny ever since she was a little girl. This particular brought a smile of approval to the razor lips of Madame de Sabran, who, after a moment's silence, brought up the subject of that very odd couple who never spoke to anyone. Who were those people, where did they come from, what did the man do? The desk-clerk had told her the name, but she had forgotten it.

'Was it Solal?' asked Mrs Forbes, with hope ashine in her eyes.

'Yes, that's it. I remember now.'

'To be avoided like the plague,' said Mrs Forbes with an obsequious smile. 'Ah, here's our tea. First, let's quench our thirst and then I'll tell you all about it, it's quite a tale, you'll see. I have it from the horse's mouth. Heard all about it from my cousin Robert Huxley, who is an adviser with the League of Nations, a great friend of Sir John Cheyne, whom you probably know. (As she did not in fact know him, Madame de Sabran's face moved not a muscle.) Bob got here yesterday with my husband and will be spending a few days with us, a charming boy, I would be delighted to introduce him to you. Oh yes, those two should be avoided like the plague.'

He wiped the perspiration from his forehead. This morning, in her tennis shorts, so pleased, all ready and waiting for her date with la Forbes. What had he let her in for? Mrs Forbes put down her empty cup, sighed pleasantly, said that there was nothing like tea for quenching one's thirst, settled back into the divan, gave a contented smile, and embarked upon her good deed for the day.

'To be avoided like the plague, dear Baroness,' she said again. (She was burning to say simply my dear, but judged that she would be better advised to wait until tomorrow, until the game of tennis, which would furnish a more propitious moment.) 'They are living in sin. In sin,' she repeated. 'My cousin has put me fully in the picture. The woman is the wife of one of his colleagues at the League of Nations. It all came out straight away, because the poor husband tried to kill himself the very day the guilty couple ran away together. Fortunately they got to him just in time. But when I think she had the gall to tell me that she was the man's wife while all the time she has a lawful husband alive and well in Geneva!'

'I'm surprised that they put up with that sort of thing here,' said Madame de Sabran.

'Especially since they were required to register under their real names, since they had to show their passports. I made enquiries at the desk. But that's not all, there's more. You won't credit it, but the man had a top job in the League of Nations. I should add that he's a Jew.'

'Doesn't surprise me in the least,' said Madame de Sabran. 'Their sort worm their way into everything. Do you know, there are even a couple at the Quai d'Orsay! We live in strange times.'

'A very top job, I was saying . . .'

'It's a mafia,' said Madame de Sabran knowingly. 'Really, I'd rather have Hitler than Blum any day. At least the Chancellor is someone who stands for order and a firm hand, a real leader. But please go on.'

'Well, I've been put fully in the picture by my cousin Bob. Sir John is extremely fond of him. Now, three or four months ago the man was dismissed, or rather forced to resign, which comes to the same thing of course, for conduct, how shall I put it, unbecoming.'

'For conduct disgraceful,' said Madame de Sabran, relishing her saliva. 'But there, given the background, what else would you expect? And what did he do, exactly?'

'Unfortunately Bob wasn't able to give me the details. Normally he's terribly well-informed, given the very friendly personal footing he's on with Sir John and Lady Cheyne. But the whole business was hushed up. Apparently only a very few highly placed people are in the know. The man did something so serious and so dishonourable (Madame de Sabran nodded approvingly) that the scandal was covered up so that it wouldn't reflect on the League of Nations! All that anyone knows is that he was kicked out.'

'I'm glad to hear it,' said Madame de Sabran. 'A case of treason, I dare say. One could expect anything from a co-religionist of Dreyfus. Ah, poor Colonel Henry!'

'Turfed out ignominiously. (Madame de Sabran greeted this intelligence appropriately.) It was then, according to my cousin, that he rushed back to Geneva and ran away with his partner in crime. So he's not anything any more. He's a nobody. When I think that the hussy had the impertinence yesterday to ask me if I'd like a game of tennis! She was so insistent and, because I'm so good-natured, I more or less accepted for this morning, believing that I was dealing with pukka people, people of our sort, with credentials, persons of good standing. Naturally, the instant Bob put us in the picture and opened our eyes we decided to have nothing to do with them. My husband rang the man this morning and told him I was unwell. That's him all over, he's too kind, it's the way he is. It's not for nothing that Viscountess Layton calls him the consul-generous instead of general! Dear Patricia, always so witty, with just that hint of mischief!'

'In my opinion, kindness should not exclude firmness,' said Madame de Sabran. 'In your husband's place I would have dotted the i's and crossed the t's.'

'But I must say that when he was on the phone his tone was sufficiently pointed.'

'I'm glad to hear it,' said Madame de Sabran.

The two worthy ladies, the one gushing damply and the other as dry as a stick, went on discussing the succulent topic, squeezing the very last drop of pleasure from this instance of social proscription, a pleasure enhanced by the knowledge that they were ladies of unimpeachable credentials, who received and were received. From time to time, communing in their own uprightness, they exchanged smiles. There is nothing like a common hatred for bringing people together.

Meanwhile he was thinking of his innocent girl, and in his mind's eye he saw her excited face when she had come to tell him yesterday about la Forbes's invitation. She had begun to come alive again, had felt an interest in living. She had banged on his door and burst in, surer of herself than usual, without her customary diffidence. And then almost immediately there had followed a thoroughgoing kiss, the first for weeks. And suddenly she adored tennis and said the ghastly woman with red hair was a very nice person. And she'd shot off to Cannes to buy a tennis outfit. She had come back with two, poor goose, one practical with shorts, one quite impractical with a little skirt, and had tried on both in front of him. So excited that she had done an imitation of the podgy doll jumping up and down and shrieking that she wanted a Chrysler. And last night as passionate as in the Geneva days. Oh the power of social conformity! This morning at nine she was already dressed for tennis, two hours early, practising strokes with her racket, tossing up imaginary balls in front of the mirror. Then the ring of the phone, and the social mills had begun to grind.

After a further smile cementing their alliance in the cause of virtue, Madame de Sabran moved on to another agreeable matter, to wit the charity ball which she organized each year at the Royal for the benefit and succour of assorted poor but dear families at Agay and Saint-Raphaël, whose appalling destitution she described in some detail, relishing the feeling of her own goodness and her certainty that no misfortune could befall her.

Yes, each year a wonderful friend at Cannes, who entertained a great deal, provided her with an up-to-date list of persons in residence in the area who were likely to be interested in doing their bit for a good cause. Tomorrow she would be sending out invitations to everyone who mattered on the Riviera, and that included a Royal Highness who was currently at Monte. What could be better than to do good and enjoy oneself into the bargain? Moreover, one sometimes met such interesting, congenial people at charity balls. But naturally that was incidental. Doing good was the important thing.

Mrs Forbes grew excited, insisted that she adored charity balls and anything, really, that had to do with philanthropy, altruism and taking an interest in the poor. So she announced that she was prepared to do everything in her power to assist Madame de Sabran in issuing the invitations. She could already see herself being presented to the Royal Highness.

At this juncture the consul-general and his cousin turned up, both dressed for golf. After the introductions, the baring of teeth and the mention of Dear Sacha, the quite delightful Huxley added a few finishing touches to the tale his aunt had told, spoke warmly in support of the poor deceived husband, who was a distinguished official, a hard-working chap who enjoyed the good opinion of his colleagues. He'd got over his injury quite quickly, because fortunately the bullet had gone through the temporal bone without touching the brain. He must have been holding the gun awkwardly, or perhaps his hand had been shaking, which was understandable enough. He was a really charming young man, who improved on acquaintance. He had been back at work at the Palais for almost two months, and all his colleagues had been delighted to see him again. They had been very decent to him, had rallied round and asked him out a great deal. His boss had been very good to him too, and had sent him on a long official visit to Africa to take his mind off things. He had flown out to Dakar last Monday.

Turning next to his former boss and punctuating each seedy detail with an avid smile followed by a flick of a reptilian, spite-laden tongue, which was immediately withdrawn after a quick lick of his upper lip, he explained how friends of his at the Quai d'Orsay, alerted by the dismissal of Monsieur Solal for reasons which had not been made public, had discovered an irregularity in the naturalization papers of the said Solal, to wit a shortfall in the qualifying period of continuous residence. The result had been withdrawal of French nationality by a decree published in the *Journal Officiel*. What, on top of everything else he'd been a naturalized Frenchman? That was the last straw! protested Madame de Sabran. Well, the Republican government had behaved properly for once in its life, and she was not afraid to say so, though she was the daughter, wife and mother of army officers! Having neither citizenship nor a profession, the fellow is socially dead, concluded Solal's former principal private secretary and protégé with a final flick of his tongue.

Whereupon, being not indifferent to the male body beautiful (a fact of which the Forbeses pretended to be unaware, since there had never been any hint of scandal), he shot a curious but cautious glance at a startlingly handsome adolescent boy who had just walked into the hotel carrying a tennis-racket under one arm. There followed a brief silence, which he filled by mentioning the recent appeal made by the physicist Einstein on behalf of the Jews in Germany. At this, Madame de Sabran's hackles rose.

'Oh no, not the old refrain about persecution! The whole thing has been blown up out of all proportion. Chancellor Hitler has put them in their place, and that's that. And what does this physicist think should be done?'

'He would like various countries to open their frontiers to these people, so that they might leave Germany.'

'Doesn't surprise me in the least,' said Madame de Sabran: 'they all stick together. It's really too much, these people are so full of themselves, they think they can do exactly as they please!'

'But his appeal has received a cool reception from the great powers,' smiled Bob the Charmer.

'I'm glad to hear it!' said Madame de Sabran. 'Things would have come to a pretty pass if all the co-religionists of Dreyfus had ended up on our doorstep! After all, they are German, they should stay where they belong. And if they are kept somewhat out of the public view, that's as it should be!'

After another silence, there was an exchange of smiling, cultured views, and naturally the talk ran to music, a circumstance which at last gave Madame de Sabran the opportunity to mention a duchess, a dear childhood friend who had music in her bones and whom she was looking forward to joining on a cruise in the spring. The Forbeses countered this with another cruise in the company of the inevitable Sir Alfred Tucker and Viscountess Layton, which gave Huxley a chance to say that he had run into the latter's niece when calling on a very sweet and intelligent queen-in-exile whom he often visited in her delightful house at Vevey, a revelation which drew a look of interest from Madame de Sabran, who said that she hoped she could count on seeing him at her charity ball, which naturally led the lady to quote with approval something Tolstoy once said about the spiritual pleasure of loving, which furnished the Consul, as generous as he was general, with an opportunity to get his word in by evoking the dignity of the human person.

This was the signal for a survey of the noblest vistas. The company gorged itself on those realities which remained helpfully invisible and declared itself convinced there was a life to come in the hereafter, with the two ladies appearing particularly keen that their souls should endure for ever, the debate being marked by forceful displays of canines and incisors, for it was pleasant to feel that one was with people from one's own milieu, who shared one's aspirations and ideals.

In his room, he paced up and down with the majesty of the solitary exile, pausing occasionally at the mirror-fronted wardrobe, running his hand across his forehead, then resuming his pacing, with a permanent mental picture of the husband holding the gun to his temple. The poor wretch had suffered on his account, suffered so much that he had wanted to die. Poor Deume, so keen to get on. Yes, he had sinned against him, but he had been punished. For henceforth he was an outcast, a man walled up inside love. Whereas young Deume, ringed by his own kind, well integrated, well supported, presently on a mission to Africa with a pith helmet on his head, was a figure of authority, a representative of officialdom, a man who could strut his hour. I'm happy for you, young Deume.

She would be back soon with the records, their pathetic records. What could he do to save her? Go downstairs and beg la Forbes to send her an invitation to something? Just once, Mrs Forbes, so that she does not suspect that she has been ostracized on my account. Afterwards we'll leave, we'll move to another hotel, you'll have seen the last of us. She is all I have now, and I need her to go on loving me. Take pity on her, Mrs Forbes, she's not Jewish, she's not used to the treatment. In the name of Christ, Mrs Forbes.

Sheer madness. He could go down on bended knee to both women and they would still be what they were, utterly sure of their truths, strong in the knowledge that they were the majority and the norm, shielded by the buckler of society, having no heart, putting no foot wrong, strangers to tribulation, and convinced, of course, that there is a God. Charmed lives, with the added luxury of believing that they were good women.

Still, shouldn't he try? Bring himself to look at them, smile at them, smile at them with tears in his eyes, tell them that their time on earth was short enough and that they should not spend it in hating? Sheer madness. Christ Himself had not succeeded in changing them. Enough. Soon she would be back. What could he do to hide the fact that he was a leper, a beaten man? What could he do to keep her love? Their love was all they had left. Their poor, frail love.

CHAPTER 86

Freshly bathed yet again and newly shaved and nobly dressing-gowned once more. Yes, he needed to be handsome now more than ever. All an outcast could count on was biology. O Naileater, O Solomon, O Saltiel. He kissed his hand as though it were his absent uncle's cheek. Should he run away? Run away and live with them?

Dark outside. Ten o'clock. His poor darling had been left to her own devices for hours, not daring to disturb him, for was he not supposed to have a headache? She had merely let him know she was back by slipping a note under his door, in her best writing, for she had evidently taken pains to make it look neat. 'I'm ready and waiting, but don't come unless you're feeling better. I managed to get hold of all six concertos.' All alone with her records, waiting to play them for him, waiting upon his good pleasure. His darling, his own darling, what, oh what had he let her in for? What, oh what lay in store for his innocent girl? Yes, he'd have to go, he'd have to do his duty. He paused by the wardrobe.

'Got it!' he told the mirror.

When he walked into her room, an implacable Brandenburg Concerto was grinding on. Wearing an evening gown and a smile, his poor girl stood with one hand resting on the infernal machine. He pretended to be entranced, to listen with rapt attention to the long-distance sawyers and wood-borers of the Almighty. When the record stopped, he switched off the light and said he had something to tell her. No, nothing dire, darling.

In the dark, when she was lying by his side, he kissed her hand and began to speak. So what it came down to was that he had decided to make a clean break, once and for all, with everything and anything that did not impinge directly upon them, sever all ties with the world outside, with other people. Only one thing mattered: their love. How unconvincing the words sounded, he thought, and he held her close to make her see things his way.

'You think the same, don't you?'

'Yes,' she breathed.

'I don't want anything to come between us and our love,' he whispered. 'The only danger we run here is the Forbes woman, who is not going to let matters rest where they are. But I've sorted it out. I ran into Huxley earlier on. He was very civil. (He felt a pang of shame at these words which had slipped out naturally, they smacked of the underling, the underling he had become.) He offered to introduce me to his cousin. I saw what would happen if I accepted. Invitations, tennis doubles, bridge parties, so much time stolen from love.'

'So?'

'So I asked him to convey our apologies to his cousin and say she'd better not count on us for tennis. Was I right? Are you cross?'

'Of course I'm not cross. She's the one who'll be cross. She'll cut us dead, but it can't be helped. What matters is us.'

They had pulled back from the brink. He kissed the eyes of his sweet, compliant girl, so wholehearted in her support and so devastated in her unconscious. Some reward was called for. He held her closer, and their lips met in the dark. No need to look for another hotel, the Forbeses were neutralized now, and she wouldn't try to get to know anyone else, he told himself during their embrace, which, in the absence of anything to talk about, was long and unrestrained.

Yes, henceforth keep her constantly entertained, give her plenty to think about. Go to Cannes in the morning and load her with substitutes to make up for her disappointed social expectations. Buy her lots of expensive new outfits, designer dresses. Then take her to lunch at the Moscow. Caviare and champagne were other good substitutes for a proper social life. During lunch at the Moscow, discuss the dresses she had bought. Then buy her diamonds. Then a visit to the theatre or the cinema. Then an hour's riding or a spin in a motor boat.

So ran his thoughts while his lips persecuted the lips of her innocence. And travel and cruises, all the paltry joys I can give her, he thought during that endless embrace. Yes, he would do everything he could to conceal their leper state, he promised her with all his soul. He would do everything he could to make the desert of their love bloom, he promised her with all his soul, lips still joined to the lips of She-Who-Must-Be-Protected. But for how long could he stand the strain? Oh let me be the one to be unhappy, he thought.

'Undress me,' she said. 'I love it when you undress me. But put the light on. I love it when you look at me.'

He switched on the light. He undressed her. Yes, take her now, give her the petty joy of being taken, the pitiful pleasure which a leperman could still give his leperwoman, he thought, his handsome face above the beautiful, ecstatic face of the smiling unhappy darling beneath him. What, oh what had he let her in for? My little girl, my child, he whispered to her in his soul while cheerlessly did he use her as a woman.

CHAPTER 87

Two days later they had got to the coffee in their sitting-room, where they had been served lunch. Unspeaking, brows furrowed, he was totally absorbed in the flotilla he was making. He stuck a still smoking cigarette plus two matches for masts in the last hull of orange peel, then launched all three ships on to the whipped-cream sea of the meringues.

'Arctic vessels,' he explained after watching her for a moment in silence.

She gave a hurried smile and said: 'How sweet', which made him glance up at her suspiciously. But no, she was being quite serious, quite genuine in what she said. Oh woman's unconquerable love, oh the mysterious power of sex! If one day he took it into his head to make mud pies or crow like a rooster, she would be quite capable of throwing up her hands in delight and detecting signs of genius in such antics.

'Very sweet. Really it is,' she repeated. 'It's as if they'd been trapped by the polar ice. (Raising one hand to his temple, he acknowledged this with a grim salute. Reassured, she gathered the trailing flaps of her dressing-gown around her and got to her feet, politely diffident.) I think it's time I was getting ready. Still want to go out riding?'

'Why not?'

'In that case I'll ring the stables at Cannes. Are you going to get ready too?'

'I'll get ready too.'

'See you shortly. I shan't be long.'

Left to himself, he sighed. He saw her in her nakedness every day, and yet she still thought she had to be polite and formal with him. Poor girl, she so wanted to be the ideal mistress, she did her level best to keep the temperature of passion stoked to fever pitch.

At last she had gone off to get dressed. Hooray. Ten minutes of being his own man. Always worth having. True, but when she got back she would put the dread question, hang the sword of Damocles over his head: she would ask what plans did he have for this afternoon, after they'd finished riding? What new pleasures could he devise to camouflage their isolation? There were no new ones left. The same never-ending substitutes for a social life, the same old pathetic pleasures still open to the outcast – visits to the theatre, the cinema or the roulette tables, horse-racing, pigeon-shooting, *thés dansants*, buying new clothes, and presents.

And after the outings to Cannes, Nice and Monte-Carlo there followed the inevitable, depressingly good dinner and obligatory conversation and the effort of coming up with new things to talk about when there weren't any new things left to talk about. He knew all the Ariane stories backwards, such as the rare soul of Fluffy her cat and the sweet character of Magali her owl, and all those Chinese-torture childhood memories, the little song she'd made up, the chant of the gutter on the roof and the raindrops dripping on the orange awning, and the trips out to Annemasse to see Catholics, and reciting poems in the attic with her sister and all the rest of it, and she always told everything in exactly the same words. They couldn't go on resurrecting the same old stuff everlastingly. So what did they do? They talked about the other people in the restaurant.

Oh yes, though they never saw anybody else and could not discuss friends, which pukka people found such a pleasant way of passing the time, and though there was no longer any job to talk about, because, as Mrs Forbes put it, he had been turfed out ignominiously, they were nevertheless amorous mammals endowed with the power of speech and had therefore to find something to fuel their conversations. So they discussed fellow diners they did not know from Adam, tried to guess what jobs they did, what they were like, and how they felt about the people they were with. The dismal occupation for all who, besieged by loneliness, reluctantly become snoopers and psychologists.

And when they had finished analysing these desirable, inaccessible strangers whom they despised, they cast round for other things to say. So they talked about the dress she'd just bought or the characters in the novels she read to him each evening. Was she aware of the tragic nature of their predicament? No, for she was a lady, and resolute in the cause of love.

But today he did not feel up to force-feeding her on surrogate pap. Too bad, Cannes was off the menu, he'd pull the one about having a headache and then stagger back to his room and twiddle his thumbs in peace until it was time for dinner. No, that wasn't on, he couldn't leave her to stew all by herself in her apartment. But what on earth was he going to tell her when she reappeared all noble and loving and perfumed, so ready, so willing? He had absolutely nothing to say. Oh, if he were a postman he'd tell her about his round. If he were a policeman on the beat he would tell her how he'd given a suspect a good going-over! That sort of thing was real, true, solid. Or he'd see her get all excited because they'd been invited out that evening by his sergeant or the chief-postman or whatever. Oh, if only women would settle for a man's tenderness! But he'd been enrolled for services to passion. Should he put a bun in her oven to give her something to take her mind off him and also something to do? But having children presupposed marriage, and marriage presupposed an existence within the social pale. Whereas he was an outcast, an untouchable. In any case, they couldn't get married because she already had a husband. And, anyway, she had given up everything to be able to live a spangled life, not so that she could start breeding. So he had no option but to be a passionate lover in the heroic mould.

'Come in.'

It was, unexpectedly got up in white jacket and black tie, a red-faced Paolo, who, after almost falling over himself, asked if he could clear the table. Thank you, sir. No, sir, he'd been taken off lift duty that morning. He'd been replaced by a coloured man. Yes, sir, he'd been promoted, praise the Lord. Under questioning, he swabbed his forehead. Plans? Well, he wanted to put some money by and go back to his village, San Bernardo delle Acque, and buy a piece of land, and then, God willing, get married and settle down. He said thank you sir again and started to leave. But from his finger Solal took a ring set with a large stone which flashed white and blue, held it out to the dazed Paolo, hugged him, and bundled him out into the corridor.

'Oh to be Paolo!'

Yes, he envied the simple-minded clod who hadn't been sacked, had got himself promoted, wasn't stateless and would soon be married. Happy Paolo, restored to San Bernardo, respected by his fellow citizens and perhaps even the next Mayor of San Bernardo. In reality he was a lot smarter than Solal, for he found the world a kindly place, got on and believed in God.

'Come in.'

When he saw her in jodhpurs and riding boots, he felt a surge of pity. She had clearly been through every quality-control check imaginable, including full inspection of the seat of her breeches to ensure it wasn't baggy and lumpish but hugged her hindquarters correctly and gave her curves their proper due. Right, fair enough, they'd go riding. Fruit of the tree of Aaron the brother of Moses, he would perform like a chinless English wonder on a horse which out-girthed Naileater and would shake him to bits while his poor girl forced him to admire flowers, so much inedible vegetable matter which she found so terribly interesting, or pointed out some pointless hue in the sky above. 'A murrain on whomsoever pauseth to contemplate a tree in its splendour, saith the Talmud,' he improvised. And afterwards there'd be tea at the Casino and racking his brains to think of some new present he could buy her, and then the restaurant and whispering remarks about the other diners, and then finding words to say how beautiful and elegant she looked and how much he loved her, new words, for the old ones, the words he'd used in Geneva, no longer had the same impact. And all the while there were Jews in Germany who lived in fear.

'Not Cannes,' he said. 'I'm sorry.'

'It doesn't matter a bit,' she said. 'We'll go to my room. It'll be nice to have a quiet afternoon to ourselves. We'll make ourselves comfortable. (And chat, he thought.) And then we'll have tea.' (A glorious prospect this, he mused. He felt sorry for her for trying to liven things up and mask defeat by announcing this ghastly tea business two hours in advance, as though it were something to look forward to. Whatever had happened to Isolde?)

In her room, which she ordered to be filled with fresh flowers each day, she sat herself down comfortably and he sat himself down comfortably, with death in his soul. Next she smiled at him. He smiled back. When she'd finished smiling, she stood and said she had a surprise for him. That morning she'd got up early and popped over to Saint-Raphaël to get some more records. She'd got some magnificent things, top of the list being a chorale from Bach's St John Passion. She burbled on about it excitedly. Oh, those opening notes, the tonic G, repeated three times, which gave the start of the chorale a sorrowing, meditative feel, and the F sharp, where the voice hung suspended, seemed to ask an anguished question, and so on, and he felt pity for the wretched girl who tried so hard to give meaning to their life in their goldfish bowl.

'Would you like to hear the chorale?'

'Yes. Love to, darling.'

When the record had spun to its fearsome close, he bravely asked to hear '*Voi che sapete*'. She gave him a grateful look, happy because he had asked, without needing to be prompted, for their tune, their love's own call-sign. While the Viennese soprano did her worst, he told himself that instead of sitting here listening to a record he might at this very instant have been a minister or at the very least an ambassador, while with another part of his mind he wondered what new line he could dream up shortly to put new life into the poor girl who would have been blissfully happy to be an ambassador's wife and enjoy the respect of morons. Of course, being an ambassador, who was just another useless member of the official in-crowd, meant very little and was even rather pathetic, though to be able to say so with conviction you really needed to be an ambassador. It was only very important to be an ambassador if you weren't one. When the Mozart aria died away, he said he thought it was wonderful, such tender music, it sort of bled with happiness. He was aware that he was talking rubbish, but it didn't matter. With her, it was the tone that was all-important.

'Can we have "*Voi che sapete*" again?' he asked, to be on the safe side, and he suppressed a sorrowing, nervous laugh when he saw her leap into action.

When she'd wound up the gramophone, she stretched out on the bed and looked at him. He did what was expected of him. Equipped with long nose and dark-ringed eyes, he lay down beside her, acutely conscious of the emptiness of their life, while the Mozart aria, their national anthem, filled Ariane with fine feelings, made her aware of how much she loved her magnificent man. Suddenly, in rich, deep notes, the soprano began to give her view on what love was, and then groaned on about it in accents of the profoundest melancholy, as though she were going to be sick. Ariane said sorry, she hadn't wound the gramophone up enough. Seizing the opportunity with alacrity, he prevented her from getting up, leaped off the bed, turned the handle with such venom that the spring snapped. He said sorry, said he was really sorry. Good riddance. Gorgon bites dust.

Coming back to her side, he was at a loss for words. Should he let her speak? If he did, there'd be childhood memories or stories about her pets. The practical solution was to make love to her.

Now that she's been pleasured and gone to sleep my time's my own and I can fill it by telling myself stories sort of cinema-in-the-head just for me he does out the dining-room in the inn with the garden roller but it's time for breakfast he beats the gong to tell himself it's time for breakfast he comes running looking surprised and delighted he phones his cow Brunette who doesn't need to be told twice he is ever so careful not to offend her modesty he milks her with the greatest tact he puts sugar into milky coffee the sugar-lumps are like butterflies in his fingers his employer Jeroboam the innkeeper appears holding a Bible visibly stirred by verse eighteen, he kicks Charlie Chaplin who grabs a slice of bread and butter wolfs it down then bowler-hat tilted over one eye and proud as a Spanish nobleman he puts on a pair of gloves with holes in he goes out into the road wilily waddling a drum-major armed with a merrily whirling prod-stick he drives Jeroboam's cows he stops he lingers tearfully over the letter which is being read by a stranger sitting on a milestone who shouts angrily at Charlie who bows and goes on his way skipping and shrugging his shoulders benignly but where have the cows got to he looks for them behind a tree behind a rose-bush then surrendering to the flower-filled morning he dances a Prince Charming with a carnation between his teeth he dances a fidgety king condemned to hobnailed boots he skips from girl to girl from rose to rosebud on he goes on he flies a black sylph a puppet on a string kicking his legs for all he's worth with no thought now for lost cows and nasty men oh I'm getting sick of this he gets to Mary's house he whiles away an unforgettable hour making eyes his curly locks crazily bobbing he cranes his neck wildly like a tenor in a concert and sings a serenade then flirting deliciously he unwittingly pockets a brooch belonging to his lady-love but Jeroboam turns up and Charlie makes himself scarce with courage in his moustache and fear in his rear end while his boss bursting with virtuous outrage takes a stick to his niece Mary who struggles and her skirt falls down also her bloomers much to the indignation of Jeroboam who wields his stick even more furiously back at the inn Charlie forgets his troubles by losing himself in a great mission an occult labour he catches flies he reappears at rapid intervals brandishing a new victim and each time he succeeds in his task he lowers his eyes modestly and revels in a halo of gravity of saintly modesty of duty done he puts each fly in the cage with graceful assurance he tests his biceps and congratulates himself but now an injured toff is brought in Charlie falls over himself to help he takes the young man's watch waves it about to shake the mercury down puts it in the patient's mouth then with a look of medical concentration takes the pulse of the unconscious young man alack and alas by the next day Mary's heart has been won over by the spats and cane mounted with a cigarette-lighter of the well-to-do patient who is able to whisk a heavy silk handkerchief from his sleeve with practised ease oh poor Charlie one elbow in a lump of lard he suffers agonies but Jeroboam gives him no time for noble sorrowing gives him capitalist kicks instead and Charlie dashes off at high speed zigzagging wildly wondering in fits and starts which way to go switching directions suddenly lurching and staggering he careers through the stock-still fields and all of a sudden a corking idea brings a sober smile to his lips a quick-winged black and white butterfly to his face how vulnerable he seems with his eyes made up like a Tunisian dancing-girl and his hair ethereal in the mellow sunlight now he's wearing a tailcoat suffering agonies in a high starched collar done up to the nines to win back his fickle girl the stitches of his ingenious sock-and-spats combined come undone and the wool stretches out in a line along the length of several streets Guileless Charlie shakes one tangled foot with artless patience a dandy dandily dawdling whose dreams are full of angels dressed like policemen and pugilists with wings oh the sublime craziness which allows him to ignore the woolly tangle and go on shaking his triumph-of-hope-over-reality hobnailed boot but now to win back to dazzle Mary he guilelessly pulls a torn handkerchief from the tattered sleeve of his coat but notwithstanding the poignant cane with a candle stuck in the top he does not melt Mary's heart and all at once he looks at her and he understands and his moustache stiffens as if stung and an intellijew-ish smile widens his left nostril and lifts a corner of one lip over a wealth of knowledge of human heartache he shuffles off slowly lonely picking a flea off his coat he strokes it and lets it go at this point he spots a policeman coming towards him with his hands placidly and menacingly behind his back so to demonstrate his innocence he polishes his nails but the guardian of law and order bears down fearsomely on the pea-brained prince who doffs his hat and retreats in a flurry of Spanish *entrechats* taking bows like a lady circus-rider receiving an ovation before finally making off taking care not to lose the habit of face-saving by leaving the policeman with the memory of having been made to fall flat on his face the next day his little dog brings him a wallet containing a thousand dollars whereupon Napoleon Charlie walks into the saloon where he was a regular when he was still poor and downtrodden he disdainfully rolls a cigarette between his millionaire fingers he has a brow like Nietzsche and sinks glass after rapid glass of port one after the other in quick staccato succession like punches then solidly armed with bewitching teeth he smiles at the simple trusting girl who works as a singer and next moment the happy man and his darling wife have set off on their honeymoon and with them go the trusting girl's three little brothers plus two widows and five orphaned girls who have been adopted by filthy-wealthy Charlie the boat pitches and tosses as in a dream though he is seasick Charlie nevertheless attempts to solve the enigma of the deck-chair he goes at it with a will, with mild-mannered persistence he folds unfolds turns reassembles analyses and pensively arranges the articulated lounger which is far too complicated for ordinary decent mortals and in the end realizing that he will never master these contraptions and that superhuman tasks await him on the morrow he pitches the whole sophisticated shoot over the side the next day he has settled in the country he is wearing a floppy straw hat he is sowing he makes holes in the field with one finger he puts a seed in each hole and then covers it patting the earth carefully and stands back like an artist to see the effect but the defenders of the rules tear him away from his great endeavour he is lifted by the scruff of the neck led off with his feet dangling and dragged before the committee of public safety presided over by Jeroboam and the good judges pass the death sentence on the hopeless little man who says thank you two nasty academicians carry him off in a cart drawn by an old horse to the guillotine there a silvery-toned Charlie forgives Jeroboam who is present with his little boy whom he has brought along to see an example being set the condemned man raises his exquisite eyes to heaven sighs for the sake of appearances gives the horse a goodbye kiss consults a pocket barometer gives his two parakeets into the care of the executioner and then embraces him and smiling like a virgin heads for the retribution-machine and the blade swishes and lops off that pretty head which as it rolls into the sawdust-filled basket winks affectionately at Jeroboam's fair-haired little boy hello she's stirring she's opened her eyes she's looking at me she's smiling she's snuggling closer what shall we do dunno go out perhaps no it's going to rain watch out childhood memories looming yes make love to her again.

When she'd finished moaning in that special way of hers (which never varied), after passing certain tender judgements (which were always the same), she dozed by his side, sticky in her nakedness, while he summarized the day's events. Woke up, had bath, shaved, turned up in her room after the Mozart summons, kisses, had breakfast in dignified dressing-gown, kisses, talk of books and art, first coupling, unambiguous moans interspersed with assurances that she loved him, exchange of sweet nothings, rest, had second bath, change of dressing-gown, records, music on the wireless, listening to her read, records, kisses, lunch in their rooms, coffee, the polar vessels, then coupling number two after removal of riding outfit which ended up at the foot of the bed, then coupling number three after cinema-in-head. Watching her sleep, he silently conjugated the verb to love in the past, present and, alas, future tenses. He had just started on the subjunctive when, waking suddenly, she kissed his hand and then looked up at him, staggeringly trusting and eagerly expectant.

'What shall we do now, darling?'

Always the same old refrain, he screamed inwardly. What do we ever do? We love each other, that's what we do! When they'd been in Geneva she wouldn't have dared ask that awful question. In Geneva, being together was enough, that was happiness. Whereas nowadays she was always wanting to know what little treats he was thinking of giving her as a reward. Should he make love to her again? No, didn't feel like it. Anyway, she didn't either. Say something tender? That would hardly be enough to make her jump out of her socks. Still, why not give it a go.

'I love you,' he said one more time that day, which was a day for love, like all their days.

To thank him, she took his hand and on it dropped a curiously small but noisy kiss. Words, the very words which had made her drunk with happiness at the Ritz, those self-same words now merely earned a stunted dwarf of a kiss which made a faintly rude noise.

Outside, the universal, unrelenting rain articulated their unhappi-ness. Trapped in their love-nest, sentenced for life to love's hard labour, they lay side by side, handsome, tender, loving and utterly aimless. What could be done to stir their torpor? He held her close to give their torpor a stir. She curled up into a ball against him. What now? They had long ago unwound the very last strand of their cocoon of memories, thoughts, and shared tastes. The cocoon of their sensuality too: there was not really much mileage in sex. She snuggled up closer to the man of her life, and he felt sick with pity. He had not answered her question, and the poor creature did not dare ask again. Oh, what they needed now was a good couple of hours of adultery at the Ritz! Coming to him secretly, at four, heart thumping and eyes aflutter, with the pain and joy of knowing that come what may she would have to tear herself away at six, she wouldn't dream of asking him what they were going to do!

'Darling, the rain's easing off. Don't you think we ought to go out just for a little while? It would do you good.'

If they'd still been in Geneva, and she had still been living with Deume, and she were due back in Cologny two hours from now, would she be suggesting a healthy stroll outside? No, she'd cling to him like a limpet until the very last moment, stimulated, alive! And when she got back to Cologny she would be quite beastly to poor Deume, she would focus the whole of her affective being on the lover she saw so rarely, concentrate all her feelings on him until their next meeting. And how delicious to think that next month the husband would be away and they'd be able to make the most of it by spending three days at Agay, three whole days which she would pat and pet in anticipation, three winged days which she would stroke and caress during the bleak and cheerless evenings spent in her husband's company. But now he was the husband, a husband to be kissed noisily on the cheek, like a baby. She even talked to him like a husband sometimes. Hadn't she said only the other day that she had *one of her headaches?*

'They're dancing downstairs,' she said.

'Yes, they're dancing.'

'That music is so vulgar.'

'Terribly.' (Peeved because she's not down there too, she's doing her level best to get her own back, he thought.)

'They've put a notice up in the lobby,' she said after a moment's silence. 'From now on there'll be dancing every afternoon.'

'Good.'

He sharpened his nose with his fingers. So, she was keeping abreast of what went on in the hotel, was she? Showing an interest in the world that was out of bounds, yearning for green pastures whereon the general grazed. And why not, poor thing? She was a normal, healthy girl. He pictured her standing with lips half open reading the notice in the lobby, like a beggar with her nose pressed against a cakeshop window. He kissed her on both cheeks. 'Thank you,' she said, and her little thank-you made him ache inside.

'Listen darling, what say if we went down? I feel like dancing with you.'

So that was it! She hungered to be among other people! If all she wanted was to dance with him, why didn't she simply suggest tripping the light fantastic here, in her room, to the sound of her damned gramophone? Oh no, he wasn't enough, she needed other people! She needed to see and be seen by other people! In Geneva, when he'd asked if she would be prepared to be cast away with him on a desert island, she'd looked thrilled! He resisted the temptation to remind her how thrilled she'd been. No, it would only ferment inside her and she'd end up realizing that he was not the be-all and end-all, indispensable and all-sufficing. There were truths which were best left unsaid.

Should they wander down and join the dance? For the people downstairs, dancing was a legitimate sexual game, a kind of time-off from a strictly ordered social existence. But the two of them had coupled times without number: surely they didn't still have to go in for all that jigging and prancing? Ridiculous idea! It was also out of the question. Downstairs were the Forbeses, downstairs was Society. The Forbes fracas had happened the day before yesterday. In two days the ghastly redhead must have gossiped to any number of her own kind. By now they must all be in the know. Of course, all the people downstairs were stupid and vulgar. There were only middle middle-class people in the hotel, and he'd chosen it deliberately to avoid running the risk of meeting anyone from the old days. In the old days he would not have condescended to rub shoulders with such riff-raff. Now that he was in no position to do so, these common people became important, desirable, an aristocracy.

He turned and looked at her. She was waiting submissively. She was waiting importunately. I'll do whatever you wish. But I insist on being happy. Come on, show me a good time, improvise, prove to me that I didn't ruin my life by rushing headlong into this love of ours.

What could he come up with to avoid seeing her wilt and droop? What had a mind worthy of higher tasks been doing for weeks and weeks? Finding ways of preventing her being bored, or at least of preventing her knowing that she was bored. What titbit could he throw her today? Cannes again, and buying new dresses, and the rest of the social substitutes? She'd soon get tired of that. And nothing he could do would ever be as good as a stupid conversation with the Forbeses of this world. Was it worth reviving the dodge he'd used the other day and say he was bored? No. He couldn't bear to see her cry.

'Darling, what are you thinking about?'

'The Treaty of Versailles.'

'Oh, I'm sorry.'

He bit his lip. Oh the look of respect on her face! The girl was stupid enough to believe that he could be bothered to waste time thinking about such a piece of stupidity, even respected him for it! And why was she so respectful? Because the treaty, the product of impoverished brains, fell within the ambit of the great social world, and also because she still thought he was Under-Clown-General. Poor, honest Protestant girl, who'd believed him at once when he told her he'd arranged to go on leave for eighteen months, which sounded more plausible than a year.

The music which rose from downstairs in celebration of the spirit of fraternal communion was intolerable. She wouldn't even have noticed it the first night they'd spent together at Agay. Of course, with her poor, loyal conscious mind she worshipped her darling, wanted no one else but him, relied on him alone. But her unconscious was drawn by the tom-tom beat of the tribal dance. Poor girl, she was suffocating and did not know it, suffocating behind the prison bars of love. Should he make a sudden grab for her, as though he intended to ravish her? She might like that. Oh what a sorry business! Oh the humiliation! Oh those times in Geneva, so impatient to see each other again, the joy of being together, of being alone together! The laughter of the corporate crowd downstairs was an abomination! It floated up, and she listened to the terrible laughter which reminded them of their isolation. Quick, a substitute!

'Darling, let's go see a film.'

'Oooh yes!' she cried. 'But close your eyes. I'll get dressed. Shan't be long.'

He shut his eyes since coyness was the order of the day. The darling girl, so ready to fall in with his plans, had been instantly overjoyed. Yes, but in the old days in Geneva she would have been appalled if he'd suggested going to the cinema instead of staying in her little sitting-room kissing and ogling and talking endlessly. Solal of Agay had been ousted by a rival: Solal of Geneva.

★

739

In the taxi ferrying them to Saint-Raphaël she took his hand and scattered tiny kisses on the silk of his shirt cuff. That was because they were on their way to a change of scenery, he thought, heading towards something other than love, towards an ersatz version of a social life. But there was something else, something much more deplorable. The woman now stupidly pecking at his heavy silk cuff was kissing elegance, which meant wealth, which implied social distinction and therefore power. But if he were to tell her that, she would protest vehemently and talk about souls and never understand, far less admit, that deep-down she regarded the sumptuous silk wristband of his shirt as an extension of her Solal's soul. She was far too noble-minded for that and not nearly bright enough, thank God on both counts. Oh, she might not know it, but what she really admired about him was the fact that he was the powerful embodiment of social orthodoxy. He was a man who had risen high and would rise higher yet, she thought with her unconscious mind, which, as snobbish as anyone else's, yearned to be the wife of an ambassador. Woe betide the man he would be later on. He yanked on the wristband of his shirt which she had kissed and tore it, then smiled at the trailing silk tatter and pressed it to his eyes.

'Darling, why . . . ?' she said in a scared voice.

'Me juve,' he said in the accent of the Jews of Poland. 'Me like destructions, me like destructions wery much.'

To reassure her, he kissed her lips once more, and then again, marvelling inwardly at this strange custom which was so widely practised by men and women. The taxi stopped outside the Chic Cinema. He told the driver to wait and smiled mysteriously, congratulating himself on having speculated so successfully on the stock market during his years of Under-Clowning-General. Being rich was his revenge. He was a tramp, but a tramp with money. He enjoyed letting the torn silk of his shirt-cuff trail across the marble counter of the ticket office.

They made their way into the small auditorium, which smelled of sweat and garlic, sat down and waited. Eventually the elderly house lights flickered, faltered, and then went out. In the darkness, which rustled with the chomping of peanuts, she took his hand and asked in a whisper if he was happy. He assented with an equine toss of his head, and she snuggled up to him, for the second feature was just beginning. An American penitentiary. Prisoners behind bars. He envied them, because they had hierarchies, a social life: they were a criminal fraternity, but a fraternity for all that. Out of the corner of his eye, he glanced at the only social life he had, she so pure in profile that it broke his heart. What were they doing in this awful cinema which stank of plebeian feet? They'd come looking for happiness. And was it to experience the bliss of being in this reeking flea-pit that they had both ruined their lives? She squeezed his hand. So she can feel how much she loves me, he thought. But there was no life in her grip; it was mere politeness. The wonder of their sublimely joined hands as they stood at the window of her sitting-room on that first night, after the Ritz, would never return.

Throughout the entire film, he chewed on his obsession. Sentenced to passion for life. Other people were smart, they committed adultery on the quiet. Which meant obstacles, infrequent meetings, rapture. Whereas they, fools that they were, were buried alive under their love. Some were even smarter, they managed the thing honourably. The woman arranged to get a divorce, then the pair of them remarried, respected by friends and neighbours who all knew exactly where they stood on what had happened. Should he marry her? That was a solution which he'd already ruled out.

The interval. The house lights flickered and brashly splashed a milky glare over the numbed audience, who blinked as reality returned, then roused themselves as a greasy crone with kiss-curls went among them chanting 'Hices, loverly choc-hices, confeckshunry.' Disengaging their hands, the two lovers talked about the film to escape the awkwardness of silence, and, as they prattled on vacuously, Solal was overcome by a sense of his own decline and fall from grace. There they sat, quietly discussing the film, two beings apart, smartly dressed, cut off from the carefree, chummy, babbling, confident, slobbering, ice-cream-licking rabble. He was suddenly aware that an apologetic note had crept into his voice, as though he were a ghetto Jew afraid of drawing attention to himself. She was making herself inconspicuous too, speaking in whispers just as he did, and he realized that in her unconscious mind the poor girl knew that they were outcasts.

Abandoning humility and going on the attack, he began talking too loudly, beckoned to the usherette with her tray, bought a bag of sweets, handed it to Ariane, who smiled, said thank you, helped herself to a mint, and popped it into her mouth after removing the paper. So it had all been for this! The wonder of dancing together at the Ritz had been for this! The fervour of their first night had led him here, to a dirty little cinema where he sat prosaically sucking mints, feeling sick at heart, dismally sucking mints and listening while his lovely girl, once so wild, so crazy, talked shyly about a second-rate film, visibly awkward and ill at ease, his darling, morbidly self-conscious, his darling girl, and refusing to admit it. Why not go all the way and buy a couple of choc-ices now, so that they could suck them together, for the masochistic pleasure of sinking even lower?

As darkness returned to the auditorium which now filled with the plebeian smell of orange peel, the second half of the programme began. She took his hand gently once more, and the newsreel unwound. Dromedaries with their minds on loftier things sailed supercili-ously along a Cairo street then disappeared behind a police checkpoint on the Friedrichstrasse which dissolved to a fire-ball engulfing a factory in California which was rapidly extinguished by a Parisian downpour through which sprinted runners sponsored by a daily newspaper, and the winner stood panting, a broad smile all over his face, not knowing what to do with his hands, and swigged champagne proffered by a solicitous interviewer, and Hitler barked like a dog, and in Rio de Janeiro grinning Negro beggars climbed on their knees up the steps of a baroque church pursued by a slow-motion demonstra-tion of football action, the forwards kicking the ball through an unreal, weightless world in which strength and power were lazily protracted, endlessly booting the ball with an unhurried balletic sureness of touch, and Miss Arkansas panicked when she realized that she only had six seconds to impress the judges and did her tragic best to look attractive only to be replaced by two crashed Canadian trains and the Sultan of Morocco walking up the ship's gangplank to greet Marshal Lyautey and as he went holding the hem of his robes behind which Mussolini bawled defiance, hands on hips and chin almost touching his forehead, and cars skidded in an arc as they entered a corner where there was a gang of kids wearing jumpers advertising

Menier Chocolate, and Oxford beat Cambridge in the Boat Race, and Marshal Pilsudski bowed his drooping moustache to a tall Romanian queen, and a twitching French cabinet minister pinned a medal to a velvet cushion then disagreeably yapped a speech under an umbrella, and had he not himself, had he not too been a cabinet minister, and was now a nobody who sucked mints?

Then the first of the main features began to roll. Holding hands once more (like two drowning persons clinging to each other, he thought), they were subjected to a display of flesh belonging to a young female star of the silvery screen who had animal lips, alarming, Hottentot-thick lips, like the sucker of some gigantic tapeworm or the maw of a sea monster, and enormous breasts, which were the mainstay of her talent, ten kilos of constantly bared fat which had made her world-famous. After a few minutes he got up, and they left just as the revolting trollop was exhibiting her large posterior, which was her secondary talent.

'We'll go back to the hotel and dance for a while,' he said, as they got into the taxi.

She snuggled up to him. Like at the Ritz, like on their first evening, she thought, and she took his hand again and raised it to her lips while he brooded over the curse which doomed them perpetually to their own company, condemned them to possess nothing but their love. Should he move out and see her just once a week to allow her to experience the joy of being together again? But what would they both find to do on the other six days?

They danced among the other couples in the main ballroom of the Royal. Whenever the band stopped playing, they went back to their table, dignified and silent, while the in-crowd chatted animatedly, for they were all acquainted and none of them was having, at least not overtly, an affair with any of the others. Each time the band struck up again, the gentlemen, all lawyers or in the silk business or the army and graceful despite hernias and varicose ulcers, rose and courteously approached the wives of recorders and members of the bench and begged the honour. Certain ladies, some with hairy chins, accepted with girlish delight and got coquettishly to their feet. Others refused in the time-honoured manner, with refined, modest, wistful smiles, like grateful but quite untouchable maidens. Each and every one was asked to dance, except the celestial Ariane Cassandre Corisande, née d'Auble.

'I have a slight headache,' she said after their sixth dance. 'Would you like to go up?'

They rose and left. But when they got to the lift she asked him if he felt like casting an eye over the magazines in the lobby. There was an issue of *Vogue* that she would rather like to look at. She doesn't realize that in reality she's afraid to go back to her room and be alone with me, he thought. He acquiesced, and they sat down at the table where the magazines and newspapers were kept. Keeping her voice down, she asked him if she could hold his hand and said that he meant everything in the world to her. That's true, he thought, and she means all the world to me too, though it does not get us very far.

At the far end of the lobby, ten large, imposing ladies of the middling station were sturdily ensconced. Stoutly settled on their behinds, entrenched in their armchairs, fully accoutred and queens of all they surveyed, they were knitting voraciously and actively conversing in pairs. The hands and mouths of these aged hellish guardians of the proprieties worked unceasingly, implacably, for they were in no doubt of their fitness to sit thus in judgement. Poring over their magazines, intermittent objects of the scrutiny of the knitting hell-cats, the two lovers held hands, pretended to read, and, over the interference from the dance-band nearby, listened to the muddled snatches of conversation which reached them in discrete bursts and fragments, like some potent litany.

Seeing a Marshal of France standing not three metres from me I mean to say it brought tears to my eyes Fact is my rheumatism's playing up again It's not so much the cold but the rawness in the atmosphere that does it You never can tell with the English In any case you're better off indoors than outside You were lucky because it's not every day of the week that you get to see a Marshal of France Three metres imagine it The whole international money system has sold out to the communists it's a well-known fact Now knit four purl The Marshal had such a radiant look in his eye that I was knocked completely sideways it was the most beautiful moment of my entire life When you've said foreigners you've said it all When I think that in 1914 grapes were twenty centimes a kilo A look of such unworldliness one could sense that here was a man of honour And grapes like you never see nowadays Now knit six plain He looked every inch a leader of men but one could tell he had a heart of gold And in restaurants you could get a very decent meal for three francs or three francs fifty and wine thrown in And was your husband there that time with the Marshal I wonder what's on the menu for tonight No unfortunately and afterwards he bitterly regretted it In any case I do hope they're not going to give us chicken if it's anything like that old broiler they served up the other day They are quite delightful people Did you see the sun come out all at once Really the weather has gone completely haywire There aren't any seasons any more What can you expect hotel cooking is hotel cooking We see a great deal of them Oh dear I've got it wrong again it should have been six purl that's me all over True but at the prices they charge they could give us a decent bit of chicken The days are drawing in They don't invite just anybody Still I suppose you can say that every day is one day nearer spring Everyone likes them And they have tremendous pull It's narsty sorry nice to be in their company It's no good I'm going to have to undo it all and I haven't brought the right needles It happens a lot these days my tongue slips Roast chicken skin done nice and crisp is what I like best of all When I'm knitting kiddies' clothes I always start the sleeves from the top that way I can always lengthen them if I have to All the major inventions are ours but it's always foreigners who find ways of exploiting them Between you and me I get awfully constipated The Jews are to blame I start on my summer jumpers in the spring and my winter jumpers in the summer that way I can be sure of having them ready at the right time Yes it's always foreigners who make money out of them You've got to be organized It's the financiers who rule the world And they're all foreign She was out of mourning before six months were up The dreadful thing is that farmworkers are deserting the countryside It's all the fault of the Jews And what did the Marshal do They're drawn to the factories It's all the fault of the Jews He smiled and one sensed that here was such a kindly man And even more to the cinemas A magnificent soldier and a God-fearing man the two always go together I think these modern dances are quite disgusting Marvellous blue eyes you know straightforwardness itself The government should ban them A Jew's a Jew and you'll not persuade me otherwise Oh with the government we've got at the moment And it was so sweet when he kissed that little girl a great man but so kind so simple The entire race gives me the shivers I learned a great deal from that lecture the English consul gave and he had such presence too I rather like Il Duce there's something so martial about him a great man And so witty into the bargain His wife is very nice too ever so refined Yes both of them are very proper Not like certain people not a million miles from here I know exactly what you mean The governess actually wanted the same as us for dessert He was killed in action you know such a consolation for his poor mother Whenever I hear a regimental band I can't help it my heart goes pit-a-pat Anyway it was the brother-in-law who designed the war memorial he has an art diploma War brings out the best in men The working classes were made to obey orders you'll never persuade me otherwise The important thing is to be respected abroad Dreyfus was a traitor it's a well-known fact In any case Colonel Henry gave his word as an officer and a gentleman What else is there to say A colonel is a colonel there's no getting away from that Degenerate art is what my son calls it We've been too soft Doctor Schweitzer is a great man I have a photo of him hanging over my bed Though it's odd him not being a member of the Academy I've finished *The Ripening Corn* I must let you have it back Did you like it Loved it thought it was wonderful I'll lend you another René Bazin and *The Blue Teal* as well it's ever so genteel Socialist and Jew is six of one and half a dozen of the other You know I only read novels by authors who are members of the Academy They're always so well written such an attractive style And I'm very fond of Alphonse Daudet too such a distinguished writer Dr Schweitzer is wonderful A book written by a member of the Academy is a copper-bottomed guarantee A divorcée's a divorcée They're the sort of books that give you food for thought You're so right such an uplifting type of book So you reckon linseed does the trick better You'll see it works wonders Lovely people A very well-paid job So nice to be in their company You soak the seeds overnight and you take them first thing in the morning on an empty stomach The ins and outs Anyhow it works better with me than prunes All doors are closed to them I'll try because truth to tell things might have been easier this morning You're wrong she's not his wife And then a short stroll after lunch there's nothing better for helping things along Oh that ring on her finger doesn't mean a thing I always go wrong when I'm decreasing International finance is now entirely in their hands A clean sweep with a broom Servants in the old days were just like members of the family Stayed in service with the family till the day they died I always keep a note of invitations so I can return them Mussolini has such a nice smile Whereas the maids you get today I always note down my menus so there's no risk of serving the same things to the same people And they say that Il Duce plays the violin beautifully The chits you get these days are light-fingered Ooh that's lovely Deep down he's very soft-hearted And they're so demanding with it The Italians are really very fortunate Say what you will bricks and mortar are the best investment Blum is in cahoots with Stalin Jews always get on with each other like a house on fire A solid piece of property Noble thoughts An unimpeachable reputation Speaking for myself I prefer prunes on an empty stomach They say teacake gives you energy I don't mind admitting I prefer enemas It made me smell a rat They don't have just anybody around A fine soul Pretty well-off He lost his job and it was his own fault We broke off relations at once I'd go as far as to say extremely well-off We've been friendly with the parents for thirty years To be avoided like the plague was what the consul's wife told me Say consul-general dear it's a higher rank altogether You've got to show charity though It's also excellent for constipation They're Protestants but they invite people round and get invited back Yes we go to Switzerland every year You simply avoid talking about religion He said now you listen to me Mummy You can't just ignore people with an uncle who is a three-star general Swiss banks are very discreet The mother is a charming woman you know she was a Bomboin before she married With taxes the way they are you have no choice it's a matter of self-preservation Doctor Schweitzer It's hard to credit but he weighs ten pounds already There was such a crowd at the wedding And what put me on my guard straight away It remains to be seen whether the family will give its consent We put it all in trust in Swiss francs or dollars We put all our trust in God An engraved wedding card My husband is very fond of Nestlé shares They were given wonderful presents Bearer bonds are most convenient for you know what You can say it till you're blue in the face And they have the same social background There was a crowd at the funeral it was a grand sight And that way you avoid ghastly death duties Honesty personified You know who you're dealing with Beautiful family vault Moreover they have that system of anonymous I mean numbered accounts it's most agreeable Money is their god it's a well-known fact They're revolutionaries too I can smell them at ten paces And you also have joint accounts which are a great help I can pick them out just by their noses The money belongs to both father and son The Protocols of the Elders of Zion Only the father can touch it during his lifetime When you're a Miss Sphincter you don't marry any Tom, Dick or Harry Then when the father dies there's no bother with the tax people They didn't return our invitation so we don't have anything more to do with them It'll help the young man to get a seat on the Privy Council Oh he knows how to stand up for himself Acquests means that property owned by either spouse before marriage remains in their name They're Nîmes's leading family Anyway the next step is up to them we shan't budge an inch Or again you can use the bank's safe-deposit boxes Direct expectations in the near future You go once a year and cut out your coupons She leads a very intense spiritual life It's very good for colds They have these little booths in the safe-deposit vault with everything you need scissors pins Especially since socially speaking it's pretty second-rate When the father dies all the children have to do is open the safe-deposit since they've got the key and power of attorney and no one's any the wiser Yes in the very near future too because the grandmother has already had two seizures A trip to Switzerland comes a lot cheaper than having to pay all those outrageous taxes With a dispensation from fasting and abstinence which was only right Eight stocking-stitches for a cable-stitch One enormous table in the shape of a horseshoe With his father-in-law behind him he'll be a senior member of the Privy Council in next to no time I think small tables arranged separately are much smarter Sacha Guitry is so witty On the smutty side but so very French At root it all comes down to constipation Honeymoons are all very well but after the glamour fades you come down to earth with a bump Edmond Rostand is so subtle never a hint of smut and always terribly patriotic especially that play *L'Aiglon* He stuck to his guns and now he's a consul One spoonful of liquid paraffin before retiring at night The survival of the soul It's very good for constipation My motto is always put other people first He's Greek or something similar Especially since it always pays to give other people a helping hand Yes the son is in the diplomatic dear Still it might have been an Armenian Though the grandfather was a pork-butcher But dear there's a cardinal who is Armenian That's not the same thing at all a cardinal's a cardinal She comes of very ordinary stock but she more than made up for it when she married him My son who is a hospital registrar It's a scream to watch her eating a peach with her fingers my daughter nearly died laughing Dances are essential for helping young people to get acquainted What's bred in the bone will come out in the flesh He said I may travel second-class but I'm still Monsieur Bomboin for all that There's nothing to beat early training A good name is worth more than gold Especially as having a good name helps you get on in life The father insisted on a meeting of both lawyers and it was then that it all came out A good solidly built property is a copper-bottomed guarantee When she found out that he didn't believe in the afterlife she gave him back his engagement ring Bricks and mortar are always bricks and mortar Oh you can see who she takes after You can get such good imitation pearls nowadays that it's hardly worth bothering Religion is a copper-bottomed guarantee Say what you like a diamond's a diamond Myself I'm in favour of the guillotine Yes but it doesn't pay He said I've seen my king now I can die happy And with all these devaluations diamonds are not to be sniffed at As I was saying he's brother-in-law to the admiral And if there's a revolution they're easy to take across the frontier Doctor Schweitzer But you always lose money if you resell She wouldn't even feed the child herself When you use a private clearing-bank you can transfer whatever you like The guillotine is more humane There was just the Prefect his wife and us That way they don't have to be kept at the taxpayer's expense The working classes don't have the same needs as we do The Queen of England has such a kindly face The traditional dress of our own dear region Nor the same worries The traditional folk-dances The tax-collector's aunt Now you couldn't wish for anything more becoming Her mother drew the line at that and told her she wouldn't get another penny He's a general and lives at Le Mans just like his father which I think is very sweet They're the only ones who can afford tenderloin Just family heirlooms And of course he wants his own car It's all the fault of the Jews With the kind of example he's always been set New Year visits are a tiresome chore The sunrise was as beautiful as a picture postcard Still they're vital if you want to keep up with people The parents' apartment has ten front windows so I said it was all right for her to dance with him You'll not credit it but mine said she wanted to use our bathroom Moscow is where they get their orders Moscow's behind it all But he's a friend of my son's We just won't put up with that sort of thing here We've been too soft Love thy neighbour You needn't worry because I never repeat anything She's living in sin with her fancy man the husband refused her a divorce Thank God there are still people with backbone in France And to think that her parents were such respectable people Still with a character like hers anyone could have seen it coming Watch out for forged references It's hard to credit but after the father died she was seen at the theatre before she'd been in mourning three months The ins and outs of it And mark you it wasn't a classical play not the kind they put on at the Comédie-Française oh no the little madam would go to one of those modern plays you can't make head nor tail of Myself I always ring up their previous employers and make enquiries Mummy I won't marry anyone except an officer she said to me Obviously it's safer you can speak openly with people of your own background The poor don't know just how well off they are not having to pay all these outrageous taxes And when she was supposed to be in deep mourning she wore grey How awful The most restful sleep is the kind you get before midnight And with all the money she came into from her father Myself I insist on having a good character reference And naturally all the best houses are closed to her Doctor Schweitzer When you think that the prefect and all the best people went to her father's receptions it's enough to make the poor man turn in his grave In this life you need to be idealistic It's very effective for constipation To be avoided like the plague is what the consul's wife said to me.

CHAPTER 88

Two hours later, after dinner, they settled down in her room and there was a silence which she filled by offering him a cigarette and then lighting it in a scrupulous and heart-melting quest for perfection. The poor girl does her level best, he thought. Ha, now she's taking one herself. To put some life into the proceedings. To create a relaxed atmosphere. She's wearing that evening dress entirely for my benefit. We make an odd couple, she pointlessly got up in her glad-rags which would be more appropriate at Buckingham Palace, and me in a red dressing-gown, slippers and no socks.

'Those old hags downstairs were quite nauseating,' she said after another silence. 'I can't think why we stayed there listening to them. (You because you hunger for social contacts, however squalid. Me to lick the pebble of my unhappiness.) Basically, I'm beginning to think I'm becoming unsociable, that I hate other people. I only feel right when I'm with you. You are the only person who exists. (Oh yes? And what about that handsome waiter just now? When he went out, you took a good peek at yourself in the mirror above the fireplace. That little unconscious of yours just had to make sure if you'd been judged and found beautiful. But good luck to you if being considered attractive by somebody else made you feel happy.) Tomorrow I'll whizz over to Saint-Raphaël and get the gramophone repaired,' she said, after a third silence. 'If they can't mend it while I wait, I'll buy another one. (He kissed her hand.) And while I'm there I'll try to get hold of the Mozart Horn Concerto. It's not terribly well known but it's very fine. Do you know it?'

751

'Oh yes,' he lied. 'The horn part is astounding.'

She gave an approving smile. When she'd used up all her smile, she said she'd forgotten to show him the surprise she'd got for him, a box of Turkish nougat she'd found yesterday in a little shop in Saint-Raphaël.

'It rejoices in the name of halva, I believe. (She pronounced it "chalva" for the local colour of it. This irritated Solal almost as much as the 'rejoices in the name of", which she evidently considered nobler than "is called" '.) I thought it might take your fancy.'

Inflated language everywhere, he thought. She asked him if he'd like to taste some halva. He said he'd love to, but not now, later. Then she produced another surprise, an electric coffee-maker, also bought yesterday, plus all the necessary: ground coffee, sugar, cups and spoons. Now she'd be able to make him coffee herself, which would be better than the hotel's. He said she was very clever to have thought of it and, as it happened, he felt like a cup of coffee.

'In that case I think I'm entitled to a little kiss,' she said. (Continuing fall in the value of the Palestinian pound, he thought as he gave her a little kiss on the cheek. They had started giving each other more and more little kisses. And actually they were sincerely meant.)

In high spirits, she set to with a will and assembled the coffee-maker according to the instructions in the leaflet. As he raised the cup to his lips, she peered at him to see if he liked it. 'Excellent,' he said, and once more she inhaled through her nose. But when the coffee had been drunk it was drunk, and there wasn't anything else to drink, or do, and silence fell again. So she suggested reading out the last two chapters of the novel she'd started some days before. He agreed with alacrity.

She settled herself comfortably – to establish a cosy, natural, relaxed atmosphere, he thought – removed one of his slippers, then proceeded to massage his naked foot as she read. As usual, she tried to breathe life into the dialogue, putting on a gruff, soldierly voice when it was the hero of the tale who was speaking. That's how she liked them, he thought, men with positive attitudes, the sort who didn't duck a challenge. That's the sort she ought to have had really, a modern, dynamic clergyman say, or a legation secretary who played polo, or an English lord who went exploring in the Himalayas. She had no luck, poor kid.

When she had finished reading, they moved on to a pointlessly intelligent analysis of the novel, smoking expensive cigarettes as they talked. Then she suggested that they might start another book by the same author. He indicated that he'd rather not. He'd had enough of geometrically constructed novels which were nauseatingly clever and drier than dust. So she suggested she should read him a biography of Disraeli instead. Oh no, not that sly old fox who, possessing no talents beyond a certain low cunning, had taken good care not to make a mess of his life. After a silence, she mentioned how dull the weather had been that day, which led her on to observe that she felt cheered that it would soon be spring, in about ten weeks actually, which prompted her to speak of the strange, almost religious, awe she experienced when she saw little green shoots appear out of the earth, humbly reaching out for life. He nodded in earnest agreement, but thought to himself that this was the third time since they'd been at Agay that she had dredged up green shoots and almost religious awe. It wasn't easy to renew the stock. Again he felt pity, but that solved nothing. She was doing her best to share things with him. Very well, let's share. So he was very sharing and understanding and said that he too felt deeply moved every time he saw little green shoots. At this point she would probably expatiate on crows (underestimated intelligence of), a subject to which he braced himself to tip his hat as it flew by. But he was spared the crows, and there was a silence.

What could they do now? Should he kiss her like a tempest, like in the Geneva days? Have a care, that could be dangerous. If the kiss were passionate enough, and she responded conscientiously and doubtless out of a sense of duty, the snag was that she would wonder why there was no follow-up. Best make it just an affectionate brush on her eyes with his lips. So he kissed her eyes, and she expressed her gratitude with a ghastly, petted, schoolgirly 'Thank you.' There followed a silence. Unable to come up with a new topic of conversation or a novel way of telling her either that she was beautiful or that he loved her, which being new would make some impact on her, he decided nevertheless to press ahead with an ardent, long-distance embrace. The which he did, and during the performance he marvelled yet again at this practice to which men and women were given, a quite ludicrous custom really, the peculiar notion of seeking some furious conjoining through orifices designed for eating. When the conjoining was over, the silence returned and she smiled at him, compliant, perfect, game for anything, for kisses or dominoes or childhood memories or bed. Absolutely perfect. Still, when they'd played dominoes last night she'd had to bite her lip to stifle a yawn.

'How about a game of dominoes?' she said playfully. 'I insist on having my revenge. I just know I'll win tonight.'

Returning from the sitting-room carrying the box of games, she got out the dominoes and they divided them. But just as she was putting down her first double-six the music struck up below. Once more the happy crowd down there would be dancing now, mocking the two lonely lovers. His poor girl was excluded from all the fun. He said he didn't want to play any more and pushed away the dominoes, which ended up on the floor. She bent down to pick them up. Quick, think up something to compete with the social world downstairs, anything to stop the poor creature dwelling on the contrast between their anaemic life among the dominoes and the offensive gaiety which floated up to them, the wholesome gaiety of the herd of morons who were now clapping and laughing. Anything, but make it alive, exciting, riveting. How about slapping her across the face? But those waiting, lustrous eyes unmanned him. The best and simplest way of course was to want her and have her. Easier said than done. But in Geneva it was easier done than said. He stood up suddenly, and she started.

'What if I were torso-man?' he asked, and she licked her fear-dried lips.

'I don't follow you,' she said with an attempt at a smile.

'Sit down, noble lady and loyal companion. You aren't cold, are you, feeling all right, everything ticking over as should be? We'll come to torso-man in a moment. But first let's settle another problem. The other day, before we went out riding, because you were so keen to go, you came up to me, you smoothed the lapels of my jacket, and you said how handsome I was and how well I looked in my riding clothes. Well?'

'But I don't understand.'

'"My darling is so handsome, he looks so well in his riding clothes," that's what you said, and then you started fiddling some more with my lapels. Answer me!'

'What am I supposed to say?'

'Do you admit saying those words?'

'Yes, of course. What harm was there in that?'

'A great deal! Because it's not me you love but a man, any man, provided he was good-looking! So, if you hadn't met me, you'd have now been slobbering over somebody else my size and telling him the same revolting things! Clucking and cooing, head back, eyes gazing up inanely at some blond Viking with a commanding manner and a pipe stuck in his mouth, stroking his lapels in the same nauseating way, only too anxious to open that mouth of yours! Be quiet!'

'But I didn't say anything.'

'Hold your tongue, I said! And if the man were to take the pipe out of his mouth, you are not repelled by the foul taste of tobacco spittle on his lips. I know, I know, that main clause needs a conditional tense, but it's all the same in the end! Whoever would not be repelled is already not repelled! And you also said my boots suited me! Women always get excited about boots! Boots mean virility, military glory, the victory of the strong over the weak, and the rest of the gorilla chest-beating rigmarole women love so much! You and your kind are worshippers of nature and its ignoble laws! And there's worse to come: to a pagan like you, boots are a symbol of social power! Oh yes, a man who rides is invariably a gentleman, a grandee, a headman of the tribe, in other words a descendant of the robber-barons of the Middle Ages, a knight on a charger, a receptacle of power and might, a noble! Noble! A squalid, double-edged word which speaks volumes about the sordid glorification of might, a squalid word which means both oppressor of the weak and man worthy of respect. Have I said all this before? Quite possibly. But did not the prophets too play tunes on the same strings? In a word, the woman who worships boots is a plucked and trussed oven-ready fascist! Knight, chivalry, man of honour, ugh! Ask Naileater to tell you what lies behind honour, that same honour which you laud to the skies! Hold your tongue!

'Poor, good, mild-mannered Deume, whom she deserted for me –

for me! – simply because I flexed my muscles at the Ritz, casually beat my chest like a gorilla, and humiliated poor, inoffensive Deume! And while I was humiliating him by phone I felt totally and utterly ashamed, but I had no choice, because that was the despicable price she demanded for her love! How ironic: I denounced strength and virility, but it was with strength and virility that I won her, ignobly swept her off her feet! I feel ashamed each time I think of myself swaggering that night at the Ritz, like a gorilla, strutting like a peacock, prancing about like some rutting wild beast! But what else could I have done? I had offered her a mild-mannered, inoffensive old man, but she wouldn't have him and threw a tooth-glass or something of the kind in his face! Hold your tongue!

'Am I mad? Am I crazy with my talk of the animal worship of strength, of strength which is the power to kill? I don't think so, for I see her now – oh yes I see you, my sweet – in my mind's eye I see her that day in Nice, between the acts at the circus, looking strangely aroused and submissive, staring into the tiger's cage! And what a gleam of sensuality there was in that look! In her excitement she grabbed my hand, making do with mine because she could not hold the hand of the tiger! Oh yes, I know, I should have said paw. Excited, aroused by the tiger, just as good Europa was of yore by the bull from the sea! Jupiter was no fool: he knew women! Europa, the virgin with the flowing hair, doubtless lowered her eyes chastely and spake thus to the bull: "Ooh! What big muscles you have, sweetikins." And consider that other good woman, the señorita in the play, who tells her man that he is her proud and noble-hearted lion! Her lion! So you see that the word which to that lickerish trollop Doña Sol, the very word which to her seemed the most tender, the most adoring, the most agreeable of all words, is the word which stands for a brutish beast with enormous teeth and claws and deadly power! "You are my proud, my noble-hearted lion!" O unclean, impure creature!

'Moreover, did not this woman, this same silent woman who now stands before me putting such a noble face on things, did she not have the effrontery that day in Nice as we paused before the tiger's cage to say that she would love to touch the tiger's fur? Yes, touch it! A clear case of sexual attraction! Sin begins with the work of hands! Hold your tongue! Who knows, maybe she prefers the fur of the tiger to the skin of Solal! And the way you flirt with all the cats you meet! That one yesterday, a miniature tiger, lethal to birds, you tickled its belly with a pleasure that was so very revealing. Hold your tongue, daughter of Moab! But she doesn't stroke slugs, oh no! She turns up her nose at slugs! Why such revulsion, why not flirt with slugs? Because they are soft and non-erectile, because they have no muscles or teeth, because they are harmless and incapable of murder! But a tiger or a generalissimo or a dictator or a Solal being arrogant and forceful at the Ritz is a different matter altogether: he carries all before him, his hand is kissed on that first evening, until such time as his lapels can be patted! Is there no end to this base worship of the power of life and death, the base worship of sordid virility! Hold your tongue!'

Trembling-lipped, he glared for a moment at the guilty woman before him, then picked up the riding-crop where it lay and thwacked an armchair so violently that she recoiled in fear.

'And if I had them cut off,' he asked. 'Answer me!'

'I don't know what you mean,' she replied.

'Don't be evasive! You know very well what I mean! If I had both of those two loathsome testifiers removed, would you still stroke my lapels so lovingly, you know, lovingly as in Mozart, as in "*Voi che sapete*"? And would your soul still be twinned with mine? Answer me!'

'Listen, darling, let's not go on with this.'

'Why?'

'You know very well why.'

'Tell me why.'

'Because it's such an unlikely idea.'

'Unlikely is it? Go tell that to the birds, or your cats if you prefer. Unlikely? And what, pray, do you know about what's unlikely and what isn't? How do you know that I'm not tempted by the prospect of saying goodbye to virility?'

'Darling, don't let's talk about this any more.'

'I take it, then, that you refuse to commit yourself. Give praise to those two humble spheroids so dear to the hearts of Ophelias everywhere, and let us guard them as jealously as a treasure without price! (He looked at her closely, and his eyes shone with the joy of

757

knowing.) I know exactly what you are thinking at this moment! You're hesitating between "Jewish mind goes to pieces" and "Jewish mind hell-bent on destruction", isn't that so? You women keep your brains wrapped in a cosy cocoon of romantic platitudes, that's how you always deal with awkward truths! Lucifer was the angel who came bearing light, so you turned him into the devil! But let us now come to torso-man. Would you still love me if I were torso-man?'

A sudden pang, an ache, a pain: the other evening in Nice, the sight of ship's colours being struck at sunset on a French destroyer. The flag was hauled down reverently and he had watched, envying the sailors standing stiffly to attention, envying the officer who gave the salute while the colours were slowly lowered in the gathering dusk. Farewell, sweet France, for he was now no son of hers. A few days after arriving in Saint-Raphaël he had received the letter on flimsy paper from the police department begging to inform him that by a decree published in the *Journal Officiel* Monsieur Solal was stripped of his French nationality; that motive for loss of entitlement was not, according to the terms of the law, required to be given, but that the person concerned was allowed a period of two months in which to lodge an appeal; that, the aforementioned decree being immediately applicable regardless of the entering of any such appeal, the above-mentioned person was invited to present himself at the above-named police station for the purpose of returning all French identity papers and, in particular, of surrendering his passport. Solal knew the letter by heart. He had duly presented himself at the police station. He had sat for hours on a squalid bench, waiting upon the good pleasure of a paunchy inspector. He remembered the leer of pleasure on the face of the seedy policeman, and his dirty fingernails, as he had examined the diplomatic passport. And now the only papers he had were a temporary residence permit and the identity and travel document issued to all stateless persons. He was nothing now: he was only a lover. And what was he doing at this moment? He was trying to save their love from its anaemia, he was inflicting pain on a hapless woman. Meek she was and submissive, and once more respectful of his silence. She believed in him, had forsaken all for him, caring nothing for what other people said and thought, and she lived only for him, she was his, defenceless she was, and absurdly clothed in grace and weakness when she went naked, so beautiful and destined to die and lie stiff and white in her coffin. Oh, the ghastly laughter downstairs, the applause to which she was listening.

. 'I'm waiting for an answer. Torso-man!'

'I don't know what you're talking about.'

'Then I shall spell it out. Here I am, all of a sudden, not handsome any more, I'm hideous to look at, I'm torso-man as the result of some unavoidable operation. What are your feelings towards me? Are they feelings of love? I'm waiting for your answer.'

'But I haven't got an answer. It's such a ridiculous idea.'

He felt the impact as though he had been punched. Gone was the respect she had shown him during their first days together. He was now ridiculous. He decided to make the affront an excuse to walk out on her. After a while she would come knocking, begging to be forgiven, and there would be making-up and their love would be regilded for another hour or two.

'Good-night,' he said, getting to his feet. But she held him back.

'Listen Sol, I'll be frank. I'm feeling pretty rotten, didn't get much sleep last night. So let's put a stop to all this, because I don't think I've got the strength to give you much of an answer, I'm whacked. Listen, don't let's spoil this evening. (Even supposing we don't spoil this one, there are three thousand six hundred and fifty other evenings which we mustn't spoil either, he thought.) Listen Sol, it's not because you're handsome that I love you, though I'm glad you are. It would be sad if you ever got ugly, but, good-looking or hideous, you'll always be my dearest love.'

'But why should I be your dearest love without legs or toes? Why should I be so dear to you?'

'Because I have given you my heart, because you are who you are, because you are capable of asking all these crazy questions, because you are my fretting child, my ailing boy.'

He sat down, the wind quite taken out of his sails. The thrust had gone home. Damn! If it was love you wanted, then what was this but love? He scratched his temple, pulled a face by moving his closed mouth from side to side, felt to see if his nose was still where it should be, and stroked it. Then, reaching out to the gramophone, he began absent-mindedly winding the handle. Suddenly aware that it was meeting no resistance, he remembered the broken spring and looked round warily. No, she hadn't noticed anything. He cleared his throat to give himself confidence, and stood up. But it simply couldn't be: she was lying and didn't know it. If she believed she would still love him if he were hideous, a mutilated trunk of a man, it was merely because at this moment in time he was handsome, disgustingly handsome.

God, what did he think he was playing at? Everywhere in the world there were liberation movements, hopes, struggles to create greater happiness among men. And what was he doing? He was fully occupied creating a miserable climate of passion, had a full-time job relieving the boredom of a wretched woman by tormenting her! She was obviously bored with him. But that first evening at the Ritz she hadn't been at all bored. Oh no, she had been dizzy with bliss that first evening at the Ritz. And who had made her dizzy? A man named Solal whom she did not know. And now he was a man she did know, a man who had sneezed maritally this afternoon, after their coupling, and in the silence of the post-coital intermission she had, to his mortification, heard him sneeze. Oh yes, she had deceived him in advance with the Solal she had known that first night, the Solal of the Ritz who had not sneezed, Solal the Romantic.

'Solal cuckolded by Solal,' he murmured, and he twisted his curly mane left and right into cuckold horns, and he waved to the cuckold in the mirror, while she, head bowed, sat and shivered. To be sure, she had deceived him with that other Solal-self, for had she not dared to love him that very first evening? She had deceived the man she knew now with a stranger she had met at the Ritz! And she had immediately kissed the hand of the very first man who had shown his face – a Solal substitute, a stand-in, not the real Solal! And why? For all the reasons he despised, for the same animal reasons which had operated in the times of the primeval forest! And that first evening, at Cologny, she had not shrunk from giving her lips to the lips of a stranger! Brazen and wanton! Oh women! Brazen, wanton lovers of men! It was unbelievable, but they who were so delicate loved men, beyond a shadow of a doubt they loved men, they loved the braggarts, they loved the louts, they loved revoltingly hairy boors! Incredibly, they accepted male sensuality, yearned for it, gorged on it! It was past all belief, yet it was true! And no one was shocked!

He turned to face her, only to be utterly disconcerted by the purity of her expression, the innocence of her demurely lowered eyes. Pure! She who had given herself to a stranger at the Ritz, a Jew from God knew where, was also purity! Yet she had needed no bidding to give her lips, her tongue, to a man she did not know! Oh, women would drive him insane, for who could understand them? They would make him mad: Madonnas one moment, lewd Bacchantes the next! And yet they spoke such noble words when they were dressed! But suddenly riding on the wild wings of night they spoke words which would strike you dead on the spot, my poor little Solomon!

'Listen, darling,' she said. 'Don't let's stay here. Let's do something. Let's go downstairs.'

He was stabbed to the heart by a dagger of despair. Her tender words were a judgement. 'Don't let's stay here. Let's do something!' So being together meant not doing anything. 'Let's do something!' But what? Why not just carry on from where you left off?

'Let's go back to torso-man. Again I put the question, which is not the least ridiculous. (He spoke slowly, savouring each word.) Let's suppose advanced gas gangrene left the doctors with no option but to amputate my arms and both my legs to the groin, that is to say to leave me a human torso, and to which add that I also stink and am covered with pustules from the effects of the gangrene,' he smiled sweetly, and his cup of joy overflowed. 'It could happen. Such disorders do exist. Well then, if I were just an abridged torso, an immobilized, fetid, reeking heap, would you still love me in the grand poetic manner, along the lines of Cherubino and the Brandenburg Concertos? And would you still shower me with sublime, amour-piercing kisses? Answer me!'

'Stop this, stop it!' she begged. 'I can't take any more of this, I'm so tired. You can say whatever you like, but you won't get another word out of me.'

'Clerk of the court!' he barked, pointing with his forefinger. 'You will take note that the accused again refuses to answer the question. What would really happen, my dear, if I were an abbreviated, foul-smelling torso, is that you would manage to think up perfectly valid reasons for finding that my soul is no longer what it was, that it has gone off, and you would stop loving me for good. Which is hardly fair. Am I to blame for gangrene? There I am, stretched out on a table, a poor, stinking lump, with no arms, no legs, not even stumps, but with my masculinity unimpaired, laid out for your despair and disgust, picture it, poor me, not much left of me to speak of, flat out on my table, head aching, a single punch would knock me off on to the floor and I'd never be able to pick myself up again unaided! But God in heaven, there's no need to go to the trouble of being lopped and butchered! A couple of missing front teeth would do the trick as well and make quite sure that your soul suddenly ceased to find delight in mine.'

He rubbed his hands and smiled as he thought of a pretty prank to play on her. A first-class jape! He'd go out first thing in the morning, get his head shaved by a barber, and then all his teeth pulled out by a dentist! Oh the look on her face when he showed up looking like some comic-opera convict with a wide, empty grin! It would be worth doing as a homage to truth!

'Darling,' she said. 'Don't go on. Why do you want to spoil everything? (He gave a despairing laugh. So she too was an anti-Semite!) Please, darling,' she begged. (How easily she said 'darling', when her darling could just as well have been somebody else!) 'Darling, drop it. Wouldn't you rather tell me about when you were a little boy, or about your uncle you love so much? What does he look like? Describe him to me.'

'He's very ugly,' he said brusquely. 'Nothing doing there.'

Why did women hanker so after good looks? The other day she had told him he had beautiful eyes. Ought he now to be jealous of his own eyes? You have beautiful eyes: that meant that later on, when his eyes had become dull and rheumy, it would be all up with him! He got to his feet.

'Women are serpents with angel faces, for one fine day they suddenly, swooningly decide that they have fallen out of love! Then imitate the action of the spider! Bring on the spider we know so well! "Dear human torso," they say to the poor heap on the table, "what's the point of lying, I just don't love you any more! My mouth must remain as pure as my inner being, nor must it with pointless name-calling defile the noble memory of our past happiness!" (She bit her lip to ward off a heavy-hearted attack of giggles at the thought of the poetess haranguing her truncated lover.) Behold the spider at work! Still, who knows,' he went on mellifluously, 'perhaps you would go on loving me after all, torso notwithstanding, though that would be infinitely worse. For then you would turn into the Heroine Who Sacrifices All to her human torso, who takes care not to breathe in too much when she's near him, because he stinks to high heaven, who washes him, has to carry him about, and with a saintly smile sits him on the lavatory. But in reality your damned human torso would be a devil of a nuisance! And beneath your oh-so-heroic conscious mind your much more sensible unconscious would be busy wishing that the useless lump would die and have done with it! And that, my dear, is the top and bottom of it!'

Sure of himself, tall in his long, red dressing-gown, he crossed his arms challengingly, awaiting her reply which he would then proceed to demolish. But her head remained bowed and she said nothing. At length he unfolded his arms and began to speak in a kindly, smooth, lecturing voice.

'There is another problem which we failed to thrash out last night. With your permission, I shall raise it now.'

'No, stop, please stop! Look at me. I love you, you know I do. So why are you tormenting me? Why do you go on torturing yourself? My love, kiss me!'

He felt a sudden desire, oh yes such a desire, to kiss her cheeks and hold her close! But, when the kissing stopped, there would still be music playing downstairs and the two of them would still be up here, alone with their dominoes. Billing and cooing wasn't exactly an all-consuming pastime; kissing and cuddling was no match for the clapping at the end of a tango and the applause of a happy crowd of dancers clamouring for an encore. There was no choice but to go on.

'And that other problem is: you and sex.'

He nodded knowingly and stared. It had been obvious during these last weeks at Agay that she had taken only a theoretical interest in sex, had forced herself to show a certain enthusiasm for it without being aware that she wasn't really all that keen any more. But back in Geneva, when he'd been new – a novelty – she had been very interested in sex indeed. *Ergo*, quite likely to be interested in sex with some other novelty newcomer! In Geneva, oh the kissing she had given him, her tongue turning and twisting like a flailing aeroplane propeller!

Still holding her in his stare, he pictured her during those first nights, moaning, urging him on, suddenly bold with her words, with her touch, with her bucking body. She was still like that at Agay sometimes. The other evening, after the scene when he'd told her it was all over and then asked her to forgive him, she had flailed with her tongue just as she used to in the old days. Because a scene made him into a novelty again for an hour or two. 'Which means . . .' he murmured, and he glared at her with wild eyes. She licked her lips. Don't argue, let him get it off his chest, don't cross him.

'Interested in sex and therefore doomed to be unfaithful!' he declared. 'Which means that there'll be some kicking over of traces once I'm dead. Oh yes, when I'm dead you'll be devastated of course, and you'll think of ending it all and you'll go back to Geneva feeling very sorry for yourself. And then what happens? I'll tell you. You're bound to run across Christian Cuza, you remember him, my last PPS, I introduced you, handsome, urbane, dreamy Christian who also happens to be a Romanian prince. Oh you'll see him again because I always said very nice things about him to you and because he was genuinely fond of me. And you won't mind his being there because then you'll be able to talk about me, because only Cuza will understand how you feel, understand what pearl of great price you have lost. To cut a long story short, the pleasure of a grief shared, the hours of friendship spent communing over the memory of the dear departed, going through old photos of him together on a sofa, sitting side by side with a gap of six flimsy inches between the two of you, six respectable inches which do not bode well! Am I right? Not going to answer, eh? As you wish! And then one warm evening, with the summer lightning puncturing the sky and the thunder growling, you will burst into tears when you're discussing something the dear departed used to say or do. Then Cuza will comfort you, he'll say he wants to be a brother to you, that you can always rely on him. And he'll believe it too, he's a very decent sort, thought the world of me. And then he'll put his arm around your waist so that he feels sure and you feel sure that you can rely on him. And now raise the floodgates! And all at once, because good, kind friend Cuza has brought his cheek nearer, to comfort you, there is a sudden outbreak of triple-turbine, full-throttled kisses, just like the ones you used to give me, only now they come tasselled with tears! (To avoid seeing the kisses, he closed his eyes, then opened them again.) The tears and the sobbing are genuine enough, but they were unleashed by your unconscious as a way of prodding dear Christian, who is a slow starter. You don't believe me? Please yourself! But the worst of it is that you will give Cuza not merely your body, that much I am resigned to, but also your love, and that I find unbearable! But that's women for you. They will give their sweetness, that most precious part of themselves, exclusively to a man with pawing hands, and only then if they have first been pawed! And poor Solal a corpse, so soon forgotten!'

He glared at her accusingly. Oh yes, she was interested in sex, alas! For proof, you needed to look no further than the air of respectability she kept up when not stormily probing with her tongue, the demure way she behaved with other men, the keep-off-the-grass signals she gave out, which were an indication of her fear of other men, who were all a threat if they were young enough to serve, to serve her. Such unbearable coyness! And that unbearably prim way in which she was now sitting there on her chair, with her knees unbearably together! What right did she have to make herself out to be so very proper when she was the same woman who would proceed with Cuza from tears to the commingling of tongues, while he, the poor discarded lover six feet under, would be left to his own devices in his wooden box! Naturally, her conscience would prick her, all the Aubles enjoyed healthy consciences, of course it would, but she would find some noble justification for dancing on his grave, she would even think of a way of making the poor corpse contribute to his own eclipse! It was Solal, my Solal, our Solal who brought us together, she would murmur, and the pass would be sold, and to Cuza she would speak the same words she had spoken to her previous lover-man when he was alive. I like it when you undress me, I like you to see me naked, she would say. Oh stop it, I can't take much more of this.

'Actually, there's no need to wait until I'm dead,' he said, smiling grimly, not noticing that she was trembling. 'With a little nudge from me, you could be unfaithful to me while I'm still alive! All I'd have to do is force you to spend a whole night in a narrow bed, naked, by the side of some lusty young athlete, also naked, and you'd see! Oh, the two of you there side by side! And such a narrow bed! And I'd have brought it all on myself! Of course, you'd resist the temptation. Naturally, you'd want to be faithful, but the bed is awfully narrow and your thigh presses deliciously against another brawny young thigh! And what happens next, my sweet? Answer me!'

'Let me be!' she cried.

'What happens next?'

'I'd get up and go,' she cried. 'I wouldn't stay there in that bed!'

He gave a bitter laugh. Aha! She was afraid of temptation! Aha! She was incapable of remaining unstirred by the side of a lusty young athlete! He turned quickly and stared at this virtuoso of the pelvic thrust whose thrusting was, for the time being, reserved for his exclusive use.

'And now I have another question for you,' he began gently. 'Tell me, darling, if you had to be raped, who would you prefer to be raped by, a man who was good-looking or a man who was ugly? Just supposing. Let's say you've been captured by bandits and they sit in a circle in their cave, all shaggy and hairy, and give you the choice. Go on, tell me which you'd rather: an ugly man or a good-looking man? You can't avoid being raped, the bandit chief has ordered it done, and orders are orders. But he's willing to let you choose. So what's it to be? Ugly or good-looking?'

'God, you're mad! I never heard such an idea!'

'It's the bandit chief's idea. Ugly or good-looking? Come, my sweet, be a good girl and answer.'

'I won't answer! It's too absurd!'

Aha! Dodged the issue again! She wouldn't say! Suddenly another picture came into his head. Ariane and a young, married Protestant clergyman cast away on a desert isle after their ship had gone down! She would obviously deny it if he told her that within three months she and her cleric would be bouncing up and down on the bed of dried leaves in the hut built by the said cleric's own hand! No, make that two months! Or even one month if there chanced to come a summer's night and the breeze was warm and the smell of the sea was rising and the hut comfortable and no cold in the head and a myriad stars in the firmament or a crimson sunset with clouds of green and pink, just the way she liked them.

'A fortnight would be enough!'

And even if there were no desert isle, even if she were to remain faithful for ever, there were any number of ways open to her in which she might be unfaithful. At least the brazen ones did it openly. They slept with another man, which was straightforward, honest in a way, at least it was not hypocritical. But with her, even if desert islands never came into it, there were so many lures, so many openings for sly little adulterous betrayals! A sidelong glance would do it! One glance in the direction of some Greek god or a gleaming-toothed Algerian or a Spanish dancing-girl or a regiment marching by or a boy scout or even a tree which re-minded her of virile man, not to mention tigers! And the tickle of the hairdresser's snipping scissors spelled danger too, for they unques-tionably started pleasant tinglings on the nape of the neck! It was impossible to love this woman and keep your peace of mind! Should he lock her away and allow her to see only hunchbacks who weren't hairdressers? The dreams, the memories would stay with her! No, he wasn't overstating the case! All women were unfaithful, at least in their unconscious minds. He was so stricken by the thought that when he put the Calabrian question to her again, his heart wasn't in it.

'The ugly man,' she replied, for the sake of peace and quiet, to have done with it.

He could not bear to hear the word 'man' from the mouth of this woman! So barefaced! Oh, the foul reek of the word, the male-hairy word on such pretty lips! What did she mean by saying 'ugly'? She obviously felt that the good-looking man was dangerous, temptingly dangerous! He pictured her pulsating beneath the weight of a hand-some Calabrian bandit wearing green leggings and soft moccasins with curved toes! The lusty bandit stank! But she was not put off by the Calabrian bandit! Women were all so indulgent towards the roughness of the male and his attributes! He looked away to blot out the sight of the bandits' camp-follower. He found the young Calabrian's large nose especially offensive, for it was a distressingly suggestive nose, enormous and full of promise! The female's weakness for virility, worse, the way women worshipped virility and anything which was its badge and bestial affirmation, such loathsome indulgence angered and shocked him. He found it hard to believe, yet he had to bow to the facts. These creatures, so delicate, so gentle, had a taste for male crudeness! So why, then, in street or drawing-room, did they pose, why did they act so prim and pretty? The duplicity of it was enough to unhinge him. Enough!

'That'll do for this time. I'm gentle as a lamb now. Observe: I even kiss your hand. Kiss me. Here, on the neck, on the left. And now the right. Thank you. And now let's go out, it's stopped raining. That's right, I shall keep my dressing-gown on. It's late, there won't be anyone about outside.'

Meekly walking along the corridor by his side, she felt worthless, drained, a tailor's dummy in an evening gown. In the lift, she smiled wanly at the Negro attendant with the kindly face, and Sol bore this whiff of adultery in silence. But then, seeing her drop her gaze, he toyed with the idea that it was her way of overcoming the attraction she felt. Oh yes, all women covertly lusted after black men. A black man was their secret ideal. Only social prejudice and inherited custom prevented them performing symphonies in black and white. Regrettable, but there it was. The old lift finally creaked to a halt. In the lobby, people were chatting quietly or playing patience: they were not living on love alone.

'Take us up again,' he said to the Negro lift attendant.

'That dress looks very nice on you,' he said, being kind, as he sat cross-legged on the sofa. 'And now, darling, I'm all ears. Get the Conrad novel. Read me the beginning again.'

She fetched the book, cleared her throat, and gave it all she had. Unfortunately the novel began badly from her point of view, for the hero was the dynamic captain of an ocean-going vessel and, in her eagerness to read with all the right intonations, she gave him a gruff, manly voice. This was torture to Solal. Aha! A deep voice, a sensual voice! She was admitting, more brazenly than ever, what kind of men she loved, what she wanted men to be like!

'Stop it!' he barked in an unbearably shrill voice. 'Stop! I insist on a modicum of decency and restraint! But don't be alarmed,' he added in his normal voice, 'you can still go on loving me. I can still kill and I am still good for fathering offspring! Don't worry, I'm fully functional, I'm as fit as any three of Conrad's captains! Right then, let's get back to the shipwreck. There you are, on your desert island. Now what if the only other survivor was the hotel waiter who was here a while back, or another man of the cloth, or even, perish the thought, a rabbi, and you and this other castaway could never escape from your island? What then?'

'Darling, please. I'm so tired.'

'Quite. There's not much point in asking you anyway. You won't give me a straight answer, you'll never give me the satisfaction of admitting the truth, though it's as plain as a pikestaff! I know exactly what would happen. At first not much, obviously. You'll stay faithful to me because you'll still be hoping to be picked up by some passing ship. So you light fires as beacons at night, and by day you hoist a flag made out of a shirt belonging to the waiter, who as a result will become deliciously tanned. So to begin with, then, nothing happens. Especially since the waiter isn't somebody you can discuss Proust with, perish the thought! But within a few weeks, when hopes of being rescued by that passing ship have faded and you know beyond doubt that you and he are doomed to be stuck on your desert island, sentenced to living together far from other people and civilized rules, you start putting Tahitian flowers in your hair! (Carried away, elated by the truth, he strode round the room, oblivious of the fact that she was shaking.) And you'll make him tasty things to eat with the fish he's caught and the various kinds of aromatic herbs which you go out to pick in a sarong! It's all innocent enough, but already you are living like man and wife! I know beyond a shadow of a doubt that what I'm saying is the truth! You think I'm mad, but I'm not mad at all! And so time passes, until finally, one sweet-scented night, what was bound to happen will surely come to pass in your palm-thatched hut, in, out, in, out! Or maybe,' he went on lyrically and with much feeling, 'maybe at the end of one fine day there you are, sitting side by side, barefoot, holding hands, on the shore of an indigo and purple sea, watching the sun go down in a blaze of romantic, conniving colours, and then it happens. This woman, who lives and breathes for me alone – and this she believes in all sincerity – will lay her flowered head on the tanned and gleaming shoulder of the waiter or the rabbi, whichever, who has become her lord, just as I am now, her man in the warmth of the night and the fragrance of the mangrove tree. And she will murmur "*Tvoya zhena*,"' he exclaimed, and he went over to the window and looked out.

Leaning his brow against the glass, he closed his eyes and pictured her lying with her head on a large, smooth chest. There it was: on her perfumed isle, she had forgotten him completely, was giving her new man the same kisses she had lavished on him during their first days together! Perhaps, given the climate, her kisses were even more abandoned, kisses with snaking, probing tongue, all quite exceptionally obscene! He was beginning to feel a surge of desire for her when, turning round, he saw that the unhappy girl was lying on the carpet, face down, body convulsed with sobs.

He took her in his arms, picked her up, laid her on the bed, and threw a fur coat over her, for her teeth were chattering with cold. He tiptoed into the bathroom and came back with a hot-water bottle, which he put under the fur coat. He turned out the ceiling light, switched on her bedside lamp, knelt but did not dare kiss her hand, whispered that she was to call if she needed him, and then, feeling none too proud of himself, he tiptoed out.

In the sitting-room, he stood in the darkness by the door he had quietly closed, pacing, listening for sounds, thinking about the wretched life they led, smoking and touching his chest at intervals with the glowing end of his cigarette. Finally he made up his mind, opened the door carefully, padded across to the bed, leaned over the innocent girl who in sleep was released from her misery, his woman whom he had hurt, she who had given him her heart, she who had danced in wonderment at the Ritz, she who had wanted nothing more than to go away and live with him for ever, his trusting girl who believed her happiness would have no end, who had grown thin believing. Kneeling, his cheeks lit by tears, he watched over his blameless girl who slept like a child, his woman whom he had hurt. 'I will never, ever hurt you again,' he told her to himself, 'and I will love you with all my might and you shall be happy, you'll see.'

CHAPTER 89

Next morning, after a melancholy shave, he lit a cigarette to get himself back into an optimistic frame of mind, and forced a smile to convince himself that he had found the answer. Of course! They must sever all social links, because constantly rubbing shoulders with other people reminded them that they were outcasts and therefore alone, walled up inside their love. If they had a house of their own, they would have no contact with others and wouldn't be troubled by the contrast, by reminders of the life which went on outside. They would live in their own world and, seeing nobody, would not need other people. And he would do all he could to make their house a temple where he could set before her a life of perfect love.

It was all quite absurd, but he had gone too far down the road to turn back now. The major task ahead was to make her happy, he told himself as he strode breezily into her room, twirling his beads to make himself look keen, like a man whose mind was made up. He kissed her at once on her forehead, her eyes, her hands, to infect her with hope.

'Hello, my angel, my only love! It's all over, *finis*, I'm cured: no more scenes ever again! All things are new made! Glory to God in the Highest! And there's something else,' he announced, with well-feigned exhilaration, and he took both her hands in his. 'Listen. How would you like to have a house of our very own? The one you looked at the other day and said was sweet?'

'Near La Baumette? The one that's to let?'

'Yes, my love.'

She nuzzled up close to him and laughed in the elusive, tremulous way she had that night at the Ritz. A house of their own! And one with such a pretty name: Belle de Mai! (She could already picture herself as Queen of the May.) He looked at her, touched by her resilience, by her youthful capacity for hope! She leaped out of bed.

'I want to see it at once! Let me have my bath! Off you go, darling! Order the taxi while you're waiting! It won't take me long to dress!'

The moment the taxi drew up outside Belle de Mai she fell head over heels in love with the house, which backed on to a modest pine-grove and boasted a lawn which ran down to the sea edge. Oh, those four cypresses! After a tour, punctuated by much excited whooping, of this gem of a house, she came running back to him, covered his hand with kisses, complained that he wasn't admiring it enough, that he wasn't saying with sufficient enthusiasm that Belle de Mai was fairyland, declared that she already felt utterly at home and read out what was written on the notice fixed to the gate. 'House to Let. All enquiries to Maître Simiand, Solicitor, Cannes.' She dragged him by the hand to make him hurry up, threw herself into the taxi, and kissed his silk cuffs. Imitating the doll-woman at the Royal, she sang out that what she wanted was Belle de Mai, so there, Belle de Mai, yah-boo-sucks!

Still dragging him by the hand, she went up the steps leading to the solicitor's office two at a time. Oh, it was the only house worthy of them! She burst through the door and spoke to the oldest of the clerks. 'We'd like to rent Belle de Mai.' The elderly chief clerk, a tall smoked eel in a celluloid wing-collar, asked what this Belle de Mai was. She explained, said that she and her husband had decided that the house was just what they wanted and that they would like to take it. The way the chief clerk shook his head filled her with panic. Was it already let? 'I couldn't rightly say.'

They sat down. 'Perhaps we could buy it?' she said, prompting him. He did not have time to reply, because at that moment Maître Simiand himself suddenly appeared at the door of his office, perfectly groomed and exuding clouds of royal fern. He made way for them with the courteous deference which earned him the lasting respect of

773

his fellow citizens until the day when, several years later, he was charged with misappropriation and fraud. She sat facing him across his Empire desk and, shaking slightly, spoke her little speech, giving a delightful description of the house, to which the young solicitor listened appreciatively.

'I felt immediately at home there,' the poor girl repeated. (She's happy now she's having dealings with someone other than myself, thought Solal.) 'The two cypresses on either side are absolutely marvellous,' she said with a social smile. (A whiff of adultery there, thought Solal.) 'I hope it isn't let already?'

'Well, negotiations are under way with a second party.'

Solal saw through his little game but said nothing. The rent would be put up, but what did it matter? It wasn't much of a sacrifice to pay slightly over the odds so that she could have the pleasure of a sham conversation with someone other than the hotel waiter or her hairdresser, someone almost of her own sort. Go ahead, make the most of it, my darling.

'But nothing's been signed yet?' she asked.

'No, but the party concerned are personal friends of the owner.'

She wanted to say something bold along the lines of business is business, but didn't dare. Instead, she made do with remarking that she would be prepared to offer more than these other people, well just a little more. He watched his innocent girl, who was born to be swindled. Who would look after her later on, when he was no longer there to do it?

'Such is not our practice,' said the solicitor with impressive coolness. 'The figure quoted to the other party is forty-eight thousand francs per annum. In all honesty, we cannot ask you to pay more. That is the price. (He normally asks for half that and gets no takers, thought Solal.) But the other party are having second thoughts, hedging, haggling.'

'I see,' she said with a smile. 'But don't you think it's rather expensive?'

'Not at all.'

'And you're quite sure that the house is satisfactory from all points of view?' asked the woman of business. 'Because we haven't seen round inside yet.'

'Quite sure.' (She inhaled contentedly, sensing that here was a bargain not to be missed.)

'We'll take it.'

The solicitor yielded with a nod, and she told herself that really it wasn't expensive at all. In fact everything was cheap in France, since all you had to do was divide by six. Eight thousand Swiss francs wasn't dear. Excellent, a snip. The solicitor concluded their business by saying that the key was with the estate agent, who was located just a few doors up the street, at number twenty. He would draw up a tenancy agreement for them to sign, it being understood, of course, that a full year's rental was to be paid in advance.

The agent was a vast, verbose shark on whose desk were a three-inch shell, a picture of Marshal Foch and a statuette of the Virgin, all designed to inspire confidence. The solicitor had just phoned and he knew what sort of people he was dealing with. While his mute, myopic assistant sat at his desk opposite, beavering away with a quill beneath the low, smoke-begrimed ceiling, he spent a quarter of an hour drawing freely on a copious stock of platitudes, expatiating on divers complex matters concerning the leasing and sale of property which had absolutely nothing to do with Belle de Mai. In the end he declared that, unfortunately for them, the other party had telephoned him that very morning to say that they were prepared to accept the figure of forty-eight thousand, a development of which Maître Simiand was unaware. And naturally, given that they were friends of the owner. 'Oh no,' she murmured. There might just be a way round it, added the agent. Yes, their rivals were baulking at the prospect of having to pay the land tax, though it came to a mere six thousand francs. The estate shark would have quoted a somewhat higher figure had it not been for the impenetrable attitude of the husband. He was wondering whether he was really as stupid as he seemed, or whether he would put his oar in at the last moment.

'Done,' she said.

The agent inserted his little finger into one ear and asked Ariane if the fifty-four thousand francs could be paid then and there. She turned to Solal, who reached for his cheque-book.

'And naturally, there are the costs of drawing up the tenancy agreement, the registration fee and sundry other expenses to be considered.'

'Naturally,' she said, 'I quite see that. So can we sign the contract at once? Because we'd like the key so that we can see inside.'

She jumped out of the taxi, opened the gate, unlocked the front door, and stopped dead in her tracks, bowled over by the spacious hall and the high gallery which circled it. Oh, she would turn Belle de Mai into such a delightful home that it would be a pleasure to live there. And it was such a fine day too! The first of December and the sun so hot! She took both his hands and, leaning her head back, made him wheel round and round with her until the two of them were quite dizzy. She stopped suddenly, overwhelmed by a feeling of tender compassion for him. He had whirled round clumsily, like a child being taught a marvellous new game, and it struck her that he could not have played much when he was a boy.

They wandered from room to room. Forcefully, her voice ringing loudly through the empty, echoing rooms, she pointed out where their bedrooms would be, and the drawing-room and the dining-room. When she realized that there were two bathrooms, she gave a delighted little shriek. Really, fifty-four thousand francs, which was nine thousand francs in real money, wasn't a lot. After a quick inspection of the cellar and the attic, she decided they must go back to Cannes to choose furniture and carpets, or at least get some ideas.

'We'll spend the whole afternoon at it, all right?' she said in the taxi. 'That won't be too long, because there are so many things that need to be decided. But first we'll have lunch. I'm absolutely ravenous! Look, darling, let's not go to the Moscow this time. We'll go to some little restaurant, if that's all right with you. To start, I'll order a huge *omelette aux fines herbes*, or maybe one with ham in it, but only if you promise you won't think too badly of me. Happy? Me too! Ecstatic!'

That evening at the Royal they talked endlessly about their very own Belle de Mai, sang its praises, discussed the furniture they'd already bought, drew up plans, and kissed a great deal. At midnight they separated. But shortly afterwards he heard a shy knock, saw a sheet of paper which had been slipped under his door, picked it up, and read: 'Doth it please my Lord to share the bed of his servant?'

An hour later, as he slept pressed up against her, she was busily thinking in the dark. It would have to look very grand, very attractive inside, because they'd be spending the rest of their lives there. Two bathrooms was perfect, and Sol's room connected with one of them. It was annoying that there was only one lavatory, which would be awkward. That's it, have a lavatory installed in each of the bathrooms while Sol was away. Yes, get him out of the way while the house was being done out, so that she would have peace to get on with various not very romantic improvements. Oh yes, an absolute must, a lavatory in each bathroom, that was the answer. That way there'd be no embarrassing moments.

At eight next morning, already bathed and dressed, they went downstairs. After having breakfast in the dining-room, much to the surprise of the hotel staff, they set off. Taking his arm, she reverted to her brisk, social voice.

'Darling, I have something serious to say, which is that I'd rather you left everything to me and didn't see the work on the house being done in bits and pieces. You see, I want it to be like a wave of a magic wand for you, I don't want you back here until everything is good and ready. I'll wire Mariette and ask her to come at once. She'll come all right. She does everything I want her to. But you mustn't stay in Agay, because if you do we'll be tempted to see each other.'

And besides, though this she did not mention to him, there was the crucial issue of the two lavatories which were to be put in, and she must make absolutely sure that he didn't get wind of the scheme nor the briefest glimpse, even a distant peek, of the two china pedestals being delivered. And, furthermore, she also wanted to feel free to be a bit hoydenish and wind-blown while everything was being got ready, to feel she could gossip with Mariette without anyone peering over her shoulder, and polish and scrub to her heart's content: it would be such fun.

'So, darling, you'll shoot off to Cannes tonight, won't you? You'll stay at the best hotel, of course: you can let me know which. I'll give you a ring as soon as everything is ready here. I reckon it'll all be done and dusted in a couple of weeks. We won't write, and it will be heavenly when you get back! But now I've got something rather important to say, darling. I've made up my mind to be your Chancellor of the Exchequer. I don't want you to have to bother with money matters. Now that we have our very own house, I shall be the one who looks after the accounts.'

It was agreed that he would give her a cheque each month and that she would take care of everything. But she did not tell him that she intended to write to her bank in Geneva and ask them to send a hundred thousand French francs after they'd sold the requisite number of shares. In this way, by using the Chancellor of the Exchequer subterfuge, she would be able to contribute to their expenses without his being any the wiser. Was a hundred thousand French francs too much? No, not when it was divided by six. Oh yes, she'd turn the house into a temple where they would lead a life devoted entirely to love. She took his hand in hers and looked at him with all her soul.

'Darling, this is the beginning of a new life, our real life, isn't it?'

CHAPTER 90

'How time flies, fourth of Febbry today, and Febbry hath only twenty
eight, like it says in the rhyme, and is the bad-temperedest month of
the lot, two months I been here already at this Agay place, they don't
give poor ole Mariette a second thought unless they need her, and she
was lucky to catch me before I left Geneva, if she'd sent that
terrygram a week later she'd have found me gone seeing as how I had
this fancy to pop up to see my sister and have a look round Paris 'cos
I'm very strong on Family, why on the very morning the terrygram
come I was only saying just before the terrygram was delivered I was
saying to meself Mariette you got to enjoy yourself a bit 'cos you're
not getting any younger it'll soon be time you started thinking of
getting measured for your box there are times when I'm right down
in the dumps you'd never believe how low I get, anyroad I was ready
for the off seeing as how I'd already handed ole Face-Ache my notice
what with Monsieur Adrien being over his upset and just about to go
off to Africa on his political travels it was mainly on his account that
I'd stayed so long but to have to put up with ole Face-Ache going on
all hours of the day saying how Madame Ariane had no morals
calling her a tart was the bally limit, of course it upset me to go on
account of Monsieur Hippolyte never a word from him against
Madame Ariane, but that's how things go love's got a mind of its
own love's a bird that grows up wild like the song says, but anyroad
as soon as Monsieur Adrien went off to Africa I felt easy in my mind
that I could go for a bit of a look round Paris and have a chance to
get over the turn I had what a shock seeing him there with his head

covered in blood, 'cos late that night I thought to meself it's no good I just gotter go and find out how things stand, it's what they call a premonitition 'cos when I'd been as usual that morning not suspecting anything was up not even knowing he was back he said he didn't need me 'cos Madame Ariane had gone away and was never coming back then he shut the door in my face but in a sad way not an angry way, all day long I kept asking meself shall I go back or shan't I but I didn't dare go on account of the look on his face and then about eleven at night I thought it's no good I'm going, so I get dressed quickly put my hat on the black one that's so pretty and I fetch the key she gave me a key so as I wouldn't go ringing the doorbell of a morning, in I go everything quiet as the grave nobody downstairs so I go upstairs, nobody in his room, I go into his washroom, there he was, poor lad, on his knees on the floor looking like a corpse with his head covered in blood on the stool poor lamb, it fair knocked the stuffing out of me, the gun on the floor and me not knowing what to do for the best, I thought get the police so I tried to call the police straight away on the terryphone but terryphones are awkward beggars the receiver thing shook in my hand something terrible so quick I run round to get my friend who works as a maid for the neighbours next door, no oil-painting but ever so nice and well-spoken, she throws a coat over her nightie and runs back with me to the scene of the tragedy to phone for the police, she's ejucated knows how to put things, then for the doctor as a matter of fact it was the one from Cologny just up the road which was handy, Dr Saladin, nice-looking man, anyway to cut a long story short the doctor just took one look at him and saw he wasn't a goner but he needed treating pretty sharpish, so quick send for the ambulance, in fact it was my idea to call round that saved his bacon, You saved his life, my dear, Dr Saladin says to me, his very words, now just picture the sort of tizz I was in being caught up in the tragical middle of a love story gone wrong but you gotter hand it to me I was quick off the mark with the right ideas such as telling my friend the maid to send a terrygram straight away to ole Face-Ache to say she was to come back spit-spot on the double, she was away in Belgium looking after some rich ole biddy prob'ly to get her name put down in her will she don't miss a trick that one take it from me, but anyroad she comes rushing back 'cos give her her due she thinks the sun shines out of her Didi, you should have heard her going on something chronic about Madame Ariane to Monsieur Hippolyte, a tigress wasn't in it, of course I had to tell Madame Ariane all about it 'cos she hadn't heard a thing seeing as how nobody knew her address, so the minute I got here I'd hardly got my coat off before she was asking me how Monsieur Adrien was, meaning how he'd taken her going off like that, 'cos she didn't know anything about the tragedy of love at the end of its tether, asking after his health looking a bit shamefaced but caring too, so then I just had to tell her everything 'cos she had no idea, his head covered in blood, the whole lot, the bullet in his temple, just think, but it hadn't gone in very deep, she wept buckets, eyes all puffy and red as if they'd had paprika put in them, the strong sort, blowing her nose all the time blaming herself, you see her conscience was telling her it was all her fault, the wages of sin as they say, anyroad I calmed her down, he's fine now I said, I even told a lie by making out he'd put on weight, she said that Monsieur Solal mustn't know, that I wasn't to mention the tragedy, so as I was saying her terrygram upset all my plans seeing as how after Paris at my sister's I was counting on finding meself a new position got to I need the money and besides I get so down when I don't keep on the go, oh I wouldn't have liked being a princess, I think I'll make meself a nice little cup of coffee, so I was thinking that when I got back from my sister's, she's got a very nice job, caretaker for the Aga Khan, I'd look around for another position I was thinking that even before I went off to Paris to see my sister, we're very fond of each other closer than twins we are and besides there was the business of the Spaniard and I wanted to see her to talk it through with her 'cos my niece has been put in the family way by a Spaniard he's a waiter in a café very dark-skinned seems he's got a bit of the Arab in the background and now that he's got her into trouble he don't want to marry her they're all the same so I says to meself I'd better go and sort it out, give the dago a piece of my mind seems he's an ugly devil got hair all over him even got hairs sprouting in his ears, that's how they like them these days, that's modern girls for you, now if you'd have seen my hubby, but anyway as I was saying even before I went off to Paris to sort out this business of my niece I was thinking of going over and telling Monsieur Agrippa that when I got back from seeing my sister and her daughter who's been left in the lurch by a rotter, my niece that is, that I'd be free to do for him but only on condition that he gives that Euphrosine the elbow because I just won't be bossed around by a jumped-up nobody, but just then Madame Ariane's terrygram arrives and when it comes to choosing she'll always come first 'cos I powdered her little botty when she was a baby, I'd hardly got the terrygram when I thought quick get yourself round to Monsieur Agrippa's and tell him his niece's address but then I says to meself hold your horses my girl in the first place it's delicate seeing as how Monsieur Agrippa is so very proper and in the second maybe she don't want anybody to know where she's gone to not even her uncle but later on she told me she'd written to him and put him in the picture, it must have been a shock to the poor man what with him being so proper and religious to find out that his darling niece had been carrying on something chronic, anyway to get back to the beginning and what I was saying about how quick off the mark I am, speedy is my middle name, the day after I got the terrygram I was already settled in here helping Madame Ariane in all sorts of ways, chipping in with advice about furniture fittings and carpets, she had to have the finest sheets, I daren't think of the cost, and all this time he didn't show his face seeing as how she'd told him he was to stay in Cannes, his lordship was above such things, couldn't bear to see all the scrubbing and that, but she did go to Cannes twice, no I tell a lie, three times she went, for a bit of slap and tickle of course though she reckoned it was to talk about furniture, but not more than three times seeing as how she was so set on getting everything good and ready here for her fancy man, everything had to look very grand, just like on the stage, what took most time was the two extra lavs, no shut up don't make me larf, I'll tell you all about it, I don't like it here, all that sea water in wintertime is ever so gloomy, good job they got the central heating 'cos though it's supposed to be hot all the time on your Riviera it's not true, with the wind they get here take it from me hot it isn't, and besides it's too near the sea, I just can't get used to the noise of the sea, at night it's like dead men singing, I came here for her sake, good job the hotel I'm staying in said I could have a room without board, oh it's quite small, a sort of working man's hotel, it's just got six rooms and a café downstairs, good job it's a fair way from the sea, you don't get the noise of the waves yowling like souls in torment, it was her that didn't want me here at night, said there wasn't enough room, oh there's plenty of room but I know the real reason, she wants her big romance with tall dark Mr Handsome to be a secret, with nobody to see them at night when they're spooning and lovey-doveying, you know love's old dream love's sweet dream, I'll tell you all about it, there's heaps of time 'cos I got everything ready and besides Romeo and Juliet are out for a stroll, but there's stacks of work to do here I even worked Xmas Day just like it was an ordinary day, I even come in on Sundays, 'cos everything has to be just so for his nibs the Prince of Passion, just like on the films, poor Didi nobody ever did as much for you, though come to think of it if I didn't come in on a Sunday I'd only get bored all by meself in my room, 'cos I haven't got to know a soul in the hotel don't want to they're a common lot, but as I was saying every day it's temple-of-love stuff with the pair of them priesting and priestessing nineteen to the dozen, and the way she runs round tending him hand and foot, always telling me mind he don't see that, mind he don't find out, watch out for this, watch out for that, he don't like this and he don't like that, oh no nobody ever got so soppy over poor ole Didi though he was always nice to me always had a kind word for me, but Prince Charming don't talk to me much don't even look at me, mark my words her uncle, I mean Monsieur Agrippa, will leave her everything house the lot in his will, the house at Champel that is, and she'll sell it see if she don't, 'cos she won't dare go back to Geneva to live, she'll get thousands and thousands for it seeing as how it's the old style of house very grand and all them grounds and in the poshest part of town land don't come cheap, not that she'll get all it fetches seeing as how the bank and lawyers and the rest have sticky fingers and eyes that's bigger than their bellies, to my mind Monsieur Agrippa hasn't got long to go, he's as thin as I don't know thin as a stick of wild asparagus the spindly green sort that's got more flavour than the cultivated kind, to my mind going by how he behaves he can't ever have touched a woman, oh no he's not got long for this world, so when it comes down to it even doctors snuff it for all the knowing airs they put on, 'cos when your time is up it's up, ah poor ole

Mariette your turn will come, you didn't make the most of your chances when you were young and now you've got big swelled-up legs like a elephant in the circus, but as I was saying she'd hardly sent the terrygram before I was here, that was on the fourth of December, the pair of us set to and by the eighteenth everything was shipshape mind you she was handing out the tips right left and centre I just shut my eyes so I wouldn't know how much she was giving away, both of us slaved harder than darky women, everything looks fine now all except the kitchen which is too white makes the place look like a horspital, I don't care for it meself, and another thing, that electric stove isn't much cop for frying on, and you can't turn the heat down low low like you can with gas, and it takes ages to get hot, and then the hotplate stays hot as anything after you've finished with it, no I can't get on with it, but I didn't say anything, he who pays the piper calls the tune like Monsieur Pasteur used to say, the drawing-room the dining-room all very tasty in a plain sort of way, but no ornaments and suchlike, knick-knacks do cheer a place up make it cosy, now his bedroom is all white carpet and white velvet I don't care for that, and the lighting is the kind where you can't see where the bulbs are, and as for that bed of hers it's so low I get backache with bending over when I make it, it's a proper musolino-leum, very showy you could get a couple of camels in it and still have room left, it beats me, the best thing about this place is that every-thing's on the ground floor, no stairs and that suits my various veins, anyway on the eighteenth, an hour before he was due back Are you comfy in your room at the hotel Mariette she says to me, no shut up now it was her way of leading up to getting me out of the way, Yes says I but being one to speak my mind I says I'd have rather been staying here 'specially 'cos me being there means you've got the hotel bill to pay, Yes but there's no room here she says, I didn't say anything to that but it's not true that there isn't room here, in the first place there's the box-room, and in the second there's the attic which could have been done out very nice except that to get there it's ladder not stairs, Get away with you you two-faced little monkey says I to meself, that's all flummery the truth of the matter is that you don't want me around spying on your secret kissing and canoodling when he gets back, Look Mariette says she he'll be here in half an

hour so I'm giving you the rest of the day off, But I don't mind
staying says I, so then she says It's a special day we haven't seen each
other for two weeks, I could have said And what about the three
times you went to see him then but I didn't lower meself, Very well
says I, all dignified like, You can have your dinner at the hotel says
she, I can't stand throwing money down the drain says I politely, you
know how nose-in-the-air I can be, I'll have a bit of cheese on my
way out says I, my pride was hurt you see, being turned out like that
as if I was some stranger, 'cos in my mind's eye lying in bed at night,
as good as the flicks is my bed, I'd been seeing the two of us there on
the welcome mat together, me being part of the family in a way,
wearing my best, saying Pleased to meet you I'm sure 'cos in fact I
had yet to set eyes on her handsome caballero, anyway without more
ado I put my hat on the pretty one black with shiny spangles on and
tied the string so tight I all but throttled meself, she was taking it all
in, then I took my black-pearl handbag with A Present from the
Exhibition picked out in white pearl on it, Good-night says I and she
must have known what I was getting at 'cos I was that vexed I rushed
here all the way from Geneva almost the minute she wired for me to
come, quick hat on catch the train which I almost missed, 'cos to my
mind you were Family, I bathed and dried her when she was a baby,
patting her little baby's botty even giving her a kiss on her little
botty-bum-bum which isn't so little any more well you see she didn't
treat me like one of the family now, turning me out like a African
slave, special day indeed seeing as how they hadn't clapped eyes on
each other for a fortnight, you could have seen Sir Gorgeous every
day, but oh no Madame had to put on a show, Sir Sensitive mustn't
see this, mustn't see that before everything's hunky and dory, and me
having brought from Geneva specially for her the best piece I made
during my time at the factory, even the boss complimented me on it,
an ashtray made out of ceramic paste, very artistic, with a snake
coiled all round it looked almost alive and a frog with its mouth open
for the ash from the cigarettes, yes dried her and put talcum powder
on her morning and night, so to get my own back that night I had
dinner in the hotel café, a real slap-up do to pay her out, sardines
in oil and garlic sausage for first course, and then pig's trotters in
breadcrumbs, they had some as it happened, there was cold chicken

too but I didn't fancy any, chicken's got no taste, the only nice part of the chicken is the parson's nose, but now that's all blown over I've forgiven her, she gets such la-di-da ideas, you'd never believe, take them two washrooms, she says you gotter call them bathrooms, I always say washrooms 'cos it's where you get washed though you don't always have a bath, that's my story and I'm sticking to it so there, anyway one washroom for him with a connecting door to his bedroom and the other washroom for her done out with all mod cons as they say, but her washroom didn't have a connecting door to her bedroom, and then there was a separate lav, a convenience is what they call it, all white with luxury fittings and tiled so you could almost eat off the floor, but oh no that wasn't good enough for her she must have a special convenience for each of them, so she had one put into each washroom, so if you count the separate one that was there already that nobody uses and the servants' one in the cellar which is for me that makes four conveniences in all, no stop don't make me larf, of course I cottoned on straight away, the lavs in the two washrooms are to make sure the one don't know when the other has gone to spend a penny, or even tuppence, they can think that they've just gone to rinse their hands in the basin or take a dip in the bath seeing as how the noise of the taps drowns out everything else, but that's not all, she had an opening made in the wall and a door put in to connect her room with her washroom where she's got her convenience, it's so she can be even more secret about going to spend a penny 'cos no one will even see her going into her washroom, nobody any the wiser, I'll fox you I can spend a penny behind your back is the idea, now the way I see it there's nothing to be ashamed about in spending a penny, that's how the good Lord made us, even kings and queens go the same as me, my hubby always knew when I was going and it didn't stop us loving each other believe you me, but not her, she keeps it all a state secret and on top of that you know the flush on conveniences well she's had a special de-luxe one fitted that's silent, it's so he can't hear anything, so the romance is kept up, while she was about it she should have had a musical box thing put in singing Star of love and love's sweet light which came on when you pulled the chain, that would have been even more romantic, you've no idea all the work it made, there was three men came all the way from Nice, even worked Sundays, just think how much that cost, I looked the other way so I wouldn't see the tips she gave them to keep them sweet, of course it all took time, making the opening in Madame's wall to put in a door to the washroom, and then the conveniences to install, great big pipes to lay under the tiles on the floor of both washrooms, the Swiss say mosaics but that don't mean the same they don't speak proper French, except my friend the maid I was telling you about, she's ejucated, when she talks it's like music in your ears, and also under the beautiful parky in the hall, and then it all had to be put back straight again, and all that trouble so that his nibs wouldn't know when she's spending a penny, as I was saying every blessed day they put on a beauty parade like they was on the stage or in the pictures, you know paradise-of-love stuff, Your heart stole mine that day of rapture divine, like Monsieur Victor Hugo says in one of his pomes, they say that even when he was eighty he didn't turn his nose up at a bit of the other white whiskers or no white whiskers kept a slip of a girl locked up all to himself, had a weakness for it all his life forever chasing skirts he was, mind you his wife wasn't best pleased she got her own back she played him fast and loose, it's in a book they lent me when I was in the horspital, she knocked about with this other one who did writing too, Monsieur Sainte-Beuve he was called, funny-looking sort, and then they stay in bed all afternoon Having Relations all very hush-hush in that great big bed it's miles wide it's the size of the Place de la Concorde, and they're ever so proper with each other when they talk it's like a bishop having a natter with a cardinal, and they have baths all bally day long, and that's not counting dips in the sea, if the sun's shining they go swimming even though it's wintertime, now speaking for myself I don't care much for the sea, you can't drink it you can't wash in it 'cos you can't get a lather going with it, it don't make suds, oh I don't like it round here, it's all rocks and stones, if it was me I'd call it the Dustiera not the Riviera, and there's mosquitoes every-where, what's the use of mosquitoes, they were put on this earth to bother folks that's what, and then this wind hear it? it just goes on moaning all the blessed time, it's just like the proverb says when Febbry's calm, there'll be gusts in May, proverbs are always right, it's the wisdom of the ages, I know 'em all, one swallow don't make a summer, north winds do blow and we shall have snow, March in like a lion out like a lamb, red sky at night shepherd's delight red sky in morning shepherd's warning, winter breezes bring coughs and sneezes, if Febbry don't March then April May, ne'er cast a clout till May is out, Christmas warm Easter storm, April showers bring forth the flowers, I know all the other ones as well, I'll tell them to you some other time, haven't the heart for it today 'cos I feel down in the dumps like they say, and then the way them bells keep ringing is getting on my wick, drives me up the wall, I'm going potty in this house they carry on like lovey-dovey dolls, like as if they was acting in a play, only see each other when they're all spruced up, she wrote down all the different rings on the card you see there pinned up over that beggar of an electric stove, three shorts and one long, three longs and one short, two longs, one long, two shorts, if she thinks it's easy telling the difference when you're getting on a bit, there are rings for me and rings for them and sometimes when it's for them I think it's for me and I rush off to see what she wants and then it turns out it wasn't for me after all, there are rings for when Sir Adorable Prince wants her to come and talk but only through the door, there are rings for when she asks if she can move around the place without him seeing her 'cos she's not finished titivating yet, rings for when he answers yes, rings for when he tells her to go to her room 'cos he's got to fetch a book from the drawing-room and isn't what they call presentable seeing as how he hasn't shaved, so then she rings in reply to say yes she'll go to her room, rings for when he wants to let her know he's back in his room and now she can move about even if she does look a fright seeing as how he won't catch sight of her, and every time it rings I jump out of my boots, at first there were times when I had to put my hand in my mouth I got such a fright, what the dickens is going on I thought, the house is full of electric ghosts, but now I'm used to it, it makes me larf, I dance the polka in my kitchen when they start their ringing, you'd think you were in a bell-factory and all the bells were being tested to see if they're working proper, they have rings for when he gets back from his walks, he's a good-looking man no question a real good-looking man, he rings the front doorbell four times so she can scoot off and hide if she hasn't powdered her nose enough, then there's a ring for when she asks if she can come and talk through the door, I mean the door to his room, but without him seeing her 'cos she's not finished making herself beautiful enough, there's a ring for when he says yes, and that means he has to stay shut up a prisoner of love in his cage and keep out of the way sometimes until lunch-time while Madame goes round giving orders in a white overall you'd think she was a nurse in a horspital, oh I'd hate to die in horspital, they're so unfeeling don't care about folk they think they're better than you are 'cos they aren't ill but just you wait your turn will come, and then sometimes she clarts her face up with what they call a mask, to make her look pretty, it scares me when I see her walking around with that stuff on her face not talking, looks like mud the same colour as the battleships you can see from here, I'm against war, all it does is make a lot of folk unhappy on both sides, and the big noises just stay put and shout to the young ones Come on lads show 'em what you're made of you gotter lay down your lives for your country that's the spirit, you gotter be heroes and fight for your country we'll give you a lovely grave with a bit of a flambo on top from a gas ring that never goes out not that it'll do you much good but us big noises will just snuggle down here in our comfy billets, and then there's three longs for when she calls me to do her room, but she stays in it in case she's seen by Sir Charlie Darling 'cos he's all shaved and ready and has let her know that he's ready and presentable but she's not presentable seeing as how she's not tarted her face up enough, so three longs, oh and a lot of others that I can never remember, and then if she's got a bit of a cold she won't come out at all if you please so that he won't see her looking a fright and she won't see him again until her cold's passed off, which means me taking her food to her room on a tray so she's a prisoner of love too, and sometimes when the bells aren't working on account of the electricity being off it's Go and ask if it's all right for me to come out, 'cos she won't let herself be seen unless she's properly dolled up, and it's the same thing with him, so then I have to rush around from one to the other like a racehorse skidding and sliding about in my slippers and sometimes I shout gee-up horsey to keep myself going, quick now off you go and tell Madame not to show her face seeing as how Sir Gorgeous has to come out for something, now and then a bit of tripping and sliding does me good, bucks me up no end, but then poor ole Mariette's got to go scurrying off to tell Sir Handsome righty-oh Madame won't come out now but would Sir Handsome let her know when she can 'cos Madame has got to go to Cannes to do some shopping and mind you tell him she's very sorry it's urgent and don't forget to say very sorry, 'cos that's how it is with them polite as kings at court they are, in the mornings it's all toing and froing, like in the animal house at the circus where they raise the cage doors to let the wild creatures in and out, 'cos the lion must never be with the tiger, no hobnobbing between lions and tigers allowed, they're born enemies, oh but sometimes I just gotter larf, one time she had something special to say urgent couldn't wait but neither of them was presentable enough yet seeing as how it was so early in the morning, so she slips on her fetchingest dress and goes into his room backwards to have a hush-hush palaver with him, I don't miss a trick of course I don't let on oh yes I have a squint through the keyhole now and then just to keep abreast, anyway in she reverses and talks with her back to him, that way get it she didn't see him looking a fright and he didn't see her looking a fright, or put it this way he could see her all right but from the back and the back view don't matter like the view from the front, specially the face, but they don't carry on like that very often, only the twice, what it all adds up to you see is that they don't like it when one of them knows that the other one isn't looking what they call implacable, that means not a hair out of place from head to foot, another time I saw her, through the keyhole again it was, nothing else for it I'm entitled I'm duty-bound to keep an eye open so she don't come to no harm if they was ever to have a tiff besides it's not much fun being here, there's times when I get really low, I feel all alone forgotten by the whole yuman race as they say, well anyway I seen her with this blindfold over her eyes, 'cos she had to talk to him but wasn't allowed to see him, and he was guiding her like she was blind so she could sit down on a chair, she had a blindfold on 'cos this time she was presentable and it was him that wasn't presentable as they call it, so there she was on her chair with this blindfold on looking like a sleepwalker or one of them gyppos you meet in the street and they tell your fortune sometimes what they tell you really happens especially Madame Petroska she's got the gift, but the sight of her there talking so po-faced with a blindfold over her eyes well it was so daft I couldn't stand it no more and had to take myself off to my pantry I was nearly splitting my sides I opened the chute for the kitchen-waste wide and stuck my head in it so I could let it all out in peace without them hearing, p'raps one of these days I'll put a blindfold over my eyes like Madame Petroska so I can't see his nibs, but then how on earth could I see to wax the floor and polish the parky, but that time he was away on his travels she really let her hair down with me in the kitchen, had a good ole plateful of sauerkraut with smoked cutlets sausage salt bacon the lot enjoyed it licked her chops afterwards but said on no account was his lordship to know she'd been eating sauerkraut, and they're always going at it like fighting lobsters in that great bed, I can hear them, a little of what you fancy does you good but you can have too much of a good thing, and the sheets on the big bed I've got to change them two three times a week on washing days there's three of us on with it me and two women who come in, but mark you when it's just the two of us together of a morning she's ever so sweet, we have a laugh real good pals thick as thieves, and with her chattering nineteen to the dozen so you'd think she'd been inoculated with a grammyphone needle, no side with her, but when I wait on the pair of them at table she looks down her nose at me like a princess as if I was just a potato peeling, oh mark my words she's not easy when Mr Tall-and-Curly's about, the other day she went red as a beetroot got up on her high hobby-horse 'cos I'd said while they was having dinner that the plumber had made a rattling good job of her lav, she could have strangled me, and now I haven't to speak when they're having their dinners, not even to tell her we're out of onions, and when I'm serving out I gotter be careful not to cough, and I'm not allowed to wait at table in my slippers, not allowed to say anything about the meat, even if it's overcooked and it's not my fault they was late prob'ly on account of overdoing it in that king-size bed, the upshot being that I gotter have a face like the waiters you see in posh hotels, I put my poker face on before I go into the dining-room I start by closing my mouth tight as if I'm going to a funeral though sometimes I want to laugh fit to bust I get red as a beetroot just as I'm going in through the door and there they are, sat at the table although not five minutes before they were giving the bed-springs a good going-over, at table they're so la-di-da it makes me see red, saying yes please no thank you, talking just like they was two presidents of France, and with her just taking little mouthfuls that are hardly worth bothering with, but in the mornings if we're having our breakfast coffee together she tucks into enough bread and butter and jam to sink a hippopotamouse, and she takes good care to keep the kitchen door shut when she's having her coffee with me 'cos she's dead scared he might see her simpling herself by having breakfast with her ole Mariette who changed her nappies when she was little, and sometimes all of a sudden she rushes in panic-stricken, quick I gotter drop everything and iron one of her silk dresses 'cos them nights-of-passion dresses of hers mustn't be creased they're a bit like blouses but also like tailor-made evening gowns, I'll have to show you, then it's on with the music on the grammyphone it gives me the willies when they shut themselves away in their room to worship love in the temple, but there won't be any kiddies, no fear of that, I know what I'm talking about I keep my eyes skinned, and then when they've finished their goings-on they go to sleep, then they wake up again, and they have baths, they go out for walks and they always wear their best, and then for ole Mariette it's off with you and get that master bedroom tidied up, and sometimes when I collect her dirty smalls I've gotter hide them in my apron for fear the king of kings might come out of his room at the wrong moment and catch sight of her dirty smalls though her smalls are always clean, poor Didi you had your good points after all, and if I go for his nibs's underthings she mustn't ever see any of them before they go into the washing-machine, I can't get on with these newfangled washers you know I liked the old ones better they were straightforward, his nibs's things aren't ever dirty either, mind you I'm not allowed to say dirty underwear to her if he's about or might hear, I mustn't say dirty either, If you must mention the linen she tells me say soiled, and if now and again she gives me a hand about the house, folding sheets or whatever, it's always got to be done on the sly, and when it's not bed it's bath and titivating and the rest of it, and they only use words like you find in books, always so polite and smiling you'd think there was something the matter with them, never a tiff never a pet name, p'raps they'll go on play-acting Great Love Scenes and the rest of the tommy-rot until the pair of them grow white whiskers, now I say it isn't right, it's no sort of life, and for a man it's not healthy, a man's not got a woman's stamina, it's a medical fact, and what I can't forgive is the way she's so nice to me when it's just the two of us, talking about the housework saying how well I cope, how I'm ever so good at keeping the dust down, dust's something you gotter do battle with every blessed day, anyway taking an interest in everything like a lady should, but once Sir Priceless shows his face it's goodbye to all that she looks down her nose at me and puts on her face like a statue, I don't exist, and what really gets me is how they never kiss each other if I'm there, it's as if they was saying You don't count, now I'd thought everything would be quite different, if I wasn't so fond of her I wouldn't stay here another minute, why on earth don't they ever say nice things to each other when I'm there, instead of which they go off serious as bishops for their carryings-on in their musolinoleum, and me forever stuck in the kitchen like in prison while they're playing riddles upstairs in ole Charlemagne's bedroom, and all the time they're in there the grammyphone's blaring so if they do ever have a kiddy he'll be a big opera singer you can take my word for it, and all that blindman's buff carry-on Come in but close your eyes I'm not presentable turn round, if that's love then I want no part of it, why me and my hubby would have rather had to spend a penny together than be parted and that's what real love is say I. Watch out, they're coming.'

CHAPTER 91

The days of exquisite love uncoiled slowly, each one like the one before. The two supreme lovers never met in the morning, which was set aside by Ariane for domestic duties. Ever determined to provide the man she loved with a setting characterized by order and beauty, she gave Mariette her instructions, oversaw all cleaning operations, drew up menus, wrote lists for tradesmen, and saw to the flower arrangements. She came and went freely, for they had agreed that from the moment she gave two rings from her room he wasn't to show his face. He in turn was to respond with two rings to confirm that he had heard and thus ensure that she ran no risk of being taken unawares in a too-too-shaming state of aesthetic disarray. Most days he simply stayed out of the way until lunch-time while Ariane, not yet bathed and hair not done, moved hither and thither in a white housecoat conscientiously discharging her scene-setting function.

At the end of the morning, after issuing her final instructions, she would repair to her room and read a literary magazine or a novel praised by the critics or a few pages of a history of philosophy. All this she did for his sake, so that she might have intellectual conversations with him. When she'd finished reading, she would stretch out on the sofa, empty her thoughts of all material considerations, close her eyes, and force herself to concentrate on their love, so that her mind would be protean and cleansed, two of her favourite words, so that she would exist only for him when she saw him again. When she'd had her bath, she would seek him out, hair set and with perfumes anointed. And then would unfurl what she called their 'Prime Time'. Gravely he would kiss her hand, in full knowledge of how false and absurd was the life they led. After lunch, if he sensed that a move in the direction of sexual congress was called for on psychological grounds, he would say that he would like to lie next to her for a while, for there were proprieties to respect. She would take his meaning and kiss his hand. With a little song of victory in her heart she would say: 'I'll call you', and go to her room. There she closed the shutters, drew the curtains, covered her bedside lamp with a red scarf to create a suitably voluptuous atmosphere but also perhaps to neutralize any post-prandial flushing of her cheek, undressed, covered her nakedness with a robe of love, a kind of silky peplum designed by herself and intended to be put on so that it could be taken off, ensured that she was unimpeachable in her beauty, then slipped on her finger the platinum wedding ring she had asked him to buy her, wound up the ghastly gramophone, and the Mozart aria would go forth just as it used to at the Royal. Then he would make his entrance, a rather reluctant priest of love, sometimes biting his lip to hold back a fit of giggles, and the priestess in her consecrated robes would tense the muscles of her jaw as a way of convincing herself that desire moved within her. 'My pet lamb,' she had murmured one day as she undressed him slowly. 'Pet lamb, bed-lamb. To the bed-slaughter,' he had replied to himself. A feeble retaliation.

For the wretched girl was so damned precious. She used such choice language, even when she had no clothes on. In the tender and all too familiar remarks which followed what she called a 'consecration', the word 'ecstasy' had always to figure, because it was more elevated. Oh how Solal squirmed whenever she said in tones verging on the stern: 'Hold back, let's know ecstasy together!' It made him blush in the red-tinged semi-dark, though he was genuinely touched by her concern to preserve intact something which gave life a real point, the simultaneousness which she interpreted as an indication that love was still alive.

Yes, she got through enormous quantities of choice words at Belle de Mai. For instance, she said 'centre' rather than use another word which she considered too medical. And so on, and he felt ashamed. He also felt ashamed of the kiss on the forehead she gave him after each aforementioned ecstasy, which inwardly, imitating the accent of a famous clown, he took pathetic pleasure in pronouncing eggstasy. It's to demonstrate what colossal amounts of soul have gone into it, he would muse after the peck on his forehead, and then would feel instantly contrite and silently ask his poor girl to forgive him, for she genuinely yearned after style, fine feeling and beauty, especially beauty, which they sprayed over areas where life was extinct.

At the end of the afternoon they would take a stroll or drive over to Cannes. Then they returned home. After a candlelit dinner, he wearing dinner-jacket and she in an evening gown, they would proceed to the drawing-room, where they admired the pointless whorl and surge of the sea framed in the bay window. Just as they had done at the Royal, they smoked expensive cigarettes and talked of lofty subjects, music or painting or the beauties of nature. Sometimes there were silences. Whenever this happened she would talk animatedly about the tiny velvet animals they'd bought at Cannes, arrange them to better effect on the table specially set aside for them, and gaze at them fondly. 'Our little world,' she would say as she stroked the little donkey which was her favourite. Heigh-ho, he thought, you have to make the most of whatever social openings come your way. Or else she would ask what he would like to go on tomorrow's menus. They would discuss this at some length, because, though she was not aware of it, she had in fact become rather greedy. Or else she would sit herself down at the piano and sing while he listened, with a faint smile on his face for the absurdity of the life they led. Or else they talked about literature. They were alarmingly interested in literature. Sombrely he chewed on the emptiness of their talk. Art was a means of communing with others, a social act, an act of fraternization. On a desert island there was neither art nor literature.

If by chance the conversation descended to some banal topic, she who stood for Values persisted in using her noble language. Which is why she always said 'photograph' never 'photo', 'cinema' not 'the pictures' and certainly not 'the flicks'. Which is also why she always referred to her lawn undergarments as her 'heavenlies', even 'pantalettes' being unspeakable. Which, lastly, is why as she was telling him one day about what one of the tradesmen had said – nothing was beneath reporting in the solitary life they led – and the man having said something about laughing fit to bust, she spelt this last word out so as not to sully her lips with it. She's becoming halfwitted, he thought. A further symptom of her mania for the noble mode: the system of rings pinned up in the kitchen for the edification of Mariette had been written out in capitals, so as not to devalue her handwriting in her lover's eyes should he, exceptionally, stray into the kitchen one day.

She would often complain of feeling tired in the evening. When this happened they took their leave of each other early. Come along, he would tell himself, get a move on, get your poor little self off to bed, you've earned it. Another day gone, he would tell himself when he was in bed, a hard day's work balancing on the high wire. But at least it's all going along smoothly for the time being, he'd say. Another day's march stolen on unhappiness.

On one of the last days in May, the gong for lunch had just sounded when he suddenly clapped his hands, once, very loudly. He'd just come up with the answer. Time for a holiday! And it would mean a break for her too! Throwing his dressing-gown over a chair, he put on his pyjama top, slipped into bed, waggled his toes contentedly, and gave the rings which summoned her to him. Entering his room, she asked him what was the matter. He closed his eyes, fighting the pain.

'Liver attack,' he murmured gloomily.

She bit her lip. It was her fault, obviously the crayfish they'd eaten last night, she and her silly notions about mayonnaise. Her eyes were hot with unhappiness. Because of her, he was in pain. She took his hand and asked if it hurt a lot. He turned two dull eyes to her, wondering how he should reply. A plain 'a bit', which would be manly and very Jack London? He opted for a silent nod of the head, slightly remote, then closed his eyes again, looking like a statue of Pain Endured. He was delighted. They now had two or three good days ahead of them. The pressure was off him, and she would have something absorbing to keep her busy. She kissed his hand.

'Shall I phone for a doctor? (A doctor who might see through the pretence? And, more seriously, a man who had an occupation other than love whom she might well be capable of fancying? He opened his eyes again and said no with a shake of his head.) I'll look after you, my darling, I know all about treating liver upsets, my aunt was a martyr to her liver. The first thing to do is to apply poultices, but you'll have to have them very hot, all right? I'll go this minute and make one,' she smiled, and she hurried off.

All through the afternoon she scampered from kitchen to bedroom bearing endless supplies of fresh poultices. Scalding her fingers, she ran all the way so that they would be as hot as possible. She was firing on all pistons, alive, with her mind fully on her task, revelling in the absence of Mariette, who had gone to Paris for the wedding of a niece. She was free to look after him all by herself, in her own way. For his part he was happy knowing that she was happy. Her poultices were too fiery and raised blisters, but how marvellous not to have to deck her with garlands of love.

And so they spent two exquisite days with no oral suctions, just affectionate pecks on the forehead. She forgot her noble style, plumped up his pillows, brought healing herbal infusions, and read to him. He enjoyed listening to her read now, for now she expected nothing of him, treated him like a sick man. He was so happy that sometimes he quite forgot to wince on cue. She scuttled about in buoyant spirits, delighted to hear that it wasn't hurting as much. He smiled when he heard her singing in the kitchen as she prepared another of her appalling poultices. Never mind the blisters and the healing teas, never mind her not allowing him to eat anything. It was a small price to pay for giving her so much happiness.

But on the third morning she became worried because the pain was not getting any better, pleaded with him to let her call the doctor, and pressed him so hard that it was agreed that if there were no sign of improvement by evening she would ring. He had no choice but to surrender. At the start of the afternoon he announced that he was cured. Their life of love would now get under way once more and the priestess of the swelling jaw muscles would oust the loving mother. Farewell herbal infusions, goodbye lovely poultices!

PART SIX

CHAPTER 92

He sat in one of the armchairs in the drawing-room, with both hands occupied with *Country Life*, a magazine to which she subscribed, peering gloomily at pictures of prize bulls and ducks. The day before yesterday, the twenty-sixth of August, they had celebrated the first anniversary of their arrival at Agay with special kisses, choicest glances, best-quality words, and a gourmet menu. A year of love at Agay, a year of nothing but love. The celebration had been her idea. She was very keen on anniversaries, she had a long list of them. What was she doing now? He turned his head. She was standing in the bay window watching the noisy crew in the garden of the house across the way playing blind man's buff. The women pretended to be afraid and let out little sexual squeals.

'Those women really are vulgar,' she said with a smile as she rejoined him, and he knew that he would have to console her, to jolly her along by being extra nice.

'You are beautiful,' he told her. 'Come and sit on my knee.'

She did not have to be asked twice, and held out her cheek for a peck. Alas, an abdominal rumbling swelled to an accompaniment of grace notes played on a double bass. It died away abruptly, and she gave a cough designed to drown and counter it retroactively with a competing diversion. He kissed her cheek naturally, as though he had noticed nothing, to lessen her embarrassment. But, following rapidly and majestically on the heels of the first, there rose a second rumble, which she camouflaged by clearing her throat. Against a third, cavernous at first but graduating through warble to rill, she fought by applying discreet but firm pressure with her hand in a vain attempt to contain and muffle. A fourth followed, in a minor key, sad and subtle. Staking her all on a change of position, she moved to an armchair facing him and said in a ringing voice that it was a lovely day. In an equally ringing voice, he said that it was a glorious day and warmed to his theme while she squirmed furtively in an attempt to find a posture which would silence the uproar provoked by the displacement of gases and juices in her blameless stomach. But to no avail, and new generations of gurgles rose thunderously from her depths, vociferous in stating their claims to be heard. He anticipated their coming, gave them a sympathetic welcome, felt for the poor girl, yet could not help but note their several characters, which ranged from the mysterious, sprightly, humble, proud, sly, and venial to the funereal. In the end she hit on the sensible ploy of standing up and rewinding the gramophone, which for once served a useful purpose. And so the Brandenburg Concerto in F major blared forth, drowning all intestinal hubbub, and Solal gave thanks for the music, the ideal damper for unseemly rumbles.

Alas, just as the last strains of the concerto for long-distance wood-saws died away, a new rumble declared itself, a king among rumbles, a beauty, shooting-starred and varied, a thing of spirals and whorls, like the capital on a Corinthian column. Others followed where it had led, and came now in twos and threes, striking great organ notes with accompaniment of bassoon, bombardon, cor anglais, flageolet, bagpipe and clarinet. Upon which she gave up the unequal struggle and said it was time she started seeing about dinner. She had two reasons for this decision, he thought. The first met an immediate need: to slip away to the kitchen and rumble in peace, with no one to hear. The second, aimed at producing a longer-term result, was to get something into her stomach in double-quick time, so as to crush and quell the rumbling, which, flattened and choked by the food ingested, would be prevented from rising to the surface, there to burst and frolic unconstrained.

'Won't be a jiffy,' she said sweetly, and made a dignified exit which made up for her humiliation.

He gave a shrug the moment the door closed behind her. Oh dear, so it was to end up listening to a sequence of abdominal growls that he had ruined his own life and also the life of an innocent whose unconscious must be feeling rather let down now that it had discovered that a grand passion was not a many-splendoured thing after all. He was quite aware that for the last few months only her conscious mind had been in love with him. Those weeks in Geneva, dodo-dead weeks of true passion, had started a myth which the poor, loyal creature had tried to live up to by playing to the hilt the role of adoring mistress. But her unconscious was now weary of the role. Poor darling! So unhappy, yet not wanting to admit it, refusing to see that their ship was on the rocks. As a result, her unhappiness showed itself as and when it could, in headaches, fits of absent-mindedness, mysterious onsets of tiredness, an enhanced love of nature and a suspect horror of snobbery. Whatever happens, never tell her the truth. It would kill her.

Their miserable life together. The pretentious ritual which meant that they saw each other only as miraculous lovers, priests and ministrators of their love, a love supposedly unchanged since those first heady days. The farcical game of seeing each other only as beautiful and nauseatingly noble, without blot or stain, always freshly bathed and always pretending to be driven by identical desires. Day after day, their grimly anaemic need for beauty, the solemn hardening of sublime, unremitting passion, like the scabs of scurvy. The bogus life which she had both wanted and organized for the preservation of what she called 'higher values', the whole pathetic farce of which she was both author and director, a brave show but a farce for all that, the farce of unalterable love, in which the poor dear girl ardently believed and which she acted out with all her soul, and he ached with pity and he admired her faith. Oh my darling, for as long as I live and breathe I shall go on acting out the farce of our love, our poor love wilting in this forced solitude, our moth-eaten love, until the ending of my days, and you will never know the truth, this I promise. Thus he spake to her in his heart.

The miserable life they led together. The shame he had felt that day in Cannes when he had observed himself sitting with her at a table on the terrace of the Casino, each silently ingesting an enormous chocolate ice with too much whipped cream. The Liégois ice-cream had been his idea. And in this wise did they find consolation for their life: they overate. Though she was not aware of it, she too was seeking ways of curing the beriberi of love. The ludicrous erotic teasing, her constant recourse to the full-length mirror, baths, kissing beneath the pines, and all the other fruits of the poor creature's ingenuity. 'Darling, it's so hot today and I'm not wearing a thing under my dress.' It made his teeth ache with shame and pity. Or else, as she read Proust to him, she would cross her legs too high while he told himself that a discussion with half a dozen of the cretins who worked at the League of Nations would have had a damn sight more red corpuscles in it. An exchange of simpering inanities, of course, but at least it would have been shared with an inanely smiling brother, a moron but still a brother, a brother indispensable. What was the point of Proust, what was the point of knowing what men did and thought if you had stopped living in their midst? Poor sweet, she went on reading and crossed her legs even higher. For his part, Proustian appraisals of the ways of the fashionable crowd made him feel queasy, and, as one of the excluded, it pained him to have to sit and listen to base but serviceable hints for getting on in society. 'Proust was a homosexual snob and his chatter bores me,' he would say, and to force her to make herself decent, would suggest a game of chess. She would stand up to get the board and the hem of her dress would come down again. Saved! Gone, those flashing thighs!

The miserable life they led. Sometimes he would force himself to be spiteful, though he had no wish to be spiteful, but their love had to be made exciting, turned into an interesting drama, with surprise twists, misunderstandings and making up. He also resorted to giving her imaginary grounds for jealousy, so that she wouldn't be bored and he shouldn't be bored himself, hoping to inject a little zest into their life, with scenes and accusations and ensuing carnalities. Making her suffer was a way of putting an end to the migraines and the drowsiness which always overpowered her after ten thirty at night, the politely stifled yawns and the rest of the symptoms through which her unconscious conveyed its disappointment and its dissatisfaction with the love which now languished so dully, the love from which she had expected so much. Yes, her unconscious, for she was not consciously aware of any of this. But, sweet, demanding slave, it was making her ill.

The miserable life they led. Yet at the start of June, after his bogus liver attack, there had been a couple of almost happy weeks while the work she had wanted done to make their useless drawing-room even more attractive was being carried out. They had met early each morning, without any prior ringing of bells, in their ordinary clothes. After having breakfast together, they would look in to see how things were progressing, chat with the workmen, and get Mariette, who had perked up visibly when they arrived, to take them drinks and something to eat. The three workmen had made all the difference. During those two weeks they had had a kind of social life, there had been a purpose to things.

The miserable life they led. At the end of the second week, when the workmen had left, she and he had admired their refurbished home and had been thrilled with the new fireplace, which she had insisted on inaugurating with a roaring fire in spite of the mildness of the weather. 'Darling, it's lovely, don't you think?' Then, to try them out, they'd sat down in their new armchairs, which were massive and English, soft and dark brown, like a pair of immense chocolate mousses. 'Lovely, isn't it?' she had repeated, and, casting a satisfied eye around her, had taken a deep, proprietorial breath. And then, after a silence, she had begun reading out the memoirs of a great English lady, breaking off to protest and say how much she despised that whole snobbish clan. After dinner there had been a ring at the front door. She had jumped, and then said coolly that it was probably the people who'd taken the villa across the way who had come to pay a courtesy call. After pushing back a stray wisp of hair, and wearing a measured smile, she had gone to answer the door. Returning to the drawing-room, she'd said in a small, unaffected voice that it was a mistake, sat down in one of the chocolate mousses, and averred that they were so much more comfortable than the old ones. He had agreed, and she'd opened the *Revue de Paris* and begun reading an article about Byzantine art.

The miserable life they led. Every morning the poor creature put herself through a secret routine of exercises. She lay on the carpet in her swimming-costume with no idea that he was watching through the keyhole as she raised her legs, bicycled gravely, slowly lowered her legs, concentrating on breathing in and breathing out, then repeated the process, looking to her clandestine drill to overcome her torpor, which she doubtless attributed to a lack of exercise, for she was much too decent to see the truth, which was that they were bored with each other, that the ship of their love had sprung a leak and that it was making her ill. After her gymnastics she would sometimes stand and surreptitiously don a Swiss cowherd's cap embroidered with edelweiss and would then proceed to yodel while she tidied her wardrobe, would quietly yodel a song of the mountains, a song of her native land, which was another of her wretched little secrets.

The miserable life they led. The other evening, after dinner, she'd announced yet again that she would bake him a nice cake in the morning, and once more she'd asked him what kind he preferred, chocolate or coffee *crème*. Then, after a silence, she'd said she'd like a dog. 'A dog would be nice company when we go out walking, don't you think?' He'd agreed, because (a) it would be something to talk about and (b) it would give them something to do next day. She had written down the different breeds which she considered possibilities on a sheet of paper divided into two columns, one for pros and the other for cons. Subsequently the subject had never come up again. Maybe she thought a dog might bark in the middle of their consecrations, as she called them, or perhaps going walkies with it might get a teeny bit embarrassing on account of certain little habits dogs have.

The miserable life they led. Last night, at ten thirty, though she had felt an imperious need for sleep, she had bravely hidden it. But he knew the signs. The subtle itching of the nose, minimally and elegantly assuaged by discreet attentions to her nostrils. Eyes now wide and staring, now furtively closed and immediately reopened. Nostrils flaring, teeth gritted, and breasts held high for that smuggled yawn. The poor girl was sleepy but, because he was talking, she bravely insisted on staying, sincerely insisted on listening with interest, for she loved him, was firm of purpose and, moreover, polite. So she listened on, with a smile on her face, but in her eyes was a worried, almost frantic, look, a fear that she would be too late to bed if he went on talking, the morbid fear that she would certainly spend a sleepless night if she wasn't tucked up by eleven at the latest, a fear which she kept to herself but had confided to her private diary, which he had read in secret. Oh, that pleasant, well-brought-up smile with which she listened, a fixed smile, painted on, permanently pinned to her lips, stiff and unmoving, sweetly framing her listening teeth, the smile of a tailor's dummy, a ghastly dead smile with which she lovingly beat him into submission. And so, to banish the sight of her smile-festooned panic, he had stood up as he did every evening and said it was time they were saying good-night. 'Just five minutes more,' she had suggested magnanimously now that she was sure she would soon be in bed. Five polite minutes, just five and not one more! Oh their nights in Geneva! There, at two in the morning, when he wished to leave and let her sleep, how distraught his passionate girl used to be! 'Stay, don't go yet!' she would say in her gold-flecked voice, a voice which had now grown silent. 'It's not late!' she would say, and she would cling to him.

What could he do to put the life back in her? How about resuscitating the ploy he'd used a few months back, by making out that Elizabeth Vanstead was in Cannes threatening suicide if he didn't come, and then go to Cannes and see her as he had that other time, allegedly to spend a few days with her, all proper and above board, to prevent a crisis? Truth to tell, he'd got bored kicking his heels in Cannes all alone in a room in the Carlton, reading detective novels and, as his only comfort, having lavish meals brought up. Eating and reading, the twin mammaries which suckled solitude. But that last evening in the Carlton he'd felt a sudden need for jubilation, for conquest. There had been a Danish nurse. Result: muted jubilation, conquest turned to ashes. Next day, when he'd returned to Belle de Mai, she had bubbled over with life once more. She had wept, had plied her handkerchief tragically, had fired damply nasal questions and given him searching looks suddenly filled with the madness of certainty. 'You're lying! I'm sure you went to bed with her! Tell me the truth, I'd prefer to know, I'll forgive you if you tell me everything.' And so on. And when he had solemnly sworn that there was nothing between him and E. Vanstead, that he'd only agreed to go and see her because he'd felt sorry for her, because she had literally begged him to, oh such furious kisses and another instalment of waterworks. Then another session of question-and-answer. So what had they done all day? What had they talked about? Did their rooms have a connecting door? How was she dressed? Did she wear a dressing-gown in the mornings? And because he had said yes to this she'd cried and sobbed even more and clung to him, and then there had been kisses in the grandest style, the result of which was that she could sense he'd been telling her the truth, that he had been faithful to her all along. And then the predictable continuation had followed, with the poor girl triumphing in the certain knowledge that he still belonged to her because, and then she was holding him between her gripping legs, and then was bestowing allegedly bewitching caresses on the bare shoulder of her man. In ecstasy had she gazed upon him as in the days of Geneva, for he was precious and he was fascinating. Regaining her breath and fully reassured, she even allowed herself the moral satisfaction of feeling sorry for the rival she had seen off. Poor girl, you've been diddled. But the subterfuge had been for her benefit, to rekindle the happiness of loving in her.

Yes, she had bubbled with life, but it had only lasted a few days. Thereafter, E. Vanstead having disappeared over the horizon, the business of chocolate cake versus coffee-*crème* cake had resurfaced and, after the ten-thirty watershed, the evening panics had returned. So they had resorted to that other staple ploy: making up their minds to travel, they had completed a gruesome tour of Italy. So many monuments and museums visited without interest, since they both existed outside the community of men and women. Persons of refinement who took an interest in books, painting and sculpture did so in the last analysis so that they could talk about them later with other people, so that they might build up a stock of impressions they could share with others, those others on whom they depended. The notion that art was denied to the lonely was one which he had pondered time and time again. People who are cut off from human kind are much given to rumination.

After Italy, there was their week in Geneva. That evening at the Donon, when she had attempted to cobble together an interesting conversation. Which obviously meant wheeling out childhood memories. For of course they had nothing concerning their present to tell each other. Next she had diffidently suggested they might dance. 'Darling, let's dance too.' Her meek 'too', an admission of defeat, had cut him to the quick. After they'd danced a second time and had returned to their table, she had opened her handbag. 'I'm terribly sorry but I seem to have forgotten to bring a handkerchief. Could you lend me one?' 'Sorry, darling, I didn't bring one myself.' So she had sniffed discreetly, sweetly, dismayed but smiling, while he looked the other way so as not to compound her nasally induced indignity. She smiled and died a thousand deaths, and he loved her, loved his poor girl who was so wretched because her nose was blocked and because he knew it was, at her wits' end because she could not rid herself of the blockage. Pretending to be unaware of her awful predicament, and in an attempt to reassure her with a display of affection and respect, he had kissed her hand. After the fifth or sixth furtive sniff, she muttered that she was sorry but she was going to have to go back to the hotel for a handkerchief. 'I'll come with you, darling,' he said. 'No, I'd rather you stayed, I'll be back soon, it's not far to the hotel.' He knew very well why she wanted to go by herself. She was afraid some catastrophe might happen on the way, given the size of the blockage and the risk of a sudden sneeze with all the consequences which that might entail. 'Come back soon, darling.' Tormented by her cargo and anxious to offload it, she had flashed him a refined smile of farewell – oh to what wretchedness does the loving state reduce poor mortals forced to act it out! – and she had hurried off, doubtless hating the nose which had chosen to fill up and block at the very same Donon where, many moons previously, on the night of their elopement, they had wondrously danced until dawn. Once outside, she had probably run all the way to the redeeming handkerchief. O my darling, how happy I would make you if you were ill for years and years and you were my little girl and I could look after you in bed and serve you and wash you and comb your hair. Alas, they were sentenced to be extraordinary and sublime. Then he'd told himself that when she got back he'd act desire as he danced with her, to please her. The drawback there was that, being a pragmatist, she'd expect a practical follow-up when they got back to the hotel. Oh, if only she knew how much he'd loved her, how delightful he'd found her because she was all hot and bothered on account of her blocked nose. But no, he couldn't tell her that, she would be mortified. He was obliged to keep the best of what he felt for her to himself. My love! Oh to be able to call you silly little names, honey, or honey-bunch, or even, when you're in pyjamas, droopy-drawers. But that was ruled out. It was a crime against love. She returned to the Donon, poetic and unblocked, but had scarcely sat down before she started sniffing again. Prolific was hardly the word for it. He'd offered her a cigarette in the hope it would produce a restricting effect on her nasal passages. Alas, this proved not to be so. Go on, have a good blow and clear it! But no, she merely dabbed at her nose with the elegance and subtle grace of a kitten and gave a series of pretty, ineffectual, pretty ineffectual nff-nffs. That's no good, he said to himself, best start again from the top, you haven't a clue. He so wanted to explain that there was plenty left up there, that she should blow hard, and he cursed the damnable demands of beauty. In the end she'd made up her mind and, deciding to leave nothing to chance, had brayed through her nose with all her might. Her elephant-ine trumpeting had, praise the Lord, elicited a complete discharge and established a consequential aridity: he curbed an urge to applaud. Now safely delivered, she took him by the hand so that she could feel just how much she loved him, how much they loved each other. It was sad. But that's enough of that.

And now they'd been back at Belle de Mai for weeks. The day they'd arrived, there on the kitchen table they'd found a note from Mariette to say that she'd had to rush off suddenly to Paris to look after her sister, who was ill. Obviously a fabrication. The old girl couldn't take any more of the hothouse life they led and had left their unhappiness behind her. Good for you, Mariette! Then there had been the telegram from the solicitor saying that Ariane's uncle had died. In her grief, she had clung to him. Tears, kisses and a particularly memorable coupling, worthy of the old Geneva days. Oh yes, something new and interesting had happened. She loved her uncle, and her grief ran deep, but above all there had been the input of all those anti-anaemic vitamins from outside. On top of which they were to be parted for a few days and that made him exist for her. He had taken her to the station at Cannes, where a welter of kisses had preceded the train's departure. She had shown the same furious ardour on her return from Geneva. But within days they were back in the noble mire, wading through the listless ritual of Amazing Love.

She had not found another servant, not even a daily, and had taken charge of everything herself, alternating the roles of furtive housewife and priestess of love. He spent the mornings more determinedly shut up in his room than ever, while she peeled vegetables or, turban on head to protect her hair, leaned over a frying-pan or tried to retrieve a mayonnaise. 'May I do your room now?' At this point he took refuge in the drawing-room, so that he would not see the broomstress at work. He would have very much liked to sweep and polish with her. But he had to go on being a Prince of Passion. Not for his sake but for hers. Having to behave like a drone all the time was very trying. But, when she went out to the shops at Saint-Raphaël or Cannes, he raced round doing whatever he could to help, sweeping rooms, washing and scrubbing the kitchen floor, polishing the brass, waxing the parquet. And did it all in secret, so as not to tarnish his image as lover, the stupid image she was so intent on preserving. And she was so absent-minded and scatty that when she got back she never suspected a thing. Casting an eye over her spotless kitchen or her sparkling dining-room, she would tell herself with no little pride that she kept their house looking very nice, and with no one to help her either, and she would take a deep, satisfied breath. His adorable, unsuspecting girl.

Once these chores were out of the way she did her secret exercises, had her bath, then put on her Passion Dress which she had washed the night before and ironed early that morning, and only then, sacerdotally, with jaw muscles jutting, did the vestal, exuding waftures of a fragrance marketed as Antic Amber, step into the land of the living. At this juncture they would lunch on the damned terrace so that they could enjoy the view of the damned sea. She went to considerable trouble over their meals. The day before yesterday, such a sumptuous lunch to celebrate their anniversary. His whimsical girl had even done out a menu in her own fair hand, taking great delight in writing (correctly, for his benefit) lobster à l'armoricaine (and not à l'américaine) and jacket (not baked) potatoes. So a girl with a poetic turn and not the least whit Jewish. But the lobster was inedible.

Damn, the first gong. A quarter of an hour from now he'd have to sally forth on to the terrace and eat with taste and discernment and get himself stung by mosquitoes, vile little brutes, which were not only after his blood but out to do him violence. What pleasure could they possibly get from injecting pepper into his skin? It was a quite gratuitous piece of beastliness. Go ahead, you're welcome to the blood, but don't give me a bad time afterwards! The thought of old Madame Sarles suddenly came into his mind, and he whiled away a pleasant moment imagining that she had left money in her will for starting a retirement home for elderly, devout mosquitoes. Yes, that pious lady would undoubtedly have approved of the habits of mosquitoes. They sang you an alluring little song and then poisoned your blood, raising bumps and making you scratch for hours and hours. And if you got cross they said: 'Dearly beloved, we pray constantly for thee, for we bear thee great love! Hear our dainty, sounding bells, hear us as we pray to God to make thee to prosper so that we can sting thee in abundance, and this we do with love and with eyes ashine with spiritual fervour!' But if understanding that a mosquito could not help sticking his Cayenne-tipped barb into you meant forgiving it, then he gladly forgave old Madame Sarles, the great mosquito in his life, a dazzling virtuoso of the pinprick who had never been able to resist the pleasure of poisoning him day after day. God rest her soul.

Oh yes, venture out on to the terrace in his black tie and get bitten on the ankles and prattle on about the colours in the sea and be prodigious and look her hot and deep in the eye and find brand-new ways of saying that he loved her. And yet he did: he loved her. No woman had ever been as close to him. With the others, Adrienne, Aude, Isolde and the ones in between, he had always felt apart. Strangers seen through a wall of glass. They were capable of movement, and sometimes he could quite see that they existed independently, just as he did, and then he asked himself by what right these women moved around in his world. But Ariane was his second skin, his congenial, simple, trusting girl. He loved to watch her when she wasn't looking, and tried to hide his tenderness, that crime against passion. How many times had he resisted the temptation to take her in his arms and kiss her hard on the cheek, kiss her cheek a score of times, and only her cheek. Everything about her was a delight, even when she was being silly. The menu she'd naïvely edged with little flowers the day before yesterday had been a delight. Delightful too was the appalling lobster which she'd decorated but oversalted, and he'd helped himself to more, just to jolly her along.

For, as his affection for her grew and grew, so he desired her less and less, though she set great store by being desired and doubtless believed that such was her right, which was very irritating. Oh their monotonous couplings, each one like the one before! In Cannes, on the last evening of operation Vanstead, with the Danish nurse whom he had called to the Carlton on the pretext that he was unwell, with his nurse, who had meant nothing to him and whose first name he did not even know, the pleasure had been intense. Not a word had passed between them. Absolute physical bliss in a silence disturbed only by her gasps. At midnight, when she was dressed again, his unspeaking partner of moments before had fastened her blue, reproachless eyes on him and, prim in starched collar and stiff cuffs, had asked if she was to come back the next day at the same time. When he said no, she had left without a knowing smile or look, a respectable nurse in low heels, with her white cap perched on top of her flaxen hair.

The second gong made him jump. Damn, he'd forgotten to dress. Quickly now, on with the pointless dinner-jacket, but she insisted on it just as she herself insisted on wearing an evening gown which made her look like an opera singer. 'Let's hope we are spared a recital of rumblings abdominal,' he muttered, and was ashamed to take such revenge against the miserable life they led.

After dinner on the terrace, they moved to the drawing-room. They sat before the open bay window, she ironically in a low-cut gown and he in a white dinner-jacket, and watched with seeming casualness the thrilling spectacle of the noisy crew across the way stuffing themselves and talking and chatting to each other from one end of the long table to the other. They sat on, smoking exquisite cigarettes, distinguished and silent in their sumptuous, flower-filled drawing-room, alone and beautiful, excluded but so elegant. When the junior member of the Council of State came back wearing a woman's hat, a great cheer went up and everyone applauded. At which point she said that she had bought a brand of caffeine-free tea which did not prevent one from sleeping. So that's the level of news to which we have now sunk.

'Perhaps we could try it later,' she said. 'But I don't think it will be as nice as ordinary tea. Oh, I forgot to show you,' she said after a moment's silence. 'This morning, among those old papers Mariette brought back from Geneva, I came across a photograph of me aged thirteen. Shall I get it?'

Returning from her room, she handed him a small square of stiff paper, sat excitedly at his side, on the arm of his chair, and looked admiringly at the little girl in socks and sandals, so delightful with those ringlets, that big bow in her hair, the short skirt and those gorgeous bare legs.

'You were pretty then.'

'And now?' she asked, bringing her cheek nearer.

'And now too.'

'But which do you prefer? Her or me?'

'Both are exquisite.'

Oh, change and decay, he thought, and handed her back the photo. And now what could he talk to her about? They had already pretty well exhausted the sea and its hues, the sky and its moon. Everything that could possibly be said about Proust had been said, and about how they'd both sensed that Albertine was in fact a young man. The reason, respectable observers would say, was that their love was not rich enough. He would like to see those respectable observers change places with them and watch them cope with being shackled within the cell-like confines of a great love. Talk to her about animals? They'd done that. He knew by heart all the animals she liked and why. How about the war in Spain? Too painful, now that he was no longer part of all that. Tell her for the ten-thousandth time that he loved her, just like that, without dressing it up? Now a man who had a proper social life coming home with his wife after an evening spent with their friends, the unlikeable but indispensable Dumardins, was in a good position to say something sparkling and loving, such as Madame Dumardin doesn't dress half as well as you do, my pet. Over the way, the happy neighbours danced to a tinkling piano and allowed themselves a shoal of minor adulteries.

'In Cannes,' said Ariane, 'there's a woman who gives Hawaiian guitar lessons. I've a good mind to go.'

After a moment's silence she mentioned the odd couple she'd

noticed on the bus to Cannes, described what they looked like, and repeated what they'd said. He put on his understanding face and forced a smile. As usual, the poor girl was trying to be witty and amusing. Actually she was an acute observer. People who sat on their lonely shelf, hungering for the company of others, were always acute observers. But these two strangers on a bus were the only pickings she could bring him from the world outside. There was another silence.

How about slapping her face suddenly, giving no reason, and then stomping off to his room? It would be a good deed: her evening wouldn't be so tedious, she'd have something to think about, could wonder why and in what way she had offended him, could cry and think how they might have spent such a pleasant evening together if only he hadn't been beastly to her. Give her a spot of drama, all the fun of the fair. And then she would move to hope and expectation and finally to reconciliation. No. Hadn't the heart for it.

But he'd had the heart the other evening. He'd slapped her hard and then locked himself in his room, where he'd gashed his thigh to redress the balance. Oh it was tragicomic: hitting a sweet creature of whom he was so genuinely fond, out of kindness! Yes, kindness! To wipe that pleasant smile off the face of a well-bred girl who refused to acknowledge that she was bored silly and probably attributed her lowness of spirit to some non-specific physical cause. Yes, kindness! To restore her to life, to prevent her seeing the wreck of their love. But he hadn't been able to bear it when he'd seen her in the road outside, holding her hand to her smarting cheek, and he had gone running to her, 'I'm sorry, my love, my sweet, my angel, I'm sorry, I don't know what came over me.' She had looked at him the way she had at the Ritz, with believer's eyes. How could he do it again?

'Yes, I really think I will go and see that woman. It seems all it takes is a dozen lessons. Then I'll be able to play you Hawaiian music in the evening, it's terribly catchy.'

Aha, she didn't say nostalgic. That'll come in time. How could he even think of slapping a poor girl who was planning to bewitch him with Hawaiian music and trying vaguely to replace or combat the missing social dimension with the twang of a Hawaiian guitar? Anyway, was he going to have to slap her face every evening? It was a tonic which would eventually lose its effectiveness. Should he go and have a word with the podgy member of the Council of State over the road, beg him to invite them round, maybe even offer him money? No, that was simply not done. And the most heartbreaking aspect of the whole case, and the most unfair, was that being constantly shut up in his deep-sea diving-bell with only her for company simply got on his nerves. Her rumbling stomach got on his nerves. Her ethereal, post-coital caresses got on his nerves. Her Genevan accent and vocabulary got on his nerves. Why did she have to say 'fertl' rather than 'fertile', why the devil did she say 'store' not 'shop'? Why 'motor', not 'car'? It made her sound so affected.

And the strong whiff of capitalist attitudes which she exuded. He recalled the day when, her lip curling with mild contempt, she had said that it was amazing how much Mariette thought about money, set such store by money, talked about money all the time, and was forever wanting to know how much Madame Ariane had paid for those shoes, this bag, that dress. 'Odd, anyone being so keen to know how much everything costs,' she had added with an indulgent display of her mild contempt. Quite, Madame, you and your kind can afford the luxury of not caring for money, of never mentioning money, of being uninterested. All you have to do is pop to the bank. And she always spoke to servants in that pleasant lady-of-the-manor way of hers. And only the other evening, how eloquent she had grown when expatiating on tea, the sacred drink of her clique who were the owners of the means of production. 'People react very sensitively to tea, don't you find, darling? It's all a question of physical make-up. For instance, if one is not feeling well, one finds it less palatable. But if one has not tasted tea for three whole days it strikes one as being amazingly good, don't you think?' She had chopped the 'amazingly' into four distinct parts to give it all due prominence, and he had looked at her curiously. How changed, the crazy, inspired girl he'd known in Geneva! And then there was her morbid passion for flowers. She was forever sticking their dying remains all over the house, in the drawing-room, in the hall, in her bedroom. Only yesterday, she had harangued him about autumn flowers, she liked them best, and had launched into a full description of dahlias, asters and other makes of vegetable matter. The dahlia, ah, a sensual bloom, heavy, rich, which made her think of Titian: 'Do you find that too, darling?' And her morbid obsession with the beauties of nature. 'Darling, do come and see the colour of that mountain.' Very well, and he'd gone, but all he'd seen was a mountain, a large lump of rock. Oh for his own Ionian Sea, in age-old springtime, tender touch of clear water. 'Darling, do come and see the sunset.' It bored him rigid. And her obsession too with views, a preoccupation doubtless peculiar to the Swiss, who were a mountain people. Always asking if there was a good view from some station or other, or even just simply A View. Incidentally, she always said 'station' for 'spot', and that was Swiss too, perhaps. And now she used make-up, which didn't suit her. And what had happened at the Donon now recurred frequently. She blew her nose far too genteelly, and it got on his nerves. 'Go on, have a good clear out,' he murmured to himself. And, immediately afterwards, shame, pity, remorse: remorse so deep that he felt an urge to go down on his knees to her. But the nasal blockage persisted and was noticeable in the poor girl's voice, and it was absolutely maddening. And sometimes she had bad breath. I'm sorry, darling, forgive me. Yes, please forgive me, though your breath really does smell today, there's nothing I can do about it and there's no way I can avoid being aware of it. But worst of all was that sometimes, all of a sudden, for no reason, he felt a strange aversion for her, perhaps because she was a woman.

Oh poor girl, pretending unconcern yet never for a moment taking her eyes off the antics of the moronic neighbours, disappointed because she was not one of them, humiliated because they had not come to call. Of course, all the time they'd been at Agay the only kind of social life she had known had been having breakfast in secret with Mariette. Another burst of laughter from across the way. Some attractive, silly girl had stuck a man's hat on her head and everyone was clapping and shouting 'Good old Jeanne, go on Jeanne, let her rip!' But here, in the elegant drawing-room with its splendid flowers, was deathly silence.

'Do you think I should go for the Hawaiian-guitar lessons?'

'Yes, darling. Good idea.'

'In that case I'll make a start tomorrow. I'll soon be singing Hawaiian songs for you to my own accompaniment.'

'Fine,' he said with a smile, then suddenly got to his feet. 'I'll go and pack. There are people I must see about my affairs.'

'When are you leaving?'

'Tonight. It's urgent. Financial matters.'

'But where are you going?'

'Paris. Friends to see.'

'Oh darling! Do let me come with you! (How eagerly she had spoken the words! Thirsting for any sort of a change! She was already picturing their arrival in Paris, the new faces in the station, in the streets and, above all, oh yes, above all the friends he'd be seeing to whom he would introduce her. Attracted by his friends like flies by the honeypot! Others, not just him; others, not just him: it was her motto. Because he was staring at her, she thought he was hesitating.) O darling, I'll be terribly good, I'll wait until you've finished all your business, and then we'll . . .'

'We'll what?' he interrupted sternly. (Cold-eyed, he waited for the terrible ending: 'call on friends in the evening'.)

'I was going to say that we'll be so looking forward to seeing each other again in the evening, it would be lovely,' she said, frightened by the fixed, wild, calculating look in his eye.

Aha, she had admitted her secret desire! To be rid of her damned beloved at least for several hours each day, to watch him go, and stop having him cluttering up the place, not to be always seeing him at home wandering around in one of his everlasting dressing-gowns! Actually she was quite right. They were suffocating because they spent all their time together being extraordinarily beautiful so that they could tell each other every minute of the day how extraordinarily in love with each other they were. In reality, though she did not know it, she longed, yearned to be the wife of an Under-Clown-General and give parties every evening, with carefully graded smiles, for large numbers of revitalizing, self-important, bemedalled morons, preferably in formal evening dress.

In the neighbours' garden another game of blind man's buff was in progress. Oh yes, he envied them too, he also wanted to be on good terms with a miserable junior member of the Council of State, he who once . . . Oh the sexual screams of the stupid women as they ran away. He turned to look at her. She and her Hawaiian guitar, poor girl. Well then, he'd go to Paris alone, he'd leave this very night, and he would triumph in Paris, triumph for her, and he would return bringing back happiness, happiness at last for his darling, loads of happiness for his darling love.

CHAPTER 93

He lies awake thinking of the unhappy woman who waits for him at Agay, patiently waits, not daring to ask why she must write to him poste restante or why he does not tell her the name of his hotel. Too right, darling, it's the George V for this super-tramp. 'Restored to the land of the living,' he had said out loud as he had climbed into his sleeper, and he had smiled at an attractive woman passenger in the corridor, and she had smiled back, and oh such kissing with her in the night, such kissing with Béatrice.

He rubs his chin where the sprouting bristles itch. Not shaved since being turned down by the albino, an umpteen- maybe sixteen-day-old beard. What's the date today? He leans over, picks up the paper and reads the date. Monday, 10 September 1936. That makes it a thirteen-day-old beard. The albino had a face like a tapir. The day after he got into Paris, Béatrice Riùlzi having left for London, he'd gone to the Rue de l'Université. He'd insisted on being seen by the head man, the Director, insisted like a man down on his luck, insisted like a Jew. He had been so sure of himself on the train with Béatrice, had been what women call a charmer, so sure of himself on sexual ground. But sitting before the Director he had suddenly felt awkward, had smiled too much. The razor-edged words of the albino after the glance through his dossier. An irregularity in his naturalization papers, insufficient qualifying residence. He had left and wandered through the streets, stateless and with no function, a chemically pure Jew.

★

He stares at his hand. It moves. He kisses it so as not to be alone. Should he go back to speculating on the stock market and take his revenge by being rich? Pariahs are allowed to speculate. A pariah can be debarred from everything except making money by his wits, the ultimate consolation. No, heart not in it. But his heart had been in it all right after the set-back. Yes, darling, I had the heart to traipse round knocking on doors, begging for help. Delarue, who in the old days he'd rescued from a wretched fate as a down-at-heel journalist and had appointed as his principal private secretary at the Ministry of Labour, was now an inspector general. His former subordinate had adopted such a patronizing tone. 'Sorry, old man, you can't un-denaturalize somebody just like that.' After saying there was absolutely nothing he could do, he had offered the unshaven down-and-out a glass of Scotch and proceeded to tell him about his fascinating work as government delegate to the International Labour Office. He'd got even less change out of his other old chums. Never invited across the doors of their offices, never asked to sit down. They all knew about the scandal. They all knew he had been sacked. They all knew his French citizenship had been withdrawn. They all used the same excuses. 'Haven't the authority to intervene. There are no new facts to justify an application to have the decision overturned. So there you are, old man, you've only yourself to blame.' Some even allowed themselves the luxury of feeling sorry for him as they gently steered him towards the exit. 'It really is such a shame.' And in the eyes of all of them he read mistrust, hostility, fear. Men do not care for the sight of misfortune.

He has eased himself back into the warmth of his bed. He puts a smile on his face to cover his misery. His bare feet caress the sheets, luxuriating in their smoothness, delighting in them. This much at least remains to him: the ease and comfort which money can buy. The day before yesterday he'd gone back to the Rue de l'Université to try again. Speech written out the night before, case learned by heart, all rehearsed in the mirror. Hoped his umpteen-day-old beard would soften the albino's heart. And then, after spending hours kicking his heels in a waiting-room reciting his heart-softening arguments to himself, he had been seen. The man was clearly irritated by the sheer persistence of the lunatic he was dealing with. 'You people, you know, you get kicked out of the front door and you climb back in through the window.' 'You people.' Ah! We know who you mean. And he had made the most of his opportunity to humiliate a former government minister, a man who was now powerless. 'All you need do is take up official residence in France and then submit a new application when the formal qualifying period has expired. Since, that is, you seem so very keen on becoming French.' Heartless, that 'so very keen'. The heartlessness of those who have a place in the sun, the cruel irony of the sated who find it odd that a man should actually be hungry.

Aloud, he mimics the odd way the albino spoke. 'Shinche, vat ish, you sheem sho very keen on becoming Frencha.' An underdog jibe, a feeble riposte. Misfortune demeans, but it also dulls the brain. He'd been so stupid, turning up like that with a prepared speech and thinking stubble would melt hearts. He'd spoken of his isolation and his hunger to belong in a country he could call his own, and the man had replied with official residence in France and formal qualifying period, and while he spoke had looked at the framed photographs of his two well-groomed children and his legally-signed-and-sealed wife who was eminently presentable and probably had money of her own. Oh, the indifference of the fortunate! Oh, the smugness on the face of the man behind the desk as he looked at his photos, looked with unassailable certainty at the evidence of the unimpeachability of his life! A bastard with a clear conscience, with his feet firmly under the social table. Not intelligent, but smart. Whereas he was intelligent but not smart at all. And then the man got up and said he had other people to shee.

He smiles as he ponders his fate. He'd succeeded once on the strength of his intelligence. Member of Parliament, government minister, et cetera. A success built on sand, because it had come through the exercise of his intelligence. Success on the high wire, with no safety-net. Unable to count on family or connections, the old-school tie, chums from childhood and adolescence, or any of the natural helping hands which weave the snugly fitting garment of solidarity with one's milieu, he had had only himself to rely on. He had been brought down by a princely blunder. And now he is a man alone. The rest of them, firmly embedded in the establishment, are all connected by a maze of protective threads to natural allies. Life is sweet for those who follow the normal path, so sweet that they do not realize quite how much they owe to their background and believe that their success is due entirely to their own efforts. The part played by family and long-standing friendships is vital to the extensive silver-spoon club of privy counsellors, Treasury officials and diplomats who never passed an examination in their lives. He would like to see how they would have fared in his shoes, clods who had been mollycoddled from birth and borne along from cradle to grave on the gentle social stream. If Proust had so wished, his papa could have calmly and with no trouble at all wangled a job for him in the Quai d'Orsay, because the moron Norpois, a chum of Proust the Father, was standing by ready to introduce Proust the Sprog to a collection of other morons. Oh, of course he knows they aren't morons and weren't hopeless at exams. He says morons, he says they can't pass exams because he, well, just let it go. Yes, he'd succeeded without the safety-net of clubbability. And then he'd made his blunder at the meeting of the Council of their League of Nations and had come a cropper. And the very next day he'd made an even more serious blunder: he'd sent an anonymous letter disclosing the irregularity in his naturalization papers. From that day on he has been a man alone and his country is a woman. He takes the packet sealed with sealing-wax from the drawer of his bedside table. Should he open it? Why not, he is entitled to a little happiness. But no. His father was Gamaliel of the Solals, the revered Chief Rabbi. He puts the packet back into the drawer.

Quickly now, find a Purpose. He rings for the waiter, then gets out of bed, checks that the door is locked, and waits. When the two knocks come, he orders the full breakfast through the door. Three fried eggs, bacon, coffee, toast, butter, croissants and English marmalade. Then he returns to bed, forces a smile and a contented sigh. Oh yes, old friend, I have a nice bed, very comfortable. The albino had cut him short, stood up and said he had other people to shee. Then he'd smiled to earn the nonentity's goodwill and a few extra minutes in which to plead his cause, and he'd given him the end of his speech, carefully rehearsed in the mirror the night before, had produced his arguments, which were clumsy and earnest. The kind of life he has inflicted on the woman he loves. His love of France and even his reasons for loving France. But the man is too French to understand his fervour, his need. So his speech got him nowhere and the man opened the door without saying a word. So then he told him he was finished. 'Sho shorry,' the man said.

Two knocks at the door. He is afraid to confront the waiter, a man of purpose from the world outside, a messenger from the land of the living, one of the lucky devils who has a place in the brotherhood of men. 'Leave the tray by the door, I'll come for it.' He waits for the sound of footsteps to die away, carefully opens the door a few inches, and looks left and right. No one watching. He gathers up the tray, quickly double-locks the door, removes the key, puts it under the pillow, and gets back into bed.

Sitting up in bed with the friendly tray in front of him, he smiles. Mmm. These eggs and bacon smell good. Three little chums. Well, he's got his breakfast too, and it's bigger and better than the average lucky devil gets. Yes, but for the lucky devils the first meal of the day is a prelude to what goes on outside, provides them with the calories they need for intermingling with others of their own kind. Whereas in his case breakfast is just something to do, a short-term goal, ten minutes of solitary, sticky happiness. He opens *Le Temps* and gives audience to the world outside while at the same time surrendering to the dismal sensuality of food. He is quite aware that within a year at the outside he will commit suicide, and yet he calmly bites into his croissants, which he takes with lashings of butter and mounds of marmalade. Pity they hadn't brought the jar it had come in, with the Scottish soldier on the label. It's interesting to look at pictures on labels as you eat. It's company.

His short-lived pleasure now a thing of the past, he gets up. Where's the key? He looks for it here and then there, and as he looks he rolls his wrist in the action of turning a key, as a help to finding it.

Eventually he comes across it under his pillow and half opens the door. He stares at all the shoes lined up in the corridor outside the other doors. The feet of the carefree are his social connections. Last night, at around two o'clock, he felt crazily tempted to borrow some of them and lay them out on his bed. He leans out further for a better view. How happy all these well-polished, neatly arranged, self-confident shoes look. Yes, precisely: self-confident. Their owners staying in the hotel have a purpose in life. In his case it's the opposite.

Footsteps. He shuts the door hurriedly and turns the key in the lock. A knock. It's the valet asking if it's all right to clean the room. 'No. Later.' When everything is silent once more, he executes a dance step in the wardrobe mirror and snaps his fingers like castanets. It doesn't really matter if he isn't happy. The happy die too. Having checked that the corridor is now empty again, he quickly puts the tray down outside the door, smartly hangs the 'Do not disturb' sign on the knob, turns the key twice in the lock, and pokes out his tongue. Saved!

He makes the bed carefully, then sets about tidying the room, using a face-towel for a duster. 'We look after our little ghetto, must keep our little ghetto looking nice,' he mutters, as though he is telling a secret. He moves two armchairs which are too close together, clears away a jumble of books, and sets out the cigarette-boxes in a symmetrical pattern, with the ashtray in the middle. 'Oh yes, here in the ghetto we have a mania for tidiness. The point is that we can go on thinking everything's all right. We have tidiness as a substitute for happiness.' And such, gentlemen, he murmurs, are the amusements of the lonely. And then he croons that the pleasure of love lasts but a moment, deliberately sings in a shrill, effeminate falsetto, to while away the time, to put on a performance for himself, sings with feeling to decant his presently unemployed love into his song. What's this? Dust on the bedside table! He gives the marble top a quick wipe with the towel, which he shakes out of the window. Those tiny humans far below: all rushing, all with a purpose, all hurrying towards others of their own kind. He lowers the blind to blot them out. He draws the curtains so that he is not aware that there is a world outside, a world of hope and success. Ah yes, there was a time when he went forth to conquer, to captivate, to be loved. He had been one of them.

In the near dark he prowls around the room, furrow-browed, tweaking the occasional hair out of his scalp. Banished. Excluded. Of all the avocations existing outside, the only one now remaining to him is business, the manipulation of money, as it had been for his medieval forebears. Tomorrow, open a shop and set up as a pawnbroker, and on the door of the shop put up a brass plate. Have 'Patrician Moneylender' engraved on the brass plate. No, stay cooped up here in the George V and settle for living a life of luxury. Here, in this room, he can do whatever he wants – speak Hebrew, recite Ronsard, shout out that he is a monster with two heads and two hearts, that he belongs exclusively to the Jewish nation, exclusively to the French nation. Here, all alone, he can cover his shoulders with the sublime synagogue prayer-shawl and, if he feels like it, stick a tricolour rosette on his forehead. Here, gone to earth and alone, he will not see the mistrust in the eyes of those whom he loves but who do not love him. Go to the synagogue every day? But what does he have in common with all those respectable mumblers in bowler hats who fidget while they wait for the service to end, make sure they never neglect their business affairs and their outside interests, touch the brims of their hats when persons of influence pass by, and shed copious tears when, during the ceremony to mark his religious coming-of-age, they watch their boy reading the Prophets dressed like a proper little gentleman with a tiny bowler on his head. Trembling suddenly in the presence of the Almighty, he recites the eighteen blessings from the sabbath-day order of service.

'We are in love with you, my heart and I,' he says smilingly to the mirror, and then crosses the room and inspects the lock. Yes, locked. For added safety he pushes home the bolt, then checks that it is secure by turning the knob and trying to open the door. The door holds firm. Good, safe and sound. 'It's just the two of us now,' he says, and he gets into the disgustingly warm bed and smiles to ward off interruptions, though he has the sign hanging outside his door to protect him. He pulls the covers up to his chin, waggles his bare feet to feel how soft the sheets are, and gives another smile. Beds are not anti-Semitic.

He switches on his bedside lamp, picks up *Le Temps*, which is a window on the life from which he is excluded, and carefully avoids the society page and the diary of diplomatic receptions. But on every page his eye is drawn to ministers, generals, ambassadors. There are far too many ambassadors, there are ambassadors everywhere. Take a shot of veronal to blot out the crafty swine, canny hangers-on every man jack of them, former private secretaries who got where they are by licking the boots of gullible foreign ministers. He smiles, recalling that Naileater had said exactly the same thing about ambassadors he had encountered in thé pages of newspapers. Anyway, thirty years from now the whole crawling clique will all be dead. Yes, but in the meantime they are happy, they busy themselves with their supremely unimportant affairs, bustling, dynamic, telephoning, giving orders, ensuring that things are done which are almost immediately undone, forgetting that they will die.

He closes his eyes and tries to sleep. The telegram he'd sent yesterday must have set her mind at rest. Full of lies, saying his affairs are well on the way to being sorted out, that he'll be home soon. Leaning across to his bedside table, he opens the drawer again, takes out the packet with the sealing-wax on it, stares at it, and then puts it back. Not sleepy, the veronal hasn't worked. He gets up and inspects the room. Finger-marks on the wardrobe mirror. He rubs them with a handkerchief. Not very pretty, his unmade bed. Let's make it again properly, let's do it right, Jews together, with love. Pull the sheets smooth, and the blankets, tuck the ends in properly and straighten the counterpane, make it neat.

Having remade his bed, he looks for guidance in the mirror over the wash-basin. Staring at his bearded face, he feels at a loss, so he smiles to encourage cheerful thoughts which refuse to come. He washes his hands with soap and water, taking his time, to make time pass, to hook into hope by performing a trivial, everyday ritual. Next, he splashes himself with amber-coloured eau-de-Cologne to recapture the will to live, to give himself new heart. Poor Deume. Serves me right, I'm suffering too. He takes a penknife and scrapes the hard skin on the soles of his feet, scrupulously scrapes, and enjoys seeing the white flecks fall and build into a small heap. A meagre diversion. Best go out, walk about the streets. Yes, let's dip a toe into the social water. He sniggers; that way there are two of him.

Dressed now, he goes and says goodbye to himself in the mirror. The beard is appalling, makes him look like a convict. Can't be bothered to shave. They can hardly arrest him for having a beard. Anyway, the suit is Savile Row, which makes up for the beard. He opens the door and then shuts it hurriedly. What will the valet and the chambermaid think when they see that the bed has been made? Mustn't put their backs up. He hastily unmakes the bed, opens the door a few inches, and peers out. Nobody about in the corridor. He steps out and sets off, holding a handkerchief to his mouth as though he has toothache, his hat pulled well down to hide those awful, lustrous, betraying eyes. Ring for the lift? No, they stare at you more in lifts, because they are bored, on the lookout for anything to help pass the time. Fewer risks on the stairs. He runs down them, his unambiguous nose concealed by the handkerchief. He accelerates through the lobby with his eyes on the ground to avoid the danger of bumping into acquaintances from the old days.

In the Rue Marbeuf, spotting an inscription chalked on a wall, he walks past it, looking the other way. Best not to know. But, irresistibly drawn, he stops, turns and looks. Such large numbers of citizens in these love-thy-neighbour cities who wished death to the Jews. Perhaps whoever is asking for him to be put to death is a nice lad, a good son who buys flowers for his old mother. To avoid seeing any more walls, he walks into a brasserie. Hoping to catch snippets of conversation, he sits near a pleasant-looking old couple and orders a double whisky. Yes, look cheerful. He picks up the copy of *L'Illustration* lying on his table, opens it, and gives a start. No, they didn't say 'Jew', they said 'June'. The nice old man whispers something in the ear of his wife, who reacts with the unconcern which indicates that something is afoot and peers all round the room before letting her eyes settle on the well-dressed man with the beard. She looks at her husband and gives him a wink of complicity, a knowing, hungry, colluding, foxy wink which sparkles with malice and cunning. 'Yes, of course,' she says, displaying two rows of crenellated teeth covered with green moss. He has been spotted. He gets up, leaves money on the table, and throws himself out, forgetting his whisky.

Through the streets he goes, those rivers which irrigate the parched lives of the lonely, and as he goes he nibbles roasted peanuts bought from one of his own kind, an elderly Jew from Salonika with white, wavy hair and eyes as tender as any odalisque's, on he wanders, pausing from time to time outside the windows of dress shops, dipping into the bag of peanuts, dropping brown bits all over the lapels of his jacket, staring at the prettily painted wax dummies, so elegant, so obviously glad to be alive, so unremittingly delighted with life, then moving on, muttering under his breath, sometimes smiling to himself, going into shops and emerging with objects which will keep him company in his room, acquaintances to look at, to love.

In a toyshop, he buys a little articulated skier and a set of brightly coloured cornelian marbles. His eye is drawn by a false nose made out of cardboard. He buys that too, telling the assistant that his little boy will love it. Once outside, he takes the skier out of his paper bag, holds him by the arm, and swings him round and round. We're strolling along together. A bookshop. He stops, goes in, and buys a copy of *The Case of the Painted Parrot*, a detective novel spawned by the small brain of a large and elderly Englishwoman. A florist's. He stops, goes in, and orders three dozen roses to be delivered to the George V but dares not give his name. Room three-three-oh. Urgent. They're for a friend. 'I love you, you know,' he mutters reaching the street once more. Overall, he'd been treated quite decently by the florist. He claps his hands once. 'Come on, let's have some fun,' he murmurs.

All alone in the big city, he walks on, dragging his heart, dragging himself down the long streets, and watches as two army officers pass gaily by, talking in loud voices, for they have an absolute right to talk in loud voices. To comfort himself, for the companionship of it, he buys a bar of milk chocolate. When the chocolate is all gone, he moves on again, alone once more. Dull-eyed and slack-mouthed, he stumbles on, feet uncertain, humming a happy tune in a low but expressive voice, to fill the emptiness. He takes *The Case of the Painted Parrot* out of his pocket and reads as he walks, so that there is no need to think.

A crowd outside a church. He stops, puts his book under his arm, and watches. There is a red carpet on the steps. Self-important assistants are arranging the display of potted plants. Now the fat church verger appears with his wand. A notable marriage is about to be celebrated. Large limousines. A lady in sky blue holds out her hand to a general in white gloves. Humiliated, he flees, humming an exorcising song, swinging his little skier.

He gives a start when he spots a policeman away to his left who is keeping pace with him. He whistles out of tune to demonstrate that he has nothing on his conscience, puts on a nonchalant little smile, he's not worried, the picture of innocence. I hate your guts, he tells him to himself. Go up to him straightforwardly and ask the way to the Madeleine to allay his suspicions? No, the best policy is to have nothing at all to do with the police. Quickening his step, he crosses from one pavement to the other. 'Foxed you,' he murmurs and walks on, clearing his throat at regular intervals, a man alone beating time to his thoughts with glottal clearings of his throat.

A photographer's shop window. He stops to look at the faces caught in a state of grace, free of the meanness of daily life. When people pose for a photograph, they smile, they are kindly disposed, their soul is garbed in its finest raiment. They are a pleasure to look at, they are seen at their best. A pleasure to behold, that workman there in his new suit, standing beside a table holding a book, with one leg hooked round the other and one foot arched. That's enough of that. He crosses the road, drawn to trees. He sits on a bench. All these people who pass by are going about occasions which though lawful are utterly pointless, such as going to the barber's or paying visits to electricity or gas showrooms. But if he were to ask them to save him, for instance by signing a petition, no chance. Chat to a barber? Yes. Spend hours looking at vacuum cleaners? You bet. But lift a finger to save a man's life? No. And all these women walking along, prettily mincing, heels tapping as they go, serenely believing that they will live for ever.

A little old man has just sat down on the bench and says: 'Morning.' You say 'Morning' because you don't know who I am. 'Nice day today,' the old man says, but the rain last week played the devil with his rheumatics. At his age, what with his rheumatics and his stomach that's playing up, he's not fit for doing skilled work any more. Just raising his arm makes him dizzy, but you got to when you're a decorator, not up to doing ceilings any more, the minute he gets anywhere near a ladder, that's it, he goes all giddy, everything goes round and round, so now all he does is a bit of odd-jobbing. 'And what line are you in, then?' he says. 'I'm a violinist,' says Solal. 'Ah, it's a gift is fiddling, you either got it or you haven't.' The conversation continues, takes a friendly turn. Oh yes, from now on all his friendships will be temporary. A quarter of an hour with a stranger and that's it. Can't be helped, grateful for whatever crumbs come his way, listen to what the old fool is saying. For more than a year she has been the only person he has talked to. 'Now your average Frenchman is a individdlest,' the old man says. And that too is friendship: the old man lays a table for him spread with the finest contents of his little brain, a posh word which he's read somewhere or heard a mate of his say. He puts it on display, rolls it round his tongue. It feels good when you can use words above your station. 'Myself, I reckon the Jews are to blame,' he ends. It was bound to come, of course. Oh poor innocent! Like a pickpocket in reverse, he quietly slips a banknote into the pocket of the jacket of the old man who is unsuspectingly cataloguing the crimes of the Jews. He stands up, shakes his roughened hand, smiles into his blue eyes, and moves on. There is a philosopher, Sartre, who has written that man is absolutely free and personally responsible for his moral actions. It is a middle-class idea, the idea of someone who has led a sheltered life, who has never had to stand on his own two feet.

★

Streets and yet more streets. Suddenly, two crashed cars, a policeman writing an accident report, onlookers arguing about the incident. He listens, joins in, ashamed for falling so low, but it's a good feeling. A group is anonymous, it's not like a someone you sense is hostile, a person who makes your blood run cold. Besides, it puts you in touch with the collective. You are part of it, you belong, you can say your piece, you can agree about the cause of the accident, you can smile at the others, you are all equal, you rub shoulders, you can criticize the driver who is to blame, you love each other.

The group has broken up. Goodbye love. He resumes his walking and crosses a square. A toddler staggering like a drunken man. A toddler is delightful, for a toddler is not dangerous, a toddler does not judge Jews. He feels like kissing him. No, his hair is too fair. Twenty years from now and he'll be a raging anti-Semite. He leaves the square. A regiment of soldiers. Must be the Foreign Legion, since they have white markings on their caps. Now legionnaires are happy men. Obeying orders, giving orders, never alone. He suddenly realizes that he is marching along with them, has fallen in with their despicable military step which brings disgrace on the whole human race, is keeping time to the band just yards from a gallows-faced lieutenant with long sideboards. What if he enlisted? He wouldn't be asked to show his papers, he could give a false name. How about 'Jacques Christian'?

The church he passed a while back. The red carpet's gone. Tonight there'll be one virgin less. Pity. There aren't that many around. The church bells ring out, but not for him. They are summoning the fortunate, those whose cup of communion runneth over, calling them to their delectable duty, bidding them come warm themselves, inviting them to be together, to come out of the cold, to mingle like the sounds of the tolling bells, sounds that tell of gladness and community, sounds that merge and blend in joy. Should he convert? He could never convert from conviction, but he might if it meant he would be one of them, if it meant being accepted. His intelligence and drive would make him be more Catholic than they, though he would not believe in their dogma. But he would exemplify and magnify their dogma once he'd taken holy orders and become a famed preacher of the Word, widely respected and loved by all. What acquaintances would he not have then, what friendships! Yes, loved by all, that was the thing. Another policeman watches him with the fixed, inane, dumbly insolent look usually seen on the faces of cows. He crosses the road to the pavement opposite.

Streets and yet more streets. On he goes with hunger in his heart and mistrust in his eye, on and on, a Jew humming a sad song, humming out of key, rolling his eyes like a lunatic to make the time pass, dipping into another bag of oily, roasted, companionable peanuts, wandering into an amusement arcade to watch the balls crashing around the electric pin-tables, but most often muttering to himself and swinging his arms in time to his thoughts. At Easter, go to Rome and join the crowd cheering the Pope. No one will know what he is, he'll be able to shout 'Long live the Pope!' with the rest of them. He'd heard the 'Song of the Volga Boatmen' on the wireless the other day. Oh for a land where men would welcome him with open arms and kiss him on the lips! Stir yourself, speak, walk, don't stop, say something, anything. A writer's eccentricities fuel his writing. If an author has a neurotic obsession with trifles which leads him to attach vast importance to such small matters as, say, the knotting of his tie, it is this self-same absurd attention to minutiae which gives his work its particular charm, its ripeness, its wealth of detail. He is afraid to attract attention. He keeps his eyes down, believing that by doing so he will be invisible. A born suspect. Will they turn him into an anti-Semite? Is he one already? Is his pride merely a cover for shame and loathing? Is he proud because there is nothing else he can be? Come on, speak, say something, so that he shall not know his fate, say something quickly, oh why don't the words come? How serious Ariane looks when she is being praised for her beauty, she takes it all in and sighs happily and puts on her good-little-girl face. Darling girl, so faithful, so gullible, and destined to be deceived. She would have been better off with the lord who climbed mountains, an oaf with Character. Poor kid. She has no luck.

★

Quick, more words, anything, paper over the misery with words. Each day when he was Under-Clown-General he would go among ersatz versions of his fellow men and find a kind of brotherhood, for though they did stupid things at least they did them together, and the brotherliness was wholesome. Quick, more words: if you stop talking the misery breaks through. He can't make out the change he is given, can't work out if it is right. He pretends to check so that the shopkeeper is not surprised. When that girl assistant in the grocer's realized she'd given him too much change, she smiled nicely just to say she didn't hold him to blame for the close shave she'd had. And the look that man had given him the other day when he'd said he'd forgotten his wallet, such a suspicious look, the look an honest man gives when confronted by a shady customer. Be an officer, but just a lieutenant. Obey, give orders, belong, know your place, have uncomplicated dealings with other people. Or else live alone with a kitten, which will have no idea that he is a pariah and will be happy to be with him and won't be troubled by a discontented, censorious, adulterous unconscious. Keep her in his room in the George V and kiss her fondly all the time and say: 'Pretty pussy, we're happy together you and I, you don't need anyone but me.' The sealed packet. All the care she'd taken to work out her plan. The large envelope which he'd received poste restante containing the sealed packet and her little note. He knows the little note by heart. He's going to recite it. 'Darling, In the enclosed packet sealed with sealing-wax are photographs of me. I took them all by myself: they're time exposures. I warn you now. They're a weeny bit risqué. If you don't care for the idea, please, please tear them up without looking at them. If you do look at them and you like them, wire and tell me. Naturally I developed and printed them myself. Don't open the sealed packet until you are all by yourself, and then only if you really want to.' Crossing the street will bring him luck. Cross now. No, green light, have to wait. If it turns red before you get to seven it'll be a sign that everything will turn out right. Six. Red light. He shrugs his shoulders and crosses. A group of building workers sitting with their backs to the wall eating their snap. Chatting together as they chew their sausage. An act of communion, a ritual to warm the heart.

★

Streets and yet more streets. Wake up, more words, words to fill the vacuum. Despair is waiting in the wings to pounce at the first drop of silence. How about going to see a doctor? He'll have to sit in the waiting-room under the fierce eye of some wounded tigress, but then he'll have a friend for a quarter of an hour, a brother who will take an interest in him and lay a perfumed head on his bare chest for twenty or maybe a hundred francs. A hundred francs isn't a lot for a quarter of an hour's kindness. No, the doc will tell him to strip so that he can examine him and he'll see, he'll notice. Doctors are all anti-Semites. Like lawyers. Maybe he is too. Yes, when he gets back to the hotel, tear them up without looking at them. Or maybe go to a barber who will look after him, shave him, talk to him, love him. Barbers are less anti-Semitic than people in the liberal professions, except if your hair crinkles too much. The newspaper report about the body of the child found in Fontainebleau forest. They'll make out it was a ritual murder, and he has no alibi. The good-looking newspaper-boy on the boulevard the other day had yelled: 'Read all abaht it! Get your *Antijuif* 'ere!' And lots of people had bought *L'Antijuif*. He had too, couldn't resist it. He read it as he walked along, bumping into passers-by while looking at a cartoon showing a pot-bellied banker with a top-hat and a large nose. Heal thyself, stop thinking about their hate all the time. Ask someone the way to the Place de la Concorde, to get back into the way of having normal relations with others, to get into the habit, to get over it. Perhaps the man he asks will answer him civilly. Or should he ask him for a light? The man smiles benevolently while another man uses his flame to light a cigarette.

Streets and yet more streets. In his mouth is the cheap, unclean fetor, the depressing, cloying after-taste of peanuts. On he goes, with shoulders hunched and eyes like two narrow slits. Another square. A dog sniffing round the base of a tree for a smell which will catch his fancy. O happy dog! Quickly now, have some thoughts, any thoughts. How can you believe what they say if you only see things from the outside? 'God, it's a joke,' he mutters and looks round to see if anyone is listening. In reality the fear of dying has given them mental dyspepsia and they wallow in the diarrhoea it produces. 'Their patriotism, what a joke,' he mutters, and looks round to see if anyone is listening. To die defending your hot-water bottle is the best, the most enviable of fates. The way they pause for One Minute's Silence (just the one) to honour their dead and then go off to lunch. The cleric on the wireless who spoke of grief, a decidedly cold fish who said mere words, paused to clear his throat, and talked of grief in a comfortable voice. The other day he'd felt so alone there in the street, was swamped by such pain that before he could go back to his hotel he had needed to be stayed by chocolate cakes, which he bought in cakeshops along his way. Only those fortunate enough to have a regular place in society hanker after solitude, and they do so with such stupid smugness. Last Sunday morning the bells of the nearby church had rung out, and he had heard them ring even though he had put his head under the pillow so that he would not hear their summons, their tolling happiness.

A bistro. At the next table, a couple of workmen. 'Nah, the pictures ain't my line at all, what I go for is anythin' that's ejucational, the sights, museums, Napoleon's tomb and that. I go to see Napoleon's tomb at least once a year, on me tod, jes' to remind meself what it's all abaht, sometimes I go more often, to show a pal around and explain it to 'im. Yus, mate, these two 'ands you see 'ere 'ave 'eld the Emprer's 'at and I tell you it gives you a shivery feelin'. I touched 'is weskit an' all, the bloke on the door said I could on account of us 'aving 'ad a bit of a chin-wag, but the Emprer's sword I din't touch, couldn't bring meself to, out of regard. Been round the Pantheon too, very interestin', all them great men they buried there in the nation's 'onner. But gettin' back to Napoleon, 'e said I wants to be laid to rest on the banks of the Seine, near to the people of France wot I always loved. Now that, mate, brings a lump to your froat. A real man, 'e was. When I was a kid I took a proper shine to 'im, you'd never believe. And 'is son, L'Aiglon, likewise. Now, no officers ever got anywhere near that one, otherwise 'e'd 'ave been put on the throne, but 'e'd never 'ave been 'alf the man 'is father was, oh no, they broke the mould when 'e died, 'eroes like the father is one-offs! To start with, 'e was king of Rome but 'is grandfather saw to it 'e was booted out on account of the way 'e 'ated 'is father, an' after that 'e was jes'

Duke of Raikstag.' 'I bet Napoleon 'ad the pick of all the girls 'e fancied?' asked the other man. 'Too right 'e did. If 'e 'ad an eye to one, 'e jes' gave the order and it was leg-over time at midnight.' 'Strikes me Napoleon was a sort of 'Itler in a way.' 'Don't be darft! Napoleon was Master of the World! No two ways abaht it! Nowadays, your modern generals 'ave 'ad all the trainin' an' that, of course, but what I say is that with your modern weapons they got it a lot easier, while Napoleon done it all with cold steel!' 'Napoleon was famous in 'is day, I ain't sayin' 'e wasn't, but 'e 'ad a lot on 'is conscience, such as three million pushin' up the daisies,' the other man said. 'Napoleon's Napoleon, say what you like! Listen, mate, if 'e 'adn't run up agin' that Wellington! An' stabbed in the back by that Grouchy an' all! What you gotter remember is that 'e was a soddin' genius! And don't you go forgettin' that Napoleon allus put 'is country first, all 'e done 'e done it for France, so other nations would look up to us, take all them battles 'e won! Besides which 'e done a lot of good, it's a fact. If 'e'd done bad things, 'e wouldn't 'ave been loved. All 'is grenadiers blubbed like kids when 'e told 'em goodbye at Fontainebleau and kissed the flag of France and 'eld it fast against 'is 'eart. 'E was speshul, take it from me!' 'I'm not sayin' any different, but you gotter remember that in them days France 'ad more people than anybody else!' 'Don't be darft! Napoleon will allus be Napoleon!' 'Very true, but all the same 'e done for a good few!' 'Listen, mate, that don't count compared with your 'Itler, now there's one who'll do for quite a few more before 'e's finished, see if 'e don't, because you can take it from me that we're 'eaded for war on account of the Jews! They're the ones who want it! Not 'im!' 'Now that's a fact, but it's us who'll be done in and all on account of them buggers!' 'Bloody Yids, we oughter kick 'em all out, that's what,' calls the lady at the till. He obeys, pays, and leaves.

'Death to the Jews,' clamour the walls. 'Life to Christians,' he replies. Oh yes, he wants nothing better than to love them. But couldn't they make a start, to give him some encouragement? From time to time he glances up uncertainly at the walls, and when he spots the slogan he stares at the ground. 'Death to the Jews.' The same words everywhere, in all countries. Is he really that repulsive? Maybe he is, for they're always saying so. 'If that's what you think, come on, do it, finish me off,' he murmurs. A handbill stuck on a down-pipe. Better not read it. To avoid the temptation, he crosses the street to the other side. But in a while he crosses again, to check. Yes, there it is again, though this time it's just 'Down with the Jews', which is better. It's progress.

On he goes, dipping into his bag of peanuts – peanuts are friends with Jews – and suddenly pulls up short. Another 'Death to the Jews', another swastika. He is afraid of the vicious words and the vicious symbol and yet he goes seeking them out, tracking them down, waiting for them to appear, he is the slogan-hunter and he wallows in the idea, but his eyes hurt. What do the people who scrawl these words have for hearts? Do they not have mothers? Have they never known kindness? Are they unaware that when Jews read the words they look at the ground or, if they are with a friend who is a Christian or a wife who is a Christian, simply pretend they haven't noticed them? Are they unaware of how much pain they cause, of how cruel they are? No, they are not aware of any such thing. Little boys who pull the wings off flies are not aware of it either. He stares at the four words, goes up close, and rubs out one letter with his finger. It's better in the singular. 'Death to the Jew' it reads now. The nose on that banker in *L'Antijuif*. He touches his own nose. If every day was carnival time he could hide it. Easy.

Standing motionless with his back to the wall, he moves his lips. 'Christians, I thirst for your love. Christians, let me love you. Christians, fellow creatures doomed to die, companions on this earth, children of Christ whose blood I share, let us love one another,' he murmurs, and he stares at those who pass by and love him not, and furtively he holds out a begging hand, and knows that he is acting foolishly, that nothing will do any good. He begins walking once more, buys a newspaper to read, to read so as not to think. Head down, he reads, cannons into other people, and nearly gets himself run over. Rue Caumartin. The walls which are his enemies shout out at him, follow him wherever he goes. Boulevard de la Madeleine. Should he duck down into the Metro and hide? Stand against a wall in the passages of the Metro, empty his mind under the ground, declare that he is flotsam, a man without responsibility, a man without hope. No, the Metro is worse. Louder than the walls above the ground, the walls of the Metro call for blood. His blood.

The Place de la Madeleine. A cakeshop. He goes in, buys six chocolate truffles, leaves, continues on his way, swinging the box containing the truffles while his shoes glide majestically over the paving-stones. Six truffles, gentlemen, there'll be a crowd. Six friendly little Christians in the ghetto, in a sense they're already there waiting for him. That's it, go back to the hotel, get into bed, get into bed with himself, with his good friend Solal, and while away the time reading anti-Semitic obscenities and scoffing truffles. Oh yes, back in the ghetto is a whole suitcaseful of anti-Semitic obscenities, and suddenly in the night he gets out of bed, feverishly opens the case, and begins reading their obscenities standing up, avidly, continues through the night, goes on reading their obscenities, each one read with interest, a dead man's interest. No, men are not kind. But soon, in his room, such a lovely room to be in when the door is locked behind him, he won't read their obscenities, he'll read a detective novel instead. A detective novel is an agreeable thing: it gives an entirely false picture of life which isn't a reminder of the world outside, and besides some people are unhappy in detective novels, which is a comfort, it means you don't feel so alone. Hello, he doesn't seem to have that book by the old Englishwoman. Must have left it somewhere. *The Case of the Painted Parrot*. Stupid old hag.

On the Quai Malaquais. The quayside booksellers. That's it, that's the solution! Shut himself up in a hotel room and read novels, only go out to buy more, dabble in the stock market now and then, and read, spend his whole life reading and waiting for death. Yes, but what about her, all alone at Agay? Must make up mind tonight, without fail. Meanwhile, buy this volume of Saint-Simon's *Memoirs*. No, since alone in a world swarming with enemies, steal it. There's no reason why he should obey the laws of a world which wants him dead. Death to the Jews? Fine. In that case he'll steal. There are no rules in war. He picks up the book, peruses it idly, calmly puts it under his arm, and then walks off, sleek of foot, swinging his box of chocolate truffles.

In the Place Saint-Germain-des-Prés. By the church steps, the paper-boy is selling his papers. 'Read all abaht it! Get your *Antijuif* 'ere! Latest edition!' Ah, another issue. No, don't buy it. Putting his handkerchief over his nose, he goes up to the paper-boy, asks for *L'Antijuif*, and pays. The paper-boy smiles. Should he remove his handkerchief, talk to him, make him see? Brother, don't you under-stand you put me on the rack? You are intelligent, you have a nice face, why can't we love one another. 'Read all abaht it! Get your *Antijuif* 'ere!' He flees, crosses the road, turns into a side-street and waves the hate-sheet. 'Read all abaht it! Get your *Antijuif* 'ere!' he shouts to the empty street. 'Death to the Jews!' he screams wildly. 'Death to me!' he shouts, his face bright with tears.

A taxi. He hails it and jumps in. 'The George V,' he says. Pretend to be mad so they'll shut him away in an asylum? That way he could go on living, without belonging and without suffering because he did not belong. When the taxi stops outside the hotel, don't go straight in, hang about on the other side of the street and wait. When the time's right, go through the revolving doors and make a beeline across the lobby, pretending to be blowing your nose. In the lift, appear calm and read the menu. The menu is always displayed in the lift.

Hat pulled down, handkerchief covering his nose, he bursts in, pushes the door shut, drops the book, and flops on to the bed. In his prone position, he whistles Schumann's *Rêverie* off-key while with his finger he writes 'Death to the Jews' in the air, then he presses the same finger between one eyeball and its socket so that he sees double. It passes the time. But that's enough. He stands, looks around him, smiles to see his room looking so immaculate, with no slogans at all chalked anywhere on the walls. Suddenly elated, he crosses to the door in a series of absurd little standing jumps and double-locks it. Alone at last, really alone! He feels sorry for the poor old bookseller with the long beard that fluttered in the wind. Tomorrow he'll give him back his Saint-Simon, he'll give him dollars so that he doesn't have to work any more in the open air, in the cold. A thousand-dollar note. Several, if he doesn't look too amazed. Oh yes, speculator emeritus, adept at using his brains, buying when the market's down and selling when it's on the up. With the profits he's made over the last few months, he has over a hundred thousand dollars on him, a buckler athwart his chest, and so easy to carry should he ever be deported.

He tries the lighter he's just bought. The little devil is in good shape, gives a very fine flame. Now for the little skier. He puts him on the pillow, which is perfect as a snowy slope, makes him perform slaloms and christianias, decides he's a sweetie, picks him up and gives him a kiss. 'We two get on just fine together,' he says. And now the suitcase. From the luggage cupboard he fetches the handsome case he'd bought the other day and inhales the luxurious smell of leather. Tomorrow, get some special cream to keep it supple. He frowns, for he has just noticed a stain on the carpet. He wets a face-towel, gets down on hands and knees, and rubs. Excellent. Stain gone. Oh yes, must look after your little ghetto. You can't live if you don't love. No, don't open the packet. 'Everything will turn out fine, you'll see,' he says, and he gives a wry smile, for such is the motto of the desperate. What next? Jerusalem? Or the cellar of the Silbersteins and Rachel? Yes, but how can he leave her alone? He stares at himself in the shaving-mirror. An hairy man. Tonight, make a will in her favour. Yes, burn some of it, that'll teach them. From the inside pocket of his jacket he produces a thousand-dollar note, strikes a match, burns the note, then another, and another. It's no fun.

Come on, break out the false nose! He takes it out of the bag, raises it to his lips and stands in front of the mirror to put it on, arranges the elastic and looks at himself admiringly. There! He is now complete and unabridged, for he is endowed with the majestic appendage signifying the will to survive, which grew to its present size because it was always used to sniff out enemies and detect traps. Carrying the suitcase, sign and symbol of the ancient wanderer, ennobled by the cardboard nose of royal authority which smells of glue and a cellar –

O Silbersteins! O Rachel! – he shuffles, shoulders bent, God's crook-back, eyes watchful, feet dragging and case swinging, shuffles through the centuries and many lands, arguing immoderately, his hands waving and protean, his lips spreading in resigned, torpidly knowing smiles, on and on he goes, suddenly falling silent but thoughtful-eyed, suddenly the holiness of the Almighty proclaiming, suddenly his head and shoulders rocking, suddenly a keen glance sideways casting, frightened, frightening in his beauty, the chosen one. Yes! Standing there in his mirror is Israel entire.

Naked now and smooth-cheeked, he opens the old case and from it takes the shawl of the synagogue. He kisses its fringes, drapes his nakedness with it, and says the blessing. He winds the phylacteries around his arm and says the blessing. Then from the case he takes the crown of the Feast of Lots, Rachel's crown, the cardboard crown which travels with him everywhere in his wanderings, the battered crown set with glass diamonds. He puts it on his head and sets off down the nights and through the ages, sorrowing as he goes, blessed with ancient beauty, halts in front of the solitary king who stands before him in the mirror, smiles at his reflection, his companion through life, keeper of his secrets, his reflection which alone knows that he is a king in Israel. 'Yes,' he murmurs to his reflection, 'they will build the Laughing Wall, and in the blue temple the bright water will sing.'

He jumps. Is it the police? He asks who is it. The florist's delivery-man. He puts on a dressing-gown, removes the false nose, half opens the door, shuts it quickly, and puts the bouquet in the bath. What next? But of course, he can eat, that's it, fellow-me-lad, eat. He can still eat, eating never lets you down. His Majesty is about to eat. He picks up the phone; orders cakes so that he doesn't have to wait for anything to be made, so that he can feel instant happiness.

He picks up the tray from outside the door, quickly turns the key in the lock, lowers the blinds, and draws the curtains to cancel the world outside. Next he switches on the lights, sets down the tray of cakes on the table, which he pushes up against the wardrobe mirror so that he has a guest, and then begins to eat while perusing the Saint-Simon. Sometimes he glances up at the mirror, smiles at himself, smiles at the down-and-out eating alone, quietly eating, reading as he eats, accepting his lot, making the most of it. Then he resumes his perusal of Saint-Simon, who, he discovers, was a well-integrated little crawler who knew everybody and was fawned on by the whole court because he had once been honoured by a remark by His Majesty, who had assured him that the royal favour shown to his father would also be bestowed on him. Dukes and peers were up and about from early morning, eagerly discussing His Majesty's mood and his still steaming stools, finding out who was in favour and who disgraced ingratiating themselves with the former and avoiding the latter, and above all determined to be noticed by the Great Excretor seated on his close-stool and be found pleasing in his sight. Crafty tail-wagging curs, the lot of them. Including Racine, grovellingly confessing his faults on the steps of the throne in the hope of being reinstated in the royal favour. Curs. But happy curs.

A sudden burst of the 'Marseillaise' on the radio, sung by a crowd. His heart misses a beat, he rises and stands motionless, stands to attention, his hand absurdly poking his temple in a military salute, tremulous with love, a true son of France, and he lends his voice to the voices of those who were once his compatriots. When the last echo dies away, he turns the radio off and he is alone and a Jew in a room with lowered blinds, lit by electricity, though the sun shines bright outside.

To avoid dwelling on his existence, he gets into bed and picks up a best-selling novel, the author of which is a woman and the heroine a little bitch, a splendid product of the middle classes, who is bored and sleeps with all and sundry for something to do and, after going to bed whisky-drunk with this one and then with that one, who may have syphilis, drives off at ninety miles an hour, for something to do. He tosses the nauseating little trollop into the waste-paper basket.

The radio. A Protestant service. Heart-sad, he listens to the singing of the faithful. Oh those voices! So sure, so hopeful, so gentle, so good:

at least they're good for the time being. He gets out of bed, goes over to the radio, and kneels before it to belong, to be with brother human beings. A hard lump in his throat, difficulty breathing. He knows that he is grotesque, a solitary outsider, grotesque for singing their hymns of praise with them, grotesque for singing along with those who reject and mistrust him. But all the same he joins with them and sings their noble hymn, oh the joy of singing with them, of singing that their God is a bulwark, a stout shield and defender, the joy of making the sign of the cross to belong with them, to love them and be loved by them, the joy of saying the sacred words with brother human beings. For Thine is the kingdom, the power and the glory, for ever and ever, amen. 'Receive God's holy blessing,' the minister says. Whereupon he bows his head to receive the blessing, like them, with them. Then he stands up, alone and a Jew, and he remembers the walls.

He puts his cardboard nose on again and sniggers. Why not give the walls outside exactly what they want? Hateful his vitality; stupid this will to live. Jerusalem or Rachel? But for the moment the chocolate truffles, quickly now. 'I'm going to eat you all up, my little treasures,' he says. 'Sorry, but I'd forgotten all about you.' He observes himself masticating in the mirror, masticating with pitiful glee. But when the truffles are all gone the despair has not gone away.

'Death to the Jews.' His cardboard nose is uncomfortable, he chokes on his loneliness, on the suffocating smell of glue and cellar, but no, keep it on, his false nose is his honour. Cornered, behaving like a man cornered, he rolls his eyes and suddenly he is a French army captain and the wall-daubers are going to send him to Devil's Island. He snaps to attention. The whole battalion has assembled at his back, while before him stands the officer charged with ensuring that justice is seen to be done, an officer with a large moustache, reeking of garlic, who rips off his stripes and breaks his sword over his knee. He shouts at the mirror, in a voice made nasal by his fancy-dress nose, shouts that he is innocent, that he is not a traitor. *'Vive la France!'* he shouts.

★

Why not take the flowers and lay them at the tomb of the Unknown Soldier under the Arc de Triomphe? They'll laugh. In her letter, she said not to open the packet until he was alone. Well, he certainly is alone: alone is the word for it! Suddenly he decides: Yes he'll open it and look. A grubby pleasure owing to him. He can stop worrying about his destiny for whole minutes. Because what's in the packet is a breath of life, a privilege granted only to him. Leper he may be, but few happy men have wives more beautiful and loving. For love, to keep her man, she has dared, demeaned by solitude, dared, she the daughter of unspotted lineage, dared, for his sake, dared to brave the degradation of dirty pictures. Well then, very well then, he now has a Purpose, which is to look at her dirty pictures, love them one by one, painstakingly, find her desirable and to hell with Deuteronomy. Yes, my love, let us be degraded together.

Don't open it straight away. Order a good dinner first. Oh yes, misfortune demeans, but here's one way of fighting back against misfortune. Oh yes, absolutely, a first-class dinner, with champagne. The cooks will pull out all the stops for him. The dirty pictures will keep. No one can deprive him of that pleasure! He may not have the 'Marseillaise' and brothers to sing it with, nor the Coldstream Guards presenting arms to him, to France's representative, but he does have dirty pictures! We have our own ways of being happy, gentlemen, just as you have!

No, not dinner. Not hungry. Can't face it. Quickly now, a quick fix of happiness. He breaks the seals, opens the packet, closes his eyes, and chooses at random. Don't look at once, work up to it slowly, keep telling yourself a glimpse of happiness lies just around the corner. He places one hand flat on the photograph then opens his eyes. Slowly he draws his hand downwards. Oh! Horrible! He slides his hand up again so that only the face is visible. Lo, an aristocratic face, the face of a daughter of those who spurn him. A respectable face, a decent face, but take your hand away and what a contrast! Try some of the others. Ariane as a lusting nun. Ariane as a little girl in a short skirt, with bare legs, beckoning crudely. And this one, even worse. Very well, be degraded, Solal. Poor darling girl, unhinged by solitude, this appalling talent of hers spawned by the seething ferment of her solitude. He stares hard at the photos, spreads them all out, feels desire for them, for his harem. Good, he may have reached the depths of his unhappiness but he can still take an interest in something, can still desire. Oh, the albino with the neatly trimmed hair goes home contentedly to his wife and children and does not need degrading photographs to make him happy. He gets to his feet and tears them up. But what can he do now. Love! Go to Ariane! Go to her, his country and his home! Yes, leave tonight! Pack bags, dress, taxi to the station!

He leaves his bags at the luggage counter and wanders idly out into the Boulevard Diderot, waiting for his train to form. Suddenly, in the night, under the misty lights, he knows them as they file out of the station in twos and threes, some wearing black, wide-brimmed, ear-splaying, head-cramming Homburgs, others in flat, fur-trimmed velvet skullcaps, but all garbed in interminable black coats, the older ones clutching furled umbrellas, but all carrying suitcases, shoulders hunched, feet dragging, and debating excitedly as they go. He knows them, knows them for his well-beloved fathers and subjects, meek and majestic, the devout of strict observance, the firm of purpose, the faithful with black beards and dangling earlocks, self-contained and absolute, strangers in their exile, unshakeable in their otherness, scorned and scorning, indifferent to mockery, fabulously, undeviatingly themselves, going their own upright way, proud of their truth, scorned and mocked, the exalted of his people, issued forth from the Lord and His Sinai, bearers of His Law.

He has drawn closer the better to see them, the better to feast his eyes. He follows them through the dark night streets, rounding his shoulders like theirs, head down like theirs, and like them screwing up his eyes and darting quick, furtive glances around him, follows God's crook-backs, spellbound by their bent backs and their black coats and their beards, follows the bearded of God, feeling love for his people and filling his heart with his love, walks in the wake of the centuries and the dragging coats and the dragging steps and the everlastingly carried possessions, walks and murmurs 'Thy tents are beautiful, O

Jacob, and thy dwellings, O Israel', walks in the wake of his well-beloved black priests of God, fathers and sons of prophets, walks in the wake of his chosen people and fills his heart with his people, Israel, his love.

They halt outside Kohn's Restaurant, debate, make up their minds, enter, find tables, and sit with their cases between their legs, for safety. He remains outside and watches them through the window, through the curtains, watches his languid-eyed wanderers, his well-beloved fathers and subjects stroking their beards and caressing their passports, prodding their aching backs and their overloaded livers, all arguing vociferously, hands gesticulating, hands thinking. Incisive looks probe, deduce and know, fingers curl pensive beards, noses compute, brows impute, lowered eyes conclude. Pink with life against the black of their beards, too pink and fleshy, lips spread in resigned, torpidly knowing smiles, then shut, tremble, tighten, calculate, ponder, cogitate, ruminate and deliberate while diamonds in tissue paper circulate.

Still wearing their hats – for hair is a form of nakedness – the bearded band he loves are now eating with gusto, hunched over their plates, studiously feeding on cold stuffed fish, chopped liver, aubergine caviare and meatballs served on fried onion rings. At the back of the room, an old man with an immeasurable beard sits hunched over the Holy Law, which takes precedence over God himself, reads and rocks as he reads.

Then, outside in the dark night where fine, cold rain drizzles down, their solitary king stands at the curtain-hung window and he too rocks his head and shoulders, rocks in time to the immemorial rhythm, chants a hymn to the Almighty in the old tongue, the hymn which Moses and the children of Israel sang to the Almighty who delivered them from the hand of Pharaoh, who cast the Egyptians into the Red Sea, and the waters covered the chariots and the horsemen and all the host of Pharaoh, and there remained not so much as one of them, but the children of Israel walked upon the dry land in the midst of the sea, and the waters were a wall unto them on their right hand and on their left, and Israel saw the Egyptians dead upon the sea shore, and it was well. Praise to the Almighty, for who is more magnificent in holiness and more worthy of praise than He? Sing praises to the Almighty, for He has made His glory to shine! Horses and horsemen all did He cast into the sea! Hallelujah!

CHAPTER 94

'We had dinner in our dining-room around a table which seats twenty-four and now we are settled in our spacious and quite useless drawing-room sitting in our appallingly comfortable chocolate-mousse armchairs, I am pretending to read so that I shan't have to talk to the poor girl while she is sewing up all the hems which I unpicked on the quiet to give her something to do she told me it would take her quite a while perhaps a couple of hours because first she'll have to remove the old threads and after that she intends putting in some fine needlework poor darling she said she wants to make the stitches even and tiny so they won't show or gape very well darling go ahead make it perfect poor kitten she can't be much of a hand at sewing but at least her life has some point for the time being on no account stop pretending to read under pain of conversation let's hope we're not in for a recital of rumblings tonight, I'm sorry darling but you do realize that I've been doing my level best since I got back from Paris, she was so sweet the other night when I called in on her to say good-night she was reading and I said come along it's time to go to sleep now she shut her book at once she said yes all right in such a way that my heart missed a beat an angel's yes a good little girl's yes heart-stopping and so meek I felt myself melt with love melt with the pity that is love, Ariane my child who cries so bitterly when I get angry her searing anguish her eyes puffy with so much crying her nose swollen with so much wiping but if I say I'm sorry she forgives me at once shows no resentment and in no time at all I hear her in her room singing and the bitter anguish is all gone, I feel such pity for my

849

child so quickly restored to hope so eager to be happy, darling your sex frightens me frightened me when you bent down in your nakedness to pick up something off the floor, this morning you went out shopping and I was alone in the house and I kissed your pretty grey blazer it was hanging up in the hall I kissed it several times I even kissed the lining, and now I'm going to tell you everything without running any risk of making myself look small since you cannot hear me alas oh yes I must absolutely keep face so you can go on being proud to love me but even so some day I may tell you all about the Silbersteins' cellar, I wanted to stay on with them but they asked me to save them so on the fourth day I left only to fail in each and every capital failed in London failed in Washington failed in the Council of their damned L of N when I asked the self-important clowns to take in my German Jews to divide them among themselves, they said my plan was utopian that if they took them all there would be an upsurge of anti-Semitism in the countries which accepted them in other words they threw them to their butchers because they loathe anti-Semitism, for which I arraigned both them and their love-thy-neighbour cant O great Christ betrayed whereupon ructions and to put it simply I was turfed out as the Forbes woman put it ignominiously instant dismissal for conduct prejudicial to the interests of the League of Nations said the letter which old Cheyne wrote to me and then followed the decree rescinding my nationality on grounds of procedural irregularity and then a few days ago my stupid attempts to get the decree withdrawn and the pathetic comfort of her photos, poor girl thinking up her next pose yes that one too he'll like that one me with no clothes on standing in front of the mirror that way he'll have a view of both sides of me left hand raised touching the mirror and right hand between my as if I'm about to yes he'll like that, poor girl standing in position for the time exposure hurriedly getting into her deplorable pose, and then the decision to go back to her to seek comfort in our miserable bodies but suddenly hope dawns yes stop off first at Geneva, persuade the Clown-General to take me back, ah my serene seamstress behold! behold Solal the Cretin in Geneva drafting a letter to give to old Cheyne when he goes to see him a twenty-page letter in which he sets out his misery the wretched life we lead a long letter ensure he reads it when I'm there, yes best make it a letter because I'm afraid I'll forget what to say if I say it face to face yes a letter because I'm feeling low and not at all sure if I can say it properly and make him see melt his heart whereas with a letter you can put things properly, darling look upon your poor believer who spent days composing his make-or-break weighty deadly serious letter seven days and seven nights spent looking for arguments to melt his heart scribbling words starting again then typing the letter on a typewriter bought specially for the purpose a Royal the fool typing with two fingers shut up in a hotel room preparing his pitiful big move yes typing a letter so the old man can read it easily and get the message and be lulled into a kindly frame of mind and feel sorry yes a letter typed with two fingers in front of a mirror for company so that the mirror is company for this solitary rootless man this Jew a letter typed by a despairing man who sweats and can't type and sometimes glances up and stares at his reflection and feels deep pity for the pathetic figure before him, yes darling with two fingers but it was neatly typed no typing errors at all when I made a mistake I rubbed it out just like a proper typist with a special rubber a round thin eraser which kept me company for a week I would look at the eraser and think it was aiding and abetting and helping to save me I loved it I can remember exactly what was printed on it Weldon Roberts Eraser I rubbed gently so I wouldn't leave marks on the exquisite paper or dirty it yes aim for a really beautifully typed letter to put Cheyne in a good mood these little things can make all the difference at least that is what the no-hopers of this world always say anyway by sticking at it I ended up a pretty competent typist that's the way play the highest cards you have in your hand win him round with a letter moving in content and impeccable in form oh yes dwelling on your misfortunes can addle the brain, and lo came the evening when I called at the Cheyne residence at seven incredibly clean-shaven and feeling awkward almost forced my way in I handed him the letter so impeccable in form and he glanced casually at the letter so moving in content read it turning the pages so quickly that I felt sick felt my Jew face flush angry purple, oh yes darling it took him just four or five minutes to read the letter I had sweated over for days and nights he gave it back to me held it between thumb and forefinger as if it were dirty my lovely letter my beautiful letter so beautifully typed with two fingers he said there was nothing he could do for me, and then just listen to this the fool produced another letter from his pocket a brief note in case the first met with a rebuff a fall-back letter in which the poor fool his wits turned by loneliness dared offer the old man all the money he had the pathetic fool stating the exact amount in dollars yes every penny I had if the old man would agree to give me a job any job even a minor job so long as I would be a part of things so long as I could shake the pariah dust from my feet whereupon the fool was turned away indignantly by Cheyne the sterling multimillionaire Cheyne the incorruptible, outside I tramped the streets dragging my misery with me wanting my Uncle Saltiel oh to see him again and go back and live with him but that's out of the question he would be so distressed to see how low I have fallen I won't make him unhappy stopping by the lake tearing up both letters my two brilliant ploys my great hopes and throwing them into the lake and watching them float away on the current, street after street after street thinking of how to rid you of me and leave you all my dollars putting them in a bank in your name and then going back to live in the cellar with them, I was exhausted I hadn't eaten anything the whole of the time I'd spent sweating over my typewriter so I wandered into a café and I talked to you over coffee and croissants and there were tears in my eyes I whispered to you with tears in my eyes for the unhappiness I have brought upon you the misery of love in quarantine a love so chemically pure, at the table to my left was an old man who didn't notice that I was crying a little old man with a nose like a strawberry he was drinking white wine then a grim-voiced newsboy appeared hawking the *Tribune* his voice was portentous clamorous urgent and he rattled the change in his bag he called out special edition Swiss franc devalued which made a stir everyone bought a paper, the three who came and sat at the table of the man with the grog-blossom nose and the rest of them all started talking about the devaluation some being for and some against, I drew closer the stateless person drew closer and argued strongly that devaluation meant salvation for our country the old man agreed with me he said quite right all decent people should think like this gentleman and he shook my hand and afterwards they all rushed home to pass on the news I left too outside in the street I saw the old man who'd already gone a fair way I ran to catch him but when I was almost up with him I felt awkward and slowed down so he wouldn't realize that I needed him needed the company needed the brotherhood, we talked some more about the devaluation he told me he'd be worse off as a result that the cost of living would go up but too bad the general interest had got to come first so I repeated what matters most is saving our country it was nice to be able to say our country he introduced himself Sallaz schoolteacher retired I felt uncomfortable saying my name so I just babbled on talked about our country the Switzerland we loved the old man was delighted and suggested a drink said it's on me one for all and all for one, we went into a brasserie and sat down next to a fat man and his fat wife who were unfolding their serviettes as the gourmet hors-d'œuvres arrived settling into their chairs with well-bred complacency and healthy appetites about to be satisfied and exchanging unexpectedly good-humoured smiles, the old man and I clinked our glasses he started asking questions I said I was the Swiss consul in Athens I described the consulate and the Swiss flag hanging from a balcony on national holidays what you've got to understand Monsieur Sallaz is that when you're far from home it's a comfort to see your country's flag flying he asked if the Swiss consul's standing was the same as that of the consuls of the major powers I said it's higher because we are straight as a die everybody knows it and respects us for it he gave a proud little laugh and said by Jove that's right we Swiss aren't a pack of rogues like that lot in the Balkans so I upped the ante I said in Switzerland we don't fiddle the income tax he offered me an alarming black cigar I smoked it all the way down for love of our own Swiss country, I don't want to pry sir but may I know your name well now that we've had a drink together I think you're perfectly entitled to ask the name's Motta you wouldn't by any chance be related to the Federal Councillor Motta I'm his nephew said I whereupon he gave me a look so respectful so fond that it hurt he finished his glass of white wine well you can be very proud of your uncle because Federal Councillor Motta is a great man a true son of Ticino a true son of Switzerland the spearhead of our diplomacy as they say ah what we need is more men of his calibre it's true you do look like him, he suggested another round of white wine to cement the friendship we drank up I spoke fulsomely in praise of liberal Swiss institutions with special reference to their stability and prudence adding a word about the independent Alps and the *ranz-des-vaches*, did you know Monsieur Sallaz that Louis XIV banned the singing of the *ranz* and those caught *in flagrante delicto* were sentenced to life imprisonment that's right when our soldiers in the service of the French king heard the *ranz-des-vaches* they deserted by the dozen which only goes to show how much we love our country and how much we pine for our beloved mountains and our beloved Alpine slopes, I wasn't joking I was quite carried away I was thinking of you my darling when you're by yourself humming one of your mountain songs, at this point the old man broke into the *ranz-des-vaches* and I sang along with him the other customers joined in too and next we sang the Swiss national anthem hail to thee fair Switzerland the blood the lives of thy children, then Sallaz got shakily to his feet and announced to all the customers that his friend was the nephew of Federal Councillor Motta Head of the Ministry of Foreign Affairs at which several came up to me and shook me by the hand and people shouted three cheers for Motta I thanked them all feeling the warmth of my fellow men yes there were tears in the eyes of this descendant of Aaron brother of Moses, I say Monsieur Motta it would give me the greatest pleasure if you would do me the honour of coming to my house tomorrow evening for a fondue with my family, I accepted he gave me his address and we separated I'm delighted to have met you sir take care we'll expect you tomorrow night I knew I wouldn't go it would be too painful to sit round the family table under false pretences, I was afraid to go back to my hotel afraid of going back to myself so I went to another café where they were also talking about the devaluation I sat down near them the bony *béret basque* with the blotchy face said it's the Jews that's been angling for a devaluation and all your department stores and your fixed-price emporiums is owned by Jew-boys they're driving corner shops to the wall they're taking the bread out of our mouths nobody asked them to come here to my way of thinking they oughter be treated a bit like the way they get treated in Germany if you see what I mean though we didn't oughter be too hard on them because they're yuman when all is said and done, whenever I encounter a little boy my heart does not leap up when I see him smile because I am haunted by the spectre of the man he'll grow up to be a man with long teeth sly sickeningly gregarious another Jew-hater, she sits silent and reserved asking for nothing happy to sew for me I love you I love your clumsiness your childish gestures, Proust had the peculiar habit of dunking little sponge cakes in lime-blossom tea two sweetish tastes combined in one disgusting taste of sponge cake mixed with the even more disgusting taste of the lime tea a kind of perverse femininity which tells me as much about him as the hysterically flattering things he wrote to Anna de Noailles in reality he didn't think that much of her had no reason to he flattered her because she was a star of polite society no don't tell her she'd be hurt she's so very fond of the little Vinteuil phrase and the bells of Martinville and the Vivonne and the hawthorns at Méséglise and the rest of the exquisiteries, Laure Laure Laure Laure in the chalet the little mountain hotel the children got to know me quickly adopted me I played with them and after a few days she decided to call me Uncle she was beautiful very beautiful she was fourteen years old no thirteen and already her breasts her thighs oh so beautiful a woman already but with the grace of a child, when the only way down was over the tangle of fallen tree-trunks I asked her if she was afraid oh no I'm never afraid when I'm with you but hold me tight and I held her close and then she said oh yes and in her upturned eyes was love unadulterated love, the next day she behaved more naturally with me she blurted out you know I like you more than people usually like uncles, O Laure at thirteen what games we played we played on a see-saw so we could face one another so we could go on looking at each other without the others knowing but we never admitted anything to each other about what we felt on the see-sawing yee-yawing plank we stared at one another unsmiling dumb with love grave with love I thought she was so beautiful and she thought I was handsome we stared we drank each other's nearness I can't for the life of me think what you can see in bobbing up and down like you've been doing this past hour said her mother and when her mother had gone we started staring at each other again she and I so serious, with the other children we played Siberian sledging so that we could hold hands under the sledge blanket, we loved each other but never said so we were pure or as good as, every afternoon she would come and ask me to play and I had to try to catch her and her little brother and her friend Isabelle who'd come to spend a week with her in the chalet, Laure O Laure she loved being caught by me she let out little frightened squeals when I grabbed her and held her breathless against me and once she murmured it's awful but I like it, and one evening she sulked because that afternoon I had caught Isabelle too often oh the way she looked when on another evening she and I got back late it was dark in the forest she said hold me I'm scared and I held her by the waist but she removed my arm from her waist and put my hand on her breast she pressed my hand hard on her breast and I heard a salivary intake of breath, every evening after dinner when she and her little brother went to say good-night to the grown-ups before going to bed Laure made sure she kissed everybody but everybody for the sake of appearances and me the last just a peck on the cheek awfully proper with eyes averted and just a tiny bit frightened, we'd both been looking forward so much to that pure kiss throughout the whole of dinner we knew it was coming and we kept glancing at each other throughout the meal the others never suspected a thing and when the marvellous moment came we feigned indifference I was twenty she was thirteen Laure Laure a single summer's love I was twenty she was thirteen after lunch she'd come looking for me I say Uncle let's play siestas come on let's climb up to that grassy ledge up there we can have forty winks together it'll be fun we'll take a rug I was twenty she was thirteen when we got there we lay down on the grass under the tall pine me her and her little brother he got dragged along too for the sake of appearances too but we never said so indeed we never admitted anything openly to each other I was twenty she was thirteen ah those high-altitude siestas the weather was always glorious and the air full of the buzz of summer I was twenty she was thirteen she always insisted that the three of us should get under the rug and she would take my hand and lay her head on my hand and close her eyes and sleep or pretend to sleep on my hand and her burning lips were on my hand but her lips did not move because she did not dare to kiss my hand I was twenty she was thirteen or else she would wrap herself up in the rug oh rugs of our love of our great love of a single summer then she would rest her head on my knee supposedly to go to sleep then she would lift her head and look at me

I was twenty she was thirteen and I loved her I loved her Laure O
Laure O child yet woman, when the holidays were over the day she
was leaving in the little cable-car station her mother was at the ticket
window Laure in socks Laure at thirteen suddenly said I know why
you always wanted us to be with the others and never alone I know
what you were afraid of you were afraid that there were other things
for just the two of us to do and I wouldn't have minded those other
things I would have liked us to be alone together for a whole day for
a whole night farewell Laure who was thirteen oh the love of a single
summer's length my great love oh my Cephalonian boyhood oh
Passover on the eve of Passover my lord and father would fill the first
cup and then say the blessing in Thy love for us has Thou given us
this feast of unleavened bread in commemoration of our deliverance
and as a token of our going out of Egypt blessed be Thou O Lord
who sanctifieth Thy people Israel, I admired his voice and next came
the cleansing of the hands and then the dipping of the chervil in
vinegar then the breaking of unleavened bread and after that was the
telling of the story my lord and father raised the salver aloft and
would say here is the bread of affliction which our forefathers did
once eat in Egypt's land whoever hungers let him come and eat with
us whoever is in need let him come and celebrate Passover with us
this year we are here but next may we be in the land of Israel this
year we are slaves but next year may we be a free people, and then
because I was the youngest I put the prescribed question how does
this night differ from other nights why on every other night do we
eat leavened bread and why on this night unleavened bread I was
deeply moved when I put the question to my lord and father who
then would remove the cloth that covered the unleavened bread and
begin the reply looking directly at me and I would blush with pride
he would say we were slaves to Pharaoh in Egypt and the Eternal our
God brought us forth with His powerful hand and His outstretched
arm, my solitary Jewish wandering through the streets of Geneva
after the Cheyne fiasco, first to Devaluation Café then to the brasserie
with Sallaz and then the café featuring the *béret basque* and they're
yuman when all is said and done, then a third café and the four
workmen at the next table who'd finished their game of cards, don't
it just make yer sick though exclaimed the loser he threw his cards

down with feigned indignation which he intended to be funny to show that he wasn't bothered about losing that he was above such things and also to make out that he was a good sport who took it all in good part he turned to the winner and said you allus turn up aces but me the only thing I ever turn up is the gas which got a laugh, encouraged he went on and said to the winner you're wasted in your job you should have become a croupier, come a cropper more like replied the winner and there was another round of solid working-class guffaws, o' course said the oldest a chap likes winnin' it's only yuman nature but when you lose it don't do to grouse, quite right said the loser and he calmly produced the sum he had lost and handed it to the winner and said oh it don't do any good getting all hot and bothered and said it in a straight serious way to show he wasn't hiding how cut up he was the fourth member of the group who had red hair said to the winner we'd better phone the bank and tell 'em to fetch a van over to carry your winnin's away in but nobody laughed because he was a shy man and told his jokes with none of the authority of the strong, after a while I left I went into one of those little cafés where they have music-hall turns to entertain the customers I went in because of its name the San Fairy Ann the little curtain went up on the little stage and Damien came on Damien was down on the bill for Comic Songs poor Damien with his paunch large dyed moustache poached eyes jacket too tight key-chain hanging out of a dignified white waistcoat Damien was wearing the Military Cross he rubbed and wrung his large red hands to display his elegance and poise as he waited for the band to finish his introduction and then began singing articulating carefully poor conscientious failure who washed his feet once a week began singing a satirical song about rich people who give a lavish party and he pulled a posh face featuring demurely pouting lips, but nary a crust in the larder for my poor little ones and he raised both heavily ringed hands and clasped his head in despair, so to feed my pretty bairns I took to a life of crime and he waggled his ringed and tastefully thieving fingers, and when the song was over he made more washing motions with his hands while the band played the introduction for the next ditty which was another social protest involving the son of a rich mill-owner who seduces an honest factory-girl by showering her with kisses here Damien caressed his backside, and she was intoxicated by love here Damien's sausage fingers spiralled upwards like smoke, and the poor weak little thing got carried away here he raised one hand to his forehead and closed his eyes, and it all ended up with a lot of being sorry for girls who get into trouble girls who go wrong, yes darling your yes your frightens me, next on the bill was an enormously stout lady with very fat white hands who sang earthy songs she laughed as she came on to suggest that she was a card she beamed at the audience to suggest that she had them just where she wanted them to let them know that she had them in the palm of her hand then with the air of one accustomed to carrying all before her announced the title of the song she was about to sing The Cigarette Waltz dedicated to all smokers then said Maestro to the pianist to indicate that he could start, the last verse was devoted to the cigarette rolled by the man in the condemned cell and the tears of his grief-stricken mother, Hear, O Israel: the Lord our God, the Lord is One, O God whom I love I miss Thee every hour, if I forget Thee O Jerusalem let my right hand forget its cunning, next came Yamina the Oriental Dancer the net over her bosom was designed rather to prevent her breasts sagging than to hide them I felt so depressed my darling I thought of you Yamina's two girl assistants clapped their hands extravagantly but managed to do it silently, during the interval Yamina had a drink with the earthy songstress she said I'd give my eye-teeth for a really unusual dance routine you know costume with great big ostrich feathers and the rest of it what would make it a really big hit is that me and Marcel have both got fair hair, then afterwards streets and yet more streets and feeling ashamed as I walked through the door, the four girls sitting in the bar downstairs in negligées all stood up no I want to be left alone I gave them some money I drank a glass of rum two other girls at the next table to mine were sitting on the knees of a couple of soldiers the older one was being saucy to make herself seem younger poking her tongue out at her soldier pinching his ear, no that's what it costs to go upstairs that's separate from tips us girls depend on the generosity of our gentlemen see all we get is what the customers give us go on make it a round figure go on be nice and after we'll give you a good time me and my friend know all the tricks you just see if we don't, in

Geneva the letter she read out to me to make me laugh a letter her husband Deume had got from his mother she had the brass-faced nerve to read it out to me, women will do anything to please the man they love, a letter about somebody called Adhémar van Offel who asks his aunt if God loves servants shall I imagine Adhémar talking to his aunt no use it as the basis of a little scene between the Countess de Surville and her son Patrice on a fine morning in summer in the spacious red and gold drawing-room of the ancestral castle a handsome boy of nine was sitting pensively beside his mother who was modestly bent over her needlework suddenly he made up his mind and tiptoed over to her Mother dear tell me does God love servants as much as he loves us who are pukka crust Madame de Surville buried her yearning face in her hands and remained thus for some time reflecting in silence while the boy with blond curls knelt trembling before his one-eyed mother staring radiantly at her then at length the Countess surfacing from her prolonged meditation held out both hands Yes my child God loves servants just as much as he loves us she replied simply and with a strange pallor in her face and eyes cast down, it was a bitter blow but the noble boy bore it without flinching yet as he tried to smile at his mother large tears could be seen trickling down his rosy cheeks, whereupon the Countess held him close Child child she said you stand upon the threshold of life you will encounter many rude surprises but I am confident that you will be able to meet them with courage like a man like a patriot like a true believer like a worthy son of your dear father who fell on the glorious field of battle, Yes Mother replied little Patrice who suddenly giving vent to his despair shook with great racking sobs I am grateful to you he added for thinking sufficiently well of me to tell me the honest truth please forgive me mother dear for momentarily showing something of the cruel disappointment I felt on hearing your words but you will concede Mother dear that God moves in mysterious ways, Dear child went on Madame de Surville I admit it gladly for the lower classes are sometimes such a disappointment and so terribly lacking in spirituality and other-worldly radiance, That I too in turn will concede the blond boy replied eagerly and would even go so far as to add that the crass materialism of humble folk has frequently offended my native delicacy of feeling the Prince of Wales being my ideal and also Marshal Foch and that it has only been by resorting to prayer that I have been able to overcome my revulsion but then you know who I take after he added cleverly catching the eye of his dear mother who blushed modestly, there followed a lengthy silence during which both mother and son seemed to gather new strength through the intense power of concentration little Patrice standing with his eyes turned heavenwards as though listening to choirs of angels through which he thought he could detect the voice of Dear Grandpapa who had also fallen gloriously on the field of battle, then at length patting his blond curls he asked his mother's permission to speak and waited with a delicate smile and well-bred deference, disturbed in her pious thoughts Madame de Surville started clasped her hand tremblingly to her heart and gave a half-stifled but gracious cry then acquiesced with such a sweet look on her ringlet-framed face, Mother dear another and even graver question torments me a question which perhaps Satan has whispered in my ear which is do you truly believe that God also loves those who have only recently taken out French nationality asked the child whose heart was beating so fast that he thought he would faint, the Countess de Surville collected her thoughts for a moment then looked at her son with her one good but luminous eye, Let us pray she said simply, and after letting her soul soar lengthily up to her Maker and having received an answer from on high she stood up suddenly and so fiercely that her hair came undone and her skirt unhitched itself and fell to the floor revealing a camisole and a pair of rather long frilly bloomers, Yes she cried impetuous and flame-cheeked, yes He loves naturalized persons He even loves strikers and strike-fomenters and the ring-leaders who have all come here from abroad He also loves those who have no roof over their heads stateless persons and even Jews and people in concentration camps, at these words Patrice sprang forward and kneeling before his mother kissed her hand passionately, You are a saint dear Mama he exclaimed, they talk about the destructive mind of the Jews but what can I do about it if they have turned Lucifer the bringer of light into the devil himself what can I do about it if barefoot in a long cymar with a lance in my hand the lance on which perch the moon-owl and all the birds of knowledge and of disquiet what can I do about it if my left eye is half-closed while the other is wide open and second-sighted what can I do about it if I see and know, they say destructive mind but what can I do about it if the dances they dance in their balls are pseudo-couplings the young men press the young women close against them and the mothers look on fondly oh the pure joy of the dance they say but in that case why sex to sex male against female they also say moral uplift because the dancers rub against each other to raise money for the benefit of needy folk who are not made millionaires thereby and wives go home with husbands after clinging to an assortment of strange men against whom they have rubbed while conversing politely on assorted elevated subjects, all's well in the world and they are not ashamed because it was only a dance the word being a sufficient alibi oh the sweet reek of rottenness, they say destructive mind but what can I do about it if they have decked with plumes of grandeur and beauty the strength which is the power to kill, oh the baboonish respect for strength for instance their passion for sport or the pure baboonish homage of mealy-mouthed ceremonial words which are tantamount to saying to the powerful You are the face of the Establishment you have the might of society behind you and are therefore dangerous being many whereas I am one and stand alone before you who represent the might of the many and are therefore able to break me at will and that is why I bend my knee, and what are the bowings and scrapings and obeisance of lesser mortals in the presence of greater men but a substitute and echo of baboonish submission which is none other than the posture of the female deferring on all fours to the dominant male, they say destructive mind but what can I do about it if I have seen and judged their esteemed statesmen, oh the pathetic lives led by politicians courting the moronic masses making them laugh now and then to be popular shaking unwashed hands doing deals with crooks and thieves always watching their step always watching their backs seeking ever greater influence or as the poor clowns put it rising up the ladder laying waste their energies in stratagems setting traps arranging the downfall of rivals losing sleep over it taking a hand in disputes between mortal nations which are as sordid as any family quarrel and all this so that they may rise above the crowd in other words that they may enjoy the respect of the mediocre oh the vulgar thirst for power, they say destructive mind but what can I do about it if disciples follow all too ready to step into the shoes of their revered masters, what can I do if cast away on a desert island, but that's enough about desert islands we know what happens on desert islands, what can I do about it if the peerless wife puts on lipstick and silk stockings the day after the funeral of the husband she adored and will remarry which is a thought too horrible to contemplate, what can I do if my poor girl yielded to animal persuasion and abandoned her Deume who was a decent man, what can I do if men are not good and gentle and make it impossible for me to love them, what can I do if vile servile apes go bed-hopping their way up the social ladder, I feel a sudden pity for the vileness the servility of the tribe of gorillas who don the clothes of men but keep their fangs sharpened poor fools they are afraid because this world of ours is a dangerous place a world of nature red in tooth and claw where a man must either bite or fawn on the biters and have money good jobs contacts protectors the vileness the servileness stem from fear poor clowns, they say destructive mind but what can I do about it if there is no point to the universe neither rhyme nor reason say I with the passion of the true believer what can I do about it if I know that all religions are empty childish magic and mumbo-jumbo because men do not have the courage to see nor do they wish to see that they are alone that they are cast adrift that there is nothing for them neither purpose here below nor life hereafter and what can I do about it if God does not exist it isn't my fault nor is it for want of loving Him and awaiting His coming, for the God I deny each day and love each day I feel a pride which is bottomless and comes down to me through all the length of centuries I am His priest and His Levite and in the synagogue with the fringed silk shawl upon my arm as a shield I proclaim day after day that my God liveth despite all my despairing unbelief, I proclaim Thee the Eternal God of my fathers God of earth and God of sea by the blast of the breath of Thy nostrils were the mountains overturned by Thy right hand was the thunder unleashed and Thy commands were borne upon the winds God of Abraham God of Isaac God of Jacob that didst grant the patriarchs a blessed old age and didst dwell in the tents pitched at eventide in the plains of the valleys God who was worshipped at the rising of the sun by my fathers amid the clamour of ox goat and camel God of the storm and

God of the whirling wind God the unforgiving God the chider Thou didst rain down brimstone and fire upon the cities of the unjust Thou didst crush the impure Thou didst cast down the evil-doer Eternal God who didst bring us out of the house of bondage Thou didst chastise Pharaoh with Thy mighty hand Thou didst perform great marvels Thou didst put aside the waters like an unclean woman that Thy beloved people Israel might go out Eternal God of my fathers with fire lit on their lips didst Thou consecrate the clamouring madmen that stood at the crossroads and shouted threats at kings and smote the mighty and roared Thy ordinances wrathful God of Israel God of my fathers who gave Thee praise dressed in gold and fine linen who did make Thee offerings of lambs and wheat and wine, but what can I do about it if I lack the innocent guile to call truth those things which comfort me nor am I sufficiently afraid of dying to need a paradise populated by irritating old women with moustaches who though spiritual are not alas invisible and praise the Almighty without end and cling to the hairs of His beard which He shakes with a toss of His head to be rid of them for He hates them, they say you've got it wrong there is no paradise no one bothers with paradise nowadays smart modern souls go to the hereafter, ah yes the hereafter I had forgotten, the hereafter inhabited only by invisible shades which have no flavour no smell no eyes to see nor lips to smile sorry wraiths bloodlessly floating, ah yes life eternal correct me if I'm wrong means that I shall apparently still be able to see though my eyes are pools of deliquescent slime, ah yes you're trotting out the good old invisible realities again, so very handy these realities which have the good taste to be invisible, and where do I stand in all this, and what am I supposed to do in the hereafter surrounded by invisible exhalations and puny charmless shades, I who am addicted to seeing and hearing seeing with real eyes of flesh and blood hearing with ears that are visible and fitted with Eustachian tubes, the way I see it I'll be more or less lost in the crowd in a set-up designed for souls I who love loving with my loving loved lips, and it would appear that in this hereafter my billions of thoughts and images and feelings for yes in these areas I am a billionaire will go on existing in the ether without any help from my eyes or the workings of my brain beneath the vulnerable shell of my soon-to-be-decomposed skull, so it seems that I

shall see without eyes and love without lips, oh no the whole idea is
barbarous and fantastical and childish, come let's discuss it seriously
like grown men and not like quibblerians, now sexuality is a rather
basic ingredient of the human personality and of what you call the
soul, so where does this prime ingredient and its physical well-spring
figure in your paradise and what happens to it in your hereafter
where for obvious reasons angels cannot even sit down, and are not
your vasodilators and vasoconstrictors the condition or cause of your
excitements and affects and what is a soul without affects and what is
meant by living without a body, I hear them protest but in such
sweet tones with such pity for the vulgar upstart that I am and they
speak to me of disembodied eyes and immaterial ears, but armour-
plated by my obtuseness of which I am reasonably proud I say it
won't wash with me for ears that aren't ears are hilarious nonsense
and as notions go pretty feeble to boot, vulgar upstart you say, I'm
only too happy to be vulgar, only vulgar people are afraid of vulgarity,
so in a word gentlemen I simply do not believe all this nonsense
about ears that vanish up some hey-prestoing conjuror's sleeve, oh yes
I'm up with the latest thinking I know that the aficionados of the
incorporeal state don't talk nowadays about disembodied eyes and
immaterial ears they prefer to talk about an extremely genteel world
inhabited solely by gaggles of unearthly presences that are neither fish
nor fowl principles essences insubstantialities taradiddles the fundamen-
tal quality and attribute of which is to be non-existent, a very proper
very smart very exclusive world where souls circulate safely without
ever colliding innumerable intangible souls little diaphanous monsters
the plenipotentiary representatives of their owners who have popped
their clogs, a very fashionable refined snobbish world where there is
neither seeing nor hearing but only spiritually being, but enough for I
fear my wits will turn that's more than enough about invisible
realities they stick in my craw cut it out away with the rotting stench
of the fear of dying, they can think whatever they like let them
believe that I'm an infidel that I'm spiritually far too illiterate ever to
be at home with their subtleties, oh I see them so knowing but quite
incapable of explaining anything to my squalid intellect, expatiating
on forces and sources and emanations and fluids and tidal flows of
spirit would that be all Madame shall I wrap them for you, expatiating

on spiritual experiences which is the name they give to their auto-suggestions, when faced by my gross materiality they are visibly embarrassed by an awareness of their own superiority of the loftiness of their spirituality which is never explained but invariably carries all before it, and this spirituality of theirs serves as an extra hot-water bottle and additional central heating and is an anaesthetic and an alibi too, this spirituality of theirs justifies injustice and enables them to reconcile a clear conscience with a private income, spirituality with a bank account, yes God exists but is so inconspicuous that I feel ashamed on His account, but this elderly lady assures me that He thaved her and that she ith conthtantly filled by Hith Prethenthe but what's the point of arguing with the poor old girl let's leave her in peace leave her to be happy another old biddy this one has a beard and the stubborn stern intimidating look of the obtuse informs me that there is a plan in creation and therefore a mind which devised the plan and that it follows that I should pay the author royalties on His handiwork let's leave her alone too, actually in their heart of hearts men don't believe in God all men including those who do believe in God and pious people about to embark for the hereafter are afraid of dying and much prefer the here below, O sweet seamstress of mine so patient so discreet shall I tell her my Rosenfeld story to entertain her no that's one to keep all to myself you see darling my Rosenfeld story isn't true at all there's no such person as Rosenfeld and I feel rather ashamed about the story which isn't true I feel guilty but I can't get it out of my mind I shall tell it to myself all of it leaving nothing out I've plenty of time because she'll be kept fully occupied for a couple of hours with my dressing-gown which I deliberately sabotaged pretty sneaky really but anyhow a good hour I've bags of time, here goes if you were to invite Rosenfeld something which you'd do reluctantly but let's say you had no choice that day when you met him for the first time if you were to invite him round for tea at four you could be sure he'll turn up at three or five wearing a dinner-jacket and escorted by various members of his family none of whom you know and none of whom you have of course invited, now describe the antics of Rosenfeld and company, the minute he arrives he makes straight for your grand piano and on it deposits little Benjamin who is six wears a miniature grown-up's suit and a dinky bowler hat which he makes no attempt to remove, Benjamin stands on the piano and immediately starts talking to you in English and Spanish and even Russian which he informs you is the language of the future and all the Rosenfelds swell with pride meanwhile Rosenfeld senior watches you like a hawk does not take his eyes off you trying to guess how you are reacting trying to see if you are admiring too, I can already speak four languages says Benjamin but I'll be even cleverer when I'm older because a command of languages shows what a man is made of and helps you to get to the top with a car servants marry the boss's daughter wedding breakfast in a five-star hotel with smoked salmon and everybody wearing morning coats, then at a sign from his father Benjamin who is still standing on the piano sings a Hebrew prayer then a Swiss folk-song, hums a Russian dance and recites an unsolicited fable which he introduces in these terms And now I shall recite the ant and the grasshopper by our great French poet La Fontaine, and when he has recited it he asks which you like best Corneille or Racine and immediately argues with what you've said while his aunts read your personal diaries and laugh uproariously at the naïvety of your jottings and then compare the prescriptions issued by your doctors and discuss your constipation which has emerged in the process and advise you what to do about it while the little sister who wants to show how clever she is and be admired too scrapes away on the fiddle she has brought for that very purpose and the thin oldest sister with the coal-black eyes flicks through the books on your shelves which she makes no secret of despising and then delivers a lecturette in a Romanian accent on Rimbaud who she tells your appalled mother was a young homosexual god or rather a yunk homosessual gott while placid Sara sixteen hair like shoe-polish and mountain-breasted makes periodic forays to the sideboard from which she takes a cream cake and leaning her elbows on the table and cupping her cheek in one hand like a fat Queen of Sheba nibbles the cake half-heartedly and says it isn't very fresh and promptly moves on to the sandwiches which she opens discarding the ones made with ham which she puts to one side for you whispering that Grandma mustn't know that there's pork because she'd be dreadfully cross and if you say that you have been very careful not to serve pork she shakes her head in a sceptical but placatory way and says yes yes yes or rather yay yay yay while Rosenfeld weighs up your cigarette-case in his hand to see if it's made of solid gold or just gold-plated tries to put a value on your carpets blows on his tea which he has poured into his saucer to cool before swallowing it to an earnest accompaniment of gurgles says it's not bad but it would be a lot better if you served it with cherry jam old man to sweeten it the thing to do is pop a spoonful into your mouth and take a quick swig he expresses surprise at your ignorance in the matter of tea raises his arms to heaven knocks over a large Chinese vase of ancient vintage says not to worry he's quite all right thank God and in any case the vase was very badly placed it was far too close to people what a peculiar idea to put it there and anyway who told you it was authentic it's a fake you can take that from me old man and while he's on the subject he tells you a boring story which amuses him immensely about a member of the Romanian cabinet who was a friend of a rabbi a really close friend you have my word on it may I lose the sight of my eyes if I tell a lie who even used to have the odd meal with the rabbi in his house so you can see he had a taste for kasha tzimmus cholent essigfleisch lokschen verenikas kneidlach very partial to anything like that was the Christian politician you understand, at which point he asks you if you believe in God and how much rent you pay for your flat which he says is very tasteful though it's a pity it has a view over that horrible backyard, and then he asks if you declare all your earnings to the taxman and if you say yes of course he smiles sceptically and says yay yay yay just like his daughter, then he asks you if you're a touch anti-Semitic or rather anti-Semitical and tries to get you to admit it with all sorts of friendly knowing conniving cheery kindly head-wagging encouragements and he rounds this off by saying that surely you have polyps in your nose and adenoids too which is why your voice is so flat and nasal and he mimics it and roars with laughter but since he has a kind heart he adds that you shouldn't waste any time but get it seen to by a surgeon whose address he lets you have no better still old man I'll put in a word with him myself and while you stand helplessly by in your own living-room which he has dismissed as being dark and as he says a bit tatty as you stand helplessly in your own living-room amid the debris of

Chinese vases shattered by this stumbling fumbling gesticulating athletically ungifted family and while the younger members of the tribe read dog-ear and write all over your books Rosenfeld phones the surgeon embarks on lengthy negotiations over the price of the operation which he enthusiastically haggles down in a welter of chummy conspiratorial winks he tells the surgeon that you are a friend and friends are entitled to a discount yay yay yay a friend I think a great deal of because he's a gent but ha ha not much of a head for business not got much go a bit of a weak character really, whereupon his oldest daughter passes remarks about you and says sniggeringly that you are an introvert what are you talking about protests a cousin recently arrived from England he's an extrovert read Jung read Stekel read Ranck read Ferenczi read Karl Abraham read Jones read Adler rubbish he's a schizophrenic shouts Benjamin and the moist-eyed Rosenfeld looks on admiringly I advise a course of electric-shock treatment says a young Jacob in a shrill voice whereupon his father a Greek Jew who holds a Turkish passport glares triumphantly at Rosenfeld while his eleven-year-old offspring announces in the same shrill voice that next year he intends sitting the baccalaureate given the fact that my teachers have such a high opinion of me and after that I shall be the most brilliant student in medical school where I shall specialize in gynaecology which is a very lucrative trade because of all the deliveries involved but on the other hand I may very well decide to go into the French diplomatic service or the Turkish diplomatic service if pater hasn't yet got himself naturalized French whereupon Rosenfeld uninterested in the doings of everyone except his Benjamin picks up your phone and uses it to make a number of calls in the course of which he buys and resells a second-hand car while an obscure quarrel breaks out between members of the tribe and an old woman lets down her hair and ululates and Rosenfeld's brother-in-law plays your guitar and a child is sick all over your bed and his hysterical mother makes him a cup of herb tea while Madame Rosenfeld wearing a toothpaste-pink dress opens all your kitchen cupboards and passes remarks about how few provisions they contain and Great-Grandma sings in Russian that love is not a crime as she makes Romanian cakes in the kitchen and explains that she's doing it to teach your wife how meanwhile a female cousin with a face like an ibis and a great mop of hair gives lessons in personal hygiene to your daughter and unidentified relatives taste all the tonics and pick-me-ups in your medicine chest or try your aftershave and a woolly-headed infant pops up in the living-room yelling that the gas company is diddling you because the meter in the cellar which he has just inspected has definitely been tampered with and an aged forebear raves to you about the Old Testament in words which emerge from a beard as long as the fur-lined overcoat he has insisted on keeping on and various ladies wearing jewellery and carrying their shoes in their hands walk about unshod in clammy silk stockings and waggle their toes to rest their feet and complain about the heat which makes their tired little fat tootsies swell and one of them tells you that it's odd you should have chosen a house so far from the underground but obviously it's cheaper to live in an area as derelict as this and maybe you haven't got the cash to move to a better area don't talk rubbish exclaims Rosenfeld suddenly reappearing he's a lot better off than you think so there's no need to worry on that score maybe he's got more than me I'll make enquiries I have this friend who works in a bank but anyhow you needn't worry he's very well off but he's discreet I like a man who's discreet and he slaps you on the back so hard it makes you choke while young girls in green and yellow ball-gowns details of whose respective dowries he has whispered in your ear just in case noisily tuck into successive waves of oily Romanian cakes borne in from the kitchen by the beaming perspiring great-grandma assisted by mute but curly-haired cousins and a nonagenarian fans himself and chuckles inwardly at some obscure joke in the Talmud and a wrinkly-faced but young gnome rattles off incomprehensible Jewish stories which only he finds hilarious and all around you the mob drink noisily congratulate you on your breeding but criticize your plumbing and in particular the flush eat with lips greasy and mouths open and talk as they eat and talk only about themselves and they know everything and they scoff and patronize meanwhile a tiny wily hundred-year-old with a face like a kid goat and a rabbi's skullcap who locked himself in your bathroom the moment he arrived is using your Sandow Elastic Chest-Expander to tone himself up and develop his muscles at the expense of the Gentile whose bathing-trunks he unearthed and immediately put on and at intervals he trots into the living-room to show you his new biceps

and makes you feel them makes remarks in Hebrew displays colossal
vitality and showers heart-warming blessings on his swarming pro-
geny while one of his aged sons splashes about in your scalding bath
and fills your house with steam and singing and you are comatose by
midnight when Rosenfeld who you invited to tea by himself suggests
having a bite of supper old man we'll start with a vat of bortsch
followed by piroshki or if you prefer maybe Pojarski cutlets which he
pronounces cutterlets look lively old man don't be like that not
saying anything nodding off you're a real sleepyhead come on perk
up please we'll ask the womenfolk to see to it we'll ask your ladies
and my ladies but my ladies will be in charge because my ladies are
better at cooking which he pronounces cushion and we'll lend a hand
we'll sing and you mustn't worry about a thing we brought everything we need with us salted cucumbers gefilte fish applestrudel
tzibbele kugel nice chopped liver the whole works because it's good
manners and we'll stay up all night chatting like old friends and you
can put mattresses down on the living-room floor just like in Romania
and Rooshia ah Rooshia before was much nicer we'll sleep like tops
now you're not to worry the kiddies are used to it and it's no good
being all down in the mouth and going all psychautomatic on me
you might drop dead tomorrow so you've got to laugh and have fun
and to encourage you to relax and cheer up he becomes very familiar
and says shape yourself start getting your papers together so you can
register which he pronounces rochester, but why in God's name have
I told myself this ridiculous made-up tale which has no basis in reality
why oh why because I've never met any such crowd of grotesques
nor have I ever been present at any such masquerade on the contrary
it has always been among my Jewish brethren that I have encountered
human beings with the noblest hearts and the most courteous manners,
why so fascinated by the minor eccentricities of the handful of
Rosenfelds who do exist why did I exaggerate inflate give them such
a free rein why did I join so willingly in the festivities oh yes it's
because I am unhappy that I said all those horrible things which aren't
true it's perhaps because I want to convince myself convince other
people that I'm not a Jew like other Jews that I am an exceptional Jew
to make it absolutely clear that I am different from those who are
reviled of men because I make mock of them to let it be known oh

shame on me that I am not a very Jewish Jew and that it's quite all right for you to like me maybe there is in me some terrible hidden wish to disown the greatest people on earth some terrible wish to be free of them maybe it's a way of hitting back at my unhappiness to punish it because it is what makes me unhappy for it is a constant source of unhappiness not to be liked always to be suspect yes a form of retaliation against the noble misery that belonging to the chosen people brings me or worse still it is perhaps attributable to some ignoble resentment that I feel against my people but no I revere my people who bear the mark of suffering my people Israel who saves, a saviour who saves through eyes, through eyes that know through eyes which have wept tears for the jeers of crowds who saves through its face its face twisted by suffering through its suffering face through its mute face through its face spattered with the lingering spittle of the derision and hatred of men who are its sons oh shame it is perhaps an ignoble unconscious rejection of my companions in misery who partake of the same cruel banquet at which we swallow the same insults and it may be that I resent them for the same reasons that prisoners who share the same cell hate each other no no I venerate my beloved my kind-hearted intelligent Jews it was fear of danger that made them so intelligent it was the ever-present need to be alert to the machinations of the enemy that made them such remarkable psychologists perhaps it is also because I have been contaminated by the derision of those who hate us and am merely imitating their unjust ways maybe it is also an attempt to have a little fun at the expense of my unhappiness and find a measure of consolation it is also because I have been infected by their hatred yes we have been hearing their ugly accusations for so long that they have filled us with a temptation born of despair to take them at their word and it is their most devilish sin to have filled us with the temptation born of despair to hate ourselves wrongfully the temptation born of despair to be ashamed of our great people the temptation born of despair to accept the wicked thought that since they hate us so much everywhere then we deserve to be hated and by God I know that we deserve nothing of the sort I know that their hatred is the inane tribal hatred of those who are different and also the hatred born of envy and also the animal hatred of the weak for in numbers we are weak everywhere

and men are not good and weakness attracts excites their hidden
congenital bestial cruelty and it is no doubt satisfying to hate the
weak when you can insult and beat them with impunity O my
people my suffering people I am your son who loves and venerates
you your son who will never tire of praising his people Israel a loyal
people a courageous people a stiff-necked people who in a holy
citadel braved Rome under the Caesars and for seven years made the
most powerful of empires tremble O my nine hundred and sixty
heroes besieged at Masada who all took their own lives on the first
day of Passover in the year seventy-three rather than submit to the
Roman conqueror and bow down to his contemptible gods O my
starving wanderers held captive in so many foreign fields hauling
their dogged hope down the centuries and eternally refusing to
disperse and be absorbed by the nations where they lived in exile O
my proud people bent on survival and jealously guarding its soul a
people who stood firm and resisted resisted not for a year not for five
years not for ten years but a people who stood firm for two thousand
years what other people stood firm for so long yes two thousand
years of resistance a beacon to light the way of all other peoples O
my forefathers down the length of the centuries who preferred
massacre to betrayal and the stake to apostasy licked by flames and
proclaiming unto their last breath the Oneness of God and the
greatness of their faith O my medieval kinsmen who chose death over
conversion in Verdun-sur-Garonne in Carentan in Bray in Burgos in
Barcelona in Toledo in Trent in Nuremberg in Worms in Frankfurt
in Spires in Oppenheim in Mainz through the length and breadth of
Germany from the Alps to the North Sea all my indomitable resisters
who cut the throats of their women and children and then killed
themselves or entrusted to the most worthy of their number the task
of killing them one by one or set fire to their houses and cast
themselves into the flames clutching their babes in their arms singing
psalms as they burned O my obstinate forebears who for centuries
tolerated lives far worse than death lives of degradation and ignominy
sacred degradation holy ignominy which was the price they paid for
their stiff-backed insistence on keeping faith with a God who is One
and Holy and a Pope Innocent III punished their stiff-backed resistance
by requiring them to wear a yellow disc forbade them under pain

of death to show themselves in the street unless the emblem was sewn to their coats the emblem of infamy which for six centuries was to expose them throughout the whole of Europe to jeers and insults an ever-present visible badge of shame and inferiority which was as an invitation to the mob to heap outrage and violence on their heads but that wasn't enough and fifty years later the Council of Vienna judged that the yellow disc was insufficiently degrading and decided to make us even more ridiculous by making us wear a funny hat which could be either pointed or cocked and thus accoutred did we make our way from province to province and we went in distress in fear obstinate mocked reviled unyielding we went patient grotesque sublime in our pointed or as the case may be cocked hats and the crowd laughed we went branded marked rejected by all stigmatized beaten with sticks a target for every outrage the thought of it makes my stomach heave my eyes sting I feel the nails of it in my heart we went pelted with filth shoulders sunk backs bent eyes wary we went clothed in dirty rags outwardly humble inwardly proud and unbending we went down the centuries the ragged heralds and curators of the true God and the cocked and pointed hats decreed by the Christians' council were our chosen crowns O wonder of wonders the miserable and despised creature that was a Jew became august a patriarch once more in the peace of his home lavished on his wife and his children all the love which the world outside rejected and his home was a temple and the family table an altar and on the sabbath day he was a prince and a member of a nation of priests and on that holy day he was happy for he knew that soon the Almighty would set his feet on the road back to Jerusalem O my living people and while he waited his powerful enemies fell and perished down the length of centuries dead are the peoples who devoured us whole dead the Assyrians so proud of their battle scars so proud in their broad armour dead the Pharaohs and their chariots of war dead the august great-buttocked Whore of Babylon pestle of the protesting earth dead Rome and its legions in grave battle order aligned but Israel lives on and if Rosenfeld exists I claim him as mine as a brother and I give him the limelight and I delight in him and why not he is a good man of business a good father a loving husband a friend always ready to do a good turn

874

enthusiastic ingenious and ebullient no great breeding of course but when would he have had the time the opportunity to become domesticated and learn manners for that requires a modicum of settled contentment it takes roots not expulsions not perpetual upheavals not the drab expectation of misery in each generation not living in an atmosphere of hate not wearing cocked or pointed hats in your heart because insecurity and the habit of humiliation do not breed fine manners the manners which matter so much to you and your kind my darling girl but which are no more than conditioned reflexes and it takes just two or three generations for the reflexes to become second nature see for instance the delightful manners of Disraeli and certain members of the Rothschild family not that such things mean much to me because I know that my lovely boorish brethren are the sons and fathers of mankind's princes are the most luxuriant kind of compost and in any case why shouldn't we have our boors other peoples have them too not all their farmers and workers and shop-keepers are models of refinement we are entitled to our boors I claim our right to have boors for why do we have to be perfect and to be quite frank I secretly dote on Rosenfeld and anyway Rosenfeld isn't any worse than any other nation's undomesticated unfortunates it's just that he's more spectacular more passionate more eager to live life to the full more impetuously and whimsically ill-mannered more inventively and quite brilliantly ill-mannered and no one can deny him a fond combustible heart or cast doubt on the touching concern he shows when his wife whom he calls his capital is ill at the first sign of illness it's quick send for the most famous doctors to attend to his better half or to Benjamin who is his dearly beloved son and close to being his Messiah oh the tender heart of a Jew is beyond compare O Rosenfeld of my heart I was really very happy back there surrounded by Rosenfelds I was part of a family I had come home I loved them and if I exaggerated them caricatured them multiplied their little eccentricities it was perhaps for love of them to enjoy the taste of them just as a man who likes pepper will sprinkle generous quantities will sprinkle too much will sprinkle enough to take the skin off his tongue so that he gets the full benefit but I know that if I exaggerated their outlandishness so that I might savour and love it more I realize that I must also honour it for I know that such strange antics are the sores and wounds of a persecuted people the sores and wounds of an unhappy people racked by centuries of torment bravely borne sores and wounds which are the sorry products of the unkillable steadfastness of my people and that they remind me of this remind me of their staunch refusal to accept annihilation remind me of how they were condemned to perform daily acts of heroism to react with the ingenuity on which life itself depended to devise uneasy torpid strategies for enduring and surviving in a hostile world so sing praises to the sores of my people they are the unsightly jewels in their crown I will treasure my people and everything about my people even the large and lovely much-mocked noses of my people yes noses that bristle with panic so keen in scenting danger and I will treasure the bent backs of my people their backs bent by fear by flight by desperate wandering backs bent to make them less visible smaller as they venture down dangerous alleyways backs bent too by centuries of heads lowered over the holy book and its Commandments noble heads of an ancient people forever reading the Testament O my Christian brothers you will see how my people will regain their youth when they return in freedom to Jerusalem and they will exemplify justice and courage they will be a witness for other nations who will look and stand amazed and beneath the sun in that sky there will be no more boors my lovely pathetic boors the luckless offspring of centuries of pain and you will see how the sons of my people restored to the land of Israel will be serene and proud and handsome and noble in bearing and brave in war if need be and when at last you see our true face Hallelujah you will love my people you will love Israel which gave you God which gave you the wisest of books which gave you the prophet who was love and in truth why should it be a cause for astonishment that the Germans a people who live under the sway of nature should have always detested Israel a people who live under the rule of anti-nature for behold the German has heard and he has listened more attentively than others he has heard the youthful forceful voice which speaks in the fearsome forests of the night in the silent rustling forests a siren voice feral as the dawn sings beneath the moonbeams sings that nature's law is arrogant might and rampant egoism and rude health and youthful grappling and assertiveness and domination and quick cunning and sharp-toothed malice and unbridled lust and the joyous cruelty of the young who destroy with a smile on their lips the insistent voice sings sweetly frenziedly of war and its overlords sings of strong naked bodies tanned by the sun of muscles like coiled serpents writhing in the athlete's back sings of beauty and youth which are might the might which is the power of life and death all alone and crazed it sings on it glorifies noble conquest pours scorn on women and contempt on the needy it sings of callousness violence the warlike virtues of military supremacy which is the daughter of might and cunning the exuberant splendour of injustice the sacredness of blood spilt for the cause and the nobility of arms and the enslavement of the weak and the slaughter of the infirm and the sacred rights of the strong in other words of those best equipped to commit murder sings and glorifies the man of nature who is pure ravening animal the beauty of the wild beast which is a noble and perfect creature a lord unfettered by the hypocrisy that is born of weakness on and on sings the alluring irresistible voice in the German forest it sings the praises of the dominant the intrepid and the brutal harden your hearts the voice sings blithely be like beasts comes the Bacchic echo and the Germanic voice accompanied by a chorus of voices of poets and philosophers mocks at justice mocks at pity mocks at freedom and it sings sweetly beguilingly of the tyranny of nature of the inegalitarianism of nature of the hatred endemic in nature behold it says I bring you new tablets and a new law which decrees that there is no law evoe! the Commandments of the Jew Moses are rescinded and everything is permitted and I am beautiful and my breasts are young cries the Dionysian voice in a howl of drunken mirth that rings through the forest where now the puny bustle of creation begins to stir and with the rising sun all the scraps and crumbs of nature irresponsibly writhe and rise to murder and survive oh yes that is the voice of nature and Hitler sheds a tear for animals and says they are his brothers and he tells Rauschning that nature is cruel and that man must therefore be cruel too in truth when Hitler's henchmen worship armies and war what are they worshipping if not the threatening teeth of the gorilla who stands squat and bow-legged squaring up to another gorilla and when they sing of their ancient legends and of their ancestors with long blond hair and horned helmets oh yes horned for it is vital to look like an animal and it is doubtless a most pleasant thing to go forth in the guise of a bull what are they celebrating if not a cruel past to which they are nostalgically committed and attracted and when they fill their mouths with swaggering talk of their race talk of the one blood by which they are joined what are they doing if not reverting to notions of animality which wolves understand well enough though even wolves do not devour their own kind and when they exalt strength or the exercise of body and flesh in the sunlight when like their Hitler or their Nietzsche they boast of being inexorable and implacable what are they boasting of if not their return to the great apedom of the primeval forest and in truth when they massacre and torture Jews they are punishing the people of the Holy Law and of the prophets the people who strove to establish the reign of the human on earth oh yes they know or sense that they are the people who live under the sway of nature and that Israel is the people who combat the laws of nature and the bearer of a crazy hope which nature abhors and they instinctively abominate the people which opposes them and which upon Sinai's top did declare war upon the natural upon the animal in man and to this war both the religion of Jews and the religion of Christians have borne witness hosanna hallelujah hosanna in the old religion God whose mettle is the mettle of the Jewish prophet irritable benign and naïvely earnest God issues decrees without cease He specifies what man must do and more particularly must not do if he is to expunge the taint of nature and animality and thou shalt not kill is the first of His Commandments the first battle-cry in the war on nature oh in my bones I feel the pride of it and in the synagogue I tremble when the descendant of Aaron opens the Ark and brings forth the Scrolls of the Holy Law and holds them out to the people hosanna hallelujah hosanna the Christian religion which descended from my people transformed Gentiledom and through it man has become human across vast tracts of this earth hosanna hallelujah hosanna a new birth a new man Adam a new salvation through faith the Imitation of Christ saving grace which redeems original sin which is at bottom the taint of nature and animality and all these lofty Christian concepts stem directly from the same Jewish determination to change natural man into a child of God into a soul which has been saved in other words into a being who is human hosanna hallelujah hosanna and thus by other more inward paths is the same end achieved which is the humanization of man hosanna hallelujah hosanna two daughters of Jerusalem one Jewish and one Christian and Hitler from the height from which he loves to look down upon nature which he worships hates them both in equal measure for both are queens of mankind and eternal enemies of the laws of nature and whether they know it or not whether they wish it or not men's noblest qualities are rooted in the Jewish soul and the rock on which they stand is the Bible O my lovely Jews to whom I speak in silence know your people Israel venerate your people Israel for seeking schism and separation for having taken up arms against nature and nature's laws but alas men do not and will not see the truth I speak and I remain cold and alone with my royal truth alas all truths unshared and unloved by men are pitiful and become madness O my glorious pitiful girl O my crazy darling girl let us be mad together let us keep each other warm far from them a little while back I looked at myself in the mirror and felt pity for the lonely figure I cut that day wandering through Paris a king without a people the only man who truly loves his people felt pity for myself for I shall die one year ten years from now and my crazy truth will die with me a year hence ten years hence die for ever O my brothers in this earthly life companions from whom I keep my distance fellow galley-slaves tell me oh tell me while she sits sewing and I hold aloft an invisible cup pray tell me what I am doing here a guest at this undistinguished banquet which has been laid since the earliest point of unrecorded time I came I am here but why am I here and what is the point and is there really a point my time has come the hour has come for all of us moving particles and it will pass absurdly pass but where will it go and why perhaps the unmoving dead know ah so much knowledge buried deep poor Solal man or beast I shall die I shall be returned to nature for ever and then where will be my joy and the song I sang as I went to her in our beginnings in a motor car went to her who waited in her Romanian dress and she stood at the door beneath the roses waiting for me in her perfect dress and where will be the exquisite evening when I was a schoolboy of ten and had just begun a new exercise book with such absurd enthusiasm such pointless trust I sat by my serene mother who watched her little boy as he lovingly did his homework in the pool of light cast by the oil-lamp and where tell me pray where has that happiness gone give it a rest come Solal return to your unhinged mode yes it pleases me that my brothers the pious Jews of the ghettos give spangled names to their Law calling it Betrothed and Crowned it pleases me that their parchment Scrolls on which the Holy Law is writ in the ancient script of my people are decorated with unpretentious crowns and wrapped in unlovely velvet and gold for they have no talent for comely abominations but they love their Law with every fibre of their beings oh the Scrolls of the Law in the synagogue in grave procession borne the faithful kiss them and with all my soul I bow before them and feel my heart quicken in my chest quicken for the majesty which passes by and I kiss them too and such is our only act of adoration in the house of the God in whom I do not believe but revere O my dead of ancient days O you who by your Law and your Commandments and your prophets took up arms against nature and her animal laws laws of murder and pillage laws of impurity and injustice O my dead of ancient days holy tribe O my sublime stammering prophets my towering simple impassioned indefatigable spouters of threats and promises fierce defenders of Israel unceasingly lashing a people they would make holy a people whose like is not in nature and such is love such is our love O my dead of ancient days I fervently praise you praise your Law for it is our glory as primates sprung from time without memory our claim to royalty and our divine homeland to fashion our clay into figures of men through obedience to the Law to be metamorphosed into the gnarled and twisted but miraculous bent-backed wanderer a creature monstrous and sublime a new being who may at times be loathsome for these are merely his first faltering steps and he will be imperfect and a failure and a hypocrite for thousands of years this twisted miraculous divine-eyed being this non-animal non-natural monster that is man the product of our own heroic handiwork and in sooth it is our last-ditch heroism to refuse to be what we are that is beasts subject to the rules of nature and to want to be what we are not which is men and this we did without urging for there is nothing that forces us to do it nothing for the universe is not governed nor does it have any meaning beyond its pointless existence in the stark eye of the void and in truth our greatness lies in this obedience to the Law which nothing justifies nor sanctions save our own crazy will and there is neither hope nor reward oh to be in the cellar oh to proclaim the coming of the land of sun and sea our homeland granted to us by the Almighty blessed be His name proclaim the flight from captivity and the mountains will crack and give vent to their joy and beneath the sun of our sky we will establish the everlasting reign of justice whereupon the uncle-in-majesty blesses me he winds the thongs of the Law about my arm and about my head and the no-neck midget with the lustrous eyes places the crown on my head then leads me by the hand to the open coach inlaid with antic gold and sparkling with many-faceted mirrors oh the splendour of the royal coach as it proceeds bumpily through the slippery cobbled streets ah through the German streets goes the coach of the Law drawn by Isaac and Jacob the centenarian solemn-bearded horses with long oval faces watchful faces thoughtful faces striving to be human while I stand in the coach king of the race which challenged nature and nature's laws king of the loving race beloved of the Lord and chosen by Him a king upright in the old coach adorned with cherubim bearing flaming torches lurching through the German streets a pitching tossing battered coach followed by the midget walking with difficulty on her twisted legs accompanied by her wondrous blind sister and the uncle-in-majesty and behind them come the halt with shining eyes epileptics noble old men astoundingly handsome adolescents all pied-pipered by the king of rubies and sapphires who stands in the open coach the priest and king who holds aloft the Scrolls of the Commandments and smiles with joy unconfined for behold oh miracle wrought by the Law the Germans are magically metamorphosed into men and cease singing of the joy of seeing their knives stream with the blood of Israel cease proclaiming their murderous joy and instead acclaim the king they smile at him oh miracle wrought by the Law they love the king of the Jews who greets them with gentleness and raises on high the Law that is Mother and Betrothed and raimented in velvet and gold and crowned with silver who unremittingly holds out the Holy Law to them while two crookbacked but princely boys with saucer eyes garlanded in blue support his arms for heavy is the Law and from time to time the two ancient nags stop and turn their gentle fearful heads turn their enormous eyes lovingly on their king then resume their trembling careful progress but why do I now find myself in this forest alive with whispering fears the rustling starts a cold sweat and enemies lurk behind trees and icy fingers of fear run up and down my spine and there are dangerous footsteps behind me in this forest on this mountain and why am I nailed no I nail myself to the door of this cathedral on this mountain I pierce my own side with a nail from the cellar one of the long nails she gave me as a souvenir I who proclaim undyingly into the dark wind that the day of the never-ending kiss will dawn who nail myself oh those naked dead men yonder the skeletal incinerated dead with faces pain-twisted by torture who now quicken and rise up in the flames resuscitated helpless hapless victims O my lovely dead dears and yonder the empty coach goes on its doomed way threatening to overturn but pressing ever onwards eternally bearing the august Mother of the Jews raimented in velvet and gold and crowned with silver and the two gaunt horses advance indefatig-ably their hooves slipping in a shower of sparks and they stumble and drop to their knees then struggle bravely to their feet ancient asthmatic broken obedient stubborn creatures painfully plodding and now and then turning their gentle faces to behold their bloody king and still the two sublime palfreys lathered by the sweat of death trudge along the everlastingly windswept road suddenly taking fright and the horse Isaac coughs like a man while the midget with the large round eyes pretends to laugh at the man nailed to the wart-studded door and then wipes the tears from his cheeks for he cannot bear the pain of leaving his earthly children all alone and the midget weeps now weeps openly and suddenly bids him ringingly to offer up the prayer laid down in the ritual for the hour has come and the king has nailed his throat to the wart-studded door and blood spurts black and red and he intones the last prayer proclaims the Oneness of God Hear O Israel the Lord our God the Lord is One and his body arches convulsively and his eyes are upturned and white for ever yes my darling I love you more and more and silently I shout it from the rooftops of my heart while you sit there quietly restitching the hems which I unpicked to give your life a brief point I worship you who sit there sewing making damp little spittly noises as do all needlewomen intent on the task in hand I love the even rhythm of your breathing as you sew I love your serene and demure face as you sew for your face is so kind and gentle that it makes me kind and gentle too makes me a schoolboy once more hello a rumble never mind I can live with a few rumbles I can even respect rumbling and greet it with a smile because it comes from my sweet seamstress I watch lovingly as you wet your finger and twist the cotton to make it fine enough to thread lovingly through the needle eyes asquint and lips placidly pursed as you lovingly ply the looping needle so serious so thoughtful and I feel at peace as I watch you sew I sit in the lee of a mother hunched over her sacred toil sweet slave and mother oh how your task becomes you oh how noble and natural your face seems now but why must I forever be spread-eagling myself on you to make you happy such a shame my love my soothing seamstress the way you ply your needle your fingers moving with a purpose have a quality of such resigned pensive sweetness and I adore you but why must I always be straddling you like an animal to keep you happy and talking of which the two-backed beast has made only one appearance in the week since my return and that was the night I got back and you are probably starting to worry because you want my love you women are obsessed with the need to be shown proof that you are loved by having your man climb all over you anyway I'll try but not tonight maybe tomorrow of course you love me your conscious even worships me and goes on worshipping me but your unconscious isn't as crazy for me as it used to be oh no darling your unconscious would much prefer to be the lawful wedded wife of that English lord who has just got back to London after leading an expedition to the Himalayas would much prefer to be able to throw a party and invite delightful influential well-bred friends to celebrate the absurd mountain triumph of dear manly hubby so calm a man of few words poised universally popular a man with an ideal a man who loves animals and strong tea and gravely inhales aromatic tobacco through manfully clenched teeth from the briar pipe you bought for him you took a good long look at that photo of him in your magazine twenty seconds at least oh yes my darling your unconscious has its knife in me for being exotic but not very sporty not swimming enough talking too much not leaping around enough in the open air and being far too much of an infidel furthermore your unconscious doesn't care at all for my dressing-gowns which it thinks are too long though your conscious mind thinks them aristocratic your unconscious also loathes my whirling worry-beads and my silk socks it would much prefer the thick woolly sort and the hobnailed boots as worn by the aforementioned peer and mountain-climber and then again your unconscious has it in for me for not saying I liked the thesis your late brother wrote about those two pretentious prigs Madame de Staël and that insufferable George Sand sorry but it's not my fault if your brother was a donnish pedant but above all your unconscious will never forgive me for making you live in a goldfish bowl of course you'd kill yourself if I were to leave you but deep-down you're heartily sick of me and who knows maybe your heart of hearts has never really loved me as required by the standards of your pedigree and class oh yes you came to me because I made you but I'm not your type sweetie I swept you off your feet because I'm clever in any case you were ripe for plucking by the first man who came along and offered to take you away from poor Deume and when your unconscious fell in love with me because it felt trapped and had no choice it loved me mainly to spite your husband loved me because it fancied the role of mistress extraordinaire a part which you couldn't wait to get your teeth into and which I offered you hello she's stopped sewing so she can scratch her nose on the sly her itching nose may very well be a sublimation of her desire to be married to the English lord an itch she can soothe by scratching but of course that's not true it's just a playful little joke to cover my drooping spirits darling what can I say or do to make you feel once more what you felt that first night when we danced at the Ritz because that is what your unconscious requires she's not saying anything at the minute because she thinks I'm concentrating on my book and is far too polite to disturb me but when she's finished sewing I'll have to stop pretending I'm reading and when that happens what topic of conversation can I float perhaps she'll come up with some poetic thoughts along the lines of the pervasive sense she sometimes has of the joy of leafless trees which commune with mother earth yes she'll say pervasive or possibly how the branch of some tree suddenly seemed to her to have a soul she was so intelligent in Geneva but that soon wore off oh outside the wind shrieks like a posse of mad women screaming in terror for help crazy women with their hair hanging down when she's finished sewing the dressing-gown which I deliberately ruined she might well suggest a game of dominoes she'll suggest it in her brightest most animated manner something along the lines of I want my revenge I'm sure I'll win tonight the noise she makes as she mixes the dominoes before the game starts is terrifying the sound of it scares me it's the knell of our love tolling or maybe she'll say yet again how clever she was to get a record-player that works off electricity it's so much nicer don't you think darling or maybe she'll suggest listening to some new thing by Bach and explain that the recording she says pressing which I find very irritating is really of much much better quality than the previous pressings she's bought all those damned Bach records I'm quite aware of course that Bach is a great musician I only call him a metronome for long-distance wood-saws to get my own back for all the anti-anaemic force-feeding that goes on poor girl she does her best never forget that she will die and therefore cherish her without stint or maybe she'll suggest reading me a novel will she never get over her mania for massaging my feet while she reads what did my feet ever do to her to make her want to be forever fiddling with them and she's so irritating when she says darling I think I've improved my massage technique and so grave when she starts on the talc actually she isn't as good at it as Isolde when she reads she emphasizes the words to breathe life into the thing it's ghastly when she puts on that damned gruff voice for the hero that's how she likes them assertive dynamic outgoing sporty morons she gets on my nerves and she melts my heart she is delightful and absurd when she's imitating a man and she rubs my feet the right way but she rubs me up the wrong way I'm sorry my dear I love you and I tell you so when I'm alone in my room I love you but I get bored being with you and I honestly feel no desire for you she'll soon be finished with her sewing she'll say there all mended now and she'll smile and then I'll say she's sweet and she'll probably turn pert and demand a little kiss as a reward and I will give her a kiss and be scared she'll go for my lips but I'm good at evasive action and then there'll be some anti-anaemic brainwave such as pausing and then saying that she's thinking of taking up painting again darling I'd so love to paint a portrait of you how splendid what a good idea but perhaps you'll get bored posing not at all on the contrary oh the tedium of it all in the old days I only had to turn on the charm and conquered and was loved but I never belonged it was all pretence I've never gone along with it all never believed in their standards and values and categories always the odd man out never part of the crowd I was always on my own even when I was playing the role of government minister even when I was cast as Under-Clown-General Solal solitary solecism oh how bored I am oh I am pursued by boatfuls of skeletons which skim a river that runs past banks lined with temples with many windows through which poke countless tiny laughing faces I am also followed by lions wearing mitres men burning incense old women holding aloft little girls transfixed on long bamboo poles and then I tear out my eyes and throw them into the precipice where they bounce and burst in a shower of little green flames when I reach the palace I yank the bell-pull which makes a sound like a man guffawing and the door opens it's a lift which whisks me down into the depths of the Middle Ages then I have to change lifts and I step into the room with a false window I open the shutters but beyond is still a landscape painted on canvas and I enter the room where the horse gallops non-stop but stays in the same place and the tall woman endlessly arranges her hair with a comb which picks up little green men and I go into the room full of gesticulating bodies piled high one on top of the other in a pyramid in a hullabalooing mound the tongues of those below lick the heels of those above while the heels tread on the heads of the lickers below and spittle runs down the pyramid collects in the basin which overflows and behind the altar made of clay and granite is the goat which strains desperately in a frenzy of copulation oh the tall empress in a blonde wig embraces the nakedness of a slave-girl with great round eyes I am afraid of what lies in store for me later and to avoid finding out I leave and wander through corridors suffering because of the cruel walls there is so much going on in the corridors of the centuries which swarm with actresses dancers circus-performers sacred animals painted harlots bear-tamers raddled queens a bare-backed horse galloping with its long thick mane flowing in the wind of its passage and behind it at full stretch and decked with vines run two tigers which keep up a hell-for-leather pace and sometimes weave and pass beneath the magnificent steed the smell of intrigue is palpable there are revolts in burning palaces and century follows century and conquerors come and the conquerors are conquered in turn pass O ye races tribes and empires I remain hello she's all but finished if I tell her it's time for bed she's bound to say no not yet it's only just ten best adopt the fatherly approach darling you look tired better get some rest but do make a special point of saying I'm feeling pretty bushed too that will clinch it with her and then no hanging about get up give her a quick kiss on one eye no make that both eyes the effect is altogether more loving so make it a double kiss make your move now let's get shot of her it's only being cruel to be kind.'

CHAPTER 95

Supine, with the family photograph album propped up against her, twisting and untwisting a ribbon like a bed-fast convalescent with nothing to do, she lay playing with her ribbon, alone with the sound of the sea, alone with her ribbon. Abruptly she tossed it aside and opened the album, a weighty tome bound in leather and buckram with metal corners and clasps, and began leafing through it. Sitting at a little cloth-draped table, a great-grandmama in a crinoline, with unforgiving eyes, armed with a Bible in which she keeps her place with one finger. A short great-uncle in a colonel's uniform, elbow leaning on a wreathed column, standing impishly in front of a palm-tree on a painted backdrop, legs raffishly crossed and one foot resting on a roguishly arched toe. Herself at six months, a well-fed, sunny-faced credit of a baby on a cushion. Daddy getting an honorary doctorate. Uncle Agrippa chairing a meeting of the synod of the Swiss Protestant Church. Herself at thirteen with bare legs and ankle-socks. Cousin Aymon, Swiss Minister in Paris, with the legation staff. Tantlérie having tea with some chichi English lady. A garden party at Tantlérie's.

She closed the album, quelled the silver clasps, popped a chocolate into her mouth, and let the resulting bitter mud slowly dissolve. All of Genevan high society was there, at the garden party. Charming people, people with taste. She fiddled with her hair, curling it with one finger then uncurling it. The corners of her mouth drooped in a childish scowl, her diaphragm contracted, and the air in her lungs was expelled sharply. A sob, in other words. Outside, the immortal sea.

Oh the Swiss mountains, those summer holidays in the mountains with Éliane. Lying under a buzzing pine-tree, holding hands, how happily they had listened to the distant tapping, to the sound of a peasant sharpening the blade of his scythe with a hammer, a regular tapping borne on the diamond air, clear and resonant in the hot summer sun and so reassuring. Oh her mountain pulsating with life in high summer, insects busy in the sun, ceaselessly going about their business, families to feed, ants scurrying, the simple, strong men cutting the hay, simple, good men with long moustaches cutting the hay, hardworking men, honest Swiss mountainfolk, simple and true. Christians.

She switched off the light, turned on her side, immediately caught the smell of dust and hot sun, and saw once more Tantlérie's attic where in the holidays she and her sister were secretly great actresses dressed up in old clothes purloined from trunks, two skinny adolescent girls too tall for their age, declaiming a tragedy, dying deaths and snorting with passion, she as Phèdre amorously hoarse-voiced, Éliane as faithful Hippolyte, and then suddenly collapsing in a fit of giggles and the laughter of youth. She switched the light back on to see what time it was. Nearly midnight and not sleepy. She had another look at the photo of herself when she was thirteen. A pretty little thing with those curls and her great big bow.

In the bathroom, wearing a short tennis skirt and a close-fitting top which showed the shape of her full breasts, bare-legged, with ankle-socks and tennis shoes, she made up her lips and her eyes, dampened her hair, which she arranged in ringlets and tied up in a big blue ribbon, then took a step back to get a better view of herself in the mirror. There was something disturbing about the little girl with a made-up face who stared back at her. She sat down, crossed her legs, stuck out her tongue, moistened her top lip, and crossed her legs higher.

'Oh no,' she murmured and suddenly stood up, wiped off the make-up, uncurled her ringlets, removed all trace of her little-girl disguise, and then stopped absolutely still. Yes, go and speak to him, tell him everything, unburden herself. It was vile of her to have kept him in the dark all this time. She combed her hair, put on her dressing-gown and stepped into her white sandals, applied perfume to give herself courage, and consulted the mirror mirror on the wall.

CHAPTER 96

'That's it that's the answer pretend I'm mad pretend she's my mother
the Queen and I'm the King her son the King with the crown which
Rachel the midget my lovely midget Rachel gave me that day in the
coach in the cellar as I was leaving she said I was to take it with me
the battered cardboard crown with imitation rubies from the Feast of
Lots the Feast of Queen Esther blessings be upon her yes I'll put on
the crown and I'll go cross-eyed and doolally to make it look genuine
to make her think I've gone mad but then I'll suddenly switch to
warm smiles to make her think everything's fine yes as madman and
son I shall be able to love her absolutely without having to play the
lover play the animal game of the lover without any of that regulation
bumping and grinding and groaning and shunting and pummelling
yes no more having to dominate and subdue her through the sweaty
collision of two rumpling crumpling bodies yes free of passion free of
having to humiliate her free of having to take the wind out of her
poor sails a son is not expected to share a bed all that's required of a
son is to cherish oh I'll do all the cherishing that's needed oh miracle
no more striving to turn each day into love's sweet dawn a son is not
expected to breathe fire oh miracle no more having to be prodigious
all the time no more having to be a sloe-eyed exciting lover no more
having to be tall and dark and enigmatic oh miracle no more of those
wild tonguing kisses which make both participants look so moronic
that they'd die laughing or curl up with shame if they could only see
the doggy expressions they had on their faces O darling darling at last
I'd be free to be tenderly loving and not be afraid that you'd find my

tenderness dull afraid that you'd see it as a sign of weakness the sort of weakness that women despise because they all go wild for gorilla muscles and then my darling you could catch as many colds as you liked you could rumble away to your heart's content rumble your fill rumble all you wanted a sneezing nose-wiping rumbling mother or even a mother with bad breath is no less loved yes loved just as much and even more if she sneezes nicely or rather pretend I'm mad a mad father and she's my daughter no a mother and a mad son is heaps better a mother never deserts her son but a daughter always ends up running away with a gorilla carried off in the long hairy arms of a gorilla and she stops loving her father and on her wedding day she spits in his face and says go to hell and drop dead for she is counting on what he'll leave her in his will and also if I were a son I could serve and honour and respect her I so want to respect her oh yes I'd respect her yes I would if I were her son for ever and ever oh miracle not feeling bored with her any more and helping in all sorts of ways a man who is mad is entitled to yes sweep the floor together do the cooking together cook and talk about salt and winter savory yes and summer savory too doing the cooking together getting on with it quietly like friends oh miracle to be two friends and even up to a point two girls together oh miracle to go shopping in the market at Saint-Raphaël a man who is mad is perfectly in his rights to go shopping in the market with his mother his pretty mother yes and I'll carry the bags yes one day if she's tired I'll say that although I'm King I'll do the shopping by myself and she'll agree to avoid upsetting the madman and if she's tired she'll also let me sweep the floor all by myself I shall insist on it such is my good pleasure Madame but I'll do the sweeping right royally I'll always wear my crown wear my cardboard crown tilted slightly to one side to make myself look like a dotty sort of king but nice with it yes while she takes a bath I who am King and son will make the beds as a nice surprise yes get a move on with the beds do them properly pull the underthingumajig straight no creases a surprise for the Queen-mother and then as a reward for giving her a surprise she'll give me a kiss oh miracle just a peck on the cheek on both cheeks we can kiss all the time with no more need to be afraid of surfeit no more need to be afraid of losing face no more need to be beastly no more need to pretend to be one of those heartless types women always fall for just to please her and prevent her being bored yes starting tomorrow it's son and mother for ever and ever and an end to juices flowing boot out the man the beast the swine the father she deceived me with deceived her son I'll ask her if she loves me more if she loves her son more than she loves the man who died and is no more and she will say why of course I do and I'll tell her to send to Cannes and order me a golden throne and I shall always be dignified and royal and royally enthroned when she comes knocking on my door I shall say that at the King's court etiquette requires that you scratch on the door as at the court of Louis XIV when she comes in I'll order her to curtsy true Madame you may be my mother but you are also a subject so pray Madame curtsy thrice to your King and after you've dropped your curtsies I shall stand and in turn shall bow three times to my lady mother as behoves a loving son a mad son yes I shan't mind pretending to be mad until the day I die if it means that I can at last love her truly O my love I shall love you with the love which never dies.'

CHAPTER 97

She closed the door behind her, approached him slowly, and stopped at the foot of the bed. He sensed from her tightly clenched hands and the solemn way she stood that she had steeled herself to take an unprecedented step. She stared at the floor, very tense, and asked if she could lie down by his side. He moved to make room for her.

'I've something serious to say,' she said, and she took his hand in hers. 'It's a secret. I can't keep it to myself any more. Darling, don't think too badly of me. I didn't love my husband, I used to think I wasn't normal, I was so alone. Can I tell you everything?'

He did not reply. A sudden rush of blood oppressed his lungs, interfered with his breathing, prevented his speaking. He knew that she was waiting for some word of encouragement before going on, but he also knew that if he said anything she would be frightened by the snarl in his voice and wouldn't say another word. He nodded a yes and stroked her shoulder.

'Tell me, darling, things won't go all sour between us afterwards, will they?'

He nodded a no and squeezed her hand. But he sensed that he was going to have to say something to reassure her, to ensure that she told him everything. After taking several deep breaths to calm himself, he smiled.

'No, darling, things won't go sour between us.'

'You'll listen like a friend?'

'Yes, darling, like a friend.'

'It was before I met you, you know.'

He felt repelled by the body lying next to his. But he stroked her hair.

'I dare say life with a man you didn't love must have been pretty miserable.'

'Thanks for understanding,' she said, and she gave him a wan, dignified, hurt little smile which irritated him beyond endurance.

'And it lasted how long?' he asked, still caressing her hair.

'Till the day after the Ritz. Naturally I wrote and told him it was all over.'

'Have you seen him since?'

'Never!' she exclaimed.

Teeth on edge, he bit his lip to divert his anger. As if all this wasn't enough, she was allowing herself the luxury of virtuous indignation! She wasn't going to get away with any of this.

'When was the last time you saw him?'

She did not speak but took his hand in hers. Her noble silence filled him with fury. But patience. First the facts.

'I wasn't to know,' she said, looking away.

'The day we met at the Ritz?' he asked gently.

'Yes,' she breathed, and she gripped his hand tightly.

'What time that day?'

'Is it really all right for me to talk?'

'Of course, my love.'

She looked at him, gave him a faint, grateful smile, and kissed his hand.

'Just before I left Cologny. I rang him just to say hello, to tell him I had to go to the Ritz to be with my husband. He wanted me to come, begged me to go round and see him, just for a moment.'

'And you went?'

'Yes.'

'And what happened?'

She did not answer and looked away. He pushed her out of bed and she fell on the floor, where she remained in an absurd sitting position, the skirt of her dressing-gown gaping and exposing her half-opened thighs. Her sex revolted him: it had been used, others had been there.

Without getting up, she straightened her dressing-gown, and he bunched his fists and closed his eyes. Embarrassed! She dared to be embarrassed! So by the time they'd met that night at the Ritz she had already been to bed with this other man, and three hours later she'd had the effrontery to kiss his hand, the hand of a stranger, for a perfect stranger is what he had been then, and her lips still wet with the other man's kisses! Slept with him, she had slept with him, and three or four hours later, when they had gone back to her house, in the little sitting-room, she'd sat down all maidenly modesty at the piano and played him a chorale, the music of purity, and only four hours earlier she who now tinkled Bach's keys had been on her back with her legs open! 'Leave me, leave me to think about what's happening to me,' she had said, the easy virgin had had the nerve to say, that night as they separated, and had accompanied the words with an expression of noble fervour. A virgin sacred and untouchable who had been touching God knew what just five hours before! Oh, how modestly she wrapped herself in her dressing-gown!

'Open it up!'

'I won't!'

'Open it! Just like you did for him!'

'No!' she said, and she looked at him stupidly, slack-jawed.

She stood up and fastened the belt of her dressing-gown. He gave a bitter laugh. The lady covered her nakedness for him alone! Only he was not entitled to see her in the flesh! Leaping out of bed, he grabbed her flimsy wrap and yanked till it ripped from top to bottom. He tore away the flapping remnants and saw her beat a buttock-bobbing, humiliated retreat. He followed her into her room at once and was filled with pity for her distress as she clumsily donned another dressing-gown, a creature of weakness, a victim fingered by fate. That was all very well, but the other man had seen her delectable rump too, the same rump, she hadn't been fitted with a new one in the meantime. 'Always,' she had whispered to him in the Ritz as they danced. And only three hours before she'd been all welcoming thighs and beckoning smiles!

'Had you just slept with him the night we met at the Ritz?'

'No.'

'But you were his mistress?'

She shook her head stubbornly, mulishly, and opened her eyes wide. Losing control had been a mistake, he shouldn't have kicked her out of bed. She was scared now, and wouldn't admit anything else.

'Tell me you were his mistress.'

'I wasn't his mistress.'

Like an animal playing dead. It hurt him to see her so abject. But there had been kissing at the very least, just three hours before! Just three hours before the most beautiful moment in the whole of their life together!

'So you weren't his mistress?'

'No.'

'In that case, why did you say you had something serious to tell me?'

'Because it's serious that there's been something in my life.'

Something? He pictured a colossal phallus, and recoiled from the bestial spectacle. And here she was, at this moment, so pure of face, so demure, so poised! It was horrible!

'Go on. Explain what you mean.'

'There's nothing to explain. We were just friends, maybe a bit too close, but that's all.'

'You said: "Can I tell you everything?" And would this everything be just that you were very close friends?'

'Yes.'

'You went to bed with him!'

'No! As God is my witness!'

Her solemn fervour made him feel sick to his stomach. Why did women attach such enormous importance to carnimality! And why drag God into the chafings of the flesh! Why set their itches and urges before the Almighty!

'Did he ever come to your husband's house?'

'Sometimes. Not often.'

He shuddered. Oh the slut! She'd had the nerve to show her lover off to her husband! Whereas with him, that first evening, it had been all Bach, raptures over a nightingale, solemn words, and the awkward fumblings of the beginner as their lips first met, and on the evenings that followed there had been all sorts of oh-so-sublime posturing when he arrived and a great deal of kneeling. And this same woman

897

had coolly introduced her lover to the husband she was deceiving! That was probably what was meant by the Mystery of Woman.

'Did you go to his place? (She looked up at him and coughed. Giving herself time to think, he mused.) Did you go to his place?'

'In the beginning, yes. Later on I wouldn't. We used to meet in town, in cafés.'

He whirled his beads. Oh how much more mouth-watering those secret rendezvous must have been than a long dull day at Belle de Mai! Oh the trouble she must have taken getting ready to meet her man! Oh the way she'd walked into the café and, seeing him from a distance, had smiled!

'Why did you stop wanting to go to his place?'

'Because the third time I went he got a bit too . . . attentive.'

Attentive! He was lost in admiration. She certainly had a way with words, genteel words, words which papered over the cracks. Attentive was innocent, it suggested minuets and admirers and gentlemanly courtships and Mozart. She never forgot her manners, not even with sex. And, besides, it was a way of ennobling the other man's lust, it was part of the revolting way women had of tolerating male lechery.

'You said you thought you loved him, yet you stopped wanting to go calling? (She looked at him and then at the floor. Had she really said that she thought she loved him?) Come on now, surely you realize how implausible that sounds.'

After a silence she looked up again.

'I was scared to tell the truth because you'd have assumed I was his mistress. Yes, I used to go to see him. But I wasn't his mistress.'

'We'll come back to that. Who exactly was this self-restraining but attentive friend?'

'Oh God, what's the point?'

'Tell me his name! I want his name and I want it now!'

His heart raced as he waited for the enemy to make his entrance. Afraid to see him. Had to know.

'Dietsch.'

'Nationality?'

'German.'

'Just my luck. Christian name?'

'Serge.'

'Why "Serge"? Serge isn't a German name.'

'His mother was Russian.'

'I see you have it all at the tips of your fingers. What does he do?'

'He conducts orchestras. He's the maestro.'

'You mean he's a maestro.'

'I don't understand.'

'Ah, very quick to defend him aren't we?'

'I've absolutely no idea of what you are implying.'

'Why so hoity-toity with me?'

'Sorry, but I really don't know.'

'That's better. I don't suppose you were hoity-toity with Dietsch. Well, darling, I'll explain. In your book he's *the* maestro. In mine, though I do not know Urge, sorry Serge, he is merely a maestro, a conductor. Compare Einstein the physicist! Freud the psychoanalyst!'

Nostrils flaring and wearing an expression of glee on his face, he strode round the room, the ends of his dressing-gown flapping in his slipstream. Suddenly he stopped, turned, and lit a cigarette.

'Poor kid, you're so clumsy,' he began, to soften her up.

'Clumsy in what way?'

'Like that for example: asking in what way you've been clumsy. It proves you know you're on shaky ground. Anyway, though you weren't aware you were doing it, you've told me on seven separate occasions that you were his mistress.'

'I haven't said I was his mistress.'

'That makes eight! If you really weren't his mistress, then instead of saying that you never said you were his mistress you'd have made do with saying that you weren't his mistress. (He clapped his hands.) Gotcha!'

'No, no! I swear it's not true! We were just good friends!'

'You've admitted it eight times,' he smiled, and he twirled his cigarette between his fingers. 'The first time was when you came to my room, so noble and contrite, and you mentioned a secret you couldn't keep to yourself any more. Tell me, what's so terrible about being just good friends? Second admission: when I asked you if you'd been to bed with him that evening just before we met at the Ritz, you said "No". What did that "No" mean? It meant that you'd slept with him lots of times before! Otherwise your reaction would have been not to answer "No" but to say "I've never ever slept with him"! I'll put the rest of your admissions in cold storage, though they're there if you want them. Ergo you were his mistress. Actually I'm fully aware that you intended to admit it at the start. But I made the mistake of kicking you out of bed. But, come to think of it, why did you want to tell me about this man?'

'So I wouldn't have anything to hide from you.'

He felt a surge of pity. Poor girl, she genuinely believed that was the real reason. It was quite true: women were driven by their unconscious.

'So this man kisses you forty times, this way, that way, all ways, and you let him, and there's a smile on your face. (He wanted her.) In the receiving and giving of kisses of every variety, even the category of what Michael calls the inside reverse double-columbine, you raise no objections and even say thank you for every columbine you get! But if he starts getting attentive, as you nobly put it, by which I mean he has a mind to proceed to the logical sequel to the forty kisses, you take umbrage, you come over all virtuous, you shy away from the sequel! Come now, Ariane, earn my good opinion! Tell me the truth! You were his mistress! You know it, and so do I!'

He had spoken so quickly that she had not understood everything, a circumstance which convinced her that what he said must therefore be true. Besides, he had spoken with such certainty. And since it was patently obvious that he knew, she might as well make a clean breast of it.

'Yes,' she breathed, head bowed.

'Yes what?'

'Yes to what you said.'

'His mistress?'

She nodded a yes. He closed his eyes as he registered the shock, and realized that it was only now that he believed it. A hairy man, a man with a tail, crouching over the woman he loved!

'But only once,' she said.

'We'll come back to that later. Did you?'

'No,' she breathed.

How quickly she caught on! Oh, so sly! So shameless! He put the question more clearly. She blushed, and he lost his temper. What right did she have to blush? Indefatigably he repeated his question, and on each occasion she said no. But when he put the question for the twentieth or thirtieth time, defeated and with tears brimming in her eyes she shouted 'Yes, yes!' 'But not much,' she added after a pause, and she burned with shame and felt foolish. Outside, an amorous tom-cat wooed his lady-love. 'That's enough, Dietsch!' shouted Solal. A she-cat responded in an assertive contralto. 'That's enough, Ariane!' shouted Solal. At this point she decided to cry properly, which she did without having to try very hard, for she had only to feel sorry for herself, which was something that came to her easily.

'Why are you crying? We've been talking about a passing moment of happiness and that makes you cry?'

'Yes.'

'Why?'

She blew her nose, her tears withered by the unsympathetic welcome they had been given. He observed that her nose was red and swollen. Oddly enough, he felt no resentment at this moment and stared at her puffy nose in a not unkindly way. He repeated his 'Why?' several times, without thinking, mechanically.

'I don't know what you're saying. Why what?'

'Why are you crying?'

'Because I'm sorry.'

'But why? You did what you did.'

'It all seems so hateful now.'

'But presumably you didn't hate it when you were biting his neck. Incidentally, did you bite his neck every day?'

'What are you trying to say? I never bit his neck.'

'Well, that's good to know. Thanks. I shall have to start asking you to bite my neck. At least that's something you won't have done with him. In any case, it's the only thing I'll ever ask you to do for me from now on. (She bit her lip to stifle a mirthless, nervous giggle.) How many times did you sleep with each other? I'll keep on asking until tomorrow if I have to.'

'I gave myself to him just that one time.'

'Gave myself'! The words made him grip the glass he was holding so hard that it broke and blood flowed. She came closer and asked him to let her disinfect it for him.

'To hell with antiseptics! Why just the one time?'

'I told him what we were doing was wrong.'

He burst out laughing. Like a schoolmistress explaining to the little boy that what he'd done wasn't very nice and really quite naughty! Suddenly he felt inexpressibly happy. He put two cigarettes in his mouth, lit both, pulled on them hard and heartily, walked up and down, highly pleased with himself. Stopping in front of her, his two cigarettes held between his second and third fingers, he glared at her defiantly, elatedly. The light of battle lit his mouth.

'So then and there, still moist and clammy, you told him.'

'No, next day.'

'You went back to see him, you were in love with him, you'd enjoyed it first time round, felt what you nobly call ecstasy, eggstatic eggstasy, and then you decided you'd had enough, right? But one time or a hundred times, it's all the same! Did you sleep with him a hundred times?'

'No, I swear!'

'Fifty?'

'No.'

'Nine hundred times?'

'No.'

'Fifteen?'

'Good God, do you think I kept a tally?'

Appalled, he sat down, wiped his forehead with his bleeding hand. She hadn't counted! That meant it must have happened lots of times! Fifteen times at least, it seemed: fifteen would be a minimum!

'Go on.'

'What do you want me to say?'

'What I am waiting for you to say. Out with it!'

'I never felt anything after that first time,' she said after a pause.

Tainted, diminished, she looked away. Oh, he would stop loving her now. He stared at her with interest. Never felt anything! She certainly had a way with words!

'Why?'

'Why what?'

'Why didn't you feel anything the other times? You felt something the first time.'

'How should I know, for goodness' sake! I just didn't feel anything.'

'So why did you go on with it?'

'To avoid upsetting him. Oh leave me alone,' she groaned.

He sensed that she was telling the truth and looked at her with curiosity. A completely different species. To avoid upsetting him! How polite could you get!

'Why did he used to come to your house?'

'That was just at the start.'

'Wasn't it good enough for him where he lived? Why did he have to turn up on your husband's doorstep?'

'Because I liked seeing him. Because my husband was boring.'

She coughed liked a consumptive, louder and longer than was strictly necessary. He felt a stab of pain. Liked seeing another man! That was worse than going to bed with him. He pictured her sitting at her window, waiting for Dietsch to appear on the horizon!

'And whenever your husband left the room you would kiss?'

'No, never!' she exclaimed, and again he knew that she was telling the truth.

'Why not?'

'Because it wouldn't have been right,' she sobbed.

He began spinning round and round like a dervish, arms outstretched, forehead streaked with blood. Her reply took his breath away. He stopped whirling, faced the wall, beat his head against it, beat his cut hand against it and began counting silently. He stopped when there were six bloody hand-prints on the wall. Poor darling, what you must be going through, she thought. Oh, if only he would at least let her see to his hand. Was it badly cut? And his forehead, it was all covered in blood. Her poor darling, and all on account of Dietsch. He turned, looked at her disconsolately, seeing another man's woman. Then he went away.

CHAPTER 98

He poured eau-de-Cologne over his cut hand, decided that as gashed hands went he'd made a pretty good job of things, then felt bored. Surely she wasn't not going to come, was she, and leave him all by himself? For something to do, he thought about dying, imagined himself lying in his coffin with all the grisly details, then he inflicted assorted poses on the furry teddy-bear, turning him into a lover declaring his passion and then into a dictator haranguing a crowd. He was making him play football with a jade marble when he heard two knocks. He turned and saw that a sheet of paper had been slipped under the door. He picked it up.

'All the people I knew had dropped me. The only person I was really close to, my uncle, was in Africa. I was so isolated, my life was empty. I only went to bed with you know who so that I could have him as a friend, so I wouldn't feel all alone. I never loved him. He was my refuge from the poor devil I married. The moment you appeared on the scene and wanted me, he simply ceased to exist. Don't laugh if I say that I came to you virgin in mind and body. You mustn't laugh because it's true. Oh yes, virgin in body too, because I never knew what physical joy was until I met you. Don't leave me. If you're tired of me there's only one thing left for me to do. I'm so unhappy. Please let me come in.'

Behind the door he heard muffled sobs. He put on a pair of white gloves, gashed hand first, and got into a fresh dressing-gown, a black one, to contrast with the gloves. After a look at himself in the mirror, he opened the door. She was sitting on the floor, hair in a tangle, with her head against the jamb and a little handkerchief in one hand. He took her by both arms and helped her to her feet. She was shivering, so he opened his wardrobe, took out one of his coats, and put it over her. Standing there lost in a man's overcoat which was far too big and long and left only her ankles showing, she seemed very small, like a little girl. She kept her hands hidden in the sleeves, her teeth chattered and she looked waifish, swamped by his enormous coat.

'Sit down,' he said. 'I'll make you some tea.'

As soon as she was alone, she got up, felt in the pocket of her dressing-gown for her comb and compact, tidied her hair, blew her nose, powdered her face, sat down again, waited, looked around the room, and was surprised to see the teddy-bear: he'd never mentioned any teddy-bear to her, it was the twin of the one he'd given her. She ran her finger through its fur. When he returned, carrying a tray, she began shivering again.

'Drink this, darling,' he said when he'd poured her a cup. (She sniffled, looked up at him with eyes like a beaten dog, swallowed a mouthful, and shivered some more.) 'Want a biscuit? (She said no with a meek little shake of her head.) Have some more tea.'

She steeled herself and said: 'Do you still love me?'

He smiled, and she took his gloved hand and kissed it gingerly.

'Did you disinfect it?'

'Yes.'

'Won't you have some tea too? I'll get you a cup.'

'No, don't bother.'

'Drink out of mine, then.'

He took a sip and then sat down facing her. The sound of dance music floated in from the neighbours' house across the way, and there was a burst of happy voices. They paid no attention. It was late, but she did not feel sleepy. Nobody's bored tonight, he thought. She picked up a cigarette-box off the table, held it out to him, and gave him a light. He took two pulls on the cigarette, then stubbed it out. He smiled again, and she sat on his knee and held out her lips. Their kiss lasted some time. She wanted him, and in no time at all, as though nothing untoward had happened, she knew that he wanted her too. Women sometimes have a way of catching on. But, suddenly remembering that these lips had been offered to another, he freed himself, but calmly and without fuss.

'It's over now, darling girl, and I want to say I'm sorry. But, if you really want it to be over for good, you must tell me everything.'

'But afterwards things would be worse, not better.'

'On the contrary, it'll make me easier in my mind: I won't have this unbearable feeling that you're hiding things from me. I was impossible back there, and I'm truly sorry. It's just that I felt excluded from a part of your life, I felt like a stranger who had no right to know. It was too hurtful.'

He gently rearranged a lock of her hair.

'Are you sure it'll be all right afterwards?'

'Afterwards you will be a sweet girl who's made a clean breast of everything to the man she loves. Besides, after all, so what, dull as Dietsch-water, all passed under the bridge now, right? (He's so sweet, she thought, still so young, very loving, if a little shell-shocked.) We mustn't let him loom so large: he's not worth it. Oh, I know that the a conductor/the conductor business wasn't important. And anyway you broke it off with him at once. (He rearranged another lock of her hair.) Actually I'm not in any hurry, just knowing that you'll tell me everything sooner or later has eased my mind. You see, I'm quite a different person already. If you don't want to talk about it tonight, you can tell me when you're good and ready: tomorrow, the day after, next week.'

'I'd rather get it over with now,' she said.

Now in buoyant mood, he kissed her, all smiles, surrendering to the anticipated pleasure of hearing the tale. Like a boy at the circus waiting for the clowns to be brought on. Fussing over her, he brought her another, warmer, coat, his vicuña, which he spread over her legs, and then offered to make more tea. He danced attendance, treating her as though she were pregnant or a genius about to deliver herself of a masterpiece and not to be ruffled at any cost. He turned off the ceiling light, lit the bedside lamp, and even suggested that she had a lie-down, but this she refused.

'I'd prefer it if you asked me questions,' she said, taking his hand.

'How did you get to know him?'

'Through Alix de Boygne, a friend of mine, the only one I had left, much older than me, middle-aged. (Enter the Bawd, he thought.) She was very kind to me.'

'Tell me about her,' he said warmly, all ears.

'Good society background, but there had been someone in her life, a married man whose wife wouldn't give him a divorce, it all caused a bit of a stir in Geneva at the time. But all that was ages ago, and it's forgotten now. (The hypocrisy of that "someone in her life" filled him with anger, and he felt a sudden hatred for the lascivious old tart. But he didn't let it show, and nodded understandingly.) She's very generous, keeps an open mind. (And that's not all she keeps open, he thought.) She was very interested in art, helped to fund a chamber orchestra and invited budding musicians down to stay at her house in the country. (A taste for young flesh, he thought.) She was tremendously cross with the people we knew for dropping me. She rallied round and rather spoilt me.'

She sniffed and wiped her nose.

'Was she fat?'

'A bit,' she said awkwardly. (He smiled, thrilled by her obesity.) 'But terribly elegant. (Courtesy of steel-boned stays, he thought, and a maid to pull the draw-strings tight.) And tremendously cultured too.'

'You never mentioned her when we were in Geneva.'

'That was because I'd stopped seeing her. She left town just before I, before I got to know you. She went off to Kenya to live with her married sister.' (And with black men, he thought.)

'And you met him at her house?'

'Yes,' she said, underlining the word with an affirmative but restrained nod.

The respectable, conventional gesture set his teeth on edge, but he overrode his irritation. After all, she wasn't going to launch into the dance of the seven veils just because the man had crept into the conversation.

'How old was he?' he asked with a twinge of unease.

'Fifty-five.'

He smiled faintly. That meant he'd be about fifty-six now. Good. And four years from now, sixty. Even better.

'Tall?'

'Not tall, but not short either. Middling.'

'What sort of middling? Middling to tall or middling to short?'

'A bit shorter than average height. (He smiled benignly. He was almost getting to like comrade Dietsch.) Look, can't we drop this now?'

'No. Describe him some more.'

'If I do, it won't all turn nasty, will it?'

'On the contrary, darling. I told you. What about his hair, for example?'

'White, combed straight back,' she said, looking at her sandals. (He put his hands on her knees and squeezed gently.) 'Now that's enough describing, if you don't mind.'

'And his moustache. Also white?'

'No.'

'Black?'

'Yes.'

He relaxed his grip, changed his mind, and squeezed again. He did not dare ask for further details. Comrade Dietsch was quite capable of being trim and well-proportioned. Stick to his head. Not bald, unfortunately. But at least his hair was white, thank God.

'Yes,' he said earnestly, 'I can quite see that the contrast between the black moustache and the white hair must have been quite striking. (She coughed.) Sorry?'

'I didn't say anything. Throat tickling a bit.'

'But the contrast was striking?'

'At first, I found him off-putting. (Fine, but let's get on to later!) It was his moustache, it looked dyed. But I soon realized ... I can tell you everything, can't I?'

'Darling, look at me. I'm calm as can be, and that's because you've stopped holding me at arm's length. You were saying that you soon realized.'

'That he was an intelligent man, cultured, refined and a bit shrinking. (Not in every department, he thought.) We just talked.'

'Yes, darling. And then?'

'Well, as I went home I felt quite happy. Then a few days later Alix and I went to see him conduct. The Pastoral was on the programme.'

He frowned. Of course, the lady was artistic and so one simply said 'the Pastoral': it gave the impression that one was close to Beethoven. And to Dietsch. She'd have to pay for 'the Pastoral'.

'Go on, darling.'

'Well, anyhow, he was standing in for the regular conductor, whose name I've forgotten. (Couldn't remember the name of the regular conductor. But she remembered the name of the stand-in perfectly. She wouldn't get away with any of this.) I liked the way he conducted.'

In his mind's eye he saw Dietsch the genius twitching like a puppet, conducting without a baton, and the two dim-witted women swooning, convinced that here was Beethoven himself before their very eyes! Beethoven and Mozart were never admired the way people admired conductors, who were the fleas of genius, the ticks of genius, bloodsuckers of genius who took themselves so seriously and had a ridiculously inflated sense of their own importance and had the nerve to let themselves be called maestros and took bows as though they were actually Beethoven and Mozart and earned so much more than Beethoven and Mozart ever did! And why did she admire the leech Dietsch? Because he could read music written by someone else! Dietsch, the little tick, was just about up to writing, at a pinch, a short military march.

'I can see that he was a more interesting proposition than your husband.'

'True,' she conceded, giving the matter her serious and objective consideration. He was so angry that he bit his lip until it bled.

'Tell me just a little more about him, darling, and then it will all be over.'

'Well, he was Principal Conductor with the Dresden Philharmonic. When the Nazis came to power he resigned. Actually he was a member of the Social Democratic Party.'

'That's nice. And?'

'Well, he came to Switzerland and had to settle for being Second Conductor of the Geneva Symphony, although he had been Principal

Conductor of the leading orchestra in Germany. (She was obviously crazy about Dietsch! So what on earth was she doing at Belle de Mai with a man who couldn't read a note of music?) There, I think that's plenty for now, if you don't mind.'

'Just one last thing, darling, and then we'll draw a line under it all. Did you sometimes spend the whole night with him?'

The question was crude, so he squeezed her hands lovingly, kissed her hands.

'No, but can we please stop? All that is dead and buried, and I don't like thinking about it.'

'It's absolutely the last question. Did you ever spend the night together?'

'Very infrequently,' she said in her angel voice.

'There, you see? Nothing dreadful happens when you give me a straight answer. But how did you manage it?' he smiled, amused and teasing.

'Through Alix,' she said, smoothing her dressing-gown over her knee. But please let's just leave it there.'

He took a long, hard pull on his cigarette so that his voice would be steady when he spoke. Then he gave her a nodding, winking smile of complicity.

'Ah, I get it! You were supposed to have gone to see her, whereas in reality you were with him, and you rang your husband to say it was too late to get back and that she insisted you stay the night! That's how it was, right, sly little minx?'

'Yes,' she breathed, head down, and there was a silence.

'Tell me, darling, have you had any other men?'

'God, what sort of woman do you take me for?'

'A whore, of course,' he said sweetly. 'A very sly little whore.'

'It's not true!' she exclaimed, rising to her feet, hackles raised. 'I forbid you to say that!'

'But why? You don't mean to tell me that you really believe you're an honest woman?'

'Certainly I do! And you know very well that it's true! I was trapped in my horrible marriage, didn't know which way to turn. (Enter spiderwoman, he thought.) I am an honest woman!'

'Pardon me, but . . . (He gave a polite, hesitant shrug.) But when you got back to your husband you were . . . (He pretended to search for a suitably polite adjective.) Damp after what you'd been up to with Dietsch and, well anyhow, it struck me that you weren't being entirely honest.'

'I admit I was wrong not to have told him everything, but I was afraid of hurting him. It's the only thing I did that was wrong. I'm not ashamed of any of the rest of it. My husband was an oaf. And I met a man who had a soul, yes, a soul!'

'A big one, was it?'

She gawped at him, nonplussed. Then the penny dropped.

'You are disgusting!'

He clapped his hands and raised his eyes to take heaven as his witness. That beat everything! She had done it three maybe four times a night with her bandleader, gone at it hammer and tongs, and he was the one who was disgusting! It was enough to make a chap want to run away and hide his face.

To hide his face, he yanked a sheet off the bed and put it over himself. Draped in his white winding-sheet, he stalked around the room. As she watched his ghostly figure striding to and fro, she told herself she wasn't to laugh and said sobering things to herself. It's very serious, my life is at the crossroads, she said to herself. Eventually he abandoned his shroud and lit a cigarette. She wasn't laughing now. Yes, she was at the crossroads.

'Listen, darling,' she said, 'all that's dead and done with now.'

'On the contrary, it's very much alive. Dietsch will always lie between you and me. And of course on you. He's there now. He's at it all the time. I can't live with you any more. Go! Get out of this house!'

CHAPTER 99

No, it was impossible. He could not bear to be alone, he needed her, needed to see her. If only she would smile at him, that would be the end of it, everything would be all right again. He stepped out into the hall, sounded his chest, tweaked his hair, sharpened his nose with thumb and forefinger, and made up his mind. To avoid losing face, he didn't knock but just walked in masterfully. She did not look up but went on putting clothes into the open case on the bed, first folding them neatly, absorbed, impassive. She was enjoying making him suffer. This was it, he'd see that she'd made up her mind and was going.

To hide how much he needed her, to show her how little he cared, he said sarcastically: 'So it's goodbye then, not *au revoir*?'

She nodded a yes and carried on with her careful packing. To make her suffer, to show her that he was fully expecting her to leave, he lent a hand and passed a dress from the wardrobe.

'That'll do, my case is just about full,' she said as he held out another dress. 'I'm not taking everything. I'll write and let you know where to send the rest.'

'Let me give you some money.'

'No thanks. I've got all I need.'

'What train are you catching?'

'It doesn't matter. The first one that comes along.'

'It's almost three in the morning. The first train out is the Marseilles train, and it doesn't leave until seven.'

'I'll wait at the station.'

Brows knitted and forehead furrowed, she stuffed shoes into one corner of the case.

'Mistral's blowing. It'll be cold hanging about in the waiting-room. Don't forget to take a coat.'

'I'm not bothered about the cold. Catching pneumonia would be one way out.'

She forced the family photograph album into another corner of the case. He whistled under his breath.

'I suppose you'll make for Geneva. Is that so you can go to more symphony concerts?'

She turned on him belligerently, fists clenched.

'You lied when you said it would be all right if I told you everything. I trusted you: I don't have a suspicious mind.'

She was quite right, of course. She was an honest woman. Still, that honest mouth of hers had been intimate with a moustache.

'You shouldn't have made bed-spring music with your bandleader three hours before you turned up and kissed my hand!'

His breath rasped in his throat. It was intolerable to be perpetually confronted by the spectacle of the most loving, the noblest of women, so pure in face, and have to picture her incomprehensibly impaled beneath the weight of an orchestra-conducting chimpanzee, gasping, panting beneath her chimpanzee. Yes, the most loving of women. What other woman had ever loved him as much as she had? That night at the Ritz, as she kissed his hand, she had seemed so pure. And afterwards, at her house, she had looked so young and so innocent sitting at her piano, so gravely robed in love. And yet only hours before, sprawled under the chimp!

'You ought to be ashamed of yourself, talking to me like that! What harm did I ever do you? It all happened before I met you.'

'Get on with it. Shut your case.'

'So it doesn't bother you at all to let me walk out by myself into the night and the cold?'

'It's a pity, of course. But there it is. We can't go on living together. Don't forget your coat.'

He was pleased with his answer. The cool manner was the most convincing, it made the fact that they were going their separate ways crystal clear. She was crying and blowing her nose. Fine. At least at this moment she preferred him to Dietsch. She snapped the case shut, blew her nose again, and turned to face him.

'You know, don't you, that there's no one in the world I can turn to?'

'Just keep a firm grip on your conductor's baton. (Oh, if she would only take one step forward, if she would only hold out her hand, he'd take her in his arms and all this would be over. Why didn't she come to him?) So you think I'm coarse?'

'I didn't say a word.'

'No, but that's what you were thinking! You believe that being noble means using quality words, avoiding words which are supposed to be cheap and vulgar, and doing exactly and as often as possible the things the cheap, vulgar words describe. I said "keep a firm grip on your conductor's baton" and that makes me vulgar, I can see it in the curl of your eyelashes! But, if you're so noble, what precisely were you up to on the quiet behind locked doors in a bedroom with Dietsch while your poor husband waited for you trustingly, lovingly?'

'If what I did with D was wrong . . .'

He gave an amused, pained laugh. So modest, so decent! She'd gone to bed with an initial! She had deceived him, was still deceiving him, with an initial!

'Oh, I get it. If what you did with Dietsch was wrong, then what you did with me was also wrong. As if I didn't know! I've had to pay a high enough price for it.'

'What do you mean?'

Yes, he at least paid for adultery in the hell of a love lived in quarantine, a hell that had lasted thirteen months, twenty-four hours a day, the hell of living with the knowledge that each day she loved him a little less. Whereas her bandleader was a lucky man, for every time they met was wonderful because they did not meet often, every time was party time, and the presence in the background of her grindingly boring husband added spice to the proceedings.

'What do you mean?' she repeated.

Should he scream at her that this was the first time in an age that they were free of their anaemia, that at last being together actually meant something? But if he did, what would the poor girl have left? No, he must spare her the humiliation.

'I don't know what I meant.'

'Well, in that case I'd be grateful if you'd go away. I must get dressed.'

'Does it bother you to put a skirt on in front of the man who succeeded your bandleader?' he said, listlessly, mechanically, feeling no pain, for he was weary.

'Please go.'

He went. In the hall he felt a twinge of anxiety. Surely she wouldn't call his bluff and actually leave? She appeared, suitcase in hand, wearing a smart grey suit, the one he liked her in best, and face made up. How beautiful she looked. She made slowly for the door and slowly opened it.

'Goodbye,' she said, and she looked at him for the last time.

'I can't say I'm happy at the idea of your leaving at three in the morning. What will you do in the station until seven? It's only a halt, and the waiting-room is locked at night. It would be more sensible to leave just before the train is due, at least that way it won't be as tiring for you as standing around in the cold.'

'Very well, I'll wait in my room until twenty to seven,' she said when he'd been sufficiently insistent for her to feel that she could accept with honour.

'Get some rest, try and get some sleep, but set the alarm in case you go off into a deep sleep. Set it for six thirty, or even twenty past six, it's a fair way to the station from here. Well then, I'll say goodbye now. Sure you don't want any money?'

'Positive, thanks.'

'Right then, that's it. Goodbye.'

Back in his own room, he removed his white gloves, picked up the teddy-bear, and changed its boots for green espadrilles and its sombrero for a little straw boater. The charm of this soon wore off. Telling himself he was thirsty, he went into the kitchen, got a bottle of lime cordial from a cupboard, and then put it back again. He returned to his room to put his gloves on again, then knocked on her door. She was standing by her case, with her arms crossed and her hands on her shoulders, and wearing a dressing-gown, which reassured him.

'Sorry to disturb you, but I'm thirsty. Where's the lime cordial?'

'In the big cupboard in the kitchen, bottom shelf, left-hand side.'

It struck her immediately that if he went and got it himself she wouldn't see him again. So she offered to go and fetch the juice of the lime herself. He said thank you. She asked him where he wanted it, here or in his room? It struck him that if she brought it to his room she'd go away again at once.

'Well, I'm here,' he said coolly.

Alone, he checked in the mirror. The white gloves looked very well against the black dressing-gown. When she returned from the kitchen, she set the silver tray gracefully on the table, poured the lime cordial, topped it up with mineral water, added two ice-cubes with a pair of silver tongs, stirred, handed him the glass and sat down. She pulled her dressing-gown down modestly so that it hid her legs. He tipped the contents of the glass on to the carpet.

'Raise your dressing-gown!'

'No!'

'Raise it!'

'No!'

'If Dietsch was allowed to see, then I want to see too!'

Holding one hand firmly on her knees, she began to sob, her face crumpled, and this made him furiously angry. She wouldn't show him what she had shown another man and she had the nerve to be coy! Why should he be the only one who was never shown anything? He went on and on repeating his monotonous request that she lift her dressing-gown, until the relentlessly repeated words lost all meaning. 'Raise it, raise it, raise it, raise it!' At last, to make the voice stop, distraught and humiliated, she raised her dressing-gown and revealed her long, silky legs and her thighs.

'There, you brute, you horrible, cruel brute, are you satisfied now?'

Her whole body shook, and her face, traversed by waves of conflicting emotion, was a thing of terror and beauty. He started towards her.

'I am your woman,' she said through her tears as she lay, marvellously lay, under him, and he washed over her like breaking waves and she broke over him and said that he mustn't be unkind to her any more, said again that she was his woman, and he adored his woman and broke over her like waves. Oh chafing love, song of contending flesh, primal rhythm, overmastering rhythm, sacred rhythm. Oh the deep thrusting, the shuddering release, the despairing smile of life which at last breaks free and makes life eternal.

First Dietsch, now me! he thought, their two bodies still joined. Dietsch before him in these same latitudes! 'Not much,' she'd said, but that 'not much' was a lie, 'not much' didn't mean feeling nothing, he thought, their two bodies still joined. And if she had felt once, why not the other times too? Besides, if it were true that she'd felt no pleasure after the first time, she wouldn't have persisted. Therefore, oh yes, each time with Dietsch. He rolled off her. She saw the madness in his eyes and jumped naked out of bed, opened the French window, fled into the garden, and fell over. A brightness of smooth flesh agleam with moonlight. He gave a start. She would catch her death lying naked in the damp grass!

'Come back! I won't hurt you!'

As he approached, she scrambled to her feet and made off at a run towards the rose-hedge. In the still black trees, the first little stout-hearted birds were greeting the coming dawn, lovingly greeting each other, whereas she was running, running away from him, afraid of him. He went back into the house, reappeared carrying the vicuña coat, put it down on the gravel of the drive, shouted that she was not to be afraid, that he would shut himself in his room, that she was to put the coat on.

He watched for her behind his bedroom curtains, saw her at last make up her mind to come in, saw her wearing the coat, submissive. But why didn't she button it up? Her pitiful vulnerability glimpsed through the chink of the flapping coat. 'Button it up, my darling, button up, my precious, don't catch cold, you are so fragile,' he murmured against the glass.

Moments later he went into her room and found her pale and motionless, her blue-ringed eyes staring unblinkingly at the ruins of her life. He winced to see her hurt and suffering through his fault. A brute, he was a brute, and he was accursed. To alleviate her distress, he feigned a grief which in fact he felt quite genuinely, sat down heavily to attract her attention, and let his head rest on the table-top.

He knew her, her heart was kind. When she saw him suffering, she would want to comfort him, would draw near and comfort him, would come close and take away her lover's pain, and in so doing she would forget her own pain and feel better. But she did not come immediately, and he heaved a sigh. At last she came to him, leaned over him, stroked his hair, appeased by her mission to comfort him. Suddenly an image of Dietsch in full manhood leaped fully formed into his mind. Oh the slut! He looked up.

'How big?'

'How big what?'

'How big was he?'

'O God, what's the point? What is the point?' she exclaimed with a grimace of despair.

'There's a great deal of point!' he said solemnly. 'It's the whole point of my life! Say: how big!'

'I've no idea. Five foot five, I think.'

Taking a perverse pleasure in believing that Dietsch was possessed of mighty attributes, he recoiled in horror and put one hand to his lips. What sort of monster was this man!

'I understand everything now,' he said, and he began pacing to and fro, arms raised in total stupefaction while she cried and gave nervous laughs and hated herself for laughing. Was she in hell? The damned probably laughed as they burned.

'This is too awful,' she said.

'As you say, five feet and five inches is awful,' he said. 'Whatever complexion you put on it, I can quite see it's too awful. It's also too big.'

Broad daylight outside. He was standing in front of her. She sat as though turned to stone, not moving a muscle and rocked from time to time by fits of shivering. He had been talking at her indefatigably for hours. He stood there, his dressing-gown lying on the floor, still wearing his gloves but otherwise completely naked, for he felt hot, with three lighted cigarettes between his lips, and smoked, wreathed in a fug which made her sinner's eyes sting, smoked greedily and talked non-stop, with the smell of Dietsch sweat in his nostrils, his eyes filled by the image of his darling's lips touching

918

filthy Dietsch lips, oh, those four small loathsome steaklets in perpetual motion. Oratorical and prophetic, absurd and high-minded, he talked and talked, and his head pounded and his eyes ached with the constant spectacle of their adulterous bodies and their wantoning tongues, and he accused, denounced, catalogued the foulness of the sinful woman who sat before him, invoked the example of his respectable grand-mothers who chastely hid their hair in beaded nets, for hair is a form of nakedness saith the Talmud, and praised to the skies the virtuous sexual ineptitude of the Jewesses of Cephalonia, for whom a handsome man meant a man of girth and presence. And faithful to their lords and husbands every one!

Motionless, head bowed, she heard him through the swirls of cigarette smoke, barely understanding, numbed by sleep and unhappi-ness, while he, sick at heart, gave clownish impersonations of Dietsch and Ariane locked in fond embrace, made mock to demean them, to break the spell cast by Dietsch the distant, Dietsch the desirable. In the end she struggled to her feet, determined to make her escape. But she hadn't the strength to catch trains. Check in at the Royal instead. Oh to be free of this, to hear the sound of his voice no more, to sleep.

'Let me go.'

He came close and pinched her ear, but there was no venom in the gesture. He had no wish to harm her. But beg her to stay? Out of the question. His arm was limp and his fingers felt unreal, but he pinched her ear again in the hope that the scene would continue, for then she would stay.

'Stop it! Don't touch me!'

'Didn't he touch you?'

'The way he touched me was different,' she muttered, stupid with sleep and lassitude.

Different! Oh, how could she be so shameless! And she had the nerve to say it to his face! He resisted the temptation to hit her. If he hit her, she would leave. The alarm went off. Six thirty. At all costs stop her thinking about the seven o'clock train.

'Repeat what you just said.'

'What did I say?'

'You said the way he touched you was different.'

'All right. "The way he touched me was different."'

'What do you mean "different"?'

'He didn't pinch my ear.'

'Why not?' he asked mechanically, with nothing particular in mind, for the show had to go on.

'Why not what?'

'Why didn't he pinch your ear?'

'Because he wasn't common.'

He glanced at himself in the mirror. Ah, so he was common, in spite of the white gloves.

'How did he touch you, then?'

'I don't remember.'

'Tell me how he touched you.'

'But you know already! (He stopped himself from hitting her.) Good God, don't you see that you're turning our love into something dirty?'

'That's all to the good. But I forbid you to speak of our love. There's no such thing as our love any more. You've thrown it away, dietsched it.'

'In that case, let me go.'

'And did you say that you were his woman too? Probably said it in German. *"Ich bin deine Frau."'*

'I never spoke German to him.'

'Did you say it in French?'

'I didn't say anything to him.'

'Not true. You couldn't have not talked to each other. Tell me what you said to him during those special moments.'

'I don't remember.'

'So you did speak words to him. I must know what words.'

'God, why do you go on and on about him?'

It was true. By talking about Dietsch so much, by constantly bringing up the way he'd held her in his arms, all he'd achieved was to gild his image and strengthen his distant spell: he had made Dietsch attractive, alluring. And now, her mind teeming with Dietsch, reliving past happiness because her lover who felt betrayed had put the idea into her head with his garrulousness, it might very well turn out that she would want to go back to Dietsch, who was now an exciting novelty once more, and resume the close combat of yore. Too bad, couldn't be helped. Get the facts.

'Tell me what you used to say to him,' he said, stressing each word.

'I don't know. Nothing really.'

'Did you call him "My love"?'

'Certainly not. I didn't love him.'

'In that case, why did you let him do as he liked with you?'

'Because he was gentle and very polite.'

'Polite? With all that exploring of your nether latitudes?'

'You are disgusting.'

'So a man who goes exploring is automatically polite?' he shouted in a rage. 'But put it into words and it's disgusting. I'm the one who is despicable, and he is respectable! Do you respect him?'

'Yes, I respect him.'

Both of them were scarcely able to stand, were like malfunctioning machines, ground down by fatigue and incoherence. Outside, the birds were now singing their small hymns of praise to the sun. Dazed, still naked, still smoking, he stared incredulously at this woman who dared to respect a man with whom she had done the foulest things. With one limp arm, he gave her the lightest of pushes, as though he were dreaming. She went down like a sack of potatoes, though she put her hands out to break the fall. She lay face down and motionless, her forehead resting on one arm. Her flimsy dressing-gown had ridden up to her waist, exposing her nakedness. She uttered a long moan, called for her father, and sobbed. Her rump moved, rising and falling to the rhythm of her sobs. He drew closer.

CHAPTER 100

Leaving his suitcase on a bench, he walked along the platform, stopped at the slot-machine, inserted the required coins, pulled handles, watched the little paper packets pop out, whistled, and, staring up at the sky, sauntered back the way he'd come. At eleven o'clock he started worrying. Was she going to call his bluff and not come to the station to stop him leaving? If it wasn't running late, the Marseilles train would be here in eight minutes. Eventually he saw a car he recognized. It was Agay's other taxi. She got out of it carrying a case. Their eyes met, but each stifled an urge to laugh, a purely nervous reaction which had no mirth in it.

'Are you leaving too?' he said, frowning and staring at the ground.

'I'm leaving too.'

'Where will you go?'

'Anywhere, so long as it's far away from you. Where are you going?'

'Marseilles,' he said, his eyes still on the ground to keep a tight rein on his impulse to laugh.

'In that case I'll get the train after yours.'

'Did you lock up properly? Did you turn off the gas?'

She shrugged to indicate that such petty matters did not figure high on her agenda, and moved away to the other bench on the platform. They sat with their cases, six feet apart, and proceeded to ignore each other. At five minutes past eleven he stood up, made his way to the ticket office, and asked for two first-class tickets to Marseilles. Then he returned to the platform, where he stood waiting, suitcase in hand, still avoiding her eye. At last the train puffed indignantly into the station, expired, and disgorged a knot of commuters. As he got in, he peered out of the corner of his eye. If she didn't get in too, he'd jump out on to the platform at the last minute.

'What do you think you're doing?' he asked as she stepped into his compartment.

'Catching a train.'

'You haven't got a ticket.'

'I'll get one from the ticket-inspector.'

'You could at least go and sit in another compartment.'

'There's plenty of room in this one.'

Whistles blew and the train groaned, protested, snorted in a huff of steam and a screech of metal, then rolled backwards, shook itself, and began to creep smoothly forward. Then, taking its courage in both hands, it charged, hurling itself bodily forward, yanking its chained and tortured coaches behind it, spluttering to the rhythm of its relentless wheels. When she stood up to put her suitcase on the rack, he let her, and sat watching her clumsy efforts with satisfaction. Yes, she'd just have to get on with it. When the case was safely stowed away, she sat down on the seat opposite. Both of them kept staring at the floor, because they knew that if they caught each other trying to be serious they wouldn't be able to help smiling and then laughing outright, and that would involve considerable loss of face.

In the rocking corridor, a gaggle of English passengers bumped along laughing apologetically, and they were followed by a raucous gang of American youths, gaudy, gum-chewing, manly morons in the making, convinced of their own importance and nasally braying their mastery of the world, and they in turn were followed by their gangling sisters in knee-socks, sexually aware and precociously lip-sticked, who also whinnied at the world through vibrantly nasal passages, unstoppably vulgar, endlessly, bovinely chomping on chewing-gum, tomorrow's majorettes.

They both continued to ignore each other, while outside hunched trees reared up and then were gone, and telegraph poles streaked past in reverse on scalloped wires, and a village bell rang, and a dog with its tongue hanging out strained comically to the top of a grassy knoll, and the train gave a sudden lurch and squealed with fright, and the gravel gleamed between the rails, and another locomotive roared snootily past belching obscenely, and a level-crossing keeper stood like a tailor's dummy, and far off a toy yacht was a white fleck on Mediterranean silk.

Enter three budding adolescent girls. After a lot of silly giggling, because they had decided that he was awfully handsome, they began chattering away, using words which they considered very smart to make themselves seem interesting and original, to attract his attention. One mentioned a crooner and said that he was dishy, another mentioned this fantastic cold she'd had last week, and the third said she'd had one too and it made her cough like, well, like anything. He stood up, left the compartment, and negotiated the concertina-sided passage which linked coaches and smelled of sheep's wool. He found himself in the third-class, opened the door of the last compartment along, and sat down.

Intoxicated by its own speed, constantly threatening to leave the rails, the panicking, clumsy, streaking train thundered into a tunnel with a screech of fear, and smoke whitened the windows, and clanking pandemonium bounced back off the oozing walls, and then the countryside was suddenly there again, serene and green. From time to time the other passengers watched the well-dressed intruder in silence, and then eventually resumed their conversations. A heavily made-up factory-girl with darned silk stockings gave the cold shoulder to a farmworker who, as he sweet-talked her, stroked his stubbly chin to cover his shyness. A fat motherly body wearing a tam and a coat with a rabbit-fur collar answered a question put by the woman sitting next to her, then yawned to disguise the lie still fresh on her lips, after which she wiped the long candle dangling from the nose of her three-year-old cherub and began chatting to him in a false, showy way for the edification of the other passengers, asking him things in a peculiar, formal voice so as to extract unexpected grown-up answers which would amaze the onlookers, on whom she kept a keen weather eye, while the brat, sensing that he had been granted unusual licence, made the most of the opportunity to scream his head off, stamp his feet, dribble, and regurgitate bits of garlic sausage. An engaged couple, in a world of their own at the far end of one of the bench-seats, sat with their red, dirty-nailed fingers intertwined. She sported a crop of pustules on her forehead. He had a tiny nose and wore a light-brown dog-tooth jacket, a stiff collar, a jumper zipped up the front, patent-leather shoes and purple socks. A propelling-pencil and a pen were clipped to his top pocket, which also boasted a lace-edged handkerchief and a chain holding a 13 in a circle. He kept plying her with whispered questions, purring amorous entreaties to which she, highly delighted, merely replied with stifled giggles or little wheedling oohs. A fully paid-up member of society's great club, within his rights, confident of his bona fides, he pawed his girl's backside while she simpered smugly, hummed 'The Chapel in the Moonlight' to bind him in her spell, and, as she did so, laid her pustule-studded forehead smoochily on his manly, heavily padded shoulder.

Saint-Raphaël. Recoiling, lurching, wheels protesting like a pack of yelping, tormented puppies, the train ground to a halt with a long, weary sigh and a series of spasms, metallic growls and hisses which culminated in one expiring gasp. A bold influx of new passengers. Room reluctantly, suspiciously made for them by the old. A whole family trooped in, led by an elderly red-faced matron in a black veil, and the train set off, endlessly asthmatically wheezing, in a clangour of panicking metal. In the distance a river gleamed briefly and was immediately extinguished, and the elderly matron handed all her brood's tickets to the inspector with that little self-satisfied smirk which is the trade mark of persons whose papers are in order and who are members of a group. Then she struck up a conversation with the motherly party in the tam, to whom she said outright that she could not bear to see animals suffer, then another with the girl with the fiancé with the still wandering hands, who, before replying to the forceful virago, licked her downy top lip. After which the engaged couple fed their inner selves with brawn and saveloys, the girl sucking at filaments of meat stuck between her teeth with sophistication and the last word in bird noises. When they had finished their repast, she peeled an orange with her thumbnail and passed it to her man, who absorbed it leaning forward, legs apart, to avoid making a mess on his clothes, then belched, wiped his hands on the handkerchief she gave him, and wrestled with the zip of his new jumper, while the train bolted, lurched, and careered along at an alarming speed. Flushed with wine, perspiring freely, the girl decided it would be a lark to say goo'bye goo'bye goo'bye to all the people they passed, and she waved her hand at them excitedly. This made all the other passengers laugh. Proud of his fiancée's success and his thoughts turning again to love, he began nibbling an ear graced with an earring in the shape of a ship's anchor, a proceeding which drew a fit of giggles from the delectable creature, who exclaimed: 'Stop it, you're driving me crazy!' and followed this up with: 'Give over, pack it in!' When her young suitor, now red in the face, persisted in notifying her of his passion, the pimply damsel gave him a saucy slap, poked out a well-coated tongue, and then cast a coal-black eye over her audience to see what effect this had produced. Solal stood up. He'd rubbed shoulders with proles for quite long enough. Safe now to go back to where the money was, for the three stupid girls had got off at Saint-Raphaël, chattering and giggling.

In her best little-girl voice, she said that she'd been wrong about there being an early-morning train for Marseilles that stopped at Agay. According to the timetable the three girls had let her see, this was the first train of the day for Marseilles. 'Good,' he said, without looking at her, and he lit a cigarette as a barrier between them. There was a pause, and then she said that this train was very fast and they'd be in Marseilles early, they were due in at one thirty-nine. 'Good,' he said. After another pause, she said it was a pity they'd caught the train at Cannes, because there was a scheduled stop at Saint-Raphaël. It was the fault of the first taxi-driver, who had misled him, done it on purpose probably, to have the longer fare. He did not reply. Then she got up and came and sat down beside him. 'May I?' she asked. He did not answer. She put her arm through the arm of her great big shamefaced Mr Wolf and asked if he was all right. 'Yes, fine,' he said. 'Me too,' she said, and she kissed his cut hand and laid her head on the shoulder of the man she loved.

When the train pulled into the station at Toulon, she woke with a start and whispered yes she'd turned the gas off. A white-jacketed waiter from the dining-car walked by ringing his bell and announced the second service of lunch. She said she was hungry. He said that he was hungry too.

CHAPTER 101

They had just got back to the hotel from an afternoon spent roaming round the city hand in hand. She had loved everything about Marseilles: the barrows in the Rue Longue-des-Capucins bright with food-mountains and raucous with the cries of the street traders, the fish market and the loud-mouthed fishwives, the Rue de Rome, the Rue Saint-Ferréol, the Canebière, the Vieux-Port, the narrow, ominous, spontaneous streets where sinister men sidled with feline grace and pock-marked faces.

Happy because she could hear him singing in the bath, she smiled at herself in the mirror. Such a good idea remembering to bring the pretty slippers and the pearl necklace which went so well with her dressing-gown. Holding her smile, she proceeded to inspect the cold dinner which had just been laid out on the table and gave herself a mental pat on the back for ordering the kind of meal he liked best: hors-d'œuvres, salmon steaks, assorted cold meats, chocolate mousse, petits fours and champagne. Another good idea had been to ask for a five-branched candelabra. They would dine by candlelight, so much cosier. Everything was fine. He had been ever so gentle with her from the moment they had arrived.

She was about to open the box of candles and dress the candelabra when he came in, looking quite superb in his raw-silk dressing-gown. She pushed back a strand of hair from her forehead and motioned to the table with a gracious, effeminate wave of her hand.

'Just look at these hors-d'œuvres. Such wonderful colours. There are Swedish starters and Russian salad: they were my idea. Those little straw-coloured things are called *supions*, it's a Provençal speciality so the waiter told me, and delicious by all accounts, but you have to dunk them in this green dip. Listen, darling, you know what? You are going to go and lie down and I shall bring you dinner in bed. And, while you're tucking in to all these delicious goodies, I'll read to you. What do you say?'

'No, we'll sit down to dinner here. You can read to me after we've eaten, when I'm in bed. And, while you read, I'll be ruthless with the petits fours. But I'll let you have some if you like.'

'All right, darling, that's fine by me,' she said, and on her face appeared such a look of maternal love. (How could I ever be angry with him, she thought.) And now I'm going to light the candelabra, you'll see, it'll make a lovely glow. (She opened the box and took out a candle.) It's very fat, I don't know if it'll fit.'

He stiffened like a startled leopard. Oh, her hand, her pure hand, around the candle! Oh, that horrible, angelic smile!

'Please put that candle down,' he said, looking at the floor. 'No candles, I don't want candles, I hate candles. Put them out of sight somewhere. Thank you. Now listen, I'm going to ask you a question, just one, it won't hurt. If you answer, I won't get angry, I promise. Did you used to take a bag with you on those evenings when you were going to spend the night. (He broke off. He could not bring himself to say with Dietsch.) An overnight bag?'

'Yes,' she said, trembling, and he raised his head ruefully and all of a sudden looked like a sick dog.

'A small bag, was it?'

'Yes.'

'Of course it was.'

In his mind's eye he pictured with horror the contents of the bag. A very fetching pair of silk pyjamas or maybe a flimsy nightie, though it would have been no sooner on than off again. Comb, toothbrush, creams, powder, toothpaste, all the paraphernalia she'd need when she woke up, and she would wake up happy. Oh, those waking kisses. Damn that disgusting Boygne woman. And almost certainly a book that she particularly liked and would want to read out to her man when the earth had stopped moving. She liked sharing, it was in her nature. Besides, reading to him was refined, a shared experience which would ease her conscience by casting a veil of nobility over the sordidness of adultery. And did she call him 'Serge'? She would certainly have said 'dear' as she did to him, and 'darling' as she did to him, and would have spoken the self-same secret words in the shadow of the night. Perhaps she had even been taught to say them by her man. And maybe in the bag was a little box of cachous designed to give the impression that her breath was perennially sweet. Surreptitiously, in the pause between two pro-tracted kisses, quick reach for a cachou, but keep it casual, and then quick as a flash tuck it into her cheek, left-hand side, behind the wisdom tooth, so that it was undetectable to the probing tongue of her bandleader.

'Did you put just one or several in your mouth?'

'One or several what?'

'Cachous.'

'I've never eaten a cachou in my life,' she sighed. 'Oh come on, let's eat. Or, if you don't want to eat, we'll go out instead.'

'One last thing, and then I shan't ask you anything else. When you got to his place, did you take all your clothes off at once? (His blood pressure rose alarmingly. She, undressing unblushingly or, worse, blushingly, and Dietsch standing there with his tongue already hang-ing out lecherously!) Answer me, darling. You see, I'm perfectly calm, I'm holding your hand. All I want to know is did you undress the instant you got there?'

'Of course not. Don't be silly!'

Oh the shame of that 'Don't be silly'! A 'Don't be silly' which meant 'I am far too pure to take my clothes off all at once, it simply isn't done, it has to be taken in stages, in a kind of seraphic striptease punctuated by high-carat oglings and large inputs of soul.' Naturally: all the idealistic abominations of her class. She needed romantic gradations, whipped cream, needed whipped cream to hide the pig's trotters! She was a hypocrite, because the only reason she'd gone there in the first place was to undress!

Stop, stop, don't think any more, and more to the point don't imagine any more. Take pity on her, so unhappy, pale as death, jelly-kneed, awaiting sentence, head bowed, not daring to look him in the eye. Think that one day she will die. Think about that day at Belle de

Mai when he had asked her casually if there was any more of some sort of sweet, he couldn't remember what sort, and she'd gone to Saint-Raphaël to buy some in the pouring rain, on foot, because there weren't any trains or taxis. Eleven kilometres there and eleven kilometres back, a six-hour walk in all. And he had not known what she'd done, because he'd gone up to his room to rest. And the note she'd left for him when he woke up: 'I can't bear it when you don't have everything you want.' Oh yes, it was halva. And the state she was in when she'd got home that evening, and it was only then that he'd found out that she'd walked all the way there and back. Yes, but that was exactly what made everything so terrible – a woman who loved him so absolutely had allowed Dietsch's hairy paw to unbutton her blouse. Oh, how she must have loved his white hair and black moustache!

She looked up at him with her pleading, lustrous, loving eyes. So why had she countenanced the hairy paw? And by what right had she told him on that first night at Cologny, just as he was leaving, that she wasn't going to sleep, instead she was going to think about what was happening to her, about the miracle that had happened? She'd been good and dietsched, and would have been far better off sticking with dishy Dietsch.

'There's just one thing that surprises me, though,' he started mellifluously, and he began putting the little silver boat containing the green dip for the fried *supions* through a series of threatening manœuvres, 'the only thing that surprises me is that you never call me "Adrien" or "Serge". It's odd you never get muddled: I mean to say there's quite a crowd of us, yet you always call me "Sol". Don't you ever get fed up with the same name all the time? It would be nicer if you called me "Adrisergeolal", don't you think? That way you could enjoy having us all at the same time.'

'Please don't go on. I know you don't really mean to be cruel. Get a grip on yourself, Sol.'

'That's not my name. If you don't call me by my real name I won't ever kiss you again, I'll never Adrisergeolalize you again. Or, better still, call me "Monsieur Three-in-One".'

'No.'

'Why not?'

'Because I won't let you sink so low. Because you're my only love.'

'I'm not your only love. I don't want to be called by names that have already been used for somebody else. I want a name all to myself, an honest name. Come, my little stockpiler, let's have a little honesty! Call me "Monsieur Three-in-One"!'

'No,' she said, and looked him straight in the eye, stared back at him, beautiful and aggressive.

She was wonderful. Which was why he toyed with the notion of throwing the sauce-boat and its contents at the wall. But that would only cause unpleasantness with the hotel management. He abandoned the idea and turned on the radio. That swine Mussolini was speaking, and a whole nation listened adoringly. And meanwhile what was he doing? Tormenting a defenceless woman, that's what. If only she would suddenly shout out that Dietsch disgusted her, that she'd never felt anything when she was with him. But she did not say the only words, even if they were untrue words, that would have calmed him, nor would she ever, for she was too decent a girl to repudiate or blacken or ridicule an old flame. He respected her for that. But he also hated her for it.

'Get a grip on yourself, darling,' she said, holding out both hands. (He frowned. What right did she have to call him "darling"?) You must get a grip on yourself, Sol,' she repeated.

'That's not my name. I'll get a grip on myself if you ask properly. Come on, make an effort!'

'Get a grip on yourself, Monsieur Three-in-One,' she said softly, after a moment's silence.

He rubbed his hands. At last a glimmer of honesty! He gave her a little thank-you smile. But suddenly her conductor in tails and white tie was unbuttoning her silk blouse. Oh, that black moustache nuzzling her golden breasts! And she cooing and crooning while the mouth belonging to her white-maned moustachioed baby suckled at her and his head drove greedily and aggressively against her. Oh, the nipple held between those front teeth, and that tongue maypoling around the nipple! And she had the gall to sit there looking innocent and so modest! Now the orchestra-conducting baby unclenched its teeth and ran its hairy tongue, its rasping ox-tongue, over a breast that was spikier than a Prussian helmet! And as the bull licked, the mistress of the keyboard chorale smiled! Oh, now one hairy paw was lifting her skirt! He shuddered with horror and dropped his amber beads. She bent down to pick them up, and as she did so the top of her dressing-gown yawned and revealed her breasts. The same breasts, not replacements, which had been offered to her other man! The full set! All that was missing now was the man and his hairiness!

'Did he use any fancy German techniques when he fornicated?'

She did not answer. So he picked up the dish of chocolate mousse and threw the contents at the fornicatee, deliberately pulling his aim to avoid hitting her. But, having little or no talent for slapstick, he misjudged it. The missile hit the target, and her luminous face was spattered with chocolate mousse. She did not move, deriving a not unenjoyable sense of self-righteousness from letting the brown goo dribble unchecked, then touched her cheek and stared at her messy hand. So it was to end up like this that she had led love's march of triumph on the day she had waited for him to return to Geneva! He made a dash for the bathroom, came back with a towel, applied one damp end to her sticky face, and wiped it gently. He knelt before her, kissed the hem of her dressing-gown, kissed her feet, and then looked up at her. 'Go to bed,' she said, 'I'll come to you, I'll stroke your hair and you'll sleep.'

Suddenly waking in the dark, they held hands. 'I'm a brute,' he murmured. 'Hush, it's not true, you are my sick boy,' she said, and he kissed her hand, wet her hand with his tears, put it to her that he should slash his face, cut himself with one of the table-knives, to prove it to her. He'd do it now if she wanted! 'No, darling, no, my sick boy,' she said, 'save your face for me, save all your love for me,' she said.

All of a sudden he got out of bed, lit the ceiling light and a cigarette, inhaled deeply, frowned deeply, strode round the room, tall and slim, pouring smoke from his nostrils and poison from his eyes, tossing his tufted hair like angry snakes. He approached the bed like the Archangel of Wrath and, turning the cord of his dressing-gown into a sling, made as if to threaten her.

'On your feet,' he said. She obeyed and got up. 'Call Geneva. Get him on the phone.'

'No, don't make me. I couldn't possibly phone him.'

'But you could get into his bed easily enough! That's a lot harder than phoning! Go on, ring him. You must know his number by heart! Go on, remind him of the good old days!'

'He doesn't mean a thing to me any more.'

Suddenly aware of his liver, he stared at her in horror. So, she simply drifted from one man to the next, had the gall just to write off a man to whom she had been so very close! What were women made of? The eyes which had gazed on Dietsch were now brazenly turned on him! And, only moments before, she who had explored secret latitudes of Dietschland had dared to hold his hand!

'Pick up the phone!'

'Please don't make me. It's past midnight, and I'm so tired. You can't have forgotten what last night was like at Agay. I'm exhausted, I've got nothing left,' she sobbed, and she fell back on the bed.

'Not on your back,' he barked, and she turned over, broken, on to her stomach. 'That's even worse,' he bellowed. 'Get out! Go to your room: I don't want to see either of you ever again! Get out, you bitch!'

Shrunken and gaunt, the bitch went. Disconcerted, he stared at his hands. He needed her, for she was all he had. He called her back. She came, and stood motionless and white-faced in the doorway.

'Well? Here I am.' (He loved her little clenched fists.)

'Did you go studding in the afternoons?'

'O God, why are we living together? Is this what love is?'

'Did you go studding in the afternoons? Answer me. Did you go studding in the afternoons? Answer me! Did you go studding in the afternoons? Answer me! I'll go on asking until you answer. Did you go studding in the afternoons? Answer me!'

'Yes, sometimes.'

'Where?'

'At the stud-farm,' she said and fled.

To make her come back without having to call her, he picked up the brass inkstand and threw it at the wardrobe mirror. Then he proceeded to annihilate the wineglasses and next the crockery. She did not budge, and that made him angry. The noise made by the bottle of champagne exploding against the wall was more successful. She came back, appalled.

'What do you want now? Get out!'

She turned on her heel and made a quick exit. Disappointed, he tore down the curtains and then looked around him. Hm. The room wasn't exactly inviting now, too much mess. All this broken glass lying about glassassinated on the floor. He ruffled his hair and whistled '*Voi che sapete*' under his breath. The best thing would be to see if they could patch things up. Agreed. Attempt reconciliation. He tapped on the communicating door. Yes, when she came he would tell her that he would sign in her presence, there and then, a binding pledge by which he undertook never to mention the other man again. 'Darling, it's all over, that's the end of it. After all, it's quite true, you didn't know me in those days.' He knocked again and cleared his throat.

She came and halted before him, dignified and defenceless, a victim who stood her ground. He admired her. Noble, yes. Honest, yes. But, if so honest, why had she lied so consistently to her husband? Damn that Boygne woman, a dyspeptic old trollop whose own frolicking days were over and who made up for it by making beds for young women to lie on! And when poor Deume used to phone in the morning and ask to speak to his wife, the lying old harridan would tell him pleasantly that Ariane was still asleep and then, quick, ring Dietsch's number! Oh, the life of romance and variety which she had lived with Dietsch and would never know with him! Furthermore, Dietsch must have been tremendously attractive with all that silver hair. So how could he compete? His hair was black just like everybody else's.

'Well?' she said. 'I'm here.'

What right did she have to such an honest face? Her face was a provocation.

'Say you're a whore.'

'It's not true, as you very well know,' she said calmly.

'You paid him! You told me!'

'All I said was that I loaned him money to bale him out.'

'Did he pay you back?'

'I never mentioned it, and he must have forgotten.'

Angered by her feminine indulgence for her sometime stallion, he grabbed her by the hair. The idea that this stupid woman should have let herself be cheated made him mad with rage. Oh, he ought to take the first plane out and force her musical pimp to cough up!

'Say you're a tart.'

'It's not true, I'm a respectable woman. Let go of me!'

Still holding her by the hair, but not too roughly, because he pitied her, because he did not want to hurt her, he yanked her head from side to side, infuriated by the thought that she had let herself be swindled because she was grateful for sex, infuriated because he felt powerless to make her see that the man was a swindler. She'd never admit it! Oh, the tried and tested indulgence of women! Such stupid creatures, letting themselves be taken in by any suitably equipped male capable of satisfying them! 'I am a respectable woman, and he was a decent man,' she repeated, head see-sawing, eyes popping, teeth chattering, and beautiful. She was defending his rival! Saying that she preferred his rival! Still holding her by the hair, he slapped her beautiful face. 'Stop it,' she said in her miraculous little-girl voice. 'Stop it! Don't hit me again! For your sake, for the sake of what we mean to each other, don't hit me!' To cover his shame by an even more shameful act, he hit her again. 'Sol, O my darling love!' she cried. He let go of her hair, utterly deflated by her words. 'No, my love, you must never,' she sobbed, 'you mustn't ever do that again, my love, for your sake, not for mine, my darling love! Be a man I can respect!' she sobbed.

Once more he took her in his arms, once more he held her close. Never again, never again. They stood tear-wet cheek to tear-wet cheek. He had been a brute, an utter brute, to have struck such innocence, such saintly innocence. 'Help me, help me,' he pleaded, 'I don't want to hurt you any more, you are my own darling, help me.'

He drew away from her, and she was suddenly afraid of his seeing eyes. Another man had dishonoured her far more and yet she respected him, and called him a decent man! Dietsch had struck her in far more shameful ways but she had not greeted his blows with tears, she had not pleaded with Dietsch to stop, she had not said 'Stop it! don't do it again!' to him. All these months the two of them had been together and she had kept all this carefully hidden from him! And most of all, oh yes, most of all, during those first nights in Geneva, she had behaved like some inexperienced virgin, she who had pawed and patted Dietsch!

'Pawed and patted, pawed and patted!' he cried, and he pushed her away.

She collapsed on to the floor, holding her smarting face in her hands. She had stopped crying and was staring at the broken plates, the shattered wineglasses, the cigarette-ends which littered the carpet, staring at her life. Her love, the only love of her life, was coming to a squalid end. Oh the day she had waited for him to return, oh her ducky dress flapping in the breeze as she walked. And now she was just another woman knocked about by her lover.

Kneeling down, one elbow propped on an armchair, she picked up the pearl necklace he had given her, which had fallen on the floor. He had looked like a delighted little boy when he'd opened the case to show her. She wound the necklace around one finger, unwound it, put it on the carpet, made it into a triangle, then a square. She was numb with misery, a little girl playing. But maybe the playing is in part play-acting, he thought, to show her tormentor just how pale and drawn unhappiness made her look.

'Get out.'

She stood up and shuffled back to her room, shoulders drooping. Suddenly he felt terrified of being all alone. Oh, if only she would come back of her own accord, give some sign that she forgave him! Call her, yes, but without showing how much he needed her.

'Hey, bitch!'

She returned, elegant, weary, shivering.

'Here I am.'

'Get out!'

'Very well,' she said, and left.

He felt a surge of self-loathing, threw away a half-smoked cigarette, lit another, stubbed it out. From his suitcase he took the damascene dagger which was a present from Michael, tossed it high in the air, caught it, put it back in its sheath, and called her again.

'Hey, whore!'

She appeared at once, and it crossed his mind that she was using submission as a form of retaliation.

'Here I am,' she said.

'Tidy this mess up!'

Whether the room was a mess or not mattered little to him. What he wanted was to be able to see the face he loved. She went down on hands and knees and picked up the cigarette-ends, the pieces of mirror, and the remains of the broken plates and glasses. He wanted to tell her to take care, to be careful she didn't cut herself. But he didn't dare. To hide his shame, he pretended to watch her with the cold eyes of the torturer who leaves no stone unturned. Oh that pliant neck! The proud girl of yore, the laughing girl of Geneva, was now on all fours picking up cigarette-ends like a charwoman. He coughed to clear his throat.

'That's enough tidying. You're too tired.'

Still on her knees, she turned and said she'd soon be done, and resumed her chore. Aha, thinks she can get round me by showing willing, he thought. Poor kid, life hasn't finally got to her yet, hope still springs eternal in her. And maybe she was also being a bit of a martyr. But mostly she was feeling grateful for the few kindly words he had just thrown her way, and wanted to thank him by gathering up the debris. Still on her knees, reaching out with her hands, she went on carefully picking up the pieces. Suddenly he saw her kneeling for Dietsch! Her face was the face of a child and a saint – but a saint accustomed to be on the receiving end of missionary zeal! No. No more of that.

'Nearly finished,' she said with a voice like that of the model pupil who is always good and invariably gets top marks for conduct.

'Thank you,' he said. 'All nice and tidy now. It's one in the morning. Go to your room, get some rest.'

She got to her feet: 'In that case I'll say good-night,' she said. 'Good-night,' she repeated, begging for a crumb of kindness.

'Wait. Wouldn't you like to take something to eat with you?' he asked, watching the smoke spiralling up from his cigarette.

'I don't think so,' she said.

He sensed that she felt awkward about taking food away with her, that she did not want to be thought in any way shallow or unfeeling. But she must be absolutely starving. To save her face and preserve her dignity as a woman in torment, to make it crystal clear that it was not she who wanted to eat but he who was forcing her to, he said in his most categorical manner:

'I want you to eat something.'

'All right,' she said obediently.

Choosing what seemed to him the most wholesome, he held out the plate of cold meats, the tomato salad and two rolls.

'That's plenty, thank you,' she said sheepishly, and closed the door behind her.

He stared at the hole in the mirror and the pile of broken shards she had left in one corner. Passion, alias love, was a complete and utter shambles too. If unaccompanied by jealousy, it meant boredom. If attended by jealousy, then it was sheer, animal hell. She was a slave, and he was a brute. Novelists were a disgrace: a gang of liars who dressed up passion and made brainless males and females chase after it. Novelists were a disgrace: they were the suppliers and flatterers of the owning classes. And stupid women revelled in their filthy lies and double-dealing and lapped it all up. And worst of all was the real reason why she had brought the Dietsch business into the open, why she had felt a sudden rush of honesty. He knew exactly why she had wanted, in all self-deceiving good faith, to be unburdened of the famous secret she simply could not keep to herself any longer. When they'd been out for walks these last few days, he hadn't been able to think of anything to say and had hardly spoken. Add to which they'd shared a bed only once since he'd got back, the first night, and since then nothing. And on top of that, last night at Agay, he'd said good-night to her far too early, a mistake which had given her unconscious time to work, assert itself, whip up a storm of jealousy, not the real thing of course, more a fit of pique really, at an acceptable, controllable level. Just enough to make her seem interesting again. When she'd come to his room, she had been ready to tell all, but in a non-specific, noble sort of way, with no physical details, along the lines of there'd-been-another-man-in-her-life. Poor girl. She had meant well.

Two knocks, ladylike and polite, at the door. She came in. In a pathetic little voice which made her sound like a half-drowned kitten, she said she'd forgotten a knife and fork, took what she needed, then went away again, head bowed. She did not dare go back to ask for a napkin, which she had also forgotten. Instead, she made do with a face-towel from the bathroom. She attacked the food ravenously, and as she ate she read the woman's page of an old newspaper which she had found in a drawer. Oh what a pitiable thing is a human, dear brothers in man.

A little while later he asked her through the door if there was anything else she wanted. She wiped her mouth with the face-towel, patted her hair, and said no thank you. But shortly after this the door opened a little way and a plate was pushed along the carpet bearing petits fours arranged in a circle on a paper doily. 'No chocolate mousse, it's all gone,' murmured the invisible victualler for his own benefit. Whereupon he closed the door, sat down, crossed his legs, and, removing the damascene blade from its sheath, slowly began making incisions in the sole of his right foot.

CHAPTER 102

A little before three in the morning he went to her, fully dressed, apologized for waking her, said that he felt uncomfortable in his room, jittery, on account of the wrecked curtains and all that broken glass lying around and the cracked mirror. The room was, frankly, off-putting. The obvious solution was to move to another hotel. There was one fairly near, the Splendide. But what story could they spin the people in the Noailles to explain the mess? She sat up in bed, rubbed her eyes, and paused for a moment without speaking. If she said: 'No, not the Splendide', he would guess why and there'd be another scene. Whey-faced, her eyes ringed with blue, she stared at him for a moment, then said she'd take care of everything, that all he need do was to go on ahead to the Splendide and she would join him there as soon as she could. She smiled weakly, and asked him to remember to take his overcoat. It would be quite cold outside at this time of night.

He did as he was bid with alacrity, only too happy to obey, cleared his throat to say well in that case he'd be off, that he'd left his wallet with enough to cover the hotel bill, so toodle-oo for now, thanks, see you shortly, and he went, feeling none too proud of himself, eyes on the ground and hat pulled well down, limping a little, for his gashed foot was hurting. 'So sweet-natured, so willing, and ready to take care of everything,' he murmured in the fourth-floor corridor.

He had been a brute, he had behaved disgracefully, quite disgracefully, he told himself firmly as he went down the stairs. On reaching the third floor, he slapped his face twice, hard, and then gave himself an upper-cut under the chin which proved so hefty that he had to sit down for a moment on a stair. When his head cleared, he stood up and continued his cautious way down. When he got to the first floor, he paused, for it dawned on him that leaving her to sort out everything with the hotel management all by herself was an absolutely vile thing to have done. Hating himself, he punched himself very hard in the right eye, which swelled up immediately. On the ground floor, where the night man was snoring, he made a furtive exit on tiptoe, crossed the now almost deserted Canebière, waving his arms as though addressing a public meeting and still limping. 'My poor boy, my poor mad boy,' she murmured, leaning over the narrow balcony, from which vantage point she followed his progress. What was wrong? Why was he limping? 'Be nice to me, don't be nasty any more,' she murmured.

She shut the window and phoned down to the desk, said that they'd been called away to an illness and were leaving immediately, so could their bill be made up? After shutting the cases, she drafted several versions of a letter, made a clean copy, and read it over in a whisper: 'Dear Sir, Please find enclosed reimbursement together with our sincere apologies for the damage occasioned by circumstances beyond our control.' Should she finish with a thank-you? Certainly not. Several thousand francs said it all. She put the letter and the banknotes into an envelope on which she wrote: 'Personal. For the attention of the Manager of the Hotel Noailles. Urgent.'

She dared not call the lift but walked down the four flights of stairs carrying both the cases. On reaching the ground floor, she smiled at the night man, gave him a large tip to get on the right side of him, and found an opportunity while he was busy receipting the bill to slip the envelope furtively under a newspaper spread out on the counter.

Taxi. An elderly driver, with a white Pomeranian on the seat beside him. 'Station, please,' she said for the benefit of the night man, who was putting the cases into the boot. That way the hotel people wouldn't know where to start looking for them when they discovered the mess in their room. Two minutes later, she leaned forward, tapped the glass, told the driver she'd changed her mind, and asked him to take her to the 'Sordide, sorry, Splendide. Thank you so much.'

She felt a sudden stabbing pain in her chest and had the odd feeling that something very similar had already happened to her before, in another life, something very dreadful, with the police on her tail, with her switching hotels and covering her tracks like a hunted criminal. They were alone in the great wide world. He a dot some place in the great city, and she another dot at a different place. Two dots joined by a very thin thread. Two destinies which would fuse. If he hadn't gone to the other hotel, how would she ever find him again? Why didn't he go back to his job at the League of Nations? Why had he asked to have his leave extended? What was he hiding? Ah, here's the Splendide. What else could she have done? She could hardly have refused out of hand: he would have guessed. She got out of the taxi, paid, stroked the white pom, and asked if it had had distemper. 'Yes, lady, had it twelve years ago,' answered the old man in a voice which sounded as though it had not yet broken.

At five in the morning, remembering she had told him in Geneva that she knew Marseilles, he slipped quietly into her room and leaned over her sleeping form, which exuded a smell of warm biscuits. No, let her be, leave the questions till later, when she was awake.

'Who were you with that time you came to Marseilles?'

She opened one eye then the other, her mouth gaped, stupid with sleep.

'Oh there you are. What's the matter?'

'Who did you come with that time you were here in Marseilles?'

She raised herself, sat up, and drew her hand clumsily across her forehead: it was the same harrowing gesture that he'd seen from the sick chimpanzee at Basle Zoo the day he'd taken Saltiel and Solomon there, the same gesture that Rachel made too.

'No,' she murmured foolishly.

'Was it Dietsch?' he asked, and she looked away, no longer having the strength to deny it. 'When your husband was away on an official visit?'

'Yes,' she breathed.

'Why Marseilles?'

'A concert, he was conducting here. I didn't know you then.'

'He was conducting here! How splendid! How very splendid that he was able to read a musical score written by someone else! And how did he conduct, with a baton or without a button? Unbuttoned was he? No flies on him, eh? And which hotel did you stay at? Answer me!' he ordered, and once more she raised her hand to her brow and made the face which was a sign of tears to come. 'Here? Was it this hotel? Get dressed.'

She threw back the bedcovers, stepped barefoot on to the carpet, and then proceeded as though sleepwalking to put on a slip and her stockings, took some time to fasten her suspenders, failed to shut her case by the lock and did up the straps instead. O God! She was with a madman, a raving lunatic who had beat himself up and was proud of his swollen, black eye. He glared at her with his good eye. So she had been in this hotel with Dietsch, perhaps in this very bed, two noble-souled fish twisting and squirming, and the bed had groaned, and the manager had come and put his hands together and pleaded with them not to wreck his furniture! But they had gone on broncoing, and the manager had turned them out! Bed-smashers and mattress-wreckers, known to all the taverns of Marseilles, blacklisted by all the hotels in Marseilles! Just then she sneezed twice, and he felt a surge of pity, searing pity, pity for a frail human creature doomed to sickness and death. He took her by the hand.

'Come, my sweet.'

They went down by the stairs, hand in hand, each carrying a suitcase, he with a coat over his pyjamas and she wearing only a slip under her mackintosh. On the ground floor she put down her case and mechanically hitched up her drooping, wrinkled stockings, while the deskman was hard put to understand why this client with higgledy-piggledy hair and a tie in one hand should be telling him that the Splendide was too old for his taste, that he wanted a young hotel, as young as possible. A banknote was instrumental in persuading him to mention the Bristol, which hadn't been up long.

'Built when?'

'Last year, sir.'

'Perfect,' said Solal, and he gave him another note.

The cases were stowed into a taxi. It was the same driver with the white pom. From Ariane's case strayed half of one stocking and a strong fragrance of eau-de-Cologne. He watched her once more out of the corner of his left eye. Should he leave her, so that she was rid of him? But what would she do then? Their love was all the poor girl had left. Besides, he loved her. Oh, that wonderful first evening together! 'Spare me,' she'd said on that first night. But had Dietsch spared her only hours before? He would never know. *'Tvoya zhena,'* she had whispered that night, *'tvoya zhena'*, while only hours before her mouth had been pressed to the mouth of a man with white hair. And wavy white hair, at that! Yes, her mouth, the same mouth that was now next to him in this taxi, exactly the same identical mouth. His angel was trembling. She was afraid of him. What could he do to stop making her suffer? How could he fight the pair of them, loins joined, groins grinding? Try and make her repulsive? Imagine her thirty feet of intestines? Imagine her skeleton? Imagine the food passing through her oesophagus and entering her stomach and its progress thence through to the end of the process? Imagine her lungs, soft and red, like offal in a butcher's shop? It was no good. She was his beautiful, his pure, his saintly love. But his saintly love had reached out her hand and touched a man's abomination, felt the bestial desire of a man, and had done so without revulsion. What could he do about it if his mind was filled with a constant picture of her with her male, an ineradicable image of his saintly love with a male ape who was not loathsome in her sight, a male ape who did not disgust her: that was what amazed him, shocked him. Yes, she was good to him, of course, kind and loving, walking miles to bring him halva, yet all the same she'd scrubbed herself clean before going to see her male ape, scrubadubdub and soapysudsud, to be a tasty dish for Dietsch, to get herself thoroughly dietsched, but there it was, that was the size of it, so don't think about it any more. I promise. You have my word on it.

'So now it's the Hotel Bristol,' she murmured, sitting on the edge of the bath, still wearing her mackintosh, not having the strength to get undressed. The bathroom was hideous. They'd been much better off at the Noailles. The stupid porter had dumped their bags in the bathroom. Serge had been weak, a bit spineless really, but at least he was gentle and attentive. A fly landed on her and made her flinch. She sniffed, rummaged through her handbag, but found only a small, torn handkerchief which was quite useless. She bent down and opened her case. No handkerchiefs. Left them all behind at the Noailles. Never mind. She blew her nose on a stiff, shiny face-towel then tossed it under the bath. The door opened. Enter, limping, a lord with a black eye which was swollen and half closed. She shivered. Why was he limping? Oh, never mind, it didn't matter.

'There is a man in your eyes. Hide your eyes.'

Don't struggle, do whatever he said. What could she hide her eyes with? He stood over her like an implacable torturer. Actually he was hoping for a miracle, for a wondrous reconciliation. She unfolded another towel and placed it on her warm-gold hair. The starched cloth dangled down.

'Not big enough. Your lips are visible and I don't want to see your lips. They've been used too much.'

She found a large hand-towel and draped it over her head. 'Thank you,' he said. Then, as she sheltered under her white tent, she was seized by the most excruciating fit of giggles, which she camouflaged as sobs to sidetrack the lunatic she could see through a chink, who was staring with his one good eye at the hiccuping towel, disappointed that she'd acquiesced without putting up a fight. What was he supposed to do with a woman disguised as a towel? He couldn't talk to her, because he couldn't see her. To start a conversation, should he begin with a hello? Eventually her fake sobs died away. He found the veiled, unspeaking figure rather eerie. He scratched his head. How long was she going to sit there under her burnous, like a ghost? And why didn't she move? He felt intimidated, confused, felt he had somehow been diddled. How could he break the deadlock?

'Can I take it off now?' asked a muffled voice.

'If you wish,' he said with an air of unconcern.

'We're absolutely worn out, both of us,' she said, shrugging off her mantle and not looking at her one-eyed jailer to avoid any risk of another appalling fit of giggles. 'Don't you want to go to bed and sleep? It's after six in the morning.'

'It is sixty o'clock in the morning. I'm waiting.'

'What are you waiting for?'

'I'm waiting for you to say what I'm waiting for you to say.'

'How am I supposed to know what that is? Just tell me what you want me to say.'

'If I told you, there wouldn't be any point. I want it to be spontaneous. So I'm waiting.'

'I can't guess.'

'If you are who I still hope you are, in spite of all that's happened, you must guess. Either guess or shut up.'

'Well, I'll just have to shut up then, it's all the same to me, everything's all the same to me, I'm exhausted.'

He stared at her as she perched once more on the edge of the bath, head bowed, contemplating her stockings, which had collapsed around her ankles. How could she be so dim that she couldn't guess, would never guess what he expected from her, which was to hear her say that Dietsch made her feel sick, that he was ugly, that he was stupid, that she'd never really enjoyed doing it with him? But, alas, she was far too much of a lady for that. She would never dream of disowning her baton-waver, a leech who lived off musical geniuses, sucked their blood, and bowed at the end of a symphony as if he'd actually written the damned thing himself!

Searching through his case for a packet of cigarettes, he came across the black monocle he hadn't worn since Geneva. He immediately screwed it into his bruised, swollen, half-closed eye, glanced at himself in the mirror, approved of the effect, lit a cigarette, and sighed. How could he go on living with her? There was nothing she could say that she hadn't already said to her other lover-man or been told by him. Since her other lover-man was apparently so cultured, it was very likely that it was from him she had got all those long words she was so fond of. 'Integration', 'slippage', 'exemplarity', and the nauseating 'explicate' so beloved of pedants everywhere – all those words came from Dietsch. From this day forth, each 'explicate' would stick in his gullet like a fishbone. Oh yes, very cultured was Dietsch. Yesterday in the train, when they had still been on speaking terms, she had mentioned that Dietsch also taught the history of music at the University of Lausanne. Which made him the compleat leech. But far worse than that were all the little things, the gestures, the habits of intimacy which she had picked up from him. She had done it all with Dietsch. She had eaten with him, gone for walks with him. Never eat with her again, no more walks with her! He scratched his head. At a pinch, he could always make her walk on her hands, upside down, with her legs in the air. It was most unlikely that she'd ever done that with Dietsch. But he could hardly make her walk on her hands all the time. No, but he would never go to bed with her again. The two of them had done everything. Though maybe they hadn't done it swinging on a chandelier. Not a very comfortable prospect.

'You look absolutely whacked. Come and sleep by me. Come into my room,' she said, and she took his hand.

In her room, he sat down, lit another cigarette, inhaled deeply, felt a sudden rush of inexpressible happiness, but then remembered. The most awful aspect of the whole predicament was that with him she had experienced, and would experience again, long hours of unadulterated but far from adulterous tedium. And his idiot girl, her head filled with romantic longings, vulnerable to regrets like all her sex, ever questing like all her sisters, would make unconscious comparisons. Under time's forgiving spell, Dietsch would be remembered only for the happy days. But he, a complete fool who had turned into a mere spouse, went on and on about Dietsch, and in doing so had in fact appointed himself his spokesman, magnified his attraction, and carved out for himself the role of retrospectively hoodwinked husband. Oh, all that plotting arranged by the Boygne woman! Oh, how exciting to rush off on the sly to be with Dietsch and spend an illicit night of love with him! And, then next morning, la Boygne would dial the number of Dietsch the Leech of Beethoven: 'Daahling, your husband's just this minute rung from his office, I told him you were still asleep, that I didn't want to wake you, but do try to phone him so that he doesn't bother me again.' Big, bad Boygne! O hapless Solal, the tiresome gooseberry, not up to providing vibrant, illicit nights of love, the no-hope challenger in the ring with a conductor of symphonies who had the starry weight advantage of not being there. There was only one way of making her sick of him and that was to order her back to Geneva to live with him for a few months. Then he, Solal, would revert to being the lover. Yes! Tell her she must leave for Geneva at once!

But, straightening up and catching her in the act of wiping her nose, he was disarmed by the modest scale of her nasal emissions, which sacrificed efficacy to the cause of unobtrusiveness. Poor shiny nose, it was quite swollen now and not very pretty. Poor eyes, all puffy with tears. He wanted to kiss her but did not dare: too daunting. Poor little torn handkerchief which she used for her dainty discharges. He would get a better one for her.

When he returned from the bathroom with a large, spanking-new cambric handkerchief which he'd got from his suitcase, he came close so that he could give it to her, and was struck by her vulnerability. Oh, the way she looked up at him, so humble, like a dog begging for a bone. Then he took a sudden step back. The fact was that, if her bandleader's hands had been granted the power to leave indelible prints, then at this moment she would be black and blue, blue and black all over, except maybe for the soles of her feet. And was he supposed to be content with the soles of her feet? He put the clean handkerchief in his pocket.

'Know what I think?' he asked, after screwing his black monocle more firmly into his eye. 'Not going to ask? Then I'll tell you. I think that all things considered, and thanks to your most helpful brokering, I've come to know your gentleman friend very well. Intimately in fact. My lover in a sense. What do you say to that?'

'Oh please, please, stop it,' she moaned, and she reached for his hand. But he shook her off, flinching from any touch of Dietsch.

'What do you say?'

'I don't know anything any more, I just want to sleep. It's half past six.'

He fumed inwardly. Who did she think she was: the speaking clock? He gave himself the once-over in the mirror, noted that the black monocle made him look like a jolly-rogering buccaneer and righter of wrongs, then resumed his station facing her, legs splayed and hands akimbo.

'And when you were with him, were you never awake at half past six?'

'No. At half past six I was always asleep.'

The laughter of the buccaneering lord scored the silence of the room. Asleep! And she had the gall, the effrontery, to tell him to his face! Of course she'd been asleep! But who had she been asleep next to, and after doing what? Oh vile, the man's maleness! And she hadn't shrunk from the sight! And she hadn't shrunk from a lot worse than that! Oh, the soft touch of those hands!

'You like men, don't you?'

'No. Men disgust me!'

'Me included?'

'Yes, you too!'

'So we've got there at last,' he said with a smile, and he sharpened his nose between thumb and forefinger, not without a certain satisfaction, for this at least was simple and clear-cut.

'O God, if only you knew how little that man Dietsch meant to me.'

'"That man"! My, my! And why "that man"? Why this sudden animosity for somebody you used to visit with an overnight bag and a certain end in view? Want to try again?'

'I said: "If only you knew how little Monsieur Dietsch meant to me."'

'Monsieur'! She called a man who had sprawled naked on top of her 'Monsieur'? He grabbed her by one ear, though he was moved to pity by her pale face and blue-ringed eyes.

'Ah, so it's "Monsieur" now, is it! "O sir, my legs are open, do come in, pray, and oblige your infinitely obedient"!'

'You're horrible, horrible, horrible!' she cried, the little girl in her surfacing from the past. 'I'd never have taken from him what I take from you!'

'Who is this "him"?'

'Dietsch!'

'I will not tolerate the way you talk about him as if he were a friend of mine. Who are you talking about?'

'D.'

'You didn't call him "D" to his face! Say "Serge"!'

'I never used his Christian name.'

'Then what did you call him?'

'I don't remember!'

'In that case, call him "Monsieur Urge". You see, I'm being nice, I could make you call him far worse things than that, but "Monsieur Urge" will do. And what about Monsieur Urge?'

'I won't say it. Let him be.'

'Whowhowho? Answer me! Whowhowho?'

'God, you're mad!' she cried, and she squeezed her temples with both hands, exaggerating her panic. 'I'm spending the night with a madman!'

'I would draw your attention to the fact that it's light outside. But no matter, we'll let that pass. So you would prefer to spend the night with a man in his right mind? Isn't that so, whore?'

'I can't take any more of this!' she cried. 'I hate everybody!'

She picked up the glass inkwell, checked an impulse to fling it at the wall, put it down, and vented her hatred first on the blotting-pad, which she attempted to twist and bend, and then on the hotel notepaper, which she tore into little pieces.

'What did that paper ever do to you?'

'It's whore's confetti!'

'There's one sheet left, don't tear it up. Write down that you slept with Dietsch and sign it. Here's a pen. And don't break the nib.'

She did as she was told and appended her signature, Ariane d'Auble, three times. He was satisfied with what she had written. It was definite now. No more doubts. He folded the paper and put it in his pocket. Now he had proof. Say what you like, though, he mused, she was a sweet girl. Any other woman in her position would have walked out on him long before this. She stretched out on the bed, her teeth chattering, glared at him angrily, and coughed quite unnecessarily several times. At which he forced himself to cough too, and coughed long and loud like a sick animal.

'What's the matter?' she asked. 'Why are you coughing like that?'

He coughed louder, great baying, hacking coughs, shuddered like a tubercular lion, and kept it up for so long that eventually she realized that he was doing it on purpose, to frighten her. She got up.

'That's enough!' she said firmly. 'Stop it, do you hear? Don't cough any more!'

But as he persisted with his infuriating coughing, she went up to him and slapped his face. He smiled and crossed his arms, looking strangely serene. Normal service had been restored.

'Ariane, my Aryan! I should have known,' he said with a satisfied smile.

'I'm sorry,' she said, 'I don't know what came over me. I really am sorry.'

'I forgive you, but on one condition. That we return to Geneva and you go to bed with him.'

'Never!'

'But why not? You've done it before!' he shouted. 'Ah! I see!' he said after a silence. 'I get it! You're afraid you might like it! Well, whether you want to or not, you're going to do it! I insist that you go to bed with Dietsch, so that the three of us can all walk in the light of truth! And also so that you realize that doing it with him isn't so wonderful as you think. Will you sleep with him, yes or no? Our love hangs on it. Say: will you sleep with him?'

'All right, all right! I'll go to bed with him!'

She went over to the window and leaned out. It wasn't the dying that scared her but the void. And the thought of knowing as she fell through the air that her head would split open when she hit the ground. She put one knee on the window-sill. He sprang into action. She swayed wildly backwards and forwards, to give him time to stop her. The moment he grabbed her she began struggling, quite determined now to die. But he held her fast. She turned her head and faced him, with hate in her eyes. He resisted the temptation to kiss those lips which were now so close, and shut the window.

'So, you reckon you are an honest, respectable woman?'

'No! I am neither honest nor respectable!'

'In that case, why didn't you warn me? Why didn't you tell me at the Ritz that before we went on seeing each other it would have been a good idea to have had my predecessor tested for the pox? I was taking a big risk.'

She threw herself face down on the bed and sobbed into her pillow, thighs and buttocks pumping. Oh the pumping with Dietsch, the arching and bucking of an honest, respectable woman, a woman who loved him. For he knew full well that she was an honest woman and that she loved him, and there lay his agony. This woman now filthily broncoing before his very eyes with her other lover-man was a good woman and she loved him, the same innocent girl who had with such childish delight told him the tale of the farm-girl from Savoy who pretended to be sorry for her cow Buttercup and kept saying: 'Poor Buttercup, who's been smacking Buttercup, then?' to which the clever cow would respond with a martyred moo, and this very same woman whose thighs and buttocks, oh those thighs and buttocks which pumped to the rhythm of the thighs and buttocks of a man with white hair who was a member of the race of Jew-killers, this self-same woman had told her innocent tale with such relish, he remembered exactly how she had told it, ah yes, for authenticity she said: 'Pore Boottercoop', just as the farm-girl had: 'Pore Boottercoop, who's been smacking Boottercoop, then?' and then his adorable little girl, his Ariane, would imitate the cow, which, to say yes they'd been smacking her, had said: 'Moo Moo', and that was the best part of the whole story, though the really best bit of all was in Geneva when the two of them went 'Moo Moo' together so they could share the point of the story and see what a smart cow old Buttercup really was. Oh, they'd been silly and happy in those days, and such good friends, like brother and sister. And yet that same sister, that same little girl, had given sanctuary to the loathsome virility of another man and had enjoyed it!

'On your feet!' he ordered, and she turned over and got up slowly. 'Come on! Stir every fibre of your being!'

'What else do you want from me?' she asked.

'The belly-dance!'

She shook her head in refusal, looking him in the eye, hands clenched. Trembling with rage, he bit his lip. So, when he asked her to perform a modest belly-dance, a dance of the belly only, all he got was a blank refusal. But her other lover-man had only to ask and there was lap-dancing galore! Oh the expert pumping of her thighs and buttocks beneath the white-maned chimpanzee, and oh how she clung to that mane of white! Oh, foul couple coupling! A bitch and her dog, two rasping-breathed beasts, their sweaty conjoinings, their smells, their juices.

She coughed, and he was aware of her standing before him. She who once had been a panting bitch on heat, Dietsch's more than willing partner, now cut a sorry figure, pale-faced and thin, as she stood before him, weary unto death, hands clenched, poor brave little hands, such a sorry figure with her mackintosh, her slip, her collapsed stockings, her puffy nose, her eyes swollen with tears, her lustrous eyes ringed with sickly blue. His darling, his own darling. Oh cursèd physical love! Cursèd passion!

PART SEVEN

The ceiling light had been left on and burned lugubriously in the room where the noon sun seeped through the drawn curtains. Lying motionless in bed, eyes staring, he listened to the sounds of life outside and watched the little bustling shadows toing and froing upside down on the ceiling in the gap above the curtains, feet first, heads inverted, miniature silhouettes going about their lawful occasions. Here they were again in Geneva, back at the Ritz.

Careful to avoid touching her, he leaned across to look at the absurd little girl with the made-up face who was sleeping at his side, or pretending to sleep, doped to the eyeballs with ether, pathetic in her little tennis skirt which had ridden halfway up her thighs, bare-legged, with those little socks, the slippers intended to make her look like a little girl, the childish ringlets and the bow of pink ribbon.

He took the ether bottle which she was holding close to her chest, removed the stopper, and inhaled. She turned over, murmured she wanted some too, inhaled in turn, several times, then handed the bottle back to him. 'Don't look at me,' she said, and she turned over again and shut her eyes. Oh those holidays she'd spent in the mountains with Éliane, the chalet, the tapping of someone sharpening a scythe. Oh the clear, far-off sound, the pure sound in the diamond air, the sound of summer, the sound of childhood.

She sat up, careful to avoid touching him, glanced across at the little alarm clock, picked up the phone, and ordered lunch. 'No, not a table, just a tray, thank you.' She put the receiver down, took the ether bottle from him, and inhaled deeply, eyes closed, surrendering

957

to the cool sweetness invading her. Yesterday, Kanakis's wife had stared curiously in the street but had not acknowledged her. The day before, her cousin Saladin had pretended she hadn't seen her. They used to play together when they were little. She never returned that dolly I loaned her. Should I phone and ask for it back?

'Leave the tray by the door. I'll come for it.'

She got out of bed, opened the door, picked up the tray, put it on the bed, and got back between the sheets. Keeping their distance, they ate in silence in the stifling semi-darkness while a heavy, insistent bluebottle zig-zagged witlessly over them, droned on and on, unbearably superior, furious, obstinate, bold, asserting its right to be a nuisance and only too happy to be exercising it. In the silence broken only by the scrape of fork on knife or the occasional clink of a wineglass, they chewed with the faint, unflattering sounds of masticating teeth. In front of them a bar of sunlight, in which slow diamonds of dust danced decorously, struck a silver tureen lid, which bounced it on to the wall. She moved her knee to alter the angle of the tray and redirect the bright disc on to the ceiling. Éliane, their childhood games. They'd played dazzling each other with mirrors. They'd called it 'having sun-fights'.

Still taking care to avoid touching him, she got out of bed, a phoney schoolgirl with smudgy make-up, and dumped the tray on the floor, while he, still in bed, hastily stuffed under the counterpane the lacy brassière which Ingrid Groning had left behind.

As she got back into bed, she brushed against his leg, which he removed at once. Snuggling down with her face to the wall, she closed her eyes. The hidey-hole she'd made with Éliane in Tantlérie's garden, for what they'd called their 'desert-island treasure'. They'd dug the hole next to a tree, and written secret instructions for finding it again in Éliane's Bible. They'd buried little bits of glass, chocolate-paper, coins, sweets, a chocolate bear, and a curtain ring which was supposed to be a wedding ring for when she grew up. Then they'd fallen out and she'd punched Éliane on the nose and then they'd made up and they'd used the blood from her nose to write a tragic letter supposedly written after the wreck of the three-masted schooner *The Shark*, they'd collected the drips in a spoon and dipped the pen in it and they'd taken turns to write. She had written that she would only dig up the desert-island treasure on the day she got married and she'd put the ring on her loving husband's finger. And then there had been resolutions, written backwards so no one would be able to decipher them, about going in for Spiritual Uplift and about leading a noble life in future. Well, the future had come, the future was now, and it was she who had phoned Ingrid last night and had willed what had happened. I did it to keep you, she said to herself, and her lips silently shaped the words as she half-buried her head under her pillow.

He took the dish of confectionery and put it between them. They helped themselves in the semi-darkness, she to the fondants and he to the Turkish delight, which he munched slowly, occasionally sniffing ether, reviewing their life together, the wretched life they'd lived together for more than two years. Today was the ninth of September. Two years and three months since that first night at the Ritz. Nearly a year since the jealous-of-Dietsch crises. He had been genuinely jealous, though he'd also fanned the flames, for he derived pleasure from torturing himself with visions, conjuring up images, embroidering them, using them as a stick to beat himself with, to make himself suffer, to make her suffer, hoping to drag them out of the quagmire and fashion a life of passion which banished the tedium. It had been a godsend for their anaemia. Exit boredom; enter drama! The dire delight of being able to make love again as though they meant it, she once more desirable and desiring. Those scenes, first at Agay and then in Marseilles. The jealousy had continued after they got back to Belle de Mai. Then the interlude of the slashed wrists: he'd done it because he felt so ashamed for making her unhappy, and it had meant being carted off to hospital. Then she'd caught pneumonia. She'd been looked after by him, just him, without a nurse, against the doctor's advice. Day and night for weeks on end he had cared for her and washed her like a child, had put her on the bedpan several times a day and emptied it and wafted the mephitic stench away. Blessed weeks. No more jealousy, wafted away for ever by the enamel bedpan. Sights and smells he would never forget. Blessed weeks. He had watched over his patient and felt glad that her poor suffering body, demeaned by sickness, had known fleeting joys with Dietsch, a decent man, who now seemed not so bad after all. Alas, as she convalesced and her health returned, he had sensed amorous stirrings in her, felt the gaze of the sweet enchantress on him. And so once again he had been forced to cast himself as the irresistible-eyed cock-of-the-walk, and she had been delighted and had rushed off to do her hair and slip into something pointlessly voluptuous and cover the lamp in her bedroom with gallows red to create a climate of sensuality, desperately hoping a successful rogering would constitute an unambiguous test, and, deciding post-coitally that high marks could indeed be awarded, she proceeded at once to hang nauseatingly sentimental caresses on his neck and hair, like crawling spiders of gratitude, and made his flesh creep with fond little questions and fonder appreciative endorsements. And he'd reverted to taking several baths a day and shaving at least twice, to racking his brains for poetic ways of praising his angel's beauty and the various parts of her anatomy, to having to come up with new words each day because she was insatiable, because he cherished her, and because he loved to see her inhaling contentment with the air she breathed. And once more those daunting records of Mozart and Bach, more sunsets and pointless couplings followed by remorseless debriefings which involved massive expenditures of soul. And after that? After that, they'd travelled. Now and then he had manufactured little green-eyed Dietschodramas out of the goodness of his heart, to keep her happy, and then he had grown weary and Dietsch sank without trace, Dietsch's parts were left in peace. Their decision, after they got back from Egypt, to settle in Geneva, in the house at Bellevue. Excited, her head full of fancies, she had bloomed afresh as she threw herself into the task of creating a harmonious setting. 'No, darling, you must have this room, it's much more elegantly proportioned and the view is so expansive.' Acquisition of Persian carpets and period Spanish furniture. A score of vivid, vital days. But, once the harmonious setting had been created, the unacknowledged claustrophobia, the need for other people, people at any price, the need to have people around, even strangers, even those who were not clubbable. At Belle de Mai their love had been younger and they had held out longer against their lonely lighthouse-keeping existence. But in Bellevue the asthma of solitude had set in unbearably by the third week. Hiding their mortification, they had gone back to the Ritz. Oh, their bleak conjunctions, she faking pleasure, oh yes, out of consideration, poor girl. Oh, the way the both of them, equally wretched, had resorted to pathetic stimuli, in unspoken complicity. They had looked to their mirrors. At certain junctures they had resorted to using dirty words, like whips. They had looked to books. 'Darling, I've bought a book, it's a bit naughty but terribly well done: there's no harm in both of us reading it together, is there?' And she had brought home others, even naughtier, as she said, unhappy daughter of an austere line. And thence, gradually, to practices which she found to her taste, or pretended to find to her taste. Sometimes, seeking reassurance, she would mutter to him in the near-dark of their nights. 'Tell me, it's not wrong, is it, if I get a bit infernal, if I do those things, tell me, when two people love each other everything is beautiful, isn't that right?' She was fond of saying 'infernal', a word which had succeeded the coy 'naughty' and raised a flicker of sulphurous flames over their unadventurous expedients. And after that? After that were her dreams, she'd probably made them up, which she told him as she lay close to him in the night, in their bed, in a whisper. 'Darling, I had such a peculiar dream last night: I was yours, and there was a beautiful young woman by the side of the bed, watching.' A few days later, another and bolder dream. Then there'd been others, still worse, and she'd always told them in the night, in the dark. He had listened to her fabrications with shame and despair. 'Darling, I dreamt I was being loved by two men, but each of the men was you.' The last statement was intended to safeguard appearances, so that she could be faithful and infernal at the same time. Next Ingrid Groning had returned to the Ritz. Suddenly it was the friendship stakes between the two women. She began talking to him far too much about how beautiful Ingrid was, about what beautiful breasts she had. Last night she had dressed up like a schoolgirl. Then, at midnight, she had suggested inviting Ingrid along. The horror of it. 'Be pure, for our God is pure,' the Chief Rabbi had always told him, while his hand still lay heavy on his head after the sabbath-day blessing. Forgive me, my lord and father. Oh the synagogue of his childhood, the steps leading up to the dais enclosed by the marble balustrade, and at its centre the lectern used by the presiding cantor. Upstairs, the gallery. There the women sat, fenced in by lattice-work screens behind which figures stirred. Downstairs, on a kind of throne, his father, and he standing by his side, by the side of the revered Chief Rabbi, proud to be his son. Oh sweet joy of hearing the cantor sing in the tongue of their ancestors. And at the far end, facing the dais, the velvet and gold of the Ark of the Holy Commandments, and he was in Israel, with brothers joined.

In their bathroom, she squatted on the white japanned seat and then changed her mind. No, he might hear. How bizarre, still going out of my way to avoid anything that might upset him. Throwing a dressing-gown over her schoolgirl get-up, she went out into the corridor, opened the door of one of the bathrooms further down the hall, pushed the bolt home, lifted the skirt of her dressing-gown, sat down on the white japanned seat, put the ether bottle she had brought with her on the floor, stood up, pulled the chain, stood watching the miniature cataract frothing in the china bowl, sat down again, tore off a sheet of lavatory paper and folded it once, then twice. Oh, Tantlérie's garden, the young quince-tree hung with little pink fruit like lanterns, the split mirabelle-tree with mahogany-dark resin which oozed from a crack and which she worked with her fingers, the bench by the little fountain which never quite stopped running where the blue-tits came to drink, the old green bench which had wrinkled in the rain and picking off its flaking green scales had been such fun. Oh, Tantlérie's garden, the kindly old sequoia swaying as though it had a mind of its own, the three blossom-wreathed branches of the apricot-tree reaching airily out across the window panes, the bird that warned of coming rain repeating its monotonous call. Oh, the summer rain in the garden, the rhythms in the drainpipes when it rained, water dripping from the eaves on to the canvas of the awning below, the large stained patch which had formed where it fell, falling with an expansive, rhythmic beat which rose above the steady rustling continuum of the summer rain as a solo instrument floats above the sound of the orchestra, and she stayed where she was for some time and listened, listened to the falling rain, happy.

'I was happy,' she murmured, ensconced on her throne.

She tore off another sheet of lavatory paper and made it into a cone, which she immediately tossed aside. She stood up and looked at herself in the mirror. She wasn't a little girl any more. Two lines there, running upwards from the sides of her mouth. She sat down once more on the white japanned seat, bent down and picked up the cone. 'Tsk, tsk! Where are your manners, Ariane? That's the sort of thing common children do.' Tantlérie had said that to her the day she'd wanted to buy an ice-cream cone in the street, and had also said it that time she'd wanted to put coins in the slot-machines at Cornavin station. Oh, her childhood! When she was thirteen she'd had a crush on Pastor Ferrier, who had replaced Pastor Oltramare at Sunday School. When they'd sung her favourite hymn, 'Jesu, Thou joy of loving hearts', she had sung 'Ferrier, thou joy of loving hearts' instead, and no one ever noticed. Instead of 'Jesu, our hope, our heart's desire', she sang 'Ferrier, our hope, our heart's desire', and no one ever noticed that either. And when she had finished Sunday School she had written him a letter which ended: 'Through you I have seen the Light', and she had signed it simply 'A grateful Sunday Scholar'. All that, and then last night there'd been Ingrid. It was ridiculous sitting all this time on a toilet seat. It's because I'm scared. One of the earliest photos of her, a toothless baby in a tub of water under a tree in the garden, laughing gummily. Another photo when she was two and roly-poly and sitting on the grass half-hidden by a clump of marguerites much taller than she was. Another, of her riding on the back of the Candolles' huge St Bernard. Her little cousin André hitting her when she was seven. Mariette had told her to stick up for herself, that she was just as tough as her cousin. Next day, she had stuck up for herself, had fought André and won, and went home with her dress torn, but victorious. The photo of her and Éliane wearing Arab costumes for a fancy-dress party at the house of their cousins, the de Lulles.

'I was happy,' she murmured, ensconced on her throne, and she leaned over and reached for the ether bottle, inhaled, and smiled as the cool breath flowed into her. 'It's freezing hard the ice is on the pool,' she hummed to the old tune, the tune of her childhood, and she sobbed suddenly, deliberately, barkingly. Oh, the games she'd played with Éliane. They'd played persecuting Christians, and she'd been St Blandine, thrown to the lions by the pagans, and Éliane as the lion had used a funnel to roar louder. Sometimes she had been a heroic Christian virgin, chained to the banisters on the attic stairs, and

Éliane was a Roman soldier torturing her by sticking a pin in her leg, but not very deep, and afterwards they'd put iodine on the pricks. They'd also played falling down. They let themselves fall off the swing to hurt themselves a bit, or climbed on to a table and on to a chair on the table to reach the round window near the ceiling, and then they'd squirmed through the round window and let themselves drop into the bathroom on the other side. Once, they'd filled the bath and she'd let herself drop into the water with all her clothes on. I was happy, I had no idea of what lay in wait for me. Later on, when Éliane was fifteen and she was sixteen, spouting verse at the old, tarnished Venetian mirror. Ah! Tantlérie's attic! The smell of dust and hot sun on wood, their very own sanctuary in the summer holidays, where she and her sister could be great actresses throatily declaiming tragedies. Éliane was always the hero and she was always the heroine, and she would alternate weeping and wailing with striking regal poses, but the grandest gesture of all, the one they considered to be the ultimate expression of love, was to press one hand to the brow and then take ages dying. Darling Éliane! How awful they'd felt when they found out that a cousin of theirs, a student, had got himself drunk. She'd gone to Éliane's room in the middle of the night and woken her up, and they'd both got down on their knees and prayed for him. 'Lord, please make him grow to be a decent man, and see that he does not partake of strong waters.' All that, and then last night there'd been Ingrid. Later on, when Éliane was sixteen and she was seventeen, those innocent evening dances with other girls. They'd set such store by doing the steps right. They didn't say 'doing the right steps' but 'doing the steps right', with the emphasis on 'right'. They had wanted those evenings to be perfect, a work of art. Empty-headed but happy, self-assured, such proper young ladies, the flower of the finest Genevan society, and very highly thought of. All that, and then last night there'd been Ingrid. She'd done it for him, to keep him. Heigh-ho, on your feet.

Back in her bedroom, stretched out on the bed with a box of chocolates propped up against her ribs, she put a fondant in her mouth, unstopped the bottle of ether, and inhaled, smiling at the surgical iciness which seeped into her. Geneva, when their love was new, the charity show organized by the people from the Secretariat. He had asked her to be in it, it was a tragedy, saying that he wanted to be in the audience and be like a total stranger who didn't know her from Eve, that he wanted to see her as if she were a stranger, remote and distant up there on stage, and know that after the performance she would be his all through the night, and no one in the auditorium would have the slightest inkling. After each act, when the spectators applauded and she took her bow with the rest of the cast, it was at him that she had looked, it was to him that she had bowed. Oh, the vibrant joy of their secret love! Before the play began, she'd told him that when she came down the steps in Act One her hand would move across her groin to gather the cloth of her dress and lift her skirt an inch or so, it was a dark-blue dress, such a pretty blue, and by this gesture he would know that at that instant the remote stranger up there on the stage would be thinking of him, thinking of their nights.

She pressed one nostril with her forefinger to block it and allow the other nostril to suck at the ether fumes more greedily, to increase the flow. She reached for two chocolates, put them in her mouth, and felt queasy as she chewed on them. Her march of triumph on the day of his return. Striding along, wearing nothing under her ducky dress which flapped in the breeze, eagerly striding out on her march of love, the snap of her dress was exhilarating, the wind on her face was exhilarating, the wind on her face and her head held high, the wind on her young face alive with love. She inhaled again, smiled, and there were tears on her little-girl face, on her face which had aged, and the tears redistributed the mascara over her cheeks.

Suddenly she got out of bed, padded heavily around the airless room, ether bottle in hand, stamping her feet, deliberately clumping, wilfully old, grotesquely skipping a step, poking her tongue out, and then she began muttering that this was the march of love, the march of her love, the squalid march of love.

CHAPTER 104

Late evening. She came to him, approached the bed, and asked if she could stay. He motioned to her to lie down next to him, reached for the bottle she was holding, removed the stopper, and inhaled deeply. She lay down by his side without removing her dressing-gown. He turned out the light and asked if she wanted the ether. In the darkened room, she felt for the bottle, inhaled deeply, then inhaled some more, and all at once from the ballroom rose a summons, Hawaiian guitars reluctantly releasing their long, pure lamentation, a lament from the heart, a long-drawn, sweet lament, liquid to liquidate the soul, an infinite keening of farewell. It was the same music, exactly the same, that they had heard on that first night; then she had bowed her head, had looked at him, icy-cold, trembling with fear and love. Now she lay there and listened, clutching the bottle, cradling it like a baby.

She inhaled again, closed her eyes, and smiled. Now they were playing a waltz downstairs, their first waltz. Solemnly did they dance, with eyes only for each other did they dance, with eyes feasting on the other, solicitous, intense, engrossed. Locked in his arms and happy to follow his lead, oblivious to her surroundings, she listened to the happiness coursing through her veins, glancing up at intervals to admire herself in the tall mirrors on the walls, was elegant, heart-stopping, exceptional, a woman loved, a woman fair and beloved of her lord.

He took the ether bottle from her and held it under his nose. In those first days, the wild joy he had felt as he readied himself to go to her, the glory of shaving for her, of bathing for her, and in the car which took him to her he sang in triumph that he was loved, looked at the man who was loved reflected in the glass of the car window, the happy owner of perfect teeth, smiling at his teeth, happy to be handsome, happy to be going to her, to the woman who stood waiting robed in love at her door beneath the roses, waiting in her white dress with the wide sleeves nipped at the wrist. 'What are you thinking about?' she asked. 'Your Romanian dress,' he said. 'You liked it, didn't you?' she asked. 'You looked wonderful in it,' he said, and in the dark she breathed more easily, just as she used to when he said nice things to her. 'I've still got it: it's in my trunk,' she said, and she switched on the light so that she could look at him, and she ran her finger along the line of his eyebrows.

She reached once more for the ether bottle, inhaled, and smiled. On that first evening, when she'd danced with him, she had drawn back the better to see him as he whispered wondrous words which she did not always understand for she was too busy drinking him with her eyes. But when he'd said that they were in love, then she'd understood, she'd given a little laugh of joy, and then he had told her that he was dying to kiss and bless her long curved lashes. Whereas now . . .

She inhaled more ether and smiled at the easeful coolness sluicing into her. Ah, the little sitting-room that first evening, her little sitting-room which she had insisted on showing him straight away, after the Ritz. They had stood at the open window looking out over the garden, breathing the star-spangled night, listening to the softly stirring leaves of the trees, which whispered their love. 'Always,' she had whispered. Then she had played a chorale for him. Then the sofa, kisses on the sofa, the first true kisses of her life. 'Your woman,' she had said to him each time they stopped to get their breath. Over and over they had declared that they loved each other, then they had laughed for joy and joined their lips, and then broken off so that they could proclaim the wondrous tidings times without number. Whereas now . . .

She inhaled the ether and smiled. Ah, those first days of their loving, Genevan days, the making shift to be beautiful, the joy of being beautiful for him, the joy of waiting, the moment of his coming at nine and she invariably at the door, impatient, with the healthy bloom of youth on her, waiting at the door beneath the roses round the door, in the Romanian dress he liked, white it was with wide sleeves nipped at the wrist, the ecstatic greetings when they saw each other again, the evenings spent together, the hours spent gazing at each other, talking to each other, telling each other everything about themselves, innumerable kisses offered and received, yes, the only true kisses of her entire life, and when he left her in the small hours, left her in a star-burst of kisses, deep and endless kisses, sometimes he came back, an hour later, two minutes later, oh the wonder of seeing her once more, oh his passionate homecoming, 'I can't live without you,' he said, 'it's impossible', and for love's sake would kneel before her, just as she for love's sake knelt before him, and then there was kissing, she and he devout and pious, a shoal, a mountain of kisses, sincere kisses, love's true kisses, a great flapping of winged kisses, 'I can't live without you,' he had said between the kisses, and he had stayed, her miracle who could not, no he could not live without her, stayed for hours on end, stayed until the dawn broke and the birds began to sing, and it was love. Whereas now they had stopped wanting each other, they were bored with each other. This she now knew.

She inhaled the ether and smiled. When he went away on official business, ah what telegrams he had sent her, in code if the words were too passionate, and oh the joy of deciphering his words, and the long telegrams she had sent in reply, telegrams hundreds of words long, always telegrams, so that there should be no delay in his knowing how much she loved him, and oh all the preparations she had made for his sacred return, the clothes she'd ordered from the dress shop, the hours spent perfecting her beauty, and she had sung the Whitsun hymn, sung of the coming of a heavenly king. And now they were bored with each other, they had stopped wanting each other, felt no desire for each other, they forced themselves, they strained after desire, and this she now knew, had long known.

'What are you thinking?' she asked.

'Nothing,' he said, and he kissed her hand and looked at her. Last night she had come to him dressed as a schoolgirl and been horribly cute, saying 'Hello Uncle' and sitting bare-thighed on her uncle's knee and whispering that if she didn't behave properly then he'd have to smack her. Oh the sorrow of it and the foolishness, and yet there was nobility, there was grandeur behind the grotesquerie, which was nothing less than the revolt of their threadbare passion against the dying of the flame: their stupid obscenities were a last, desperate attempt to rekindle it. At midnight she had suggested asking Ingrid to come, and he had agreed, capitulated out of desperation, because she wanted it, to breathe life into the embers. They were in paradise, and they suffered the torments of the damned. She took his hand.

'Want to, darling?'

He squeezed her hand and intimated yes, he wanted to. Whereupon she got out of bed and left him.

CHAPTER 105

In her room, she picked up a book which lay on the table, opened it, read a few lines without understanding a word, put it down again, removed the cord of her dressing-gown, and dropped it on the floor. Perspiring, she bent down and picked it up again, cracked it several times, like a whip, with a dazed look in her eye and a smile on her lips, then she dropped it again and touched her cheek. It was her, no doubt about it, her cheeks were warm, her hands could move, she was in charge of her hands. Oh this love of mine inside me, eternally enclosed within me and perpetually released so that I may contemplate it, and then folded away once more and shut up and kept safe in my heart. She had liked that sentence so much that she had written it down so she would never forget it. One evening he had walked into her little sitting-room and they had both suddenly received such an illumination of the purity of their love that they had fallen to their knees, had suddenly knelt before each other.

She sat down at the writing-table, took the powders out of their box, and counted them. Thirty. Three times more than was required for the both of them. The chemist at Saint-Raphaël had warned her to take good care, since just five of these powders constituted a lethal dose. She arranged them in a circle, then in a cross. But what was she thinking of, keeping him waiting like this? Start, had to make a start. She stood up, scratched her cheek, dazed, a smile playing on her lips. Yes, do it in the bathroom, use all the powders, take no chances.

Standing at the wash-basin, she tore the flimsy paper envelope and opened the first powder. When she was little, she used to ask if she could have the white paper wrappers the nougat came in: it was a minor miracle, the wrappers simply melted on her tongue. She opened all the little envelopes one after the other, tipped the contents of each into a glass of water which she stirred with the handle of a toothbrush, to ensure an even distribution of the transparent particles, and then poured half the liquid into another glass. One glass for her, one glass for him.

When she'd had her bath, she carefully redid her hair, applied perfume and powder, and got into the Romanian dress, the dress with the wide sleeves nipped at the wrist, the dress she had worn as she had waited at her door beneath the roses round the door. In the mirror she was beautiful. She raised both glasses and held them side by side to see if there was the same amount in each. She also used to hold up glasses side by side to see if she had been given as much pear squash as Éliane. They would often drink it neat, it was lovely. She had never seen pear squash anywhere else, Tantlérie's was the only place where it was made, it was scrumptious, with just a hint of cloves. They used to have it in summer especially, diluted with delicious cool water from the well. The buzzing of the bees on the hot summer days. Swig it down, without a second thought. She used to make all sorts of fuss if she had to take any kind of medicine. Tantlérie used to jolly her along. 'Come on, don't shilly-shally, down the red lane, be a good girl, you'll be glad afterwards.'

She raised the glass to her lips but barely wet them. There were bits in the bottom. She stirred the mixture with the handle of the toothbrush, closed her eyes, drank half, stopped with a little scared smile, heard the bees buzzing in the heavy heat, saw poppies waving in the cornfields, gave another stir, drank the other half in one gulp, and with it quaffed all the beauty of the world. There, she'd been a good girl, all gone, Tantlérie used to say. Yes, all gone, nothing left in the glass, she had drunk it all, even the sludge at the bottom, she could taste it bitter on her tongue. Quickly now, go and see him.

CHAPTER 106

'Come ladies, come buy my sweet poppies,' sang an antic voice as she entered his room carrying the other glass in her hand. He stood waiting for her, archangelic in his long dressing-gown, and handsome, as handsome as on that first night. She set the glass down on the bedside table. He picked it up and stared at the sediment at the bottom. In that mud lay his quietude. In that mud lay the annihilation of the trees, the dissolution of the sea which he had loved so much, the sea of his native land, pellucid and warm over its crystal-clear bed, but never more for him. In that mud lay the extinction of his voice, the stilling of his laughter so loved by all the women he had loved. 'Such a tender, cruel laugh,' they had said. The fat bluebottle was back on station, erratically circling, busy, bustling, grimly buzzing, making ready, exulting.

He drank deeply, then stopped. The goodness had stayed at the bottom, and he must finish it all. He swirled the glass, raised it to his lips, drank the lees which would still him for ever. He put the glass down, got into bed, and she lay down by his side. 'Together,' she said. 'Take me in your arms, hold me close,' she said. 'Kiss my eyes, there is no greater love,' she said, chilled and strangely trembling.

And so he took her in his arms and held her close, and he kissed her long curved lashes, and they were suddenly transported back to their first night, and he held her close with all his mortal love. 'Closer,' she said, 'hold me closer and closer still.' Oh, she hungered for his love, needed it now, mountains of it, for soon the gate would open, and she clung to him, needing to feel his nearness, clung to him with all her mortal strength. Fevered, her voice no more than a whisper, she asked him if they would be together again, afterwards, on the other side, and she smiled at him as if to say but of course they would be together again, afterwards, on the other side, and flecks of froth collected in the corners of her smile as she smiled to say that they would be together always on the other side, and there would be real love there, there was only true love on the other side, and now the spittle ran down her neck and on to the dress she had worn as she stood and waited at her door for his coming.

And then once more the waltz struck up downstairs, the waltz that had on that first night unfurled its slow, lingering refrain, and she grew dizzy as she danced with her lord, who held her in his arms and led her, danced oblivious to her surroundings, glancing up to admire herself in the tall mirrors as she whirled, elegant, heart-stopping, a woman who was loved, for she was fair and beloved of her lord.

But her feet grew leaden, and now she was not dancing, could dance no more. What had happened to her feet? Had they gone first, gone over to the other side, were they waiting for her there in the church shaped like a mountain, the mountain church where the black wind blew? Oh, what summons was this, and the gate opened. Oh, wide was the gate and inky the blackness beyond, and the wind blew through the gate, the unceasing wind from the other side, a dank wind smelling of earth, the cold wind of blackness. 'Darling, you'd better take a coat.'

Ah, there was a crooning now in the cypress-trees, the keening of those who take their leave and look no more. Who was holding her legs fast? The numbness worked upwards, and as it rose it spread a chill before it and her breathing grew laboured and there were dewy pearls on her cheeks and a taste in her mouth. 'You won't forget,' she murmured. 'Tonight at nine,' she murmured, and her mouth filled with spittle and her lips smiled dully and she tried to lean her head back to see him but could not, and on the other side someone was sharpening a scythe with a hammer. She tried to move her hand in a gesture of farewell, but could not, her hand had gone before her. 'Wait for me,' he said to her from a great distance. 'For see, there comes my heavenly king!' she smiled, and she stepped into the mountain church.

Then he closed her eyes, and stood up, and took her in his arms, and lifted her heavy, empty deadness, and circled the room carrying her in his arms, holding her close and cradling her with all his love, cradling and gazing at the silent, serene, loving woman who had given so generously of her lips, had slipped such fervent notes under doors at break of day, cradling and gazing at his pallid-faced queen, his lovely innocent who had kept her trysts beneath the polestar.

Suddenly his legs buckled and a cold hand nudged him, and he set her down on the bed and lay by her side and kissed her virginal face, softened now by just the shadow of a smile and as beautiful as it had been on that first of their nights, kissed her hand, which was still warm but heavy now, held her hand in his, kept her hand in his until he reached the cellar where a midget was weeping, weeping openly for her comely king who was dying transfixed with nails to the wart-studded door, her doomed king who was weeping too, weeping for forsaking his children on earth, his children whom he had not saved, what would they do without him, and suddenly the midget enjoined him in ringing tones, ordered him to offer up the last prayer in accordance with the ritual, for the hour had come.